MW01203902

Stephen Crane

The Complete Short Stories of Stephen Crane

e-artnow 2021

Stephen Crane

The Complete Short Stories of Stephen Crane

100+ Tales & Novellas: Maggie, The Open Boat, Blue Hotel, The Monster, The Little Regiment…

e-artnow, 2021
Contact: info@e-artnow.org

ISBN 978-80-273-4177-1

Contents

The Little Regiment and Other Episodes from the American Civil War

THE LITTLE REGIMENT

I

The fog made the clothes of the men of the column in the roadway seem of a luminous quality. It imparted to the heavy infantry overcoats a new colour, a kind of blue which was so pale that a regiment might have been merely a long, low shadow in the mist. However, a muttering, one part grumble, three parts joke, hovered in the air above the thick ranks, and blended in an undertoned roar, which was the voice of the column.

The town on the southern shore of the little river loomed spectrally, a faint etching upon the grey cloud-masses which were shifting with oily languor. A long row of guns upon the northern bank had been pitiless in their hatred, but a little battered belfry could be dimly seen still pointing with invincible resolution toward the heavens.

The enclouded air vibrated with noises made by hidden colossal things. The infantry tramplings, the heavy rumbling of the artillery, made the earth speak of gigantic preparation. Guns on distant heights thundered from time to time with sudden, nervous roar, as if unable to endure in silence a knowledge of hostile troops massing, other guns going to position. These sounds, near and remote, defined an immense battle-ground, described the tremendous width of the stage of the prospective drama. The voices of the guns, slightly casual, unexcited in their challenges and warnings, could not destroy the unutterable eloquence of the word in the air, a meaning of impending struggle which made the breath halt at the lips.

The column in the roadway was ankle-deep in mud. The men swore piously at the rain which drizzled upon them, compelling them to stand always very erect in fear of the drops that would sweep in under their coat-collars. The fog was as cold as wet cloths. The men stuffed their hands deep in their pockets, and huddled their muskets in their arms. The machinery of orders had rooted these soldiers deeply into the mud, precisely as almighty nature roots mullein stalks.

They listened and speculated when a tumult of fighting came from the dim town across the river. When the noise lulled for a time they resumed their descriptions of the mud and graphically exaggerated the number of hours they had been kept waiting. The general commanding their division rode along the ranks, and they cheered admiringly, affectionately, crying out to him gleeful prophecies of the coming battle. Each man scanned him with a peculiarly keen personal interest, and afterward spoke of him with unquestioning devotion and confidence, narrating anecdotes which were mainly untrue.

When the jokers lifted the shrill voices which invariably belonged to them, flinging witticisms at their comrades, a loud laugh would sweep from rank to rank, and soldiers who had not heard would lean forward and demand repetition. When were borne past them some wounded men with grey and blood-smeared faces, and eyes that rolled in that helpless beseeching for assistance from the sky which comes with supreme pain, the soldiers in the mud watched intently, and from time to time asked of the bearers an account of the affair. Frequently they bragged of their corps, their division, their brigade, their regiment. Anon they referred to the mud and the cold drizzle. Upon this threshold of a wild scene of death they, in short, defied the proportion of events with that splendour of heedlessness which belongs only to veterans.

"Like a lot of wooden soldiers," swore Billie Dempster, moving his feet in the thick mass, and casting a vindictive glance indefinitely: "standing in the mud for a hundred years."

"Oh, shut up!" murmured his brother Dan. The manner of his words implied that this fraternal voice near him was an indescribable bore.

"Why should I shut up?" demanded Billie.

"Because you're a fool," cried Dan, taking no time to debate it; "the biggest fool in the regiment."

There was but one man between them, and he was habituated. These insults from brother to brother had swept across his chest, flown past his face, many times during two long campaigns. Upon this occasion he simply grinned first at one, then at the other.

The way of these brothers was not an unknown topic in regimental gossip. They had enlisted simultaneously, with each sneering loudly at the other for doing it. They left their little town, and went forward with the flag, exchanging protestations of undying suspicion. In the camp life they so openly despised each other that, when entertaining quarrels were lacking, their companions often contrived situations calculated to bring forth display of this fraternal dislike.

Both were large-limbed, strong young men, and often fought with friends in camp unless one was near to interfere with the other. This latter happened rather frequently, because Dan, preposterously willing for any manner of combat, had a very great horror of seeing Billie in a fight; and Billie, almost odiously ready himself, simply refused to see Dan stripped to his shirt and with his fists aloft. This sat queerly upon them, and made them the objects of plots.

When Dan jumped through a ring of eager soldiers and dragged forth his raving brother by the arm, a thing often predicted would almost come to pass. When Billie performed the same office for Dan, the prediction would again miss fulfilment by an inch. But indeed they never fought together, although they were perpetually upon the verge.

They expressed longing for such conflict. As a matter of truth, they had at one time made full arrangement for it, but even with the encouragement and interest of half of the regiment they somehow failed to achieve collision.

If Dan became a victim of police duty, no jeering was so destructive to the feelings as Billie's comment. If Billie got a call to appear at the headquarters, none would so genially prophesy his complete undoing as Dan. Small misfortunes to one were, in truth, invariably greeted with hilarity by the other, who seemed to see in them great re-enforcement of his opinion.

As soldiers, they expressed each for each a scorn intense and blasting. After a certain battle, Billie was promoted to corporal. When Dan was told of it, he seemed smitten dumb with astonishment and patriotic indignation. He stared in silence, while the dark blood rushed to Billie's forehead, and he shifted his weight from foot to foot. Dan at last found his tongue, and said: "Well, I'm durned!" If he had heard that an army mule had been appointed to the post of corps commander, his tone could not have had more derision in it. Afterward, he adopted a fervid insubordination, an almost religious reluctance to obey the new corporal's orders, which came near to developing the desired strife.

It is here finally to be recorded also that Dan, most ferociously profane in speech, very rarely swore in the presence of his brother; and that Billie, whose oaths came from his lips with the grace of falling pebbles, was seldom known to express himself in this manner when near his brother Dan.

At last the afternoon contained a suggestion of evening. Metallic cries rang suddenly from end to end of the column. They inspired at once a quick, business-like adjustment. The long thing stirred in the mud. The men had hushed, and were looking across the river. A moment later the shadowy mass of pale blue figures was moving steadily toward the stream. There could be heard from the town a clash of swift fighting and cheering. The noise of the shooting coming through the heavy air had its sharpness taken from it, and sounded in thuds.

There was a halt upon the bank above the pontoons. When the column went winding down the incline, and streamed out upon the bridge, the fog had faded to a great degree, and in the clearer dusk the guns on a distant ridge were enabled to perceive the crossing. The long whirling outcries of the shells came into the air above the men. An occasional solid shot struck the surface of the river, and dashed into view a sudden vertical jet. The distance was subtly illuminated by the lightning from the deep-booming guns. One by one the batteries on the northern shore aroused, the innumerable guns bellowing in angry oration at the distant ridge. The rolling thunder crashed and reverberated as a wild surf sounds on a still night, and to this music the column marched across the pontoons.

The waters of the grim river curled away in a smile from the ends of the great boats, and slid swiftly beneath the planking. The dark, riddled walls of the town upreared before the troops, and from a region hidden by these hammered and tumbled houses came incessantly the yells and firings of a prolonged and close skirmish.

When Dan had called his brother a fool, his voice had been so decisive, so brightly assured, that many men had laughed, considering it to be great humour under the circumstances. The incident happened to rankle deep in Billie. It was not any strange thing that his brother had called him a fool. In fact, he often called him a fool with exactly the same amount of cheerful and prompt conviction, and before large audiences, too. Billie wondered in his own mind why he took such profound offence in this case; but, at any rate, as he slid down the bank and on to the bridge with his regiment, he was searching his knowledge for something that would pierce Dan's blithesome spirit. But he could contrive nothing at this time, and his impotency made the glance which he was once able to give his brother still more malignant.

The guns far and near were roaring a fearful and grand introduction for this column which was marching upon the stage of death. Billie felt it, but only in a numb way. His heart was cased in that curious dissonant metal which covers a man's emotions at such times. The terrible voices from the hills told him that in this wide conflict his life was an insignificant fact, and that his death would be an insignificant fact. They portended the whirlwind to which he would be as necessary as a butterfly's waved wing. The solemnity, the sadness of it came near enough to make him wonder why he was neither solemn nor sad. When his mind vaguely adjusted events according to their importance to him, it appeared that the uppermost thing was the fact that upon the eve of battle, and before many comrades, his brother had called him a fool.

Dan was in a particularly happy mood. "Hurray! Look at 'em shoot," he said, when the long witches' croon of the shells came into the air. It enraged Billie when he felt the little thorn in him, and saw at the same time that his brother had completely forgotten it.

The column went from the bridge into more mud. At this southern end there was a chaos of hoarse directions and commands. Darkness was coming upon the earth, and regiments were being hurried up the slippery bank. As Billie floundered in the black mud, amid the swearing, sliding crowd, he suddenly resolved that, in the absence of other means of hurting Dan, he would avoid looking at him, refrain from speaking to him, pay absolutely no heed to his existence; and this done skilfully would, he imagined, soon reduce his brother to a poignant sensitiveness.

At the top of the bank the column again halted and rearranged itself, as a man after a climb rearranges his clothing. Presently the great steel-backed brigade, an infinitely graceful thing in the rhythm and ease of its veteran movement, swung up a little narrow, slanting street.

Evening had come so swiftly that the fighting on the remote borders of the town was indicated by thin flashes of flame. Some building was on fire, and its reflection upon the clouds was an oval of delicate pink.

All demeanour of rural serenity had been wrenched violently from the little town by the guns and by the waves of men which had surged through it. The hand of war laid upon this village had in an instant changed it to a thing of remnants. It resembled the place of a monstrous shaking of the earth itself. The windows, now mere unsightly holes, made the tumbled and blackened dwellings seem skeletons. Doors lay splintered to fragments. Chimneys had flung their bricks everywhere. The artillery fire had not neglected the rows of gentle shade-trees which had lined the streets. Branches and heavy trunks cluttered the mud in driftwood tangles, while a few shattered forms had contrived to remain dejectedly, mournfully upright. They expressed an innocence, a helplessness, which perforce created a pity for their happening into this caldron of battle. Furthermore, there was under foot a vast collection of odd things reminiscent of the charge, the fight, the retreat. There were boxes and barrels filled with earth, behind which riflemen had lain snugly, and in these little trenches were the dead in blue with the dead in grey, the poses eloquent of the struggles for possession of the town, until the history of the whole conflict was written plainly in the streets.

And yet the spirit of this little city, its quaint individuality, poised in the air above the ruins, defying the guns, the sweeping volleys; holding in contempt those avaricious blazes which had attacked many dwellings. The hard earthen sidewalks proclaimed the games that had been played there during long lazy days, in the careful, shadows of the trees. "General Merchandise," in faint letters upon a long board, had to be read with a slanted glance, for the sign dangled by one end; but the porch of the old store was a palpable legend of wide-hatted men, smoking.

This subtle essence, this soul of the life that had been, brushed like invisible wings the thoughts of the men in the swift columns that came up from the river.

In the darkness a loud and endless humming arose from the great blue crowds bivouacked in the streets. From time to time a sharp spatter of firing from far picket lines entered this bass chorus. The smell from the smouldering ruins floated on the cold night breeze.

Dan, seated ruefully upon the doorstep of a shot-pierced house, was proclaiming the campaign badly managed. Orders had been issued forbidding camp-fires.

Suddenly he ceased his oration, and scanning the group of his comrades, said: "Where's Billie? Do you know?"

"Gone on picket."

"Get out! Has he?" said Dan. "No business to go on picket. Why don't some of them other corporals take their turn?"

A bearded private was smoking his pipe of confiscated tobacco, seated comfortably upon a horse-hair trunk which he had dragged from the house. He observed: "Was his turn."

"No such thing," cried Dan. He and the man on the horse-hair trunk held discussion in which Dan stoutly maintained that if his brother had been sent on picket it was an injustice. He ceased his argument when another soldier, upon whose arms could faintly be seen the two stripes of a corporal, entered the circle. "Humph," said Dan, "where you been?"

The corporal made no answer. Presently Dan said: "Billie, where you been?"

His brother did not seem to hear these inquiries. He glanced at the house which towered above them, and remarked casually to the man on the horse-hair trunk: "Funny, ain't it? After the pelting this town got, you'd think there wouldn't be one brick left on another."

"Oh," said Dan, glowering at his brother's back. "Getting mighty smart, ain't you?"

The absence of camp-fires allowed the evening to make apparent its quality of faint silver light in which the blue clothes of the throng became black, and the faces became white expanses, void of expression. There was considerable excitement a short distance from the group around the doorstep. A soldier had chanced upon a hoop-skirt, and arrayed in it he was performing a dance amid the applause of his companions. Billie and a greater part of the men immediately poured over there to witness the exhibition.

"What's the matter with Billie?" demanded Dan of the man upon the horse-hair trunk.

"How do I know?" rejoined the other in mild resentment. He arose and walked away. When he returned he said briefly, in a weather-wise tone, that it would rain during the night.

Dan took a seat upon one end of the horse-hair trunk. He was facing the crowd around the dancer, which in its hilarity swung this way and that way. At times he imagined that he could recognise his brother's face.

He and the man on the other end of the trunk thoughtfully talked of the army's position. To their minds, infantry and artillery were in a most precarious jumble in the streets of the town; but they did not grow nervous over it, for they were used to having the army appear in a precarious jumble to their minds. They had learned to accept such puzzling situations as a consequence of their position in the ranks, and were now usually in possession of a simple but perfectly immovable faith that somebody understood the jumble. Even if they had been convinced that the army was a headless monster, they would merely have nodded with the veteran's singular cynicism. It was none of their business as soldiers. Their duty was to grab sleep and food when occasion permitted, and cheerfully fight wherever their feet were planted until more orders came. This was a task sufficiently absorbing.

They spoke of other corps, and this talk being confidential, their voices dropped to tones of awe. "The Ninth" — "The First" — "The Fifth" — "The Sixth" — "The Third" — the simple numerals rang with eloquence, each having a meaning which was to float through many years as no intangible arithmetical mist, but as pregnant with individuality as the names of cities.

Of their own corps they spoke with a deep veneration, an idolatry, a supreme confidence which apparently would not blanch to see it match against everything.

It was as if their respect for other corps was due partly to a wonder that organisations not blessed with their own famous numeral could take such an interest in war. They could prove that their division was the best in the corps, and that their brigade was the best in the division. And their regiment-it was plain that no fortune of life was equal to the chance which caused a man to be born, so to speak, into this command, the keystone of the defending arch.

At times Dan covered with insults the character of a vague, unnamed general to whose petulance and busy-body spirit he ascribed the order which made hot coffee impossible.

Dan said that victory was certain in the coming battle. The other man seemed rather dubious. He remarked upon the fortified line of hills, which had impressed him even from the other side of the river. "Shucks," said Dan. "Why, we — —" He pictured a splendid overflowing of these hills by the sea of men in blue. During the period of this conversation Dan's glance searched the merry throng about the dancer. Above the babble of voices in the street a far-away thunder could sometimes be heard-evidently from the very edge of the horizon-the boom-boom of restless guns.

III

Ultimately the night deepened to the tone of black velvet. The outlines of the fireless camp were like the faint drawings upon ancient tapestry. The glint of a rifle, the shine of a button, might have been of threads of silver and gold sewn upon the fabric of the night. There was little presented to the vision, but to a sense more subtle there was discernible in the atmosphere something like a pulse; a mystic beating which would have told a stranger of the presence of a giant thing-the slumbering mass of regiments and batteries.

With fires forbidden, the floor of a dry old kitchen was thought to be a good exchange for the cold earth of December, even if a shell had exploded in it, and knocked it so out of shape that when a man lay curled in his blanket his last waking thought was likely to be of the wall that bellied out above him, as if strongly anxious to topple upon the score of soldiers.

Billie looked at the bricks ever about to descend in a shower upon his face, listened to the industrious pickets plying their rifles on the border of the town, imagined some measure of the din of the coming battle, thought of Dan and Dan's chagrin, and rolling over in his blanket went to sleep with satisfaction.

At an unknown hour he was aroused by the creaking of boards. Lifting himself upon his elbow, he saw a sergeant prowling among the sleeping forms. The sergeant carried a candle in an old brass candlestick. He would have resembled some old farmer on an unusual midnight tour if it were not for the significance of his gleaming buttons and striped sleeves.

Billie blinked stupidly at the light until his mind returned from the journeys of slumber. The sergeant stooped among the unconscious soldiers, holding the candle close, and peering into each face.

"Hello, Haines," said Billie. "Relief?"

"Hello, Billie," said the sergeant. "Special duty."

"Dan got to go?"

"Jameson, Hunter, McCormack, D. Dempster. Yes. Where is he?"

"Over there by the winder," said Billie, gesturing. "What is it for, Haines?"

"You don't think I know, do you?" demanded the sergeant. He began to pipe sharply but cheerily at men upon the floor. "Come, Mac, get up here. Here's a special for you. Wake up, Jameson. Come along, Dannie, me boy."

Each man at once took this call to duty as a personal affront. They pulled themselves out of their blankets, rubbed their eyes, and swore at whoever was responsible. "Them's orders," cried the sergeant. "Come! Get out of here." An undetailed head with dishevelled hair thrust out from a blanket, and a sleepy voice said: "Shut up, Haines, and go home."

When the detail clanked out of the kitchen, all but one of the remaining men seemed to be again asleep. Billie, leaning on his elbow, was gazing into darkness. When the footsteps died to silence, he curled himself into his blanket.

At the first cool lavender lights of daybreak he aroused again, and scanned his recumbent companions. Seeing a wakeful one he asked: "Is Dan back yet?"

The man said: "Hain't seen 'im."

Billie put both hands behind his head, and scowled into the air. "Can't see the use of these cussed details in the night-time," he muttered in his most unreasonable tones. "Darn nuisances. Why can't they — —" He grumbled at length and graphically.

When Dan entered with the squad, however, Billie was convincingly asleep.

IV

The regiment trotted in double time along the street, and the colonel seemed to quarrel over the right of way with many artillery officers. Batteries were waiting in the mud, and the men of them, exasperated by the bustle of this ambitious infantry, shook their fists from saddle and caisson, exchanging all manner of taunts and jests. The slanted guns continued to look reflectively at the ground.

On the outskirts of the crumbled town a fringe of blue figures were firing into the fog. The regiment swung out into skirmish lines, and the fringe of blue figures departed, turning their backs and going joyfully around the flank.

The bullets began a low moan off toward a ridge which loomed faintly in the heavy mist. When the swift crescendo had reached its climax, the missiles zipped just overhead, as if piercing an invisible curtain. A battery on the hill was crashing with such tumult that it was as if the guns had quarrelled and had fallen pell-mell and snarling upon each other. The shells howled on their journey toward the town. From short-range distance there came a spatter of musketry, sweeping along an invisible line, and making faint sheets of orange light.

Some in the new skirmish lines were beginning to fire at various shadows discerned in the vapour, forms of men suddenly revealed by some humour of the laggard masses of clouds. The crackle of musketry began to dominate the purring of the hostile bullets. Dan, in the front rank, held his rifle poised, and looked into the fog keenly, coldly, with the air of a sportsman. His nerves were so steady that it was as if they had been drawn from his body, leaving him merely a muscular machine; but his numb heart was somehow beating to the pealing march of the fight.

The waving skirmish line went backward and forward, ran this way and that way. Men got lost in the fog, and men were found again. Once they got too close to the formidable ridge, and the thing burst out as if repulsing a general attack. Once another blue regiment was apprehended on the very edge of firing into them. Once a friendly battery began an elaborate and scientific process of extermination. Always as busy as brokers, the men slid here and there over the plain, fighting their foes, escaping from their friends, leaving a history of many movements in the wet yellow turf, cursing the atmosphere, blazing away every time they could identify the enemy.

In one mystic changing of the fog as if the fingers of spirits were drawing aside these draperies, a small group of the grey skirmishers, silent, statuesque, were suddenly disclosed to Dan and those about him. So vivid and near were they that there was something uncanny in the revelation.

There might have been a second of mutual staring. Then each rifle in each group was at the shoulder. As Dan's glance flashed along the barrel of his weapon, the figure of a man suddenly loomed as if the musket had been a telescope. The short black beard, the slouch hat, the pose of the man as he sighted to shoot, made a quick picture in Dan's mind. The same moment, it would seem, he pulled his own trigger, and the man, smitten, lurched forward, while his exploding rifle made a slanting crimson streak in the air, and the slouch hat fell before the body. The billows of the fog, governed by singular impulses, rolled between.

"You got that feller sure enough," said a comrade to Dan. Dan looked at him absent-mindedly.

V

When the next morning calmly displayed another fog, the men of the regiment exchanged eloquent comments; but they did not abuse it at length, because the streets of the town now contained enough galloping aides to make three troops of cavalry, and they knew that they had come to the verge of the great fight.

Dan conversed with the man who had once possessed a horse-hair trunk; but they did not mention the line of hills which had furnished them in more careless moments with an agreeable topic. They avoided it now as condemned men do the subject of death, and yet the thought of it stayed in their eyes as they looked at each other and talked gravely of other things.

The expectant regiment heaved a long sigh of relief when the sharp call: "Fall in," repeated indefinitely, arose in the streets. It was inevitable that a bloody battle was to be fought, and they wanted to get it off their minds. They were, however, doomed again to spend a long period planted firmly in the mud. They craned their necks, and wondered where some of the other regiments were going.

At last the mists rolled carelessly away. Nature made at this time all provisions to enable foes to see each other, and immediately the roar of guns resounded from every hill. The endless cracking of the skirmishers swelled to rolling crashes of musketry. Shells screamed with panther-like noises at the houses. Dan looked at the man of the horse-hair trunk, and the man said: "Well, here she comes!"

The tenor voices of younger officers and the deep and hoarse voices of the older ones rang in the streets. These cries pricked like spurs. The masses of men vibrated from the suddenness with which they were plunged into the situation of troops about to fight. That the orders were long-expected did not concern the emotion.

Simultaneous movement was imparted to all these thick bodies of men and horses that lay in the town. Regiment after regiment swung rapidly into the streets that faced the sinister ridge.

This exodus was theatrical. The little sober-hued village had been like the cloak which disguises the king of drama. It was now put aside, and an army, splendid thing of steel and blue, stood forth in the sunlight.

Even the soldiers in the heavy columns drew deep breaths at the sight, more majestic than they had dreamed. The heights of the enemy's position were crowded with men who resembled people come to witness some mighty pageant. But as the column moved steadily to their positions, the guns, matter-of-fact warriors, doubled their number, and shells burst with red thrilling tumult on the crowded plain. One came into the ranks of the regiment, and after the smoke and the wrath of it had faded, leaving motionless figures, every one stormed according to the limits of his vocabulary, for veterans detest being killed when they are not busy.

The regiment sometimes looked sideways at its brigade companions composed of men who had never been in battle; but no frozen blood could withstand the heat of the splendour of this army before the eyes on the plain, these lines so long that the flanks were little streaks, this mass of men of one intention. The recruits carried themselves heedlessly. At the rear was an idle battery, and three artillerymen in a foolish row on a caisson nudged each other and grinned at the recruits. "You'll catch it pretty soon," they called out. They were impersonally gleeful, as if they themselves were not also likely to catch it pretty soon. But with this picture of an army in their hearts, the new men perhaps felt the devotion which the drops may feel for the wave; they were of its power and glory; they smiled jauntily at the foolish row of gunners, and told them to go to blazes.

The column trotted across some little bridges, and spread quickly into lines of battle. Before them was a bit of plain, and back of the plain was the ridge. There was no time left for considerations. The men were staring at the plain, mightily wondering how it would feel to be out there, when a brigade in advance yelled and charged. The hill was all grey smoke and fire-points.

That fierce elation in the terrors of war, catching a man's heart and making it burn with such ardour that he becomes capable of dying, flashed in the faces of the men like coloured lights, and made them resemble leashed animals, eager, ferocious, daunting at nothing. The line was really in its first leap before the wild, hoarse crying of the orders.

The greed for close quarters, which is the emotion of a bayonet charge, came then into the minds of the men and developed until it was a madness. The field, with its faded grass of a Southern winter, seemed to this fury miles in width.

High, slow-moving masses of smoke, with an odour of burning cotton, engulfed the line until the men might have been swimmers. Before them the ridge, the shore of this grey sea, was outlined, crossed, and recrossed by sheets of flame. The howl of the battle arose to the noise of innumerable wind demons.

The line, galloping, scrambling, plunging like a herd of wounded horses, went over a field that was sown with corpses, the records of other charges.

Directly in front of the black-faced, whooping Dan, carousing in this onward sweep like a new kind of fiend, a wounded man appeared, raising his shattered body, and staring at this rush of men down upon him. It seemed to occur to him that he was to be trampled; he made a desperate, piteous effort to escape; then finally huddled in a waiting heap. Dan and the soldier near him widened the interval between them without looking down, without appearing to heed the wounded man. This little clump of blue seemed to reel past them as boulders reel past a train.

Bursting through a smoke-wave, the scampering, unformed bunches came upon the wreck of the brigade that had preceded them, a floundering mass stopped afar from the hill by the swirling volleys.

It was as if a necromancer had suddenly shown them a picture of the fate which awaited them; but the line with muscular spasm hurled itself over this wreckage and onward, until men were stumbling amid the relics of other assaults, the point where the fire from the ridge consumed.

The men, panting, perspiring, with crazed faces, tried to push against it; but it was as if they had come to a wall. The wave halted, shuddered in an agony from the quick struggle of its two desires, then toppled, and broke into a fragmentary thing which has no name.

Veterans could now at last be distinguished from recruits. The new regiments were instantly gone, lost, scattered, as if they never had been. But the sweeping failure of the charge, the battle, could not make the veterans forget their business. With a last throe, the band of maniacs drew itself up and blazed a volley at the hill, insignificant to those iron entrenchments, but nevertheless expressing that singular final despair which enables men coolly to defy the walls of a city of death.

After this episode the men renamed their command. They called it the Little Regiment.

"I seen Dan shoot a feller yesterday. Yes, sir. I'm sure it was him that done it. And maybe he thinks about that feller now, and wonders if he tumbled down just about the same way. Them things come up in a man's mind."

Bivouac fires upon the sidewalks, in the streets, in the yards, threw high their wavering reflections, which examined, like slim, red fingers, the dingy, scarred walls and the piles of tumbled brick. The droning of voices again arose from great blue crowds.

The odour of frying bacon, the fragrance from countless little coffee-pails floated among the ruins. The rifles, stacked in the shadows, emitted flashes of steely light. Wherever a flag lay horizontally from one stack to another was the bed of an eagle which had led men into the mystic smoke.

The men about a particular fire were engaged in holding in check their jovial spirits. They moved whispering around the blaze, although they looked at it with a certain fine contentment, like labourers after a day's hard work.

There was one who sat apart. They did not address him save in tones suddenly changed. They did not regard him directly, but always in little sidelong glances.

At last a soldier from a distant fire came into this circle of light. He studied for a time the man who sat apart. Then he hesitatingly stepped closer, and said: "Got any news, Dan?"

"No," said Dan.

The new-comer shifted his feet. He looked at the fire, at the sky, at the other men, at Dan. His face expressed a curious despair; his tongue was plainly in rebellion. Finally, however, he contrived to say: "Well, there's some chance yet, Dan. Lots of the wounded are still lying out there, you know. There's some chance yet."

"Yes," said Dan.

The soldier shifted his feet again, and looked miserably into the air.

After another struggle he said: "Well, there's some chance yet, Dan."

He moved hastily away.

One of the men of the squad, perhaps encouraged by this example, now approached the still figure. "No news yet, hey?" he said, after coughing behind his hand.

"No," said Dan.

"Well," said the man, "I've been thinking of how he was fretting about you the night you went on special duty. You recollect? Well, sir, I was surprised. He couldn't say enough about it. I swan, I don't believe he slep' a wink after you left, but just lay awake cussing special duty and worrying. I was surprised. But there he lay cussing. He — —"

Dan made a curious sound, as if a stone had wedged in his throat. He said: "Shut up, will you?"

Afterward the men would not allow this moody contemplation of the fire to be interrupted.

"Oh, let him alone, can't you?"

"Come away from there, Casey!"

"Say, can't you leave him be?"

They moved with reverence about the immovable figure, with its countenance of mask-like invulnerability.

VII

After the red round eye of the sun had stared long at the little plain and its burden, darkness, a sable mercy, came heavily upon it, and the wan hands of the dead were no longer seen in strange frozen gestures.

The heights in front of the plain shone with tiny camp-fires, and from the town in the rear, small shimmerings ascended from the blazes of the bivouac. The plain was a black expanse upon which, from time to time, dots of light, lanterns, floated slowly here and there. These fields were long steeped in grim mystery.

Suddenly, upon one dark spot, there was a resurrection. A strange thing had been groaning there, prostrate. Then it suddenly dragged itself to a sitting posture, and became a man.

The man stared stupidly for a moment at the lights on the hill, then turned and contemplated the faint colouring over the town. For some moments he remained thus, staring with dull eyes, his face unemotional, wooden.

Finally he looked around him at the corpses dimly to be seen. No change flashed into his face upon viewing these men. They seemed to suggest merely that his information concerning himself was not too complete. He ran his fingers over his arms and chest, bearing always the air of an idiot upon a bench at an almshouse door.

Finding no wound in his arms nor in his chest, he raised his hand to his head, and the fingers came away with some dark liquid upon them. Holding these fingers close to his eyes, he scanned them in the same stupid fashion, while his body gently swayed.

The soldier rolled his eyes again toward the town. When he arose, his clothing peeled from the frozen ground like wet paper. Hearing the sound of it, he seemed to see reason for deliberation. He paused and looked at the ground, then at his trousers, then at the ground.

Finally he went slowly off toward the faint reflection, holding his hands palm outward before him, and walking in the manner of a blind man.

VIII

The immovable Dan again sat unaddressed in the midst of comrades, who did not joke aloud. The dampness of the usual morning fog seemed to make the little camp-fires furious.

Suddenly a cry arose in the streets, a shout of amazement and delight. The men making breakfast at the fire looked up quickly. They broke forth in clamorous exclamation: "Well! Of all things! Dan! Dan! Look who's coming! Oh, Dan!"

Dan the silent raised his eyes and saw a man, with a bandage of the size of a helmet about his head, receiving a furious demonstration from the company. He was shaking hands, and explaining, and haranguing to a high degree.

Dan started. His face of bronze flushed to his temples. He seemed about to leap from the ground, but then suddenly he sank back, and resumed his impassive gazing.

The men were in a flurry. They looked from one to the other. "Dan!
Look! See who's coming!" some cried again. "Dan! Look!"

He scowled at last, and moved his shoulders sullenly. "Well, don't I know it?"

But they could not be convinced that his eyes were in service. "Dan, why can't you look! See who's coming!"

He made a gesture then of irritation and rage. "Curse it! Don't I know it?"

The man with a bandage of the size of a helmet moved forward, always shaking hands and explaining. At times his glance wandered to Dan, who saw with his eyes riveted.

After a series of shiftings, it occurred naturally that the man with the bandage was very near to the man who saw the flames. He paused, and there was a little silence. Finally he said: "Hello, Dan."

"Hello, Billie."

THREE MIRACULOUS SOLDIERS

I

The girl was in the front room on the second floor, peering through the blinds. It was the "best room." There was a very new rag carpet on the floor. The edges of it had been dyed with alternate stripes of red and green. Upon the wooden mantel there were two little puffy figures in clay—a shepherd and a shepherdess probably. A triangle of pink and white wool hung carefully over the edge of this shelf. Upon the bureau there was nothing at all save a spread newspaper, with edges folded to make it into a mat. The quilts and sheets had been removed from the bed and were stacked upon a chair. The pillows and the great feather mattress were muffled and tumbled until they resembled great dumplings. The picture of a man terribly leaden in complexion hung in an oval frame on one white wall and steadily confronted the bureau.

From between the slats of the blinds she had a view of the road as it wended across the meadow to the woods, and again where it reappeared crossing the hill, half a mile away. It lay yellow and warm in the summer sunshine. From the long grasses of the meadow came the rhythmic click of the insects. Occasional frogs in the hidden brook made a peculiar chug-chug sound, as if somebody throttled them. The leaves of the wood swung in gentle winds. Through the dark-green branches of the pines that grew in the front yard could be seen the mountains, far to the south-east, and inexpressibly blue.

Mary's eyes were fastened upon the little streak of road that appeared on the distant hill. Her face was flushed with excitement, and the hand which stretched in a strained pose on the sill trembled because of the nervous shaking of the wrist. The pines whisked their green needles with a soft, hissing sound against the house.

At last the girl turned from the window and went to the head of the stairs. "Well, I just know they're coming, anyhow," she cried argumentatively to the depths.

A voice from below called to her angrily: "They ain't. We've never seen one yet. They never come into this neighbourhood. You just come down here and 'tend to your work insteader watching for soldiers."

"Well, ma, I just know they're coming."

A voice retorted with the shrillness and mechanical violence of occasional housewives. The girl swished her skirts defiantly and returned to the window.

Upon the yellow streak of road that lay across the hillside there now was a handful of black dots-horsemen. A cloud of dust floated away. The girl flew to the head of the stairs and whirled down into the kitchen.

"They're coming! They're coming!"

It was as if she had cried "Fire!" Her mother had been peeling potatoes while seated comfortably at the table. She sprang to her feet. "No-it can't be-how you know it's them-where?" The stubby knife fell from her hand, and two or three curls of potato skin dropped from her apron to the floor.

The girl turned and dashed upstairs. Her mother followed, gasping for breath, and yet contriving to fill the air with questions, reproach, and remonstrance. The girl was already at the window, eagerly pointing. "There! There! See 'em! See 'em!"

Rushing to the window, the mother scanned for an instant the road on the hill. She crouched back with a groan. "It's them, sure as the world! It's them!" She waved her hands in despairing gestures.

The black dots vanished into the wood. The girl at the window was quivering and her eyes were shining like water when the sun flashes. "Hush! They're in the woods! They'll be here directly." She bent down and intently watched the green archway whence the road emerged. "Hush! I hear 'em coming," she swiftly whispered to her mother, for the elder woman had dropped dolefully upon the mattress and was sobbing. And, indeed, the girl could hear the quick, dull trample of horses. She stepped aside with sudden apprehension, but she bent her head forward in order to still scan the road.

"Here they are!"

There was something very theatrical in the sudden appearance of these men to the eyes of the girl. It was as if a scene had been shifted. The forest suddenly disclosed them —a dozen brown-faced troopers in blue-galloping.

"Oh, look!" breathed the girl. Her mouth was puckered into an expression of strange fascination, as if she had expected to see the troopers change into demons and gloat at her. She was at last looking upon those curious beings who rode down from the North-those men of legend and colossal tale-they who were possessed of such marvellous hallucinations.

The little troop rode in silence. At its head was a youthful fellow with some dim yellow stripes upon his arm. In his right hand he held his carbine, slanting upward, with the stock resting upon his knee. He was absorbed in a scrutiny of the country before him.

At the heels of the sergeant the rest of the squad rode in thin column, with creak of leather and tinkle of steel and tin. The girl scanned the faces of the horsemen, seeming astonished vaguely to find them of the type she knew.

The lad at the head of the troop comprehended the house and its environments in two glances. He did not check the long, swinging stride of his horse. The troopers glanced for a moment like casual tourists, and then returned to their study of the region in front. The heavy thudding of the hoofs became a small noise. The dust, hanging in sheets, slowly sank.

The sobs of the woman on the bed took form in words which, while strong in their note of calamity, yet expressed a querulous mental reaching for some near thing to blame. "And it'll be lucky fer us if we ain't both butchered in our sleep-plundering and running off horses-old Santo's gone-you see if he ain't —plundering —"

"But, ma," said the girl, perplexed and terrified in the same moment, "they've gone."

"Oh, but they'll come back!" cried the mother, without pausing her wail. "They'll come back-trust them for that-running off horses. O John, John! why did you, why did you?" She suddenly lifted herself and sat rigid, staring at her daughter. "Mary," she said in tragic whisper, "the kitchen door isn't locked!" Already she was bended forward to listen, her mouth agape, her eyes fixed upon her daughter.

"Mother," faltered the girl.

Her mother again whispered, "The kitchen door isn't locked."

Motionless and mute they stared into each other's eyes.

At last the girl quavered, "We better-we better go and lock it." The mother nodded. Hanging arm in arm they stole across the floor toward the head of the stairs. A board of the floor creaked. They halted and exchanged a look of dumb agony.

At last they reached the head of the stairs. From the kitchen came the bass humming of the kettle and frequent sputterings and cracklings from the fire. These sounds were sinister. The mother and the girl stood incapable of movement. "There's somebody down there!" whispered the elder woman.

Finally, the girl made a gesture of resolution. She twisted her arm from her mother's hands and went two steps downward. She addressed the kitchen: "Who's there?" Her tone was intended to be dauntless. It rang so dramatically in the silence that a sudden new panic seized them as if the suspected presence in the kitchen had cried out to them. But the girl ventured again: "Is there anybody there?" No reply was made save by the kettle and the fire.

With a stealthy tread the girl continued her journey. As she neared the last step the fire crackled explosively and the girl screamed. But the mystic presence had not swept around the corner to grab her, so she dropped to a seat on the step and laughed. "It was-was only the-the fire," she said, stammering hysterically.

Then she arose with sudden fortitude and cried: "Why, there isn't anybody there! I know there isn't." She marched down into the kitchen. In her face was dread, as if she half expected to confront something, but the room was empty. She cried joyously: "There's nobody here! Come on down, ma." She ran to the kitchen door and locked it.

The mother came down to the kitchen. "Oh, dear, what a fright I've had! It's given me the sick headache. I know it has."

"Oh, ma," said the girl.

"I know it has—I know it. Oh, if your father was only here! He'd settle those Yankees mighty quick-he'd settle 'em! Two poor helpless women—"

"Why, ma, what makes you act so? The Yankees haven't—"

"Oh, they'll be back-they'll be back. Two poor helpless women! Your father and your uncle Asa and Bill off galavanting around and fighting when they ought to be protecting their home! That's the kind of men they are. Didn't I say to your father just before he left—"

"Ma," said the girl, coming suddenly from the window, "the barn door is open. I wonder if they took old Santo?"

"Oh, of course they have-of course-Mary, I don't see what we are going to do—I don't see what we are going to do."

The girl said, "Ma, I'm going to see if they took old Santo."

"Mary," cried the mother, "don't you dare!"

"But think of poor old Sant, ma."

"Never you mind old Santo. We're lucky to be safe ourselves, I tell you. Never mind old Santo. Don't you dare to go out there, Mary-Mary!"

The girl had unlocked the door and stepped out upon the porch. The mother cried in despair, "Mary!"

"Why, there isn't anybody out here," the girl called in response. She stood for a moment with a curious smile upon her face as of gleeful satisfaction at her daring.

The breeze was waving the boughs of the apple trees. A rooster with an air importantly courteous was conducting three hens upon a foraging tour. On the hillside at the rear of the grey old barn the red leaves of a creeper flamed amid the summer foliage. High in the sky clouds rolled toward the north. The girl swung impulsively from the little stoop and ran toward the barn.

The great door was open, and the carved peg which usually performed the office of a catch lay on the ground. The girl could not see into the barn because of the heavy shadows. She paused in a listening attitude and heard a horse munching placidly. She gave a cry of delight and sprang across the threshold. Then she suddenly shrank back and gasped. She had confronted three men in grey seated upon the floor with their legs stretched out and their backs against Santo's manger. Their dust-covered countenances were expanded in grins.

II

As Mary sprang backward and screamed, one of the calm men in grey, still grinning, announced, "I knowed you'd holler." Sitting there comfortably the three surveyed her with amusement.

Mary caught her breath, throwing her hand up to her throat. "Oh!" she said, "you-you frightened me!"

"We're sorry, lady, but couldn't help it no way," cheerfully responded another. "I knowed you'd holler when I seen you coming yere, but I raikoned we couldn't help it no way. We hain't a-troubling this yere barn, I don't guess. We been doing some mighty tall sleeping yere. We done woke when them Yanks loped past."

"Where did you come from? Did-did you escape from the-the Yankees?" The girl still stammered and trembled.

The three soldiers laughed. "No, m'm. No, m'm. They never cotch us. We was in a muss down the road yere about two mile. And Bill yere they gin it to him in the arm, kehplunk. And they pasted me thar, too. Curious, And Sim yere, he didn't get nothing, but they chased us all quite a little piece, and we done lose track of our boys."

"Was it-was it those who passed here just now? Did they chase you?"

The men in grey laughed again. "What-them? No, indeedee! There was a mighty big swarm of Yanks and a mighty big swarm of our boys, too. What-that little passel? No, m'm."

She became calm enough to scan them more attentively. They were much begrimed and very dusty. Their grey clothes were tattered. Splashed mud had dried upon them in reddish spots. It appeared, too, that the men had not shaved in many days. In the hats there was a singular diversity. One soldier wore the little blue cap of the Northern infantry, with corps emblem and regimental number; one wore a great slouch hat with a wide hole in the crown; and the other wore no hat at all. The left sleeve of one man and the right sleeve of another had been slit, and the arms were neatly bandaged with clean cloths. "These hain't no more than two little cuts," explained one. "We stopped up yere to Mis' Leavitts-she said her name was-and she bind them for us. Bill yere, he had the thirst come on him. And the fever too. We — —"

"Did you ever see my father in the army?" asked Mary. "John Hinckson-his name is."

The three soldiers grinned again, but they replied kindly: "No, m'm. No, m'm, we hain't never. What is he-in the cavalry?"

"No," said the girl. "He and my uncle Asa and my cousin-his name is Bill Parker-they are all with Longstreet-they call him."

"Oh," said the soldiers. "Longstreet? Oh, they're a good smart ways from yere. 'Way off up nawtheast. There hain't nothing but cavalry down yere. They're in the infantry, probably."

"We haven't heard anything from them for days and days," said Mary.

"Oh, they're all right in the infantry," said one man, to be consoling. "The infantry don't do much fighting. They go bellering out in a big swarm and only a few of 'em get hurt. But if they was in the cavalry-the cavalry —"

Mary interrupted him without intention. "Are you hungry?" she asked.

The soldiers looked at each other, struck by some sudden and singular shame. They hung their heads. "No, m'm," replied one at last.

Santo, in his stall, was tranquilly chewing and chewing. Sometimes he looked benevolently over at them. He was an old horse, and there was something about his eyes and his forelock which created the impression that he wore spectacles. Mary went and patted his nose. "Well, if you are hungry, I can get you something," she told the men. "Or you might come to the house."

"We wouldn't dast go to the house," said one. "That passel of Yanks was only a scouting crowd, most like. Just an advance. More coming, likely."

"Well, I can bring you something," cried the girl eagerly. "Won't you let me bring you something?"

"Well," said a soldier with embarrassment, "we hain't had much. If you could bring us a little snack-like-just a snack-we'd —"

Without waiting for him to cease, the girl turned toward the door. But before she had reached it she stopped abruptly. "Listen!" she whispered. Her form was bent forward, her head turned and lowered, her hand extended toward the men, in a command for silence.

They could faintly hear the thudding of many hoofs, the clank of arms, and frequent calling voices.

"By cracky, it's the Yanks!" The soldiers scrambled to their feet and came toward the door. "I knowed that first crowd was only an advance."

The girl and the three men peered from the shadows of the barn. The view of the road was intersected by tree trunks and a little henhouse. However, they could see many horsemen streaming down the road. The horsemen were in blue. "Oh, hide-hide-hide!" cried the girl, with a sob in her voice.

"Wait a minute," whispered a grey soldier excitedly. "Maybe they're going along by. No, by thunder, they hain't! They're halting. Scoot, boys!"

They made a noiseless dash into the dark end of the barn. The girl, standing by the door, heard them break forth an instant later in clamorous whispers. "Where'll we hide? Where'll we hide? There hain't a place to hide!" The girl turned and glanced wildly about the barn. It seemed true. The stock of hay had grown low under Santo's endless munching, and from occasional levyings by passing troopers in grey. The poles of the mow were barely covered, save in one corner where there was a little bunch.

The girl espied the great feed-box. She ran to it and lifted the lid. "Here! here!" she called. "Get in here."

They had been tearing noiselessly around the rear part of the barn. At her low call they came and plunged at the box. They did not all get in at the same moment without a good deal of a tangle. The wounded men gasped and muttered, but they at last were flopped down on the layer of feed which covered the bottom. Swiftly and softly the girl lowered the lid and then turned like a flash toward the door.

No one appeared there, so she went close to survey the situation. The troopers had dismounted, and stood in silence by their horses.

A grey-bearded man, whose red cheeks and nose shone vividly above the whiskers, was strolling about with two or three others. They wore double-breasted coats, and faded yellow sashes were wound under their black leather sword-belts. The grey-bearded soldier was apparently giving orders, pointing here and there.

Mary tiptoed to the feed-box. "They've all got off their horses," she said to it. A finger projected from a knot-hole near the top, and said to her very plainly, "Come closer." She obeyed, and then a muffled voice could be heard: "Scoot for the house, lady, and if we don't see you again, why, much obliged for what you done."

"Good-bye," she said to the feed-box.

She made two attempts to walk dauntlessly from the barn, but each time she faltered and failed just before she reached the point where she could have been seen by the blue-coated troopers. At last, however, she made a sort of a rush forward and went out into the bright sunshine.

The group of men in double-breasted coats wheeled in her direction at the instant. The grey-bearded officer forgot to lower his arm which had been stretched forth in giving an order.

She felt that her feet were touching the ground in a most unnatural manner. Her bearing, she believed, was suddenly grown awkward and ungainly. Upon her face she thought that this sentence was plainly written: "There are three men hidden in the feed-box."

The grey-bearded soldier came toward her. She stopped; she seemed about to run away. But the soldier doffed his little blue cap and looked amiable. "You live here, I presume?" he said.

"Yes," she answered.

"Well, we are obliged to camp here for the night, and as we've got two wounded men with us I don't suppose you'd mind if we put them in the barn."

"In-in the barn?"

He became aware that she was agitated. He smiled assuringly. "You needn't be frightened. We won't hurt anything around here. You'll all be safe enough."

The girl balanced on one foot and swung the other to and fro in the grass. She was looking down at it. "But-but I don't think ma would like it if-if you took the barn."

The old officer laughed. "Wouldn't she?" said he. "That's so. Maybe she wouldn't." He reflected for a time and then decided cheerfully: "Well, we will have to go ask her, anyhow. Where is she? In the house?"

"Yes," replied the girl, "she's in the house. She-she'll be scared to death when she sees you!"

"Well, you go and ask her then," said the soldier, always wearing a benign smile. "You go ask her and then come and tell me."

When the girl pushed open the door and entered the kitchen, she found it empty. "Ma!" she called softly. There was no answer. The kettle still was humming its low song. The knife and the curl of potato-skin lay on the floor.

She went to her mother's room and entered timidly. The new, lonely aspect of the house shook her nerves. Upon the bed was a confusion of coverings. "Ma!" called the girl, quaking in fear that her mother was not there to reply. But there was a sudden turmoil of the quilts, and her mother's head was thrust forth. "Mary!" she cried, in what seemed to be a supreme astonishment, "I thought —I thought — —"

"Oh, ma," blurted the girl, "there's over a thousand Yankees in the yard, and I've hidden three of our men in the feed-box!"

The elder woman, however, upon the appearance of her daughter had begun to thrash hysterically about on the bed and wail.

"Ma!" the girl exclaimed, "and now they want to use the barn-and our men in the feed-box! What shall I do, ma? What shall I do?"

Her mother did not seem to hear, so absorbed was she in her grievous flounderings and tears. "Ma!" appealed the girl. "Ma!"

For a moment Mary stood silently debating, her lips apart, her eyes fixed. Then she went to the kitchen window and peeked.

The old officer and the others were staring up the road. She went to another window in order to get a proper view of the road, and saw that they were gazing at a small body of horsemen approaching at a trot and raising much dust. Presently she recognised them as the squad that had passed the house earlier, for the young man with the dim yellow chevron still rode at their head. An unarmed horseman in grey was receiving their close attention.

As they came very near to the house she darted to the first window again. The grey-bearded officer was smiling a fine broad smile of satisfaction. "So you got him?" he called out. The young sergeant sprang from his horse and his brown hand moved in a salute. The girl could not hear his reply. She saw the unarmed horseman in grey stroking a very black moustache and looking about him coolly and with an interested air. He appeared so indifferent that she did not understand he was a prisoner until she heard the grey-beard call out: "Well, put him in the barn. He'll be safe there, I guess." A party of troopers moved with the prisoner toward the barn.

The girl made a sudden gesture of horror, remembering the three men in the feed-box.

III

The busy troopers in blue scurried about the long lines of stamping horses. Men crooked their backs and perspired in order to rub with cloths or bunches of grass these slim equine legs, upon whose splendid machinery they depended so greatly. The lips of the horses were still wet and frothy from the steel bars which had wrenched at their mouths all day. Over their backs and about their noses sped the talk of the men.

"Moind where yer plug is steppin', Finerty! Keep 'im aff me!"

"An ould elephant! He shtrides like a school-house."

"Bill's little mar' —she was plum beat when she come in with Crawford's crowd."

"Crawford's the hardest-ridin' cavalryman in the army. An' he don't use up a horse, neither— much. They stay fresh when the others are most a-droppin'."

"Finerty, will yeh moind that cow a yours?"

Amid a bustle of gossip and banter, the horses retained their air of solemn rumination, twisting their lower jaws from side to side and sometimes rubbing noses dreamfully.

Over in front of the barn three troopers sat talking comfortably. Their carbines were leaned against the wall. At their side and outlined in the black of the open door stood a sentry, his weapon resting in the hollow of his arm. Four horses, saddled and accoutred, were conferring with their heads close together. The four bridle-reins were flung over a post.

Upon the calm green of the land, typical in every way of peace, the hues of war brought thither by the troops shone strangely. Mary, gazing curiously, did not feel that she was contemplating a familiar scene. It was no longer the home acres. The new blue, steel, and faded yellow thoroughly dominated the old green and brown. She could hear the voices of the men, and it seemed from their tone that they had camped there for years. Everything with them was usual. They had taken possession of the landscape in such a way that even the old marks appeared strange and formidable to the girl.

Mary had intended to go and tell the commander in blue that her mother did not wish his men to use the barn at all, but she paused when she heard him speak to the sergeant. She thought she perceived then that it mattered little to him what her mother wished, and that an objection by her or by anybody would be futile. She saw the soldiers conduct the prisoner in grey into the barn, and for a long time she watched the three chatting guards and the pondering sentry. Upon her mind in desolate weight was the recollection of the three men in the feed-box.

It seemed to her that in a case of this description it was her duty to be a heroine. In all the stories she had read when at boarding-school in Pennsylvania, the girl characters, confronted with such difficulties, invariably did hair-breadth things. True, they were usually bent upon rescuing and recovering their lovers, and neither the calm man in grey, nor any of the three in the feed-box, was lover of hers, but then a real heroine would not pause over this minor question. Plainly a heroine would take measures to rescue the four men. If she did not at least make the attempt, she would be false to those carefully constructed ideals which were the accumulation of years of dreaming.

But the situation puzzled her. There was the barn with only one door, and with four armed troopers in front of this door, one of them with his back to the rest of the world, engaged, no doubt, in a steadfast contemplation of the calm man, and incidentally, of the feed-box. She knew, too, that even if she should open the kitchen door, three heads, and perhaps four, would turn casually in her direction. Their ears were real ears.

Heroines, she knew, conducted these matters with infinite precision and despatch. They severed the hero's bonds, cried a dramatic sentence, and stood between him and his enemies until he had run far enough away. She saw well, however, that even should she achieve all things up to the point where she might take glorious stand between the escaping and the pursuers, those grim troopers in blue would not pause. They would run around her, make a circuit. One by one she saw the gorgeous contrivances and expedients of fiction fall before the plain, homely difficulties of this situation. They were of no service. Sadly, ruefully, she thought of the calm man and of the contents of the feed-box.

The sum of her invention was that she could sally forth to the commander of the blue cavalry, and confessing to him that there were three of her friends and his enemies secreted in the feed-box, pray him to let them depart unmolested. But she was beginning to believe the old greybeard to be a bear. It was hardly probable that he would give this plan his support. It was more probable that he and some of his men would at once descend upon the feed-box and confiscate her three friends. The difficulty with her idea was that she could not learn its value without trying it, and then in case of failure it would be too late for remedies and other plans. She reflected that war made men very unreasonable.

All that she could do was to stand at the window and mournfully regard the barn. She admitted this to herself with a sense of deep humiliation. She was not, then, made of that fine stuff, that mental satin, which enabled some other beings to be of such mighty service to the distressed. She was defeated by a barn with one door, by four men with eight eyes and eight ears-trivialities that would not impede the real heroine.

The vivid white light of broad day began slowly to fade. Tones of grey came upon the fields, and the shadows were of lead. In this more sombre atmosphere the fires built by the troops down in the far end of the orchard grew more brilliant, becoming spots of crimson colour in the dark grove.

The girl heard a fretting voice from her mother's room. "Mary!" She hastily obeyed the call. She perceived that she had quite forgotten her mother's existence in this time of excitement.

The elder woman still lay upon the bed. Her face was flushed and perspiration stood amid new wrinkles upon her forehead. Weaving wild glances from side to side, she began to whimper. "Oh, I'm just sick —I'm just sick! Have those men gone yet? Have they gone?"

The girl smoothed a pillow carefully for her mother's head. "No, ma.
They're here yet. But they haven't hurt anything-it doesn't seem. Will
I get you something to eat?"

Her mother gestured her away with the impatience of the ill. "No-no-just don't bother me. My head is splitting, and you know very well that nothing can be done for me when I get one of these spells. It's trouble-that's what makes them. When are those men going? Look here, don't you go 'way. You stick close to the house now."

"I'll stay right here," said the girl. She sat in the gloom and listened to her mother's incessant moaning. When she attempted to move, her mother cried out at her. When she desired to ask if she might try to alleviate the pain, she was interrupted shortly. Somehow her sitting in passive silence within hearing of this illness seemed to contribute to her mother's relief. She assumed a posture of submission. Sometimes her mother projected questions concerning the local condition, and although she laboured to be graphic and at the same time soothing, unalarming, her form of reply was always displeasing to the sick woman, and brought forth ejaculations of angry impatience.

Eventually the woman slept in the manner of one worn from terrible labour. The girl went slowly and softly to the kitchen. When she looked from the window, she saw the four soldiers still at the barn door. In the west, the sky was yellow. Some tree-trunks intersecting it appeared black as streaks of ink. Soldiers hovered in blue clouds about the bright splendour of the fires in the orchard. There were glimmers of steel.

The girl sat in the new gloom of the kitchen and watched. The soldiers lit a lantern and hung it in the barn. Its rays made the form of the sentry seem gigantic. Horses whinnied from the orchard. There was a low hum of human voices. Sometimes small detachments of troopers rode past the front of the house. The girl heard the abrupt calls of sentries. She fetched some food and ate it from her hand, standing by the window. She was so afraid that something would occur that she barely left her post for an instant.

A picture of the interior of the barn hung vividly in her mind. She recalled the knot-holes in the boards at the rear, but she admitted that the prisoners could not escape through them. She remembered some inadequacies of the roof, but these also counted for nothing. When confronting the problem, she felt her ambitions, her ideals tumbling headlong like cottages of straw.

Once she felt that she had decided to reconnoitre at any rate. It was night; the lantern at the barn and the camp fires made everything without their circle into masses of heavy mystic blackness. She took two steps toward the door. But there she paused. Innumerable possibilities of danger had assailed her mind. She returned to the window and stood wavering. At last, she went swiftly to the door, opened it, and slid noiselessly into the darkness.

For a moment she regarded the shadows. Down in the orchard the camp fires of the troops appeared precisely like a great painting, all in reds upon a black cloth. The voices of the troopers still hummed. The girl started slowly off in the opposite direction. Her eyes were fixed in a stare; she studied the darkness in front for a moment, before she ventured upon a forward step. Unconsciously, her throat was arranged for a sudden shrill scream. High in the tree-branches she could hear the voice of the wind, a melody of the night, low and sad, the plaint of an endless, incommunicable sorrow. Her own distress, the plight of the men in grey-these near matters as well as all she had known or imagined of grief-everything was expressed in this soft mourning of the wind in the trees. At first she felt like weeping. This sound told her of human impotency and doom. Then later the trees and the wind breathed strength to her, sang of sacrifice, of dauntless effort, of hard carven faces that did not blanch when Duty came at midnight or at noon.

She turned often to scan the shadowy figures that moved from time to time in the light at the barn door. Once she trod upon a stick, and it flopped, crackling in the intolerable manner of all sticks. At this noise, however, the guards at the barn made no sign. Finally, she was where she could see the knot-holes in the rear of the structure gleaming like pieces of metal from the effect of the light within. Scarcely breathing in her excitement she glided close and applied an eye to a knot-hole. She had barely achieved one glance at the interior before she sprang back shuddering.

For the unconscious and cheerful sentry at the door was swearing away in flaming sentences, heaping one gorgeous oath upon another, making a conflagration of his description of his troop-horse. "Why," he was declaring to the calm prisoner in grey, "you ain't got a horse in your hull — — army that can run forty rod with that there little mar'!"

As in the outer darkness Mary cautiously returned to the knot-hole, the three guards in front suddenly called in low tones: "S-s-s-h!" "Quit, Pete; here comes the lieutenant." The sentry had apparently been about to resume his declamation, but at these warnings he suddenly posed in a soldierly manner.

A tall and lean officer with a smooth face entered the barn. The sentry saluted primly. The officer flashed a comprehensive glance about him. "Everything all right?"

"All right, sir."

This officer had eyes like the points of stilettos. The lines from his nose to the corners of his mouth were deep, and gave him a slightly disagreeable aspect, but somewhere in his face there was a quality of singular thoughtfulness, as of the absorbed student dealing in generalities, which was utterly in opposition to the rapacious keenness of the eyes which saw everything.

Suddenly he lifted a long finger and pointed. "What's that?"

"That? That's a feed-box, I suppose."

"What's in it?"

"I don't know. I—"

"You ought to know," said the officer sharply. He walked over to the feed-box and flung up the lid. With a sweeping gesture he reached down and scooped a handful of feed. "You ought to know what's in everything when you have prisoners in your care," he added, scowling.

During the time of this incident, the girl had nearly swooned. Her hands searched weakly over the boards for something to which to cling. With the pallor of the dying she had watched the downward sweep of the officer's arm, which after all had only brought forth a handful of feed. The result was a stupefaction of her mind. She was astonished out of her senses at this spectacle of three large men metamorphosed into a handful of feed.

IV

It is perhaps a singular thing that this absence of the three men from the feed-box at the time of the sharp lieutenant's investigation should terrify the girl more than it should joy her. That for which she had prayed had come to pass. Apparently the escape of these men in the face of every improbability had been granted her, but her dominating emotion was fright. The feed-box was a mystic and terrible machine, like some dark magician's trap. She felt it almost possible that she should see the three weird man floating spectrally away through the air. She glanced with swift apprehension behind her, and when the dazzle from the lantern's light had left her eyes, saw only the dim hillside stretched in solemn silence.

The interior of the barn possessed for her another fascination because it was now uncanny. It contained that extraordinary feed-box. When she peeped again at the knot-hole, the calm, grey prisoner was seated upon the feed-box, thumping it with his dangling, careless heels as if it were in nowise his conception of a remarkable feed-box. The sentry also stood facing it. His carbine he held in the hollow of his arm. His legs were spread apart, and he mused. From without came the low mumble of the three other troopers. The sharp lieutenant had vanished.

The trembling yellow light of the lantern caused the figures of the men to cast monstrous wavering shadows. There were spaces of gloom which shrouded ordinary things in impressive garb. The roof presented an inscrutable blackness, save where small rifts in the shingles glowed phosphorescently. Frequently old Santo put down a thunderous hoof. The heels of the prisoner made a sound like the booming of a wild kind of drum. When the men moved their heads, their eyes shone with ghoulish whiteness, and their complexions were always waxen and unreal. And there was that profoundly strange feed-box, imperturbable with its burden of fantastic mystery.

Suddenly from down near her feet the girl heard a crunching sound, a sort of a nibbling, as if some silent and very discreet terrier was at work upon the turf. She faltered back; here was no doubt another grotesque detail of this most unnatural episode. She did not run, because physically she was in the power of these events. Her feet chained her to the ground in submission to this march of terror after terror. As she stared at the spot from which this sound seemed to come, there floated through her mind a vague, sweet vision —a vision of her safe little room, in which at this hour she usually was sleeping.

The scratching continued faintly and with frequent pauses, as if the terrier was then listening. When the girl first removed her eyes from the knot-hole the scene appeared of one velvet blackness; then gradually objects loomed with a dim lustre. She could see now where the tops of the trees joined the sky and the form of the barn was before her dyed in heavy purple. She was ever about to shriek, but no sound came from her constricted throat. She gazed at the ground with the expression of countenance of one who watches the sinister-moving grass where a serpent approaches.

Dimly she saw a piece of sod wrenched free and drawn under the great foundation-beam of the barn. Once she imagined that she saw human hands, not outlined at all, but sufficient, in colour, form, or movement to make subtle suggestion.

Then suddenly a thought that illuminated the entire situation flashed in her mind like a light. The three men, late of the feed-box, were beneath the floor of the barn and were now scraping their way under this beam. She did not consider for a moment how they could come there. They were marvellous creatures. The supernatural was to be expected of them. She no longer trembled, for she was possessed upon this instant of the most unchangeable species of conviction. The evidence before her amounted to no evidence at all, but nevertheless her opinion grew in an instant from an irresponsible acorn to a rooted and immovable tree. It was as if she was on a jury.

She stooped down hastily and scanned the ground. There she indeed saw a pair of hands hauling at the dirt where the sod had been displaced. Softly, in a whisper like a breath, she said, "Hey!"

The dim hands were drawn hastily under the barn. The girl reflected for a moment. Then she stooped and whispered: "Hey! It's me!"

After a time there was a resumption of the digging. The ghostly hands began once more their cautious mining. She waited. In hollow reverberations from the interior of the barn came the frequent sounds of old Santo's lazy movements. The sentry conversed with the prisoner.

At last the girl saw a head thrust slowly from under the beam. She perceived the face of one of the miraculous soldiers from the feed-box. A pair of eyes glintered and wavered, then finally settled upon her, a pale statue of a girl. The eyes became lit with a kind of humorous greeting. An arm gestured at her.

Stooping, she breathed, "All right." The man drew himself silently back under the beam. A moment later the pair of hands resumed their cautious task. Ultimately the head and arms of the man were thrust strangely from the earth. He was lying on his back. The girl thought of the dirt in his hair. Wriggling slowly and pushing at the beam above him he forced his way out of the curious little passage. He twisted his body and raised himself upon his hands. He grinned at the girl and drew his feet carefully from under the beam. When he at last stood erect beside her, he at once began mechanically to brush the dirt from his clothes with his hands. In the barn the sentry and his prisoner were evidently engaged in an argument.

The girl and the first miraculous soldier signalled warily. It seemed that they feared that their arms would make noises in passing through the air. Their lips moved, conveying dim meanings.

In this sign-language the girl described the situation in the barn. With guarded motions, she told him of the importance of absolute stillness. He nodded, and then in the same manner he told her of his two companions under the barn floor. He informed her again of their wounded state, and wagged his head to express his despair. He contorted his face, to tell how sore were their arms; and jabbed the air mournfully, to express their remote geographical position.

This signalling was interrupted by the sound of a body being dragged or dragging itself with slow, swishing sound under the barn. The sound was too loud for safety. They rushed to the hole and began to semaphore until a shaggy head appeared with rolling eyes and quick grin.

With frantic downward motions of their arms they suppressed this grin and with it the swishing noise. In dramatic pantomime they informed this head of the terrible consequences of so much noise. The head nodded, and painfully, but with extreme care, the second man pushed and pulled himself from the hole.

In a faint whisper the first man said, "Where's Sim?"

The second man made low reply: "He's right here." He motioned reassuringly toward the hole.

When the third head appeared, a soft smile of glee came upon each face, and the mute group exchanged expressive glances.

When they all stood together, free from this tragic barn, they breathed a long sigh that was contemporaneous with another smile and another exchange of glances.

One of the men tiptoed to a knot-hole and peered into the barn. The sentry was at that moment speaking. "Yes, we know 'em all. There isn't a house in this region that we don't know who is in it most of the time. We collar 'em once in a while—like we did you. Now, that house out yonder, we ——"

The man suddenly left the knot-hole and returned to the others. Upon his face, dimly discerned, there was an indication that he had made an astonishing discovery. The others questioned him with their eyes, but he simply waved an arm to express his inability to speak at that spot. He led them back toward the hill, prowling carefully. At a safe distance from the barn he halted, and as they grouped eagerly about him, he exploded in an intense undertone: "Why, that-that's Cap'n Sawyer they got in yonder."

"Cap'n Sawyer!" incredulously whispered the other men.

But the girl had something to ask. "How did you get out of that feed-box?" He smiled. "Well, when you put us in there, we was just in a minute when we allowed it wasn't a mighty safe place, and we allowed we'd get out. And we did. We skedaddled 'round and 'round until it 'peared like we was going to get cotched, and then we flung ourselves down in the cow-stalls where it's low-like —just dirt floor-and then we just naturally went a-whooping under the barn floor when the Yanks come. And we didn't know Cap'n Sawyer by his voice nohow. We heard 'im discoursing, and we allowed it was a mighty pert man, but we didn't know that it was him. No, m'm."

These three men, so recently from a situation of peril, seemed suddenly to have dropped all thought of it. They stood with sad faces looking at the barn. They seemed to be making no plans at all to reach a place of more complete safety. They were halted and stupefied by some unknown calamity.

"How do you raikon they cotch him, Sim?" one whispered mournfully.

"I don't know," replied another in the same tone.

Another with a low snarl expressed in two words his opinion of the methods of Fate: "Oh, hell!"

The three men started then as if simultaneously stung, and gazed at the young girl who stood silently near them. The man who had sworn began to make agitated apology: "Pardon, miss! 'Pon my soul, I clean forgot you was by. 'Deed, and I wouldn't swear like that if I had knowed. 'Deed, I wouldn't."

The girl did not seem to hear him. She was staring at the barn.

Suddenly she turned and whispered, "Who is he?"

"He's Cap'n Sawyer, m'm," they told her sorrowfully. "He's our own cap'n. He's been in command of us yere since a long time. He's got folks about yere. Raikon they cotch him while he was a-visiting."

She was still for a time, and then, awed, she said: "Will they-will they hang him?"

"No, m'm. Oh no, m'm. Don't raikon no such thing. No, m'm."

The group became absorbed in a contemplation of the barn. For a time no one moved nor spoke. At last the girl was aroused by slight sounds, and turning, she perceived that the three men who had so recently escaped from the barn were now advancing toward it.

V

The girl, waiting in the darkness, expected to hear the sudden crash and uproar of a fight as soon as the three creeping men should reach the barn. She reflected in an agony upon the swift disaster that would befall any enterprise so desperate. She had an impulse to beg them to come away. The grass rustled in silken movements as she sped toward the barn.

When she arrived, however, she gazed about her bewildered. The men were gone. She searched with her eyes, trying to detect some moving thing, but she could see nothing.

Left alone again, she began to be afraid of the night. The great stretches of darkness could hide crawling dangers. From sheer desire to see a human, she was obliged to peep again at the knot-hole. The sentry had apparently wearied of talking. Instead, he was reflecting. The prisoner still sat on the feed-box, moodily staring at the floor. The girl felt in one way that she was looking at a ghastly group in wax. She started when the old horse put down an echoing hoof. She wished the men would speak; their silence re-enforced the strange aspect. They might have been two dead men.

The girl felt impelled to look at the corner of the interior where were the cow-stalls. There was no light there save the appearance of peculiar grey haze which marked the track of the dimming rays of the lantern. All else was sombre shadow. At last she saw something move there. It might have been as small as a rat, or it might have been a part of something as large as a man. At any rate, it proclaimed that something in that spot was alive. At one time she saw it plainly, and at other times it vanished, because her fixture of gaze caused her occasionally to greatly tangle and blur those peculiar shadows and faint lights. At last, however, she perceived a human head. It was monstrously dishevelled and wild. It moved slowly forward until its glance could fall upon the prisoner and then upon the sentry. The wandering rays caused the eyes to glitter like silver. The girl's heart pounded so that she put her hand over it.

The sentry and the prisoner remained immovably waxen, and over in the gloom the head thrust from the floor watched them with its silver eyes.

Finally, the prisoner slipped from the feed-box, and raising his arms, yawned at great length. "Oh, well," he remarked, "you boys will get a good licking if you fool around here much longer. That's some satisfaction, anyhow, even if you did bag me. You'll get a good walloping." He reflected for a moment, and decided: "I'm sort of willing to be captured if you fellows only get a d——d good licking for being so smart."

The sentry looked up and smiled a superior smile. "Licking, hey? Nixey!" He winked exasperatingly at the prisoner. "You fellows are not fast enough, my boy. Why didn't you lick us at ——? and at ——? and at ——?" He named some of the great battles.

To this the captive officer blurted in angry astonishment: "Why, we did!"

The sentry winked again in profound irony. "Yes, I know you did. Of course. You whipped us, didn't you? Fine kind of whipping that was! Why, we——"

He suddenly ceased, smitten mute by a sound that broke the stillness of the night. It was the sharp crack of a distant shot that made wild echoes among the hills. It was instantly followed by the hoarse cry of a human voice, a far-away yell of warning, singing of surprise, peril, fear of death. A moment later there was a distant, fierce spattering of shots. The sentry and the prisoner stood facing each other, their lips apart, listening.

The orchard at that instant awoke to sudden tumult. There were the thud and scramble and scamper of feet, the mellow, swift clash of arms, men's voices in question, oath, command, hurried and unhurried, resolute and frantic. A horse sped along the road at a raging gallop. A loud voice shouted, "What is it, Ferguson?" Another voice yelled something incoherent. There was a sharp, discordant chorus of command. An uproarious volley suddenly rang from the orchard. The prisoner in grey moved from his intent, listening attitude. Instantly the eyes of the sentry blazed, and he said with a new and terrible sternness: "Stand where you are!"

The prisoner trembled in his excitement. Expressions of delight and triumph bubbled to his lips. "A surprise, by Gawd! Now-now, you'll see!"

The sentry stolidly swung his carbine to his shoulder. He sighted carefully along the barrel until it pointed at the prisoner's head, about at his nose. "Well, I've got you, anyhow. Remember that! Don't move!"

The prisoner could not keep his arms from nervously gesturing. "I won't; but — —"

"And shut your mouth!"

The three comrades of the sentry flung themselves into view.

"Pete-devil of a row! —can you — —"

"I've got him," said the sentry calmly and without moving. It was as if the barrel of the carbine rested on piers of stone. The three comrades turned and plunged into the darkness.

In the orchard it seemed as if two gigantic animals were engaged in a mad, floundering encounter, snarling, howling in a whirling chaos of noise and motion. In the barn the prisoner and his guard faced each other in silence.

As for the girl at the knot-hole, the sky had fallen at the beginning of this clamour. She would not have been astonished to see the stars swinging from their abodes, and the vegetation, the barn, all blow away. It was the end of everything, the grand universal murder. When two of the three miraculous soldiers who formed the original feed-box corps emerged in detail from the hole under the beam, and slid away into the darkness, she did no more than glance at them.

Suddenly she recollected the head with silver eyes. She started forward and again applied her eyes to the knot-hole. Even with the din resounding from the orchard, from up the road and down the road, from the heavens and from the deep earth, the central fascination was this mystic head. There, to her, was the dark god of the tragedy.

The prisoner in grey at this moment burst into a laugh that was no more than a hysterical gurgle. "Well, you can't hold that gun out for ever! Pretty soon you'll have to lower it."

The sentry's voice sounded slightly muffled, for his cheek was pressed against the weapon. "I won't be tired for some time yet."

The girl saw the head slowly rise, the eyes fixed upon the sentry's face. A tall, black figure slunk across the cow-stalls and vanished back of old Santo's quarters. She knew what was to come to pass. She knew this grim thing was upon a terrible mission, and that it would reappear again at the head of the little passage between Santo's stall and the wall, almost at the sentry's elbow; and yet when she saw a faint indication as of a form crouching there, a scream from an utterly new alarm almost escaped her.

The sentry's arms, after all, were not of granite. He moved restively. At last he spoke in his even, unchanging tone: "Well, I guess you'll have to climb into that feed-box. Step back and lift the lid."

"Why, you don't mean — —"

"Step back!"

The girl felt a cry of warning arising to her lips as she gazed at this sentry. She noted every detail of his facial expression. She saw, moreover, his mass of brown hair bunching disgracefully about his ears, his clear eyes lit now with a hard, cold light, his forehead puckered in a mighty scowl, the ring upon the third finger of the left hand. "Oh, they won't kill him! Surely they won't kill him!" The noise of the fight in the orchard was the loud music, the thunder and lightning, the rioting of the tempest which people love during the critical scene of a tragedy.

When the prisoner moved back in reluctant obedience, he faced for an instant the entrance of the little passage, and what he saw there must have been written swiftly, graphically in his eyes. And the sentry read it and knew then that he was upon the threshold of his death. In a fraction of time, certain information went from the grim thing in the passage to the prisoner, and from the prisoner to the sentry. But at that instant the black formidable figure arose, towered, and made its leap. A new shadow flashed across the floor when the blow was struck.

As for the girl at the knot-hole, when she returned to sense she found herself standing with clenched hands and screaming with her might.

As if her reason had again departed from her, she ran around the barn, in at the door, and flung herself sobbing beside the body of the soldier in blue.

The uproar of the fight became at last coherent, inasmuch as one party was giving shouts of supreme exultation. The firing no longer sounded in crashes; it was now expressed in spiteful crackles, the last words of the combat, spoken with feminine vindictiveness.

Presently there was a thud of flying feet. A grimy, panting, red-faced mob of troopers in blue plunged into the barn, became instantly frozen to attitudes of amazement and rage, and then roared in one great chorus: "He's gone!"

The girl who knelt beside the body upon the floor turned toward them her lamenting eyes and cried: "He's not dead, is he? He can't be dead?"

They thronged forward. The sharp lieutenant who had been so particular about the feed-box knelt by the side of the girl, and laid his head against the chest of the prostrate soldier. "Why, no," he said, rising and looking at the man. "He's all right. Some of you boys throw some water on him."

"Are you sure?" demanded the girl feverishly.

"Of course! He'll be better after awhile."

"Oh!" said she softly, and then looked down at the sentry. She started to arise, and the lieutenant reached down and hoisted rather awkwardly at her arm.

"Don't you worry about him. He's all right."

She turned her face with its curving lips and shining eyes once more toward the unconscious soldier upon the floor. The troopers made a lane to the door, the lieutenant bowed, the girl vanished.

"Queer," said a young officer. "Girl very clearly worst kind of rebel, and yet she falls to weeping and wailing like mad over one of her enemies. Be around in the morning with all sorts of doctoring-you see if she ain't. Queer."

The sharp lieutenant shrugged his shoulders. After reflection he shrugged his shoulders again. He said: "War changes many things; but it doesn't change everything, thank God!"

A MYSTERY OF HEROISM

The dark uniforms of the men were so coated with dust from the incessant wrestling of the two armies that the regiment almost seemed a part of the clay bank which shielded them from the shells. On the top of the hill a battery was arguing in tremendous roars with some other guns, and to the eye of the infantry, the artillerymen, the guns, the caissons, the horses, were distinctly outlined upon the blue sky. When a piece was fired, a red streak as round as a log flashed low in the heavens, like a monstrous bolt of lightning. The men of the battery wore white duck trousers, which somehow emphasised their legs: and when they ran and crowded in little groups at the bidding of the shouting officers, it was more impressive than usual to the infantry.

Fred Collins, of A Company, was saying: "Thunder, I wisht I had a drink. Ain't there any water round here?" Then, somebody yelled: "There goes th' bugler!"

As the eyes of half the regiment swept in one machine-like movement, there was an instant's picture of a horse in a great convulsive leap of a death-wound and a rider leaning back with a crooked arm and spread fingers before his face. On the ground was the crimson terror of an exploding shell, with fibres of flame that seemed like lances. A glittering bugle swung clear of the rider's back as fell headlong the horse and the man. In the air was an odour as from a conflagration.

Sometimes they of the infantry looked down at a fair little meadow which spread at their feet. Its long, green grass was rippling gently in a breeze. Beyond it was the grey form of a house half torn to pieces by shells and by the busy axes of soldiers who had pursued firewood. The line of an old fence was now dimly marked by long weeds and by an occasional post. A shell had blown the well-house to fragments. Little lines of grey smoke ribboning upward from some embers indicated the place where had stood the barn.

From beyond a curtain of green woods there came the sound of some stupendous scuffle, as if two animals of the size of islands were fighting. At a distance there were occasional appearances of swift-moving men, horses, batteries, flags, and, with the crashing of infantry volleys were heard, often, wild and frenzied cheers. In the midst of it all Smith and Ferguson, two privates of A Company, were engaged in a heated discussion, which involved the greatest questions of the national existence.

The battery on the hill presently engaged in a frightful duel. The white legs of the gunners scampered this way and that way, and the officers redoubled their shouts. The guns, with their demeanours of stolidity and courage, were typical of something infinitely self-possessed in this clamour of death that swirled around the hill.

One of a "swing" team was suddenly smitten quivering to the ground, and his maddened brethren dragged his torn body in their struggle to escape from this turmoil and danger. A young soldier astride one of the leaders swore and fumed in his saddle, and furiously jerked at the bridle. An officer screamed out an order so violently that his voice broke and ended the sentence in a falsetto shriek.

The leading company of the infantry regiment was somewhat exposed, and the colonel ordered it moved more fully under the shelter of the hill. There was the clank of steel against steel.

A lieutenant of the battery rode down and passed them, holding his right arm carefully in his left hand. And it was as if this arm was not at all a part of him, but belonged to another man. His sober and reflective charger went slowly. The officer's face was grimy and perspiring, and his uniform was tousled as if he had been in direct grapple with an enemy. He smiled grimly when the men stared at him. He turned his horse toward the meadow.

Collins, of A Company, said: "I wisht I had a drink. I bet there's water in that there ol' well yonder!"

"Yes; but how you goin' to git it?"

For the little meadow which intervened was now suffering a terrible onslaught of shells. Its green and beautiful calm had vanished utterly. Brown earth was being flung in monstrous handfuls. And there was a massacre of the young blades of grass. They were being torn, burned, obliterated. Some curious fortune of the battle had made this gentle little meadow the object of the red hate of the shells, and each one as it exploded seemed like an imprecation in the face of a maiden.

The wounded officer who was riding across this expanse said to himself: "Why, they couldn't shoot any harder if the whole army was massed here!"

A shell struck the grey ruins of the house, and as, after the roar, the shattered wall fell in fragments, there was a noise which resembled the flapping of shutters during a wild gale of winter. Indeed, the infantry paused in the shelter of the bank appeared as men standing upon a shore contemplating a madness of the sea. The angel of calamity had under its glance the battery upon the hill. Fewer white-legged men laboured about the guns. A shell had smitten one of the pieces, and after the flare, the smoke, the dust, the wrath of this blow were gone, it was possible to see white lugs stretched horizontally upon the ground. And at that interval to the rear, where it is the business of battery horses to stand with their noses to the fight awaiting the command to drag their guns out of the destruction, or into it, or wheresoever these incomprehensible humans demanded with whip and spur-in this line of passive and dumb spectators, whose fluttering hearts yet would not let them forget the iron laws of man's control of them-in this rank of brute-soldiers there had been relentless and hideous carnage. From the ruck of bleeding and prostrate horses, the men of the infantry could see one animal raising its stricken body with its fore legs, and turning its nose with mystic and profound eloquence toward the sky.

Some comrades joked Collins about his thirst. "Well, if yeh want a drink so bad, why don't yeh go git it?"

"Well, I will in a minnet, if yeh don't shut up!"

A lieutenant of artillery floundered his horse straight down the hill with as little concern as if it were level ground. As he galloped past the colonel of the infantry, he threw up his hand in swift salute. "We've got to get out of that," he roared angrily. He was a black-bearded officer, and his eyes, which resembled beads, sparkled like those of an insane man. His jumping horse sped along the column of infantry.

The fat major, standing carelessly with his sword held horizontally behind him and with his legs far apart, looked after the receding horseman and laughed. "He wants to get back with orders pretty quick, or there'll be no batt'ry left," he observed.

The wise young captain of the second company hazarded to the lieutenant-colonel that the enemy's infantry would probably soon attack the hill, and the lieutenant-colonel snubbed him.

A private in one of the rear companies looked out over the meadow, and then turned to a companion and said, "Look there, Jim!" It was the wounded officer from the battery, who some time before had started to ride across the meadow, supporting his right arm carefully with his left hand. This man had encountered a shell apparently at a time when no one perceived him, and he could now be seen lying face downward with a stirruped foot stretched across the body of his dead horse. A leg of the charger extended slantingly upward precisely as stiff as a stake. Around this motionless pair the shells still howled.

There was a quarrel in A Company. Collins was shaking his fist in the faces of some laughing comrades. "Dern yeh! I ain't afraid t' go. If yeh say much, I will go!"

"Of course, yeh will! You'll run through that there medder, won't yeh?"

Collins said, in a terrible voice: "You see now!" At this ominous threat his comrades broke into renewed jeers.

Collins gave them a dark scowl, and went to find his captain. The latter was conversing with the colonel of the regiment.

"Captain," said Collins, saluting and standing at attention-in those days all trousers bagged at the knees —"Captain, I wan't t' get permission to go git some water from that there well over yonder!"

The colonel and the captain swung about simultaneously and stared across the meadow. The captain laughed. "You must be pretty thirsty, Collins?"

"Yes, sir, I am."

"Well-ah," said the captain. After a moment, he asked, "Can't you wait?"

"No, sir."

The colonel was watching Collins's face. "Look here, my lad," he said, in a pious sort of a voice —"Look here, my lad" —Collins was not a lad —"don't you think that's taking pretty big risks for a little drink of water."

"I dunno," said Collins uncomfortably. Some of the resentment toward his companions, which perhaps had forced him into this affair, was beginning to fade. "I dunno wether 'tis."

The colonel and the captain contemplated him for a time.

"Well," said the captain finally.

"Well," said the colonel, "if you want to go, why, go."

Collins saluted. "Much obliged t' yeh."

As he moved away the colonel called after him. "Take some of the other boys' canteens with you an' hurry back now."

"Yes, sir, I will."

The colonel and the captain looked at each other then, for it had suddenly occurred that they could not for the life of them tell whether Collins wanted to go or whether he did not.

They turned to regard Collins, and as they perceived him surrounded by gesticulating comrades, the colonel said: "Well, by thunder! I guess he's going."

Collins appeared as a man dreaming. In the midst of the questions, the advice, the warnings, all the excited talk of his company mates, he maintained a curious silence.

They were very busy in preparing him for his ordeal. When they inspected him carefully, it was somewhat like the examination that grooms give a horse before a race; and they were amazed, staggered by the whole affair. Their astonishment found vent in strange repetitions.

"Are yeh sure a-goin'?" they demanded again and again.

"Certainly I am," cried Collins at last furiously.

He strode sullenly away from them. He was swinging five or six canteens by their cords. It seemed that his cap would not remain firmly on his head, and often he reached and pulled it down over his brow.

There was a general movement in the compact column. The long animal-like thing moved slightly. Its four hundred eyes were turned upon the figure of Collins.

"Well, sir, if that ain't th' derndest thing! I never thought Fred

Collins had the blood in him for that kind of business."

"What's he goin' to do, anyhow?"

"He's goin' to that well there after water."

"We ain't dyin' of thirst, are we? That's foolishness."

"Well, somebody put him up to it, an' he's doin' it."

"Say, he must be a desperate cuss."

When Collins faced the meadow and walked away from the regiment, he was vaguely conscious that a chasm, the deep valley of all prides, was suddenly between him and his comrades. It was provisional, but the provision was that he return as a victor. He had blindly been led by quaint emotions, and laid himself under an obligation to walk squarely up to the face of death.

But he was not sure that he wished to make a retraction, even if he could do so without shame. As a matter of truth, he was sure of very little. He was mainly surprised.

It seemed to him supernaturally strange that he had allowed his mind to manoeuvre his body into such a situation. He understood that it might be called dramatically great.

However, he had no full appreciation of anything, excepting that he was actually conscious of being dazed. He could feel his dulled mid groping after the form and colour of this incident. He wondered why he did not feel some keen agony of fear cutting his sense like a knife. He wondered at this, because human expression had said loudly for centuries that men should feel afraid of certain things, and that all men who did not feel this fear were phenomena-heroes.

He was, then, a hero. He suffered that disappointment which we would all have if we discovered that we were ourselves capable of those deeds which we most admire in history and legend. This, then, was a hero. After all, heroes were not much.

No, it could not be true. He was not a hero. Heroes had no shames in their lives, and, as for him, he remembered borrowing fifteen dollars from a friend and promising to pay it back the next day, and then avoiding that friend for ten months. When at home his mother had aroused him for the early labour of his life on the farm, it had often been his fashion to be irritable, childish, diabolical; and his mother had died since he had come to the war.

He saw that, in this matter of the well, the canteens, the shells, he was an intruder in the land of fine deeds.

He was now about thirty paces from his comrades. The regiment had just turned its many faces toward him.

From the forest of terrific noises there suddenly emerged a little uneven line of men. They fired fiercely and rapidly at distant foliage on which appeared little puffs of white smoke. The spatter of skirmish firing was added to the thunder of the guns on the hill. The little line of men ran forward. A colour-sergeant fell flat with his flag as if he had slipped on ice. There was hoarse cheering from this distant field.

Collins suddenly felt that two demon fingers were pressed into his ears. He could see nothing but flying arrows, flaming red. He lurched from the shock of this explosion, but he made a mad rush for the house, which he viewed as a man submerged to the neck in a boiling surf might view the shore. In the air, little pieces of shell howled and the earthquake explosions drove him insane with the menace of their roar. As he ran the canteens knocked together with a rhythmical tinkling.

As he neared the house, each detail of the scene became vivid to him.

He was aware of some bricks of the vanished chimney lying on the sod.

There was a door which hung by one hinge.

Rifle bullets called forth by the insistent skirmishers came from the far-off bank of foliage. They mingled with the shells and the pieces of shells until the air was torn in all directions by hootings, yells, howls. The sky was full of fiends who directed all their wild rage at his head.

When he came to the well, he flung himself face downward and peered into its darkness. There were furtive silver glintings some feet from the surface. He grabbed one of the canteens, and, unfastening its cap, swung it down by the cord. The water flowed slowly in with an indolent gurgle.

And now as he lay with his face turned away he was suddenly smitten with the terror. It came upon his heart like the grasp of claws. All the power faded from his muscles. For an instant he was no more than a dead man.

The canteen filled with a maddening slowness, in the manner of all bottles. Presently he recovered his strength and addressed a screaming oath to it. He leaned over until it seemed as if he intended to try to push water into it with his hands. His eyes as he gazed down into the well shone like two pieces of metal, and in their expression was a great appeal and a great curse. The stupid water derided him.

There was the blaring thunder of a shell. Crimson light shone through the swift-boiling smoke, and made a pink reflection on part of the wall of the well. Collins jerked out his arm and canteen with the same motion that a man would use in withdrawing his head from a furnace.

He scrambled erect and glared and hesitated. On the ground near him lay the old well bucket, with a length of rusty chain. He lowered it swiftly into the well. The bucket struck the water and then, turning lazily over, sank. When, with hand reaching tremblingly over hand, he hauled it out, it knocked often against the walls of the well and spilled some of its contents.

In running with a filled bucket, a man can adopt but one kind of gait. So through this terrible field, over which screamed practical angels of death, Collins ran in the manner of a farmer chased out of a dairy by a bull.

His face went staring white with anticipation-anticipation of a blow that would whirl him around and down. He would fall as he had seen other men fall, the life knocked out of them so suddenly that their knees were no more quick to touch the ground than their heads. He saw the long blue line of the regiment, but his comrades were standing looking at him from the edge of an impossible star. He was aware of some deep wheel-ruts and hoof-prints in the sod beneath his feet.

The artillery officer who had fallen in this meadow had been making groans in the teeth of the tempest of sound. These futile cries, wrenched from him by his agony, were heard only by shells, bullets. When wild-eyed Collins came running, this officer raised himself. His face contorted and blanched from pain, he was about to utter some great beseeching cry. But suddenly his face straightened and he called:

"Say, young man, give me a drink of water, will you?"

Collins had no room amid his emotions for surprise. He was mad from the threats of destruction.

"I can't!" he screamed, and in his reply was a full description of his quaking apprehension. His cap was gone and his hair was riotous. His clothes made it appear that he had been dragged over the ground by the heels. He ran on.

The officer's head sank down, and one elbow crooked. His foot in its brass-bound stirrup still stretched over the body of his horse, and the other leg was under the steed.

But Collins turned. He came dashing back. His face had now turned grey, and in his eyes was all terror. "Here it is! here it is!"

The officer was as a man gone in drink. His arm bent like a twig. His head drooped as if his neck were of willow. He was sinking to the ground, to lie face downward.

Collins grabbed him by the shoulder. "Here it is. Here's your drink.
Turn over. Turn over, man, for God's sake!"

With Collins hauling at his shoulder, the officer twisted his body and fell with his face turned toward that region where lived the unspeakable noises of the swirling missiles. There was the faintest shadow of a smile on his lips as he looked at Collins. He gave a sigh, a little primitive breath like that from a child.

Collins tried to hold the bucket steadily, but his shaking hands caused the water to splash all over the face of the dying man. Then he jerked it away and ran on.

The regiment gave him a welcoming roar. The grimed faces were wrinkled in laughter.

His captain waved the bucket away. "Give it to the men!"

The two genial, skylarking young lieutenants were the first to gain possession of it. They played over it in their fashion.

When one tried to drink the other teasingly knocked his elbow. "Don't,
Billie! You'll make me spill it," said the one. The other laughed.

Suddenly there was an oath, the thud of wood on the ground, and a swift murmur of astonishment among the ranks. The two lieutenants glared at each other. The bucket lay on the ground empty.

AN INDIANA CAMPAIGN

I

When the able-bodied citizens of the village formed a company and marched away to the war, Major Tom Boldin assumed in a manner the burden of the village cares. Everybody ran to him when they felt obliged to discuss their affairs. The sorrows of the town were dragged before him. His little bench at the sunny side of Migglesville tavern became a sort of an open court where people came to speak resentfully of their grievances. He accepted his position and struggled manfully under the load. It behoved him, as a man who had seen the sky red over the quaint, low cities of Mexico, and the compact Northern bayonets gleaming on the narrow roads.

One warm summer day the major sat asleep on his little bench. There was a lull in the tempest of discussion which usually enveloped him. His cane, by use of which he could make the most tremendous and impressive gestures, reposed beside him. His hat lay upon the bench, and his old bald head had swung far forward until his nose actually touched the first button of his waistcoat.

The sparrows wrangled desperately in the road, defying perspiration. Once a team went jangling and creaking past, raising a yellow blur of dust before the soft tones of the field and sky. In the long grass of the meadow across the road the insects chirped and clacked eternally.

Suddenly a frouzy-headed boy appeared in the roadway, his bare feet pattering rapidly. He was extremely excited. He gave a shrill whoop as he discovered the sleeping major and rushed toward him. He created a terrific panic among some chickens who had been scratching intently near the major's feet. They clamoured in an insanity of fear, and rushed hither and thither seeking a way of escape, whereas in reality all ways lay plainly open to them.

This tumult caused the major to arouse with a sudden little jump of amazement and apprehension. He rubbed his eyes and gazed about him. Meanwhile, some clever chicken had discovered a passage to safety, and led the flock into the garden, where they squawked in sustained alarm.

Panting from his run and choked with terror, the little boy stood before the major, struggling with a tale that was ever upon the tip of his tongue.

"Major-now-major——"

The old man, roused from a delicious slumber, glared impatiently at the little boy. "Come, come! What's th' matter with yeh?" he demanded. "What's th' matter? Don't stand there shaking! Speak up!"

"Lots is th' matter!" the little boy shouted valiantly, with a courage born of the importance of his tale. "My ma's chickens 'uz all stole, an' —now-he's over in th' woods!"

"Who is? Who is over in the woods? Go ahead!"

"Now-th' rebel is!"

"What?" roared the major.

"Th' rebel!" cried the little boy, with the last of his breath.

The major pounced from his bench in tempestuous excitement. He seized the little boy by the collar and gave him a great jerk. "Where? Are yeh sure? Who saw 'im? How long ago? Where is he now? Did you see 'im?"

The little boy, frightened at the major's fury, began to sob. After a moment he managed to stammer: "He-now-he's in the woods. I saw 'im. He looks uglier'n anythin'."

The major released his hold upon the boy, and pausing for a time, indulged in a glorious dream. Then he said: "By thunder! we'll ketch th' cuss. You wait here," he told the boy, "and don't say a word t' anybody. Do you hear?"

The boy, still weeping, nodded, and the major hurriedly entered the inn. He took down from its pegs an awkward smooth-bore rifle and carefully examined the enormous percussion cap that was fitted over the nipple. Mistrusting the cap, he removed it and replaced it with a new one. He scrutinised the gun keenly, as if he could judge in this manner of the condition of the load. All his movements were deliberate and deadly.

When he arrived upon the porch of the tavern he beheld the yard filled with people. Peter Witheby, sooty-faced and grinning, was in the van. He looked at the major. "Well?" he said.

"Well?" returned the major, bridling.

"Well, what's 'che got?" said old Peter.

"'Got?' Got a rebel over in th' woods!" roared the major.

At this sentence the women and boys, who had gathered eagerly about him, gave vent to startled cries. The women had come from adjacent houses, but the little boys represented the entire village. They had miraculously heard the first whisper of rumour, and they performed wonders in getting to the spot. They clustered around the important figure of the major and gazed in silent awe. The women, however, burst forth. At the word "rebel," which represented to them all terrible things, they deluged the major with questions which were obviously unanswerable.

He shook them off with violent impatience. Meanwhile Peter Witheby was trying to force exasperating interrogations through the tumult to the major's ears. "What? No! Yes! How d' I know?" the maddened veteran snarled as he struggled with his friends. "No! Yes! What? How in thunder d' I know?" Upon the steps of the tavern the landlady sat, weeping forlornly.

At last the major burst through the crowd, and went to the roadway. There, as they all streamed after him, he turned and faced them. "Now, look a' here, I don't know any more about this than you do," he told them forcibly. "All that I know is that there's a rebel over in Smith's woods, an' all I know is that I'm agoin' after 'im."

"But hol' on a minnet," said old Peter. "How do yeh know he's a rebel?"

"I know he is!" cried the major. "Don't yeh think I know what a rebel is?"

Then, with a gesture of disdain at the babbling crowd, he marched determinedly away, his rifle held in the hollow of his arm. At this heroic moment a new clamour arose, half admiration, half dismay. Old Peter hobbled after the major, continually repeating, "Hol' on a minnet."

The little boy who had given the alarm was the centre of a throng of lads who gazed with envy and awe, discovering in him a new quality. He held forth to them eloquently. The women stared after the figure of the major and old Peter, his pursuer. Jerozel Bronson, a half-witted lad who comprehended nothing save an occasional genial word, leaned against the fence and grinned like a skull. The major and the pursuer passed out of view around the turn in the road where the great maples lazily shook the dust that lay on their leaves.

For a moment the little group of women listened intently as if they expected to hear a sudden shot and cries from the distance. They looked at each other, their lips a little way apart. The trees sighed softly in the heat of the summer sun. The insects in the meadow continued their monotonous humming, and, somewhere, a hen had been stricken with fear and was cackling loudly.

Finally, Mrs. Goodwin said: "Well, I'm goin' up to th' turn a' th' road, anyhow." Mrs. Willets and Mrs. Joe Peterson, her particular friends, cried out at this temerity, but she said: "Well, I'm goin', anyhow."

She called Bronson. "Come on, Jerozel. You're a man, an' if he should chase us, why, you mus' pitch inteh 'im. Hey?"

Bronson always obeyed everybody. He grinned an assent, and went with her down the road.

A little boy attempted to follow them, but a shrill scream from his mother made him halt.

The remaining women stood motionless, their eyes fixed upon Mrs. Goodwin and Jerozel. Then at last one gave a laugh of triumph at her conquest of caution and fear, and cried: "Well, I'm goin' too!"

Another instantly said, "So am I." There began a general movement. Some of the little boys had already ventured a hundred feet away from the main body, and at this unanimous advance they spread out ahead in little groups. Some recounted terrible stories of rebel ferocity. Their eyes were large with excitement. The whole thing, with its possible dangers, had for them a delicious element. Johnnie Peterson, who could whip any boy present, explained what he would do in case the enemy should happen to pounce out at him.

The familiar scene suddenly assumed a new aspect. The field of corn, which met the road upon the left, was no longer a mere field of corn. It was a darkly mystic place whose recesses could contain all manner of dangers. The long green leaves, waving in the breeze, rustled from the passing of men. In the song of the insects there were now omens, threats.

There was a warning in the enamel blue of the sky, in the stretch of yellow road, in the very atmosphere. Above the tops of the corn loomed the distant foliage of Smith's woods, curtaining the silent action of a tragedy whose horrors they imagined.

The women and the little boys came to a halt, overwhelmed by the impressiveness of the landscape. They waited silently.

Mrs. Goodwin suddenly said: "I'm goin' back." The others, who all wished to return, cried at once disdainfully:

"Well, go back, if yeh want to!"

A cricket at the roadside exploded suddenly in his shrill song, and a woman, who had been standing near, shrieked in startled terror. An electric movement went through the group of women. They jumped and gave vent to sudden screams. With the fears still upon their agitated faces, they turned to berate the one who had shrieked. "My! what a goose you are, Sallie! Why, it took my breath away. Goodness sakes, don't holler like that again!"

"Hol' on a minnet!" Peter Witheby was crying to the major, as the latter, full of the importance and dignity of his position as protector of Migglesville, paced forward swiftly. The veteran already felt upon his brow a wreath formed of the flowers of gratitude, and as he strode he was absorbed in planning a calm and self-contained manner of wearing it. "Hol' on a minnet!" piped old Peter in the rear.

At last the major, aroused from his dream of triumph, turned about wrathfully. "Well, what?"

"Now, look a' here," said Peter. "What 'che goin' t' do?"

The major, with a gesture of supreme exasperation, wheeled again and went on. When he arrived at the cornfield he halted and waited for Peter. He had suddenly felt that indefinable menace in the landscape.

"Well?" demanded Peter, panting.

The major's eyes wavered a trifle. "Well," he repeated —"well, I'm goin' in there an' bring out that there rebel."

They both paused and studied the gently swaying masses of corn, and behind them the looming woods, sinister with possible secrets.

"Well," said old Peter.

The major moved uneasily and put his hand to his brow. Peter waited in obvious expectation.

The major crossed through the grass at the roadside and climbed the fence. He put both legs over the topmost rail and then sat perched there, facing the woods. Once he turned his head and asked, "What?"

"I hain't said anythin'," answered Peter.

The major clambered down from the fence and went slowly into the corn, his gun held in readiness. Peter stood in the road.

Presently the major returned and said, in a cautious whisper: "If yeh hear anythin', you come a-runnin', will yeh?"

"Well, I hain't got no gun nor nuthin'," said Peter, in the same low tone; "what good 'ud I do?"

"Well, yeh might come along with me an' watch," said the major. "Four eyes is better'n two."

"If I had a gun —" began Peter.

"Oh, yeh don't need no gun," interrupted the major, waving his hand: "All I'm afraid of is that I won't find 'im. My eyes ain't so good as they was."

"Well —"

"Come along," whispered the major. "Yeh hain't afraid, are yeh?"

"No, but —"

"Well, come along, then. What's th' matter with yeh?"

Peter climbed the fence. He paused on the top rail and took a prolonged stare at the inscrutable woods. When he joined the major in the cornfield he said, with a touch of anger:

"Well, you got the gun. Remember that. If he comes for me, I hain't got a blame thing!"

"Shucks!" answered the major. "He ain't agoin' t' come for yeh."

The two then began a wary journey through the corn. One by one the long aisles between the rows appeared. As they glanced along each of them it seemed as if some gruesome thing had just previously vacated it. Old Peter halted once and whispered: "Say, look a' here; supposin' — supposin' —"

"Supposin' what?" demanded the major.

"Supposin' —" said Peter. "Well, remember you got th' gun, an' I hain't got anythin'.'"

"Thunder!" said the major.

When they got to where the stalks were very short because of the shade cast by the trees of the wood, they halted again. The leaves were gently swishing in the breeze. Before them stretched the mystic green wall of the forest, and there seemed to be in it eyes which followed each of their movements.

Peter at last said, "I don't believe there's anybody in there."

"Yes, there is, too," said the major. "I'll bet anythin' he's in there."

"How d' yeh know?" asked Peter. "I'll bet he ain't within a mile o' here."

The major suddenly ejaculated, "Listen!"

They bent forward, scarce breathing, their mouths agape, their eyes glinting. Finally, the major turned his head. "Did yeh hear that?" he said hoarsely.

"No," said Peter in a low voice. "What was it?"

The major listened for a moment. Then he turned again. "I thought I heerd somebody holler!" he explained cautiously.

They both bent forward and listened once more. Peter, in the intentness of his attitude, lost his balance, and was obliged to lift his foot hastily and with noise. "S-s-sh!" hissed the major.

After a minute Peter spoke quite loudly: "Oh, shucks! I don't believe yeh heerd anythin'."

The major made a frantic downward gesture with his hand. "Shet up, will yeh!" he said in an angry undertone.

Peter became silent for a moment, but presently he said again: "Oh, yeh didn't hear anythin'."

The major turned to glare at his companion in despair and wrath.

"What's th' matter with yeh? Can't yeh shet up?"

"Oh, this here ain't no use. If you're goin' in after 'im, why don't yeh go in after 'im?"

"Well, gimme time, can't yeh?" said the major in a growl. And, as if to add more to this reproach, he climbed the fence that compassed the woods, looking resentfully back at his companion.

"Well," said Peter, when the major paused.

The major stepped down upon the thick carpet of brown leaves that stretched under the trees. He turned then to whisper: "You wait here, will yeh?" His face was red with determination.

"Well, hol' on a minnet!" said Peter. "You —I —we'd better —"

"No," said the major. "You wait here."

He went stealthily into the thickets. Peter watched him until he grew to be a vague, slow-moving shadow. From time to time he could hear the leaves crackle and twigs snap under the major's awkward tread. Peter, intent, breathless, waited for the peal of sudden tragedy. Finally, the woods grew silent in a solemn and impressive hush that caused Peter to feel the thumping of his heart. He began to look about him to make sure that nothing should spring upon him from the sombre shadows. He scrutinised this cool gloom before him, and at times he thought he could perceive the moving of swift silent shapes. He concluded that he had better go back and try to muster some assistance to the major.

As Peter came through the corn, the women in the road caught sight of the glittering figure and screamed. Many of them began to run. The little boys, with all their valour, scurried away in clouds. Mrs. Joe Peterson, however, cast a glance over her shoulders as she, with her skirts gathered up, was running as best she could. She instantly stopped and, in tones of deepest scorn, called out to the others, "Why, it's on'y Pete Witheby!" They came faltering back then, those who had been naturally swiftest in the race avoiding the eyes of those whose limbs had enabled them to flee a short distance.

Peter came rapidly, appreciating the glances of vivid interest in the eyes of the women. To their lightning-like questions, which hit all sides of the episode, he opposed a new tranquillity, gained from his sudden ascent in importance. He made no answer to their clamour. When he had reached the top of the fence he called out commandingly: "Here you, Johnnie, you and George, run an' git my gun! It's hangin' on th' pegs over th' bench in th' shop."

At this terrible sentence, a shuddering cry broke from the women. The boys named sped down the road, accompanied by a retinue of envious companions.

Peter swung his legs over the rail and faced the woods again. He twisted his head once to say: "Keep still, can't yeh? Quit scufflin' aroun'!" They could see by his manner that this was a supreme moment. The group became motionless and still. Later, Peter turned to say, "S-s-sh!" to a restless boy, and the air with which he said it smote them all with awe.

The little boys who had gone after the gun came pattering along hurriedly, the weapon borne in the midst of them. Each was anxious to share in the honour. The one who had been delegated to bring it was bullying and directing his comrades.

Peter said, "S-s-sh!" He took the gun and poised it in readiness to sweep the cornfield. He scowled at the boys and whispered angrily: "Why didn't yeh bring th' powder-horn an' th' thing with th' bullets in? I told yeh t' bring 'em. I'll send somebody else next time."

"Yeh didn't tell us!" cried the two boys shrilly.

"S-s-sh! Quit yeh noise," said Peter, with a violent gesture.

However, this reproof enabled other boys to recover that peace of mind which they had lost when seeing their friends loaded with honours.

The women had cautiously approached the fence, and, from time to time, whispered feverish questions; but Peter repulsed them savagely, with an air of being infinitely bothered by their interference in his intent watch. They were forced to listen again in silence to the weird and prophetic chanting of the insects and the mystic silken rustling of the corn.

At last the thud of hurrying feet in the soft soil of the field came to their ears. A dark form sped toward them. A wave of a mighty fear swept over the group, and the screams of the women came hoarsely from their choked throats. Peter swung madly from his perch, and turned to use the fence as a rampart.

But it was the major. His face was inflamed and his eyes were glaring. He clutched his rifle by the middle and swung it wildly. He was bounding at a great speed for his fat, short body.

"It's all right! it's all right!" he began to yell some distance away.
"It's all right! It's on'y ol' Milt' Jacoby!"

When he arrived at the top of the fence he paused, and mopped his brow.

"What?" they thundered, in an agony of sudden, unreasoning disappointment.

Mrs. Joe Peterson, who was a distant connection of Milton Jacoby, thought to forestall any damage to her social position by saying at once disdainfully, "Drunk, I s'pose!"

"Yep," said the major, still on the fence, and mopping his brow. "Drunk as a fool. Thunder! I was surprised. I—I—thought it was a rebel, sure."

The thoughts of all these women wavered for a time. They were at a loss for precise expression of their emotion. At last, however, they hurled this superior sentence at the major:

"Well, yeh might have known."

A GREY SLEEVE

I

"It looks as if it might rain this afternoon," remarked the lieutenant of artillery.

"So it does," the infantry captain assented. He glanced casually at the sky. When his eyes had lowered to the green-shadowed landscape before him, he said fretfully: "I wish those fellows out yonder would quit pelting at us. They've been at it since noon."

At the edge of a grove of maples, across wide fields, there occasionally appeared little puffs of smoke of a dull hue in this gloom of sky which expressed an impending rain. The long wave of blue and steel in the field moved uneasily at the eternal barking of the far-away sharpshooters, and the men, leaning upon their rifles, stared at the grove of maples. Once a private turned to borrow some tobacco from a comrade in the rear rank, but, with his hand still stretched out, he continued to twist his head and glance at the distant trees. He was afraid the enemy would shoot him at a time when he was not looking.

Suddenly the artillery officer said: "See what's coming!"

Along the rear of the brigade of infantry a column of cavalry was sweeping at a hard gallop. A lieutenant, riding some yards to the right of the column, bawled furiously at the four troopers just at the rear of the colours. They had lost distance and made a little gap, but at the shouts of the lieutenant they urged their horses forward. The bugler, careering along behind the captain of the troop, fought and tugged like a wrestler to keep his frantic animal from bolting far ahead of the column.

On the springy turf the innumerable hoofs thundered in a swift storm of sound. In the brown faces of the troopers their eyes were set like bits of flashing steel.

The long line of the infantry regiments standing at ease underwent a sudden movement at the rush of the passing squadron. The foot soldiers turned their heads to gaze at the torrent of horses and men.

The yellow folds of the flag fluttered back in silken, shuddering waves, as if it were a reluctant thing. Occasionally a giant spring of a charger would rear the firm and sturdy figure of a soldier suddenly head and shoulders above his comrades. Over the noise of the scudding hoofs could be heard the creaking of leather trappings, the jingle and clank of steel, and the tense, low-toned commands or appeals of the men to their horses; and the horses were mad with the headlong sweep of this movement. Powerful under jaws bent back and straightened, so that the bits were clamped as rigidly as vices upon the teeth, and glistening necks arched in desperate resistance to the hands at the bridles. Swinging their heads in rage at the granite laws of their lives, which compelled even their angers and their ardours to chosen directions and chosen faces, their flight was as a flight of harnessed demons.

The captain's bay kept its pace at the head of the squadron with the lithe bounds of a thoroughbred, and this horse was proud as a chief at the roaring trample of his fellows behind him. The captain's glance was calmly upon the grove of maples whence the sharpshooters of the enemy had been picking at the blue line. He seemed to be reflecting. He stolidly rose and fell with the plunges of his horse in all the indifference of a deacon's figure seated plumply in church. And it occurred to many of the watching infantry to wonder why this officer could remain imperturbable and reflective when his squadron was thundering and swarming behind him like the rushing of a flood.

The column swung in a sabre-curve toward a break in a fence, and dashed into a roadway. Once a little plank bridge was encountered, and the sound of the hoofs upon it was like the long roll of many drums. An old captain in the infantry turned to his first lieutenant and made a remark, which was a compound of bitter disparagement of cavalry in general and soldierly admiration of this particular troop.

Suddenly the bugle sounded, and the column halted with a jolting upheaval amid sharp, brief cries. A moment later the men had tumbled from their horses, and, carbines in hand, were running in a swarm toward the grove of maples. In the road one of every four of the troopers was standing with braced legs, and pulling and hauling at the bridles of four frenzied horses.

The captain was running awkwardly in his boots. He held his sabre low, so that the point often threatened to catch in the turf. His yellow hair ruffled out from under his faded cap. "Go in hard now!" he roared, in a voice of hoarse fury. His face was violently red.

The troopers threw themselves upon the grove like wolves upon a great animal. Along the whole front of woods there was the dry crackling of musketry, with bitter, swift flashes and smoke that writhed like stung phantoms. The troopers yelled shrilly and spanged bullets low into the foliage.

For a moment, when near the woods, the line almost halted. The men struggled and fought for a time like swimmers encountering a powerful current. Then with a supreme effort they went on again. They dashed madly at the grove, whose foliage from the high light of the field was as inscrutable as a wall.

Then suddenly each detail of the calm trees became apparent, and with a few more frantic leaps the men were in the cool gloom of the woods. There was a heavy odour as from burned paper. Wisps of grey smoke wound upward. The men halted and, grimy, perspiring, and puffing, they searched the recesses of the woods with eager, fierce glances. Figures could be seen flitting afar off. A dozen carbines rattled at them in an angry volley.

During this pause the captain strode along the line, his face lit with a broad smile of contentment. "When he sends this crowd to do anything, I guess he'll find we do it pretty sharp," he said to the grinning lieutenant.

"Say, they didn't stand that rush a minute, did they?" said the subaltern. Both officers were profoundly dusty in their uniforms, and their faces were soiled like those of two urchins.

Out in the grass behind them were three tumbled and silent forms.

Presently the line moved forward again. The men went from tree to tree like hunters stalking game. Some at the left of the line fired occasionally, and those at the right gazed curiously in that direction. The men still breathed heavily from their scramble across the field.

Of a sudden a trooper halted and said: "Hello! there's a house!" Every one paused. The men turned to look at their leader.

The captain stretched his neck and swung his head from side to side.
"By George, it is a house!" he said.

Through the wealth of leaves there vaguely loomed the form of a large white house. These troopers, brown-faced from many days of campaigning, each feature of them telling of their placid confidence and courage, were stopped abruptly by the appearance of this house. There was some subtle suggestion-some tale of an unknown thing-which watched them from they knew not what part of it.

A rail fence girded a wide lawn of tangled grass. Seven pines stood along a drive-way which led from two distant posts of a vanished gate. The blue-clothed troopers moved forward until they stood at the fence peering over it.

The captain put one hand on the top rail and seemed to be about to climb the fence, when suddenly he hesitated, and said in a low voice: "Watson, what do you think of it?"

The lieutenant stared at the house. "Derned if I know!" he replied.

The captain pondered. It happened that the whole company had turned a gaze of profound awe and doubt upon this edifice which confronted them. The men were very silent.

At last the captain swore and said: "We are certainly a pack of fools. Derned old deserted house halting a company of Union cavalry, and making us gape like babies!"

"Yes, but there's something-something — —" insisted the subaltern in a half stammer.

"Well, if there's 'something-something' in there, I'll get it out," said the captain. "Send Sharpe clean around to the other side with about twelve men, so we will sure bag your 'something-something,' and I'll take a few of the boys and find out what's in the d — —d old thing!"

He chose the nearest eight men for his "storming party," as the lieutenant called it. After he had waited some minutes for the others to get into position, he said "Come ahead" to his eight men, and climbed the fence.

The brighter light of the tangled lawn made him suddenly feel tremendously apparent, and he wondered if there could be some mystic thing in the house which was regarding this approach. His men trudged silently at his back. They stared at the windows and lost themselves in deep speculations as to the probability of there being, perhaps, eyes behind the blinds-malignant eyes, piercing eyes.

Suddenly a corporal in the party gave vent to a startled exclamation, and half threw his carbine into position. The captain turned quickly, and the corporal said: "I saw an arm move the blinds-an arm with a grey sleeve!"

"Don't be a fool, Jones, now," said the captain sharply.

"I swear t' —" began the corporal, but the captain silenced him.

When they arrived at the front of the house, the troopers paused, while the captain went softly up the front steps. He stood before the large front door and studied it. Some crickets chirped in the long grass, and the nearest pine could be heard in its endless sighs. One of the privates moved uneasily, and his foot crunched the gravel. Suddenly the captain swore angrily and kicked the door with a loud crash. It flew open.

The bright lights of the day flashed into the old house when the captain angrily kicked open the door. He was aware of a wide hallway, carpeted with matting and extending deep into the dwelling. There was also an old walnut hat-rack and a little marble-topped table with a vase and two books upon it. Farther back was a great, venerable fireplace containing dreary ashes.

But directly in front of the captain was a young girl. The flying open of the door had obviously been an utter astonishment to her, and she remained transfixed there in the middle of the floor, staring at the captain with wide eyes.

She was like a child caught at the time of a raid upon the cake. She wavered to and fro upon her feet, and held her hands behind her. There were two little points of terror in her eyes, as she gazed up at the young captain in dusty blue, with his reddish, bronze complexion, his yellow hair, his bright sabre held threateningly.

These two remained motionless and silent, simply staring at each other for some moments.

The captain felt his rage fade out of him and leave his mind limp. He had been violently angry, because this house had made him feel hesitant, wary. He did not like to be wary. He liked to feel confident, sure. So he had kicked the door open, and had been prepared, to march in like a soldier of wrath.

But now he began, for one thing, to wonder if his uniform was so dusty and old in appearance. Moreover, he had a feeling that his face was covered with a compound of dust, grime, and perspiration. He took a step forward and said: "I didn't mean to frighten you." But his voice was coarse from his battle-howling. It seemed to him to have hempen fibres in it.

The girl's breath came in little, quick gasps, and she looked at him as she would have looked at a serpent.

"I didn't mean to frighten you," he said again.

The girl, still with her hands behind her, began to back away.

"Is there any one else in the house?" he went on, while slowly following her. "I don't wish to disturb you, but we had a fight with some rebel skirmishers in the woods, and I thought maybe some of them might have come in here. In fact, I was pretty sure of it. Are there any of them here?"

The girl looked at him and said, "No!" He wondered why extreme agitation made the eyes of some women so limpid and bright.

"Who is here besides yourself?"

By this time his pursuit had driven her to the end of the hall, and she remained there with her back to the wall and her hands still behind her. When she answered this question, she did not look at him but down at the floor. She cleared her voice and then said: "There is no one here."

"No one?"

She lifted her eyes to him in that appeal that the human being must make even to falling trees, crashing boulders, the sea in a storm, and said, "No, no, there is no one here." He could plainly see her tremble.

Of a sudden he bethought him that she continually kept her hands behind her. As he recalled her air when first discovered, he remembered she appeared precisely as a child detected at one of the crimes of childhood. Moreover, she had always backed away from him. He thought now that she was concealing something which was an evidence of the presence of the enemy in the house.

"What are you holding behind you?" he said suddenly.

She gave a little quick moan, as if some grim hand had throttled her.

"What are you holding behind you?"

"Oh, nothing-please. I am not holding anything behind me; indeed I'm not."

"Very well. Hold your hands out in front of you, then."

"Oh, indeed, I'm not holding anything behind me. Indeed I'm not."

"Well," he began. Then he paused, and remained for a moment dubious. Finally, he laughed. "Well, I shall have my men search the house, anyhow. I'm sorry to trouble you, but I feel sure that there is some one here whom we want." He turned to the corporal, who with the other men was gaping quietly in at the door, and said: "Jones, go through the house."

As for himself, he remained planted in front of the girl, for she evidently did not dare to move and allow him to see what she held so carefully behind her back. So she was his prisoner.

The men rummaged around on the ground floor of the house. Sometimes the captain called to them, "Try that closet," "Is there any cellar?" But they found no one, and at last they went trooping toward the stairs which led to the second floor.

But at this movement on the part of the men the girl uttered a cry —a cry of such fright and appeal that the men paused. "Oh, don't go up there! Please don't go up there! —ple-ease! There is no one there! Indeed-indeed there is not! Oh, ple-ease!"

"Go on, Jones," said the captain calmly.

The obedient corporal made a preliminary step, and the girl bounded toward the stairs with another cry.

As she passed him, the captain caught sight of that which she had concealed behind her back, and which she had forgotten in this supreme moment. It was a pistol.

She ran to the first step, and standing there, faced the men, one hand extended with perpendicular palm, and the other holding the pistol at her side. "Oh, please, don't go up there! Nobody is there-indeed, there is not! P-l-e-a-s-e!" Then suddenly she sank swiftly down upon the step, and, huddling forlornly, began to weep in the agony and with the convulsive tremors of an infant. The pistol fell from her fingers and rattled down to the floor.

The astonished troopers looked at their astonished captain. There was a short silence.

Finally, the captain stooped and picked up the pistol. It was a heavy weapon of the army pattern. He ascertained that it was empty.

He leaned toward the shaking girl, and said gently: "Will you tell me what you were going to do with this pistol?"

He had to repeat the question a number of times, but at last a muffled voice said, "Nothing."

"Nothing!" He insisted quietly upon a further answer. At the tender tones of the captain's voice, the phlegmatic corporal turned and winked gravely at the man next to him.

"Won't you tell me?"

The girl shook her head.

"Please tell me!"

The silent privates were moving their feet uneasily and wondering how long they were to wait. The captain said: "Please, won't you tell me?"

Then this girl's voice began in stricken tones half coherent, and amid violent sobbing: "It was grandpa's. He-he-he said he was going to shoot anybody who came in here-he didn't care if there were thousands of 'em. And-and I know he would, and I was afraid they'd kill him. And so-and so I stole away his pistol-and I was going to hide it when you-you-you kicked open the door."

The men straightened up and looked at each other. The girl began to weep again.

The captain mopped his brow. He peered down at the girl. He mopped his brow again. Suddenly he said: "Ah, don't cry like that."

He moved restlessly and looked down at his boots. He mopped his brow again.

Then he gripped the corporal by the arm and dragged him some yards back from the others. "Jones," he said, in an intensely earnest voice, "will you tell me what in the devil I am going to do?"

The corporal's countenance became illuminated with satisfaction at being thus requested to advise his superior officer. He adopted an air of great thought, and finally said: "Well, of course, the feller with the grey sleeve must be upstairs, and we must get past the girl and up there somehow. Suppose I take her by the arm and lead her —"

"What!" interrupted the captain from between his clinched teeth. As he turned away from the corporal, he said fiercely over his shoulder: "You touch that girl and I'll split your skull!"

The corporal looked after his captain with an expression of mingled amazement, grief, and philosophy. He seemed to be saying to himself that there unfortunately were times, after all, when one could not rely upon the most reliable of men. When he returned to the group he found the captain bending over the girl and saying: "Why is it that you don't want us to search upstairs?"

The girl's head was buried in her crossed arms. Locks of her hair had escaped from their fastenings, and these fell upon her shoulder.

"Won't you tell me?"

The corporal here winked again at the man next to him.

"Because," the girl moaned —"because-there isn't anybody up there."

The captain at last said timidly: "Well, I'm afraid —I'm afraid we'll have to — —"

The girl sprang to her feet again, and implored him with her hands. She looked deep into his eyes with her glance, which was at this time like that of the fawn when it says to the hunter, "Have mercy upon me!"

These two stood regarding each other. The captain's foot was on the bottom step, but he seemed to be shrinking. He wore an air of being deeply wretched and ashamed. There was a silence!

Suddenly the corporal said in a quick, low tone: "Look out, captain!"

All turned their eyes swiftly toward the head of the stairs. There had appeared there a youth in a grey uniform. He stood looking coolly down at them. No word was said by the troopers. The girl gave vent to a little wail of desolation, "O Harry!"

He began slowly to descend the stairs. His right arm was in a white sling, and there were some fresh blood-stains upon the cloth. His face was rigid and deathly pale, but his eyes flashed like lights. The girl was again moaning in an utterly dreary fashion, as the youth came slowly down toward the silent men in blue.

Six steps from the bottom of the flight he halted and said: "I reckon it's me you're looking for."

The troopers had crowded forward a trifle and, posed in lithe, nervous attitudes, were watching him like cats. The captain remained unmoved. At the youth's question he merely nodded his head and said, "Yes."

The young man in grey looked down at the girl, and then, in the same even tone which now, however, seemed to vibrate with suppressed fury, he said: "And is that any reason why you should insult my sister?"

At this sentence, the girl intervened, desperately, between the young man in grey and the officer in blue. "Oh, don't, Harry, don't! He was good to me! He was good to me, Harry-indeed he was!"

The youth came on in his quiet, erect fashion, until the girl could have touched either of the men with her hand, for the captain still remained with his foot upon the first step. She continually repeated: "O Harry! O Harry!"

The youth in grey manoeuvred to glare into the captain's face, first over one shoulder of the girl and then over the other. In a voice that rang like metal, he said: "You are armed and unwounded, while I have no weapons and am wounded; but —"

The captain had stepped back and sheathed his sabre. The eyes of these two men were gleaming fire, but otherwise the captain's countenance was imperturbable. He said: "You are mistaken. You have no reason to —"

"You lie!"

All save the captain and the youth in grey started in an electric movement. These two words crackled in the air like shattered glass. There was a breathless silence.

The captain cleared his throat. His look at the youth contained a quality of singular and terrible ferocity, but he said in his stolid tone: "I don't suppose you mean what you say now."

Upon his arm he had felt the pressure of some unconscious little fingers. The girl was leaning against the wall as if she no longer knew how to keep her balance, but those fingers-he held his arm very still. She murmured: "O Harry, don't! He was good to me-indeed he was!"

The corporal had come forward until he in a measure confronted the youth in grey, for he saw those fingers upon the captain's arm, and he knew that sometimes very strong men were not able to move hand nor foot under such conditions.

The youth had suddenly seemed to become weak. He breathed heavily and clung to the rail. He was glaring at the captain, and apparently summoning all his will power to combat his weakness. The corporal addressed him with profound straightforwardness: "Don't you be a derned fool!" The youth turned toward him so fiercely that the corporal threw up a knee and an elbow like a boy who expects to be cuffed.

The girl pleaded with the captain. "You won't hurt him, will you? He don't know what he's saying. He's wounded, you know. Please don't mind him!"

"I won't touch him," said the captain, with rather extraordinary earnestness; "don't you worry about him at all. I won't touch him!"

Then he looked at her, and the girl suddenly withdrew her fingers from his arm.

The corporal contemplated the top of the stairs, and remarked without surprise: "There's another of 'em coming!"

An old man was clambering down the stairs with much speed. He waved a cane wildly. "Get out of my house, you thieves! Get out! I won't have you cross my threshold! Get out!" He mumbled and wagged his head in an old man's fury. It was plainly his intention to assault them.

And so it occurred that a young girl became engaged in protecting a stalwart captain, fully armed, and with eight grim troopers at his back, from the attack of an old man with a walking-stick!

A blush passed over the temples and brow of the captain, and he looked particularly savage and weary. Despite the girl's efforts, he suddenly faced the old man.

"Look here," he said distinctly, "we came in because we had been fighting in the woods yonder, and we concluded that some of the enemy were in this house, especially when we saw a grey sleeve at the window. But this young man is wounded, and I have nothing to say to him. I will even take it for granted that there are no others like him upstairs. We will go away, leaving your d —-d old house just as we found it! And we are no more thieves and rascals than you are!"

The old man simply roared: "I haven't got a cow nor a pig nor a chicken on the place! Your soldiers have stolen everything they could carry away. They have torn down half my fences for firewood. This afternoon some of your accursed bullets even broke my window panes!"

The girl had been faltering: "Grandpa! O grandpa!"

The captain looked at the girl. She returned his glance from the shadow of the old man's shoulder. After studying her face a moment, he said: "Well, we will go now." He strode toward the door, and his men clanked docilely after him.

At this time there was the sound of harsh cries and rushing footsteps from without. The door flew open, and a whirlwind composed of blue-coated troopers came in with a swoop. It was headed by the lieutenant. "Oh, here you are!" he cried, catching his breath. "We thought —
—Oh, look at the girl!"

The captain said intensely: "Shut up, you fool!"

The men settled to a halt with a clash and a bang. There could be heard the dulled sound of many hoofs outside of the house.

"Did you order up the horses?" inquired the captain.

"Yes. We thought — —"

"Well, then, let's get out of here," interrupted the captain morosely.

The men began to filter out into the open air. The youth in grey had been hanging dismally to the railing of the stairway. He now was climbing slowly up to the second floor. The old man was addressing himself directly to the serene corporal.

"Not a chicken on the place!" he cried.

"Well, I didn't take your chickens, did I?"

"No, maybe you didn't, but — —"

The captain crossed the hall and stood before the girl in rather a culprit's fashion. "You are not angry at me, are you?" he asked timidly.

"No," she said. She hesitated a moment, and then suddenly held out her hand. "You were good to me-and I'm —much obliged."

The captain took her hand, and then he blushed, for he found himself unable to formulate a sentence that applied in any way to the situation.

She did not seem to heed that hand for a time.

He loosened his grasp presently, for he was ashamed to hold it so long without saying anything clever. At last, with an air of charging an intrenched brigade, he contrived to say: "I would rather do anything than frighten or trouble you."

His brow was warmly perspiring. He had a sense of being hideous in his dusty uniform and with his grimy face.

She said, "Oh, I'm so glad it was you instead of somebody who might have-might have hurt brother Harry and grandpa!"

He told her, "I wouldn't have hurt em for anything!"

There was a little silence.

"Well, good-bye!" he said at last.

"Good-bye!"

He walked toward the door past the old man, who was scolding at the vanishing figure of the corporal. The captain looked back. She had remained there watching him.

At the bugle's order, the troopers standing beside their horses swung briskly into the saddle. The lieutenant said to the first sergeant:

"Williams, did they ever meet before?"

"Hanged if I know!"

"Well, say —-"

The captain saw a curtain move at one of the windows. He cantered from his position at the head of the column and steered his horse between two flower-beds.

"Well, good-bye!"

The squadron trampled slowly past.

"Good-bye!"

They shook hands.

He evidently had something enormously important to say to her, but it seems that he could not manage it. He struggled heroically. The bay charger, with his great mystically solemn eyes, looked around the corner of his shoulder at the girl.

The captain studied a pine tree. The girl inspected the grass beneath the window. The captain said hoarsely: "I don't suppose —I don't suppose —I'll ever see you again!"

She looked at him affrightedly and shrank back from the window. He seemed to have woefully expected a reception of this kind for his question. He gave her instantly a glance of appeal.

She said: "Why, no, I don't suppose you will."

"Never?"

"Why, no, 'tain't possible. You-you are a —Yankee!"

"Oh, I know it, but — —" Eventually he continued: "Well, some day, you know, when there's no more fighting, we might — —" He observed that she had again withdrawn suddenly into the shadow, so he said: "Well, good-bye!"

When he held her fingers she bowed her head, and he saw a pink blush steal over the curves of her cheek and neck.

"Am I never going to see you again?"

She made no reply.

"Never?" he repeated.

After a long time, he bent over to hear a faint reply: "Sometimes-when there are no troops in the neighbourhood-grandpa don't mind if I —walk over as far as that old oak tree yonder-in the afternoons."

It appeared that the captain's grip was very strong, for she uttered an exclamation and looked at her fingers as if she expected to find them mere fragments. He rode away.

The bay horse leaped a flower-bed. They were almost to the drive, when the girl uttered a panic-stricken cry.

The captain wheeled his horse violently, and upon his return journey went straight through a flower-bed.

The girl had clasped her hands. She beseeched him wildly with her eyes.
"Oh, please, don't believe it! I never walk to the old oak tree. Indeed
I don't! I never-never-never walk there."

The bridle drooped on the bay charger's neck. The captain's figure seemed limp. With an expression of profound dejection and gloom he stared off at where the leaden sky met the dark green line of the woods. The long-impending rain began to fall with a mournful patter, drop and drop. There was a silence.

At last a low voice said, "Well —I might-sometimes I might-perhaps-but only once in a great while —I might walk to the old tree-in the afternoons."

THE VETERAN

Out of the low window could be seen three hickory trees placed irregularly in a meadow that was resplendent in spring-time green. Farther away, the old, dismal belfry of the village church loomed over the pines. A horse, meditating in the shade of one of the hickories, lazily swished his tail. The warm sunshine made an oblong of vivid yellow on the floor of the grocery.

"Could you see the whites of their eyes?" said the man, who was seated on a soap box.

"Nothing of the kind," replied old Henry warmly. "Just a lot of flitting figures, and I let go at where they 'peared to be the thickest. Bang!"

"Mr. Fleming," said the grocer-his deferential voice expressed somehow the old man's exact social weight —"Mr. Fleming, you never was frightened much in them battles, was you?"

The veteran looked down and grinned. Observing his manner, the entire group tittered. "Well, I guess I was," he answered finally. "Pretty well scared, sometimes. Why, in my first battle I thought the sky was falling down. I thought the world was coming to an end. You bet I was scared."

Every one laughed. Perhaps it seemed strange and rather wonderful to them that a man should admit the thing, and in the tone of their laughter there was probably more admiration than if old Fleming had declared that he had always been a lion. Moreover, they knew that he had ranked as an orderly sergeant, and so their opinion of his heroism was fixed. None, to be sure, knew how an orderly sergeant ranked, but then it was understood to be somewhere just shy of a major-general's stars. So, when old Henry admitted that he had been frightened, there was a laugh.

"The trouble was," said the old man, "I thought they were all shooting at me. Yes, sir, I thought every man in the other army was aiming at me in particular, and only me. And it seemed so darned unreasonable, you know. I wanted to explain to 'em what an almighty good fellow I was, because I thought then they might quit all trying to hit me. But I couldn't explain, and they kept on being unreasonable-blim! —blam! bang! So I run!"

Two little triangles of wrinkles appeared at the corners of his eyes. Evidently he appreciated some comedy in this recital. Down near his feet, however, little Jim, his grandson, was visibly horror-stricken. His hands were clasped nervously, and his eyes were wide with astonishment at this terrible scandal, his most magnificent grandfather telling such a thing.

"That was at Chancellorsville. Of course, afterward I got kind of used to it. A man does. Lots of men, though, seem to feel all right from the start. I did, as soon as I 'got on to it,' as they say now; but at first I was pretty well flustered. Now, there was young Jim Conklin, old Si Conklin's son-that used to keep the tannery-you none of you recollect him-well, he went into it from the start just as if he was born to it. But with me it was different. I had to get used to it."

When little Jim walked with his grandfather he was in the habit of skipping along on the stone pavement, in front of the three stores and the hotel of the town, and betting that he could avoid the cracks. But upon this day he walked soberly, with his hand gripping two of his grandfather's fingers. Sometimes he kicked abstractedly at dandelions that curved over the walk. Any one could see that he was much troubled.

"There's Sickles's colt over in the medder, Jimmie," said the old man. "Don't you wish you owned one like him?"

"Um," said the boy, with a strange lack of interest. He continued his reflections. Then finally he ventured: "Grandpa-now-was that true what you was telling those men?"

"What?" asked the grandfather. "What was I telling them?"

"Oh, about your running."

"Why, yes, that was true enough, Jimmie. It was my first fight, and there was an awful lot of noise, you know."

Jimmie seemed dazed that this idol, of its own will, should so totter. His stout boyish idealism was injured.

Presently the grandfather said: "Sickles's colt is going for a drink. Don't you wish you owned Sickles's colt, Jimmie?"

The boy merely answered: "He ain't as nice as our'n." He lapsed then into another moody silence.

* * * * *

One of the hired men, a Swede, desired to drive to the county seat for purposes of his own. The old man loaned a horse and an unwashed buggy. It appeared later that one of the purposes of the Swede was to get drunk.

After quelling some boisterous frolic of the farm hands and boys in the garret, the old man had that night gone peacefully to sleep, when he was aroused by clamouring at the kitchen door. He grabbed his trousers, and they waved out behind as he dashed forward. He could hear the voice of the Swede, screaming and blubbering. He pushed the wooden button, and, as the door flew open, the Swede, a maniac, stumbled inward, chattering, weeping, still screaming: "De barn fire! Fire! Fire! De barn fire! Fire! Fire! Fire!"

There was a swift and indescribable change in the old man. His face ceased instantly to be a face; it became a mask, a grey thing, with horror written about the mouth and eyes. He hoarsely shouted at the foot of the little rickety stairs, and immediately, it seemed, there came down an avalanche of men. No one knew that during this time the old lady had been standing in her night-clothes at the bedroom door, yelling: "What's th' matter? What's th' matter? What's th' matter?"

When they dashed toward the barn it presented to their eyes its usual appearance, solemn, rather mystic in the black night. The Swede's lantern was overturned at a point some yards in front of the barn doors. It contained a wild little conflagration of its own, and even in their excitement some of those who ran felt a gentle secondary vibration of the thrifty part of their minds at sight of this overturned lantern. Under ordinary circumstances it would have been a calamity.

But the cattle in the barn were trampling, trampling, trampling, and above this noise could be heard a humming like the song of innumerable bees. The old man hurled aside the great doors, and a yellow flame leaped out at one corner and sped and wavered frantically up the old grey wall. It was glad, terrible, this single flame, like the wild banner of deadly and triumphant foes.

The motley crowd from the garret had come with all the pails of the farm. They flung themselves upon the well. It was a leisurely old machine, long dwelling in indolence. It was in the habit of giving out water with a sort of reluctance. The men stormed at it, cursed it; but it continued to allow the buckets to be filled only after the wheezy windlass had howled many protests at the mad-handed men.

With his opened knife in his hand old Fleming himself had gone headlong into the barn, where the stifling smoke swirled with the air currents, and where could be heard in its fulness the terrible chorus of the flames, laden with tones of hate and death, a hymn of wonderful ferocity.

He flung a blanket over an old mare's head, cut the halter close to the manger, led the mare to the door, and fairly kicked her out to safety. He returned with the same blanket, and rescued one of the work horses. He took five horses out, and then came out himself, with his clothes bravely on fire. He had no whiskers, and very little hair on his head. They soused five pailfuls of water on him. His eldest son made a clean miss with the sixth pailful, because the old man had turned and was running down the decline and around to the basement of the barn, where were the stanchions of the cows. Some one noticed at the time that he ran very lamely, as if one of the frenzied horses had smashed his hip.

The cows, with their heads held in the heavy stanchions, had thrown themselves, strangled themselves, tangled themselves-done everything which the ingenuity of their exuberant fear could suggest to them.

Here, as at the well, the same thing happened to every man save one. Their hands went mad. They became incapable of everything save the power to rush into dangerous situations.

The old man released the cow nearest the door, and she, blind drunk with terror, crashed into the Swede. The Swede had been running to and fro babbling. He carried an empty milk-pail, to which he clung with an unconscious, fierce enthusiasm. He shrieked like one lost as he went under the cow's hoofs, and the milk-pail, rolling across the floor, made a flash of silver in the gloom.

Old Fleming took a fork, beat off the cow, and dragged the paralysed Swede to the open air. When they had rescued all the cows save one, which had so fastened herself that she could not be moved an inch, they returned to the front of the barn, and stood sadly, breathing like men who had reached the final point of human effort.

Many people had come running. Some one had even gone to the church, and now, from the distance, rang the tocsin note of the old bell. There was a long flare of crimson on the sky, which made remote people speculate as to the whereabouts of the fire.

The long flames sang their drumming chorus in voices of the heaviest bass. The wind whirled clouds of smoke and cinders into the faces of the spectators. The form of the old barn was outlined in black amid these masses of orange-hued flames.

And then came this Swede again, crying as one who is the weapon of the sinister fates: "De colts! De colts! You have forgot de colts!"

Old Fleming staggered. It was true: they had forgotten the two colts in the box-stalls at the back of the barn. "Boys," he said, "I must try to get 'em out." They clamoured about him then, afraid for him, afraid of what they should see. Then they talked wildly each to each. "Why, it's sure death!" "He would never get out!" "Why, it's suicide for a man to go in there!" Old Fleming stared absent-mindedly at the open doors. "The poor little things!" he said. He rushed into the barn.

When the roof fell in, a great funnel of smoke swarmed toward the sky, as if the old man's mighty spirit, released from its body—a little bottle-had swelled like the genie of fable. The smoke was tinted rose-hue from the flames, and perhaps the unutterable midnights of the universe will have no power to daunt the colour of this soul.

The Open Boat and Other Stories

Part I
Minor Conflicts

The Open Boat

A Tale intended to be after the Fact. Being the Experience of Four Men from the Sunk Steamer 'Commodore'

None of them knew the colour of the sky. Their eyes glanced level, and were fastened upon the waves that swept toward them. These waves were of the hue of slate, save for the tops, which were of foaming white, and all of the men knew the colours of the sea. The horizon narrowed and widened, and dipped and rose, and at all times its edge was jagged with waves that seemed thrust up in points like rocks.

Many a man ought to have a bath-tub larger than the boat which here rode upon the sea. These waves were most wrongfully and barbarously abrupt and tall, and each froth-top was a problem in small boat navigation.

The cook squatted in the bottom and looked with both eyes at the six inches of gunwale which separated him from the ocean. His sleeves were rolled over his fat forearms, and the two flaps of his unbuttoned vest dangled as he bent to bail out the boat. Often he said: "Gawd! That was a narrow clip." As he remarked it he invariably gazed eastward over the broken sea.

The oiler, steering with one of the two oars in the boat, sometimes raised himself suddenly to keep clear of water that swirled in over the stern. It was a thin little oar and it seemed often ready to snap.

The correspondent, pulling at the other oar, watched the waves and wondered why he was there.

The injured captain, lying in the bow, was at this time buried in that profound dejection and indifference which comes, temporarily at least, to even the bravest and most enduring when, willy nilly, the firm fails, the army loses, the ship goes down. The mind of the master of a vessel is rooted deep in the timbers of her, though he commanded for a day or a decade, and this captain had on him the stern impression of a scene in the greys of dawn of seven turned faces, and later a stump of a top-mast with a white ball on it that slashed to and fro at the waves, went low and lower, and down. Thereafter there was something strange in his voice. Although steady, it was deep with mourning, and of a quality beyond oration or tears.

"Keep 'er a little more south, Billie," said he.

"'A little more south,' sir," said the oiler in the stern.

A seat in this boat was not unlike a seat upon a bucking broncho, and, by the same token, a broncho is not much smaller. The craft pranced and reared, and plunged like an animal. As each wave came, and she rose for it, she seemed like a horse making at a fence outrageously high. The manner of her scramble over these walls of water is a mystic thing, and, moreover, at the top of them were ordinarily these problems in white water, the foam racing down from the summit of each wave, requiring a new leap, and a leap from the air. Then, after scornfully bumping a crest, she would slide, and race, and splash down a long incline, and arrive bobbing and nodding in front of the next menace.

A singular disadvantage of the sea lies in the fact that after successfully surmounting one wave you discover that there is another behind it just as important and just as nervously anxious to do something effective in the way of swamping boats. In a ten-foot dingey one can get an idea of the resources of the sea in the line of waves that is not probable to the average experience which is never at sea in a dingey. As each slaty wall of water approached, it shut all else from the view of the men in the boat, and it was not difficult to imagine that this particular wave was the final outburst of the ocean, the last effort of the grim water. There was a terrible grace in the move of the waves, and they came in silence, save for the snarling of the crests.

In the wan light, the faces of the men must have been grey. Their eyes must have glinted in strange ways as they gazed steadily astern. Viewed from a balcony, the whole thing would doubtlessly have been weirdly picturesque. But the men in the boat had no time to see it, and if they had had leisure there were other things to occupy their minds. The sun swung steadily up the sky, and they knew it was broad day because the colour of the sea changed from slate to emerald-green, streaked with amber lights, and the foam was like tumbling snow. The process of the breaking day was unknown to them. They were aware only of this effect upon the colour of the waves that rolled toward them.

In disjointed sentences the cook and the correspondent argued as to the difference between a life-saving station and a house of refuge. The cook had said: "There's a house of refuge just north of the Mosquito Inlet Light, and as soon as they see us, they'll come off in their boat and pick us up."

"As soon as who see us?" said the correspondent.

"The crew," said the cook.

"Houses of refuge don't have crews," said the correspondent. "As I understand them, they are only places where clothes and grub are stored for the benefit of shipwrecked people. They don't carry crews."

"Oh, yes, they do," said the cook.

"No, they don't," said the correspondent.

"Well, we're not there yet, anyhow," said the oiler, in the stern.

"Well," said the cook, "perhaps it's not a house of refuge that I'm thinking of as being near Mosquito Inlet Light. Perhaps it's a life-saving station."

"We're not there yet," said the oiler, in the stern.

II

As the boat bounced from the top of each wave, the wind tore through the hair of the hatless men, and as the craft plopped her stern down again the spray slashed past them. The crest of each of these waves was a hill, from the top of which the men surveyed, for a moment, a broad tumultuous expanse, shining and wind-riven. It was probably splendid. It was probably glorious, this play of the free sea, wild with lights of emerald and white and amber.

"Bully good thing it's an on-shore wind," said the cook. "If not, where would we be? Wouldn't have a show."

"That's right," said the correspondent.

The busy oiler nodded his assent.

Then the captain, in the bow, chuckled in a way that expressed humour, contempt, tragedy, all in one. "Do you think we've got much of a show now, boys?" said he.

Whereupon the three were silent, save for a trifle of hemming and hawing. To express any particular optimism at this time they felt to be childish and stupid, but they all doubtless possessed this sense of the situation in their mind. A young man thinks doggedly at such times. On the other hand, the ethics of their condition was decidedly against any open suggestion of hopelessness. So they were silent.

"Oh, well," said the captain, soothing his children, "we'll get ashore all right."

But there was that in his tone which made them think, so the oiler quoth: "Yes! If this wind holds!"

The cook was bailing: "Yes! If we don't catch hell in the surf."

Canton flannel gulls flew near and far. Sometimes they sat down on the sea, near patches of brown sea-weed that rolled over the waves with a movement like carpets on a line in a gale. The birds sat comfortably in groups, and they were envied by some in the dingey, for the wrath of the sea was no more to them than it was to a covey of prairie chickens a thousand miles inland. Often they came very close and stared at the men with black bead-like eyes. At these times they were uncanny and sinister in their unblinking scrutiny, and the men hooted angrily at them, telling them to be gone. One came, and evidently decided to alight on the top of the captain's head. The bird flew parallel to the boat and did not circle, but made short sidelong jumps in the air in chicken-fashion. His black eyes were wistfully fixed upon the captain's head. "Ugly brute," said the oiler to the bird. "You look as if you were made with a jack-knife." The cook and the correspondent swore darkly at the creature. The captain naturally wished to knock it away with the end of the heavy painter; but he did not dare do it, because anything resembling an emphatic gesture would have capsized this freighted boat, and so with his open hand, the captain gently and carefully waved the gull away. After it had been discouraged from the pursuit the captain breathed easier on account of his hair, and others breathed easier because the bird struck their minds at this time as being somehow grewsome and ominous.

In the meantime the oiler and the correspondent rowed. And also they rowed.

They sat together in the same seat, and each rowed an oar. Then the oiler took both oars; then the correspondent took both oars; then the oiler; then the correspondent. They rowed and they rowed. The very ticklish part of the business was when the time came for the reclining one in the stern to take his turn at the oars. By the very last star of truth, it is easier to steal eggs from under a hen than it was to change seats in the dingey. First the man in the stern slid his hand along the thwart and moved with care, as if he were of Sèvres. Then the man in the rowing seat slid his hand along the other thwart. It was all done with the most extraordinary care. As the two sidled past each other, the whole party kept watchful eyes on the coming wave, and the captain cried: "Look out now! Steady there!"

The brown mats of sea-weed that appeared from time to time were like islands, bits of earth. They were travelling, apparently, neither one way nor the other. They were, to all intents, stationary. They informed the men in the boat that it was making progress slowly toward the land.

The captain, rearing cautiously in the bow, after the dingey soared on a great swell, said that he had seen the lighthouse at Mosquito Inlet. Presently the cook remarked that he had seen it. The correspondent was at the oars then, and for some reason he too wished to look at the lighthouse, but his back was toward the far shore and the waves were important, and for some time he could not seize an opportunity to turn his head. But at last there came a wave more gentle than the others, and when at the crest of it he swiftly scoured the western horizon.

"See it?" said the captain.

"No," said the correspondent slowly, "I didn't see anything."

"Look again," said the captain. He pointed. "It's exactly in that direction."

At the top of another wave, the correspondent did as he was bid, and this time his eyes chanced on a small still thing on the edge of the swaying horizon. It was precisely like the point of a pin. It took an anxious eye to find a lighthouse so tiny.

"Think we'll make it, captain?"

"If this wind holds and the boat don't swamp, we can't do much else," said the captain.

The little boat, lifted by each towering sea, and splashed viciously by the crests, made progress that in the absence of sea-weed was not apparent to those in her. She seemed just a wee thing wallowing, miraculously top-up, at the mercy of five oceans. Occasionally, a great spread of water, like white flames, swarmed into her.

"Bail her, cook," said the captain serenely.

"All right, captain," said the cheerful cook.

It would be difficult to describe the subtle brotherhood of men that was here established on the seas. No one said that it was so. No one mentioned it. But it dwelt in the boat, and each man felt it warm him. They were a captain, an oiler, a cook, and a correspondent, and they were friends, friends in a more curiously iron-bound degree than may be common. The hurt captain, lying against the water-jar in the bow, spoke always in a low voice and calmly, but he could never command a more ready and swiftly obedient crew than the motley three of the dingey. It was more than a mere recognition of what was best for the common safety. There was surely in it a quality that was personal and heartfelt. And after this devotion to the commander of the boat there was this comradeship that the correspondent, for instance, who had been taught to be cynical of men, knew even at the time was the best experience of his life. But no one said that it was so. No one mentioned it.

"I wish we had a sail," remarked the captain. "We might try my overcoat on the end of an oar and give you two boys a chance to rest." So the cook and the correspondent held the mast and spread wide the overcoat. The oiler steered, and the little boat made good way with her new rig. Sometimes the oiler had to scull sharply to keep a sea from breaking into the boat, but otherwise sailing was a success.

Meanwhile the lighthouse had been growing slowly larger. It had now almost assumed colour, and appeared like a little grey shadow on the sky. The man at the oars could not be prevented from turning his head rather often to try for a glimpse of this little grey shadow.

At last, from the top of each wave the men in the tossing boat could see land. Even as the lighthouse was an upright shadow on the sky, this land seemed but a long black shadow on the sea. It certainly was thinner than paper. "We must be about opposite New Smyrna," said the cook, who had coasted this shore often in schooners. "Captain, by the way, I believe they abandoned that life-saving station there about a year ago."

"Did they?" said the captain.

The wind slowly died away. The cook and the correspondent were not now obliged to slave in order to hold high the oar. But the waves continued their old impetuous swooping at the dingey, and the little craft, no longer under way, struggled woundily over them. The oiler or the correspondent took the oars again.

Shipwrecks are *à propos* of nothing. If men could only train for them and have them occur when the men had reached pink condition, there would be less drowning at sea. Of the four in the dingey none had slept any time worth mentioning for two days and two nights previous to embarking in the dingey, and in the excitement of clambering about the deck of a foundering ship they had also forgotten to eat heartily.

For these reasons, and for others, neither the oiler nor the correspondent was fond of rowing at this time. The correspondent wondered ingenuously how in the name of all that was sane could there be people who thought it amusing to row a boat. It was not an amusement; it was a diabolical punishment, and even a genius of mental aberrations could never conclude that it was anything but a horror to the muscles and a crime against the back. He mentioned to the boat in general how the amusement of rowing struck him, and the weary-faced oiler smiled in full sympathy. Previously to the foundering, by the way, the oiler had worked double-watch in the engine-room of the ship.

"Take her easy, now, boys," said the captain. "Don't spend yourselves. If we have to run a surf you'll need all your strength, because we'll sure have to swim for it. Take your time."

Slowly the land arose from the sea. From a black line it became a line of black and a line of white, trees and sand. Finally, the captain said that he could make out a house on the shore. "That's the house of refuge, sure," said the cook. "They'll see us before long, and come out after us."

The distant lighthouse reared high. "The keeper ought to be able to make us out now, if he's looking through a glass," said the captain. "He'll notify the life-saving people."

"None of those other boats could have got ashore to give word of the wreck," said the oiler, in a low voice. "Else the life-boat would be out hunting us."

Slowly and beautifully the land loomed out of the sea. The wind came again. It had veered from the north-east to the south-east. Finally, a new sound struck the ears of the men in the boat. It was the low thunder of the surf on the shore. "We'll never be able to make the lighthouse now," said the captain. "Swing her head a little more north, Billie," said he.

"'A little more north,' sir," said the oiler.

Whereupon the little boat turned her nose once more down the wind, and all but the oarsman watched the shore grow. Under the influence of this expansion doubt and direful apprehension was leaving the minds of the men. The management of the boat was still most absorbing, but it could not prevent a quiet cheerfulness. In an hour, perhaps, they would be ashore.

Their backbones had become thoroughly used to balancing in the boat, and they now rode this wild colt of a dingey like circus men. The correspondent thought that he had been drenched to the skin, but happening to feel in the top pocket of his coat, he found therein eight cigars. Four of them were soaked with sea-water; four were perfectly scatheless. After a search, somebody produced three dry matches, and thereupon the four waifs rode impudently in their little boat, and with an assurance of an impending rescue shining in their eyes, puffed at the big cigars and judged well and ill of all men. Everybody took a drink of water.

IV

"Cook," remarked the captain, "there don't seem to be any signs of life about your house of refuge."

"No," replied the cook. "Funny they don't see us!"

A broad stretch of lowly coast lay before the eyes of the men. It was of dunes topped with dark vegetation. The roar of the surf was plain, and sometimes they could see the white lip of a wave as it spun up the beach. A tiny house was blocked out black upon the sky. Southward, the slim lighthouse lifted its little grey length.

Tide, wind, and waves were swinging the dingey northward. "Funny they don't see us," said the men.

The surf's roar was here dulled, but its tone was, nevertheless, thunderous and mighty. As the boat swam over the great rollers, the men sat listening to this roar. "We'll swamp sure," said everybody.

It is fair to say here that there was not a life-saving station within twenty miles in either direction, but the men did not know this fact, and in consequence they made dark and opprobrious remarks concerning the eyesight of the nation's life-savers. Four scowling men sat in the dingey and surpassed records in the invention of epithets.

"Funny they don't see us."

The light-heartedness of a former time had completely faded. To their sharpened minds it was easy to conjure pictures of all kinds of incompetency and blindness and, indeed, cowardice. There was the shore of the populous land, and it was bitter and bitter to them that from it came no sign.

"Well," said the captain, ultimately, "I suppose we'll have to make a try for ourselves. If we stay out here too long, we'll none of us have strength left to swim after the boat swamps."

And so the oiler, who was at the oars, turned the boat straight for the shore. There was a sudden tightening of muscles. There was some thinking.

"If we don't all get ashore —" said the captain. "If we don't all get ashore, I suppose you fellows know where to send news of my finish?"

They then briefly exchanged some addresses and admonitions. As for the reflections of the men, there was a great deal of rage in them. Perchance they might be formulated thus: "If I am going to be drowned-if I am going to be drowned-if I am going to be drowned, why, in the name of the seven mad gods who rule the sea, was I allowed to come thus far and contemplate sand and trees? Was I brought here merely to have my nose dragged away as I was about to nibble the sacred cheese of life? It is preposterous. If this old ninny-woman, Fate, cannot do better than this, she should be deprived of the management of men's fortunes. She is an old hen who knows not her intention. If she has decided to drown me, why did she not do it in the beginning and save me all this trouble? The whole affair is absurd....But no, she cannot mean to drown me. She dare not drown me. She cannot drown me. Not after all this work." Afterward the man might have had an impulse to shake his fist at the clouds: "Just you drown me, now, and then hear what I call you!"

The billows that came at this time were more formidable. They seemed always just about to break and roll over the little boat in a turmoil of foam. There was a preparatory and long growl in the speech of them. No mind unused to the sea would have concluded that the dingey could ascend these sheer heights in time. The shore was still afar. The oiler was a wily surfman. "Boys," he said swiftly, "she won't live three minutes more, and we're too far out to swim. Shall I take her to sea again, captain?"

"Yes! Go ahead!" said the captain.

This oiler, by a series of quick miracles, and fast and steady oarsmanship, turned the boat in the middle of the surf and took her safely to sea again.

There was a considerable silence as the boat bumped over the furrowed sea to deeper water. Then somebody in gloom spoke. "Well, anyhow, they must have seen us from the shore by now."

The gulls went in slanting flight up the wind toward the grey desolate east. A squall, marked by dingy clouds, and clouds brick-red, like smoke from a burning building, appeared from the south-east.

"What do you think of those life-saving people? Ain't they peaches?"

"Funny they haven't seen us."

"Maybe they think we're out here for sport! Maybe they think we're fishin'. Maybe they think we're damned fools."

It was a long afternoon. A changed tide tried to force them southward, but wind and wave said northward. Far ahead, where coast-line, sea, and sky formed their mighty angle, there were little dots which seemed to indicate a city on the shore.

"St. Augustine?"

The captain shook his head. "Too near Mosquito Inlet."

And the oiler rowed, and then the correspondent rowed. Then the oiler rowed. It was a weary business. The human back can become the seat of more aches and pains than are registered in books for the composite anatomy of a regiment. It is a limited area, but it can become the theatre of innumerable muscular conflicts, tangles, wrenches, knots, and other comforts.

"Did you ever like to row, Billie?" asked the correspondent.

"No," said the oiler. "Hang it."

When one exchanged the rowing-seat for a place in the bottom of the boat, he suffered a bodily depression that caused him to be careless of everything save an obligation to wiggle one finger. There was cold sea-water swashing to and fro in the boat, and he lay in it. His head, pillowed on a thwart, was within an inch of the swirl of a wave crest, and sometimes a particularly obstreperous sea came in-board and drenched him once more. But these matters did not annoy him. It is almost certain that if the boat had capsized he would have tumbled comfortably out upon the ocean as if he felt sure that it was a great soft mattress.

"Look! There's a man on the shore!"

"Where?"

"There! See 'im? See 'im?"

"Yes, sure! He's walking along."

"Now he's stopped. Look! He's facing us!"

"He's waving at us!"

"So he is! By thunder!"

"Ah, now we're all right! Now we're all right! There'll be a boat out here for us in half-an-hour."

"He's going on. He's running. He's going up to that house there."

The remote beach seemed lower than the sea, and it required a searching glance to discern the little black figure. The captain saw a floating stick and they rowed to it. A bath-towel was by some weird chance in the boat, and, tying this on the stick, the captain waved it. The oarsman did not dare turn his head, so he was obliged to ask questions.

"What's he doing now?"

"He's standing still again. He's looking, I think.... There he goes again. Towards the house.... Now he's stopped again."

"Is he waving at us?"

"No, not now! he was, though."

"Look! There comes another man!"

"He's running."

"Look at him go, would you."

"Why, he's on a bicycle. Now he's met the other man. They're both waving at us. Look!"

"There comes something up the beach."

"What the devil is that thing?"

"Why, it looks like a boat."

"Why, certainly it's a boat."

"No, it's on wheels."

"Yes, so it is. Well, that must be the life-boat. They drag them along shore on a wagon."

"That's the life-boat, sure."

"No, by —— , it's —it's an omnibus."

"I tell you it's a life-boat."

"It is not! It's an omnibus. I can see it plain. See? One of these big hotel omnibuses."

"By thunder, you're right. It's an omnibus, sure as fate. What do you suppose they are doing with an omnibus? Maybe they are going around collecting the life-crew, hey?"

"That's it, likely. Look! There's a fellow waving a little black flag. He's standing on the steps of the omnibus. There come those other two fellows. Now they're all talking together. Look at the fellow with the flag. Maybe he ain't waving it."

"That ain't a flag, is it? That's his coat. Why certainly, that's his coat."

"So it is. It's his coat. He's taken it off and is waving it around his head. But would you look at him swing it."

"Oh, say, there isn't any life-saving station there. That's just a winter resort hotel omnibus that has brought over some of the boarders to see us drown."

"What's that idiot with the coat mean? What's he signaling, anyhow?"

"It looks as if he were trying to tell us to go north. There must be a life-saving station up there."

"No! He thinks we're fishing. Just giving us a merry hand. See? Ah, there, Willie."

"Well, I wish I could make something out of those signals. What do you suppose he means?"

"He don't mean anything. He's just playing."

"Well, if he'd just signal us to try the surf again, or to go to sea and wait, or go north, or go south, or go to hell-there would be some reason in it. But look at him. He just stands there and keeps his coat revolving like a wheel. The ass!"

"There come more people."

"Now there's quite a mob. Look! Isn't that a boat?"

"Where? Oh, I see where you mean. No, that's no boat."

"That fellow is still waving his coat."

"He must think we like to see him do that. Why don't he quit it? It don't mean anything."

"I don't know. I think he is trying to make us go north. It must be that there's a life-saving station there somewhere."

"Say, he ain't tired yet. Look at 'im wave."

"Wonder how long he can keep that up. He's been revolving his coat ever since he caught sight of us. He's an idiot. Why aren't they getting men to bring a boat out? A fishing boat-one of those big yawls-could come out here all right. Why don't he do something?"

"Oh, it's all right, now."

"They'll have a boat out here for us in less than no time, now that they've seen us."

A faint yellow tone came into the sky over the low land. The shadows on the sea slowly deepened. The wind bore coldness with it, and the men began to shiver.

"Holy smoke!" said one, allowing his voice to express his impious mood, "if we keep on monkeying out here! If we've got to flounder out here all night!"

"Oh, we'll never have to stay here all night! Don't you worry. They've seen us now, and it won't be long before they'll come chasing out after us."

The shore grew dusky. The man waving a coat blended gradually into this gloom, and it swallowed in the same manner the omnibus and the group of people. The spray, when it dashed uproariously over the side, made the voyagers shrink and swear like men who were being branded.

"I'd like to catch the chump who waved the coat. I feel like soaking him one, just for luck."

"Why? What did he do?"

"Oh, nothing, but then he seemed so damned cheerful."

In the meantime the oiler rowed, and then the correspondent rowed, and then the oiler rowed. Grey-faced and bowed forward, they mechanically, turn by turn, plied the leaden oars. The form of the lighthouse had vanished from the southern horizon, but finally a pale star appeared, just lifting from the sea. The streaked saffron in the west passed before the all-merging darkness, and the sea to the east was black. The land had vanished, and was expressed only by the low and drear thunder of the surf.

"If I am going to be drowned-if I am going to be drowned-if I am going to be drowned, why, in the name of the seven mad gods who rule the sea, was I allowed to come thus far and contemplate sand and trees? Was I brought here merely to have my nose dragged away as I was about to nibble the sacred cheese of life?"

The patient captain, drooped over the water-jar, was sometimes obliged to speak to the oarsman.

"Keep her head up! Keep her head up!"

" 'Keep her head up,' sir." The voices were weary and low.

This was surely a quiet evening. All save the oarsman lay heavily and listlessly in the boat's bottom. As for him, his eyes were just capable of noting the tall black waves that swept forward in a most sinister silence, save for an occasional subdued growl of a crest.

The cook's head was on a thwart, and he looked without interest at the water under his nose. He was deep in other scenes. Finally he spoke. "Billie," he murmured, dreamfully, "what kind of pie do you like best?"

V

"Pie," said the oiler and the correspondent, agitatedly. "Don't talk about those things, blast you!"

"Well," said the cook, "I was just thinking about ham sandwiches, and — —"

A night on the sea in an open boat is a long night. As darkness settled finally, the shine of the light, lifting from the sea in the south, changed to full gold. On the northern horizon a new light appeared, a small bluish gleam on the edge of the waters. These two lights were the furniture of the world. Otherwise there was nothing but waves.

Two men huddled in the stern, and distances were so magnificent in the dingey that the rower was enabled to keep his feet partly warmed by thrusting them under his companions. Their legs indeed extended far under the rowing-seat until they touched the feet of the captain forward. Sometimes, despite the efforts of the tired oarsman, a wave came piling into the boat, an icy wave of the night, and the chilling water soaked them anew. They would twist their bodies for a moment and groan, and sleep the dead sleep once more, while the water in the boat gurgled about them as the craft rocked.

The plan of the oiler and the correspondent was for one to row until he lost the ability, and then arouse the other from his sea-water couch in the bottom of the boat.

The oiler plied the oars until his head drooped forward, and the overpowering sleep blinded him. And he rowed yet afterward. Then he touched a man in the bottom of the boat, and called his name. "Will you spell me for a little while?" he said, meekly.

"Sure, Billie," said the correspondent, awakening and dragging himself to a sitting position. They exchanged places carefully, and the oiler, cuddling down in the sea-water at the cook's side, seemed to go to sleep instantly.

The particular violence of the sea had ceased. The waves came without snarling. The obligation of the man at the oars was to keep the boat headed so that the tilt of the rollers would not capsize her, and to preserve her from filling when the crests rushed past. The black waves were silent and hard to be seen in the darkness. Often one was almost upon the boat before the oarsman was aware.

In a low voice the correspondent addressed the captain. He was not sure that the captain was awake, although this iron man seemed to be always awake. "Captain, shall I keep her making for that light north, sir?"

The same steady voice answered him. "Yes. Keep it about two points off the port bow."

The cook had tied a life-belt around himself in order to get even the warmth which this clumsy cork contrivance could donate, and he seemed almost stove-like when a rower, whose teeth invariably chattered wildly as soon as he ceased his labour, dropped down to sleep.

The correspondent, as he rowed, looked down at the two men sleeping under-foot. The cook's arm was around the oiler's shoulders, and, with their fragmentary clothing and haggard faces, they were the babes of the sea, a grotesque rendering of the old babes in the wood.

Later he must have grown stupid at his work, for suddenly there was a growling of water, and a crest came with a roar and a swash into the boat, and it was a wonder that it did not set the cook afloat in his life-belt. The cook continued to sleep, but the oiler sat up, blinking his eyes and shaking with the new cold.

"Oh, I'm awful sorry, Billie," said the correspondent contritely.

"That's all right, old boy," said the oiler, and lay down again and was asleep.

Presently it seemed that even the captain dozed, and the correspondent thought that he was the one man afloat on all the oceans. The wind had a voice as it came over the waves, and it was sadder than the end.

There was a long, loud swishing astern of the boat, and a gleaming trail of phosphorescence, like blue flame, was furrowed on the black waters. It might have been made by a monstrous knife.

Then there came a stillness, while the correspondent breathed with the open mouth and looked at the sea.

Suddenly there was another swish and another long flash of bluish light, and this time it was alongside the boat, and might almost have been reached with an oar. The correspondent saw an enormous fin speed like a shadow through the water, hurling the crystalline spray and leaving the long glowing trail.

The correspondent looked over his shoulder at the captain. His face was hidden, and he seemed to be asleep. He looked at the babes of the sea. They certainly were asleep. So, being bereft of sympathy, he leaned a little way to one side and swore softly into the sea.

But the thing did not then leave the vicinity of the boat. Ahead or astern, on one side or the other, at intervals long or short, fled the long sparkling streak, and there was to be heard the whiroo of the dark fin. The speed and power of the thing was greatly to be admired. It cut the water like a gigantic and keen projectile.

The presence of this biding thing did not affect the man with the same horror that it would if he had been a picnicker. He simply looked at the sea dully and swore in an undertone.

Nevertheless, it is true that he did not wish to be alone. He wished one of his companions to awaken by chance and keep him company with it. But the captain hung motionless over the water-jar, and the oiler and the cook in the bottom of the boat were plunged in slumber.

"If I am going to be drowned-if I am going to be drowned-if I am going to be drowned, why, in the name of the seven mad gods who rule the sea, was I allowed to come thus far and contemplate sand and trees?"

During this dismal night, it may be remarked that a man would conclude that it was really the intention of the seven mad gods to drown him, despite the abominable injustice of it. For it was certainly an abominable injustice to drown a man who had worked so hard, so hard. The man felt it would be a crime most unnatural. Other people had drowned at sea since galleys swarmed with painted sails, but still — —

When it occurs to a man that nature does not regard him as important, and that she feels she would not maim the universe by disposing of him, he at first wishes to throw bricks at the temple, and he hates deeply the fact that there are no bricks and no temples. Any visible expression of nature would surely be pelleted with his jeers.

Then, if there be no tangible thing to hoot he feels, perhaps, the desire to confront a personification and indulge in pleas, bowed to one knee, and with hands supplicant, saying: "Yes, but I love myself."

A high cold star on a winter's night is the word he feels that she says to him. Thereafter he knows the pathos of his situation.

The men in the dingey had not discussed these matters, but each had, no doubt, reflected upon them in silence and according to his mind. There was seldom any expression upon their faces save the general one of complete weariness. Speech was devoted to the business of the boat.

To chime the notes of his emotion, a verse mysteriously entered the correspondent's head. He had even forgotten that he had forgotten this verse, but it suddenly was in his mind.

"A soldier of the Legion lay dying in Algiers,
There was lack of woman's nursing, there was dearth of woman's tears;
But a comrade stood beside him, and he took that comrade's hand,
And he said: 'I shall never see my own, my native land.'"

In his childhood, the correspondent had been made acquainted with the fact that a soldier of the Legion lay dying in Algiers, but he had never regarded the fact as important. Myriads of his school-fellows had informed him of the soldier's plight, but the dinning had naturally ended by making him perfectly indifferent. He had never considered it his affair that a soldier of the Legion lay dying in Algiers, nor had it appeared to him as a matter for sorrow. It was less to him than the breaking of a pencil's point.

Now, however, it quaintly came to him as a human, living thing. It was no longer merely a picture of a few throes in the breast of a poet, meanwhile drinking tea and warming his feet at the grate; it was an actuality-stern, mournful, and fine.

The correspondent plainly saw the soldier. He lay on the sand with his feet out straight and still. While his pale left hand was upon his chest in an attempt to thwart the going of his life, the blood came between his fingers. In the far Algerian distance, a city of low square forms was set against a sky that was faint with the last sunset hues. The correspondent, plying the oars and dreaming of the slow and slower movements of the lips of the soldier, was moved by a profound and perfectly impersonal comprehension. He was sorry for the soldier of the Legion who lay dying in Algiers.

The thing which had followed the boat and waited, had evidently grown bored at the delay. There was no longer to be heard the slash of the cut-water, and there was no longer the flame of the long trail. The light in the north still glimmered, but it was apparently no nearer to the boat. Sometimes the boom of the surf rang in the correspondent's ears, and he turned the craft seaward then and rowed harder. Southward, some one had evidently built a watch-fire on the beach. It was too low and too far to be seen, but it made a shimmering, roseate reflection upon the bluff back of it, and this could be discerned from the boat. The wind came stronger, and sometimes a wave suddenly raged out like a mountain-cat, and there was to be seen the sheen and sparkle of a broken crest.

The captain, in the bow, moved on his water-jar and sat erect. "Pretty long night," he observed to the correspondent. He looked at the shore. "Those life-saving people take their time."

"Did you see that shark playing around?"

"Yes, I saw him. He was a big fellow, all right."

"Wish I had known you were awake."

Later the correspondent spoke into the bottom of the boat.

"Billie!" There was a slow and gradual disentanglement. "Billie, will you spell me?"

"Sure," said the oiler.

As soon as the correspondent touched the cold comfortable sea-water in the bottom of the boat, and had huddled close to the cook's life-belt he was deep in sleep, despite the fact that his teeth played all the popular airs. This sleep was so good to him that it was but a moment before he heard a voice call his name in a tone that demonstrated the last stages of exhaustion. "Will you spell me?"

"Sure, Billie."

The light in the north had mysteriously vanished, but the correspondent took his course from the wide-awake captain.

Later in the night they took the boat farther out to sea, and the captain directed the cook to take one oar at the stern and keep the boat facing the seas. He was to call out if he should hear the thunder of the surf. This plan enabled the oiler and the correspondent to get respite together. "We'll give those boys a chance to get into shape again," said the captain. They curled down and, after a few preliminary chatterings and trembles, slept once more the dead sleep. Neither knew they had bequeathed to the cook the company of another shark, or perhaps the same shark.

As the boat caroused on the waves, spray occasionally bumped over the side and gave them a fresh soaking, but this had no power to break their repose. The ominous slash of the wind and the water affected them as it would have affected mummies.

"Boys," said the cook, with the notes of every reluctance in his voice, "she's drifted in pretty close. I guess one of you had better take her to sea again." The correspondent, aroused, heard the crash of the toppled crests.

As he was rowing, the captain gave him some whisky-and-water, and this steadied the chills out of him. "If I ever get ashore and anybody shows me even a photograph of an oar — —"

At last there was a short conversation.

"Billie.... Billie, will you spell me?"

"Sure," said the oiler.

VII

When the correspondent again opened his eyes, the sea and the sky were each of the grey hue of the dawning. Later, carmine and gold was painted upon the waters. The morning appeared finally, in its splendour, with a sky of pure blue, and the sunlight flamed on the tips of the waves.

On the distant dunes were set many little black cottages, and a tall white windmill reared above them. No man, nor dog, nor bicycle appeared on the beach. The cottages might have formed a deserted village.

The voyagers scanned the shore. A conference was held in the boat. "Well," said the captain, "if no help is coming we might better try a run through the surf right away. If we stay out here much longer we will be too weak to do anything for ourselves at all." The others silently acquiesced in this reasoning. The boat was headed for the beach. The correspondent wondered if none ever ascended the tall wind-tower, and if then they never looked seaward. This tower was a giant, standing with its back to the plight of the ants. It represented in a degree, to the correspondent, the serenity of nature amid the struggles of the individual-nature in the wind, and nature in the vision of men. She did not seem cruel to him then, nor beneficent, nor treacherous, nor wise. But she was indifferent, flatly indifferent. It is, perhaps, plausible that a man in this situation, impressed with the unconcern of the universe, should see the innumerable flaws of his life, and have them taste wickedly in his mind and wish for another chance. A distinction between right and wrong seems absurdly clear to him, then, in this new ignorance of the grave-edge, and he understands that if he were given another opportunity he would mend his conduct and his words, and be better and brighter during an introduction or at a tea.

"Now, boys," said the captain, "she is going to swamp, sure. All we can do is to work her in as far as possible, and then when she swamps, pile out and scramble for the beach. Keep cool now, and don't jump until she swamps sure."

The oiler took the oars. Over his shoulders he scanned the surf. "Captain," he said, "I think I'd better bring her about, and keep her head-on to the seas and back her in."

"All right, Billie," said the captain. "Back her in." The oiler swung the boat then and, seated in the stern, the cook and the correspondent were obliged to look over their shoulders to contemplate the lonely and indifferent shore.

The monstrous in-shore rollers heaved the boat high until the men were again enabled to see the white sheets of water scudding up the slanted beach. "We won't get in very close," said the captain. Each time a man could wrest his attention from the rollers, he turned his glance toward the shore, and in the expression of the eyes during this contemplation there was a singular quality. The correspondent, observing the others, knew that they were not afraid, but the full meaning of their glances was shrouded.

As for himself, he was too tired to grapple fundamentally with the fact. He tried to coerce his mind into thinking of it, but the mind was dominated at this time by the muscles, and the muscles said they did not care. It merely occurred to him that if he should drown it would be a shame.

There were no hurried words, no pallor, no plain agitation. The men simply looked at the shore. "Now, remember to get well clear of the boat when you jump," said the captain.

Seaward the crest of a roller suddenly fell with a thunderous crash, and the long white comber came roaring down upon the boat.

"Steady now," said the captain. The men were silent. They turned their eyes from the shore to the comber and waited. The boat slid up the incline, leaped at the furious top, bounced over it, and swung down the long back of the wave. Some water had been shipped and the cook bailed it out.

But the next crest crashed also. The tumbling boiling flood of white water caught the boat and whirled it almost perpendicular. Water swarmed in from all sides. The correspondent had his hands on the gunwale at this time, and when the water entered at that place he swiftly withdrew his fingers, as if he objected to wetting them.

The little boat, drunken with this weight of water, reeled and snuggled deeper into the sea.

"Bail her out, cook! Bail her out," said the captain.

"All right, captain," said the cook.

"Now, boys, the next one will do for us, sure," said the oiler. "Mind to jump clear of the boat."

The third wave moved forward, huge, furious, implacable. It fairly swallowed the dingey, and almost simultaneously the men tumbled into the sea. A piece of life-belt had lain in the bottom of the boat, and as the correspondent went overboard he held this to his chest with his left hand.

The January water was icy, and he reflected immediately that it was colder than he had expected to find it off the coast of Florida. This appeared to his dazed mind as a fact important enough to be noted at the time. The coldness of the water was sad; it was tragic. This fact was somehow so mixed and confused with his opinion of his own situation that it seemed almost a proper reason for tears. The water was cold.

When he came to the surface he was conscious of little but the noisy water. Afterward he saw his companions in the sea. The oiler was ahead in the race. He was swimming strongly and rapidly. Off to the correspondent's left, the cook's great white and corked back bulged out of the water, and in the rear the captain was hanging with his one good hand to the keel of the overturned dingey.

There is a certain immovable quality to a shore, and the correspondent wondered at it amid the confusion of the sea.

It seemed also very attractive, but the correspondent knew that it was a long journey, and he paddled leisurely. The piece of life-preserver lay under him, and sometimes he whirled down the incline of a wave as if he were on a hand-sled.

But finally he arrived at a place in the sea where travel was beset with difficulty. He did not pause swimming to inquire what manner of current had caught him, but there his progress ceased. The shore was set before him like a bit of scenery on a stage, and he looked at it and understood with his eyes each detail of it.

As the cook passed, much farther to the left, the captain was calling to him, "Turn over on your back, cook! Turn over on your back and use the oar."

"All right, sir." The cook turned on his back, and, paddling with an oar, went ahead as if he were a canoe.

Presently the boat also passed to the left of the correspondent with the captain clinging with one hand to the keel. He would have appeared like a man raising himself to look over a board fence, if it were not for the extraordinary gymnastics of the boat. The correspondent marvelled that the captain could still hold to it.

They passed on, nearer to shore-the oiler, the cook, the captain-and following them went the water-jar, bouncing gaily over the seas.

The correspondent remained in the grip of this strange new enemy —a current. The shore, with its white slope of sand and its green bluff, topped with little silent cottages, was spread like a picture before him. It was very near to him then, but he was impressed as one who in a gallery looks at a scene from Brittany or Holland.

He thought: "I am going to drown? Can it be possible? Can it be possible? Can it be possible?" Perhaps an individual must consider his own death to be the final phenomenon of nature.

But later a wave perhaps whirled him out of this small deadly current, for he found suddenly that he could again make progress toward the shore. Later still, he was aware that the captain, clinging with one hand to the keel of the dingey, had his face turned away from the shore and toward him, and was calling his name. "Come to the boat! Come to the boat!"

In his struggle to reach the captain and the boat, he reflected that when one gets properly wearied, drowning must really be a comfortable arrangement, a cessation of hostilities accompanied by a large degree of relief, and he was glad of it, for the main thing in his mind for some moments had been horror of the temporary agony. He did not wish to be hurt.

Presently he saw a man running along the shore. He was undressing with most remarkable speed. Coat, trousers, shirt, everything flew magically off him.

"Come to the boat," called the captain.

"All right, captain." As the correspondent paddled, he saw the captain let himself down to bottom and leave the boat. Then the correspondent performed his one little marvel of the voyage. A large wave caught him and flung him with ease and supreme speed completely over the boat and far beyond it. It struck him even then as an event in gymnastics, and a true miracle of the sea. An overturned boat in the surf is not a plaything to a swimming man.

The correspondent arrived in water that reached only to his waist, but his condition did not enable him to stand for more than a moment. Each wave knocked him into a heap, and the under-tow pulled at him.

Then he saw the man who had been running and undressing, and undressing and running, come bounding into the water. He dragged ashore the cook, and then waded towards the captain, but the captain waved him away, and sent him to the correspondent. He was naked, naked as a tree in winter, but a halo was about his head, and he shone like a saint. He gave a strong pull, and a long drag, and a bully heave at the correspondent's hand. The correspondent, schooled in the minor formulæ, said: "Thanks, old man." But suddenly the man cried: "What's that?" He pointed a swift finger. The correspondent said: "Go."

In the shallows, face downward, lay the oiler. His forehead touched sand that was periodically, between each wave, clear of the sea.

The correspondent did not know all that transpired afterward. When he achieved safe ground he fell, striking the sand with each particular part of his body. It was as if he had dropped from a roof, but the thud was grateful to him.

It seems that instantly the beach was populated with men with blankets, clothes, and flasks, and women with coffee-pots and all the remedies sacred to their minds. The welcome of the land to the men from the sea was warm and generous, but a still and dripping shape was carried slowly up the beach, and the land's welcome for it could only be the different and sinister hospitality of the grave.

When it came night, the white waves paced to and fro in the moonlight, and the wind brought the sound of the great sea's voice to the men on shore, and they felt that they could then be interpreters.

A Man and Some Others

I

Dark mesquit spread from horizon to horizon. There was no house or horseman from which a mind could evolve a city or a crowd. The world was declared to be a desert and unpeopled. Sometimes, however, on days when no heat-mist arose, a blue shape, dim, of the substance of a spectre's veil, appeared in the south-west, and a pondering sheep-herder might remember that there were mountains.

In the silence of these plains the sudden and childish banging of a tin pan could have made an iron-nerved man leap into the air. The sky was ever flawless; the manoeuvring of clouds was an unknown pageant; but at times a sheep-herder could see, miles away, the long, white streamers of dust rising from the feet of another's flock, and the interest became intense.

Bill was arduously cooking his dinner, bending over the fire, and toiling like a blacksmith. A movement, a flash of strange colour, perhaps, off in the bushes, caused him suddenly to turn his head. Presently he arose, and, shading his eyes with his hand, stood motionless and gazing. He perceived at last a Mexican sheep-herder winding through the brush toward his camp.

"Hello!" shouted Bill.

The Mexican made no answer, but came steadily forward until he was within some twenty yards. There he paused, and, folding his arms, drew himself up in the manner affected by the villain in the play. His serape muffled the lower part of his face, and his great sombrero shaded his brow. Being unexpected and also silent, he had something of the quality of an apparition; moreover, it was clearly his intention to be mysterious and devilish.

The American's pipe, sticking carelessly in the corner of his mouth, was twisted until the wrong side was uppermost, and he held his frying-pan poised in the air. He surveyed with evident surprise this apparition in the mesquit. "Hello, José!" he said; "what's the matter?"

The Mexican spoke with the solemnity of funeral tollings: "Beel, you mus' geet off range. We want you geet off range. We no like. Un'erstan'? We no like."

"What you talking about?" said Bill. "No like what?"

"We no like you here. Un'erstan'? Too mooch. You mus' geet out. We no like. Un'erstan'?"

"Understand? No; I don't know what the blazes you're gittin' at." Bill's eyes wavered in bewilderment, and his jaw fell. "I must git out? I must git off the range? What you givin' us?"

The Mexican unfolded his serape with his small yellow hand. Upon his face was then to be seen a smile that was gently, almost caressingly murderous. "Beel," he said, "geet out!"

Bill's arm dropped until the frying-pan was at his knee. Finally he turned again toward the fire. "Go on, you dog-gone little yaller rat!" he said over his shoulder. "You fellers can't chase me off this range. I got as much right here as anybody."

"Beel," answered the other in a vibrant tone, thrusting his head forward and moving one foot, "you geet out or we keel you."

"Who will?" said Bill.

"I —and the others." The Mexican tapped his breast gracefully.

Bill reflected for a time, and then he said: "You ain't got no manner of license to warn me off'n this range, and I won't move a rod. Understand? I've got rights, and I suppose if I don't see 'em through, no one is likely to give me a good hand and help me lick you fellers, since I'm the only white man in half a day's ride. Now, look; if you fellers try to rush this camp, I'm goin' to plug about fifty per cent. of the gentlemen present, sure. I'm goin' in for trouble, an' I'll git a lot of you. 'Nuther thing: if I was a fine valuable caballero like you, I'd stay in the rear till the shootin' was done, because I'm goin' to make a particular p'int of shootin' you through the chest." He grinned affably, and made a gesture of dismissal.

As for the Mexican, he waved his hands in a consummate expression of indifference. "Oh, all right," he said. Then, in a tone of deep menace and glee, he added: "We will keel you eef you no geet. They have decide'."

"They have, have they?" said Bill. "Well, you tell them to go to the devil!"

Bill had been a mine-owner in Wyoming, a great man, an aristocrat, one who possessed un-limited credit in the saloons down the gulch. He had the social weight that could interrupt a lynching or advise a bad man of the particular merits of a remote geographical point. However, the fates exploded the toy balloon with which they had amused Bill, and on the evening of the same day he was a professional gambler with ill-fortune dealing him unspeakable irritation in the shape of three big cards whenever another fellow stood pat. It is well here to inform the world that Bill considered his calamities of life all dwarfs in comparison with the excitement of one particular evening, when three kings came to him with criminal regularity against a man who always filled a straight. Later he became a cow-boy, more weirdly abandoned than if he had never been an aristocrat. By this time all that remained of his former splendour was his pride, or his vanity, which was one thing which need not have remained. He killed the foreman of the ranch over an inconsequent matter as to which of them was a liar, and the midnight train carried him eastward. He became a brakeman on the Union Pacific, and really gained high honours in the hobo war that for many years has devastated the beautiful railroads of our country. A creature of ill-fortune himself, he practised all the ordinary cruelties upon these other creatures of ill-fortune. He was of so fierce a mien that tramps usually surrendered at once whatever coin or tobacco they had in their possession; and if afterward he kicked them from the train, it was only because this was a recognized treachery of the war upon the hoboes. In a famous battle fought in Nebraska in 1879, he would have achieved a lasting distinction if it had not been for a deserter from the United States army. He was at the head of a heroic and sweeping charge, which really broke the power of the hoboes in that country for three months; he had already worsted four tramps with his own coupling-stick, when a stone thrown by the ex-third baseman of F Troop's nine laid him flat on the prairie, and later enforced a stay in the hospital in Omaha. After his recovery he engaged with other railroads, and shuffled cars in countless yards. An order to strike came upon him in Michigan, and afterward the vengeance of the railroad pursued him until he assumed a name. This mask is like the darkness in which the burglar chooses to move. It destroys many of the healthy fears. It is a small thing, but it eats that which we call our conscience. The conductor of No. 419 stood in the caboose within two feet of Bill's nose, and called him a liar. Bill requested him to use a milder term. He had not bored the foreman of Tin Can Ranch with any such request, but had killed him with expedition. The conductor seemed to insist, and so Bill let the matter drop.

He became the bouncer of a saloon on the Bowery in New York. Here most of his fights were as successful as had been his brushes with the hoboes in the West. He gained the complete admiration of the four clean bar-tenders who stood behind the great and glittering bar. He was an honoured man. He nearly killed Bad Hennessy, who, as a matter of fact, had more reputation than ability, and his fame moved up the Bowery and down the Bowery.

But let a man adopt fighting as his business, and the thought grows constantly within him that it is his business to fight. These phrases became mixed in Bill's mind precisely as they are here mixed; and let a man get this idea in his mind, and defeat begins to move toward him over the unknown ways of circumstances. One summer night three sailors from the U.S.S. *Seattle* sat in the saloon drinking and attending to other people's affairs in an amiable fashion. Bill was a proud man since he had thrashed so many citizens, and it suddenly occurred to him that the loud talk of the sailors was very offensive. So he swaggered upon their attention, and warned them that the saloon was the flowery abode of peace and gentle silence. They glanced at him in surprise, and without a moment's pause consigned him to a worse place than any stoker of them knew. Whereupon he flung one of them through the side door before the others could prevent it. On the sidewalk there was a short struggle, with many hoarse epithets in the air, and then Bill slid into the saloon again. A frown of false rage was upon his brow, and he strutted like a savage king. He took a long yellow night-stick from behind the lunch-counter, and started importantly toward the main doors to see that the incensed seamen did not again enter.

The ways of sailormen are without speech, and, together in the street, the three sailors exchanged no word, but they moved at once. Landsmen would have required two years of discussion to gain such unanimity. In silence, and immediately, they seized a long piece of scantling that lay handily. With one forward to guide the battering-ram, and with two behind him to furnish the power, they made a beautiful curve, and came down like the Assyrians on the front door of that saloon.

Mystic and still mystic are the laws of fate. Bill, with his kingly frown and his long night-stick, appeared at precisely that moment in the doorway. He stood like a statue of victory; his pride was at its zenith; and in the same second this atrocious piece of scantling punched him in the bulwarks of his stomach, and he vanished like a mist. Opinions differed as to where the end of the scantling landed him, but it was ultimately clear that it landed him in south-western Texas, where he became a sheep-herder.

The sailors charged three times upon the plate-glass front of the saloon, and when they had finished, it looked as if it had been the victim of a rural fire company's success in saving it from the flames. As the proprietor of the place surveyed the ruins, he remarked that Bill was a very zealous guardian of property. As the ambulance surgeon surveyed Bill, he remarked that the wound was really an excavation.

As his Mexican friend tripped blithely away, Bill turned with a thoughtful face to his frying-pan and his fire. After dinner he drew his revolver from its scarred old holster, and examined every part of it. It was the revolver that had dealt death to the foreman, and it had also been in free fights in which it had dealt death to several or none. Bill loved it because its allegiance was more than that of man, horse, or dog. It questioned neither social nor moral position; it obeyed alike the saint and the assassin. It was the claw of the eagle, the tooth of the lion, the poison of the snake; and when he swept it from its holster, this minion smote where he listed, even to the battering of a far penny. Wherefore it was his dearest possession, and was not to be exchanged in south-western Texas for a handful of rubies, nor even the shame and homage of the conductor of No. 419.

During the afternoon he moved through his monotony of work and leisure with the same air of deep meditation. The smoke of his supper-time fire was curling across the shadowy sea of mesquit when the instinct of the plainsman warned him that the stillness, the desolation, was again invaded. He saw a motionless horseman in black outline against the pallid sky. The silhouette displayed serape and sombrero, and even the Mexican spurs as large as pies. When this black figure began to move toward the camp, Bill's hand dropped to his revolver.

The horseman approached until Bill was enabled to see pronounced American features, and a skin too red to grow on a Mexican face. Bill released his grip on his revolver.

"Hello!" called the horseman.

"Hello!" answered Bill.

The horseman cantered forward. "Good evening," he said, as he again drew rein.

"Good evenin'," answered Bill, without committing himself by too much courtesy.

For a moment the two men scanned each other in a way that is not ill-mannered on the plains, where one is in danger of meeting horse-thieves or tourists.

Bill saw a type which did not belong in the mesquit. The young fellow had invested in some Mexican trappings of an expensive kind. Bill's eyes searched the outfit for some sign of craft, but there was none. Even with his local regalia, it was clear that the young man was of a far, black Northern city. He had discarded the enormous stirrups of his Mexican saddle; he used the small English stirrup, and his feet were thrust forward until the steel tightly gripped his ankles. As Bill's eyes travelled over the stranger, they lighted suddenly upon the stirrups and the thrust feet, and immediately he smiled in a friendly way. No dark purpose could dwell in the innocent heart of a man who rode thus on the plains.

As for the stranger, he saw a tattered individual with a tangle of hair and beard, and with a complexion turned brick-colour from the sun and whisky. He saw a pair of eyes that at first looked at him as the wolf looks at the wolf, and then became childlike, almost timid, in their glance. Here was evidently a man who had often stormed the iron walls of the city of success, and who now sometimes valued himself as the rabbit values his prowess.

The stranger smiled genially, and sprang from his horse. "Well, sir, I suppose you will let me camp here with you to-night?"

"Eh?" said Bill.

"I suppose you will let me camp here with you to-night?"

Bill for a time seemed too astonished for words. "Well," —he answered, scowling in inhospitable annoyance —"well, I don't believe this here is a good place to camp to-night, mister."

The stranger turned quickly from his saddle-girth.

"What?" he said in surprise. "You don't want me here? You don't want me to camp here?"

Bill's feet scuffled awkwardly, and he looked steadily at a cactus plant. "Well, you see, mister," he said, "I'd like your company well enough, but-you see, some of these here greasers are goin' to chase me off the range to-night; and while I might like a man's company all right, I couldn't let him in for no such game when he ain't got nothin' to do with the trouble."

"Going to chase you off the range?" cried the stranger.

"Well, they said they were goin' to do it," said Bill.

"And-great heavens! will they kill you, do you think?"

"Don't know. Can't tell till afterwards. You see, they take some feller that's alone like me, and then they rush his camp when he ain't quite ready for 'em, and ginerally plug 'im with a sawed-off shot-gun load before he has a chance to git at 'em. They lay around and wait for their chance, and it comes soon enough. Of course a feller alone like me has got to let up watching some time. Maybe they ketch 'im asleep. Maybe the feller gits tired waiting, and goes out in broad day, and kills two or three just to make the whole crowd pile on him and settle the thing. I heard of a case like that once. It's awful hard on a man's mind-to git a gang after him."

"And so they're going to rush your camp to-night?" cried the stranger. "How do you know? Who told you?"

"Feller come and told me."

"And what are you going to do? Fight?"

"Don't see nothin' else to do," answered Bill gloomily, still staring at the cactus plant.

There was a silence. Finally the stranger burst out in an amazed cry. "Well, I never heard of such a thing in my life! How many of them are there?"

"Eight," answered Bill. "And now look-a-here; you ain't got no manner of business foolin' around here just now, and you might better lope off before dark. I don't ask no help in this here row. I know your happening along here just now don't give me no call on you, and you better hit the trail."

"Well, why in the name of wonder don't you go get the sheriff?" cried the stranger.

"Oh, h——!" said Bill.

IV

Long, smoldering clouds spread in the western sky, and to the east silver mists lay on the purple gloom of the wilderness.

Finally, when the great moon climbed the heavens and cast its ghastly radiance upon the bushes, it made a new and more brilliant crimson of the campfire, where the flames capered merrily through its mesquit branches, filling the silence with the fire chorus, an ancient melody which surely bears a message of the inconsequence of individual tragedy —a message that is in the boom of the sea, the sliver of the wind through the grass-blades, the silken clash of hemlock boughs.

No figures moved in the rosy space of the camp, and the search of the moonbeams failed to disclose a living thing in the bushes. There was no owl-faced clock to chant the weariness of the long silence that brooded upon the plain.

The dew gave the darkness under the mesquit a velvet quality that made air seem nearer to water, and no eye could have seen through it the black things that moved like monster lizards toward the camp. The branches, the leaves, that are fain to cry out when death approaches in the wilds, were frustrated by these uncanny bodies gliding with the finesse of the escaping serpent. They crept forward to the last point where assuredly no frantic attempt of the fire could discover them, and there they paused to locate the prey. A romance relates the tale of the black cell hidden deep in the earth, where, upon entering, one sees only the little eyes of snakes fixing him in menaces. If a man could have approached a certain spot in the bushes, he would not have found it romantically necessary to have his hair rise. There would have been a sufficient expression of horror in the feeling of the death-hand at the nape of his neck and in his rubber knee-joints.

Two of these bodies finally moved toward each other until for each there grew out of the darkness a face placidly smiling with tender dreams of assassination. "The fool is asleep by the fire, God be praised!" The lips of the other widened in a grin of affectionate appreciation of the fool and his plight. There was some signaling in the gloom, and then began a series of subtle rustlings, interjected often with pauses, during which no sound arose but the sound of faint breathing.

A bush stood like a rock in the stream of firelight, sending its long shadow backward. With painful caution the little company travelled along this shadow, and finally arrived at the rear of the bush. Through its branches they surveyed for a moment of comfortable satisfaction a form in a grey blanket extended on the ground near the fire. The smile of joyful anticipation fled quickly, to give place to a quiet air of business. Two men lifted shot-guns with much of the barrels gone, and sighting these weapons through the branches, pulled trigger together.

The noise of the explosions roared over the lonely mesquit as if these guns wished to inform the entire world; and as the grey smoke fled, the dodging company back of the bush saw the blanketed form twitching; whereupon they burst out in chorus in a laugh, and arose as merry as a lot of banqueters. They gleefully gestured congratulations, and strode bravely into the light of the fire.

Then suddenly a new laugh rang from some unknown spot in the darkness. It was a fearsome laugh of ridicule, hatred, ferocity. It might have been demoniac. It smote them motionless in their gleeful prowl, as the stern voice from the sky smites the legendary malefactor. They might have been a weird group in wax, the light of the dying fire on their yellow faces, and shining athwart their eyes turned toward the darkness whence might come the unknown and the terrible.

The thing in the grey blanket no longer twitched; but if the knives in their hands had been thrust toward it, each knife was now drawn back, and its owner's elbow was thrown upward, as if he expected death from the clouds.

This laugh had so chained their reason that for a moment they had no wit to flee. They were prisoners to their terror. Then suddenly the belated decision arrived, and with bubbling cries they turned to run; but at that instant there was a long flash of red in the darkness, and with the report one of the men shouted a bitter shout, spun once, and tumbled headlong. The thick bushes failed to impede the route of the others.

The silence returned to the wilderness. The tired flames faintly illumined the blanketed thing and the flung corpse of the marauder, and sang the fire chorus, the ancient melody which bears the message of the inconsequence of human tragedy.

V

"Now you are worse off than ever," said the young man, dry-voiced and awed.

"No, I ain't," said Bill rebelliously. "I'm one ahead."

After reflection, the stranger remarked, "Well, there's seven more."

They were cautiously and slowly approaching the camp. The sun was flaring its first warming rays over the grey wilderness. Upreared twigs, prominent branches, shone with golden light, while the shadows under the mesquit were heavily blue.

Suddenly the stranger uttered a frightened cry. He had arrived at a point whence he had, through openings in the thicket, a clear view of a dead face.

"Gosh!" said Bill, who at the next instant had seen the thing; "I thought at first it was that there José. That would have been queer, after what I told 'im yesterday."

They continued their way, the stranger wincing in his walk, and Bill exhibiting considerable curiosity.

The yellow beams of the new sun were touching the grim hues of the dead Mexican's face, and creating there an inhuman effect, which made his countenance more like a mask of dulled brass. One hand, grown curiously thinner, had been flung out regardlessly to a cactus bush.

Bill walked forward and stood looking respectfully at the body. "I know that feller; his name is Miguel. He — —"

The stranger's nerves might have been in that condition when there is no backbone to the body, only a long groove. "Good heavens!" he exclaimed, much agitated; "don't speak that way!"

"What way?" said Bill. "I only said his name was Miguel."

After a pause the stranger said:

"Oh, I know; but — —" He waved his hand. "Lower your voice, or something. I don't know. This part of the business rattles me, don't you see?"

"Oh, all right," replied Bill, bowing to the other's mysterious mood. But in a moment he burst out violently and loud in the most extraordinary profanity, the oaths winging from him as the sparks go from the funnel.

He had been examining the contents of the bundled grey blanket, and he had brought forth, among other things, his frying-pan. It was now only a rim with a handle; the Mexican volley had centered upon it. A Mexican shot-gun of the abbreviated description is ordinarily loaded with flat-irons, stove-lids, lead pipe, old horseshoes, sections of chain, window weights, railroad sleepers and spikes, dumb-bells, and any other junk which may be at hand. When one of these loads encounters a man vitally, it is likely to make an impression upon him, and a cooking-utensil may be supposed to subside before such an assault of curiosities.

Bill held high his desecrated frying-pan, turning it this way and that way. He swore until he happened to note the absence of the stranger. A moment later he saw him leading his horse from the bushes. In silence and sullenly the young man went about saddling the animal. Bill said, "Well, goin' to pull out?"

The stranger's hands fumbled uncertainly at the throat-latch. Once he exclaimed irritably, blaming the buckle for the trembling of his fingers. Once he turned to look at the dead face with the light of the morning sun upon it. At last he cried, "Oh, I know the whole thing was all square enough-couldn't be squarer-but somehow or other, that man there takes the heart out of me." He turned his troubled face for another look. "He seems to be all the time calling me a —he makes me feel like a murderer."

"But," said Bill, puzzling, "you didn't shoot him, mister; I shot him."

"I know; but I feel that way, somehow. I can't get rid of it."

Bill considered for a time; then he said diffidently, "Mister, you're a eddycated man, ain't you?"

"What?"

"You're what they call a —a eddycated man, ain't you?"

The young man, perplexed, evidently had a question upon his lips, when there was a roar of guns, bright flashes, and in the air such hooting and whistling as would come from a swift flock of steam-boilers. The stranger's horse gave a mighty, convulsive spring, snorting wildly in its sudden anguish, fell upon its knees, scrambled afoot again, and was away in the uncanny death run known to men who have seen the finish of brave horses.

"This comes from discussin' things," cried Bill angrily.

He had thrown himself flat on the ground facing the thicket whence had come the firing. He could see the smoke winding over the bush-tops. He lifted his revolver, and the weapon came slowly up from the ground and poised like the glittering crest of a snake. Somewhere on his face there was a kind of smile, cynical, wicked, deadly, of a ferocity which at the same time had brought a deep flush to his face, and had caused two upright lines to glow in his eyes.

"Hello, José!" he called, amiable for satire's sake. "Got your old blunderbusses loaded up again yet?"

The stillness had returned to the plain. The sun's brilliant rays swept over the sea of mesquit, painting the far mists of the west with faint rosy light, and high in the air some great bird fled toward the south.

"You come out here," called Bill, again addressing the landscape, "and I'll give you some shootin' lessons. That ain't the way to shoot." Receiving no reply, he began to invent epithets and yell them at the thicket. He was something of a master of insult, and, moreover, he dived into his memory to bring forth imprecations tarnished with age, unused since fluent Bowery days. The occupation amused him, and sometimes he laughed so that it was uncomfortable for his chest to be against the ground.

Finally the stranger, prostrate near him, said wearily, "Oh, they've gone."

"Don't you believe it," replied Bill, sobering swiftly. "They're there yet-every man of 'em."

"How do you know?"

"Because I do. They won't shake us so soon. Don't put your head up, or they'll get you, sure." Bill's eyes, meanwhile, had not wavered from their scrutiny of the thicket in front. "They're there all right; don't you forget it. Now you listen." So he called out: "José! Ojo, José! Speak up, *hombre*! I want have talk. Speak up, you yaller cuss, you!"

Whereupon a mocking voice from off in the bushes said, "Señor?"

"There," said Bill to his ally; "didn't I tell you? The whole batch." Again he lifted his voice. "José-look-ain't you gittin' kinder tired? You better go home, you fellers, and git some rest."

The answer was a sudden furious chatter of Spanish, eloquent with hatred, calling down upon Bill all the calamities which life holds. It was as if some one had suddenly enraged a cageful of wild cats. The spirits of all the revenges which they had imagined were loosened at this time, and filled the air.

"They're in a holler," said Bill, chuckling, "or there'd be shootin'."

Presently he began to grow angry. His hidden enemies called him nine kinds of coward, a man who could fight only in the dark, a baby who would run from the shadows of such noble Mexican gentlemen, a dog that sneaked. They described the affair of the previous night, and informed him of the base advantage he had taken of their friend. In fact, they in all sincerity endowed him with every quality which he no less earnestly believed them to possess. One could have seen the phrases bite him as he lay there on the ground fingering his revolver.

VI

It is sometimes taught that men do the furious and desperate thing from an emotion that is as even and placid as the thoughts of a village clergyman on Sunday afternoon. Usually, however, it is to be believed that a panther is at the time born in the heart, and that the subject does not resemble a man picking mulberries.

"B' G——!" said Bill, speaking as from a throat filled with dust, "I'll go after 'em in a minute."

"Don't you budge an inch!" cried the stranger, sternly. "Don't you budge!"

"Well," said Bill, glaring at the bushes —"well —"

"Put your head down!" suddenly screamed the stranger, in white alarm. As the guns roared, Bill uttered a loud grunt, and for a moment leaned panting on his elbow, while his arm shook like a twig. Then he upreared like a great and bloody spirit of vengeance, his face lighted with the blaze of his last passion. The Mexicans came swiftly and in silence.

The lightning action of the next few moments was of the fabric of dreams to the stranger. The muscular struggle may not be real to the drowning man. His mind may be fixed on the far, straight shadows back of the stars, and the terror of them. And so the fight, and his part in it, had to the stranger only the quality of a picture half drawn. The rush of feet, the spatter of shots, the cries, the swollen faces seen like masks on the smoke, resembled a happening of the night.

And yet afterward certain lines, forms, lived out so strongly from the incoherence that they were always in his memory.

He killed a man, and the thought went swiftly by him, like the feather on the gale, that it was easy to kill a man.

Moreover, he suddenly felt for Bill, this grimy sheep-herder, some deep form of idolatry. Bill was dying, and the dignity of last defeat, the superiority of him who stands in his grave, was in the pose of the lost sheep-herder.

The stranger sat on the ground idly mopping the sweat and powder-stain from his brow. He wore the gentle idiot smile of an aged beggar as he watched three Mexicans limping and staggering in the distance. He noted at this time that one who still possessed a serape had from it none of the grandeur of the cloaked Spaniard, but that against the sky the silhouette resembled a cornucopia of childhood's Christmas.

They turned to look at him, and he lifted his weary arm to menace them with his revolver. They stood for a moment banded together, and hooted curses at him.

Finally he arose, and, walking some paces, stooped to loosen Bill's grey hands from a throat. Swaying as if slightly drunk, he stood looking down into the still face.

Struck suddenly with a thought, he went about with dulled eyes on the ground, until he plucked his gaudy blanket from where it lay dirty from trampling feet. He dusted it carefully, and then returned and laid it over Bill's form. There he again stood motionless, his mouth just agape and the same stupid glance in his eyes, when all at once he made a gesture of fright and looked wildly about him.

He had almost reached the thicket when he stopped, smitten with alarm. A body contorted, with one arm stiff in the air, lay in his path. Slowly and warily he moved around it, and in a moment the bushes, nodding and whispering, their leaf-faces turned toward the scene behind him, swung and swung again into stillness and the peace of the wilderness.

The Bride Comes to Yellow Sky

I

The great Pullman was whirling onward with such dignity of motion that a glance from the window seemed simply to prove that the plains of Texas were pouring eastward. Vast flats of green grass, dull-hued spaces of mesquit and cactus, little groups of frame houses, woods of light and tender trees, all were sweeping into the east, sweeping over the horizon, a precipice.

A newly-married pair had boarded this train at San Antonio. The man's face was reddened from many days in the wind and sun, and a direct result of his new black clothes was that his brick-coloured hands were constantly performing in a most conscious fashion. From time to time he looked down respectfully at his attire. He sat with a hand on each knee, like a man waiting in a barber's shop. The glances he devoted to other passengers were furtive and shy.

The bride was not pretty, nor was she very young. She wore a dress of blue cashmere, with small reservations of velvet here and there, and with steel buttons abounding. She continually twisted her head to regard her puff-sleeves, very stiff, straight, and high. They embarrassed her. It was quite apparent that she had cooked, and that she expected to cook, dutifully. The blushes caused by the careless scrutiny of some passengers as she had entered the car were strange to see upon this plain, under-class countenance, which was drawn in placid, almost emotionless lines.

They were evidently very happy. "Ever been in a parlour-car before?" he asked, smiling with delight.

"No," she answered; "I never was. It's fine, ain't it?"

"Great. And then, after a while, we'll go forward to the diner, and get a big lay-out. Finest meal in the world. Charge, a dollar."

"Oh, do they?" cried the bride. "Charge a dollar? Why, that's too much-for us-ain't it, Jack?"

"Not this trip, anyhow," he answered bravely. "We're going to go the whole thing."

Later, he explained to her about the train. "You see, it's a thousand miles from one end of Texas to the other, and this train runs right across it, and never stops but four times."

He had the pride of an owner. He pointed out to her the dazzling fittings of the coach, and, in truth, her eyes opened wider as she contemplated the sea-green figured velvet, the shining brass, silver, and glass, the wood that gleamed as darkly brilliant as the surface of a pool of oil. At one end a bronze figure sturdily held a support for a separated chamber, and at convenient places on the ceiling were frescoes in olive and silver.

To the minds of the pair, their surroundings reflected the glory of their marriage that morning in San Antonio. This was the environment of their new estate, and the man's face, in particular, beamed with an elation that made him appear ridiculous to the negro porter. This individual at times surveyed them from afar with an amused and superior grin. On other occasions he bullied them with skill in ways that did not make it exactly plain to them that they were being bullied. He subtly used all the manners of the most unconquerable kind of snobbery. He oppressed them, but of this oppression they had small knowledge, and they speedily forgot that unfrequently a number of travellers covered them with stares of derisive enjoyment. Historically there was supposed to be something infinitely humorous in their situation.

"We are due in Yellow Sky at 3.42," he said, looking tenderly into her eyes.

"Oh, are we?" she said, as if she had not been aware of it.

To evince surprise at her husband's statement was part of her wifely amiability. She took from a pocket a little silver watch, and as she held it before her, and stared at it with a frown of attention, the new husband's face shone.

"I bought it in San Anton' from a friend of mine," he told her gleefully.

"It's seventeen minutes past twelve," she said, looking up at him with a kind of shy and clumsy coquetry.

A passenger, noting this play, grew excessively sardonic, and winked at himself in one of the numerous mirrors.

At last they went to the dining-car. Two rows of negro waiters in dazzling white suits surveyed their entrance with the interest, and also the equanimity, of men who had been forewarned. The pair fell to the lot of a waiter who happened to feel pleasure in steering them through their meal. He viewed them with the manner of a fatherly pilot, his countenance radiant with benevolence. The patronage entwined with the ordinary deference was not palpable to them. And yet as they returned to their coach they showed in their faces a sense of escape.

To the left, miles down a long purple slope, was a little ribbon of mist, where moved the keening Rio Grande. The train was approaching it at an angle, and the apex was Yellow Sky. Presently it was apparent that as the distance from Yellow Sky grew shorter, the husband became commensurately restless. His brick-red hands were more insistent in their prominence. Occasionally he was even rather absent-minded and far away when the bride leaned forward and addressed him.

As a matter of truth, Jack Potter was beginning to find the shadow of a deed weigh upon him like a leaden slab. He, the town-marshal of Yellow Sky, a man known, liked, and feared in his corner, a prominent person, had gone to San Antonio to meet a girl he believed he loved, and there, after the usual prayers, had actually induced her to marry him without consulting Yellow Sky for any part of the transaction. He was now bringing his bride before an innocent and unsuspecting community.

Of course, people in Yellow Sky married as it pleased them in accordance with a general custom, but such was Potter's thought of his duty to his friends, or of their idea of his duty, or of an unspoken form which does not control men in these matters, that he felt he was heinous. He had committed an extraordinary crime. Face to face with this girl in San Antonio, and spurred by his sharp impulse, he had gone headlong over all the social hedges. At San Antonio he was like a man hidden in the dark. A knife to sever any friendly duty, any form, was easy to his hand in that remote city. But the hour of Yellow Sky, the hour of daylight, was approaching.

He knew full well that his marriage was an important thing to his town. It could only be exceeded by the burning of the new hotel. His friends would not forgive him. Frequently he had reflected upon the advisability of telling them by telegraph, but a new cowardice had been upon him. He feared to do it. And now the train was hurrying him toward a scene of amazement, glee, reproach. He glanced out of the window at the line of haze swinging slowly in toward the train.

Yellow Sky had a kind of brass band which played painfully to the delight of the populace. He laughed without heart as he thought of it. If the citizens could dream of his prospective arrival with his bride, they would parade the band at the station, and escort them, amid cheers and laughing congratulations, to his adobe home.

He resolved that he would use all the devices of speed and plainscraft in making the journey from the station to his house. Once within that safe citadel, he could issue some sort of a vocal bulletin, and then not go among the citizens until they had time to wear off a little of their enthusiasm.

The bride looked anxiously at him. "What's worrying you, Jack?"

He laughed again. "I'm not worrying, girl. I'm only thinking of Yellow Sky."

She flushed in comprehension.

A sense of mutual guilt invaded their minds, and developed a finer tenderness. They looked at each other with eyes softly aglow. But Potter often laughed the same nervous laugh. The flush upon the bride's face seemed quite permanent.

The traitor to the feelings of Yellow Sky narrowly watched the speeding landscape. "We're nearly there," he said.

Presently the porter came and announced the proximity of Potter's home. He held a brush in his hand, and, with all his airy superiority gone, he brushed Potter's new clothes, as the latter slowly turned this way and that way. Potter fumbled out a coin, and gave it to the porter as he had seen others do. It was a heavy and muscle-bound business, as that of a man shoeing his first horse.

The porter took their bag, and, as the train began to slow, they moved forward to the hooded platform of the car. Presently the two engines and their long string of coaches rushed into the station of Yellow Sky.

"They have to take water here," said Potter, from a constricted throat, and in mournful cadence as one announcing death. Before the train stopped his eye had swept the length of the platform, and he was glad and astonished to see there was no one upon it but the station-agent, who, with a slightly hurried and anxious air, was walking toward the water-tanks. When the train had halted, the porter alighted first and placed in position a little temporary step.

"Come on, girl," said Potter, hoarsely.

As he helped her down, they each laughed on a false note. He took the bag from the negro, and bade his wife cling to his arm. As they slunk rapidly away, his hang-dog glance perceived that they were unloading the two trunks, and also that the station-agent, far ahead, near the baggage-car, had turned, and was running toward him, making gestures. He laughed, and groaned as he laughed, when he noted the first effect of his marital bliss upon Yellow Sky. He gripped his wife's arm firmly to his side, and they fled. Behind them the porter stood chuckling fatuously.

II

The California Express on the Southron Railway was due at Yellow Sky in twenty-one minutes. There were six men at the bar of the Weary Gentleman saloon. One was a drummer, who talked a great deal and rapidly; three were Texans, who did not care to talk at that time; and two were Mexican sheep-herders, who did not talk as a general practice in the Weary Gentleman saloon. The bar-keeper's dog lay on the board-walk that crossed in front of the door. His head was on his paws, and he glanced drowsily here and there with the constant vigilance of a dog that is kicked on occasion. Across the sandy street were some vivid green grass plots, so wonderful in appearance amid the sands that burned near them in a blazing sun, that they caused a doubt in the mind. They exactly resembled the grass-mats used to represent lawns on the stage. At the cooler end of the railway-station a man without a coat sat in a tilted chair and smoked his pipe. The fresh-cut bank of the Rio Grande circled near the town, and there could be seen beyond it a great plum-coloured plain of mesquit.

Save for the busy drummer and his companions in the saloon, Yellow Sky was dozing. The new-comer leaned gracefully upon the bar, and recited many tales with the confidence of a bard who has come upon a new field.

"And at the moment that the old man fell down-stairs, with the bureau in his arms, the old woman was coming up with two scuttles of coal, and, of course — —"

The drummer's tale was interrupted by a young man who suddenly appeared in the open door. He cried —

"Scratchy Wilson's drunk, and has turned loose with both hands."

The two Mexicans at once set down their glasses, and faded out of the rear entrance of the saloon.

The drummer, innocent and jocular, answered —

"All right, old man. S'pose he has. Come and have a drink, anyhow."

But the information had made such an obvious cleft in every skull in the room, that the drummer was obliged to see its importance. All had become instantly morose.

"Say," said he, mystified, "what is this?"

His three companions made the introductory gesture of eloquent speech, but the young man at the door forestalled them.

"It means, my friend," he answered, as he came into the saloon, "that for the next two hours this town won't be a health resort."

The bar-keeper went to the door, and locked and barred it. Reaching out of the window, he pulled in heavy wooden shutters and barred them. Immediately a solemn, chapel-like gloom was upon the place. The drummer was looking from one to another.

"But say," he cried, "what is this, anyhow? You don't mean there is going to be a gun-fight?"

"Don't know whether there'll be a fight or not," answered one man grimly. "But there'll be some shootin' —some good shootin'."

The young man who had warned them waved his hand. "Oh, there'll be a fight, fast enough, if any one wants it. Anybody can get a fight out there in the street. There's a fight just waiting."

The drummer seemed to be swayed between the interest of a foreigner, and a perception of personal danger.

"What did you say his name was?" he asked.

"Scratchy Wilson," they answered in chorus.

"And will he kill anybody? What are you going to do? Does this happen often? Does he rampage round like this once a week or so? Can he break in that door?"

"No, he can't break down that door," replied the bar-keeper. "He's tried it three times. But when he comes you'd better lay down on the floor, stranger. He's dead sure to shoot at it, and a bullet may come through."

Thereafter the drummer kept a strict eye on the door. The time had not yet been called for him to hug the floor, but as a minor precaution he sidled near to the wall.

"Will he kill anybody?" he said again.

The men laughed low and scornfully at the question.

"He's out to shoot, and he's out for trouble. Don't see any good in experimentin' with him."

"But what do you do in a case like this? What do you do?"

A man responded —"Why, he and Jack Potter — —"

But, in chorus, the other men interrupted —"Jack Potter's in San Anton'."

"Well, who is he? What's he got to do with it?"

"Oh, he's the town-marshal. He goes out and fights Scratchy when he gets on one of these tears."

"Whow!" said the drummer, mopping his brow. "Nice job he's got."

The voices had toned away to mere whisperings. The drummer wished to ask further questions, which were born of an increasing anxiety and bewilderment, but when he attempted them, the men merely looked at him in irritation, and motioned him to remain silent. A tense waiting hush was upon them. In the deep shadows of the room their eyes shone as they listened for sounds from the street. One man made three gestures at the bar-keeper, and the latter, moving like a ghost, handed him a glass and a bottle. The man poured a full glass of whisky, and set down the bottle noiselessly. He gulped the whisky in a swallow, and turned again toward the door in immovable silence. The drummer saw that the bar-keeper, without a sound, had taken a Winchester from beneath the bar. Later, he saw this individual beckoning to him, so he tip-toed across the room.

"You better come with me back of the bar."

"No, thanks," said the drummer, perspiring. "I'd rather be where I can make a break for the back-door."

Whereupon the man of bottles made a kindly but peremptory gesture. The drummer obeyed it, and finding himself seated on a box, with his head below the level of the bar, balm was laid upon his soul at sight of various zinc and copper fittings that bore a resemblance to plate armour. The bar-keeper took a seat comfortably upon an adjacent box.

"You see," he whispered, "this here Scratchy Wilson is a wonder with a gun —a perfect wonder-and when he goes on the war-trail, we hunt our holes-naturally. He's about the last one of the old gang that used to hang out along the river here. He's a terror when he's drunk. When he's sober he's all right-kind of simple-wouldn't hurt a fly-nicest fellow in town. But when he's drunk-whoo!"

There were periods of stillness.

"I wish Jack Potter was back from San Anton'," said the bar-keeper. "He shot Wilson up once-in the leg-and he would sail in and pull out the kinks in this thing."

Presently they heard from a distance the sound of a shot, followed by three wild yells. It instantly removed a bond from the men in the darkened saloon. There was a shuffling of feet. They looked at each other.

"Here he comes," they said.

III

A man in a maroon-coloured flannel shirt, which had been purchased for purposes of decoration, and made, principally, by some Jewish women on the east side of New York, rounded a corner and walked into the middle of the main street of Yellow Sky. In either hand the man held a long, heavy blue-black revolver. Often he yelled, and these cries rang through a semblance of a deserted village, shrilly flying over the roofs in a volume that seemed to have no relation to the ordinary vocal strength of a man. It was as if the surrounding stillness formed the arch of a tomb over him. These cries of ferocious challenge rang against walls of silence. And his boots had red tops with gilded imprints, of the kind beloved in winter by little sledging boys on the hillsides of New England.

The man's face flamed in a rage begot of whisky. His eyes, rolling and yet keen for ambush, hunted the still door-ways and windows. He walked with the creeping movement of the mid-night cat. As it occurred to him, he roared menacing information. The long revolvers in his hands were as easy as straws; they were moved with an electric swiftness. The little fingers of each hand played sometimes in a musician's way. Plain from the low collar of the shirt, the cords of his neck straightened and sank as passion moved him. The only sounds were his terrible invitations. The calm adobes preserved their demeanour at the passing of this small thing in the middle of the street.

There was no offer of fight-no offer of fight. The man called to the sky. There were no attractions. He bellowed and fumed and swayed his revolver here and everywhere.

The dog of the bar-keeper of the Weary Gentleman saloon had not appreciated the advance of events. He yet lay dozing in front of his master's door. At sight of the dog, the man paused and raised his revolver humorously. At sight of the man, the dog sprang up and walked diagonally away, with a sullen head and growling. The man yelled, and the dog broke into a gallop. As it was about to enter an alley, there was a loud noise, a whistling, and something spat the ground directly before it. The dog screamed, and, wheeling in terror, galloped headlong in a new direction. Again there was a noise, a whistling, and sand was kicked viciously before it. Fear-stricken, the dog turned and flurried like an animal in a pen. The man stood laughing, his weapons at his hips.

Ultimately the man was attracted by the closed door of the Weary Gentleman saloon. He went to it, and, hammering with a revolver, demanded drink.

The door remaining imperturbable, he picked a bit of paper from the walk, and nailed it to the framework with a knife. He then turned his back contemptuously upon this popular resort, and, walking to the opposite side of the street and spinning there on his heel quickly and lithely, fired at the bit of paper. He missed it by a half-inch. He swore at himself, and went away. Later, he comfortably fusiladed the windows of his most intimate friend. The man was playing with this town. It was a toy for him.

But still there was no offer of fight. The name of Jack Potter, his ancient antagonist, entered his mind, and he concluded that it would be a glad thing if he should go to Potter's house, and, by bombardment, induce him to come out and fight. He moved in the direction of his desire, chanting Apache scalp music.

When he arrived at it, Potter's house presented the same still, calm front as had the other adobes. Taking up a strategic position, the man howled a challenge. But this house regarded him as might a great stone god. It gave no sign. After a decent wait, the man howled further challenges, mingling with them wonderful epithets.

Presently there came the spectacle of a man churning himself into deepest rage over the immobility of a house. He fumed at it as the winter wind attacks a prairie cabin in the north. To the distance there should have gone the sound of a tumult like the fighting of two hundred Mexicans. As necessity bade him, he paused for breath or to reload his revolvers.

Potter and his bride walked sheepishly and with speed. Sometimes they laughed together shame-facedly and low.

"Next corner, dear," he said finally.

They put forth the efforts of a pair walking bowed against a strong wind. Potter was about to raise a finger to point the first appearance of the new home, when, as they circled the corner, they came face to face with a man in a maroon-coloured shirt, who was feverishly pushing cartridges into a large revolver. Upon the instant the man dropped this revolver to the ground, and, like lightning, whipped another from its holster. The second weapon was aimed at the bridegroom's chest.

There was a silence. Potter's mouth seemed to be merely a grave for his tongue. He exhibited an instinct to at once loosen his arm from the woman's grip, and he dropped the bag to the sand. As for the bride, her face had gone as yellow as old cloth. She was a slave to hideous rites, gazing at the apparitional snake.

The two men faced each other at a distance of three paces. He of the revolver smiled with a new and quiet ferocity. "Tried to sneak up on me!" he said. "Tried to sneak up on me!" His eyes grew more baleful. As Potter made a slight movement, the man thrust his revolver venomously forward. "No; don't you do it, Jack Potter. Don't you move a finger towards a gun just yet. Don't you move an eyelash. The time has come for me to settle with you, and I'm going to do it my own way, and loaf along with no interferin'. So if you don't want a gun bent on you, just mind what I tell you."

Potter looked at his enemy. "I ain't got a gun on me, Scratchy," he said. "Honest, I ain't." He was stiffening and steadying, but yet somewhere at the back of his mind a vision of the Pullman floated-the sea-green figured velvet, the shining brass, silver, and glass, the wood that gleamed as darkly brilliant as the surface of a pool of oil-all the glory of their marriage, the environment of the new estate.

"You know I fight when it comes to fighting, Scratchy Wilson, but I ain't got a gun on me. You'll have to do all the shootin' yourself."

His enemy's face went livid. He stepped forward, and lashed his weapon to and fro before Potter's chest.

"Don't you tell me you ain't got no gun on you, you whelp. Don't tell me no lie like that. There ain't a man in Texas ever seen you without no gun. Don't take me for no kid."

His eyes blazed with light and his throat worked like a pump.

"I ain't takin' you for no kid," answered Potter. His heels had not moved an inch backward. "I'm takin' you for a —— fool. I tell you I ain't got a gun, and I ain't. If you're goin' to shoot me up, you'd better begin now. You'll never get a chance like this again."

So much enforced reasoning had told on Wilson's rage. He was calmer.

"If you ain't got a gun, why ain't you got a gun?" he sneered. "Been to Sunday school?"

"I ain't got a gun because I've just come from San Anton' with my wife. I'm married," said Potter. "And if I'd thought there was going to be any galoots like you prowling around when I brought my wife home, I'd had a gun, and don't you forget it."

"Married!" said Scratchy, not at all comprehending.

"Yes, married! I'm married," said Potter, distinctly.

"Married!" said Scratchy; seeming for the first time he saw the drooping drowning woman at the other man's side. "No!" he said. He was like a creature allowed a glimpse of another world. He moved a pace backward, and his arm with the revolver dropped to his side. "Is this-is this the lady?" he asked.

"Yes, this is the lady," answered Potter.

There was another period of silence.

"Well," said Wilson at last, slowly, "I s'pose it's all off now?"

"It's all off if you say so, Scratchy. You know I didn't make the trouble."

Potter lifted his valise.

"Well, I 'low it's off, Jack," said Wilson. He was looking at the ground. "Married!" He was not a student of chivalry; it was merely that in the presence of this foreign condition he was a simple child of the earlier plains. He picked up his starboard revolver, and placing both weapons in their holsters, he went away. His feet made funnel-shaped tracks in the heavy sand.

The Wise Men

They were youths of subtle mind. They were very wicked according to report, and yet they managed to have it reflect great credit upon them. They often had the well-informed and the great talkers of the American colony engaged in reciting their misdeeds, and facts relating to their sins were usually told with a flourish of awe and fine admiration.

One was from San Francisco and one was from New York, but they resembled each other in appearance. This is an idiosyncrasy of geography.

They were never apart in the City of Mexico, at any rate, excepting perhaps when one had retired to his hotel for a respite, and then the other was usually camped down at the office sending up servants with clamorous messages. "Oh, get up and come on down."

They were two lads-they were called the kids-and far from their mothers. Occasionally some wise man pitied them, but he usually was alone in his wisdom. The other folk frankly were transfixed at the splendour of the audacity and endurance of these kids.

"When do those boys ever sleep?" murmured a man as he viewed them entering a café about eight o'clock one morning. Their smooth infantile faces looked bright and fresh enough, at any rate. "Jim told me he saw them still at it about 4.30 this morning."

"Sleep!" ejaculated a companion in a glowing voice. "They never sleep! They go to bed once in every two weeks." His boast of it seemed almost a personal pride.

"They'll end with a crash, though, if they keep it up at this pace," said a gloomy voice from behind a newspaper.

The Café Colorado has a front of white and gold, in which is set larger plate-glass windows than are commonly to be found in Mexico. Two little wings of willow flip-flapping incessantly serve as doors. Under them small stray dogs go furtively into the café, and are shied into the street again by the waiters. On the side-walk there is always a decorative effect of loungers, ranging from the newly-arrived and superior tourist to the old veteran of the silver mines bronzed by violent suns. They contemplate with various shades of interest the show of the street-the red, purple, dusty white, glaring forth against the walls in the furious sunshine.

One afternoon the kids strolled into the Café Colorado. A half-dozen of the men who sat smoking and reading with a sort of Parisian effect at the little tables which lined two sides of the room, looked up and bowed smiling, and although this coming of the kids was anything but an unusual event, at least a dozen men wheeled in their chairs to stare after them. Three waiters polished tables, and moved chairs noisily, and appeared to be eager. Distinctly these kids were of importance.

Behind the distant bar, the tall form of old Pop himself awaited them smiling with broad geniality. "Well, my boys, how are you?" he cried in a voice of profound solicitude. He allowed five or six of his customers to languish in the care of Mexican bartenders, while he himself gave his eloquent attention to the kids, lending all the dignity of a great event to their arrival. "How are the boys to-day, eh?"

"You're a smooth old guy," said one, eying him. "Are you giving us this welcome so we won't notice it when you push your worst whisky at us?"

Pop turned in appeal from one kid to the other kid. "There, now, hear that, will you?" He assumed an oratorical pose. "Why, my boys, you always get the best that this house has got."

"Yes, we do!" The kids laughed. "Well, bring it out, anyhow, and if it's the same you sold us last night, we'll grab your cash register and run."

Pop whirled a bottle along the bar and then gazed at it with a rapt expression. "Fine as silk," he murmured. "Now just taste that, and if it isn't the best whisky you ever put in your face, why I'm a liar, that's all."

The kids surveyed him with scorn, and poured their allowances. Then they stood for a time insulting Pop about his whisky. "Usually it tastes exactly like new parlour furniture," said the San Francisco kid. "Well, here goes, and you want to look out for your cash register."

"Your health, gentlemen," said Pop with a grand air, and as he wiped his bristling grey moustaches he wagged his head with reference to the cash register question. "I could catch you before you got very far."

"Why, are you a runner?" said one derisively.

"You just bank on me, my boy," said Pop, with deep emphasis. "I'm a flier."

The kids sat down their glasses suddenly and looked at him. "You must be," they said. Pop was tall and graceful and magnificent in manner, but he did not display those qualities of form which mean speed in the animal. His hair was grey; his face was round and fat from much living. The buttons of his glittering white waistcoat formed a fine curve, so that if the concave surface of a piece of barrel-hoop had been laid against Pop it would have touched every button. "You must be," observed the kids again.

"Well, you can laugh all you like, but-no jolly now, boys, I tell you I'm a winner. Why, I bet you I can skin anything in this town on a square go. When I kept my place in Eagle Pass there wasn't anybody who could touch me. One of these sure things came down from San Anton'. Oh, he was a runner he was. One of these people with wings. Well, I skinned 'im. What? Certainly I did. Never touched me."

The kids had been regarding him in grave silence, but at this moment they grinned, and said quite in chorus, "Oh, you old liar!"

Pop's voice took on a whining tone of earnestness. "Boys, I'm telling it to you straight. I'm a flier."

One of the kids had had a dreamy cloud in his eye and he cried out suddenly —"Say, what a joke to play this on Freddie."

The other jumped ecstatically. "Oh, wouldn't it though. Say he wouldn't do a thing but howl! He'd go crazy."

They looked at Pop as if they longed to be certain that he was, after all, a runner. "Now, Pop, on the level," said one of them wistfully, "can you run?"

"Boys," swore Pop, "I'm a peach! On the dead level, I'm a peach."

"By golly, I believe the old Indian can run," said one to the other, as if they were alone in confidence.

"That's what I can," cried Pop.

The kids said —"Well, so long, old man." They went to a table and sat down. They ordered a salad. They were always ordering salads. This was because one kid had a wild passion for salads, and the other didn't care. So at any hour of the day they might be seen ordering a salad. When this one came they went into a sort of executive session. It was a very long consultation. Men noted it. Occasionally the kids laughed in supreme enjoyment of something unknown. The low rumble of wheels came from the street. Often could be heard the parrot-like cries of distant vendors. The sunlight streamed through the green curtains, and made little amber-coloured flitterings on the marble floor. High up among the severe decorations of the ceiling-reminiscent of the days when the great building was a palace —a small white butterfly was wending through the cool air spaces. The long billiard hall led back to a vague gloom. The balls were always clicking, and one could see countless crooked elbows. Beggars slunk through the wicker doors, and were ejected by the nearest waiter. At last the kids called Pop to them.

"Sit down, Pop. Have a drink." They scanned him carefully. "Say now, Pop, on your solemn oath, can you run?"

"Boys," said Pop piously, and raising his hand, "I can run like a rabbit."

"On your oath?"

"On my oath."

"Can you beat Freddie?"

Pop appeared to look at the matter from all sides. "Well, boys, I'll tell you. No man is ever cock-sure of anything in this world, and I don't want to say that I can best any man, but I've seen Freddie run, and I'm ready to swear I can beat him. In a hundred yards I'd just

about skin 'im neat-you understand, just about neat. Freddie is a good average runner, but I —
you understand —I'm just —a little-bit-better." The kids had been listening with the utmost
attention. Pop spoke the latter part slowly and meanfully. They thought he intended them to
see his great confidence.

One said —"Pop, if you throw us in this thing, we'll come here and drink for two weeks
without paying. We'll back you and work a josh on Freddie! But O! —if you throw us!"

To this menace Pop cried —"Boys, I'll make the run of my life! On my oath!"

The salad having vanished, the kids arose. "All right, now," they warned him. "If you play
us for duffers, we'll get square. Don't you forget it."

"Boys, I'll give you a race for your money. Book on that. I may lose-understand, I may
lose-no man can help meeting a better man. But I think I can skin him, and I'll give you a
run for your money, you bet."

"All right, then. But, look here," they told him, "you keep your face closed. Nobody gets
in on this but us. Understand?"

"Not a soul," Pop declared. They left him, gesturing a last warning from the wicker doors.

In the street they saw Benson, his cane gripped in the middle, strolling through the white-
clothed jabbering natives on the shady side. They semaphored to him eagerly. He came across
cautiously, like a man who ventures into dangerous company.

"We're going to get up a race. Pop and Fred. Pop swears he can skin 'im. This is a tip. Keep
it dark. Say, won't Freddie be hot?"

Benson looked as if he had been compelled to endure these exhibitions of insanity for a
century. "Oh, you fellows are off. Pop can't beat Freddie. He's an old bat. Why, it's impossible.
Pop can't beat Freddie."

"Can't he? Want to bet he can't?" said the kids. "There now, let's see-you're talking so large."

"Well, you — —"

"Oh, bet. Bet or else close your trap. That's the way."

"How do you know you can pull off the race? Seen Freddie?"

"No, but — —"

"Well, see him then. Can't bet with no race arranged. I'll bet with you all right-all right.
I'll give you fellows a tip though-you're a pair of asses. Pop can't run any faster than a brick
school-house."

The kids scowled at him and defiantly said —"Can't he?" They left him and went to the Casa
Verde. Freddie, beautiful in his white jacket, was holding one of his innumerable conversations
across the bar. He smiled when he saw them. "Where you boys been?" he demanded, in a
paternal tone. Almost all the proprietors of American cafés in the city used to adopt a paternal
tone when they spoke to the kids.

"Oh, been 'round,'" they replied.

"Have a drink?" said the proprietor of the Casa Verde, forgetting his other social obligations.
During the course of this ceremony one of the kids remarked —

"Freddie, Pop says he can beat you running."

"Does he?" observed Freddie without excitement. He was used to various snares of the kids.

"That's what. He says he can leave you at the wire and not see you again."

"Well, he lies," replied Freddie placidly.

"And I'll bet you a bottle of wine that he can do it, too."

"Rats!" said Freddie.

"Oh, that's all right," pursued a kid. "You can throw bluffs all you like, but he can lose you
in a hundred yards' dash, you bet."

Freddie drank his whisky, and then settled his elbows on the bar.

"Say, now, what do you boys keep coming in here with some pipe-story all the time for? You
can't josh me. Do you think you can scare me about Pop? Why, I know I can beat him. He
can't run with me. Certainly not. Why, you fellows are just jollying me."

"Are we though!" said the kids. "You daren't bet the bottle of wine."

"Oh, of course I can bet you a bottle of wine," said Freddie disdainfully. "Nobody cares about a bottle of wine, but — —"

"Well, make it five then," advised one of the kids.

Freddie hunched his shoulders. "Why, certainly I will. Make it ten if you like, but — —"

"We do," they said.

"Ten, is it? All right; that goes." A look of weariness came over Freddie's face. "But you boys are foolish. I tell you Pop is an old man. How can you expect him to run? Of course, I'm no great runner, but then I'm young and healthy and-and a pretty smooth runner too. Pop is old and fat, and then he doesn't do a thing but tank all day. It's a cinch."

The kids looked at him and laughed rapturously. They waved their fingers at him. "Ah, there!" they cried. They meant that they had made a victim of him.

But Freddie continued to expostulate. "I tell you he couldn't win-an old man like him. You're crazy. Of course, I know you don't care about ten bottles of wine, but, then-to make such bets as that. You're twisted."

"Are we, though?" cried the kids in mockery. They had precipitated Freddie into a long and thoughtful treatise on every possible chance of the thing as he saw it. They disputed with him from time to time, and jeered at him. He laboured on through his argument. Their childish faces were bright with glee.

In the midst of it Wilburson entered. Wilburson worked; not too much, though. He had hold of the Mexican end of a great importing house of New York, and as he was a junior partner, he worked. But not too much, though. "What's the howl?" he said.

The kids giggled. "We've got Freddie rattled."

"Why," said Freddie, turning to him, "these two Indians are trying to tell me that Pop can beat me running."

"Like the devil," said Wilburson, incredulously.

"Well, can't he?" demanded a kid.

"Why, certainly not," said Wilburson, dismissing every possibility of it with a gesture. "That old bat? Certainly not. I'll bet fifty dollars that Freddie — —"

"Take you," said a kid.

"What?" said Wilburson, "that Freddie won't beat Pop?"

The kid that had spoken now nodded his head.

"That Freddie won't beat Pop?" repeated Wilburson.

"Yes. It's a go?"

"Why, certainly," retorted Wilburson. "Fifty? All right."

"Bet you five bottles on the side," ventured the other kid.

"Why, certainly," exploded Wilburson wrathfully. "You fellows must take me for something easy. I'll take all those kinds of bets I can get. Cer-tain-ly."

They settled the details. The course was to be paced off on the asphalt of one of the adjacent side-streets, and then, at about eleven o'clock in the evening, the match would be run. Usually in Mexico the streets of a city grow lonely and dark but a little after nine o'clock. There are occasional lurking figures, perhaps, but no crowds, lights and noise. The course would doubtless be undisturbed. As for the policeman in the vicinity, they-well, they were conditionally amiable.

The kids went to see Pop; they told him of the arrangement, and then in deep tones they said, "Oh, Pop, if you throw us!"

Pop appeared to be a trifle shaken by the weight of responsibility thrust upon him, but he spoke out bravely. "Boys, I'll pinch that race. Now you watch me. I'll pinch it."

The kids went then on some business of their own, for they were not seen again till evening. When they returned to the neighbourhood of the Café Colorado the usual stream of carriages was whirling along the calle. The wheels hummed on the asphalt, and the coachmen towered in their great sombreros. On the sidewalk a gazing crowd sauntered, the better class self-satisfied and proud, in their Derby hats and cut-away coats, the lower classes muffling their dark faces in their blankets, slipping along in leather sandals. An electric light sputtered and fumed over the throng. The afternoon shower had left the pave wet and glittering. The air was still laden with the odour of rain on flowers, grass, leaves.

In the Café Colorado a cosmopolitan crowd ate, drank, played billiards, gossiped, or read in the glaring yellow light. When the kids entered a large circle of men that had been gesticulating near the bar greeted them with a roar.

"Here they are now!"

"Oh, you pair of peaches!"

"Say, got any more money to bet with?" Colonel Hammigan, grinning, pushed his way to them. "Say, boys, we'll all have a drink on you now because you won't have any money after eleven o'clock. You'll be going down the back stairs in your stocking feet."

Although the kids remained unnaturally serene and quiet, argument in the Café Colorado became tumultuous. Here and there a man who did not intend to bet ventured meekly that perchance Pop might win, and the others swarmed upon him in a whirlwind of angry denial and ridicule.

Pop, enthroned behind the bar, looked over at this storm with a shadow of anxiety upon his face. This widespread flouting affected him, but the kids looked blissfully satisfied with the tumult they had stirred.

Blanco, honest man, ever worrying for his friends, came to them. "Say, you fellows, you aren't betting too much? This thing looks kind of shaky, don't it?"

The faces of the kids grew sober, and after consideration one said —"No, I guess we've got a good thing, Blanco. Pop is going to surprise them, I think."

"Well, don't — —"

"All right, old boy. We'll watch out."

From time to time the kids had much business with certain orange, red, blue, purple, and green bills. They were making little memoranda on the back of visiting cards. Pop watched them closely, the shadow still upon his face. Once he called to them, and when they came he leaned over the bar and said intensely —"Say, boys, remember, now —I might lose this race. Nobody can ever say for sure, and if I do, why — —"

"Oh, that's all right, Pop," said the kids, reassuringly. "Don't mind it. Do your derndest, and let it go at that."

When they had left him, however, they went to a corner to consult. "Say, this is getting interesting. Are you in deep?" asked one anxiously of his friend.

"Yes, pretty deep," said the other stolidly. "Are you?"

"Deep as the devil," replied the other in the same tone.

They looked at each other stonily and went back to the crowd. Benson had just entered the café. He approached them with a gloating smile of victory. "Well, where's all that money you were going to bet?"

"Right here," said the kids, thrusting into their waistcoat pockets.

At eleven o'clock a curious thing was learned. When Pop and Freddie, the kids and all, came to the little side street, it was thick with people. It seemed that the news of this race had spread like the wind among the Americans, and they had come to witness the event. In the darkness the crowd moved, mumbling in argument.

The principals-the kids and those with them-surveyed this scene with some dismay. "Say-here's a go." Even then a policeman might be seen approaching, the light from his little lantern flickering on his white cap, gloves, brass buttons, and on the butt of the old-fashioned Colt's revolver which hung at his belt. He addressed Freddie in swift Mexican. Freddie listened, nodding from time to time. Finally Freddie turned to the others to translate. "He says he'll get into trouble if he allows this race when all this crowd is here."

There was a murmur of discontent. The policeman looked at them with an expression of anxiety on his broad, brown face.

"Oh, come on. We'll go hold it on some other fellow's beat," said one of the kids. The group moved slowly away debating. Suddenly the other kid cried, "I know! The Paseo!"

"By jiminy," said Freddie, "just the thing. We'll get a cab and go out to the Paseo. S-s-h! Keep it quiet; we don't want all this mob."

Later they tumbled into a cab-Pop, Freddie, the kids, old Colonel Hammigan and Benson. They whispered to the men who had wagered, "The Paseo." The cab whirled away up the black street. There were occasional grunts and groans, cries of "Oh, get off me feet," and of "Quit! you're killing me." Six people do not have fun in one cab. The principals spoke to each other with the respect and friendliness which comes to good men at such times. Once a kid put his head out of the window and looked backward. He pulled it in again and cried, "Great Scott! Look at that, would you!"

The others struggled to do as they were bid, and afterwards shouted, "Holy smoke! Well, I'll be blowed! Thunder and turf!"

Galloping after them came innumerable cabs, their lights twinkling, streaming in a great procession through the night.

"The street is full of them," ejaculated the old colonel.

The Paseo de la Reforma is the famous drive of the city of Mexico, leading to the Castle of Chapultepec, which last ought to be well known in the United States.

It is a fine broad avenue of macadam with a much greater quality of dignity than anything of the kind we possess in our own land. It seems of the old world, where to the beauty of the thing itself is added the solemnity of tradition and history, the knowledge that feet in buskins trod the same stones, that cavalcades of steel thundered there before the coming of carriages.

When the Americans tumbled out of their cabs the giant bronzes of Aztec and Spaniard loomed dimly above them like towers. The four roads of poplar trees rustled weirdly off there in the darkness. Pop took out his watch and struck a match. "Well, hurry up this thing. It's almost midnight."

The other cabs came swarming, the drivers lashing their horses, for these Americans, who did all manner of strange things, nevertheless always paid well for it. There was a mighty hubbub then in the darkness. Five or six men began to pace the distance and quarrel. Others knotted their handkerchiefs together to make a tape. Men were swearing over bets, fussing and fuming about the odds. Benson came to the kids swaggering. "You're a pair of asses." The cabs waited in a solid block down the avenue. Above the crowd the tall statues hid their visages in the night.

At last a voice floated through the darkness. "Are you ready there?" Everybody yelled excitedly. The men at the tape pulled it out straight. "Hold it higher, Jim, you fool," and silence fell then upon the throng. Men bended down trying to pierce the deep gloom with their eyes. From out at the starting point came muffled voices. The crowd swayed and jostled.

The racers did not come. The crowd began to fret, its nerves burning. "Oh, hurry up," shrilled some one.

The voice called again —"Ready there?" Everybody replied —"Yes, all ready. Hurry up!"

There was a more muffled discussion at the starting point. In the crowd a man began to make a proposition. "I'll bet twenty —" but the crowd interrupted with a howl. "Here they come!" The thickly-packed body of men swung as if the ground had moved. The men at the tape shouldered madly at their fellows, bawling, "Keep back! Keep back!"

From the distance came the noise of feet pattering furiously. Vague forms flashed into view for an instant. A hoarse roar broke from the crowd. Men bended and swayed and fought. The kids back near the tape exchanged another stolid look. A white form shone forth. It grew like a spectre. Always could be heard the wild patter. A scream broke from the crowd. "By Gawd, it's Pop! Pop! Pop's ahead!"

The old man spun towards the tape like a madman, his chin thrown back, his grey hair flying. His legs moved like oiled machinery. And as he shot forward a howl as from forty cages of wild animals went toward the imperturbable chieftains in bronze. The crowd flung themselves forward. "Oh, you old Indian! You savage! Did anybody ever see such running?"

"Ain't he a peach! Well!"

"Where's the kids? H-e-y, kids!"

109

"Look at him, would you? Did you ever think?" These cries flew in the air blended in a vast shout of astonishment and laughter.

For an instant the whole tragedy was in view. Freddie, desperate, his teeth shining, his face contorted, whirling along in deadly effort, was twenty feet behind the tall form of old Pop, who, dressed only in his-only in his underclothes-gained with each stride. One grand insane moment, and then Pop had hurled himself against the tape-victor!

Freddie, fallen into the arms of some men, struggled with his breath, and at last managed to stammer —

"Say, can't —can't —that old-old-man run!"

Pop, puffing and heaving, could only gasp —"Where's my shoes? Who's got my shoes?"

Later Freddie scrambled panting through the crowd, and held out his hand. "Good man, Pop!" And then he looked up and down the tall, stout form. "Hell! who would think you could run like that?"

The kids were surrounded by a crowd, laughing tempestuously.

"How did you know he could run?"

"Why didn't you give me a line on him?"

"Say-great snakes! —you fellows had a nerve to bet on Pop."

"Why, I was cock-sure he couldn't win."

"Oh, you fellows must have seen him run before."

"Who would ever think it?"

Benson came by, filling the midnight air with curses. They turned to jibe him.

"What's the matter, Benson?"

"Somebody pinched my handkerchief. I tied it up in that string. Damn it."

The kids laughed blithely. "Why, hello! Benson," they said.

There was a great rush for cabs. Shouting, laughing, wondering, the crowd hustled into their conveyances, and the drivers flogged their horses toward the city again.

"Won't Freddie be crazy! Say, he'll be guyed about this for years."

"But who would ever think that old tank could run so?"

One cab had to wait while Pop and Freddie resumed various parts of their clothing.

As they drove home, Freddie said —"Well, Pop, you beat me."

Pop said —"That's all right, old man."

The kids, grinning, said —"How much did you lose, Benson?"

Benson said defiantly —"Oh, not so much. How much did you win?"

"Oh, not so much."

Old Colonel Hammigan, squeezed down in a corner, had apparently been reviewing the event in his mind, for he suddenly remarked, "Well, I'm damned!"

They were late in reaching the Café Colorado, but when they did, the bottles were on the bar as thick as pickets on a fence.

The Five White Mice

Freddie was mixing a cock-tail. His hand with the long spoon was whirling swiftly, and the ice in the glass hummed and rattled like a cheap watch. Over by the window, a gambler, a millionaire, a railway conductor, and the agent of a vast American syndicate were playing seven-up. Freddie surveyed them with the ironical glance of a man who is mixing a cock-tail.

From time to time a swarthy Mexican waiter came with his tray from the rooms at the rear, and called his orders across the bar. The sounds of the indolent stir of the city, awakening from its siesta, floated over the screens which barred the sun and the inquisitive eye. From the far-away kitchen could be heard the roar of the old French *chef*, driving, herding, and abusing his Mexican helpers.

A string of men came suddenly in from the street. They stormed up to the bar. There were impatient shouts. "Come now, Freddie, don't stand there like a portrait of yourself. Wiggle!" Drinks of many kinds and colours, amber, green, mahogany, strong and mild, began to swarm upon the bar with all the attendants of lemon, sugar, mint and ice. Freddie, with Mexican support, worked like a sailor in the provision of them, sometimes talking with that scorn for drink and admiration for those who drink which is the attribute of a good bar-keeper.

At last a man was afflicted with a stroke of dice-shaking. A herculean discussion was waging, and he was deeply engaged in it, but at the same time he lazily flirted the dice. Occasionally he made great combinations. "Look at that, would you?" he cried proudly. The others paid little heed. Then violently the craving took them. It went along the line like an epidemic, and involved them all. In a moment they had arranged a carnival of dice-shaking with money penalties and liquid prizes. They clamorously made it a point of honour with Freddie that he should play and take his chance of sometimes providing this large group with free refreshment. With bended heads like football players, they surged over the tinkling dice, jostling, cheering, and bitterly arguing. One of the quiet company playing seven-up at the corner table said profanely that the row reminded him of a bowling contest at a picnic.

After the regular shower, many carriages rolled over the smooth calle, and sent a musical thunder through the Casa Verde. The shop-windows became aglow with light, and the walks were crowded with youths, callow and ogling, dressed vainly according to superstitious fashions. The policemen had muffled themselves in their gnome-like cloaks, and placed their lanterns as obstacles for the carriages in the middle of the street. The city of Mexico gave forth the deep organ-mellow tones of its evening resurrection.

But still the group at the bar of the Casa Verde were shaking dice. They had passed beyond shaking for drinks for the crowd, for Mexican dollars, for dinners, for the wine at dinner. They had even gone to the trouble of separating the cigars and cigarettes from the dinner's bill, and causing a distinct man to be responsible for them. Finally they were aghast. Nothing remained in sight of their minds which even remotely suggested further gambling. There was a pause for deep consideration.

"Well — —"

"Well — —"

A man called out in the exuberance of creation. "I know! Let's shake for a box to-night at the circus! A box at the circus!" The group was profoundly edified. "That's it! That's it! Come on now! Box at the circus!" A dominating voice cried —"Three dashes-high man out!" An American, tall, and with a face of copper red from the rays that flash among the Sierra Madres and burn on the cactus deserts, took the little leathern cup and spun the dice out upon the polished wood. A fascinated assemblage hung upon the bar-rail. Three kings turned their pink faces upward. The tall man flourished the cup, burlesquing, and flung the two other dice. From them he ultimately extracted one more pink king. "There," he said. "Now, let's see! Four kings!" He began to swagger in a sort of provisional way.

The next man took the cup, and blew softly in the top of it. Poising it in his hand, he then surveyed the company with a stony eye and paused. They knew perfectly well that he was applying the magic of deliberation and ostentatious indifference, but they could not wait in tranquillity during the performance of all these rites. They began to call out impatiently. "Come now-hurry up." At last the man, with a gesture that was singularly impressive, threw the dice. The others set up a howl of joy. "Not a pair!" There was another solemn pause. The men moved restlessly. "Come, now, go ahead!" In the end, the man, induced and abused, achieved something that was nothing in the presence of four kings. The tall man climbed on the foot-rail and leaned hazardously forward. "Four kings! My four kings are good to go out," he bellowed into the middle of the mob, and although in a moment he did pass into the radiant region of exemption, he continued to bawl advice and scorn.

The mirrors and oiled woods of the Casa Verde were now dancing with blue flashes from a great buzzing electric lamp. A host of quiet members of the Anglo-Saxon colony had come in for their pre-dinner cock-tails. An amiable person was exhibiting to some tourists this popular American saloon. It was a very sober and respectable time of day. Freddie reproved courageously the dice-shaking brawlers, and, in return, he received the choicest advice in a tumult of seven combined vocabularies. He laughed; he had been compelled to retire from the game, but he was keeping an interested, if furtive, eye upon it.

Down at the end of the line there was a youth at whom everybody railed for his flaming ill-luck. At each disaster, Freddie swore from behind the bar in a sort of affectionate contempt. "Why, this kid has had no luck for two days. Did you ever see such throwin'?"

The contest narrowed eventually to the New York kid and an individual who swung about placidly on legs that moved in nefarious circles. He had a grin that resembled a bit of carving. He was obliged to lean down and blink rapidly to ascertain the facts of his venture, but fate presented him with five queens. His smile did not change, but he puffed gently like a man who has been running.

The others, having emerged unscathed from this part of the conflict, waxed hilarious with the kid. They smote him on either shoulders. "We've got you stuck for it, kid! You can't beat that game! Five queens!"

Up to this time the kid had displayed only the temper of the gambler, but the cheerful hoots of the players, supplemented now by a ring of guying non-combatants, caused him to feel profoundly that it would be fine to beat the five queens. He addressed a gambler's slogan to the interior of the cup.

> "Oh, five white mice of chance,
> Shirts of wool and corduroy pants,
> Gold and wine, women and sin,
> All for you if you let me come in —
> Into the house of chance."

Flashing the dice sardonically out upon the bar, he displayed three aces. From two dice in the next throw he achieved one more ace. For his last throw, he rattled the single dice for a long time. He already had four aces; if he accomplished another one, the five queens were vanquished and the box at the circus came from the drunken man's pocket. All the kid's movements were slow and elaborate. For the last throw he planted the cup bottom-down on the bar with the one dice hidden under it. Then he turned and faced the crowd with the air of a conjuror or a cheat.

"Oh, maybe it's an ace," he said in boastful calm. "Maybe it's an ace."

Instantly he was presiding over a little drama in which every man was absorbed. The kid leaned with his back against the bar-rail and with his elbows upon it.

"Maybe it's an ace," he repeated.

A jeering voice in the background said —"Yes, maybe it is, kid!"

The kid's eyes searched for a moment among the men. "I'll bet fifty dollars it is an ace," he said.

Another voice asked —"American money?"

"Yes," answered the kid.

"Oh!" There was a genial laugh at this discomfiture. However, no one came forward at the kid's challenge, and presently he turned to the cup. "Now, I'll show you." With the manner of a mayor unveiling a statue, he lifted the cup. There was revealed naught but a ten-spot. In the roar which arose could be heard each man ridiculing the cowardice of his neighbour, and above all the din rang the voice of Freddie be-rating every one. "Why, there isn't one liver to every five men in the outfit. That was the greatest cold bluff I ever saw worked. He wouldn't know how to cheat with dice if he wanted to. Don't know the first thing about it. I could hardly keep from laughin' when I seen him drillin' you around. Why, I tell you, I had that fifty dollars right in my pocket if I wanted to be a chump. You're an easy lot — —"

Nevertheless the group who had won in the theatre-box game did not relinquish their triumph. They burst like a storm about the head of the kid, swinging at him with their fists. "'Five white mice'!" they quoted, choking. "'Five white mice'!"

"Oh, they are not so bad," said the kid.

Afterward it often occurred that a man would jeer a finger at the kid and derisively say — "'Five white mice.'"

On the route from the dinner to the circus, others of the party often asked the kid if he had really intended to make his appeal to mice. They suggested other animals-rabbits, dogs, hedgehogs, snakes, opossums. To this banter the kid replied with a serious expression of his belief in the fidelity and wisdom of the five white mice. He presented a most eloquent case, decorated with fine language and insults, in which he proved that if one was going to believe in anything at all, one might as well choose the five white mice. His companions, however, at once and unanimously pointed out to him that his recent exploit did not place him in the light of a convincing advocate.

The kid discerned two figures in the street. They were making imperious signs at him. He waited for them to approach, for he recognized one as the other kid-the Frisco kid: there were two kids. With the Frisco kid was Benson. They arrived almost breathless. "Where you been?" cried the Frisco kid. It was an arrangement that upon a meeting the one that could first ask this question was entitled to use a tone of limitless injury. "What you been doing? Where you going? Come on with us. Benson and I have got a little scheme."

The New York kid pulled his arm from the grapple of the other. "I can't. I've got to take these sutlers to the circus. They stuck me for it shaking dice at Freddie's. I can't, I tell you."

The two did not at first attend to his remarks. "Come on! We've got a little scheme."

"I can't. They stuck me. I've got to take'm to the circus."

At this time it did not suit the men with the scheme to recognize these objections as important. "Oh, take'm some other time. Well, can't you take'm some other time? Let 'em go. Damn the circus. Get cold feet. What did you get stuck for? Get cold feet."

But despite their fighting, the New York kid broke away from them. "I can't, I tell you. They stuck me." As he left them, they yelled with rage. "Well, meet us, now, do you hear? In the Casa Verde as soon as the circus quits! Hear?" They threw maledictions after him.

In the city of Mexico, a man goes to the circus without descending in any way to infant amusements, because the Circo Teatro Orrin is one of the best in the world, and too easily surpasses anything of the kind in the United States, where it is merely a matter of a number of rings, if possible, and a great professional agreement to lie to the public. Moreover, the American clown, who in the Mexican arena prances and gabbles, is the clown to whom writers refer as the delight of their childhood, and lament that he is dead. At this circus the kid was not debased by the sight of mournful prisoner elephants and caged animals forlorn and sickly. He sat in his box until late, and laughed and swore when past laughing at the comic foolish-wise clown.

When he returned to the Casa Verde there was no display of the Frisco kid and Benson. Freddie was leaning on the bar listening to four men terribly discuss a question that was not plain. There was a card-game in the corner, of course. Sounds of revelry pealed from the rear rooms.

When the kid asked Freddie if he had seen his friend and Benson, Freddie looked bored. "Oh, yes, they were in here just a minute ago, but I don't know where they went. They've got their skates on. Where've they been? Came in here rolling across the floor like two little gilt gods. They wobbled around for a time, and then Frisco wanted me to send six bottles of wine around to Benson's rooms, but I didn't have anybody to send this time of night, and so they got mad and went out. Where did they get their loads?"

In the first deep gloom of the street the kid paused a moment debating. But presently he heard quavering voices. "Oh, kid! kid! Com'ere!" Peering, he recognized two vague figures against the opposite wall. He crossed the street, and they said —"Hello-kid."

"Say, where did you get it?" he demanded sternly. "You Indians better go home. What did you want to get scragged for?" His face was luminous with virtue.

As they swung to and fro, they made angry denials. "We ain' load'! We ain' load'. Big chump. Comonangetadrink."

The sober youth turned then to his friend. "Hadn't you better go home, kid? Come on, it's late. You'd better break away."

The Frisco kid wagged his head decisively. "Got take Benson home first. He'll be wallowing around in a minute. Don't mind me. I'm all right."

"Cerly, he's all right," said Benson, arousing from deep thought. "He's all right. But better take'm home, though. That's ri-right. He's load'. But he's all right. No need go home any more'n you. But better take'm home. He's load'." He looked at his companion with compassion. "Kid, you're load'."

The sober kid spoke abruptly to his friend from San Francisco. "Kid, pull yourself together, now. Don't fool. We've got to brace this ass of a Benson all the way home. Get hold of his other arm."

The Frisco kid immediately obeyed his comrade without a word or a glower. He seized Benson and came to attention like a soldier. Later, indeed, he meekly ventured —"Can't we take cab?" But when the New York kid snapped out that there were no convenient cabs he subsided to an impassive silence. He seemed to be reflecting upon his state, without astonishment, dismay, or any particular emotion. He submitted himself woodenly to the direction of his friend.

Benson had protested when they had grasped his arms. "Washa doing?" he said in a new and guttural voice. "Washa doing? I ain' load'. Comonangetadrink. I——"

"Oh, come along, you idiot," said the New York kid. The Frisco kid merely presented the mien of a stoic to the appeal of Benson, and in silence dragged away at one of his arms. Benson's feet came from that particular spot on the pavement with the reluctance of roots and also with the ultimate suddenness of roots. The three of them lurched out into the street in the abandon of tumbling chimneys. Benson was meanwhile noisily challenging the others to produce any reasons for his being taken home. His toes clashed into the kerb when they reached the other side of the calle, and for a moment the kids hauled him along with the points of his shoes scraping musically on the pavement. He balked formidably as they were about to pass the Casa Verde. "No! No! Leshavanothdrink! Anothdrink! Onemore!"

But the Frisco kid obeyed the voice of his partner in a manner that was blind but absolute, and they scummed Benson on past the door. Locked together the three swung into a dark street. The sober kid's flank was continually careering ahead of the other wing. He harshly admonished the Frisco child, and the latter promptly improved in the same manner of unthinking complete obedience. Benson began to recite the tale of a love affair, a tale that didn't even have a middle. Occasionally the New York kid swore. They toppled on their way like three comedians playing at it on the stage.

At midnight a little Mexican street burrowing among the walls of the city is as dark as a whale's throat at deep sea. Upon this occasion heavy clouds hung over the capital and the sky was a pall. The projecting balconies could make no shadows.

114

"Shay," said Benson, breaking away from his escort suddenly, "what want gome for? I ain't load'. You got reg'lar spool-fact'ry in your head-you N' York kid there. Thish oth' kid, he's mos' proper shober, mos' proper shober. He's drunk, but-but he's shober."

"Ah, shup up, Benson," said the New York kid. "Come along now. We can't stay here all night." Benson refused to be corralled, but spread his legs and twirled like a dervish, meanwhile under the evident impression that he was conducting himself most handsomely. It was not long before he gained the opinion that he was laughing at the others. "Eight purple dogsh-dogs! Eight purple dogs. Thas what kid'll see in the morn'. Look ou' for 'em. They —"

As Benson, describing the canine phenomena, swung wildly across the sidewalk, it chanced that three other pedestrians were passing in shadowy rank. Benson's shoulder jostled one of them.

A Mexican wheeled upon the instant. His hand flashed to his hip. There was a moment of silence, during which Benson's voice was not heard raised in apology. Then an indescribable comment, one burning word, came from between the Mexican's teeth.

Benson, rolling about in a semi-detached manner, stared vacantly at the Mexican, who thrust his lean face forward while his fingers played nervously at his hip. The New York kid could not follow Spanish well, but he understood when the Mexican breathed softly: "Does the señor want to fight?"

Benson simply gazed in gentle surprise. The woman next to him at dinner had said something inventive. His tailor had presented his bill. Something had occurred which was mildly out of the ordinary, and his surcharged brain refused to cope with it. He displayed only the agitation of a smoker temporarily without a light.

The New York kid had almost instantly grasped Benson's arm, and was about to jerk him away, when the other kid, who up to this time had been an automaton, suddenly projected himself forward, thrust the rubber Benson aside, and said —"Yes."

There was no sound nor light in the world. The wall at the left happened to be of the common prison-like construction-no door, no window, no opening at all. Humanity was enclosed and asleep. Into the mouth of the sober kid came a wretched bitter taste as if it had filled with blood. He was transfixed as if he was already seeing the lightning ripples on the knife-blade.

But the Mexican's hand did not move at that time. His face went still further forward and he whispered —"So?" The sober kid saw this face as if he and it were alone in space —a yellow mask smiling in eager cruelty, in satisfaction, and above all it was lit with sinister decision. As for the features, they were reminiscent of an unplaced, a forgotten type, which really resembled with precision those of a man who had shaved him three times in Boston in 1888. But the expression burned his mind as sealing-wax burns the palm, and fascinated, stupefied, he actually watched the progress of the man's thought toward the point where a knife would be wrenched from its sheath. The emotion, a sort of mechanical fury, a breeze made by electric fans, a rage made by vanity, smote the dark countenance in wave after wave.

Then the New York kid took a sudden step forward. His hand was at his hip. He was gripping there a revolver of robust size. He recalled that upon its black handle was stamped a hunting scene in which a sportsman in fine leggings and a peaked cap was taking aim at a stag less than one-eighth of an inch away.

His pace forward caused instant movement of the Mexicans. One immediately took two steps to face him squarely. There was a general adjustment, pair and pair. This opponent of the New York kid was a tall man and quite stout. His sombrero was drawn low over his eyes. His serape was flung on his left shoulder. His back was bended in the supposed manner of a Spanish grandee. This concave gentleman cut a fine and terrible figure. The lad, moved by the spirits of his modest and perpendicular ancestors, had time to feel his blood roar at sight of the pose.

He was aware that the third Mexican was over on the left fronting Benson, and he was aware that Benson was leaning against the wall sleepily and peacefully eying the convention. So it happened that these six men stood, side fronting side, five of them with their right hands at their hips and with their bodies lifted nervously, while the central pair exchanged a crescendo of provocations. The meaning of their words rose and rose. They were travelling in a straight line toward collision.

The New York kid contemplated his Spanish grandee. He drew his revolver upward until the hammer was surely free of the holster. He waited immovable and watchful while the garrulous Frisco kid expended two and a half lexicons on the middle Mexican.

The eastern lad suddenly decided that he was going to be killed. His mind leaped forward and studied the aftermath. The story would be a marvel of brevity when first it reached the far New York home, written in a careful hand on a bit of cheap paper, topped and footed and backed by the printed fortifications of the cable company. But they are often as stones flung into mirrors, these bits of paper upon which are laconically written all the most terrible chronicles of the times. He witnessed the uprising of his mother and sister, and the invincible calm of his hard-mouthed old father, who would probably shut himself in his library and smoke alone. Then his father would come, and they would bring him here and say —"This is the place." Then, very likely, each would remove his hat. They would stand quietly with their hats in their hands for a decent minute. He pitied his old financing father, unyielding and millioned, a man who commonly spoke twenty-two words a year to his beloved son. The kid under stood it at this time. If his fate was not impregnable, he might have turned out to be a man and have been liked by his father.

The other kid would mourn his death. He would be preternaturally correct for some weeks, and recite the tale without swearing. But it would not bore him. For the sake of his dead comrade he would be glad to be preternaturally correct, and to recite the tale without swearing.

These views were perfectly stereopticon, flashing in and away from his thought with an in-conceivable rapidity until after all they were simply one quick dismal impression. And now here is the unreal real: into this kid's nostrils, at the expectant moment of slaughter, had come the scent of new-mown hay, a fragrance from a field of prostrate grass, a fragrance which contained the sunshine, the bees, the peace of meadows, and the wonder of a distant crooning stream. It had no right to be supreme, but it was supreme, and he breathed it as he waited for pain and a sight of the unknown.

But in the same instant, it may be, his thought flew to the Frisco kid, and it came upon him like a flicker of lightning that the Frisco kid was not going to be there to perform, for instance, the extraordinary office of respectable mourner. The other kid's head was muddled, his hand was unsteady, his agility was gone. This other kid was facing the determined and most ferocious gentleman of the enemy. The New York kid became convinced that his friend was lost. There was going to be a screaming murder. He was so certain of it that he wanted to shield his eyes from sight of the leaping arm and the knife. It was sickening, utterly sickening. The New York kid might have been taking his first sea-voyage. A combination of honourable manhood and inability prevented him from running away.

He suddenly knew that it was possible to draw his own revolver, and by a swift manoeuvre face down all three Mexicans. If he was quick enough he would probably be victor. If any hitch occurred in the draw he would undoubtedly be dead with his friends. It was a new game; he had never been obliged to face a situation of this kind in the Beacon Club in New York. In this test, the lungs of the kid still continued to perform their duty.

"Oh, five white mice of chance,
Shirts of wool and corduroy pants,
Gold and wine, women and sin,
All for you if you let me come in —
Into the house of chance."

He thought of the weight and size of his revolver, and dismay pierced him. He feared that in his hands it would be as unwieldy as a sewing-machine for this quick work. He imagined, too, that some singular providence might cause him to lose his grip as he raised his weapon.

Or it might get fatally entangled in the tails of his coat. Some of the eels of despair lay wet and cold against his back.

But at the supreme moment the revolver came forth as if it were greased and it arose like a feather. This somnolent machine, after months of repose, was finally looking at the breasts of men.

Perhaps in this one series of movements, the kid had unconsciously used nervous force sufficient to raise a bale of hay. Before he comprehended it he was standing behind his revolver glaring over the barrel at the Mexicans, menacing first one and then another. His finger was tremoring on the trigger. The revolver gleamed in the darkness with a fine silver light.

The fulsome grandee sprang backward with a low cry. The man who had been facing the Frisco kid took a quick step away. The beautiful array of Mexicans was suddenly disorganized.

The cry and the backward steps revealed something of great importance to the New York kid. He had never dreamed that he did not have a complete monopoly of all possible trepidations. The cry of the grandee was that of a man who suddenly sees a poisonous snake. Thus the kid was able to understand swiftly that they were all human beings. They were unanimous in not wishing for too bloody combat. There was a sudden expression of the equality. He had vaguely believed that they were not going to evince much consideration for his dramatic development as an active factor. They even might be exasperated into an onslaught by it. Instead, they had respected his movement with a respect as great even as an ejaculation of fear and backward steps. Upon the instant he pounced forward and began to swear, unreeling great English oaths as thick as ropes, and lashing the faces of the Mexicans with them. He was bursting with rage, because these men had not previously confided to him that they were vulnerable. The whole thing had been an absurd imposition. He had been seduced into respectful alarm by the concave attitude of the grandee. And after all there had been an equality of emotion, an equality: he was furious. He wanted to take the serape of the grandee and swaddle him in it.

The Mexicans slunk back, their eyes burning wistfully. The kid took aim first at one and then at another. After they had achieved a certain distance they paused and drew up in a rank. They then resumed some of their old splendour of manner. A voice hailed him in a tone of cynical bravado as if it had come from between lips of smiling mockery. "Well, señor, it is finished?"

The kid scowled into the darkness, his revolver drooping at his side. After a moment he answered —"I am willing." He found it strange that he should be able to speak after this silence of years.

"Good-night, señor."

"Good-night."

When he turned to look at the Frisco kid he found him in his original position, his hand upon his hip. He was blinking in perplexity at the point from whence the Mexicans had vanished.

"Well," said the sober kid crossly, "are you ready to go home now?"

The Frisco kid said —"Where they gone?" His voice was undisturbed but inquisitive.

Benson suddenly propelled himself from his dreamful position against the wall. "Frishco kid's all right. He's drunk's fool and he's all right. But you New York kid, you're shober." He passed into a state of profound investigation. "Kid shober 'cause didn't go with us. Didn't go with us 'cause went to damn circus. Went to damn circus 'cause lose shakin' dice. Lose shakin' dice 'cause-what make lose shakin' dice, kid?"

The New York kid eyed the senile youth. "I don't know. The five white mice, maybe."

Benson puzzled so over this reply that he had to be held erect by his friends. Finally the Frisco kid said —"Let's go home."

Nothing had happened.

Flanagan and His Short Filibustering Adventure

I

"I have got twenty men at me back who will fight to the death," said the warrior to the old filibuster.

"And they can be blowed for all me," replied the old filibuster. "Common as sparrows. Cheap as cigarettes. Show me twenty men with steel clamps on their mouths, with holes in their heads where memory ought to be, and I want 'em. But twenty brave men merely? I'd rather have twenty brave onions."

Thereupon the warrior removed sadly, feeling that no salaams were paid to valour in these days of mechanical excellence.

Valour, in truth, is no bad thing to have when filibustering; but many medals are to be won by the man who knows not the meaning of "pow-wow," before or afterwards. Twenty brave men with tongues hung lightly may make trouble rise from the ground like smoke from grass, because of their subsequent fiery pride; whereas twenty cow-eyed villains who accept unrighteous and far-compelling kicks as they do the rain from heaven may halo the ultimate history of an expedition with gold, and plentifully bedeck their names, winning forty years of gratitude from patriots, simply by remaining silent. As for the cause, it may be only that they have no friends or other credulous furniture.

If it were not for the curse of the swinging tongue, it is surely to be said that the filibustering industry, flourishing now in the United States, would be pie. Under correct conditions, it is merely a matter of dealing with some little detectives whose skill at search is rated by those who pay them at a value of twelve or twenty dollars each week. It is nearly axiomatic that normally a twelve dollar per week detective cannot defeat a one hundred thousand dollar filibustering excursion. Against the criminal, the detective represents the commonwealth, but in this other case he represents his desire to show cause why his salary should be paid. He represents himself merely, and he counts no more than a grocer's clerk.

But the pride of the successful filibuster often smites him and his cause like an axe, and men who have not confided in their mothers go prone with him. It can make the dome of the Capitol tremble and incite the Senators to over-turning benches. It can increase the salaries of detectives who could not detect the location of a pain in the chest. It is a wonderful thing, this pride.

Filibustering was once such a simple game. It was managed blandly by gentle captains and smooth and undisturbed gentlemen, who at other times dealt in law, soap, medicine, and bananas. It was a great pity that the little cote of doves in Washington were obliged to rustle officially, and naval men were kept from their berths at night, and sundry Custom House people got wiggings, all because the returned adventurer pow-wowed in his pride. A yellow and red banner would have been long since smothered in a shame of defeat if a contract to filibuster had been let to some admirable organization like one of our trusts.

And yet the game is not obsolete. It is still played by the wise and the silent men whose names are not display-typed and blathered from one end of the country to the other.

There is in mind now a man who knew one side of a fence from the other side when he looked sharply. They were hunting for captains then to command the first vessels of what has since become a famous little fleet. One was recommended to this man, and he said, "Send him down to my office and I'll look him over." He was an attorney, and he liked to lean back in his chair, twirl a paper-knife, and let the other fellow talk.

The sea-faring man came and stood and appeared confounded. The attorney asked the terrible first question of the filibuster to the applicant. He said, "Why do you want to go?"

The captain reflected, changed his attitude three times, and decided ultimately that he didn't know. He seemed greatly ashamed. The attorney, looking at him, saw that he had eyes that resembled a lambkin's eyes.

"Glory?" said the attorney at last.

"No-o," said the captain.

"Pay?"

"No-o. Not that so much."

"Think they'll give you a land grant when they win out?"

"No; never thought."

"No glory; no immense pay; no land grant. What are you going for, then?"

"Well, I don't know," said the captain, with his glance on the floor and shifting his position again. "I don't know. I guess it's just for fun mostly." The attorney asked him out to have a drink.

When he stood on the bridge of his out-going steamer, the attorney saw him again. His shore meekness and uncertainty were gone. He was clear-eyed and strong, aroused like a mastiff at night. He took his cigar out of his mouth and yelled some sudden language at the deck.

This steamer had about her a quality of unholy mediæval disrepair, which is usually accounted the principal prerogative of the United States Revenue Marine. There is many a seaworthy ice-house if she were a good ship. She swashed through the seas as genially as an old wooden clock, burying her head under waves that came only like children at play, and, on board, it cost a ducking to go from anywhere to anywhere.

The captain had commanded vessels that shore-people thought were liners; but when a man gets the ant of desire-to-see-what-it's-like stirring in his heart, he will wallow out to sea in a pail. The thing surpasses a man's love for his sweetheart. The great tank-steamer *Thunder-Voice* had long been Flanagan's sweetheart, but he was far happier off Hatteras watching this wretched little portmanteau boom down the slant of a wave.

The crew scraped acquaintance one with another gradually. Each man came ultimately to ask his neighbour what particular turn of ill-fortune or inherited deviltry caused him to try this voyage. When one frank, bold man saw another frank, bold man aboard, he smiled, and they became friends. There was not a mind on board the ship that was not fastened to the dangers of the coast of Cuba, and taking wonder at this prospect and delight in it. Still, in jovial moments they termed each other accursed idiots.

At first there was some trouble in the engine-room, where there were many steel animals, for the most part painted red and in other places very shiny-bewildering, complex, incomprehensible to any one who don't care, usually thumping, thumping, thumping with the monotony of a snore.

It seems that this engine was as whimsical as a gas-meter. The chief engineer was a fine old fellow with a grey moustache, but the engine told him that it didn't intend to budge until it felt better. He came to the bridge and said, "The blamed old thing has laid down on us, sir."

"Who was on duty?" roared the captain.

"The second, sir."

"Why didn't he call you?"

"Don't know, sir." Later the stokers had occasion to thank the stars that they were not second engineers.

The *Foundling* was soundly thrashed by the waves for loitering while the captain and the engineers fought the obstinate machinery. During this wait on the sea, the first gloom came to the faces of the company. The ocean is wide, and a ship is a small place for the feet, and an ill ship is worriment. Even when she was again under way, the gloom was still upon the crew. From time to time men went to the engine-room doors, and looking down, wanted to ask questions of the chief engineer, who slowly prowled to and fro, and watched with careful eye his red-painted mysteries. No man wished to have a companion know that he was anxious, and so questions were caught at the lips. Perhaps none commented save the first mate, who remarked to the captain, "Wonder what the bally old thing will do, sir, when we're chased by a Spanish cruiser?"

The captain merely grinned. Later he looked over the side and said to himself with scorn, "Sixteen knots! sixteen knots! Sixteen hinges on the inner gates of Hades! Sixteen knots! Seven is her gait, and nine if you crack her up to it."

There may never be a captain whose crew can't sniff his misgivings. They scent it as a herd scents the menace far through the trees and over the ridges. A captain that does not know that he is on a foundering ship sometimes can take his men to tea and buttered toast twelve minutes before the disaster, but let him fret for a moment in the loneliness of his cabin, and in no time it affects the liver of a distant and sensitive seaman. Even as Flanagan reflected on the *Foundling*, viewing her as a filibuster, word arrived that a winter of discontent had come to the stoke-room.

The captain knew that it requires sky to give a man courage. He sent for a stoker and talked to him on the bridge. The man, standing under the sky, instantly and shamefacedly denied all knowledge of the business; nevertheless, a jaw had presently to be broken by a fist because the *Foundling* could only steam nine knots, and because the stoke-room has no sky, no wind, no bright horizon.

When the *Foundling* was somewhere off Savannah a blow came from the north-east, and the steamer, headed south-east, rolled like a boiling potato. The first mate was a fine officer, and so a wave crashed him into the deck-house and broke his arm. The cook was a good cook, and so the heave of the ship flung him heels over head with a pot of boiling water, and caused him to lose interest in everything save his legs. "By the piper," said Flanagan to himself, "this filibustering is no trick with cards."

Later there was more trouble in the stoke-room. All the stokers participated save the one with a broken jaw, who had become discouraged. The captain had an excellent chest development. When he went aft, roaring, it was plain that a man could beat carpets with a voice like that one.

One night the *Foundling* was off the southern coast of Florida, and running at half-speed towards the shore. The captain was on the bridge. "Four flashes at intervals of one minute," he said to himself, gazing steadfastly towards the beach. Suddenly a yellow eye opened in the black face of the night, and looked at the *Foundling* and closed again. The captain studied his watch and the shore. Three times more the eye opened and looked at the *Foundling* and closed again. The captain called to the vague figures on the deck below him. "Answer it." The flash of a light from the bow of the steamer displayed for a moment in golden colour the crests of the inriding waves.

The *Foundling* lay to and waited. The long swells rolled her gracefully, and her two stub masts reaching into the darkness swung with the solemnity of batons timing a dirge. When the ship had left Boston she had been as encrusted with ice as a Dakota stage-driver's beard, but now the gentle wind of Florida softly swayed the lock on the forehead of the coatless Flanagan, and he lit a new cigar without troubling to make a shield of his hands.

Finally a dark boat came plashing over the waves. As it came very near, the captain leaned forward and perceived that the men in her rowed like seamstresses, and at the same time a voice hailed him in bad English. "It's a dead sure connection," said he to himself.

At sea, to load two hundred thousand rounds of rifle ammunition, seven hundred and fifty rifles, two rapid-fire field guns with a hundred shells, forty bundles of machetes, and a hundred pounds of dynamite, from yawls, and by men who are not born stevedores, and in a heavy ground swell, and with the searchlight of a United States cruiser sometimes flashing like lightning in the sky to the southward, is no business for a Sunday-school class. When at last the *Foundling* was steaming for the open over the grey sea at dawn, there was not a man of the forty come aboard from the Florida shore, nor of the fifteen sailed from Boston, who was not glad, standing with his hair matted to his forehead with sweat, smiling at the broad wake of the *Foundling* and the dim streak on the horizon which was Florida.

But there is a point of the compass in these waters men call the north-east. When the strong winds come from that direction they kick up a turmoil that is not good for a *Foundling* stuffed with coals and war-stores. In the gale which came, this ship was no more than a drunken soldier.

The Cuban leader, standing on the bridge with the captain, was presently informed that of his men, thirty-nine out of a possible thirty-nine were sea-sick. And in truth they were sea-sick. There are degrees in this complaint, but that matter was waived between them. They were all sick to the limits. They strewed the deck in every posture of human anguish, and when the *Foundling* ducked and water came sluicing down from the bows, they let it sluice. They were satisfied if they could keep their heads clear of the wash; and if they could not keep their heads clear of the wash, they didn't care. Presently the *Foundling* swung her course to the south-east, and the waves pounded her broadside. The patriots were all ordered below decks, and there they howled and measured their misery one against another. All day the *Foundling* plopped and floundered over a blazing bright meadow of an ocean whereon the white foam was like flowers.

The captain on the bridge mused and studied the bare horizon. "Hell!" said he to himself, and the word was more in amazement than in indignation or sorrow. "Thirty-nine sea-sick passengers, the mate with a broken arm, a stoker with a broken jaw, the cook with a pair of scalded legs, and an engine likely to be taken with all these diseases, if not more! If I get back to a home port with a spoke of the wheel gripped in my hands, it'll be fair luck!"

There is a kind of corn-whisky bred in Florida which the natives declare is potent in the proportion of seven fights to a drink. Some of the Cuban volunteers had had the forethought to bring a small quantity of this whisky aboard with them, and being now in the fire-room and sea-sick, feeling that they would not care to drink liquor for two or three years to come, they gracefully tendered their portions to the stokers. The stokers accepted these gifts without avidity, but with a certain earnestness of manner.

As they were stokers, and toiling, the whirl of emotion was delayed, but it arrived ultimately, and with emphasis. One stoker called another stoker a weird name, and the latter, righteously inflamed at it, smote his mate with an iron shovel, and the man fell headlong over a heap of coal, which crashed gently while piece after piece rattled down upon the deck.

A third stoker was providently enraged at the scene, and assailed the second stoker. They fought for some moments, while the sea-sick Cubans sprawled on the deck watched with languid rolling glances the ferocity of this scuffle. One was so indifferent to the strategic importance of the space he occupied that he was kicked on the shins.

When the second engineer came to separating the combatants, he was sincere in his efforts, and he came near to disabling them for life.

The captain said, "I'll go down there and — —" But the leader of the Cubans restrained him. "No, no," he cried, "you must not. We must treat them like children, very gently, all the time, you see, or else when we get back to a United States port they will-what you call? Spring? Yes, spring the whole business. We must-jolly them, you see?"

"You mean," said the captain thoughtfully, "they are likely to get mad, and give the expedition dead away when we reach port again unless we blarney them now?"

"Yes, yes," cried the Cuban leader, "unless we are so very gentle with them they will make many troubles afterwards for us in the newspapers and then in court."

"Well, but I won't have my crew — —" began the captain.

"But you must," interrupted the Cuban, "you must. It is the only thing. You are like the captain of a pirate ship. You see? Only you can't throw them overboard like him. You see?"

"Hum," said the captain, "this here filibustering business has got a lot to it when you come to look it over."

He called the fighting stokers to the bridge, and the three came, meek and considerably battered. He was lecturing them soundly but sensibly, when he suddenly tripped a sentence and cried —"Here! Where's that other fellow? How does it come he wasn't in the fight?"

The row of stokers cried at once eagerly, "He's hurt, sir. He's got a broken jaw, sir."

"So he has; so he has," murmured the captain, much embarrassed.

And because of all these affairs, the *Foundling* steamed toward Cuba with its crew in a sling, if one may be allowed to speak in that way.

At night the *Foundling* approached the coast like a thief. Her lights were muffled, so that from the deck the sea shone with its own radiance, like the faint shimmer of some kinds of silk. The men on deck spoke in whispers, and even down in the fire-room the hidden stokers working before the blood-red furnace doors used no words and walked on tip-toe. The stars were out in the blue-velvet sky, and their light with the soft shine of the sea caused the coast to appear black as the side of a coffin. The surf boomed in low thunder on the distant beach.

The *Foundling's* engines ceased their thumping for a time. She glided quietly forward until a bell chimed faintly in the engine-room. Then she paused with a flourish of phosphorescent waters.

"Give the signal," said the captain. Three times a flash of light went from the bow. There was a moment of waiting. Then an eye like the one on the coast of Florida opened and closed, opened and closed, opened and closed. The Cubans, grouped in a great shadow on deck, burst into a low chatter of delight. A hiss from their leader silenced them.

"Well?" said the captain.

"All right," said the leader.

At the giving of the word it was not apparent that any one on board of the *Foundling* had ever been sea-sick. The boats were lowered swiftly-too swiftly. Boxes of cartridges were dragged from the hold and passed over the side with a rapidity that made men in the boats exclaim against it. They were being bombarded. When a boat headed for shore its rowers pulled like madmen. The captain paced slowly to and fro on the bridge. In the engine-room the engineers stood at their station, and in the stoke-hold the firemen fidgeted silently around the furnace doors.

On the bridge Flanagan reflected. "Oh, I don't know!" he observed. "This filibustering business isn't so bad. Pretty soon it'll be off to sea again with nothing to do but some big lying when I get into port."

In one of the boats returning from shore came twelve Cuban officers, the greater number of them convalescing from wounds, while two or three of them had been ordered to America on commissions from the insurgents. The captain welcomed them, and assured them of a speedy and safe voyage.

Presently he went again to the bridge and scanned the horizon. The sea was lonely like the spaces amid the suns. The captain grinned and softly smote his chest. "It's dead easy," he said.

It was near the end of the cargo, and the men were breathing like spent horses, although their elation grew with each moment, when suddenly a voice spoke from the sky. It was not a loud voice, but the quality of it brought every man on deck to full stop and motionless, as if they had all been changed to wax. "Captain," said the man at the masthead, "there's a light to the west'ard, sir. Think it's a steamer, sir."

There was a still moment until the captain called, "Well, keep your eye on it now." Speaking to the deck, he said, "Go ahead with your unloading."

The second engineer went to the galley to borrow a tin cup. "Hear the news, second?" asked the cook. "Steamer coming up from the west'ard."

"Gee!" said the second engineer. In the engine-room he said to the chief, "Steamer coming up from the west'ard, sir." The chief engineer began to test various little machines with which his domain was decorated. Finally he addressed the stoke-room. "Boys, I want you to look sharp now. There's a steamer coming up to the west'ard."

"All right, sir," said the stoke-room.

From time to time the captain hailed the masthead. "How is she now?"

"Seems to be coming down on us pretty fast, sir."

The Cuban leader came anxiously to the captain. "Do you think we can save all the cargo? It is rather delicate business. No?"

"Go ahead," said Flanagan. "Fire away! I'll wait."

There continued the hurried shuffling of feet on deck, and the low cries of the men unloading the cargo. In the engine-room the chief and his assistant were staring at the gong. In the stoke-room the firemen breathed through their teeth. A shovel slipped from where it leaned against the side and banged on the floor. The stokers started and looked around quickly.

Climbing to the rail and holding on to a stay, the captain gazed westward. A light had raised out of the deep. After watching this light for a time he called to the Cuban leader. "Well, as soon as you're ready now, we might as well be skipping out."

Finally, the Cuban leader told him, "Well, this is the last load. As soon as the boats come back you can be off."

"Shan't wait for all the boats," said the captain. "That fellow is too close." As the second boat came aboard, the *Foundling* turned, and like a black shadow stole seaward to cross the bows of the oncoming steamer. "Waited about ten minutes too long," said the captain to himself.

Suddenly the light in the west vanished. "Hum!" said Flanagan, "he's up to some meanness." Every one outside of the engine-rooms was set on watch. The *Foundling*, going at full speed into the north-east, slashed a wonderful trail of blue silver on the dark bosom of the sea.

A man on deck cried out hurriedly, "There she is, sir." Many eyes searched the western gloom, and one after another the glances of the men found a tiny shadow on the deep with a line of white beneath it. "He couldn't be heading better if he had a line to us," said Flanagan.

There was a thin flash of red in the darkness. It was long and keen like a crimson rapier. A short, sharp report sounded, and then a shot whined swiftly in the air and blipped into the sea. The captain had been about to take a bite of plug tobacco at the beginning of this incident, and his arm was raised. He remained like a frozen figure while the shot whined, and then, as it blipped into the sea, his hand went to his mouth and he bit the plug. He looked wide-eyed at the shadow with its line of white.

The senior Cuban officer came hurriedly to the bridge. "It is no good to surrender," he cried. "They would only shoot or hang all of us."

There was another thin red flash and a report. A loud whirring noise passed over the ship.

"I'm not going to surrender," said the captain, hanging with both hands to the rail. He appeared like a man whose traditions of peace are clinched in his heart. He was as astonished as if his hat had turned into a dog. Presently he wheeled quickly and said —"What kind of a gun is that?"

"It is a one-pounder," cried the Cuban officer. "The boat is one of those little gunboats made from a yacht. You see?"

"Well, if it's only a yawl, he'll sink us in five more minutes," said Flanagan. For a moment he looked helplessly off at the horizon. His under-jaw hung low. But a moment later, something touched him, like a stiletto point of inspiration. He leaped to the pilothouse and roared at the man at the wheel. The *Foundling* sheered suddenly to starboard, made a clumsy turn, and Flanagan was bellowing through the tube to the engine-room before everybody discovered that the old basket was heading straight for the Spanish gun-boat. The ship lunged forward like a draught-horse on the gallop.

This strange manoeuvre by the *Foundling* first dealt consternation on board of the *Foundling*. Men instinctively crouched on the instant, and then swore their supreme oath, which was un-heard by their own ears.

Later the manoeuvre of the *Foundling* dealt consternation on board of the gunboat. She had been going victoriously forward dim-eyed from the fury of her pursuit. Then this tall threatening shape had suddenly loomed over her like a giant apparition.

The people on board the *Foundling* heard panic shouts, hoarse orders. The little gunboat was paralyzed with astonishment.

Suddenly Flanagan yelled with rage and sprang for the wheel. The helmsman had turned his eyes away. As the captain whirled the wheel far to starboard he heard a crunch as the *Foundling*, lifted on a wave, smashed her shoulder against the gunboat, and he saw shooting past a little launch sort of a thing with men on her that ran this way and that way. The Cuban officers, joined by the cook and a seaman, emptied their revolvers into the surprised terror of the seas.

There was naturally no pursuit. Under comfortable speed the *Foundling* stood to the northwards.

The captain went to his berth chuckling. "There, by God!" he said. "There now!"

IV

When Flanagan came again on deck, the first mate, his arm in a sling, walked the bridge. Flanagan was smiling a wide smile. The bridge of the *Foundling* was dipping afar and then afar. With each lunge of the little steamer the water seethed and boomed alongside, and the spray dashed high and swiftly.

"Well," said Flanagan, inflating himself, "we've had a great deal of a time, and we've come through it all right, and thank Heaven it is all over."

The sky in the north-east was of a dull brick-red in tone, shaded here and there by black masses that billowed out in some fashion from the flat heavens.

"Look there," said the mate.

"Hum!" said the captain. "Looks like a blow, don't it?"

Later the surface of the water rippled and flickered in the preliminary wind. The sea had become the colour of lead. The swashing sound of the waves on the sides of the *Foundling* was now provided with some manner of ominous significance. The men's shouts were hoarse.

A squall struck the *Foundling* on her starboard quarter, and she leaned under the force of it as if she were never to return to the even keel. "I'll be glad when we get in," said the mate. "I'm going to quit then. I've got enough."

"Hell!" said the beaming Flanagan.

The steamer crawled on into the north-west. The white water, sweeping out from her, deadened the chug-chug-chug of the tired old engines.

Once, when the boat careened, she laid her shoulder flat on the sea and rested in that manner. The mate, looking down the bridge, which slanted more than a coal-shute, whistled softly to himself. Slowly, heavily, the *Foundling* arose to meet another sea.

At night waves thundered mightily on the bows of the steamer, and water lit with the beautiful phosphorescent glamour went boiling and howling along deck.

By good fortune the chief engineer crawled safely, but utterly drenched, to the galley for coffee. "Well, how goes it, chief?" said the cook, standing with his fat arms folded in order to prove that he could balance himself under any conditions.

The engineer shook his head dejectedly. "This old biscuit-box will never see port again. Why, she'll fall to pieces."

Finally at night the captain said, "Launch the boats." The Cubans hovered about him. "Is the ship going to sink?" The captain addressed them politely. "Gentlemen, we are in trouble, but all I ask of you is that you just do what I tell you, and no harm will come to anybody."

The mate directed the lowering of the first boat, and the men performed this task with all decency, like people at the side of a grave.

A young oiler came to the captain. "The chief sends word, sir, that the water is almost up to the fires."

"Keep at it as long as you can."

"Keep at it as long as we can, sir?"

Flanagan took the senior Cuban officer to the rail, and, as the steamer sheered high on a great sea, showed him a yellow dot on the horizon. It was smaller than a needle when its point is towards you.

"There," said the captain. The wind-driven spray was lashing his face. "That's Jupiter Light on the Florida coast. Put your men in the boat we've just launched, and the mate will take you to that light."

Afterwards Flanagan turned to the chief engineer. "We can never beach," said the old man. "The stokers have got to quit in a minute." Tears were in his eyes.

The *Foundling* was a wounded thing. She lay on the water with gasping engines, and each wave resembled her death-blow.

Now the way of a good ship on the sea is finer than sword-play. But this is when she is alive. If a time comes that the ship dies, then her way is the way of a floating old glove, and she has that much vim, spirit, buoyancy. At this time many men on the *Foundling* suddenly came to know that they were clinging to a corpse.

The captain went to the stoke-room, and what he saw as he swung down the companion suddenly turned him hesitant and dumb. Water was swirling to and fro with the roll of the ship, fuming greasily around half-strangled machinery that still attempted to perform its duty. Steam arose from the water, and through its clouds shone the red glare of the dying fires. As for the stokers, death might have been with silence in this room. One lay in his berth, his hands under his head, staring moodily at the wall. One sat near the foot of the companion, his face hidden in his arms. One leaned against the side and gazed at the snarling water as it rose, and its mad eddies among the machinery. In the unholy red light and grey mist of this stifling dim Inferno they were strange figures with their silence and their immobility. The wretched *Foundling* groaned deeply as she lifted, and groaned deeply as she sank into the trough, while hurried waves then thundered over her with the noise of landslides. The terrified machinery was making gestures.

But Flanagan took control of himself suddenly. Then he stirred the fire-room. The stillness had been so unearthly that he was not altogether inapprehensive of strange and grim deeds when he charged into them; but precisely as they had submitted to the sea so they submitted to Flanagan. For a moment they rolled their eyes like hurt cows, but they obeyed the Voice. The situation simply required a Voice.

When the captain returned to the deck the hue of this fire-room was in his mind, and then he understood doom and its weight and complexion.

When finally the *Foundling* sank she shifted and settled as calmly as an animal curls down in the bush grass. Away over the waves two bobbing boats paused to witness this quiet death. It was a slow manoeuvre, altogether without the pageantry of uproar, but it flashed pallor into the faces of all men who saw it, and they groaned when they said, "There she goes!" Suddenly the captain whirled and knocked his hand on the gunwale. He sobbed for a time, and then he sobbed and swore also.

There was a dance at the Imperial Inn. During the evening some irresponsible young men came from the beach bringing the statement that several boatloads of people had been perceived off shore. It was a charming dance, and none cared to take time to believe this tale. The fountain in the court-yard splashed softly, and couple after couple paraded through the aisles of palms, where lamps with red shades threw a rose light upon the gleaming leaves. The band played its waltzes slumberously, and its music came faintly to the people among the palms.

Sometimes a woman said —"Oh, it is not really true, is it, that there was a wreck out at sea?"

A man usually said —"No, of course not."

At last, however, a youth came violently from the beach. He was triumphant in manner. "They're out there," he cried. "A whole boat-load!" He received eager attention, and he told all that he supposed. His news destroyed the dance. After a time the band was playing beautifully to space. The guests had hurried to the beach. One little girl cried, "Oh, mamma, may I go too?" Being refused permission she pouted.

As they came from the shelter of the great hotel, the wind was blowing swiftly from the sea, and at intervals a breaker shone livid. The women shuddered, and their bending companions seized the opportunity to draw the cloaks closer.

"Oh, dear!" said a girl; "supposin' they were out there drowning while we were dancing!"

"Oh, nonsense!" said her younger brother; "that don't happen."

"Well, it might, you know, Roger. How can you tell?"

A man who was not her brother gazed at her then with profound admiration. Later, she complained of the damp sand, and, drawing back her skirts, looked ruefully at her little feet.

A mother's son was venturing too near to the water in his interest and excitement. Occasionally she cautioned and reproached him from the background.

Save for the white glare of the breakers, the sea was a great wind-crossed void. From the throng of charming women floated the perfume of many flowers. Later there floated to them a body with a calm face of an Irish type. The expedition of the *Foundling* will never be historic.

Horses

Richardson pulled up his horse, and looked back over the trail where the crimson serape of his servant flamed amid the dusk of the mesquit. The hills in the west were carved into peaks, and were painted the most profound blue. Above them the sky was of that marvellous tone of green-like still, sun-shot water-which people denounce in pictures.

José was muffled deep in his blanket, and his great toppling sombrero was drawn low over his brow. He shadowed his master along the dimming trail in the fashion of an assassin. A cold wind of the impending night swept over the wilderness of mesquit.

"Man," said Richardson in lame Mexican as the servant drew near, "I want eat! I want sleep! Understand-no? Quickly! Understand?"

"Si, señor," said José, nodding. He stretched one arm out of his blanket and pointed a yellow finger into the gloom. "Over there, small village. Si, señor."

They rode forward again. Once the American's horse shied and breathed quiveringly at something which he saw or imagined in the darkness, and the rider drew a steady, patient rein, and leaned over to speak tenderly as if he were addressing a frightened woman. The sky had faded to white over the mountains, and the plain was a vast, pointless ocean of black.

Suddenly some low houses appeared squatting amid the bushes. The horsemen rode into a hollow until the houses rose against the sombre sundown sky, and then up a small hillock, causing these habitations to sink like boats in the sea of shadow.

A beam of red firelight fell across the trail. Richardson sat sleepily on his horse while his servant quarrelled with somebody —a mere voice in the gloom-over the price of bed and board. The houses about him were for the most part like tombs in their whiteness and silence, but there were scudding black figures that seemed interested in his arrival.

José came at last to the horses' heads, and the American slid stiffly from his seat. He muttered a greeting, as with his spurred feet he clicked into the adobe house that confronted him. The brown stolid face of a woman shone in the light of the fire. He seated himself on the earthen floor and blinked drowsily at the blaze. He was aware that the woman was clinking earthenware, and hieing here and everywhere in the manoeuvres of the housewife. From a dark corner there came the sound of two or three snores twining together.

The woman handed him a bowl of tortillas. She was a submissive creature, timid and large-eyed. She gazed at his enormous silver spurs, his large and impressive revolver, with the interest and admiration of the highly-privileged cat of the adage. When he ate, she seemed transfixed off there in the gloom, her white teeth shining.

José entered, staggering under two Mexican saddles, large enough for building-sites. Richardson decided to smoke a cigarette, and then changed his mind. It would be much finer to go to sleep. His blanket hung over his left shoulder, furled into a long pipe of cloth, according to the Mexican fashion. By doffing his sombrero, unfastening his spurs and his revolver belt, he made himself ready for the slow, blissful twist into the blanket. Like a cautious man he lay close to the wall, and all his property was very near his hand.

The mesquit brush burned long. José threw two gigantic wings of shadow as he flapped his blanket about him-first across his chest under his arms, and then around his neck and across his chest again-this time over his arms, with the end tossed on his right shoulder. A Mexican thus snugly enveloped can nevertheless free his fighting arm in a beautifully brisk way, merely shrugging his shoulder as he grabs for the weapon at his belt. (They always wear their serapes in this manner.)

The firelight smothered the rays which, streaming from a moon as large as a drum-head, were struggling at the open door. Richardson heard from the plain the fine, rhythmical trample of the hoofs of hurried horses. He went to sleep wondering who rode so fast and so late. And in the deep silence the pale rays of the moon must have prevailed against the red spears of the fire until the room was slowly flooded to its middle with a rectangle of silver light.

Richardson was awakened by the sound of a guitar. It was badly played-in this land of Mexico, from which the romance of the instrument ascends to us like a perfume. The guitar was groaning and whining like a badgered soul. A noise of scuffling feet accompanied the music. Sometimes laughter arose, and often the voices of men saying bitter things to each other, but always the guitar cried on, the treble sounding as if some one were beating iron, and the bass humming like bees. "Damn it-they're having a dance," he muttered, fretfully. He heard two men quarrelling in short, sharp words, like pistol shots; they were calling each other worse names than common people know in other countries. He wondered why the noise was so loud. Raising his head from his saddle pillow, he saw, with the help of the valiant moonbeams, a blanket hanging flat against the wall at the further end of the room. Being of opinion that it concealed a door, and remembering that Mexican drink made men very drunk, he pulled his revolver closer to him and prepared for sudden disaster.

Richardson was dreaming of his far and beloved north.

"Well, I would kill him, then!"

"No, you must not!"

"Yes, I will kill him! Listen! I will ask this American beast for his beautiful pistol and spurs and money and saddle, and if he will not give them-you will see!"

"But these Americans-they are a strange people. Look out, señor."

Then twenty voices took part in the discussion. They rose in quavering shrillness, as from men badly drunk. Richardson felt the skin draw tight around his mouth, and his knee-joints turned to bread. He slowly came to a sitting posture, glaring at the motionless blanket at the far end of the room. This stiff and mechanical movement, accomplished entirely by the muscles of the waist, must have looked like the rising of a corpse in the wan moonlight, which gave everything a hue of the grave.

My friend, take my advice and never be executed by a hangman who doesn't talk the English language. It, or anything that resembles it, is the most difficult of deaths. The tumultuous emotions of Richardson's terror destroyed that slow and careful process of thought by means of which he understood Mexican. Then he used his instinctive comprehension of the first and universal language, which is tone. Still, it is disheartening not to be able to understand the detail of threats against the blood of your body.

Suddenly, the clamour of voices ceased. There was a silence —a silence of decision. The blanket was flung aside, and the red light of a torch flared into the room. It was held high by a fat, round-faced Mexican, whose little snake-like moustache was as black as his eyes, and whose eyes were black as jet. He was insane with the wild rage of a man whose liquor is dully burning at his brain. Five or six of his fellows crowded after him. The guitar, which had been thrummed doggedly during the time of the high words, now suddenly stopped. They contemplated each other. Richardson sat very straight and still, his right hand lost in his blanket. The Mexicans jostled in the light of the torch, their eyes blinking and glittering.

The fat one posed in the manner of a grandee. Presently his hand dropped to his belt, and from his lips there spun an epithet —a hideous word which often foreshadows knife-blows, a word peculiarly of Mexico, where people have to dig deep to find an insult that has not lost its savour. The American did not move. He was staring at the fat Mexican with a strange fixedness of gaze, not fearful, not dauntless, not anything that could be interpreted. He simply stared.

The fat Mexican must have been disconcerted, for he continued to pose as a grandee, with more and more sublimity, until it would have been easy for him to have fallen over backward. His companions were swaying very drunkenly. They still blinked their little beady eyes at Richardson. Ah, well, sirs, here was a mystery! At the approach of their menacing company, why did not this American cry out and turn pale, or run, or pray them mercy? The animal merely sat still, and stared, and waited for them to begin. Well, evidently he was a great fighter! Or perhaps he was an idiot? Indeed, this was an embarrassing situation, for who was going forward to discover whether he was a great fighter or an idiot?

To Richardson, whose nerves were tingling and twitching like live wires, and whose heart jolted inside him, this pause was a long horror; and for these men, who could so frighten him, there began to swell in him a fierce hatred—a hatred that made him long to be capable of fighting all of them, a hatred that made him capable of fighting all of them. A 44-calibre revolver can make a hole large enough for little boys to shoot marbles through; and there was a certain fat Mexican with a moustache like a snake who came extremely near to have eaten his last tomale merely because he frightened a man too much.

José had slept the first part of the night in his fashion, his body hunched into a heap, his legs crooked, his head touching his knees. Shadows had obscured him from the sight of the invaders. At this point he arose, and began to prowl quakingly over toward Richardson, as if he meant to hide behind him.

Of a sudden the fat Mexican gave a howl of glee. José had come within the torch's circle of light. With roars of ferocity the whole group of Mexicans pounced on the American's servant. He shrank shuddering away from them, beseeching by every device of word and gesture. They pushed him this way and that. They beat him with their fists. They stung him with their curses. As he grovelled on his knees, the fat Mexican took him by the throat and said—"I am going to kill you!" And continually they turned their eyes to see if they were to succeed in causing the initial demonstration by the American. But he looked on impassively. Under the blanket his fingers were clenched, as iron, upon the handle of his revolver.

Here suddenly two brilliant clashing chords from the guitar were heard, and a woman's voice, full of laughter and confidence, cried from without—"Hello! hello! Where are you?" The lurching company of Mexicans instantly paused and looked at the ground. One said, as he stood with his legs wide apart in order to balance himself—"It is the girls. They have come!" He screamed in answer to the question of the woman—"Here!" And without waiting he started on a pilgrimage toward the blanket-covered door. One could now hear a number of female voices giggling and chattering.

Two other Mexicans said—"Yes, it is the girls! Yes!" They also started quietly away. Even the fat Mexican's ferocity seemed to be affected. He looked uncertainly at the still immovable American. Two of his friends grasped him gaily—"Come, the girls are here! Come!" He cast another glower at Richardson. "But this ——," he began. Laughing, his comrades hustled him toward the door. On its threshold, and holding back the blanket, with one hand, he turned his yellow face with a last challenging glare toward the American. José, bewailing his state in little sobs of utter despair and woe, crept to Richardson and huddled near his knee. Then the cries of the Mexicans meeting the girls were heard, and the guitar burst out in joyous humming.

The moon clouded, and but a faint square of light fell through the open main door of the house. The coals of the fire were silent, save for occasional sputters. Richardson did not change his position. He remained staring at the blanket which hid the strategic door in the far end. At his knees José was arguing, in a low, aggrieved tone, with the saints. Without, the Mexicans laughed and danced, and-it would appear from the sound-drank more.

In the stillness and the night Richardson sat wondering if some serpent-like Mexican were sliding towards him in the darkness, and if the first thing he knew of it would be the deadly sting of a knife. "Sssh," he whispered, to José. He drew his revolver from under the blanket, and held it on his leg. The blanket over the door fascinated him. It was a vague form, black and unmoving. Through the opening it shielded were to come, probably, threats, death. Sometimes he thought he saw it move. As grim white sheets, the black and silver of coffins, all the panoply of death, affect us, because of that which they hide, so this blanket, dangling before a hole in an adobe wall, was to Richardson a horrible emblem, and a horrible thing in itself. In his present mood he could not have been brought to touch it with his finger.

The celebrating Mexicans occasionally howled in song. The guitarist played with speed and enthusiasm. Richardson longed to run. But in this vibrating and threatening gloom his terror convinced him that a move on his part would be a signal for the pounce of death. José, crouching abjectly, mumbled now and again. Slowly, and ponderous as stars, the minutes went.

Suddenly Richardson thrilled and started. His breath for a moment left him. In sleep his nerveless fingers had allowed his revolver to fall and clang upon the hard floor. He grabbed it up hastily, and his glance swept apprehensively over the room. A chill blue light of dawn was in the place. Every outline was slowly growing; detail was following detail. The dread blanket did not move. The riotous company had gone or fallen silent. He felt the effect of this cold dawn in his blood. The candour of breaking day brought his nerve. He touched José. "Come," he said. His servant lifted his lined yellow face, and comprehended. Richardson buckled on his spurs and strode up; José obediently lifted the two great saddles. Richardson held two bridles and a blanket on his left arm; in his right hand he had his revolver. They sneaked toward the door.

The man who said that spurs jingled was insane. Spurs have a mellow clash-clash-clash. Walking in spurs-notably Mexican spurs-you remind yourself vaguely of a telegraphic linesman. Richardson was inexpressibly shocked when he came to walk. He sounded to himself like a pair of cymbals. He would have known of this if he had reflected; but then, he was escaping, not reflecting. He made a gesture of despair, and from under the two saddles José tried to make one of hopeless horror. Richardson stooped, and with shaking fingers unfastened the spurs. Taking them in his left hand, he picked up his revolver, and they slunk on toward the door. On the threshold he looked back. In a corner he saw, watching him with large eyes, the Indian man and woman who had been his hosts. Throughout the night they had made no sign, and now they neither spoke nor moved. Yet Richardson thought he detected meek satisfaction at his departure.

The street was still and deserted. In the eastern sky there was a lemon-coloured patch. José had picketed the horses at the side of the house. As the two men came round the corner Richardson's beast set up a whinny of welcome. The little horse had heard them coming. He stood facing them, his ears cocked forward, his eyes bright with welcome.

Richardson made a frantic gesture, but the horse, in his happiness at the appearance of his friends, whinnied with enthusiasm. The American felt that he could have strangled his well-beloved steed. Upon the threshold of safety, he was being betrayed by his horse, his friend! He felt the same hate that he would have felt for a dragon. And yet, as he glanced wildly about him, he could see nothing stirring in the street, nothing at the doors of the tomb-like houses.

José had his own saddle-girth and both bridles buckled in a moment. He curled the picket-ropes with a few sweeps of his arm. The American's fingers, however, were shaking so that he could hardly buckle the girth. His hands were in invisible mittens. He was wondering, calculating, hoping about his horse. He knew the little animal's willingness and courage under all circumstances up to this time; but then-here it was different. Who could tell if some wretched instance of equine perversity was not about to develop? Maybe the little fellow would not feel like smoking over the plain at express speed this morning, and so he would rebel, and kick, and be wicked. Maybe he would be without feeling of interest, and run listlessly. All riders who have had to hurry in the saddle know what it is to be on a horse who does not understand the dramatic situation. Riding a lame sheep is bliss to it. Richardson, fumbling furiously at the girth, thought of these things.

Presently he had it fastened. He swung into the saddle, and as he did so his horse made a mad jump forward. The spurs of José scratched and tore the flanks of his great black beast, and side by side the two horses raced down the village street. The American heard his horse breathe a quivering sigh of excitement. Those four feet skimmed. They were as light as fairy puff balls. The houses glided past in a moment, and the great, clear, silent plain appeared like a pale blue sea of mist and wet bushes. Above the mountains the colours of the sunlight were like the first tones, the opening chords of the mighty hymn of the morning.

The American looked down at his horse. He felt in his heart the first thrill of confidence. The little animal, unurged and quite tranquil, moving his ears this way and that way with an air of interest in the scenery, was nevertheless bounding into the eye of the breaking day with the speed of a frightened antelope. Richardson, looking down, saw the long, fine reach of forelimb as steady as steel machinery. As the ground reeled past, the long, dried grasses hissed, and cactus plants were dull blurs. A wind whirled the horse's mane over his rider's bridle hand.

José's profile was lined against the pale sky. It was as that of a man who swims alone in an ocean. His eyes glinted like metal, fastened on some unknown point ahead of him, some fabulous place of safety. Occasionally his mouth puckered in a little unheard cry; and his legs, bended back, worked spasmodically as his spurred heels sliced his charger's sides.

Richardson consulted the gloom in the west for signs of a hard-riding, yelling cavalcade. He knew that, whereas his friends the enemy had not attacked him when he had sat still and with apparent calmness confronted them, they would take furiously after him now that he had run from them-now that he had confessed himself the weaker. Their valour would grow like weeds in the spring, and upon discovering his escape they would ride forth dauntless warriors. Sometimes he was sure he saw them. Sometimes he was sure he heard them. Continually looking backward over his shoulder, he studied the purple expanses where the night was marching away. José rolled and shuddered in his saddle, persistently disturbing the stride of the black horse, fretting and worrying him until the white foam flew, and the great shoulders shone like satin from the sweat.

At last, Richardson drew his horse carefully down to a walk. José wished to rush insanely on, but the American spoke to him sternly. As the two paced forward side by side, Richardson's little horse thrust over his soft nose and inquired into the black's condition.

Riding with José was like riding with a corpse. His face resembled a cast in lead. Sometimes he swung forward and almost pitched from his seat. Richardson was too frightened himself to do anything but hate this man for his fear. Finally, he issued a mandate which nearly caused José's eyes to slide out of his head and fall to the ground, like two coins: —"Ride behind me-about fifty paces."

"Señor — —" stuttered the servant. "Go," cried the American furiously. He glared at the other and laid his hand on his revolver. José looked at his master wildly. He made a piteous gesture. Then slowly he fell back, watching the hard face of the American for a sign of mercy. But Richardson had resolved in his rage that at any rate he was going to use the eyes and ears of extreme fear to detect the approach of danger; so he established his panic-stricken servant as a sort of outpost.

As they proceeded, he was obliged to watch sharply to see that the servant did not slink forward and join him. When José made beseeching circles in the air with his arm, he replied by menacingly gripping his revolver. José had a revolver too; nevertheless it was very clear in his mind that the revolver was distinctly an American weapon. He had been educated in the Rio Grande country.

Richardson lost the trail once. He was recalled to it by the loud sobs of his servant.

Then at last José came clattering forward, gesticulating and wailing. The little horse sprang to the shoulder of the black. They were off.

Richardson, again looking backward, could see a slanting flare of dust on the whitening plain. He thought that he could detect small moving figures in it.

José's moans and cries amounted to a university course in theology. They broke continually from his quivering lips. His spurs were as motors. They forced the black horse over the plain in great headlong leaps. But under Richardson there was a little insignificant rat-coloured beast who was running apparently with almost as much effort as it takes a bronze statue to stand still. The ground seemed merely something to be touched from time to time with hoofs that were as light as blown leaves. Occasionally Richardson lay back and pulled stoutly at the bridle to keep from abandoning his servant. José harried at his horse's mouth, flopped about in the saddle, and made his two heels beat like flails. The black ran like a horse in despair.

Crimson serapes in the distance resemble drops of blood on the great cloth of plain. Richardson began to dream of all possible chances. Although quite a humane man, he did not once think of his servant. José being a Mexican, it was natural that he should be killed in Mexico;

but for himself, a New Yorker— —! He remembered all the tales of such races for life, and he thought them badly written.

The great black horse was growing indifferent. The jabs of José's spurs no longer caused him to bound forward in wild leaps of pain. José had at last succeeded in teaching him that spurring was to be expected, speed or no speed, and now he took the pain of it dully and stolidly, as an animal who finds that doing his best gains him no respite. José was turned into a raving maniac. He bellowed and screamed, working his arms and his heels like one in a fit. He resembled a man on a sinking ship, who appeals to the ship. Richardson, too, cried madly to the black horse. The spirit of the horse responded to these calls, and quivering and breathing heavily he made a great effort, a sort of a final rush, not for himself apparently, but because he understood that his life's sacrifice, perhaps, had been invoked by these two men who cried to him in the universal tongue. Richardson had no sense of appreciation at this time-he was too frightened; but often now he remembers a certain black horse.

From the rear could be heard a yelling, and once a shot was fired-in the air, evidently. Richardson moaned as he looked back. He kept his hand on his revolver. He tried to imagine the brief tumult of his capture-the flurry of dust from the hoofs of horses pulled suddenly to their haunches, the shrill, biting curses of the men, the ring of the shots, his own last contortion. He wondered, too, if he could not somehow manage to pelt that fat Mexican, just to cure his abominable egotism.

It was José, the terror-stricken, who at last discovered safety. Suddenly he gave a howl of delight and astonished his horse into a new burst of speed. They were on a little ridge at the time, and the American at the top of it saw his servant gallop down the slope and into the arms, so to speak, of a small column of horsemen in grey and silver clothes. In the dim light of the early morning they were as vague as shadows, but Richardson knew them at once for a detachment of Rurales, that crack cavalry corps of the Mexican army which polices the plain so zealously, being of themselves the law and the arm of it —a fierce and swift-moving body that knows little of prevention but much of vengeance. They drew up suddenly, and the rows of great silver-trimmed sombreros bobbed in surprise.

Richardson saw José throw himself from his horse and begin to jabber at the leader. When he arrived he found that his servant had already outlined the entire situation, and was then engaged in describing him, Richardson, as an American señor of vast wealth, who was the friend of almost every governmental potentate within two hundred miles. This seemed profoundly to impress the officer. He bowed gravely to Richardson and smiled significantly at his men, who unslung their carbines.

The little ridge hid the pursuers from view, but the rapid thud of their horses' feet could be heard. Occasionally they yelled and called to each other. Then at last they swept over the brow of the hill, a wild mob of almost fifty drunken horsemen. When they discerned the pale-uniformed Rurales, they were sailing down the slope at top speed.

If toboggans half-way down a hill should suddenly make up their minds to turn round and go back, there would be an effect something like that produced by the drunken horsemen. Richardson saw the Rurales serenely swing their carbines forward, and, peculiar-minded person that he was, felt his heart leap into his throat at the prospective volley. But the officer rode forward alone.

It appeared that the man who owned the best horse in this astonished company was the fat Mexican with the snaky moustache, and, in consequence, this gentleman was quite a distance in the van. He tried to pull up, wheel his horse, and scuttle back over the hill as some of his companions had done, but the officer called to him in a voice harsh with rage. " — —!" howled the officer. "This señor is my friend, the friend of my friends. Do you dare pursue him, — —? — —! — —! — —! — —!" These dashes represent terrible names, all different, used by the officer.

The fat Mexican simply grovelled on his horse's neck. His face was green: it could be seen that he expected death. The officer stormed with magnificent intensity: " — —! — —! — —!"

Finally he sprang from his saddle, and, running to the fat Mexican's side, yelled —"Go!" and kicked the horse in the belly with all his might. The animal gave a mighty leap into the air, and the fat Mexican, with one wretched glance at the contemplative Rurales, aimed his steed for the top of the ridge. Richardson gulped again in expectation of a volley, for-it is said-this is a favourite method for disposing of objectionable people. The fat, green Mexican also thought that he was to be killed on the run, from the miserable look he cast at the troops. Nevertheless, he was allowed to vanish in a cloud of yellow dust at the ridge-top.

José was exultant, defiant, and, oh! bristling with courage. The black horse was drooping sadly, his nose to the ground. Richardson's little animal, with his ears bent forward, was staring at the horses of the Rurales as if in an intense study. Richardson longed for speech, but he could only bend forward and pat the shining, silken shoulders. The little horse turned his head and looked back gravely.

Death and the Child

The peasants who were streaming down the mountain trail had in their sharp terror evidently lost their ability to count. The cattle and the huge round bundles seemed to suffice to the minds of the crowd if there were now two in each case where there had been three. This brown stream poured on with a constant wastage of goods and beasts. A goat fell behind to scout the dried grass and its owner, howling, flogging his donkeys, passed far ahead. A colt, suddenly frightened, made a stumbling charge up the hill-side. The expenditure was always profligate and always unnamed, unnoted. It was as if fear was a river, and this horde had simply been caught in the torrent, man tumbling over beast, beast over man, as helpless in it as the logs that fall and shoulder grindingly through the gorges of a lumber country. It was a freshet that might sear the face of the tall quiet mountain; it might draw a livid line across the land, this downpour of fear with a thousand homes adrift in the current-men, women, babes, animals. From it there arose a constant babble of tongues, shrill, broken, and sometimes choking as from men drowning. Many made gestures, painting their agonies on the air with fingers that twirled swiftly.

The blue bay with its pointed ships and the white town lay below them, distant, flat, serene. There was upon this vista a peace that a bird knows when high in the air it surveys the world, a great calm thing rolling noiselessly toward the end of the mystery. Here on the height one felt the existence of the universe scornfully defining the pain in ten thousand minds. The sky was an arch of stolid sapphire. Even to the mountains raising their mighty shapes from the valley, this headlong rush of the fugitives was too minute. The sea, the sky, and the hills combined in their grandeur to term this misery inconsequent. Then too it sometimes happened that a face seen as it passed on the flood reflected curiously the spirit of them all and still more. One saw then a woman of the opinion of the vaults above the clouds. When a child cried it cried always because of some adjacent misfortune, some discomfort of a pack-saddle or rudeness of an encircling arm. In the dismal melody of this flight there were often sounding chords of apathy. Into these preoccupied countenances, one felt that needles could be thrust without purchasing a scream. The trail wound here and there as the sheep had willed in the making of it.

Although this throng seemed to prove that the whole of humanity was fleeing in one direction-with every tie severed that binds us to the soil —a young man was walking rapidly up the mountain, hastening to a side of the path from time to time to avoid some particularly wide rush of people and cattle. He looked at everything in agitation and pity. Frequently he called admonitions to maniacal fugitives, and at other moments he exchanged strange stares with the imperturbable ones. They seemed to him to wear merely the expressions of so many boulders rolling down the hill. He exhibited wonder and awe with his pitying glances.

Turning once toward the rear, he saw a man in the uniform of a lieutenant of infantry marching the same way. He waited then, subconsciously elate at a prospect of being able to make into words the emotion which heretofore had only been expressed in the flash of eyes and sensitive movements of his flexible mouth. He spoke to the officer in rapid French, waving his arms wildly, and often pointing with a dramatic finger. "Ah, this is too cruel, too cruel, too cruel. Is it not? I did not think it would be as bad as this. I did not think-God's mercy —I did not think at all. And yet I am a Greek. Or at least my father was a Greek. I did not come here to fight. I am really a correspondent, you see? I was to write for an Italian paper. I have been educated in Italy. I have spent nearly all my life in Italy. At the schools and universities! I knew nothing of war! I was a student —a student. I came here merely because my father was a Greek, and for his sake I thought of Greece —I loved Greece. But I did not dream — —"

He paused, breathing heavily. His eyes glistened from that soft overflow which comes on occasion to the glance of a young woman. Eager, passionate, profoundly moved, his first words, while facing the procession of fugitives, had been an active definition of his own dimension, his personal relation to men, geography, life. Throughout he had preserved the fiery dignity of a tragedian.

The officer's manner at once deferred to this outburst. "Yes," he said, polite but mournful, "these poor people! These poor people! I do not know what is to become of these poor people."

The young man declaimed again. "I had no dream —I had no dream that it would be like this! This is too cruel! Too cruel! Now I want to be a soldier. Now I want to fight. Now I want to do battle for the land of my father." He made a sweeping gesture into the north-west.

The officer was also a young man, but he was very bronzed and steady. Above his high military collar of crimson cloth with one silver star upon it, appeared a profile stern, quiet, and confident, respecting fate, fearing only opinion. His clothes were covered with dust; the only bright spot was the flame of the crimson collar. At the violent cries of his companion he smiled as if to himself, meanwhile keeping his eyes fixed in a glance ahead.

From a land toward which their faces were bent came a continuous boom of artillery fire. It was sounding in regular measures like the beating of a colossal clock, a clock that was counting the seconds in the lives of the stars, and men had time to die between the ticks. Solemn, oracular, inexorable, the great seconds tolled over the hills as if God fronted this dial rimmed by the horizon. The soldier and the correspondent found themselves silent. The latter in particular was sunk in a great mournfulness, as if he had resolved willy-nilly to swing to the bottom of the abyss where dwell secrets of his kind, and had learned beforehand that all to be met there was cruelty and hopelessness. A strap of his bright new leather leggings came unfastened, and he bowed over it slowly, impressively, as one bending over the grave of a child.

Then suddenly, the reverberations mingled until one could not separate an explosion from another, and into the hubbub came the drawling sound of a leisurely musketry fire. Instantly, for some reason of cadence, the noise was irritating, silly, infantile. This uproar was childish. It forced the nerves to object, to protest against this racket which was as idle as the din of a lad with a drum.

The lieutenant lifted his finger and pointed. He spoke in vexed tones, as if he held the other man personally responsible for the noise. "Well, there!" he said. "If you wish for war you now have an opportunity magnificent."

The correspondent raised himself upon his toes. He tapped his chest with gloomy pride. "Yes! There is war! There is the war I wish to enter. I fling myself in. I am a Greek, a Greek, you understand. I wish to fight for my country. You know the way. Lead me. I offer myself." Struck by a sudden thought he brought a case from his pocket, and extracting a card handed it to the officer with a bow. "My name is Peza," he said simply.

A strange smile passed over the soldier's face. There was pity and pride-the vanity of experience-and contempt in it. "Very well," he said, returning the bow. "If my company is in the middle of the fight I shall be glad for the honour of your companionship. If my company is not in the middle of the fight —I will make other arrangements for you."

Peza bowed once more, very stiffly, and correctly spoke his thanks. On the edge of what he took to be a great venture toward death, he discovered that he was annoyed at something in the lieutenant's tone. Things immediately assumed new and extraordinary proportions. The battle, the great carnival of woe, was sunk at once to an equation with a vexation by a stranger. He wanted to ask the lieutenant what was his meaning. He bowed again majestically; the lieutenant bowed. They flung a shadow of manners, of capering tinsel ceremony across a land that groaned, and it satisfied something within themselves completely.

In the meantime, the river of fleeing villagers had changed to simply a last dropping of belated creatures, who fled past stammering and flinging their hands high. The two men had come to the top of the great hill. Before them was a green plain as level as an inland sea. It swept northward, and merged finally into a length of silvery mist. Upon the near part of this plain, and upon two grey treeless mountains at the side of it, were little black lines from which floated slanting sheets of smoke. It was not a battle to the nerves. One could survey it with equanimity, as if it were a tea-table; but upon Peza's mind it struck a loud clanging blow. It was war. Edified, aghast, triumphant, he paused suddenly, his lips apart. He remembered the pageants of carnage that had marched through the dreams of his childhood. Love he knew that he had confronted, alone, isolated, wondering, an individual, an atom taking the hand of a titanic principle. But, like the faintest breeze on his forehead, he felt here the vibration from the hearts of forty thousand men.

The lieutenant's nostrils were moving. "I must go at once," he said. "I must go at once."

"I will go with you wherever you go," shouted Peza loudly.

A primitive track wound down the side of the mountain, and in their rush they bounded from here to there, choosing risks which in the ordinary caution of man would surely have seemed of remarkable danger. The ardour of the correspondent surpassed the full energy of the soldier. Several times he turned and shouted, "Come on! Come on!"

At the foot of the path they came to a wide road, which extended toward the battle in a yellow and straight line. Some men were trudging wearily to the rear. They were without rifles; their clumsy uniforms were dirty and all awry. They turned eyes dully aglow with fever upon the pair striding toward the battle. Others were bandaged with the triangular kerchief upon which one could still see through bloodstains the little explanatory pictures illustrating the ways to bind various wounds. "Fig. 1." —"Fig. 2." —"Fig. 7." Mingled with the pacing soldiers were peasants, indifferent, capable of smiling, gibbering about the battle, which was to them an ulterior drama. A man was leading a string of three donkeys to the rear, and at intervals he was accosted by wounded or fevered soldiers, from whom he defended his animals with ape-like cries and mad gesticulation. After much chattering they usually subsided gloomily, and allowed him to go with his sleek little beasts unburdened. Finally he encountered a soldier who walked slowly with the assistance of a staff. His head was bound with a wide bandage, grimey from blood and mud. He made application to the peasant, and immediately they were involved in a hideous Levantine discussion. The peasant whined and clamoured, sometimes spitting like a kitten. The wounded soldier jawed on thunderously, his great hands stretched in claw-like graspings over the peasant's head. Once he raised his staff and made threat with it. Then suddenly the row was at an end. The other sick men saw their comrade mount the leading donkey and at once begin to drum with his heels. None attempted to gain the backs of the remaining animals. They gazed after them dully. Finally they saw the caravan outlined for a moment against the sky. The soldier was still waving his arms passionately, having it out with the peasant.

Peza was alive with despair for these men who looked at him with such doleful, quiet eyes. "Ah, my God!" he cried to the lieutenant, "these poor souls! These poor souls!"

The officer faced about angrily. "If you are coming with me there is no time for this." Peza obeyed instantly and with a sudden meekness. In the moment some portion of egotism left him, and he modestly wondered if the universe took cognizance of him to an important degree. This theatre for slaughter, built by the inscrutable needs of the earth, was an enormous affair, and he reflected that the accidental destruction of an individual, Peza by name, would perhaps be nothing at all.

With the lieutenant he was soon walking along behind a series of little crescent-shape trenches, in which were soldiers, tranquilly interested, gossiping with the hum of a tea-party. Although these men were not at this time under fire, he concluded that they were fabulously brave. Else they would not be so comfortable, so at home in their sticky brown trenches. They were certain to be heavily attacked before the day was old. The universities had not taught him to understand this attitude.

At the passing of the young man in very nice tweed, with his new leggings, his new white helmet, his new field-glass case, his new revolver holster, the soiled soldiers turned with the same curiosity which a being in strange garb meets at the corners of streets. He might as well have been promenading a populous avenue. The soldiers volubly discussed his identity.

To Peza there was something awful in the absolute familiarity of each tone, expression, gesture. These men, menaced with battle, displayed the curiosity of the café. Then, on the verge of his great encounter toward death, he found himself extremely embar rassed, composing his face with difficulty, wondering what to do with his hands, like a gawk at a levée.

He felt ridiculous, and also he felt awed, aghast, at these men who could turn their faces from the ominous front and debate his clothes, his business. There was an element which was new born into his theory of war. He was not averse to the brisk pace at which the lieutenant moved along the line.

The roar of fighting was always in Peza's ears. It came from some short hills ahead and to the left. The road curved suddenly and entered a wood. The trees stretched their luxuriant and graceful branches over grassy slopes. A breeze made all this verdure gently rustle and speak in long silken sighs. Absorbed in listening to the hurricane racket from the front, he still remembered that these trees were growing, the grass-blades were extending according to their process. He inhaled a deep breath of moisture and fragrance from the grove, a wet odour which expressed all the opulent fecundity of unmoved nature, marching on with her million plans for multiple life, multiple death.

Further on, they came to a place where the Turkish shells were landing. There was a long hurtling sound in the air, and then one had sight of a shell. To Peza it was of the conical missiles which friendly officers had displayed to him on board warships. Curiously enough, too, this first shell smacked of the foundry, of men with smudged faces, of the blare of furnace fires. It brought machinery immediately into his mind. He thought that if he was killed there at that time it would be as romantic, to the old standards, as death by a bit of falling iron in a factory.

A child was playing on a mountain and disregarding a battle that was waging on the plain. Behind him was the little cobbled hut of his fled parents. It was now occupied by a pearl-coloured cow that stared out from the darkness thoughtful and tender-eyed. The child ran to and fro, fumbling with sticks and making great machinations with pebbles. By a striking exercise of artistic license the sticks were ponies, cows, and dogs, and the pebbles were sheep. He was managing large agricultural and herding affairs. He was too intent on them to pay much heed to the fight four miles away, which at that distance resembled in sound the beating of surf upon rocks. However, there were occasions when some louder outbreak of that thunder stirred him from his serious occupation, and he turned then a questioning eye upon the battle, a small stick poised in his hand, interrupted in the act of sending his dog after his sheep. His tranquillity in regard to the death on the plain was as invincible as that of the mountain on which he stood.

It was evident that fear had swept the parents away from their home in a manner that could make them forget this child, the first-born. Nevertheless, the hut was clean bare. The cow had committed no impropriety in billeting herself at the domicile of her masters. This smoke-coloured and odorous interior contained nothing as large as a humming-bird. Terror had operated on these runaway people in its sinister fashion, elevating details to enormous heights, causing a man to remember a button while he forgot a coat, overpowering every one with recollections of a broken coffee-cup, deluging them with fears for the safety of an old pipe, and causing them to forget their first-born. Meanwhile the child played soberly with his trinkets.

He was solitary; engrossed in his own pursuits, it was seldom that he lifted his head to inquire of the world why it made so much noise. The stick in his hand was much larger to him than was an army corps of the distance. It was too childish for the mind of the child. He was dealing with sticks.

The battle lines writhed at times in the agony of a sea-creature on the sands. These tentacles flung and waved in a supreme excitement of pain, and the struggles of the great outlined body brought it nearer and nearer to the child. Once he looked at the plain and saw some men running wildly across a field. He had seen people chasing obdurate beasts in such fashion, and it struck him immediately that it was a manly thing which he would incorporate in his game. Consequently he raced furiously at his stone sheep, flourishing a cudgel, crying the shepherd calls. He paused frequently to get a cue of manner from the soldiers fighting on the plain. He reproduced, to a degree, any movements which he accounted rational to his theory of sheep-herding, the business of men, the traditional and exalted living of his father.

It was as if Peza was a corpse walking on the bottom of the sea, and finding there fields of grain, groves, weeds, the faces of men, voices. War, a strange employment of the race, presented to him a scene crowded with familiar objects which wore the livery of their commonness, placidly, undauntedly. He was smitten with keen astonishment; a spread of green grass lit with the flames of poppies was too old for the company of this new ogre. If he had been devoting the full lens of his mind to this phase, he would have known he was amazed that the trees, the flowers, the grass, all tender and peaceful nature had not taken to heels at once upon the outbreak of battle. He venerated the immovable poppies.

The road seemed to lead into the apex of an angle formed by the two defensive lines of the Greeks. There was a straggle of wounded men and of gunless and jaded men. These latter did not seem to be frightened. They remained very cool, walking with unhurried steps and busy in gossip. Peza tried to define them. Perhaps during the fight they had reached the limit of their mental storage, their capacity for excitement, for tragedy, and had then simply come away. Peza remembered his visit to a certain place of pictures, where he had found himself amid heavenly skies and diabolic midnights-the sunshine beating red upon desert sands, nude bodies flung to the shore in the green moon-glow, ghastly and starving men clawing at a wall in darkness, a girl at her bath with screened rays falling upon her pearly shoulders, a dance, a funeral, a review, an execution, all the strength of argus-eyed art: and he had whirled and whirled amid this universe with cries of woe and joy, sin and beauty piercing his ears until he had been obliged to simply come away. He remembered that as he had emerged he had lit a cigarette with unction and advanced promptly to a café. A great hollow quiet seemed to be upon the earth.

This was a different case, but in his thoughts he conceded the same causes to many of these gunless wanderers. They too may have dreamed at lightning speed until the capacity for it was overwhelmed. As he watched them, he again saw himself walking toward the café, puffing upon his cigarette. As if to reinforce his theory, a soldier stopped him with an eager but polite inquiry for a match. He watched the man light his little roll of tobacco and paper and begin to smoke ravenously.

Peza no longer was torn with sorrow at the sight of wounded men. Evidently he found that pity had a numerical limit, and when this was passed the emotion became another thing. Now, as he viewed them, he merely felt himself very lucky, and beseeched the continuance of his superior fortune. At the passing of these slouched and stained figures he now heard a reiteration of warning. A part of himself was appealing through the medium of these grim shapes. It was plucking at his sleeve and pointing, telling him to beware; and so it had come to pass that he cared for the implacable misery of these soldiers only as he would have cared for the harms of broken dolls. His whole vision was focussed upon his own chance.

The lieutenant suddenly halted. "Look," he said. "I find that my duty is in another direction. I must go another way. But if you wish to fight you have only to go forward, and any officer of the fighting line will give you opportunity." He raised his cap ceremoniously; Peza raised his new white helmet. The stranger to battles uttered thanks to his chaperon, the one who had presented him. They bowed punctiliously, staring at each other with civil eyes.

The lieutenant moved quietly away through a field. In an instant it flashed upon Peza's mind that this desertion was perfidious. He had been subjected to a criminal discourtesy. The officer had fetched him into the middle of the thing, and then left him to wander helplessly toward death. At one time he was upon the point of shouting at the officer.

In the vale there was an effect as if one was then beneath the battle. It was going on above somewhere. Alone, unguided, Peza felt like a man groping in a cellar. He reflected too that one should always see the beginning of a fight. It was too difficult to thus approach it when the affair was in full swing. The trees hid all movements of troops from him, and he thought he might be walking out to the very spot which chance had provided for the reception of a fool. He asked eager questions of passing soldiers. Some paid no heed to him; others shook their heads mournfully. They knew nothing save that war was hard work. If they talked at all it was in testimony of having fought well, savagely. They did not know if the army was going to advance, hold its ground, or retreat; they were weary.

A long pointed shell flashed through the air and struck near the base of a tree, with a fierce upheaval, compounded of earth and flames. Looking back, Peza could see the shattered tree quivering from head to foot. Its whole being underwent a convulsive tremor which was an exhibition of pain, and, furthermore, deep amazement. As he advanced through the vale, the shells continued to hiss and hurtle in long low flights, and the bullets purred in the air. The missiles were flying into the breast of an astounded nature. The landscape, bewildered, agonized, was suffering a rain of infamous shots, and Peza imagined a million eyes gazing at him with the gaze of startled antelopes.

There was a resolute crashing of musketry from the tall hill on the left, and from directly in front there was a mingled din of artillery and musketry firing. Peza felt that his pride was playing a great trick in forcing him forward in this manner under conditions of strangeness, isolation, and ignorance. But he recalled the manner of the lieutenant, the smile on the hill-top among the flying peasants. Peza blushed and pulled the peak of his helmet down on his forehead. He strode onward firmly. Nevertheless he hated the lieutenant, and he resolved that on some future occasion he would take much trouble to arrange a stinging social revenge upon that grinning jackanapes. It did not occur to him until later that he was now going to battle mainly because at a previous time a certain man had smiled.

IV

The road curved round the base of a little hill, and on this hill a battery of mountain guns was leisurely shelling something unseen. In the lee of the height the mules, contented under their heavy saddles, were quietly browsing the long grass. Peza ascended the hill by a slanting path. He felt his heart beat swiftly; once at the top of the hill he would be obliged to look this phenomenon in the face. He hurried, with a mysterious idea of preventing by this strategy the battle from making his appearance a signal for some tremendous renewal. This vague thought seemed logical at the time. Certainly this living thing had knowledge of his coming. He endowed it with the intelligence of a barbaric deity. And so he hurried; he wished to surprise war, this terrible emperor, when it was growling on its throne. The ferocious and horrible sovereign was not to be allowed to make the arrival a pretext for some fit of smoky rage and blood. In this half-lull, Peza had distinctly the sense of stealing upon the battle unawares.

The soldiers watching the mules did not seem to be impressed by anything august. Two of them sat side by side and talked comfortably; another lay flat upon his back staring dreamily at the sky; another cursed a mule for certain refractions. Despite their uniforms, their bandoliers and rifles, they were dwelling in the peace of hostlers. However, the long shells were whooping from time to time over the brow of the hill, and swirling in almost straight lines toward the vale of trees, flowers, and grass. Peza, hearing and seeing the shells, and seeing the pensive guardians of the mules, felt reassured. They were accepting the condition of war as easily as an old sailor accepts the chair behind the counter of a tobacco-shop. Or, it was merely that the farm-boy had gone to sea, and he had adjusted himself to the circumstances immediately, and with only the usual first misadventures in conduct. Peza was proud and ashamed that he was not of them, these stupid peasants, who, throughout the world, hold potentates on their thrones, make statesmen illustrious, provide generals with lasting victories, all with ignorance, indifference, or half-witted hatred, moving the world with the strength of their arms and getting their heads knocked together in the name of God, the king, or the Stock Exchange; immortal, dreaming, hopeless asses who surrender their reason to the care of a shining puppet, and persuade some toy to carry their lives in his purse. Peza mentally abased himself before them, and wished to stir them with furious kicks.

As his eyes ranged above the rim of the plateau, he saw a group of artillery officers talking busily. They turned at once and regarded his ascent. A moment later a row of infantry soldiers in a trench beyond the little guns all faced him. Peza bowed to the officers. He understood at the time that he had made a good and cool bow, and he wondered at it, for his breath was coming in gasps, he was stifling from sheer excitement. He felt like a tipsy man trying to conceal his muscular uncertainty from the people in the street. But the officers did not display any knowledge. They bowed. Behind them Peza saw the plain, glittering green, with three lines of black marked upon it heavily. The front of the first of these lines was frothy with smoke. To the left of this hill was a craggy mountain, from which came a continual dull rattle of musketry. Its summit was ringed with the white smoke. The black lines on the plain slowly moved. The shells that came from there passed overhead with the sound of great birds frantically flapping their wings. Peza thought of the first sight of the sea during a storm. He seemed to feel against his face the wind that races over the tops of cold and tumultuous billows.

He heard a voice afar off—"Sir, what would you?" He turned, and saw the dapper captain of the battery standing beside him. Only a moment had elapsed. "Pardon me, sir," said Peza, bowing again. The officer was evidently reserving his bows; he scanned the new-comer attentively. "Are you a correspondent?" he asked. Peza produced a card. "Yes, I came as a correspondent," he replied, "but now, sir, I have other thoughts. I wish to help. You see? I wish to help."

"What do you mean?" said the captain. "Are you a Greek? Do you wish to fight?"

"Yes, I am a Greek. I wish to fight." Peza's voice surprised him by coming from his lips in even and deliberate tones. He thought with gratification that he was behaving rather well. Another shell travelling from some unknown point on the plain whirled close and furiously in the air, pursuing an apparently horizontal course as if it were never going to touch the earth. The dark shape swished across the sky.

"Ah," cried the captain, now smiling, "I am not sure that we will be able to accommodate you with a fierce affair here just at this time, but — —" He walked gaily to and fro behind the guns with Peza, pointing out to him the lines of the Greeks, and describing his opinion of the general plan of defence. He wore the air of an amiable host. Other officers questioned Peza in regard to the politics of the war. The king, the ministry, Germany, England, Russia, all these huge words were continually upon their tongues. "And the people in Athens? Were they — —" Amid this vivacious babble Peza, seated upon an ammunition box, kept his glance high, watching the appearance of shell after shell. These officers were like men who had been lost for days in the forest. They were thirsty for any scrap of news. Nevertheless, one of them would occasionally dispute their informant courteously. What would Servia have to say to that? No, no, France and Russia could never allow it. Peza was elated. The shells killed no one; war was not so bad. He was simply having coffee in the smoking-room of some embassy where reverberate the names of nations.

A rumour had passed along the motley line of privates in the trench. The new arrival with the clean white helmet was a famous English cavalry officer come to assist the army with his counsel. They stared at the figure of him, surrounded by officers. Peza, gaining sense of the glances and whispers, felt that his coming was an event.

Later, he resolved that he could with temerity do something finer. He contemplated the mountain where the Greek infantry was engaged, and announced leisurely to the captain of the battery that he thought presently of going in that direction and getting into the fight. He re-affirmed the sentiments of a patriot. The captain seemed surprised. "Oh, there will be fighting here at this knoll in a few minutes," he said orientally. "That will be sufficient? You had better stay with us. Besides, I have been ordered to resume fire." The officers all tried to dissuade him from departing. It was really not worth the trouble. The battery would begin again directly. Then it would be amusing for him.

Peza felt that he was wandering with his protestations of high patriotism through a desert of sensible men. These officers gave no heed to his exalted declarations. They seemed too jaded. They were fighting the men who were fighting them. Palaver of the particular kind had subsided before their intense pre-occupation in war as a craft. Moreover, many men had talked in that manner and only talked.

Peza believed at first that they were treating him delicately. They were considerate of his inexperience. War had turned out to be such a gentle business that Peza concluded he could scorn this idea. He bade them a heroic farewell despite their objections.

However, when he reflected upon their ways afterward, he saw dimly that they were actuated principally by some universal childish desire for a spectator of their fine things. They were going into action, and they wished to be seen at war, precise and fearless.

V

Climbing slowly to the high infantry position, Peza was amazed to meet a soldier whose jaw had been half shot away, and who was being helped down the sheep track by two tearful comrades. The man's breast was drenched with blood, and from a cloth which he held to the wound drops were splashing wildly upon the stones of the path. He gazed at Peza for a moment. It was a mystic gaze, which Peza withstood with difficulty. He was exchanging looks with a spectre; all aspect of the man was somehow gone from this victim. As Peza went on, one of the unwounded soldiers loudly shouted to him to return and assist in this tragic march. But even Peza's fingers revolted; he was afraid of the spectre; he would not have dared to touch it. He was surely craven in the movement of refusal he made to them. He scrambled hastily on up the path. He was running away.

At the top of the hill he came immediately upon a part of the line that was in action. Another battery of mountain guns was here firing at the streaks of black on the plain. There were trenches filled with men lining parts of the crest, and near the base were other trenches, all crashing away mightily. The plain stretched as far as the eye can see, and from where silver mist ended this emerald ocean of grass, a great ridge of snow-topped mountains poised against a fleckless blue sky. Two knolls, green and yellow with grain, sat on the prairie confronting the dark hills of the Greek position. Between them were the lines of the enemy. A row of trees, a village, a stretch of road, showed faintly on this great canvas, this tremendous picture, but men, the Turkish battalions, were emphasized startlingly upon it. The ranks of troops between the knolls and the Greek position were as black as ink.

The first line of course was muffled in smoke, but at the rear of it battalions crawled up and to and fro plainer than beetles on a plate. Peza had never understood that masses of men were so declarative, so unmistakable, as if nature makes every arrangement to give information of the coming and the presence of destruction, the end, oblivion. The firing was full, complete, a roar of cataracts, and this pealing of connected volleys was adjusted to the grandeur of the far-off range of snowy mountains. Peza, breathless, pale, felt that he had been set upon a pillar and was surveying mankind, the world. In the meantime dust had got in his eye. He took his handkerchief and mechanically administered to it.

An officer with a double stripe of purple on his trousers paced in the rear of the battery of howitzers. He waved a little cane. Sometimes he paused in his promenade to study the field through his glasses. "A fine scene, sir," he cried airily, upon the approach of Peza. It was like a blow in the chest to the wide-eyed volunteer. It revealed to him a point of view. "Yes, sir, it is a fine scene," he answered. They spoke in French. "I am happy to be able to entertain monsieur with a little practice," continued the officer. "I am firing upon that mass of troops you see there a little to the right. They are probably forming for another attack." Peza smiled; here again appeared manners, manners erect by the side of death.

The right-flank gun of the battery thundered; there was a belch of fire and smoke; the shell flung swiftly and afar was known only to the ear in which rang a broadening hooting wake of sound. The howitzer had thrown itself backward convulsively, and lay with its wheels moving in the air as a squad of men rushed toward it. And later, it seemed as if each little gun had made the supreme effort of its being in each particular shot. They roared with voices far too loud, and the thunderous effort caused a gun to bound as in a dying convulsion. And then occasionally one was hurled with wheels in air. These shuddering howitzers presented an appearance of so many cowards always longing to bolt to the rear, but being implacably held to their business by this throng of soldiers who ran in squads to drag them up again to their obligation. The guns were herded and cajoled and bullied interminably. One by one, in relentless program, they were dragged forward to contribute a profound vibration of steel and wood, a flash and a roar, to the important happiness of man.

The adjacent infantry celebrated a good shot with smiles and an outburst of gleeful talk.

"Look, sir," cried an officer to Peza. Thin smoke was drifting lazily before Peza, and dodging impatiently he brought his eyes to bear upon that part of the plain indicated by the officer's finger. The enemy's infantry was advancing to attack. From the black lines had come forth an inky mass which was shaped much like a human tongue. It advanced slowly, casually, without apparent spirit, but with an insolent confidence that was like a proclamation of the inevitable.

The impetuous part was all played by the defensive side. Officers called, men plucked each other by the sleeve; there were shouts, motions, all eyes were turned upon the inky mass which was flowing toward the base of the hills, heavily, languorously, as oily and thick as one of the streams that ooze through a swamp.

Peza was chattering a question at every one. In the way, pushed aside, or in the way again, he continued to repeat it. "Can they take the position? Can they take the position? Can they take the position?" He was apparently addressing an assemblage of deaf men. Every eye was busy watching every hand. The soldiers did not even seem to see the interesting stranger in the white helmet who was crying out so feverishly.

Finally, however, the hurried captain of the battery espied him and heeded his question. "No, sir! no, sir! It is impossible," he shouted angrily. His manner seemed to denote that if he had sufficient time he would have completely insulted Peza. The latter swallowed the crumb of news without regard to the coating of scorn, and, waving his hand in adieu, he began to run along the crest of the hill toward the part of the Greek line against which the attack was directed.

VI

Peza, as he ran along the crest of the mountain, believed that his action was receiving the wrathful attention of the hosts of the foe. To him then it was incredible foolhardiness thus to call to himself the stares of thousands of hateful eyes. He was like a lad induced by playmates to commit some indiscretion in a cathedral. He was abashed; perhaps he even blushed as he ran. It seemed to him that the whole solemn ceremony of war had paused during this commission. So he scrambled wildly over the rocks in his haste to end the embarrassing ordeal. When he came among the crowning rifle-pits filled with eager soldiers he wanted to yell with joy. None noticed him save a young officer of infantry, who said —"Sir, what do you want?" It was obvious that people had devoted some attention to their own affairs.

Peza asserted, in Greek, that he wished above everything to battle for the fatherland. The officer nodded; with a smile he pointed to some dead men covered with blankets, from which were thrust upturned dusty shoes.

"Yes, I know, I know," cried Peza. He thought the officer was poetically alluding to the danger.

"No," said the officer at once. "I mean cartridges —a bandolier. Take a bandolier from one of them."

Peza went cautiously toward a body. He moved a hand toward the corner of a blanket. There he hesitated, stuck, as if his arm had turned to plaster. Hearing a rustle behind him he spun quickly. Three soldiers of the close rank in the trench were regarding him. The officer came again and tapped him on the shoulder. "Have you any tobacco?" Peza looked at him in bewilderment. His hand was still extended toward the blanket which covered the dead soldier. "Yes," he said, "I have some tobacco." He gave the officer his pouch. As if in compensation, the other directed a soldier to strip the bandolier from the corpse. Peza, having crossed the long cartridge belt on his breast, felt that the dead man had flung his two arms around him.

A soldier with a polite nod and smile gave Peza a rifle, a relic of another dead man. Thus, he felt, besides the clutch of a corpse about his neck, that the rifle was as inhumanly horrible as a snake that lives in a tomb. He heard at his ear something that was in effect like the voices of those two dead men, their low voices speaking to him of bloody death, mutilation. The bandolier gripped him tighter; he wished to raise his hands to his throat like a man who is choking. The rifle was clammy; upon his palms he felt the movement of the sluggish currents of a serpent's life; it was crawling and frightful.

All about him were these peasants, with their interested countenances, gibbering of the fight. From time to time a soldier cried out in semi-humorous lamentations descriptive of his thirst. One bearded man sat munching a great bit of hard bread. Fat, greasy, squat, he was like an idol made of tallow. Peza felt dimly that there was a distinction between this man and a young student who could write sonnets and play the piano quite well. This old blockhead was coolly gnawing at the bread, while he, Peza, was being throttled by a dead man's arms.

He looked behind him, and saw that a head by some chance had been uncovered from its blanket. Two liquid-like eyes were staring into his face. The head was turned a little sideways as if to get better opportunity for the scrutiny. Peza could feel himself blanch; he was being drawn and drawn by these dead men slowly, firmly down as to some mystic chamber under the earth where they could walk, dreadful figures, swollen and blood-marked. He was bidden; they had commanded him; he was going, going, going.

When the man in the new white helmet bolted for the rear, many of the soldiers in the trench thought that he had been struck, but those who had been nearest to him knew better. Otherwise they would have heard the silken sliding tender noise of the bullet and the thud of its impact. They bawled after him curses, and also outbursts of self-congratulation and vanity. Despite the prominence of the cowardly part, they were enabled to see in this exhibition a fine comment upon their own fortitude. The other soldiers thought that Peza had been wounded somewhere in the neck, because as he ran he was tearing madly at the bandolier, the dead man's arms. The soldier with the bread paused in his eating and cynically remarked upon the speed of the runaway.

An officer's voice was suddenly heard calling out the calculation of the distance to the enemy, the readjustment of the sights. There was a stirring rattle along the line. The men turned their eyes to the front. Other trenches beneath them to the right were already heavily in action. The smoke was lifting toward the blue sky. The soldier with the bread placed it carefully on a bit of paper beside him as he turned to kneel in the trench.

VII

In the late afternoon, the child ceased his play on the mountain with his flocks and his dogs. Part of the battle had whirled very near to the base of his hill, and the noise was great. Sometimes he could see fantastic smoky shapes which resembled the curious figures in foam which one sees on the slant of a rough sea. The plain indeed was etched in white circles and whirligigs like the slope of a colossal wave. The child took seat on a stone and contemplated the fight. He was beginning to be astonished; he had never before seen cattle herded with such uproar. Lines of flame flashed out here and there. It was mystery.

Finally, without any preliminary indication, he began to weep. If the men struggling on the plain had had time and greater vision, they could have seen this strange tiny figure seated on a boulder, surveying them while the tears streamed. It was as simple as some powerful symbol.

As the magic clear light of day amid the mountains dimmed the distances, and the plain shone as a pallid blue cloth marked by the red threads of the firing, the child arose and moved off to the unwelcoming door of his home. He called softly for his mother, and complained of his hunger in the familiar formula. The pearl-coloured cow, grinding her jaws thoughtfully, stared at him with her large eyes. The peaceful gloom of evening was slowly draping the hills.

The child heard a rattle of loose stones on the hillside, and facing the sound, saw a moment later a man drag himself up to the crest of the hill and fall panting. Forgetting his mother and his hunger, filled with calm interest, the child walked forward and stood over the heaving form. His eyes too were now large and inscrutably wise and sad like those of the animal in the house.

After a silence he spoke inquiringly. "Are you a man?"

Peza rolled over quickly and gazed up into the fearless cherubic countenance. He did not attempt to reply. He breathed as if life was about to leave his body. He was covered with dust; his face had been cut in some way, and his cheek was ribboned with blood. All the spick of his former appearance had vanished in a general dishevelment, in which he resembled a creature that had been flung to and fro, up and down, by cliffs and prairies during an earthquake. He rolled his eye glassily at the child.

They remained thus until the child repeated his words. "Are you a man?"

Peza gasped in the manner of a fish. Palsied, windless, and abject, he confronted the primitive courage, the sovereign child, the brother of the mountains, the sky and the sea, and he knew that the definition of his misery could be written on a grass-blade.

Part II
Midnight Sketches

An Experiment in Misery

(From the Press, New York.)

It was late at night, and a fine rain was swirling softly down, causing the pavements to glisten with hue of steel and blue and yellow in the rays of the innumerable lights. A youth was trudging slowly, without enthusiasm, with his hands buried deep in his trouser's pockets, towards the down-town places where beds can be hired for coppers. He was clothed in an aged and tattered suit, and his derby was a marvel of dust-covered crown and torn rim. He was going forth to eat as the wanderer may eat, and sleep as the homeless sleep. By the time he had reached City Hall Park he was so completely plastered with yells of "bum" and "hobo," and with various unholy epithets that small boys had applied to him at intervals, that he was in a state of the most profound dejection. The sifting rain saturated the old velvet collar of his overcoat, and as the wet cloth pressed against his neck, he felt that there no longer could be pleasure in life. He looked about him searching for an outcast of highest degree that they too might share miseries, but the lights threw a quivering glare over rows and circles of deserted benches that glistened damply, showing patches of wet sod behind them. It seemed that their usual freights had fled on this night to better things. There were only squads of well-dressed Brooklyn people who swarmed towards the bridge.

The young man loitered about for a time and then went shuffling off down Park Row. In the sudden descent in style of the dress of the crowd he felt relief, and as if he were at last in his own country. He began to see tatters that matched his tatters. In Chatham Square there were aimless men strewn in front of saloons and lodging-houses, standing sadly, patiently, reminding one vaguely of the attitudes of chickens in a storm. He aligned himself with these men, and turned slowly to occupy himself with the flowing life of the great street.

Through the mists of the cold and storming night, the cable cars went in silent procession, great affairs shining with red and brass, moving with formidable power, calm and irresistible, dangerful and gloomy, breaking silence only by the loud fierce cry of the gong. Two rivers of people swarmed along the side walks, spattered with black mud, which made each shoe leave a scar-like impression. Overhead elevated trains with a shrill grinding of the wheels stopped at the station, which upon its leg-like pillars seemed to resemble some monstrous kind of crab squatting over the street. The quick fat puffings of the engines could be heard. Down an alley there were sombre curtains of purple and black, on which street lamps dully glittered like embroidered flowers.

A saloon stood with a voracious air on a corner. A sign leaning against the front of the door-post announced "Free hot soup to-night!" The swing doors, snapping to and fro like ravenous lips, made gratified smacks as the saloon gorged itself with plump men, eating with astounding and endless appetite, smiling in some indescribable manner as the men came from all directions like sacrifices to a heathenish superstition.

Caught by the delectable sign the young man allowed himself to be swallowed. A bar-tender placed a schooner of dark and portentous beer on the bar. Its monumental form up-reared until the froth a-top was above the crown of the young man's brown derby.

"Soup over there, gents," said the bar-tender affably. A little yellow man in rags and the youth grasped their schooners and went with speed toward a lunch counter, where a man with oily but imposing whiskers ladled genially from a kettle until he had furnished his two mendicants with a soup that was steaming hot, and in which there were little floating suggestions of chicken. The young man, sipping his broth, felt the cordiality expressed by the warmth of the mixture, and he beamed at the man with oily but imposing whiskers, who was presiding like a priest behind an altar. "Have some more, gents?" he inquired of the two sorry figures before him. The little yellow man accepted with a swift gesture, but the youth shook his head and went out, following a man whose wondrous seediness promised that he would have a knowledge of cheap lodging-houses.

On the side-walk he accosted the seedy man. "Say, do you know a cheap place to sleep?"

The other hesitated for a time gazing sideways. Finally he nodded in the direction of the street, "I sleep up there," he said, "when I've got the price."

"How much?"

"Ten cents."

The young man shook his head dolefully. "That's too rich for me."

At that moment there approached the two a reeling man in strange garments. His head was a fuddle of bushy hair and whiskers, from which his eyes peered with a guilty slant. In a close scrutiny it was possible to distinguish the cruel lines of a mouth which looked as if its lips had just closed with satisfaction over some tender and piteous morsel. He appeared like an assassin steeped in crimes performed awkwardly.

But at this time his voice was tuned to the coaxing key of an affectionate puppy. He looked at the men with wheedling eyes, and began to sing a little melody for charity.

"Say, gents, can't yeh give a poor feller a couple of cents t' git a bed. I got five, and I gits anudder two I gits me a bed. Now, on th' square, gents, can't yeh jest gimme two cents t' git a bed? Now, yeh know how a respecter'ble gentlem'n feels when he's down on his luck, an' I — —"

The seedy man, staring with imperturbable countenance at a train which clattered overhead, interrupted in an expressionless voice —"Ah, go t' h —!"

But the youth spoke to the prayerful assassin in tones of astonishment and inquiry. "Say, you must be crazy! Why don't yeh strike somebody that looks as if they had money?"

The assassin, tottering about on his uncertain legs, and at intervals brushing imaginary obstacles from before his nose, entered into a long explanation of the psychology of the situation. It was so profound that it was unintelligible.

When he had exhausted the subject, the young man said to him —

"Let's see th' five cents."

The assassin wore an expression of drunken woe at this sentence, filled with suspicion of him. With a deeply pained air he began to fumble in his clothing, his red hands trembling. Presently he announced in a voice of bitter grief, as if he had been betrayed —"There's on'y four."

"Four," said the young man thoughtfully. "Well, look-a-here, I'm a stranger here, an' if ye'll steer me to your cheap joint I'll find the other three."

The assassin's countenance became instantly radiant with joy. His whiskers quivered with the wealth of his alleged emotions. He seized the young man's hand in a transport of delight and friendliness.

"B' Gawd," he cried, "if ye'll do that, b' Gawd, I'd say yeh was a damned good fellow, I would, an' I'd remember yeh all m' life, I would, b' Gawd, an' if I ever got a chance I'd return the compliment" —he spoke with drunken dignity, —"b' Gawd, I'd treat yeh white, I would, an' I'd allus remember yeh."

The young man drew back, looking at the assassin coldly. "Oh, that's all right," he said. "You show me th' joint-that's all you've got t' do."

The assassin, gesticulating gratitude, led the young man along a dark street. Finally he stopped before a little dusty door. He raised his hand impressively. "Look-a-here," he said, and there was a thrill of deep and ancient wisdom upon his face, "I've brought yeh here, an' that's my part, ain't it? If th' place don't suit yeh, yeh needn't git mad at me, need yeh? There won't be no bad feelin', will there?"

"No," said the young man.

The assassin waved his arm tragically, and led the march up the steep stairway. On the way the young man furnished the assassin with three pennies. At the top a man with benevolent spectacles looked at them through a hole in a board. He collected their money, wrote some names on a register, and speedily was leading the two men along a gloom-shrouded corridor.

Shortly after the beginning of this journey the young man felt his liver turn white, for from the dark and secret places of the building there suddenly came to his nostrils strange and unspeakable odours, that assailed him like malignant diseases with wings. They seemed to be from human bodies closely packed in dens; the exhalations from a hundred pairs of reeking lips; the fumes from a thousand bygone debauches; the expression of a thousand present miseries.

A man, naked save for a little snuff-coloured undershirt, was parading sleepily along the corridor. He rubbed his eyes, and, giving vent to a prodigious yawn, demanded to be told the time.

"Half-past one."

The man yawned again. He opened a door, and for a moment his form was outlined against a black, opaque interior. To this door came the three men, and as it was again opened the unholy odours rushed out like fiends, so that the young man was obliged to struggle as against an overpowering wind.

It was some time before the youth's eyes were good in the intense gloom within, but the man with benevolent spectacles led him skilfully, pausing but a moment to deposit the limp assassin upon a cot. He took the youth to a cot that lay tranquilly by the window, and showing him a tall locker for clothes that stood near the head with the ominous air of a tombstone, left him.

The youth sat on his cot and peered about him. There was a gas-jet in a distant part of the room, that burned a small flickering orange-hued flame. It caused vast masses of tumbled shadows in all parts of the place, save where, immediately about it, there was a little grey haze. As the young man's eyes became used to the darkness, he could see upon the cots that thickly littered the floor the forms of men sprawled out, lying in death-like silence, or heaving and snoring with tremendous effort, like stabbed fish.

The youth locked his derby and his shoes in the mummy case near him, and then lay down with an old and familiar coat around his shoulders. A blanket he handed gingerly, drawing it over part of the coat. The cot was covered with leather, and as cold as melting snow. The youth was obliged to shiver for some time on this affair, which was like a slab. Presently, however, his chill gave him peace, and during this period of leisure from it he turned his head to stare at his friend the assassin, whom he could dimly discern where he lay sprawled on a cot in the abandon of a man filled with drink. He was snoring with incredible vigour. His wet hair and beard dimly glistened, and his inflamed nose shone with subdued lustre like a red light in a fog.

Within reach of the youth's hand was one who lay with yellow breast and shoulders bare to the cold drafts. One arm hung over the side of the cot, and the fingers lay full length upon the wet cement floor of the room. Beneath the inky brows could be seen the eyes of the man exposed by the partly opened lids. To the youth it seemed that he and this corpse-like being were exchanging a prolonged stare, and that the other threatened with his eyes. He drew back watching his neighbour from the shadows of his blanket edge. The man did not move once through the night, but lay in this stillness as of death like a body stretched out expectant of the surgeon's knife.

And all through the room could be seen the tawny hues of naked flesh, limbs thrust into the darkness, projecting beyond the cots; upreared knees, arms hanging long and thin over the cot edges. For the most part they were statuesque, carven, dead. With the curious lockers standing all about like tombstones, there was a strange effect of a graveyard where bodies were merely flung.

Yet occasionally could be seen limbs wildly tossing in fantastic nightmare gestures, accompanied by guttural cries, grunts, oaths. And there was one fellow off in a gloomy corner, who in his dreams was oppressed by some frightful calamity, for of a sudden he began to utter long wails that went almost like yells from a hound, echoing wailfully and weird through this chill place of tombstones where men lay like the dead.

The sound in its high piercing beginnings, that dwindled to final melancholy moans, expressed a red and grim tragedy of the unfathomable possibilities of the man's dreams. But to the youth these were not merely the shrieks of a vision-pierced man: they were an utterance of the meaning of the room and its occupants. It was to him the protest of the wretch who feels the touch of the imperturbable granite wheels, and who then cries with an impersonal eloquence, with a strength not from him, giving voice to the wail of a whole section, a class, a people. This, weaving into the young man's brain, and mingling with his views of the vast and sombre shadows that, like mighty black fingers, curled around the naked bodies, made the young man so that he did not sleep, but lay carving the biographies for these men from his meagre experience. At times the fellow in the corner howled in a writhing agony of his imaginations.

Finally a long lance-point of grey light shot through the dusty panes of the window. Without, the young man could see roofs drearily white in the dawning. The point of light yellowed and grew brighter, until the golden rays of the morning sun came in bravely and strong. They touched with radiant colour the form of a small fat man, who snored in stuttering fashion. His round and shiny bald head glowed suddenly with the valour of a decoration. He sat up, blinked at the sun, swore fretfully, and pulled his blanket over the ornamental splendours of his head.

The youth contentedly watched this rout of the shadows before the bright spears of the sun, and presently he slumbered. When he awoke he heard the voice of the assassin raised in valiant curses. Putting up his head, he perceived his comrade seated on the side of the cot engaged in scratching his neck with long finger-nails that rasped like files.

"Hully Jee, dis is a new breed. They've got can-openers on their feet." He continued in a violent tirade.

The young man hastily unlocked his closet and took out his shoes and hat. As he sat on the side of the cot lacing his shoes, he glanced about and saw that daylight had made the room comparatively common-place and uninteresting. The men, whose faces seemed stolid, serene or absent, were engaged in dressing, while a great crackle of bantering conversation arose.

A few were parading in unconcerned nakedness. Here and there were men of brawn, whose skins shone clear and ruddy. They took splendid poses, standing massively like chiefs. When they had dressed in their ungainly garments there was an extraordinary change. They then showed bumps and deficiencies of all kinds.

There were others who exhibited many deformities. Shoulders were slanting, humped, pulled this way and pulled that way. And notable among these latter men was the little fat man, who had refused to allow his head to be glorified. His pudgy form, builded like a pear, bustled to and fro, while he swore in fish-wife fashion. It appeared that some article of his apparel had vanished.

The young man attired speedily, and went to his friend the assassin. At first the latter looked dazed at the sight of the youth. This face seemed to be appealing to him through the cloud wastes of his memory. He scratched his neck and reflected. At last he grinned, a broad smile gradually spreading until his countenance was a round illumination. "Hello, Willie," he cried cheerily.

"Hello," said the young man. "Are yeh ready t' fly?"

"Sure." The assassin tied his shoe carefully with some twine and came ambling.

When he reached the street the young man experienced no sudden relief from unholy atmospheres. He had forgotten all about them, and had been breathing naturally, and with no sensation of discomfort or distress.

He was thinking of these things as he walked along the street, when he was suddenly startled by feeling the assassin's hand, trembling with excitement, clutching his arm, and when the assassin spoke, his voice went into quavers from a supreme agitation.

"I'll be hully, bloomin' blowed if there wasn't a feller with a nightshirt on up there in that joint."

The youth was bewildered for a moment, but presently he turned to smile indulgently at the assassin's humour.

"Oh, you're a d — —d liar," he merely said.

Whereupon the assassin began to gesture extravagantly, and take oath by strange gods. He frantically placed himself at the mercy of remarkable fates if his tale were not true.

"Yes, he did! I cross m'heart thousan' times!" he protested, and at the moment his eyes were large with amazement, his mouth wrinkled in unnatural glee.

"Yessir! A nightshirt! A hully white nightshirt!"

"You lie!"

"No, sir! I hope ter die b'fore I kin git anudder ball if there wasn't a jay wid a hully, bloomin' white nightshirt!"

His face was filled with the infinite wonder of it. "A hully white nightshirt," he continually repeated.

The young man saw the dark entrance to a basement restaurant. There was a sign which read "No mystery about our hash!" and there were other age-stained and world-battered legends which told him that the place was within his means. He stopped before it and spoke to the assassin. "I guess I'll git somethin' t' eat."

At this the assassin, for some reason, appeared to be quite embarrassed. He gazed at the seductive front of the eating place for a moment. Then he started slowly up the street. "Well, good-bye, Willie," he said bravely.

For an instant the youth studied the departing figure. Then he called out, "Hol' on a minnet." As they came together he spoke in a certain fierce way, as if he feared that the other would think him to be charitable. "Look-a-here, if yeh wanta git some breakfas' I'll lend yeh three cents t' do it with. But say, look-a-here, you've gota git out an' hustle. I ain't goin' t' support yeh, or I'll go broke b'fore night. I ain't no millionaire."

"I take me oath, Willie," said the assassin earnestly, "th' on'y thing I really needs is a ball. Me t'roat feels like a fryin'-pan. But as I can't get a ball, why, th' next bes' thing is breakfast, an' if yeh do that for me, b' Gawd, I say yeh was th' whitest lad I ever see."

They spent a few moments in dexterous exchanges of phrases, in which they each protested that the other was, as the assassin had originally said, "a respecter'ble gentlem'n." And they concluded with mutual assurances that they were the souls of intelligence and virtue. Then they went into the restaurant.

There was a long counter, dimly lighted from hidden sources. Two or three men in soiled white aprons rushed here and there.

The youth bought a bowl of coffee for two cents and a roll for one cent. The assassin purchased the same. The bowls were webbed with brown seams, and the tin spoons wore an air of having emerged from the first pyramid. Upon them were black moss-like encrustations of age, and they were bent and scarred from the attacks of long-forgotten teeth. But over their repast the wanderers waxed warm and mellow. The assassin grew affable as the hot mixture went soothingly down his parched throat, and the young man felt courage flow in his veins.

Memories began to throng in on the assassin, and he brought forth long tales, intricate, incoherent, delivered with a chattering swiftness as from an old woman. " — — great job out'n Orange. Boss keep yeh hustlin' though all time. I was there three days, and then I went an' ask 'im t' lend me a dollar. 'G-g-go ter the devil,' he ses, an' I lose me job."

"South no good. Damn niggers work for twenty-five an' thirty cents a day. Run white man out. Good grub though. Easy livin'."

"Yas; useter work little in Toledo, raftin' logs. Make two or three dollars er day in the spring. Lived high. Cold as ice though in the winter."

"I was raised in northern N'York. O-o-oh, yeh jest oughto live there. No beer ner whisky though, way off in the woods. But all th' good hot grub yeh can eat. B' Gawd, I hung around there long as I could till th' ol' man fired me. 'Git t' hell outa here, yeh wuthless skunk, git t' hell outa here, an' go die,' he ses. 'You're a hell of a father,' I ses, 'you are,' an' I quit 'im."

As they were passing from the dim eating place, they encountered an old man who was trying to steal forth with a tiny package of food, but a tall man with an indomitable moustache stood dragon fashion, barring the way of escape. They heard the old man raise a plaintive protest.

"Ah, you always want to know what I take out, and you never see that I usually bring a package in here from my place of business."

As the wanderers trudged slowly along Park Row, the assassin began to expand and grow blithe. "B' Gawd, we've been livin' like kings," he said, smacking appreciative lips.

"Look out, or we'll have t' pay fer it t'night," said the youth with gloomy warning.

But the assassin refused to turn his gaze toward the future. He went with a limping step, into which he injected a suggestion of lamblike gambols. His mouth was wreathed in a red grin.

In the City Hall Park the two wanderers sat down in the little circle of benches sanctified by traditions of their class. They huddled in their old garments, slumbrously conscious of the march of the hours which for them had no meaning.

The people of the street hurrying hither and thither made a blend of black figures changing yet frieze-like. They walked in their good clothes as upon important missions, giving no gaze to the two wanderers seated upon the benches. They expressed to the young man his infinite distance from all that he valued. Social position, comfort, the pleasures of living, were unconquerable kingdoms. He felt a sudden awe.

And in the background a multitude of buildings, of pitiless hues and sternly high, were to him emblematic of a nation forcing its regal head into the clouds, throwing no downward glances; in the sublimity of its aspirations ignoring the wretches who may flounder at its feet. The roar of the city in his ear was to him the confusion of strange tongues, babbling heedlessly; it was the clink of coin, the voice of the city's hopes which were to him no hopes.

He confessed himself an outcast, and his eyes from under the lowered rim of his hat began to glance guiltily, wearing the criminal expression that comes with certain convictions.

The Men in the Storm

The blizzard began to swirl great clouds of snow along the streets, sweeping it down from the roofs, and up from the pavements, until the faces of pedestrians tingled and burned as from a thousand needle-prickings. Those on the walks huddled their necks closely in the collars of their coats, and went along stooping like a race of aged people. The drivers of vehicles hurried their horses furiously on their way. They were made more cruel by the exposure of their position, aloft on high seats. The street cars, bound up town, went slowly, the horses slipping and straining in the spongy brown mass that lay between the rails. The drivers, muffled to the eyes, stood erect, facing the wind, models of grim philosophy. Overhead trains rumbled and roared, and the dark structure of the elevated railroad, stretching over the avenue, dripped little streams and drops of water upon the mud and snow beneath.

All the clatter of the street was softened by the masses that lay upon the cobbles, until, even to one who looked from a window, it became important music, a melody of life made necessary to the ear by the dreariness of the pitiless beat and sweep of the storm. Occasionally one could see black figures of men busily shovelling the white drifts from the walks. The sounds from their labour created new recollections of rural experiences which every man manages to have in a measure. Later, the immense windows of the shops became aglow with light, throwing great beams of orange and yellow upon the pavement. They were infinitely cheerful, yet in a way they accentuated the force and discomfort of the storm, and gave a meaning to the pace of the people and the vehicles, scores of pedestrians and drivers, wretched with cold faces, necks and feet, speeding for scores of unknown doors and entrances, scattering to an infinite variety of shelters, to places which the imagination made warm with the familiar colours of home.

There was an absolute expression of hot dinners in the pace of the people. If one dared to speculate upon the destination of those who came trooping, he lost himself in a maze of social calculation; he might fling a handful of sand and attempt to follow the flight of each particular grain. But as to the suggestion of hot dinners, he was in firm lines of thought, for it was upon every hurrying face. It is a matter of tradition; it is from the tales of childhood. It comes forth with every storm.

However, in a certain part of a dark west-side street, there was a collection of men to whom these things were as if they were not. In this street was located a charitable house, where for five cents the homeless of the city could get a bed at night, and in the morning coffee and bread.

During the afternoon of the storm, the whirling snows acted as drivers, as men with whips, and at half-past three the walk before the closed doors of the house was covered with wanderers of the street, waiting. For some distance on either side of the place they could be seen lurking in the doorways and behind projecting parts of buildings, gathering in close bunches in an effort to get warm. A covered wagon drawn up near the curb sheltered a dozen of them. Under the stairs that led to the elevated railway station, there were six or eight, their hands stuffed deep in their pockets, their shoulders stooped, jiggling their feet. Others always could be seen coming, a strange procession, some slouching along with the characteristic hopeless gait of professional strays, some coming with hesitating steps, wearing the air of men to whom this sort of thing was new.

It was an afternoon of incredible length. The snow, blowing in twisting clouds, sought out the men in their meagre hiding-places, and skilfully beat in among them, drenching their persons with showers of fine stinging flakes. They crowded together, muttering, and fumbling in their pockets to get their red inflamed wrists covered by the cloth.

New-comers usually halted at one end of the groups and addressed a question, perhaps much as a matter of form, "Is it open yet?"

Those who had been waiting inclined to take the questioner seriously and became contemptuous. "No; do yeh think we'd be standin' here?"

The gathering swelled in numbers steadily and persistently. One could always see them coming, trudging slowly through the storm.

Finally, the little snow plains in the street began to assume a leaden hue from the shadows of evening. The buildings upreared gloomily save where various windows became brilliant figures of light, that made shimmers and splashes of yellow on the snow. A street lamp on the curb struggled to illuminate, but it was reduced to impotent blindness by the swift gusts of sleet crusting its panes.

In this half-darkness, the men began to come from their shelter places and mass in front of the doors of charity. They were of all types, but the nationalities were mostly American, German, and Irish. Many were strong, healthy, clear-skinned fellows, with that stamp of countenance which is not frequently seen upon seekers after charity. There were men of undoubted patience, industry, and temperance, who, in time of ill-fortune, do not habitually turn to rail at the state of society, snarling at the arrogance of the rich, and bemoaning the cowardice of the poor, but who at these times are apt to wear a sudden and singular meekness, as if they saw the world's progress marching from them, and were trying to perceive where they had failed, what they had lacked, to be thus vanquished in the race. Then there were others of the shifting, Bowery element, who were used to paying ten cents for a place to sleep, but who now came here because it was cheaper.

But they were all mixed in one mass so thoroughly that one could not have discerned the different elements, but for the fact that the labouring men, for the most part, remained silent and impassive in the blizzard, their eyes fixed on the windows of the house, statues of patience.

The sidewalk soon became completely blocked by the bodies of the men. They pressed close to one another like sheep in a winter's gale, keeping one another warm by the heat of their bodies. The snow came down upon this compressed group of men until, directly from above, it might have appeared like a heap of snow-covered merchandise, if it were not for the fact that the crowd swayed gently with a unanimous, rhythmical motion. It was wonderful to see how the snow lay upon the heads and shoulders of these men, in little ridges an inch thick perhaps in places, the flakes steadily adding drop and drop, precisely as they fall upon the unresisting grass of the fields. The feet of the men were all wet and cold, and the wish to warm them accounted for the slow, gentle, rhythmical motion. Occasionally some man whose ear or nose tingled acutely from the cold winds would wriggle down until his head was protected by the shoulders of his companions.

There was a continuous murmuring discussion as to the probability of the doors being speedily opened. They persistently lifted their eyes towards the windows. One could hear little combats of opinion.

"There's a light in th' winder!"

"Naw; it's a reflection f'm across th' way."

"Well, didn't I see 'em light it?"

"You did?"

"I did!"

"Well, then, that settles it!"

As the time approached when they expected to be allowed to enter, the men crowded to the doors in an unspeakable crush, jamming and wedging in a way that it seemed would crack bones. They surged heavily against the building in a powerful wave of pushing shoulders. Once a rumour flitted among all the tossing heads.

"They can't open th' door! Th' fellers er smack up agin 'em."

Then a dull roar of rage came from the men on the outskirts; but all the time they strained and pushed until it appeared to be impossible for those that they cried out against to do anything but be crushed into pulp.

"Ah, git away f'm th' door!"

"Git outa that!"

"Throw 'em out!"

"Kill 'em!"

"Say, fellers, now, what th' 'ell? G've 'em a chance t' open th' door!"

"Yeh dam pigs, give 'em a chance t' open th' door!"

Men in the outskirts of the crowd occasionally yelled when a boot-heel of one of trampling feet crushed on their freezing extremities.

"Git off me feet, yeh clumsy tarrier!"

"Say, don't stand on me feet! Walk on th' ground!"

A man near the doors suddenly shouted —"O-o-oh! Le' me out-le' me out!" And another, a man of infinite valour, once twisted his head so as to half face those who were pushing behind him. "Quit yer shovin', yeh" —and he delivered a volley of the most powerful and singular invective, straight into the faces of the men behind him. It was as if he was hammering the noses of them with curses of triple brass. His face, red with rage, could be seen upon it, an expression of sublime disregard of consequences. But nobody cared to reply to his imprecations; it was too cold. Many of them snickered, and all continued to push.

In occasional pauses of the crowd's movement the men had opportunities to make jokes; usually grim things, and no doubt very uncouth. Nevertheless, they were notable-one does not expect to find the quality of humour in a heap of old clothes under a snow-drift.

The winds seemed to grow fiercer as time wore on. Some of the gusts of snow that came down on the close collection of heads, cut like knives and needles, and the men huddled, and swore, not like dark assassins, but in a sort of American fashion, grimly and desperately, it is true, but yet with a wondrous under-effect, indefinable and mystic, as if there was some kind of humour in this catastrophe, in this situation in a night of snow-laden winds.

Once the window of the huge dry-goods shop across the street furnished material for a few moments of forgetfulness. In the brilliantly-lighted space appeared the figure of a man. He was rather stout and very well clothed. His beard was fashioned charmingly after that of the Prince of Wales. He stood in an attitude of magnificent reflection. He slowly stroked his moustache with a certain grandeur of manner, and looked down at the snow-encrusted mob. From below, there was denoted a supreme complacence in him. It seemed that the sight operated inversely, and enabled him to more clearly regard his own delightful environment.

One of the mob chanced to turn his head, and perceived the figure in the window. "Hello, lookit 'is whiskers," he said genially.

Many of the men turned then, and a shout went up. They called to him in all strange keys. They addressed him in every manner, from familiar and cordial greetings, to carefully-worded advice concerning changes in his personal appearance. The man presently fled, and the mob chuckled ferociously, like ogres who had just devoured something.

They turned then to serious business. Often they addressed the stolid front of the house.

"Oh, let us in fer Gawd's sake!"

"Let us in, or we'll all drop dead!"

"Say, what's th' use o' keepin' us poor Indians out in th' cold?"

And always some one was saying, "Keep off my feet."

The crushing of the crowd grew terrific toward the last. The men, in keen pain from the blasts, began almost to fight. With the pitiless whirl of snow upon them, the battle for shelter was going to the strong. It became known that the basement door at the foot of a little steep flight of stairs was the one to be opened, and they jostled and heaved in this direction like labouring fiends. One could hear them panting and groaning in their fierce exertion.

Usually some one in the front ranks was protesting to those in the rear —"O-o-ow! Oh, say now, fellers, let up, will yeh? Do yeh wanta kill somebody!"

A policeman arrived and went into the midst of them, scolding and be-rating, occasionally threatening, but using no force but that of his hands and shoulders against these men who were only struggling to get in out of the storm. His decisive tones rang out sharply —"Stop that pushin' back there! Come, boys, don't push! Stop that! Here you, quit yer shovin'! Cheese that!"

When the door below was opened, a thick stream of men forced a way down the stairs, which were of an extraordinary narrowness, and seemed only wide enough for one at a time. Yet they somehow went down almost three abreast. It was a difficult and painful operation. The crowd was like a turbulent water forcing itself through one tiny outlet. The men in the rear, excited by the success of the others, made frantic exertions, for it seemed that this large band would more than fill the quarters, and that many would be left upon the pavements. It would be disastrous to be of the last, and accordingly men with the snow biting their faces, writhed and twisted with their might. One expected that from the tremendous pressure, the narrow passage to the basement door would be so choked and clogged with human limbs and bodies that movement would be impossible. Once indeed the crowd was forced to stop, and a cry went along that a man had been injured at the foot of the stairs. But presently the slow movement began again, and the policeman fought at the top of the flight to ease the pressure of those that were going down.

A reddish light from a window fell upon the faces of the men, when they, in turn, arrived at the last three steps, and were about to enter. One could then note a change of expression that had come over their features. As they stood thus upon the threshold of their hopes, they looked suddenly contented and complacent. The fire had passed from their eyes and the snarl had vanished from their lips. The very force of the crowd in the rear, which had previously vexed them, was regarded from another point of view, for it now made it inevitable that they should go through the little doors into the place that was cheery and warm with light.

The tossing crowd on the sidewalk grew smaller and smaller. The snow beat with merciless persistence upon the bowed heads of those who waited. The wind drove it up from the pavements in frantic forms of winding white, and it seethed in circles about the huddled forms passing in one by one, three by three, out of the storm.

The Duel That Was Not Fought

Patsy Tulligan was not as wise as seven owls, but his courage could throw a shadow as long as the steeple of a cathedral. There were men on Cherry Street who had whipped him five times, but they all knew that Patsy would be as ready for the sixth time as if nothing had happened.

Once he and two friends had been away up on Eighth Avenue, far out of their country, and upon their return journey that evening they stopped frequently in saloons until they were as independent of their surroundings as eagles, and cared much less about thirty days on Blackwell's.

On Lower Sixth Avenue they paused in a saloon where there was a good deal of lamp-glare and polished wood to be seen from the outside, and within, the mellow light shone on much furbished brass and more polished wood. It was a better saloon than they were in the habit of seeing, but they did not mind it. They sat down at one of the little tables that were in a row parallel to the bar and ordered beer. They blinked stolidly at the decorations, the bar-tender, and the other customers. When anything transpired they discussed it with dazzling frankness, and what they said of it was as free as air to the other people in the place.

At midnight there were few people in the saloon. Patsy and his friends still sat drinking. Two well-dressed men were at another table, smoking cigars slowly and swinging back in their chairs. They occupied themselves with themselves in the usual manner, never betraying by a wink of an eyelid that they knew that other folk existed. At another table directly behind Patsy and his companions was a slim little Cuban, with miraculously small feet and hands, and with a youthful touch of down upon his lip. As he lifted his cigarette from time to time his little finger was bended in dainty fashion, and there was a green flash when a huge emerald ring caught the light. The bar-tender came often with his little brass tray. Occasionally Patsy and his two friends quarrelled.

Once this little Cuban happened to make some slight noise and Patsy turned his head to observe him. Then Patsy made a careless and rather loud comment to his two friends. He used a word which is no more than passing the time of day down in Cherry Street, but to the Cuban it was a dagger-point. There was a harsh scraping sound as a chair was pushed swiftly back.

The little Cuban was upon his feet. His eyes were shining with a rage that flashed there like sparks as he glared at Patsy. His olive face had turned a shade of grey from his anger. Withal his chest was thrust out in portentous dignity, and his hand, still grasping his wine-glass, was cool and steady, the little finger still bended, the great emerald gleaming upon it. The others, motionless, stared at him.

"Sir," he began ceremoniously. He spoke gravely and in a slow way, his tone coming in a marvel of self-possessed cadences from between those lips which quivered with wrath. "You have insult me. You are a dog, a hound, a cur. I spit upon you. I must have some of your blood."

Patsy looked at him over his shoulder.

"What's th' matter wi' che?" he demanded. He did not quite understand the words of this little man who glared at him steadily, but he knew that it was something about fighting. He snarled with the readiness of his class and heaved his shoulders contemptuously. "Ah, what's eatin' yeh? Take a walk! You h'ain't got nothin' t' do with me, have yeh? Well, den, go sit on yerself."

And his companions leaned back valorously in their chairs, and scrutinized this slim young fellow who was addressing Patsy.

"What's de little Dago chewin' about?"

"He wants t' scrap!"

"What!"

The Cuban listened with apparent composure. It was only when they laughed that his body cringed as if he was receiving lashes. Presently he put down his glass and walked over to their table. He proceeded always with the most impressive deliberation.

"Sir," he began again. "You have insult me. I must have s-s-satisfac-shone. I must have your body upon the point of my sword. In my country you would already be dead. I must have s-s-satisfac-shone."

Patsy had looked at the Cuban with a trifle of bewilderment. But at last his face began to grow dark with belligerency, his mouth curve in that wide sneer with which he would confront an angel of darkness. He arose suddenly in his seat and came towards the little Cuban. He was going to be impressive too.

"Say, young feller, if yeh go shootin' off fer face at me, I'll wipe d' joint wid yeh. What'cher gaffin' about, hey? Are yeh givin' me er jolly? Say, if yeh pick me up fer a cinch, I'll fool yeh. Dat's what! Don't take me fer no dead easy mug." And as he glowered at the little Cuban, he ended his oration with one eloquent word, "Nit!"

The bar-tender nervously polished his bar with a towel, and kept his eyes fastened upon the men. Occasionally he became transfixed with interest, leaning forward with one hand upon the edge of the bar and the other holding the towel grabbed in a lump, as if he had been turned into bronze when in the very act of polishing.

The Cuban did not move when Patsy came toward him and delivered his oration. At its conclusion he turned his livid face toward where, above him, Patsy was swaggering and heaving his shoulders in a consummate display of bravery and readiness. The Cuban, in his clear, tense tones, spoke one word. It was the bitter insult. It seemed to fairly spin from his lips and crackle in the air like breaking glass.

Every man save the little Cuban made an electric movement. Patsy roared a black oath and thrust himself forward until he towered almost directly above the other man. His fists were doubled into knots of bone and hard flesh. The Cuban had raised a steady finger.

"If you touch me wis your hand, I will keel you."

The two well-dressed men had come swiftly, uttering protesting cries. They suddenly intervened in this second of time in which Patsy had sprung forward and the Cuban had uttered his threat. The four men were now a tossing, arguing, violent group, one well-dressed man lecturing the Cuban, and the other holding off Patsy, who was now wild with rage, loudly repeating the Cuban's threat, and manoeuvring and struggling to get at him for revenge's sake.

The bar-tender, feverishly scouring away with his towel, and at times pacing to and fro with nervous and excited tread, shouted out —

"Say, for heaven's sake, don't fight in here. If yeh wanta fight, go out in the street and fight all yeh please. But don't fight in here."

Patsy knew only one thing, and this he kept repeating —

"Well, he wants t' scrap! I didn't begin dis! He wants t' scrap."

The well-dressed man confronting him continually replied —

"Oh, well, now, look here, he's only a lad. He don't know what he's doing. He's crazy mad. You wouldn't slug a kid like that."

Patsy and his aroused companions, who cursed and growled, were persistent with their argument. "Well, he wants t' scrap!" The whole affair was as plain as daylight when one saw this great fact. The interference and intolerable discussion brought the three of them forward, battleful and fierce.

"What's eatin' you, anyhow?" they demanded. "Dis ain't your business, is it? What business you got shootin' off your face?"

The other peacemaker was trying to restrain the little Cuban, who had grown shrill and violent.

"If he touch me wis his hand I will keel him. We must fight like gentlemen or else I keel him when he touch me wis his hand."

The man who was fending off Patsy comprehended these sentences that were screamed behind his back, and he explained to Patsy —

"But he wants to fight you with swords. With swords, you know."

The Cuban, dodging around the peacemakers, yelled in Patsy's face —

162

"Ah, if I could get you before me wis my sword! Ah! Ah! A-a-ah!" Patsy made a furious blow with a swift fist, but the peacemakers bucked against his body suddenly like football players.

Patsy was greatly puzzled. He continued doggedly to try to get near enough to the Cuban to punch him. To these attempts the Cuban replied savagely —

"If you touch me wis your hand, I will cut your heart in two piece."

At last Patsy said —"Well, if he's so dead stuck on fightin' wid swords, I'll fight 'im. Soitenly! I'll fight 'im." All this palaver had evidently tired him, and he now puffed out his lips with the air of a man who is willing to submit to any conditions if he can only bring on the row soon enough. He swaggered, "I'll fight 'im wid swords. Let 'im bring on his swords, an' I'll fight 'im 'til he's ready t' quit."

The two well-dressed men grinned. "Why, look here," they said to Patsy, "he'd punch you full of holes. Why, he's a fencer. You can't fight him with swords. He'd kill you in 'bout a minute."

"Well, I'll giv' 'im a go at it, anyhow," said Patsy, stout-hearted and resolute. "I'll giv' 'im a go at it, anyhow, an' I'll stay wid 'im long as I kin."

As for the Cuban, his lithe little body was quivering in an ecstasy of the muscles. His face radiant with a savage joy, he fastened his glance upon Patsy, his eyes gleaming with a gloating, murderous light. A most unspeakable, animal-like rage was in his expression.

"Ah! ah! He will fight me! Ah!" He bended unconsciously in the posture of a fencer. He had all the quick, springy movements of a skilful swordsman. "Ah, the b-r-r-rute! The b-r-r-rute! I will stick him like a pig!"

The two peacemakers, still grinning broadly, were having a great time with Patsy.

"Why, you infernal idiot, this man would slice you all up. You better jump off the bridge if you want to commit suicide. You wouldn't stand a ghost of a chance to live ten seconds."

Patsy was as unshaken as granite. "Well, if he wants t' fight wid swords, he'll get it. I'll giv' 'im a go at it, anyhow."

One man said —"Well, have you got a sword? Do you know what a sword is? Have you got a sword?"

"No, I ain't got none," said Patsy honestly, "but I kin git one." Then he added valiantly —"An' quick too."

The two men laughed. "Why, can't you understand it would be sure death to fight a sword duel with this fellow?"

"Dat's all right! See? I know me own business. If he wants t' fight one of dees d —n duels, I'm in it, understan'?"

"Have you ever fought one, you fool?"

"No, I ain't. But I will fight one, dough! I ain't no muff. If he want t' fight a duel, by Gawd, I'm wid 'im! D'yeh understan' dat!" Patsy cocked his hat and swaggered. He was getting very serious.

The little Cuban burst out —"Ah, come on, sirs: come on! We can take cab. Ah, you big cow, I will stick you, I will stick you. Ah, you will look very beautiful, very beautiful. Ah, come on, sirs. We will stop at hotel-my hotel. I there have weapons."

"Yeh will, will yeh? Yeh bloomin' little black Dago," cried Patsy in hoarse and maddened reply to the personal part of the Cuban's speech. He stepped forward. "Git yer d —n swords," he commanded. "Git yer swords. Git 'em quick! I'll fight wi' che! I'll fight wid anyting, too! See? I'll fight yeh wid a knife an' fork if yeh say so! I'll fight yer standin' up er sittin' down!" Patsy delivered this intense oration with sweeping, intensely emphatic gestures, his hands stretched out eloquently, his jaw thrust forward, his eyes glaring.

"Ah," cried the little Cuban joyously. "Ah, you are in very pretty temper. Ah, how I will cut your heart in two piece, my dear, d-e-a-r friend." His eyes, too, shone like carbuncles, with a swift, changing glitter, always fastened upon Patsy's face.

The two peacemakers were perspiring and in despair. One of them blurted out —

"Well, I'll be blamed if this ain't the most ridiculous thing I ever saw."

The other said —"For ten dollars I'd be tempted to let these two infernal blockheads have their duel."

Patsy was strutting to and fro, and conferring grandly with his friends.

"He took me for a muff. He tought he was goin' t' bluff me out, talkin' 'bout swords. He'll get fooled." He addressed the Cuban —"You're a fine little dirty picter of a scrapper, ain't che? I'll chew yez up, dat's what I will."

There began then some rapid action. The patience of well-dressed men is not an eternal thing. It began to look as if it would at last be a fight with six corners to it. The faces of the men were shining red with anger. They jostled each other defiantly, and almost every one blazed out at three or four of the others. The bar-tender had given up protesting. He swore for a time, and banged his glasses. Then he jumped the bar and ran out of the saloon, cursing sullenly.

When he came back with a policeman, Patsy and the Cuban were preparing to depart together. Patsy was delivering his last oration —

"I'll fight yer wid swords! Sure I will! Come ahead, Dago! I'll fight yeh anywheres wid anyting! We'll have a large, juicy scrap, an' don't yeh forgit dat! I'm right wid yez. I ain't no muff! I scrap wid a man jest as soon as he ses scrap, an' if yeh wanta scrap, I'm yer kitten. Understan' dat?"

The policeman said sharply —"Come, now; what's all this?" He had a distinctly business air.

The little Cuban stepped forward calmly. "It is none of your business."

The policeman flushed to his ears. "What?"

One well-dressed man touched the other on the sleeve. "Here's the time to skip," he whispered. They halted a block away from the saloon and watched the policeman pull the Cuban through the door. There was a minute of scuffle on the sidewalk, and into this deserted street at midnight fifty people appeared at once as if from the sky to watch it.

At last the three Cherry Hill men came from the saloon, and swaggered with all their old valour toward the peacemakers.

"Ah," said Patsy to them, "he was so hot talkin' about this duel business, but I would a-given 'im a great scrap, an' don't yeh forgit it."

For Patsy was not as wise as seven owls, but his courage could throw a shadow as long as the steeple of a cathedral.

An Ominous Baby

A baby was wandering in a strange country. He was a tattered child with a frowsled wealth of yellow hair. His dress, of a checked stuff, was soiled, and showed the marks of many conflicts, like the chain-shirt of a warrior. His sun-tanned knees shone above wrinkled stockings, which he pulled up occasionally with an impatient movement when they entangled his feet. From a gaping shoe there appeared an array of tiny toes.

He was toddling along an avenue between rows of stolid brown houses. He went slowly, with a look of absorbed interest on his small flushed face. His blue eyes stared curiously. Carriages went with a musical rumble over the smooth asphalt. A man with a chrysanthemum was going up steps. Two nursery maids chatted as they walked slowly, while their charges hobnobbed amiably between perambulators. A truck wagon roared thunderously in the distance.

The child from the poor district made his way along the brown street filled with dull grey shadows. High up, near the roofs, glancing sun-rays changed cornices to blazing gold and silvered the fronts of windows. The wandering baby stopped and stared at the two children laughing and playing in their carriages among the heaps of rugs and cushions. He braced his legs apart in an attitude of earnest attention. His lower jaw fell, and disclosed his small, even teeth. As they moved on, he followed the carriages with awe in his face as if contemplating a pageant. Once one of the babies, with twittering laughter, shook a gorgeous rattle at him. He smiled jovially in return.

Finally a nursery maid ceased conversation and, turning, made a gesture of annoyance.

"Go 'way, little boy," she said to him. "Go 'way. You're all dirty."

He gazed at her with infant tranquillity for a moment, and then went slowly off dragging behind him a bit of rope he had acquired in another street. He continued to investigate the new scenes. The people and houses struck him with interest as would flowers and trees. Passengers had to avoid the small, absorbed figure in the middle of the sidewalk. They glanced at the intent baby face covered with scratches and dust as with scars and with powder smoke.

After a time, the wanderer discovered upon the pavement a pretty child in fine clothes playing with a toy. It was a tiny fire-engine, painted brilliantly in crimson and gold. The wheels rattled as its small owner dragged it uproariously about by means of a string. The babe with his bit of rope trailing behind him paused and regarded the child and the toy. For a long while he remained motionless, save for his eyes, which followed all movements of the glittering thing. The owner paid no attention to the spectator, but continued his joyous imitations of phases of the career of a fire-engine. His gleeful baby laugh rang against the calm fronts of the houses. After a little the wandering baby began quietly to sidle nearer. His bit of rope, now forgotten, dropped at his feet. He removed his eyes from the toy and glanced expectantly at the other child.

"Say," he breathed softly.

The owner of the toy was running down the walk at top speed. His tongue was clanging like a bell and his legs were galloping. He did not look around at the coaxing call from the small tattered figure on the curb.

The wandering baby approached still nearer, and presently spoke again.

"Say," he murmured, "le' me play wif it?"

The other child interrupted some shrill tootings. He bended his head and spoke disdainfully over his shoulder.

"No," he said.

The wanderer retreated to the curb. He failed to notice the bit of rope, once treasured. His eyes followed as before the winding course of the engine, and his tender mouth twitched.

"Say," he ventured at last, "is dat yours?"

"Yes," said the other, tilting his round chin. He drew his property suddenly behind him as if it were menaced. "Yes," he repeated, "it's mine."

"Well, le' me play wif it?" said the wandering baby, with a trembling note of desire in his voice.

"No," cried the pretty child with determined lips. "It's mine. My ma-ma buyed it."

"Well, tan't I play wif it?" His voice was a sob. He stretched forth little covetous hands.

"No," the pretty child continued to repeat. "No, it's mine."

"Well, I want to play wif it," wailed the other. A sudden fierce frown mantled his baby face. He clenched his fat hands and advanced with a formidable gesture. He looked some wee battler in a war.

"It's mine! It's mine," cried the pretty child, his voice in the treble of outraged rights.

"I want it," roared the wanderer.

"It's mine! It's mine!"

"I want it!"

"It's mine!"

The pretty child retreated to the fence, and there paused at bay. He protected his property with outstretched arms. The small vandal made a charge. There was a short scuffle at the fence. Each grasped the string to the toy and tugged. Their faces were wrinkled with baby rage, the verge of tears. Finally, the child in tatters gave a supreme tug and wrenched the string from the other's hands. He set off rapidly down the street, bearing the toy in his arms. He was weeping with the air of a wronged one who has at last succeeded in achieving his rights. The other baby was squalling lustily. He seemed quite helpless. He rung his chubby hands and railed.

After the small barbarian had got some distance away, he paused and regarded his booty. His little form curved with pride. A soft, gleeful smile loomed through the storm of tears. With great care he prepared the toy for travelling. He stopped a moment on a corner and gazed at the pretty child, whose small figure was quivering with sobs. As the latter began to show signs of beginning pursuit, the little vandal turned and vanished down a dark side street as into a cavern.

A Great Mistake

An Italian kept a fruit-stand on a corner where he had good aim at the people who came down from the elevated station, and at those who went along two thronged streets. He sat most of the day in a backless chair that was placed strategically.

There was a babe living hard by, up five flights of stairs, who regarded this Italian as a tremendous being. The babe had investigated this fruit-stand. It had thrilled him as few things he had met with in his travels had thrilled him. The sweets of the world had laid there in dazzling rows, tumbled in luxurious heaps. When he gazed at this Italian seated amid such splendid treasures, his lower lip hung low and his eyes, raised to the vendor's face, were filled with deep respect, worship, as if he saw omnipotence.

The babe came often to this corner. He hovered about the stand and watched each detail of the business. He was fascinated by the tranquillity of the vendor, the majesty of power and possession. At times he was so engrossed in his contemplation that people, hurrying, had to use care to avoid bumping him down.

He had never ventured very near to the stand. It was his habit to hang warily about the curb. Even there he resembled a babe who looks unbidden at a feast of gods.

One day, however, as the baby was thus staring, the vendor arose, and going along the front of the stand, began to polish oranges with a red pocket handkerchief. The breathless spectator moved across the side walk until his small face almost touched the vendor's sleeve. His fingers were gripped in a fold of his dress.

At last, the Italian finished with the oranges and returned to his chair. He drew a newspaper printed in his language from behind a bunch of bananas. He settled himself in a comfortable position, and began to glare savagely at the print. The babe was left face to face with the massed joys of the world. For a time he was a simple worshipper at this golden shrine. Then tumultuous desires began to shake him. His dreams were of conquest. His lips moved. Presently into his head there came a little plan. He sidled nearer, throwing swift and cunning glances at the Italian. He strove to maintain his conventional manner, but the whole plot was written upon his countenance.

At last he had come near enough to touch the fruit. From the tattered skirt came slowly his small dirty hand. His eyes were still fixed upon the vendor. His features were set, save for the under lip, which had a faint fluttering movement. The hand went forward.

Elevated trains thundered to the station and the stairway poured people upon the sidewalks. There was a deep sea roar from feet and wheels going ceaselessly. None seemed to perceive the babe engaged in a great venture.

The Italian turned his paper. Sudden panic smote the babe. His hand dropped, and he gave vent to a cry of dismay. He remained for a moment staring at the vendor. There was evidently a great debate in his mind. His infant intellect had defined this Italian. The latter was undoubtedly a man who would eat babes that provoked him. And the alarm in the babe when this monarch had turned his newspaper brought vividly before him the consequences if he were detected. But at this moment the vendor gave a blissful grunt, and tilting his chair against a wall, closed his eyes. His paper dropped unheeded.

The babe ceased his scrutiny and again raised his hand. It was moved with supreme caution toward the fruit. The fingers were bent, claw-like, in the manner of great heart-shaking greed. Once he stopped and chattered convulsively, because the vendor moved in his sleep. The babe, with his eyes still upon the Italian, again put forth his hand, and the rapacious fingers closed over a round bulb.

And it was written that the Italian should at this moment open his eyes. He glared at the babe a fierce question. Thereupon the babe thrust the round bulb behind him, and with a face expressive of the deepest guilt, began a wild but elaborate series of gestures declaring his innocence. The Italian howled. He sprang to his feet, and with three steps overtook the babe. He whirled him fiercely, and took from the little fingers a lemon.

An Eloquence of Grief

The windows were high and saintly, of the shape that is found in churches. From time to time a policeman at the door spoke sharply to some incoming person. "Take your hat off!" He displayed in his voice the horror of a priest when the sanctity of a chapel is defied or forgotten. The court-room was crowded with people who sloped back comfortably in their chairs, regarding with undeviating glances the procession and its attendant and guardian policemen that moved slowly inside the spear-topped railing. All persons connected with a case went close to the magistrate's desk before a word was spoken in the matter, and then their voices were toned to the ordinary talking strength. The crowd in the court-room could not hear a sentence; they could merely see shifting figures, men that gestured quietly, women that sometimes raised an eager eloquent arm. They could not always see the judge, although they were able to estimate his location by the tall stands surmounted by white globes that were at either hand of him. And so those who had come for curiosity's sweet sake wore an air of being in wait for a cry of anguish, some loud painful protestation that would bring the proper thrill to their jaded, world-weary nerves-wires that refused to vibrate for ordinary affairs.

Inside the railing the court officers shuffled the various groups with speed and skill; and behind the desk the magistrate patiently toiled his way through mazes of wonderful testimony.

In a corner of this space, devoted to those who had business before the judge, an officer in plain clothes stood with a girl that wept constantly. None seemed to notice the girl, and there was no reason why she should be noticed, if the curious in the body of the court-room were not interested in the devastation which tears bring upon some complexions. Her tears seemed to burn like acid, and they left fierce pink marks on her face. Occasionally the girl looked across the room, where two well-dressed young women and a man stood waiting with the serenity of people who are not concerned as to the interior fittings of a jail.

The business of the court progressed, and presently the girl, the officer, and the well-dressed contingent stood before the judge. Thereupon two lawyers engaged in some preliminary fire-wheels, which were endured generally in silence. The girl, it appeared, was accused of stealing fifty dollars' worth of silk clothing from the room of one of the well-dressed women. She had been a servant in the house.

In a clear way, and with none of the ferocity that an accuser often exhibits in a police-court, calmly and moderately, the two young women gave their testimony. Behind them stood their escort, always mute. His part, evidently, was to furnish the dignity, and he furnished it heavily, almost massively.

When they had finished, the girl told her part. She had full, almost Afric, lips, and they had turned quite white. The lawyer for the others asked some questions, which he did-be it said, in passing-with the air of a man throwing flower-pots at a stone house.

It was a short case and soon finished. At the end of it the judge said that, considering the evidence, he would have to commit the girl for trial. Instantly the quick-eyed court officer began to clear the way for the next case. The well-dressed women and their escort turned one way and the girl turned another, toward a door with an austere arch leading into a stone-paved passage. Then it was that a great cry rang through the court-room, the cry of this girl who believed that she was lost.

The loungers, many of them, underwent a spasmodic movement as if they had been knived. The court officers rallied quickly. The girl fell back opportunely for the arms of one of them, and her wild heels clicked twice on the floor. "I am innocent! Oh, I am innocent!"

People pity those who need none, and the guilty sob alone; but innocent or guilty, this girl's scream described such a profound depth of woe-it was so graphic of grief, that it slit with a dagger's sweep the curtain of common-place, and disclosed the gloom-shrouded spectre that sat in the young girl's heart so plainly, in so universal a tone of the mind, that a man heard expressed some far-off midnight terror of his own thought.

The cries died away down the stone-paved passage. A patrol-man leaned one arm composedly on the railing, and down below him stood an aged, almost toothless wanderer, tottering and grinning.

"Plase, yer honer," said the old man as the time arrived for him to speak, "if ye'll lave me go this time, I've niver been dhrunk befoor, sir."

A court officer lifted his hand to hide a smile.

The Auction

Some said that Ferguson gave up sailoring because he was tired of the sea. Some said that it was because he loved a woman. In truth it was because he was tired of the sea and because he loved a woman.

He saw the woman once, and immediately she became for him the symbol of all things unconnected with the sea. He did not trouble to look again at the grey old goddess, the muttering slave of the moon. Her splendours, her treacheries, her smiles, her rages, her vanities, were no longer on his mind. He took heels after a little human being, and the woman made his thought spin at all times like a top; whereas the ocean had only made him think when he was on watch.

He developed a grin for the power of the sea, and, in derision, he wanted to sell the red and green parrot which had sailed four voyages with him. The woman, however, had a sentiment concerning the bird's plumage, and she commanded Ferguson to keep it in order, as it happened, that she might forget to put food in its cage.

The parrot did not attend the wedding. It stayed at home and blasphemed at a stock of furniture, bought on the installment plan, and arrayed for the reception of the bride and groom.

As a sailor, Ferguson had suffered the acute hankering for port; and being now always in port, he tried to force life to become an endless picnic. He was not an example of diligent and peaceful citizenship. Ablution became difficult in the little apartment, because Ferguson kept the wash-basin filled with ice and bottles of beer: and so, finally, the dealer in second-hand furniture agreed to auction the household goods on commission. Owing to an exceedingly liberal definition of a term, the parrot and cage were included. "On the level?" cried the parrot, "On the level? On the level? On the level?"

On the way to the sale, Ferguson's wife spoke hopefully. "You can't tell, Jim," she said. "Perhaps some of 'em will get to biddin', and we might get almost as much as we paid for the things."

The auction room was in a cellar. It was crowded with people and with house furniture; so that as the auctioneer's assistant moved from one piece to another he caused a great shuffling. There was an astounding number of old women in curious bonnets. The rickety stairway was thronged with men who wished to smoke and be free from the old women. Two lamps made all the faces appear yellow as parchment. Incidentally they could impart a lustre of value to very poor furniture.

The auctioneer was a fat, shrewd-looking individual, who seemed also to be a great bully. The assistant was the most imperturbable of beings, moving with the dignity of an image on rollers. As the Fergusons forced their way down the stair-way, the assistant roared: "Number twenty-one!"

"Number twenty-one!" cried the auctioneer. "Number twenty-one! A fine new handsome bureau! Two dollars? Two dollars is bid! Two and a half! Two and a half! Three? Three is bid. Four! Four dollars! A fine new handsome bureau at four dollars! Four dollars! Four dollars! F-o-u-r d-o-l-l-a-r-s! Sold at four dollars."

"On the level?" cried the parrot, muffled somewhere among furniture and carpets. "On the level? On the level?" Every one tittered.

Mrs. Ferguson had turned pale, and gripped her husband's arm. "Jim! Did you hear? The bureau-four dollars —"

Ferguson glowered at her with the swift brutality of a man afraid of a scene. "Shut up, can't you!"

Mrs. Ferguson took a seat upon the steps; and hidden there by the thick ranks of men, she began to softly sob. Through her tears appeared the yellowish mist of the lamplight, streaming about the monstrous shadows of the spectators. From time to time these latter whispered eagerly: "See, that went cheap!" In fact when anything was bought at a particularly low price, a murmur of admiration arose for the successful bidder.

The bedstead was sold for two dollars, the mattresses and springs for one dollar and sixty cents. This figure seemed to go through the woman's heart. There was derision in the sound of it. She bowed her head in her hands. "Oh, God, a dollar-sixty! Oh, God, a dollar-sixty!"

The parrot was evidently under heaps of carpet, but the dauntless bird still raised the cry, "On the level?"

Some of the men near Mrs. Ferguson moved timidly away upon hearing her low sobs. They perfectly understood that a woman in tears is formidable.

The shrill voice went like a hammer, beat and beat, upon the woman's heart. An odour of varnish, of the dust of old carpets, assailed her and seemed to possess a sinister meaning. The golden haze from the two lamps was an atmosphere of shame, sorrow, greed. But it was when the parrot called that a terror of the place and of the eyes of the people arose in her so strongly that she could not have lifted her head any more than if her neck had been of iron.

At last came the parrot's turn. The assistant fumbled until he found the ring of the cage, and the bird was drawn into view. It adjusted its feathers calmly and cast a rolling wicked eye over the crowd.

"Oh, the good ship Sarah sailed the seas,
And the wind it blew all day —"

This was the part of a ballad which Ferguson had tried to teach it. With a singular audacity and scorn, the parrot bawled these lines at the auctioneer as if it considered them to bear some particular insult.

The throng in the cellar burst into laughter. The auctioneer attempted to start the bidding, and the parrot interrupted with a repetition of the lines. It swaggered to and fro on its perch, and gazed at the faces of the crowd, with so much rowdy understanding and derision that even the auctioneer could not confront it. The auction was brought to a halt; a wild hilarity developed, and every one gave jeering advice.

Ferguson looked down at his wife and groaned. She had cowered against the wall, hiding her face. He touched her shoulder and she arose. They sneaked softly up the stairs with heads bowed.

Out in the street, Ferguson gripped his fists and said: "Oh, but wouldn't I like to strangle it!"

His wife cried in a voice of wild grief: "It-it m —made us a laughing-stock in-in front of all that crowd!"

For the auctioning of their household goods, the sale of their home-this financial calamity lost its power in the presence of the social shame contained in a crowd's laughter.

The Pace of Youth

I

Stimson stood in a corner and glowered. He was a fierce man and had indomitable whiskers, albeit he was very small.

"That young tarrier," he whispered to himself. "He wants to quit makin' eyes at Lizzie. This is too much of a good thing. First thing you know, he'll get fired."

His brow creased in a frown, he strode over to the huge open doors and looked at a sign. "Stimson's Mammoth Merry-Go-Round," it read, and the glory of it was great. Stimson stood and contemplated the sign. It was an enormous affair; the letters were as large as men. The glow of it, the grandeur of it was very apparent to Stimson. At the end of his contemplation, he shook his head thoughtfully, determinedly. "No, no," he muttered. "This is too much of a good thing. First thing you know, he'll get fired."

A soft booming sound of surf, mingled with the cries of bathers, came from the beach. There was a vista of sand and sky and sea that drew to a mystic point far away in the northward. In the mighty angle, a girl in a red dress was crawling slowly like some kind of a spider on the fabric of nature. A few flags hung lazily above where the bath-houses were marshalled in compact squares. Upon the edge of the sea stood a ship with its shadowy sails painted dimly upon the sky, and high overhead in the still, sun-shot air a great hawk swung and drifted slowly.

Within the Merry-Go-Round there was a whirling circle of ornamental lions, giraffes, camels, ponies, goats, glittering with varnish and metal that caught swift reflections from windows high above them. With stiff wooden legs, they swept on in a never-ending race, while a great orchestrion clamoured in wild speed. The summer sunlight sprinkled its gold upon the garnet canopies carried by the tireless racers and upon all the devices of decoration that made Stimson's machine magnificent and famous. A host of laughing children bestrode the animals, bending forward like charging cavalrymen, and shaking reins and whooping in glee. At intervals they leaned out perilously to clutch at iron rings that were tendered to them by a long wooden arm. At the intense moment before the swift grab for the rings one could see their little nervous bodies quiver with eagerness; the laughter rang shrill and excited. Down in the long rows of benches, crowds of people sat watching the game, while occasionally a father might arise and go near to shout encouragement, cautionary commands, or applause at his flying offspring. Frequently mothers called out: "Be careful, Georgie!" The orchestrion bellowed and thundered on its platform, filling the ears with its long monotonous song. Over in a corner, a man in a white apron and behind a counter roared above the tumult: "Pop corn! Pop corn!"

A young man stood upon a small, raised platform, erected in a manner of a pulpit, and just without the line of the circling figures. It was his duty to manipulate the wooden arm and affix the rings. When all were gone into the hands of the triumphant children, he held forth a basket, into which they returned all save the coveted brass one, which meant another ride free and made the holder very illustrious. The young man stood all day upon his narrow platform, affixing rings or holding forth the basket. He was a sort of general squire in these lists of childhood. He was very busy.

And yet Stimson, the astute, had noticed that the young man frequently found time to twist about on his platform and smile at a girl who shyly sold tickets behind a silvered netting. This, indeed, was the great reason of Stimson's glowering. The young man upon the raised platform had no manner of licence to smile at the girl behind the silvered netting. It was a most gigantic insolence. Stimson was amazed at it. "By Jiminy," he said to himself again, "that fellow is smiling at my daughter." Even in this tone of great wrath it could be discerned that Stimson was filled with wonder that any youth should dare smile at the daughter in the presence of the august father.

Often the dark-eyed girl peered between the shining wires, and, upon being detected by the young man, she usually turned her head away quickly to prove to him that she was not interested. At other times, however, her eyes seemed filled with a tender fear lest he should fall from that exceedingly dangerous platform. As for the young man, it was plain that these glances filled him with valour, and he stood carelessly upon his perch, as if he deemed it of no consequence that he might fall from it. In all the complexities of his daily life and duties he found opportunity to gaze ardently at the vision behind the netting.

This silent courtship was conducted over the heads of the crowd who thronged about the bright machine. The swift eloquent glances of the young man went noiselessly and unseen with their message. There had finally become established between the two in this manner a subtle understanding and companionship. They communicated accurately all that they felt. The boy told his love, his reverence, his hope in the changes of the future. The girl told him that she loved him, that she did not love him, that she did not know if she loved him, that she loved him. Sometimes a little sign saying "cashier" in gold letters, and hanging upon the silvered netting, got directly in range and interfered with the tender message.

The love affair had not continued without anger, unhappiness, despair. The girl had once smiled brightly upon a youth who came to buy some tickets for his little sister, and the young man upon the platform observing this smile had been filled with gloomy rage. He stood like a dark statue of vengeance upon his pedestal and thrust out the basket to the children with a gesture that was full of scorn for their hollow happiness, for their insecure and temporary joy. For five hours he did not once look at the girl when she was looking at him. He was going to crush her with his indifference; he was going to demonstrate that he had never been serious. However, when he narrowly observed her in secret he discovered that she seemed more blythe than was usual with her. When he found that his apparent indifference had not crushed her he suffered greatly. She did not love him, he concluded. If she had loved him she would have been crushed. For two days he lived a miserable existence upon his high perch. He consoled himself by thinking of how unhappy he was, and by swift, furtive glances at the loved face. At any rate he was in her presence, and he could get a good view from his perch when there was no interference by the little sign: "Cashier."

But suddenly, swiftly, these clouds vanished, and under the imperial blue sky of the restored confidence they dwelt in peace, a peace that was satisfaction, a peace that, like a babe, put its trust in the treachery of the future. This confidence endured until the next day, when she, for an unknown cause, suddenly refused to look at him. Mechanically he continued his task, his brain dazed, a tortured victim of doubt, fear, suspicion. With his eyes he supplicated her to telegraph an explanation. She replied with a stony glance that froze his blood. There was a great difference in their respective reasons for becoming angry. His were always foolish, but apparent, plain as the moon. Hers were subtle, feminine, as incomprehensible as the stars, as mysterious as the shadows at night.

They fell and soared, and soared and fell in this manner until they knew that to live without each other would be a wandering in deserts. They had grown so intent upon the uncertainties, the variations, the guessings of their affair that the world had become but a huge immaterial background. In time of peace their smiles were soft and prayerful, caresses confided to the air. In time of war, their youthful hearts, capable of profound agony, were wrung by the intricate emotions of doubt. They were the victims of the dread angel of affectionate speculation that forces the brain endlessly on roads that lead nowhere.

At night, the problem of whether she loved him confronted the young man like a spectre, looming as high as a hill and telling him not to delude himself. Upon the following day, this battle of the night displayed itself in the renewed fervour of his glances and in their increased number. Whenever he thought he could detect that she too was suffering, he felt a thrill of joy.

But there came a time when the young man looked back upon these contortions with contempt. He believed then that he had imagined his pain. This came about when the redoubtable Stimson marched forward to participate.

"This has got to stop," Stimson had said to himself, as he stood and watched them. They had grown careless of the light world that clattered about them; they were become so engrossed in their personal drama that the language of their eyes was almost as obvious as gestures. And Stimson, through his keenness, his wonderful, infallible penetration, suddenly came into possession of these obvious facts. "Well, of all the nerves," he said, regarding with a new interest the young man upon the perch.

He was a resolute man. He never hesitated to grapple with a crisis. He decided to overturn everything at once, for, although small, he was very fierce and impetuous. He resolved to crush this dreaming.

He strode over to the silvered netting. "Say, you want to quit your everlasting grinning at that idiot," he said, grimly.

The girl cast down her eyes and made a little heap of quarters into a stack. She was unable to withstand the terrible scrutiny of her small and fierce father.

Stimson turned from his daughter and went to a spot beneath the platform. He fixed his eyes upon the young man and said —

"I've been speakin' to Lizzie. You better attend strictly to your own business or there'll be a new man here next week." It was as if he had blazed away with a shot-gun. The young man reeled upon his perch. At last he in a measure regained his composure and managed to stammer: "A —all right, sir." He knew that denials would be futile with the terrible Stimson. He agitatedly began to rattle the rings in the basket, and pretend that he was obliged to count them or inspect them in some way. He, too, was unable to face the great Stimson.

For a moment, Stimson stood in fine satisfaction and gloated over the effect of his threat.

"I've fixed them," he said complacently, and went out to smoke a cigar and revel in himself. Through his mind went the proud reflection that people who came in contact with his granite will usually ended in quick and abject submission.

II

One evening, a week after Stimson had indulged in the proud reflection that people who came in contact with his granite will usually ended in quick and abject submission, a young feminine friend of the girl behind the silvered netting came to her there and asked her to walk on the beach after "Stimson's Mammoth Merry-Go-Round" was closed for the night. The girl assented with a nod.

The young man upon the perch holding the rings saw this nod and judged its meaning. Into his mind came an idea of defeating the watchfulness of the redoubtable Stimson.

When the Merry-Go-Round was closed and the two girls started for the beach, he wandered off aimlessly in another direction, but he kept them in view, and as soon as he was assured that he had escaped the vigilance of Stimson, he followed them.

The electric lights on the beach made a broad band of tremoring light, extending parallel to the sea, and upon the wide walk there slowly paraded a great crowd, intermingling, intertwining, sometimes colliding. In the darkness stretched the vast purple expanse of the ocean, and the deep indigo sky above was peopled with yellow stars. Occasionally out upon the water a whirling mass of froth suddenly flashed into view, like a great ghostly robe appearing, and then vanished, leaving the sea in its darkness, from whence came those bass tones of the water's unknown emotion. A wind, cool, reminiscent of the wave wastes, made the women hold their wraps about their throats, and caused the men to grip the rims of their straw hats. It carried the noise of the band in the pavilion in gusts. Sometimes people unable to hear the music, glanced up at the pavilion and were reassured upon beholding the distant leader still gesticulating and bobbing, and the other members of the band with their lips glued to their instruments. High in the sky soared an unassuming moon, faintly silver.

For a time the young man was afraid to approach the two girls; he followed them at a distance and called himself a coward. At last, however, he saw them stop on the outer edge of the crowd and stand silently listening to the voices of the sea. When he came to where they stood, he was trembling in his agitation. They had not seen him.

"Lizzie," he began. "I——"

The girl wheeled instantly and put her hand to her throat.

"Oh, Frank, how you frightened me," she said-inevitably.

"Well, you know I—I——" he stuttered.

But the other girl was one of those beings who are born to attend at tragedies. She had for love a reverence, an admiration that was greater the more that she contemplated the fact that she knew nothing of it. This couple, with their emotions, awed her and made her humbly wish that she might be destined to be of some service to them. She was very homely.

When the young man faltered before them, she, in her sympathy, actually over-estimated the crisis, and felt that he might fall dying at their feet. Shyly, but with courage, she marched to the rescue.

"Won't you come and walk on the beach with us?" she said.

The young woman gave her a glance of deep gratitude which was not without the patronage which a man in his condition naturally feels for one who pities it. The three walked on.

Finally, the being who was born to attend at this tragedy, said that she wished to sit down and gaze at the sea, alone.

They politely urged her to walk on with them, but she was obstinate. She wished to gaze at the sea, alone. The young man swore to himself that he would be her friend until he died.

And so the two young lovers went on without her. They turned once to look at her.

"Jennie's awful nice," said the girl.

"You bet she is," replied the young man, ardently.

They were silent for a little time.

At last the girl said —

"You were angry at me yesterday."

"No, I wasn't."

"Yes, you were, too. You wouldn't look at me once all day."

"No, I wasn't angry. I was only putting on."

Though she had, of course, known it, this confession seemed to make her very indignant. She flashed a resentful glance at him.

"Oh, were you, indeed?" she said with a great air.

For a few minutes she was so haughty with him that he loved her to madness. And directly this poem, which stuck at his lips, came forth lamely in fragments.

When they walked back toward the other girl and saw the patience of her attitude, their hearts swelled in a patronizing and secondary tenderness for her.

They were very happy. If they had been miserable they would have charged this fairy scene of the night with a criminal heartlessness; but as they were joyous, they vaguely wondered how the purple sea, the yellow stars, the changing crowds under the electric lights could be so phlegmatic and stolid.

They walked home by the lake-side way, and out upon the water those gay paper lanterns, flashing, fleeting, and careering, sang to them, sang a chorus of red and violet, and green and gold; a song of mystic bands of the future.

One day, when business paused during a dull sultry afternoon, Stimson went up town. Upon his return, he found that the popcorn man, from his stand over in a corner, was keeping an eye upon the cashier's cage, and that nobody at all was attending to the wooden arm and the iron rings. He strode forward like a sergeant of grenadiers.

"Where in thunder is Lizzie?" he demanded, a cloud of rage in his eyes.

The popcorn man, although associated long with Stimson, had never got over being dazed.

"They've-they've-gone round to th'—th'—house," he said with difficulty, as if he had just been stunned.

"Whose house?" snapped Stimson.

"Your-your house, I 'spose," said the popcorn man.

Stimson marched round to his home. Kingly denunciations surged, already formulated, to the tip of his tongue, and he bided the moment when his anger could fall upon the heads of that pair of children. He found his wife convulsive and in tears.

"Where's Lizzie?"

And then she burst forth —"Oh-John-John-they've run away, I know they have. They drove by here not three minutes ago. They must have done it on purpose to bid me good-bye, for Lizzie waved her hand sad-like; and then, before I could get out to ask where they were going or what, Frank whipped up the horse."

Stimson gave vent to a dreadful roar.

"Get my revolver-get a hack-get my revolver, do you hear-what the devil — —" His voice became incoherent.

He had always ordered his wife about as if she were a battalion of infantry, and despite her misery, the training of years forced her to spring mechanically to obey; but suddenly she turned to him with a shrill appeal.

"Oh, John-not-the-revolver."

"Confound it, let go of me," he roared again, and shook her from him.

He ran hatless upon the street. There were a mul titude of hacks at the summer resort, but it was ages to him before he could find one. Then he charged it like a bull.

"Uptown," he yelled, as he tumbled into the rear seat.

The hackman thought of severed arteries. His galloping horse distanced a large number of citizens who had been running to find what caused such contortions by the little hatless man.

It chanced as the bouncing hack went along near the lake, Stimson gazed across the calm grey expanse and recognized a colour in a bonnet and a pose of a head. A buggy was travelling along a highway that led to Sorington. Stimson bellowed —"There-there-there they are-in that buggy."

The hackman became inspired with the full knowledge of the situation. He struck a delirious blow with the whip. His mouth expanded in a grin of excitement and joy. It came to pass that this old vehicle, with its drowsy horse and its dusty-eyed and tranquil driver, seemed suddenly to awaken, to become animated and fleet. The horse ceased to ruminate on his state, his air of reflection vanished. He became intent upon his aged legs and spread them in quaint and ridiculous devices for speed. The driver, his eyes shining, sat critically in his seat. He watched each motion of this rattling machine down before him. He resembled an engineer. He used the whip with judgment and deliberation as the engineer would have used coal or oil. The horse clacked swiftly upon the macadam, the wheels hummed, the body of the vehicle wheezed and groaned.

Stimson, in the rear seat, was erect in that impassive attitude that comes sometimes to the furious man when he is obliged to leave the battle to others. Frequently, however, the tempest in his breast came to his face and he howled —

"Go it-go it-you're gaining; pound 'im! Thump the life out of 'im; hit 'im hard, you fool." His hand grasped the rod that supported the carriage top, and it was clenched so that the nails were faintly blue.

Ahead, that other carriage had been flying with speed, as from realization of the menace in the rear. It bowled away rapidly, drawn by the eager spirit of a young and modern horse. Stimson could see the buggy-top bobbing, bobbing. That little pane, like an eye, was a derision to him. Once he leaned forward and bawled angry sentences. He began to feel impotent; his whole expedition was a tottering of an old man upon a trail of birds. A sense of age made him choke again with wrath. That other vehicle, that was youth, with youth's pace; it was swift-flying with the hope of dreams. He began to comprehend those two children ahead of him, and he knew a sudden and strange awe, because he understood the power of their young blood, the power to fly strongly into the future and feel and hope again, even at that time when his bones must be laid in the earth. The dust rose easily from the hot road and stifled the nostrils of Stimson.

The highway vanished far away in a point with a suggestion of intolerable length. The other vehicle was becoming so small that Stimson could no longer see the derisive eye.

At last the hackman drew rein to his horse and turned to look at Stimson.

"No use, I guess," he said.

Stimson made a gesture of acquiescence, rage, despair. As the hackman turned his dripping horse about, Stimson sank back with the astonishment and grief of a man who has been defied by the universe. He had been in a great perspiration, and now his bald head felt cool and uncomfortable. He put up his hand with a sudden recollection that he had forgotten his hat.

At last he made a gesture. It meant that at any rate he was not responsible.

A Detail

The tiny old lady in the black dress and curious little black bonnet had at first seemed alarmed at the sound made by her feet upon the stone pavements. But later she forgot about it, for she suddenly came into the tempest of the Sixth Avenue shopping district, where from the streams of people and vehicles went up a roar like that from headlong mountain torrents.

She seemed then like a chip that catches, recoils, turns and wheels, a reluctant thing in the clutch of the impetuous river. She hesitated, faltered, debated with herself. Frequently she seemed about to address people; then of a sudden she would evidently lose her courage. Meanwhile the torrent jostled her, swung her this and that way.

At last, however, she saw two young women gazing in at a shop-window. They were well-dressed girls; they wore gowns with enormous sleeves that made them look like full-rigged ships with all sails set. They seemed to have plenty of time; they leisurely scanned the goods in the window. Other people had made the tiny old woman much afraid because obviously they were speeding to keep such tremendously important engagements. She went close to the girls and peered in at the same window. She watched them furtively for a time. Then finally she said —

"Excuse me!"

The girls looked down at this old face with its two large eyes turned towards them.

"Excuse me, can you tell me where I can get any work?"

For an instant the two girls stared. Then they seemed about to exchange a smile, but, at the last moment, they checked it. The tiny old lady's eyes were upon them. She was quaintly serious, silently expectant. She made one marvel that in that face the wrinkles showed no trace of experience, knowledge; they were simply little, soft, innocent creases. As for her glance, it had the trustfulness of ignorance and the candour of babyhood.

"I want to get something to do, because I need the money," she continued since, in their astonishment, they had not replied to her first question. "Of course I'm not strong and I couldn't do very much, but I can sew well; and in a house where there was a good many men folks, I could do all the mending. Do you know any place where they would like me to come?"

The young women did then exchange a smile, but it was a subtle tender smile, the edge of personal grief.

"Well, no, madame," hesitatingly said one of them at last; "I don't think I know any one."

A shade passed over the tiny old lady's face, a shadow of the wing of disappointment.

"Don't you?" she said, with a little struggle to be brave, in her voice.

Then the girl hastily continued —"But if you will give me your address, I may find some one, and if I do, I will surely let you know of it."

The tiny old lady dictated her address, bending over to watch the girl write on a visiting card with a little silver pencil. Then she said —

"I thank you very much." She bowed to them, smiling, and went on down the avenue.

As for the two girls, they walked to the curb and watched this aged figure, small and frail, in its black gown and curious black bonnet. At last, the crowd, the innumerable wagons, intermingling and changing with uproar and riot, suddenly engulfed it.

Blue Hotel & His New Mittens

The Blue Hotel

The Palace Hotel at Fort Romper was painted a light blue, a shade that is on the legs of a kind of heron, causing the bird to declare its position against any background. The Palace Hotel, then, was always screaming and howling in a way that made the dazzling winter landscape of Nebraska seem only a gray swampish hush. It stood alone on the prairie, and when the snow was falling the town two hundred yards away was not visible. But when the traveller alighted at the railway station he was obliged to pass the Palace Hotel before he could come upon the company of low clapboard houses which composed Fort Romper, and it was not to be thought that any traveller could pass the Palace Hotel without looking at it. Pat Scully, the proprietor, had proved himself a master of strategy when he chose his paints. It is true that on clear days, when the great trans-continental expresses, long lines of swaying Pullmans, swept through Fort Romper, passengers were overcome at the sight, and the cult that knows the brown-reds and the subdivisions of the dark greens of the East expressed shame, pity, horror, in a laugh. But to the citizens of this prairie town and to the people who would naturally stop there, Pat Scully had performed a feat. With this opulence and splendor, these creeds, classes, egotisms, that streamed through Romper on the rails day after day, they had no color in common.

As if the displayed delights of such a blue hotel were not sufficiently enticing, it was Scully's habit to go every morning and evening to meet the leisurely trains that stopped at Romper and work his seductions upon any man that he might see wavering, gripsack in hand.

One morning, when a snow-crusted engine dragged its long string of freight cars and its one passenger coach to the station, Scully performed the marvel of catching three men. One was a shaky and quick-eyed Swede, with a great shining cheap valise; one was a tall bronzed cowboy, who was on his way to a ranch near the Dakota line; one was a little silent man from the East, who didn't look it, and didn't announce it. Scully practically made them prisoners. He was so nimble and merry and kindly that each probably felt it would be the height of brutality to try to escape. They trudged off over the creaking board sidewalks in the wake of the eager little Irishman. He wore a heavy fur cap squeezed tightly down on his head. It caused his two red ears to stick out stiffly, as if they were made of tin.

At last, Scully, elaborately, with boisterous hospitality, conducted them through the portals of the blue hotel. The room which they entered was small. It seemed to be merely a proper temple for an enormous stove, which, in the centre, was humming with godlike violence. At various points on its surface the iron had become luminous and glowed yellow from the heat. Beside the stove Scully's son Johnnie was playing High-Five with an old farmer who had whiskers both gray and sandy. They were quarrelling. Frequently the old farmer turned his face towards a box of sawdust-colored brown from tobacco juice-that was behind the stove, and spat with an air of great impatience and irritation. With a loud flourish of words Scully destroyed the game of cards, and bustled his son up-stairs with part of the baggage of the new guests. He himself conducted them to three basins of the coldest water in the world. The cowboy and the Easterner burnished themselves fiery-red with this water, until it seemed to be some kind of a metal polish. The Swede, however, merely dipped his fingers gingerly and with trepidation. It was notable that throughout this series of small ceremonies the three travellers were made to feel that Scully was very benevolent. He was conferring great favors upon them. He handed the towel from one to the other with an air of philanthropic impulse.

Afterwards they went to the first room, and, sitting about the stove, listened to Scully's officious clamor at his daughters, who were preparing the mid-day meal. They reflected in the silence of experienced men who tread carefully amid new people. Nevertheless, the old farmer, stationary, invincible in his chair near the warmest part of the stove, turned his face from the sawdust box frequently and addressed a glowing commonplace to the strangers. Usually he was answered in short but adequate sentences by either the cowboy or the Easterner. The Swede said nothing. He seemed to be occupied in making furtive estimates of each man in the room.

One might have thought that he had the sense of silly suspicion which comes to guilt. He resembled a badly frightened man.

Later, at dinner, he spoke a little, addressing his conversation entirely to Scully. He volunteered that he had come from New York, where for ten years he had worked as a tailor. These facts seemed to strike Scully as fascinating, and afterwards he volunteered that he had lived at Romper for fourteen years. The Swede asked about the crops and the price of labor. He seemed barely to listen to Scully's extended replies. His eyes continued to rove from man to man.

Finally, with a laugh and a wink, he said that some of these Western communities were very dangerous; and after his statement he straightened his legs under the table, tilted his head, and laughed again, loudly. It was plain that the demonstration had no meaning to the others. They looked at him wondering and in silence.

II

As the men trooped heavily back into the front-room, the two little windows presented views of a turmoiling sea of snow. The huge arms of the wind were making attempts-mighty, circular, futile-to embrace the flakes as they sped. A gate-post like a still man with a blanched face stood aghast amid this profligate fury. In a hearty voice Scully announced the presence of a blizzard. The guests of the blue hotel, lighting their pipes, assented with grunts of lazy masculine contentment. No island of the sea could be exempt in the degree of this little room with its humming stove. Johnnie, son of Scully, in a tone which defined his opinion of his ability as a card-player, challenged the old farmer of both gray and sandy whiskers to a game of High-Five. The farmer agreed with a contemptuous and bitter scoff. They sat close to the stove, and squared their knees under a wide board. The cowboy and the Easterner watched the game with interest. The Swede remained near the window, aloof, but with a countenance that showed signs of an inexplicable excitement.

The play of Johnnie and the gray-beard was suddenly ended by another quarrel. The old man arose while casting a look of heated scorn at his adversary. He slowly buttoned his coat, and then stalked with fabulous dignity from the room. In the discreet silence of all other men the Swede laughed. His laughter rang somehow childish. Men by this time had begun to look at him askance, as if they wished to inquire what ailed him.

A new game was formed jocosely. The cowboy volunteered to become the partner of Johnnie, and they all then turned to ask the Swede to throw in his lot with the little Easterner, He asked some questions about the game, and, learning that it wore many names, and that he had played it when it was under an alias, he accepted the invitation. He strode towards the men nervously, as if he expected to be assaulted. Finally, seated, he gazed from face to face and laughed shrilly. This laugh was so strange that the Easterner looked up quickly, the cowboy sat intent and with his mouth open, and Johnnie paused, holding the cards with still fingers.

Afterwards there was a short silence. Then Johnnie said, "Well, let's get at it. Come on now!" They pulled their chairs forward until their knees were bunched under the board. They began to play, and their interest in the game caused the others to forget the manner of the Swede.

The cowboy was a board-whacker. Each time that he held superior cards he whanged them, one by one, with exceeding force, down upon the improvised table, and took the tricks with a glowing air of prowess and pride that sent thrills of indignation into the hearts of his opponents. A game with a board-whacker in it is sure to become intense. The countenances of the Easterner and the Swede were miserable whenever the cowboy thundered down his aces and kings, while Johnnie, his eyes gleaming with joy, chuckled and chuckled.

Because of the absorbing play none considered the strange ways of the Swede. They paid strict heed to the game. Finally, during a lull caused by a new deal, the Swede suddenly addressed Johnnie: "I suppose there have been a good many men killed in this room." The jaws of the others dropped and they looked at him.

"What in hell are you talking about?" said Johnnie.

The Swede laughed again his blatant laugh, full of a kind of false courage and defiance. "Oh, you know what I mean all right," he answered.

"I'm a liar if I do!" Johnnie protested. The card was halted, and the men stared at the Swede. Johnnie evidently felt that as the son of the proprietor he should make a direct inquiry. "Now, what might you be drivin' at, mister?" he asked. The Swede winked at him. It was a wink full of cunning. His fingers shook on the edge of the board. "Oh, maybe you think I have been to nowheres. Maybe you think I'm a tenderfoot?"

"I don't know nothin' about you," answered Johnnie, "and I don't give a damn where you've been. All I got to say is that I don't know what you're driving at. There hain't never been nobody killed in this room."

The cowboy, who had been steadily gazing at the Swede, then spoke: "What's wrong with you, mister?"

Apparently it seemed to the Swede that he was formidably menaced. He shivered and turned white near the corners of his mouth. He sent an appealing glance in the direction of the little Easterner. During these moments he did not forget to wear his air of advanced pot-valor. "They say they don't know what I mean," he remarked mockingly to the Easterner.

The latter answered after prolonged and cautious reflection. "I don't understand you," he said, impassively.

The Swede made a movement then which announced that he thought he had encountered treachery from the only quarter where he had expected sympathy, if not help. "Oh, I see you are all against me. I see —"

The cowboy was in a state of deep stupefaction. "Say." he cried, as he tumbled the deck violently down upon the board " —say, what are you gittin' at, hey?"

The Swede sprang up with the celerity of a man escaping from a snake on the floor. "I don't want to fight!" he shouted. "I don't want to fight!"

The cowboy stretched his long legs indolently and deliberately. His hands were in his pockets. He spat into the sawdust box. "Well, who the hell thought you did?" he inquired.

The Swede backed rapidly towards a corner of the room. His hands were out protectingly in front of his chest, but he was making an obvious struggle to control his fright. "Gentlemen," he quavered, "I suppose I am going to be killed before I can leave this house! I suppose I am going to be killed before I can leave this house!" In his eyes was the dying-swan look. Through the windows could be seen the snow turning blue in the shadow of dusk. The wind tore at the house and some loose thing beat regularly against the clap-boards like a spirit tapping.

A door opened, and Scully himself entered. He paused in surprise as he noted the tragic attitude of the Swede. Then he said, "What's the matter here?"

The Swede answered him swiftly and eagerly: "These men are going to kill me."

"Kill you!" ejaculated Scully. "Kill you! What are you talkin'?"

The Swede made the gesture of a martyr.

Scully wheeled sternly upon his son. "What is this, Johnnie?"

The lad had grown sullen. "Damned if I know," he answered. "I can't make no sense to it." He began to shuffle the cards, fluttering them together with an angry snap. "He says a good many men have been killed in this room, or something like that. And he says he's goin' to be killed here too. I don't know what ails him. He's crazy, I shouldn't wonder."

Scully then looked for explanation to the cowboy, but the cowboy simply shrugged his shoulders.

"Kill you?" said Scully again to the Swede. "Kill you? Man, you're off your nut."

"Oh, I know." burst out the Swede. "I know what will happen. Yes, I'm crazy-yes. Yes, of course, I'm crazy-yes. But I know one thing —" There was a sort of sweat of misery and terror upon his face. "I know I won't get out of here alive."

The cowboy drew a deep breath, as if his mind was passing into the last stages of dissolution. "Well, I'm dog-goned," he whispered to himself.

Scully wheeled suddenly and faced his son. "You've been troublin' this man!"

Johnnie's voice was loud with its burden of grievance. "Why, good Gawd, I ain't done nothin' to 'im."

The Swede broke in. "Gentlemen, do not disturb yourselves. I will leave this house. I will go away because" —he accused them dramatically with his glance —"because I do not want to be killed."

Scully was furious with his son. "Will you tell me what is the matter, you young divil? What's the matter, anyhow? Speak out!"

"Blame it!" cried Johnnie in despair, "don't I tell you I don't know. He-he says we want to kill him, and that's all I know. I can't tell what ails him."

The Swede continued to repeat: "Never mind, Mr. Scully; nevermind. I will leave this house. I will go away, because I do not wish to be killed. Yes, of course, I am crazy-yes. But I know one thing! I will go away. I will leave this house. Never mind, Mr. Scully; never mind. I will go away."

"You will not go 'way," said Scully. "You will not go 'way until I hear the reason of this business. If anybody has troubled you I will take care of him. This is my house. You are under my roof, and I will not allow any peaceable man to be troubled here." He cast a terrible eye upon Johnnie, the cowboy, and the Easterner.

"Never mind, Mr. Scully; never mind. I will go away. I do not wish to be killed." The Swede moved towards the door, which opened upon the stairs. It was evidently his intention to go at once for his baggage.

"No, no," shouted Scully peremptorily; but the white-faced man slid by him and disappeared. "Now," said Scully severely, "what does this mane?"

Johnnie and the cowboy cried together: "Why, we didn't do nothin' to 'im!"

Scully's eyes were cold. "No," he said, "you didn't?"

Johnnie swore a deep oath. "Why this is the wildest loon I ever see. We didn't do nothin' at all. We were jest sittin' here play in' cards, and he —"

The father suddenly spoke to the Easterner. "Mr. Blanc," he asked, "what has these boys been doin'?"

The Easterner reflected again. "I didn't see anything wrong at all," he said at last, slowly.

Scully began to howl. "But what does it mane?" He stared ferociously at his son. "I have a mind to lather you for this, me boy."

Johnnie was frantic. "Well, what have I done?" he bawled at his father.

III

"I think you are tongue-tied," said Scully finally to his son, the cowboy, and the Easterner; and at the end of this scornful sentence he left the room.

Up-stairs the Swede was swiftly fastening the straps of his great valise. Once his back happened to be half turned towards the door, and, hearing a noise there, he wheeled and sprang up, uttering a loud cry. Scully's wrinkled visage showed grimly in the light of the small lamp he carried. This yellow effulgence, streaming upward, colored only his prominent features, and left his eyes, for instance, in mysterious shadow. He resembled a murderer.

"Man! man!" he exclaimed, "have you gone daffy?"

"Oh, no! Oh, no!" rejoined the other. "There are people in this world who know pretty nearly as much as you do-understand?"

For a moment they stood gazing at each other. Upon the Swede's deathly pale checks were two spots brightly crimson and sharply edged, as if they had been carefully painted. Scully placed the light on the table and sat himself on the edge of the bed. He spoke ruminatively. "By cracky, I never heard of such a thing in my life. It's a complete muddle. I can't, for the soul of me, think how you ever got this idea into your head." Presently he lifted his eyes and asked: "And did you sure think they were going to kill you?"

The Swede scanned the old man as if he wished to see into his mind. "I did," he said at last. He obviously suspected that this answer might precipitate an outbreak. As he pulled on a strap his whole arm shook, the elbow wavering like a bit of paper.

Scully banged his hand impressively on the foot-board of the bed. "Why, man, we're goin' to have a line of ilictric street-cars in this town next spring."

"'A line of electric street-cars,'" repeated the Swede, stupidly.

"And," said Scully, "there's a new railroad goin' to be built down from Broken Arm to here. Not to mintion the four churches and the smashin' big brick school-house. Then there's the big factory, too. Why, in two years Romper 'll be a *metropolis*."

Having finished the preparation of his baggage, the Swede straightened himself. "Mr. Scully," he said, with sudden hardihood, "how much do I owe you?"

"You don't owe me anythin'," said the old man, angrily.

"Yes, I do," retorted the Swede. He took seventy-five cents from his pocket and tendered it to Scully; but the latter snapped his fingers in disdainful refusal. However, it happened that they both stood gazing in a strange fashion at three silver pieces on the Swede's open palm.

"I'll not take your money," said Scully at last. "Not after what's been goin' on here." Then a plan seemed to strike him. "Here," he cried, picking up his lamp and moving towards the door. "Here! Come with me a minute."

"No," said the Swede, in overwhelming alarm.

"Yes," urged the old man. "Come on! I want you to come and see a picter-just across the hall-in my room."

The Swede must have concluded that his hour was come. His jaw dropped and his teeth showed like a dead man's. He ultimately followed Scully across the corridor, but he had the step of one hung in chains.

Scully flashed the light high on the wall of his own chamber. There was revealed a ridiculous photograph of a little girl. She was leaning against a balustrade of gorgeous decoration, and the formidable bang to her hair was prominent. The figure was as graceful as an upright sled-stake, and, withal, it was of the hue of lead. "There," said Scully, tenderly, "that's the picter of my little girl that died. Her name was Carrie. She had the purtiest hair you ever saw! I was that fond of her, she —"

Turning then, he saw that the Swede was not contemplating the picture at all, but, instead, was keeping keen watch on the gloom in the rear.

"Look, man!" cried Scully, heartily. "That's the picter of my little gal that died. Her name was Carrie. And then here's the picter of my oldest boy, Michael. He's a lawyer in Lincoln, an' doin' well. I gave that boy a grand eddycation, and I'm glad for it now. He's a fine boy. Look at 'im now. Ain't he bold as blazes, him there in Lincoln, an honored an' respicted gintleman. An honored an' respicted gintleman," concluded Scully with a flourish. And, so saying, he smote the Swede jovially on the back.

The Swede faintly smiled.

"Now," said the old man, "there's only one more thing." He dropped suddenly to the floor and thrust his head beneath the bed. The Swede could hear his muffled voice. "I'd keep it under me piller if it wasn't for that boy Johnnie. Then there's the old woman-Where is it now? I never put it twice in the same place. Ah, now come out with you!"

Presently he backed clumsily from under the bed, dragging with him an old coat rolled into a bundle. "I've fetched him," he muttered. Kneeling on the floor, he unrolled the coat and extracted from its heart a large yellow-brown whiskey bottle.

His first maneuver was to hold the bottle up to the light. Reassured, apparently, that nobody had been tampering with it, he thrust it with a generous movement towards the Swede.

The weak-kneed Swede was about to eagerly clutch this element of strength, but he suddenly jerked his hand away and cast a look of horror upon Scully.

"Drink," said the old man affectionately. He had risen to his feet, and now stood facing the Swede.

There was a silence. Then again Scully said: "Drink!"

The Swede laughed wildly. He grabbed the bottle, put it to his mouth, and as his lips curled absurdly around the opening and his throat worked, he kept his glance, burning with hatred, upon the old man's face.

IV

After the departure of Scully the three men, with the card-board still upon their knees, preserved for a long time an astounded silence. Then Johnnie said: "That's the dod-dangest Swede I ever see."

"He ain't no Swede," said the cowboy, scornfully.

"Well, what is he then?" cried Johnnie. "What is he then?"

"It's my opinion," replied the cowboy deliberately, "he's some kind of a Dutchman." It was a venerable custom of the country to entitle as Swedes all light-haired men who spoke with a heavy tongue. In consequence the idea of the cowboy was not without its daring. "Yes, sir," he repeated. "It's my opinion this feller is some kind of a Dutchman."

"Well, he says he's a Swede, anyhow," muttered Johnnie, sulkily. He turned to the Easterner: "What do you think, Mr. Blanc?"

"Oh, I don't know," replied the Easterner.

"Well, what do you think makes him act that way?" asked the cowboy.

"Why, he's frightened." The Easterner knocked his pipe against a rim of the stove. "He's clear frightened out of his boots."

"What at?" cried Johnnie and cowboy together.

The Easterner reflected over his answer.

"What at?" cried the others again.

"Oh, I don't know, but it seems to me this man has been reading dime-novels, and he thinks he's right out in the middle of it-the shootin' and stabbin' and all."

"But," said the cowboy, deeply scandalized, "this ain't Wyoming, ner none of them places. This is Nebrasker."

"Yes," added Johnnie, "an' why don't he wait till he gits *out West?*"

The travelled Easterner laughed. "It isn't different there even-not in these days. But he thinks he's right in the middle of hell."

Johnnie and the cowboy mused long.

"It's awful funny," remarked Johnnie at last.

"Yes," said the cowboy. "This is a queer game. I hope we don't git snowed in, because then we'd have to stand this here man bein' around with us all the time. That wouldn't be no good."

"I wish pop would throw him out," said Johnnie.

Presently they heard a loud stamping on the stairs, accompanied by ringing jokes in the voice of old Scully, and laughter, evidently from the Swede. The men around the stove stared vacantly at each other. "Gosh!" said the cowboy. The door flew open, and old Scully, flushed and anecdotal, came into the room. He was jabbering at the Swede, who followed him, laughing bravely. It was the entry of two roisterers from a banquet-hall.

"Come now," said Scully sharply to the three seated men, "move up and give us a chance at the stove." The cowboy and the Easterner obediently sidled their chairs to make room for the new-comers. Johnnie, however, simply arranged himself in a more indolent attitude, and then remained motionless.

"Come! Git over, there," said Scully.

"Plenty of room on the other side of the stove," said Johnnie.

"Do you think we want to sit in the draught?" roared the father.

But the Swede here interposed with a grandeur of confidence. "No, no. Let the boy sit where he likes," he cried in a bullying voice to the father.

"All right! All right!" said Scully, deferentially. The cowboy and the Easterner exchanged glances of wonder.

The five chairs were formed in a crescent about one side of the stove. The Swede began to talk; he talked arrogantly, profanely, angrily. Johnnie, the cowboy, and the Easterner maintained a morose silence, while old Scully appeared to be receptive and eager, breaking in constantly with sympathetic ejaculations.

Finally the Swede announced that he was thirsty. He moved in his chair, and said that he would go for a drink of water.

"I'll git it for you," cried Scully at once.

"No," said the Swede, contemptuously. "I'll get it for myself." He arose and stalked with the air of an owner off into the executive parts of the hotel.

As soon as the Swede was out of hearing Scully sprang to his feet and whispered intensely to the others: "Up-stairs he thought I was tryin' to poison 'im."

"Say," said Johnnie, "this makes me sick. Why don't you throw 'im out in the snow?"

"Why, he's all right now," declared Scully. "It was only that he was from the East, and he thought this was a tough place. That's all. He's all right now."

The cowboy looked with admiration upon the Easterner. "You were straight," he said. "You were on to that there Dutchman."

"Well," said Johnnie to his father, "he may be all right now, but I don't see it. Other time he was scared, but now he's too fresh."

Scully's speech was always a combination of Irish brogue and idiom, Western twang and idiom, and scraps of curiously formal diction taken from the story-books and newspapers. He now hurled a strange mass of language at the head of his son. "What do I keep? What do I keep? What do I keep?" he demanded, in a voice of thunder. He slapped his knee impressively, to indicate that he himself was going to make reply, and that all should heed. "I keep a hotel," he shouted. "A hotel, do you mind? A guest under my roof has sacred privileges. He is to be intimidated by none. Not one word shall he hear that would prejudice him in favor of goin' away. I'll not have it. There's no place in this here town where they can say they iver took in a guest of mine because he was afraid to stay here." He wheeled suddenly upon the cowboy and the Easterner. "Am I right?"

"Yes, Mr. Scully," said the cowboy, "I think you're right."

"Yes, Mr. Scully," said the Easterner, "I think you're right."

At six-o'clock supper, the Swede fizzed like a fire-wheel. He sometimes seemed on the point of bursting into riotous song, and in all his madness he was encouraged by old Scully. The Easterner was incased in reserve; the cowboy sat in wide-mouthed amazement, forgetting to eat, while Johnnie wrathily demolished great plates of food. The daughters of the house, when they were obliged to replenish the biscuits, approached as warily as Indians, and, having succeeded in their purpose, fled with ill-concealed trepidation. The Swede domineered the whole feast, and he gave it the appearance of a cruel bacchanal. He seemed to have grown suddenly taller; he gazed, brutally disdainful, into every face. His voice rang through the room. Once when he jabbed out harpoon-fashion with his fork to pinion a biscuit, the weapon nearly impaled the hand of the Easterner which had been stretched quietly out for the same biscuit.

After supper, as the men filed towards the other room, the Swede smote Scully ruthlessly on the shoulder. "Well, old boy, that was a good, square meal." Johnnie looked hopefully at his father; he knew that shoulder was tender from an old fall; and, indeed, it appeared for a moment as if Scully was going to flame out over the matter, but in the end he smiled a sickly smile and remained silent. The others understood from his manner that he was admitting his responsibility for the Swede's new view-point.

Johnnie, however, addressed his parent in an aside. "Why don't you license somebody to kick you down-stairs?" Scully scowled darkly by way of reply.

When they were gathered about the stove, the Swede insisted on another game of High Five. Scully gently deprecated the plan at first, but the Swede turned a wolfish glare upon him. The old man subsided, and the Swede canvassed the others. In his tone there was always a great threat. The cowboy and the Easterner both remarked indifferently that they would play. Scully said that he would presently have to go to meet the 6.58 train, and so the Swede turned menacingly upon Johnnie. For a moment their glances crossed like blades, and then Johnnie smiled and said, "Yes, I'll play."

They formed a square, with the little board on their knees. The Easterner and the Swede were again partners. As the play went on, it was noticeable that the cowboy was not board-whacking as usual. Meanwhile, Scully, near the lamp, had put on his spectacles and, with an appearance curiously like an old priest, was reading a newspaper. In time he went out to meet the 6.58 train, and, despite his precautions, a gust of polar wind whirled into the room as he opened the door. Besides scattering the cards, it dulled the players to the marrow. The Swede cursed frightfully. When Scully returned, his entrance disturbed a cosey and friendly scene. The Swede again cursed. But presently they were once more intent, their heads bent forward and their hands moving swiftly. The Swede had adopted the fashion of board-whacking.

Scully took up his paper and for a long time remained immersed in matters which were extraordinarily remote from him. The lamp burned badly, and once he stopped to adjust the wick. The newspaper, as he turned from page to page, rustled with a slow and comfortable sound. Then suddenly he heard three terrible words: "You are cheatin'!"

Such scenes often prove that there can be little of dramatic import in environment. Any room can present a tragic front; any room can be comic. This little den was now hideous as a torture-chamber. The new faces of the men themselves had changed it upon the instant. The Swede held a huge fist in front of Johnnie's face, while the latter looked steadily over it into the blazing orbs of his accuser. The Easterner had grown pallid; the cowboy's jaw had dropped in that expression of bovine amazement which was one of his important mannerisms. After the three words, the first sound in the room was made by Scully's paper as it floated forgotten to his feet. His spectacles had also fallen from his nose, but by a clutch he had saved them in air. His hand, grasping the spectacles, now remained poised awkwardly and near his shoulder. He stared at the card-players.

Probably the silence was while a second elapsed. Then, if the floor had been suddenly twitched out from under the men they could not have moved quicker. The five had projected themselves headlong towards a common point. It happened that Johnnie, in rising to hurl himself upon the Swede, had stumbled slightly because of his curiously instinctive care for the cards and the board. The loss of the moment allowed time for the arrival of Scully, and also allowed the cowboy time to give the Swede a great push which sent him staggering back. The men found tongue together, and hoarse shouts of rage, appeal, or fear burst from every throat. The cowboy pushed and jostled feverishly at the Swede, and the Easterner and Scully clung wildly to Johnnie; but, through the smoky air, above the swaying bodies of the peace-compellers, the eyes of the two warriors ever sought each other in glances of challenge that were at once hot and steely.

Of course the board had been overturned, and now the whole company of cards was scattered over the floor, where the boots of the men trampled the fat and painted kings and queens as they gazed with their silly eyes at the war that was waging above them.

Scully's voice was dominating the yells. "Stop now? Stop, I say! Stop, now —"

Johnnie, as he struggled to burst through the rank formed by Scully and the Easterner, was crying, "Well, he says I cheated! He says I cheated! I won't allow no man to say I cheated! If he says I cheated, he's a — — — — — —!"

The cowboy was telling the Swede, "Quit, now! Quit, d'ye hear —"

The screams of the Swede never ceased: "He did cheat! I saw him! I saw him —"

As for the Easterner, he was importuning in a voice that was not heeded: "Wait a moment, can't you? Oh, wait a moment. What's the good of a fight over a game of cards? Wait a moment —"

In this tumult no complete sentences were clear. "Cheat" — "Quit" — "He says" — these fragments pierced the uproar and rang out sharply. It was remarkable that, whereas Scully undoubtedly made the most noise, he was the least heard of any of the riotous band.

Then suddenly there was a great cessation. It was as if each man had paused for breath; and although the room was still lighted with the anger of men, it could be seen that there was no danger of immediate conflict, and at once Johnnie, shouldering his way forward, almost succeeded in confronting the Swede. "What did you say I cheated for? What did you say I cheated for? I don't cheat, and I won't let no man say I do!"

The Swede said, "I saw you! I saw you!"

"Well," cried Johnnie, "I'll fight any man what says I cheat!"

"No, you won't," said the cowboy. "Not here."

"Ah, be still, can't you?" said Scully, coming between them.

The quiet was sufficient to allow the Easterner's voice to be heard. He was repeating, "Oh, wait a moment, can't you? What's the good of a fight over a game of cards? Wait a moment!"

Johnnie, his red face appearing above his father's shoulder, hailed the Swede again. "Did you say I cheated?"

The Swede showed his teeth. "Yes."

"Then," said Johnnie, "we must fight."

"Yes, fight," roared the Swede. He was like a demoniac. "Yes, fight! I'll show you what kind of a man I am! I'll show you who you want to fight! Maybe you think I can't fight! Maybe you think I can't! I'll show you, you skin, you card-sharp! Yes, you cheated! You cheated! You cheated!"

"Well, let's go at it, then, mister," said Johnnie, coolly.

The cowboy's brow was beaded with sweat from his efforts in intercepting all sorts of raids. He turned in despair to Scully. "What are you goin' to do now?"

A change had come over the Celtic visage of the old man. He now seemed all eagerness; his eyes glowed.

"We'll let them fight," he answered, stalwartly. "I can't put up with it any longer. I've stood this damned Swede till I'm sick. We'll let them fight."

The men prepared to go out-of-doors. The Easterner was so nervous that he had great difficulty in getting his arms into the sleeves of his new leather coat. As the cowboy drew his fur cap down over his ears his hands trembled. In fact, Johnnie and old Scully were the only ones who displayed no agitation. These preliminaries were conducted without words.

Scully threw open the door. "Well, come on," he said. Instantly a terrific wind caused the flame of the lamp to struggle at its wick, while a puff of black smoke sprang from the chimney-top. The stove was in mid-current of the blast, and its voice swelled to equal the roar of the storm. Some of the scarred and bedabbled cards were caught up from the floor and dashed helplessly against the farther wall. The men lowered their heads and plunged into the tempest as into a sea.

No snow was falling, but great whirls and clouds of flakes, swept up from the ground by the frantic winds, were streaming southward with the speed of bullets. The covered land was blue with the sheen of an unearthly satin, and there was no other hue save where, at the low, black railway station-which seemed incredibly distant-one light gleamed like a tiny jewel. As the men floundered into a thigh deep drift, it was known that the Swede was bawling out something. Scully went to him, put a hand on his shoulder and projected an ear. "What's that you say?" he shouted.

"I say," bawled the Swede again, "I won't stand much show against this gang. I know you'll all pitch on me."

Scully smote him reproachfully on the arm. "Tut, man!" he yelled. The wind tore the words from Scully's lips and scattered them far alee.

"You are all a gang of—" boomed the Swede, but the storm also seized the remainder of this sentence.

Immediately turning their backs upon the wind, the men had swung around a corner to the sheltered side of the hotel. It was the function of the little house to preserve here, amid this great devastation of snow, an irregular V-shape of heavily incrusted grass, which crackled beneath the feet. One could imagine the great drifts piled against the windward side. When the party reached the comparative peace of this spot it was found that the Swede was still bellowing.

"Oh, I know what kind of a thing this is! I know you'll all pitch on me. I can't lick you all!"

Scully turned upon him panther fashion. "You'll not have to whip all of us. You'll have to whip my son Johnnie. An' the man what troubles you durin' that time will have me to dale with."

The arrangements were swiftly made. The two men faced each other, obedient to the harsh commands of Scully, whose face, in the subtly luminous gloom, could be seen set in the austere impersonal lines that are pictured on the countenances of the Roman veterans. The Easterner's teeth were chattering, and he was hopping up and down like a mechanical toy. The cowboy stood rock-like.

The contestants had not stripped off any clothing. Each was in his ordinary attire. Their fists were up, and they eyed each other in a calm that had the elements of leonine cruelty in it.

During this pause, the Easterner's mind, like a film, took lasting impressions of three men-the iron-nerved master of the ceremony; the Swede, pale, motionless, terrible; and Johnnie, serene yet ferocious, brutish yet heroic. The entire prelude had in it a tragedy greater than the tragedy of action, and this aspect was accentuated by the long, mellow cry of the blizzard, as it sped the tumbling and wailing flakes into the black abyss of the south.

"Now!" said Scully.

The two combatants leaped forward and crashed together like bullocks. There was heard the cushioned sound of blows, and of a curse squeezing out from between the tight teeth of one.

As for the spectators, the Easterner's pent-up breath exploded from him with a pop of relief, absolute relief from the tension of the preliminaries. The cowboy bounded into the air with a yowl. Scully was immovable as from supreme amazement and fear at the fury of the fight which he himself had permitted and arranged.

For a time the encounter in the darkness was such a perplexity of flying arms that it presented no more detail than would a swiftly revolving wheel. Occasionally a face, as if illumined by a flash of light, would shine out, ghastly and marked with pink spots. A moment later, the men might have been known as shadows, if it were not for the involuntary utterance of oaths that came from them in whispers.

Suddenly a holocaust of warlike desire caught the cowboy, and he bolted forward with the speed of a broncho. "Go it, Johnnie! go it! Kill him! Kill him!"

Scully confronted him. "Kape back," he said; and by his glance the cowboy could tell that this man was Johnnie's father.

To the Easterner there was a monotony of unchangeable fighting that was an abomination. This confused mingling was eternal to his sense, which was concentrated in a longing for the end, the priceless end. Once the fighters lurched near him, and as he scrambled hastily backward he heard them breathe like men on the rack.

"Kill him, Johnnie! Kill him! Kill him! Kill him!" The cowboy's face was contorted like one of those agony masks in museums.

"Keep still," said Scully, icily.

Then there was a sudden loud grunt, incomplete, cut short, and Johnnie's body swung away from the Swede and fell with sickening heaviness to the grass. The cowboy was barely in time to prevent the mad Swede from flinging himself upon his prone adversary. "No, you don't," said the cowboy, interposing an arm. "Wait a second."

Scully was at his son's side. "Johnnie! Johnnie, me boy!" His voice had a quality of melancholy tenderness. "Johnnie! Can you go on with it?" He looked anxiously down into the bloody, pulpy face of his son.

There was a moment of silence, and then Johnnie answered in his ordinary voice, "Yes, I—it-yes."

Assisted by his father he struggled to his feet. "Wait a bit now till you git your wind," said the old man.

A few paces away the cowboy was lecturing the Swede. "No, you don't! Wait a second!"

The Easterner was plucking at Scully's sleeve. "Oh, this is enough," he pleaded. "This is enough! Let it go as it stands. This is enough!"

"Bill," said Scully, "git out of the road." The cowboy stepped aside. "Now." The combatants were actuated by a new caution as they advanced towards collision. They glared at each other, and then the Swede aimed a lightning blow that carried with it his entire weight. Johnnie was evidently half stupid from weakness, but he miraculously dodged, and his fist sent the over-balanced Swede sprawling.

The cowboy, Scully, and the Easterner burst into a cheer that was like a chorus of triumphant soldiery, but before its conclusion the Swede had scuffled agilely to his feet and come in berserk abandon at his foe. There was another perplexity of flying arms, and Johnnie's body again swung away and fell, even as a bundle might fall from a roof. The Swede instantly staggered to a little wind-waved tree and leaned upon it, breathing like an engine, while his savage and flame-lit eyes roamed from face to face as the men bent over Johnnie. There was a splendor of isolation in his situation at this time which the Easterner felt once when, lifting his eyes from the man on the ground, he beheld that mysterious and lonely figure, waiting.

"Arc you any good yet, Johnnie?" asked Scully in a broken voice.

The son gasped and opened his eyes languidly. After a moment he answered, "No—I ain't—any good-any-more." Then, from shame and bodily ill he began to weep, the tears furrowing down through the blood-stains on his face. "He was too-too-too heavy for me."

Scully straightened and addressed the waiting figure. "Stranger," he said, evenly, "it's all up with our side." Then his voice changed into that vibrant huskiness which is commonly the tone of the most simple and deadly announcements. "Johnnie is whipped."

Without replying, the victor moved off on the route to the front door of the hotel.

The cowboy was formulating new and un-spellable blasphemies. The Easterner was startled to find that they were out in a wind that seemed to come direct from the shadowed arctic floes. He heard again the wail of the snow as it was flung to its grave in the south. He knew now that all this time the cold had been sinking into him deeper and deeper, and he wondered that he had not perished. He felt indifferent to the condition of the vanquished man.

"Johnnie, can you walk?" asked Scully.

"Did I hurt-hurt him any?" asked the son.

"Can you walk, boy? Can you walk?"

Johnnie's voice was suddenly strong. There was a robust impatience in it. "I asked you whether I hurt him any!"

"Yes, yes, Johnnie," answered the cowboy, consolingly; "he's hurt a good deal."

They raised him from the ground, and as soon as he was on his feet he went tottering off, re-buffing all attempts at assistance. When the party rounded the corner they were fairly blinded by the pelting of the snow. It burned their faces like fire. The cowboy carried Johnnie through the drift to the door. As they entered some cards again rose from the floor and beat against the wall.

The Easterner rushed to the stove. He was so profoundly chilled that he almost dared to embrace the glowing iron. The Swede was not in the room. Johnnie sank into a chair, and, folding his arms on his knees, buried his face in them. Scully, warming one foot and then the other at a rim of the stove, muttered to himself with Celtic mournfulness. The cowboy had removed his fur cap, and with a dazed and rueful air he was running one hand through his tousled locks. From overhead they could hear the creaking of boards, as the Swede tramped here and there in his room.

The sad quiet was broken by the sudden flinging open of a door that led towards the kitchen. It was instantly followed by an inrush of women. They precipitated themselves upon Johnnie amid a chorus of lamentation. Before they carried their prey off to the kitchen, there to be bathed and harangued with that mixture of sympathy and abuse which is a feat of their sex, the mother straightened herself and fixed old Scully with an eye of stern reproach. "Shame be upon you, Patrick Scully!" she cried. "Your own son, too. Shame be upon you!"

"There, now! Be quiet, now!" said the old man, weakly.

"Shame be upon you, Patrick Scully!" The girls, rallying to this slogan, sniffed disdainfully in the direction of those trembling accomplices, the cowboy and the Easterner. Presently they bore Johnnie away, and left the three men to dismal reflection.

"I'd like to fight this here Dutchman myself," said the cowboy, breaking a long silence.

Scully wagged his head sadly. "No, that wouldn't do. It wouldn't be right. It wouldn't be right."

"Well, why wouldn't it?" argued the cowboy. "I don't see no harm in it."

"No," answered Scully, with mournful heroism. "It wouldn't be right. It was Johnnie's fight, and now we mustn't whip the man just because he whipped Johnnie."

"Yes, that's true enough," said the cowboy; "but-he better not get fresh with me, because I couldn't stand no more of it."

"You'll not say a word to him," commanded Scully, and even then they heard the tread of the Swede on the stairs. His entrance was made theatric. He swept the door back with a bang and swaggered to the middle of the room. No one looked at him. "Well," he cried, insolently, at Scully, "I s'pose you'll tell me now how much I owe you?"

The old man remained stolid. "You don't owe me nothin'."

"Huh!" said the Swede, "huh! Don't owe 'im nothin'."

The cowboy addressed the Swede. "Stranger, I don't see how you come to be so gay around here."

Old Scully was instantly alert. "Stop!" he shouted, holding his hand forth, fingers upward. "Bill, you shut up!"

The cowboy spat carelessly into the sawdust box. "I didn't say a word, did I?" he asked.

"Mr. Scully," called the Swede, "how much do I owe you?" It was seen that he was attired for departure, and that he had his valise in his hand.

"You don't owe me nothin'," repeated Scully in his same imperturbable way.

"Huh!" said the Swede. "I guess you're right. I guess if it was any way at all, you'd owe me somethin'. That's what I guess." He turned to the cowboy. "'Kill him! Kill him! Kill him!'" he mimicked, and then guffawed victoriously. "'Kill him!'" He was convulsed with ironical humor.

But he might have been jeering the dead. The three men were immovable and silent, staring with glassy eyes at the stove.

The Swede opened the door and passed into the storm, giving one derisive glance backward at the still group.

As soon as the door was closed, Scully and the cowboy leaped to their feet and began to curse. They trampled to and fro, waving their arms and smashing into the air with their fists. "Oh, but that was a hard minute!" wailed Scully. "That was a hard minute! Him there leerin' and scoffin'! One bang at his nose was worth forty dollars to me that minute! How did you stand it, Bill?"

"How did I stand it?" cried the cowboy in a quivering voice. "How did I stand it? Oh!"

The old man burst into sudden brogue. "I'd loike to take that Swade," he wailed, "and hould 'im down on a shtone flure and bate 'im to a jelly wid a shtick!"

The cowboy groaned in sympathy. "I'd like to git him by the neck and ha-ammer him " — he brought his hand down on a chair with a noise like a pistol-shot —"hammer that there Dutchman until he couldn't tell himself from a dead coyote!"

"I'd bate 'im until he —"

"I'd show *him* some things —"

And then together they raised a yearning, fanatic cry —"Oh-o-oh! if we only could —"

"Yes!"

"Yes!"

"And then I'd —"

"O-o-oh!"

The Swede, tightly gripping his valise, tacked across the face of the storm as if he carried sails. He was following a line of little naked, gasping trees, which he knew must mark the way of the road. His face, fresh from the pounding of Johnnie's fists, felt more pleasure than pain in the wind and the driving snow. A number of square shapes loomed upon him finally, and he knew them as the houses of the main body of the town. He found a street and made travel along it, leaning heavily upon the wind whenever, at a corner, a terrific blast caught him.

He might have been in a deserted village. We picture the world as thick with conquering and elate humanity, but here, with the bugles of the tempest pealing, it was hard to imagine a peopled earth. One viewed the existence of man then as a marvel, and conceded a glamour of wonder to these lice which were caused to cling to a whirling, fire-smote, ice-locked, disease-stricken, space-lost bulb. The conceit of man was explained by this storm to be the very engine of life. One was a coxcomb not to die in it. However, the Swede found a saloon.

In front of it an indomitable red light was burning, and the snow-flakes were made blood color as they flew through the circumscribed territory of the lamp's shining. The Swede pushed open the door of the saloon and entered. A sanded expanse was before him, and at the end of it four men sat about a table drinking. Down one side of the room extended a radiant bar, and its guardian was leaning upon his elbows listening to the talk of the men at the table. The Swede dropped his valise upon the floor, and, smiling fraternally upon the barkeeper, said, "Gimme some whiskey, will you?" The man placed a bottle, a whiskey-glass, and a glass of ice-thick water upon the bar. The Swede poured himself an abnormal portion of whiskey and drank it in three gulps. "Pretty bad night," remarked the bartender, indifferently. He was making the pretension of blindness which is usually a distinction of his class; but it could have been seen that he was furtively studying the half-erased blood-stains on the face of the Swede. "Bad night," he said again.

"Oh, it's good enough for me," replied the Swede, hardily, as he poured himself some more whiskey. The barkeeper took his coin and maneuvered it through its reception by the highly nickelled cash-machine. A bell rang; a card labelled "20 cts." had appeared.

"No," continued the Swede, "this isn't too bad weather. It's good enough for me."

"So?" murmured the barkeeper, languidly.

The copious drams made the Swede's eyes swim, and he breathed a trifle heavier. "Yes, I like this weather. I like it. It suits me." It was apparently his design to impart a deep significance to these words.

"So?" murmured the bartender again. He turned to gaze dreamily at the scroll-like birds and bird-like scrolls which had been drawn with soap upon the mirrors back of the bar.

"Well, I guess I'll take another drink," said the Swede, presently. "Have something?"

"No, thanks; I'm not drinkin'," answered the bartender. Afterwards he asked, "How did you hurt your face?"

The Swede immediately began to boast loudly. "Why, in a fight. I thumped the soul out of a man down here at Scully's hotel."

The interest of the four men at the table was at last aroused.

"Who was it?" said one.

"Johnnie Scully," blustered the Swede. "Son of the man what runs it. He will be pretty near dead for some weeks, I can tell you. I made a nice thing of him, I did. He couldn't get up. They carried him in the house. Have a drink?"

Instantly the men in some subtle way incased themselves in reserve. "No, thanks," said one. The group was of curious formation. Two were prominent local business men; one was the district-attorney; and one was a professional gambler of the kind known as "square." But a scrutiny of the group would not have enabled an observer to pick the gambler from the men of more reputable pursuits. He was, in fact, a man so delicate in manner, when among people of fair class, and so judicious in his choice of victims, that in the strictly masculine part of the town's life he had come to be explicitly trusted and admired. People called him a thoroughbred. The fear and contempt with which his craft was regarded was undoubtedly the reason that his quiet dignity shone conspicuous above the quiet dignity of men who might be merely hatters, billiard markers, or grocery-clerks. Beyond an occasional unwary traveller, who came by rail, this gambler was supposed to prey solely upon reckless and senile farmers, who, when flush with good crops, drove into town in all the pride and confidence of an absolutely invulnerable stupidity. Hearing at times in circuitous fashion of the despoilment of such a farmer, the important men of Romper invariably laughed in contempt of the victim, and, if they thought of the wolf at all, it was with a kind of pride at the knowledge that he would never dare think of attacking their wisdom and courage. Besides, it was popular that this gambler had a real wife and two real children in a neat cottage in a suburb, where he led an exemplary home life; and when any one even suggested a discrepancy in his character, the crowd immediately vociferated descriptions of this virtuous family circle. Then men who led exemplary home lives, and men who did not lead exemplary home lives, all subsided in a bunch, remarking that there was nothing more to be said.

However, when a restriction was placed upon him-as, for instance, when a strong clique of members of the new Pollywog Club refused to permit him, even as a spectator, to appear in the rooms of the organization-the candor and gentleness with which he accepted the judgment disarmed many of his foes and made his friends more desperately partisan. He invariably distinguished between himself and a respectable Romper man so quickly and frankly that his manner actually appeared to be a continual broadcast compliment.

And one must not forget to declare the fundamental fact of his entire position in Romper. It is irrefutable that in all affairs outside of his business, in all matters that occur eternally and commonly between man and man, this thieving card-player was so generous, so just, so moral, that, in a contest, he could have put to flight the consciences of nine-tenths of the citizens of Romper.

And so it happened that he was seated in this saloon with the two prominent local merchants and the district-attorney.

The Swede continued to drink raw whiskey, meanwhile babbling at the barkeeper and trying to induce him to indulge in potations. "Come on. Have a drink. Come on. What-no? Well, have a little one, then. By gawd, I've whipped a man to-night, and I want to celebrate. I whipped him good, too. Gentlemen," the Swede cried to the men at the table, "have a drink?"

"Ssh!" said the barkeeper.

The group at the table, although furtively attentive, had been pretending to be deep in talk, but now a man lifted his eyes towards the Swede and said, shortly, "Thanks. We don't want any more."

At this reply the Swede ruffled out his chest like a rooster. "Well," he exploded, "it seems I can't get anybody to drink with me in this town. Seems so, don't it? Well!"

"Ssh!" said the barkeeper.

"Say," snarled the Swede, "don't you try to shut me up. I won't have it. I'm a gentleman, and I want people to drink with me. And I want 'em to drink with me now. *Now* —do you understand?" He rapped the bar with his knuckles.

Years of experience had calloused the bartender. He merely grew sulky. "I hear you," he answered.

"Well," cried the Swede, "listen hard then. See those men over there? Well, they're going to drink with me, and don't you forget it. Now you watch."

"Hi!" yelled the barkeeper, "this won't do!"

"Why won't it?" demanded the Swede. He stalked over to the table, and by chance laid his hand upon the shoulder of the gambler. "How about this?" he asked, wrathfully. "I asked you to drink with me."

The gambler simply twisted his head and spoke over his shoulder. "My friend, I don't know you."

"Oh, hell!" answered the Swede, "come and have a drink."

"Now, my boy," advised the gambler, kindly, "take your hand off my shoulder and go 'way and mind your own business." He was a little, slim man, and it seemed strange to hear him use this tone of heroic patronage to the burly Swede. The other men at the table said nothing.

"What! You won't drink with me, you little dude? I'll make you then! I'll make you!" The Swede had grasped the gambler frenziedly at the throat, and was dragging him from his chair. The other men sprang up. The barkeeper dashed around the corner of his bar. There was a great tumult, and then was seen a long blade in the hand of the gambler. It shot forward, and a human body, this citadel of virtue, wisdom, power, was pierced as easily as if it had been a melon. The Swede fell with a cry of supreme astonishment.

The prominent merchants and the district attorney must have at once tumbled out of the place backward. The bartender found himself hanging limply to the arm of a chair and gazing into the eyes of a murderer.

"Henry," said the latter, as he wiped his knife on one of the towels that hung beneath the bar-rail, "you tell 'em where to find me. I'll be home, waiting for 'em." Then he vanished. A moment afterwards the barkeeper was in the street dinning through the storm for help, and, moreover, companionship.

The corpse of the Swede, alone in the saloon, had its eyes fixed upon a dreadful legend that dwelt atop of the cash-machine: "This registers the amount of your purchase."

198

IX

Months later, the cowboy was frying pork over the stove of a little ranch near the Dakota line, when there was a quick thud of hoofs outside, and presently the Easterner entered with the letters and the papers.

"Well," said the Easterner at once, "the chap that killed the Swede has got three years. Wasn't much, was it?"

"He has? Three years?" The cowboy poised his pan of pork, while he ruminated upon the news. "Three years. That ain't much."

"No. It was a light sentence," replied the Easterner as he unbuckled his spurs. "Seems there was a good deal of sympathy for him in Romper."

"If the bartender had been any good," observed the cowboy, thoughtfully, "he would have gone in and cracked that there Dutchman on the head with a bottle in the beginnin' of it and stopped all this here murderin'."

"Yes, a thousand things might have happened," said the Easterner, tartly.

The cowboy returned his pan of pork to the fire, but his philosophy continued. "It's funny, ain't it? If he hadn't said Johnnie was cheatin' he'd be alive this minute. He was an awful fool. Game played for fun, too. Not for money. I believe he was crazy."

"I feel sorry for that gambler," said the Easterner.

"Oh, so do I," said the cowboy. "He don't deserve none of it for killin' who he did."

"The Swede might not have been killed if everything had been square."

"Might not have been killed?" exclaimed the cowboy. "Everythin' square? Why, when he said that Johnnie was cheatin' and acted like such a jackass? And then in the saloon he fairly walked up to git hurt?" With these arguments the cowboy browbeat the Easterner and reduced him to rage.

"You're a fool!" cried the Easterner, viciously. "You're a bigger jackass than the Swede by a million majority. Now let me tell you one thing. Let me tell you something. Listen! Johnnie *was* cheating!"

"'Johnnie,'" said the cowboy, blankly. There was a minute of silence, and then he said, robustly, "Why, no. The game was only for fun."

"Fun or not," said the Easterner, "Johnnie was cheating. I saw him. I know it. I saw him. And I refused to stand up and be a man. I let the Swede fight it out alone. And you-you were simply puffing around the place and wanting to fight. And then old Scully himself! We are all in it! This poor gambler isn't even a noun. He is kind of an adverb. Every sin is the result of a collaboration. We, five of us, have collaborated in the murder of this Swede. Usually there are from a dozen to forty women really involved in every murder, but in this case it seems to be only five men-you, I, Johnnie, old Scully, and that fool of an unfortunate gambler came merely as a culmination, the apex of a human movement, and gets all the punishment."

The cowboy, injured and rebellious, cried out blindly into this fog of mysterious theory: "Well, I didn't do anythin', did I?"

His New Mittens

Little Horace was walking home from school, brilliantly decorated by a pair of new red mittens. A number of boys were snowballing gleefully in a field. They hailed him. "Come on, Horace! We're having a battle."

Horace was sad. "No," he said, "I can't. I've got to go home." At noon his mother had admonished him: "Now, Horace, you come straight home as soon as school is out. Do you hear? And don't you get them nice new mittens all wet, either. Do you hear?" Also his aunt had said: "I declare, Emily, it's a shame the way you allow that child to ruin his things." She had meant mittens. To his mother, Horace had dutifully replied, "Yes'm." But he now loitered in the vicinity of the group of uproarious boys, who were yelling like hawks as the white balls flew.

Some of them immediately analyzed this extraordinary hesitancy. "Hah!" they paused to scoff, "afraid of your new mittens, ain't you?" Some smaller boys, who were not yet so wise in discerning motives, applauded this attack with unreasonable vehemence. "A-fray-ed of his mit-tens! A-fray-ed of his mit-tens." They sang these lines to cruel and monotonous music which is as old perhaps as American childhood, and which it is the privilege of the emancipated adult to completely forget. "Afray-ed of his mit-tens!"

Horace cast a tortured glance towards his playmates, and then dropped his eyes to the snow at his feet. Presently he turned to the trunk of one of the great maple-trees that lined the curb. He made a pretence of closely examining the rough and virile bark. To his mind, this familiar street of Whilomville seemed to grow dark in the thick shadow of shame. The trees and the houses were now palled in purple.

"A-fray-ed of his mit-tens!" The terrible music had in it a meaning from the moonlit war-drums of chanting cannibals.

At last Horace, with supreme effort, raised his head. "'Tain't them I care about," he said, gruffly. "I've got to go home. That's all."

Whereupon each boy held his left forefinger as if it were a pencil and began to sharpen it derisively with his right forefinger. They came closer, and sang like a trained chorus, "A-fray-ed of his mittens!"

When he raised his voice to deny the charge it was simply lost in the screams of the mob. He was alone, fronting all the traditions of boyhood held before him by inexorable representatives. To such a low state had he fallen that one lad, a mere baby, outflanked him and then struck him in the cheek with a heavy snowball. The act was acclaimed with loud jeers. Horace turned to dart at his assailant, but there was an immediate demonstration on the other flank, and he found himself obliged to keep his face towards the hilarious crew of tormentors. The baby retreated in safety to the rear of the crowd, where he was received with fulsome compliments upon his daring. Horace retreated slowly up the walk. He continually tried to make them heed him, but the only sound was the chant, "A-fray-ed of his mit-tens!" In this desperate withdrawal the beset and haggard boy suffered more than is the common lot of man.

Being a boy himself, he did not understand boys at all. He had, of course, the dismal conviction that they were going to dog him to his grave. But near the corner of the field they suddenly seemed to forget all about it. Indeed, they possessed only the malevolence of so many flitter-headed sparrows. The interest had swung capriciously to some other matter. In a moment they were off in the field again, carousing amid the snow. Some authoritative boy had probably said, "Aw, come on!"

As the pursuit ceased, Horace ceased his retreat. He spent some time in what was evidently an attempt to adjust his self respect, and then began to wander furtively down towards the group. He, too, had undergone an important change. Perhaps his sharp agony was only as durable as the malevolence of the others. In this boyish life obedience to some unformulated creed of manners was enforced with capricious but merciless rigor. However, they were, after all, his comrades, his friends.

They did not heed his return. They were engaged in an altercation. It had evidently been planned that this battle was between Indians and soldiers. The smaller and weaker boys had been induced to appear as Indians in the initial skirmish, but they were now very sick of it, and were reluctantly but steadfastly, affirming their desire for a change of caste. The larger boys had all won great distinction, devastating Indians materially, and they wished the war to go on as planned. They explained vociferously that it was proper for the soldiers always to thrash the Indians. The little boys did not pretend to deny the truth of this argument; they confined themselves to the simple statement that, in that case, they wished to be soldiers. Each little boy willingly appealed to the others to remain Indians, but as for himself he reiterated his desire to enlist as a soldier. The larger boys were in despair over this dearth of enthusiasm in the small Indians. They alternately wheedled and bullied, but they could not persuade the little boys, who were really suffering dreadful humiliation rather than submit to another onslaught of soldiers. They were called all the baby names that had the power of stinging deep into their pride, but they remained firm.

Then a formidable lad, a leader of reputation, one who could whip many boys that wore long trousers, suddenly blew out his cheeks and shouted, "Well, all right then. I'll be an Indian myself. Now." The little boys greeted with cheers this addition to their wearied ranks, and seemed then content. But matters were not mended in the least, because all of the personal following of the formidable lad, with the addition of every outsider, spontaneously forsook the flag and declared themselves Indians. There were now no soldiers. The Indians had carried everything unanimously. The formidable lad used his influence, but his influence could not shake the loyalty of his friends, who refused to fight under any colors but his colors.

Plainly there was nothing for it but to coerce the little ones. The formidable lad again became a soldier, and then graciously permitted to join him all the real fighting strength of the crowd, leaving behind a most forlorn band of little Indians. Then the soldiers attacked the Indians, exhorting them to opposition at the same time.

The Indians at first adopted a policy of hurried surrender, but this had no success, as none of the surrenders were accepted. They then turned to flee, bawling out protests. The ferocious soldiers pursued them amid shouts. The battle widened, developing all manner of marvellous detail.

Horace had turned towards home several times, but, as a matter of fact, this scene held him in a spell. It was fascinating beyond anything which the grown man understands. He had always in the back of his head a sense of guilt, even a sense of impending punishment for disobedience, but they could not weigh with the delirium of this snow-battle.

One of the raiding soldiers, espying Horace, called out in passing, "A-fray-ed of his mit-tens!" Horace flinched at this renewal, and the other lad paused to taunt him again. Horace scooped some snow, moulded it into a ball, and flung it at the other. "Ho!" cried the boy, "you're an Indian, are you? Hey, fellers, here's an Indian that ain't been killed yet." He and Horace engaged in a duel in which both were in such haste to mould snowballs that they had little time for aiming.

Horace once struck his opponent squarely in the chest. "Hey," he shouted, "you're dead. You can't fight any more, Pete. I killed you. You're dead."

The other boy flushed red, but he continued frantically to make ammunition. "You never touched me!" he retorted, glowering. "You never touched me! Where, now?" he added, defiantly. "Where did you hit me?"

"On the coat! Right on your breast! You can't fight any more! You're dead!"

"You never!"

"I did, too! Hey, fellers, ain't he dead? I hit 'im square!"

"He never!"

Nobody had seen the affair, but some of the boys took sides in absolute accordance with their friendship for one of the concerned parties. Horace's opponent went about contending, "He never touched me! He never came near me! He never came near me!"

The formidable leader now came forward and accosted Horace. "What was you? An Indian? Well, then, you're dead-that's all. He hit you. I saw him."

"Me?" shrieked Horace. "He never came within a mile of me — —"

At that moment he heard his name called in a certain familiar tune of two notes, with the last note shrill and prolonged. He looked towards the sidewalk, and saw his mother standing there in her widow's weeds, with two brown paper parcels under her arm. A silence had fallen upon all the boys. Horace moved slowly towards his mother. She did not seem to note his approach; she was gazing austerely off through the naked branches of the maples where two crimson sunset bars lay on the deep blue sky.

At a distance of ten paces Horace made a desperate venture. "Oh, ma," he whined, "can't I stay out for a while?"

"No," she answered solemnly, "you come with me." Horace knew that profile; it was the inexorable profile. But he continued to plead, because it was not beyond his mind that a great show of suffering now might diminish his suffering later.

He did not dare to look back at his playmates. It was already a public scandal that he could not stay out as late as other boys, and he could imagine his standing now that he had been again dragged off by his mother in sight of the whole world. He was a profoundly miserable human being.

Aunt Martha opened the door for them. Light streamed about her straight skirt. "Oh," she said, "so you found him on the road, eh? Well, I declare! It was about time!"

Horace slunk into the kitchen. The stove, straddling out on its four iron legs, was gently humming. Aunt Martha had evidently just lighted the lamp, for she went to it and began to twist the wick experimentally.

"Now," said the mother, "let's see them mittens."

Horace's chin sank. The aspiration of the criminal, the passionate desire for an asylum from retribution, from justice, was aflame in his heart. "I —I —don't —don't know where they are." he gasped finally, as he passed his hand over his pockets.

"Horace," intoned his mother, "you are tellin' me a story!"

"'Tain't a story," he answered, just above his breath. He looked like a sheep-stealer.

His mother held him by the arm, and began to search his pockets. Almost at once she was able to bring forth a pair of very wet mittens. "Well, I declare!" cried Aunt Martha. The two women went close to the lamp, and minutely examined the mittens, turning them over and over.

Afterwards, when Horace looked up, his mother's sad-lined, homely face was turned towards him. He burst into tears.

His mother drew a chair near the stove. "Just you sit there now, until I tell you to git off." He sidled meekly into the chair. His mother and his aunt went briskly about the business of preparing supper. They did not display a knowledge of his existence; they carried an effect of oblivion so far that they even did not speak to each other. Presently they went into the dining and living room; Horace could hear the dishes rattling. His Aunt Martha brought a plate of food, placed it on a chair near him, and went away without a word.

Horace instantly decided that he would not touch a morsel of the food. He had often used this ruse in dealing with his mother. He did not know why it brought her to terms, but certainly it sometimes did.

The mother looked up when the aunt returned to the other room. "Is he eatin' his supper?" she asked.

The maiden aunt, fortified in ignorance, gazed with pity and contempt upon this interest. "Well, now, Emily, how do I know?" she queried. "Was I goin' to stand over 'im? Of all the worryin' you do about that child! It's a shame the way you're bringin' up that child."

"Well, he ought to eat somethin'. It won't do fer him to go without eatin'," the mother retorted, weakly.

Aunt Martha, profoundly scorning the policy of concession which these words meant, uttered a long, contemptuous sigh.

Alone in the kitchen, Horace stared with sombre eyes at the plate of food. For a long time he betrayed no sign of yielding. His mood was adamantine. He was resolved not to sell his vengeance for bread, cold ham, and a pickle, and yet it must be known that the sight of them affected him powerfully. The pickle in particular was notable for its seductive charm. He surveyed it darkly.

But at last, unable to longer endure his state, his attitude in the presence of the pickle, he put out an inquisitive finger and touched it, and it was cool and green and plump. Then a full conception of the cruel woe of his situation swept upon him suddenly, and his eyes filled with tears, which began to move down his cheeks. He sniffled. His heart was black with hatred. He painted in his mind scenes of deadly retribution. His mother would be taught that he was not one to endure persecution meekly, without raising an arm in his defence. And so his dreams were of a slaughter of feelings, and near the end of them his mother was pictured as coming, bowed with pain, to his feet. Weeping, she implored his charity. Would he forgive her? No; his once tender heart had been turned to stone by her injustice. He could not forgive her. She must pay the inexorable penalty.

The first item in this horrible plan was the refusal of the food. This he knew by experience would work havoc in his mother's heart. And so he grimly waited.

But suddenly it occurred to him that the first part of his revenge was in danger of failing. The thought struck him that his mother might not capitulate in the usual way. According to his recollection, the time was more than due when she should come in, worried, sadly affectionate, and ask him if he was ill. It had then been his custom to hint in a resigned voice that he was the victim of secret disease, but that he preferred to suffer in silence and alone. If she was obdurate in her anxiety, he always asked her in a gloomy, low voice to go away and leave him to suffer in silence and alone in the darkness without food. He had known this maneuvering to result even in pie.

But what was the meaning of the long pause and the stillness? Had his old and valued ruse betrayed him? As the truth sank into his mind, he supremely loathed life, the world, his mother. Her heart was beating back the besiegers; he was a defeated child.

He wept for a time before deciding upon the final stroke. He would run away. In a remote corner of the world he would become some sort of bloody-handed person driven to a life of crime by the barbarity of his mother. She should never know his fate. He would torture her for years with doubts and doubts, and drive her implacably to a repentant grave. Nor would Aunt Martha escape. Some day, a century hence, when his mother was dead, he would write to his Aunt Martha, and point out her part in the blighting of his life. For one blow against him now he would, in time, deal back a thousand-aye, ten thousand.

He arose and took his coat and cap. As he moved stealthily towards the door he cast a glance backward at the pickle. He was tempted to take it, but he knew that if he left the plate inviolate his mother would feel even worse.

A blue snow was falling. People, bowed forward, were moving briskly along the walks. The electric lamps hummed amid showers of flakes. As Horace emerged from the kitchen, a shrill squall drove the flakes around the corner of the house. He cowered away from it, and its violence illumined his mind vaguely in new directions. He deliberated upon a choice of remote corners of the globe. He found that he had no plans which were definite enough in a geographical way, but without much loss of time he decided upon California. He moved briskly as far as his mother's front gate on the road to California. He was off at last. His success was a trifle dreadful; his throat choked.

But at the gate he paused. He did not know if his journey to California would be shorter if he went down Niagara Avenue or off through Hogan Street. As the storm was very cold and the point was very important, he decided to withdraw for reflection to the wood-shed. He entered the dark shanty, and took seat upon the old chopping-block upon which he was supposed to perform for a few minutes every afternoon when he returned from school. The wind screamed and shouted at the loose boards, and there was a rift of snow on the floor to leeward of a crack.

Here the idea of starting for California on such a night departed from his mind, leaving him ruminating miserably upon his martyrdom. He saw nothing for it but to sleep all night in the wood-shed and start for California in the morning bright and early. Thinking of his bed, he kicked over the floor and found that the innumerable chips were all frozen tightly, bedded in ice.

Later he viewed with joy some signs of excitement in the house. The flare of a lamp moved rapidly from window to window. Then the kitchen door slammed loudly and a shawled figure sped towards the gate. At last he was making them feel his power. The shivering child's face was lit with saturnine glee as in the darkness of the wood-shed he gloated over the evidences of consternation in his home. The shawled figure had been his Aunt Martha dashing with the alarm to the neighbors.

The cold of the wood-shed was tormenting him. He endured only because of the terror he was causing. But then it occurred to him that, if they instituted a search for him, they would probably examine the wood-shed. He knew that it would not be manful to be caught so soon. He was not positive now that he was going to remain away forever, but at any rate he was bound to inflict some more damage before allowing himself to be captured. If he merely succeeded in making his mother angry, she would thrash him on sight. He must prolong the time in order to be safe. If he held out properly, he was sure of a welcome of love, even though he should drip with crimes.

Evidently the storm had increased, for when he went out it swung him violently with its rough and merciless strength. Panting, stung, half blinded with the driving flakes, he was now a waif, exiled, friendless, and poor. With a bursting heart, he thought of his home and his mother. To his forlorn vision they were as far away as heaven.

IV

Horace was undergoing changes of feeling so rapidly that he was merely moved hither and then thither like a kite. He was now aghast at the merciless ferocity of his mother. It was she who had thrust him into this wild storm, and she was perfectly indifferent to his fate, perfectly indifferent. The forlorn wanderer could no longer weep. The strong sobs caught at his throat, making his breath come in short, quick snuffles. All in him was conquered save the enigmatical childish ideal of form, manner. This principle still held out, and it was the only thing between him and submission. When he surrendered, he must surrender in a way that deferred to the undefined code. He longed simply to go to the kitchen and stumble in, but his unfathomable sense of fitness forbade him.

Presently he found himself at the head of Niagara Avenue, staring through the snow into the blazing windows of Stickney's butcher-shop. Stickney was the family butcher, not so much because of a superiority to other Whilomville butchers as because he lived next door and had been an intimate friend of the father of Horace. Rows of glowing pigs hung head downward back of the tables, which bore huge pieces of red beef. Clumps of attenuated turkeys were suspended here and there. Stickney, hale and smiling, was bantering with a woman in a cloak, who, with a monster basket on her arm, was dickering for eight cents' worth of some thing. Horace watched them through a crusted pane. When the woman came out and passed him, he went towards the door. He touched the latch with his finger, but withdrew again suddenly to the sidewalk. Inside Stickney was whistling cheerily and assorting his knives.

Finally Horace went desperately forward, opened the door, and entered the shop. His head hung low. Stickney stopped whistling. "Hello, young man," he cried, "what brings you here?"

Horace halted, but said nothing. He swung one foot to and fro over the saw-dust floor.

Stickney had placed his two fat hands palms downward and wide apart on the table, in the attitude of a butcher facing a customer, but now he straightened.

"Here," he said, "what's wrong? What's wrong, kid?"

"Nothin'," answered Horace, huskily. He labored for a moment with something in his throat, and afterwards added, "O'ny — —I've — —I've run away, and —"

"Run away!" shouted Stickney. "Run away from what? Who?"

"From — —home," answered Horace. "I don't like it there any more. I — —" He had arranged an oration to win the sympathy of the butcher; he had prepared a table setting forth the merits of his case in the most logical fashion, but it was as if the wind had been knocked out of his mind. "I've run away. I — —"

Stickney reached an enormous hand over the array of beef, and firmly grappled the emigrant. Then he swung himself to Horace's side. His face was stretched with laughter, and he playfully shook his prisoner. "Come — —come — —come. What dashed nonsense is this? Run away, hey? Run away?" Whereupon the child's long-tried spirit found vent in howls.

"Come, come," said Stickney, busily. "Never mind now, never mind. You just come along with me. It'll be all right. I'll fix it. Never you mind."

Five minutes later the butcher, with a great ulster over his apron, was leading the boy homeward.

At the very threshold, Horace raised his last flag of pride. "No — —no," he sobbed. "I don't want to. I don't want to go in there." He braced his foot against the step and made a very respectable resistance.

"Now, Horace," cried the butcher. He thrust open the door with a bang. "Hello there!" Across the dark kitchen the door to the living-room opened and Aunt Martha appeared. "You've found him!" she screamed.

"We've come to make a call," roared the butcher. At the entrance to the living-room a silence fell upon them all. Upon a couch Horace saw his mother lying limp, pale as death, her eyes gleaming with pain. There was an electric pause before she swung a waxen hand towards Horace. "My child," she murmured, tremulously. Whereupon the sinister person addressed, with a prolonged wail of grief and joy, ran to her with speed. "Mam-ma! Mam-ma! Oh, mam-ma!" She was not able to speak in a known tongue as she folded him in her weak arms.

Aunt Martha turned defiantly upon the butcher because her face betrayed her. She was crying. She made a gesture half military, half feminine. "Won't you have a glass of our root-beer, Mr. Stickney? We make it ourselves."

Whilomville Stories

I
The Angel Child

I

ALTHOUGH Whilomville was in no sense a summer resort, the advent of the warm season meant much to it, for then came visitors from the city-people of considerable confidence-alighting upon their country cousins. Moreover, many citizens who could afford to do so escaped at this time to the sea-side. The town, with the commercial life quite taken out of it, drawled and drowsed through long months, during which nothing was worse than the white dust which arose behind every vehicle at blinding noon, and nothing was finer than the cool sheen of the hose sprays over the cropped lawns under the many maples in the twilight.

One summer the Trescotts had a visitation. Mrs. Trescott owned a cousin who was a painter of high degree. I had almost said that he was of national reputation, but, come to think of it, it is better to say that almost everybody in the United States who knew about art and its travail knew about him. He had picked out a wife, and naturally, looking at him, one wondered how he had done it. She was quick, beautiful, imperious, while he was quiet, slow, and misty. She was a veritable queen of health, while he, apparently, was of a most brittle constitution. When he played tennis, particularly, he looked every minute as if he were going to break.

They lived in New York, in awesome apartments wherein Japan and Persia, and indeed all the world, confounded the observer. At the end was a cathedral-like studio. They had one child. Perhaps it would be better to say that they had one CHILD. It was a girl. When she came to Whilomville with her parents, it was patent that she had an inexhaustible store of white frocks, and that her voice was high and commanding. These things the town knew quickly. Other things it was doomed to discover by a process.

Her effect upon the children of the Trescott neighborhood was singular. They at first feared, then admired, then embraced. In two days she was a Begum. All day long her voice could be heard directing, drilling, and compelling those free-born children; and to say that they felt oppression would be wrong, for they really fought for records of loyal obedience.

All went well until one day was her birthday.

On the morning of this day she walked out into the Trescott garden and said to her father, confidently, "Papa, give me some money, because this is my birthday."

He looked dreamily up from his easel. "Your birthday?" he murmured. Her envisioned father was never energetic enough to be irritable unless some one broke through into that place where he lived with the desires of his life. But neither wife nor child ever heeded or even understood the temperamental values, and so some part of him had grown hardened to their inroads. "Money?" he said. "Here." He handed her a five-dollar bill. It was that he did not at all understand the nature of a five-dollar bill. He was deaf to it. He had it; he gave it; that was all.

She sallied forth to a waiting people-Jimmie Trescott, Dan Earl, Ella Earl, the Margate twins, the three Phelps children, and others. "I've got some pennies now," she cried, waving the bill, "and I am going to buy some candy." They were deeply stirred by this announcement. Most children are penniless three hundred days in the year, and to another possessing five pennies they pay deference. To little Cora waving a bright green note these children paid heathenish homage. In some disorder they thronged after her to a small shop on Bridge Street hill. First of all came ice-cream. Seated in the comic little back parlor, they clamored shrilly over plates of various flavors, and the shopkeeper marvelled that cream could vanish so quickly down throats that seemed wide open, always, for the making of excited screams.

These children represented the families of most excellent people. They were all born in whatever purple there was to be had in the vicinity of Whilomville. The Margate twins, for example, were out-and-out prize-winners. With their long golden curls and their countenances of similar vacuity, they shone upon the front bench of all Sunday-school functions, hand in hand, while their uplifted mother felt about her the envy of a hundred other parents, and less heavenly children scoffed from near the door.

Then there was little Dan Earl, probably the nicest boy in the world, gentle, fine-grained, obedient to the point where he obeyed anybody. Jimmie Trescott himself was, indeed, the only child who was at all versed in villany, but in these particular days he was on his very good behavior. As a matter of fact, he was in love. The beauty of his regal little cousin had stolen his manly heart.

Yes, they were all most excellent children, but, loosened upon this candy-shop with five dollars, they resembled, in a tiny way, drunken revelling soldiers within the walls of a stormed city. Upon the heels of ice-cream and cake came chocolate mice, butter-scotch, "everlastings," chocolate cigars, taffy-on-a-stick, taffy-on-a-slate-pencil, and many semi-transparent devices resembling lions, tigers, elephants, horses, cats, dogs, cows, sheep, tables, chairs, engines (both railway and for the fighting of fire), soldiers, fine ladies, odd-looking men, clocks, watches, revolvers, rabbits, and bedsteads. A cent was the price of a single wonder.

Some of the children, going quite daft, soon had thought to make fight over the spoils, but their queen ruled with an iron grip. Her first inspiration was to satisfy her own fancies, but as soon as that was done she mingled prodigality with a fine justice, dividing, balancing, bestowing, and sometimes taking away from somebody even that which he had.

It was an orgy. In thirty-five minutes those respectable children looked as if they had been dragged at the tail of a chariot. The sacred Margate twins, blinking and grunting, wished to take seat upon the floor, and even the most durable Jimmie Trescott found occasion to lean against the counter, wearing at the time a solemn and abstracted air, as if he expected something to happen to him shortly.

Of course their belief had been in an unlimited capacity, but they found there was an end. The shopkeeper handed the queen her change.

"Two seventy-three from five leaves two twenty-seven, Miss Cora," he said, looking upon her with admiration.

She turned swiftly to her clan. "O-oh!" she cried, in amazement. "Look how much I have left!" They gazed at the coins in her palm. They knew then that it was not their capacities which were endless; it was the five dollars.

The queen led the way to the street. "We must think up some way of spending more money," she said, frowning. They stood in silence, awaiting her further speech.

Suddenly she clapped her hands and screamed with delight. "Come on!" she cried. "I know what let's do." Now behold, she had discovered the red and white pole in front of the shop of one William Neeltje, a barber by trade.

It becomes necessary to say a few words concerning Neeltje. He was new to the town. He had come and opened a dusty little shop on dusty Bridge Street hill, and although the neighborhood knew from the courier winds that his diet was mainly cabbage, they were satisfied with that meagre data. Of course Riefsnyder came to investigate him for the local Barbers' Union, but he found in him only sweetness and light, with a willingness to charge any price at all for a shave or a haircut. In fact, the advent of Neeltje would have made barely a ripple upon the placid bosom of Whilomville if it were not that his name was Neeltje.

At first the people looked at his sign-board out of the eye corner, and wondered lazily why any one should bear the name of Neeltje; but as time went on, men spoke to other men, saying, "How do you pronounce the name of that barber up there on Bridge Street hill?" And then, before any could prevent it, the best minds of the town were splintering their lances against William Neeltje's sign-board. If a man had a mental superior, he guided him seductively to this name, and watched with glee his wrecking. The clergy of the town even entered the lists. There was one among them who had taken a collegiate prize in Syriac, as well as in several less opaque languages, and the other clergymen-at one of their weekly meetings-sought to betray him into this ambush. He pronounced the name correctly, but that mattered little, since none of them knew whether he did or did not; and so they took triumph according to their ignorance. Under these arduous circumstances it was certain that the town should look for a nickname, and at this time the nickname was in process of formation. So William Neeltje lived on with his secret, smiling foolishly towards the world.

"Come on," cried little Cora. "Let's all get our hair cut. That's what let's do. Let's all get our hair cut! Come on! Come on! Come on!" The others were carried off their feet by the fury of this assault. To get their hair cut! What joy! Little did they know if this were fun; they only knew that their small leader said it was fun. Chocolate-stained but confident, the band marched into William Neeltje's barber shop.

"We wish to get our hair cut," said little Cora, haughtily.

Neeltje, in his shirt-sleeves, stood looking at them with his half-idiot smile.

"Hurry, now!" commanded the queen. A dray-horse toiled step by step, step by step, up Bridge Street hill; a far woman's voice arose; there could be heard the ceaseless hammers of shingling carpenters; all was summer peace. "Come on, now. Who's goin' first? Come on, Ella; you go first. Gettin' our hair cut! Oh what fun!"

Little Ella Earl would not, however, be first in the chair. She was drawn towards it by a singular fascination, but at the same time she was afraid of it, and so she hung back, saying: "No! You go first! No! You go first!" The question was precipitated by the twins and one of the Phelps children. They made simultaneous rush for the chair, and screamed and kicked, each pair preventing the third child. The queen entered this mêlée, and decided in favor of the Phelps boy. He ascended the chair. Thereat an awed silence fell upon the band. And always William Neeltje smiled fatuously.

He tucked a cloth in the neck of the Phelps boy, and taking scissors, began to cut his hair. The group of children came closer and closer. Even the queen was deeply moved. "Does it hurt any?" she asked, in a wee voice.

"Naw," said the Phelps boy, with dignity. "Anyhow, I've had m' hair cut afore."

When he appeared to them looking very soldierly with his cropped little head, there was a tumult over the chair. The Margate twins howled; Jimmie Trescott was kicking them on the shins. It was a fight.

But the twins could not prevail, being the smallest of all the children. The queen herself took the chair, and ordered Neeltje as if he were a lady's-maid. To the floor there fell proud ringlets, blazing even there in their humiliation with a full fine bronze light. Then Jimmie Trescott, then Ella Earl (two long ash-colored plaits), then a Phelps girl, then another Phelps girl; and so on from head to head. The ceremony received unexpected check when the turn came to Dan Earl. This lad, usually docile to any rein, had suddenly grown mulishly obstinate. No, he would not, he would not. He himself did not seem to know why he refused to have his hair cut, but, despite the shrill derision of the company, he remained obdurate. Anyhow, the twins, long held in check, and now feverishly eager, were already struggling for the chair.

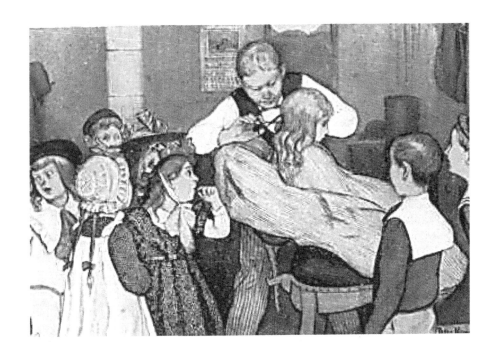

"THE QUEEN HERSELF TOOK THE CHAIR"

And so to the floor at last came the golden Margate curls, the heart treasure and glory of a mother, three aunts, and some feminine cousins.

All having been finished, the children, highly elate, thronged out into the street. They crowed and cackled with pride and joy, anon turning to scorn the cowardly Dan Earl.

Ella Earl was an exception. She had been pensive for some time, and now the shorn little maiden began vaguely to weep. In the door of his shop William Neeltje stood watching them, upon his face a grin of almost inhuman idiocy.

It now becomes the duty of the unfortunate writer to exhibit these children to their fond parents. "Come on, Jimmie," cried little Cora, "let's go show mamma." And they hurried off, these happy children, to show mamma.

The Trescotts and their guests were assembled indolently awaiting the luncheon-bell. Jimmie and the angel child burst in upon them. "Oh, mamma," shrieked little Cora, "see how fine I am! I've had my hair cut! Isn't it splendid? And Jimmie too!"

The wretched mother took one sight, emitted one yell, and fell into a chair. Mrs. Trescott dropped a large lady's journal and made a nerveless mechanical clutch at it. The painter gripped the arms of his chair and leaned forward, staring until his eyes were like two little clock faces. Dr. Trescott did not move or speak.

To the children the next moments were chaotic. There was a loudly wailing mother, and a pale-faced, aghast mother; a stammering father, and a grim and terrible father. The angel child did not understand anything of it save the voice of calamity, and in a moment all her little imperialism went to the winds. She ran sobbing to her mother. "Oh, mamma! mamma! mamma!"

The desolate Jimmie heard out of this inexplicable situation a voice which he knew well, a sort of colonel's voice, and he obeyed like any good soldier. "Jimmie!"

He stepped three paces to the front. "Yes, sir."

"How did this-how did this happen?" said Trescott.

Now Jimmie could have explained how had happened anything which had happened, but he did not know what had happened, so he said, "I—I —nothin'."

"And, oh, look at her frock!" said Mrs. Trescott, brokenly.

"'LOOK!' SHE DECLAIMED"

The words turned the mind of the mother of the angel child. She looked up, her eyes blazing. "Frock!" she repeated. "Frock! What do I care for her frock? Frock!" she choked out again from the depths of her bitterness. Then she arose suddenly, and whirled tragically upon her husband. "Look!" she declaimed. "All-her-lovely-hair-all her lovely hair-gone-gone!" The painter was apparently in a fit; his jaw was set, his eyes were glazed, his body was stiff and straight. "All gone-all-her lovely hair-all gone-my poor little darlin' —my-poor-little-darlin'!" And the angel child added her heart-broken voice to her mother's wail as they fled into each other's arms.

In the mean time Trescott was patiently unravelling some skeins of Jimmie's tangled intellect. "And then you went to this barber's on the hill. Yes. And where did you get the money? Yes. I see. And who besides you and Cora had their hair cut? The Margate twi-Oh, lord!"

Over at the Margate place old Eldridge Margate, the grandfather of the twins, was in the back garden picking pease and smoking ruminatively to himself. Suddenly he heard from the house great noises. Doors slammed, women rushed up-stairs and down-stairs calling to each other in voices of agony. And then full and mellow upon the still air arose the roar of the twins in pain.

Old Eldridge stepped out of the pea-patch and moved towards the house, puzzled, staring, not yet having decided that it was his duty to rush forward. Then around the corner of the house shot his daughter Mollie, her face pale with horror.

"What's the matter?" he cried.

"Oh, father," she gasped, "the children! They —"

Then around the corner of the house came the twins, howling at the top of their power, their faces flowing with tears. They were still hand in hand, the ruling passion being strong even in this suffering. At sight of them old Eldridge took his pipe hastily out of his mouth. "Good God!" he said.

And now what befell one William Neeltje, a barber by trade? And what was said by angry parents of the mother of such an angel child? And what was the fate of the angel child herself?

There was surely a tempest. With the exception of the Margate twins, the boys could well be eliminated from the affair. Of course it didn't matter if their hair was cut. Also the two little Phelps girls had had very short hair, anyhow, and their parents were not too greatly incensed. In the case of Ella Earl, it was mainly the pathos of the little girl's own grieving; but her mother played a most generous part, and called upon Mrs. Trescott, and condoled with the mother of the angel child over their equivalent losses. But the Margate contingent! They simply screeched.

"AROUND THE CORNER OF THE HOUSE CAME THE TWINS"

Trescott, composed and cool-blooded, was in the middle of a giddy whirl. He was not going to allow the mobbing of his wife's cousins, nor was he going to pretend that the spoliation of the Margate twins was a virtuous and beautiful act. He was elected, gratuitously, to the position of a buffer.

But, curiously enough, the one who achieved the bulk of the misery was old Eldridge Margate, who had been picking pease at the time. The feminine Margates stormed his position as individuals, in pairs, in teams, and *en masse*. In two days they may have aged him seven years. He must destroy the utter Neeltje. He must midnightly massacre the angel child and her mother. He must dip his arms in blood to the elbows.

Trescott took the first opportunity to express to him his concern over the affair, but when the subject of the disaster was mentioned, old Eldridge, to the doctor's great surprise, actually chuckled long and deeply. "Oh, well, look-a-here," he said. "I never was so much in love with them there damn curls. The curls was purty-yes-but then I'd a darn sight rather see boys look more like boys than like two little wax figgers. An', ye know, the little cusses like it themselves. *They* never took no stock in all this washin' an' combin' an' fixin' an' goin' to church an' paradin' an' showin' off. They stood it because they were told to. That's all. Of course this here Neel-te-gee, er whatever his name is, is a plumb dumb ijit, but I don't see what's to be done, now that the kids is full well cropped. I might go and burn his shop over his head, but that wouldn't bring no hair back onto the kids. They're even kicking on sashes now, and that's all right, 'cause what fer does a boy want a sash?"

Whereupon Trescott perceived that the old man wore his brains above his shoulders, and Trescott departed from him rejoicing greatly that it was only women who could not know that there was finality to most disasters, and that when a thing was fully done, no amount of door-slammings, rushing up-stairs and down-stairs, calls, lamentations, tears, could bring back a single hair to the heads of twins.

AT THE RAILWAY STATION

But the rains came and the winds blew in the most biblical way when a certain fact came to light in the Trescott household. Little Cora, corroborated by Jimmie, innocently remarked that five dollars had been given her by her father on her birthday, and with this money the evil had been wrought. Trescott had known it, but he-thoughtful man-had said nothing. For her part, the mother of the angel child had up to that moment never reflected that the consummation of the wickedness must have cost a small sum of money. But now it was all clear to her. He was the guilty one-he! "My angel child!"

The scene which ensued was inspiriting. A few days later, loungers at the railway station saw a lady leading a shorn and still undaunted lamb. Attached to them was a husband and father, who was plainly bewildered, but still more plainly vexed, as if he would be saying: "Damn 'em! Why can't they leave me alone?"

II
Lynx-Hunting

JIMMIE lounged about the dining-room and watched his mother with large, serious eyes. Suddenly he said, "Ma-now-can I borrow pa's gun?"

She was overcome with the feminine horror which is able to mistake preliminary words for the full accomplishment of the dread thing. "Why, Jimmie!" she cried. "Of al-l wonders! Your father's gun! No indeed you can't!"

He was fairly well crushed, but he managed to mutter, sullenly, "Well, Willie Dalzel, he's got a gun." In reality his heart had previously been beating with such tumult-he had himself been so impressed with the daring and sin of his request-that he was glad that all was over now, and his mother could do very little further harm to his sensibilities. He had been influenced into the venture by the larger boys.

"'MA-NOW-CAN I BORROW PA'S GUN?'"

"Huh!" the Dalzel urchin had said; "your father's got a gun, hasn't he? Well, why don't you bring that?"

Puffing himself, Jimmie had replied, "Well, I can, if I want to." It was a black lie, but really the Dalzel boy was too outrageous with his eternal bill-posting about the gun which a beaming uncle had intrusted to him. Its possession made him superior in manfulness to most boys in the neighborhood-or at least they enviously conceded him such position-but he was so overbearing, and stuffed the fact of his treasure so relentlessly down their throats, that on this occasion the miserable Jimmie had lied as naturally as most animals swim.

Willie Dalzel had not been checkmated, for he had instantly retorted, "Why don't you get it, then?"

"Well, I can, if I want to."

"Well, get it, then!"

"Well, I can, if I want to."

Thereupon Jimmie had paced away with great airs of surety as far as the door of his home, where his manner changed to one of tremulous misgiving as it came upon him to address his mother in the dining-room. There had happened that which had happened.

When Jimmie returned to his two distinguished companions he was blown out with a singular pomposity. He spoke these noble words: "Oh, well, I guess I don't want to take the gun out to-day."

They had been watching him with gleaming ferret eyes, and they detected his falsity at once. They challenged him with shouted gibes, but it was not in the rules for the conduct of boys that one should admit anything whatsoever, and so Jimmie, backed into an ethical corner, lied as stupidly, as desperately, as hopelessly as ever lone savage fights when surrounded at last in his jungle.

Such accusations were never known to come to any point, for the reason that the number and kind of denials always equalled or exceeded the number of accusations, and no boy was ever brought really to book for these misdeeds.

In the end they went off together, Willie Dalzel with his gun being a trifle in advance and discoursing upon his various works. They passed along a maple-lined avenue, a highway common to boys bound for that free land of hills and woods in which they lived in some part their romance of the moment, whether it was of Indians, miners, smugglers, soldiers, or outlaws. The paths were their paths, and much was known to them of the secrets of the dark green hemlock thickets, the wastes of sweet-fern and huckleberry, the cliffs of gaunt bluestone with the sumach burning red at their feet. Each boy had, I am sure, a conviction that some day the wilderness was to give forth to him a marvellous secret. They felt that the hills and the forest knew much, and they heard a voice of it in the silence. It was vague, thrilling, fearful, and altogether fabulous. The grown folk seemed to regard these wastes merely as so much distance between one place and another place, or as a rabbit-cover, or as a district to be judged according to the value of the timber; but to the boys it spoke some great inspiring word, which they knew even as those who pace the shore know the enigmatic speech of the surf. In the mean time they lived there, in season, lives of ringing adventure-by dint of imagination.

The boys left the avenue, skirted hastily through some private grounds, climbed a fence, and entered the thickets. It happened that at school the previous day Willie Dalzel had been forced to read and acquire in some part a solemn description of a lynx. The meagre information thrust upon him had caused him grimaces of suffering, but now he said, suddenly, "I'm goin' to shoot a lynx."

The other boys admired this statement, but they were silent for a time. Finally Jimmie said, meekly, "What's a lynx?" He had endured his ignorance as long as he was able.

The Dalzel boy mocked him. "Why, don't you know what a lynx is? A lynx? Why, a lynx is a animal somethin' like a cat, an' it's got great big green eyes, and it sits on the limb of a tree an' jus' glares at you. It's a pretty bad animal, I tell you. Why, when I —"

"Huh!" said the third boy. "Where'd you ever see a lynx?"

"Oh, I've seen 'em-plenty of 'em. I bet you'd be scared if you seen one once."

Jimmie and the other boy each demanded, "How do you know I would?"

They penetrated deeper into the wood. They climbed a rocky zigzag path which led them at times where with their hands they could almost touch the tops of giant pines. The gray cliffs sprang sheer towards the sky. Willie Dalzel babbled about his impossible lynx, and they stalked the mountain-side like chamois-hunters, although no noise of bird or beast broke the stillness of the hills. Below them Whilomville was spread out somewhat like the cheap green and black lithograph of the time —"A Bird's-eye View of Whilomville, N. Y."

THE DALZEL BOY TAKING THE PART OF A BANDIT CHIEF

In the end the boys reached the top of the mountain and scouted off among wild and desolate ridges. They were burning with the desire to slay large animals. They thought continually of elephants, lions, tigers, crocodiles. They discoursed upon their immaculate conduct in case such monsters confronted them, and they all lied carefully about their courage.

The breeze was heavy with the smell of sweet-fern. The pines and hemlocks sighed as they waved their branches. In the hollows the leaves of the laurels were lacquered where the sunlight found them. No matter the weather, it would be impossible to long continue an expedition of this kind without a fire, and presently they built one, snapping down for fuel the brittle under-branches of the pines. About this fire they were willed to conduct a sort of play, the Dalzel boy taking the part of a bandit chief, and the other boys being his trusty lieutenants. They stalked to and fro, long-strided, stern yet devil-may-care, three terrible little figures.

Jimmie had an uncle who made game of him whenever he caught him in this kind of play, and often this uncle quoted derisively the following classic: "Once aboard the lugger, Bill, and the girl is mine. Now to burn the château and destroy all evidence of our crime. But, hark'e, Bill, no wiolence." Wheeling abruptly, he addressed these dramatic words to his comrades. They were impressed; they decided at once to be smugglers, and in the most ribald fashion they talked about carrying off young women.

At last they continued their march through the woods. The smuggling *motif* was now grafted fantastically upon the original lynx idea, which Willie Dalzel refused to abandon at any price.

Once they came upon an innocent bird who happened to be looking another way at the time. After a great deal of manœvering and big words, Willie Dalzel reared his fowling-piece and blew this poor thing into a mere rag of wet feathers, of which he was proud.

Afterwards the other big boy had a turn at another bird. Then it was plainly Jimmie's chance. The two others had, of course, some thought of cheating him out of this chance, but of a truth he was timid to explode such a thunderous weapon, and as soon as they detected this fear they simply overbore him, and made it clearly understood that if he refused to shoot he would lose his caste, his scalp-lock, his girdle, his honor.

They had reached the old death-colored snake-fence which marked the limits of the upper pasture of the Fleming farm. Under some hickory-trees the path ran parallel to the fence. Behold! a small priestly chipmonk came to a rail, and folding his hands on his abdomen, addressed them in his own tongue. It was Jimmie's shot. Adjured by the others, he took the gun. His face was stiff with apprehension. The Dalzel boy was giving forth fine words. "Go ahead. Aw, don't be afraid. It's nothin' to do. Why, I've done it a million times. Don't shut both your eyes, now. Jus' keep one open and shut the other one. He'll get away if you don't watch out. Now you're all right. Why don't you let'er go? Go ahead."

"THERE WAS A FRIGHTFUL ROAR"

Jimmie, with his legs braced apart, was in the centre of the path. His back was greatly bent, owing to the mechanics of supporting the heavy gun. His companions were screeching in the rear. There was a wait.

Then he pulled trigger. To him there was a frightful roar, his cheek and his shoulder took a stunning blow, his face felt a hot flush of fire, and opening his two eyes, he found that he was still alive. He was not too dazed to instantly adopt a becoming egotism. It had been the first shot of his life.

But directly after the well-mannered celebration of this victory a certain cow, which had been grazing in the line of fire, was seen to break wildly across the pasture, bellowing and bucking. The three smugglers and lynx-hunters looked at each other out of blanched faces. Jimmie had hit the cow. The first evidence of his comprehension of this fact was in the celerity with which he returned the discharged gun to Willie Dalzel.

They turned to flee. The land was black, as if it had been overshadowed suddenly with thick storm-clouds, and even as they fled in their horror a gigantic Swedish farm-hand came from the heavens and fell upon them, shrieking in eerie triumph. In a twinkle they were clouted prostrate. The Swede was elate and ferocious in a foreign and fulsome way. He continued to beat them and yell.

From the ground they raised their dismal appeal. "Oh, please, mister, we didn't do it! He did it! I didn't do it! We didn't do it! We didn't mean to do it! Oh, please, mister!"

In these moments of childish terror little lads go half-blind, and it is possible that few moments of their after-life made them suffer as they did when the Swede flung them over the fence and marched them towards the farm-house. They begged like cowards on the scaffold, and each one was for himself. "Oh, please let me go, mister! I didn't do it, mister! He did it! Oh, p-l-ease let me go, mister!"

" 'I THOUGHT SHE WAS A LYNX' "

The boyish view belongs to boys alone, and if this tall and knotted laborer was needlessly without charity, none of the three lads questioned it. Usually when they were punished they decided that they deserved it, and the more they were punished the more they were convinced that they were criminals of a most subterranean type. As to the hitting of the cow being a pure accident, and therefore not of necessity a criminal matter, such reading never entered their heads. When things happened and they were caught, they commonly paid dire consequences, and they were accustomed to measure the probabilities of woe utterly by the damage done, and not in any way by the culpability. The shooting of the cow was plainly heinous, and undoubtedly their dungeons would be knee-deep in water.

"He did it, mister!" This was a general outcry. Jimmie used it as often as did the others. As for them, it is certain that they had no direct thought of betraying their comrade for their own salvation. They thought themselves guilty because they were caught; when boys were not caught they might possibly be innocent. But captured boys were guilty. When they cried out that Jimmie was the culprit, it was principally a simple expression of terror.

Old Henry Fleming, the owner of the farm, strode across the pasture towards them. He had in his hand a most cruel whip. This whip he flourished. At his approach the boys suffered the agonies of the fire regions. And yet anybody with half an eye could see that the whip in his hand was a mere accident, and that he was a kind old man-when he cared.

When he had come near he spoke crisply. "What you boys ben doin' to my cow?" The tone had deep threat in it. They all answered by saying that none of them had shot the cow. Their denials were tearful and clamorous, and they crawled knee by knee. The vision of it was like three martyrs being dragged towards the stake. Old Fleming stood there, grim, tight-lipped. After a time he said, "Which boy done it?"

There was some confusion, and then Jimmie spake. "I done it, mister."

Fleming looked at him. Then he asked, "Well, what did you shoot 'er fer?"

Jimmie thought, hesitated, decided, faltered, and then formulated this: "I thought she was a lynx."

Old Fleming and his Swede at once lay down in the grass and laughed themselves helpless.

The Lover and the Telltale

WHEN the angel child returned with her parents to New York, the fond heart of Jimmie Trescott felt its bruise greatly. For two days he simply moped, becoming a stranger to all former joys. When his old comrades yelled invitation, as they swept off on some interesting quest, he replied with mournful gestures of disillusion.

He thought often of writing to her, but of course the shame of it made him pause. Write a letter to a girl? The mere enormity of the idea caused him shudders. Persons of his quality never wrote letters to girls. Such was the occupation of mollycoddles and snivellers. He knew that if his acquaintances and friends found in him evidences of such weakness and general milkiness, they would fling themselves upon him like so many wolves, and bait him beyond the borders of sanity.

However, one day at school, in that time of the morning session when children of his age were allowed fifteen minutes of play in the school-grounds, he did not as usual rush forth ferociously to his games. Commonly he was of the worst hoodlums, preying upon his weaker brethren with all the cruel disregard of a grown man. On this particular morning he stayed in the school-room, and with his tongue stuck from the corner of his mouth, and his head twisting in a painful way, he wrote to little Cora, pouring out to her all the poetry of his hungry soul, as follows: "My dear Cora I love thee with all my hart oh come bac again, bac, bac gain for I love thee best of all oh come bac again When the spring come again we'l fly and we'l fly like a brid."

As for the last word, he knew under normal circumstances perfectly well how to spell "bird," but in this case he had transposed two of the letters through excitement, supreme agitation.

Nor had this letter been composed without fear and furtive glancing. There was always a number of children who, for the time, cared more for the quiet of the school-room than for the tempest of the play-ground, and there was always that dismal company who were being forcibly deprived of their recess-who were being "kept in." More than one curious eye was turned upon the desperate and lawless Jimmie Trescott suddenly taken to ways of peace, and as he felt these eyes he flushed guiltily, with felonious glances from side to side.

It happened that a certain vigilant little girl had a seat directly across the aisle from Jimmie's seat, and she had remained in the room during the intermission, because of her interest in some absurd domestic details concerning her desk. Parenthetically it might be stated that she was in the habit of imagining this desk to be a house, and at this time, with an important little frown, indicative of a proper matron, she was engaged in dramatizing her ideas of a household.

But this small Rose Goldege happened to be of a family which numbered few males. It was, in fact, one of those curious middle-class families that hold much of their ground, retain most of their position, after all their visible means of support have been dropped in the grave. It contained now only a collection of women who existed submissively, defiantly, securely, mysteriously, in a pretentious and often exasperating virtue. It was often too triumphantly clear that they were free of bad habits. However, bad habits is a term here used in a commoner meaning, because it is certainly true that the principal and indeed solitary joy which entered their lonely lives was the joy of talking wickedly and busily about their neighbors. It was all done without dream of its being of the vulgarity of the alleys. Indeed it was simply a constitutional but not incredible chastity and honesty expressing itself in its ordinary superior way of the whirling circles of life, and the vehemence of the criticism was not lessened by a further infusion of an acid of worldly defeat, worldly suffering, and worldly hopelessness.

Out of this family circle had sprung the typical little girl who discovered Jimmie Trescott agonizingly writing a letter to his sweetheart. Of course all the children were the most abandoned gossips, but she was peculiarly adapted to the purpose of making Jimmie miserable over this particular point. It was her life to sit of evenings about the stove and hearken to her mother and a lot of spinsters talk of many things. During these evenings she was never licensed to utter an opinion either one way or the other way. She was then simply a very little girl sitting open-eyed in the gloom, and listening to many things which she often interpreted wrongly. They on their part kept up a kind of a smug-faced pretence of concealing from her information in detail of the widespread crime, which pretence may have been more elaborately dangerous than no pretence at all. Thus all her home-teaching fitted her to recognize at once in Jimmie Trescott's manner that he was concealing something that would properly interest the world. She set up a scream. "Oh! Oh! Oh! Jimmie Trescott's writing to his girl! Oh! Oh!"

Jimmie cast a miserable glance upon her —a glance in which hatred mingled with despair. Through the open window he could hear the boisterous cries of his friends-his hoodlum friends-who would no more understand the utter poetry of his position than they would understand an ancient tribal sign-language. His face was set in a truer expression of horror than any of the romances describe upon the features of a man flung into a moat, a man shot in the breast with an arrow, a man cleft in the neck with a battle-axe. He was suppedaneous of the fullest power of childish pain. His one course was to rush upon her and attempt, by an impossible means of strangulation, to keep her important news from the public.

The teacher, a thoughtful young woman at her desk upon the platform, saw a little scuffle which informed her that two of her scholars were larking. She called out sharply. The command penetrated to the middle of an early world struggle. In Jimmie's age there was no particular scruple in the minds of the male sex against laying warrior hands upon their weaker sisters. But, of course, this voice from the throne hindered Jimmie in what might have been a berserk attack.

Even the little girl was retarded by the voice, but, without being unlawful, she managed soon to shy through the door and out upon the play-ground, yelling, "Oh, Jimmie Trescott's been writing to his girl!"

The unhappy Jimmie was following as closely as he was allowed by his knowledge of the decencies to be preserved under the eye of the teacher.

Jimmie himself was mainly responsible for the scene which ensued on the play-ground. It is possible that the little girl might have run, shrieking his infamy, without exciting more than a general but unmilitant interest. These barbarians were excited only by the actual appearance of human woe; in that event they cheered and danced. Jimmie made the strategic mistake of pursuing little Rose, and thus exposed his thin skin to the whole school. He had in his cowering mind a vision of a hundred children turning from their play under the maple-trees and speeding towards him over the gravel with sudden wild taunts. Upon him drove a yelping demoniac mob, to which his words were futile. He saw in this mob boys that he dimly knew, and his deadly enemies, and his retainers, and his most intimate friends. The virulence of his deadly enemy was no greater than the virulence of his intimate friend. From the outskirts the little informer could be heard still screaming the news, like a toy parrot with clock-work inside of it. It broke up all sorts of games, not so much because of the mere fact of the letter-writing, as because the children knew that some sufferer was at the last point, and, like little blood-fanged wolves, they thronged to the scene of his destruction. They galloped about him shrilly chanting insults. He turned from one to another, only to meet with howls. He was baited.

Then, in one instant, he changed all this with a blow. Bang! The most pitiless of the boys near him received a punch, fairly and skilfully, which made him bellow out like a walrus, and then Jimmie laid desperately into the whole world, striking out frenziedly in all directions. Boys who could handily whip him, and knew it, backed away from this onslaught. Here was intention-serious intention. They themselves were not in frenzy, and their cooler judgment respected Jimmie's efforts when he ran amuck. They saw that it really was none of their affair. In the mean time the wretched little girl who had caused the bloody riot was away, by the fence, weeping because boys were fighting.

"THEY GALLOPED ABOUT HIM, SHRILLY CHANTING INSULTS."

Jimmie several times hit the wrong boy-that is to say, he several times hit a wrong boy hard enough to arouse also in him a spirit of strife. Jimmie wore a little shirt-waist. It was passing now rapidly into oblivion. He was sobbing, and there was one blood stain upon his cheek. The school-ground sounded like a pinetree when a hundred crows roost in it at night.

Then upon the situation there pealed a brazen bell. It was a bell that these children obeyed, even as older nations obey the formal law which is printed in calf-skin. It smote them into some sort of inaction; even Jimmie was influenced by its potency, although, as a finale, he kicked out lustily into the legs of an intimate friend who had been one of the foremost in the torture.

When they came to form into line for the march into the school-room it was curious that Jimmie had many admirers. It was not his prowess; it was the soul he had infused into his gymnastics; and he, still panting, looked about him with a stern and challenging glare.

And yet when the long tramping line had entered the school-room his status had again changed. The other children then began to regard him as a boy in disrepair, and boys in disrepair were always accosted ominously from the throne. Jimmie's march towards his seat was a feat. It was composed partly of a most slinking attempt to dodge the perception of the teacher and partly of pure braggadocio erected for the benefit of his observant fellow-men.

The teacher looked carefully down at him. "Jimmie Trescott," she said.

"Yes'm," he answered, with businesslike briskness, which really spelled out falsity in all its letters.

"Come up to the desk."

He rose amid the awe of the entire school-room. When he arrived she said,

"Jimmie, you've been fighting."

"Yes'm," he answered. This was not so much an admission of the fact as it was a concessional answer to anything she might say.

"Who have you been fighting?" she asked.

"I dunno', 'm."

Whereupon the empress blazed out in wrath. "You don't know who you've been fighting?"

Jimmie looked at her gloomily. "No, 'm."

She seemed about to disintegrate to mere flaming fagots of anger. "You don't know who you've been fighting?" she demanded, blazing. "Well, you stay in after school until you find out."

As he returned to his place all the children knew by his vanquished air that sorrow had fallen upon the house of Trescott. When he took his seat he saw gloating upon him the satanic black eyes of the little Goldege girl.

IV
"Showin' Off"

JIMMIE TRESCOTT'S new velocipede had the largest front wheel of any velocipede in Whilomville. When it first arrived from New York he wished to sacrifice school, food, and sleep to it. Evidently he wished to become a sort of a perpetual velocipede-rider. But the powers of the family laid a number of judicious embargoes upon him, and he was prevented from becoming a fanatic. Of course this caused him to retain a fondness for the three-wheeled thing much longer than if he had been allowed to debauch himself for a span of days. But in the end it was an immaterial machine to him. For long periods he left it idle in the stable.

One day he loitered from school towards home by a very circuitous route. He was accompanied by only one of his retainers. The object of this détour was the wooing of a little girl in a red hood. He had been in love with her for some three weeks. His desk was near her desk in school, but he had never spoken to her. He had been afraid to take such a radical step. It was not customary to speak to girls. Even boys who had school-going sisters seldom addressed them during that part of a day which was devoted to education.

The reasons for this conduct were very plain. First, the more robust boys considered talking with girls an unmanly occupation; second, the greater part of the boys were afraid; third, they had no idea of what to say, because they esteemed the proper sentences should be supernaturally incisive and eloquent. In consequence, a small contingent of blue-eyed weaklings were the sole intimates of the frail sex, and for it they were boisterously and disdainfully called "girl-boys."

But this situation did not prevent serious and ardent wooing. For instance, Jimmie and the little girl who wore the red hood must have exchanged glances at least two hundred times in every school-hour, and this exchange of glances accomplished everything. In them the two children renewed their curious inarticulate vows.

Jimmie had developed a devotion to school which was the admiration of his father and mother. In the mornings he was so impatient to have it made known to him that no misfortune had befallen his romance during the night that he was actually detected at times feverishly listening for the "first bell." Dr. Trescott was exceedingly complacent of the change, and as for Mrs. Trescott, she had ecstatic visions of a white-haired Jimmie leading the nations in knowledge, comprehending all from bugs to comets. It was merely the doing of the little girl in the red hood.

When Jimmie made up his mind to follow his sweetheart home from school, the project seemed such an arbitrary and shameless innovation that he hastily lied to himself about it. No, he was not following Abbie. He was merely making his way homeward through the new and rather longer route of Bryant Street and Oakland Park. It had nothing at all to do with a girl. It was a mere eccentric notion.

"Come on," said Jimmie, gruffly, to his retainer. "Let's go home this way."

"What fer?" demanded the retainer.

"Oh, b'cause."

"Huh?"

"Oh, it's more fun-goin' this way."

The retainer was bored and loath, but that mattered very little. He did not know how to disobey his chief. Together they followed the trail of red-hooded Abbie and another small girl. These latter at once understood the object of the chase, and looking back giggling, they pretended to quicken their pace. But they were always looking back. Jimmie now began his courtship in earnest. The first thing to do was to prove his strength in battle. This was transacted by means of the retainer. He took that devoted boy and flung him heavily to the ground, meanwhile mouthing a preposterous ferocity.

The retainer accepted this behavior with a sort of bland resignation. After his overthrow he raised himself, coolly brushed some dust and dead leaves from his clothes, and then seemed to forget the incident.

"I can jump farther'n you can," said Jimmie, in a loud voice.

"I know it," responded the retainer, simply.

But this would not do. There must be a contest.

"Come on," shouted Jimmie, imperiously. "Let's see you jump."

The retainer selected a footing on the curb, balanced and calculated a moment, and jumped without enthusiasm. Jimmie's leap of course was longer.

"There!" he cried, blowing out his lips. "I beat you, didn't I? Easy. I beat you." He made a great hubbub, as if the affair was unprecedented.

"Yes," admitted the other, emotionless.

Later, Jimmie forced his retainer to run a race with him, held more jumping matches, flung him twice to earth, and generally behaved as if a retainer was indestructible. If the retainer had been in the plot, it is conceivable that he would have endured this treatment with mere whispered, half-laughing protests. But he was not in the plot at all, and so he became enigmatic. One cannot often sound the profound well in which lie the meanings of boyhood.

Following the two little girls, Jimmie eventually passed into that suburb of Whilomville which is called Oakland Park. At his heels came a badly battered retainer. Oakland Park was a somewhat strange country to the boys. They were dubious of the manners and customs, and of course they would have to meet the local chieftains, who might look askance upon this invasion.

Jimmie's girl departed into her home with a last backward glance that almost blinded the thrilling boy. On this pretext and that pretext, he kept his retainer in play before the house. He had hopes that she would emerge as soon as she had deposited her school-bag.

A boy came along the walk. Jimmie knew him at school. He was Tommie Semple, one of the weaklings who made friends with the fair sex. "Hello, Tom," said Jimmie. "You live round here?"

"Yeh," said Tom, with composed pride. At school he was afraid of Jimmie, but he did not evince any of this fear as he strolled well inside his own frontiers. Jimmie and his retainer had not expected this boy to display the manners of a minor chief, and they contemplated him attentively. There was a silence. Finally Jimmie said:

"I can put you down." He moved forward briskly. "Can't I?" he demanded.

The challenged boy backed away. "I know you can," he declared, frankly and promptly.

The little girl in the red hood had come out with a hoop. She looked at Jimmie with an air of insolent surprise in the fact that he still existed, and began to trundle her hoop off towards some other little girls who were shrilly playing near a nurse-maid and a perambulator.

Jimmie adroitly shifted his position until he too was playing near the perambulator, pretentiously making mince-meat out of his retainer and Tommie Semple.

Of course little Abbie had defined the meaning of Jimmie's appearance in Oakland Park. Despite this nonchalance and grand air of accident, nothing could have been more plain. Whereupon she of course became insufferably vain in manner, and whenever Jimmie came near her she tossed her head and turned away her face, and daintily swished her skirts as if he were contagion itself. But Jimmie was happy. His soul was satisfied with the mere presence of the beloved object so long as he could feel that she furtively gazed upon him from time to time and noted his extraordinary prowess, which he was proving upon the persons of his retainer and Tommie Semple. And he was making an impression. There could be no doubt of it. He had many times caught her eye fixed admiringly upon him as he mauled the retainer. Indeed, all the little girls gave attention to his deeds, and he was the hero of the hour.

Presently a boy on a velocipede was seen to be tooling down towards them. "Who's this comin'?" said Jimmie, bluntly, to the Semple boy.

"That's Horace Glenn," said Tommie, "an' he's got a new velocipede, an' he can ride it like anything."

"Can you lick him?" asked Jimmie.

"I don't —I never fought with 'im," answered the other. He bravely tried to appear as a man of respectable achievement, but with Horace coming towards them the risk was too great. However, he added, *"Maybe* I could."

The advent of Horace on his new velocipede created a sensation which he haughtily accepted as a familiar thing. Only Jimmie and his retainer remained silent and impassive. Horace eyed the two invaders.

"Hello, Jimmie!"

"Hello, Horace!"

After the typical silence Jimmie said, pompously, "I got a velocipede."

"Have you?" asked Horace, anxiously. He did not wish anybody in the world but himself to possess a velocipede.

"Yes," sang Jimmie. "An' it's a bigger one than that, too! A good deal bigger! An' it's a better one, too!"

"Huh!" retorted Horace, sceptically.

"'Ain't I, Clarence? 'Ain't I? 'Ain't I got one bigger'n that?"

The retainer answered with alacrity:

"Yes, he has! A good deal bigger! An' it's a dindy, too!"

This corroboration rather disconcerted Horace, but he continued to scoff at any statement that Jimmie also owned a velocipede. As for the contention that this supposed velocipede could be larger than his own, he simply wouldn't hear of it.

Jimmie had been a very gallant figure before the coming of Horace, but the new velocipede had relegated him to a squalid secondary position. So he affected to look with contempt upon it. Voluminously he bragged of the velocipede in the stable at home. He painted its virtues and beauty in loud and extravagant words, flaming words. And the retainer stood by, glibly endorsing everything.

The little company heeded him, and he passed on vociferously from extravagance to utter impossibility. Horace was very sick of it. His defence was reduced to a mere mechanical grumbling: "Don't believe you got one 'tall. Don't believe you got one 'tall."

Jimmie turned upon him suddenly. "How fast can you go? How fast can you go?" he demanded. "Let's see. I bet you can't go fast."

Horace lifted his spirits and answered with proper defiance. "Can't I?" he mocked. "Can't I?"

"No, you can't," said Jimmie. "You can't go fast."

Horace cried: "Well, you see me now! I'll show you! I'll show you if I can't go fast!" Taking a firm seat on his vermilion machine, he pedalled furiously up the walk, turned, and pedalled back again. "There, now!" he shouted, triumphantly. "Ain't that fast? There, now!" There was a low murmur of appreciation from the little girls. Jimmie saw with pain that even his divinity was smiling upon his rival. "There! Ain't that fast? Ain't that fast?" He strove to pin Jimmie down to an admission. He was exuberant with victory.

Notwithstanding a feeling of discomfiture, Jimmie did not lose a moment of time. "Why," he yelled, "that ain't goin' fast 'tall! That ain't goin' fast 'tall! Why, I can go almost *twice* as fast as that! Almost *twice* as fast! Can't I, Clarence?"

The royal retainer nodded solemnly at the wide-eyed group. "Course you can!"

"Why," spouted Jimmie, "you just ought to see me ride once! You just ought to see me! Why, I can go like the wind! Can't I, Clarence? And I can ride far, too-oh, awful far! Can't I, Clarence? Why, I wouldn't have that one! 'Tain't any good! You just ought to see mine once!"

The overwhelmed Horace attempted to reconstruct his battered glories. "I can ride right over the curb-stone —at some of the crossin's," he announced, brightly.

Jimmie's derision was a splendid sight. *"Right over the curb-stone!"* Why, that wouldn't be *nothin'* for me to do! I've rode mine down Bridge Street hill. Yessir! 'Ain't I, Clarence? Why, it ain't nothin' to ride over a curb-stone —not for *me*! Is it, Clarence?"

"Down Bridge Street hill? You never!" said Horace, hopelessly.

"Well, didn't I, Clarence? Didn't I, now?"

The faithful retainer again nodded solemnly at the assemblage.

At last Horace, having fallen as low as was possible, began to display a spirit for climbing up again. "Oh, you can do wonders!" he said, laughing. "You can do wonders! I s'pose you could ride down that bank there?" he asked, with art. He had indicated a grassy terrace some six feet in height which bounded one side of the walk. At the bottom was a small ravine in which the reckless had flung ashes and tins. "I s'pose you could ride down that bank?"

"'I —' HE BEGAN. THEN HE VANISHED FROM THE EDGE OF THE WALK."

All eyes now turned upon Jimmie to detect a sign of his weakening, but he instantly and sublimely arose to the occasion. "That bank?" he asked, scornfully. "Why, I've ridden down banks like that many a time. 'Ain't I, Clarence?"

This was too much for the company. A sound like the wind in the leaves arose; it was the song of incredulity and ridicule. "O —o —o —o —o!" And on the outskirts a little girl suddenly shrieked out, "Story-teller!"

Horace had certainly won a skirmish. He was gleeful. "Oh, you can do wonders!" he gurgled. "You can do wonders!" The neighborhood's superficial hostility to foreigners arose like magic under the influence of his sudden success, and Horace had the delight of seeing Jimmie persecuted in that manner known only to children and insects.

Jimmie called angrily to the boy on the velocipede, "If you'll lend me yours, I'll show you whether I can or not."

Horace turned his superior nose in the air. "Oh no! I don't ever lend it." Then he thought of a blow which would make Jimmie's humiliation complete. "Besides," he said, airily, "'tain't really anything hard to do. I could do it-easy-if I wanted to."

But his supposed adherents, instead of receiving this boast with cheers, looked upon him in a sudden blank silence. Jimmie and his retainer pounced like cats upon their advantage.

"Oh," they yelled, "you *could*, eh? Well, let's see you do it, then! Let's see you do it! Let's see you do it! Now!" In a moment the crew of little spectators were gibing at Horace.

The blow that would make Jimmie's humiliation complete! Instead, it had boomeranged Horace into the mud. He kept up a sullen muttering:

"'Tain't really anything! I could if I wanted to!"

"Dare you to!" screeched Jimmie and his partisans. "Dare you to! Dare you to! Dare you to!"

There were two things to be done-to make gallant effort or to retreat. Somewhat to their amazement, the children at last found Horace moving through their clamor to the edge of the bank. Sitting on the velocipede, he looked at the ravine, and then, with gloomy pride, at the other children. A hush came upon them, for it was seen that he was intending to make some kind of an ante-mortem statement.

"I —" he began. Then he vanished from the edge of the walk. The start had been unintentional-an accident.

The stupefied Jimmie saw the calamity through a haze. His first clear vision was when Horace, with a face as red as a red flag, arose bawling from his tangled velocipede. He and his retainer exchanged a glance of horror and fled the neighborhood. They did not look back until they had reached the top of the hill near the lake. They could see Horace walking slowly under the maples towards his home, pushing his shattered velocipede before him. His chin was thrown high, and the breeze bore them the sound of his howls.

V

Making an Orator

IN the school at Whilomville it was the habit, when children had progressed to a certain class, to have them devote Friday afternoon to what was called elocution. This was in the piteously ignorant belief that orators were thus made. By process of school law, unfortunate boys and girls were dragged up to address their fellow-scholars in the literature of the mid-century. Probably the children who were most capable of expressing themselves, the children who were most sensitive to the power of speech, suffered the most wrong. Little blockheads who could learn eight lines of conventional poetry, and could get up and spin it rapidly at their classmates, did not undergo a single pang. The plan operated mainly to agonize many children permanently against arising to speak their thought to fellow-creatures.

Jimmie Trescott had an idea that by exhibition of undue ignorance he could escape from being promoted into the first class room which exacted such penalty from its inmates. He preferred to dwell in a less classic shade rather than venture into a domain where he was obliged to perform a certain duty which struck him as being worse than death. However, willy-nilly, he was somehow sent ahead into the place of torture.

Every Friday at least ten of the little children had to mount the stage beside the teacher's desk and babble something which none of them understood. This was to make them orators. If it had been ordered that they should croak like frogs, it would have advanced most of them just as far towards oratory.

Alphabetically Jimmie Trescott was near the end of the list of victims, but his time was none the less inevitable. "Tanner, Timmens, Trass, Trescott —" He saw his downfall approaching.

He was passive to the teacher while she drove into his mind the incomprehensible lines of "The Charge of the Light Brigade":

> Half a league, half a league,
> Half a league onward —

He had no conception of a league. If in the ordinary course of life somebody had told him that he was half a league from home, he might have been frightened that half a league was fifty miles; but he struggled manfully with the valley of death and a mystic six hundred, who were performing something there which was very fine, he had been told. He learned all the verses.

But as his own Friday afternoon approached he was moved to make known to his family that a dreadful disease was upon him, and was likely at any time to prevent him from going to his beloved school.

On the great Friday when the children of his initials were to speak their pieces Dr. Trescott was away from home, and the mother of the boy was alarmed beyond measure at Jimmie's curious illness, which caused him to lie on the rug in front of the fire and groan cavernously.

She bathed his feet in hot mustard water until they were lobster-red. She also placed a mustard plaster on his chest.

He announced that these remedies did him no good at all-no good at all. With an air of martyrdom he endured a perfect downpour of motherly attention all that day. Thus the first Friday was passed in safety.

With singular patience he sat before the fire in the dining-room and looked at picture-books, only complaining of pain when he suspected his mother of thinking that he was getting better.

The next day being Saturday and a holiday, he was miraculously delivered from the arms of disease, and went forth to play, a blatantly healthy boy.

He had no further attack until Thursday night of the next week, when he announced that he felt very, very poorly. The mother was already chronically alarmed over the condition of her son, but Dr. Trescott asked him questions which denoted some incredulity. On the third Friday Jimmie was dropped at the door of the school from the doctor's buggy. The other children, notably those who had already passed over the mountain of distress, looked at him with glee, seeing in him another lamb brought to butchery. Seated at his desk in the school-room, Jimmie sometimes remembered with dreadful distinctness every line of "The Charge of the Light Brigade," and at other times his mind was utterly empty of it. Geography, arithmetic, and spelling-usually great tasks-quite rolled off him. His mind was dwelling with terror upon the time when his name should be called and he was obliged to go up to the platform, turn, bow, and recite his message to his fellow-men.

Desperate expedients for delay came to him. If he could have engaged the services of a real pain, he would have been glad. But steadily, inexorably, the minutes marched on towards his great crisis, and all his plans for escape blended into a mere panic fear.

The maples outside were defeating the weakening rays of the afternoon sun, and in the shadowed school-room had come a stillness, in which, nevertheless, one could feel the complacence of the little pupils who had already passed through the flames. They were calmly prepared to recognize as a spectacle the torture of others.

Little Johnnie Tanner opened the ceremony. He stamped heavily up to the platform, and bowed in such a manner that he almost fell down. He blurted out that it would ill befit him to sit silent while the name of his fair Ireland was being reproached, and he appealed to the gallant soldier before him if every British battle-field was not sown with the bones of sons of the Emerald Isle. He was also heard to say that he had listened with deepening surprise and scorn to the insinuation of the honorable member from North Glenmorganshire that the loyalty of the Irish regiments in her Majesty's service could be questioned. To what purpose, then, he asked, had the blood of Irishmen flowed on a hundred fields? To what purpose had Irishmen gone to their death with bravery and devotion in every part of the world where the victorious flag of England had been carried? If the honorable member for North Glenmorganshire insisted upon construing a mere pothouse row between soldiers in Dublin into a grand treachery to the colors and to her Majesty's uniform, then it was time for Ireland to think bitterly of her dead sons, whose graves now marked every step of England's progress, and yet who could have their honors stripped from them so easily by the honorable member for North Glenmorganshire. Furthermore, the honorable member for North Glenmorganshire —

It is needless to say that little Johnnie Tanner's language made it exceedingly hot for the honorable member for North Glenmorganshire. But Johnnie was not angry. He was only in haste. He finished the honorable member for North Glenmorganshire in what might be called a gallop.

Susie Timmens then went to the platform, and with a face as pale as death whisperingly reiterated that she would be Queen of the May. The child represented there a perfect picture of unnecessary suffering. Her small lips were quite blue, and her eyes, opened wide, stared with a look of horror at nothing.

The phlegmatic Trass boy, with his moon face only expressing peasant parentage, calmly spoke some undeniably true words concerning destiny.

In his seat Jimmie Trescott was going half blind with fear of his approaching doom. He wished that the Trass boy would talk forever about destiny. If the school-house had taken fire he thought that he would have felt simply relief. Anything was better. Death amid the flames was preferable to a recital of "The Charge of the Light Brigade."

But the Trass boy finished his remarks about destiny in a very short time. Jimmie heard the teacher call his name, and he felt the whole world look at him. He did not know how he made his way to the stage. Parts of him seemed to be of lead, and at the same time parts of him seemed to be light as air, detached. His face had gone as pale as had been the face of Susie Timmens. He was simply a child in torment; that is all there is to be said specifically about it; and to intelligent people the exhibition would have been not more edifying than a dog-fight.

"AND THEN HE SUDDENLY SAID, 'HALF A LEG —'"

He bowed precariously, choked, made an inarticulate sound, and then he suddenly said,

"Half a leg —"

"*League*," said the teacher, coolly.

"Half a leg —"

236

"League," said the teacher.

"League," repeated Jimmie, wildly.

> "Half a league, half a league, half a league onward."

He paused here and looked wretchedly at the teacher.

"Half a league," he muttered —"half a league —"

He seemed likely to keep continuing this phrase indefinitely, so after a time the teacher said, "Well, go on."

"Half a league," responded Jimmie.

The teacher had the opened book before her, and she read from it:

> "'All in the valley of Death
> Rode the —'

Go on," she concluded.

Jimmie said,

> "All in the valley of Death
> Rode the-the-the —"

He cast a glance of supreme appeal upon the teacher, and breathlessly whispered, "Rode the what?"

The young woman flushed with indignation to the roots of her hair.

> "Rode the six hundred,"

she snapped at him.

The class was arustle with delight at this cruel display. They were no better than a Roman populace in Nero's time.

Jimmie started off again:

> "Half a leg-league, half a league, half a league onward.
> All in the valley of death rode the six hundred.
> Forward-forward-forward —"

"The Light Brigade," suggested the teacher, sharply.

"The Light Brigade," said Jimmie. He was about to die of the ignoble pain of his position. As for Tennyson's lines, they had all gone grandly out of his mind, leaving it a whited wall.

The teacher's indignation was still rampant. She looked at the miserable wretch before her with an angry stare.

"You stay in after school and learn that all over again," she commanded. "And be prepared to speak it next Friday. I am astonished at you, Jimmie. Go to your seat."

If she had suddenly and magically made a spirit of him and left him free to soar high above all the travail of our earthly lives she could not have overjoyed him more. He fled back to his seat without hearing the low-toned gibes of his schoolmates. He gave no thought to the terrors of the next Friday. The evils of the day had been sufficient, and to a childish mind a week is a great space of time.

With the delightful inconsistency of his age he sat in blissful calm, and watched the sufferings of an unfortunate boy named Zimmerman, who was the next victim of education. Jimmie, of course, did not know that on this day there had been laid for him the foundation of a finished incapacity for public speaking which would be his until he died.

VI
Shame

DON'T come in here botherin' me," said the cook, intolerantly. "What with your mother bein' away on a visit, an' your father comin' home soon to lunch, I have enough on my mind-and that without bein' bothered with *you*. The kitchen is no place for little boys, anyhow. Run away, and don't be interferin' with my work." She frowned and made a grand pretence of being deep in herculean labors; but Jimmie did not run away.

"Now-they're goin' to have a picnic," he said, half audibly.

"What?"

"Now-they're goin' to have a picnic."

"Who's goin' to have a picnic?" demanded the cook, loudly. Her accent could have led one to suppose that if the projectors did not turn out to be the proper parties, she immediately would forbid this picnic.

Jimmie looked at her with more hopefulness. After twenty minutes of futile skirmishing, he had at least succeeded in introducing the subject. To her question he answered, eagerly:

"Oh, everybody! Lots and lots of boys and girls. Everybody."

"Who's everybody?"

According to custom, Jimmie began to singsong through his nose in a quite indescribable fashion an enumeration of the prospective picnickers: "Willie Dalzel an' Dan Earl an' Ella Earl an' Wolcott Margate an' Reeves Margate an' Walter Phelps an' Homer Phelps an' Minnie Phelps an'—oh-lots more girls an'—everybody. An' their mothers an' big sisters too." Then he announced a new bit of information: "They're goin' to have a picnic."

"Well, let them," said the cook, blandly.

Jimmie fidgeted for a time in silence. At last he murmured, "I—now—I thought maybe you'd let me go."

The cook turned from her work with an air of irritation and amazement that Jimmie should still be in the kitchen. "Who's stoppin' you?" she asked, sharply. "I ain't stoppin' you, am I?"

"No," admitted Jimmie, in a low voice.

"Well, why don't you go, then? Nobody's stoppin' you."

"But," said Jimmie, "I—you-now-each fellow has got to take somethin' to eat with 'm."

"Oh ho!" cried the cook, triumphantly. "So that's it, is it? So that's what you've been shyin' round here fer, eh? Well, you may as well take yourself off without more words. What with your mother bein' away on a visit, an' your father comin' home soon to his lunch, I have enough on my mind-an' that without being bothered with *you!*"

Jimmie made no reply, but moved in grief towards the door. The cook continued: "Some people in this house seem to think there's 'bout a thousand cooks in this kitchen. Where I used to work b'fore, there was some reason in 'em. I ain't a horse. A picnic!"

Jimmie said nothing, but he loitered.

"Seems as if I had enough to do, without havin' *you* come round talkin' about picnics. Nobody ever seems to think of the work I have to do. Nobody ever seems to think of it. Then they come and talk to me about picnics! What do I care about picnics?"

Jimmie loitered.

"Where I used to work b'fore, there was some reason in 'em. I never heard tell of no picnics right on top of your mother bein' away on a visit an' your father comin' home soon to his lunch. It's all foolishness."

Little Jimmie leaned his head flat against the wall and began to weep. She stared at him scornfully. "Cryin', eh? Cryin'? What are you cryin' fer?"

"N-n-nothin'," sobbed Jimmie.

There was a silence, save for Jimmie's convulsive breathing. At length the cook said: "Stop that blubberin', now. Stop it! This kitchen ain't no place fer it. Stop it!...Very well! If you don't stop, I won't give you nothin' to go to the picnic with-there!"

For the moment he could not end his tears. "You never said," he sputtered —"you never said you'd give me anything."

"An' why would I?" she cried, angrily. "Why would I —with you in here a-cryin' an' a-blubberin' an' a-bleatin' round? Enough to drive a woman crazy! I don't see how you could expect me to! The idea!"

Suddenly Jimmie announced: "I've stopped cryin'. I ain't goin' to cry no more 'tall."

"Well, then," grumbled the cook —"well, then, stop it. I've got enough on my mind." It chanced that she was making for luncheon some salmon croquettes. A tin still half full of pinky prepared fish was beside her on the table. Still grumbling, she seized a loaf of bread and, wielding a knife, she cut from this loaf four slices, each of which was as big as a six-shilling novel. She profligately spread them with butter, and jabbing the point of her knife into the salmon-tin, she brought up bits of salmon, which she flung and flattened upon the bread. Then she crashed the pieces of bread together in pairs, much as one would clash cymbals. There was no doubt in her own mind but that she had created two sandwiches.

"There," she cried. "That'll do you all right. Lemme see. What 'll I put 'em in? There — I've got it." She thrust the sandwiches into a small pail and jammed on the lid. Jimmie was ready for the picnic. "Oh, thank you, Mary!" he cried, joyfully, and in a moment he was off, running swiftly.

The picnickers had started nearly half an hour earlier, owing to his inability to quickly attack and subdue the cook, but he knew that the rendezvous was in the grove of tall, pillarlike hemlocks and pines that grew on a rocky knoll at the lake shore. His heart was very light as he sped, swinging his pail. But a few minutes previously his soul had been gloomed in despair; now he was happy. He was going to the picnic, where privilege of participation was to be bought by the contents of the little tin pail.

When he arrived in the outskirts of the grove he heard a merry clamor, and when he reached the top of the knoll he looked down the slope upon a scene which almost made his little breast burst with joy. They actually had two camp-fires! Two camp-fires! At one of them Mrs. Earl was making something-chocolate, no doubt-and at the other a young lady in white duck and a sailor hat was dropping eggs into boiling water. Other grown-up people had spread a white cloth and were laying upon it things from baskets. In the deep cool shadow of the trees the children scurried, laughing. Jimmie hastened forward to join his friends.

Homer Phelps caught first sight of him. "Ho!" he shouted; "here comes Jimmie Trescott! Come on, Jimmie; you be on our side!" The children had divided themselves into two bands for some purpose of play. The others of Homer Phelps's party loudly endorsed his plan. "Yes, Jimmie, you be on *our* side." Then arose the usual dispute. "Well, we got the weakest side."

"'Tain't any weaker'n ours."

Homer Phelps suddenly started, and looking hard, said, "What you got in the pail, Jim?"

Jimmie answered, somewhat uneasily, "Got m' lunch in it."

Instantly that brat of a Minnie Phelps simply tore down the sky with her shrieks of derision. "Got his *lunch* in it! In a *pail*!" She ran screaming to her mother. "Oh, mamma! Oh, mamma! Jimmie Trescott's got his picnic in a pail!"

Now there was nothing in the nature of this fact to particularly move the others-notably the boys, who were not competent to care if he had brought his luncheon in a coal-bin; but such is the instinct of childish society that they all immediately moved away from him. In a moment he had been made a social leper. All old intimacies were flung into the lake, so to speak. They dared not compromise themselves. At safe distances the boys shouted, scornfully: "Huh! Got his picnic in a pail!" Never again during that picnic did the little girls speak of him as Jimmie Trescott. His name now was Him.

His mind was dark with pain as he stood, the hangdog, kicking the gravel, and muttering as defiantly as he was able, "Well, I can have it in a pail if I want to." This statement of freedom was of no importance, and he knew it, but it was the only idea in his head.

"'JIMMY TRESCOTT'S GOT HIS PICNIC IN A PAIL!'"

He had been baited at school for being detected in writing a letter to little Cora, the angel child, and he had known how to defend himself, but this situation was in no way similar. This was a social affair, with grown people on all sides. It would be sweet to catch the Margate twins, for instance, and hammer them into a state of bleating respect for his pail; but that was a matter for the jungles of childhood, where grown folk seldom penetrated. He could only glower.

The amiable voice of Mrs. Earl suddenly called: "Come, children! Everything's ready!" They scampered away, glancing back for one last gloat at Jimmie standing there with his pail.

He did not know what to do. He knew that the grown folk expected him at the spread, but if he approached he would be greeted by a shameful chorus from the children-more especially from some of those damnable little girls. Still, luxuries beyond all dreaming were heaped on that cloth. One could not forget them. Perhaps if he crept up modestly, and was very gentle and very nice to the little girls, they would allow him peace. Of course it had been dreadful to come with a pail to such a grand picnic, but they might forgive him.

Oh no, they would not! He knew them better. And then suddenly he remembered with what delightful expectations he had raced to this grove, and self-pity overwhelmed him, and he thought he wanted to die and make every one feel sorry.

The young lady in white duck and a sailor hat looked at him, and then spoke to her sister, Mrs. Earl. "Who's that hovering in the distance, Emily?"

Mrs. Earl peered. "Why, it's Jimmie Trescott! Jimmie, come to the picnic! Why don't you come to the picnic, Jimmie?" He began to sidle towards the cloth.

But at Mrs. Earl's call there was another outburst from many of the children. "He's got his picnic in a pail! In a *pail*! Got it in a pail!"

Minnie Phelps was a shrill fiend. "Oh, mamma, he's got it in that pail! See! Isn't it funny? Isn't it dreadful funny?"

"What ghastly prigs children are, Emily!" said the young lady. "They are spoiling that boy's whole day, breaking his heart, the little cats! I think I'll go over and talk to him."

"Maybe you had better not," answered Mrs. Earl, dubiously. "Somehow these things arrange themselves. If you interfere, you are likely to prolong everything."

"Well, I'll try, at least," said the young lady.

At the second outburst against him Jimmie had crouched down by a tree, half hiding behind it, half pretending that he was not hiding behind it. He turned his sad gaze towards the lake. The bit of water seen through the shadows seemed perpendicular, a slate-colored wall. He heard a noise near him, and turning, he perceived the young lady looking down at him. In her hand she held plates. "May I sit near you?" she asked, coolly.

Jimmie could hardly believe his ears. After disposing herself and the plates upon the pine needles, she made brief explanation. "They're rather crowded, you see, over there. I don't like to be crowded at a picnic, so I thought I'd come here. I hope you don't mind."

Jimmie made haste to find his tongue. "Oh, I don't mind! I *like* to have you here." The ingenuous emphasis made it appear that the fact of his liking to have her there was in the nature of a law-dispelling phenomenon, but she did not smile.

"How large is that lake?" she asked.

Jimmie, falling into the snare, at once began to talk in the manner of a proprietor of the lake. "Oh, it's almost twenty miles long, an' in one place it's almost four miles wide! an' it's *deep* too-awful deep-an' it's got real steamboats on it, an' —oh-lots of other boats, an' —an' —an' —"

"Do you go out on it sometimes?"

"Oh, lots of times! My father's got a boat," he said, eying her to note the effect of his words. She was correctly pleased and struck with wonder. "Oh, has he?" she cried, as if she never before had heard of a man owning a boat.

Jimmie continued: "Yes, an' it's a grea' big boat, too, with sails, real sails; an' sometimes he takes me out in her, too; an' once he took me fishin', an' we had sandwiches, plenty of 'em, an' my father he drank beer right out of the bottle —*right out of the bottle*!"

The young lady was properly overwhelmed by this amazing intelligence. Jimmie saw the impression he had created, and he enthusiastically resumed his narrative: "An' after, he let me throw the bottles in the water, and I throwed 'em 'way, 'way, 'way out. An' they sank, an' —never comed up," he concluded, dramatically.

His face was glorified; he had forgotten all about the pail; he was absorbed in this communion with a beautiful lady who was so interested in what he had to say.

She indicated one of the plates, and said, indifferently: "Perhaps you would like some of those sandwiches. I made them. Do you like olives? And there's a deviled egg. I made that also."

"Did you really?" said Jimmie, politely. His face gloomed for a moment because the pail was recalled to his mind, but he timidly possessed himself of a sandwich.

"Hope you are not going to scorn my deviled egg," said his goddess. "I am very proud of it." He did not; he scorned little that was on the plate.

Their gentle intimacy was ineffable to the boy. He thought he had a friend, a beautiful lady, who liked him more than she did anybody at the picnic, to say the least. This was proved by the fact that she had flung aside the luxuries of the spread cloth to sit with him, the exile. Thus early did he fall a victim to woman's wiles.

"Where do you live?" he asked, suddenly.

"Oh, a long way from here! In New York."

His next question was put very bluntly. "Are you married?"

"Oh no!" she answered, gravely.

Jimmie was silent for a time, during which he glanced shyly and furtively up at her face. It was evident that he was somewhat embarrassed. Finally he said, "When I grow up to be a man—"

"Oh, that is some time yet!" said the beautiful lady.

"But when I *do*, I—I should like to marry you."

"Well, I will remember it," she answered; "but don't talk of it now, because it's such a long time; and—I wouldn't wish you to consider yourself bound." She smiled at him.

He began to brag. "When I grow up to be a man, I'm goin' to have lots an' lots of money, an' I'm goin' to have a grea' big house, an' a horse an' a shot-gun, an' lots an' lots of books 'bout elephants an' tigers, an' lots an' lots of ice-cream an' pie an'—caramels." As before, she was impressed; he could see it. "An' I'm goin' to have lots an' lots of children—'bout three hundred, I guess-an' there won't none of 'em be girls. They'll all be boys-like me."

"Oh, my!" she said.

His garment of shame was gone from him. The pail was dead and well buried. It seemed to him that months elapsed as he dwelt in happiness near the beautiful lady and trumpeted his vanity.

At last there was a shout. "Come on! we're going home." The picnickers trooped out of the grove. The children wished to resume their jeering, for Jimmie still gripped his pail, but they were restrained by the circumstances. He was walking at the side of the beautiful lady.

During this journey he abandoned many of his habits. For instance, he never travelled without skipping gracefully from crack to crack between the stones, or without pretending that he was a train of cars, or without some mumming device of childhood. But now he behaved with dignity. He made no more noise than a little mouse. He escorted the beautiful lady to the gate of the Earl home, where he awkwardly, solemnly, and wistfully shook hands in good-by. He watched her go up the walk; the door clanged.

On his way home he dreamed. One of these dreams was fascinating. Supposing the beautiful lady was his teacher in school! Oh, my! wouldn't he be a good boy, sitting like a statuette all day long, and knowing every lesson to perfection, and-everything. And then supposing that a boy should sass her. Jimmie painted himself waylaying that boy on the homeward road, and the fate of the boy was a thing to make strong men cover their eyes with their hands. And she would like him more and more-more and more. And he-he would be a little god.

But as he was entering his father's grounds an appalling recollection came to him. He was returning with the bread-and-butter and the salmon untouched in the pail! He could imagine the cook, nine feet tall, waving her fist. "An' so that's what I took trouble for, is it? So's you could bring it back? So's you could bring it back?" He skulked towards the house like a marauding bushranger. When he neared the kitchen door he made a desperate rush past it, aiming to gain the stables and there secrete his guilt. He was nearing them, when a thunderous voice hailed him from the rear:

"Jimmie Trescott, where you goin' with that pail?"

It was the cook. He made no reply, but plunged into the shelter of the stables. He whirled the lid from the pail and dashed its contents beneath a heap of blankets. Then he stood panting, his eyes on the door. The cook did not pursue, but she was bawling:

"Jimmie Trescott, what you doin' with that pail?"

He came forth, swinging it. "Nothin'," he said, in virtuous protest.

"I know better," she said, sharply, as she relieved him of his curse.

In the morning Jimmie was playing near the stable, when he heard a shout from Peter Washington, who attended Dr. Trescott's horse:

"Jim! Oh, Jim!"

"What?"

"Come yah."

Jimmie went reluctantly to the door of the stable, and Peter Washington asked:

"Wut's dish yere fish an' brade doin' unner dese yer blankups?"

"I don't know. I didn't have nothin' to do with it," answered Jimmie, indignantly.

"Don' tell *me*!" cried Peter Washington, as he flung it all away —"don' tell *me*! When I fin' fish an' brade unner dese yer blankups, I don' go an' think dese yer ho'ses er yer pop's put 'em. I *know*. An' if I caitch enny more dish yer fish an' brade in dish yer stable, *I'll* tell yer pop."

VII
The Carriage-Lamps

IT was the fault of a small nickel-plated revolver, a most incompetent weapon, which, wherever one aimed, would fling the bullet as the devil willed, and no man, when about to use it, could tell exactly what was in store for the surrounding country. This treasure had been acquired by Jimmie Trescott after arduous bargaining with another small boy. Jimmie wended homeward, patting his hip pocket at every three paces.

Peter Washington, working in the carriage-house, looked out upon him with a shrewd eye. "Oh, Jim," he called, "wut you got in yer hind pocket?"

"Nothin'," said Jimmie, feeling carefully under his jacket to make sure that the revolver wouldn't fall out.

Peter chuckled. "S'more foolishness, I raikon. You gwine be hung one day, Jim, you keep up all dish yer nonsense."

Jimmie made no reply, but went into the back garden, where he hid the revolver in a box under a lilac-bush. Then he returned to the vicinity of Peter, and began to cruise to and fro in the offing, showing all the signals of one wishing to open treaty. "Pete," he said, "how much does a box of cartridges cost?"

Peter raised himself violently, holding in one hand a piece of harness, and in the other an old rag. "Ca'tridgers! *Ca'tridgers!* Lan'sake! wut the kid want with ca'tridgers? Knew it! Knew it! Come home er-holdin' on to his hind pocket like he got money in it. An' now he want ca'tridgers."

Jimmie, after viewing with dismay the excitement caused by his question, began to move warily out of the reach of a possible hostile movement.

"Ca'tridgers!" continued Peter, in scorn and horror. "Kid like you! No bigger'n er minute! Look yah, Jim, you done been swappin' round, an' you done got hol' of er pistol!" The charge was dramatic.

The wind was almost knocked out of Jimmie by this display of Peter's terrible miraculous power, and as he backed away his feeble denials were more convincing than a confession.

"I'll tell yer pop!" cried Peter, in virtuous grandeur. "I'll tell yer pop!"

In the distance Jimmie stood appalled. He knew not what to do. The dread adult wisdom of Peter Washington had laid bare the sin, and disgrace stared at Jimmie.

There was a whirl of wheels, and a high, lean trotting-mare spun Doctor Trescott's buggy towards Peter, who ran forward busily. As the doctor climbed out, Peter, holding the mare's head, began his denunciation:

"Docteh, I gwine tell on Jim. He come home er-holdin' on to his hind pocket, an' proud like he won a tuhkey-raffle, an' I sure know what he been up to, an' I done challenge him, an' he nev' say he didn't."

"Why, what do you mean?" said the doctor. "What's this, Jimmie?"

The boy came forward, glaring wrathfully at Peter. In fact, he suddenly was so filled with rage at Peter that he forgot all precautions. "It's about a pistol," he said, bluntly. "I've got a pistol. I swapped for it."

"I done tol' 'im his pop wouldn' stand no fiah-awms, an' him a kid like he is. I done tol' 'im. Lan' sake! he strut like he was a soldier! Come in yere proud, an' er-holdin' on to his hind pocket. He think he was Jesse James, I raikon. But I done tol' 'im his pop stan' no sech foolishness. First thing —*blam* —he shoot his haid off. No, seh, he too tinety t' come in yere er-struttin' like he jest bought Main Street. I tol' 'im. I done tol' 'im-shawp. I don' wanter be loafin' round dis yer stable if Jim he gwine go shootin' round an' shootin' round —*blim-blam-blim-blam*! No, seh. I retiahs. I retiahs. It's all right if er grown man got er gun, but ain't no kids come foolishin' round *me* with fiah-awms. No, seh. I retiahs."

"Oh, be quiet, Peter!" said the doctor. "Where is this thing, Jimmie?"

The boy went sulkily to the box under the lilac-bush and returned with the revolver. "Here 'tis," he said, with a glare over his shoulder at Peter. The doctor looked at the silly weapon in critical contempt.

"It's not much of a thing, Jimmie, but I don't think you are quite old enough for it yet. I'll keep it for you in one of the drawers of my desk."

Peter Washington burst out proudly: "I done tol' 'im th' docteh wouldn' stan' no traffickin' round yere with fiah-awms. I done tol' 'im."

Jimmie and his father went together into the house, and as Peter unharnessed the mare he continued his comments on the boy and the revolver. He was not cast down by the absence of hearers. In fact, he usually talked better when there was no one to listen save the horses. But now his observations bore small resemblance to his earlier and public statements. Admiration and the keen family pride of a Southern negro who has been long in one place were now in his tone.

"That boy! He's er devil! When he get to be er man-wow! He'll jes take an' make things whirl round yere. Raikon we'll all take er back seat when he come erlong er-raisin' Cain."

He had unharnessed the mare, and with his back bent was pushing the buggy into the carriage-house.

"Er pistol! An' him no bigger than er minute!"

A small stone whizzed past Peter's head and clattered on the stable. He hastily dropped all occupation and struck a curious attitude. His right knee was almost up to his chin, and his arms were wreathed protectingly about his head. He had not looked in the direction from which the stone had come, but he had begun immediately to yell:

"'YOU JIM! QUIT! QUIT, I TELL YER!'"

"You Jim! Quit! Quit, I tell yer, Jim! Watch out! You gwine break somethin', Jim!"

"Yah!" taunted the boy, as with the speed and ease of a light-cavalryman he manœuvred in the distance. "Yah! Told on me, did you! Told on me, hey! There! How do you like that?" The missiles resounded against the stable.

"Watch out, Jim! You gwine break something, Jim, I tell yer! Quit yer foolishness, Jim! Ow! Watch out, boy! I —"

There was a crash. With diabolic ingenuity, one of Jimmie's pebbles had entered the carriage-house and had landed among a row of carriage-lamps on a shelf, creating havoc which was apparently beyond all reason of physical law. It seemed to Jimmie that the racket of falling glass could have been heard in an adjacent county.

Peter was a prophet who after persecution was suffered to recall everything to the mind of the persecutor. "*There!* Knew it! Knew it! *Now* I raikon you'll quit. Hi! jes look ut dese yer lamps! Fer lan' sake! Oh, now yer pop jes break ev'ry bone in yer body!"

In the doorway of the kitchen the cook appeared with a startled face. Jimmie's father and mother came suddenly out on the front veranda. "What was that noise?" called the the doctor.

Peter went forward to explain. "Jim he was er-heavin' rocks at me, docteh, an' erlong come one rock an' go *blam* inter all th' lamps an' jes skitter 'em t' bits. I declayah —"

Jimmie, half blinded with emotion, was nevertheless aware of a lightning glance from his father, a glance which cowed and frightened him to the ends of his toes. He heard the steady but deadly tones of his father in a fury: "Go into the house and wait until I come."

Bowed in anguish, the boy moved across the lawn and up the steps. His mother was standing on the veranda still gazing towards the stable. He loitered in the faint hope that she might take some small pity on his state. But she could have heeded him no less if he had been invisible. He entered the house.

When the doctor returned from his investigation of the harm done by Jimmie's hand, Mrs. Trescott looked at him anxiously, for she knew that he was concealing some volcanic impulses. "Well?" she asked.

"It isn't the lamps," he said at first. He seated himself on the rail. "I don't know what we are going to do with that boy. It isn't so much the lamps as it is the other thing. He was throwing stones at Peter because Peter told me about the revolver. What are we going to do with him?"

"I'm sure I don't know," replied the mother. "We've tried almost everything. Of course much of it is pure animal spirits. Jimmie is not naturally vicious —"

"Oh, I know," interrupted the doctor, impatiently. "Do you suppose, when the stones were singing about Peter's ears, he cared whether they were flung by a boy who was naturally vicious or a boy who was not? The question might interest him afterward, but at the time he was mainly occupied in dodging these effects of pure animal spirits."

"Don't be too hard on the boy, Ned. There's lots of time yet. He's so young yet, and — I believe he gets most of his naughtiness from that wretched Dalzel boy. That Dalzel boy-well, he's simply awful!" Then, with true motherly instinct to shift blame from her own boy's shoulders, she proceeded to sketch the character of the Dalzel boy in lines that would have made that talented young vagabond stare. It was not admittedly her feeling that the doctor's attention should be diverted from the main issue and his indignation divided among the camps, but presently the doctor felt himself burn with wrath for the Dalzel boy.

"Why don't you keep Jimmie away from him?" he demanded. "Jimmie has no business consorting with abandoned little predestined jail-birds like him. If I catch him on the place I'll box his ears."

"It is simply impossible, unless we kept Jimmie shut up all the time," said Mrs. Trescott. "I can't watch him every minute of the day, and the moment my back is turned, he's off."

"I should think those Dalzel people would hire somebody to bring up their child for them," said the doctor. "They don't seem to know how to do it themselves."

Presently you would have thought from the talk that one Willie Dalzel had been throwing stones at Peter Washington because Peter Washington had told Doctor Trescott that Willie Dalzel had come into possession of a revolver.

In the mean time Jimmie had gone into the house to await the coming of his father. He was in a rebellious mood. He had not intended to destroy the carriage-lamps. He had been merely hurling stones at a creature whose perfidy deserved such action, and the hitting of the lamps had been merely another move of the great conspirator Fate to force one Jimmie Trescott into dark and troublous ways. The boy was beginning to find the world a bitter place. He couldn't win appreciation for a single virtue; he could only achieve quick, rigorous punishment for his misdemeanors. Everything was an enemy. Now there were those silly old lamps-what were they doing up on that shelf, anyhow? It would have been just as easy for them at the time to have been in some other place. But no; there they had been, like the crowd that is passing under the wall when the mason for the first time in twenty years lets fall a brick. Furthermore, the flight of that stone had been perfectly unreasonable. It had been a sort of freak in physical law. Jimmie understood that he might have thrown stones from the same fatal spot for an hour without hurting a single lamp. He was a victim-that was it. Fate had conspired with the detail of his environment to simply hound him into a grave or into a cell.

But who would understand? Who would understand? And here the boy turned his mental glance in every direction, and found nothing but what was to him the black of cruel ignorance. Very well; some day they would —

From somewhere out in the street he heard a peculiar whistle of two notes. It was the common signal of the boys in the neighborhood, and judging from the direction of the sound, it was apparently intended to summon him. He moved immediately to one of the windows of the sitting-room. It opened upon a part of the grounds remote from the stables and cut off from the veranda by a wing. He perceived Willie Dalzel loitering in the street. Jimmie whistled the signal after having pushed up the window-sash some inches. He saw the Dalzel boy turn and regard him, and then call several other boys. They stood in a group and gestured. These gestures plainly said: "Come out. We've got something on hand." Jimmie sadly shook his head.

But they did not go away. They held a long consultation. Presently Jimmie saw the intrepid Dalzel boy climb the fence and begin to creep among the shrubbery, in elaborate imitation of an Indian scout. In time he arrived under Jimmie's window, and raised his face to whisper: "Come on out! We're going on a bear-hunt."

A bear-hunt! Of course Jimmie knew that it would not be a real bear-hunt, but would be a sort of carouse of pretension and big talking and preposterous lying and valor, wherein each boy would strive to have himself called Kit Carson by the others. He was profoundly affected. However, the parental word was upon him, and he could not move. "No," he answered, "I can't. I've got to stay in."

"Are you a prisoner?" demanded the Dalzel boy, eagerly.

"No-o —yes —I s'pose I am."

The other lad became much excited, but he did not lose his wariness. "Don't you want to be rescued?"

"Why-no —I dun'no'," replied Jimmie, dubiously.

Willie Dalzel was indignant. "Why, of course you want to be rescued! We'll rescue you. I'll go and get my men." And thinking this a good sentence, he repeated, pompously, "I'll go and get my men." He began to crawl away, but when he was distant some ten paces he turned to say: "Keep up a stout heart. Remember that you have friends who will be faithful unto death. The time is not now far off when you will again view the blessed sunlight."

The poetry of these remarks filled Jimmie with ecstasy, and he watched eagerly for the coming of the friends who would be faithful unto death. They delayed some time, for the reason that Willie Dalzel was making a speech.

"Now, men," he said, "our comrade is a prisoner in yon-in yond-in that there fortress. We must to the rescue. Who volunteers to go with me?" He fixed them with a stern eye.

There was a silence, and then one of the smaller boys remarked,

"If Doc Trescott ketches us trackin' over his lawn —"

Willie Dalzel pounced upon the speaker and took him by the throat. The two presented a sort of a burlesque of the wood-cut on the cover of a dime novel which Willie had just been reading — *The Red Captain: A Tale of the Pirates of the Spanish Main.*

"You are a coward!" said Willie, through his clinched teeth.

"No, I ain't, Willie," piped the other, as best he could.

"I say you are," cried the great chieftain, indignantly. "Don't tell *me* I'm a liar." He relinquished his hold upon the coward and resumed his speech. "You know me, men. Many of you have been my followers for long years. You saw me slay Six-handed Dick with my own hand. You know I never falter. Our comrade is a prisoner in the cruel hands of our enemies. Aw, Pete Washington? He dassent. My pa says if Pete ever troubles me he'll brain 'im. Come on! To the rescue! Who will go with me to the rescue? Aw, come on! What are you afraid of?"

"HE TURNED TO SAY: 'KEEP UP A STOUT HEART'"

It was another instance of the power of eloquence upon the human mind. There was only one boy who was not thrilled by this oration, and he was a boy whose favorite reading had been of the road-agents and gun-fighters of the great West, and he thought the whole thing should be conducted in the Deadwood Dick manner. This talk of a "comrade" was silly; "pard" was the proper word. He resolved that he would make a show of being a pirate, and keep secret the fact that he really was Hold-up Harry, the Terror of the Sierras.

But the others were knit close in piratical bonds. One by one they climbed the fence at a point hidden from the house by tall shrubs. With many a low-breathed caution they went upon their perilous adventure.

Jimmie was grown tired of waiting for his friends who would be faithful unto death. Finally he decided that he would rescue himself. It would be a gross breach of rule, but he couldn't sit there all the rest of the day waiting for his faithful-unto-death friends. The window was only five feet from the ground. He softly raised the sash and threw one leg over the sill. But at the same time he perceived his friends snaking among the bushes. He withdrew his leg and waited, seeing that he was now to be rescued in an orthodox way. The brave pirates came nearer and nearer.

Jimmie heard a noise of a closing door, and turning, he saw his father in the room looking at him and the open window in angry surprise. Boys never faint, but Jimmie probably came as near to it as may the average boy.

"What's all this?" asked the doctor, staring. Involuntarily Jimmie glanced over his shoulder through the window. His father saw the creeping figures. "What are those boys doing?" he said, sharply, and he knit his brows.

"Nothin'."

"Nothing! Don't tell me that. Are they coming here to the window?"

"Y-e-s, sir."

"What for?"

"To-to see me."

"What about?"

"About-about nothin'."

"What about?"

Jimmie knew that he could conceal nothing.

"THE BOY TURNED AGAIN TO HIS FRIEND"

He said, "They're comin' to-to-to rescue me." He began to whimper.

The doctor sat down heavily.

"What? To rescue you?" he gasped.

"Y-yes, sir."

The doctor's eyes began to twinkle. "Very well," he said presently. "I will sit here and observe this rescue. And on no account do you warn them that I am here. Understand?"

Of course Jimmie understood. He had been mad to warn his friends, but his father's mere presence had frightened him from doing it. He stood trembling at the window, while the doctor stretched in an easy-chair near at hand. They waited. The doctor could tell by his son's increasing agitation that the great moment was near. Suddenly he heard Willie Dalzel's voice hiss out a word: "S-s-silence!" Then the same voice addressed Jimmie at the window: "Good cheer, my comrade. The time is now at hand. I have come. Never did the Red Captain turn his back on a friend. One minute more and you will be free. Once aboard my gallant craft and you can bid defiance to your haughty enemies. Why don't you hurry up? What are you standin' there lookin' like a cow for?"

"I —er-now-you —" stammered Jimmie.

Here Hold-up Harry, the Terror of the Sierras, evidently concluded that Willie Dalzel had had enough of the premier part, so he said:

"Brace up, pard. Don't ye turn white-livered now, fer ye know that Hold-up Harry, the Terrar of the Sarahs, ain't the man ter —"

"Oh, stop it!" said Willie Dalzel. "He won't understand that, you know. He's a pirate. Now, Jimmie, come on. Be of light heart, my comrade. Soon you —"

"I 'low arter all this here long time in jail ye thought ye had no friends mebbe, but I tell ye Hold-up Harry, the Terrar of the Sarahs —"

"A boat is waitin' —"

"I have ready a trusty horse —"

Willie Dalzel could endure his rival no longer.

"Look here, Henry, you're spoilin' the whole thing. We're all pirates, don't you see, and you're a pirate too."

"I ain't a pirate. I'm Hold-up Harry, the Terrar of the Sarahs."

"You ain't, I say," said Willie, in despair. "You're spoilin' everything, you are. All right, now. You wait. I'll fix you for this, see if I don't! Oh, come on, Jimmie. A boat awaits us at the foot of the rocks. In one short hour you'll be free forever from your ex-exewable enemies, and their vile plots. Hasten, for the dawn approaches."

"THEY WHIRLED AND SCAMPERED AWAY LIKE DEER"

The suffering Jimmie looked at his father, and was surprised at what he saw. The doctor was doubled up like a man with the colic. He was breathing heavily. The boy turned again to his friends. "I —now-look here," he began, stumbling among the words. "You —I —I don't think I'll be rescued to-day."

The pirates were scandalized. "What?" they whispered, angrily. "Ain't you goin' to be rescued? Well, all right for you, Jimmie Trescott. That's a nice way to act, that is!" Their upturned eyes glowered at Jimmie.

Suddenly Doctor Trescott appeared at the window with Jimmie. "Oh, go home, boys!" he gasped, but they did not hear him. Upon the instant they had whirled and scampered away like deer. The first lad to reach the fence was the Red Captain, but Hold-up Harry, the Terror of the Sierras, was so close that there was little to choose between them.

Doctor Trescott lowered the window, and then spoke to his son in his usual quiet way. "Jimmie, I wish you would go and tell Peter to have the buggy ready at seven o'clock."

"Yes, sir," said Jimmie, and he swaggered out to the stables. "Pete, father wants the buggy ready at seven o'clock."

Peter paid no heed to this order, but with the tender sympathy of a true friend he inquired, "Hu't?"

"Hurt? Did what hurt?"

"Yer trouncin'."

"Trouncin'!" said Jimmie, contemptuously. "I didn't get any trouncin'."

"No?" said Peter. He gave Jimmie a quick shrewd glance, and saw that he was telling the truth. He began to mutter and mumble over his work. "Ump! Ump! Dese yer white folks act like they think er boy's made er glass. No trouncin'! Ump!" He was consumed with curiosity to learn why Jimmie had not felt a heavy parental hand, but he did not care to lower his dignity by asking questions about it. At last, however, he reached the limits of his endurance, and in a voice pretentiously careless he asked, "Didn' yer pop take on like mad er-bout dese yer cay'ge-lamps?"

"Carriage-lamps?" inquired Jimmie.

"Ump."

"No, he didn't say anything about carriage-lamps —not that I remember. Maybe he did, though. Lemme see....No, he never mentioned 'em."

VIII
The Knife

I

SI BRYANT'S place was on the shore of the lake, and his garden-patch, shielded from the north by a bold little promontory and a higher ridge inland, was accounted the most successful and surprising in all Whilomville township. One afternoon Si was working in the garden-patch, when Doctor Trescott's man, Peter Washington, came trudging slowly along the road, observing nature. He scanned the white man's fine agricultural results. "Take your eye off them there mellons, you rascal," said Si, placidly.

The negro's face widened in a grin of delight. "Well, Mist' Bryant, I raikon I ain't on'y make m'se'f covertous er-lookin' at dem yere mellums, sure 'nough. Dey suhtainly is grand."

"That's all right," responded Si, with affected bitterness of spirit. "That's all right. Just don't you admire 'em too much, that's all." Peter chuckled and chuckled. "Ma Lode! Mist' Bryant, y-y-you don' think I'm gwine come prowlin' in dish yer gawden?"

"No, I know you hain't," said Si, with solemnity. "B'cause, if you did, I'd shoot you so full of holes you couldn't tell yourself from a sponge."

"Um-no, seh! No, seh! I don' raikon you'll get chance at Pete, Mist' Bryant. No, seh. I'll take an' run 'long an' rob er bank 'fore I'll come foolishin' 'round *your* gawden, Mist' Bryant."

Bryant, gnarled and strong as an old tree, leaned on his hoe, and laughed a Yankee laugh. His mouth remained tightly closed, but the sinister lines which ran from the sides of his nose to the meetings of his lips developed to form a comic oval, and he emitted a series of grunts, while his eyes gleamed merrily and his shoulders shook. Pete, on the contrary, threw back his head and guffawed thunderously. The effete joke in regard to an American negro's fondness for watermelons was still an admirable pleasantry to them, and this was not the first time they had engaged in badinage over it. In fact, this venerable survival had formed between them a friendship of casual roadside quality.

Afterwards Peter went on up the road. He continued to chuckle until he was far away. He was going to pay a visit to old Alek Williams, a negro who lived with a large family in a hut clinging to the side of a mountain. The scattered colony of negroes which hovered near Whilomville was of interesting origin, being the result of some contrabands who had drifted as far north as Whilomville during the great civil war. The descendants of these adventurers were mainly conspicuous for their bewildering number, and the facility which they possessed for adding even to this number. Speaking, for example, of the Jacksons-one couldn't hurl a stone into the hills about Whilomville without having it land on the roof of a hut full of Jacksons. The town reaped little in labor from these curious suburbs. There were a few men who came in regularly to work in gardens, to drive teams, to care for horses, and there were a few women who came in to cook or to wash. These latter had usually drunken husbands. In the main the colony loafed in high spirits, and the industrious minority gained no direct honor from their fellows, unless they spent their earnings on raiment, in which case they were naturally treated with distinction. On the whole, the hardships of these people were the wind, the rain, the snow, and any other physical difficulties which they could cultivate. About twice a year the lady philanthropists of Whilomville went up against them, and came away poorer in goods but rich in complacence. After one of these attacks the colony would preserve a comic air of rectitude for two days, and then relapse again to the genial irresponsibility of a crew of monkeys.

Peter Washington was one of the industrious class who occupied a position of distinction, for he surely spent his money on personal decoration. On occasion he could dress better than the Mayor of Whilomville himself, or at least in more colors, which was the main thing to the minds of his admirers. His ideal had been the late gallant Henry Johnson, whose conquests in

Watermelon Alley, as well as in the hill shanties, had proved him the equal if not the superior of any Pullman-car porter in the country. Perhaps Peter had too much Virginia laziness and humor in him to be a wholly adequate successor to the fastidious Henry Johnson, but, at any rate, he admired his memory so attentively as to be openly termed a dude by envious people.

"HE HEAVED ONE OF HIS EIGHT-OUNCE ROCKS"

On this afternoon he was going to call on old Alek Williams because Alek's eldest girl was just turned seventeen, and, to Peter's mind, was a triumph of beauty. He was not wearing his best clothes, because on his last visit Alek's half-breed hound Susie had taken occasion to forcefully extract a quite large and valuable part of the visitor's trousers. When Peter arrived at the end of the rocky field which contained old Alek's shanty he stooped and provided himself with several large stones, weighing them carefully in his hand, and finally continuing his journey with three stones of about eight ounces each. When he was near the house, three gaunt hounds, Rover and Carlo and Susie, came sweeping down upon him. His impression was that they were going to climb him as if he were a tree, but at the critical moment they swerved and went growling and snapping around him, their heads low, their eyes malignant. The afternoon caller waited until Susie presented her side to him, then he heaved one of his eight-ounce rocks. When it landed, her hollow ribs gave forth a drumlike sound, and she was knocked sprawling, her legs in the air. The other hounds at once fled in horror, and she followed as soon as she was able, yelping at the top of her lungs. The afternoon caller resumed his march.

At the wild expressions of Susie's anguish old Alek had flung open the door and come hastily into the sunshine. "Yah, you Suse, come erlong outa dat now. What fer you-Oh, how do, how do, Mist' Wash'ton-how do?"

"How do, Mist' Willums? I done foun' it necessa'y fer ter damnearkill dish yer dawg a yourn, Mist' Willums."

"Come in, come in, Mist' Wash'ton. Dawg no 'count, Mist' Wash'ton." Then he turned to address the unfortunate animal. "Hu't, did it? Hu't? 'Pears like you gwine dun some saince by time somebody brek yer back. 'Pears like I gwine club yer inter er frazzle 'fore you fin' out some saince. Gw'on 'way f'm yah!"

As the old man and his guest entered the shanty a body of black children spread out in crescent-shape formation and observed Peter with awe. Fat old Mrs. Williams greeted him turbulently, while the eldest girl, Mollie, lurked in a corner and giggled with finished imbecility, gazing at the visitor with eyes that were shy and bold by turns. She seemed at times absurdly over-confident, at times foolishly afraid; but her giggle consistently endured. It was a giggle on which an irascible but right-minded judge would have ordered her forthwith to be buried alive.

"MOLLIE LURKED IN A CORNER AND GIGGLED"

254

Amid a great deal of hospitable gabbling, Peter was conducted to the best chair out of the three that the house contained. Enthroned therein, he made himself charming in talk to the old people, who beamed upon him joyously. As for Mollie, he affected to be unaware of her existence. This may have been a method for entrapping the sentimental interest of that young gazelle, or it may be that the giggle had worked upon him.

He was absolutely fascinating to the old people. They could talk like rotary snow-ploughs, and he gave them every chance, while his face was illumined with appreciation. They pressed him to stay for supper, and he consented, after a glance at the pot on the stove which was too furtive to be noted.

During the meal old Alek recounted the high state of Judge Oglethorpe's kitchen-garden, which Alek said was due to his unremitting industry and fine intelligence. Alek was a gardener, whenever impending starvation forced him to cease temporarily from being a lily of the field.

"Mist' Bryant he suhtainly got er grand gawden," observed Peter.

"Dat so, dat so, Mist' Wash'ton," assented Alek. "He got fine gawden."

"Seems like I nev' *did* see sech mellums, big as er bar'l, layin' dere. I don't raikon an'body in dish yer county kin hol' it with Mist' Bryant when comes ter mellums."

"Dat so, Mist' Wash'ton."

They did not talk of watermelons until their heads held nothing else, as the phrase goes. But they talked of watermelons until, when Peter started for home that night over a lonely road, they held a certain dominant position in his mind. Alek had come with him as far as the fence, in order to protect him from a possible attack by the mongrels. There they had cheerfully parted, two honest men.

The night was dark, and heavy with moisture. Peter found it uncomfortable to walk rapidly. He merely loitered on the road. When opposite Si Bryant's place he paused and looked over the fence into the garden. He imagined he could see the form of a huge melon lying in dim stateliness not ten yards away. He looked at the Bryant house. Two windows, down-stairs, were lighted. The Bryants kept no dog, old Si's favorite child having once been bitten by a dog, and having since died, within that year, of pneumonia.

Peering over the fence, Peter fancied that if any low-minded night-prowler should happen to note the melon, he would not find it difficult to possess himself of it. This person would merely wait until the lights were out in the house, and the people presumably asleep. Then he would climb the fence, reach the melon in a few strides, sever the stem with his ready knife, and in a trice be back in the road with his prize. There need be no noise, and, after all, the house was some distance.

Selecting a smooth bit of turf, Peter took a seat by the road-side. From time to time he glanced at the lighted window.

When Peter and Alek had said good-bye, the old man turned back in the rocky field and shaped a slow course towards that high dim light which marked the little window of his shanty. It would be incorrect to say that Alek could think of nothing but watermelons. But it was true that Si Bryant's watermelon-patch occupied a certain conspicuous position in his thoughts.

He sighed; he almost wished that he was again a conscienceless pickaninny, instead of being one of the most ornate, solemn, and look-at-me-sinner deacons that ever graced the handle of a collection-basket. At this time it made him quite sad to reflect upon his granite integrity. A weaker man might perhaps bow his moral head to the temptation, but for him such a fall was impossible. He was a prince of the church, and if he had been nine princes of the church he could not have been more proud. In fact, religion was to the old man a sort of personal dignity. And he was on Sundays so obtrusively good that you could see his sanctity through a door. He forced it on you until you would have felt its influence even in a forecastle.

It was clear in his mind that he must put watermelon thoughts from him, and after a moment he told himself, with much ostentation, that he had done so. But it was cooler under the sky than in the shanty, and as he was not sleepy, he decided to take a stroll down to Si Bryant's place and look at the melons from a pinnacle of spotless innocence. Reaching the road, he paused to listen. It would not do to let Peter hear him, because that graceless rapscallion would probably misunderstand him. But, assuring himself that Peter was well on his way, he set out, walking briskly until he was within four hundred yards of Bryant's place. Here he went to the side of the road, and walked thereafter on the damp, yielding turf. He made no sound.

He did not go on to that point in the main road which was directly opposite the water-melon-patch. He did not wish to have his ascetic contemplation disturbed by some chance wayfarer. He turned off along a short lane which led to Si Bryant's barn. Here he reached a place where he could see, over the fence, the faint shapes of the melons.

Alek was affected. The house was some distance away, there was no dog, and doubtless the Bryants would soon extinguish their lights and go to bed. Then some poor lost lamb of sin might come and scale the fence, reach a melon in a moment, sever the stem with his ready knife, and in a trice be back in the road with his prize. And this poor lost lamb of sin might even be a bishop, but no one would ever know it. Alek singled out with his eye a very large melon, and thought that the lamb would prove his judgment if he took that one.

He found a soft place in the grass, and arranged himself comfortably. He watched the lights in the windows.

It seemed to Peter Washington that the Bryants absolutely consulted their own wishes in regard to the time for retiring; but at last he saw the lighted windows fade briskly from left to right, and after a moment a window on the second floor blazed out against the darkness. Si was going to bed. In five minutes this window abruptly vanished, and all the world was night.

Peter spent the ensuing quarter-hour in no mental debate. His mind was fixed. He was here, and the melon was there. He would have it. But an idea of being caught appalled him. He thought of his position. He was the beau of his community, honored right and left. He pictured the consternation of his friends and the cheers of his enemies if the hands of the redoubtable Si Bryant should grip him in his shame.

He arose, and going to the fence, listened. No sound broke the stillness, save the rhythmical incessant clicking of myriad insects, and the guttural chanting of the frogs in the reeds at the lake-side. Moved by sudden decision, he climbed the fence and crept silently and swiftly down upon the melon. His open knife was in his hand. There was the melon, cool, fair to see, as pompous in its fatness as the cook in a monastery.

Peter put out a hand to steady it while he cut the stem. But at the instant he was aware that a black form had dropped over the fence lining the lane in front of him and was coming stealthily towards him. In a palsy of terror he dropped flat upon the ground, not having strength enough to run away. The next moment he was looking into the amazed and agonized face of old Alek Williams.

There was a moment of loaded silence, and then Peter was overcome by a mad inspiration. He suddenly dropped his knife and leaped upon Alek. "I got che!" he hissed. "I got che! I got che!" The old man sank down as limp as rags. "I got che! I got che! Steal Mist' Bryant's mellums, hey?"

Alek, in a low voice, began to beg. "Oh, Mist' Peter Wash'ton, don' go fer ter be too ha'd on er ole man! I nev' come yere fer ter steal 'em. 'Deed I didn't, Mist' Wash'ton! I come yere jes fer ter *feel* 'em. Oh, please, Mist' Wash'ton —"

"Come erlong outa yere, you ol' rip," said Peter, "an' don' trumple on dese yer baids. I gwine put you wah you won' ketch col'."

Without difficulty he tumbled the whining Alek over the fence to the roadway, and followed him with sheriff-like expedition! He took him by the scruff. "Come erlong, deacon. I raikon I gwine put you wah you kin pray, deacon. Come erlong, deacon."

The emphasis and reiteration of his layman's title in the church produced a deadly effect upon Alek. He felt to his marrow the heinous crime into which this treacherous night had betrayed him. As Peter marched his prisoner up the road towards the mouth of the lane, he continued his remarks: "Come erlong, deacon. Nev' see er man so anxious like erbout er mellum-paitch, deacon. Seem like you jes must see'em er-growin' an' *feel* 'em, deacon. Mist' Bryant he'll be s'prised, deacon, findin' out you come fer ter *feel* his mellums. Come erlong, deacon. Mist' Bryant he expectin' some ole rip like you come soon."

They had almost reached the lane when Alek's cur Susie, who had followed her master, approached in the silence which attends dangerous dogs; and seeing indications of what she took to be war, she appended herself swiftly but firmly to the calf of Peter's left leg. The mêlée was short, but spirited. Alek had no wish to have his dog complicate his already serious misfortunes, and went manfully to the defence of his captor. He procured a large stone, and by beating this with both hands down upon the resounding skull of the animal, he induced her to quit her grip. Breathing heavily, Peter dropped into the long grass at the road-side. He said nothing.

"THE NEXT MOMENT HE WAS LOOKING INTO THE AMAZED AND AGONIZED
FACE OF OLD ALEK"

"Mist' Wash'ton," said Alek at last, in a quavering voice, "I raikon I gwine wait yere see what you gwine do ter me."

Whereupon Peter passed into a spasmodic state, in which he rolled to and fro and shook.

"Mist' Wash'ton, I hope dish yer dog 'ain't gone an' give you fitses?"

Peter sat up suddenly. "No, she 'ain't," he answered; "but she gin me er big skeer; an' fer yer 'sistance with er cobblestone, Mist' Willums, I tell you what I gwine do —I tell you what I gwine do." He waited an impressive moment. "I gwine 'lease you!"

Old Alek trembled like a little bush in a wind. "Mist' Wash'ton?"

Quoth Peter, deliberately, "I gwine 'lease you."

The old man was filled with a desire to negotiate this statement at once, but he felt the necessity of carrying off the event without an appearance of haste. "Yes, seh; thank 'e, seh; thank 'e, Mist' Wash'ton. I raikon I ramble home pressenly." He waited an interval, and then dubiously said, "Good-evenin', Mist' Wash'ton."

"Good-evenin', deacon. Don' come foolin' roun' *feelin'* no mellums, and I say troof. Good-evenin', deacon."

Alek took off his hat and made three profound bows. "Thank 'e, seh. Thank 'e, seh. Thank 'e, seh."

Peter underwent another severe spasm, but the old man walked off towards his home with a humble and contrite heart.

IV

The next morning Alek proceeded from his shanty under the complete but customary illusion that he was going to work. He trudged manfully along until he reached the vicinity of Si Bryant's place. Then, by stages, he relapsed into a slink. He was passing the garden-patch under full steam, when, at some distance ahead of him, he saw Si Bryant leaning casually on the garden fence.

"Good-mornin', Alek."

"Good-mawnin', Mist' Bryant," answered Alek, with a new deference. He was marching on, when he was halted by a word —"Alek!"

He stopped. "Yes, seh."

"I found a knife this mornin' in th' road," drawled Si, "an' I thought maybe it was yourn."

Improved in mind by this divergence from the direct line of attack, Alek stepped up easily to look at the knife. "No, seh," he said, scanning it as it lay in Si's palm, while the cold steel-blue eyes of the white man looked down into his stomach, "'tain't no knife er mine." But he knew the knife. He knew it as if it had been his mother. And at the same moment a spark flashed through his head and made wise his understanding. He knew everything. "'Tain't much of er knife, Mist' Bryant," he said, deprecatingly.

"'Tain't much of a knife, I know that," cried Si, in sudden heat, "but I found it this mornin' in my watermelon-patch —hear?"

"Watahmellum-paitch?" yelled Alek, not astounded.

"Yes, in my watermelon-patch," sneered Si, "an' I think you know something about it, too!"

"Me?" cried Alek. "Me?"

"Yes-you!" said Si, with icy ferocity. "Yes-you!" He had become convinced that Alek was not in any way guilty, but he was certain that the old man knew the owner of the knife, and so he pressed him at first on criminal lines. "Alek, you might as well own up now. You've been meddlin' with my watermelons!"

"Me?" cried Alek again. "Yah's *ma* knife. I done cah'e it foh yeahs."

Bryant changed his ways. "Look here, Alek," he said, confidentially: "I know you and you know me, and there ain't no use in any more skirmishin'. *I* know that *you* know whose knife that is. Now whose is it?"

This challenge was so formidable in character that Alek temporarily quailed and began to stammer. "Er-now-Mist' Bryant-you-you-frien' er mine —"

"I know I'm a friend of yours, but," said Bryant, inexorably, "who owns this knife?"

Alek gathered unto himself some remnants of dignity and spoke with reproach: "Mist' Bryant, dish yer knife ain' mine."

"No," said Bryant, "it ain't. But you know who it belongs to, an' I want you to tell me-quick."

"Well, Mist' Bryant," answered Alek, scratching his wool, "I won't say 's I *do* know who b'longs ter dish yer knife, an' I won't say 's I *don't*."

Bryant again laughed his Yankee laugh, but this time there was little humor in it. It was dangerous.

Alek, seeing that he had gotten himself into hot water by the fine diplomacy of his last sentence, immediately began to flounder and totally submerge himself. "No, Mist' Bryant," he repeated, "I won't say 's I *do* know who b'longs ter dish yer knife, an' I won't say 's I *don't*." And he began to parrot this fatal sentence again and again. It seemed wound about his tongue. He could not rid himself of it. Its very power to make trouble for him seemed to originate the mysterious Afric reason for its repetition.

"Is he a very close friend of yourn?" said Bryant, softly.

"F-frien'?" stuttered Alek. He appeared to weigh this question with much care. "Well, seems like he *was* er frien', an' then agin, it seems like he —"

"It seems like he *wasn't*?" asked Bryant.

"Yes, seh, jest so, jest so," cried Alek. "Sometimes it seems like he *wasn't*. Then agin —" He stopped for profound meditation.

The patience of the white man seemed inexhaustible. At length his low and oily voice broke the stillness. "Oh, well, of course if he's a friend of yourn, Alek! You know I wouldn't want to make no trouble for a friend of yourn."

"Yes, seh," cried the negro at once. "He's er frien' er mine. He is dat."

"Well, then, it seems as if about the only thing to do is for you to tell me his name so's I can send him his knife, and that's all there is to it."

Alek took off his hat, and in perplexity ran his hand over his wool. He studied the ground. But several times he raised his eyes to take a sly peep at the imperturbable visage of the white man. "Y —y —yes, Mist' Bryant....I raikon dat's erbout all what kin be done. I gwine tell you who b'longs ter dish yer knife."

"Of course," said the smooth Bryant, "it ain't a very nice thing to have to do, but —"

"No, seh," cried Alek, brightly; "I'm gwine tell you, Mist' Bryant. I gwine tell you erbout dat knife. Mist' Bryant," he asked, solemnly, "does you know who b'longs ter dat knife?"

"No, I —"

"Well, I gwine tell. I gwine tell who, Mr Bryant —" The old man drew himself to a stately pose and held forth his arm. "I gwine tell who, Mist' Bryant, *dish yer knife b'longs ter Sam Jackson!*"

"THE OLD MAN DREW HIMSELF TO A STATELY POSE"

Bryant was startled into indignation. "Who in hell is Sam Jackson?" he growled.

"He's a nigger," said Alek, impressively, "and he wuks in er lumber-yawd up yere in Hoswego."

IX
The Stove

I

THEY'LL bring her," said Mrs. Trescott, dubiously. Her cousin, the painter, the bewildered father of the angel child, had written to say that if they were asked, he and his wife would come to the Trescotts for the Christmas holidays. But he had not officially stated that the angel child would form part of the expedition. "But of course they'll bring her," said Mrs. Trescott to her husband.

The doctor assented. "Yes, they'll have to bring her. They wouldn't dare leave New York at her mercy."

"Well," sighed Mrs. Trescott, after a pause, "the neighbors will be pleased. When they see her they'll immediately lock up their children for safety."

"Anyhow," said Trescott, "the devastation of the Margate twins was complete. She can't do that particular thing again. I shall be interested to note what form her energy will take this time."

"Oh yes! that's it!" cried the wife. "You'll be *interested*. You've hit it exactly. You'll be interested to note what form her energy will take this time. And then, when the real crisis comes, you'll put on your hat and walk out of the house and leave *me* to straighten things out. This is not a scientific question; this is a practical matter."

"Well, as a practical man, I advocate chaining her out in the stable," answered the doctor.

When Jimmie Trescott was told that his old flame was again to appear, he remained calm. In fact, time had so mended his youthful heart that it was a regular apple of oblivion and peace. Her image in his thought was as the track of a bird on deep snow-it was an impression, but it did not concern the depths. However, he did what befitted his state. He went out and bragged in the street: "My cousin is comin' next week f'om New York."..."My cousin is comin' to-morrow f'om New York."

"Girl or boy?" said the populace, bluntly; but, when enlightened, they speedily cried, "Oh, we remember *her*!" They were charmed, for they thought of her as an outlaw, and they surmised that she could lead them into a very ecstasy of sin. They thought of her as a brave bandit, because they had been whipped for various pranks into which she had led them. When Jimmie made his declaration, they fell into a state of pleased and shuddering expectancy.

Mrs. Trescott pronounced her point of view: "The child is a nice child, if only Caroline had some sense. But she hasn't. And Willis is like a wax figure. I don't see what can be done, unless-unless you simply go to Willis and put the whole thing right at him." Then, for purposes of indication, she improvised a speech: "Look here, Willis, you've got a little daughter, haven't you? But, confound it, man, she is not the only girl child ever brought into the sunlight. There are a lot of children. Children are an ordinary phenomenon. In China they drown girl babies. If you wish to submit to this frightful impostor and tyrant, that is all very well, but why in the name of humanity do you make us submit to it?"

Doctor Trescott laughed. "I wouldn't dare say it to him."

"Anyhow," said Mrs. Trescott, determinedly, "that is what you *should* say to him."

"It wouldn't do the slightest good. It would only make him very angry, and I would lay myself perfectly open to a suggestion that I had better attend to my own affairs with more rigor."

"Well, I suppose you are right," Mrs. Trescott again said.

"Why don't you speak to Caroline?" asked the doctor, humorously.

"Speak to Caroline! Why, I wouldn't for the *world*! She'd fly through the roof. She'd snap my head off! Speak to Caroline! You must be mad!"

One afternoon the doctor went to await his visitors on the platform of the railway station. He was thoughtfully smiling. For some quaint reason he was convinced that he was to be treated to a quick manifestation of little Cora's peculiar and interesting powers. And yet, when the train paused at the station, there appeared to him only a pretty little girl in a fur-lined hood, and with her nose reddening from the sudden cold, and-attended respectfully by her parents. He smiled again, reflecting that he had comically exaggerated the dangers of dear little Cora. It amused his philosophy to note that he had really been perturbed.

As the big sleigh sped homeward there was a sudden shrill outcry from the angel child: "Oh, mamma! mamma! They've forgotten my stove!"

"Hush, dear; hush!" said the mother. "It's all right."

"Oh, but, mamma, they've forgotten my stove!"

The doctor thrust his chin suddenly out of his top-coat collar. "Stove?" he said. "Stove? What stove?"

"Oh, just a toy of the child's," explained the mother. "She's grown so fond of it, she loves it so, that if we didn't take it everywhere with her she'd suffer dreadfully. So we always bring it."

"Oh!" said the doctor. He pictured a little tin trinket. But when the stove was really unmasked, it turned out to be an affair of cast iron, as big as a portmanteau, and, as the stage people say, practicable. There was some trouble that evening when came the hour of children's bedtime. Little Cora burst into a wild declaration that she could not retire for the night unless the stove was carried up-stairs and placed, at her bedside. While the mother was trying to dissuade the child, the Trescott's held their peace and gazed with awe. The incident closed when the lamb-eyed father gathered the stove in his arms and preceded the angel child to her chamber.

"THE LAMB-EYED FATHER PRECEDED THE ANGEL CHILD TO HER CHAMBER"

In the morning, Trescott was standing with his back to the dining room fire, awaiting breakfast, when he heard a noise of descending guests. Presently the door opened, and the party entered in regular order. First came the angel child, then the cooing mother, and last the great painter with his arm full of the stove. He deposited it gently in a corner, and sighed. Trescott wore a wide grin.

"What are you carting that thing all over the house for?" he said, brutally. "Why don't you put it some place where she can play with it, and leave it there?"

The mother rebuked him with a look. "Well, if it gives her pleasure, Ned?" she expostulated, softly. "If it makes the child happy to have the stove with her, why shouldn't she have it?"

"Just so," said the doctor, with calmness.

Jimmie's idea was the roaring fireplace in the cabin of the lone mountaineer. At first he was not able to admire a girl's stove built on well-known domestic lines. He eyed it and thought it was very pretty, but it did not move him immediately. But a certain respect grew to an interest, and he became the angel child's accomplice. And even if he had not had an interest grow upon him, he was certain to have been implicated sooner or later, because of the imperious way of little Cora, who made a serf of him in a few swift sentences. Together they carried the stove out into the desolate garden and squatted it in the snow. Jimmie's snug little muscles had been pitted against the sheer nervous vigor of this little golden-haired girl, and he had not won great honors. When the mind blazed inside the small body, the angel child was pure force. She began to speak: "Now, Jim, get some paper. Get some wood-little sticks at first. Now we want a match. You got a match? Well, go get a match. Get some more wood. Hurry up, now! No. *No!* I'll light it my own self. You get some more wood. There! Isn't that splendid? You get a whole lot of wood an' pile it up here by the stove. An' now what'll we cook? We must have somethin' to cook, you know, else it ain't like the real."

"Potatoes," said Jimmie, at once.

The day was clear, cold, bright. An icy wind sped from over the waters of the lake. A grown person would hardly have been abroad save on compulsion of a kind, and yet, when they were called to luncheon, the two little simpletons protested with great cries.

The ladies of Whilomville were somewhat given to the pagan habit of tea parties. When a tea party was to befall a certain house one could read it in the manner of the prospective hostess, who for some previous days would go about twitching this and twisting that, and dusting here and polishing there; the ordinary habits of the household began then to disagree with her, and her unfortunate husband and children fled to the lengths of their tethers. Then there was a hush. Then there was a tea party. On the fatal afternoon a small picked company of latent enemies would meet. There would be a fanfare of affectionate greetings, during which everybody would measure to an inch the importance of what everybody else was wearing. Those who wore old dresses would wish then that they had not come; and those who saw that, in the company, they were well clad, would be pleased or exalted, or filled with the joys of cruelty. Then they had tea, which was a habit and a delight with none of them, their usual beverage being coffee with milk.

Usually the party jerked horribly in the beginning, while the hostess strove and pulled and pushed to make its progress smooth. Then suddenly it would be off like the wind, eight, fifteen, or twenty-five tongues clattering, with a noise like a cotton-mill combined with the noise of a few penny whistles. Then the hostess had nothing to do but to look glad, and see that everybody had enough tea and cake. When the door was closed behind the last guest, the hostess would usually drop into a chair and say: "Thank Heaven! They're gone!" There would be no malice in this expression. It simply would be that, womanlike, she had flung herself headlong at the accomplishment of a pleasure which she could not even define, and at the end she felt only weariness.

The value and beauty, or oddity, of the tea-cups was another element which entered largely into the spirit of these terrible enterprises. The quality of the tea was an element which did not enter at all. Uniformly it was rather bad. But the cups! Some of the more ambitious people aspired to have cups each of a different pattern, possessing, in fact, the sole similarity that with their odd curves and dips of form they each resembled anything but a teacup. Others of the more ambitious aspired to a quite severe and godly "set," which, when viewed, appalled one with its austere and rigid family resemblances, and made one desire to ask the hostess if the teapot was not the father of all the little cups, and at the same time protesting gallantly that such a young and charming cream-jug surely could not be their mother.

But of course the serious part is that these collections so differed in style and the obvious amount paid for them that nobody could be happy. The poorer ones envied; the richer ones feared; the poorer ones continually striving to overtake the leaders; the leaders always with their heads turned back to hear overtaking footsteps. And none of these things here written did they know. Instead of seeing that they were very stupid, they thought they were very fine. And they gave and took heart-bruises —fierce, deep heart-bruises —under the clear impression that of such kind of rubbish was the kingdom of nice people. The characteristics of outsiders of course emerged in shreds from these tea parties, and it is doubtful if the characteristics of insiders escaped entirely. In fact, these tea parties were in the large way the result of a conspiracy of certain unenlightened people to make life still more uncomfortable.

Mrs. Trescott was in the circle of tea-fighters largely through a sort of artificial necessity —a necessity, in short, which she had herself created in a spirit of femininity.

When the painter and his family came for the holidays, Mrs. Trescott had for some time been feeling that it was her turn to give a tea party, and she was resolved upon it now that she was reinforced by the beautiful wife of the painter, whose charms would make all the other women feel badly. And Mrs. Trescott further resolved that the affair should be notable in more than one way. The painter's wife suggested that, as an innovation, they give the people good tea; but Mrs. Trescott shook her head; she was quite sure they would not like it.

It was an impressive gathering. A few came to see if they could not find out the faults of the painter's wife, and these, added to those who would have attended even without that attractive prospect, swelled the company to a number quite large for Whilomville. There were the usual preliminary jolts, and then suddenly the tea party was in full swing, and looked like an unprecedented success.

Mrs. Trescott exchanged a glance with the painter's wife. They felt proud and superior. This tea party was almost perfection.

III

Jimmie and the angel child, after being oppressed by innumerable admonitions to behave correctly during the afternoon, succeeded in reaching the garden, where the stove awaited them. They were enjoying themselves grandly, when snow began to fall so heavily that it gradually dampened their ardor as well as extinguished the fire in the stove. They stood ruefully until the angel child devised the plan of carrying the stove into the stable, and there, safe from the storm, to continue the festivities. But they were met at the door of the stable by Peter Washington.

"What you 'bout, Jim?"

"Now-it's snowin' so hard, we thought we'd take the stove into the stable."

"An' have er fiah in it? No, seh! G'w'on 'way f'm heh! —g'w'on! Don' 'low no sech foolishin' round yer. No, seh!"

"Well, we ain't goin' to hurt your old stable, are we?" asked Jimmie, ironically.

"Dat you ain't, Jim! Not so long's I keep my two eyes right plumb squaah pinted at ol' Jim. No, seh!" Peter began to chuckle in derision.

The two vagabonds stood before him while he informed them of their iniquities as well as their absurdities, and further made clear his own masterly grasp of the spirit of their devices. Nothing affects children so much as rhetoric. It may not involve any definite presentation of common-sense, but if it is picturesque they surrender decently to its influence. Peter was by all means a rhetorician, and it was not long before the two children had dismally succumbed to him. They went away.

Depositing the stove in the snow, they straightened to look at each other. It did not enter either head to relinquish the idea of continuing the game. But the situation seemed invulnerable.

The angel child went on a scouting tour. Presently she returned, flying. "I know! Let's have it in the cellar! In the cellar! Oh, it'll be lovely!"

The outer door of the cellar was open, and they proceeded down some steps with their treasure. There was plenty of light; the cellar was high-walled, warm, and dry. They named it an ideal place. Two huge cylindrical furnaces were humming away, one at either end. Overhead the beams detonated with the different emotions which agitated the tea party.

Jimmie worked like a stoker, and soon there was a fine bright fire in the stove. The fuel was of small brittle sticks which did not make a great deal of smoke.

"Now what'll we cook?" cried little Cora. "What'll we cook, Jim? We must have something to cook, you know."

"Potatoes?" said Jimmie.

But the angel child made a scornful gesture. "No. I've cooked 'bout a million potatoes, I guess. Potatoes aren't nice any more."

Jimmie's mind was all said and done when the question of potatoes had been passed, and he looked weakly at his companion.

"Haven't you got any turnips in your house?" she inquired, contemptuously. "In *my* house we have *turnips.*"

"Oh, turnips!" exclaimed Jimmie, immensely relieved to find that the honor of his family was safe. "Turnips? Oh, bushels an' bushels an' bushels! Out in the shed."

"Well, go an' get a whole lot," commanded the angel child. "Go an' get a whole lot. Grea' big ones. *We* always have grea' big ones."

Jimmie went to the shed and kicked gently at a company of turnips which the frost had amalgamated. He made three journeys to and from the cellar, carrying always the very largest types from his father's store. Four of them filled the oven of little Cora's stove. This fact did not please her, so they placed three rows of turnips on the hot top. Then the angel child, profoundly moved by an inspiration, suddenly cried out,

"Oh, Jimmie, let's play we're keepin' a hotel, an' have got to cook for 'bout a thousand people, an' those two furnaces will be the ovens, an' I'll be the chief cook —"

"No; I want to be chief cook some of the time," interrupted Jimmie.

"No; I'll be chief cook my own self. You must be my 'sistant. Now I'll prepare 'em—see? An' then you put 'em in the ovens. Get the shovel. We'll play that's the pan. I'll fix 'em, an' then you put 'em in the oven. Hold it still now."

Jim held the coal-shovel while little Cora, with a frown of importance, arranged turnips in rows upon it. She patted each one daintily, and then backed away to view it, with her head critically sideways.

"There!" she shouted at last. "That'll do, I guess. Put 'em in the oven."

Jimmie marched with his shovelful of turnips to one of the furnaces. The door was already open, and he slid the shovel in upon the red coals.

"Come on," cried little Cora. "I've got another batch nearly ready."

"But what am I goin' to do with these?" asked Jimmie. "There ain't only one shovel."

"Leave 'm in there," retorted the girl, passionately. "Leave 'm in there, an' then play you're comin' with another pan. 'Tain't right to stand there an' *hold* the pan, you goose."

So Jimmie expelled all his turnips from his shovel out upon the furnace fire, and returned obediently for another batch.

"These are puddings," yelled the angel child, gleefully. "Dozens an' dozens of puddings for the thousand people at our grea' big hotel."

IV

At the first alarm the painter had fled to the doctor's office, where he hid his face behind a book and pretended that he did not hear the noise of feminine revelling. When the doctor came from a round of calls, he too retreated upon the office, and the men consoled each other as well as they were able. Once Mrs. Trescott dashed in to say delightedly that her tea party was not only the success of the season, but it was probably the very nicest tea party that had ever been held in Whilomville. After vainly beseeching them to return with her, she dashed away again, her face bright with happiness.

The doctor and the painter remained for a long time in silence, Trescott tapping reflectively upon the window-pane. Finally he turned to the painter, and sniffing, said: "What is that, Willis? Don't you smell something?"

The painter also sniffed. "Why, yes! It's like—it's like turnips."

"Turnips? No; it can't be.

"Well, it's very much like it."

The puzzled doctor opened the door into the hall, and at first it appeared that he was going to give back two paces. A result of frizzling turnips, which was almost as tangible as mist, had blown in upon his face and made him gasp. "Good God! Willis, what can this be?" he cried.

"Whee!" said the painter. "It's awful, isn't it?"

The doctor made his way hurriedly to his wife, but before he could speak with her he had to endure the business of greeting a score of women. Then he whispered, "Out in the hall there's an awful —"

"THE SOLEMN ODOR OF BURNING TURNIPS ROLLED IN LIKE A SEA-FOG"

But at that moment it came to them on the wings of a sudden draught. The solemn odor of burning turnips rolled in like a sea-fog, and fell upon that dainty, perfumed tea party. It was almost a personality; if some unbidden and extremely odious guest had entered the room, the effect would have been much the same. The sprightly talk stopped with a jolt, and people looked at each other. Then a few brave and considerate persons made the usual attempt to talk away as if nothing had happened. They all looked at their hostess, who wore an air of stupefaction.

The odor of burning turnips grew and grew. To Trescott it seemed to make a noise. He thought he could hear the dull roar of this outrage. Under some circumstances he might have been able to take the situation from a point of view of comedy, but the agony of his wife was too acute, and, for him, too visible. She was saying: "Yes, we saw the play the last time we were in New York. I liked it very much. That scene in the second act-the gloomy church, you know, and all that-and the organ playing-and then when the four singing little girls came in —" But Trescott comprehended that she did not know if she was talking of a play or a parachute.

He had not been in the room twenty seconds before his brow suddenly flushed with an angry inspiration. He left the room hastily, leaving behind him an incoherent phrase of apology, and charged upon his office, where he found the painter somnolent.

"Willis!" he cried, sternly, "come with me. It's that damn kid of yours!"

The painter was immediately agitated. He always seemed to feel more than any one else in the world the peculiar ability of his child to create resounding excitement, but he seemed always to exhibit his feelings very late. He arose hastily, and hurried after Trescott to the top of the inside cellar stairway. Trescott motioned him to pause, and for an instant they listened.

"Hurry up, Jim," cried the busy little Cora. "Here's another whole batch of lovely puddings. Hurry up now, an' put 'em in the oven."

Trescott looked at the painter; the painter groaned. Then they appeared violently in the middle of the great kitchen of the hotel with a thousand people in it. "Jimmie, go up-stairs!" said Trescott, and then he turned to watch the painter deal with the angel child.

With some imitation of wrath, the painter stalked to his daughter's side and grasped her by the arm.

"'HERE'S ANOTHER BATCH OF LOVELY PUDDINGS'"

"Oh, papa! papa!" she screamed. "You're pinching me! You're pinching me! You're pinching me, papa!"

270

At first the painter had seemed resolved to keep his grip, but suddenly he let go her arm in a panic. "I've hurt her," he said, turning to Trescott.

Trescott had swiftly done much towards the obliteration of the hotel kitchen, but he looked up now and spoke, after a short period of reflection. "You've hurt her, have you? Well, hurt her again. Spank her!" he cried, enthusiastically. "Spank her, confound you, man! She needs it. Here's your chance. Spank her, and spank her good. Spank her!"

The painter naturally wavered over this incendiary proposition, but at last, in one supreme burst of daring, he shut his eyes and again grabbed his precious offspring.

The spanking was lamentably the work of a perfect bungler. It couldn't have hurt at all; but the angel child raised to heaven a loud, clear soprano howl that expressed the last word in even mediæval anguish. Soon the painter was aghast. "Stop it, darling! I didn't mean —I didn't mean to-to hurt you so much, you know." He danced nervously. Trescott sat on a box, and devilishly smiled.

But the pasture call of suffering motherhood came down to them, and a moment later a splendid apparition appeared on the cellar stairs. She understood the scene at a glance. "Willis! What have you been doing?"

Trescott sat on his box, the painter guiltily moved from foot to foot, and the angel child advanced to her mother with arms outstretched, making a piteous wail of amazed and pained pride that would have moved Peter the Great. Regardless of her frock, the panting mother knelt on the stone floor and took her child to her bosom, and looked, then, bitterly, scornfully, at the cowering father and husband.

The painter, for his part, at once looked reproachfully at Trescott, as if to say: "There! You see?"

Trescott arose and extended his hands in a quiet but magnificent gesture of despair and weariness. He seemed about to say something classic, and, quite instinctively, they waited. The stillness was deep, and the wait was longer than a moment. "Well," he said, "we can't live in the cellar. Let's go up-stairs."

X

The Trial, Execution, and Burial of Homer Phelps

FROM time to time an enwearied pine bough let fall to the earth its load of melting snow, and the branch swung back glistening in the faint wintry sunlight. Down the gulch a brook clattered amid its ice with the sound of a perpetual breaking of glass. All the forest looked drenched and forlorn.

The sky-line was a ragged enclosure of gray cliffs and hemlocks and pines. If one had been miraculously set down in this gulch one could have imagined easily that the nearest human habitation was hundreds of miles away, if it were not for an old half-discernible wood-road that led towards the brook.

"Halt! Who's there?"

This low and gruff cry suddenly dispelled the stillness which lay upon the lonely gulch, but the hush which followed it seemed even more profound. The hush endured for some seconds, and then the voice of the challenger was again raised, this time with a distinctly querulous note in it.

"Halt! Who's there? Why don't you answer when I holler? Don't you know you're likely to get shot?"

A second voice answered, "Oh, you knew who I was easy enough."

"That don't make no diff'rence." One of the Margate twins stepped from a thicket and confronted Homer Phelps on the old wood-road. The majestic scowl of official wrath was upon the brow of Reeves Margate, a long stick was held in the hollow of his arm as one would hold a rifle, and he strode grimly to the other boy. "That don't make no diff'rence. You've got to answer when I holler, anyhow. Willie says so."

At the mention of the dread chieftain's name the Phelps boy daunted a trifle, but he still sulkily murmured, "Well, you knew it was me."

He started on his way through the snow, but the twin sturdily blocked the path. "You can't pass less'n you give the countersign."

"Huh?" said the Phelps boy. "Countersign?"

"Yes-countersign," sneered the twin, strong in his sense of virtue.

But the Phelps boy became very angry. "Can't I, hey? Can't I, hey? I'll show you whether I can or not! I'll show you, Reeves Margate!"

There was a short scuffle, and then arose the anguished clamor of the sentry: "Hey, fellers! Here's a man tryin' to run a-past the guard. Hey, fellers! Hey!"

There was a great noise in the adjacent underbrush. The voice of Willie could be heard exhorting his followers to charge swiftly and bravely. Then they appeared-Willie Dalzel, Jimmie Trescott, the other Margate twin, and Dan Earl. The chieftain's face was dark with wrath. "What's the matter? Can't you play it right? 'Ain't you got any sense?" he asked the Phelps boy.

The sentry was yelling out his grievance. "Now-he came along an' I hollered at 'im, an' he didn't pay no 'tention, an' when I ast 'im for the countersign, he wouldn't say nothin'. That ain't no way."

"Can't you play it right?" asked the chief again, with gloomy scorn.

"He knew it was me easy enough," said the Phelps boy.

"That 'ain't got nothin' to do with it," cried the chief, furiously. "That 'ain't got nothin' to do with it. If you're goin' to play, you've got to play it right. It ain't no fun if you go spoilin' the whole thing this way. Can't you play it right?"

"I forgot the countersign," lied the culprit, weakly.

Whereupon the remainder of the band yelled out, with one triumphant voice: "War to the knife! War to the knife! I remember it, Willie. Don't I, Willie?"

The leader was puzzled. Evidently he was trying to develop in his mind a plan for dealing correctly with this unusual incident. He felt, no doubt, that he must proceed according to the books, but unfortunately the books did not cover the point precisely. However, he finally said to Homer Phelps, "You are under arrest." Then with a stentorian voice he shouted, "Seize him!"

His loyal followers looked startled for a brief moment, but directly they began to move upon the Phelps boy. The latter clearly did not intend to be seized. He backed away, expostulating wildly. He even seemed somewhat frightened. "No, no; don't you touch me, I tell you; don't you dare touch me."

The others did not seem anxious to engage. They moved slowly, watching the desperate light in his eyes. The chieftain stood with folded arms, his face growing darker and darker with impatience. At length he burst out: "Oh, seize him, I tell you! Why don't you seize him? Grab him by the leg, Dannie! Hurry up, all of you! Seize him, I keep a-say-in'!"

Thus adjured, the Margate twins and Dan Earl made another pained effort, while Jimmie Trescott manœuvred to cut off a retreat. But, to tell the truth, there was a boyish law which held them back from laying hands of violence upon little Phelps under these conditions. Perhaps it was because they were only playing, whereas he was now undeniably serious. At any rate, they looked very sick of their occupation.

"Don't you dare!" snarled the Phelps boy, facing first one and then the other; he was almost in tears —"don't you dare touch me!"

The chieftain was now hopping with exasperation. "Oh, seize him, can't you? You're no good at all!" Then he loosed his wrath upon the Phelps boy: "Stand still, Homer, can't you? You've got to be seized, you know. That ain't the way. It ain't any fun if you keep a-dodgin' that way. Stand still, can't you! You've got to be seized."

"I don't *want* to be seized," retorted the Phelps boy, obstinate and bitter.

"But you've *got* to be seized!" yelled the maddened chief. "Don't you see? That's the way to play it."

The Phelps boy answered, promptly, "But I don't want to play that way."

"But that's the *right* way to play it. Don't you see? You've got to play it the right way. You've got to be seized, an' then we'll hold a trial on you, an' —an' all sorts of things."

But this prospect held no illusions for the Phelps boy. He continued doggedly to repeat, "I don't want to play that way!"

Of course in the end the chief stooped to beg and beseech this unreasonable lad. "Oh, come on, Homer! Don't be so mean. You're a-spoilin' everything. We won't hurt you any. Not the tintiest bit. It's all just playin'. What's the matter with you?"

The different tone of the leader made an immediate impression upon the other. He showed some signs of the beginning of weakness. "Well," he asked, "what you goin' to do?"

"Why, first we're goin' to put you in a dungeon, or tie you to a stake, or something like that-just pertend, you know," added the chief, hurriedly, "an' then we'll hold a trial, awful solemn, but there won't be anything what'll hurt you. Not a thing."

"FROM THIS BOOT HE EMPTIED ABOUT A QUART OF SNOW"

And so the game was readjusted. The Phelps boy was marched off between Dan Earl and a Margate twin. The party proceeded to their camp, which was hidden some hundred feet back in the thickets. There was a miserable little hut with a pine-bark roof, which so frankly and constantly leaked that existence in the open air was always preferable. At present it was noisily dripping melted snow into the black mouldy interior. In front of this hut a feeble fire was flickering through its unhappy career. Underfoot, the watery snow was of the color of lead.

The party having arrived at the camp, the chief leaned against a tree, and balancing on one foot, drew off a rubber boot. From this boot he emptied about a quart of snow. He squeezed his stocking, which had a hole from which protruded a lobster-red toe. He resumed his boot. "Bring up the prisoner," said he. They did it. "Guilty or not guilty?" he asked.

"Huh?" said the Phelps boy.

"Guilty or not guilty?" demanded the chief, peremptorily. "Guilty or not guilty? Don't you understand?"

Homer Phelps looked profoundly puzzled. "Guilty or not guilty?" he asked, slowly and weakly.

The chief made a swift gesture, and turned in despair to the others. "Oh, he don't do it right! He does it all wrong!" He again faced the prisoner with an air of making a last attempt, "Now look-a-here, Homer, when I say, 'Guilty or not guilty?' you want to up an' say, 'Not Guilty.' Don't you see?"

"Not guilty," said Homer, at once.

"No, no, no. Wait till I ask you. Now wait." He called out, pompously, "Pards, if this prisoner before us is guilty, what shall be his fate?"

All those well-trained little infants with one voice sung out, "*Death!*"

"Prisoner," continued the chief, "are you guilty or not guilty?"

"But look-a-here," argued Homer, "you said it wouldn't be nothin' that would hurt. I —"

"Thunder an' lightnin'!" roared the wretched chief. "Keep your mouth shut, can't ye? What in the mischief —"

But there was an interruption from Jimmie Trescott, who shouldered a twin aside and stepped to the front. "Here," he said, very contemptuously, "let me be the prisoner. I'll show 'im how to do it."

"All right, Jim," cried the chief, delighted; "you be the prisoner, then. Now all you fellers with guns stand there in a row! Get out of the way, Homer!" He cleared his throat, and addressed Jimmie. "Prisoner, are you guilty or not guilty?"

"Not guilty," answered Jimmie, firmly. Standing there before his judge-unarmed, slim, quiet, modest-he was ideal.

The chief beamed upon him, and looked aside to cast a triumphant and withering glance upon Homer Phelps. He said: "There! That's the way to do it."

The twins and Dan Earl also much admired Jimmie.

"That's all right so far, anyhow," said the satisfied chief. "An' now we'll-now we'll-we'll perceed with the execution."

"That ain't right," said the new prisoner, suddenly. "That ain't the next thing. You've got to have a trial first. You've got to fetch up a lot of people first who'll say I done it."

"That's so," said the chief. "I didn't think. Here, Reeves, you be first witness. Did the prisoner do it?"

The twin gulped for a moment in his anxiety to make the proper reply. He was at the point where the roads forked. Finally he hazarded, "Yes."

"There," said the chief, "that's one of 'em. Now, Dan, you be a witness. Did he do it?"

Dan Earl, having before him the twin's example, did not hesitate. "Yes," he said.

"Well, then, pards, what shall be his fate?"

Again came the ringing answer, "*Death!*"

With Jimmie in the principal rôle, this drama, hidden deep in the hemlock thicket neared a kind of perfection. "You must blind-fold me," cried the condemned lad, briskly, "an' then I'll go off an' stand, an' you must all get in a row an' shoot me."

The chief gave this plan his urbane countenance, and the twins and Dan Earl were greatly pleased. They blindfolded Jimmie under his careful directions. He waded a few paces into snow, and then turned and stood with quiet dignity, awaiting his fate. The chief marshalled the twins and Dan Earl in line with their sticks. He gave the necessary commands: "Load! Ready! Aim! Fire!" At the last command the firing party all together yelled, "Bang!"

Jimmie threw his hands high, tottered in agony for a moment, and then crashed full length into the snow-into, one would think, a serious case of pneumonia. It was beautiful.

THE EXECUTION

He arose almost immediately and came back to them, wondrously pleased with himself. They acclaimed him joyously.

The chief was particularly grateful. He was always trying to bring off these little romantic affairs, and it seemed, after all, that the only boy who could ever really help him was Jimmie Trescott. "There," he said to the others, "that's the way it ought to be done."

They were touched to the heart by the whole thing, and they looked at Jimmie with big, smiling eyes. Jimmie, blown out like a balloon-fish with pride of his performance, swaggered to the fire and took seat on some wet hemlock boughs. "Fetch some more wood, one of you kids," he murmured, negligently. One of the twins came fortunately upon a small cedar-tree the lower branches of which were dead and dry. An armful of these branches flung upon the sick fire soon made a high, ruddy, warm blaze, which was like an illumination in honor of Jimmie's success.

The boys sprawled about the fire and talked the regular language of the game. "Waal, pards," remarked the chief, "it's many a night we've had together here in the Rockies among the b'ars an' the Indyuns, hey?"

"Yes, pard," replied Jimmie Trescott, "I reckon you're right. Our wild, free life is-there ain't nothin' to compare with our wild, free life."

Whereupon the two lads arose and magnificently shook hands, while the others watched them in an ecstasy. "I'll allus stick by ye, pard," said Jimmie, earnestly. "When yer in trouble, don't forget that Lightnin' Lou is at yer back."

"Thanky, pard," quoth Willie Dalzel, deeply affected. "I'll not forget it, pard. An' don't you forget, either, that Dead-shot Demon, the leader of the Red Raiders, never forgits a friend."

But Homer Phelps was having none of this great fun. Since his disgraceful refusal to be seized and executed he had been hovering unheeded on the outskirts of the band. He seemed very sorry; he cast a wistful eye at the romantic scene. He knew too well that if he went near at that particular time he would be certain to encounter a pitiless snubbing. So he vacillated modestly in the background.

At last the moment came when he dared venture near enough to the fire to gain some warmth, for he was now bitterly suffering with the cold. He sidled close to Willie Dalzel. No one heeded him. Eventually he looked at his chief, and with a bright face said,

"Now-if I was seized now to be executed, I could do it as well as Jimmie Trescott, I could."

The chief gave a crow of scorn, in which he was followed by the other boys. "Ho!" he cried, "why didn't you do it, then? Why didn't you do it?" Homer Phelps felt upon him many pairs of disdainful eyes. He wagged his shoulders in misery.

"You're dead," said the chief, frankly. "That's what you are. We executed you, we did."

"When?" demanded the Phelps boy, with some spirit.

"Just a little while ago. Didn't we, fellers? Hey, fellers, didn't we?"

The trained chorus cried: "Yes, of course we did. You're dead, Homer. You can't play any more. You're dead."

"That wasn't me. It was Jimmie Trescott," he said, in a low and bitter voice, his eyes on the ground. He would have given the world if he could have retracted his mad refusals of the early part of the drama.

"No," said the chief, "it was you. We're playin' it was you, an' it *was* you. You're dead, you are." And seeing the cruel effect of his words, he did not refrain from administering some advice: "The next time, don't be such a chuckle-head."

Presently the camp imagined that it was attacked by Indians, and the boys dodged behind trees with their stick-rifles, shouting out, "Bang!" and encouraging each other to resist until the last. In the mean time the dead lad hovered near the fire, looking moodily at the gay and exciting scene. After the fight the gallant defenders returned one by one to the fire, where they grandly clasped hands, calling each other "old pard," and boasting of their deeds.

Parenthetically, one of the twins had an unfortunate inspiration. "I killed the Indy-un chief, fellers. Did you see me kill the Indy-un chief?"

But Willie Dalzel, his own chief, turned upon him wrathfully: "*You* didn't kill no chief. *I* killed 'im with me own hand."

"Oh!" said the twin, apologetically, at once. "It must have been some other Indy-un."

"Who's wounded?" cried Willie Dalzel. "Ain't anybody wounded?" The party professed themselves well and sound. The roving and inventive eye of the chief chanced upon Homer Phelps. "Ho! Here's a dead man! Come on, fellers, here's a dead man! We've got to bury him, you know." And at his bidding they pounced upon the dead Phelps lad. The unhappy boy saw clearly his road to rehabilitation, but mind and body revolted at the idea of burial, even as they had revolted at the thought of execution. "No!" he said, stubbornly. "No! I don't want to be buried! I don't want to be buried!"

THE FUNERAL ORATION

"You've *got* to be buried!" yelled the chief, passionately. "'Tain't goin' to hurt ye, is it? Think you're made of glass? Come on, fellers, get the grave ready!"

They scattered hemlock boughs upon the snow in the form of a rectangle, and piled other boughs near at hand. The victim surveyed these preparations with a glassy eye. When all was ready, the chief turned determinedly to him: "Come on now, Homer. We've got to carry you to the grave. Get him by the legs, Jim!"

Little Phelps had now passed into that state which may be described as a curious and temporary childish fatalism. He still objected, but it was only feeble muttering, as if he did not know what he spoke. In some confusion they carried him to the rectangle of hemlock boughs and dropped him. Then they piled other boughs upon him until he was not to be seen. The chief stepped forward to make a short address, but before proceeding with it he thought it expedient, from certain indications, to speak to the grave itself. "Lie still, can't ye? Lie still until I get through." There was a faint movement of the boughs, and then a perfect silence.

The chief took off his hat. Those who watched him could see that his face was harrowed with emotion. "Pards," he began, brokenly —"pards, we've got one more debt to pay them murderin' red-skins. Bowie-knife Joe was a brave man an' a good pard, but-he's gone now-gone." He paused for a moment, overcome, and the stillness was only broken by the deep manly grief of Jimmie Trescott.

XI
The Fight

I

THE child life of the neighborhood was sometimes moved in its deeps at the sight of wagon-loads of furniture arriving in front of some house which, with closed blinds and barred doors, had been for a time a mystery, or even a fear. The boys often expressed this fear by stamping bravely and noisily on the porch of the house, and then suddenly darting away with screams of nervous laughter, as if they expected to be pursued by something uncanny. There was a group who held that the cellar of a vacant house was certainly the abode of robbers, smugglers, assassins, mysterious masked men in council about the dim rays of a candle, and possessing skulls, emblematic bloody daggers, and owls. Then, near the first of April, would come along a wagon-load of furniture, and children would assemble on the walk by the gate and make serious examination of everything that passed into the house, and taking no thought whatever of masked men.

One day it was announced in the neighborhood that a family was actually moving into the Hannigan house, next door to Dr. Trescott's. Jimmie was one of the first to be informed, and by the time some of his friends came dashing up he was versed in much.

"Any boys?" they demanded, eagerly.

"Yes," answered Jimmie, proudly. "One's a little feller, and one's most as big as me. I saw 'em, I did."

"Where are they?" asked Willie Dalzel, as if under the circumstances he could not take Jimmie's word, but must have the evidence of his senses.

"Oh, they're in there," said Jimmie, carelessly. It was evident he owned these new boys.

Willie Dalzel resented Jimmie's proprietary way.

"Ho!" he cried, scornfully. "Why don't they come out, then? Why don't they come out?"

"How d' I know?" said Jimmie.

"STAMPING BRAVELY AND NOISILY ON THE PORCH"

"Well," retorted Willie Dalzel, "you seemed to know so thundering much about 'em."

At the moment a boy came strolling down the gravel walk which led from the front door to the gate. He was about the height and age of Jimmie Trescott, but he was thick through the chest and had fat legs. His face was round and rosy and plump, but his hair was curly black, and his brows were naturally darkling, so that he resembled both a pudding and a young bull.

He approached slowly the group of older inhabitants, and they had grown profoundly silent. They looked him over; he looked them over. They might have been savages observing the first white man, or white men observing the first savage. The silence held steady.

As he neared the gate the strange boy wandered off to the left in a definite way, which proved his instinct to make a circular voyage when in doubt. The motionless group stared at him. In time this unsmiling scrutiny worked upon him somewhat, and he leaned against the fence and fastidiously examined one shoe.

In the end Willie Dalzel authoritatively broke the stillness. "What's your name?" said he, gruffly.

"Johnnie Hedge 'tis," answered the new boy. Then came another great silence while Whilomville pondered this intelligence.

Again came the voice of authority —"Where'd you live b'fore?"

"Jersey City."

These two sentences completed the first section of the formal code. The second section concerned itself with the establishment of the new-comer's exact position in the neighborhood.

"I kin lick you," announced Willie Dalzel, and awaited the answer.

The Hedge boy had stared at Willie Dalzel, but he stared at him again. After a pause he said, "I know you kin."

"Well," demanded Willie, "kin *he* lick you?" And he indicated Jimmie Trescott with a sweep which announced plainly that Jimmie was the next in prowess.

Whereupon the new boy looked at Jimmie respectfully but carefully, and at length said, "I dun'no'."

This was the signal for an outburst of shrill screaming, and everybody pushed Jimmie forward. He knew what he had to say, and, as befitted the occasion, he said it fiercely: "Kin you lick me?"

The new boy also understood what he had to say, and, despite his unhappy and lonely state, he said it bravely: "Yes."

"Well," retorted Jimmie, bluntly, "come out and do it, then! Jest come out and do it!" And these words were greeted with cheers. These little rascals yelled that there should be a fight at once. They were in bliss over the prospect. "Go on, Jim! Make 'im come out. He said he could lick you. Aw-aw-aw! He said he could lick you!" There probably never was a fight among this class in Whilomville which was not the result of the goading and guying of two proud lads by a populace of urchins who simply wished to see a show.

Willie Dalzel was very busy. He turned first to the one and then to the other. "You said you could lick him. Well, why don't you come out and do it, then? You said you could lick him, didn't you?"

"Yes," answered the new boy, dogged and dubious.

Willie tried to drag Jimmie by the arm. "Aw, go on, Jimmie! You ain't afraid, are you?"

"No," said Jimmie.

The two victims opened wide eyes at each other. The fence separated them, and so it was impossible for them to immediately engage; but they seemed to understand that they were ultimately to be sacrificed to the ferocious aspirations of the other boys, and each scanned the other to learn something of his spirit. They were not angry at all. They were merely two little gladiators who were being clamorously told to hurt each other. Each displayed hesitation and doubt without displaying fear. They did not exactly understand what were their feelings, and they moodily kicked the ground and made low and sullen answers to Willie Dalzel, who worked like a circus-manager.

"Aw, go on, Jim! What's the matter with you? You ain't afraid, are you? Well, then, say something." This sentiment received more cheering from the abandoned little wretches who wished to be entertained, and in this cheering there could be heard notes of derision of Jimmie Trescott. The latter had a position to sustain; he was well known; he often bragged of his willingness and ability to thrash other boys; well, then, here was a boy of his size who said that he could not thrash him. What was he going to do about it? The crowd made these arguments very clear, and repeated them again and again.

Finally Jimmie, driven to aggression, walked close to the fence and said to the new boy, "The first time I catch you out of your own yard I'll lam the head off'n you!" This was received with wild plaudits by the Whilomville urchins.

But the new boy stepped back from the fence. He was awed by Jimmie's formidable mien. But he managed to get out a semi-defiant sentence. "Maybe you will, and maybe you won't," said he.

However, his short retreat was taken as a practical victory for Jimmie, and the boys hooted him bitterly. He remained inside the fence, swinging one foot and scowling, while Jimmie was escorted off down the street amid acclamations. The new boy turned and walked back towards the house, his face gloomy, lined deep with discouragement, as if he felt that the new environment's antagonism and palpable cruelty were sure to prove too much for him.

II

The mother of Johnnie Hedge was a widow, and the chief theory of her life was that her boy should be in school on the greatest possible number of days. He himself had no sympathy with this ambition, but she detected the truth of his diseases with an unerring eye, and he was required to be really ill before he could win the right to disregard the first bell, morning and noon. The chicken-pox and the mumps had given him vacations-vacations of misery, wherein he nearly died between pain and nursing. But bad colds in the head did nothing for him, and he was not able to invent a satisfactory hacking cough. His mother was not consistently a tartar. In most things he swayed her to his will. He was allowed to have more jam, pickles, and pie than most boys; she respected his profound loathing of Sunday-school; on summer evenings he could remain out-of-doors until 8.30; but in this matter of school she was inexorable. This single point in her character was of steel.

The Hedges arrived in Whilomville on a Saturday, and on the following Monday Johnnie wended his way to school with a note to the principal and his Jersey City school-books. He knew perfectly well that he would be told to buy new and different books, but in those days mothers always had an idea that old books would "do," and they invariably sent boys off to a new school with books which would not meet the selected and unchangeable views of the new administration. The old books never would "do." Then the boys brought them home to annoyed mothers and asked for ninety cents or sixty cents or eighty-five cents or some number of cents for another outfit. In the garret of every house holding a large family there was a collection of effete school-books, with mother rebellious because James could not inherit his books from Paul, who should properly be Peter's heir, while Peter should be a beneficiary under Henry's will.

"'THE FIRST TIME I CATCH YOU I'LL LAM THE HEAD OFF'N YOU'"

But the matter of the books was not the measure of Johnnie Hedge's unhappiness. This whole business of changing schools was a complete torture. Alone he had to go among a new people, a new tribe, and he apprehended his serious time. There were only two fates for him. One meant victory. One meant a kind of serfdom in which he would subscribe to every word of some superior boy and support his every word. It was not anything like an English system of fagging, because boys invariably drifted into the figurative service of other boys whom they devotedly admired, and if they were obliged to subscribe to everything, it is true that they would have done so freely in any case. One means to suggest that Johnnie Hedge had to find his place. Willie Dalzel was a type of the little chieftain, and Willie was a master, but he was not a bully in a special physical sense. He did not drag little boys by the ears until they cried, nor make them tearfully fetch and carry for him. They fetched and carried, but it was because of their worship of his prowess and genius. And so all through the strata of boy life were chieftains and subchieftains and assistant subchieftains. There was no question of little Hedge being towed about by the nose; it was, as one has said, that he had to find his place in a new school. And this in itself was a problem which awed his boyish heart. He was a stranger cast away upon the moon. None knew him, understood him, felt for him. He would be surrounded for this initiative time by a horde of jackal creatures who might turn out in the end to be little boys like himself, but this last point his philosophy could not understand in its fulness.

He came to a white meeting-house sort of a place, in the squat tower of which a great bell was clanging impressively. He passed through an iron gate into a play-ground worn bare as the bed of a mountain brook by the endless runnings and scufflings of little children. There was still a half-hour before the final clangor in the squat tower, but the play-ground held a number of frolicsome imps. A loitering boy espied Johnnie Hedge, and he howled: "Oh! oh! Here's a new feller! Here's a new feller!" He advanced upon the strange arrival. "What's your name?" he demanded, belligerently, like a particularly offensive custom-house officer.

"Johnnie Hedge," responded the new-comer, shyly.

This name struck the other boy as being very comic. All new names strike boys as being comic. He laughed noisily.

"Oh, fellers, he says his name is Johnnie Hedge! Haw! haw! haw!"

The new boy felt that his name was the most disgraceful thing which had ever been attached to a human being.

"Johnnie Hedge! Haw! haw! What room you in?" said the other lad.

"I dun'no'," said Johnnie. In the mean time a small flock of interested vultures had gathered about him. The main thing was his absolute strangeness. He even would have welcomed the sight of his tormentors of Saturday; he had seen them before at least. These creatures were only so many incomprehensible problems. He diffidently began to make his way towards the main door of the school, and the other boys followed him. They demanded information.

"Are you through subtraction yet? We study jogerfre-did you, ever? You live here now? You goin' to school here now?"

To many questions he made answer as well as the clamor would permit, and at length he reached the main door and went quaking unto his new kings. As befitted them, the rabble stopped at the door. A teacher strolling along a corridor found a small boy holding in his hand a note. The boy palpably did not know what to do with the note, but the teacher knew, and took it. Thereafter this little boy was in harness.

A splendid lady in gorgeous robes gave him a seat at a double desk, at the end of which sat a hoodlum with grimy finger-nails, who eyed the inauguration with an extreme and personal curiosity. The other desks were gradually occupied by children, who first were told of the new boy, and then turned upon him a speculative and somewhat derisive eye. The school opened; little classes went forward to a position in front of the teacher's platform and tried to explain that they knew something. The new boy was not requisitioned a great deal; he was allowed to lie dormant until he became used to the scenes and until the teacher found, approximately, his mental position. In the mean time he suffered a shower of stares and whispers and giggles, as if he were a man-ape, whereas he was precisely like other children. From time to time he made funny and pathetic little overtures to other boys, but these overtures could not yet be received; he was not known; he was a foreigner. The village school was like a nation. It was tight. Its amiability or friendship must be won in certain ways.

At recess he hovered in the school-room around the weak lights of society and around the teacher, in the hope that somebody might be good to him, but none considered him save as some sort of a specimen. The teacher of course had a secondary interest in the fact that he was an additional one to a class of sixty-three.

At twelve o'clock, when the ordered files of boys and girls marched towards the door, he exhibited-to no eye-the tremblings of a coward in a charge. He exaggerated the lawlessness of the play-ground and the street.

But the reality was hard enough. A shout greeted him:

"Oh, here's the new feller! Here's the new feller!"

Small and utterly obscure boys teased him. He had a hard time of it to get to the gate. There never was any actual hurt, but everything was competent to smite the lad with shame. It was a curious, groundless shame, but nevertheless it was shame. He was a new-comer, and he definitely felt the disgrace of the fact. In the street he was seen and recognized by some lads who had formed part of the group of Saturday. They shouted:

"Oh, Jimmie! Jimmie! Here he is! Here's that new feller!"

Jimmie Trescott was going virtuously towards his luncheon when he heard these cries behind him. He pretended not to hear, and in this deception he was assisted by the fact that he was engaged at the time in a furious argument with a friend over the relative merits of two "Uncle Tom's Cabin" companies. It appeared that one company had only two bloodhounds, while the other had ten. On the other hand, the first company had two Topsys and two Uncle Toms, while the second had only one Topsy and one Uncle Tom.

But the shouting little boys were hard after him. Finally they were even pulling at his arms.

"Jimmie —"

"What?" he demanded, turning with a snarl. "What d'you want? Leggo my arm!"

"Here he is! Here's the new feller! Here's the new feller! Now!"

"I don't care if he is," said Jimmie, with grand impatience. He tilted his chin. "I don't care if he is."

Then they reviled him. "Thought you was goin' to lick him first time you caught him! Yah! You're a 'fraid-cat!" They began to sing "'Fraid-cat! 'Fraidcat! 'Fraid-cat!" He expostulated hotly, turning from one to the other, but they would not listen. In the mean time the Hedge boy slunk on his way, looking with deep anxiety upon this attempt to send Jimmie against him. But Jimmie would have none of the plan.

When the children met again on the play-ground, Jimmie was openly challenged with cowardice. He had made a big threat in the hearing of comrades, and when invited by them to take advantage of an opportunity, he had refused. They had been fairly sure of their amusement, and they were indignant. Jimmie was finally driven to declare that as soon as school was out for the day, he would thrash the Hedge boy.

When finally the children came rushing out of the iron gate, filled with the delights of freedom, a hundred boys surrounded Jimmie in high spirits, for he had said that he was determined. They waited for the lone lad from Jersey City. When he appeared, Jimmie wasted no time. He walked straight to him and said, "Did you say you kin lick me?"

Johnnie Hedge was cowed, shrinking, affrighted, and the roars of a hundred boys thundered in his ears, but again he knew what he had to say. "Yes," he gasped, in anguish.

"Then," said Jimmie, resolutely, "you've got to fight." There was a joyous clamor by the mob. The beleaguered lad looked this way and that way for succor, as Willie Dalzel and other officious youngsters policed an irregular circle in the crowd. He saw Jimmie facing him; there was no help for it; he dropped his books-the old books which would not "do."

Now it was the fashion among tiny Whilomville belligerents to fight much in the manner of little bear cubs. Two boys would rush upon each other, immediately grapple, and-the best boy having probably succeeded in getting the coveted "under hold" —there would presently be a crash to the earth of the inferior boy, and he would probably be mopped around in the dust, or the mud, or the snow, or whatever the material happened to be, until the engagement was over. Whatever havoc was dealt out to him was ordinarily the result of his wild endeavors to throw off his opponent and arise. Both infants wept during the fight, as a common thing, and if they wept very hard, the fight was a harder fight. The result was never very bloody, but the complete dishevelment of both victor and vanquished was extraordinary. As for the spectacle, it more resembled a collision of boys in a fog than it did the manly art of hammering another human being into speechless inability.

The fight began when Jimmie made a mad, bear-cub rush at the new boy, amid savage cries of encouragement. Willie Dalzel, for instance, almost howled his head off. Very timid boys on the outskirts of the throng felt their hearts leap to their throats. It was a time when certain natures were impressed that only man is vile.

But it appeared that bear-cub rushing was no part of the instruction received by boys in Jersey City. Boys in Jersey City were apparently schooled curiously. Upon the onslaught of Jimmie, the stranger had gone wild with rage-boylike. Some spark had touched his fighting-blood, and in a moment he was a cornered, desperate, fire-eyed little man. He began to swing his arms, to revolve them so swiftly that one might have considered him a small, working model of an extra-fine patented windmill which was caught in a gale. For a moment this defence surprised Jimmie more than it damaged him, but two moments later a small, knotty fist caught him squarely in the eye, and with a shriek he went down in defeat. He lay on the ground so stunned that he could not even cry; but if he had been able to cry, he would have cried over his prestige-or something-not over his eye.

There was a dreadful tumult. The boys cast glances of amazement and terror upon the victor, and thronged upon the beaten Jimmie Trescott. It was a moment of excitement so intense that one cannot say what happened. Never before had Whilomville seen such a thing-not the little tots. They were aghast, dumfounded, and they glanced often over their shoulders at the new boy, who stood alone, his clinched fists at his side, his face crimson, his lips still working with the fury of battle.

But there was another surprise for Whilomville. It might have been seen that the little victor was silently debating against an impulse.

"NO TIME FOR ACADEMICS-HE RAN"

But the impulse won, for the lone lad from Jersey City suddenly wheeled, sprang like a demon, and struck another boy.

A curtain should be drawn before this deed. A knowledge of it is really too much for the heart to bear. The other boy was Willie Dalzel. The lone lad from Jersey City had smitten him full sore.

There is little to say of it. It must have been that a feeling worked gradually to the top of the little stranger's wrath that Jimmie Trescott had been a mere tool, that the front and centre of his persecutors had been Willie Dalzel, and being rendered temporarily lawless by his fighting-blood, he raised his hand and smote for revenge.

Willie Dalzel had been in the middle of a vandal's cry, which screeched out over the voices of everybody. The new boy's fist cut it in half, so to say. And then arose the howl of an amazed and terrorized walrus.

One wishes to draw a second curtain. Without discussion or inquiry or brief retort, Willie Dalzel ran away. He ran like a hare straight for home, this redoubtable chieftain. Following him at a heavy and slow pace ran the impassioned new boy. The scene was long remembered.

Willie Dalzel was no coward; he had been panic-stricken into running away from a new thing. He ran as a man might run from the sudden appearance of a vampire or a ghoul or a gorilla. This was no time for academics-he ran.

Jimmie slowly gathered himself and came to his feet. "Where's Willie?" said he, first of all. The crowd sniggered. "Where's Willie?" said Jimmie again.

"Why, he licked him *too*!" answered a boy suddenly.

"He did?" said Jimmie. He sat weakly down on the roadway. "He did?" After allowing a moment for the fact to sink into him, he looked up at the crowd with his one good eye and his one bunged eye, and smiled cheerfully.

XII
The City Urchin and the Chaste Villagers

AFTER the brief encounters between the Hedge boy and Jimmie Trescott and the Hedge boy and Willie Dalzel, the neighborhood which contained the homes of the boys was, as far as child life is concerned, in a state resembling anarchy. This was owing to the signal overthrow and shameful retreat of the boy who had for several years led a certain little clan by the nose. The adherence of the little community did not go necessarily to the boy who could whip all the others, but it certainly could not go to a boy who had run away in a manner that made his shame patent to the whole world. Willie Dalzel found himself in a painful position. This tiny tribe which had followed him with such unwavering faith was now largely engaged in whistling and catcalling and hooting. He chased a number of them into the sanctity of their own yards, but from these coigns they continued to ridicule him.

But it must not be supposed that the fickle tribe went over in a body to the new light. They did nothing of the sort. They occupied themselves with avenging all which they had endured-gladly enough, too-for many months. As for the Hedge boy, he maintained a curious timid reserve, minding his own business with extreme care, and going to school with that deadly punctuality of which his mother was the genius. Jimmie Trescott suffered no adverse criticism from his fellows. He was entitled to be beaten by a boy who had made Willie Dalzel bellow like a bull-calf and run away. Indeed, he received some honors. He had confronted a very superior boy and received a bang in the eye which for a time was the wonder of the children, and he had not bellowed like a bull-calf. As a matter of fact, he was often invited to tell how it had felt, and this he did with some pride, claiming arrogantly that he had been superior to any particular pain.

Early in the episode he and the Hedge boy had patched up a treaty. Living next door to each other, they could not fail to have each other often in sight. One afternoon they wandered together in the strange indefinite diplomacy of boyhood. As they drew close the new boy suddenly said, "Napple?"

"Yes," said Jimmie, and the new boy bestowed upon him an apple. It was one of those green-coated winter-apples which lie for many months in safe and dry places, and can at any time be brought forth for the persecution of the unwary and inexperienced. An older age would have fled from this apple, but to the unguided youth of Jimmie Trescott it was a thing to be possessed and cherished. Wherefore this apple was the emblem of something more than a truce, despite the fact that it tasted like wet Indian meal; and Jimmie looked at the Hedge boy out of one good eye and one bunged eye. The long-drawn animosities of men have no place in the life of a boy. The boy's mind is flexible; he readjusts his position with an ease which is derived from the fact-simply-that he is not yet a man.

But there were other and more important matters. Johnnie Hedge's exploits had brought him into such prominence among the school-boys that it was necessary to settle a number of points once and for all. There was the usual number of boys in the school who were popularly known to be champions in their various classes. Among these Johnnie Hedge now had to thread his way, every boy taking it upon himself to feel anxious that Johnnie's exact position should be soon established. His fame as a fighter had gone forth to the world, but there were other boys who had fame as fighters, and the world was extremely anxious to know where to place the new-comer. Various heroes were urged to attempt this classification. Usually it was not accounted a matter of supreme importance, but in this boy life it was essential.

In all cases the heroes were backward enough. It was their followings who agitated the question. And so Johnnie Hedge was more or less beset.

He maintained his bashfulness. He backed away from altercation. It was plain that to bring matters to a point he must be forced into a quarrel. It was also plain that the proper person for the business was some boy who could whip Willie Dalzel, and these formidable warriors were distinctly averse to undertaking the new contract. It is a kind of a law in boy life that a quiet, decent, peace-loving lad is able to thrash a wide-mouthed talker. And so it had transpired that by a peculiar system of elimination most of the real chiefs were quiet, decent, peace-loving boys, and they had no desire to engage in a fight with a boy on the sole grounds that it was not known who could whip. Johnnie Hedge attended his affairs, they attended their affairs, and around them waged this discussion of relative merit. Jimmie Trescott took a prominent part in these arguments. He contended that Johnnie Hedge could thrash any boy in the world. He was certain of it, and to any one who opposed him he said, "You just get one of those smashes in the eye, and then you'll see." In the mean time there was a grand and impressive silence in the direction of Willie Dalzel. He had gathered remnants of his clan, but the main parts of his sovereignty were scattered to the winds. He was an enemy.

Owing to the circumspect behavior of the new boy, the commotions on the school grounds came to nothing. He was often asked, "Kin you lick him?" And he invariably replied, "I dun'no'." This idea of waging battle with the entire world appalled him.

A war for complete supremacy of the tribe which had been headed by Willie Dalzel was fought out in the country of the tribe. It came to pass that a certain half-dime blood-and-thunder pamphlet had a great vogue in the tribe at this particular time. This story relates the experience of a lad who began his career as cabin-boy on a pirate ship. Throughout the first fifteen chapters he was rope's-ended from one end of the ship to the other end, and very often he was felled to the deck by a heavy fist. He lived through enough hardships to have killed a battalion of Turkish soldiers, but in the end he rose upon them. Yes, he rose upon them. Hordes of pirates fell before his intrepid arm, and in the last chapters of the book he is seen jauntily careering on his own hook as one of the most gallous pirate captains that ever sailed the seas.

Naturally, when this tale was thoroughly understood by the tribe, they had to dramatize it, although it was a dramatization that would gain no royalties for the author. Now it was plain that the urchin who was cast for the cabin-boy's part would lead a life throughout the first fifteen chapters which would attract few actors. Willie Dalzel developed a scheme by which some small lad would play cabin-boy during this period of misfortune and abuse, and then, when the cabin-boy came to the part where he slew all his enemies and reached his zenith, that he, Willie Dalzel, should take the part.

This fugitive and disconnected rendering of a great play opened in Jimmie Trescott's back garden. The path between the two lines of gooseberry-bushes was elected unanimously to be the ship. Then Willie Dalzel insisted that Homer Phelps should be the cabin-boy. Homer tried the position for a time, and then elected that he would resign in favor of some other victim. There was no other applicant to succeed him, whereupon it became necessary to press some boy. Jimmie Trescott was a great actor, as is well known, but he steadfastly refused to engage for the part. Ultimately they seized upon little Dan Earl, whose disposition was so milky and docile that he would do whatever anybody asked of him. But Dan Earl made the one firm revolt of his life after trying existence as cabin-boy for some ten minutes. Willie Dalzel was in despair. Then he suddenly sighted the little brother of Johnnie Hedge, who had come into the garden, and in a poor-little-stranger sort of fashion was looking wistfully at the play. When he was invited to become the cabin-boy he accepted joyfully, thinking that it was his initiation into the tribe. Then they proceeded to give him the rope's end and to punch him with a realism which was not altogether painless. Directly he began to cry out. They exhorted him not to cry out, not to mind it, but still they continued to hurt him.

There was a commotion among the gooseberry-bushes, two branches were swept aside, and Johnnie Hedge walked down upon them. Every boy stopped in his tracks. Johnnie was boiling with rage.

"Who hurt him?" he said, ferociously. "Did you?" He had looked at Willie Dalzel.

Willie Dalzel began to mumble: "We was on'y playin'. Wasn't nothin' fer him to cry fer."

The new boy had at his command some big phrases, and he used them. "I am goin' to whip you within an inch of your life. I am goin' to tan the hide off'n you." And immediately there was a mixture-an infusion of two boys which looked as if it had been done by a chemist. The other children stood back, stricken with horror. But out of this whirl they presently perceived the figure of Willie Dalzel seated upon the chest of the Hedge boy.

"Got enough?" asked Willie, hoarsely.

"No," choked out the Hedge boy. Then there was another flapping and floundering, and finally another calm.

"'WHO HURT HIM?' HE SAID FEROCIOUSLY"

"Got enough?" asked Willie.

"No," said the Hedge boy. A sort of war-cloud again puzzled the sight of the observers. Both combatants were breathless, bloodless in their faces, and very weak.

"Got enough?" said Willie.

"No," said the Hedge boy. The carnage was again renewed. All the spectators were silent but Johnnie Hedge's little brother, who shrilly exhorted him to continue the struggle. But it was not plain that the Hedge boy needed any encouragement, for he was crying bitterly, and it has been explained that when a boy cried it was a bad time to hope for peace. He had managed to wriggle over upon his hands and knees. But Willie Dalzel was tenaciously gripping him from the back, and it seemed that his strength would spend itself in futility. The bear cub seemed to have the advantage of the working model of the windmill. They heaved, uttered strange words, wept, and the sun looked down upon them with steady, unwinking eye.

Peter Washington came out of the stable and observed this tragedy of the back garden. He stood transfixed for a moment, and then ran towards it, shouting: "Hi! What's all dish yere? Hi! Stopper dat, stopper dat, you two! For lan' sake, what's all dish yere?" He grabbed the struggling boys and pulled them apart. He was stormy and fine in his indignation. "For lan' sake! You two kids act like you gwine mad dogs. Stopper dat!" The whitened, tearful, soiled combatants, their clothing all awry, glared fiercely at each other as Peter stood between them, lecturing. They made several futile attempts to circumvent him and again come to battle. As he fended them off with his open hands he delivered his reproaches at Jimmie. "I's s'prised at *you*! I suhtainly is!"

"Why?" said Jimmie. "I 'ain't done nothin'. What have I done?"

"Y-y-you done 'courage dese yere kids ter scrap," said Peter, virtuously.

"Me?" cried Jimmie. "I 'ain't had nothin' to do with it."

"I raikon you 'ain't," retorted Peter, with heavy sarcasm. "I raikon you been er-prayin', 'ain't you?" Turning to Willie Dalzel, he said, "You jest take an' run erlong outer dish yere or I'll jest nachually take an' damnearkill you." Willie Dalzel went. To the new boy Peter said: "You look like you had some saince, but I raikon you don't know no more'n er rabbit. You jest take an' trot erlong off home, an' don' lemme caitch you round yere er-fightin' or I'll break yer back." The Hedge boy moved away with dignity, followed by his little brother. The latter, when he had placed a sufficient distance between himself and Peter, played his fingers at his nose and called out:

"'NIG-GER-R-R! NIG-GER-R-R!'"

"Nig-ger-r-r! Nig-ger-r-r!"

Peter Washington's resentment poured out upon Jimmie.

"'Pears like you never would understan' you ain't reg'lar common trash. You take an' 'sociate with an'body what done come erlong."

"Aw, go on," retorted Jimmie, profanely. "Go soak your head, Pete."

The remaining boys retired to the street, whereupon they perceived Willie Dalzel in the distance. He ran to them.

"I licked him!" he shouted, exultantly. "I licked him! Didn't I, now?"

From the Whilomville point of view he was entitled to a favorable answer. They made it. "Yes," they said, "you did."

"I run in," cried Willie, "an' I grabbed 'im, an' afore he knew what it was I throwed 'im. An' then it was easy." He puffed out his chest and smiled like an English recruiting-sergeant. "An' now," said he, suddenly facing Jimmie Trescott, "whose side were you on?"

The question was direct and startling. Jimmie gave back two paces. "He licked you once," he explained, haltingly.

"He never saw the day when he could lick one side of me. I could lick him with my left hand tied behind me. Why, I could lick him when I was asleep." Willie Dalzel was magnificent.

A gate clicked, and Johnnie Hedge was seen to be strolling towards them.

"You said," he remarked, coldly, "you licked me, didn't you?"

Willie Dalzel stood his ground. "Yes," he said, stoutly.

"Well, you're a liar," said the Hedge boy.

"You're another," retorted Willie.

"No, I ain't, either, but *you're* a liar."

"You're another," retorted Willie.

"Don't you dare tell *me* I'm a liar, or I'll smack your mouth for you," said the Hedge boy.

"Well, I did, didn't I?" barked Willie. "An' whatche goin' to do about it?"

"I'm goin' to lam you," said the Hedge boy.

He approached to attack warily, and the other boys held their breaths. Willie Dalzel winced back a pace. "Hol' on a minute," he cried, raising his palm. "I'm not —"

"ONE APPROACHING FROM BEHIND LAID HOLD OF HIS EAR"

But the comic windmill was again in motion, and between gasps from his exertions Johnnie Hedge remarked, "I'll-show-you-whether-you kin-lick me-or not."

The first blows did not reach home on Willie, for he backed away with expedition, keeping up his futile cry, "Hol' on a minute." Soon enough a swinging fist landed on his cheek. It did not knock him down, but it hurt him a little and frightened him a great deal. He suddenly opened his mouth to an amazing and startling extent, tilted back his head, and howled, while his eyes, glittering with tears, were fixed upon this scowling butcher of a Johnnie Hedge. The latter was making slow and vicious circles, evidently intending to renew the massacre.

But the spectators really had been desolated and shocked by the terrible thing which had happened to Willie Dalzel. They now cried out: "No, no; don't hit 'im any more! Don't hit 'im any more!"

Jimmie Trescott, in a panic of bravery, yelled, "We'll all jump on you if you do."

The Hedge boy paused, at bay. He breathed angrily, and flashed his glance from lad to lad. They still protested: "No, no; don't hit 'im any more. Don't hit 'im no more."

"I'll hammer him until he can't stand up," said Johnnie, observing that they all feared him. "I'll fix him so he won't know hisself, an' if any of you kids bother with *me* —"

Suddenly he ceased, he trembled, he collapsed. The hand of one approaching from behind had laid hold upon his ear, and it was the hand of one whom he knew.

The other lads heard a loud, iron-filing voice say, "Caught ye at it again, ye brat, ye." They saw a dreadful woman with gray hair, with a sharp red nose, with bare arms, with spectacles of such magnifying quality that her eyes shone through them like two fierce white moons. She was Johnnie Hedge's mother. Still holding Johnnie by the ear, she swung out swiftly and dexterously, and succeeded in boxing the ears of two boys before the crowd regained its presence of mind and stampeded. Yes, the war for supremacy was over, and the question was never again disputed. The supreme power was Mrs. Hedge.

XIII
A Little Pilgrimage

ONE November it became clear to childish minds in certain parts of Whilomville that the Sunday-school of the Presbyterian church would not have for the children the usual tree on Christmas eve. The funds free for that ancient festival would be used for the relief of suffering among the victims of the Charleston earthquake.

The plan had been born in the generous head of the superintendent of the Sunday-school, and during one session he had made a strong plea that the children should forego the vain pleasures of a tree and, in glorious application of the Golden Rule, refuse a local use of the fund, and will that it be sent where dire pain might be alleviated. At the end of a tearfully eloquent speech the question was put fairly to a vote, and the children in a burst of virtuous abandon carried the question for Charleston. Many of the teachers had been careful to preserve a finely neutral attitude, but even if they had cautioned the children against being too impetuous they could not have checked the wild impulses.

But this was a long time before Christmas.

Very early, boys held important speech together. "Huh! you ain't goin' to have no Christmas tree at the Presbyterian Sunday-school."

Sullenly the victim answered, "No, we ain't."

"Huh!" scoffed the other denomination, "we are goin' to have the all-firedest biggest tree that you ever saw in the world."

The little Presbyterians were greatly downcast.

It happened that Jimmie Trescott had regularly attended the Presbyterian Sunday-school. The Trescotts were consistently undenominational, but they had sent their lad on Sundays to one of the places where they thought he would receive benefits. However, on one day in December, Jimmie appeared before his father and made a strong spiritual appeal to be forth-with attached to the Sunday-school of the Big Progressive church. Doctor Trescott mused this question considerably. "Well, Jim," he said, "why do you conclude that the Big Progressive Sunday-school is better for you than the Presbyterian Sunday-school?"

"Now-it's nicer," answered Jimmie, looking at his father with an anxious eye.

"How do you mean?"

"Why-now-some of the boys what go to the Presbyterian place, they ain't very nice," explained the flagrant Jimmie.

Trescott mused the question considerably once more. In the end he said: "Well, you may change if you wish, this one time, but you must not be changing to and fro. You decide now, and then you must abide by your decision."

"Yessir," said Jimmie, brightly. "Big Progressive."

"All right," said the father. "But remember what I've told you."

On the following Sunday morning Jimmie presented himself at the door of the basement of the Big Progressive church. He was conspicuously washed, notably raimented, prominently polished. And, incidentally, he was very uncomfortable because of all these virtues.

A number of acquaintances greeted him contemptuously. "Hello, Jimmie! What you doin' here? Thought you was a Presbyterian?"

Jimmie cast down his eyes and made no reply. He was too cowed by the change. However, Homer Phelps, who was a regular patron of the Big Progressive Sunday-school, suddenly appeared and said, "Hello, Jim!" Jimmie seized upon him. Homer Phelps was amenable to Trescott laws, tribal if you like, but iron-bound, almost compulsory.

"Hello, Homer!" said Jimmie, and his manner was so good that Homer felt a great thrill in being able to show his superior a new condition of life.

"You 'ain't never come here afore, have you?" he demanded, with a new arrogance.

"No, I 'ain't," said Jimmie. Then they stared at each other and manœuvred.

"You don't know *my* teacher," said Homer.

"No, I don't know *her*" admitted Jimmie, but in a way which contended, modestly, that he knew countless other Sunday-school teachers.

"Better join our class," said Homer, sagely. "She wears spectacles; don't see very well. Sometimes we do almost what we like."

"All right," said Jimmie, glad to place himself in the hands of his friends. In due time they entered the Sunday-school room, where a man with benevolent whiskers stood on a platform and said, "We will now sing No. 33 —'Pull for the Shore, Sailor, Pull for the Shore.'" And as the obedient throng burst into melody the man on the platform indicated the time with a fat, white, and graceful hand. He was an ideal Sunday-school superintendent-one who had never felt hunger or thirst or the wound of the challenge of dishonor; a man, indeed, with beautiful flat hands who waved them in greasy victorious beneficence over a crowd of children.

Jimmie, walking carefully on his toes, followed Homer Phelps. He felt that the kingly superintendent might cry out and blast him to ashes before he could reach a chair. It was a desperate journey. But at last he heard Homer muttering to a young lady, who looked at him through glasses which greatly magnified her eyes. "A new boy," she said, in an oily and deeply religious voice.

"Yes'm," said Jimmie, trembling. The five other boys of the class scanned him keenly and derided his condition.

"We will proceed to the lesson," said the young lady. Then she cried sternly, like a sergeant, "The seventh chapter of Jeremiah!"

There was a swift fluttering of leaflets. Then the name of Jeremiah, a wise man, towered over the feelings of these boys. Homer Phelps was doomed to read the fourth verse. He took a deep breath, he puffed out his lips, he gathered his strength for a great effort. His beginning was childishly explosive. He hurriedly said:

"Trust ye not in lying words, saying The temple of the Lord, the temple of the Lord, the temple of the Lord, are these."

"Now," said the teacher, "Johnnie Scanlan, tell us what these words mean." The Scanlan boy shamefacedly muttered that he did not know. The teacher's countenance saddened. Her heart was in her work; she wanted to make a success of this Sunday-school class. "Perhaps Homer Phelps can tell us," she remarked.

Homer gulped; he looked at Jimmie. Through the great room hummed a steady hum. A little circle, very near, was being told about Daniel in the lion's den. They were deeply moved. At the moment they liked Sunday-school.

"Why-now-it means," said Homer, with a grand pomposity born of a sense of hopeless ignorance —"it means-why it means that they were in the wrong place."

"No," said the teacher, profoundly; "it means that we should be good, very good indeed. That is what it means. It means that we should love the Lord and be good. Love the Lord and be good. That is what it means."

"THE PROFESSIONAL BRIGHT BOY OF THE CLASS SUDDENLY AWOKE"

The little boys suddenly had a sense of black wickedness as their teacher looked austerely upon them. They gazed at her with the wide-open eyes of simplicity. They were stirred again. This thing of being good-this great business of life-apparently it was always successful. They knew from the fairy tales. But it was difficult, wasn't it? It was said to be the most heart-breaking task to be generous, wasn't it? One had to pay the price of one's eyes in order to be pacific, didn't one? As for patience, it was tortured martyrdom to be patient, wasn't it? Sin was simple, wasn't it? But virtue was so difficult that it could only be practised by heavenly beings, wasn't it?

And the angels, the Sunday-school superintendent, and the teacher swam in the high visions of the little boys as beings so good that if a boy scratched his shin in the same room he was a profane and sentenced devil.

"And," said the teacher, "'The temple of the Lord'—what does that mean? I'll ask the new boy. What does that mean?"

"I dun'no'," said Jimmie, blankly.

But here the professional bright boy of the class suddenly awoke to his obligations. "Teacher," he cried, "it means church, same as this."

"Exactly," said the teacher, deeply satisfied with this reply. "You know your lesson well, Clarence. I am much pleased."

The other boys, instead of being envious, looked with admiration upon Clarence, while he adopted an air of being habituated to perform such feats every day of his life. Still, he was not much of a boy. He had the virtue of being able to walk on very high stilts, but when the season of stilts had passed he possessed no rank save this Sunday-school rank, this clever-little-Clarence business of knowing the Bible and the lesson better than the other boys. The other boys, sometimes looking at him meditatively, did not actually decide to thrash him as soon as he cleared the portals of the church, but they certainly decided to molest him in such ways as would re-establish their self-respect. Back of the superintendent's chair hung a lithograph of the martyrdom of St. Stephen.

Jimmie, feeling stiff and encased in his best clothes, waited for the ordeal to end. A bell pealed: the fat hand of the superintendent had tapped a bell. Slowly the rustling and murmuring dwindled to silence. The benevolent man faced the school. "I have to announce," he began, waving his body from side to side in the conventional bows of his kind, "that—" Bang went the bell. "Give me your attention, please, children. I have to announce that the Board has decided that this year there will be no Christmas tree, but the—"

Instantly the room buzzed with the subdued clamor of the children. Jimmie was speechless. He stood morosely during the singing of the closing hymn. He passed out into the street with the others, pushing no more than was required.

Speedily the whole idea left him. If he remembered Sunday-school at all, it was to remember that he did not like it.

Wounds in the Rain: War Stories

The Price of the Harness

I

Twenty-five men were making a road out of a path up the hillside. The light batteries in the rear were impatient to advance, but first must be done all that digging and smoothing which gains no encrusted medals from war. The men worked like gardeners, and a road was growing from the old pack-animal trail.

Trees arched from a field of guinea-grass which resembled young wild corn. The day was still and dry. The men working were dressed in the consistent blue of United States regulars. They looked indifferent, almost stolid, despite the heat and the labour. There was little talking. From time to time a Government pack-train, led by a sleek-sided tender bell-mare, came from one way or the other way, and the men stood aside as the strong, hard, black-and-tan animals crowded eagerly after their curious little feminine leader.

A volunteer staff-officer appeared, and, sitting on his horse in the middle of the work, asked the sergeant in command some questions which were apparently not relevant to any military business. Men straggling along on various duties almost invariably spun some kind of a joke as they passed.

A corporal and four men were guarding boxes of spare ammunition at the top of the hill, and one of the number often went to the foot of the hill swinging canteens.

The day wore down to the Cuban dusk, in which the shadows are all grim and of ghostly shape. The men began to lift their eyes from the shovels and picks, and glance in the direction of their camp. The sun threw his last lance through the foliage. The steep mountain-range on the right turned blue and as without detail as a curtain. The tiny ruby of light ahead meant that the ammunition-guard were cooking their supper. From somewhere in the world came a single rifle-shot.

Figures appeared, dim in the shadow of the trees. A murmur, a sigh of quiet relief, arose from the working party. Later, they swung up the hill in an unformed formation, being always like soldiers, and unable even to carry a spade save like United States regular soldiers. As they passed through some fields, the bland white light of the end of the day feebly touched each hard bronze profile.

"Wonder if we'll git anythin' to eat," said Watkins, in a low voice.

"Should think so," said Nolan, in the same tone. They betrayed no impatience; they seemed to feel a kind of awe of the situation.

The sergeant turned. One could see the cool grey eye flashing under the brim of the campaign hat. "What in hell you fellers kickin' about?" he asked. They made no reply, understanding that they were being suppressed.

As they moved on, a murmur arose from the tall grass on either hand. It was the noise from the bivouac of ten thousand men, although one saw practically nothing from the low-cart roadway. The sergeant led his party up a wet clay bank and into a trampled field. Here were scattered tiny white shelter tents, and in the darkness they were luminous like the rearing stones in a graveyard. A few fires burned blood-red, and the shadowy figures of men moved with no more expression of detail than there is in the swaying of foliage on a windy night.

The working party felt their way to where their tents were pitched. A man suddenly cursed; he had mislaid something, and he knew he was not going to find it that night. Watkins spoke again with the monotony of a clock, "Wonder if we'll git anythin' to eat."

Martin, with eyes turned pensively to the stars, began a treatise. "Them Spaniards — —"

"Oh, quit it," cried Nolan. "What th' piper do you know about th' Spaniards, you fat-headed Dutchman? Better think of your belly, you blunderin' swine, an' what you're goin' to put in it, grass or dirt."

A laugh, a sort of a deep growl, arose from the prostrate men. In the meantime the sergeant had reappeared and was standing over them. "No rations to-night," he said gruffly, and turning on his heel, walked away.

This announcement was received in silence. But Watkins had flung himself face downward, and putting his lips close to a tuft of grass, he formulated oaths. Martin arose and, going to his shelter, crawled in sulkily. After a long interval Nolan said aloud, "Hell!" Grierson, enlisted for the war, raised a querulous voice. "Well, I wonder when we *will* git fed?"

From the ground about him came a low chuckle, full of ironical comment upon Grierson's lack of certain qualities which the other men felt themselves to possess.

In the cold light of dawn the men were on their knees, packing, strapping, and buckling. The comic toy hamlet of shelter-tents had been wiped out as if by a cyclone. Through the trees could be seen the crimson of a light battery's blankets, and the wheels creaked like the sound of a musketry fight. Nolan, well gripped by his shelter tent, his blanket, and his cartridge-belt, and bearing his rifle, advanced upon a small group of men who were hastily finishing a can of coffee.

"Say, give us a drink, will yeh?" he asked, wistfully. He was as sad-eyed as an orphan beggar.

Every man in the group turned to look him straight in the face. He had asked for the principal ruby out of each one's crown. There was a grim silence. Then one said, "What fer?" Nolan cast his glance to the ground, and went away abashed.

But he espied Watkins and Martin surrounding Grierson, who had gained three pieces of hard-tack by mere force of his audacious inexperience. Grierson was fending his comrades off tearfully.

"Now, don't be damn pigs," he cried. "Hold on a minute." Here Nolan asserted a claim. Grierson groaned. Kneeling piously, he divided the hard-tack with minute care into four portions. The men, who had had their heads together like players watching a wheel of fortune, arose suddenly, each chewing. Nolan interpolated a drink of water, and sighed contentedly.

The whole forest seemed to be moving. From the field on the other side of the road a column of men in blue was slowly pouring; the battery had creaked on ahead; from the rear came a hum of advancing regiments. Then from a mile away rang the noise of a shot; then another shot; in a moment the rifles there were drumming, drumming, drumming. The artillery boomed out suddenly. A day of battle was begun.

The men made no exclamations. They rolled their eyes in the direction of the sound, and then swept with a calm glance the forests and the hills which surrounded them, implacably mysterious forests and hills which lent to every rifle-shot the ominous quality which belongs to secret assassination. The whole scene would have spoken to the private soldiers of ambushes, sudden flank attacks, terrible disasters, if it were not for those cool gentlemen with shoulder-straps and swords who, the private soldiers knew, were of another world and omnipotent for the business.

The battalions moved out into the mud and began a leisurely march in the damp shade of the trees. The advance of two batteries had churned the black soil into a formidable paste. The brown leggings of the men, stained with the mud of other days, took on a deeper colour. Perspiration broke gently out on the reddish faces. With his heavy roll of blanket and the half of a shelter-tent crossing his right shoulder and under his left arm, each man presented the appearance of being clasped from behind, wrestler fashion, by a pair of thick white arms.

There was something distinctive in the way they carried their rifles. There was the grace of an old hunter somewhere in it, the grace of a man whose rifle has become absolutely a part of himself. Furthermore, almost every blue shirt sleeve was rolled to the elbow, disclosing fore-arms of almost incredible brawn. The rifles seemed light, almost fragile, in the hands that were at the end of these arms, never fat but always with rolling muscles and veins that seemed on the point of bursting. And another thing was the silence and the marvellous impassivity of the faces as the column made its slow way toward where the whole forest spluttered and fluttered with battle.

Opportunely, the battalion was halted a-straddle of a stream, and before it again moved, most of the men had filled their canteens. The firing increased. Ahead and to the left a battery was booming at methodical intervals, while the infantry racket was that continual drumming which, after all, often sounds like rain on a roof. Directly ahead one could hear the deep voices of field-pieces.

Some wounded Cubans were carried by in litters improvised from hammocks swung on poles. One had a ghastly cut in the throat, probably from a fragment of shell, and his head was turned as if Providence particularly wished to display this wide and lapping gash to the long column that was winding toward the front. And another Cuban, shot through the groin, kept up a continual wail as he swung from the tread of his bearers. "Ay-ee! Ay-ee! Madre mia! Madre mia!" He sang this bitter ballad into the ears of at least three thousand men as they slowly made way for his bearers on the narrow wood-path. These wounded insurgents were, then, to a large part of the advancing army, the visible messengers of bloodshed and death, and the men regarded them with thoughtful awe. This doleful sobbing cry —"Madre mia" —was a tangible consequent misery of all that firing on in front into which the men knew they were soon to be plunged. Some of them wished to inquire of the bearers the details of what had happened; but they could not speak Spanish, and so it was as if fate had intentionally sealed the lips of all in order that even meagre information might not leak out concerning this mystery-battle. On the other hand, many unversed private soldiers looked upon the unfortunate as men who had seen thousands maimed and bleeding, and absolutely could not conjure any further interest in such scenes.

A young staff-officer passed on horseback. The vocal Cuban was always wailing, but the officer wheeled past the bearers without heeding anything. And yet he never before had seen such a sight. His case was different from that of the private soldiers. He heeded nothing because he was busy-immensely busy and hurried with a multitude of reasons and desires for doing his duty perfectly. His whole life had been a mere period of preliminary reflection for this situation, and he had no clear idea of anything save his obligation as an officer. A man of this kind might be stupid; it is conceivable that in remote cases certain bumps on his head might be composed entirely of wood; but those traditions of fidelity and courage which have been handed to him from generation to generation, and which he has tenaciously preserved despite the persecution of legislators and the indifference of his country, make it incredible that in battle he should ever fail to give his best blood and his best thought for his general, for his men, and for himself. And so this young officer in the shapeless hat and the torn and dirty shirt failed to heed the wails of the wounded man, even as the pilgrim fails to heed the world as he raises his illumined face toward his purpose-rightly or wrongly, his purpose-his sky of the ideal of duty; and the wonderful part of it is, that he is guided by an ideal which he has himself created, and has alone protected from attack. The young man was merely an officer in the United States regular army.

The column swung across a shallow ford and took a road which passed the right flank of one of the American batteries. On a hill it was booming and belching great clouds of white smoke. The infantry looked up with interest. Arrayed below the hill and behind the battery were the horses and limbers, the riders checking their pawing mounts, and behind each rider a red blanket flamed against the fervent green of the bushes. As the infantry moved along the road, some of the battery horses turned at the noise of the trampling feet and surveyed the men with eyes as deep as wells, serene, mournful, generous eyes, lit heart-breakingly with something that was akin to a philosophy, a religion of self-sacrifice —oh, gallant, gallant horses!

"I know a feller in that battery," said Nolan, musingly. "A driver."

"Dam sight rather be a gunner," said Martin.

"Why would ye?" said Nolan, opposingly.

"Well, I'd take my chances as a gunner b'fore I'd sit way up in th' air on a raw-boned plug an' git shot at."

"Aw — —" began Nolan.

"They've had some losses t'-day all right," interrupted Grierson.

"Horses?" asked Watkins.

"Horses and men too," said Grierson.

"How d'yeh know?"

"A feller told me there by the ford."

They kept only a part of their minds bearing on this discussion because they could already hear high in the air the wire-string note of the enemy's bullets.

The road taken by this battalion as it followed other battalions is something less than a mile long in its journey across a heavily-wooded plain. It is greatly changed now, —in fact it was metamorphosed in two days; but at that time it was a mere track through dense shrubbery, from which rose great dignified arching trees. It was, in fact, a path through a jungle.

The battalion had no sooner left the battery in rear when bullets began to drive overhead. They made several different sounds, but as these were mainly high shots it was usual for them to make the faint note of a vibrant string, touched elusively, half-dreamily.

The military balloon, a fat, wavering, yellow thing, was leading the advance like some new conception of war-god. Its bloated mass shone above the trees, and served incidentally to indicate to the men at the rear that comrades were in advance. The track itself exhibited for all its visible length a closely-knit procession of soldiers in blue with breasts crossed with white shelter-tents. The first ominous order of battle came down the line. "Use the cut-off. Don't use the magazine until you're ordered." Non-commissioned officers repeated the command gruffly. A sound of clicking locks rattled along the columns. All men knew that the time had come.

The front had burst out with a roar like a brush-fire. The balloon was dying, dying a gigantic and public death before the eyes of two armies. It quivered, sank, faded into the trees amid the flurry of a battle that was suddenly and tremendously like a storm.

The American battery thundered behind the men with a shock that seemed likely to tear the backs of their heads off. The Spanish shrapnel fled on a line to their left, swirling and swishing in supernatural velocity. The noise of the rifle bullets broke in their faces like the noise of so many lamp-chimneys or sped overhead in swift cruel spitting. And at the front the battle-sound, as if it were simply music, was beginning to swell and swell until the volleys rolled like a surf.

The officers shouted hoarsely, "Come on, men! Hurry up, boys! Come on now! Hurry up!" The soldiers, running heavily in their accoutrements, dashed forward. A baggage guard was swiftly detailed; the men tore their rolls from their shoulders as if the things were afire. The battalion, stripped for action, again dashed forward.

"Come on, men! Come on!" To them the battle was as yet merely a road through the woods crowded with troops, who lowered their heads anxiously as the bullets fled high. But a moment later the column wheeled abruptly to the left and entered a field of tall green grass. The line scattered to a skirmish formation. In front was a series of knolls treed sparsely like orchards; and although no enemy was visible, these knolls were all popping and spitting with rifle-fire. In some places there were to be seen long grey lines of dirt, intrenchments. The American shells were kicking up reddish clouds of dust from the brow of one of the knolls, where stood a pagoda-like house. It was not much like a battle with men; it was a battle with a bit of charming scenery, enigmatically potent for death.

Nolan knew that Martin had suddenly fallen. "What — —" he began.

"They've hit me," said Martin.

"Jesus!" said Nolan.

Martin lay on the ground, clutching his left forearm just below the elbow with all the strength of his right hand. His lips were pursed ruefully. He did not seem to know what to do. He continued to stare at his arm.

Then suddenly the bullets drove at them low and hard. The men flung themselves face downward in the grass. Nolan lost all thought of his friend. Oddly enough, he felt somewhat like a man hiding under a bed, and he was just as sure that he could not raise his head high without being shot as a man hiding under a bed is sure that he cannot raise his head without bumping it.

A lieutenant was seated in the grass just behind him. He was in the careless and yet rigid pose of a man balancing a loaded plate on his knee at a picnic. He was talking in soothing paternal tones.

"Now, don't get rattled. We're all right here. Just as safe as being in church.... They're all going high. Don't mind them.... Don't mind them.... They're all going high. We've got them rattled and they can't shoot straight. Don't mind them."

The sun burned down steadily from a pale blue sky upon the crackling woods and knolls and fields. From the roar of musketry it might have been that the celestial heat was frying this part of the world.

Nolan snuggled close to the grass. He watched a grey line of intrenchments, above which floated the veriest gossamer of smoke. A flag lolled on a staff behind it. The men in the trench volleyed whenever an American shell exploded near them. It was some kind of infantile defiance. Frequently a bullet came from the woods directly behind Nolan and his comrades. They thought at the time that these bullets were from the rifle of some incompetent soldier of their own side.

There was no cheering. The men would have looked about them, wondering where was the army, if it were not that the crash of the fighting for the distance of a mile denoted plainly enough where was the army.

Officially, the battalion had not yet fired a shot; there had been merely some irresponsible popping by men on the extreme left flank. But it was known that the lieutenant-colonel who had been in command was dead-shot through the heart-and that the captains were thinned down to two. At the rear went on a long tragedy, in which men, bent and hasty, hurried to shelter with other men, helpless, dazed, and bloody. Nolan knew of it all from the hoarse and affrighted voices which he heard as he lay flattened in the grass. There came to him a sense of exultation. Here, then, was one of those dread and lurid situations, which in a nation's history stand out in crimson letters, becoming a tale of blood to stir generation after generation. And he was in it, and unharmed. If he lived through the battle, he would be a hero of the desperate fight at — —; and here he wondered for a second what fate would be pleased to bestow as a name for this battle.

But it is quite sure that hardly another man in the battalion was engaged in any thoughts concerning the historic. On the contrary, they deemed it ill that they were being badly cut up on a most unimportant occasion. It would have benefited the conduct of whoever were weak if they had known that they were engaged in a battle that would be famous for ever.

Martin had picked himself up from where the bullet had knocked him and addressed the lieu-tenant. "I'm hit, sir," he said.

The lieutenant was very busy. "All right, all right," he said, just heeding the man enough to learn where he was wounded. "Go over that way. You ought to see a dressing-station under those trees."

Martin found himself dizzy and sick. The sensation in his arm was distinctly galvanic. The feeling was so strange that he could wonder at times if a wound was really what ailed him. Once, in this dazed way, he examined his arm; he saw the hole. Yes, he was shot; that was it. And more than in any other way it affected him with a profound sadness.

As directed by the lieutenant, he went to the clump of trees, but he found no dressing-station there. He found only a dead soldier lying with his face buried in his arms and with his shoulders humped high as if he were convulsively sobbing. Martin decided to make his way to the road, deeming that he thus would better his chances of getting to a surgeon. But he suddenly found his way blocked by a fence of barbed wire. Such was his mental condition that he brought up at a rigid halt before this fence, and stared stupidly at it. It did not seem to him possible that this obstacle could be defeated by any means. The fence was there, and it stopped his progress. He could not go in that direction.

But as he turned he espied that procession of wounded men, strange pilgrims, that had al-ready worn a path in the tall grass. They were passing through a gap in the fence. Martin joined them. The bullets were flying over them in sheets, but many of them bore themselves as men who had now exacted from fate a singular immunity. Generally there were no outcries, no kick-ing, no talk at all. They too, like Martin, seemed buried in a vague but profound melancholy.

But there was one who cried out loudly. A man shot in the head was being carried ardu-ously by four comrades, and he continually yelled one word that was terrible in its primitive strength, —"Bread! Bread! Bread!" Following him and his bearers were a limping crowd of men less cruelly wounded, who kept their eyes always fixed on him, as if they gained from his extreme agony some balm for their own sufferings.

"Bread! Give me bread!"

Martin plucked a man by the sleeve. The man had been shot in the foot, and was making his way with the help of a curved, incompetent stick. It is an axiom of war that wounded men can never find straight sticks.

"What's the matter with that feller?" asked Martin.

"Nutty," said the man.

"Why is he?"

"Shot in th' head," answered the other, impatiently.

The wail of the sufferer arose in the field amid the swift rasp of bullets and the boom and shatter of shrapnel. "Bread! Bread! Oh, God, can't you give me bread? Bread!" The bearers of him were suffering exquisite agony, and often they exchanged glances which exhibited their despair of ever getting free of this tragedy. It seemed endless.

"Bread! Bread! Bread!"

But despite the fact that there was always in the way of this crowd a wistful melancholy, one must know that there were plenty of men who laughed, laughed at their wounds whimsically, quaintly inventing odd humours concerning bicycles and cabs, extracting from this shedding of their blood a wonderful amount of material for cheerful badinage, and, with their faces twisted from pain as they stepped, they often joked like music-hall stars. And perhaps this was the most tearful part of all.

They trudged along a road until they reached a ford. Here under the eave of the bank lay a dismal company. In the mud and in the damp shade of some bushes were a half-hundred pale-faced men prostrate. Two or three surgeons were working there. Also, there was a chaplain, grim-mouthed, resolute, his surtout discarded. Overhead always was that incessant maddening wail of bullets.

Martin was standing gazing drowsily at the scene when a surgeon grabbed him. "Here, what's the matter with you?" Martin was daunted. He wondered what he had done that the surgeon should be so angry with him.

"In the arm," he muttered, half-shamefacedly.

After the surgeon had hastily and irritably bandaged the injured member he glared at Martin and said, "You can walk all right, can't you?"

"Yes, sir," said Martin.

"Well, now, you just make tracks down that road."

"Yes, sir." Martin went meekly off. The doctor had seemed exasperated almost to the point of madness.

The road was at this time swept with the fire of a body of Spanish sharpshooters who had come cunningly around the flanks of the American army, and were now hidden in the dense foliage that lined both sides of the road. They were shooting at everything. The road was as crowded as a street in a city, and at an absurdly short range they emptied their rifles at the passing people. They were aided always by the over-sweep from the regular Spanish line of battle.

Martin was sleepy from his wound. He saw tragedy follow tragedy, but they created in him no feeling of horror.

A man with a red cross on his arm was leaning against a great tree. Suddenly he tumbled to the ground, and writhed for a moment in the way of a child oppressed with colic. A comrade immediately began to bustle importantly. "Here," he called to Martin, "help me carry this man, will you?"

Martin looked at him with dull scorn. "I'll be damned if I do," he said. "Can't carry myself, let alone somebody else."

This answer, which rings now so inhuman, pitiless, did not affect the other man. "Well, all right," he said. "Here comes some other fellers." The wounded man had now turned blue-grey; his eyes were closed; his body shook in a gentle, persistent chill.

Occasionally Martin came upon dead horses, their limbs sticking out and up like stakes. One beast mortally shot, was besieged by three or four men who were trying to push it into the bushes, where it could live its brief time of anguish without thrashing to death any of the wounded men in the gloomy procession.

The mule train, with extra ammunition, charged toward the front, still led by the tinkling bell-mare.

An ambulance was stuck momentarily in the mud, and above the crack of battle one could hear the familiar objurgations of the driver as he whirled his lash.

Two privates were having a hard time with a wounded captain, whom they were supporting to the rear, He was half cursing, half wailing out the information that he not only would not go another step toward the rear, but that he was certainly going to return at once to the front. They begged, pleaded at great length as they continually headed him off. They were not unlike two nurses with an exceptionally bad and headstrong little duke.

The wounded soldiers paused to look impassively upon this struggle. They were always like men who could not be aroused by anything further.

The visible hospital was mainly straggling thickets intersected with narrow paths, the ground being covered with men. Martin saw a busy person with a book and a pencil, but he did not approach him to become officially a member of the hospital. All he desired was rest and immunity from nagging. He took seat painfully under a bush and leaned his back upon the trunk. There he remained thinking, his face wooden.

V

"My Gawd," said Nolan, squirming on his belly in the grass, "I can't stand this much longer."

Then suddenly every rifle in the firing line seemed to go off of its own accord. It was the result of an order, but few men heard the order; in the main they had fired because they heard others fire, and their sense was so quick that the volley did not sound too ragged. These marksmen had been lying for nearly an hour in stony silence, their sights adjusted, their fingers fondling their rifles, their eyes staring at the intrenchments of the enemy. The battalion had suffered heavy losses, and these losses had been hard to bear, for a soldier always reasons that men lost during a period of inaction are men badly lost.

The line now sounded like a great machine set to running frantically in the open air, the bright sunshine of a green field. To the prut of the magazine rifles was added the under-chorus of the clicking mechanism, steady and swift, as if the hand of one operator was controlling it all. It reminds one always of a loom, a great grand steel loom, clinking, clanking, plunking, plinking, to weave a woof of thin red threads, the cloth of death. By the men's shoulders under their eager hands dropped continually the yellow empty shells, spinning into the crushed grass blades to remain there and mark for the belated eye the line of a battalion's fight.

All impatience, all rebellious feeling, had passed out of the men as soon as they had been allowed to use their weapons against the enemy. They now were absorbed in this business of hitting something, and all the long training at the rifle ranges, all the pride of the marksman which had been so long alive in them, made them forget for the time everything but shooting. They were as deliberate and exact as so many watchmakers.

A new sense of safety was rightfully upon them. They knew that those mysterious men in the high far trenches in front were having the bullets sping in their faces with relentless and remarkable precision; they knew, in fact, that they were now doing the thing which they had been trained endlessly to do, and they knew they were doing it well. Nolan, for instance, was overjoyed. "Plug 'em," he said: "Plug 'em." He laid his face to his rifle as if it were his mistress. He was aiming under the shadow of a certain portico of a fortified house: there he could faintly see a long black line which he knew to be a loop-hole cut for riflemen, and he knew that every shot of his was going there under the portico, mayhap through the loop-hole to the brain of another man like himself. He loaded the awkward magazine of his rifle again and again. He was so intent that he did not know of new orders until he saw the men about him scrambling to their feet and running forward, crouching low as they ran.

He heard a shout. "Come on, boys! We can't be last! We're going up! We're going up." He sprang to his feet and, stooping, ran with the others. Something fine, soft, gentle, touched his heart as he ran. He had loved the regiment, the army, because the regiment, the army, was his life, —he had no other outlook; and now these men, his comrades, were performing his dream-scenes for him; they were doing as he had ordained in his visions. It is curious that in this charge he considered himself as rather unworthy. Although he himself was in the assault with the rest of them, it seemed to him that his comrades were dazzlingly courageous. His part, to his mind, was merely that of a man who was going along with the crowd.

He saw Grierson biting madly with his pincers at a barbed-wire fence. They were half-way up the beautiful sylvan slope; there was no enemy to be seen, and yet the landscape rained bullets. Somebody punched him violently in the stomach. He thought dully to lie down and rest, but instead he fell with a crash.

The sparse line of men in blue shirts and dirty slouch hats swept on up the hill. He decided to shut his eyes for a moment because he felt very dreamy and peaceful. It seemed only a minute before he heard a voice say, "There he is." Grierson and Watkins had come to look for him. He searched their faces at once and keenly, for he had a thought that the line might be driven down the hill and leave him in Spanish hands. But he saw that everything was secure, and he prepared no questions.

"Nolan," said Grierson clumsily, "do you know me?"

The man on the ground smiled softly. "Of course I know you, you chowder-faced monkey. Why wouldn't I know you?"

Watkins knelt beside him. "Where did they plug you, old boy?"

Nolan was somewhat dubious. "It ain't much. I don't think but it's somewheres there." He laid a finger on the pit of his stomach. They lifted his shirt, and then privately they exchanged a glance of horror.

"Does it hurt, Jimmie?" said Grierson, hoarsely.

"No," said Nolan, "it don't hurt any, but I feel sort of dead-to-the-world and numb all over. I don't think it's very bad."

"Oh, it's all right," said Watkins.

"What I need is a drink," said Nolan, grinning at them. "I'm chilly-lying on this damp ground."

"It ain't very damp, Jimmie," said Grierson.

"Well, it is damp," said Nolan, with sudden irritability. "I can feel it. I'm wet, I tell you-wet through-just from lying here."

They answered hastily. "Yes, that's so, Jimmie. It *is* damp. That's so."

"Just put your hand under my back and see how wet the ground is," he said.

"No," they answered. "That's all right, Jimmie. We know it's wet."

"Well, put your hand under and see," he cried, stubbornly.

"Oh, never mind, Jimmie."

"No," he said, in a temper. "See for yourself." Grierson seemed to be afraid of Nolan's agitation, and so he slipped a hand under the prostrate man, and presently withdrew it covered with blood. "Yes," he said, hiding his hand carefully from Nolan's eyes, "you were right, Jimmie."

"Of course I was," said Nolan, contentedly closing his eyes. "This hillside holds water like a swamp." After a moment he said, "Guess I ought to know. I'm flat here on it, and you fellers are standing up."

He did not know he was dying. He thought he was holding an argument on the condition of the turf.

"Cover his face," said Grierson, in a low and husky voice afterwards.

"What'll I cover it with?" said Watkins.

They looked at themselves. They stood in their shirts, trousers, leggings, shoes; they had nothing.

"Oh," said Grierson, "here's his hat." He brought it and laid it on the face of the dead man. They stood for a time. It was apparent that they thought it essential and decent to say or do something. Finally Watkins said in a broken voice, "Aw, it's a dam shame." They moved slowly off toward the firing line.

In the blue gloom of evening, in one of the fever-tents, the two rows of still figures became hideous, charnel. The languid movement of a hand was surrounded with spectral mystery, and the occasional painful twisting of a body under a blanket was terrifying, as if dead men were moving in their graves under the sod. A heavy odour of sickness and medicine hung in the air.

"What regiment are you in?" said a feeble voice.

"Twenty-ninth Infantry," answered another voice.

"Twenty-ninth! Why, the man on the other side of me is in the Twenty-ninth."

"He is?...Hey, there, partner, are you in the Twenty-ninth?"

A third voice merely answered wearily. "Martin of C Company."

"What? Jack, is that you?"

"It's part of me.... Who are you?"

"Grierson, you fat-head. I thought you were wounded."

There was the noise of a man gulping a great drink of water, and at its conclusion Martin said, "I am."

"Well, what you doin' in the fever-place, then?"

Martin replied with drowsy impatience. "Got the fever too."

"Gee!" said Grierson.

Thereafter there was silence in the fever-tent, save for the noise made by a man over in a corner —a kind of man always found in an American crowd —a heroic, implacable comedian and patriot, of a humour that has bitterness and ferocity and love in it, and he was wringing from the situation a grim meaning by singing the "Star-Spangled Banner" with all the ardour which could be procured from his fever-stricken body.

"Billie," called Martin in a low voice, "where's Jimmy Nolan?"

"He's dead," said Grierson.

A triangle of raw gold light shone on a side of the tent. Somewhere in the valley an engine's bell was ringing, and it sounded of peace and home as if it hung on a cow's neck.

"And where's Ike Watkins?"

"Well, he ain't dead, but he got shot through the lungs. They say he ain't got much show."

Through the clouded odours of sickness and medicine rang the dauntless voice of the man in the corner.

The Lone Charge of William B. Perkins

He could not distinguish between a five-inch quick-firing gun and a nickle-plated ice-pick, and so, naturally, he had been elected to fill the position of war-correspondent. The responsible party was the editor of the "Minnesota Herald." Perkins had no information of war, and no particular rapidity of mind for acquiring it, but he had that rank and fibrous quality of courage which springs from the thick soil of Western America.

It was morning in Guantanamo Bay. If the marines encamped on the hill had had time to turn their gaze seaward, they might have seen a small newspaper despatch-boat wending its way toward the entrance of the harbour over the blue, sunlit waters of the Caribbean. In the stern of this tug Perkins was seated upon some coal bags, while the breeze gently ruffled his greasy pajamas. He was staring at a brown line of entrenchments surmounted by a flag, which was Camp McCalla. In the harbour were anchored two or three grim, grey cruisers and a transport. As the tug steamed up the radiant channel, Perkins could see men moving on shore near the charred ruins of a village. Perkins was deeply moved; here already was more war than he had ever known in Minnesota. Presently he, clothed in the essential garments of a war-correspondent, was rowed to the sandy beach. Marines in yellow linen were handling an ammunition supply. They paid no attention to the visitor, being morose from the inconveniences of two days and nights of fighting. Perkins toiled up the zigzag path to the top of the hill, and looked with eager eyes at the trenches, the field-pieces, the funny little Colts, the flag, the grim marines lying wearily on their arms. And still more, he looked through the clear air over 1,000 yards of mysterious woods from which emanated at inopportune times repeated flocks of Mauser bullets.

Perkins was delighted. He was filled with admiration for these jaded and smoky men who lay so quietly in the trenches waiting for a resumption of guerilla enterprise. But he wished they would heed him. He wanted to talk about it. Save for sharp inquiring glances, no one acknowledged his existence.

Finally he approached two young lieutenants, and in his innocent Western way he asked them if they would like a drink. The effect on the two young lieutenants was immediate and astonishing. With one voice they answered, "Yes, we would." Perkins almost wept with joy at this amiable response, and he exclaimed that he would immediately board the tug and bring off a bottle of Scotch. This attracted the officers, and in a burst of confidence one explained that there had not been a drop in camp. Perkins lunged down the hill, and fled to his boat, where in his exuberance he engaged in a preliminary altercation with some whisky. Consequently he toiled again up the hill in the blasting sun with his enthusiasm in no ways abated. The parched officers were very gracious, and such was the state of mind of Perkins that he did not note properly how serious and solemn was his engagement with the whisky. And because of this fact, and because of his antecedents, there happened the lone charge of William B. Perkins.

Now, as Perkins went down the hill, something happened. A private in those high trenches found that a cartridge was clogged in his rifle. It then becomes necessary with most kinds of rifles to explode the cartridge. The private took the rifle to his captain, and explained the case. But it would not do in that camp to fire a rifle for mechanical purposes and without warning, because the eloquent sound would bring six hundred tired marines to tension and high expectancy. So the captain turned, and in a loud voice announced to the camp that he found it necessary to shoot into the air. The communication rang sharply from voice to voice. Then the captain raised the weapon and fired. Whereupon-and whereupon—a large line of guerillas lying in the bushes decided swiftly that their presence and position were discovered, and swiftly they volleyed.

In a moment the woods and the hills were alive with the crack and sputter of rifles. Men on the warships in the harbour heard the old familiar flut-flut-fluttery-fluttery-flut-flut-flut from the entrenchments. Incidentally the launch of the "Marblehead," commanded by one of our headlong American ensigns, streaked for the strategic woods like a galloping marine dragoon, peppering away with its blunderbuss in the bow.

Perkins had arrived at the foot of the hill, where began the arrangement of 150 marines that protected the short line of communication between the main body and the beach. These men had all swarmed into line behind fortifications improvised from the boxes of provisions. And to them were gathering naked men who had been bathing, naked men who arrayed themselves speedily in cartridge belts and rifles. The woods and the hills went flut-flut-flut-fluttery-fluttery-flut-fllllluttery-flut. Under the boughs of a beautiful tree lay five wounded men thinking vividly.

And now it befell Perkins to discover a Spaniard in the bush. The distance was some five hundred yards. In a loud voice he announced his perception. He also declared hoarsely, that if he only had a rifle, he would go and possess himself of this particular enemy. Immediately an amiable lad shot in the arm said: "Well, take mine." Perkins thus acquired a rifle and a clip of five cartridges.

"Come on!" he shouted. This part of the battalion was lying very tight, not yet being engaged, but not knowing when the business would swirl around to them.

To Perkins they replied with a roar. "Come back here, you — — fool. Do you want to get shot by your own crowd? Come back, — — — —!" As a detail, it might be mentioned that the fire from a part of the hill swept the journey upon which Perkins had started.

Now behold the solitary Perkins adrift in the storm of fighting, even as a champagne jacket of straw is lost in a great surf. He found it out quickly. Four seconds elapsed before he discovered that he was an almshouse idiot plunging through hot, crackling thickets on a June morning in Cuba. Sss-s-swing-sing-ing-pop went the lightning-swift metal grasshoppers over him and beside him. The beauties of rural Minnesota illuminated his conscience with the gold of lazy corn, with the sleeping green of meadows, with the cathedral gloom of pine forests. Sshsh-swing-pop! Perkins decided that if he cared to extract himself from a tangle of imbecility he must shoot. The entire situation was that he must shoot. It was necessary that he should shoot. Nothing would save him but shooting. It is a law that men thus decide when the waters of battle close over their minds. So with a prayer that the Americans would not hit him in the back nor the left side, and that the Spaniards would not hit him in the front, he knelt like a supplicant alone in the desert of chaparral, and emptied his magazine at his Spaniard before he discovered that his Spaniard was a bit of dried palm branch.

Then Perkins flurried like a fish. His reason for being was a Spaniard in the bush. When the Spaniard turned into a dried palm branch, he could no longer furnish himself with one adequate reason.

Then did he dream frantically of some anthracite hiding-place, some profound dungeon of peace where blind mules live placidly chewing the far-gathered hay.

"Sss-swing-win-pop! Prut-prut-prrrut!" Then a field-gun spoke. "Boom-ra-swow-ow-ow-ow-pum." Then a Colt automatic began to bark. "Crack-crk-crk-crk-crk-crk" endlessly. Raked, enfiladed, flanked, surrounded, and overwhelmed, what hope was there for William B. Perkins of the "Minnesota Herald?"

But war is a spirit. War provides for those that it loves. It provides sometimes death and sometimes a singular and incredible safety. There were few ways in which it was possible to preserve Perkins. One way was by means of a steam-boiler.

Perkins espied near him an old, rusty steam-boiler lying in the bushes. War only knows how it was there, but there it was, a temple shining resplendent with safety. With a moan of haste, Perkins flung himself through that hole which expressed the absence of the steam-pipe.

Then ensconced in his boiler, Perkins comfortably listened to the ring of a fight which seemed to be in the air above him. Sometimes bullets struck their strong, swift blow against the boiler's sides, but none entered to interfere with Perkins's rest.

Time passed. The fight, short anyhow, dwindled to prut... prut... prut-prut... prut. And when the silence came, Perkins might have been seen cautiously protruding from the boiler. Presently he strolled back toward the marine lines with his hat not able to fit his head for the new bumps of wisdom that were on it.

The marines, with an annoyed air, were settling down again when an apparitional figure came from the bushes. There was great excitement.

"It's that crazy man," they shouted, and as he drew near they gathered tumultuously about him and demanded to know how he had accomplished it.

Perkins made a gesture, the gesture of a man escaping from an unintentional mud-bath, the gesture of a man coming out of battle, and then he told them.

The incredulity was immediate and general. "Yes, you did! What? In an old boiler? An old boiler? Out in that brush? Well, we guess not." They did not believe him until two days later, when a patrol happened to find the rusty boiler, relic of some curious transaction in the ruin of the Cuban sugar industry. The patrol then marvelled at the truthfulness of war-correspondents until they were almost blind.

Soon after his adventure Perkins boarded the tug, wearing a countenance of poignant thought-fulness.

The Clan of No-Name

Unwind my riddle.
Cruel as hawks the hours fly;
Wounded men seldom come home to die;
The hard waves see an arm flung high;
Scorn hits strong because of a lie;
Yet there exists a mystic tie.
Unwind my riddle.

She was out in the garden. Her mother came to her rapidly. "Margharita! Margharita, Mister Smith is here! Come!" Her mother was fat and commercially excited. Mister Smith was a matter of some importance to all Tampa people, and since he was really in love with Margharita he was distinctly of more importance to this particular household.

Palm trees tossed their sprays over the fence toward the rutted sand of the street. A little foolish fish-pond in the centre of the garden emitted a sound of red-fins flipping, flipping. "No, mamma," said the girl, "let Mr. Smith wait. I like the garden in the moonlight."

Her mother threw herself into that state of virtuous astonishment which is the weapon of her kind. "Margharita!"

The girl evidently considered herself to be a privileged belle, for she answered quite carelessly, "Oh, let him wait."

The mother threw abroad her arms with a semblance of great high-minded suffering and withdrew. Margharita walked alone in the moonlit garden. Also an electric light threw its shivering gleam over part of her parade.

There was peace for a time. Then suddenly through the faint brown palings was struck an envelope white and square. Margharita approached this envelope with an indifferent stride. She hummed a silly air, she bore herself casually, but there was something that made her grasp it hard, a peculiar muscular exhibition, not discernible to indifferent eyes. She did not clutch it, but she took it-simply took it in a way that meant everything, and, to measure it by vision, it was a picture of the most complete disregard.

She stood straight for a moment; then she drew from her bosom a photograph and thrust it through the palings. She walked rapidly into the house.

II

A man in garb of blue and white-something relating to what we call bed-ticking —was seated in a curious little cupola on the top of a Spanish blockhouse. The blockhouse sided a white military road that curved away from the man's sight into a blur of trees. On all sides of him were fields of tall grass, studded with palms and lined with fences of barbed wire. The sun beat aslant through the trees and the man sped his eyes deep into the dark tropical shadows that seemed velvet with coolness. These tranquil vistas resembled painted scenery in a theatre, and, moreover, a hot, heavy silence lay upon the land.

The soldier in the watching place leaned an unclean Mauser rifle in a corner, and, reaching down, took a glowing coal on a bit of palm bark handed up to him by a comrade. The men below were mainly asleep. The sergeant in command drowsed near the open door, the arm above his head, showing his long keen-angled chevrons attached carelessly with safety-pins. The sentry lit his cigarette and puffed languorously.

Suddenly he heard from the air around him the querulous, deadly-swift spit of rifle-bullets, and, an instant later, the poppety-pop of a small volley sounded in his face, close, as if it were fired only ten feet away. Involuntarily he threw back his head quickly as if he were protecting his nose from a falling tile. He screamed an alarm and fell into the blockhouse. In the gloom of it, men with their breaths coming sharply between their teeth, were tumbling wildly for positions at the loop-holes. The door had been slammed, but the sergeant lay just within, propped up as when he drowsed, but now with blood flowing steadily over the hand that he pressed flatly to his chest. His face was in stark yellow agony; he chokingly repeated: "Fuego! Por Dios, hombres!"

The men's ill-conditioned weapons were jammed through the loop-holes and they began to fire from all four sides of the blockhouse from the simple data, apparently, that the enemy were in the vicinity. The fumes of burnt powder grew stronger and stronger in the little square fortress. The rattling of the magazine locks was incessant, and the interior might have been that of a gloomy manufactory if it were not for the sergeant down under the feet of the men, coughing out: "Por Dios, hombres! Por Dios! Fuego!"

III

A string of five Cubans, in linen that had turned earthy brown in colour, slid through the woods at a pace that was neither a walk nor a run. It was a kind of rack. In fact the whole manner of the men, as they thus moved, bore a rather comic resemblance to the American pacing horse. But they had come many miles since sun-up over mountainous and half-marked paths, and were plainly still fresh. The men were all practicos-guides. They made no sound in their swift travel, but moved their half-shod feet with the skill of cats. The woods lay around them in a deep silence, such as one might find at the bottom of a lake.

Suddenly the leading practico raised his hand. The others pulled up short and dropped the butts of their weapons calmly and noiselessly to the ground. The leader whistled a low note and immediately another practico appeared from the bushes. He moved close to the leader without a word, and then they spoke in whispers.

"There are twenty men and a sergeant in the blockhouse."

"And the road?"

"One company of cavalry passed to the east this morning at seven o'clock. They were escorting four carts. An hour later, one horseman rode swiftly to the westward. About noon, ten infantry soldiers with a corporal were taken from the big fort and put in the first blockhouse, to the east of the fort. There were already twelve men there. We saw a Spanish column moving off toward Mariel."

"No more?"

"No more."

"Good. But the cavalry?"

"It is all right. They were going a long march."

"The expedition is a half league behind. Go and tell the general."

The scout disappeared. The five other men lifted their guns and resumed their rapid and noiseless progress. A moment later no sound broke the stillness save the thump of a mango, as it dropped lazily from its tree to the grass. So strange had been the apparition of these men, their dress had been so allied in colour to the soil, their passing had so little disturbed the solemn rumination of the forest, and their going had been so like a spectral dissolution, that a witness could have wondered if he dreamed.

IV

A small expedition had landed with arms from the United States, and had now come out of the hills and to the edge of a wood. Before them was a long-grassed rolling prairie marked with palms. A half-mile away was the military road, and they could see the top of a blockhouse. The insurgent scouts were moving somewhere off in the grass. The general sat comfortably under a tree, while his staff of three young officers stood about him chatting. Their linen clothing was notable from being distinctly whiter than those of the men who, one hundred and fifty in number, lay on the ground in a long brown fringe, ragged-indeed, bare in many places-but singularly reposeful, unworried, veteran-like.

The general, however, was thoughtful. He pulled continually at his little thin moustache. As far as the heavily patrolled and guarded military road was concerned, the insurgents had been in the habit of dashing across it in small bodies whenever they pleased, but to safely scoot over it with a valuable convoy of arms, was decidedly a more important thing. So the general awaited the return of his practicos with anxiety. The still pampas betrayed no sign of their existence.

The general gave some orders and an officer counted off twenty men to go with him, and delay any attempt of the troop of cavalry to return from the eastward. It was not an easy task, but it was a familiar task-checking the advance of a greatly superior force by a very hard fire from concealment. A few rifles had often bayed a strong column for sufficient length of time for all strategic purposes. The twenty men pulled themselves together tranquilly. They looked quite indifferent. Indeed, they had the supremely casual manner of old soldiers, hardened to battle as a condition of existence.

Thirty men were then told off, whose function it was to worry and rag at the blockhouse, and check any advance from the westward. A hundred men, carrying precious burdens-besides their own equipment-were to pass in as much of a rush as possible between these two wings, cross the road and skip for the hills, their retreat being covered by a combination of the two firing parties. It was a trick that needed both luck and neat arrangement. Spanish columns were for ever prowling through this province in all directions and at all times. Insurgent bands-the lightest of light infantry-were kept on the jump, even when they were not incommoded by fifty boxes, each one large enough for the coffin of a little man, and heavier than if the little man were in it; and fifty small but formidable boxes of ammunition.

The carriers stood to their boxes and the firing parties leaned on their rifles. The general arose and strolled to and fro, his hands behind him. Two of his staff were jesting at the third, a young man with a face less bronzed, and with very new accoutrements. On the strap of his cartouche were a gold star and a silver star, placed in a horizontal line, denoting that he was a second lieutenant. He seemed very happy; he laughed at all their jests, although his eye roved continually over the sunny grass-lands, where was going to happen his first fight. One of his stars was bright, like his hopes, the other was pale, like death.

Two practicos came racking out of the grass. They spoke rapidly to the general; he turned and nodded to his officers. The two firing parties filed out and diverged toward their positions. The general watched them through his glasses. It was strange to note how soon they were dim to the unaided eye. The little patches of brown in the green grass did not look like men at all.

Practicos continually ambled up to the general. Finally he turned and made a sign to the bearers. The first twenty men in line picked up their boxes, and this movement rapidly spread to the tail of the line. The weighted procession moved painfully out upon the sunny prairie. The general, marching at the head of it, glanced continually back as if he were compelled to drag behind him some ponderous iron chain. Besides the obvious mental worry, his face bore an expression of intense physical strain, and he even bent his shoulders, unconsciously tugging at the chain to hurry it through this enemy-crowded valley.

V

The fight was opened by eight men who, snuggling in the grass, within three hundred yards of the blockhouse, suddenly blazed away at the bed-ticking figure in the cupola and at the open door where they could see vague outlines. Then they laughed and yelled insulting language, for they knew that as far as the Spaniards were concerned, the surprise was as much as having a diamond bracelet turn to soap. It was this volley that smote the sergeant and caused the man in the cupola to scream and tumble from his perch.

The eight men, as well as all other insurgents within fair range, had chosen good positions for lying close, and for a time they let the blockhouse rage, although the soldiers therein could occasionally hear, above the clamour of their weapons, shrill and almost wolfish calls, coming from men whose lips were laid against the ground. But it is not in the nature of them of Spanish blood, and armed with rifles, to long endure the sight of anything so tangible as an enemy's blockhouse without shooting at it-other conditions being partly favourable. Presently the steaming soldiers in the little fort could hear the sping and shiver of bullets striking the wood that guarded their bodies.

A perfectly white smoke floated up over each firing Cuban, the penalty of the Remington rifle, but about the blockhouse there was only the lightest gossamer of blue. The blockhouse stood always for some big, clumsy and rather incompetent animal, while the insurgents, scattered on two sides of it, were little enterprising creatures of another species, too wise to come too near, but joyously raging at its easiest flanks and drilling the lead into its sides in a way to make it fume, and spit and rave like the tom-cat when the glad, free-band fox-hound pups catch him in the lane.

The men, outlying in the grass, chuckled deliriously at the fury of the Spanish fire. They howled opprobrium to encourage the Spaniards to fire more ill-used, incapable bullets. Whenever an insurgent was about to fire, he ordinarily prefixed the affair with a speech. "Do you want something to eat? Yes? All right." Bang! "Eat that." The more common expressions of the incredibly foul Spanish tongue were trifles light as air in this badinage, which was shrieked out from the grass during the spin of bullets, and the dull rattle of the shooting.

But at some time there came a series of sounds from the east that began in a few disconnected pruts and ended as if an amateur was trying to play the long roll upon a muffled drum. Those of the insurgents in the blockhouse attacking party, who had neighbours in the grass, turned and looked at them seriously. They knew what the new sound meant. It meant that the twenty men who had gone to the eastward were now engaged. A column of some kind was approaching from that direction, and they knew by the clatter that it was a solemn occasion.

In the first place, they were now on the wrong side of the road. They were obliged to cross it to rejoin the main body, provided of course that the main body succeeded itself in crossing it. To accomplish this, the party at the blockhouse would have to move to the eastward, until out of sight or good range of the maddened little fort. But judging from the heaviness of the firing, the party of twenty who protected the east were almost sure to be driven immediately back. Hence travel in that direction would become exceedingly hazardous. Hence a man looked seriously at his neighbour. It might easily be that in a moment they were to become an isolated force and woefully on the wrong side of the road.

Any retreat to the westward was absurd, since primarily they would have to widely circle the blockhouse, and more than that, they could hear, even now in that direction, Spanish bugle calling to Spanish bugle, far and near, until one would think that every man in Cuba was a trumpeter, and had come forth to parade his talent.

VI

The insurgent general stood in the middle of the road gnawing his lips. Occasionally, he stamped a foot and beat his hands passionately together. The carriers were streaming past him, patient, sweating fellows, bowed under their burdens, but they could not move fast enough for him when others of his men were engaged both to the east and to the west, and he, too, knew from the sound that those to the east were in a sore way. Moreover, he could hear that accursed bugling, bugling, bugling in the west.

He turned suddenly to the new lieutenant who stood behind him, pale and quiet. "Did you ever think a hundred men were so many?" he cried, incensed to the point of beating them. Then he said longingly: "Oh, for a half an hour! Or even twenty minutes!"

A practico racked violently up from the east. It is characteristic of these men that, although they take a certain roadster gait and hold it for ever, they cannot really run, sprint, race. "Captain Rodriguez is attacked by two hundred men, señor, and the cavalry is behind them. He wishes to know——"

The general was furious; he pointed. "Go! Tell Rodriguez to hold his place for twenty minutes, even if he leaves every man dead."

The practico shambled hastily off.

The last of the carriers were swarming across the road. The rifle-drumming in the east was swelling out and out, evidently coming slowly nearer. The general bit his nails. He wheeled suddenly upon the young lieutenant. "Go to Bas at the blockhouse. Tell him to hold the devil himself for ten minutes and then bring his men out of that place."

The long line of bearers was crawling like a dun worm toward the safety of the foot-hills. High bullets sang a faint song over the aide as he saluted. The bugles had in the west ceased, and that was more ominous than bugling. It meant that the Spanish troops were about to march, or perhaps that they had marched.

The young lieutenant ran along the road until he came to the bend which marked the range of sight from the blockhouse. He drew his machete, his stunning new machete, and hacked feverishly at the barbed wire fence which lined the north side of the road at that point. The first wire was obdurate, because it was too high for his stroke, but two more cut like candy, and he stepped over the remaining one, tearing his trousers in passing on the lively serpentine ends of the severed wires. Once out in the field and bullets seemed to know him and call for him and speak their wish to kill him. But he ran on, because it was his duty, and because he would be shamed before men if he did not do his duty, and because he was desolate out there all alone in the fields with death.

A man running in this manner from the rear was in immensely greater danger than those who lay snug and close. But he did not know it. He thought because he was five hundred-four hundred and fifty-four hundred yards away from the enemy and the others were only three hundred yards away that they were in far more peril. He ran to join them because of his opinion. He did not care to do it, but he thought that was what men of his kind would do in such a case. There was a standard and he must follow it, obey it, because it was a monarch, the Prince of Conduct.

A bewildered and alarmed face raised itself from the grass and a voice cried to him: "Drop, Manolo! Drop! Drop!" He recognised Bas and flung himself to the earth beside him.

"Why," he said panting, "what's the matter?"

"Matter?" said Bas. "You are one of the most desperate and careless officers I know. When I saw you coming I wouldn't have given a peseta for your life."

"Oh, no," said the young aide. Then he repeated his orders rapidly. But he was hugely delighted. He knew Bas well; Bas was a pupil of Maceo; Bas invariably led his men; he never was a mere spectator of their battle; he was known for it throughout the western end of the island. The new officer had early achieved a part of his ambition-to be called a brave man by established brave men.

"Well, if we get away from here quickly it will be better for us," said Bas, bitterly. "I've lost six men killed, and more wounded. Rodriguez can't hold his position there, and in a little time more than a thousand men will come from the other direction."

He hissed a low call, and later the young aide saw some of the men sneaking off with the wounded, lugging them on their backs as porters carry sacks. The fire from the blockhouse had become a-weary, and as the insurgent fire also slackened, Bas and the young lieutenant lay in the weeds listening to the approach of the eastern fight, which was sliding toward them like a door to shut them off.

Bas groaned. "I leave my dead. Look there." He swung his hand in a gesture and the lieutenant looking saw a corpse. He was not stricken as he expected; there was very little blood; it was a mere thing.

"Time to travel," said Bas suddenly. His imperative hissing brought his men near him; there were a few hurried questions and answers; then, characteristically, the men turned in the grass, lifted their rifles, and fired a last volley into the blockhouse, accompanying it with their shrill cries. Scrambling low to the ground, they were off in a winding line for safety. Breathing hard, the lieutenant stumbled his way forward. Behind him he could hear the men calling each to each: "Segue! Segue! Segue! Go on! Get out! Git!" Everybody understood that the peril of crossing the road was compounding from minute to minute.

When they reached the gap through which the expedition had passed, they fled out upon the road like scared wild-fowl tracking along a sea-beach. A cloud of blue figures far up this dignified shaded avenue, fired at once. The men already had begun to laugh as they shied one by one across the road. "Segue! Segue!" The hard part for the nerves had been the lack of information of the amount of danger. Now that they could see it, they accounted it all the more lightly for their previous anxiety.

Over in the other field, Bas and the young lieutenant found Rodriguez, his machete in one hand, his revolver in the other, smoky, dirty, sweating. He shrugged his shoulders when he saw them and pointed disconsolately to the brown thread of carriers moving toward the foot-hills. His own men were crouched in line just in front of him blazing like a prairie fire.

Now began the fight of a scant rear-guard to hold back the pressing Spaniards until the carriers could reach the top of the ridge, a mile away. This ridge by the way was more steep than any roof; it conformed, more, to the sides of a French war-ship. Trees grew vertically from it, however, and a man burdened only with his rifle usually pulled himself wheezingly up in a sort of ladder-climbing process, grabbing the slim trunks above him. How the loaded carriers were to conquer it in a hurry, no one knew. Rodriguez shrugged his shoulders as one who would say with philosophy, smiles, tears, courage: "Isn't this a mess!"

At an order, the men scattered back for four hundred yards with the rapidity and mystery of a handful of pebbles flung in the night. They left one behind who cried out, but it was now a game in which some were sure to be left behind to cry out.

The Spaniards deployed on the road and for twenty minutes remained there pouring into the field such a fire from their magazines as was hardly heard at Gettysburg. As a matter of truth the insurgents were at this time doing very little shooting, being chary of ammunition. But it is possible for the soldier to confuse himself with his own noise and undoubtedly the Spanish troops thought throughout their din that they were being fiercely engaged. Moreover, a firing-line —particularly at night or when opposed to a hidden foe-is nothing less than an emotional chord, a chord of a harp that sings because a puff of air arrives or when a bit of down touches it. This is always true of new troops or stupid troops and these troops were rather stupid troops. But, the way in which they mowed the verdure in the distance was a sight for a farmer.

Presently the insurgents slunk back to another position where they fired enough shots to stir again the Spaniards into an opinion that they were in a heavy fight. But such a misconception could only endure for a number of minutes. Presently it was plain that the Spaniards were about to advance and, moreover, word was brought to Rodriguez that a small band of guerillas were already making an attempt to worm around the right flank. Rodriguez cursed despairingly; he sent both Bas and the young lieutenant to that end of the line to hold the men to their work as long as possible.

In reality the men barely needed the presence of their officers. The kind of fighting left practically everything to the discretion of the individual and they arrived at concert of action mainly because of the equality of experience, in the wisdoms of bushwhacking.

The yells of the guerillas could plainly be heard and the insurgents answered in kind. The young lieutenant found desperate work on the right flank. The men were raving mad with it, babbling, tearful, almost frothing at the mouth. Two terrible bloody creatures passed him, creeping on all fours, and one in a whimper was calling upon God, his mother, and a saint. The guerillas, as effectually concealed as the insurgents, were driving their bullets low through the smoke at sight of a flame, a movement of the grass or sight of a patch of dirty brown coat. They were no column-o'-four soldiers; they were as slinky and snaky and quick as so many Indians. They were, moreover, native Cubans and because of their treachery to the one-star flag, they never by any chance received quarter if they fell into the hands of the insurgents. Nor, if the case was reversed, did they ever give quarter. It was life and life, death and death; there was no middle ground, no compromise. If a man's crowd was rapidly retreating and he was tumbled over by a slight hit, he should curse the sacred graves that the wound was not through the precise centre of his heart. The machete is a fine broad blade but it is not so nice as a drilled hole in the chest; no man wants his death-bed to be a shambles. The men fighting on the insurgents' right knew that if they fell they were lost.

On the extreme right, the young lieutenant found five men in a little saucer-like hollow. Two were dead, one was wounded and staring blankly at the sky and two were emptying hot rifles furiously. Some of the guerillas had snaked into positions only a hundred yards away.

The young man rolled in among the men in the saucer. He could hear the barking of the guerillas and the screams of the two insurgents. The rifles were popping and spitting in his face, it seemed, while the whole land was alive with a noise of rolling and drumming. Men could have gone drunken in all this flashing and flying and snarling and din, but at this time he was very deliberate. He knew that he was thrusting himself into a trap whose door, once closed, opened only when the black hand knocked and every part of him seemed to be in panic-stricken revolt. But something controlled him; something moved him inexorably in one direction; he perfectly understood but he was only sad, sad with a serene dignity, with the countenance of a mournful young prince. He was of a kind-that seemed to be it-and the men of his kind, on peak or plain, from the dark northern ice-fields to the hot wet jungles, through all wine and want, through all lies and unfamiliar truth, dark or light, the men of his kind were governed by their gods, and each man knew the law and yet could not give tongue to it, but it was the law and if the spirits of the men of his kind were all sitting in critical judgment upon him even then in the sky, he could not have bettered his conduct; he needs must obey the law and always with the law there is only one way. But from peak and plain, from dark northern ice-fields and hot wet jungles, through wine and want, through all lies and unfamiliar truth, dark or light, he heard breathed to him the approval and the benediction of his brethren.

He stooped and gently took a dead man's rifle and some cartridges. The battle was hurrying, hurrying, hurrying, but he was in no haste. His glance caught the staring eye of the wounded soldier, and he smiled at him quietly. The man-simple doomed peasant-was not of his kind, but the law on fidelity was clear.

He thrust a cartridge into the Remington and crept up beside the two unhurt men. Even as he did so, three or four bullets cut so close to him that all his flesh tingled. He fired carefully into the smoke. The guerillas were certainly not now more than fifty yards away.

He raised him coolly for his second shot, and almost instantly it was as if some giant had struck him in the chest with a beam. It whirled him in a great spasm back into the saucer. As he put his two hands to his breast, he could hear the guerillas screeching exultantly, every throat vomiting forth all the infamy of a language prolific in the phrasing of infamy.

One of the other men came rolling slowly down the slope, while his rifle followed him, and, striking another rifle, clanged out. Almost immediately the survivor howled and fled wildly. A whole volley missed him and then one or more shots caught him as a bird is caught on the wing.

The young lieutenant's body seemed galvanised from head to foot. He concluded that he was not hurt very badly, but when he tried to move he found that he could not lift his hands from his breast. He had turned to lead. He had had a plan of taking a photograph from his pocket and looking at it.

There was a stir in the grass at the edge of the saucer, and a man appeared there, looking where lay the four insurgents. His negro face was not an eminently ferocious one in its lines, but now it was lit with an illimitable blood-greed. He and the young lieutenant exchanged a singular glance; then he came stepping eagerly down. The young lieutenant closed his eyes, for he did not want to see the flash of the machete.

The Spanish colonel was in a rage, and yet immensely proud; immensely proud, and yet in a rage of disappointment. There had been a fight and the insurgents had retreated leaving their dead, but still a valuable expedition had broken through his lines and escaped to the mountains. As a matter of truth, he was not sure whether to be wholly delighted or wholly angry, for well he knew that the importance lay not so much in the truthful account of the action as it did in the heroic prose of the official report, and in the fight itself lay material for a purple splendid poem. The insurgents had run away; no one could deny it; it was plain even to whatever privates had fired with their eyes shut. This was worth a loud blow and splutter. However, when all was said and done, he could not help but reflect that if he had captured this expedition, he would have been a brigadier-general, if not more.

He was a short, heavy man with a beard, who walked in a manner common to all elderly Spanish officers, and to many young ones; that is to say, he walked as if his spine was a stick and a little longer than his body; as if he suffered from some disease of the backbone, which allowed him but scant use of his legs. He toddled along the road, gesticulating disdainfully and muttering: "Ca! Ca! Ca!"

He berated some soldiers for an immaterial thing, and as he approached the men stepped precipitately back as if he were a fire-engine. They were most of them young fellows, who displayed, when under orders, the manner of so many faithful dogs. At present, they were black, tongue-hanging, thirsty boys, bathed in the nervous weariness of the after-battle time.

Whatever he may truly have been in character, the colonel closely resembled a gluttonous and libidinous old pig, filled from head to foot with the pollution of a sinful life. "Ca!" he snarled, as he toddled. "Ca! Ca!" The soldiers saluted as they backed to the side of the road. The air was full of the odour of burnt rags. Over on the prairie guerillas and regulars were rummaging the grass. A few unimportant shots sounded from near the base of the hills.

A guerilla, glad with plunder, came to a Spanish captain. He held in his hand a photograph. "Mira, señor. I took this from the body of an officer whom I killed machete to machete."

The captain shot from the corner of his eye a cynical glance at the guerilla, a glance which commented upon the last part of the statement. "M-m-m," he said. He took the photograph and gazed with a slow faint smile, the smile of a man who knows bloodshed and homes and love, at the face of a girl. He turned the photograph presently, and on the back of it was written: "One lesson in English I will give you-this: I love you, Margharita." The photograph had been taken in Tampa.

The officer was silent for a half-minute, while his face still wore the slow faint smile. "Pobre-cetto," he murmured finally, with a philosophic sigh, which was brother to a shrug. Without deigning a word to the guerilla he thrust the photograph in his pocket and walked away.

High over the green earth, in the dizzy blue heights, some great birds were slowly circling with down-turned beaks.

Margharita was in the gardens. The blue electric rays shone through the plumes of the palm and shivered in feathery images on the walk. In the little foolish fish-pond some stalwart fish was apparently bullying the others, for often there sounded a frantic splashing.

Her mother came to her rapidly. "Margharita! Mister Smith is here! Come!"

"Oh, is he?" cried the girl. She followed her mother to the house. She swept into the little parlor with a grand air, the egotism of a savage. Smith had heard the whirl of her skirts in the hall, and his heart, as usual, thumped hard enough to make him gasp. Every time he called, he would sit waiting with the dull fear in his breast that her mother would enter and indifferently announce that she had gone up to heaven or off to New York, with one of his dream-rivals, and he would never see her again in this wide world. And he would conjure up tricks to then escape from the house without any one observing his face break up into furrows. It was part of his love to believe in the absolute treachery of his adored one. So whenever he heard the whirl of her skirts in the hall he felt that he had again leased happiness from a dark fate.

She was rosily beaming and all in white. "Why, Mister Smith," she exclaimed, as if he was the last man in the world she expected to see.

"Good-evenin'," he said, shaking hands nervously. He was always awkward and unlike himself, at the beginning of one of these calls. It took him some time to get into form.

She posed her figure in operatic style on a chair before him, and immediately galloped off a mile of questions, information of herself, gossip and general outcries which left him no obligation, but to look beamingly intelligent and from time to time say: "Yes?" His personal joy, however, was to stare at her beauty.

When she stopped and wandered as if uncertain which way to talk, there was a minute of silence, which each of them had been educated to feel was very incorrect; very incorrect indeed. Polite people always babbled at each other like two brooks.

He knew that the responsibility was upon him, and, although his mind was mainly upon the form of the proposal of marriage which he intended to make later, it was necessary that he should maintain his reputation as a well-bred man by saying something at once. It flashed upon him to ask: "Won't you please play?" But the time for the piano ruse was not yet; it was too early. So he said the first thing that came into his head: "Too bad about young Manolo Prat being killed over there in Cuba, wasn't it?"

"Wasn't it a pity?" she answered.

"They say his mother is heart-broken," he continued. "They're afraid she's goin' to die."

"And wasn't it queer that we didn't hear about it for almost two months?"

"Well, it's no use tryin' to git quick news from there."

Presently they advanced to matters more personal, and she used upon him a series of star-like glances which rumpled him at once to squalid slavery. He gloated upon her, afraid, afraid, yet more avaricious than a thousand misers. She fully comprehended; she laughed and taunted him with her eyes. She impressed upon him that she was like a will-o'-the-wisp, beautiful beyond compare but impossible, almost impossible, at least very difficult; then again, suddenly, impossible-impossible-impossible. He was glum; he would never dare propose to this radiance; it was like asking to be pope.

A moment later, there chimed into the room something that he knew to be a more tender note. The girl became dreamy as she looked at him; her voice lowered to a delicious intimacy of tone. He leaned forward; he was about to outpour his bully-ragged soul in fine words, when-presto-she was the most casual person he had ever laid eyes upon, and was asking him about the route of the proposed trolley line.

But nothing short of a fire could stop him now. He grabbed her hand. "Margharita," he murmured gutturally, "I want you to marry me."

She glared at him in the most perfect lie of astonishment. "What do you say?"

He arose, and she thereupon arose also and fled back a step. He could only stammer out her name. And thus they stood, defying the principles of the dramatic art.

"I love you," he said at last.

"How-how do I know you really-truly love me?" she said, raising her eyes timorously to his face and this timorous glance, this one timorous glance, made him the superior person in an instant. He went forward as confident as a grenadier, and, taking both her hands, kissed her.

That night she took a stained photograph from her dressing-table and holding it over the candle burned it to nothing, her red lips meanwhile parted with the intentness of her occupation. On the back of the photograph was written: "One lesson in English I will give you-this: I love you."

For the word is clear only to the kind who on peak or plain, from dark northern ice-fields to the hot wet jungles, through all wine and want, through lies and unfamiliar truth, dark or light, are governed by the unknown gods, and though each man knows the law, no man may give tongue to it.

God Rest Ye, Merry Gentlemen

Little Nell, sometimes called the Blessed Damosel, was a war correspondent for the *New York Eclipse*, and at sea on the despatch boats he wore pajamas, and on shore he wore whatever fate allowed him, which clothing was in the main unsuitable to the climate. He had been cruising in the Caribbean on a small tug, awash always, habitable never, wildly looking for Cervera's fleet; although what he was going to do with four armoured cruisers and two destroyers in the event of his really finding them had not been explained by the managing editor. The cable instructions read: —"Take tug; go find Cervera's fleet." If his unfortunate nine-knot craft should happen to find these great twenty-knot ships, with their two spiteful and faster attendants, Little Nell had wondered how he was going to lose them again. He had marvelled, both publicly and in secret, on the uncompromising asininity of managing editors at odd moments, but he had wasted little time. The *Jefferson G. Johnson* was already coaled, so he passed the word to his skipper, bought some tinned meats, cigars, and beer, and soon the *Johnson* sailed on her mission, tooting her whistle in graceful farewell to some friends of hers in the bay.

So the *Johnson* crawled giddily to one wave-height after another, and fell, aslant, into one valley after another for a longer period than was good for the hearts of the men, because the *Johnson* was merely a harbour-tug, with no architectural intention of parading the high-seas, and the crew had never seen the decks all white water like a mere sunken reef. As for the cook, he blasphemed hopelessly hour in and hour out, meanwhile pursuing the equipment of his trade frantically from side to side of the galley. Little Nell dealt with a great deal of grumbling, but he knew it was not the real evil grumbling. It was merely the unhappy words of men who wished expression of comradeship for their wet, forlorn, half-starved lives, to which, they explained, they were not accustomed, and for which, they explained, they were not properly paid. Little Nell condoled and condoled without difficulty. He laid words of gentle sympathy before them, and smothered his own misery behind the face of a reporter of the *New York Eclipse*. But they tossed themselves in their cockleshell even as far as Martinique; they knew many races and many flags, but they did not find Cervera's fleet. If they had found that elusive squadron this timid story would never have been written; there would probably have been a lyric. The *Johnson* limped one morning into the Mole St. Nicholas, and there Little Nell received this despatch: —"Can't understand your inaction. What are you doing with the boat? Report immediately. Fleet transports already left Tampa. Expected destination near Santiago. Proceed there immediately. Place yourself under orders. —Rogers, *Eclipse*."

One day, steaming along the high, luminous blue coast of Santiago province, they fetched into view the fleets, a knot of masts and funnels, looking incredibly inshore, as if they were glued to the mountains. Then mast left mast, and funnel left funnel, slowly, slowly, and the shore remained still, but the fleets seemed to move out toward the eager *Johnson*. At the speed of nine knots an hour the scene separated into its parts. On an easily rolling sea, under a crystal sky, black-hulled transports-erstwhile packets-lay waiting, while grey cruisers and gunboats lay near shore, shelling the beach and some woods. From their grey sides came thin red flashes, belches of white smoke, and then over the waters sounded boom-boom-boom-boom. The crew of the *Jefferson G. Johnson* forgave Little Nell all the suffering of a previous fortnight.

To the westward, about the mouth of Santiago harbour, sat a row of castellated grey battleships, their eyes turned another way, waiting.

The *Johnson* swung past a transport whose decks and rigging were aswarm with black figures, as if a tribe of bees had alighted upon a log. She swung past a cruiser indignant at being left out of the game, her deck thick with white-clothed tars watching the play of their luckier brethren. The cold blue, lifting seas tilted the big ships easily, slowly, and heaved the little ones in the usual sinful way, as if very little babes had surreptitiously mounted sixteen-hand trotting hunters. The *Johnson* leered and tumbled her way through a community of ships. The bombardment ceased, and some of the troopships edged in near the land. Soon boats black with men and towed by launches were almost lost to view in the scintillant mystery of light which appeared where the sea met the land. A disembarkation had begun. The *Johnson* sped on at her nine knots, and Little Nell chafed exceedingly, gloating upon the shore through his glasses, anon glancing irritably over the side to note the efforts of the excited tug. Then at last they were in a sort of a cove, with troopships, newspaper boats, and cruisers on all sides of them, and over the water came a great hum of human voices, punctuated frequently by the clang of engine-room gongs as the steamers manoeuvred to avoid jostling.

In reality it was the great moment-the moment for which men, ships, islands, and continents had been waiting for months; but somehow it did not look it. It was very calm; a certain strip of high, green, rocky shore was being rapidly populated from boat after boat; that was all. Like many preconceived moments, it refused to be supreme.

But nothing lessened Little Nell's frenzy. He knew that the army was landing-he could see it; and little did he care if the great moment did not look its part-it was his virtue as a correspondent to recognise the great moment in any disguise. The *Johnson* lowered a boat for him, and he dropped into it swiftly, forgetting everything. However, the mate, a bearded philanthropist, flung after him a mackintosh and a bottle of whisky. Little Nell's face was turned toward those other boats filled with men, all eyes upon the placid, gentle, noiseless shore. Little Nell saw many soldiers seated stiffly beside upright rifle barrels, their blue breasts crossed with white shelter tent and blanket-rolls. Launches screeched; jack-tars pushed or pulled with their boathooks; a beach was alive with working soldiers, some of them stark naked. Little Nell's boat touched the shore amid a babble of tongues, dominated at that time by a single stern voice, which was repeating, "Fall in, B Company!"

He took his mackintosh and his bottle of whisky and invaded Cuba. It was a trifle bewildering. Companies of those same men in blue and brown were being rapidly formed and marched off across a little open space-near a pool-near some palm trees-near a house-into the hills. At one side, a mulatto in dirty linen and an old straw hat was hospitably using a machete to cut open some green cocoanuts for a group of idle invaders. At the other side, up a bank, a block-house was burning furiously; while near it some railway sheds were smouldering, with a little Roger's engine standing amid the ruins, grey, almost white, with ashes until it resembled a ghost. Little Nell dodged the encrimsoned blockhouse, and proceeded where he saw a little village street lined with flimsy wooden cottages. Some ragged Cuban cavalrymen were tranquilly tending their horses in a shed which had not yet grown cold of the Spanish occupation. Three American soldiers were trying to explain to a Cuban that they wished to buy drinks. A native rode by, clubbing his pony, as always. The sky was blue; the sea talked with a gravelly accent at the feet of some rocks; upon its bosom the ships sat quiet as gulls. There was no mention, directly, of invasion-invasion for war-save in the roar of the flames at the blockhouse; but none even heeded this conflagration, excepting to note that it threw out a great heat. It was warm, very warm. It was really hard for Little Nell to keep from thinking of his own affairs: his debts, other misfortunes, loves, prospects of happiness. Nobody was in a flurry; the Cubans were not tearfully grateful; the American troops were visibly glad of being released from those ill transports, and the men often asked, with interest, "Where's the Spaniards?" And yet it must have been a great moment! It was a *great* moment!

It seemed made to prove that the emphatic time of history is not the emphatic time of the common man, who throughout the change of nations feels an itch on his shin, a pain in his head, hunger, thirst, a lack of sleep; the influence of his memory of past firesides, glasses of beer, girls, theatres, ideals, religions, parents, faces, hurts, joy.

Little Nell was hailed from a comfortable veranda, and, looking up, saw Walkley of the *Eclipse*, stretched in a yellow and green hammock, smoking his pipe with an air of having always lived in that house, in that village. "Oh, dear little Nell, how glad I am to see your angel face again! There! don't try to hide it; I can see it. Did you bring a corkscrew too? You're superseded as master of the slaves. Did you know it? And by Rogers, too! Rogers is a Sadducee, a cadaver and a pelican, appointed to the post of chief correspondent, no doubt, because of his rare gift of incapacity. Never mind."

"Where is he now?" asked Little Nell, taking seat on the steps.

"He is down interfering with the landing of the troops," answered Walkley, swinging a leg. "I hope you have the *Johnson* well stocked with food as well as with cigars, cigarettes and tobaccos, ales, wines and liquors. We shall need them. There is already famine in the house of Walkley. I have discovered that the system of transportation for our gallant soldiery does not strike in me the admiration which I have often felt when viewing the management of an ordinary bun-shop. A hunger, stifling, jammed together amid odours, and everybody irritable-ye gods, how irritable! And so I——Look! look!"

The *Jefferson G. Johnson*, well known to them at an incredible distance, could be seen striding the broad sea, the smoke belching from her funnel, headed for Jamaica. "The Army Lands in Cuba!" shrieked Walkley. "Shafter's Army Lands near Santiago! Special type! Half the front page! Oh, the Sadducee! The cadaver! The pelican!"

Little Nell was dumb with astonishment and fear. Walkley, however, was at least not dumb. "That's the pelican! That's Mr. Rogers making his first impression upon the situation. He has engraved himself upon us. We are tattooed with him. There will be a fight to-morrow, sure, and we will cover it even as you found Cervera's fleet. No food, no horses, no money. I am transport lame; you are sea-weak. We will never see our salaries again. Whereby Rogers is a fool."

"Anybody else here?" asked Little Nell wearily.

"Only young Point." Point was an artist on the *Eclipse*. "But he has nothing. Pity there wasn't an almshouse in this God-forsaken country. Here comes Point now." A sad-faced man came along carrying much luggage. "Hello, Point! lithographer *and* genius, have you food? Food. Well, then, you had better return yourself to Tampa by wire. You are no good here. Only one more little mouth to feed."

Point seated himself near Little Nell. "I haven't had anything to eat since daybreak," he said gloomily, "and I don't care much, for I am simply dog-tired."

"Don' tell *me* you are dog-tired, my talented friend," cried Walkley from his hammock. "Think of me. And now what's to be done?"

They stared for a time disconsolately at where, over the rim of the sea, trailed black smoke from the *Johnson*. From the landing-place below and to the right came the howls of a man who was superintending the disembarkation of some mules. The burning blockhouse still rendered its hollow roar. Suddenly the men-crowded landing set up its cheer, and the steamers all whistled long and raucously. Tiny black figures were raising an American flag over a blockhouse on the top of a great hill.

"That's mighty fine Sunday stuff," said Little Nell. "Well, I'll go and get the order in which the regiments landed, and who was first ashore, and all that. Then I'll go and try to find General Lawton's headquarters. His division has got the advance, I think."

"And, lo! I will write a burning description of the raising of the flag," said Walkley. "While the brilliant Point buskies for food-and makes damn sure he gets it," he added fiercely.

Little Nell thereupon wandered over the face of the earth, threading out the story of the landing of the regiments. He only found about fifty men who had been the first American soldier to set foot on Cuba, and of these he took the most probable. The army was going forward in detail, as soon as the pieces were landed. There was a house something like a crude country tavern-the soldiers in it were looking over their rifles and talking. There was a well of water quite hot-more palm trees-an inscrutable background.

When he arrived again at Walkley's mansion he found the verandah crowded with correspondents in khaki, duck, dungaree and flannel. They wore riding-breeches, but that was mainly forethought. They could see now that fate intended them to walk. Some were writing copy, while Walkley discoursed from his hammock. Rhodes-doomed to be shot in action some days later-was trying to borrow a canteen from men who had one, and from men who had none. Young Point, wan, utterly worn out, was asleep on the floor. Walkley pointed to him. "That is how he appears after his foraging journey, during which he ran all Cuba through a sieve. Oh, yes; a can of corn and a half-bottle of lime juice."

"Say, does anybody know, the name of the commander of the 26th Infantry?"

"Who commands the first brigade of Kent's Division?"

"What was the name of the chap that raised the flag?"

"What time is it?"

And a woeful man was wandering here and there with a cold pipe, saying plaintively, "Who's got a match? Anybody here got a match?"

Little Nell's left boot hurt him at the heel, and so he removed it, taking great care and whistling through his teeth. The heated dust was upon them all, making everybody feel that bathing was unknown and shattering their tempers. Young Point developed a snore which brought grim sarcasm from all quarters. Always below, hummed the traffic of the landing-place.

When night came Little Nell thought best not to go to bed until late, because he recognised the mackintosh as but a feeble comfort. The evening was a glory. A breeze came from the sea, fanning spurts of flame out of the ashes and charred remains of the sheds, while overhead lay a splendid summer-night sky, aflash with great tranquil stars. In the streets of the village were two or three fires, frequently and suddenly reddening with their glare the figures of low-voiced men who moved here and there. The lights of the transports blinked on the murmuring plain in front of the village; and far to the westward Little Nell could sometimes note a subtle indication of a playing search-light, which alone marked the presence of the invisible battleships, half-mooned about the entrance of Santiago Harbour, waiting-waiting-waiting.

When Little Nell returned to the veranda he stumbled along a man-strewn place, until he came to the spot where he left his mackintosh; but he found it gone. His curses mingled then with those of the men upon whose bodies he had trodden. Two English correspondents, lying awake to smoke a last pipe, reared and looked at him lazily. "What's wrong, old chap?" murmured one. "Eh? Lost it, eh? Well, look here; come here and take a bit of my blanket. It's a jolly big one. Oh, no trouble at all, man. There you are. Got enough? Comfy? Good-night."

A sleepy voice arose in the darkness. "If this hammock breaks, I shall hit at least ten of those Indians down there. Never mind. This is war."

The men slept. Once the sound of three or four shots rang across the windy night, and one head uprose swiftly from the verandah, two eyes looked dazedly at nothing, and the head as swiftly sank. Again a sleepy voice was heard. "Usual thing! Nervous sentries!" The men slept. Before dawn a pulseless, penetrating chill came into the air, and the correspondents awakened, shivering, into a blue world. Some of the fires still smouldered. Walkley and Little Nell kicked vigorously into Point's framework. "Come on, brilliance! Wake up, talent! Don't be sodgering. It's too cold to sleep, but it's not too cold to hustle." Point sat up dolefully. Upon his face was a childish expression. "Where are we going to get breakfast?" he asked, sulking.

"There's no breakfast for you, you hound! Get up and hustle." Accordingly they hustled. With exceeding difficulty they learned that nothing emotional had happened during the night, save the killing of two Cubans who were so secure in ignorance that they could not understand the challenge of two American sentries. Then Walkley ran a gamut of commanding officers, and Little Nell pumped privates for their impressions of Cuba. When his indignation at the absence of breakfast allowed him, Point made sketches. At the full break of day the *Adolphus*, and *Eclipse* despatch boat, sent a boat ashore with Tailor and Shackles in it, and Walkley departed tearfully for Jamaica, soon after he had bestowed upon his friends much tinned goods and blankets.

"Well, we've got our stuff off," said Little Nell. "Now Point and I must breakfast."

Shackles, for some reason, carried a great hunting-knife, and with it Little Nell opened a tin of beans.

"Fall to," he said amiably to Point.

There were some hard biscuits. Afterwards they-the four of them-marched off on the route of the troops. They were well loaded with luggage, particularly young Point, who had somehow made a great gathering of unnecessary things. Hills covered with verdure soon enclosed them. They heard that the army had advanced some nine miles with no fighting. Evidences of the rapid advance were here and there-coats, gauntlets, blanket rolls on the ground. Mule-trains came herding back along the narrow trail to the sound of a little tinkling bell. Cubans were appropriating the coats and blanket-rolls.

The four correspondents hurried onward. The surety of impending battle weighed upon them always, but there was a score of minor things more intimate. Little Nell's left heel had chafed until it must have been quite raw, and every moment he wished to take seat by the roadside and console himself from pain. Shackles and Point disliked each other extremely, and often they foolishly quarrelled over something, or nothing. The blanket-rolls and packages for the hand oppressed everybody. It was like being burned out of a boarding-house, and having to carry one's trunk eight miles to the nearest neighbour. Moreover, Point, since he had stupidly overloaded, with great wisdom placed various cameras and other trifles in the hands of his three less-burdened and more sensible friends. This made them fume and gnash, but in complete silence, since he was hideously youthful and innocent and unaware. They all wished to rebel, but none of them saw their way clear, because-they did not understand. But somehow it seemed a barbarous project-no one wanted to say anything-cursed him privately for a little ass, but-said nothing. For instance, Little Nell wished to remark, "Point, you are not a thoroughbred in a half of a way. You are an inconsiderate, thoughtless little swine." But, in truth, he said, "Point, when you started out you looked like a Christmas-tree. If we keep on robbing you of your bundles there soon won't be anything left for the children." Point asked dubiously, "What do you mean?" Little Nell merely laughed with deceptive good-nature.

They were always very thirsty. There was always a howl for the half-bottle of lime juice. Five or six drops from it were simply heavenly in the warm water from the canteens. Point seemed to try to keep the lime juice in his possession, in order that he might get more benefit of it. Before the war was ended the others found themselves declaring vehemently that they loathed Point, and yet when men asked them the reason they grew quite inarticulate. The reasons seemed then so small, so childish, as the reasons of a lot of women. And yet at the time his offences loomed enormous.

The surety of impending battle still weighed upon them. Then it came that Shackles turned seriously ill. Suddenly he dropped his own and much of Point's traps upon the trail, wriggled out of his blanket-roll, flung it away, and took seat heavily at the roadside. They saw with surprise that his face was pale as death, and yet streaming with sweat.

"Boys," he said in his ordinary voice, "I'm clean played out. I can't go another step. You fellows go on, and leave me to come as soon as I am able."

"Oh, no, that wouldn't do at all," said Little Nell and Tailor together.

Point moved over to a soft place, and dropped amid whatever traps he was himself carrying.

"Don't know whether it's ancestral or merely from the-sun-but I've got a stroke," said Shackles, and gently slumped over to a prostrate position before either Little Nell or Tailor could reach him.

Thereafter Shackles was parental; it was Little Nell and Tailor who were really suffering from a stroke, either ancestral or from the sun.

"Put my blanket-roll under my head, Nell, me son," he said gently. "There now! That is very nice. It is delicious. Why, I'm all right, only-only tired." He closed his eyes, and something like an easy slumber came over him. Once he opened his eyes. "Don't trouble about me," he remarked.

But the two fussed about him, nervous, worried, discussing this plan and that plan. It was Point who first made a business-like statement. Seated carelessly and indifferently upon his soft place, he finally blurted out:

"Say! Look here! Some of us have got to go on. We can't all stay here. Some of us have got to go on."

It was quite true; the *Eclipse* could take no account of strokes. In the end Point and Tailor went on, leaving Little Nell to bring on Shackles as soon as possible. The latter two spent many hours in the grass by the roadside. They made numerous abrupt acquaintances with passing staff officers, privates, muleteers, many stopping to inquire the wherefore of the death-faced figure on the ground. Favours were done often and often, by peer and peasant-small things, of no consequence, and yet warming.

It was dark when Shackles and Little Nell had come slowly to where they could hear the murmur of the army's bivouac.

"Shack," gasped Little Nell to the man leaning forlornly upon him, "I guess we'd better bunk down here where we stand."

"All right, old boy. Anything you say," replied Shackles, in the bass and hollow voice which arrives with such condition.

They crawled into some bushes, and distributed their belongings upon the ground. Little Nell spread out the blankets, and generally played housemaid. Then they lay down, supperless, being too weary to eat. The men slept.

At dawn Little Nell awakened and looked wildly for Shackles, whose empty blanket was pressed flat like a wet newspaper on the ground. But at nearly the same moment Shackles appeared, elate.

"Come on," he cried; "I've rustled an invitation for breakfast."

Little Nell came on with celerity.

"Where? Who?" he said.

"Oh! some officers," replied Shackles airily. If he had been ill the previous day, he showed it now only in some curious kind of deference he paid to Little Nell.

Shackles conducted his comrade, and soon they arrived at where a captain and his one subaltern arose courteously from where they were squatting near a fire of little sticks. They wore the wide white trouser-stripes of infantry officers, and upon the shoulders of their blue campaign shirts were the little marks of their rank; but otherwise there was little beyond their manners to render them different from the men who were busy with breakfast near them. The captain was old, grizzled—a common type of captain in the tiny American army-overjoyed at the active service, confident of his business, and yet breathing out in some way a note of pathos. The war was come too late. Age was grappling him, and honours were only for his widow and his children-merely a better life insurance policy. He had spent his life policing Indians with much labour, cold and heat, but with no glory for him nor his fellows. All he now could do was to die at the head of his men. If he had youthfully dreamed of a general's stars, they were now impossible to him, and he knew it. He was too old to leap so far; his sole honour was a new invitation to face death. And yet, with his ambitions lying half-strangled, he was going to take his men into any sort of holocaust, because his traditions were of gentlemen and soldiers, and because-he loved it for itself-the thing itself-the whirl, the unknown. If he had been degraded at that moment to be a pot-wrestler, no power could have starved him from going through the campaign as a spectator. Why, the army! It was in each drop of his blood.

The lieutenant was very young. Perhaps he had been hurried out of West Point at the last moment, upon a shortage of officers appearing. To him, all was opportunity. He was, in fact, in great luck. Instead of going off in 1898 to grill for an indefinite period on some God-forgotten heap of red-hot sand in New Mexico, he was here in Cuba, on real business, with his regiment. When the big engagement came he was sure to emerge from it either horizontally or at the head of a company, and what more could a boy ask? He was a very modest lad, and talked nothing of his frame of mind, but an expression of blissful contentment was ever upon his face. He really accounted himself the most fortunate boy of his time; and he felt almost certain that he would do well. It was necessary to do well. He would do well.

And yet in many ways these two were alike; the grizzled captain with his gently mournful countenance —"Too late"—and the elate young second lieutenant, his commission hardly dry. Here again it was the influence of the army. After all they were both children of the army.

It is possible to spring into the future here and chronicle what happened later. The captain, after thirty-five years of waiting for his chance, took his Mauser bullet through the brain at the foot of San Juan Hill in the very beginning of the battle, and the boy arrived on the crest panting, sweating, but unscratched, and not sure whether he commanded one company or a whole battalion. Thus fate dealt to the hosts of Shackles and Little Nell.

The breakfast was of canned tomatoes stewed with hard bread, more hard bread, and coffee. It was very good fare, almost royal. Shackles and Little Nell were absurdly grateful as they felt the hot bitter coffee tingle in them. But they departed joyfully before the sun was fairly up, and passed into Siboney. They never saw the captain again.

The beach at Siboney was furious with traffic, even as had been the beach at Daqueri. Launches shouted, jack-tars prodded with their boathooks, and load of men followed load of men. Straight, parade-like, on the shore stood a trumpeter playing familiar calls to the troop-horses who swam towards him eagerly through the salt seas. Crowding closely into the cove were transports of all sizes and ages. To the left and to the right of the little landing-beach green hills shot upward like the wings in a theatre. They were scarred here and there with blockhouses and rifle-pits. Up one hill a regiment was crawling, seemingly inch by inch. Shackles and Little Nell walked among palms and scrubby bushes, near pools, over spaces of sand holding little monuments of biscuit-boxes, ammunition-boxes, and supplies of all kinds. Some regiment was just collecting itself from the ships, and the men made great patches of blue on the brown sand.

Shackles asked a question of a man accidentally: "Where's that regiment going to?" He pointed to the force that was crawling up the hill. The man grinned, and said, "They're going to look for a fight!"

"Looking for a fight!" said Shackles and Little Nell together. They stared into each other's eyes. Then they set off for the foot of the hill. The hill was long and toilsome. Below them spread wider and wider a vista of ships quiet on a grey sea; a busy, black disembarkation-place; tall, still, green hills; a village of well separated cottages; palms; a bit of road; soldiers marching. They passed vacant Spanish trenches; little twelve-foot blockhouses. Soon they were on a fine upland near the sea. The path, under ordinary conditions, must have been a beautiful wooded way. It wound in the shade of thickets of fine trees, then through rank growths of bushes with revealed and fantastic roots, then through a grassy space which had all the beauty of a neglected orchard. But always from under their feet scuttled noisy land-crabs, demons to the nerves, which in some way possessed a semblance of moon-like faces upon their blue or red bodies, and these faces were turned with expressions of deepest horror upon Shackles and Little Nell as they sped to overtake the pugnacious regiment. The route was paved with coats, hats, tent and blanket rolls, ration-tins, haversacks-everything but ammunition belts, rifles and canteens.

They heard a dull noise of voices in front of them-men talking too loud for the etiquette of the forest-and presently they came upon two or three soldiers lying by the roadside, flame-faced, utterly spent from the hurried march in the heat. One man came limping back along the path. He looked to them anxiously for sympathy and comprehension. "Hurt m' knee. I swear I couldn't keep up with th' boys. I had to leave 'm. Wasn't that tough luck?" His collar rolled away from a red, muscular neck, and his bare forearms were better than stanchions. Yet he was almost babyishly tearful in his attempt to make the two correspondents feel that he had not turned back because he was afraid. They gave him scant courtesy, tinctured with one drop of sympathetic yet cynical understanding. Soon they overtook the hospital squad; men addressing chaste language to some pack-mules; a talkative sergeant; two amiable, cool-eyed young surgeons. Soon they were amid the rear troops of the dismounted volunteer cavalry regiment which was moving to attack. The men strode easily along, arguing one to another on ulterior matters. If they were going into battle, they either did not know it or they concealed it well. They were more like men going into a bar at one o'clock in the morning. Their laughter rang through the Cuban woods. And in the meantime, soft, mellow, sweet, sang the voice of the Cuban wood-dove, the Spanish guerilla calling to his mate-forest music; on the flanks, deep back on both flanks, the adorable wood-dove, singing only of love. Some of the advancing Americans said it was beautiful. It *was* beautiful. The Spanish guerilla calling to his mate. What could be more beautiful?

Shackles and Little Nell rushed precariously through waist-high bushes until they reached the centre of the single-filed regiment. The firing then broke out in front. All the woods set up a hot sputtering; the bullets sped along the path and across it from both sides. The thickets presented nothing but dense masses of light green foliage, out of which these swift steel things were born supernaturally.

It was a volunteer regiment going into its first action, against an enemy of unknown force, in a country where the vegetation was thicker than fur on a cat. There might have been a dreadful mess; but in military matters the only way to deal with a situation of this kind is to take it frankly by the throat and squeeze it to death. Shackles and Little Nell felt the thrill of the orders. "Come ahead, men! Keep right ahead, men! Come on!" The volunteer cavalry regiment, with all the willingness in the world, went ahead into the angle of V-shaped Spanish formation.

It seemed that every leaf had turned into a soda-bottle and was popping its cork. Some of the explosions seemed to be against the men's very faces, others against the backs of their necks. "Now, men! Keep goin' ahead. Keep on goin'." The forward troops were already engaged. They, at least, had something at which to shoot. "Now, captain, if you're ready." "Stop that swearing there." "Got a match?" "Steady, now, men."

A gate appeared in a barbed-wire fence. Within were billowy fields of long grass, dotted with palms and luxuriant mango trees. It was Elysian —a place for lovers, fair as Eden in its radiance of sun, under its blue sky. One might have expected to see white-robed figures walking slowly in the shadows. A dead man, with a bloody face, lay twisted in a curious contortion at the waist. Someone was shot in the leg, his pins knocked cleanly from under him.

"Keep goin', men." The air roared, and the ground fled reelingly under their feet. Light, shadow, trees, grass. Bullets spat from every side. Once they were in a thicket, and the men, blanched and bewildered, turned one way, and then another, not knowing which way to turn. "Keep goin', men." Soon they were in the sunlight again. They could see the long scant line, which was being drained man by man-one might say drop by drop. The musketry rolled forth in great full measure from the magazine carbines. "Keep goin', men." "Christ, I'm shot!" "They're flankin' us, sir." "We're bein' fired into by our own crowd, sir." "Keep goin', men." A low ridge before them was a bottling establishment blowing up in detail. From the right-it seemed at that time to be the far right-they could hear steady, crashing volleys-the United States regulars in action.

Then suddenly-to use a phrase of the street-the whole bottom of the thing fell out. It was suddenly and mysteriously ended. The Spaniards had run away, and some of the regulars were chasing them. It was a victory.

When the wounded men dropped in the tall grass they quite disappeared, as if they had sunk in water. Little Nell and Shackles were walking along through the fields, disputing.

"Well, damn it, man!" cried Shackles, "we *must* get a list of the killed and wounded."

"That is not nearly so important," quoth little Nell, academically, "as to get the first account to New York of the first action of the army in Cuba."

They came upon Tailor, lying with a bared torso and a small red hole through his left lung. He was calm, but evidently out of temper. "Good God, Tailor!" they cried, dropping to their knees like two pagans; "are you hurt, old boy?"

"Hurt?" he said gently. "No, 'tis not so deep as a well nor so wide as a church-door, but 'tis enough, d'you see? You understand, do you? Idiots!"

Then he became very official. "Shackles, feel and see what's under my leg. It's a small stone, or a burr, or something. Don't be clumsy now! Be careful! Be careful!" Then he said, angrily, "Oh, you didn't find it at all. Damn it!"

In reality there was nothing there, and so Shackles could not have removed it. "Sorry, old boy," he said, meekly.

"Well, you may observe that I can't stay here more than a year," said Tailor, with some oratory, "and the hospital people have their own work in hand. It behoves you, Nell, to fly to Siboney, arrest a despatch boat, get a cot and some other things, and some minions to carry me. If I get once down to the base I'm all right, but if I stay here I'm dead. Meantime Shackles can stay here and try to look as if he liked it."

There was no disobeying the man. Lying there with a little red hole in his left lung, he dominated them through his helplessness, and through their fear that if they angered him he would move and-bleed.

"Well?" said Little Nell.

"Yes," said Shackles, nodding.

Little Nell departed.

"That blanket you lent me," Tailor called after him, "is back there somewhere with Point."

Little Nell noted that many of the men who were wandering among the wounded seemed so spent with the toil and excitement of their first action that they could hardly drag one leg after the other. He found himself suddenly in the same condition, His face, his neck, even his mouth, felt dry as sun-baked bricks, and his legs were foreign to him. But he swung desperately into his five-mile task. On the way he passed many things: bleeding men carried by comrades; others making their way grimly, with encrimsoned arms; then the little settlement of the hospital squad; men on the ground everywhere, many in the path; one young captain dying, with great gasps, his body pale blue, and glistening, like the inside of a rabbit's skin. But the voice of the Cuban wood-dove, soft, mellow, sweet, singing only of love, was no longer heard from the wealth of foliage.

Presently the hurrying correspondent met another regiment coming to assist —a line of a thousand men in single file through the jungle. "Well, how is it going, old man?" "How is it coming on?" "Are we doin' 'em?" Then, after an interval, came other regiments, moving out. He had to take to the bush to let these long lines pass him, and he was delayed, and had to flounder amid brambles. But at last, like a successful pilgrim, he arrived at the brow of the great hill overlooking Siboney. His practised eye scanned the fine broad brow of the sea with its clustering ships, but he saw thereon no *Eclipse* despatch boats. He zigzagged heavily down the hill, and arrived finally amid the dust and outcries of the base. He seemed to ask a thousand men if they had seen an *Eclipse* boat on the water, or an *Eclipse* correspondent on the shore. They all answered, "No."

He was like a poverty-stricken and unknown suppliant at a foreign Court. Even his plea got only ill-hearings. He had expected the news of the serious wounding of Tailor to appal the other correspondents, but they took it quite calmly. It was as if their sense of an impending great battle between two large armies had quite got them out of focus for these minor tragedies. Tailor was hurt-yes? They looked at Little Nell, dazed. How curious that Tailor should be almost the first-how *very* curious-yes. But, as far as arousing them to any enthusiasm of active pity, it seemed impossible. He was lying up there in the grass, was he? Too bad, too bad, too bad!

Little Nell went alone and lay down in the sand with his back against a rock. Tailor was prostrate up there in the grass. Never mind. Nothing was to be done. The whole situation was too colossal. Then into his zone came Walkley the invincible.

"Walkley!" yelled Little Nell. Walkley came quickly, and Little Nell lay weakly against his rock and talked. In thirty seconds Walkley understood everything, had hurled a drink of whisky into Little Nell, had admonished him to lie quiet, and had gone to organise and manipulate. When he returned he was a trifle dubious and backward. Behind him was a singular squad of volunteers from the *Adolphus*, carrying among them a wire-woven bed.

"Look here, Nell!" said Walkley, in bashful accents; "I've collected a battalion here which is willing to go bring Tailor; but-they say-you-can't you show them where he is?"

"Yes," said Little Nell, arising.

When the party arrived at Siboney, and deposited Tailor in the best place, Walkley had found a house and stocked it with canned soups. Therein Shackles and Little Nell revelled for a time, and then rolled on the floor in their blankets. Little Nell tossed a great deal. "Oh, I'm so tired. Good God, I'm tired. I'm —tired."

In the morning a voice aroused them. It was a swollen, important, circus voice saying, "Where is Mr. Nell? I wish to see him immediately."

"Here I am, Rogers," cried Little Nell.

"Oh, Nell," said Rogers, "here's a despatch to me which I thought you had better read."

Little Nell took the despatch. It was: "Tell Nell can't understand his inaction; tell him come home first steamer from Port Antonio, Jamaica."

The Revenge of the Adolphus

I

"Stand by."

Shackles had come down from the bridge of the *Adolphus* and flung this command at three fellow-correspondents who in the galley were busy with pencils trying to write something exciting and interesting from four days quiet cruising. They looked up casually. "What for?" They did not intend to arouse for nothing. Ever since Shackles had heard the men of the navy directing each other to stand by for this thing and that thing, he had used the two words as his pet phrase and was continually telling his friends to stand by. Sometimes its portentous and emphatic reiteration became highly exasperating and men were apt to retort sharply. "Well, I *am* standing by, ain't I?" On this occasion they detected that he was serious. "Well, what for?" they repeated. In his answer Shackles was reproachful as well as impressive. "Stand by? Stand by for a Spanish gunboat. A Spanish gunboat in chase! Stand by for *two* Spanish gunboats —*both* of them in chase!"

The others looked at him for a brief space and were almost certain that they saw truth written upon his countenance. Whereupon they tumbled out of the galley and galloped up to the bridge. The cook with a mere inkling of tragedy was now out on deck bawling, "What's the matter? What's the matter? What's the matter?" Aft, the grimy head of a stoker was thrust suddenly up through the deck, so to speak. The eyes flashed in a quick look astern and then the head vanished. The correspondents were scrambling on the bridge. "Where's my glasses, damn it? Here-let me take a look. Are they Spaniards, Captain? Are you sure?"

The skipper of the *Adolphus* was at the wheel. The pilot-house was so arranged that he could not see astern without hanging forth from one of the side windows, but apparently he had made early investigation. He did not reply at once. At sea, he never replied at once to questions. At the very first, Shackles had discovered the merits of this deliberate manner and had taken delight in it. He invariably detailed his talk with the captain to the other correspondents. "Look here. I've just been to see the skipper. I said 'I would like to put into Cape Haytien.' Then he took a little think. Finally he said: 'All right.' Then I said: 'I suppose we'll need to take on more coal there?' He took another little think. I said: 'Ever ran into that port before?' He took another little think. Finally he said: 'Yes.' I said 'Have a cigar?' He took another little think. See? There's where I fooled 'im — —"

While the correspondents spun the hurried questions at him, the captain of the *Adolphus* stood with his brown hands on the wheel and his cold glance aligned straight over the bow of his ship.

"Are they Spanish gunboats, Captain? Are they, Captain?"

After a profound pause, he said: "Yes." The four correspondents hastily and in perfect time presented their backs to him and fastened their gaze on the pursuing foe. They saw a dull grey curve of sea going to the feet of the high green and blue coast-line of north-eastern Cuba, and on this sea were two miniature ships with clouds of iron-coloured smoke pouring from their funnels.

One of the correspondents strolled elaborately to the pilot-house. "Aw-Captain," he drawled, "do you think they can catch us?"

The captain's glance was still aligned over the bow of his ship. Ultimately he answered: "I don't know."

From the top of the little *Adolphus'* stack, thick dark smoke swept level for a few yards and then went rolling to leaward in great hot obscuring clouds. From time to time the grimy head was thrust through the deck, the eyes took the quick look astern and then the head vanished. The cook was trying to get somebody to listen to him. "Well, you know, damn it all, it won't be no fun to be ketched by them Spaniards. Be-Gawd, it won't. Look here, what do you think

336

they'll do to us, hey? Say, I don't like this, you know. I'm damned if I do." The sea, cut by the hurried bow of the *Adolphus*, flung its waters astern in the formation of a wide angle and the lines of the angle ruffled and hissed as they fled, while the thumping screw tormented the water at the stern. The frame of the steamer underwent regular convulsions as in the strenuous sobbing of a child.

The mate was standing near the pilot-house. Without looking at him, the captain spoke his name. "Ed!"

"Yes, sir," cried the mate with alacrity.

The captain reflected for a moment. Then he said: "Are they gainin' on us?"

The mate took another anxious survey of the race. "No —o —yes, I think they are —a little."

After a pause the captain said: "Tell the chief to shake her up more."

The mate, glad of an occupation in these tense minutes, flew down to the engine-room door. "Skipper says shake 'er up more!" he bawled. The head of the chief engineer appeared, a grizzly head now wet with oil and sweat. "What?" he shouted angrily. It was as if he had been propelling the ship with his own arms. Now he was told that his best was not good enough. "What? shake 'er up more? Why she can't carry another pound, I tell you! Not another ounce! We — —" Suddenly he ran forward and climbed to the bridge. "Captain," he cried in the loud harsh voice of one who lived usually amid the thunder of machinery, "she can't do it, sir! Be-Gawd, she can't! She's turning over now faster than she ever did in her life and we'll all blow to hell — —"

The low-toned, impassive voice of the captain suddenly checked the chief's clamour. "I'll blow her up," he said, "but I won't git ketched if I kin help it." Even then the listening correspondents found a second in which to marvel that the captain had actually explained his point of view to another human being.

The engineer stood blank. Then suddenly he cried: "All right, sir!" He threw a hurried look of despair at the correspondents, the deck of the *Adolphus*, the pursuing enemy, Cuba, the sky and the sea; he vanished in the direction of his post.

A correspondent was suddenly regifted with the power of prolonged speech. "Well, you see, the game is up, damn it. See? We can't get out of it. The skipper will blow up the whole bunch before he'll let his ship be taken, and the Spaniards are gaining. Well, that's what comes from going to war in an eight-knot tub." He bitterly accused himself, the others, and the dark, sightless, indifferent world.

This certainty of coming evil affected each one differently. One was made garrulous; one kept absent-mindedly snapping his fingers and gazing at the sea; another stepped nervously to and fro, looking everywhere as if for employment for his mind. As for Shackles he was silent and smiling, but it was a new smile that caused the lines about his mouth to betray quivering weakness. And each man looked at the others to discover their degree of fear and did his best to conceal his own, holding his crackling nerves with all his strength.

As the *Adolphus* rushed on, the sun suddenly emerged from behind grey clouds and its rays dealt titanic blows so that in a few minutes the sea was a glowing blue plain with the golden shine dancing at the tips of the waves. The coast of Cuba glowed with light. The pursuers displayed detail after detail in the new atmosphere. The voice of the cook was heard in high vexation. "Am I to git dinner as usual? How do I know? Nobody tells me what to do? Am I to git dinner as usual?"

The mate answered ferociously. "Of course you are! What do you s'pose? Ain't you the cook, you damn fool?"

The cook retorted in a mutinous scream. "Well, how would I know? If this ship is goin' to blow up — —"

The captain called from the pilot-house. "Mr. Shackles! Oh, Mr. Shackles!" The correspondent moved hastily to a window. "What is it, Captain?" The skipper of the *Adolphus* raised a battered finger and pointed over the bows. "See 'er?" he asked, laconic but quietly jubilant. Another steamer was smoking at full speed over the sun-lit seas. A great billow of pure white was on her bows. "Great Scott!" cried Shackles. "Another Spaniard?"

"No," said the captain, "that there is a United States cruiser!"

"What?" Shackles was dumfounded into muscular paralysis. "No! Are you *sure*?"

The captain nodded. "Sure, take the glass. See her ensign? Two funnels, two masts with fighting tops. She ought to be the *Chancellorville*."

Shackles choked. "Well, I'm blowed!"

"Ed!" said the captain.

"Yessir!"

"Tell the chief there is no hurry."

Shackles suddenly bethought him of his companions. He dashed to them and was full of quick scorn of their gloomy faces. "Hi, brace up there! Are you blind? Can't you see her?"

"See what?"

"Why, the *Chancellorville*, you blind mice!" roared Shackles. "See 'er? See 'er? See 'er?"

The others sprang, saw, and collapsed. Shackles was a madman for the purpose of distributing the news. "Cook!" he shrieked. "Don't you see 'er, cook? Good Gawd, man, don't you see 'er?" He ran to the lower deck and howled his information everywhere. Suddenly the whole ship smiled. Men clapped each other on the shoulder and joyously shouted. The captain thrust his head from the pilot-house to look back at the Spanish ships. Then he looked at the American cruiser. "Now, we'll see," he said grimly and vindictively to the mate. "Guess somebody else will do some running," the mate chuckled.

The two gunboats were still headed hard for the *Adolphus* and she kept on her way. The American cruiser was coming swiftly. "It's the *Chancellorville*!" cried Shackles. "I know her! We'll see a fight at sea, my boys! A fight at sea!" The enthusiastic correspondents pranced in Indian revels.

The *Chancellorville* —2000 tons —18.6 knots —10 five-inch guns-came on tempestuously, sheering the water high with her sharp bow. From her funnels the smoke raced away in driven sheets. She loomed with extraordinary rapidity like a ship bulging and growing out of the sea. She swept by the *Adolphus* so close that one could have thrown a walnut on board. She was a glistening grey apparition with a blood-red water-line, with brown gun-muzzles and white-clothed motionless jack-tars; and in her rush she was silent, deadly silent. Probably there entered the mind of every man on board the *Adolphus* a feeling of almost idolatry for this living thing, stern but, to their thought, incomparably beautiful. They would have cheered but that each man seemed to feel that a cheer would be too puny a tribute.

It was at first as if she did not see the *Adolphus*. She was going to pass without heeding this little vagabond of the high-seas. But suddenly a megaphone gaped over the rail of her bridge and a voice was heard measuredly, calmly intoning. "Hello-there! Keep-well-to — the-north'ard-and-out of my-way-and I'll-go-in-and-see — what-those-people-want — —" Then nothing was heard but the swirl of water. In a moment the *Adolphus* was looking at a high grey stern. On the quarter-deck, sailors were poised about the breach of the after-pivot-gun.

The correspondents were revelling. "Captain," yelled Shackles, "we can't miss this! We must see it!" But the skipper had already flung over the wheel. "Sure," he answered almost at once. "We can't miss it."

The cook was arrogantly, grossly triumphant. His voice rang along the deck. "There, now! How will the Spinachers like that? Now, it's our turn! We've been doin' the runnin' away but now we'll do the chasin'!" Apparently feeling some twinge of nerves from the former strain, he suddenly demanded: "Say, who's got any whisky? I'm near dead for a drink."

When the *Adolphus* came about, she laid her course for a position to the northward of a coming battle, but the situation suddenly became complicated. When the Spanish ships discovered the identity of the ship that was steaming toward them, they did not hesitate over their plan of action. With one accord they turned and ran for port. Laughter arose from the *Adolphus*. The captain broke his orders, and, instead of keeping to the northward, he headed in the wake of the impetuous *Chancellorville*. The correspondents crowded on the bow.

The Spaniards when their broadsides became visible were seen to be ships of no importance, mere little gunboats for work in the shallows back of the reefs, and it was certainly discreet to refuse encounter with the five-inch guns of the *Chancellorville*. But the joyful *Adolphus* took no account of this discretion. The pursuit of the Spaniards had been so ferocious that the quick change to heels-overhead flight filled that corner of the mind which is devoted to the spirit of revenge. It was this that moved Shackles to yell taunts futilely at the far-away ships. "Well, how do you like it, eh? How do you like it?" The *Adolphus* was drinking compensation for her previous agony.

The mountains of the shore now shadowed high into the sky and the square white houses of a town could be seen near a vague cleft which seemed to mark the entrance to a port. The gunboats were now near to it.

Suddenly white smoke streamed from the bow of the *Chancellorville* and developed swiftly into a great bulb which drifted in fragments down the wind. Presently the deep-throated boom of the gun came to the ears on board the *Adolphus*. The shot kicked up a high jet of water into the air astern of the last gunboat. The black smoke from the funnels of the cruiser made her look like a collier on fire, and in her desperation she tried many more long shots, but presently the *Adolphus*, murmuring disappointment, saw the *Chancellorville* sheer from the chase.

In time they came up with her and she was an indignant ship. Gloom and wrath was on the forecastle and wrath and gloom was on the quarter-deck. A sad voice from the bridge said: "Just missed 'em." Shackles gained permission to board the cruiser, and in the cabin, he talked to Lieutenant-Commander Surrey, tall, bald-headed and angry. "Shoals," said the captain of the *Chancellorville*. "I can't go any nearer and those gunboats could steam along a stone sidewalk if only it was wet." Then his bright eyes became brighter. "I tell you what! The *Chicken*, the *Holy Moses* and the *Mongolian* are on station off Nuevitas. If you will do me a favour-why, to-morrow I will give those people a game!"

The *Chancellorville* lay all night watching off the port of the two gunboats and, soon after daylight, the lookout descried three smokes to the westward and they were later made out to be the *Chicken*, the *Holy Moses* and the *Adolphus*, the latter tagging hurriedly after the United States vessels.

The *Chicken* had been a harbour tug but she was now the U.S.S. *Chicken*, by your leave. She carried a six-pounder forward and a six-pounder aft and her main point was her conspicuous vulnerability. The *Holy Moses* had been the private yacht of a Philadelphia millionaire. She carried six six-pounders and her main point was the chaste beauty of the officer's quarters.

On the bridge of the *Chancellorville*, Lieutenant-Commander Surrey surveyed his squadron with considerable satisfaction. Presently he signalled to the lieutenant who commanded the *Holy Moses* and to the boatswain who commanded the *Chicken* to come aboard the flag-ship. This was all very well for the captain of the yacht, but it was not so easy for the captain of the tug-boat who had two heavy lifeboats swung fifteen feet above the water. He had been accustomed to talking with senior officers from his own pilot house through the intercession of the blessed megaphone. However he got a lifeboat overside and was pulled to the *Chancellorville* by three men-which cut his crew almost into halves.

In the cabin of the *Chancellorville*, Surrey disclosed to his two captains his desires concerning the Spanish gunboats and they were glad for being ordered down from the Nuevitas station where life was very dull. He also announced that there was a shore battery containing, he believed, four field guns-three-point-twos. His draught-he spoke of it as *his* draught-would enable him to go in close enough to engage the battery at moderate range, but he pointed out that the main parts of the attempt to destroy the Spanish gunboats must be left to the *Holy Moses* and the *Chicken*. His business, he thought, could only be to keep the air so singing about the ears of the battery that the men at the guns would be unable to take an interest in the dash of the smaller American craft into the bay.

The officers spoke in their turns. The captain of the *Chicken* announced that he saw no difficulties. The squadron would follow the senior officer in line ahead, the S. O. would engage the batteries as soon as possible, she would turn to starboard when the depth of water forced her to do so and the *Holy Moses* and the *Chicken* would run past her into the bay and fight the Spanish ships wherever they were to be found. The captain of the *Holy Moses* after some moments of dignified thought said that he had no suggestions to make that would better this plan.

Surrey pressed an electric bell; a marine orderly appeared; he was sent with a message. The message brought the navigating officer of the *Chancellorville* to the cabin and the four men nosed over a chart.

In the end Surrey declared that he had made up his mind and the juniors remained in expectant silence for three minutes while he stared at the bulkhead. Then he said that the plan of the *Chicken's* captain seemed to him correct in the main. He would make one change. It was that he should first steam in and engage the battery and the other vessels should remain in their present positions until he signalled them to run into the bay. If the squadron steamed ahead in line, the battery could, if it chose, divide its fire between the cruiser and the gunboats constituting the more important attack. He had no doubt, he said, that he could soon silence the battery by tumbling the earth-works on to the guns and driving away the men even if he did not succeed in hitting the pieces. Of course he had no doubt of being able to silence the battery in twenty minutes. Then he would signal for the *Holy Moses* and the *Chicken* to make their rush, and of course he would support them with his fire as much as conditions enabled him. He arose then indicating that the conference was at an end. In the few moments more that all four men remained in the cabin, the talk changed its character completely. It was now unofficial, and the sharp badinage concealed furtive affections, Academy friendships, the feelings of old-time ship-mates, hiding everything under a veil of jokes. "Well, good luck to you, old boy! Don't get that valuable packet of yours sunk under you. Think how it would weaken the navy. Would you mind buying me three pairs of pajamas in the town yonder? If your engines get disabled, tote her under your arm. You can do it. Good-bye, old man, don't forget to come out all right — —"

When the captains of the *Holy Moses* and the *Chicken* emerged from the cabin, they strode the deck with a new step. They were proud men. The marine on duty above their boats looked at them curiously and with awe. He detected something which meant action, conflict, The boats' crews saw it also. As they pulled their steady stroke, they studied fleetingly the face of the officer in the stern sheets. In both cases they perceived a glad man and yet a man filled with a profound consideration of the future.

A bird-like whistle stirred the decks of the *Chancellorville*. It was followed by the hoarse bellowing of the boatswain's mate. As the cruiser turned her bow toward the shore, she happened to steam near the *Adolphus*. The usual calm voice hailed the despatch boat. "Keep-that-gauze under-shirt of yours-well-out of the-line of fire."

"Ay, ay, sir!"

The cruiser then moved slowly toward the shore, watched by every eye in the smaller American vessels. She was deliberate and steady, and this was reasonable even to the impatience of the other craft because the wooded shore was likely to suddenly develop new factors. Slowly she swung to starboard; smoke belched over her and the roar of a gun came along the water.

The battery was indicated by a long thin streak of yellow earth. The first shot went high, ploughing the chaparral on the hillside. The *Chancellorville* wore an air for a moment of being deep in meditation. She flung another shell, which landed squarely on the earth-work, making a great dun cloud. Before the smoke had settled, there was a crimson flash from the battery. To the watchers at sea, it was smaller than a needle. The shot made a geyser of crystal water, four hundred yards from the *Chancellorville*.

The cruiser, having made up her mind, suddenly went at the battery, hammer and tongs. She moved to and fro casually, but the thunder of her guns was gruff and angry. Sometimes she was quite hidden in her own smoke, but with exceeding regularity the earth of the battery spurted into the air. The Spanish shells, for the most part, went high and wide of the cruiser, jetting the water far away.

Once a Spanish gunner took a festive side-show chance at the waiting group of the three nondescripts. It went like a flash over the *Adolphus*, singing a wistful metallic note. Whereupon the *Adolphus* broke hurriedly for the open sea, and men on the *Holy Moses* and the *Chicken* laughed hoarsely and cruelly. The correspondents had been standing excitedly on top of the pilot-house, but at the passing of the shell, they promptly eliminated themselves by dropping with a thud to the deck below. The cook again was giving tongue. "Oh, say, this won't do! I'm damned if it will! We ain't no armoured cruiser, you know. If one of them shells hits us-well, we finish right there. 'Tain't like as if it was our *business*, foolin' 'round within the range of them guns. There's no sense in it. Them other fellows don't seem to mind it, but it's their *business*. If it's your *business*, you go ahead and do it, but if it ain't, you-look at that, would you!"

The *Chancellorville* had sent up a spread of flags, and the *Holy Moses* and the *Chicken* were steaming in.

They, on the *Chancellorville*, sometimes could see into the bay, and they perceived the enemy's gunboats moving out as if to give battle. Surrey feared that this impulse would not endure or that it was some mere pretence for the edification of the town's people and the garrison, so he hastily signalled the *Holy Moses* and the *Chicken* to go in. Thankful for small favours, they came on like charging bantams. The battery had ceased firing. As the two auxiliaries passed under the stern of the cruiser, the megaphone hailed them. "You-will-see-the-en-em —y — soon-as-you-round-the-point. A —fine-chance. Good-luck."

As a matter of fact, the Spanish gunboats had not been informed of the presence of the *Holy Moses* and the *Chicken* off the bar, and they were just blustering down the bay over the protective shoals to make it appear that they scorned the *Chancellorville*. But suddenly, from around the point, there burst into view a steam yacht, closely followed by a harbour tug. The gunboats took one swift look at this horrible sight and fled screaming.

Lieutenant Reigate, commanding the *Holy Moses*, had under his feet a craft that was capable of some speed, although before a solemn tribunal, one would have to admit that she conscientiously belied almost everything that the contractors had said of her, originally. Boatswain Pent, commanding the *Chicken*, was in possession of an utterly different kind. The *Holy Moses* was an antelope; the *Chicken* was a man who could carry a piano on his back. In this race Pent had the mortification of seeing his vessel outstripped badly.

The entrance of the two American craft had had a curious effect upon the shores of the bay. Apparently everyone had slept in the assurance that the *Chancellorville* could not cross the bar, and that the *Chancellorville* was the only hostile ship. Consequently, the appearance of the *Holy Moses* and the *Chicken*, created a curious and complete emotion. Reigate, on the bridge of the *Holy Moses*, laughed when he heard the bugles shrilling and saw through his glasses the wee figures of men running hither and thither on the shore. It was the panic of the china when the bull entered the shop. The whole bay was bright with sun. Every detail of the shore was plain. From a brown hut abeam of the *Holy Moses*, some little men ran out waving their arms and turning their tiny faces to look at the enemy. Directly ahead, some four miles, appeared the scattered white houses of a town with a wharf, and some schooners in front of it. The gunboats were making for the town. There was a stone fort on the hill overshadowing, but Reigate conjectured that there was no artillery in it.

There was a sense of something intimate and impudent in the minds of the Americans. It was like climbing over a wall and fighting a man in his own garden. It was not that they could be in any wise shaken in their resolve; it was simply that the overwhelmingly Spanish aspect of things made them feel like gruff intruders. Like many of the emotions of war-time, this emotion had nothing at all to do with war.

Reigate's only commissioned subordinate called up from the bow gun. "May I open fire, sir? I think I can fetch that last one."

"Yes." Immediately the six-pounder crashed, and in the air was the spinning-wire noise of the flying shot. It struck so close to the last gunboat that it appeared that the spray went aboard. The swift-handed men at the gun spoke of it. "Gave 'm a bath that time anyhow. First one they've ever had. Dry 'em off this time, Jim." The young ensign said: "Steady." And so the *Holy Moses* raced in, firing, until the whole town, fort, waterfront, and shipping were as plain as if they had been done on paper by a mechanical draftsman. The gunboats were trying to hide in the bosom of the town. One was frantically tying up to the wharf and the other was anchoring within a hundred yards of the shore. The Spanish infantry, of course, had dug trenches along the beach, and suddenly the air over the *Holy Moses* sung with bullets. The shore-line thrummed with musketry. Also some antique shells screamed.

The *Chicken* was doing her best. Pent's posture at the wheel seemed to indicate that her best was about thirty-four knots. In his eagerness he was braced as if he alone was taking in a 10,000 ton battleship through Hell Gate.

But the *Chicken* was not too far in the rear and Pent could see clearly that he was to have no minor part to play. Some of the antique shells had struck the *Holy Moses* and he could see the escaped steam shooting up from her. She lay close inshore and was lashing out with four six-pounders as if this was the last opportunity she would have to fire them. She had made the Spanish gunboats very sick. A solitary gun on the one moored to the wharf was from time to time firing wildly; otherwise the gunboats were silent. But the beach in front of the town was a line of fire. The *Chicken* headed for the *Holy Moses* and, as soon as possible, the six-pounder in her bow began to crack at the gunboat moored to the wharf.

In the meantime, the *Chancellorville* prowled off the bar, listening to the firing, anxious, acutely anxious, and feeling her impotency in every inch of her smart steel frame. And in the meantime, the *Adolphus* squatted on the waves and brazenly waited for news. One could thoughtfully count the seconds and reckon that, in this second and that second, a man had died-if one chose. But no one did it. Undoubtedly, the spirit was that the flag should come away with honour, honour complete, perfect, leaving no loose unfinished end over which the Spaniards could erect a monument of satisfaction, glorification. The distant guns boomed to the ears of the silent blue-jackets at their stations on the cruiser.

The *Chicken* steamed up to the *Holy Moses* and took into her nostrils the odour of steam, gunpowder and burnt things. Rifle bullets simply steamed over them both. In the merest flash of time, Pent took into his remembrance the body of a dead quartermaster on the bridge of his consort. The two megaphones uplifted together, but Pent's eager voice cried out first. "Are you injured, sir?"

"No, not completely. My engines can get me out after-after we have sunk those gunboats." The voice had been utterly conventional but it changed to sharpness. "Go in and sink that gunboat at anchor."

As the *Chicken* rounded the *Holy Moses* and started inshore, a man called to him from the depths of finished disgust. "They're takin' to their boats, sir." Pent looked and saw the men of the anchored gunboat lower their boats and pull like mad for shore.

The *Chicken*, assisted by the *Holy Moses*, began a methodical killing of the anchored gunboat. The Spanish infantry on shore fired frenziedly at the *Chicken*. Pent, giving the wheel to a waiting sailor, stepped out to a point where he could see the men at the guns. One bullet spanged past him and into the pilot-house. He ducked his head into the window. "That hit you, Murry?" he inquired with interest.

"No, sir," cheerfully responded the man at the wheel.

Pent became very busy superintending the fire of his absurd battery. The anchored gunboat simply would not sink. It evinced that unnatural stubbornness which is sometimes displayed by inanimate objects. The gunboat at the wharf had sunk as if she had been scuttled but this riddled thing at anchor would not even take fire. Pent began to grow flurried-privately. He could not stay there for ever. Why didn't the damned gunboat admit its destruction. Why — —

He was at the forward gun when one of his engine room force came to him and, after saluting, said serenely: "The men at the after-gun are all down, sir."

It was one of those curious lifts which an enlisted man, without in any way knowing it, can give his officer. The impudent tranquillity of the man at once set Pent to rights and the stoker departed admiring the extraordinary coolness of his captain.

The next few moments contained little but heat, an odour, applied mechanics and an expectation of death. Pent developed a fervid and amazed appreciation of the men, his men, men he knew very well, but strange men. What explained them? He was doing his best because he was captain of the *Chicken* and he lived or died by the *Chicken*. But what could move these men to watch his eye in bright anticipation of his orders and then obey them with enthusiastic rapidity? What caused them to speak of the action as some kind of a joke-particularly when they knew he could overhear them? What manner of men? And he anointed them secretly with his fullest affection.

Perhaps Pent did not think all this during the battle. Perhaps he thought it so soon after the battle that his full mind became confused as to the time. At any rate, it stands as an expression of his feeling.

The enemy had gotten a field-gun down to the shore and with it they began to throw three-inch shells at the *Chicken*. In this war it was usual that the down-trodden Spaniards in their ignorance should use smokeless powder while the Americans, by the power of the consistent everlasting three-ply, wire-woven, double back-action imbecility of a hay-seed government, used powder which on sea and on land cried their position to heaven, and, accordingly, good men got killed without reason. At first, Pent could not locate the field-gun at all, but as soon as he found it, he ran aft with one man and brought the after six-pounder again into action. He paid little heed to the old gun crew. One was lying on his face apparently dead; another was prone with a wound in the chest, while the third sat with his back to the deck-house holding a smitten arm. This last one called out huskily, "Give'm hell, sir."

The minutes of the battle were either days, years, or they were flashes of a second. Once Pent looking up was astonished to see three shell holes in the *Chicken's* funnel-made surreptitiously, so to speak.... "If we don't silence that field-gun, she'll sink us, boys."...The eyes of the man sitting with his back against the deck-house were looking from out his ghastly face at the new gun-crew. He spoke with the supreme laziness of a wounded man. "Give'm hell."...Pent felt a sudden twist of his shoulder. He was wounded-slightly.... The anchored gunboat was in flames.

Pent took his little blood-stained tow-boat out to the *Holy Moses*. The yacht was already under way for the bay entrance. As they were passing out of range the Spaniards heroically redoubled their fire-which is their custom. Pent, moving busily about the decks, stopped suddenly at the door of the engine-room. His face was set and his eyes were steely. He spoke to one of the engineers. "During the action I saw you firing at the enemy with a rifle. I told you once to stop, and then I saw you at it again. Pegging away with a rifle is no part of your business. I want you to understand that you are in trouble." The humbled man did not raise his eyes from the deck. Presently the *Holy Moses* displayed an anxiety for the *Chicken's* health.

"One killed and four wounded, sir."

"Have you enough men left to work your ship?"

After deliberation, Pent answered: "No, sir."

"Shall I send you assistance?"

"No, sir. I can get to sea all right."

As they neared the point they were edified by the sudden appearance of a serio-comic ally. The *Chancellorville* at last had been unable to stand the strain, and had sent in her launch with an ensign, five seamen and a number of marksmen marines. She swept hot-foot around the point, bent on terrible slaughter; the one-pounder of her bow presented a formidable appearance. The *Holy Moses* and the *Chicken* laughed until they brought indignation to the brow of the young ensign. But he forgot it when with some of his men he boarded the *Chicken* to do what was possible for the wounded. The nearest surgeon was aboard the *Chancellorville*. There was absolute silence on board the cruiser as the *Holy Moses* steamed up to report. The blue-jackets listened with all their ears. The commander of the yacht spoke slowly into his megaphone: "We have-destroyed-the two-gun-boats-sir." There was a burst of confused cheering on the forecastle of the *Chancellorville*, but an officer's cry quelled it.

"Very-good. Will-you-come aboard?"

Two correspondents were already on the deck of the cruiser. Before the last of the wounded were hoisted aboard the cruiser the *Adolphus* was on her way to Key West. When she arrived at that port of desolation Shackles fled to file the telegrams and the other correspondents fled to the hotel for clothes, good clothes, clean clothes; and food, good food, much food; and drink, much drink, any kind of drink.

Days afterward, when the officers of the noble squadron received the newspapers containing an account of their performance, they looked at each other somewhat dejectedly: "Heroic assault-grand daring of Boatswain Pent-superb accuracy of the *Holy Moses'* fire-gallant tars of the *Chicken* —their names should be remembered as long as America stands-terrible losses of the enemy ——"

When the Secretary of the Navy ultimately read the report of Commander Surrey, S.O.P., he had to prick himself with a dagger in order to remember that anything at all out of the ordinary had occurred.

The Sergeant's Private Madhouse

The moonlight was almost steady blue flame and all this radiance was lavished out upon a still lifeless wilderness of stunted trees and cactus plants. The shadows lay upon the ground, pools of black and sharply outlined, resembling substances, fabrics, and not shadows at all. From afar came the sound of the sea coughing among the hollows in the coral rock.

The land was very empty; one could easily imagine that Cuba was a simple vast solitude; one could wonder at the moon taking all the trouble of this splendid illumination. There was no wind; nothing seemed to live.

But in a particular large group of shadows lay an outpost of some forty United States marines. If it had been possible to approach them from any direction without encountering one of their sentries, one could have gone stumbling among sleeping men and men who sat waiting, their blankets tented over their heads; one would have been in among them before one's mind could have decided whether they were men or devils. If a marine moved, he took the care and the time of one who walks across a death-chamber. The lieutenant in command reached for his watch and the nickel chain gave forth the faintest tinkling sound. He could see the glistening five or six pairs of eyes that slowly turned to regard him. His sergeant lay near him and he bent his face down to whisper. "Who's on post behind the big cactus plant?"

"Dryden," rejoined the sergeant just over his breath.

After a pause the lieutenant murmured: "He's got too many nerves. I shouldn't have put him there." The sergeant asked if he should crawl down and look into affairs at Dryden's post. The young officer nodded assent and the sergeant, softly cocking his rifle, went away on his hands and knees. The lieutenant with his back to a dwarf tree, sat watching the sergeant's progress for the few moments that he could see him moving from one shadow to another. Afterward, the officer waited to hear Dryden's quick but low-voiced challenge, but time passed and no sound came from the direction of the post behind the cactus bush.

The sergeant, as he came nearer and nearer to this cactus bush — a number of peculiarly dignified columns throwing shadows of inky darkness-had slowed his pace, for he did not wish to trifle with the feelings of the sentry, and he was expecting the stern hail and was ready with the immediate answer which turns away wrath. He was not made anxious by the fact that he could not yet see Dryden, for he knew that the man would be hidden in a way practised by sentry marines since the time when two men had been killed by a disease of excessive confidence on picket. Indeed, as the sergeant went still nearer, he became more and more angry. Dryden was evidently a most proper sentry.

Finally he arrived at a point where he could see Dryden seated in the shadow, staring into the bushes ahead of him, his rifle ready on his knee. The sergeant in his rage longed for the peaceful precincts of the Washington Marine Barracks where there would have been no situation to prevent the most complete non-commissioned oratory. He felt indecent in his capacity of a man able to creep up to the back of a G Company member on guard duty. Never mind; in the morning back at camp — —

But, suddenly, he felt afraid. There was something wrong with Dryden. He remembered old tales of comrades creeping out to find a picket seated against a tree perhaps, upright enough but stone dead. The sergeant paused and gave the inscrutable back of the sentry a long stare. Dubious he again moved forward. At three paces, he hissed like a little snake. Dryden did not show a sign of hearing. At last, the sergeant was in a position from which he was able to reach out and touch Dryden on the arm. Whereupon was turned to him the face of a man livid with mad fright. The sergeant grabbed him by the wrist and with discreet fury shook him. "Here! Pull yourself together!"

Dryden paid no heed but turned his wild face from the newcomer to the ground in front. "Don't you see 'em, sergeant? Don't you see 'em?"

"Where?" whispered the sergeant.

"Ahead, and a little on the right flank. A reg'lar skirmish line. Don't you see 'em?"

"Naw," whispered the sergeant. Dryden began to shake. He began moving one hand from his head to his knee and from his knee to his head rapidly, in a way that is without explanation. "I don't dare fire," he wept. "If I do they'll see me, and oh, how they'll pepper me!"

The sergeant lying on his belly, understood one thing. Dryden had gone mad. Dryden was the March Hare. The old man gulped down his uproarious emotions as well as he was able and used the most simple device. "Go," he said, "and tell the lieutenant while I cover your post for you."

"No! They'd see me! They'd see me! And then they'd pepper me! O, how they'd pepper me!"

The sergeant was face to face with the biggest situation of his life. In the first place he knew that at night a large or small force of Spanish guerillas was never more than easy rifle range from any marine outpost, both sides maintaining a secrecy as absolute as possible in regard to their real position and strength. Everything was on a watch-spring foundation. A loud word might be paid for by a night-attack which would involve five hundred men who needed their earned sleep, not to speak of some of them who would need their lives. The slip of a foot and the rolling of a pint of gravel might go from consequence to consequence until various crews went to general quarters on their ships in the harbour, their batteries booming as the swift search-light flashes tore through the foliage. Men would get killed-notably the sergeant and Dryden-and outposts would be cut off and the whole night would be one pitiless turmoil. And so Sergeant George H. Peasley began to run his private madhouse behind the cactus-bush.

"Dryden," said the sergeant, "you do as I tell you and go tell the lieutenant."

"I don't dare move," shivered the man. "They'll see me if I move. They'll see me. They're almost up now. Let's hide — —"

"Well, then you stay here a moment and I'll go and — —"

Dryden turned upon him a look so tigerish that the old man felt his hair move. "Don't you stir," he hissed. "You want to give me away. You want them to see me. Don't you stir." The sergeant decided not to stir.

He became aware of the slow wheeling of eternity, its majestic incomprehensibility of movement. Seconds, minutes, were quaint little things, tangible as toys, and there were billions of them, all alike. "Dryden," he whispered at the end of a century in which, curiously, he had never joined the marine corps at all but had taken to another walk of life and prospered greatly in it. "Dryden, this is all foolishness." He thought of the expedient of smashing the man over the head with his rifle, but Dryden was so supernaturally alert that there surely would issue some small scuffle and there could be not even the fraction of a scuffle. The sergeant relapsed into the contemplation of another century.

His patient had one fine virtue. He was in such terror of the phantom skirmish line that his voice never went above a whisper, whereas his delusion might have expressed itself in hyena yells and shots from his rifle. The sergeant, shuddering, had visions of how it might have been-the mad private leaping into the air and howling and shooting at his friends and making them the centre of the enemy's eager attention. This, to his mind, would have been conventional conduct for a maniac. The trembling victim of an idea was somewhat puzzling. The sergeant decided that from time to time he would reason with his patient. "Look here, Dryden, you don't see any real Spaniards. You've been drinking or-something. Now — —"

But Dryden only glared him into silence. Dryden was inspired with such a profound contempt of him that it was become hatred. "Don't you stir!" And it was clear that if the sergeant did stir, the mad private would introduce calamity. "Now," said Peasley to himself, "if those guerillas *should* take a crack at us to-night, they'd find a lunatic asylum right in the front and it would be astonishing."

The silence of the night was broken by the quick low voice of a sentry to the left some distance. The breathless stillness brought an effect to the words as if they had been spoken in one's ear.

"Halt-who's there-halt or I'll fire!" Bang!

At the moment of sudden attack particularly at night, it is improbable that a man registers much detail of either thought or action. He may afterward say: "I was here." He may say: "I was there." "I did this." "I did that." But there remains a great incoherency because of the tumultuous thought which seethes through the head. "Is this defeat?" At night in a wilderness and against skilful foes half-seen, one does not trouble to ask if it is also Death. Defeat is Death, then, save for the miraculous. But the exaggerating magnifying first thought subsides in the ordered mind of the soldier and he knows, soon, what he is doing and how much of it. The sergeant's immediate impulse had been to squeeze close to the ground and listen-listen-above all else, listen. But the next moment he grabbed his private asylum by the scruff of its neck, jerked it to its feet and started to retreat upon the main outpost.

To the left, rifle-flashes were bursting from the shadows. To the rear, the lieutenant was giving some hoarse order or admonition. Through the air swept some Spanish bullets, very high, as if they had been fired at a man in a tree. The private asylum came on so hastily that the sergeant found he could remove his grip, and soon they were in the midst of the men of the outpost. Here there was no occasion for enlightening the lieutenant. In the first place such surprises required statement, question and answer. It is impossible to get a grossly original and fantastic idea through a man's head in less than one minute of rapid talk, and the sergeant knew the lieutenant could not spare the minute. He himself had no minutes to devote to anything but the business of the outpost. And the madman disappeared from his pen and he forgot about him.

It was a long night and the little fight was as long as the night. It was a heart-breaking work. The forty marines lay in an irregular oval. From all sides, the Mauser bullets sang low and hard. Their occupation was to prevent a rush, and to this end they potted carefully at the flash of a Mauser-save when they got excited for a moment, in which case their magazines rattled like a great Waterbury watch. Then they settled again to a systematic potting.

The enemy were not of the regular Spanish forces. They were of a corps of guerillas, native-born Cubans, who preferred the flag of Spain. They were all men who knew the craft of the woods and were all recruited from the district. They fought more like red Indians than any people but the red Indians themselves. Each seemed to possess an individuality, a fighting individuality, which is only found in the highest order of irregular soldiers. Personally they were as distinct as possible, but through equality of knowledge and experience, they arrived at concert of action. So long as they operated in the wilderness, they were formidable troops. It mattered little whether it was daylight or dark; they were mainly invisible. They had schooled from the Cubans insurgent to Spain. As the Cubans fought the Spanish troops, so would these particular Spanish troops fight the Americans. It was wisdom.

The marines thoroughly understood the game. They must lie close and fight until daylight when the guerillas promptly would go away. They had withstood other nights of this kind, and now their principal emotion was probably a sort of frantic annoyance.

Back at the main camp, whenever the roaring volleys lulled, the men in the trenches could hear their comrades of the outpost, and the guerillas pattering away interminably. The moonlight faded and left an equal darkness upon the wilderness. A man could barely see the comrade at his side. Sometimes guerillas crept so close that the flame from their rifles seemed to scorch the faces of the marines, and the reports sounded as if from two or three inches of their very noses. If a pause came, one could hear the guerillas gabbling to each other in a kind of drunken delirium. The lieutenant was praying that the ammunition would last. Everybody was praying for daybreak.

A black hour came finally, when the men were not fit to have their troubles increased. The enemy made a wild attack on one portion of the oval, which was held by about fifteen men. The remainder of the force was busy enough, and the fifteen were naturally left to their devices. Amid the whirl of it, a loud voice suddenly broke out in song:

"When shepherds guard their flocks by night,
All seated on the ground,
An angel of the Lord came down
And glory shone around."

"Who the hell is that?" demanded the lieutenant from a throat full of smoke. There was almost a full stop of the firing. The Americans were somewhat puzzled. Practical ones muttered that the fool should have a bayonet-hilt shoved down his throat. Others felt a thrill at the strangeness of the thing. Perhaps it was a sign!

"The minstrel boy to the war has gone,
In the ranks of death you'll find him,
His father's sword he has girded on
And his wild harp slung behind him."

This croak was as lugubrious as a coffin. "Who is it? Who is it?" snapped the lieutenant. "Stop him, somebody."

"It's Dryden, sir," said old Sergeant Peasley, as he felt around in the darkness for his madhouse. "I can't find him-yet."

"Please, O, please, O, do not let me fall;
You're-gurgh-ugh — —"

The sergeant had pounced upon him.

This singing had had an effect upon the Spaniards. At first they had fired frenziedly at the voice, but they soon ceased, perhaps from sheer amazement. Both sides took a spell of meditation.

The sergeant was having some difficulty with his charge. "Here, you, grab 'im. Take 'im by the throat. Be quiet, you devil."

One of the fifteen men, who had been hard-pressed, called out, "We've only got about one clip a-piece, Lieutenant. If they come again — —"

The lieutenant crawled to and fro among his men, taking clips of cartridges from those who had many. He came upon the sergeant and his madhouse. He felt Dryden's belt and found it simply stuffed with ammunition. He examined Dryden's rifle and found in it a full clip. The madhouse had not fired a shot. The lieutenant distributed these valuable prizes among the fifteen men. As the men gratefully took them, one said: "If they had come again hard enough, they would have had us, sir, —maybe."

But the Spaniards did not come again. At the first indication of daybreak, they fired their customary good-bye volley. The marines lay tight while the slow dawn crept over the land. Finally the lieutenant arose among them, and he was a bewildered man, but very angry. "Now where is that idiot, Sergeant?"

"Here he is, sir," said the old man cheerfully. He was seated on the ground beside the recumbent Dryden who, with an innocent smile on his face, was sound asleep.

"Wake him up," said the lieutenant briefly.

The sergeant shook the sleeper. "Here, Minstrel Boy, turn out. The lieutenant wants you."

Dryden climbed to his feet and saluted the officer with a dazed and childish air. "Yes, sir."

The lieutenant was obviously having difficulty in governing his feelings, but he managed to say with calmness, "You seem to be fond of singing, Dryden? Sergeant, see if he has any whisky on him."

"Sir?" said the madhouse stupefied. "Singing-fond of singing?"

Here the sergeant interposed gently, and he and the lieutenant held palaver apart from the others. The marines, hitching more comfortably their almost empty belts, spoke with grins of the madhouse. "Well, the Minstrel Boy made 'em clear out. They couldn't stand it. But—I wouldn't want to be in his boots. He'll see fireworks when the old man interviews him on the uses of grand opera in modern warfare. How do you think he managed to smuggle a bottle along without us finding it out?"

When the weary outpost was relieved and marched back to camp, the men could not rest until they had told a tale of the voice in the wilderness. In the meantime the sergeant took

Dryden aboard a ship, and to those who took charge of the man, he defined him as "the most useful —— — —— crazy man in the service of the United States."

Virtue In War

I

Gates had left the regular army in 1890, those parts of him which had not been frozen having been well fried. He took with him nothing but an oaken constitution and a knowledge of the plains and the best wishes of his fellow-officers. The Standard Oil Company differs from the United States Government in that it understands the value of the loyal and intelligent services of good men and is almost certain to reward them at the expense of incapable men. This curious practice emanates from no beneficent emotion of the Standard Oil Company, on whose feelings you could not make a scar with a hammer and chisel. It is simply that the Standard Oil Company knows more than the United States Government and makes use of virtue whenever virtue is to its advantage. In 1890 Gates really felt in his bones that, if he lived a rigorously correct life and several score of his class-mates and intimate friends died off, he would get command of a troop of horse by the time he was unfitted by age to be an active cavalry leader. He left the service of the United States and entered the service of the Standard Oil Company. In the course of time he knew that, if he lived a rigorously correct life, his position and income would develop strictly in parallel with the worth of his wisdom and experience, and he would not have to walk on the corpses of his friends.

But he was not happier. Part of his heart was in a barracks, and it was not enough to discourse of the old regiment over the port and cigars to ears which were polite enough to betray a languid ignorance. Finally came the year 1898, and Gates dropped the Standard Oil Company as if it were hot. He hit the steel trail to Washington and there fought the first serious action of the war. Like most Americans, he had a native State, and one morning he found himself major in a volunteer infantry regiment whose voice had a peculiar sharp twang to it which he could remember from childhood. The colonel welcomed the West Pointer with loud cries of joy; the lieutenant-colonel looked at him with the pebbly eye of distrust; and the senior major, having had up to this time the best battalion in the regiment, strongly disapproved of him. There were only two majors, so the lieutenant-colonel commanded the first battalion, which gave him an occupation. Lieutenant-colonels under the new rules do not always have occupations. Gates got the third battalion-four companies commanded by intelligent officers who could gauge the opinions of their men at two thousand yards and govern themselves accordingly. The battalion was immensely interested in the new major. It thought it ought to develop views about him. It thought it was its blankety-blank business to find out immediately if it liked him personally. In the company streets the talk was nothing else. Among the non-commissioned officers there were eleven old soldiers of the regular army, and they knew-and cared-that Gates had held commission in the "Sixteenth Cavalry" —as *Harper's Weekly* says. Over this fact they rejoiced and were glad, and they stood by to jump lively when he took command. He would know his work and he would know *their* work, and then in battle there would be killed only what men were absolutely necessary and the sick list would be comparatively free of fools.

The commander of the second battalion had been called by an Atlanta paper, "Major Rickets C. Carmony, the commander of the second battalion of the 307th — —, is when at home one of the biggest wholesale hardware dealers in his State. Last evening he had ice-cream, at his own expense, served out at the regular mess of the battalion, and after dinner the men gathered about his tent where three hearty cheers for the popular major were given." Carmony had bought twelve copies of this newspaper and mailed them home to his friends.

In Gates's battalion there were more kicks than ice-cream, and there was no ice-cream at all. Indignation ran high at the rapid manner in which he proceeded to make soldiers of them. Some of his officers hinted finally that the men wouldn't stand it. They were saying that they had enlisted to fight for their country-yes, but they weren't going to be bullied day in and day out by a perfect stranger. They were patriots, they were, and just as good men as ever stepped-just as good as Gates or anybody like him. But, gradually, despite itself, the battalion progressed. The men were not altogether conscious of it. They evolved rather blindly. Presently there were fights with Carmony's crowd as to which was the better battalion at drills, and at last there was no argument. It was generally admitted that Gates commanded the crack battalion. The men, believing that the beginning and the end of all soldiering was in these drills of precision, were somewhat reconciled to their major when they began to understand more of what he was trying to do for them, but they were still fiery untamed patriots of lofty pride and they resented his manner toward them. It was abrupt and sharp.

The time came when everybody knew that the Fifth Army Corps was the corps designated for the first active service in Cuba. The officers and men of the 307th observed with despair that their regiment was not in the Fifth Army Corps. The colonel was a strategist. He understood everything in a flash. Without a moment's hesitation he obtained leave and mounted the night express for Washington. There he drove Senators and Congressmen in span, tandem and four-in-hand. With the telegraph he stirred so deeply the governor, the people and the newspapers of his State that whenever on a quiet night the President put his head out of the White House he could hear the distant vast commonwealth humming with indignation. And as it is well known that the Chief Executive listens to the voice of the people, the 307th was transferred to the Fifth Army Corps. It was sent at once to Tampa, where it was brigaded with two dusty regiments of regulars, who looked at it calmly, and said nothing. The brigade commander happened to be no less a person than Gates's old colonel in the "Sixteenth Cavalry" —as Harper's Weekly says-and Gates was cheered. The old man's rather solemn look brightened when he saw Gates in the 307th. There was a great deal of battering and pounding and banging for the 307th at Tampa, but the men stood it more in wonder than in anger. The two regular regiments carried them along when they could, and when they couldn't waited impatiently for them to come up. Undoubtedly the regulars wished the volunteers were in garrison at Sitka, but they said practically nothing. They minded their own regiments. The colonel was an invaluable man in a telegraph office. When came the scramble for transports the colonel retired to a telegraph office and talked so ably to Washington that the authorities pushed a number of corps aside and made way for the 307th, as if on it depended everything. The regiment got one of the best transports, and after a series of delays and some starts, and an equal number of returns, they finally sailed for Cuba.

Now Gates had a singular adventure on the second morning after his arrival at Atlanta to take his post as a major in the 307th.

He was in his tent, writing, when suddenly the flap was flung away and a tall young private stepped inside.

"Well, Maje," said the newcomer, genially, "how goes it?"

The major's head flashed up, but he spoke without heat.

"Come to attention and salute."

"Huh!" said the private.

"Come to attention and salute."

The private looked at him in resentful amazement, and then inquired:

"Ye ain't mad, are ye? Ain't nothin' to get huffy about, is there?"

"I —— Come to attention and salute."

"Well," drawled the private, as he stared, "seein' as ye are so darn perticular, I don't care if I do-if it'll make yer meals set on yer stomick any better."

Drawing a long breath and grinning ironically, he lazily pulled his heels together and saluted with a flourish.

"There," he said, with a return to his earlier genial manner. "How's that suit ye, Maje?"

There was a silence which to an impartial observer would have seemed pregnant with dynamite and bloody death. Then the major cleared his throat and coldly said:

"And now, what is your business?"

"Who-me?" asked the private. "Oh, I just sorter dropped in." With a deeper meaning he added: "Sorter dropped in in a friendly way, thinkin' ye was mebbe a different kind of a feller from what ye be."

The inference was clearly marked.

It was now Gates's turn to stare, and stare he unfeignedly did.

"Go back to your quarters," he said at length.

The volunteer became very angry.

"Oh, ye needn't be so up-in-th'-air, need ye? Don't know's I'm dead anxious to inflict my company on yer since I've had a good look at ye. There may be men in this here battalion what's had just as much edjewcation as you have, and I'm damned if they ain't got better *manners*. Good-mornin'," he said, with dignity; and, passing out of the tent, he flung the flap back in place with an air of slamming it as if it had been a door. He made his way back to his company street, striding high. He was furious. He met a large crowd of his comrades.

"What's the matter, Lige?" asked one, who noted his temper.

"Oh, nothin'," answered Lige, with terrible feeling. "Nothin'. I jest been lookin' over the new major-that's all."

"What's he like?" asked another.

"Like?" cried Lige. "He's like nothin'. He ain't out'n the same kittle as us. No. Gawd made him all by himself-sep'rate. He's a speshul produc', he is, an' he won't have no truck with jest common —*men*, like you be."

He made a venomous gesture which included them all.

"Did he set on ye?" asked a soldier.

"Set on me? No," replied Lige, with contempt "I set on *him*. I sized 'im up in a minute. 'Oh, I don't know,' I says, as I was comin' out; 'guess you ain't the only man in the world,' I says."

For a time Lige Wigram was quite a hero. He endlessly repeated the tale of his adventure, and men admired him for so soon taking the conceit out of the new officer. Lige was proud to think of himself as a plain and simple patriot who had refused to endure any high-soaring nonsense.

But he came to believe that he had not disturbed the singular composure of the major, and this concreted his hatred. He hated Gates, not as a soldier sometimes hates an officer, a hatred half of fear. Lige hated as man to man. And he was enraged to see that so far from gaining any hatred in return, he seemed incapable of making Gates have any thought of him save as a unit in a body of three hundred men. Lige might just as well have gone and grimaced at the obelisk in Central Park.

When the battalion became the best in the regiment he had no part in the pride of the companies. He was sorry when men began to speak well of Gates. He was really a very consistent hater.

The transport occupied by the 307th was commanded by some sort of a Scandinavian, who was afraid of the shadows of his own topmasts. He would have run his steamer away from a floating Gainsborough hat, and, in fact, he ran her away from less on some occasions. The officers, wishing to arrive with the other transports, sometimes remonstrated, and to them he talked of his owners. Every officer in the convoying warships loathed him, for in case any hostile vessel should appear they did not see how they were going to protect this rabbit, who would probably manage during a fight to be in about a hundred places on the broad, broad sea, and all of them offensive to the navy's plan. When he was not talking of his owners he was remarking to the officers of the regiment that a steamer really was not like a valise, and that he was unable to take his ship under his arm and climb trees with it. He further said that "them naval fellows" were not near so smart as they thought they were.

From an indigo sea arose the lonely shore of Cuba. Ultimately, the fleet was near Santiago, and most of the transports were bidden to wait a minute while the leaders found out their minds. The skipper, to whom the 307th were prisoners, waited for thirty hours half way between Jamaica and Cuba. He explained that the Spanish fleet might emerge from Santiago Harbour at any time, and he did not propose to be caught. His owners —— Whereupon the colonel arose as one having nine hundred men at his back, and he passed up to the bridge and he spake with the captain. He explained indirectly that each individual of his nine hundred men had decided to be the first American soldier to land for this campaign, and that in order to accomplish the marvel it was necessary for the transport to be nearer than forty-five miles from the Cuban coast. If the skipper would only land the regiment the colonel would consent to his then taking his interesting old ship and going to h —— with it. And the skipper spake with the colonel. He pointed out that as far as he officially was concerned, the United States Government did not exist. He was responsible solely to his owners. The colonel pondered these sayings. He perceived that the skipper meant that he was running his ship as he deemed best, in consideration of the capital invested by his owners, and that he was not at all concerned with the feelings of a certain American military expedition to Cuba. He was a free son of the sea-he was a sovereign citizen of the republic of the waves. He was like Lige.

However, the skipper ultimately incurred the danger of taking his ship under the terrible guns of the *New York, Iowa, Oregon, Massachusetts, Indiana, Brooklyn, Texas* and a score of cruisers and gunboats. It was a brave act for the captain of a United States transport, and he was visibly nervous until he could again get to sea, where he offered praises that the accursed 307th was no longer sitting on his head. For almost a week he rambled at his cheerful will over the adjacent high seas, having in his hold a great quantity of military stores as successfully secreted as if they had been buried in a copper box in the cornerstone of a new public building in Boston. He had had his master's certificate for twenty-one years, and those people couldn't tell a marlin-spike from the starboard side of the ship.

The 307th was landed in Cuba, but to their disgust they found that about ten thousand regulars were ahead of them. They got immediate orders to move out from the base on the road to Santiago. Gates was interested to note that the only delay was caused by the fact that many men of the other battalions strayed off sight-seeing. In time the long regiment wound slowly among hills that shut them from sight of the sea.

For the men to admire, there were palm-trees, little brown huts, passive, uninterested Cuban soldiers much worn from carrying American rations inside and outside. The weather was not oppressively warm, and the journey was said to be only about seven miles. There were no rumours save that there had been one short fight and the army had advanced to within sight of Santiago. Having a peculiar faculty for the derision of the romantic, the 307th began to laugh. Actually there was not *anything* in the world which turned out to be as books describe it. Here they had landed from the transport expecting to be at once flung into line of battle and sent on some kind of furious charge, and now they were trudging along a quiet trail lined with somnolent trees and grass. The whole business so far struck them as being a highly tedious burlesque.

After a time they came to where the camps of regular regiments marked the sides of the road-little villages of tents no higher than a man's waist. The colonel found his brigade commander and the 307th was sent off into a field of long grass, where the men grew suddenly solemn with the importance of getting their supper.

In the early evening some regulars told one of Gates's companies that at daybreak this division would move to an attack upon something.

"How d'you know?" said the company, deeply awed.

"Heard it."

"Well, what are we to attack?"

"Dunno."

The 307th was not at all afraid, but each man began to imagine the morrow. The regulars seemed to have as much interest in the morrow as they did in the last Christmas. It was none of their affair, apparently.

"Look here," said Lige Wigram, to a man in the 17th Regular Infantry, "whereabouts are we goin' ter-morrow an' who do we run up against-do ye know?"

The 17th soldier replied, truculently: "If I ketch th' —— —— —— what stole my ter-baccer, I'll whirl in an' break every —— —— bone in his body."

Gates's friends in the regular regiments asked him numerous questions as to the reliability of his organisation. Would the 307th stand the racket? They were certainly not contemptuous; they simply did not seem to consider it important whether the 307th would or whether it would not.

"Well," said Gates, "they won't run the length of a tent-peg if they can gain any idea of what they're fighting; they won't bunch if they've about six acres of open ground to move in; they won't get rattled at all if they see you fellows taking it easy, and they'll fight like the devil as long as they thoroughly, completely, absolutely, satisfactorily, exhaustively understand what the business is. They're lawyers. All excepting my battalion."

Lige awakened into a world obscured by blue fog. Somebody was gently shaking him. "Git up; we're going to move." The regiment was buckling up itself. From the trail came the loud creak of a light battery moving ahead. The tones of all men were low; the faces of the officers were composed, serious. The regiment found itself moving along behind the battery before it had time to ask itself more than a hundred questions. The trail wound through a dense tall jungle, dark, heavy with dew.

The battle broke with a snap-far ahead. Presently Lige heard from the air above him a faint low note as if somebody were blowing softly in the mouth of a bottle. It was a stray bullet which had wandered a mile to tell him that war was before him. He nearly broke his neck looking upward. "Did ye hear that?" But the men were fretting to get out of this gloomy jungle. They wanted to see something. The faint rup-rup-rrrrup-rup on in the front told them that the fight had begun; death was abroad, and so the mystery of this wilderness excited them. This wilderness was portentously still and dark.

They passed the battery aligned on a hill above the trail, and they had not gone far when the gruff guns began to roar and they could hear the rocket-like swish of the flying shells. Presently everybody must have called out for the assistance of the 307th. Aides and couriers came flying back to them.

"Is this the 307th? Hurry up your men, please, Colonel. You're needed more every minute."

Oh, they were, were they? Then the regulars were not going to do *all* the fighting? The old 307th was bitterly proud or proudly bitter. They left their blanket rolls under the guard of God and pushed on, which is one of the reasons why the Cubans of that part of the country were, later, so well equipped. There began to appear fields, hot, golden-green in the sun. On some palm-dotted knolls before them they could see little lines of black dots-the American advance. A few men fell, struck down by other men who, perhaps half a mile away, were aiming at somebody else. The loss was wholly in Carmony's battalion, which immediately bunched and backed away, coming with a shock against Gates's advance company. This shock sent a tremor through all of Gates's battalion until men in the very last files cried out nervously, "Well, what in hell is up now?" There came an order to deploy and advance. An occasional hoarse yell from the regulars could be heard. The deploying made Gates's heart bleed for the colonel. The old man stood there directing the movement, straight, fearless, sombrely defiant of-everything. Carmony's four companies were like four herds. And all the time the bullets from no living man knows where kept pecking at them and pecking at them. Gates, the excellent Gates, the highly educated and strictly military Gates, grew rankly insubordinate. He knew that the regiment was suffering from nothing but the deadly range and oversweep of the modern rifle, of which many proud and confident nations know nothing save that they have killed savages with it, which is the least of all informations.

Gates rushed upon Carmony.

"— — — — it, man, if you can't get your people to deploy, for — — sake give me a chance! I'm stuck in the woods!"

Carmony gave nothing, but Gates took all he could get and his battalion deployed and advanced like men. The old colonel almost burst into tears, and he cast one quick glance of gratitude at Gates, which the younger officer wore on his heart like a secret decoration.

There was a wild scramble up hill, down dale, through thorny thickets. Death smote them with a kind of slow rhythm, leisurely taking a man now here, now there, but the cat-spit sound of the bullets was always. A large number of the men of Carmony's battalion came on with Gates. They were willing to do anything, anything. They had no real fault, unless it was that early conclusion that any brave high-minded youth was necessarily a good soldier immediately, from the beginning. In them had been born a swift feeling that the unpopular Gates knew everything, and they followed the trained soldier.

If they followed him, he certainly took them into it. As they swung heavily up one steep hill, like so many wind-blown horses, they came suddenly out into the real advance. Little blue groups of men were making frantic rushes forward and then flopping down on their bellies to fire volleys while other groups made rushes. Ahead they could see a heavy house-like fort which was inadequate to explain from whence came the myriad bullets. The remainder of the scene was landscape. Pale men, yellow men, blue men came out of this landscape quiet and sad-eyed with wounds. Often they were grimly facetious. There is nothing in the American regulars so amazing as his conduct when he is wounded-his apologetic limp, his deprecatory arm-sling, his embarrassed and ashamed shot-hole through the lungs. The men of the 307th looked at calm creatures who had divers punctures and they were made better. These men told them that it was only necessary to keep a-going. They of the 307th lay on their bellies, red, sweating and panting, and heeded the voice of the elder brother.

Gates walked back of his line, very white of face, but hard and stern past anything his men knew of him. After they had violently adjured him to lie down and he had given weak backs a cold, stiff touch, the 307th charged by rushes. The hatless colonel made frenzied speech, but the man of the time was Gates. The men seemed to feel that this was his business. Some of the regular officers said afterward that the advance of the 307th was very respectable indeed. They were rather surprised, they said. At least five of the crack regiments of the regular army were in this division, and the 307th could win no more than a feeling of kindly appreciation.

Yes, it was very good, very good indeed, but did you notice what was being done at the same moment by the 12th, the 17th, the 7th, the 8th, the 25th, the — —

Gates felt that his charge was being a success. He was carrying out a successful function. Two captains fell bang on the grass and a lieutenant slumped quietly down with a death wound. Many men sprawled suddenly. Gates was keeping his men almost even with the regulars, who were charging on his flanks. Suddenly he thought that he must have come close to the fort and that a Spaniard had tumbled a great stone block down upon his leg. Twelve hands reached out to help him, but he cried:

"No —d — — your souls-go on-go on!"

He closed his eyes for a moment, and it really was only for a moment. When he opened them he found himself alone with Lige Wigram, who lay on the ground near him.

"Maje," said Lige, "yer a good man. I've been a-follerin' ye all day an' I want to say yer a good man."

The major turned a coldly scornful eye upon the private.

"Where are you wounded? Can you walk? Well, if you can, go to the rear and leave me alone. I'm bleeding to death, and you bother me."

Lige, despite the pain in his wounded shoulder, grew indignant.

"Well," he mumbled, "you and me have been on th' outs fer a long time, an' I only wanted to tell ye that what I seen of ye t'day has made me feel mighty different."

"Go to the rear-if you can walk," said the major.

"Now, Maje, look here. A little thing like that — —"

"Go to the rear."

Lige gulped with sobs.

"Maje, I know I didn't understand ye at first, but ruther'n let a little thing like that come between us, I'd —I'd — —"

"Go to the rear."

In this reiteration Lige discovered a resemblance to that first old offensive phrase, "Come to attention and salute." He pondered over the resemblance and he saw that nothing had changed. The man bleeding to death was the same man to whom he had once paid a friendly visit with unfriendly results. He thought now that he perceived a certain hopeless gulf, a gulf which is real or unreal, according to circumstances. Sometimes all men are equal; occasionally they are not. If Gates had ever criticised Lige's manipulation of a hay fork on the farm at home, Lige would have furiously disdained his hate or blame. He saw now that he must not openly approve the major's conduct in war. The major's pride was in his business, and his, Lige's congratulations, were beyond all enduring.

The place where they were lying suddenly fell under a new heavy rain of bullets. They sputtered about the men, making the noise of large grasshoppers.

"Major!" cried Lige. "Major Gates! It won't do for ye to be left here, sir. Ye'll be killed."

"But you can't help it, lad. You take care of yourself."

"I'm damned if I do," said the private, vehemently. "If I can't git *you* out, I'll stay and wait."

The officer gazed at his man with that same icy, contemptuous gaze.

"I'm —I'm a dead man anyhow. You go to the rear, do you hear?"

"No."

The dying major drew his revolver, cocked it and aimed it unsteadily at Lige's head.

"Will you obey orders?"

"No."

"One?"

"No."

"Two?"

"No."

Gates weakly dropped his revolver.

"Go to the devil, then. You're no soldier, but —— " He tried to add something, "But —— "
He heaved a long moan. "But-you-you-oh, I'm so-o-o tired."

V

After the battle, three correspondents happened to meet on the trail. They were hot, dusty, weary, hungry and thirsty, and they repaired to the shade of a mango tree and sprawled luxuriously. Among them they mustered twoscore friends who on that day had gone to the far shore of the hereafter, but their senses were no longer resonant. Shackles was babbling plaintively about mint-juleps, and the others were bidding him to have done.

"By-the-way," said one, at last, "it's too bad about poor old Gates of the 307th. He bled to death. His men were crazy. They were blubbering and cursing around there like wild people. It seems that when they got back there to look for him they found him just about gone, and another wounded man was trying to stop the flow with his hat! His hat, mind you. Poor old Gatesie!"

"Oh, no, Shackles!" said the third man of the party. "Oh, no, you're wrong. The best mint-juleps in the world are made right in New York, Philadelphia or Boston. That Kentucky idea is only a tradition."

A wounded man approached them. He had been shot through the shoulder and his shirt had been diagonally cut away, leaving much bare skin. Over the bullet's point of entry there was a kind of a white spider, shaped from pieces of adhesive plaster. Over the point of departure there was a bloody bulb of cotton strapped to the flesh by other pieces of adhesive plaster. His eyes were dreamy, wistful, sad. "Say, gents, have any of ye got a bottle?" he asked.

A correspondent raised himself suddenly and looked with bright eyes at the soldier.

"Well, you have got a nerve," he said grinning. "Have we got a bottle, eh! Who in h — — do you think we are? If we had a bottle of good licker, do you suppose we could let the whole army drink out of it? You have too much faith in the generosity of men, my friend!"

The soldier stared, ox-like, and finally said, "Huh?"

"I say," continued the correspondent, somewhat more loudly, "that if we had had a bottle we would have probably finished it ourselves by this time."

"But," said the other, dazed, "I *meant* an empty bottle. I didn't mean no *full* bottle."

The correspondent was humorously irascible.

"An empty bottle! You must be crazy! Who ever heard of a man looking for an empty bottle? It isn't sense! I've seen a million men looking for full bottles, but you're the first man I ever saw who insisted on the bottle's being empty. What in the world do you want it for?"

"Well, ye see, mister," explained Lige, slowly, "our major he was killed this mornin' an' we're jes' goin' to bury him, an' I thought I'd jest take a look 'round an' see if I couldn't borry an empty bottle, an' then I'd take an' write his name an' reg'ment on a paper an' put it in th' bottle an' bury it with him, so's when they come fer to dig him up sometime an' take him home, there sure wouldn't be no mistake."

"Oh!"

Marines Signalling Under Fire At Guantanamo

They were four Guantanamo marines, officially known for the time as signalmen, and it was their duty to lie in the trenches of Camp McCalla, that faced the water, and, by day, signal the *Marblehead* with a flag and, by night, signal the *Marblehead* with lanterns. It was my good fortune-at that time I considered it my bad fortune, indeed-to be with them on two of the nights when a wild storm of fighting was pealing about the hill; and, of all the actions of the war, none were so hard on the nerves, none strained courage so near the panic point, as those swift nights in Camp McCalla. With a thousand rifles rattling; with the field-guns booming in your ears; with the diabolic Colt automatics clacking; with the roar of the *Marblehead* coming from the bay, and, last, with Mauser bullets sneering always in the air a few inches over one's head, and with this enduring from dusk to dawn, it is extremely doubtful if any one who was there will be able to forget it easily. The noise; the impenetrable darkness; the knowledge from the sound of the bullets that the enemy was on three sides of the camp; the infrequent bloody stumbling and death of some man with whom, perhaps, one had messed two hours previous; the weariness of the body, and the more terrible weariness of the mind, at the endlessness of the thing, made it wonderful that at least some of the men did not come out of it with their nerves hopelessly in shreds.

But, as this interesting ceremony proceeded in the darkness, it was necessary for the signal squad to coolly take and send messages. Captain McCalla always participated in the defence of the camp by raking the woods on two of its sides with the guns of the *Marblehead*. Moreover, he was the senior officer present, and he wanted to know what was happening. All night long the crews of the ships in the bay would stare sleeplessly into the blackness toward the roaring hill.

The signal squad had an old cracker-box placed on top of the trench. When not signalling they hid the lanterns in this-box; but as soon as an order to send a message was received, it became necessary for one of the men to stand up and expose the lights. And then-oh, my eye-how the guerillas hidden in the gulf of night would turn loose at those yellow gleams!

Signalling in this way is done by letting one lantern remain stationary-on top of the cracker-box, in this case-and moving the other over to the left and right and so on in the regular gestures of the wig-wagging code. It is a very simple system of night communication, but one can see that it presents rare possibilities when used in front of an enemy who, a few hundred yards away, is overjoyed at sighting so definite a mark.

How, in the name of wonders, those four men at Camp McCalla were not riddled from head to foot and sent home more as repositories of Spanish ammunition than as marines is beyond all comprehension. To make a confession-when one of these men stood up to wave his lantern, I, lying in the trench, invariably rolled a little to the right or left, in order that, when he was shot, he would not fall on me. But the squad came off scathless, despite the best efforts of the most formidable corps in the Spanish army-the Escuadra de Guantanamo. That it was the most formidable corps in the Spanish army of occupation has been told me by many Spanish officers and also by General Menocal and other insurgent officers. General Menocal was Garcia's chief-of-staff when the latter was operating busily in Santiago province. The regiment was composed solely of *practicos*, or guides, who knew every shrub and tree on the ground over which they moved.

Whenever the adjutant, Lieutenant Draper, came plunging along through the darkness with an order-such as: "Ask the *Marblehead* to please shell the woods to the left" —my heart would come into my mouth, for I knew then that one of my pals was going to stand up behind the lanterns and have all Spain shoot at him.

The answer was always upon the instant:

"Yes, sir." Then the bullets began to snap, snap, snap, at his head while all the woods began to crackle like burning straw. I could lie near and watch the face of the signalman, illumed as it was by the yellow shine of lantern light, and the absence of excitement, fright, or any emotion at all on his countenance, was something to astonish all theories out of one's mind. The face was in every instance merely that of a man intent upon his business, the business of wig-wagging into the gulf of night where a light on the *Marblehead* was seen to move slowly.

These times on the hill resembled, in some days, those terrible scenes on the stage-scenes of intense gloom, blinding lightning, with a cloaked devil or assassin or other appropriate character muttering deeply amid the awful roll of the thunder-drums. It was theatric beyond words: one felt like a leaf in this booming chaos, this prolonged tragedy of the night. Amid it all one could see from time to time the yellow light on the face of a preoccupied signalman.

Possibly no man who was there ever before understood the true eloquence of the breaking of the day. We would lie staring into the east, fairly ravenous for the dawn. Utterly worn to rags, with our nerves standing on end like so many bristles, we lay and watched the east-the unspeakably obdurate and slow east. It was a wonder that the eyes of some of us did not turn to glass balls from the fixity of our gaze.

Then there would come into the sky a patch of faint blue light. It was like a piece of moonshine. Some would say it was the beginning of daybreak; others would declare it was nothing of the kind. Men would get very disgusted with each other in these low-toned arguments held in the trenches. For my part, this development in the eastern sky destroyed many of my ideas and theories concerning the dawning of the day; but then I had never before had occasion to give it such solemn attention.

This patch widened and whitened in about the speed of a man's accomplishment if he should be in the way of painting Madison Square Garden with a camel's hair brush. The guerillas always set out to whoop it up about this time, because they knew the occasion was approaching when it would be expedient for them to elope. I, at least, always grew furious with this wretched sunrise. I thought I could have walked around the world in the time required for the old thing to get up above the horizon.

One midnight, when an important message was to be sent to the *Marblehead*, Colonel Huntington came himself to the signal place with Adjutant Draper and Captain McCauley, the quartermaster. When the man stood up to signal, the colonel stood beside him. At sight of the lights, the Spaniards performed as usual. They drove enough bullets into that immediate vicinity to kill all the marines in the corps.

Lieutenant Draper was agitated for his chief. "Colonel, won't you step down, sir?"

"Why, I guess not," said the grey old veteran in his slow, sad, always-gentle way. "I am in no more danger than the man."

"But, sir — —" began the adjutant.

"Oh, it's all right, Draper."

So the colonel and the private stood side to side and took the heavy fire without either moving a muscle.

Day was always obliged to come at last, punctuated by a final exchange of scattering shots. And the light shone on the marines, the dumb guns, the flag. Grimy yellow face looked into grimy yellow face, and grinned with weary satisfaction. Coffee!

Usually it was impossible for many of the men to sleep at once. It always took me, for instance, some hours to get my nerves combed down. But then it was great joy to lie in the trench with the four signalmen, and understand thoroughly that that night was fully over at last, and that, although the future might have in store other bad nights, that one could never escape from the prison-house which we call the past.

At the wild little fight at Cusco there were some splendid exhibitions of wig-wagging under fire. Action began when an advanced detachment of marines under Lieutenant Lucas with the Cuban guides had reached the summit of a ridge overlooking a small valley where there was a house, a well, and a thicket of some kind of shrub with great broad, oily leaves. This thicket, which was perhaps an acre in extent, contained the guerillas. The valley was open to the sea. The distance from the top of the ridge to the thicket was barely two hundred yards.

The *Dolphin* had sailed up the coast in line with the marine advance, ready with her guns to assist in any action. Captain Elliott, who commanded the two hundred marines in this fight, suddenly called out for a signalman. He wanted a man to tell the *Dolphin* to open fire on the house and the thicket. It was a blazing, bitter hot day on top of the ridge with its shrivelled chaparral and its straight, tall cactus plants. The sky was bare and blue, and hurt like brass. In two minutes the prostrate marines were red and sweating like so many hull-buried stokers in the tropics.

Captain Elliott called out:

"Where's a signalman? Who's a signalman here?"

A red-headed "mick" —I think his name was Clancy-at any rate, it will do to call him Clancy-twisted his head from where he lay on his stomach pumping his Lee, and, saluting, said that he was a signalman.

There was no regulation flag with the expedition, so Clancy was obliged to tie his blue polka-dot neckerchief on the end of his rifle. It did not make a very good flag. At first Clancy moved a ways down the safe side of the ridge and wigwagged there very busily. But what with the flag being so poor for the purpose, and the background of ridge being so dark, those on the *Dolphin* did not see it. So Clancy had to return to the top of the ridge and outline himself and his flag against the sky.

The usual thing happened. As soon as the Spaniards caught sight of this silhouette, they let go like mad at it. To make things more comfortable for Clancy, the situation demanded that he face the sea and turn his back to the Spanish bullets. This was a hard game, mark you-to stand with the small of your back to volley firing. Clancy thought so. Everybody thought so. We all cleared out of his neighbourhood. If he wanted sole possession of any particular spot on that hill, he could have it for all we would interfere with him.

It cannot be denied that Clancy was in a hurry. I watched him. He was so occupied with the bullets that snarled close to his ears that he was obliged to repeat the letters of his message softly to himself. It seemed an intolerable time before the *Dolphin* answered the little signal. Meanwhile, we gazed at him, marvelling every second that he had not yet pitched headlong. He swore at times.

Finally the *Dolphin* replied to his frantic gesticulation, and he delivered his message. As his part of the transaction was quite finished-whoop! —he dropped like a brick into the firing line and began to shoot; began to get "hunky" with all those people who had been plugging at him. The blue polka-dot neckerchief still fluttered from the barrel of his rifle. I am quite certain that he let it remain there until the end of the fight.

The shells of the *Dolphin* began to plough up the thicket, kicking the bushes, stones, and soil into the air as if somebody was blasting there.

Meanwhile, this force of two hundred marines and fifty Cubans and the force of-probably-six companies of Spanish guerillas were making such an awful din that the distant Camp McCalla was all alive with excitement. Colonel Huntington sent out strong parties to critical points on the road to facilitate, if necessary, a safe retreat, and also sent forty men under Lieutenant Magill to come up on the left flank of the two companies in action under Captain Elliott. Lieutenant Magill and his men had crowned a hill which covered entirely the flank of the fighting companies, but when the *Dolphin* opened fire, it happened that Magill was in the line of the shots. It became necessary to stop the *Dolphin* at once. Captain Elliott was not near Clancy at this time, and he called hurriedly for another signalman.

Sergeant Quick arose, and announced that he was a signalman. He produced from somewhere a blue polka-dot neckerchief as large as a quilt. He tied it on a long, crooked stick. Then he went to the top of the ridge, and turning his back to the Spanish fire, began to signal to the *Dolphin*. Again we gave a man sole possession of a particular part of the ridge. We didn't want it. He could have it and welcome. If the young sergeant had had the smallpox, the cholera, and the yellow fever, we could not have slid out with more celerity.

As men have said often, it seemed as if there was in this war a God of Battles who held His mighty hand before the Americans. As I looked at Sergeant Quick wig-wagging there against the sky, I would not have given a tin tobacco-tag for his life. Escape for him seemed impossible.

It seemed absurd to hope that he would not be hit; I only hoped that he would be hit just a little, in the arm, the shoulder, or the leg.

I watched his face, and it was as grave and serene as that of a man writing in his own library. He was the very embodiment of tranquillity in occupation. He stood there amid the animal-like babble of the Cubans, the crack of rifles, and the whistling snarl of the bullets, and wig-wagged whatever he had to wig-wag without heeding anything but his business. There was not a single trace of nervousness or haste.

To say the least, a fight at close range is absorbing as a spectacle. No man wants to take his eyes from it until that time comes when he makes up his mind to run away. To deliberately stand up and turn your back to a battle is in itself hard work. To deliberately stand up and turn your back to a battle and hear immediate evidences of the boundless enthusiasm with which a large company of the enemy shoot at you from an adjacent thicket is, to my mind at least, a very great feat. One need not dwell upon the detail of keeping the mind carefully upon a slow spelling of an important code message.

I saw Quick betray only one sign of emotion. As he swung his clumsy flag to and fro, an end of it once caught on a cactus pillar, and he looked sharply over his shoulder to see what had it. He gave the flag an impatient jerk. He looked annoyed.

This Majestic Lie

In the twilight, a great crowd was streaming up the Prado in Havana. The people had been down to the shore to laugh and twiddle their fingers at the American blockading fleet-mere colourless shapes on the edge of the sea. Gorgeous challenges had been issued to the far-away ships by little children and women while the men laughed. Havana was happy, for it was known that the illustrious sailor Don Patricio de Montojo had with his fleet met the decaying ships of one Dewey and smitten them into stuffing for a baby's pillow. Of course the American sailors were drunk at the time, but the American sailors were always drunk. Newsboys galloped among the crowd crying *La Lucha* and *La Marina*. The papers said: "This is as we foretold. How could it be otherwise when the cowardly Yankees met our brave sailors?" But the tongues of the exuberant people ran more at large. One man said in a loud voice: "How unfortunate it is that we still have to buy meat in Havana when so much pork is floating in Manila Bay!" Amid the consequent laughter, another man retorted: "Oh, never mind! That pork in Manila is rotten. It always was rotten." Still another man said: "But, little friend, it would make good manure for our fields if only we had it." And still another man said: "Ah, wait until our soldiers get with the wives of the Americans and there will be many little Yankees to serve hot on our tables. The men of the *Maine* simply made our appetites good. Never mind the pork in Manila. There will be plenty." Women laughed; children laughed because their mothers laughed; everybody laughed. And —a word with you-these people were cackling and chuckling and insulting their own dead, their own dead men of Spain, for if the poor green corpses floated then in Manila Bay they were not American corpses.

The newsboys came charging with an extra. The inhabitants of Philadelphia had fled to the forests because of a Spanish bombardment and also Boston was besieged by the Apaches who had totally invested the town. The Apache artillery had proven singularly effective and an American garrison had been unable to face it. In Chicago millionaires were giving away their palaces for two or three loaves of bread. These despatches were from Madrid and every word was truth, but they added little to the enthusiasm because the crowd-God help mankind-was greatly occupied with visions of Yankee pork floating in Manila Bay. This will be thought to be embittered writing. Very well; the writer admits its untruthfulness in one particular. It is untruthful in that it fails to reproduce one-hundredth part of the grossness and indecency of popular expression in Havana up to the time when the people knew they were beaten.

There were no lights on the Prado or in other streets because of a military order. In the slow-moving crowd, there was a young man and an old woman. Suddenly the young man laughed a strange metallic laugh and spoke in English, not cautiously. "That's damned hard to listen to."

The woman spoke quickly. "Hush, you little idiot. Do you want to be walkin' across that grass-plot in Cabanas with your arms tied behind you?" Then she murmured sadly: "Johnnie, I wonder if that's true-what they say about Manila?"

"I don't know," said Johnnie, "but I think they're lying."

As they crossed the Plaza, they could see that the Café Tacon was crowded with Spanish officers in blue and white pajama uniforms. Wine and brandy was being wildly consumed in honour of the victory at Manila. "Let's hear what they say," said Johnnie to his companion, and they moved across the street and in under the *portales*. The owner of the Café Tacon was standing on a table making a speech amid cheers. He was advocating the crucifixion of such Americans as fell into Spanish hands and-it was all very sweet and white and tender, but above all, it was chivalrous, because it is well known that the Spaniards are a chivalrous people. It has been remarked both by the English newspapers and by the bulls that are bred for the red death. And secretly the corpses in Manila Bay mocked this jubilee; the mocking, mocking corpses in Manila Bay.

To be blunt, Johnnie was an American spy. Once he had been the manager of a sugar plantation in Pinar del Rio, and during the insurrection it had been his distinguished function to pay tribute of money, food and forage alike to Spanish columns and insurgent bands. He was performing this straddle with benefit to his crops and with mildew to his conscience when Spain and the United States agreed to skirmish, both in the name of honour. It then became a military necessity that he should change his base. Whatever of the province that was still alive was sorry to see him go for he had been a very dexterous man and food and wine had been in his house even when a man with a mango could gain the envy of an entire Spanish battalion. Without doubt he had been a mere trimmer, but it was because of his crop and he always wrote the word thus: C R O P. In those days a man of peace and commerce was in a position parallel to the watchmaker who essayed a task in the midst of a drunken brawl with oaths, bottles and bullets flying about his intent bowed head. So many of them-or all of them-were trimmers, and to any armed force they fervently said: "God assist you." And behold, the trimmers dwelt safely in a tumultuous land and without effort save that their little machines for trimming ran night and day. So many a plantation became covered with a maze of lies as if thick-webbing spiders had run from stalk to stalk in the cane. So sometimes a planter incurred an equal hatred from both sides and when in trouble there was no camp to which he could flee save, straight in air, the camp of the heavenly host.

If Johnnie had not had a crop, he would have been plainly on the side of the insurgents, but his crop staked him down to the soil at a point where the Spaniards could always be sure of finding him-him or his crop-it is the same thing. But when war came between Spain and the United States he could no longer be the cleverest trimmer in Pinar del Rio. And he retreated upon Key West losing much of his baggage train, not because of panic but because of wisdom. In Key West, he was no longer the manager of a big Cuban plantation; he was a little tan-faced refugee without much money. Mainly he listened; there was nought else to do. In the first place he was a young man of extremely slow speech and in the Key West Hotel tongues ran like pin-wheels. If he had projected his methodic way of thought and speech upon this hurricane, he would have been as effective as the man who tries to smoke against the gale. This truth did not impress him. Really, he was impressed with the fact that although he knew much of Cuba, he could not talk so rapidly and wisely of it as many war-correspondents who had not yet seen the island. Usually he brooded in silence over a bottle of beer and the loss of his crop. He received no sympathy, although there was a plentitude of tender souls. War's first step is to make expectation so high that all present things are fogged and darkened in a tense wonder of the future. None cared about the collapse of Johnnie's plantation when all were thinking of the probable collapse of cities and fleets.

In the meantime, battle-ships, monitors, cruisers, gunboats and torpedo craft arrived, departed, arrived, departed. Rumours sang about the ears of warships hurriedly coaling. Rumours sang about the ears of warships leisurely coming to anchor. This happened and that happened and if the news arrived at Key West as a mouse, it was often enough cabled north as an elephant. The correspondents at Key West were perfectly capable of adjusting their perspective, but many of the editors in the United States were like deaf men at whom one has to roar. A few quiet words of information was not enough for them; one had to bawl into their ears a whirlwind tale of heroism, blood, death, victory-or defeat-at any rate, a tragedy. The papers should have sent playwrights to the first part of the war. Play-wrights are allowed to lower the curtain from time to time and say to the crowd: "Mark, ye, now! Three or four months are supposed to elapse. But the poor devils at Key West were obliged to keep the curtain up all the time." "This isn't a continuous performance." "Yes, it is; it's *got* to be a continuous performance. The welfare of the paper demands it. The people want news." Very well: continuous performance. It is strange how men of sense can go aslant at the bidding of other men of sense and combine to contribute to a general mess of exaggeration and bombast. But we did; and in the midst of the furor I remember the still figure of Johnnie, the planter, the ex-trimmer. He looked dazed.

This was in May.

We all liked him. From time to time some of us heard in his words the vibrant of a thoughtful experience. But it could not be well heard; it was only like the sound of a bell from under the floor. We were too busy with our own clatter. He was taciturn and competent while we solved the war in a babble of tongues. Soon we went about our peaceful paths saying ironically one to another: "War is hell." Meanwhile, managing editors fought us tooth and nail and we all were sent boxes of medals inscribed: "Incompetency." We became furious with ourselves. Why couldn't we send hair-raising despatches? Why couldn't we inflame the wires? All this we did. If a first-class armoured cruiser which had once been a tow-boat fired a six-pounder shot from her forward thirteen-inch gun turret, the world heard of it, you bet. We were not idle men. We had come to report the war and we did it. Our good names and our salaries depended upon it and we were urged by our managing-editors to remember that the American people were a collection of super-nervous idiots who would immediately have convulsions if we did not throw them some news-any news. It was not true, at all. The American people were anxious for things decisive to happen; they were not anxious to be lulled to satisfaction with a drug. But we lulled them. We told them this and we told them that, and I warrant you our screaming sounded like the noise of a lot of sea-birds settling for the night among the black crags.

In the meantime, Johnnie stared and meditated. In his unhurried, unstartled manner he was singularly like another man who was flying the pennant as commander-in-chief of the North Atlantic Squadron. Johnnie was a refugee; the admiral was an admiral. And yet they were much akin, these two. Their brother was the Strategy Board-the only capable political institution of the war. At Key West the naval officers spoke of their business and were devoted to it and were bound to succeed in it, but when the flag-ship was in port the only two people who were independent and sane were the admiral and Johnnie. The rest of us were lulling the public with drugs.

There was much discussion of the new batteries at Havana. Johnnie was a typical American. In Europe a typical American is a man with a hard eye, chin-whiskers and a habit of speaking through his nose. Johnnie was a young man of great energy, ready to accomplish a colossal thing for the basic reason that he was ignorant of its magnitude. In fact he attacked all obstacles in life in a spirit of contempt, seeing them smaller than they were until he had actually surmounted them-when he was likely to be immensely pleased with himself. Somewhere in him there was a sentimental tenderness, but it was like a light seen afar at night; it came, went, appeared again in a new place, flickered, flared, went out, left you in a void and angry. And if his sentimental tenderness was a light, the darkness in which it puzzled you was his irony of soul. This irony was directed first at himself; then at you; then at the nation and the flag; then at God. It was a midnight in which you searched for the little elusive, ashamed spark of tender sentiment. Sometimes, you thought this was all pretext, the manner and the way of fear of the wit of others; sometimes you thought he was a hardened savage; usually you did not think but waited in the cheerful certainty that in time the little flare of light would appear in the gloom.

Johnnie decided that he would go and spy upon the fortifications of Havana. If any one wished to know of those batteries it was the admiral of the squadron, but the admiral of the squadron knew much. I feel sure that he knew the size and position of every gun. To be sure, new guns might be mounted at any time, but they would not be big guns, and doubtless he lacked in his cabin less information than would be worth a man's life. Still, Johnnie decided to be a spy. He would go and look. We of the newspapers pinned him fast to the tail of our kite and he was taken to see the admiral. I judge that the admiral did not display much interest in the plan. But at any rate it seems that he touched Johnnie smartly enough with a brush to make him, officially, a spy. Then Johnnie bowed and left the cabin. There was no other machinery. If Johnnie was to end his life and leave a little book about it, no one cared-least of all, Johnnie and the admiral. When he came aboard the tug, he displayed his usual stalwart and rather selfish zest for fried eggs. It was all some kind of an ordinary matter. It was done every day. It was the business of packing pork, sewing shoes, binding hay. It was commonplace. No one could adjust it, get it in proportion, until-afterwards. On a dark night, they heaved him into a small boat and rowed him to the beach.

And one day he appeared at the door of a little lodging-house in Havana kept by Martha Clancy, born in Ireland, bred in New York, fifteen years married to a Spanish captain, and now a widow, keeping Cuban lodgers who had no money with which to pay her. She opened the door only a little way and looked down over her spectacles at him.

"Good-mornin' Martha," he said.

She looked a moment in silence. Then she made an indescribable gesture of weariness. "Come in," she said. He stepped inside. "And in God's name couldn't you keep your neck out of this rope? And so you had to come here, did you-to Havana? Upon my soul, Johnnie, my son, you are the biggest fool on two legs."

He moved past her into the court-yard and took his old chair at the table-between the winding stairway and the door-near the orange tree. "Why am I?" he demanded stoutly. She made no reply until she had taken seat in her rocking-chair and puffed several times upon a cigarette. Then through the smoke she said meditatively: "Everybody knows ye are a damned little mambi." Sometimes she spoke with an Irish accent.

He laughed. "I'm no more of a mambi than *you* are, anyhow."

"I'm no mambi. But your name is poison to half the Spaniards in Havana. That you know. And if you were once safe in Cayo Hueso, 'tis nobody but a born fool who would come blunderin' into Havana again. Have ye had your dinner?"

"What have you got?" he asked before committing himself.

She arose and spoke without confidence as she moved toward the cupboard. "There's some codfish salad."

"*What?*" said he.

"Codfish salad."

"*Codfish what?*"

"Codfish salad. Ain't it good enough for ye? Maybe this is Delmonico's —no? Maybe ye never heard that the Yankees have us blockaded, hey? Maybe ye think food can be picked in the streets here now, hey? I'll tell ye one thing, my son, if you stay here long you'll see the want of it and so you had best not throw it over your shoulder."

The spy settled determinedly in his chair and delivered himself his final decision. "That may all be true, but I'm *damned* if I eat codfish salad."

Old Martha was a picture of quaint despair. "You'll not?"

"No!"

"Then," she sighed piously, "may the Lord have mercy on ye, Johnnie, for you'll never do here. 'Tis not the time for you. You're due after the blockade. Will you do me the favour of translating why you won't eat codfish salad, you skinny little insurrecto?"

"Cod-fish salad!" he said with a deep sneer. "Who ever heard of it!"

Outside, on the jumbled pavement of the street, an occasional two-wheel cart passed with deafening thunder, making one think of the overturning of houses. Down from the pale sky over the patio came a heavy odour of Havana itself, a smell of old straw. The wild cries of vendors could be heard at intervals.

"You'll not?"

"No."

"And why not?"

"Cod-fish salad? Not by a blame sight!"

"Well-all right then. You are more of a pig-headed young imbecile than even I thought from seeing you come into Havana here where half the town knows you and the poorest Spaniard would give a gold piece to see you go into Cabanas and forget to come out. Did I tell you, my son Alfred is sick? Yes, poor little fellow, he lies up in the room you used to have. The fever. And did you see Woodham in Key West? Heaven save us, what quick time he made in getting out. I hear Figtree and Button are working in the cable office over there-no? And when is the war going to end? Are the Yankees going to try to take Havana? It will be a hard job, Johnnie? The Spaniards say it is impossible. Everybody is laughing at the Yankees. I hate to go into the street and hear them. Is General Lee going to lead the army? What's become of Springer? I see you've got a new pair of shoes."

In the evening there was a sudden loud knock at the outer door. Martha looked at Johnnie and Johnnie looked at Martha. He was still sitting in the patio, smoking. She took the lamp and set it on a table in the little parlour. This parlour connected the street-door with the patio, and so Johnnie would be protected from the sight of the people who knocked by the broad illuminated tract. Martha moved in pensive fashion upon the latch. "Who's there?" she asked casually.

"The police." There it was, an old melodramatic incident from the stage, from the romances. One could scarce believe it. It had all the dignity of a classic resurrection. "The police!" One sneers at its probability; it is too venerable. But so it happened.

"Who?" said Martha.

"The police!"

"What do you want here?"

"Open the door and we'll tell you."

Martha drew back the ordinary huge bolts of a Havana house and opened the door a trifle. "Tell me what you want and begone quickly," she said, "for my little boy is ill of the fever — —"

She could see four or five dim figures, and now one of these suddenly placed a foot well within the door so that she might not close it. "We have come for Johnnie. We must search your house."

"Johnnie? Johnnie? Who is Johnnie?" said Martha in her best manner.

The police inspector grinned with the light upon his face. "Don't you know Señor Johnnie from Pinar del Rio?" he asked.

"Before the war-yes. But now-where is he-he must be in Key West?"

"He is in your house."

"He? In my house? Do me the favour to think that I have some intelligence. Would I be likely to be harbouring a Yankee in these times? You must think I have no more head than an Orden Publico. And I'll not have you search my house, for there is no one here save my son-who is maybe dying of the fever-and the doctor. The doctor is with him because now is the crisis, and any one little thing may kill or cure my boy, and you will do me the favour to consider what may happen if I allow five or six heavy-footed policemen to go tramping all over my house. You may think — —"

"Stop it," said the chief police officer at last. He was laughing and weary and angry.

Martha checked her flow of Spanish. "There!" she thought, "I've done my best. He ought to fall in with it." But as the police entered she began on them again. "You will search the house whether I like it or no. Very well; but if anything happens to my boy? It is a nice way of conduct, anyhow-coming into the house of a widow at night and talking much about this Yankee and — —"

"For God's sake, señora, hold your tongue. We — —"

"Oh, yes, the señora can for God's sake very well hold her tongue, but that wouldn't assist you men into the street where you belong. Take care: if my sick boy suffers from this prowling! No, you'll find nothing in that wardrobe. And do you think he would be under the table? Don't overturn all that linen. Look you, when you go upstairs, tread lightly."

Leaving a man on guard at the street door and another in the patio, the chief policeman and the remainder of his men ascended to the gallery from which opened three sleeping-rooms. They were followed by Martha abjuring them to make no noise. The first room was empty; the second room was empty; as they approached the door of the third room, Martha whispered supplications. "Now, in the name of God, don't disturb my boy." The inspector motioned his men to pause and then he pushed open the door. Only one weak candle was burning in the room and its yellow light fell upon the bed whereon was stretched the figure of a little curly-headed boy in a white nightey. He was asleep, but his face was pink with fever and his lips were murmuring some half-coherent childish nonsense. At the head of the bed stood the motionless figure of a man. His back was to the door, but upon hearing a noise he held a solemn hand. There was an odour of medicine. Out on the balcony, Martha apparently was weeping.

The inspector hesitated for a moment; then he noiselessly entered the room and with his yellow cane prodded under the bed, in the cupboard and behind the window-curtains. Nothing came of it. He shrugged his shoulders and went out to the balcony. He was smiling sheepishly. Evidently he knew that he had been beaten. "Very good, Señora," he said. "You are clever; some day I shall be clever, too." He shook his finger at her. He was threatening her but he affected to be playful. "Then-beware! Beware!"

Martha replied blandly, "My late husband, El Capitan Señor Don Patricio de Castellon y Valladolid was a cavalier of Spain and if he was alive to-night he would now be cutting the ears from the heads of you and your miserable men who smell frightfully of cognac."

"Por Dios!" muttered the inspector as followed by his band he made his way down the spiral staircase. "It is a tongue! One vast tongue!" At the street-door they made ironical bows; they departed; they were angry men.

Johnnie came down when he heard Martha bolting the door behind the police. She brought back the lamp to the table in the patio and stood beside it, thinking. Johnnie dropped into his old chair. The expression on the spy's face was curious; it pictured glee, anxiety, self-complacency; above all it pictured self-complacency. Martha said nothing; she was still by the lamp, musing.

The long silence was suddenly broken by a tremendous guffaw from Johnnie. "Did you ever see sich a lot of fools!" He leaned his head far back and roared victorious merriment.

Martha was almost dancing in her apprehension. "Hush! Be quiet, you little demon! Hush! Do me the favour to allow them to get to the corner before you bellow like a walrus. Be quiet."

The spy ceased his laughter and spoke in indignation. "Why?" he demanded. "Ain't I got a right to laugh?"

"Not with a noise like a cow fallin' into a cucumber-frame," she answered sharply. "Do me the favour — —" Then she seemed overwhelmed with a sense of the general hopelessness of Johnnie's character. She began to wag her head. "Oh, but you are the boy for gettin' yourself into the tiger's cage without even so much as the thought of a pocket-knife in your thick head. You would be a genius of the first water if you only had a little sense. And now you're here, what are you going to do?"

He grinned at her. "I'm goin' to hold an inspection of the land and sea defences of the city of Havana."

Martha's spectacles dropped low on her nose and, looking over the rims of them in grave meditation, she said: "If you can't put up with codfish salad you had better make short work of your inspection of the land and sea defences of the city of Havana. You are likely to starve in the meantime. A man who is particular about his food has come to the wrong town if he is in Havana now."

"No, but — —" asked Johnnie seriously. "Haven't you any bread?"

"*Bread!*"

"Well, coffee then? Coffee alone will do."

"*Coffee!*"

Johnnie arose deliberately and took his hat. Martha eyed him. "And where do you think you are goin'?" she asked cuttingly.

Still deliberate, Johnnie moved in the direction of the street-door. "I'm goin' where I can get something to eat."

Martha sank into a chair with a moan which was a finished opinion-almost a definition-of Johnnie's behaviour in life. "And where will you go?" she asked faintly.

"Oh, I don't know," he rejoined. "Some café. Guess I'll go to the Café Aguacate. They feed you well there. I remember — —"

"*You* remember? *They* remember! They know you as well as if you were the sign over the door."

"Oh, they won't give me away," said Johnnie with stalwart confidence.

"Gi-give you away? Give you a-way?" stammered Martha.

The spy made no answer but went to the door, unbarred it and passed into the street. Martha caught her breath and ran after him and came face to face with him as he turned to shut the door. "Johnnie, if ye come back, bring a loaf of bread. I'm dyin' for one good honest bite in a slice of bread."

She heard his peculiar derisive laugh as she bolted the door. She returned to her chair in the patio. "Well, there," she said with affection, admiration and contempt. "There he goes! The most hard-headed little ignoramus in twenty nations! What does he care? Nothin'! And why is it? Pure bred-in-the-bone ignorance. Just because he can't stand codfish salad he goes out to a café! A café where they know him as if they had made him!... Well.... I won't see him again, probably.... But if he comes back, I hope he brings some bread. I'm near dead for it."

Johnnie strolled carelessly through dark narrow streets. Near every corner were two Orden Publicos —a kind of soldier-police —quiet in the shadow of some doorway, their Remingtons ready, their eyes shining. Johnnie walked past as if he owned them, and their eyes followed him with a sort of a lazy mechanical suspicion which was militant in none of its moods.

Johnnie was suffering from a desire to be splendidly imprudent. He wanted to make the situation gasp and thrill and tremble. From time to time he tried to conceive the idea of his being caught, but to save his eyes he could not imagine it. Such an event was impossible to his peculiar breed of fatalism which could not have conceded death until he had mouldered seven years.

He arrived at the Café Aguacate and found it much changed. The thick wooden shutters were up to keep light from shining into the street. Inside, there were only a few Spanish officers. Johnnie walked to the private rooms at the rear. He found an empty one and pressed the electric button. When he had passed through the main part of the café no one had noted him. The first to recognise him was the waiter who answered the bell. This worthy man turned to stone before the presence of Johnnie.

"Buenos noche, Francisco," said the spy, enjoying himself. "I have hunger. Bring me bread, butter, eggs and coffee." There was a silence; the waiter did not move; Johnnie smiled casually at him.

The man's throat moved; then like one suddenly re-endowed with life, he bolted from the room. After a long time, he returned with the proprietor of the place. In the wicked eye of the latter there gleamed the light of a plan. He did not respond to Johnnie's genial greeting, but at once proceeded to develop his position. "Johnnie," he said, "bread is very dear in Havana. It is very dear."

"Is it?" said Johnnie looking keenly at the speaker. He understood at once that here was some sort of an attack upon him.

"Yes," answered the proprietor of the Café Aguacate slowly and softly. "It is very dear. I think to-night one small bit of bread will cost you one centene-in advance." A centene approximates five dollars in gold.

The spy's face did not change. He appeared to reflect. "And how much for the butter?" he asked at last.

The proprietor gestured. "There is no butter. Do you think we can have everything with those Yankee pigs sitting out there on their ships?"

"And how much for the coffee?" asked Johnnie musingly.

Again the two men surveyed each other during a period of silence. Then the proprietor said gently, "I think your coffee will cost you about two centenes."

"And the eggs?"

"Eggs are very dear. I think eggs would cost you about three centenes for each one."

The new looked at the old; the North Atlantic looked at the Mediterranean; the wooden nutmeg looked at the olive. Johnnie slowly took six centenes from his pocket and laid them on the table. "That's for bread, coffee, and one egg. I don't think I could eat more than one egg to-night. I'm not so hungry as I was."

The proprietor held a perpendicular finger and tapped the table with it. "Oh, señor," he said politely, "I think you would like two eggs."

Johnnie saw the finger. He understood it. "Ye-e-es," he drawled. "I would like two eggs." He placed three more centenes on the table.

"And a little thing for the waiter? I am sure his services will be excellent, invaluable."

"Ye-e-es, for the waiter." Another centene was laid on the table.

The proprietor bowed and preceded the waiter out of the room. There was a mirror on the wall and, springing to his feet, the spy thrust his face close to the honest glass. "Well, I'm damned!" he ejaculated. "Is this me or is this the Honourable D. Hayseed Whiskers of

Kansas? Who am I, anyhow? Five dollars in gold!... Say, these people are clever. They know their business, they do. Bread, coffee and two eggs and not even sure of getting it! Fifty dol — — ... Never mind; wait until the war is over. Fifty dollars gold!" He sat for a long time; nothing happened. "Eh," he said at last, "that's the game." As the front door of the café closed upon him, he heard the proprietor and one of the waiters burst into derisive laughter.

Martha was waiting for him. "And here ye are, safe back," she said with delight as she let him enter. "And did ye bring the bread? Did ye bring the bread?"

But she saw that he was raging like a lunatic. His face was red and swollen with temper; his eyes shot forth gleams. Presently he stood before her in the patio where the light fell on him. "Don't speak to me," he choked out waving his arms. "Don't speak to me! *Damn* your bread! I went to the Café Aguacate! Oh, yes, I went there! Of course, I did! And do you know what they did to me? No! Oh, they didn't do anything to me at all! Not a thing! Fifty dollars! Ten gold pieces!"

"May the saints guard us," cried Martha. "And what was that for?"

"Because they wanted them more than I did," snarled Johnnie. "Don't you see the game. I go into the Café Aguacate. The owner of the place says to himself, 'Hello! Here's that Yankee what they call Johnnie. He's got no right here in Havana. Guess I'll peach on him to the police. They'll put him in Cabanas as a spy.' Then he does a little more thinking, and finally he says, 'No; I guess I won't peach on him just this minute. First, I'll take a small flyer myself.' So in he comes and looks me right in the eye and says, 'Excuse me but it will be a centene for the bread, a centene for the coffee, and eggs are at three centenes each. Besides there will be a small matter of another gold-piece for the waiter.' I think this over. I think it over hard.... He's clever anyhow.... When this cruel war is over, I'll be after him.... I'm a nice secret agent of the United States government, I am. I come here to be too clever for all the Spanish police, and the first thing I do is get buncoed by a rotten, little thimble-rigger in a café. Oh, yes, I'm all right."

"May the saints guard us!" cried Martha again. "I'm old enough to be your mother, or maybe, your grandmother, and I've seen a lot; but it's many a year since I laid eyes on such a ign'rant and wrong-headed little, red Indian as ye are! Why didn't ye take my advice and stay here in the house with decency and comfort. But he must be all for doing everything high and mighty. The Café Aguacate, if ye please. No plain food for his highness. He turns up his nose at cod-fish sal — —"

"Thunder and lightnin', are you going to ram that thing down my throat every two minutes, are you?" And in truth she could see that one more reference to that illustrious viand would break the back of Johnnie's gentle disposition as one breaks a twig on the knee. She shifted with Celtic ease. "Did ye bring the bread?" she asked.

He gazed at her for a moment and suddenly laughed. "I forgot to mention," he informed her impressively, "that they did not take the trouble to give me either the bread, the coffee or the eggs."

"The powers!" cried Martha.

"But it's all right. I stopped at a shop." From his pockets, he brought a small loaf, some kind of German sausage and a flask of Jamaica rum. "About all I could get. And they didn't want to sell them either. They expect presently they can exchange a box of sardines for a grand piano."

"'We are not blockaded by the Yankee warships; we are blockaded by our grocers,'" said Martha, quoting the epidemic Havana saying. But she did not delay long from the little loaf. She cut a slice from it and sat eagerly munching. Johnnie seemed more interested in the Jamaica rum. He looked up from his second glass, however, because he heard a peculiar sound. The old woman was weeping. "Hey, what's this?" he demanded in distress, but with the manner of a man who thinks gruffness is the only thing that will make people feel better and cease. "What's this anyhow? What are you cryin' for?"

"It's the bread," sobbed Martha. "It's the-the br-e-a-ddd."

"Huh? What's the matter with it?"

"It's so good, so g-good." The rain of tears did not prevent her from continuing her unusual report. "Oh, it's so good! This is the first in weeks. I didn't know bread could be so l-like heaven."

"Here," said Johnnie seriously. "Take a little mouthful of this rum. It will do you good."

"No; I only want the bub-bub-bread."

"Well, take the bread, too.... There you are. Now you feel better.... By Jove, when I think of that Café Aguacate man! Fifty dollars gold! And then not to get anything either. Say, after the war, I'm going there, and I'm just going to raze that place to the ground. You see! I'll make him think he can charge ME fifteen dollars for an egg.... And then not give me the egg."

Johnnie's subsequent activity in Havana could truthfully be related in part to a certain temporary price of eggs. It is interesting to note how close that famous event got to his eye so that,
according to the law of perspective, it was as big as the Capitol of Washington, where centres
the spirit of his nation. Around him, he felt a similar and ferocious expression of life which
informed him too plainly that if he was caught, he was doomed. Neither the garrison nor the
citizens of Havana would tolerate any nonsense in regard to him if he was caught. He would
have the steel screw against his neck in short order. And what was the main thing to bear him
up against the desire to run away before his work was done? A certain temporary price of eggs!
It not only hid the Capitol at Washington; it obscured the dangers in Havana.

Something was learned of the Santa Clara battery, because one morning an old lady in black
accompanied by a young man-evidently her son-visited a house which was to rent on the height,
in rear of the battery. The portero was too lazy and sleepy to show them over the premises,
but he granted them permission to investigate for themselves. They spent most of their time
on the flat parapeted roof of the house. At length they came down and said that the place did
not suit them. The portero went to sleep again.

Johnnie was never discouraged by the thought that his operations would be of small benefit
to the admiral commanding the fleet in adjacent waters, and to the general commanding the
army which was not going to attack Havana from the land side. At that time it was all the
world's opinion that the army from Tampa would presently appear on the Cuban beach at some
convenient point to the east or west of Havana. It turned out, of course, that the condition of
the defences of Havana was of not the slightest military importance to the United States since
the city was never attacked either by land or sea. But Johnnie could not foresee this. He
continued to take his fancy risk, continued his majestic lie, with satisfaction, sometimes with
delight, and with pride. And in the psychologic distance was old Martha dancing with fear and
shouting: "Oh, Johnnie, me son, what a born fool ye are!"

Sometimes she would address him thus: "And when ye learn all this, how are ye goin' to
get out with it?" She was contemptuous.

He would reply, as serious as a Cossack in his fatalism. "Oh, I'll get out some way."

His manœuvres in the vicinity of Regla and Guanabacoa were of a brilliant character. He
haunted the sunny long grass in the manner of a jack-rabbit. Sometimes he slept under a palm,
dreaming of the American advance fighting its way along the military road to the foot of Spanish
defences. Even when awake, he often dreamed it and thought of the all-day crash and hot roar
of an assault. Without consulting Washington, he had decided that Havana should be attacked
from the south-east. An advance from the west could be contested right up to the bar of the
Hotel Inglaterra, but when the first ridge in the south-east would be taken, the whole city
with most of its defences would lie under the American siege guns. And the approach to this
position was as reasonable as is any approach toward the muzzles of magazine rifles. Johnnie
viewed the grassy fields always as a prospective battle-ground, and one can see him lying there,
filling the landscape with visions of slow-crawling black infantry columns, galloping batteries
of artillery, streaks of faint blue smoke marking the modern firing lines, clouds of dust, a vision
of ten thousand tragedies. And his ears heard the noises.

But he was no idle shepherd boy with a head haunted by sombre and glorious fancies. On
the contrary, he was much occupied with practical matters. Some months after the close of the
war, he asked me: "Were you ever fired at from very near?" I explained some experiences which
I had stupidly esteemed as having been rather near. "But did you ever have'm fire a volley on
you from close-very close-say, thirty feet?"

Highly scandalised I answered, "No; in that case, I would not be the crowning feature of
the Smithsonian Institute."

"Well," he said, "it's a funny effect. You feel as every hair on your head had been snatched out by the roots." Questioned further he said, "I walked right up on a Spanish outpost at daybreak once, and about twenty men let go at me. Thought I was a Cuban army, I suppose."

"What did you do?"

"I run."

"Did they hit you, at all?"

"Naw."

It had been arranged that some light ship of the squadron should rendezvous with him at a certain lonely spot on the coast on a certain day and hour and pick him up. He was to wave something white. His shirt was not white, but he waved it whenever he could see the signal-tops of a war-ship. It was a very tattered banner. After a ten-mile scramble through almost pathless thickets, he had very little on him which respectable men would call a shirt, and the less one says about his trousers the better. This naked savage, then, walked all day up and down a small bit of beach waving a brown rag. At night, he slept in the sand. At full daybreak he began to wave his rag; at noon he was waving his rag; at night-fall he donned his rag and strove to think of it as a shirt. Thus passed two days, and nothing had happened. Then he retraced a twenty-five mile way to the house of old Martha. At first she took him to be one of Havana's terrible beggars and cried, "And do you come here for alms? Look out, that I do not beg of you." The one unchanged thing was his laugh of pure mockery. When she heard it, she dragged him through the door. He paid no heed to her ejaculations but went straight to where he had hidden some gold. As he was untying a bit of string from the neck of a small bag, he said, "How is little Alfred?" "Recovered, thank Heaven." He handed Martha a piece of gold. "Take this and buy what you can on the corner. I'm hungry." Martha departed with expedition. Upon her return, she was beaming. She had foraged a thin chicken, a bunch of radishes and two bottles of wine. Johnnie had finished the radishes and one bottle of wine when the chicken was still a long way from the table. He called stoutly for more, and so Martha passed again into the street with another gold piece. She bought more radishes, more wine and some cheese. They had a grand feast, with Johnnie audibly wondering until a late hour why he had waved his rag in vain.

There was no end to his suspense, no end to his work. He knew everything. He was an animate guide-book. After he knew a thing once, he verified it in several different ways in order to make sure. He fitted himself for a useful career, like a young man in a college-with the difference that the shadow of the garote fell ever upon his way, and that he was occasionally shot at, and that he could not get enough to eat, and that his existence was apparently forgotten, and that he contracted the fever. But — —

One cannot think of the terms in which to describe a futility so vast, so colossal. He had builded a little boat, and the sea had receded and left him and his boat a thousand miles inland on the top of a mountain. The war-fate had left Havana out of its plan and thus isolated Johnnie and his several pounds of useful information. The war-fate left Havana to become the somewhat indignant victim of a peaceful occupation at the close of the conflict, and Johnnie's data were worth as much as a carpenter's lien on the north pole. He had suffered and laboured for about as complete a bit of absolute nothing as one could invent. If the company which owned the sugar plantation had not generously continued his salary during the war, he would not have been able to pay his expenses on the amount allowed him by the government, which, by the way, was a more complete bit of absolute nothing than one could possibly invent.

IV

I met Johnnie in Havana in October, 1898. If I remember rightly the U.S.S. *Resolute* and the U.S.S. *Scorpion* were in the harbour, but beyond these two terrible engines of destruction there were not as yet any of the more stern signs of the American success. Many Americans were to be seen in the streets of Havana where they were not in any way molested. Among them was Johnnie in white duck and a straw hat, cool, complacent and with eyes rather more steady than ever. I addressed him upon the subject of his supreme failure, but I could not perturb his philosophy. In reply he simply asked me to dinner. "Come to the Café Aguacate at 7:30 to-night," he said. "I haven't been there in a long time. We shall see if they cook as well as ever." I turned up promptly and found Johnnie in a private room smoking a cigar in the presence of a waiter who was blue in the gills. "I've ordered the dinner," he said cheerfully. "Now I want to see if you won't be surprised how well they can do here in Havana." I was surprised. I was dumfounded. Rarely in the history of the world have two rational men sat down to such a dinner. It must have taxed the ability and endurance of the entire working force of the establishment to provide it. The variety of dishes was of course related to the markets of Havana, but the abundance and general profligacy was related only to Johnnie's imagination. Neither of us had an appetite. Our fancies fled in confusion before this puzzling luxury. I looked at Johnnie as if he were a native of Thibet. I had thought him to be a most simple man, and here I found him revelling in food like a fat, old senator of Rome's decadence. And if the dinner itself put me to open-eyed amazement, the names of the wines finished everything. Apparently Johnny had had but one standard, and that was the cost. If a wine had been very expensive, he had ordered it. I began to think him probably a maniac. At any rate, I was sure that we were both fools. Seeing my fixed stare, he spoke with affected languor: "I wish peacocks' brains and melted pearls were to be had here in Havana. We'd have 'em." Then he grinned. As a mere skirmisher I said, "In New York, we think we dine well; but really this, you know-well-Havana——"

Johnnie waved his hand pompously. "Oh, I know."

Directly after coffee, Johnnie excused himself for a moment and left the room. When he returned he said briskly, "Well, are you ready to go?" As soon as we were in a cab and safely out of hearing of the Café Aguacate, Johnnie lay back and laughed long and joyously.

But I was very serious. "Look here, Johnnie," I said to him solemnly, "when you invite me to dine with you, don't you ever do *that* again. And I'll tell you one thing-when you dine with me you will probably get the ordinary table d'hôte." I was an older man.

"Oh, that's all right," he cried. And then he too grew serious. "Well, as far as I am concerned-as far as I am concerned," he said, "the war is now over."

War Memories

"But to get the real thing!" cried Vernall, the war-correspondent. "It seems impossible! It is because war is neither magnificent nor squalid; it is simply life, and an expression of life can always evade us. We can never tell life, one to another, although sometimes we think we can."

When I climbed aboard the despatch-boat at Key West, the mate told me irritably that as soon as we crossed the bar, we would find ourselves monkey-climbing over heavy seas. It wasn't my fault, but he seemed to insinuate that it was all a result of my incapacity. There were four correspondents in the party. The leader of us came aboard with a huge bunch of bananas, which he hung like a chandelier in the centre of the tiny cabin. We made acquaintance over, around, and under this bunch of bananas, which really occupied the cabin as a soldier occupies a sentry box. But the bunch did not become really aggressive until we were well at sea. Then it began to spar. With the first roll of the ship, it launched its honest pounds at McCurdy and knocked him wildly through the door to the deck-rail, where he hung cursing hysterically. Without a moment's pause, it made for me. I flung myself head-first into my bunk and watched the demon sweep Brownlow into a corner and wedge his knee behind a sea-chest. Kary gave a shrill cry and fled. The bunch of bananas swung to and fro, silent, determined, ferocious, looking for more men. It had cleared a space for itself. My comrades looked in at the door, calling upon me to grab the thing and hold it. I pointed out to them the security and comfort of my position. They were angry. Finally the mate came and lashed the thing so that it could not prowl about the cabin and assault innocent war-correspondents. You see? War! A bunch of bananas rampant because the ship rolled.

In that early period of the war we were forced to continue our dreams. And we were all dreamers, envisioning the seas with death grapples, ship and ship. Even the navy grew cynical. Officers on the bridge lifted their megaphones and told you in resigned voices that they were out of ice, onions, and eggs. At other times, they would shoot quite casually at us with six-pounders. This industry usually progressed in the night, but it sometimes happened in the day. There was never any resentment on our side, although at moments there was some nervousness. They were impressively quick with their lanyards; our means of replying to signals were correspondingly slow. They gave you opportunity to say, "Heaven guard me!" Then they shot. But we recognised the propriety of it. Everything was correct save the war, which lagged and lagged and lagged. It did not play; it was not a gory giant; it was a bunch of bananas swung in the middle of the cabin.

Once we had the honour of being rammed at midnight by the U.S.S. *Machias*. In fact the exceeding industry of the naval commanders of the Cuban blockading fleet caused a certain liveliness to at times penetrate our mediocre existence. We were all greatly entertained over an immediate prospect of being either killed by rapid fire guns, cut in half by the ram or merely drowned, but even our great longing for diversion could not cause us to ever again go near the *Machias* on a dark night. We had sailed from Key West on a mission that had nothing to do with the coast of Cuba, and steaming due east and some thirty-five miles from the Cuban land, we did not think we were liable to an affair with any of the fierce American cruisers. Suddenly a familiar signal of red and white lights flashed like a brooch of jewels on the pall that covered the sea. It was far away and tiny, but we knew all about it. It was the electric question of an American war-ship and it demanded a swift answer in kind. The man behind the gun! What about the man in front of the gun? The war-ship signals vanished and the sea presented nothing but a smoky black stretch lit with the hissing white tops of the flying waves. A thin line of flame swept from a gun.

Thereafter followed one of those silences which had become so peculiarly instructive to the blockade-runner. Somewhere in the darkness we knew that a slate-coloured cruiser, red below the water-line and with a gold scroll on her bows, was flying over the waves toward us, while upon the dark decks the men stood at general quarters in silence about the long thin guns, and it was the law of life and death that we should make true answer in about the twelfth part of a second. Now I shall with regret disclose a certain dreadful secret of the despatch-boat service. Our signals, far from being electric, were two lanterns which we kept in a tub and covered with a tarpaulin. The tub was placed just forward of the pilot-house, and when we were accosted at night it was everybody's duty to scramble wildly for the tub and grab out the lanterns and wave them. It amounted to a slowness of speech. I remember a story of an army sentry who upon hearing a noise in his front one dark night called his usual sharp query. "Halt-who's there? Halt or I'll fire!" And getting no immediate response he fired even as he had said, killing a man with a hair-lip who unfortunately could not arrange his vocal machinery to reply in season. We were something like a boat with a hair-lip. And sometimes it was very trying to the nerves.... The pause was long. Then a voice spoke from the sea through a megaphone. It was faint but clear. "What ship is that?" No one hesitated over his answer in cases of this kind. Everybody was desirous of imparting fullest information. There was another pause. Then out of the darkness flew an American cruiser, silent as death, handled as ferociously as if the devil commanded her. Again the little voice hailed from the bridge. "What ship is that?" Evidently the reply to the first hail had been misunderstood or not heard. This time the voice rang with menace, menace of immediate and certain destruction, and the last word was intoned savagely and strangely across the windy darkness as if the officer would explain that the cruiser was after either fools or the common enemy. The yells in return did not stop her. She was hurling herself forward to ram us amidships, and the people on the little *Three Friends* looked at a tall swooping bow, and it was keener than any knife that has ever been made. As the cruiser lunged every man imagined the gallant and famous but frail *Three Friends* cut into two parts as neatly as if she had been cheese. But there was a sheer and a hard sheer to starboard, and down upon our quarter swung a monstrous thing larger than any ship in the world-the U.S.S. *Machias*. She had a freeboard of about three hundred feet and the top of her funnel was out of sight in the clouds like an Alp. I shouldn't wonder that at the top of that funnel there was a region of perpetual snow. And at a range which swiftly narrowed to nothing every gun in her port-battery swung deliberately into aim. It was closer, more deliciously intimate than a duel across a handkerchief. We all had an opportunity of looking miles down the muzzles of this festive artillery before came the collision. Then the *Machias* reeled her steel shoulder against the wooden side of the *Three Friends* and up went a roar as if a vast shingle roof had fallen. The poor little tug dipped as if she meant to pass under the war-ship, staggered and finally righted, trembling from head to foot. The cries of the splintered timbers ceased. The men on the tug gazed at each other with white faces shining faintly in the darkness. The *Machias* backed away even as the *Three Friends* drew slowly ahead, and again we were alone with the piping of the wind and the slash of the gale-driven water. Later, from some hidden part of the sea, the bullish eye of a searchlight looked at us and the widening white rays bathed us in the glare. There was another hail. "Hello there, *Three Friends*!" "Ay, ay, sir!" "Are you injured?" Our first mate had taken a lantern and was studying the side of the tug, and we held our breath for his answer. I was sure that he was going to say that we were sinking. Surely there could be no other ending to this terrific bloodthirsty assault. But the first mate said, "No, sir." Instantly the glare of the search-light was gone; the *Machias* was gone; the incident was closed.

I was dining once on board the flag-ship, the *New York*, armoured cruiser. It was the junior officers' mess, and when the coffee came, a young ensign went to the piano and began to bang out a popular tune. It was a cheerful scene, and it resembled only a cheerful scene. Suddenly we heard the whistle of the bos'n's mate, and directly above us, it seemed, a voice, hoarse as that of a sea-lion, bellowed a command: "Man the port battery." In a moment the table was vacant; the popular tune ceased in a jangle. On the quarter-deck assembled a group of officers-spectators. The quiet evening sea, lit with faint red lights, went peacefully to the feet of a verdant shore. One could hear the far-away measured tumbling of surf upon a reef. Only this sound pulsed in the air. The great grey cruiser was as still as the earth, the sea, and the sky. Then they let off a four-inch gun directly under my feet. I thought it turned me a back-somersault. That was the effect upon my mind. But it appears I did not move. The shell went carousing off to the Cuban shore, and from the vegetation there spirted a cloud of dust. Some of the officers on the quarter-deck laughed. Through their glasses they had seen a Spanish column of cavalry much agitated by the appearance of this shell among them. As far as I was concerned, there was nothing but the spirt of dust from the side of a long-suffering island. When I returned to my coffee I found that most of the young officers had also returned. Japanese boys were bringing liquors. The piano's clattering of the popular air was often interrupted by the boom of a four-inch gun. A bunch of bananas!

One day, our despatch-boat found the shores of Guantanamo Bay flowing past on either side. It was at nightfall and on the eastward point a small village was burning, and it happened that a fiery light was thrown upon some palm-trees so that it made them into enormous crimson feathers. The water was the colour of blue steel; the Cuban woods were sombre; high shivered the gory feathers. The last boatloads of the marine battalion were pulling for the beach. The marine officers gave me generous hospitality to the camp on the hill. That night there was an alarm and amid a stern calling of orders and a rushing of men, I wandered in search of some other man who had no occupation. It turned out to be the young assistant surgeon, Gibbs. We foregathered in the centre of a square of six companies of marines. There was no firing. We thought it rather comic. The next night there was an alarm; there was some firing; we lay on our bellies; it was no longer comic. On the third night the alarm came early; I went in search of Gibbs, but I soon gave over an active search for the more congenial occupation of lying flat and feeling the hot hiss of the bullets trying to cut my hair. For the moment I was no longer a cynic. I was a child who, in a fit of ignorance, had jumped into the vat of war. I heard somebody dying near me. He was dying hard. Hard. It took him a long time to die. He breathed as all noble machinery breathes when it is making its gallant strife against breaking, breaking. But he was going to break. He was going to break. It seemed to me, this breathing, the noise of a heroic pump which strives to subdue a mud which comes upon it in tons. The darkness was impenetrable. The man was lying in some depression within seven feet of me. Every wave, vibration, of his anguish beat upon my senses. He was long past groaning. There was only the bitter strife for air which pulsed out into the night in a clear penetrating whistle with intervals of terrible silence in which I held my own breath in the common unconscious aspiration to help. I thought this man would never die. I wanted him to die. Ultimately he died. At the moment the adjutant came bustling along erect amid the spitting bullets. I knew him by his voice. "Where's the doctor? There's some wounded men over there. Where's the doctor?" A man answered briskly: "Just died this minute, sir." It was as if he had said: "Just gone around the corner this minute, sir." Despite the horror of this night's business, the man's mind was somehow influenced by the coincidence of the adjutant's calling aloud for the doctor within a few seconds of the doctor's death. It-what shall I say? It interested him, this coincidence.

The day broke by inches, with an obvious and maddening reluctance. From some unfathomable source I procured an opinion that my friend was not dead at all-the wild and quivering darkness had caused me to misinterpret a few shouted words. At length the land brightened in a violent atmosphere, the perfect dawning of a tropic day, and in this light I saw a clump of men near me. At first I thought they were all dead. Then I thought they were all asleep. The truth was that a group of wan-faced, exhausted men had gone to sleep about Gibbs' body so closely and in such abandoned attitudes that one's eye could not pick the living from the dead until one saw that a certain head had beneath it a great dark pool.

In the afternoon a lot of men went bathing, and in the midst of this festivity firing was resumed. It was funny to see the men come scampering out of the water, grab at their rifles and go into action attired in nought but their cartridge-belts. The attack of the Spaniards had interrupted in some degree the services over the graves of Gibbs and some others. I remember Paine came ashore with a bottle of whisky which I took from him violently. My faithful shooting boots began to hurt me, and I went to the beach and poulticed my feet in wet clay, sitting on the little rickety pier near where the corrugated iron cable-station showed how the shells slivered through it. Some marines, desirous of mementoes, were poking with sticks in the smoking ruins of the hamlet. Down in the shallow water crabs were meandering among the weeds, and little fishes moved slowly in schools.

The next day we went shooting. It was exactly like quail shooting. I'll tell you. These guerillas who so cursed our lives had a well some five miles away, and it was the only water supply within about twelve miles of the marine camp. It was decided that it would be correct to go forth and destroy the well. Captain Elliott, of C company, was to take his men with Captain Spicer's company, D, out to the well, beat the enemy away and destroy everything. He was to start at the next daybreak. He asked me if I cared to go, and, of course, I accepted with glee; but all that night I was afraid. Bitterly afraid. The moon was very bright, shedding a magnificent radiance upon the trenches. I watched the men of C and D companies lying so tranquilly-some snoring, confound them-whereas I was certain that I could never sleep with the weight of a coming battle upon my mind, a battle in which the poor life of a war-correspondent might easily be taken by a careless enemy. But if I was frightened I was also very cold. It was a chill night and I wanted a heavy top-coat almost as much as I wanted a certificate of immunity from rifle bullets. These two feelings were of equal importance to my mind. They were twins. Elliott came and flung a tent-fly over Lieutenant Bannon and me as we lay on the ground back of the men. Then I was no longer cold, but I was still afraid, for tent-flies cannot mend a fear. In the morning I wished for some mild attack of disease, something that would incapacitate me for the business of going out gratuitously to be bombarded. But I was in an awkwardly healthy state, and so I must needs smile and look pleased with my prospects. We were to be guided by fifty Cubans, and I gave up all dreams of a postponement when I saw them shambling off in single file through the cactus. We followed presently. "Where you people goin' to?" "Don't know, Jim." "Well, good luck to you, boys." This was the world's lazy inquiry and conventional God-speed. Then the mysterious wilderness swallowed us.

The men were silent because they were ordered to be silent, but whatever faces I could observe were marked with a look of serious meditation. As they trudged slowly in single file they were reflecting upon-what? I don't know. But at length we came to ground more open. The sea appeared on our right, and we saw the gunboat *Dolphin* steaming along in a line parallel to ours. I was as glad to see her as if she had called out my name. The trail wound about the bases of some high bare spurs. If the Spaniards had occupied them I don't see how we could have gone further. But upon them were only the dove-voiced guerilla scouts calling back into the hills the news of our approach. The effect of sound is of course relative. I am sure I have never heard such a horrible sound as the beautiful cooing of the wood-dove when I was certain that it came from the yellow throat of a guerilla. Elliott sent Lieutenant Lucas with his platoon to ascend the hills and cover our advance by the trail. We halted and watched them climb, a long black streak of men in the vivid sunshine of the hillside. We did not know how tall were these hills until we saw Lucas and his men on top, and they were no larger than specks. We marched on until, at last, we heard-it seemed in the sky-the sputter of firing. This devil's dance was begun. The proper strategic movement to cover the crisis seemed to me to be to run away home and swear I had never started on this expedition. But Elliott yelled: "Now, men; straight up this hill." The men charged up against the cactus, and, because I cared for the opinion of others, I found myself tagging along close at Elliott's heels. I don't know how I got up that hill, but I think it was because I was afraid to be left behind. The immediate rear did not look safe. The crowd of strong young marines afforded the only spectacle of provisional security. So I tagged along at Elliott's heels. The hill was as steep as a Swiss roof. From it sprang out great pillars of cactus, and the human instinct was to assist one's self in the ascent by grasping cactus with one's hands. I remember the watch I had to keep upon this human instinct even when the sound of the bullets was attracting my nervous attention. However, the attractive thing to my sense at the time was the fact that every man of the marines was also climbing away like mad. It was one thing for Elliott, Spicer, Neville, Shaw and Bannon; it was another thing for me; but-what in the devil was it to the men? Not the same thing surely. It was perfectly easy for any marine to get overcome by the burning heat and, lying down, bequeath the work and the danger to his comrades. The fine thing about "the men" is that you can't explain them. I mean when you take them collectively. They do a thing, and afterward you find that they have done it because they have done it. However, when Elliott arrived at the top of the ridge, myself and many other men were with him. But there was no battle scene. Off on another ridge we could see Lucas' men and the Cubans peppering away into a valley. The bullets about our ears were really intended to lodge in them. We went over there.

I walked along the firing line and looked at the men. I kept somewhat on what I shall call the *lee* side of the ridge. Why? Because I was afraid of being shot. No other reason. Most of the men as they lay flat, shooting, looked contented, almost happy. They were pleased, these men, at the situation. I don't know. I cannot imagine. But they were pleased, at any rate. I wasn't pleased. I was picturing defeat. I was saying to myself: —"Now if the enemy should suddenly do so-and-so, or so-and-so, why-what would become of me?" During these first few moments I did not see the Spanish position because —I was afraid to look at it. Bullets were hissing and spitting over the crest of the ridge in such showers as to make observation to be a task for a brave man. No, now, look here, why the deuce should I have stuck my head up, eh? Why? Well, at any rate, I didn't until it seemed to be a far less thing than most of the men were doing as if they liked it. Then I saw nothing. At least it was only the bottom of a small valley. In this valley there was a thicket —a big thicket-and this thicket seemed to be crowded with a mysterious class of persons who were evidently trying to kill us. Our enemies? Yes-perhaps —I suppose so. Leave that to the people in the streets at home. They know and cry against the public enemy, but when men go into actual battle not one in a thousand concerns himself with an animus against the men who face him. The great desire is to beat them-beat them whoever they are as a matter, first, of personal safety, second, of personal glory. It is always safest to make the other chap quickly run away. And as he runs away, one feels, as one tries to hit him in the back and knock him sprawling, that he must be a very good and sensible fellow. But these people apparently did not mean to run away. They clung to their thicket and, amid the roar of the firing, one could sometimes hear their wild yells of insult and defiance. They were actually the most obstinate, headstrong, mulish people that you could ever imagine. The *Dolphin* was throwing shells into their immediate vicinity and the fire from the marines and Cubans was very rapid and heavy, but still those incomprehensible mortals remained in their thicket. The scene on the top of the ridge was very wild, but there was only one truly romantic figure. This was a Cuban officer who held in one hand a great glittering machete and in the other a cocked revolver. He posed like a statue of victory. Afterwards he confessed to me that he alone had been responsible for the winning of the fight. But outside of this splendid person it was simply a picture of men at work, men terribly hard at work, red-faced, sweating, gasping toilers. A Cuban negro soldier was shot though the heart and one man took the body on his back and another took it by its feet and trundled away toward the rear looking precisely like a wheelbarrow. A man in C company was shot through the ankle and he sat behind the line nursing his wound. Apparently he was pleased with it. It seemed to suit him. I don't know why. But beside him sat a comrade with a face drawn, solemn and responsible like that of a New England spinster at the bedside of a sick child.

The fight banged away with a roar like a forest fire. Suddenly a marine wriggled out of the firing line and came frantically to me. "Say, young feller, I'll give you five dollars for a drink of whisky." He tried to force into my hand a gold piece. "Go to the devil," said I, deeply scandalised. "Besides, I haven't got any whisky," "No, but look here," he beseeched me. "If I don't get a drink I'll die. And I'll give you five dollars for it. Honest, I will." I finally tried to escape from him by walking away, but he followed at my heels, importuning me with all the exasperating persistence of a professional beggar and trying to force this ghastly gold piece into my hand. I could not shake him off, and amid that clatter of furious fighting I found myself intensely embarrassed, and glancing fearfully this way and that way to make sure that people did not see me, the villain and his gold. In vain I assured him that if I had any whisky I should place it at his disposal. He could not be turned away. I thought of the European expedient in such a crisis-to jump in a cab. But unfortunately — — In the meantime I had given up my occupation of tagging at Captain Elliott's heels, because his business required that he should go into places of great danger. But from time to time I was under his attention. Once he turned to me and said: "Mr. Vernall, will you go and satisfy yourself who those people are?" Some men had appeared on a hill about six hundred yards from our left flank. "Yes, sir," cried I with, I assure you, the finest alacrity and cheerfulness, and my tone proved to me that I had inherited histrionic abilities. This tone was of course a black lie, but I went off briskly and was as jaunty as a real soldier while all the time my heart was in my boots and I was cursing the day that saw me landed on the shores of the tragic isle. If the men on the distant hill had been guerillas, my future might have been seriously jeopardised, but I had not gone far toward them when I was able to recognise the uniforms of the marine corps. Whereupon I scampered back to the firing line and with the same alacrity and cheerfulness reported my information. I mention to you that I was afraid, because there were about me that day many men who did not seem to be afraid at all, men with quiet, composed faces who went about this business as if they proceeded from a sense of habit. They were not old soldiers; they were mainly recruits, but many of them betrayed all the emotion and merely the emotion that one sees in the face of a man earnestly at work.

I don't know how long the action lasted. I remember deciding in my own mind that the Spaniards stood forty minutes. This was a mere arbitrary decision based on nothing. But at any rate we finally arrived at the satisfactory moment when the enemy began to run away. I shall never forget how my courage increased. And then began the great bird shooting. From the far side of the thicket arose an easy slope covered with plum-coloured bush. The Spaniards broke in coveys of from six to fifteen men-or birds-and swarmed up this slope. The marines on our ridge then had some fine, open field shooting. No charge could be made because the shells from the *Dolphin* were helping the Spaniards to evacuate the thicket, so the marines had to be content with this extraordinary paraphrase of a kind of sport. It was strangely like the original. The shells from the *Dolphin* were the dogs; dogs who went in and stirred out the game. The marines were suddenly gentlemen in leggings, alive with the sharp instinct which marks the hunter. The Spaniards were the birds. Yes, they were the birds, but I doubt if they would sympathise with my metaphors.

We destroyed their camp, and when the tiled roof of a burning house fell with a crash it was so like the crash of a strong volley of musketry that we all turned with a start, fearing that we would have to fight again on that same day. And this struck me at least as being an impossible thing. They gave us water from the *Dolphin* and we filled our canteens. None of the men were particularly jubilant. They did not altogether appreciate their victory. They were occupied in being glad that the fight was over. I discovered to my amazement that we were on the summit of a hill so high that our released eyes seemed to sweep over half the world. The vast stretch of sea shimmering like fragile blue silk in the breeze, lost itself ultimately in an indefinite pink haze, while in the other direction, ridge after ridge, ridge after ridge, rolled brown and arid into the north. The battle had been fought high in the air-where the rain clouds might have been. That is why everybody's face was the colour of beetroot and men lay on the ground and only swore feebly when the cactus spurs sank into them.

Finally we started for camp. Leaving our wounded, our cactus pincushions, and our heat-prostrated men on board the *Dolphin*. I did not see that the men were elate or even grinning with satisfaction. They seemed only anxious to get to food and rest. And yet it was plain that Elliott and his men had performed a service that would prove invaluable to the security and comfort of the entire battalion. They had driven the guerillas to take a road along which they would have to proceed for fifteen miles before they could get as much water as would wet the point of a pin. And by the destruction of a well at the scene of the fight, Elliott made an arid zone almost twenty miles wide between the enemy and the base camp. In Cuba this is the best of protections. However, a cup of coffee! Time enough to think of a brilliant success after one had had a cup of coffee. The long line plodded wearily through the dusky jungle which was never again to be alive with ambushes.

It was dark when we stumbled into camp, and I was sad with an ungovernable sadness, because I was too tired to remember where I had left my kit. But some of my colleagues were waiting on the beach, and they put me on a despatch-boat to take my news to a Jamaica cable-station. The appearance of this despatch-boat struck me with wonder. It was reminiscent of something with which I had been familiar in early years. I looked with dull surprise at three men of the engine-room force, who sat aft on some bags of coal smoking their pipes and talking as if there had never been any battles fought anywhere. The sudden clang of the gong made me start and listen eagerly, as if I would be asking: "What was that?" The chunking of the screw affected me also, but I seemed to relate it to a former and pleasing experience. One of the correspondents on board immediately began to tell me of the chief engineer, who, he said, was a comic old character. I was taken to see this marvel, which presented itself as a gray-bearded man with an oil can, who had the cynical, malicious, egotistic eye of proclaimed and admired ignorance. I looked dazedly at the venerable impostor. What had he to do with battles-the humming click of the locks, the odour of burnt cotton, the bullets, the firing? My friend told the scoundrel that I was just returned from the afternoon's action. He said: "That so?" And looked at me with a smile, faintly, faintly derisive. You see? I had just come out of my life's most fiery time, and that old devil looked at me with that smile. What colossal conceit. The four-times-damned doddering old head-mechanic of a derelict junk shop. The whole trouble lay in the fact that I had not shouted out with mingled awe and joy as he stood there in his wisdom and experience, with all his ancient saws and home-made epigrams ready to fire.

My friend took me to the cabin. What a squalid hole! My heart sank. The reward after the labour should have been a great airy chamber, a gigantic four-poster, iced melons, grilled birds, wine, and the delighted attendance of my friends. When I had finished my cablegram, I retired to a little shelf of a berth, which reeked of oil, while the blankets had soaked recently with sea-water. The vessel heeled to leeward in spasmodic attempts to hurl me out, and I resisted with the last of my strength. The infamous pettiness of it all! I thought the night would never end. "But never mind," I said to myself at last, "to-morrow in Fort Antonio I shall have a great bath and fine raiment, and I shall dine grandly and there will be lager beer on ice. And there will be attendants to run when I touch a bell, and I shall catch every interested romantist in the town, and spin him the story of the fight at Cusco." We reached Fort Antonio and I fled from the cable office to the hotel. I procured the bath and, as I donned whatever fine raiment I had foraged, I called the boy and pompously told him of a dinner —a real dinner, with furbelows and complications, and yet with a basis of sincerity. He looked at me calf-like for a moment, and then he went away. After a long interval, the manager himself appeared and asked me some questions which led me to see that he thought I had attempted to undermine and disintegrate the intellect of the boy, by the elocution of Arabic incantations. Well, never mind. In the end, the manager of the hotel elicited from me that great cry, that cry which during the war, rang piteously from thousands of throats, that last grand cry of anguish and despair: *"Well, then, in the name of God, can I have a cold bottle of beer?"*

Well, you see to what war brings men? War is death, and a plague of the lack of small things, and toil. Nor did I catch my sentimentalists and pour forth my tale to them, and thrill, appal, and fascinate them. However, they did feel an interest in me, for I heard a lady at the hotel ask: "Who *is* that chap in the very dirty jack-boots?" So you see, that whereas you can be very much frightened upon going into action, you can also be greatly annoyed after you have come out.

Later, I fell into the hands of one of my closest friends, and he mercilessly outlined a scheme for landing to the west of Santiago and getting through the Spanish lines to some place from which we could view the Spanish squadron lying in the harbour. There was rumour that the *Viscaya* had escaped, he said, and it would be very nice to make sure of the truth. So we steamed to a point opposite a Cuban camp which my friend knew, and flung two crop-tailed Jamaica polo ponies into the sea. We followed in a small boat and were met on the beach by a small

Cuban detachment who immediately caught our ponies and saddled them for us. I suppose we felt rather god-like. We were almost the first Americans they had seen and they looked at us with eyes of grateful affection. I don't suppose many men have the experience of being looked at with eyes of grateful affection. They guide us to a Cuban camp where, in a little palm-bark hut, a black-faced lieutenant-colonel was lolling in a hammock. I couldn't understand what was said, but at any rate he must have ordered his half-naked orderly to make coffee, for it was done. It was a dark syrup in smoky tin-cups, but it was better than the cold bottle of beer which I did not drink in Jamaica.

The Cuban camp was an expeditious affair of saplings and palm-bark tied with creepers. It could be burned to the ground in fifteen minutes and in ten reduplicated. The soldiers were in appearance an absolutely good-natured set of half-starved ragamuffins. Their breeches hung in threads about their black legs and their shirts were as nothing. They looked like a collection of real tropic savages at whom some philanthropist had flung a bundle of rags and some of the rags had stuck here and there. But their condition was now a habit. I doubt if they knew they were half-naked. Anyhow they didn't care. No more they should; the weather was warm. This lieutenant-colonel gave us an escort of five or six men and we went up into the mountains, lying flat on our Jamaica ponies while they went like rats up and down extraordinary trails. In the evening we reached the camp of a major who commanded the outposts. It was high, high in the hills. The stars were as big as cocoanuts. We lay in borrowed hammocks and watched the firelight gleam blood-red on the trees. I remember an utterly naked negro squatting, crimson, by the fire and cleaning an iron-pot. Some voices were singing an Afric wail of forsaken love and death. And at dawn we were to try to steal through the Spanish lines. I was very, very sorry.

In the cold dawn the situation was the same, but somehow courage seemed to be in the breaking day. I went off with the others quite cheerfully. We came to where the pickets stood behind bulwarks of stone in frameworks of saplings. They were peering across a narrow cloud-steeped gulch at a dull fire marking a Spanish post. There was some palaver and then, with fifteen men, we descended the side of this mountain, going down into the chill blue-and-grey clouds. We had left our horses with the Cuban pickets. We proceeded stealthily, for we were already within range of the Spanish pickets. At the bottom of the cañon it was still night. A brook, a regular salmon-stream, brawled over the rocks. There were grassy banks and most delightful trees. The whole valley was a sylvan fragrance. But the guide waved his arm and scowled warningly, and in a moment we were off, threading thickets, climbing hills, crawling through fields on our hands and knees, sometimes sweeping like seventeen phantoms across a Spanish road. I was in a dream, but I kept my eye on the guide and halted to listen when he halted to listen and ambled onward when he ambled onward. Sometimes he turned and pantomimed as ably and fiercely as a man being stung by a thousand hornets. Then we knew that the situation was extremely delicate. We were now of course well inside the Spanish lines and we ascended a great hill which overlooked the harbour of Santiago. There, tranquilly at anchor, lay the *Oquendo*, the *Maria Theresa*, the *Christobal Colon*, the *Viscaya*, the *Pluton*, the *Furor*. The bay was white in the sun and the great blacked-hull armoured cruisers were impressive in a dignity massive yet graceful. We did not know that they were all doomed ships, soon to go out to a swift death. My friend drew maps and things while I devoted myself to complete rest, blinking lazily at the Spanish squadron. We did not know that we were the last Americans to view them alive and unhurt and at peace. Then we retraced our way, at the same noiseless canter. I did not understand my condition until I considered that we were well through the Spanish lines and practically out of danger. Then I discovered that I was a dead man. The nervous force having evaporated I was a mere corpse. My limbs were of dough and my spinal cord burned within me as if it were red-hot wire. But just at this time we were discovered by a Spanish patrol, and I ascertained that I was not dead at all. We ultimately reached the foot of the mother-mountain on whose shoulders were the Cuban pickets, and here I was so sure of safety that I could not resist the temptation to die again. I think I passed into eleven distinct stupors during the ascent of that mountain while the escort stood leaning on their Remingtons.

We had done twenty-five miles at a sort of a man-gallop, never once using a beaten track, but always going promiscuously through the jungle and over the rocks. And many of the miles stood straight on end so that it was as hard to come down as it was to go up. But during my stupors, the escort *stood*, mind you, and chatted in low voices. For all the signs they showed, we might have been starting. And they had had nothing to eat but mangoes for over eight days. Previous to the eight days they had been living on mangoes and the carcase of a small lean pony. They were, in fact, of the stuff of Fenimore Cooper's Indians, only they made no preposterous orations. At the major's camp, my friend and I agreed that if our worthy escort would send down a representative with us to the coast, we would send back to them whatever we could spare from the stores of our despatch-boat. With one voice the escort answered that they themselves would go the additional four leagues, as in these starving times they did not care to trust a representative, thank you. "They can't do it; they'll peg out; there must be a limit," I said. "No," answered my friend. "They're all right; they'd run three times around the whole island for a mouthful of beer." So we saddled up and put off with our fifteen Cuban infantrymen wagging along tirelessly behind us. Sometimes, at the foot of a precipitous hill, a man asked permission to cling to my horse's tail, and then the Jamaica pony would snake him to the summit so swiftly that only his toes seemed to touch the rocks. And for this assistance the man was grateful. When we crowned the last great ridge we saw our squadron to the eastward spread in its patient semicircular about the mouth of the harbour. But as we wound towards the beach we saw a more dramatic thing-our own despatch-boat leaving the rendezvous and putting off to sea. Evidently we were late. Behind me were fifteen stomachs, empty. It was a frightful situation. My friend and I charged for the beach and those fifteen fools began to *run*.

It was no use. The despatch-boat went gaily away trailing black smoke behind her. We turned in distress wondering what we could say to that abused escort. If they massacred us, I felt that it would be merely a virtuous reply to fate and they should in no ways be blamed. There are some things which a man's feelings will not allow him to endure after a diet of mangoes and pony. However, we perceived to our amazement that they were not indignant at all. They simply smiled and made a gesture which expressed an habitual pessimism. It was a philosophy which denied the existence of everything but mangoes and pony. It was the Americans who refused to be comforted. I made a deep vow with myself that I would come as soon as possible and play a regular Santa Claus to that splendid escort. But-we put to sea in a dug-out with two black boys. The escort waved us a hearty good-bye from the shore and I never saw them again. I hope they are all on the police-force in the new Santiago.

In time we were rescued from the dug-out by our despatch-boat, and we relieved our feelings by over-rewarding the two black boys. In fact they reaped a harvest because of our emotion over our failure to fill the gallant stomachs of the escort. They were two rascals. We steamed to the flagship and were given permission to board her. Admiral Sampson is to me the most interesting personality of the war. I would not know how to sketch him for you even if I could pretend to sufficient material. Anyhow, imagine, first of all, a marble block of impassivity out of which is carved the figure of an old man. Endow this with life, and you've just begun. Then you must discard all your pictures of bluff, red-faced old gentlemen who roar against the gale, and understand that the quiet old man is a sailor and an admiral. This will be difficult; if I told you he was anything else it would be easy. He resembles other types; it is his distinction not to resemble the preconceived type of his standing. When first I met him I was impressed that he was immensely bored by the war and with the command of the North Atlantic Squadron. I perceived a manner where I thought I perceived a mood, a point of view. Later, he seemed so indifferent to small things which bore upon large things that I bowed to his apathy as a thing unprecedented, marvellous. Still I mistook a manner for a mood. Still I could not understand that this was the way of the man. I am not to blame, for my communication was slight and depended upon sufferance-upon, in fact, the traditional courtesy of the navy. But finally I saw that it was all manner, that hidden in his indifferent, even apathetic, manner, there was the alert, sure, fine mind of the best sea-captain that America has produced since-since Farragut? I don't know. I think-since Hull.

Men follow heartily when they are well led. They balk at trifles when a blockhead cries go on. For my part, an impressive thing of the war is the absolute devotion to Admiral Sampson's person-no, to his judgment and wisdom-which was paid by his ship-commanders —Evans of the *Iowa*, Taylor of the *Oregon*, Higginson of the *Massachusetts*, Phillips of the *Texas*, and all the other captains-barring one. Once, afterward, they called upon him to avenge himself upon a rival-they were there and they would have to say-but he said no-o-o, he guessed it-wouldn't do-any —g-o-oo-o-d —to the-service.

Men feared him, but he never made threats; men tumbled heels over head to obey him, but he never gave a sharp order; men loved him, but he said no word, kindly or unkindly; men cheered for him and he said: "Who are they yelling for?" Men behaved badly to him and he said nothing. Men thought of glory and he considered the management of ships. All without a sound. A noiseless campaign-on his part. No bunting, no arches, no fireworks; nothing but the perfect management of a big fleet. That is a record for you. No trumpets, no cheers of the populace. Just plain, pure, unsauced accomplishment. But ultimately he will reap his reward in-in what? In text-books on sea-campaigns. No more. The people choose their own and they choose the kind they like. Who has a better right? Anyhow he is a great man. And when you are once started you can continue to be a great man without the help of bouquets and banquets. He don't need them-bless your heart.

The flag-ship's battle-hatches were down, and between decks it was insufferable despite the electric fans. I made my way somewhat forwards, past the smart orderly, past the companion, on to the den of the junior mess. Even there they were playing cards in somebody's cabin. "Hello, old man. Been ashore? How'd it look? It's your deal, Chick." There was nothing but steamy wet heat and the decent suppression of the consequent ill-tempers. The junior officers' quarters were no more comfortable than the admiral's cabin. I had expected it to be so because of my remembrance of their gay spirits. But they were not gay. They were sweltering. Hello, old man, had I been ashore? I fled to the deck, where other officers not on duty were smoking quiet cigars. The hospitality of the officers of the flag-ship is another charming memory of the war.

I rolled into my berth on the despatch-boat that night feeling a perfect wonder of the day. Was the figure that leaned over the card-game on the flag-ship, the figure with a whisky and soda in its hand and a cigar in its teeth-was it identical with the figure scrambling, afraid of its life, through Cuban jungle? Was it the figure of the situation of the fifteen pathetic hungry men? It was the same and it went to sleep, hard sleep. I don't know where we voyaged. I think it was Jamaica. But, at any rate, upon the morning of our return to the Cuban coast, we found the sea alive with transports-United States transports from Tampa, containing the Fifth Army Corps under Major-General Shafter. The rigging and the decks of these ships were black with men and everybody wanted to land first. I landed, ultimately, and immediately began to look for an acquaintance. The boats were banged by the waves against a little flimsy dock. I fell ashore somehow, but I did not at once find an acquaintance. I talked to a private in the 2d Massachusetts Volunteers who told me that he was going to write war correspondence for a Boston newspaper. This statement did not surprise me.

There was a straggly village, but I followed the troops who at this time seemed to be moving out by companies. I found three other correspondents and it was luncheon time. Somebody had two bottles of Bass, but it was so warm that it squirted out in foam. There was no firing; no noise of any kind. An old shed was full of soldiers loafing pleasantly in the shade. It was a hot, dusty, sleepy afternoon; bees hummed. We saw Major-General Lawton standing with his staff under a tree. He was smiling as if he would say: "Well, this will be better than chasing Apaches." His division had the advance, and so he had the right to be happy. A tall man with a grey moustache, light but very strong, an ideal cavalryman. He appealed to one all the more because of the vague rumours that his superiors-some of them-were going to take mighty good care that he shouldn't get much to do. It was rather sickening to hear such talk, but later we knew that most of it must have been mere lies.

Down by the landing-place a band of correspondents were making a sort of permanent camp. They worked like Trojans, carrying wall-tents, cots, and boxes of provisions. They asked me to join them, but I looked shrewdly at the sweat on their faces and backed away. The next day the army left this permanent camp eight miles to the rear. The day became tedious. I was glad when evening came. I sat by a camp-fire and listened to a soldier of the 8th Infantry who told me that he was the first enlisted man to land. I lay pretending to appreciate him, but in fact I considered him a great shameless liar. Less than a month ago, I learned that every word he said was gospel truth. I was much surprised. We went for breakfast to the camp of the 20th Infantry, where Captain Greene and his subaltern, Exton, gave us tomatoes stewed with hard bread and coffee. Later, I discovered Greene and Exton down at the beach good-naturedly dodging the waves which seemed to be trying to prevent them from washing the breakfast dishes. I felt tremendously ashamed because my cup and my plate were there, you know, and — — Fate provides some men greased opportunities for making dizzy jackasses of themselves and I fell a victim to my flurry on this occasion. I was a blockhead. I walked away blushing. What? The battles? Yes, I saw something of all of them. I made up my mind that the next time I met Greene and Exton I'd say: "Look here; why didn't you tell me you had to wash your own dishes that morning so that I could have helped? I felt beastly when I saw you scrubbing there. And me walking around idly." But I never saw Captain Greene again. I think he is in the Philippines now fighting the Tagals. The next time I saw Exton-what? Yes, La Guasimas. That was the "rough rider fight." However, the next time I saw Exton I —what do you think? I forgot to speak about it. But if ever I meet Greene or Exton again-even if it should be twenty years —I am going to say, first thing: "Why — —" What? Yes. Roosevelt's regiment and the First and Tenth Regular Cavalry. I'll say, first thing: "Say, why didn't you tell me you had to wash your own dishes, that morning, so that I could have helped?" My stupidity will be on my conscience until I die, if, before that, I do not meet either Greene or Exton. Oh, yes, you are howling for blood, but I tell you it is more emphatic that I lost my tooth-brush. Did I tell you that? Well, I lost it, you see, and I thought of it for ten hours at a stretch. Oh, yes-he? He was shot through the heart. But, look here, I contend that the French cable company buncoed us throughout the war. What? Him? My tooth-brush I never found, but he died of his wound in time. Most of the regular soldiers carried their tooth-brushes stuck in the bands of their hats. It made a quaint military decoration. I have had a line of a thousand men pass me in the jungle and not a hat lacking the simple emblem.

The first of July? All right. My Jamaica polo-pony was not present. He was still in the hills to the westward of Santiago, but the Cubans had promised to fetch him to me. But my kit was easy to carry. It had nothing superfluous in it but a pair of spurs which made me indignant every time I looked at them. Oh, but I must tell you about a man I met directly after the La Guasimas fight. Edward Marshall, a correspondent whom I had known with a degree of intimacy for seven years, was terribly hit in that fight and asked me if I would not go to Siboney-the base-and convey the news to his colleagues of the *New York Journal* and round up some assistance. I went to Siboney, and there was not a *Journal* man to be seen, although usually you judged from appearances that the *Journal* staff was about as large as the army. Presently I met two correspondents, strangers to me, but I questioned them, saying that Marshall was badly shot and wished for such succour as *Journal* men could bring from their despatch-boat. And one of these correspondents replied. He is the man I wanted to describe. I love him as a brother. He said: "Marshall? Marshall? Why, Marshall isn't in Cuba at all. He left for New York just before the expedition sailed from Tampa." I said: "Beg pardon, but I remarked that Marshall was shot in the fight this morning, and have you seen any *Journal* people?" After a pause, he said: "I am sure Marshall is not down here at all. He's in New York." I said: "Pardon me, but I remarked that Marshall was shot in the fight this morning, and have you seen any *Journal* people?" He said: "No; now look here, you must have gotten two chaps mixed somehow.

Marshall isn't in Cuba at all. How could he be shot?" I said: "Pardon me, but I remarked that Marshall was shot in the fight this morning, and have you seen any *Journal* people?" He said: "But it can't really be Marshall, you know, for the simple reason that he's not down here." I clasped my hands to my temples, gave one piercing cry to heaven and fled from his presence. I couldn't go on with him. He excelled me at all points. I have faced death by bullets, fire, water, and disease, but to die thus-to wilfully batter myself against the ironclad opinion of this mummy-no, no, not that. In the meantime, it was admitted that a correspondent was shot, be his name Marshall, Bismarck, or Louis XIV. Now, supposing the name of this wounded correspondent had been Bishop Potter? Or Jane Austen? Or Bernhardt? Or Henri Georges Stephane Adolphe Opper de Blowitz? What effect-never mind.

We will proceed to July 1st. On that morning I marched with my kit-having everything essential save a tooth-brush —the entire army put me to shame, since there must have been at least fifteen thousand tooth-brushes in the invading force —I marched with my kit on the road to Santiago. It was a fine morning and everybody-the doomed and the immunes-how could we tell one from the other-everybody was in the highest spirits. We were enveloped in forest, but we could hear, from ahead, everybody peppering away at everybody. It was like the roll of many drums. This was Lawton over at El Caney. I reflected with complacency that Lawton's division did not concern me in a professional way. That was the affair of another man. My business was with Kent's division and Wheeler's division. We came to El Poso —a hill at nice artillery range from the Spanish defences. Here Grimes's battery was shooting a duel with one of the enemy's batteries. Scovel had established a little camp in the rear of the guns and a servant had made coffee. I invited Whigham to have coffee, and the servant added some hard biscuit and tinned tongue. I noted that Whigham was staring fixedly over my shoulder, and that he waved away the tinned tongue with some bitterness. It was a horse, a dead horse. Then a mule, which had been shot through the nose, wandered up and looked at Whigham. We ran away.

On top of the hill one had a fine view of the Spanish lines. We stared across almost a mile of jungle to ash-coloured trenches on the military crest of the ridge. A goodly distance back of this position were white buildings, all flying great red-cross flags. The jungle beneath us rattled with firing and the Spanish trenches crackled out regular volleys, but all this time there was nothing to indicate a tangible enemy. In truth, there was a man in a Panama hat strolling to and fro behind one of the Spanish trenches, gesticulating at times with a walking stick. A man in a Panama hat, walking with a stick! That was the strangest sight of my life-that symbol, that quaint figure of Mars. The battle, the thunderous row, was his possession. He was the master. He mystified us all with his infernal Panama hat and his wretched walking-stick. From near his feet came volleys and from near his side came roaring shells, but he stood there alone, visible, the one tangible thing. He was a Colossus, and he was half as high as a pin, this being. Always somebody would be saying: "Who *can* that fellow be?"

Later, the American guns shelled the trenches and a blockhouse near them, and Mars had vanished. It could not have been death. One cannot kill Mars. But there was one other figure, which arose to symbolic dignity. The balloon of our signal corps had swung over the tops of the jungle's trees toward the Spanish trenches. Whereat the balloon and the man in the Panama hat and with a walking stick-whereat these two waged tremendous battle.

Suddenly the conflict became a human thing. A little group of blue figures appeared on the green of the terrible hillside. It was some of our infantry. The attaché of a great empire was at my shoulder, and he turned to me and spoke with incredulity and scorn. "Why, they're trying to take the position," he cried, and I admitted meekly that I thought they were. "But they can't do it, you know," he protested vehemently. "It's impossible." And-good fellow that he was-he began to grieve and wail over a useless sacrifice of gallant men. "It's plucky, you know! By Gawd, it's plucky! But *they can't do it!*" He was profoundly moved; his voice was quite broken. "It will simply be a hell of a slaughter with no good coming out of it."

The trail was already crowded with stretcher-bearers and with wounded men who could walk. One had to stem a tide of mute agony. But I don't know that it was mute agony. I only know that it was mute. It was something in which the silence or, more likely, the reticence was an appalling and inexplicable fact. One's senses seemed to demand that these men should cry out. But you could really find wounded men who exhibited all the signs of a pleased and contented mood. When thinking of it now it seems strange beyond words. But at the time —I don't know-it did not attract one's wonder. A man with a hole in his arm or his shoulder, or even in the leg below the knee, was often whimsical, comic. "Well, this ain't exactly what I enlisted for, boys. If I'd been told about this in Tampa, I'd have resigned from th' army. Oh, yes, you can get the same thing if you keep on going. But I think the Spaniards may run out of ammunition in the course of a week or ten days." Then suddenly one would be confronted by the awful majesty of a man shot in the face. Particularly I remember one. He had a great dragoon moustache, and the blood streamed down his face to meet this moustache even as a torrent goes to meet the jammed log, and then swarmed out to the tips and fell in big slow drops. He looked steadily into my eyes; I was ashamed to return his glance. You understand? It is very curious-all that.

The two lines of battle were royally whacking away at each other, and there was no rest or peace in all that region. The modern bullet is a far-flying bird. It rakes the air with its hot spitting song at distances which, as a usual thing, place the whole landscape in the danger-zone. There was no direction from which they did not come. A chart of their courses over one's head would have resembled a spider's web. My friend Jimmie, the photographer, mounted to the firing line with me and we gallivanted as much as we dared. The "sense of the meeting" was curious. Most of the men seemed to have no idea of a grand historic performance, but they were grimly satisfied with themselves. "Well, begawd, we done it." Then they wanted to know about other parts of the line. "How are things looking, old man? Everything all right?" "Yes, everything is all right if you can hold this ridge." "Aw, hell," said the men, "we'll hold the ridge. Don't you worry about that, son."

It was Jimmie's first action, and, as we cautiously were making our way to the right of our lines, the crash of the Spanish fire became uproarious, and the air simply whistled. I heard a quavering voice near my shoulder, and, turning, I beheld Jimmie-Jimmie-with a face bloodless, white as paper. He looked at me with eyes opened extremely wide. "Say," he said, "this is pretty hot, ain't it?" I was delighted. I knew exactly what he meant. He wanted to have the situation defined. If I had told him that this was the occasion of some mere idle desultory firing and recommended that he wait until the real battle began, I think he would have gone in a bee-line for the rear. But I told him the truth. "Yes, Jimmie," I replied earnestly. "You can take it from me that this is patent, double-extra-what-for." And immediately he nodded. "All right." If this was a big action, then he was willing to pay in his fright as a rational price for the privilege of being present. But if this was only a penny affray, he considered the price exorbitant, and he would go away. He accepted my assurance with simple faith, and deported himself with kindly dignity as one moving amid great things. His face was still as pale as paper, but that counted for nothing. The main point was his perfect willingness to be frightened for reasons. I wonder where is Jimmie? I lent him the Jamaica polo-pony one day and it ran away with him and flung him off in the middle of a ford. He appeared to me afterward and made bitter speech concerning this horse which I had assured him was a gentle and pious animal. Then I never saw Jimmie again.

Then came the night of the first of July. A group of correspondents limped back to El Poso. It had been a day so long that the morning seemed as remote as a morning in the previous year. But I have forgotten to tell you about Reuben McNab. Many years ago, I went to school at a place called Claverack, in New York State, where there was a semi-military institution. Contemporaneous with me, as a student, was Reuben McNab, a long, lank boy, freckled, sandy-haired —an extraordinary boy in no way, and yet, I wager, a boy clearly marked in every recollection. Perhaps there is a good deal in that name. Reuben McNab. You can't fling that name carelessly over your shoulder and lose it. It follows you like the haunting memory of a sin. At any rate, Reuben McNab was identified intimately in my thought with the sunny irresponsible days at Claverack, when all the earth was a green field and all the sky was a rainless blue.

Then I looked down into a miserable huddle at Bloody Bend, a huddle of hurt men, dying men, dead men. And there I saw Reuben McNab, a corporal in the 71st New York Volunteers, and with a hole through his lung. Also, several holes through his clothing. "Well, they got me," he said in greeting. Usually they said that. There were no long speeches. "Well, they got me." That was sufficient. The duty of the upright, unhurt, man is then difficult. I doubt if many of us learned how to speak to our own wounded. In the first place, one had to play that the wound was nothing; oh, a mere nothing; a casual interference with movement, perhaps, but nothing more; oh, really nothing more. In the second place, one had to show a comrade's appreciation of this sad plight. As a result I think most of us bungled and stammered in the presence of our wounded friends. That's curious, eh? "Well, they got me," said Reuben McNab. I had looked upon five hundred wounded men with stolidity, or with a conscious indifference which filled me with amazement. But the apparition of Reuben McNab, the schoolmate, lying there in the mud, with a hole through his lung, awed me into stutterings, set me trembling with a sense of terrible intimacy with this war which theretofore I could have believed was a dream-almost. Twenty shot men rolled their eyes and looked at me. Only one man paid no heed. He was dying; he had no time. The bullets hummed low over them all. Death, having already struck, still insisted upon raising a venomous crest. "If you're goin' by the hospital, step in and see me," said Reuben McNab. That was all.

At the correspondents' camp, at El Poso, there was hot coffee. It was very good. I have a vague sense of being very selfish over my blanket and rubber coat. I have a vague sense of spasmodic firing during my sleep; it rained, and then I awoke to hear that steady drumming of an infantry fire-something which was never to cease, it seemed. They were at it again. The trail from El Poso to the positions along San Juan ridge had become an exciting thoroughfare. Shots from large-bore rifles dropped in from almost every side. At this time the safest place was the extreme front. I remember in particular the one outcry I heard. A private in the 71st, without his rifle, had gone to a stream for some water, and was returning, being but a little in rear of me. Suddenly I heard this cry —"Oh, my God, come quick" —and I was conscious then to having heard the hateful zip of a close shot. He lay on the ground, wriggling. He was hit in the hip. Two men came quickly. Presently everybody seemed to be getting knocked down. They went over like men of wet felt, quietly, calmly, with no more complaint than so many automatons. It was only that lad —"Oh, my God, come quick." Otherwise, men seemed to consider that their hurts were not worthy of particular attention. A number of people got killed very courteously, tacitly absolving the rest of us from any care in the matter. A man fell; he turned blue; his face took on an expression of deep sorrow; and then his immediate friends worried about him, if he had friends. This was July 1. I crave the permission to leap back again to that date.

On the morning of July 2, I sat on San Juan hill and watched Lawton's division come up. I was absolutely sheltered, but still where I could look into the faces of men who were trotting up under fire. There wasn't a high heroic face among them. They were all men intent on business. That was all. It may seem to you that I am trying to make everything a squalor. That would be wrong. I feel that things were often sublime. But they were *differently* sublime. They were not of our shallow and preposterous fictions. They stood out in a simple, majestic commonplace. It was the behaviour of men on the street. It was the behaviour of men. In one way, each man was just pegging along at the heels of the man before him, who was pegging along at the heels of still another man, who was pegging along at the heels of still another man who — — It was that in the flat and obvious way. In another way it was pageantry, the pageantry of the accomplishment of naked duty. One cannot speak of it-the spectacle of the common man serenely doing his work, his appointed work. It is the one thing in the universe which makes one fling expression to the winds and be satisfied to simply feel. Thus they moved at San Juan-the soldiers of the United States Regular Army. One pays them the tribute of the toast of silence.

Lying near one of the enemy's trenches was a red-headed Spanish corpse. I wonder how many hundreds were cognisant of this red-headed Spanish corpse? It arose to the dignity of a landmark. There were many corpses but only one with a red head. This red-head. He was always there. Each time I approached that part of the field I prayed that I might find that he had been buried. But he was always there-red-headed. His strong simple countenance was a malignant sneer at the system which was forever killing the credulous peasants in a sort of black night of politics, where the peasants merely followed whatever somebody had told them was lofty and good. But, nevertheless, the red-headed Spaniard was dead. He was irrevocably dead. And to what purpose? The honour of Spain? Surely the honour of Spain could have existed without the violent death of this poor red-headed peasant? Ah well, he was buried when the heavy firing ceased and men had time for such small things as funerals. The trench was turned over on top of him. It was a fine, honourable, soldierly fate-to be buried in a trench, the trench of the fight and the death. Sleep well, red-headed peasant. You came to another hemisphere to fight because-because you were told to, I suppose. Well, there you are, buried in your trench on San Juan hill. That is the end of it, your life has been taken-that is a flat, frank fact. And foreigners buried you expeditiously while speaking a strange tongue. Sleep well, red-headed mystery.

On the day before the destruction of Cervera's fleet, I steamed past our own squadron, doggedly lying in its usual semicircle, every nose pointing at the mouth of the harbour. I went to Jamaica, and on the placid evening of the next day I was again steaming past our own squadron, doggedly lying in its usual semicircle, every nose pointing at the mouth of the harbour. A megaphone-hail from the bridge of one of the yacht-gunboats came casually over the water. "Hello! hear the news?" "No; what was it?" "The Spanish fleet came out this morning." "Oh, of course, it did." "Honest, I mean." "Yes, I know; well, where are they now?" "Sunk." Was there ever such a preposterous statement? I was humiliated that my friend, the lieutenant on the yacht-gunboat, should have measured me as one likely to swallow this bad joke.

But it was all true; every word. I glanced back at our squadron, lying in its usual semicircle, every nose pointing at the mouth of the harbour. It would have been absurd to think that anything had happened. The squadron hadn't changed a button. There it sat without even a smile on the face of the tiger. And it had eaten four armoured cruisers and two torpedo-boat-destroyers while my back was turned for a moment. Courteously, but clearly, we announced across the waters that until despatch-boats came to be manned from the ranks of the celebrated horse-marines, the lieutenant's statement would probably remain unappreciated. He made a gesture, abandoning us to our scepticism. It infuriates an honourable and serious man to be taken for a liar or a joker at a time when he is supremely honourable and serious. However, when we went ashore, we found Siboney ringing with the news. It was true, then; that mishandled collection of sick ships had come out and taken the deadly thrashing which was rightfully the due of—I don't know-somebody in Spain-or perhaps nobody anywhere. One likes to wallop incapacity, but one has mingled emotions over the incapacity which is not so much personal as it is the development of centuries. This kind of incapacity cannot be centralised. You cannot hit the head which contains it all. This is the idea, I imagine, which moved the officers and men of our fleet. Almost immediately they began to speak of the Spanish Admiral as "poor old boy" with a lucid suggestion in their tones that his fate appealed to them as being undue hard, undue cruel. And yet the Spanish guns hit nothing. If a man shoots, he should hit something occasionally, and men say that from the time the Spanish ships broke clear of the harbour entrance until they were one by one overpowered, they were each a band of flame. Well, one can only mumble out that when a man shoots he should be required to hit something occasionally.

In truth, the greatest fact of the whole campaign on land and sea seems to be the fact that the Spaniards could only hit by chance, by a fluke. If he had been an able marksman, no man of our two unsupported divisions would have set foot on San Juan hill on July 1. They should have been blown to smithereens. The Spaniards had no immediate lack of ammunition, for they fired enough to kill the population of four big cities. I admit neither Velasquez nor Cervantes into this discussion, although they have appeared by authority as reasons for something which I do not clearly understand. Well, anyhow they couldn't hit anything. Velasquez? Yes. Cervantes?

Yes. But the Spanish troops seemed only to try to make a very rapid fire. Thus we lost many men. We lost them because of the simple fury of the fire; never because the fire was well-directed, intelligent. But the Americans were called upon to be whipped because of Cervantes and Velasquez. It was impossible.

Out on the slopes of San Juan the dog-tents shone white. Some kind of negotiations were going forward, and men sat on their trousers and waited. It was all rather a blur of talks with officers, and a craving for good food and good water. Once Leighton and I decided to ride over to El Caney, into which town the civilian refugees from Santiago were pouring. The road from the beleaguered city to the out-lying village was a spectacle to make one moan. There were delicate gentle families on foot, the silly French boots of the girls twisting and turning in a sort of absolute paper futility; there were sons and grandsons carrying the venerable patriarch in his own armchair; there were exhausted mothers with babes who wailed; there were young dandies with their toilettes in decay; there were puzzled, guideless women who didn't know what had happened. The first sentence one heard was the murmurous "What a damn shame." We saw a godless young trooper of the Second Cavalry sharply halt a waggon. "Hold on a minute. You must carry this woman. She's fainted twice already." The virtuous driver of the U.S. Army waggon mildly answered: "But I'm full-up now." "You can make room for her," said the private of the Second Cavalry. A young, young man with a straight mouth. It was merely a plain bit of nothing-at-all but, thank God, thank God, he seemed to have not the slightest sense of excellence. He said: "If you've got any man in there who can walk at all, you put him out and let this woman get in." "But," answered the teamster, "I'm filled up with a lot of cripples and grandmothers." Thereupon they discussed the point fairly, and ultimately the woman was lifted into the waggon.

The vivid thing was the fact that these people did not visibly suffer. Somehow they were numb. There was not a tear. There was rarely a countenance which was not wondrously casual. There was no sign of fatalistic theory. It was simply that what was happening to-day had happened yesterday, as near as one could judge. I could fancy that these people had been thrown out of their homes every day. It was utterly, utterly casual. And they accepted the ministrations of our men in the same fashion. Everything was a matter of course. I had a filled canteen. I was frightfully conscious of this fact because a filled canteen was a pearl of price; it was a great thing. It was an enormous accident which led one to offer praises that he was luckier than ten thousand better men.

As Leighton and I rode along, we came to a tree under which a refugee family had halted. They were a man, his wife, two handsome daughters and a pimply son. It was plain that they were superior people, because the girls had dressed for the exodus and wore corsets which captivated their forms with a steel-ribbed vehemence only proper for wear on a sun-blistered road to a distant town. They asked us for water. Water was the gold of the moment. Leighton was almost maudlin in his generosity. I remember being angry with him. He lavished upon them his whole canteen and he received in return not even a glance of-what? Acknowledgment? No, they didn't even admit anything. Leighton wasn't a human being; he was some sort of a mountain spring. They accepted him on a basis of pure natural phenomena. His canteen was purely an occurrence. In the meantime the pimple-faced approached me. He asked for water and held out a pint cup. My response was immediate. I tilted my canteen and poured into his cup almost a pint of my treasure. He glanced into the cup and apparently he beheld there some innocent sediment for which he alone or his people were responsible. In the American camps the men were accustomed to a sediment. Well, he glanced at my poor cupful and then negligently poured it out on the ground and held up his cup for more. I gave him more; I gave him his cup full again, but there was something within me which made me swear him out completely. But he didn't understand a word. Afterward I watched if they were capable of being moved to help on their less able fellows on this miserable journey. Not they! Nor yet anybody else. Nobody cared for anybody save my young friend of the Second Cavalry, who rode seriously to and fro doing his best for people, who took him as a result of a strange upheaval.

The fight at El Caney had been furious. General Vera del Rey with somewhat less than 1000 men-the Spanish accounts say 520 — had there made such a stand that only about 80 battered soldiers ever emerged from it. The attack cost Lawton about 400 men. The magazine rifle! But the town was now a vast parrot-cage of chattering refugees. If, on the road, they were silent, stolid and serene, in the town they found their tongues and set up such a cackle as one may seldom hear. Notably the women; it is they who invariably confuse the definition of situations, and one could wonder in amaze if this crowd of irresponsible, gabbling hens had already forgotten that this town was the deathbed, so to speak, of scores of gallant men whose blood was not yet dry; whose hands, of the hue of pale amber, stuck from the soil of the hasty burial. On the way to El Caney I had conjured a picture of the women of Santiago, proud in their pain, their despair, dealing glances of defiance, contempt, hatred at the invader; fiery ferocious ladies, so true to their vanquished and to their dead that they spurned the very existence of the low-bred churls who lacked both Velasquez and Cervantes. And instead, there was this mere noise, which reminded one alternately of a tea-party in Ireland, a village fête in the south of France, and the vacuous morning screech of a swarm of sea-gulls. "Good. There is Donna Maria. This will lower her high head. This will teach her better manners to her neighbours. She wasn't too grand to send her rascal of a servant to borrow a trifle of coffee of me in the morning, and then when I met her on the calle-por Dios, she was too blind to see me. But we are all equal here. No? Little Juan has a sore toe. Yes, Donna Maria; many thanks, many thanks. Juan, do me the favour to be quiet while Donna Maria is asking about your toe. Oh, Donna Maria, we were always poor, always. But you. My heart bleeds when I see how hard this is for you. The old cat! She gives me a head-shake."

Pushing through the throng in the plaza we came in sight of the door of the church, and here was a strange scene. The church had been turned into a hospital for Spanish wounded who had fallen into American hands. The interior of the church was too cave-like in its gloom for the eyes of the operating surgeons, so they had had the altar table carried to the doorway, where there was a bright light. Framed then in the black archway was the altar table with the figure of a man upon it. He was naked save for a breech-clout and so close, so clear was the ecclesiastic suggestion, that one's mind leaped to a phantasy that this thin, pale figure had just been torn down from a cross. The flash of the impression was like light, and for this instant it illumined all the dark recesses of one's remotest idea of sacrilege, ghastly and wanton. I bring this to you merely as an effect, an effect of mental light and shade, if you like; something done in thought similar to that which the French impressionists do in colour; something meaningless and at the same time overwhelming, crushing, monstrous. "Poor devil; I wonder if he'll pull through," said Leighton. An American surgeon and his assistants were intent over the prone figure. They wore white aprons. Something small and silvery flashed in the surgeon's hand. An assistant held the merciful sponge close to the man's nostrils, but he was writhing and moaning in some horrible dream of this artificial sleep. As the surgeon's instrument played, I fancied that the man dreamed that he was being gored by a bull. In his pleading, delirious babble occurred constantly the name of the Virgin, the Holy Mother. "Good morning," said the surgeon. He changed his knife to his left hand and gave me a wet palm. The tips of his fingers were wrinkled, shrunken, like those of a boy who has been in swimming too long. Now, in front of the door, there were three American sentries, and it was their business to-to do what? To keep this Spanish crowd from swarming over the operating table! It was perforce a public clinic. They would not be denied. The weaker women and the children jostled according to their might in the rear, while the stronger people, gaping in the front rank, cried out impatiently when the pushing disturbed their long stares. One burned with a sudden gift of public oratory. One wanted to say: "Oh, go away, go away, go away. Leave the man decently alone with his pain, you gogglers. This is not the national sport."

But within the church there was an audience of another kind. This was of the other wounded men awaiting their turn. They lay on their brown blankets in rows along the stone floor. Their eyes, too, were fastened upon the operating-table, but-that was different. Meek-eyed little yellow men lying on the floor awaiting their turns.

One afternoon I was seated with a correspondent friend, on the porch of one of the houses at Siboney. A vast man on horseback came riding along at a foot pace. When he perceived my friend, he pulled up sharply. "Whoa! Where's that mule I lent you?" My friend arose and saluted. "I've got him all right, General, thank you," said my friend. The vast man shook his finger. "Don't you lose him now." "No, sir, I won't; thank you, sir." The vast man rode away. "Who the devil is that?" said I. My friend laughed. "That's General Shafter," said he.

I gave five dollars for the Bos'n —small, black, spry imp of Jamaica sin. When I first saw him he was the property of a fireman on the *Criton*. The fireman had found him —a little wharf rat-in Port Antonio. It was not the purchase of a slave; it was that the fireman believed that he had spent about five dollars on a lot of comic supplies for the Bos'n, including a little suit of sailor clothes. The Bos'n was an adroit and fantastic black gamin. His eyes were like white lights, and his teeth were a row of little piano keys; otherwise he was black. He had both been a jockey and a cabin-boy, and he had the manners of a gentleman. After he entered my service I don't think there was ever an occasion upon which he was useful, save when he told me quaint stories of Guatemala, in which country he seemed to have lived some portion of his infantile existence. Usually he ran funny errands like little foot-races, each about fifteen yards in length. At Siboney he slept under my hammock like a poodle, and I always expected that, through the breaking of a rope, I would some night descend and obliterate him. His incompetence was spectacular. When I wanted him to do a thing, the agony of supervision was worse than the agony of personal performance. It would have been easier to have gotten my own spurs or boots or blanket than to have the bother of this little incapable's service. But the good aspect was the humorous view. He was like a boy, a mouse, a scoundrel, and a devoted servitor. He was immensely popular. His name of Bos'n became a Siboney stock-word. Everybody knew it. It was a name like President McKinley, Admiral Sampson, General Shafter. The Bos'n became a figure. One day he approached me with four one-dollar notes in United States currency. He besought me to preserve them for him, and I pompously tucked them away in my riding breeches, with an air which meant that his funds were now as safe as if they were in a national bank. Still, I asked with some surprise, where he had reaped all this money. He frankly admitted at once that it had been given to him by the enthusiastic soldiery as a tribute to his charm of person and manner. This was not astonishing for Siboney, where money was meaningless. Money was not worth carrying —"packing." However, a soldier came to our house one morning, and asked, "Got any more tobacco to sell?" As befitted men in virtuous poverty, we replied with indignation. "What tobacco?" "Why, that tobacco what the little nigger is sellin' round."

I said, "Bos'n!" He said, "Yes, mawstah." Wounded men on bloody stretchers were being carried into the hospital next door. "Bos'n, you've been stealing my tobacco." His defence was as glorious as the defence of that forlorn hope in romantic history, which drew itself up and mutely died. He lied as desperately, as savagely, as hopelessly as ever man fought.

One day a delegation from the 33d Michigan came to me and said: "Are you the proprietor of the Bos'n?" I said: "Yes." And they said: "Well, would you please be so kind as to be so good as to give him to us?" A big battle was expected for the next day. "Why," I answered, "if you want him you can have him. But he's a thief, and I won't let him go save on his personal announcement." The big battle occurred the next day, and the Bos'n did not disappear in it; but he disappeared in my interest in the battle, even as a waif might disappear in a fog. My interest in the battle made the Bos'n dissolve before my eyes. Poor little rascal! I gave him up with pain. He was such an innocent villain. He knew no more of thievery than the whole of it. Anyhow one was fond of him. He was a natural scoundrel. He was not an educated scoundrel. One cannot bear the educated scoundrel. He was ingenuous, simple, honest, abashed ruffianism.

I hope the 33d Michigan did not arrive home naked. I hope the Bos'n did not succeed in getting everything. If the Bos'n builds a palace in Detroit, I shall know where he got the money. He got it from the 33d Michigan. Poor little man. He was only eleven years old. He vanished.

I had thought to preserve him as a relic, even as one preserves forgotten bayonets and fragments of shell. And now as to the pocket of my riding-breeches. It contained four dollars in United States currency. Bos'n! Hey, Bos'n, where are you? The morning was the morning of battle.

I was on San Juan Hill when Lieutenant Hobson and the men of the *Merrimac* were exchanged and brought into the American lines. Many of us knew that the exchange was about to be made, and gathered to see the famous party. Some of our Staff officers rode out with three Spanish officers —prisoners-these latter being blindfolded before they were taken through the American position. The army was majestically minding its business in the long line of trenches when its eye caught sight of this little procession. "What's that? What they goin' to do?" "They're goin' to exchange Hobson." Wherefore every man who was foot-free staked out a claim where he could get a good view of the liberated heroes, and two bands prepared to collaborate on "The Star Spangled Banner." There was a very long wait through the sunshiny afternoon. In our impatience, we imagined them-the Americans and Spaniards-dickering away out there under the big tree like so many peddlers. Once the massed bands, misled by a rumour, stiffened themselves into that dramatic and breathless moment when each man is ready to blow. But the rumour was exploded in the nick of time. We made ill jokes, saying one to another that the negotiations had found diplomacy to be a failure, and were playing freeze-out poker for the whole batch of prisoners.

But suddenly the moment came. Along the cut roadway, toward the crowded soldiers, rode three men, and it could be seen that the central one wore the undress uniform of an officer of the United States navy. Most of the soldiers were sprawled out on the grass, bored and wearied in the sunshine. However, they aroused at the old circus-parade, torch-light procession cry, "Here they come." Then the men of the regular army did a thing. They arose *en masse* and came to "Attention." Then the men of the regular army did another thing. They slowly lifted every weather-beaten hat and drooped it until it touched the knee. Then there was a magnificent silence, broken only by the measured hoof-beats of the little company's horses as they rode through the gap. It was solemn, funereal, this splendid silent welcome of a brave man by men who stood on a hill which they had earned out of blood and death-simply, honestly, with no sense of excellence, earned out of blood and death.

Then suddenly the whole scene went to rubbish. Before he reached the bottom of the hill, Hobson was bowing to right and left like another Boulanger, and, above the thunder of the massed bands, one could hear the venerable outbreak, "Mr. Hobson, I'd like to shake the hand of the man who — —" But the real welcome was that welcome of silence. However, one could thrill again when the tail of the procession appeared-an army waggon containing the blue-jackets of the *Merrimac* adventure. I remember grinning heads stuck out from under the canvas cover of the waggon. And the army spoke to the navy. "Well, Jackie, how does it feel?" And the navy up and answered: "Great! Much obliged to you fellers for comin' here." "Say, Jackie, what did they arrest ye for anyhow? Stealin' a dawg?" The navy still grinned. Here was no rubbish. Here was the mere exchange of language between men.

Some of us fell in behind this small but royal procession and followed it to General Shafter's headquarters, some miles on the road to Siboney. I have a vague impression that I watched the meeting between Shafter and Hobson, but the impression ends there. However, I remember hearing a talk between them as to Hobson's men, and then the blue-jackets were called up to hear the congratulatory remarks of the general in command of the Fifth Army Corps. It was a scene in the fine shade of thickly-leaved trees. The general sat in his chair, his belly sticking ridiculously out before him as if he had adopted some form of artificial inflation. He looked like a joss. If the seamen had suddenly begun to burn a few sticks, most of the spectators would have exhibited no surprise. But the words he spoke were proper, clear, quiet, soldierly, the words of one man to others. The Jackies were comic. At the bidding of their officer they aligned themselves before the general, grinned with embarrassment one to the other, made funny attempts to correct the alignment, and-looked sheepish. They looked sheepish. They looked like bad little boys flagrantly caught. They had no sense of excellence. Here was no rubbish.

Very soon after this the end of the campaign came for me. I caught a fever. I am not sure to this day what kind of a fever it was. It was defined variously. I know, at any rate, that I first developed a languorous indifference to everything in the world. Then I developed a tendency to ride a horse even as a man lies on a cot. Then I—I am not sure—I think I grovelled and groaned about Siboney for several days. My colleagues, Scovel and George Rhea, found me and gave me of their best, but I didn't know whether London Bridge was falling down or whether there was a war with Spain. It was all the same. What of it? Nothing of it. Everything had happened, perhaps. But I cared not a jot. Life, death, dishonour-all were nothing to me. All I cared for was pickles. *Pickles at any price! Pickles!!*

If I had been the father of a hundred suffering daughters, I should have waved them all aside and remarked that they could be damned for all I cared. It was not a mood. One can defeat a mood. It was a physical situation. Sometimes one cannot defeat a physical situation. I heard the talk of Siboney and sometimes I answered, but I was as indifferent as the star-fish flung to die on the sands. The only fact in the universe was that my veins burned and boiled. Rhea finally staggered me down to the army-surgeon who had charge of the proceedings, and the army-surgeon looked me over with a keen healthy eye. Then he gave a permit that I should be sent home. The manipulation from the shore to the transport was something which was Rhea's affair. I am not sure whether we went in a boat or a balloon. I think it was a boat. Rhea pushed me on board and I swayed meekly and unsteadily toward the captain of the ship, a corpulent, well-conditioned, impickled person pacing noisily on the spar-deck. "Ahem, yes; well; all right. Have you got your own food? I hope, for Christ's sake, you don't expect us to feed you, do you?" Whereupon I went to the rail and weakly yelled at Rhea, but he was already afar. The captain was, meantime, remarking in bellows that, for Christ's sake, I couldn't expect him to feed me. I didn't expect to be fed. I didn't care to be fed. I wished for nothing on earth but some form of painless pause, oblivion. The insults of this old pie-stuffed scoundrel did not affect me then; they affect me now. I would like to tell him that, although I like collies, fox-terriers, and even screw-curled poodles, I do not like him. He was free to call me superfluous and throw me overboard, but he was not free to coarsely speak to a somewhat sick man. I—in fact I hate him-it is all wrong—I lose whatever ethics I possessed-but—I hate him, and I demand that you should imagine a milch cow endowed with a knowledge of navigation and in command of a ship-and perfectly capable of commanding a ship-oh, well, never mind.

I was crawling along the deck when somebody pounced violently upon me and thundered: "Who in hell are you, sir?" I said I was a correspondent. He asked me did I know that I had yellow fever. I said No. He yelled, "Well, by Gawd, you isolate yourself, sir." I said; "Where?" At this question he almost frothed at the mouth. I thought he was going to strike me. "Where?" he roared. "How in hell do I know, sir? I know as much about this ship as you do, sir. But you isolate yourself, sir." My clouded brain tried to comprehend these orders. This man was a doctor in the regular army, and it was necessary to obey him, so I bestirred myself to learn what he meant by these gorilla outcries. "All right, doctor; I'll isolate myself, but I wish you'd tell me where to go." And then he passed into such volcanic humour that I clung to the rail and gasped. "Isolate yourself, sir. Isolate yourself. That's all I've got to say, sir. I don't give a God damn where you go, but when you get there, stay there, sir." So I wandered away and ended up on the deck aft, with my head against the flagstaff and my limp body stretched on a little rug. I was not at all sorry for myself. I didn't care a tent-peg. And yet, as I look back upon it now, the situation was fairly exciting—a voyage of four or five days before me-no food-no friends-above all else, no friends-isolated on deck, and rather ill.

When I returned to the United States, I was able to move my feminine friends to tears by an account of this voyage, but, after all, it wasn't so bad. They kept me on my small reservation aft, but plenty of kindness loomed soon enough. At mess-time, they slid me a tin plate of something, usually stewed tomatoes and bread. Men are always good men. And, at any rate, most of the people were in worse condition than I—poor bandaged chaps looking sadly down at the waves. In a way, I knew the kind. First lieutenants at forty years of age, captains at fifty, majors at 102, lieutenant-colonels at 620, full colonels at 1000, and brigadiers at 9,768,295 plus. A man had to live two billion years to gain eminent rank in the regular army at that time. And, of course, they all had trembling wives at remote western posts waiting to hear the worst, the best, or the middle.

In rough weather, the officers made a sort of a common pool of all the sound legs and arms, and by dint of hanging hard to each other they managed to move from their deck chairs to their cabins and from their cabins again to their deck chairs. Thus they lived until the ship reached Hampton Roads. We slowed down opposite the curiously mingled hotels and batteries at Old Point Comfort, and at our mast-head we flew the yellow-flag, the grim ensign of the plague. Then we witnessed something which informed us that with all this ship-load of wounds and fevers and starvations we had forgotten the fourth element of war. We were flying the yellow flag, but a launch came and circled swiftly about us. There was a little woman in the launch, and she kept looking and looking and looking. Our ship was so high that she could see only those who rung at the rail, but she kept looking and looking and looking. It was plain enough-it was all plain enough-but my heart sank with the fear that she was not going to find him. But presently there was a commotion among some black dough-boys of the 24th Infantry, and two of them ran aft to Colonel Liscum, its gallant commander. Their faces were wreathed in darkey grins of delight. "Kunnel, ain't dat Mis' Liscum, Kunnel?" "What?" said the old man. He got up quickly and appeared at the rail, his arm in a sling. He cried, "Alice!" The little woman saw him, and instantly she covered up her face with her hands as if blinded with a flash of white fire. She made no outcry; it was all in this simply swift gesture, but we-we knew them. It told us. It told us the other part. And in a vision we all saw our own harbour-lights. That is to say those of us who had harbour-lights.

I was almost well, and had defeated the yellow-fever charge which had been brought against me, and so I was allowed ashore among the first. And now happened a strange thing. A hard campaign, full of wants and lacks and absences, brings a man speedily back to an appreciation of things long disregarded or forgotten. In camp, somewhere in the woods between Siboney and Santiago, I happened to think of ice-cream-soda. I had done very well without it for many years; in fact I think I loathe it; but I got to dreaming of ice-cream-soda, and I came near dying of longing for it. I couldn't get it out of my mind, try as I would to concentrate my thoughts upon the land crabs and mud with which I was surrounded. It certainly had been an institution of my childhood, but to have a ravenous longing for it in the year 1898 was about as illogical as to have a ravenous longing for kerosene. All I could do was to swear to myself that if I reached the United States again, I would immediately go to the nearest soda-water fountain and make it look like Spanish Fours. In a loud, firm voice, I would say, "Orange, please." And here is the strange thing: as soon as I was ashore I went to the nearest soda-water fountain, and in a loud, firm voice I said, "Orange, please." I remember one man who went mad that way over tinned peaches, and who wandered over the face of the earth saying plaintively, "Have you any peaches?"

Most of the wounded and sick had to be tabulated and marshalled in sections and thoroughly officialised, so that I was in time to take a position on the verandah of Chamberlain's Hotel and see my late shipmates taken to the hospital. The verandah was crowded with women in light, charming summer dresses, and with spruce officers from the Fortress. It was like a bank of flowers. It filled me with awe. All this luxury and refinement and gentle care and fragrance and colour seemed absolutely new. Then across the narrow street on the verandah of the hotel there was a similar bank of flowers. Two companies of volunteers dug a lane through the great crowd in the street and kept the way, and then through this lane there passed a curious procession. I had never known that they looked like that. Such a gang of dirty, ragged, emaciated, half-starved, bandaged cripples I had never seen. Naturally there were many men who couldn't walk, and some of these were loaded upon a big flat car which was in tow of a trolley-car. Then there were many stretchers, slow-moving. When that crowd began to pass the hotel the banks of flowers made a noise which could make one tremble. Perhaps it was a moan, perhaps it was a sob-but no, it was something beyond either a moan or a sob. Anyhow, the sound of women weeping was in it. —The sound of women weeping.

And how did these men of famous deeds appear when received thus by the people? Did they smirk and look as if they were bursting with the desire to tell everything which had happened? No they hung their heads like so many jail-birds. Most of them seemed to be suffering from something which was like stage-fright during the ordeal of this chance but supremely eloquent reception. No sense of excellence-that was it. Evidently they were willing to leave the clacking to all those natural born major-generals who after the war talked enough to make a great fall in the price of that commodity all over the world.

The episode was closed. And you can depend upon it that I have told you nothing at all, nothing at all, nothing at all.

The Second Generation

I

Caspar Cadogan resolved to go to the tropic wars and do something. The air was blue and gold with the pomp of soldiering, and in every ear rang the music of military glory. Caspar's father was a United States Senator from the great State of Skowmulligan, where the war fever ran very high. Chill is the blood of many of the sons of millionaires, but Caspar took the fever and posted to Washington. His father had never denied him anything, and this time all that Caspar wanted was a little Captaincy in the Army-just a simple little Captaincy.

The old man had been entertaining a delegation of respectable bunco-steerers from Skow-mulligan who had come to him on a matter which is none of the public's business.

Bottles of whisky and boxes of cigars were still on the table in the sumptuous private parlour. The Senator had said, "Well, gentlemen, I'll do what I can for you." By this sentence he meant whatever he meant.

Then he turned to his eager son. "Well, Caspar?" The youth poured out his modest desires. It was not altogether his fault. Life had taught him a generous faith in his own abilities. If any one had told him that he was simply an ordinary d —d fool he would have opened his eyes wide at the person's lack of judgment. All his life people had admired him.

The Skowmulligan war-horse looked with quick disapproval into the eyes of his son. "Well, Caspar," he said slowly, "I am of the opinion that they've got all the golf experts and tennis champions and cotillion leaders and piano tuners and billiard markers that they really need as officers. Now, if you were a soldier — —"

"I know," said the young man with a gesture, "but I'm not exactly a fool, I hope, and I think if I get a chance I can do something. I'd like to try. I would, indeed."

The Senator lit a cigar. He assumed an attitude of ponderous reflection. "Y —yes, but this country is full of young men who are not fools. Full of 'em."

Caspar fidgeted in the desire to answer that while he admitted the profusion of young men who were not fools, he felt that he himself possessed interesting and peculiar qualifications which would allow him to make his mark in any field of effort which he seriously challenged. But he did not make this graceful statement, for he sometimes detected something ironic in his father's temperament. The Skowmulligan war-horse had not thought of expressing an opinion of his own ability since the year 1865, when he was young, like Caspar.

"Well, well," said the Senator finally. "I'll see about it. I'll see about it." The young man was obliged to await the end of his father's characteristic method of thought. The war-horse never gave a quick answer, and if people tried to hurry him they seemed able to arouse only a feeling of irritation against making a decision at all. His mind moved like the wind, but practice had placed a Mexican bit in the mouth of his judgment. This old man of light quick thought had taught himself to move like an ox cart. Caspar said, "Yes, sir." He withdrew to his club, where, to the affectionate inquiries of some envious friends, he replied, "The old man is letting the idea soak."

The mind of the war-horse was decided far sooner than Caspar expected. In Washington a large number of well-bred handsome young men were receiving appointments as Lieutenants, as Captains, and occasionally as Majors. They were a strong, healthy, clean-eyed educated collection. They were a prime lot. A German Field-Marshal would have beamed with joy if he could have had them-to send to school. Anywhere in the world they would have made a grand show as material, but, intrinsically they were not Lieutenants, Captains and Majors. They were fine men, though manhood is only an essential part of a Lieutenant, a Captain or a Major. But at any rate, this arrangement had all the logic of going to sea in a bathing-machine.

The Senator found himself reasoning that Caspar was as good as any of them, and better than many. Presently he was bleating here and there that his boy should have a chance. "The boy's all right, I tell you, Henry. He's wild to go, and I don't see why they shouldn't give him a show. He's got plenty of nerve, and he's keen as a whiplash. I'm going to get him an appointment, and if you can do anything to help it along I wish you would."

Then he betook himself to the White House and the War Department and made a stir. People think that Administrations are always slavishly, abominably anxious to please the Machine. They are not; they wish the Machine sunk in red fire, for by the power of ten thousand past words, looks, gestures, writings, the Machine comes along and takes the Administration by the nose and twists it, and the Administration dare not even yell. The huge force which carries an election to success looks reproachfully at the Administration and says, "Give me a bun." That is a very small thing with which to reward a Colossus.

The Skowmulligan war-horse got his bun and took it to his hotel where Caspar was moodily reading war rumours. "Well, my boy, here you are." Caspar was a Captain and Commissary on the staff of Brigadier-General Reilly, commander of the Second Brigade of the First Division of the Thirtieth Army Corps.

"I had to work for it," said the Senator grimly. "They talked to me as if they thought you were some sort of empty-headed idiot. None of 'em seemed to know you personally. They just sort of took it for granted. Finally I got pretty hot in the collar." He paused a moment; his heavy, grooved face set hard; his blue eyes shone. He clapped a hand down upon the handle of his chair.

"Caspar, I've got you into this thing, and I believe you'll do all right, and I'm not saying this because I distrust either your sense or your grit. But I want you to understand you've *got to make a go of it.* I'm not going to talk any twaddle about your country and your country's flag. You understand all about that. But now you're a soldier, and there'll be this to do and that to do, and fighting to do, and you've got to do *every d ——d one of 'em* right up to the handle. I don't know how much of a shindy this thing is going to be, but any shindy is enough to show how much there is in a man. You've got your appointment, and that's all I can do for you; but I'll thrash you with my own hands if, when the Army gets back, the other fellows say my son is 'nothing but a good-looking dude.'"

He ceased, breathing heavily. Caspar looked bravely and frankly at his father, and answered in a voice which was not very tremulous. "I'll do my best. This is my chance. I'll do my best with it."

The Senator had a marvellous ability of transition from one manner to another. Suddenly he seemed very kind. "Well, that's all right, then. I guess you'll get along all right with Reilly. I know him well, and he'll see you through. I helped him along once. And now about this commissary business. As I understand it, a Commissary is a sort of caterer in a big way-that is, he looks out for a good many more things than a caterer has to bother his head about. Reilly's brigade has probably from two to three thousand men in it, and in regard to certain things you've got to look out for every man of 'em every day. I know perfectly well you couldn't successfully run a boarding-house in Ocean Grove. How are you going to manage for all these soldiers, hey? Thought about it?"

"No," said Caspar, injured. "I didn't want to be a Commissary. I wanted to be a Captain in the line."

"They wouldn't hear of it. They said you would have to take a staff appointment where people could look after you."

"Well, let them look after me," cried Caspar resentfully; "but when there's any fighting to be done I guess I won't necessarily be the last man."

"That's it," responded the Senator. "That's the spirit." They both thought that the problem of war would eliminate to an equation of actual battle.

Ultimately Caspar departed into the South to an encampment in salty grass under pine trees. Here lay an Army corps twenty thousand strong. Caspar passed into the dusty sunshine of it, and for many weeks he was lost to view.

"Of course I don't know a blamed thing about it," said Caspar frankly and modestly to a circle of his fellow staff officers. He was referring to the duties of his office.

Their faces became expressionless; they looked at him with eyes in which he could fathom nothing. After a pause one politely said, "Don't you?" It was the inevitable two words of convention.

"Why," cried Caspar, "I didn't know what a commissary officer was until I *was* one. My old Guv'nor told me. He'd looked it up in a book somewhere, I suppose; but *I* didn't know."

"Didn't you?"

The young man's face glowed with sudden humour. "Do you know, the word was intimately associated in my mind with camels. Funny, eh? I think it came from reading that rhyme of Kipling's about the commissariat camel."

"Did it?"

"Yes. Funny, isn't it? Camels!"

The brigade was ultimately landed at Siboney as part of an army to attack Santiago. The scene at the landing sometimes resembled the inspiriting daily drama at the approach to the Brooklyn Bridge. There was a great bustle, during which the wise man kept his property gripped in his hands lest it might march off into the wilderness in the pocket of one of the striding regiments. Truthfully, Caspar should have had frantic occupation, but men saw him wandering bootlessly here and there crying, "Has any one seen my saddlebags? Why, if I lose them I'm ruined. I've got everything packed away in 'em. Everything!"

They looked at him gloomily and without attention. "No," they said. It was to intimate that they would not give a rip if he had lost his nose, his teeth and his self-respect. Reilly's brigade collected itself from the boats and went off, each regiment's soul burning with anger because some other regiment was in advance of it. Moving along through the scrub and under the palms, men talked mostly of things that did not pertain to the business in hand.

General Reilly finally planted his headquarters in some tall grass under a mango tree. "Where's Cadogan?" he said suddenly as he took off his hat and smoothed the wet grey hair from his brow. Nobody knew. "I saw him looking for his saddle-bags down at the landing," said an officer dubiously. "Bother him," said the General contemptuously. "Let him stay there."

Three venerable regimental commanders came, saluted stiffly and sat in the grass. There was a pow-wow, during which Reilly explained much that the Division Commander had told him. The venerable Colonels nodded; they understood. Everything was smooth and clear to their minds. But still, the Colonel of the Forty-fourth Regular Infantry murmured about the commissariat. His men-and then he launched forth in a sentiment concerning the privations of his men in which you were confronted with his feeling that his men-his men were the only creatures of importance in the universe, which feeling was entirely correct for him. Reilly grunted. He did what most commanders did. He set the competent line to doing the work of the incompetent part of the staff.

In time Caspar came trudging along the road merrily swinging his saddle-bags. "Well, General," he cried as he saluted, "I found 'em."

"Did you?" said Reilly. Later an officer rushed to him tragically: "General, Cadogan is off there in the bushes eatin' potted ham and crackers all by himself." The officer was sent back into the bushes for Caspar, and the General sent Caspar with an order. Then Reilly and the three venerable Colonels, grinning, partook of potted ham and crackers. "Tashe a' right," said Reilly, with his mouth full. "Dorsey, see if 'e got some'n else."

"Mush be selfish young pig," said one of the Colonels, with his mouth full. "Who's he, General?"

"Son-Sen'tor Cad'gan-ol' frien' mine-dash 'im."

Caspar wrote a letter:

"Dear Father: I am sitting under a tree using the flattest part of my canteen for a desk. Even as I write the division ahead of us is moving forward and we don't know what moment the storm of battle may break out. I don't know what the plans are. General Reilly knows, but he is so good as to give me very little of his confidence. In fact, I might be part of a forlorn hope from all to the contrary I've heard from him. I understood you to say in Washington that you at one time had been of some service to him, but if that is true I can assure you he has completely forgotten it. At times his manner to me is little short of being offensive, but of course I understand that it is only the way of a crusty old soldier who has been made boorish and bearish by a long life among the Indians. I dare say I shall manage it all right without a row.

"When you hear that we have captured Santiago, please send me by first steamer a box of provisions and clothing, particularly sardines, pickles, and light-weight underwear. The other men on the staff are nice quiet chaps, but they seem a bit crude. There has been no fighting yet save the skirmish by Young's brigade. Reilly was furious because we couldn't get in it. I met General Peel yesterday. He was very nice. He said he knew you well when he was in Congress. Young Jack May is on Peel's staff. I knew him well in college. We spent an hour talking over old times. Give my love to all at home."

The march was leisurely. Reilly and his staff strolled out to the head of the long, sinuous column and entered the sultry gloom of the forest. Some less fortunate regiments had to wait among the trees at the side of the trail, and as Reilly's brigade passed them, officer called to officer, classmate to classmate, and in these greetings rang a note of everything, from West Point to Alaska. They were going into an action in which they, the officers, would lose over a hundred in killed and wounded-officers alone-and these greetings, in which many nicknames occurred, were in many cases farewells such as one pictures being given with ostentation, solemnity, fervour. "There goes Gory Widgeon! Hello, Gory! Where you starting for? Hey, Gory!"

Caspar communed with himself and decided that he was not frightened. He was eager and alert; he thought that now his obligation to his country, or himself, was to be faced, and he was mad to prove to old Reilly and the others that after all he was a very capable soldier.

Old Reilly was stumping along the line of his brigade and mumbling like a man with a mouthful of grass. The fire from the enemy's position was incredible in its swift fury, and Reilly's brigade was getting its share of a very bad ordeal. The old man's face was of the colour of a tomato, and in his rage he mouthed and sputtered strangely. As he pranced along his thin line, scornfully erect, voices arose from the grass beseeching him to take care of himself. At his heels scrambled a bugler with pallid skin and clenched teeth, a chalky, trembling youth, who kept his eye on old Reilly's back and followed it.

The old gentleman was quite mad. Apparently he thought the whole thing a dreadful mess, but now that his brigade was irrevocably in it he was full-tilting here and everywhere to establish some irreproachable, immaculate kind of behaviour on the part of every man jack in his brigade. The intentions of the three venerable Colonels were the same. They stood behind their lines, quiet, stern, courteous old fellows, admonishing their regiments to be very pretty in the face of such a hail of magazine-rifle and machine-gun fire as has never in this world been confronted save by beardless savages when the white man has found occasion to take his burden to some new place.

And the regiments were pretty. The men lay on their little stomachs and got peppered according to the law and said nothing, as the good blood pumped out into the grass, and even if a solitary rookie tried to get a decent reason to move to some haven of rational men, the cold voice of an officer made him look criminal with a shame that was a credit to his regimental education. Behind Reilly's command was a bullet-torn jungle through which it could not move as a brigade; ahead of it were Spanish trenches on hills. Reilly considered that he was in a fix no doubt, but he said this only to himself. Suddenly he saw on the right a little point of blue-shirted men already half-way up the hill. It was some pathetic fragment of the Sixth United States Infantry. Chagrined, shocked, horrified, Reilly bellowed to his bugler, and the chalked-faced youth unlocked his teeth and sounded the charge by rushes.

The men formed hastily and grimly, and rushed. Apparently there awaited them only the fate of respectable soldiers. But they went because-of the opinions of others, perhaps. They went because-no loud-mouthed lot of jail-birds such as the Twenty-Seventh Infantry could do anything that they could not do better. They went because Reilly ordered it. They went because they went.

And yet not a man of them to this day has made a public speech explaining precisely how he did the whole thing and detailing with what initiative and ability he comprehended and defeated a situation which he did not comprehend at all.

Reilly never saw the top of the hill. He was heroically striving to keep up with his men when a bullet ripped quietly through his left lung, and he fell back into the arms of the bugler, who received him as he would have received a Christmas present. The three venerable Colonels inherited the brigade in swift succession. The senior commanded for about fifty seconds, at the end of which he was mortally shot. Before they could get the news to the next in rank he, too, was shot. The junior Colonel ultimately arrived with a lean and puffing little brigade at the top of the hill. The men lay down and fired volleys at whatever was practicable.

In and out of the ditch-like trenches lay the Spanish dead, lemon-faced corpses dressed in shabby blue and white ticking. Some were huddled down comfortably like sleeping children; one had died in the attitude of a man flung back in a dentist's chair; one sat in the trench with his chin sunk despondently to his breast; few preserved a record of the agitation of battle. With the greater number it was as if death had touched them so gently, so lightly, that they had not known of it. Death had come to them rather in the form of an opiate than of a bloody blow.

But the arrived men in the blue shirts had no thought of the sallow corpses. They were eagerly exchanging a hail of shots with the Spanish second line, whose ash-coloured entrenchments barred the way to a city white amid trees. In the pauses the men talked.

"We done the best. Old E Company got there. Why, one time the hull of B Company was *behind* us."

"Jones, he was the first man up. I saw 'im."

"Which Jones?"

"Did you see ol' Two-bars runnin' like a land-crab? Made good time, too. He hit only in the high places. He's all right."

"The Lootenant s all right, too. He was a good ten yards ahead of the best of us. I hated him at the post, but for this here active service there's none of 'em can touch him."

"This is mighty different from being at the post."

"Well, we done it, an' it wasn't b'cause *I* thought it could be done. When we started, I ses to m'self: 'Well, here goes a lot o' d — —d fools.'"

"'Tain't over yet."

"Oh, they'll never git us back from here. If they start to chase us back from here we'll pile 'em up so high the last ones can't climb over. We've come this far, an' we'll stay here. I ain't done pantin'.'"

"Anything is better than packin' through that jungle an' gettin' blistered from front, rear, an' both flanks. I'd rather tackle another hill than go trailin' in them woods, so thick you can't tell whether you are one man or a division of cav'lry."

"Where's that young kitchen-soldier, Cadogan, or whatever his name is. Ain't seen him to-day."

"Well, *I* seen him. He was right in with it. He got shot, too, about half up the hill, in the leg. I seen it. He's all right. Don't worry about him. He's all right."

"I seen 'im, too. He done his stunt. As soon as I can git this piece of barbed-wire entanglement out o' me throat I'll give 'm a cheer."

"He ain't shot at all b'cause there he stands, there. See 'im?"

Rearward, the grassy slope was populous with little groups of men searching for the wounded. Reilly's brigade began to dig with its bayonets and shovel with its meat-ration cans.

IV

Senator Cadogan paced to and fro in his private parlour and smoked small, brown weak cigars. These little wisps seemed utterly inadequate to console such a ponderous satrap.

It was the evening of the 1st of July, 1898, and the Senator was immensely excited, as could be seen from the superlatively calm way in which he called out to his private secretary, who was in an adjoining room. The voice was serene, gentle, affectionate, low.

"Baker, I wish you'd go over again to the War Department and see if they've heard anything about Caspar."

A very bright-eyed, hatchet-faced young man appeared in a doorway, pen still in hand. He was hiding a nettle-like irritation behind all the finished audacity of a smirk, sharp, lying, trustworthy young politician. "I've just got back from there, sir," he suggested.

The Skowmulligan war-horse lifted his eyes and looked for a short second into the eyes of his private secretary. It was not a glare or an eagle glance; it was something beyond the practice of an actor; it was simply meaning. The clever private secretary grabbed his hat and was at once enthusiastically away. "All right, sir," he cried. "I'll find out."

The War Department was ablaze with light, and messengers were running. With the assurance of a retainer of an old house Baker made his way through much small-calibre vociferation. There was rumour of a big victory; there was rumour of a big defeat. In the corridors various watchdogs arose from their armchairs and asked him of his business in tones of uncertainty which in no wise compared with their previous habitual deference to the private secretary of the war-horse of Skowmulligan.

Ultimately Baker arrived in a room where some kind of head clerk sat writing feverishly at a roll-top desk. Baker asked a question, and the head clerk mumbled profanely without lifting his head. Apparently he said: "How in the blankety-blank blazes do I know?"

The private secretary let his jaw fall. Surely some new spirit had come suddenly upon the heart of Washington—a spirit which Baker understood to be almost defiantly indifferent to the wishes of Senator Cadogan, a spirit which was not courteously oily. What could it mean? Baker's fox-like mind sprang wildly to a conception of overturned factions, changed friends, new combinations. The assurance which had come from experience of a broad political situation suddenly left him, and he would not have been amazed if some one had told him that Senator Cadogan now controlled only six votes in the State of Skowmulligan. "Well," he stammered in his bewilderment, "well-there isn't any news of the old man's son, hey?" Again the head clerk replied blasphemously.

Eventually Baker retreated in disorder from the presence of this head clerk, having learned that the latter did not give a —— if Caspar Cadogan were sailing through Hades on an ice yacht.

Baker stormed other and more formidable officials. In fact, he struck as high as he dared. They one and all flung him short, hard words, even as men pelt an annoying cur with pebbles. He emerged from the brilliant light, from the groups of men with anxious, puzzled faces, and as he walked back to the hotel he did not know if his name were Baker or Cholmondeley.

However, as he walked up the stairs to the Senator's rooms he contrived to concentrate his intellect upon a manner of speaking.

The war-horse was still pacing his parlour and smoking. He paused at Baker's entrance. "Well?"

"Mr. Cadogan," said the private secretary coolly, "they told me at the Department that they did not give a cuss whether your son was alive or dead."

The Senator looked at Baker and smiled gently. "What's that, my boy?" he asked in a soft and considerate voice.

"They said ——" gulped Baker, with a certain tenacity. "They said that they didn't give a cuss whether your son was alive or dead."

There was a silence for the space of three seconds. Baker stood like an image; he had no machinery for balancing the issues of this kind of a situation, and he seemed to feel that if he stood as still as a stone frog he would escape the ravages of a terrible Senatorial wrath which was about to break forth in a hurricane speech which would snap off trees and sweep away barns.

"Well," drawled the Senator lazily, "who did you see, Baker?"

The private secretary resumed a certain usual manner of breathing. He told the names of the men whom he had seen.

"Ye —e —es," remarked the Senator. He took another little brown cigar and held it with a thumb and first finger, staring at it with the calm and steady scrutiny of a scientist investigating a new thing. "So they don't care whether Caspar is alive or dead, eh? Well... maybe they don't.... That's all right.... However... I think I'll just look in on 'em and state my views."

When the Senator had gone, the private secretary ran to the window and leaned afar out. Pennsylvania Avenue was gleaming silver blue in the light of many arc-lamps; the cable trains groaned along to the clangour of gongs; from the window, the walks presented a hardly diversified aspect of shirt-waists and straw hats. Sometimes a newsboy screeched.

Baker watched the tall, heavy figure of the Senator moving out to intercept a cable train. "Great Scott!" cried the private secretary to himself, "there'll be three distinct kinds of grand, plain practical fireworks. The old man is going for 'em. I wouldn't be in Lascum's boots. Ye gods, what a row there'll be."

In due time the Senator was closeted with some kind of deputy third-assistant battery-horse in the offices of the War Department. The official obviously had been told off to make a supreme effort to pacify Cadogan, and he certainly was acting according to his instructions. He was almost in tears; he spread out his hands in supplication, and his voice whined and wheedled.

"Why, really, you know, Senator, we can only beg you to look at the circumstances. Two scant divisions at the top of that hill; over a thousand men killed and wounded; the line so thin that any strong attack would smash our Army to flinders. The Spaniards have probably received reenforcements under Pando; Shafter seems to be too ill to be actively in command of our troops; Lawton can't get up with his division before to-morrow. We are actually expecting... no, I won't say expecting... but we would not be surprised... nobody in the department would be surprised if before daybreak we were compelled to give to the country the news of a disaster which would be the worst blow the National pride has ever suffered. Don't you see? Can't you see our position, Senator?"

The Senator, with a pale but composed face, contemplated the official with eyes that gleamed in a way not usual with the big, self-controlled politician.

"I'll tell you frankly, sir," continued the other. "I'll tell you frankly, that at this moment we don't know whether we are a-foot or a-horseback. Everything is in the air. We don't know whether we have won a glorious victory or simply got ourselves in a deuce of a fix."

The Senator coughed. "I suppose my boy is with the two divisions at the top of that hill? He's with Reilly."

"Yes; Reilly's brigade is up there."

"And when do you suppose the War Department can tell me if he is all right. I want to know."

"My dear Senator, frankly, I don't know. Again I beg you to think of our position. The Army is in a muddle; it's a General thinking that he must fall back, and yet not sure that he *can* fall back without losing the Army. Why, we're worrying about the lives of sixteen thousand men and the self-respect of the nation, Senator."

"I see," observed the Senator, nodding his head slowly. "And naturally the welfare of one man's son doesn't —how do they say it-doesn't cut any ice."

V

And in Cuba it rained. In a few days Reilly's brigade discovered that by their successful charge they had gained the inestimable privilege of sitting in a wet trench and slowly but surely starving to death. Men's tempers crumbled like dry bread. The soldiers who so cheerfully, quietly and decently had captured positions which the foreign experts had said were impregnable, now in turn underwent an attack which was furious as well as insidious. The heat of the sun alternated with rains which boomed and roared in their falling like mountain cataracts. It seemed as if men took the fever through sheer lack of other occupation. During the days of battle none had had time to get even a tropic headache, but no sooner was that brisk period over than men began to shiver and shudder by squads and platoons. Rations were scarce enough to make a little fat strip of bacon seem of the size of a corner lot, and coffee grains were pearls. There would have been godless quarreling over fragments if it were not that with these fevers came a great listlessness, so that men were almost content to die, if death required no exertion.

It was an occasion which distinctly separated the sheep from the goats. The goats were few enough, but their qualities glared out like crimson spots.

One morning Jameson and Ripley, two Captains in the Forty-fourth Foot, lay under a flimsy shelter of sticks and palm branches. Their dreamy, dull eyes contemplated the men in the trench which went to left and right. To them came Caspar Cadogan, moaning. "By Jove," he said, as he flung himself wearily on the ground, "I can't stand much more of this, you know. It's killing me." A bristly beard sprouted through the grime on his face; his eyelids were crimson; an indescribably dirty shirt fell away from his roughened neck; and at the same time various lines of evil and greed were deepened on his face, until he practically stood forth as a revelation, a confession. "I can't stand it. By Jove, I can't."

Stanford, a Lieutenant under Jameson, came stumbling along toward them. He was a lad of the class of '98 at West Point. It could be seen that he was flaming with fever. He rolled a calm eye at them. "Have you any water, sir?" he said to his Captain. Jameson got upon his feet and helped Stanford to lay his shaking length under the shelter. "No, boy," he answered gloomily. "Not a drop. You got any, Rip?"

"No," answered Ripley, looking with anxiety upon the young officer. "Not a drop."

"You, Cadogan?"

Here Caspar hesitated oddly for a second, and then in a tone of deep regret made answer, "No, Captain; not a mouthful."

Jameson moved off weakly. "You lay quietly, Stanford, and I'll see what I can rustle."

Presently Caspar felt that Ripley was steadily regarding him. He returned the look with one of half-guilty questioning.

"God forgive you, Cadogan," said Ripley, "but you are a damned beast. Your canteen is full of water."

Even then the apathy in their veins prevented the scene from becoming as sharp as the words sounded. Caspar sputtered like a child, and at length merely said: "No, it isn't." Stanford lifted his head to shoot a keen, proud glance at Caspar, and then turned away his face.

"You lie," said Ripley. "I can tell the sound of a full canteen as far as I can hear it."

"Well, if it is, I —I must have forgotten it."

"You lie; no man in this Army just now forgets whether his canteen is full or empty. Hand it over."

Fever is the physical counterpart of shame, and when a man has the one he accepts the other with an ease which would revolt his healthy self. However, Caspar made a desperate struggle to preserve the forms. He arose and taking the string from his shoulder, passed the canteen to Ripley. But after all there was a whine in his voice, and the assumption of dignity was really a farce. "I think I had better go, Captain. You can have the water if you want it, I'm sure. But-but I fail to see —I fail to see what reason you have for insulting me."

"Do you?" said Ripley stolidly. "That's all right."

Caspar stood for a terrible moment. He simply did not have the strength to turn his back on this-this affair. It seemed to him that he must stand forever and face it. But when he found the audacity to look again at Ripley he saw the latter was not at all concerned with the situation. Ripley, too, had the fever. The fever changes all laws of proportion. Caspar went away.

"Here, youngster; here is your drink."

Stanford made a weak gesture. "I wouldn't touch a drop from his blamed canteen if it was the last water in the world," he murmured in his high, boyish voice.

"Don't you be a young jackass," quoth Ripley tenderly.

The boy stole a glance at the canteen. He felt the propriety of arising and hurling it after Caspar, but-he, too, had the fever.

"Don't you be a young jackass," said Ripley again.

Senator Cadogan was happy. His son had returned from Cuba, and the 8:30 train that evening would bring him to the station nearest to the stone and red shingle villa which the Senator and his family occupied on the shores of Long Island Sound. The Senator's steam yacht lay some hundred yards from the beach. She had just returned from a trip to Montauk Point where the Senator had made a gallant attempt to gain his son from the transport on which he was coming from Cuba. He had fought a brave sea-fight with sundry petty little doctors and ship's officers who had raked him with broadsides, describing the laws of quarantine and had used inelegant speech to a United States Senator as he stood on the bridge of his own steam yacht. These men had grimly asked him to tell exactly how much better was Caspar than any other returning soldier.

But the Senator had not given them a long fight. In fact, the truth came to him quickly, and with almost a blush he had ordered the yacht back to her anchorage off the villa. As a matter of fact, the trip to Montauk Point had been undertaken largely from impulse. Long ago the Senator had decided that when his boy returned the greeting should have something Spartan in it. He would make a welcome such as most soldiers get. There should be no flowers and carriages when the other poor fellows got none. He should consider Caspar as a soldier. That was the way to treat a man. But in the end a sharp acid of anxiety had worked upon the iron old man, until he had ordered the yacht to take him out and make a fool of him. The result filled him with a chagrin which caused him to delegate to the mother and sisters the entire business of succouring Caspar at Montauk Point Camp. He had remained at home conducting the huge correspondence of an active National politician and waiting for this son whom he so loved and whom he so wished to be a man of a certain strong, taciturn, shrewd ideal. The recent yacht voyage he now looked upon as a kind of confession of his weakness, and he was resolved that no more signs should escape him.

But yet his boy had been down there against the enemy and among the fevers. There had been grave perils, and his boy must have faced them. And he could not prevent himself from dreaming through the poetry of fine actions in which visions his son's face shone out manly and generous. During these periods the people about him, accustomed as they were to his silence and calm in time of stress, considered that affairs in Skowmulligan might be most critical. In no other way could they account for this exaggerated phlegm.

On the night of Caspar's return he did not go to dinner, but had a tray sent to his library, where he remained writing. At last he heard the spin of the dog-cart's wheels on the gravel of the drive, and a moment later there penetrated to him the sound of joyful feminine cries. He lit another cigar; he knew that it was now his part to bide with dignity the moment when his son should shake off that other welcome and come to him. He could still hear them; in their exuberance they seemed to be capering like schoolchildren. He was impatient, but this impatience took the form of a polar stolidity.

Presently there were quick steps and a jubilant knock at his door. "Come in," he said.

In came Caspar, thin, yellow, and in soiled khaki. "They almost tore me to pieces," he cried, laughing. "They danced around like wild things." Then as they shook hands he dutifully said "How are you, sir?"

"How are you, my boy?" answered the Senator casually but kindly.

"Better than I might expect, sir," cried Caspar cheerfully. "We had a pretty hard time, you know."

"You look as if they'd given you a hard run," observed the father in a tone of slight interest.

Caspar was eager to tell. "Yes, sir," he said rapidly. "We did, indeed. Why, it was awful. We-any of us-were lucky to get out of it alive. It wasn't so much the Spaniards, you know. The Army took care of them all right. It was the fever and the-you know, we couldn't get anything to eat. And the mismanagement. Why, it was frightful."

"Yes, I've heard," said the Senator. A certain wistful look came into his eyes, but he did not allow it to become prominent. Indeed, he suppressed it. "And you, Caspar? I suppose you did your duty?"

Caspar answered with becoming modesty. "Well, I didn't do more than anybody else, I don't suppose, but-well, I got along all right, I guess."

"And this great charge up San Juan Hill?" asked, the father slowly. "Were you in that?"

"Well-yes; I was in it," replied the son.

The Senator brightened a trifle. "You were, eh? In the front of it? or just sort of going along?"

"Well—I don't know. I couldn't tell exactly. Sometimes I was in front of a lot of them, and sometimes I was-just sort of going along."

This time the Senator emphatically brightened. "That's all right, then. And of course-of course you performed your commissary duties correctly?"

The question seemed to make Caspar uncommunicative and sulky. "I did when there was anything to do," he answered. "But the whole thing was on the most unbusiness-like basis you can imagine. And they wouldn't tell you anything. Nobody would take time to instruct you in your duties, and of course if you didn't know a thing your superior officer would swoop down on you and ask you why in the deuce such and such a thing wasn't done in such and such a way. Of course I did the best I could."

The Senator's countenance had again become sombrely indifferent. "I see. But you weren't directly rebuked for incapacity, were you? No; of course you weren't. But —I mean-did any of your superior officers suggest that you were 'no good,' or anything of that sort? I mean-did you come off with a clean slate?"

Caspar took a small time to digest his father's meaning. "Oh, yes, sir," he cried at the end of his reflection. "The Commissary was in such a hopeless mess anyhow that nobody thought of doing anything but curse Washington."

"Of course," rejoined the Senator harshly. "But supposing that you had been a competent and well-trained commissary officer. What then?"

Again the son took time for consideration, and in the end deliberately replied "Well, if I had been a competent and well-trained Commissary I would have sat there and eaten up my heart and cursed Washington."

"Well, then, that's all right. And now about this charge up San Juan? Did any of the Generals speak to you afterward and say that you had done well? Didn't any of them see you?"

"Why, n —n —no, I don't suppose they did…any more than I did them. You see, this charge was a big thing and covered lots of ground, and I hardly saw anybody excepting a lot of the men."

"Well, but didn't any of the men see you? Weren't you ahead some of the time leading them on and waving your sword?"

Caspar burst into laughter. "Why, no. I had all I could do to scramble along and try to keep up. And I didn't want to go up at all."

"Why?" demanded the Senator.

"Because-because the Spaniards were shooting so much. And you could see men falling, and the bullets rushed around you in-by the bushel. And then at last it seemed that if we once drove them away from the top of the hill there would be less danger. So we all went up."

The Senator chuckled over this description. "And you didn't flinch at all?"

"Well," rejoined Caspar humorously, "I won't say I wasn't frightened."

"No, of course not. But then you did not let anybody know it?"

"Of course not."

"You understand, naturally, that I am bothering you with all these questions because I desire to hear how my only son behaved in the crisis. I don't want to worry you with it. But if you went through the San Juan charge with credit I'll have you made a Major."

"Well," said Caspar, "I wouldn't say I went through that charge with credit. I went through it all good enough, but the enlisted men around went through in the same way."

"But weren't you encouraging them and leading them on by your example?"

Caspar smirked. He began to see a point. "Well, sir," he said with a charming hesitation. "Aw-er —I —well, I dare say I was doing my share of it."

The perfect form of the reply delighted the father. He could not endure blatancy; his admiration was to be won only by a bashful hero. Now he beat his hand impulsively down upon the table. "That's what I wanted to know. That's it exactly. I'll have you made a Major next week. You've found your proper field at last. You stick to the Army, Caspar, and I'll back you up. That's the thing. In a few years it will be a great career. The United States is pretty sure to have an Army of about a hundred and fifty thousand men. And starting in when you did and with me to back you up-why, we'll make you a General in seven or eight years. That's the ticket. You stay in the Army." The Senator's cheek was flushed with enthusiasm, and he looked eagerly and confidently at his son.

But Caspar had pulled a long face. "The Army?" he said. "Stay in the Army?"

The Senator continued to outline quite rapturously his idea of the future. "The Army, evidently, is just the place for you. You know as well as I do that you have not been a howling success, exactly, in anything else which you have tried. But now the Army just suits you. It is the kind of career which especially suits you. Well, then, go in, and go at it hard. Go in to win. Go at it."

"But —" began Caspar.

The Senator interrupted swiftly. "Oh, don't worry about that part of it. I'll take care of all that. You won't get jailed in some Arizona adobe for the rest of your natural life. There won't be much more of that, anyhow; and besides, as I say, I'll look after all that end of it. The chance is splendid. A young, healthy and intelligent man, with the start you've already got, and with my backing, can do anything-anything! There will be a lot of active service-oh, yes, I'm sure of it-and everybody who — —"

"But," said Caspar, wan, desperate, heroic, "father, I don't care to stay in the Army."

The Senator lifted his eyes and darkened. "What?" he said. "What's that?" He looked at Caspar.

The son became tightened and wizened like an old miser trying to withhold gold. He replied with a sort of idiot obstinacy, "I don't care to stay in the Army."

The Senator's jaw clinched down, and he was dangerous. But, after all, there was something mournful somewhere. "Why, what do you mean?" he asked gruffly.

"Why, I couldn't get along, you know. The-the — —"

"The what?" demanded the father, suddenly uplifted with thunderous anger. "The what?"

Caspar's pain found a sort of outlet in mere irresponsible talk. "Well, you know-the other men, you know. I couldn't get along with them, you know. They're peculiar, somehow; odd; I didn't understand them, and they didn't understand me. We-we didn't hitch, somehow. They're a queer lot. They've got funny ideas. I don't know how to explain it exactly, but-somehow —I don't like 'em. That's all there is to it. They're good fellows enough, I know, but — —"

"Oh, well, Caspar," interrupted the Senator. Then he seemed to weigh a great fact in his mind. "I guess — —" He paused again in profound consideration. "I guess — —" He lit a small, brown cigar. "I guess you are no damn good."

THE END.

Great Battles of the World

VITTORIA

The campaign of 1812, which included the storming of Ciudad Rodrigo and Badajoz and the overwhelming victory of Salamanca, had apparently done so much towards destroying the Napoleonic sway in the Peninsula that the defeat of the Allies at Burgos, in October 1812, came as an embittering disappointment to England; and when Wellington, after his disastrous retreat to Ciudad Rodrigo, reported his losses as amounting to nine thousand, the usual tempest of condemnation against him was raised, and the members of the Cabinet, who were always so free with their oracular advice and so close with the nation's money, wagged their heads despairingly.

But as the whole aspect of affairs was revealed, and as Wellington coolly stated his plans for a new campaign, public opinion changed.

It was a critical juncture: Napoleon had arranged an armistice with Russia, Prussia, and Austria, which was to last until August 16, 1813, and it became known that this armistice might end in peace. Peace on the Continent would mean that Napoleon's unemployed troops might be poured into Spain in such enormous numbers as to overwhelm the Allies. So, to ensure Wellington's striking a decisive blow before this could happen, both the English Ministry and the Opposition united in supporting him, and for the first time during the war he felt sure of receiving the supplies for which he had asked.

The winter and spring were spent by Wellington in preparing for his campaign: his troops needed severe discipline after the disorder into which they had fallen during the retreat from Burgos, and the great chief entered into the matter of their equipment with most painstaking attention to detail, removing unnecessary weight from them, and supplying each infantry soldier with three extra pairs of shoes, besides heels and soles for repairs. He drew large reinforcements from England, and all were drilled to a high state of efficiency.

It is well to quote here from the letter published by Wellington on the 28th of December 1812. It was addressed to the commanders of divisions and brigades. It created a very pretty storm, as one may readily see. I quote at length, since surely no document could be more illuminative of Wellington's character, and it seems certain that this fearless letter saved the army from the happy-go-lucky feeling, very common in British field forces, that a man is a thorough soldier so long as he is willing at all times to go into action and charge, if ordered, at even the brass gates of Inferno. But Wellington knew that this was not enough. He wrote as follows:

"Gentlemen —I have ordered the army into cantonments, in which I hope that circumstances will enable me to keep them for some time, during which the troops will receive their clothing, necessaries, etc., which are already in progress by different lines of communication to the several divisions and brigades.
"But besides these objects, I must draw your attention in a very particular manner to

the state of discipline of the troops. The discipline of every army, after a long and active campaign, becomes in some degree relaxed, and requires the utmost attention on the part of general and other officers to bring it back to the state in which it ought to be for service; but I am concerned to have to observe that the army under my command has fallen off in this respect in the late campaign to a greater degree than any army with which I have ever served, or of which I have ever read.
. . . . .

"It must be obvious, however, to every officer, that from the moment the troops com-

menced their retreat from the neighbourhood of Burgos on the one hand, and from Madrid on the other, the officers lost all command over their men.
. . . . .

"I have no hesitation in attributing these evils to the habitual inattention of the officers

of the regiments to their duty as prescribed by the standing regulations of the service and by the orders of this army.

"I am far from questioning the zeal, still less the gallantry and spirit, of the officers of

the army; I am quite certain that if their minds can be convinced of the necessity of minute and constant attention to understand, recollect, and carry into execution the orders which have been issued for the performance of their duty, and that the strict performance of this duty is necessary to enable the army to serve the country as it ought to be served, they will in future give their attention to these points.

"Unfortunately, the experience of the officers of the army has induced many to con-

sider that the period during which an army is on service is one of relaxation from all rule, instead of being, as it is, the period during which of all others every rule for the regulation and control of the conduct of the soldier, for the inspection and care of his arms, ammunition, accoutrements, necessaries, and field equipments, and his horse and horse appointments, for the receipt and issue and care of his provisions and the regulation of all that belongs to his food and the forage for his horse, must be most strictly attended to by the officer of his company or troop, if it is intended that an army —a British army in particular-shall be brought into the field of battle in a state of efficiency to meet the enemy on the day of trial.

"These are points, then, to which I most earnestly entreat you to turn your attention,

and the attention of the officers of the regiments under your command, Portuguese as well as English, during the period in which it may be in my power to leave the troops in their cantonments.

. . . . .

"In regard to the food of the soldier, I have frequently observed and lamented in the

late campaign the facility and celerity with which the French soldiers cooked in comparison with those of our army.

"The cause of this disadvantage is the same with that of every other description-the

want of attention of the officers to the orders of the army and the conduct of their men, and the consequent want of authority over their conduct.

. . . . .

"But I repeat that the great object of the attention of the general and field officers must

be to get the captains and subalterns of the regiments to understand and perform the duties required from them, as the only mode by which the discipline and efficiency of the army can be restored and maintained during the next campaign."

The British general never refrained from speaking his mind, even if his ideas were certain to be contrary to the spirit of the army. I will quote from *Victories of the British Armies* as follows:

"Colborne marched with the infantry on the right; Head, with the Thirteenth Light Dragoons and two squadrons of Portuguese, on the left, and the heavy cavalry formed a reserve. Perceiving that their battering train was endangered, the French cavalry, as the ground over which they were retiring was favourable for the movement, charged the Thirteenth. But they were vigorously repulsed; and, failing in breaking the British,

417

the whole, consisting of four regiments, drew up in front, forming an imposing line. The Thirteenth instantly formed and galloped forward-and nothing could have been more splendid than their charge. They rode fairly through the French, overtook and cut down many of the gunners, and at last entirely headed the line of march, keeping up a fierce and straggling encounter with the broken horsemen of the enemy, until some of the English dragoons actually reached the gates of Badajoz."

And now I quote from Wellington's comment to Colborne:

"I wish you would call together the officers of the dragoons and point out to them the mischiefs which must result from the disorder of the troops in action. The undisciplined ardour of the Thirteenth Dragoons and First Regiment of Portuguese cavalry is not of the description of the determined bravery and steadiness of soldiers confident in their discipline and in their officers. Their conduct was that of a rabble, galloping as fast as their horses could carry them over a plain, after an enemy to whom they could do no mischief when they were broken and the pursuit had continued for a limited distance, and sacrificing substantial advantages and all the objects of your operation by their want of discipline. To this description of their conduct I add my entire conviction, that if the enemy could have thrown out of Badajoz only one hundred men regularly formed, they would have driven back these two regiments in equal haste and disorder, and would probably have taken many whose horses would have been knocked up. If the Thirteenth Dragoons are again guilty of this conduct I shall take their horses from them, and send the officers and men to do duty at Lisbon."

The incident of the dragoons' charge happened early in 1811, but it shows how Wellington dealt with the firebrands in the army. However, imagine the feelings of the Thirteenth Dragoons!

As for the Allies, they were for a long time considered quite hopeless by British officers; the Portuguese were commonly known in the ranks as the "Vamosses," from *vamos,* "let us be off," which they shouted before they ran away. (The American slang "vamoose" may have had its origin in the Mexican War.)

The Spanish and Portuguese hated each other so cordially that it was with the greatest difficulty that they could be induced to co-operate: they were continually plotting to betray each other, and, incidentally, the English. Wellington had a sufficiently hard task in keeping his English army in order and directing the civil administration of Portugal, which would otherwise have tumbled to pieces from the corruption of its government; but hardest of all was the military training of the Spanish and Portuguese. He was now in supreme command of the Spanish army, concerning which he had written:

"There is not in the whole Kingdom of Spain a depot of provisions for the support of a single battalion in operation for one day. Not a shilling of money in any military chest. To move them forward at any point now would be to ensure their certain destruction."

After that was written, however, he had been able to equip them with some degree of effectiveness, and had worked them up to a certain standard of discipline: they were brave and patient, and susceptible to improvement under systematic training. Beresford had also accomplished wonders with the Portuguese, and Wellington's army now numbered seventy thousand men, of whom forty thousand were British.

Wellington, with his lean, sharp-featured face, and dry, cold manner, was not the typical Englishman at all. He was more like the genuine Yankee of New England. He made his successes by his resourcefulness, his inability to be overpowered by circumstances. As he said: "The French plan their campaigns just as you might make a splendid set of harness. It answers very well until it gets broken, and then you are done for! Now I made my campaign of ropes; if anything went wrong I tied a knot and went on."

He was always ready, when anything broke or failed him, to "tie a knot and go on." That is the suppleness and adroitness of a great chieftain, whereas the typical English general was too magnificent for the little things; he liked to hurl his men boldly into the abyss-and then, if they perished, it had been magnificently done, at any rate. But Wellington was always practical and ready to take advantage of any opportunity that offered. He had no illusions about the grandeur of getting men killed for nothing.

There were still two hundred and thirty thousand French troops in Spain, but they were scattered across the Peninsula from Asturias to Valencia. To the extreme east was Marshal Suchet with sixty-five thou: sand men, and an expedition under General Murray was sent against him which kept him there. Clausel was prevented from leaving Biscay with his forty thousand men by the great guerilla warfare with which Wellington enveloped his forces. There remained, then, for Wellington to deal with the centre of the army under Joseph Bonaparte, whose jealous suspicions had been the means of driving from Spain Marshal Soult, a really fine and capable commander. The weak Joseph was now the head of an immense and magnificently equipped army of men and officers in the finest condition for fighting, but who were to prove of how little effect fine soldiers can be when they lack the right chief.

The army of Joseph lay in a curve from Toledo to Zamora, guarding the central valley of the Douro, and covering the great road from Madrid through Burgos and Vittoria to France. Wellington's plan was to move the left wing of his army across the Douro within the Portuguese frontier, to march it up the right bank of the Douro as far as Zamora, and then, crossing the Elsa, to unite it to the Galician forces; while the centre and right, advancing from Agueda by Salamanca, were to force the passage of the Tormes and drive the French entirely from the line of the Douro towards the Carrion.

By constantly threatening them on the flank with the left wing, which was to be always kept in advance, he thus hoped to drive the French back by Burgos into Biscay. He himself expected to establish there a new basis for the war among the numerous and well-fortified seaports on the coast. In this way, forcing the enemy back to his frontier, he would at once better his own position and intercept the whole communication of the enemy. The plan had the obvious objection that in separating his army into two forces, with great mountain ranges and impassable rivers between them, each was exposed to the risk of an attack by the whole force of the enemy.

But Wellington had resolved to take this risk. Sir Thomas Graham, in spite of his sixty-eight years, had the vigour and clear-headedness of youth, and the very genius for the difficult command given him-that of leading the left wing through virgin forests, over rugged mountains, and across deep rivers.

The march of Wellington began May 22, and an exalted spirit of enthusiasm pervaded the entire army. Even Wellington became expressive, and as he passed the stream that marks the frontier of Spain he arose in his stirrups, and, waving his hand, exclaimed, "Farewell, Portugal!"

Meanwhile Graham, on May 16, with forty thousand men, had crossed the Douro and pushed ahead, turning the French right and striking at their communications. Within ten days forty thousand men were transported through two hundred miles of the most broken and rugged country in the Peninsula, with all their artillery and baggage. Soon they were in possession of the whole crest of mountains between the Ebro and the sea. On the 31st Graham reached the Elsa. The French were astounded when Graham appeared upon their flank; they abandoned their strong position on the Douro; then they abandoned Madrid; after that, they hurried out of Burgos and Valladolid.

Wellington had crossed the Douro at Miranda on May 25, in advance of his troops, by means of a basket slung on a rope from precipice to precipice, at an immense height above the foaming torrent. The rivers were all swollen by floods.

Graham, with the left wing of the Allies, kept up his eager march. Many men were lost while fording the Elsa on May 31. The water was almost chin-deep and the bottom was covered with shifting stones. Graham hastened with fierce speed to the Ebro, eager to cross it before Joseph and break his communications with France. Joseph had wished to stop his retreat at

Burgos and give battle there, but he had been told that incredible numbers of guerillas had joined the English forces, and so he pushed on, leaving the castle at Burgos heavily mined. It was calculated that the explosion would take place just as the English entered the town, but the fuses were too quick-three thousand French soldiers, the last to leave, were crushed by the falling ruins. The allied troops marched triumphantly through the scene of their earlier struggle and defeat.

On abandoning Burgos Joseph took the road to Vittoria and sent pressing orders to Clausel to join him there, but this junction of forces was not effected-Clausel was too late.

Wellington's strategy of turning the French right has been called "the most masterly movement made during the Peninsular War." Its chief merit was that it gave Wellington the advantage of victory with hardly any loss of life. It swept the French back to the Spanish frontier. And Joseph, whose train comprised an incredible number of chariots, carriages, and waggons, bearing a helpless multitude of people of both sexes from Madrid (including the civil functionaries and officers of his court), as well as enormous stores of spoil, began to perceive that this precipitate retreat was his ruin, and that he must risk the chance of a great battle to escape being driven in hopeless confusion through the passes of the Pyrenees.

The sweep of the Allies under Graham around the French right had taken them through the wildest and most enchantingly beautiful regions. At times a hundred men had been needed to drag up one piece of artillery. Again, the guns would be lowered down a precipice by ropes, or forced up the rugged goat-paths. At length, to quote Napier, "the scarlet uniforms were to be seen in every valley, and the stream of war, descending with impetuous force down all the clefts of the mountains, burst in a hundred foaming torrents into the basin of Vittoria."

So accurately had Graham done his work in accordance with Wellington's plans, that he reached the valley just as Joseph's dejected troops were forming themselves in front of Vittoria.

The basin or valley of Vittoria, with the town in its eastern extremity, is a small plain about eight miles by six miles in extent, situated in an elevated plateau among the mountains and guarded on all sides by rugged hills.

The great road from Madrid enters the valley at the Puebla Pass, where too the river Zadora flows through a narrow mountain gorge. This road then runs up the left bank of the Zadora to Vittoria, and from there it goes on towards Bayonne and the Pyrenees. This road was Joseph's line of retreat.

King Joseph, burdened by his treasure, which included the plunder of five years of French occupation in the Peninsula, and consisted largely of priceless works of art, selected with most excellent taste by himself and other French connoisseurs, had despatched to France two great convoys, a small part of the whole treasure, along the Bayonne road. As these had to be heavily guarded against the Biscay guerillas, some thousands of troops had gone with them. Joseph's remaining forces were estimated at from sixty thousand to sixty-five thousand men.

The French were anxious above all things to keep the road open-the road to Bayonne: there are several rough mountain roads intersecting each other at Vittoria, particularly those to Pampeluna, Bilboa, and Galicia; but the great Bayonne road was the only one capable of receiving the huge train of lumbering carriages without which the army was not to move.

On the afternoon of the 20th Wellington, whose effective force was now sixty-five thousand men, surveyed the place and the enemy from the hill ranges and saw that they were making a stand. He decided then on his tactics. Instead of pushing on his combined forces to a frontal attack, he made up his mind to divide his troops; he would send Graham with the left wing, consisting of eighteen thousand men and twenty guns, around by the northern hills to the rear of the French army, there to seize the road to Bayonne. Sir Rowland Hill with twenty thousand men, including General Murillo with his Spaniards, was to move with the right wing, break through the Puebla Pass, and attack the French left.

The right centre under Wellington himself was to cross the ridges forming the southern boundary of the basin and then move straight forward to the Zadora River and attack the bridges, while the left centre was to move across the bridge of Mendoza in the direction of the town.

The French right, which Graham was to attack, occupied the heights in front of the Zadora River above the village of Abechucho, and covered Vittoria from approach by the Bilboa road; the centre extended along the left bank of the Zadora, commanding the bridges in front of it, and blocking up the great road from Madrid. The left occupied the space from Ariniz to the ridges of Puebla de Arlauzon, and guarded the Pass of Puebla, by which Hill was to enter the valley.

The early morning of June 21 was, according to one historian, "rainy and heavy with vapour," while an observer (Leith Hay) said: "The morning was extremely brilliant; a clearer or more beautiful atmosphere never favoured the progress of a gigantic conflict."

The valley, occupied by the French army, with the rich uniforms of its officers, was a superb spectacle. Marshal Jourdan, the commander, could be seen riding slowly along the line of his troops. The positions they occupied rose in steps from the centre of the valley, so that all could be seen by the English from the crest of the Morillas as they stood ready for battle. In his *Events of Military Life* Henry says:

> "The dark and formidable masses of the French were prepared at all points to repel the meditated attack-the infantry in column with loaded arms, or ambushed thickly in the low woods at the base of their position, the cavalry in lines with drawn swords, and the artillery frowning from the eminences with lighted matches; while on our side all was yet quietness and repose. The chiefs were making their observations, and the men walking about in groups amidst the piled arms, chatting and laughing and gazing, and apparently not caring a pin for the fierce hostile array in their front."

At ten o'clock Hill reached the Pass of Puebla and forced his way through with extraordinary swiftness. Murillo's Spaniards went swarming up the steep ridges to dislodge the French, but the enemy made a furious resistance, and reinforcements kept coming to their aid. General Murillo was wounded, but would not be carried from the field. Hill then sent the Seventy-first to help the Spaniards, who were showing high courage, but being terribly mown down by the French musketry. Colonel Cadogan, who led the Seventy-first, had no sooner reached the summit of the height than he fell, mortally wounded. The French were driven from their position, but the loss of Cadogan was keenly felt. The story of his strange state of exaltation the night before the battle is well known-his rapture at the prospect of taking part in it. As he lay dying on the summit he would not be moved, although the dead lay thick about him, but watched the progress of his Highlanders until he could no longer see.

While this conflict was going on, Wellington, with the right centre, had commenced his attack on the bridges over the Zadora. A Spanish peasant brought word that the bridge of Tres Puentes was negligently guarded, and offered to guide the troops to it. Kempt's Brigade soon reached it; the Fifteenth Hussars galloped over, but a shot from a French battery killed the brave peasant who had guided them.

The forces that crossed at Tres Puentes now formed under the shelter of a hill. One of the officers wrote of this position:

> "Our post was most extraordinary, as we were isolated from the rest of the army and within one hundred yards of the enemy's advance. As I looked over the bank, I could see El Rey Joseph, surrounded by at least five thousand men, within five hundred yards of us."

It has always seemed an inconceivable thing that the French should not have destroyed the seven narrow bridges across the Zadora before the 21st had dawned. Whether it was from over-confidence or sheer mental confusion, it is impossible to know.

The Third and Seventh Divisions were now moving rapidly down to the bridge of Mendoza, but the enemy's light troops and guns had opened a vigorous fire upon them, until the riflemen of the Light Division, who had crossed at Tres Puentes, charged the enemy's fire, and the bridge was carried.

Sir Thomas Picton was a picturesque figure in this part of the operations. Through some oversight he and his men, the "Fighting Third," were neglected. Orders came to other troops, bridges were being carried, but no word was sent to Picton. "D — — it!" he cried out to one of his officers, "Lord Wellington must have forgotten us!" He beat the mane of his horse with his stick in his impatience and anger. Finally, an aide-de-camp galloped up and inquired for Lord Dalhousie, who commanded the Seventh Division. In answer to Picton's inquiries he stated that he brought orders for Dalhousie to carry the bridge to the left, while the Fourth and Sixth Divisions were to support the attack. Picton rose in his stirrups, and shouted angrily to the amazed aide-de-camp:

"You may tell Lord Wellington from me, sir, that the *Third* Division, under my command, shall in less than ten minutes attack the bridge and carry it, and the Fourth and Sixth may support if they choose." Then, addressing his men with his customary blend of affection and profanity, he cried: "Come on, ye rascals! Come on, ye fighting villains!"

They carried the bridge with such fire and speed that the whole British line was animated by the sight.

Maxwell says: "The passage of the river, the movement of glittering masses from right to left as far as the eye could range, the deafening roar of cannon, the sustained fusillade of the artillery, made up a magnificent scene. The British cavalry, drawn up to support the columns, seemed a glittering line of golden helmets and sparkling swords in the keen sunshine which now shone upon the field of battle."

L'Estrange, who was with the Thirty-first, says that the men were marching through standing corn (I suppose some kind of grain that ripens early, certainly not maize) yellow for the sickle and between four and five feet high, and the hissing cannon-balls, as they rent their way through the sea of golden grain, made long furrows in it.

The hill in front of Ariniz was the key of the French line, and Wellington brought up several batteries and hurled Picton's division in a solid mass against it, while the heavy cavalry of the British came up at a gallop from the river to sustain the attack.

This hill had been the scene of a great fight in the wars of the Black Prince, where Sir William Felton, with two hundred archers and swordsmen, had been surrounded by six thousand Spaniards, and all perished, resisting doggedly. It is still called "the Englishmen's hill."

An obstinate fight now raged, for a brief space, on this spot. A long wall was held by several battalions of French infantry, whose fire was so deadly as to check the British for a time. They reached the wall, however, and for a few moments on either side of it was a seething mass of furious soldiers. "Any person," said Kincaid, who was present, "who chose to put his head over from either side, was sure of getting a sword or bayonet up his nostrils."

As the British broke over the wall, the French fell back, abandoning Ariniz for the ridge in front of Gomecha, only to be forced back again.

It was the noise of Graham's guns, booming since mid-day at their rear, that took the heart out of the French soldiery.

Graham had struck the great blow on the left; at eleven he had reached the heights above the village and bridge of Gamara Major, which were strongly occupied by the French under Reille. General Oswald commenced the attack and drove the enemy from the heights; then Major-General Robinson, at the head of a brigade of the Fifth Division, formed his men and led them forward on the run to carry the bridge and village of Gamara. But the French fire was so strong that he was compelled to fall back. Again he rallied them and crossed the bridge, but the French drove them back once more. Fresh British troops came up and the bridge was carried again; and then, for the third time, it was lost under Reille's murderous fire.

But now the panic from the centre had reached Reille. It was known that the French centre was retreating: the Frenchmen had no longer the moral strength to resist Robinson's attacks, and so the bridge was won by the English and the Bayonne road was lost to the French.

In the centre the battle had become a sort of running fight for six miles; the French were at last all thrown back into the little plain in front of Vittoria, where from the crowded throng cries of despair could be heard.

"At six o'clock," Maxwell says, "the sun was setting, and his last rays fell upon a dreadful spectacle: red masses of infantry were advancing steadily across the plain; the horse artillery came at a gallop to the front to open its fire upon the fugitives; the Hussar Brigade was charging by the Camino Real."

Of the helpless encumbrances of the French army an eye-witness said: "Behind them was the plain in which the city stood, and beyond the city thousands of carriages and animals and non-combatants, men, women, and children, were crowding together in all the madness of terror; and as the English shot went booming overhead the vast crowd started and swerved with a convulsive movement, while a dull and horrid sound of distress arose."

Joseph now ordered the retreat to be conducted by the only road left open-that to Pampeluna, but it was impossible to take away his train of carriages. He, the king, only escaped capture by jumping out of one door of his carriage as his pursuers reached the other: he left his sword of state in it, and the beautiful Correggio "Christ in the Garden," now at Apsley House, in England.

Eighty pieces of cannon, jammed close together near Vittoria on the only remaining defensible ridge near the town, had kept up a desperate fire to the last, and Reille had held his ground near the Zadora heroically, but it was useless. The great road to Bayonne was lost, and finally that to Pampeluna was choked with broken-down carriages. The British dragoons were pursuing hotly, and the frantic French soldiers plunged into morasses, over fields and hills, in the wildest rout, leaving their artillery, ammunition-waggons, and the spoil of a kingdom.

The outskirts of Vittoria were strewn with the wreckage. Never before in modern times had such a quantity of spoil fallen into the hands of a victorious army. There were objects of interest from museums, convents, and royal palaces; there were jewels of royal worth and masterpieces of Titian, Raphael, and Correggio.

The marshal's baton belonging to Jourdan had been left, with one hundred and fifty-one brass guns, four hundred and fifteen caissons of ammunition, one million three hundred thousand ball cartridges, fourteen thousand rounds of artillery ammunition, and forty thousand pounds of gunpowder. Joseph's power was gone: he was only a wretched fugitive. Six thousand of his men had been killed and wounded, and one thousand were prisoners.

It has not been possible to estimate the value of the private plunder, but five and a half millions of dollars in the military chest of the army were taken, and untold quantities of private wealth were also lost to their owners; it was all scattered-shining heaps of gold and silver-over the road, and the British soldiers reaped it. Wellington refused to make any effort to induce his men to give up the enormous sums they had absorbed: "They have earned it," he said. But he had reason to regret it. They fell into frightful orgies of intemperance that lasted for days. Wellington wrote Lord Bathurst, June 29:

> "We started with the army in the highest order, and up to the day of the battle nothing could get on better. But that event has, as usual, totally annihilated all order and discipline. The soldiers of the army have got among them about a million sterling in money, with the exception of about one hundred thousand dollars which were got in the military chest. I am convinced that we have now out of our ranks double the amount of our loss in the battle, and have lost more men in the pursuit than the enemy have."

It was calculated that seven thousand five hundred men had straggled from the effects of the plunder.

The convoys sent ahead by Joseph had contained some of the choicest works of art; they reached France safely, and are displayed in the museums of Paris. In justice to the Duke of

Wellington it must be said that he communicated with Ferdinand, offering to restore the paintings which had fallen into his hands, but Ferdinand desired him to keep them. The wives of the French officers were sent on to Pampeluna the next day by Wellington, who had treated them with great kindness.

As for the rest of the feminine army, the nuns, the actresses, and the superbly arrayed others, they made their escape with greater difficulties and hardships. Alison says: "Rich vestures of all sorts, velvet and silk brocades, gold and silver plate, noble pictures, jewels, laces, cases of claret and champagne, poodles, parrots, monkeys, and trinkets lay scattered about the fields in endless confusion, amidst weeping mothers, wailing infants, and all the unutterable miseries of warlike overthrow."

Napoleon was filled with fury at his brother for the result of Vittoria, but he instructed his ministers to say that "a somewhat brisk engagement with the English took place at Vittoria in which both sides lost equally. The French armies, however, carried out the movements in which they were engaged, but the enemy seized about one hundred guns which were left without teams at Vittoria, and it is these that the English are trying to pass off as artillery captured on the battlefield!"

One of the most important captures of the battle was a mass of documents from the archives of Madrid, including a great part of Napoleon's secret correspondence-an invaluable addition to history.

Napier's summing up of the results of the battle reads:

> "Joseph's reign was over; the crown had fallen from his head. And, after years of toils and combats, which had been rather admired than understood, the English general, emerging from the chaos of the Peninsula struggle, stood on the summit of the Pyrenees a recognised conqueror. From these lofty pinnacles the clangour of his trumpets pealed clear and loud, and the splendour of his genius appeared as a flaming beacon to warring nations."

However, Napier always was inclined to be eloquent. Perhaps it was lucky for Wellington that the worthless make-trouble, Joseph Bonaparte, had been in the place of his tremendous brother.

THE SIEGE OF PLEVNA

When the Russian army swarmed through the Shipka Pass of the Balkans there was really nothing before it but a man and an opportunity. Osman Pasha suddenly and with great dexterity took his force into Plevna, a small Bulgarian town near the Russian line of march.

The military importance of Plevna lay in the fact that this mere village of seventeen hundred people was the junction of the roads from Widin, Sophia, Biela, Zimnitza, Nikopolis, and the Shipka Pass. Osman's move was almost entirely on his own initiative. He had no great reputation, and, like Wellington in the early part of the Peninsula campaign, he was obliged to do everything with the strength of his own shoulders. The stupidity of his superiors amounted almost to an oppression.

The Russians recognised the strategic importance of Plevna a moment too late. On July 18, 1877, General Krudener at Nikopolis received orders to occupy Plevna at once. He seems to have moved promptly, but long before he could arrive Osman's tired but dogged battalions were already in the position.

The Turkish regular of that day must have resembled very closely his fellow of the present. Von Moltke, who knew the Turks well, and whose remarkable mind clearly outlined and prophesied the result of several more recent Balkan campaigns, said, "An impetuous attack may be expected from the Turks, but not an obstinate and lasting defence." Historically, the opinion of the great German field-marshal seems very curious. Even in the late war between Greece and Turkey the attacks of the Turkish troops were usually anything but impetuous. They were fearless, but very leisurely. As to the lasting and obstinate defence, one has only to regard the siege of Plevna to understand that Von Moltke was for the moment writing carelessly.

After Plevna, the word went forth that the most valuable weapon of the Turk was his shovel. When Osman arrived, the defences of Plevna consisted of an ordinary block-house, but he at once set his troops at work digging entrenchments and throwing up redoubts, which were located with great skill. Soon the vicinity of the town was one great fortress. Osman coolly was attempting to stem the Russian invasion with a force of these strange Turkish troops, patient, enduring, sweet-tempered, and ignorant, dressed in slovenly overcoats and sheep-skin sandals, living on a diet of black bread and cucumbers.

Receiving the order from the Grand Duke Nicolas, General Krudener at Nikopolis despatched at dawn of the next day six thousand five hundred men, with about seven batteries, to Plevna. No effective scouting had been done. The Russian general, Schilder-Schuldner, riding comfortably in his carriage in the customary way of Russian commanders of the time, had absolutely no information that a strong Turkish force had occupied the position. His column had been allowed to distribute itself over a distance of seventeen miles. On the morning of the 20th an attack was made with great confidence by the troops which had come up. Two Russian regiments even marched victoriously through the streets of Plevna, throwing down their heavy packs and singing for joy of the easy capture. But suddenly a frightful fusillade began from all sides. The elated regiments melted in the streets. Infuriated by religious ardour, despising the value of a Christian's life, the Turks poured out from their concealed places, and there occurred a great butchery. The Russian Nineteenth Regiment of the line was cut down to a few fragments. Much artillery ammunition was captured. The Russians lost two thousand seven hundred men. The knives of the Circassians and Bashi-Bazouks had been busy in the streets.

After this victory Osman might have whipped Krudener, but the Russian leaders had been suddenly aroused to the importance of taking Plevna, and Krudener was almost immediately reinforced with three divisions. Within the circle of defence the Turk was using his shovel. Osman gave the garrison no rest. If a man was not shooting, he was digging. The well-known Grivitza Redoubt was greatly strengthened, and some defences on the east side of the town were completed. Osman's situation was desperate, but his duty to his country was vividly defined. If he could hold this strong Turkish force on the flank of the Russians, their advance on Constantinople would hardly be possible. The Russian leaders now thoroughly understood this fact, and they tried to make the army investing Plevna more than a containing force.

The Grand Duke Nicolas had decided to order an assault on the 30th of July. Krudener telegraphed-the grand duke was thirty miles from Plevna-that he hesitated in his views of prospective success. The grand duke replied sharply, ordering that the assault be made. It seems that Krudener went into the field in the full expectation of being beaten.

Now appears in the history of the siege a figure at once sinister and foolish. Subordinate in command to Krudener was Lieutenant-General Prince Schahofskoy, who had an acute sense of his own intelligence, and in most cases dared to act independently of the orders of his chief. But to offset him there suddenly galloped into his camp a brilliant young Russian commander, a man who has set his name upon Plevna, even as the word underlies the towering reputation of Osman Pasha. General Skobeleff had come from the Grand Duke Nicolas with an order directing Prince Schahofskoy to place the young man in command of a certain brigade of Caucasian Cossacks. The prince grew stormy with outraged pride, and practically told Skobeleff to take the Cossacks and go to the devil with them.

The Russians began a heavy bombardment, to which Osman's guns replied with spirit. The key of the position was the Grivitza Redoubt. Krudener himself attacked it with eighteen battalions of infantry and ten batteries. And at the same time Prince Schahofskoy thundered away on his side. The latter at last became furious at Krudener's lack of success, and resolved to take matters into his own hands. In the afternoon he advanced with three brigades in the face of a devastating Turkish fire, took a hill, and forced the Turks to vacate their first line of entrenchments. His men were completely spent with weariness, and it is supposed that he should have waited on the hill for support from Krudener. But he urged on his tired troops and carried a second position. The Turkish batteries now concentrated their fire upon his line, and, really, the Turkish infantry whipped him soundly.

The Russians did not give up the dearly bought gain of ground without desperate fighting. Again and again they furiously charged, but only to meet failure. When night fell, the stealthy-footed irregular of the Turkish forces crept through the darkness to prey upon the route of the Russian retreat. The utter annihilation of Prince Schahofskoy's force was prevented by Skobeleff and the brigade of Cossacks with which the prince had sent him to the devil. Skobeleff's part in this assault was really a matter of clever manoeuvring.

Krudener had failed with gallantry and intelligence. Schahofskoy had failed through pig-headedness and self-confidence.

After this attempt to carry Plevna, the important Russian generals occupied themselves in mutual recriminations. Krudener bitterly blamed Schahofskoy for not obeying his orders, and Schahofskoy acidulously begged to know why Krudener had not supported him. At the same time they both claimed that the Grand Duke Nicolas, thirty miles away, should never have given an order for an assault on a position of which he had never had a view.

But even if Russian clothing and arms and trinkets were being sold for a pittance in the bazaars of Plevna, the mosques were jammed with wounded Turks, and such was the suffering that the dead in the streets and in the fields were being gnawed by the pervasive Turkish dog.

A few days later Osman Pasha received the first proper recognition from Constantinople. A small troop of cavalry had wormed its way into Plevna. It was headed by an aide-de-camp of the Sultan. In gorgeous uniform the aide appeared to Osman and presented him with the First Order of the Osmanli, the highest Turkish military decoration. And with this order came a sword, the hilt of which flamed with diamonds. Osman Pasha may have preferred a bushel of cucumbers, but at any rate he knew that the Sultan and Turkey at last understood the value of a good soldier. To the speech of the aide Osman replied with another little speech, and the soldiers in their entrenchments cheered the Sultan.

On August 31 the Turkish general made his one offensive move. He threw part of his force against a Russian redoubt and was obliged to retire with a loss of nearly three thousand men.

Afterwards he devoted his troops mainly to the business of improving the defences. He wasted no more in attempts to break out of Plevna.

At this late day of the siege, Prince Charles of Roumania was appointed to the chief command of the whole Russo-Roumanian army. But naturally this office was nominal. General Totoff had the real disposition of affairs, but he did not hold it very long. General Levitsky, the assistant chief of the Russian general staff, arrived to advise General Totoff under direct orders from the Grand Duke Nicolas. But this siege was to be very well generalled.

The Grand Duke Nicolas himself came to Plevna. One would think that the grand duke would have ended this kaleidoscopic row of superseding generals. But the Great White Czar himself appeared. Osman Pasha, shut up in Plevna, certainly was honoured with a great deal of distinguished interest.

However, Alexander I I. did his best to give no orders. He had no illusions concerning his military knowledge. With a spirit profoundly kind and gentle, he simply prayed that no more lives would be lost. It is difficult to think what he had to say to his multitudinous generals, each of whom was the genius of the only true plan for capturing Plevna.

At daylight on the 7th of September the Turks saw that the entire army of the enemy had closed in upon them. Amid fields of ripening grain shone the smart red jackets of the hussars. The Turks saw the Bulgarians in sheepskin caps, and with their broad scarlet sashes stuck full of knives and pistols. They saw the queer round oilskin shakoes of the Cossacks and the greatcoats of thick gray blanketing. They saw the uniforms of the Russian infantry, the green tunics striped with red. For five days the smoke lay heavy over Plevna.

The 11th was the fête-day of the emperor, and the general assault on that day was arranged as if it had been part of a fête. The cannonade was to begin at daybreak along the whole line and stop at eight o'clock in the morning. The artillery was to play again from eleven o'clock until one o'clock. Then it was to play again from half-past two o'clock to three o'clock.

Directly afterwards the Roumanian allies of the Russians moved in three columns against the Grivitza Redoubt. At first all three were repulsed, but with the stimulus of Russian reinforcements they rallied, and after a long time of almost hand-to-hand fighting the evening closed with them in possession of what was called the key of the Plevna position. They had lost four thousand men. The victory was fruitless, as, anticipating the attack on Grivitza, Osman had caused the building of an inner redoubt. After all their ferocious charging, the Russians were really no nearer to success.

At three o'clock of that afternoon Redoubt Number Ten had been assailed by General Schmidnikoff. The firing had been terrible, but the Russians had charged to the very walls of the redoubt. The Turks not only beat them off, but pursued with great spirit. Two of the scampering Russian battalions were then faced about to beat off the chase. They lay down at a distance of only two hundred yards of the redoubt, and sent the Turks pell-mell back into their fortifications.

At about the same time Skobeleff, wearing a white coat and mounted on a white charger, was leading his men over the "green hills" towards the Krishin Redoubt. There was a dense fog. Skobeleff's troops crossed two ridges and waded a stream. They began the ascent of a steep slope. Suddenly the fog cleared; the sun shone out brilliantly. The closely massed Russian force was exposed at short range to line after line of Turkish entrenchments. They retired once, but rallied splendidly, and before five o'clock Skobeleff found himself in possession of Redoubt Number Eleven and Redoubt Number Twelve.

His battalions were thrust like a wedge into the Turkish lines, but the Turkish commander appreciated the situation more clearly than any Russian save Skobeleff. The latter's men suffered a frightful fire. Reinforcements were refused. All during the night the faithful troops of the czar fought in darkness and without hope. They even built little ramparts of dead men. But on the morning of September 12 Skobeleff was compelled to give up all he had gained. The retreat over the "green hills" was little more than a running massacre.

After his return Skobeleff was in a state of excitement and fury. His uniform was covered with blood and mud. His Cross of St. George was twisted around over his shoulder. His face was black with powder. His eyes were bloodshot. He said, "My regiments no longer exist."

The Russian assaults had failed at all points. They had begun this last battle with thirty thousand infantry, twelve thousand cavalry, and four hundred and forty guns, and they lost over eighteen thousand men. The multitude of generals again took counsel. There were fervid animosities, and there might have been open rupture if it were not for the presence of the czar himself, whose gentleness and good-nature prevented many scenes.

It was decided that the Turks must be starved out. The Russians sent for more troops as well as for heavy supplies of clothing, ammunition, and food. The czar sent for General Todleben, who had shown great skill at Sebastopol, and the direction of the siege was put in his hands.

The Turks had been accustomed to reprovision Plevna by the skilful use of devious trails. Todleben took swift steps to put a stop to it, but he did not succeed before a huge convoy had been sent into the town through the adroit management of Chefket Pasha. But the Russian horse soon chased Chefket away, and the trails were all closed.

For the most part the September weather was fine, but this plenitude of sun made the Turkish positions about Plevna almost unbearable. Actual thousands of unburied dead lay scattered over the ridges. At one time the Russian headquarters made a polite request to be allowed to send some men to enter Grivitza and bury their own dead. But this polite request met with polite refusal.

On October 19 the Roumanians, who for weeks had been sapping their way up to the Grivitza Redoubt, made a final and desperate attack on it. They were repulsed.

In order to complete the investment, Todleben found it necessary to dislodge the Turks from four villages near Plevna.

The weeks moved by slowly with a stolid and stubborn Turk besieged by a stubborn and stolid Russian. There was occasional firing from the Russian batteries, to which the Turks did not always take occasion to reply. In Plevna there was nothing to eat but meat, and the Turkish soldiers moved about with the hoods of their dirty brown cloaks pulled over their heads. Outside Plevna there were plenty of furs and good coats, but the diet had become so plain that the sugar-loving Russian soldiers would give gold for a pot of jam.

On the cold, cloudy morning of December 11, when snow lay thickly on all the country, a sudden great booming of guns was heard, and the news flew swiftly that Osman had come out of Plevna at last, and was trying to break through the cordon his foes had spread about him. During the night he had abandoned all his defences, and by daybreak he had taken the greater part of his army across the river Vid. Advancing along the Sophia road, he charged the Russian entrenchments with such energy that the Siberian Regiment stationed at that point was almost annihilated. A desperate fight went on for four hours, with the Russians coming up battalion after battalion. Some time after noon all firing ceased, and later the Turks sent up a white flag. Cheer after cheer swelled over the dreary plain. Osman had surrendered.

The siege had lasted one hundred and forty-two days. The Russians had lost forty thousand men. The Turks had lost thirty thousand men.

The advance on Constantinople had been checked. Skobeleff said, "Osman the Victorious he will remain, in spite of his surrender."

428

THE STORMING OF BUR KERSDOR HEIGHTS

When, in 1740, Wilhelm Friedrich of Prussia died, the friends whom his heir had gathered about him at his pleasant country-house at Reinsberg were doomed to see a blight fall on their expectations such as had not been known since Poins and Falstaff congratulated themselves on having an old friend for their king.

When the young prince came to the throne as Frederick II., thought these trusting people, Prussia, instead of being a mere barracks, overrun with soldiers and ruled by a miser, would become the refuge of poets and artists. Its monarch would be a man of peace, caring for nothing beyond the joys of philosophy, poetry, music, and merry feasts-this, of course, providing for an indefinite extension of the enchanted life he and his companions led at Reinsberg.

They had the best of reasons for this belief: the antagonism between the prince and his father had begun almost as soon as the rapture of having an heir had become an old story to Friedrich Wilhelm. The tiny "Fritz," with a cocked hat and tight little soldier-clothes, drilling and being drilled with a lot of other tiny boys, —and frightfully bored with it all the time, —was a standing grievance to his rough, boorish father. "Awake him at six in the morning, and stand by to see that he does not turn over, but immediately gets up...While his hair is being combed and made into a queue, he is to have his breakfast of tea." This was the beginning of his father's instructions to his tutors when, at seven, he passed out of his governess's hands.

Notwithstanding the fine Spartan rigour of this programme, the boy came up a dainty, delicate little fellow, who turned up his nose at boar-hunting and despised his father's collection of giants, and loved to play the flute and make French verses. Friedrich Wilhelm was anything but a bad monarch; he was moral in a century when nothing of the sort was expected of monarchs; he made the Prussian army the best army in the world; he even had affections; but for a man of these virtues he was the most intolerable parent of whom there is a record.

The brilliant Wilhelmina, Frederick's dearly loved sister, whose young portraits show her as very like her brother, has this characteristic scene in her *Memoirs*. Their sister, Princess Louisa, aged fifteen, had just been betrothed to a margrave, and the king asked her-they were at table-how she would regulate her housekeeping when she was married. Louisa, a favourite, had got into the way of telling her father home-truths, which he took very well, as a rule, from her. On this occasion she told him that she would have a good table well served; "better than yours," said Louisa; "and if I have children, I will not maltreat them like you, nor force them to eat what they have an aversion to." "What do you mean by that?" said the king. "What is there wanting at my table?" "There is this wanting," she replied: "that one cannot have enough, and the little there is consists of coarse potherbs that nobody can eat." The king, who was not used to such candour, boiled with rage. "All his anger," says the Princess Wilhelmina, "fell on my brother and me. He first threw a plate at my brother's head, who ducked out of the way, then let fly another at me." After he had made the air blue with wrath, directed at Frederick, "we had to pass him in going out," and "he aimed a great blow at me with his crutch, —which, if I had not jerked away from it, would have ended me. He chased me for a while in his wheelchair, but the people drawing it gave me time to escape into the queen's chamber."

One always imagines this charming young princess in the act of dodging some sort of blow from Friedrich Wilhelm, who was nicknamed "Stumpy," privately, by his dutiful son and daughter. The habit of hating his son became an insanity; to kick him and pull his hair, break his flute, and take away his books and his brocaded dressing-gown —that was ordinary usage; it came to the point where he nearly strangled him, and later he condemned him to death for trying to run away to his uncle, George II., in England. When this sentence had been changed to a term of imprisonment, the poor young prince had a much better time of it: his gaolers were kinder than his father.

By the time he emerged from this captivity he had gained much wisdom-the cold wisdom of selfishness and dissimulation. In after years the father and son became profoundly attached to each other, but Frederick was always obliged to humour and cajole his pig-headed sire, to lie more or less, and generally adopt an insincere tone, in order to avert wrath and suspicion —a very hateful necessity to a natural truth-teller, for Frederick was by nature a great lover of facts. Although his training as a politician and a soldier included a thorough education in guile, the tutors of his childhood were simple, honest people, who gave him a good, truthful start in life.

Friedrich Wilhelm, now that his heir was twenty-one years old, thought it high time to put an end to various vague matrimonial projects, and get a wife for him straightway. Frederick having found that obedience was, on the whole, better than captivity, was submissive and silent-to his father; but his letters to his friends and his sister shrieked with protestations against a marriage in which his tastes and feelings were not so much as thought of. Above all things he wished to be allowed to travel and choose for himself, and he had a morbid horror of a dull and awkward woman. It did not much matter, he thought, what else his wife was if she were clever conversationally, with grace and charm and fine manners. Beauty was desirable, but he could get along without it, if only he could feel proud of his consort's wit and breeding. The bride of his father's choosing was the Princess Elizabeth of Brunswick-Bevern —a bashful and gawky young person, with as little distinction as a dairy-maid. But he subdued his rage and married her, and, indeed, seems always to have treated her with kindly deference, although he made no pretence of affection.

Still carrying out his father's wishes, he served in a brief campaign, and afterwards regularly devoted a portion of his time to military and political business. Friedrich Wilhelm was now pleased with his son to the extent of buying for him a delightful residence-Reinsberg-and giving him a tolerable income; and Frederick revelled in his new freedom by building conservatories, laying out pleasure-gardens, playing his flute to his heart's content, writing poor French verses, and solacing himself for the "coarse potherbs" of his childhood by exquisite dinners. They had the best musicians for their concerts at Reinsbergthe crown prince and his friends, with the crown princess and her ladies. It was here, in 1736, that Frederick began-by letter-his famous friendship with Voltaire, that survived so many phases of illusion and disillusion.

It must be said of Frederick's friends-who were mostly French-that they were men of highly trained intelligence, but they were not acute enough to know what sort of king their prince would make.

When his father passed away, Frederick felt as sincere a grief as if there had never been anything but love between them; always afterwards he spoke of him with reverence, and he learned to place a high value on the stern discipline of his early life-which is still to some extent a model for the bringing up of young Hohenzollerns.

It was a handsome young king who came to the throne in 1740. His face was round, his nose a keen aquiline, his mouth small and delicately curved, and all was dominated by those wonderful blue-gray eyes, that, as Mirabeau said, "at the bidding of his heroic soul fascinated you with seduction or with terror." Even in youth the lines of the face showed a sardonic humour. One can well imagine his replying to the optimistic Sulzer, who thought severe punishments a mistake: "Ach! meine lieber Sulzer, you don't know this-race!" In the old-age portraits the face is sharp and hatchet-like, the mouth is shrunken to a mean line, but the great eyes still flash out, commanding and clear.

The reign began with peace and philanthropy: Frederick II. started out by disbanding the giant grenadiers, the absurd monstrosities that his father had begged and bought and kidnapped from everywhere; he started a "knitting-house" for a thousand old women; abolished torture in criminal trials; set up an Academy of Sciences; summoned Voltaire and Maupertius; made Germany open its eyes at the speech, "In this country every man must get to Heaven in his own way;" and proclaimed a practical freedom of the press-all in his first week.

The fury of activity now took possession of Frederick, which lasted all his life. He had the Hohenzollern passion for doing everything himself: the three "secretaries of state" were mere clerks, who spared him only the mechanical part of secretarial duties. His system of economy was rigid. While looking over financial matters one day he found that a certain convent absorbed a considerable fund from the forest-dues, which had been bequeathed by dead dukes "for masses to be said on their behalf." He went to the place and asked the monks, "What good does anybody get out of those masses?" "Your majesty, the dukes are to be delivered out of purgatory by them." "Purgatory? And they are not out yet, poor souls, after so many hundred years of praying?" The answer was, "Not yet." "When will they be out, and the thing settled?" There was no answer to this. "Send me a courier whenever they are out!" With this sneer the king left the convent.

Stern business went on all day, and in the evening, music, dancing, theatres, suppers, till all hours; but the king was up again at four in the summer-five in winter. In early youth Frederick had known a period of gross living, from which he suffered so severely that his reaction from it was fiercely austere. After his accession, a young man who had been associated with this "mud-bath," as Carlyle has named it, begged an audience. The king received him, but rebuked him with such withering speech that he straightway went home and killed himself.

Only five months of his reign had passed when the event occurred that put an end to the ideal monarch of Frederick's subjects. Charles VI., Emperor of Germany, was dead. For years he had worked to bind together his scattered and wabbling empire, and by his "Pragmatic Sanction" secure it to his daughter, Maria Theresa, contrary to the rule that only male heirs should succeed, and she was on the day of his death (October 20) proclaimed empress.

If the young Maria Theresa had been married to the young Prince Frederick of Prussia, as their reigning parents had at one time decided, European history would undoubtedly have been different, though historians may be mistaken in thinking that much trouble would have been saved the world. In view of the fact that both these young people were extravagantly well endowed with the royal gifts of energy and decision, one must be permitted to wonder whether Frederick, as the spouse of the admirable Maria Theresa, would have ever become known as "the Great." But at all events it would have prevented him from rushing in on her domains and seizing Silesia as soon as she was left with no one but her husband —a man of the kindly inert sort-to protect her; and we should have lost the good historical scene of Maria Theresa appearing before her Hungarian Diet, with the crown on her beautiful head, thrilling every heart as she lifted her plump baby, Francis Joseph, and with tears streaming down her face implored its help against the Prussian robber.

We can still hear the thunderous roar of the loyal reply, "We will die for our sovereign, Maria Theresa!"

Nevertheless, by December the Prussian robber was in Silesia with thirty thousand men, engaged in finding out that he was really made to be a warrior. By May he held every fortified place in the province; by June Maria Theresa was forced to cede it to him-since which time it has always been a loyal part of Prussia.

"How glorious is my king, the youngest of the kings and the grandest!" chanted Voltaire in a letter to Frederick, who, one is pleased to know, found the praise rather suffocating.

The genius of Frederick was next put to a considerable test in the way of matchmaking —a delicate art, particularly when practised for the sake of providing the half-barbarous empire of Russia with mated rulers.

The Czarina Elizabeth-Great Peter's daughter-wished the king to find a German bride for her nephew-heir, who was afterwards Peter III. A true Hohenzollern, Frederick felt himself quite equal to this task-as to any other. From a bevy of young princesses he selected the daughter of the poverty-stricken Prince of Anhalt-Herbst, because of the unmistakable cleverness the girl had shown, though not fifteen. She was handsome as well, and Elizabeth renamed her "Catherine," changed her religion, and the marriage came off in 1745. Frederick had displayed great acumen, but it would puzzle a fiend to contrive a more diabolical union than that of Peter and Catherine!

Meanwhile, Maria Theresa had been preparing to fight for Silesia again. Without waiting for her, Frederick pounced upon Prague and captured it. After her armies in Silesia and Saxony had been put to flight by her adversary, at Hohenfriedberg and Sorr, and Hennersdorf and Kesselsdorf, the empress yielded. On Christmas Day, 1745, when the treaty was signed that gave

Silesia again to Prussia, —it was known as the Peace of Dresden, —Berlin went wild, and for the first time shouts were heard among the revellers, "Vivat Friedrich *der Grosse!*" The Austrians might call him "that ferocious, false, ambitious king of Prussia," but as a matter of fact he was not more false and ferocious than the other rulers, only infinitely more able. Frederick had made for himself a great name and raised his little kingdom-of only two and a half millions of people-to a noble standing among nations. The eyes of the world were fixed upon the hero to see what he would do next. What he did was to swear that he "would not fight with a cat again," and to build himself a charming country home-his palaces, and even Reinsberg, were too large. In May, 1747, he had his housewarming at little Sans Souci, where for the next forty years most of his time was spent. There were twenty boxes of German flutes in the king's cabinet at Sans Souci, and infinite boxes of Spanish snuff; and there were three arm-chairs for three favourite dogs, with low stools to make an easy step for them. There was another favourite at Sans Souci who was said to look like an ape, although he was mostly called the "skinny Apollo." How one would like to have seen the king walking the terraces, with "white shoes and stockings and red breeches, with gown and waistcoat of blue linen flowered and lined with yellow!" while men with powdered wigs and highly coloured clothes, and women whose heads bore high towers of hair unpleasantly stuffed and decorated with inconsequent dabs of finery, followed him, all talking epigrams and doing attitudes-polite people had to hold themselves in curves in the eighteenth century.

These were good years for Prussia: her law courts were reformed; her commerce flourished, and so did agriculture; potatoes were introduced-they were at first considered poisonous; a huge amount of building was done, and the army was drilled constantly under Frederick's eyes. Each year saw it a better army; its chief must have known that he was preparing for the great struggle of his life, although he took as keen an interest in keeping up the high standard of his new opera-house in Berlin, both as to music and ballet, as he did in the skilfullest manoeuvres of his troops.

Maria Theresa had never for a moment given up Silesia in her heart. She was a woman of austere virtues, but these did not stand in the way of schemes which she would have thought too despicable to be used against any one but the King of Prussia. The Czarina of Russia had been made to hate him by a series of carefully-devised plots, —she looked on him as her arch-enemy, —and within six months after the Peace of Dresden she had signed, with Maria Theresa, a treaty which actually proposed the partitioning of Frederick's kingdom, which was to be divided between Russia, Austria, and Poland, while he was to become a simple Margrave of Brandenburg!

To get the signature of Louis XV. involved harder work still for the virtuous empress-but she did it. It was to ask it of the Pompadour-in various affectionate letters, beginning "My dear cousin," or "Madame, my dearest sister." The Pompadour was also shown some stinging verses of Frederick's with herself as subject, and she (representing France) became the firm ally of Maria Theresa.

Through an Austrian clerk's treachery Frederick became aware of this stupendous conspiracy against him-but not till 1755, when it was well matured. It seemed incredible that he could think of keeping these great countries from gobbling up his little state. He could not have done it, indeed, if it had not been for a certain Englishman. It was an Englishman who saved Frederick and Prussia-the "Great Commoner," Pitt, who, having on hand a French war of his own, raised a Hanoverian army to help himself and Frederick, and granted him a welcome subsidy of six hundred and seventy thousand pounds a year.

His ten years' drilling had given Frederick a fine army of one hundred and thirty thousand men. The infantry were said to excel all others in quickness of manoeuvres and skilled shooting, while the cavalry was unsurpassed.

Frederick, without waiting for his foes to declare war and mass their mighty forces, began it by a stealthy, sudden move into Saxony in September 1756. October 1, at Lowositz, in Bohemia, he defeated von Browne, and, returning, captured the Saxon force of seventeen thousand, and took them bodily-all but the officers-into his own army.

England was delighted with this masterly act of her ally. He was known there as "the Protestant hero," which was not quite true to facts. Certainly Frederick protested against the old religion, but he was far from being on with the new one. His saying, "Every one shall go to heaven in the way he chooses," had been applauded in England, but they were not familiar with his reply when a squabble as to whether one or another set of hymn-books should be used was referred to him: "Bah! let them sing what tomfoolery they like," said the "Protestant hero." Had France and Austria, however, succeeded in obliterating Prussia, it is likely that Protestantism too would have been done for in Germany.

Frederick having himself begun the Seven Years' War, the confederated German states, with Russia, France, and Sweden, formally bound themselves to "reduce the House of Brandenburg to its former state of mediocrity," France-very rich then-paying enormous subsidies all around. England-with Hanover-alone espoused Prussia's cause. During 1757, four hundred and thirty-seven thousand men were put in the field against Frederick. Only his cat-like swiftness saved him from being overwhelmed again and again. In April he made another rush-like an avalanche-on Bohemia, and won another great victory at Prague, but he was terribly beaten by General Daun in June at Kolin. Still he kept up courage, and played the flute and wrote innumerable French verses of the usual poor quality in odd moments. In November, at Rossbach, he met an army of French and Imperialists over twice as large as his own, and by a swift, unexpected movement broke them, so that they were scattered all over the country. Every German felt proud of this French defeat, whether he were Prussian or not. It was the first time the invincible French had ever been beaten by a wholly German army, with a leader of German blood. The brilliant victory of Leuthen followed Rossbach.

But although the world was ringing with Frederick's name, and he was acknowledged to be one of the greatest generals of history, the resources of his powerful enemies were too many for him. At last it seemed that a ruinous cloud of disaster was closing around him and darkening the memory of his glorious successes.

The defeat of Kunersdorf in 1759 would have completely wiped out his army if the over-cautious Austrian General Daun had followed up his victory. "Is there no cursed bullet that can reach me!" the Prussian monarch was heard to murmur in a stupor of despair after the battle. He carried poison about him, after this, to use when affairs became too bad. A severe blow followed Kunersdorf,—George II. died in October 1760; George III. put an end to Pitt's ministry-and this was the end of England's support.

The winter of 1761-1762 saw Frederick at his lowest ebb. England's money had stopped; his own country, plundered, devastated in every direction, afforded no sufficient revenue. Fully half of the Prussian dominions were occupied by the enemy; men, horses, supplies, and transport could hardly be procured. The Prussian army was reduced to sixty thousand men, and its ranks were made up largely of vagabonds and deserters-the old, splendidly disciplined troops having been practically obliterated.

He played no more on his flute-poor Frederick! At Leipzig an old friend sighed to him, "Ach! how lean your majesty has grown!" "Lean, ja wohl," he replied; "and what wonder, with three women [Pompadour, Maria Theresa, and Czarina Elizabeth] hanging to my throat all this while!"

The Allies felt that it was only a matter of a short time before they should see their great enemy humbled to the position of Elector of Brandenburg. From this abasement Frederick was suddenly saved in January 1762. Life held another chance for him. The implacable old czarina was dead; her heir, Peter III., was not merely the friend, but the enthusiastic adorer of Frederick of Prussia. Although thirty-four years old and the husband of Catherine (the young lady Frederick had taken such pains to select for him so many years ago), Peter had been kept out of public affairs as if he were a child. Neither he nor Catherine was allowed to leave the palace without permission of the czarina; they were surrounded with spies, and kept in a gaudy and dirty semi-imprisonment the traditional style for heirs to the Russian throne. Under this system they became masters of deceit. Catherine, in her cleverly unpleasant *Memoirs,* tells how they managed to escape and visit people without being found out; how she, when ill and in bed, had a joyous company with her, who huddled behind a screen when prying ladies-in-waiting entered. But the most painful part is the account of Peter, who seems to have had more versatility in hateful ways than any one outside of Bedlam. Crazily vivacious over foolish games, brutal when drunk, and silly when sober, one wonders how for so many years Catherine endured him.

There was a saving grace, though, in him: he worshipped the King of Prussia.

Frederick adroitly rose to the occasion: releasing all his Russian prisoners, he sent them, well clad and provisioned, back to their country. On February 23 the czar responded by a public declaration of peace with Prussia and a renunciation of all conquests made during the war. His general, Czernichef, was ordered to put himself and his twenty thousand men at the disposal of the Prussian hero, and on May 5 a treaty of alliance between Prussia and Russia was announced-to the horror and disgust of France and Austria. They had relied on Czernichef, but Czernichef himself was a sincere admirer of his new commander-in-chief and delighted in the change. The Russian soldiers all shared this feeling: they called Frederick "Son of the lightning."

The French were being held by the Hanoverian army; Sweden had retired from the war; with Russia on his side, Frederick felt that he might hold out against Austria till peace was declared by the powers-peace with no provision made for the partition of his kingdom.

In planning his next campaign-the last of the war-it was evident to Frederick that nothing could be done without recapturing the fortress of Schweidnitz, recently captured by Loudon, the Austrian general. The Austrians held all Silesia, and they must be put out of it, but with Schweidnitz in their hands this was impossible.

Fortunately for Frederick, Daun was appointed commander-in-chief of the Austrians, the general who had been execrated throughout the empire for his failure to follow up Frederick after Kunersdorf. In mid-May Daun took command of the forces in Silesia, and with an army of seventy thousand men made haste to place himself in a strong position among rugged hills to guard Schweidnitz. Schweidnitz, with a garrison of twelve thousand picked men and firm defences, it was impossible to attack while Daun was there. Frederick made repeated efforts to force Daun to give up his hold on the fortress, threatening his left wing, as his right wing seemed impregnably situated; but Daun, although forced to change his position from time to time, kept firmly massed about Schweidnitz. Frederick at last, then, resolved to attempt the impossible, and, his forces now augmented by Czernichef's to eighty-one thousand, determined on storming the Heights of Burkersdorf, where Daun's right wing was firmly entrenched. The last of Frederick's notable battles of the war, —a conflict upon which the destinies of Prussia turned, —it was planned and executed by him with a consummate brightness and cleverness that more than justifies the Hohenzollern worship of their great ancestor.

Burkersdorf Height, near the village of the same name, which was also occupied by Daun, lies parallel to Kunersdorf Heights, where Frederick's army lay. It is a high hill, very steep, and half covered with rugged underbrush on the side next to Frederick's position, and Prince de Ligne and General O'Kelly-serving under Daun-had made it bristle with guns. Artillery was Daun's specialty; his guns were thick wherever the ground was not impractically steep, and palisades —"the pales strong as masts and room only for a musket-barrel between" —protected the soldiery; they were even "furnished with a lath or cross-strap all along for resting the gun-barrel on and taking aim." In fact, Burkersdorf Height was as good as a fortress. East of it was a small valley where strong entrenchments had been made and batteries placed. Farther east, two other heights had to be captured, —they were also well defended, —Ludwigsdorf and Leuthmannsdorf.

By the 17th of July Frederick had all his plans matured, and had made his very first move-that is, he had sent Generals Möllendorf and Wied on a march with their men to put the enemy on a false scent-when he received a call from Czernichef at his headquarters. It was paralysing news that Czernichef brought: Peter, the providential friend, had been dethroned by the partisans of his clever wife, Catherine.

After a reign of six months the young czar had completely disgusted his subjects: he had planned ambitious schemes of reform, and at the same time had made despotic encroachments. After delighting the Church with important concessions, he proposed virtually to take away all its lands and houses. He overdid everything, like the madman he was. He offended his army by dressing up his guards in Prussian uniforms and teaching them the Prussian drill, while he wore constantly the dress of a Prussian colonel, and sang the praises of our hero until his people were sick of the name of "my friend, the King of Prussia."

Russian morals in the eighteenth century were like snakes in Ireland-there were none. In this respect Catherine was not superior to her husband, but in mental gifts she was an extraordinary young woman. Her tact, her poise, her intelligence, would have made a noble character in a decent atmosphere. Peter had recognised her powers and relied on them, and she had endured him all these years, thinking she would one day rule Russia as his empress. But since his accession he had been completely under the dominion of the Countess Woronzow, a vicious creature, who meant to be Catherine's successor. And Catherine, when Peter threatened her and her son Paul with lifelong imprisonment, had on her side finally begun a plot, which resulted in her appealing to the guards, much as Maria Theresa had appealed to her Diet of Hungary. Every one was tired of Peter, and no voice was raised against his deposition, whereupon Catherine assumed the sovereignty of Russia, to the great relief and satisfaction of all Russians. The brutal assassination of poor Peter by Catherine's friends-not by her orders-followed in a few days.

It was the intention of Catherine, on beginning her reign, to restore Elizabeth's policy in Russian matters and recommence hostilities against Frederick; but on looking' over Peter's papers she found that Frederick had discouraged his wild schemes, and that he had begged him to rely on his wife and respect her counsels, and this produced a revulsion of feeling. She resolved that she would not fight him; nor, on the other hand, would she be his ally; the secret message that had come to Czernichef, and which he communicated to Frederick, was that Catherine reigned, and that he, her general, was ordered to return immediately to St. Petersburg.

One can only guess at Frederick's emotions at this news. Life must have seemed a lurid melodrama, presenting one hideous act after another. "This is not living," he said; "this is being killed a thousand times a day!" On the eve of the attack on Burkersdorf his ally had been taken away from him; his own forces were now weaker than those of Daun, and he did not see his way to a victory.

But the genius of Frederick could not allow him to give in to the destinies. His resourcefulness came to his rescue. He simply begged Czernichef to stay with him for three days. Three days must elapse before his official commands came. Frederick, with all the potency of his personal fascination, implored the Russian during that time to keep the matter secret, and, without one hostile act against the enemy, to *seem* to act with him as though their relations were unchanged. Czernichef consented; it was one of the most devoted acts that was ever done by a man for pure friendship; he well knew, and so did Frederick, that he might lose his head or rot in a dungeon for it, but his own heroism was great enough to make the sacrifice.

The drama accordingly went on. On the evening of the 20th, with the forces of Möllendorf and Wied, who had puzzled the enemy and returned, with Ziethen and Czernichef, —this last, of course, only for show, —Frederick silently marched into Burkersdorf village and took by storm the old Burkersdorf Castle, —an affair of a few hours, —while Daun's forces fled in all directions from the village. Then, through the night, trenches were dug and batteries built-forty guns well placed. At sunrise the whole Prussian army could be seen to be in motion by their opponents.

At four o'clock Frederick's famous cannonade began, concentrated upon the principal height of Burkersdorf. General O'Kelly's men were too high to be reached by the cannon, but it was Frederick's object to keep a furious, confusing noise going on, to help to draw attention from Wied and Möllendorf, who were doing the real fighting of the day. Möllendorf was to storm

O'Kelly's height, and Wied the Ludwigsdorf height beyond; but Frederick had arranged a spectacular drama by which the foe was to be deceived as to these intentions. It was not for nothing that Frederick had personally overlooked his theatres and operas all these years. His knowledge of scenic displays and their effect on the minds of an audience stood him in good stead this day.

The Prussian guns continued a deafening roar, hour after hour, with many blank charges, and the bewildered commanders of the allied Austrians watched from their elevation the small man on his white horse giving orders right and left. He wore a three-cornered hat with a white feather, a plain blue uniform with red facings, a yellow waistcoat liberally powdered with Spanish snuff, black velvet breeches, and high soft boots. They were shabby old clothes, but the figure had a majesty that every one recognised. The difficulty among the officers on the heights was to find out what were the orders Frederick was giving so freely. His generals, who were much smarter in their dress than he, dashed off in all directions, and marched their troops briskly about, keeping the whole line of the enemy on the alert.

Daun, ignorant of the St. Petersburg revolution and its consequences, and seeing the Russian masses drawn up threateningly opposite his left wing, which he commanded, dared not concentrate his whole force on Burkersdorf, but from time to time sent bodies of men to support de Ligne and O'Kelly. As no one could tell what spot to support, no line of action could be agreed upon. The commandant of Schweidnitz, General Guasco, with twelve thousand men, came out of the fortress to attack the Prussian rear, but, fortunately for Frederick, one of his astute superiors sent him back.

Meantime, while this uproar and these puzzling operations were going on, Wied had taken his men out of view of the Austrians by circuitous paths to the gradual eastern ascent of Ludwigsdorf and moved up in three detachments. Battery after battery he dislodged, but when he came in sight of the huge mass of guns and men at the top, it seemed wild foolishness to try to get there. It could never have been done by a straight, headlong rush; they crawled along through thickets and little valleys, creeping spirally higher and higher, dodging the fire from above, till at last a movement through a dense wood brought them to the rear and flank of the foe. Then, with a magnificent charge of bayonets, they sent them flying, and passed on to the easy rout of the troops on Leuthmannsdorf.

On Burkersdorf Height O'Kelly's men were looking for an attack on the steepest side, where they were best fortified, but Möllendorf's troops had gone by a roundabout route to the western slope, where after some searching they found a sheep-track winding up the hillside. Following this, they came to a slope so steep that horses could not draw the guns. And then the men pushed and pulled them along and up, until the Austrians spied them from above, and the cannon-balls came crashing down into them. But under this fire they planted their guns, and did such gallant work with them that they were soon at the top, dashing down the defences. It was a tough struggle: the defences were strong-there were line after line of them-and the Austrians had no idea of yielding. They fought like tigers until the fire from the muskets set the dry branches of their abatis ablaze, and Möllendorf quickly closed in around them and forced them to surrender. Frederick's orchestra still boomed on, and the show of officers on prancing steeds and parading troops kept reinforcements from coming to assist the men on Burkersdorf.

It was noon when Möllendorf had achieved his task, and Daun ordered the army to fall back. But Frederick kept his cannon going as if with a desperate intention till five, to make matters appear more dangerous than they really were to Daun. He was successful; at nightfall Daun led his entire army away, silently and in order, and he never troubled Frederick again.

He left fourteen guns behind him and over one thousand prisoners, and quite two thousand deserted to Frederick in the next few days.

And Czernichef, who had stood by him so nobly? He was full of warmest admiration for Frederick's curious tactics and their success, and the king must have been eternally grateful to him. He marched for home early next morning-and he was neither beheaded nor imprisoned by Catherine when he got there: one is very glad to know that.

Frederick was now enabled to besiege Schweidnitz; its re-conquest gave him back Silesia and left him to long years of peace at Sans Souci. It is fair to conclude that these were happy years, since his happiness lay in incessant work; it needed the most arduous toil to get his country into shape again, but Prussia deserved it —"To have achieved a Frederick the Second for king over it was Prussia's great merit," says Carlyle.

A SWEDE'S CAMPAIGN IN GERMANY

I. LEIPZIG

At the opening of the seventeenth century the prospects of Sweden must have seemed to offer less hope than those of any nation of Europe.

Only a scanty population clung to the land, whose long winters paralysed its industrial activities for many months of the year; and the deadly proximity of the insolent conqueror, Denmark, cut her off almost entirely from European commerce and made her complete subjugation seem but a question of time.

Then it was that the powerful Gustavus Vasa took charge of Sweden's destinies, delivering the country from Danish tyranny and establishing his new monarchy with the Lutheran Church for its foundation.

He was the first of a great race of kings. From the beginning of his reign, 1527, to the death of Charles XII., 1718, every monarch displayed some signal ability. But the finest flower of the line, the most original genius and hero, and one of the world's greatest conquerors, was Gustavus Adolphus, the "Northern Lion."

He was the grandson of the liberator, Gustavus Vasa, the first Protestant prince ever crowned, and the son of Charles IX., who came to the throne in his son's tenth year.

Gustavus Adolphus was born in 1594, his advent bringing great joy to the Swedes, as it shut out the possible accession of the Polish house of Vasa, who were Roman Catholics. From early childhood it was apparent that he had unusual qualities of mind, great steadfastness, and high ideals of duty, while his perceptions were swift and wonderfully luminous.

From the first he was inured to hardships-early rising, simple fare, indifference to heat and cold; much the same sort of discipline, I suppose, to which the boys of the house of Hohenzollern are now habituated. His father felt the necessity of securing the most distinguished men that were to be found for his son's education, both from Sweden and foreign lands. Count de la Gardie had charge of his military education; Helmer von Morner, of Brandenburg, was his teacher in science and languages, and John Skythe, a man of great learning, had general charge. So much severe military drill, combined with constant lessons perseveringly administered by intellectual martinets, has had the effect of crushing the spontaneity, the power of taking the initiative, out of many a callow princeling; but Gustavus was not of any ordinary princely metal. He took kindly to handling a musket and playing soldier, while at the same time he displayed a wonderful facility for learning anything that was presented to him.

Besides his mother tongue, he understood Greek, Latin, German, Dutch, Italian, Polish, and Russian, using Latin in daily speech with special fluency. His vigorous memory and brilliantly keen understanding were at the service of his natural desire to know, and all combined to make the work of teaching him a delight.

His father was proud of the promise he showed, and from his tenth year onward allowed him to take part in his councils and audiences, and sometimes even to give his answers in council. Records of reports of foreign ambassadors contain many praises of his intelligence and keen discernment in abstruse questions. When he visited Heidelberg in 1620 the Duke of Zweibrücken gave an extremely admiring account of him.

Mathematics came to him easily. His favourite subjects were the various branches of military science, and fortifications, their plans and erection, exercised his mind almost unceasingly. Grotius's treatise on the *Right of War and Peace* and Xenophon's *Anabasis* were among his favourite readings.

The family of Adolphus owed their position as the reigning power of the country to their espousal of Protestant principles, and it was therefore considered essential that the youth should be brought up to consider himself as the champion and defender of the Protestant faith.

But it seemed a part of his very being to feel sympathy with this belief only. He indeed seemed to have been born an ardent Protestant. The fine austerity of his temperament, the elevation and purity of his mind, made it impossible for him ever to relax his views. Protestantism, or Lutheranism, as the latest form of religion of which he was aware, excited his sincere devotion, which throughout his career only grew to greater heights of self-effacing enthusiasm.

Gustavus is described as being tall and slim in his early youth, with a long, thin, pale face, light hair, and pointed beard. But in after years he grew to great height and bulk, and is said to have been extremely slow and clumsy in his movements, and so heavy that no Swedish horse could carry him in armour.

It is a curious physical fact in connection with this indisputable one that his mind formed its lucid conclusions like lightning, and that much of his success as a soldier was due to the marvellous speed of his operations.

His portrait, taken at this later period by Van Dyke, shows the long face well rounded; the nose is of the prominent Roman type, while the pointed beard is still worn, also a moustache curved up at the ends. The eyes are large and beautifully shaped; they were steel-gray, and capable of fearful flashes of anger when the quick and often-repented temper of the monarch was aroused; but the brows are finely arched, and the whole face expresses justice and benevolence. Sternness is in it, but it is the face pre-eminently of a good man. One can read in it the courage of high principles and a great mind; it is absolutely unlike the portraits of the ferocious and dissolute warriors of the time.

His first campaign was undertaken when he was only in his seventeenth year. He stormed the city of Christianople, which then belonged to Denmark, and triumphantly entered the town, but afterwards, when attacking one of the Danish islands, the young leader came to grief; his horse broke through the thin ice over a morass, where he floundered for some time, surrounded by his enemies. He was finally rescued by young Baner.

In the same year Charles IX. died, and the queen-dowager, the stepmother of Gustavus, having made a full resignation of her claims to the regency, which under Swedish law she might have claimed until Gustavus had reached his twenty-fourth year, he succeeded to his father's title of "King Elect of the Swedes, Goths, and Vandals."

For a young man of eighteen it was a formidable undertaking to ascend the throne of Sweden, and he behaved with modesty and dignity at a session of the States Assembly convened to discuss the rights of succession. He spoke of his youth and inexperience, but added manfully, "Nevertheless, if the States persist in making me king, I will endeavour to acquit myself with honour and fidelity."

He was formally proclaimed king on December 31, 1611.

All the force of his character was now called into play. Among the nobility there was a great deal of jealousy; people of a certain rank felt that there was no reason why he should occupy the throne-each of them had quite as good a claim to it as this grandson of a former subject.

But here Gustavus's great personal force made itself apparent. The malcontents found it impossible to treat him otherwise than with the respect due to a sovereign. He was able to control his natural impetuosity in all matters of court usage; his nobles were first made to feel that they were kept at a distance and under the dominion of a powerful will, and then they seemed glad to serve him as he wished. His appointments of men to fill public posts, civil and military, showed remarkable acumen. For his principal counsellor he chose the famous Oxenstiern, distinguished at twenty-eight as the coldest, most practical of diplomats, and who has left a reputation as an unequalled statesman.

Two sets of questions now presented themselves to the king and the Senate: one related to the development of agriculture and mining in the country, the other to the critical condition of the kingdom, between Danes, Polanders, and Muscovites.

The king decided to continue the war with Denmark, but as King Christian got the better of him, he astutely receded, and signed a treaty of peace in 1613. He then proceeded against the Czar of Muscovy, and thereby augmented the Swedish kingdom by several provinces of importance, one of which included the ground on which St. Petersburg now stands.

In 1617 peace was concluded with Russia through the mediation of James I. of England, who was always offering himself as a peacemaker.

Gustavus now went through the ceremonies of a coronation at Upsal. It is said that this brief time of festivity was the only rest he ever enjoyed from the end of his childhood to the abrupt close of his life. At this time of so-called rest, indeed, he was concentrating all his mind on international affairs, studying the laws of commerce, and trying to lift the burden of taxation from his people as far as was possible.

He looked over his ships, which were in a wretched condition as a whole, and sent for the best mariners he could obtain from Holland and the Hanse Towns, with the idea of building up a good and sufficient navy.

His army also profited by his inventions in arms and artillery; indeed, he had at all times a watchful eye upon his soldiers, providing for their comfort and well-being. They had fur-lined coats for cold weather, and comfortable tents, and they could take the field in the bitterest winter as well as in summer.

Sweden was continually exporting steel for armour to Spain and Italy, so it occurred to Gustavus to establish home manufactories of firearms and swords that should equal those of any other country. Among his many useful improvements and inventions the leather cannon was the most curious. These pieces, being very light, were easily shifted on the battle-field and rapidly hauled over rugged country. They were made of thick layers of the hardest leather girt around with iron or brass hoops. After a dozen discharges they would fall to pieces, but they were made in camp in quantities, and could be replaced at once. Gustavus attributed many of his most brilliant victories to them and used them till the day of his death.

At this time the king and Oxenstiern were staying for a time at a castle which he had inherited from a cousin, when a fire broke out in the night and raged up all the staircases. They could only save themselves by jumping out of the windows and wading up to their shoulders through a filthy moat, but both escaped with nothing worse than bruises.

Schiller speaks admiringly of Gustavus for "a glorious triumph over himself by which he began a reign which was but one continued series of triumphs, and which was terminated by a victory."

This triumph of duty over inclination was Gustavus's yielding to the entreaties of his step-mother and other counsellors and giving up the beautiful Emma, Countess of Brahe. He was deeply in love with her, —the chroniclers assure us that his intentions were honourable, —and she had promised to be his wife; but it was represented to him that although the Countess of Brahe had all the necessary merits and virtues, marriage with a subject would seriously impair the power of his throne. So, to quote Schiller again, he "regained an absolute ascendancy over a heart which the tranquillity of a domestic life was far from being able to satisfy."

His marriage, however, although it was dictated by considerations of policy, seems to have been a successful one.

In the summer of 1620 Gustavus made a tour, incognito, of the principal towns of Germany, with the object of seeing for himself, in Berlin, the sister of the elector. His suit prospered, and it is said that in defiance of the elector's wishes the Princess Maria Eleonora, who was then in her twentieth year, accepted Gustavus and eloped with him to Sweden. They were married in Stockholm with great pomp. She was graceful and majestic, and we are assured that she made Gustavus a worthy and Christian queen.

The relations of Sweden with Poland were perpetually unsatisfactory. Sigis mund, its Catholic king, disputed the throne with his cousin Gustavus, and a tedious eight years' war resulted.

But instead of exhausting Sweden, it had the effect of developing the consummate military genius of her king; of bringing his army, by its constant exercise, to an extraordinary degree of skill, and of making ready for the coming great struggle in Germany the new principles of military art introduced by Gustavus.

Not only was he a brilliant strategist, but the king looked after his army with paternal care; it was well fed, well clad, and promptly and well paid. Every detail was attended to by him. Religious services were held, morning and evening, by every regiment. No plunder, cruelty, intemperance, no low and slanderous talk or immorality, were allowed-his officers and soldiers alike were obliged to follow his example.

It is not to be wondered at that this army was led from one victory to another, or that the fame of its discipline and its successes should be noised all over Europe. The great Thirty Years' War, that stupendous struggle of Roman Catholicism to blot out the work of the Reformation in Germany, was now raging, and in the various Protestant countries, notably England and Holland, as well as the anti-Papist states of Germany, people were beginning to look towards Gustavus as the most likely champion to give them victory. There were no such generals on the Protestant side in Europe, and it was known that Gustavus was deeply and sincerely religious, leading an upright life —a man of honour, who might be relied upon to keep his word.

Ferdinand, the Catholic Emperor of Germany, laughed at the idea of the Swedish champion; the "Snow King," he said (this being one of the favourite names for Gustavus), would melt if he tried coming south.

As for Gustavus, he had longed for years to try conclusions with Tilly and the other Imperial generals, but more particularly since Ferdinand in 1629 had promulgated the Edict of Restitution, whereby at one stroke the Archbishoprics of Magdeburg and Bremen, the Bishoprics of Minden, Verden, Halberstadt, Lubeck, Ratzeburg, Misnia, Merseburg, Naumburg, Brandenburg, H avelberg, Lebus, and Cammin, with one hundred and twenty smaller foundations, were taken away from the Protestant Church and restored to the Roman Catholic Church.

To restore these lands and dignities, which had been from fifty to eighty years in the possession of the Protestants, was of course impossible without the use of brute force. By using the armies of Tilly and Wallenstein to compel it, the Emperor Ferdinand proclaimed himself the author of a political and religious revolution, the success of which must depend entirely upon military despotism, and which was without any moral basis whatever.

There were many different motives prompting Gustavus to enter the lists against Ferdinand's forces. It was not only that there was great flattery in the appeal to help the oppressed-not only that war was his native element, wherein he felt sure of success; besides all this, he had bitter grievances to redress. In 1629 Ferdinand sent sixteen thousand Imperialist troops to take part against him in the war with Poland. To Gustavus's remonstrance Wallenstein had replied, "The Emperor has too many soldiers; he must assist his good friends with them." The envoys sent to represent Gustavus at the Congress of Lubeck were insolently turned away. Ferdinand also continued to support the claims of the Polish king, Sigismund, to the Swedish throne, refused the title of king to Gustavus Adolphus, insulted the Swedish flag, and intercepted the king's despatches.

However, Gustavus would enter the war only at his own time and on his own terms. He was far too prudent and wise, far too dutiful, to impoverish his own country or leave her exposed to the attacks of enemies. In 1624 England had approached him, wishing to know his terms for invading Germany, but England would not accede to his rather high stipulations.

The King of Denmark then underbid Gustavus, made terms with England, and rushed into the German conflict with great confidence, but he was ignominiously defeated, while Wallenstein (at that time Ferdinand's best general) established himself on the Baltic coast. This was getting dangerously near, as Gustavus felt.

In 1628 Gustavus Adolphus made an alliance with Christian of Denmark, his old enemy, but as a Protestant and a foe to Catholic rule in Germany his loyal friend-for the time. It was agreed between them that all foreign ships except the ships of the Dutch should be excluded from the Baltic. In the summer of the same year he sent two thousand men to defend Stralsund against Wallenstein.

In 1629, through the secret intervention of Cardinal Richelieu, a treaty of peace was signed with Poland at Stuhmsdorf. Again, in 1630, Cardinal Richelieu, the wily diplomatist who governed France for Louis XIII. and had a hand in all the affairs of Europe, sent Baron de Charnace to Gustavus at Stockholm and made the same proposals in the name of France that England had made in 1624. But the flippant manner of de Charnace disgusted the king, and the terms did not please him: he did not care to assume the rôle of a mercenary general paid by France and bound for a limited number of years, and so de Charnace returned home without having accomplished anything.

Richelieu, as the minister of a Catholic king and a prince himself of the Roman Catholic Church, of course did not dare to openly ally himself with Gustavus in the latter's character of defender of the Protestant faith. But in his desire to frustrate the ambitions of the House of Austria, against which he had schemed for years, he was quite willing to support any power that would directly or indirectly advance the supremacy of France.

Gustavus now felt comparatively free to leave Sweden and invade Germany. By his treaty with Denmark he was free to retreat through her territory.

After the unsuccessful attempt made by Christian of Denmark to oppose the emperor by leading the forces of the Protestant Union, Gustavus remained the only prince in Europe to whom the Germans felt they could appeal-the only one strong enough to protect them, and upright enough to ensure them religious liberty.

Pressing appeals came from all sides now to add to his own personal motives for embarking in the German war. He raised an army of forty-three thousand men in Sweden, but set out on his expedition with only thirteen thousand. On the occasion of taking his leave, Gustavus appeared before the Estates with his little daughter of four in his arms. This princess was born so "dark and ugly," with such a "rough, loud voice," that the attendants had rushed to Gustavus with the news that a son was born to him. When this was found to be a mistake they were reluctant to tell him, as his joy at having an heir to his military greatness was so openly expressed. But finally his sister, the Princess Catherine, took the child to him and explained that it was a daughter. If he felt any disappointment he did not show it; tenderly kissing the child, he said, "Let us thank God, sister; I hope this girl will be as good as a boy; I am content, and pray God to preserve the child." Then, laughing, he added, "She is an arch wench, to put a trick upon us so soon."

In this manner did the celebrated Christina of Sweden enter the world. Her father was deeply fond of her, and enjoyed taking her to his reviews; there she showed great pleasure in hearing the salutes fired, clapping her little hands, so that the king would order the firing to be repeated for her, saying, "She is a soldier's daughter."

There is a famous letter of Gustavus's still preserved in which he wrote to Oxenstiern: "I exhort and entreat you, for the love of Christ, that if all does not go on well, you will not lose courage. I conjure you to remember me and the welfare of my family, and to act towards me and mine as you would have God act towards you and yours, and as I will act to you and yours if it please God that I survive you, and that your family have need of me."

It is said that when Gustavus presented the little girl to the Estates as his heir, tears came to the eyes of those northern men, who had the name of being cold and stern, as they repeated their oath of allegiance to the young princess.

"I know," the king said to them, "the perils, the fatigues, the difficulties of the undertaking, yet neither the wealth of the House of Austria dismays me nor her veteran forces. I hold my retreat secure under the worst alternative. And if it is the will of the Supreme Being that Gustavus should die in the defence of the faith, he pays the tribute with thankful acquiescence; for it is a king's duty and his religion to obey the great Sovereign of Kings without a murmur. For the prosperity of all my subjects I offer my warmest prayers to Heaven. I bid you all a sincere-it may be an eternal-farewell."

At this time he could hardly speak for emotion. He clasped his wife to him and said "God bless you!" and then, rushing forth, he mounted his horse and galloped down to the ship that was to take him away from Sweden.

Sweden was anything but rich, yet so inspired had the people become by the exalted spirit of their monarch, that they were eager to contribute whatever they could to the campaign.

On June 24, 1630, Gustavus was the first man of his expedition to land on the Island of Usedom, where he immediately seized a pickaxe and broke the soil for the first of his entrenchments. Then, retiring a little way from his officers, he fell upon his knees and prayed.

Observing a sneering expression upon the faces of some of his officers at this, he said to them: "A good Christian will never make a bad soldier. A man that has finished his prayers has at least completed one half of his daily work."

A painting commemorating this event is said still to be in existence in a Swedish country-house belonging to the family of de la Gardie.

Hardly a month after the landing of Gustavus Ferdinand deprived himself of his most able general; he removed Wallenstein, —the Duke of Friedland, —disbanding a large part of his army, and putting the rest under the command of Tilly, who now being over seventy', was slow in getting his army ready for the field.

When Ferdinand heard of the Swedish king's arrival on German soil, he had said lightly, "I have got another little enemy!" But by Christmas time Gustavus was established firmly on the banks of the Rhine, while ambassadors and princes surrounded him.

On reaching Stettin, in Pomerania, the king found his course opposed by Boguslas, the aged and infirm Duke of Pomerania, who feared to espouse the cause of the Protestant prince. But Gustavus insisted upon entering Stettin and seeing the duke. When the latter came to meet him, borne along the street on a sedan chair, he responded to Gustavus's hearty greetings by saying lugubriously, "I must necessarily submit to superior power and the will of Providence." At which Gustavus said with gracious pleasantry, that was no doubt trying to the timid old man, "Yonder fair defendants of your garrison" (the windows were crowded with ladies) "would not hold out three minutes against one company of Dalicarnian infantry; you should behave yourself with greater prowess in the married state" (the duke was over seventy and had no children) "or else permit me to request you to adopt me for your son and successor." This was a jest in earnest, for on the death of the duke the Swedes held possession of Pomerania, which was confirmed to them by subsequent treaty.

Germany was astounded at the orderly and moral behaviour of the Swedish soldiers; nothing save "vinegar and salt" were they allowed to make any demand for outside the camp. In January a notable event occurred. Richelieu, having in view the effect that so favourable a diversion would have on the war then going on in Italy between France and the House of Austria, had at last arranged conditions that Gustavus could accept.

Richelieu, as Wakeman says, "had long fixed his eyes on Gustavus as one of the most formidable weapons capable of being used against the House of Austria, and he desired to put it in the armoury of France."

In January, 1631, Gustavus signed the treaty of Barwalde, by which he undertook to maintain an army of thirty-six thousand men, to respect the Imperial Constitution, observe neutrality towards Bavaria and the Catholic League as they observed it towards him, and to leave the Catholic religion untouched in those districts where it was established. France was to supply the king with two hundred thousand dollars yearly for six years.

In March a great gathering of Protestants was held in Leipzig; they agreed to raise troops if they themselves were attacked, but they were willing to submit to the emperor if he would but repeal the Edict of Restitution. There seemed to have been some distrust of Gustavus among them; no doubt they began to fear already that he would prove too much of a conqueror.

There had been great sympathy in England with Gustavus in his character as a Protestant champion. Charles I. himself was quite indifferent, but his subjects, particularly his Scotch subjects, were anxious to be of service in the campaign.

In July of 1631 the Marquis of Hamilton had landed on the shores of the Baltic with six thousand troops, generously raised at his own expense. The marquis was a magnificent fellow, who lived in the field like a prince, with gorgeous liveries, equipages, and table. The king received him affectionately, but although he commanded his own troops he never achieved the rank of general in the Swedish army.

It is said that the English soldiers were not of great service in the war, and that they were fearfully affected by the strange food. The German bread gave them terrible pangs (it must have been Pumpernickel); they overfed themselves dreadfully with new honey, and the German beer played havoc with them. In this way the British contingent was soon reduced to but two regiments, finally to only one, and the Marquis of Hamilton was content to follow Gustavus as a simple volunteer.

An expostulating letter from Charles I. to Gustavus in relation to Hamilton is said to be almost unintelligible except for a postscript, which reads, —

"I hope shortly you will be in a possibility to perform your promise concerning pictures and statues, therefore now in earnest do not forget it."

Gustavus Adolphus sent back to Scotland many well-trained commanders who had occasion afterwards to use their skill acquired under him. Some of these had a European reputation: Spence, of Warminster, created by Gustavus Count Orcholm; Alexander Leslie, afterwards Earl of Leven; Drummond, Governor of Pomerania; Lindsay, Earl of Crawford; Ramsay; Hepburn; Munro, and, most devoted and beloved of all the king's Scottish officers, Sir Patrick Ruthven.

Various squabbles have been recorded as taking place between the Scotchmen and the king. One relates to Colonel Seton, who was mortally offended at receiving a slap in the face from the king. He demanded instant dismissal from the Swedish service, and it was given him. He was riding off towards Denmark when the king overtook him.

"Seton," he said, "I see you are greatly offended with me, and I am sorry for what I did in haste. I have a high regard for you, and have followed you expressly to offer you all the satisfaction due to a brother officer. Here are two swords and two pistols; choose which weapon you please, and you shall avenge yourself against me."

This was too great an appeal to Seton's magnanimity; he broke out with renewed expressions of the utmost devotion to the king and his cause, and they rode back to camp together.

At one time Hepburn declared with fury to Gustavus that "he would never more unsheath his sword in the Swedish quarrel," but, nevertheless, he did do so, and was made Governor of Munich. The truth was that Gustavus had a domineering spirit and a fiery temper, but meanness or injustice had no part in him, and his noble candour won the true and everlasting attachment of those who were near him.

At one time Douglas, a Scotchman who had enrolled himself in the Swedish army in 1623, behaved in so unpardonable a fashion in Munich as to cause his arrest. Sir Henry Vane, the British ambassador to Sweden, who was greatly disliked there for his insolence and pig-head-edness, approached Gustavus and demanded the release of Douglas.

"By Heaven!" replied the king, "if you speak another syllable on the subject of that man, I will order him to be hanged." Presently, however, he said: "I now release him on *your* parole, but will not be affronted a second time. By Heaven! the fellow is a rascal, and I do not choose to be served by such sort of animals."

"May it please your majesty, I have always understood that the subjects of the king my master have rendered you the most excellent and faithful services."

"Yes, I acknowledge the people of your nation have served me well, and far better than any others, but this dog concerning whom we are talking has affronted me, and I am resolved to chastise him." Within a few moments he had grown calmer, and said: "Sir, I request you not to take exception at what has dropped from me; it was the effect of a warm and hasty temper. I am now cool again, and beseech you to pardon me."

He once spoke of this temper to his generals, saying, "You must bear with my infirmities, as I have to bear with yours."

That Gustavus had so open a way before him this far in Germany, that he had been able to walk through Pomerania and Brandenburg without encountering any opposition that he could not easily overcome, was owing to Wallenstein's Imperial command having been taken from him.

One of the cleverest strokes Richelieu had ever made was the securing the dismissal of Wallenstein from the Imperial army. It seems a miraculous piece of craft, at the very moment when Wallenstein's arms had brought glorious victory to the emperor, and when Gustavus, absolute master of his military operations, was advancing on German soil, to deprive the Imperial armies of the only leader whose authority could stand against the great talents of Gustavus.

To be sure, there was great dissatisfaction with Wallenstein among the Catholic League on account of his personal pretensions, but this of itself would not have brought about his downfall. The only effectual voice to influence Ferdinand was the voice of a priest. His own confessor wrote of Ferdinand:

"Nothing upon earth was more sacred to him than a sacerdotal head. If it should happen, he often said, that he were to meet, at the same time and place, an angel and a priest, the priest would obtain the first and the angel the second act of obeisance."

So Richelieu introduced in his court a gentle Capuchin monk, Father Joseph, who lived but to scheme for his master the cardinal. He told the emperor, among other arguments, that "It would be prudent at this time to yield to the desire of the princes the more easily to gain their suffrages for his son in the election of the King of the Romans. The storm once passed by, Wallenstein might quickly enough resume his former station."

Ferdinand piously gave in to the gentle monk, although he afterwards discovered the trickery; Wallenstein was removed and Tilly was made commander-in-chief.

Johann Tzerklas, Count von Tilly, was born in South Brabant in 1559, of an ancient and illustrious Belgian family. It is thought that he was educated for the Jesuit priesthood, and in this way became fanatically attached to Rome. At twenty-one he gave up the priesthood to enter the army of the Duke of Alva. Adopting the Imperial service, he followed the Duke of Lorraine into Hungary, where in some campaigns against the Turks he rose rapidly from one step to another.

At the conclusion of this war Maximilian of Bavaria made him commander-in-chief of his army with an unlimited power. When the unfortunate Elector Palatine Frederick accepted the crown of Bohemia and defied the emperor and his Catholic League, Maximilian took part with the emperor against him, and was rewarded, at the successful termination of the war, by having the Palatine countries given to him. The defeat of Frederick's forces in 1620 was no doubt due to Tilly's generalship. Poor Frederick, who fled from Tilly in terror and abdicated his electorate when he had two armies ready to support him, explained his poltroonery by saying philosophically: "I know now where I am; there are virtues which only misfortune can teach us; and it is in adversity alone that princes learn to know themselves."

Tilly, like Wallenstein, paid his troops on "the simple plan, that they shall get who have the power, and they shall keep who can."

But Tilly was undoubtedly more disinterested in his character than Wallenstein, who worked for his own aggrandisement, and only pretended to be at one time Protestant, at another Catholic.

Tilly was a sincere bigot, of the sort of stuff that the infamous Duke of Alva, whom he was said to resemble personally, was made. "A strange and terrific aspect," says Schiller in describing Tilly, "corresponded with this disposition: of low stature, meagre, with hollow cheeks, a long nose, a wrinkled forehead, large whiskers, and a sharp chin. He generally appeared dressed in a Spanish doublet of light green satin with open sleeves, and a small but high-crowned hat upon his head, which was ornamented with an ostrich-feather that reached down to his back."

This horrible fanatic, with his ferocious thirst for the blood of Protestants, nevertheless appreciated his adversary's powers: "The King of Sweden," he said in the assembly of the electors at Ratisbon, "is an enemy as prudent as brave; he is inured to war and in the prime of life; his measures are excellent, his resources extensive, and the states of his kingdom have shown him the greatest devotion. His army, composed of Swedes, Germans, Livonians, Finlanders,

Scotch, and English, seems to be animated by but one sentiment, that of blind obedience to his commands. He is a gamester from whom much is won even when nothing is lost."

Tilly had no fondness for parade, and appeared among his troops mounted on a wretched little palfrey. By a curious contradiction, this man, who allowed his men to perform unspeakable acts of cruelty and lust, was himself by nature both temperate and chaste.

Field Marshal Tilly was now an old man, but he could boast that he had never lost a battle. Yet he who had vanquished Mansfield, Christian of Brunswick, the Margrave of Baden, and the King of Denmark, was now to find the King of Sweden too much for him.

The progress of the "Snow King" in Pomerania and Brandenburg made the new commander-in-chief put forth all his powers to collect the military forces scattered through Germany, but it was midwinter before he appeared with twenty thousand men before Frankfort-on-the-Oder. Here he had news that Demmin and Colberg had both surrendered to the King of Sweden, and, giving up his offensive plan of attack, he retired towards the Elbe River to besiege Magdeburg.

On his way, however, he turned aside to New Brandenburg, which Gustavus had garrisoned with two thousand Swedes, Germans, and British, and, angered by their obstinate resistance, put every man of them to the sword. When Gustavus heard of this massacre he vowed that he would make Tilly behave more like a person of humanity than a savage Croatian.

Breaking up his camp at Schwedt, he marched against Frankfort-on-the-Oder, which was defended by eight thousand men-the same ferocious bands that had been devastating Pomerania and Brandenburg. The town was taken by storm after a three days' siege. Gustavus himself, helped by Hepburn and Lumsden, whom he asked to assist him with their "valiant Scots, and remember Brandenburg," placed a petard on a gate which sent it flying. The Swedish troops rushed through, and when the Imperial soldiers asked to be spared, they cried, "Brandenburg quarter!" and cut them down. Thousands were killed or drowned in the river. The remainder, excepting a number of officers who were taken prisoners, fled to Silesia. All the artillery fell into the hands of the Swedes. For the first time the king was unable wholly to restrain his men-all the stores of ill-gotten Imperialist wealth in Frankfort were grabbed by his army.

Giving Leslie charge of Frankfort, and having sent one detachment into Silesia, and another to assist Magdeburg, he then-turning aside, incidentally, to carry Landsberg-on-the-Warth — proceeded towards Berlin with troops and artillery, sending couriers in advance to explain his mission, which was to demand help from his brother-in-law, the elector.

The elector invited the king to dine and sleep at Berlin under the protection of his own guard, and consented to the temporary occupation of the fortresses of Spandau and Kustrin by the king's men, a permission which was withdrawn within a few weeks. When remonstrated with for these concessions the next day by one of his advisers, the elector said: "Mais que faire? Ils ont des canons." It is a remark which seems to explain the lazy, inconsequent character of the elector, who, however, was always ready to admit the logic of superior force.

Magdeburg, one of the richest towns of Germany, enjoyed a republican liberty under its wise magistrates. The rich archbishopric of which it was the capital had belonged for a long period to the Protestant princes of the House of Brandenburg, who had introduced their religion there. The Emperor Ferdinand had removed the Protestant administration and given the archbishopric to his own son, Leopold, but, nevertheless, the city of Magdeburg had found it possible to conclude an alliance with the King of Sweden, by which he promised to protect with all his powers its religious and civil liberties, while he obtained permission to recruit in its territory and was granted free passage through its gates.

He sent there Dietrich, of Falkenberg, an experienced soldier, to direct their military operations, and the magistrates made him governor of the city during the war.

While Gustavus was hindered from coming to its relief, Magdeburg was invested by the forces of Tilly, with those of Count Pappenheim, who served under him. Having ordered the Elector of Saxony to comply with the Edict of Restitution and to order Magdeburg to surrender, and having received a firm refusal, Tilly proceeded, March 30, 1631, to conduct the siege personally with great vigour, and finally, after a long, heroic defence, his men carried it by storm May 20.

Falkenberg was one of the first to fall. Then began the storied horrors of Magdeburg, the slaughter of the soldiers, the citizens, the children, the outrages and murder of the women, many of whom killed themselves to escape the demons let loose by Tilly.

Many Germans felt pity for the wretched women delivered into their hands, but the Walloons of Pappenheim's army were monsters of brutal fury. The scenes of crime in Magdeburg were unsurpassed in animal insanity by anything that has been recorded. When some officers of the League, sickened with these sights, appealed to Tilly to stop them, he said, "The soldier must have some reward for his danger and his labours."

The inhabitants themselves, it is said, set fire to the city in twelve different places, preferring to be buried under the walls to yielding; but some authorities say it was fired by Pappenheim. Only the Cathedral and fifty houses were left from the conflagration; the rest had gone to ruin, soot, and ashes.

At last, on May 23, Tilly walked through the ruined streets of the city. More than six thousand bodies had been thrown into the Elbe; a much greater number of living and dead had been consumed in the flames-altogether thirty thousand were killed.

On the 24th a Te Deum was chanted in the Cathedral by Tilly's orders, and he wrote to his emperor that since the taking of Troy and the destruction of Jerusalem no such victory had been seen. He then marched his men away through the Hartz Mountains, avoiding a meeting with Gustavus.

Great and bitter complaints arose in all quarters now against Gustavus for not succouring the city that depended upon him, and he was obliged to publish a justification of himself. The facts had been that the two Protestant Electors of Saxony and Brandenburg insisted, in the most cowardly spirit, upon preserving their neutrality, and would not allow the king's army to cross their territory. Had he done so in despite of them, his retreat might have been cut off. While the siege was in progress, however, Gustavus finally came to Berlin, and said to the pusillanimous elector:

"I march towards Magdeburg not for my own advantage, but for that of the Protestants. If no person will assist me I will immediately retreat, offer an accommodation to the emperor, and return to Stockholm. I am certain that Ferdinand will grant me whatever peace I desire; but let Magdeburg fall, and the emperor will have nothing more to fear from me; then behold the fate that awaits you!" The elector was frightened, but would not yield a free passage for the Swedes through his dominions, and insisted upon having Spandau given back to him, and while Gustavus was arguing the question with him the news came that Magdeburg had fallen.

The horrible fate of the city sent a shudder throughout Germany. On the strength of it Ferdinand began to make fresh exactions, clearing out more Protestant bishoprics and demanding more men and funds from the electors; but all this had the effect of opening the eyes of the members of the Protestant Union to their own foolishness in not supporting Gustavus, "and the liberties of Germany arose out of the ashes of Magdeburg," says Schiller.

It was now realised that within eight months the "Snow King" had made himself master of four cities, forts, and castles, and had cleared the whole country behind him to the shores of the Baltic —a territory one hundred and forty miles wide. But while other princes were changing their attitude, the Elector of Brandenburg remained obstinately, stupidly resolved on his own idea, —he must have Spandau back; at last Gustavus ordered his commander to evacuate the fortress, but he declared that from that day his brother-in-law should be treated as his enemy. To emphasise this, he brought his whole army before Berlin, and when the elector sent ambassadors to his camp he said to them:

"I will not be worse treated than the emperor's generals. Your master has received them in his states, has furnished them with all necessaries, surrendered every place which they desired, and, notwithstanding so much complaisance, he has not been able to prevail upon them to treat his people with more humanity. All that I require from him is security, a moderate sum of money, and bread for my troops; in return for which I promise to protect his states and to keep the war at a distance from him. I must, however, insist upon these points, and my brother the elector must quickly decide whether he will accept me for his friend or his capital plunderer."

A report of this speech, together with pointing the cannon against the town, had the effect of clearing away the elector's doubts and sweetening his fraternal relations with Gustavus. Most amiably he concluded a treaty, in which he consented to pay thirty thousand dollars monthly to the king, to allow the fortress of Spandau to remain in his hands, and engaged to open Kustrin at all times to his troops.

This decisive union of the Elector of Brandenburg with the Swedes was soon followed by others. The Elector of Saxony, who had had two hundred of his villages burned by Tilly, now joined Gustavus eagerly. When Gustavus, in order to test the Saxon ruler, who had heretofore been so shifty, sent word that he would make no alliance with him unless he would deliver up the fortress of Wittenberg, surrender as a hostage his eldest son, give the Swedish troops three months' pay, and surrender up all traitors in his ministry, the elector replied:

"Not only Wittenberg, but Torgau, all Saxony, shall be open to him; I will surrender the whole of my family to him as hostages; and if that be insufficient, I will even yield up myself to him. Hasten back, and tell him that I am ready to deliver up all the traitors he will name, to pay his army the money he desires, and to venture my life and property for the good cause."

The king, convinced of his sincerity, withdrew his severe conditions. "The mistrust," said he, "which they showed me when I wished to go to the aid of Magdeburg awakened mine; the present confidence of the elector merits an equal return from me. I am content if he will furnish my army with a month's whole pay, and I even hope to be able to indemnify him for this advance." The Landgrave of Hesse-Cassel also joined him. The Dukes of Mecklenburg and Pomerania were already his firm friends.

Shortly after these events the king summoned his allies to meet him at Torgau at a council of war, for Tilly had invested Leipzig with a large army, and was threatening it with the fate of Magdeburg. The council decided upon pursuing Tilly at once, the Saxon elector saying this vehemently. Gustavus had had a short respite from warlike labours; he had visited Pomerania in June, where great rejoicings had been held on his behalf, and where he was joined by his queen, Maria Eleonora (just a year after he had landed), who had come from Sweden with reinforcements of six thousand Swedes.

But, after all, war was the dominating thought always with Gustavus; soon he was at headquarters making active preparations for the next battle. Cust, in his *Lives of the Warriors of the Thirty Years' War,* says:

> "The bridge of Wittenberg being in his hands, he had already issued orders to Horn and Baner to meet him at this place of rendezvous, about sixteen miles from thence; Colonel Hay had been directed to occupy Havelberg; while Banditzen was now directed to remain in charge of the camp at Werben. The king, however, with the delicacy of a man of honour and station, kept all his troops on the western bank of the Elbe, that he might leave the Saxon army encamped on the right bank until he obtained from the elector his authority in writing to cross the bridge."

The united Saxon and Swedish armies joined their forces on September 7, 1631, and came within sight of Tilly's forces near Breitenfeld, a small town four miles from Leipzig. The king's governor of Leipzig had surrendered to Tilly two days before, but the "old corporal," as Gustavus called him, had inflicted no outrages upon the town.

Gustavus pushed his men forward rapidly, leaving tents and baggage behind him in his camp, thinking his men might well sleep in the fields at this season of the year. On the evening before the action Gustavus called his generals to him, explained the plan of battle to them, and told them that "they were about to fight tomorrow troops of a different stamp from Polanders or Cossacks, to whom they had hitherto been opposed.

"Fellow-soldiers," he said, "I will not dissemble the danger of the crisis. You will have a day's work that will be worthy of you. It is not my temper to diminish the merit of veteran troops like the Imperialists, but I know my own officers well, and scorn the thought of deceiving them. Our numbers are perhaps inferior, but God is just; and remember Magdeburg."

After riding about through the ranks with the sanguine, light-hearted manner that always inspired courage in his men, he retired for a few hours' sleep in his coach. And here, the chroniclers say, he dreamed that he had a pugilistic encounter with Tilly and floored him.

Tilly was waiting for them next morning on the slope of a hill, with large woods behind him, and his artillery on an eminence. His men wore white ribbons in their hats and helmets, and the allies, or confederates, as they were called, sprigs of holly or oak. The Imperial army was stretched in a single line, having neither a second line nor a reserve.

Gustavus kept his own men well separated from his Saxon troops. The Saxons were upon and behind a hill with their guns, while his own men were in separate bodies, each under its own commander, but capable of being shifted or massed according to the will of Gustavus in an incredibly short space of time. This manner of making his battle-field a chess-board, on which only his hand controlled the moves, was at that time unknown. It has been said by experts that Gustavus's tactics on the day of Leipzig added more to the art of war than any that had been invented since the days of Julius Caesar.

A strong wind raged, blowing thick dust in the faces of the Swedes, and, as the battle proceeded, the smoke of the powder. As Gustavus moved his men to the attack in compact columns, in order to pass the Loderbach, Pappenheim, at the head of two thousand cuirassiers, plunged at them with violence. The king, clad in gray, with a green plume in his gray beaver hat, and mounted on his horse of the sort called "flea-bitten,"—made a dash forward at the head of his cavalry, anxious to get the wind in his favour and to get his left flank out of range of a battery. Pappenheim, whose advance had been made without orders, received a volley from the musketeers that made him reel, and Baner at the head of the reserve cavalry, and Gustavus himself with the right wing, came on him with such impetus as to drive him fairly from the field.

Meanwhile on Tilly's extreme right Furstenberg threw himself on the Saxons; they had no such training as the king's old forces, and flew in a wild rout. The Elector of Saxony, who was in the rear, joining their flight with his body-guard, never stopped until he reached Eilenburg, where he consoled himself with deep draughts of beer, quite content to be out of the fray.

Gustavus witnessed the panic and flight of the Saxons,—from whom he had not expected too much,—and an officer he had summoned being shot dead in the saddle, the king took his place and cheered his men forward, crying "Vivat! vivat!"

The enemy fell back before the vigour of this attack. At the same time the king discovered from the thick clouds of dust about him that some large body of troops was near; he was told they were Swedes, but they were not there in accordance with his plan of battle, so he galloped up close to them, and coming back quickly organised his troops to receive an attack. "They are Imperialists," he said. "I see the Burgundian cross on their ensigns." It was here that the two Scottish regiments under Hepburn and Munro first practised firing by platoons. This was so amazing to the veteran Cronenberg and his fine Walloon infantry that they retired with all speed.

At four o'clock the king took charge of his right wing, wheeled it suddenly to the left, dashed up to the heights where the Imperial artillery was placed, and capturing it, turned the fire of their own guns on the enemy. Gustavus now swooped down upon Tilly's rear.

Caught between this cavalry attack at the rear and Horn's infantry in front, the Imperialists made a tough struggle. When the sun went down only six hundred men were left to close around Tilly and carry him from the field. With that exception the army had been destroyed. Seven thousand lay dead in the field; five thousand prisoners remained to take service with the victors, as the custom was at that time.

The king threw himself on his knees among the dead and wounded to offer up thanksgivings. He had the alarm-bells set ringing in all the villages round about to apprise the country of his victory. He encamped with his army in the deserted camp of the enemy. Almost all the baggage of the Imperialists fell into the hands of the conquerors. Hardly a soldier among the killed and wounded had less than ten ducats in his pocket or concealed within his girdle or saddle. Now that the battle was over the Elector of Saxony joined Gustavus in his camp at night. The king, who could be astutely diplomatic, gave him all the credit for having advised the battle and kept silent as to the Saxon troops. The elector, transported with joy at the issue of the day, promised to Gustavus the Roman crown. Gustavus lost no time in dallying with the Roman crown, but made new plans for action. He left Leipzig to the elector and set forward for Merseburg, which, with Halle, at once surrendered.

Here he gave his army a rest of ten days, and many Protestant princes joined him in council.

II. LUTZEN

From the day of Leipzig, Tilly's fortunes left him; his past victories were forgotten and exe-crations were heaped upon him. Though he was wounded, he went to work with all his old energy to form a new army, but the emperor expressly commanded that he should never again risk any decisive battle.

The glorious victory at Leipzig is said to have changed not only the world's opinion of Gustavus, but his own opinion of himself. He was now more confident; he took a bolder tone with his allies, a more imperious one with his enemies, and even more decision and greater speed marked his military movements, though nothing tyrannical or illiberal was seen in him.

The emperor and the Catholic League were dumfounded at the annihilation of Tilly. Richelieu was beginning to think his auxiliary too powerful; Louis XIII. even was heard to mutter, "It is time to put a limit to the progress of this Goth."

"Alone, without a rival," Schiller says, "he found himself now in the midst of Germany; nothing could arrest his course. His adversaries, the princes of the Catholic League, divided among themselves, led by different and contrary interests, acted without concert, and consequently without energy. Both statesman and general were united in the person of Gustavus. He was the only source from which all authority flowed: he alone was the soul of his party, the creator and executor of his military plans. Aided by all these advantages, at the head of such an army, endowed with a genius to profit by all these resources, conducted besides by principles of the wisest policy, it is not surprising that Gustavus Adolphus was irresistible. In not much more time than it would have taken another to make a tour of pleasure, with the sword in one hand and pardon in the other he was seen traversing Germany from one end to the other as a conqueror, lawgiver, and judge. As if he had been the legitimate sovereign, they brought him from all parts the keys of the towns and fortresses. No castle resisted him, no river stopped his victorious progress, and he often triumphed by the mere dread of his name."

Many of his advisers pressed Gustavus to attack Vienna, but after careful consideration he thought he would serve his cause best by marching straight into the heart of Germany on the Main and the Rhine.

Ten days after Leipzig the king reached Erfurt and ordered Duke William of Saxe-Weimar to take possession of the city. Proceeding through the Thuringian Forest, he reached Konigshofen Schweinfurt, which yielded to him, as did Wurzburg. Marienberg he was obliged to take by storm; a great store of treasure was here, as well as the money which the Elector of Bavaria had sent to Tilly for the purpose of replacing his shattered army.

Great quantities of provisions, corn, and wine fell into Swedish hands. A coffin filled with ducats was found, and as it was lifted the bottom gave way, and the soldiers began to help themselves to the coin in the presence of the king. "Oh, I see how it is," said he; "it is plain they must have it; let the rogues convert it to their own uses."

In truth, the character of the Swedish army was no longer beyond suspicion; the soldiers had become to some extent demoralised with their conquests; the cruelties and barbarities that they had suffered had forced upon them terrible reprisals, and the usage of looting was so universal that they could not be held back from it.

Tilly had by this time collected a new army out of the Palatinate and come back to Fulda, and here he tried to get the consent of Maximilian of Bavaria to engage Gustavus in battle again, but the duke was fearful of having another army wiped out, now the only one the Catholic League possessed, and refused him.

The Swedish king now advanced rapidly towards the Rhine by way of the Main, reducing Aschaffenburg, Seligenstadt, and the whole territory on both sides of the river. The Count of Hanau made but slight resistance when his citadel was captured, and gladly agreed to pay two thousand five hundred pounds a month for the support of the army and to recall his retainers from the Imperial service.

Nothing now kept Gustavus from marching on Frankfort-on-the-Main. The magistrates of the city begged the ambassador that he sent to entreat him to consider their legitimate oaths to the emperor, and to leave them neutral, on account of their annual fairs, which were their chief commercial enterprise. The king was not moved by these touching business considerations; he was surprised, he replied, that while the liberties of Germany were at stake and the Protestant religion in jeopardy, they should convey to his ear such an odious sentiment as neutrality, and that the citizens of Frankfort should talk of annual fairs, as if they regarded all things merely as tradesmen and merchants, rather than as men of the world with a Christian conscience. More sternly he went on to say that he had found the keys to many a town and fortress from the Isle of Rugen on the Baltic to the banks of the Main, and knew well where to find a key for Frankfort.

The magistrates were filled with alarm at this, and asked for time to consult the Elector of Mayence, their ecclesiastic sovereign, but the king replied that he was master of Aschaffenburg; he was Elector of Mayence; he would give them plenary absolution.

"The inhabitants," he said, "might desire to stretch out only their little finger to him, but he would be content with nothing but the whole hand, that he might have sufficient to grasp."

He then moved his army on Saxenhausen, a beautiful suburb of the city, and here the magistrates met him, and after taking the oath of fidelity opened the gates of the city to him. The king made a solemn public entrance into the city, leading his troops with uncovered head, as a mark of respect, and bringing in fifty-six pieces of artillery. He was welcomed by the magistracy to a great banquet in the coronation hall of the imperial palace of Braunfels. Maria Eleonora, his queen, now joined him in Frankfort, and when she met him was so overcome with joy that, throwing her arms around him, she cried, "Now is Gustavus the Great become my prisoner!"

The next event of importance in this victorious progress was the carrying of Mayence, which after a short siege capitulated on December 13. On the 14th the king celebrated his thirty-seventh birthday by entering Mayence with great pomp, and took up his residence in the palace of the elector, ordering a service of thanksgiving for his success to be held in the Roman Catholic Cathedral. Provisions, artillery, and money fell into the hands of the army. The king seized as his personal share the library of the elector, and gave it to Oxenstiern for one of the Swedish universities, but, alas! it was lost in the Baltic.

The exhausted Swedish soldiers were now allowed a space of rest to recuperate their energies. On January 10 the queen arrived in Mayence and shared with Gustavus for a short time the ceremonial splendours of a regal court, where five German princes and many foreign ambassadors had come to confer with the king and transact important negotiations with him. Among these was the Marquis de Breze, an ambassador from the French court. By his conversation Gustavus detected something of the truth, that Richelieu now feared him and was trying to undermine his power.

Accordingly, he sent word to Louis XIII. that he wished to speak with him personally. The French ambassador tried to persuade Gustavus that an interview with Richelieu would do as well, but he replied haughtily:

"All kings are equal. My predecessors have never given place to the kings of France. If your master thinks fit to despatch the cardinal half way, I will send some of my people to treat with him, but I will admit of no superiority."

When the king and queen left Mayence in mid-February, Gustavus had had a new citadel built at the confluence of the Rhine and Main, which was called at first "Gustavusburg," but in after days lapsed into "Pfaffenraube" (Priest-plunder). A lion of marble on a high marble pillar is near Mayence, holding a naked sword in his paw and wearing a helmet on his head, to mark the spot where the "Lion of the North" crossed the great river of Germany.

During February Kreutznach in the Palatinate, one of the strongest castles in Germany, and the town of Ulm surrendered to the king.

Leaving Oxenstiern, his minister and friend, to protect his conquests on the Rhine and Main, Gustavus began his advance against the enemy March 4, 1632, with an army-including his allies' forces-of one hundred thousand infantry and forty thousand cavalry under arms. The Catholic

League had been extremely active during the months since the defeat of Tilly at Breitenfeld and Leipzig, and had raised even larger forces.

By the capture of Donauwörth it was evident to Tilly that Gustavus's next move was to be towards Bavaria, for he was now master of the right bank of the Danube. Accordingly, after destroying all the bridges in the vicinity, Tilly entrenched himself in a strong position on the other side of the river Lech. Numerous garrisons defended the river as far as Augsburg. The Bavarian elector shut himself up in Tilly's camp, feeling that the issue of the coming battle must decide everything for him.

The Lech, in the month of March, is swollen to a great torrent by the melting snows from the Tyrol, and dashes furiously between high, steep banks. The officers of Gustavus considered it impossible to effect a crossing and urged him not to try it. But he exclaimed to Horn —

"What! Have we crossed the Baltic and so many great rivers of Germany, and shall we now for this Lech, this rivulet, abandon our enterprise!"

He had made the discovery that his side of the river was higher by eleven feet than the opposite bank, which would greatly favour his cannon. He immediately took advantage of this by having three batteries erected on the spot where the left bank of the Lech forms an angle opposite its right. Here seventy-two pieces kept up a constant cannonade on the enemy.

He had now to invent a bridge that would cross the torrent, and also think of means to distract the enemy from noticing its construction. He made a strong set of trestles of various heights and with unequal feet, so that they would stand upright on the uneven bed of the river; these were secured in their places by strong piles driven into the river-bed. Planks were then nailed to the trestles. While this went on, the cannonade drowned the noise of the hammers and hatchets; one thousand musketeers lined the Swedish bank and kept the Imperialist soldiers from coming near enough to discover the work, while a thick smoke, made by burning wood and wet straw, hid the workmen for the most part.

Before daybreak the bridge was finished, and an army of engineers and soldiers selected by the king soon crossed it and threw up a substantial breastwork.

Tilly saw his foes entrenched on his own side of the river and, under the tremendous firing of the guns from the higher bank, was utterly powerless to keep them from coming. For thirty-six hours the cannonade went on, the king standing most of the time at the foot of the bridge and sometimes acting as gunner himself to encourage his men. The Imperialists made a desperate effort to seize the bridge, but a large number were cut down in the attempt.

Finally, Tilly, whose courage was heroic throughout the day, fell with a shattered thigh, and had to be borne away. Maximilian, the Bavarian duke, now precipitately abandoned his impregnable position and moved the army quietly away to Ingolstadt.

When Gustavus next day found the camp vacant his astonishment was great.

"Had I been the sovereign of Bavaria," he cried, "never, though a cannon-ball had taken away my beard and chin-never would I have quitted a post like this and laid my states open to the enemy."

Bavaria, indeed, lay open to the conqueror; before occupying it, however, he rescued the Protestant town of Augsburg from the Bavarian yoke, Augsburg being in his eyes a special object of veneration on account of the famous "Confession" the place "from whence the law first proceeded from Sion." Augsburg, indeed, at first resisted him, but when he saw the dread devastation that his guns began to make on its beautiful buildings he stopped them and insisted on an interview with the governor, who, seeing the hopelessness of resistance, yielded.

Tilly died in Ingolstadt, the Elector of Bavaria sitting by his bedside. He adjured Maximilian to keep Ingolstadt with all his powers against Gustavus and to seize Ratisbon at once, begged him never to break his alliance with the emperor, and besought him to appoint General Gratz in his place. "He will conduct your troops with reputation, and, as he knows Wallenstein, will traverse the designs of that insolent man. Oh," he sighed, "would that I had expired at Leipzig and not survived my fame!"

So died Tilly-bigoted, merciless, cruel, but nevertheless faithful and zealous to his last breath in defence of his religion and the League.

Ingolstadt was a fortress considered impregnable; it had never been conquered. Gustavus had determined to take it, and made a partial investment only, for on one side of it was the whole Bavarian army under Maximilian.

While riding about the walls one day and going very near to take observations, on account of his short sight, a twenty-four pounder killed his horse-the favourite "flea-bitten" steed-under him; he rose tranquilly and, mounting another horse, continued his reconnoitring. In camp in the evening his generals in a body protested against his risking so valuable a life in this way; but he replied that he had a foolish sort of a fancy which always tempted him to imagine that he could see better for himself than others could, and that his sense of God's providence gave him the firm assurance that he had other assistance in store for so just a cause than the precarious existence of one Gustavus Adolphus.

Within a few days news came that the Bavarian troops had taken the Imperial town of Ratisbon, and this caused a change in the king's plans; he had spent eight days on Ingolstadt, but he now suddenly abandoned it, because it would have been of no special advantage to him without Ratisbon in his scheme of cutting off Maximilian from Bohemia.

Munich was his next objective point, and he now proceeded into the interior of Bavaria, where Mosburg, Landshut, all the Bishopric of Freysingen, surrendered to him. But the Bavarians looked upon Protestants as children of hell. Soldiers who did not believe in the Pope were to them accursed monsters. When they succeeded in capturing a Swedish straggler they put him to death with tortures the most refined and prolonged. When the Swedish army came upon mutilated bodies of their comrades they took vengeance into their own hands, but never by consent of Gustavus.

His approach to Munich threw the capital into an agony of terror. It had no defenders, and they feared that the treatment his soldiers had met at the hands of the country-people might lead him to use his power cruelly. Some Germans in his army begged to be allowed to repeat here the sacking of Magdeburg, but such a low revenge was impossible to the king. When the magistracy sent to implore his clemency, he answered that if they submitted readily and with good grace, care should be taken that no man should suffer with respect to life, liberty, or religion. Only one act of questionable taste accompanied his public entry, and that was the presence of a monkey in the procession —a monkey with a shaven crown and in a Capuchin's dress, with a rosary in his paw. One hopes that the king was not responsible for this.

He found an abandoned palace: the elector's treasures had been removed. There were left, though, many fine 'canvases by Flemish and Italian masters. His officers urged the king to plunder or destroy these, but he said: "Let us not imitate our ancestors, the Goths and Vandals, who destroyed everything belonging to the fine arts, which has left our nation a proverb and a byword of contempt with posterity for acts of this wanton barbarity." He had evidently forgotten the earnest request of Charles I. for "pictures and statues."

The construction of the palace —a magnificent building-caused the king to express great admiration: he asked the steward the name of the architect. "He is no other than the elector himself" was the reply. "I should like to have this architect," replied the king, "to send him to Stockholm." "That," said the steward, "he will take care to avoid."

The guns in the arsenal had been buried so carefully that they would not have been discovered if it had not been for a treacherous insider, who told the secret. "Arise from the dead," cried the king, "and come to judgment!" and one hundred and forty pieces of artillery were dug up, a large sum of gold being found in one of them.

Appointing the Scotchman Hepburn to the post of Governor of Munich, Gustavus soon started forth with his army.

Meanwhile Maximilian, although besought by his Bavarians to come and deliver them from the Swedes, could not resolve to risk a battle. The wonderful victories of Gustavus had indeed a paralysing effect upon the country. As yet no one had been found capable of resisting him.

Richelieu himself was horrorstricken at the power he had helped to raise. It was expected in France that an invasion of Swedes would be the natural continuation of the Rhine conquests; it was said that Gustavus would not rest until he had made Protestantism compulsory throughout Europe. Nothing less than the command of the German Empire was supposed to be his ultimate aim.

There is no doubt that his ambitions steadily enlarged themselves, but there is nothing to prove that he contemplated supplanting Ferdinand. His enemies were disheartened. Ferdinand was now brought to the pass of abjectly begging Wallenstein to resume his command, and Wallenstein was assuming airs of indifference and allowing himself to be persuaded only with great pressure.

This extraordinary man was the son of a Moravian baron of the ancient race of Waldstein. As a youth he was notably proud and stubborn, ambitious and conceited, often saying, "If I am not a prince, I may become one." He fell from a very high window whilst at the University of Goldben and was quite unhurt, which is said to have been the beginning of his certainty of future greatness. He was grossly superstitious always and entirely an egotist. At twenty-three he married a wealthy widow, who in a fit of jealousy gave him a "love philtre" in his wine, from which he narrowly escaped death. Dying in 1614, she left him a large property, and later he married a Countess Isabelle von Haggard, of immense fortune and of much "beauty, piety, and virtue."

Wallenstein now began to invest his great wealth in the purchase of confiscated properties, and it was said that through his knowledge of metallurgy he adulterated the coin which he paid. At all events, his wealth assumed fabulous dimensions, and through his wife's relations he mingled with the highest nobles of the empire. He always spoke with affection of his wife, but did not live with her nor write to her for years at a time.

In person Wallenstein was very tall and thin, with a yellow complexion, short red hair, and small, twinkling eyes. His cold, malignant gaze frightened his great troop of servants, who nevertheless stayed with him because they were unusually well paid. His military career had begun in his youth, when he served in Hungary.

Afterwards he raised a body of horse at his own expense for a war against the Venetians. On the breaking out of the war in Bohemia, in 1618, he was offered the post of general to the Bohemian forces, but adopted the side of the sovereign in whose family he had been brought up.

After putting down the Bohemian rebellion, in which Tilly had served Maximilian, the emperor decided that it was necessary for him to have a powerful army under his own orders. Wallenstein offered to raise an army, clothe, feed, and arm it at his own expense, if he should be made a field-general, an offer which the emperor accepted and which Wallenstein carried out.

His military activities from this time on are historical, as well as the details of his cold, pompous nature. He lived like a king, with great state, had no principles whatever about the way he acquired wealth, and spent it with magnificent lavishness.

At the time Ferdinand deprived him of his command, just as Gustavus was entering Germany, Wallenstein had become Duke of Friedland, Sagan, Glogau, and Mecklenburg, and was more insolent than if he had had royal blood in his veins. He spent an income of three millions of florins yearly, for his armies had plundered the land for years with great effect. He was able to control his rage at his sudden downfall because his Italian astrologer, Seni, who ruled him completely, assured him that the stars showed that a brilliant future awaited him, exalted beyond anything he had yet known. And so he was led on to close his career by plots against his emperor and to meet death by the hands of assassins.

All of Gustavus's successes were the source of deep satisfaction to Wallenstein; they brought nearer his inevitable recall.

Now when Tilly was dead, and the emperor was beseeching him again to take command of the Imperial troops, Wallenstein sent an envoy to convey the congratulations of the Duke of Friedland to the King of Sweden, and to invite his majesty to a close alliance with him. He undertook, in concert with Gustavus, to conquer Bohemia and Moravia and drive the emperor out of Germany.

Gustavus felt that help would be very welcome, and he seriously considered the offer; but he could not bring himself to believe in a success promised by such an unscrupulous adventurer, who so willingly offered to become a traitor. He courteously refused, and Wallenstein accepted the emperor's offer of chief command with a salary amounting to the value of one hundred and eight thousand pounds per annum. He demanded that he should have uncontrolled command of the German armies of Austria and Spain, with unlimited power to reward and punish. Neither the King of Hungary (to whom the emperor had wished to give the highest command) nor the emperor himself was ever to appear in his army or exercise the slightest authority in it. No commission or pension was to be granted without Wallenstein's approval. An Imperial hereditary estate in Austria was to be assigned to him. As the reward of success in the field he should be made lord paramount over the conquered countries, and all conquests and confiscations should be placed entirely at his disposal. All means and moneys for carrying on the war must be solely at his command.

The ambassador to whom he made these terms suggested that the emperor must have some control over his armies, and that the young King of Hungary should at least be allowed to study the art of war with Wallenstein, but the reply was: "Never will I submit to any colleague in my office; no, not even if it were God Himself with whom I should have to share my command." In his extremity the emperor accepted these conditions, April 15, 1632.

Although an avowed Jesuit, Wallenstein had no religious scruples whatever, and the Catholics feared and hated him as much as the Protestants. The gorgeous luxury of his surroundings was apparently only designed to impress the world; he was not a sensualist, but seems to have been actuated only by an insane love of power. Soldiers flocked to his standard and worshipped the mighty warrior who rewarded them with ceaseless plunder, but the princes, nobles, and peasantry of the countries through which he passed were left with a blight upon them. He seemed to be unable to see in a country any reasons for industrial prosperity or for conserving wholesome conditions of any sort; he was a brave, fearless leader-after that, a robber, and nothing else.

He distributed enormous sums among his favourites, and the amount he spent in corrupting the members of the Imperial Court was still greater. The height to which he raised the Imperial authority astonished even the emperor; but his design unquestionably was, that his sovereign should stand in fear of no one in all Germany besides himself, the source and engine of his despotic power. He cared nothing, however, himself, for popularity from his equals, and less for the detestation of the people or the complaints of the sovereigns, but was ready to bid a general defiance to all consequences.

Wallenstein raised his army. From Italy, Scotland, Ireland, as well as from every part of Germany, men flocked to him in thousands who cared little for country or religion, but were attracted by the prospects of plunder and of distinction under the renowned soldier who had made himself a dictator.

In May, 1632, his organisation was complete. He began by driving Gustavus's Saxon allies out of Bohemia, while Pappenheim scourged the Rhine country. Then he directed his forces upon rich Protestant Nuremberg.

Gustavus, before he could get there, threw himself into Nuremberg and fortified it, and then, gathering his army together, prepared to give battle to Wallenstein. But the latter had made up his mind to starve out Gustavus. With his own light cavalry, superior in number to that of the Swedes, he could more readily obtain supplies than they.

Forming a huge camp on an eminence overlooking Nuremberg, he prepared stolidly to wait until the king should be forced to go. At the end of June the camp was finished, and Gustavus held out until September.

His men were starving and dying, discipline had become relaxed, even his 160 generals becoming cruel and rapacious. On September 3 he had led his men against Wallenstein's entrenchments, but was forced to retire. A few days later he left Nuremberg, providing it with a garrison, although he had lost through battle, disease, and starvation nearly twenty thousand men. Wallenstein's loss in the same time was thirty-six thousand. No attempt at pursuit was made by Wallenstein. Turning north into Saxony, he proceeded to choose a position between the Elbe and the Saale, where he might entrench himself for the winter and carry on what to him was one of the most necessary features of a campaign-the sending of bands of marauders and requisitioners through the country.

He also had in mind detaching the Saxon elector from his alliance with Gustavus, this vacillating prince having shown symptoms of yielding to the great furore caused by Wallenstein's resumption of power.

Gustavus determined that he should not lose Saxony by want of decision. Summoning Oxenstiern and Bernhard of Saxe-Weimar to his aid, he forced his army with all speed through Thuringia, and before Wallenstein could recover from his astonishment he seized both Erfurt and Naumburg. At Erfurt he said farewell to his queen, who never saw his face again until he was in his coffin at Weissenfels.

The weather had become so bitterly cold that Wallenstein had expected no further advances from Gustavus during the winter. He was preparing to entrench himself between Merseburg and Torgau. He had sent Pappenheim again to the Rhineland. Gustavus took advantage of this division and resolved to fight before Pappenheim could return to reinforce his adversary. Wallenstein sent messenger after messenger to bring back Pappenheim, and hastily throwing up entrenchments, he awaited the onslaught of the Swedish king at the village of Lutzen, November 6.

On the southern side of the large highway leading from Lutzen to Leipzig lay the Swedes; to the north, the Imperialists. Two ditches ran by the sides of this road, and some old willow-trees bordered it. The deep, rich mould of the soil is heavy for horse and foot. On Wallenstein's right was a hill where a group of windmills waved their arms.

On the evening of the 5th the Duke of Friedland had ordered his men to deepen and widen the ditches, and he planted two large batteries on the windmill hill. Gustavus had passed the night in his coach with the Duke of Saxe-Weimar, for he owned neither tent nor field equipage. He had ordered his army to be ready two hours before daylight, but there was so solid a fog that the darkness was intense, and not a step could be taken. Gustavus had his chaplain perform divine service while waiting. He never forgot, it was said, either the time to pray or the time to pay-never leaving his men's wages in arrears. He would take no breakfast and declined to put on his steel breastplate, as a wound he had received made it uncomfortable. He was clad in a new plain cloth doublet and an elk-skin surtout.

Riding along the ranks, he encouraged each regiment, addressing Swedes and Germans in their respective tongues, and urging all to valour and steadfastness. "God with us!" was the rallying-cry of the Swedes. "Jesu Maria!" was the shout of the Imperialists.

The morning wore on, as the soldiers waited still in impenetrable darkness. At one time Gustavus threw himself on his knees and began a hymn, the military band accompanying him. His terrible weeks at Nuremberg and the hardships of the late toilsome march had seemed to bring out more strongly than ever the fervent piety of his nature. When, on his arrival a few days before at Naumburg, the people had rushed from all the country round to see him, and had prayed on their knees for the favour of touching the hem of his garment or his sword in its scabbard, he was touched by this innocent worship, but he was moved to say to those with him: "Does it not seem as if this people would deify me? Our affairs go on well without doubt, but I much fear that Divine vengeance will punish me for this rash mockery, and soon convince the foolish multitude of my weak mortality."

Towards eleven o'clock the fog began to lighten, and the enemies could see each other, while the Swedes beheld the flames of Lutzen, set on fire by Wallenstein that he might not be flanked on that side.

Gustavus now mounted his horse and drew his sword for action, placing himself at the head of the right wing. Wallenstein opened the attack with a tremendous fire of musketry and artillery, with which Gustavus's leather guns found it hard to cope. The ditches of the road made a formidable obstacle to the Swedish cavalry, being lined with musketeers. But at length the Swedish musketeers cleared the others away. The horsemen, however, under the heavy firing, now seemed to find the ditches impassable; they hesitated before them, whereupon Gustavus dashed forward to lead them across.

"If," said he sternly, "after having passed so many rivers, scaled so many walls, and fought so many battles, your old courage fails you, stand still but for a moment and see your master die in the manner we all ought to be ready to do."

He leaped the ditch, and they were after him like the wind, urging him to spare his invaluable life and promising to do everything. On the other side of the road and ditches he observed three dark masses of Imperial cuirassiers clad in iron, and turning to a colonel said:

"Charge me those black fellows, for they are men that will undo us; as for the Croats, I mind them not."

The royal order was at once executed, but the Croats suddenly swept down upon the Swedish baggage and actually reached the king's coach, which, however, they failed to capture.

Both sides fought desperately; it had to be decided whether it was Gustavus's genius that had won at the battle of the Lech and at Leipzig, or if Tilly's want of skill had been the only cause. On this day Wallenstein, Duke of Friedland, had to justify the emperor's confidence and the enormous demands he had made upon it.

Each soldier of each side seemed to feel that the honour and success of his chieftain depended solely on his individual efforts.

The Swedes advanced with such velocity and force that the first, second, and third Imperial brigades were forced to fly; but Wallenstein stopped the fugitives. Supported by three ranks of cavalry, the beaten brigades formed a new front to the Swedes and struck furiously into their ranks. A murderous series of combats then began; there was no space for even loading muskets-they fought wildly with sword and pike. At last the Swedes, exhausted, withdrew to the other side of the ditches, abandoning a battery they had gained.

In the meantime the king, at the head of his right wing, had attacked the enemy's left. His splendidly powerful cuirassiers of Finland had easily routed all the Croats and Poles covering this wing, and their flight spread confusion among the rest of the cavalry. But he then received the news that his infantry had retired, and that his left wing, under the heavy fire of the windmill hill, was about to yield.

Ordering Horn to pursue the wing which he had just defeated, he turned to fly to the assistance of his own men. His horse carried him so swiftly that no one kept up with him but the Duke of Lauenburg.

He galloped straight to the place where his men were being assailed with the greatest fury, and his near-sightedness led him too near. An Imperialist corporal noticed that all gave way before him with great respect, and shouted to a musketeer:

"Fire at him! That must be a man of distinction!" and the king's left arm was shattered.

He begged Lauenburg to help him to a place of safety, but the next moment he was shot in the back. Turning to Lauenburg he said:

"Brother, I have enough; seek only to save your own life."

As he spoke he fell to the ground, where a volley of other shots pierced him.

A desperate struggle still took place over him. A German page, refusing to tell the royal rank of his master, was mortally shot. But Gustavus still had life enough to say:

"I am the King of Sweden, and seal with my blood the Protestant religion and the liberties of Germany." Then he murmured: "My God! Alas! my poor queen!"

For a long time the Duke of Lauenburg was accused of assassinating the king, and there is a great deal to be said in support of such a charge. Among the Spanish archives were found papers showing that there was a plot in progress to kill Gustavus. Still, it is conceivable that his death was caused by the ordinary chances of war.

It was the king's charger, galloping into the Swedish lines covered with blood, that brought the news of the king's death. The Swedish cavalry came with furious speed to the place to rescue the precious remains of their king. A great conflict raged around his dead body until it was heaped with the slain. The dreadful news, spreading through the Swedish army, inflamed their courage to desperation; neither life nor death mattered to them now; the Yellow Guard of the king was nearly cut to pieces.

Bernhard, Duke of Weimar, a warrior of great skill and courage, took command of the army. The Swedish regiments under General Horn completely defeated the enemy's left wing, took possession of the windmill hill, and turned Wallenstein's cannon against him. The Swedish centre advanced and carried the battery again, and while the enemy's resistance grew more feeble, their powder-waggons blew up with fearful roars. Their courage seemed to give way, and victory was assured to the Swedes.

Then Pappenheim arrived at the head of his cuirassiers and dragoons, and there was a new battle to fight. This unexpected reinforcement renewed and fired the courage of the Imperialists. Wallenstein seized the favourable moment to form his lines again. Again he drove the Swedes back and recaptured his battery. Every man of the Yellow Regiment, which had most distinguished itself on the side of the Swedish infantry, lay dead in the order in which he had fought.

The Blue Regiment also had been blotted out by a terrific charge of the Austrian horse under Count Piccolomini, who had, during the charge, seven horses shot under him, and was hit in six places.

While the worst of the conflict was going on, Wallenstein rode through it with cold intrepidity; men and horses fell thick around him and his mantle was full of bullet-holes, but he escaped unhurt.

Pappenheim was wounded in the thigh, and the next moment a musket-ball tore his chest. He felt that he had got his death-blow, but was able to speak cheerfully to his men, who carried him away in his coach to Leipzig. He was replaced by Holk.

Duke Bernhard re-formed his men, and the fight went on with a stubborn fury that nothing could assuage. Neither side would be beaten. Again and again the Swedes were forced back; again and again they rallied and drove back their antagonists.

Ten leaders on each side had fallen. The Imperial side finally weakened with the loss of its generals. At nightfall the Swedes formed all their broken regiments into one dense mass, made their final movement across the ditches, captured the battery, and turned its guns on the enemy.

Confused as the Imperialists had become, they still fought. The bloody struggle went on until it was too dark to see anything; both armies then left the field, each claiming the victory. Pappenheim's army left their guns, being without a general and having no orders. It was said that after Pappenheim was borne away Wallenstein betook himself to a sedan chair and did not again expose himself to the enemy. He was reproached for this afterwards by his army, who also said that he retired from the field before it was necessary. Proceeding to Leipzig, he witnessed the death of Pappenheim. Piccolomini was the last of his side in the field.

The Duke of Friedland insisted on having the Te Deum sung in honour of a victory in the churches, but this deceived no one. It was no victory, but a defeat from which he never recovered. While at Leipzig he accused his officers of cowardice, and after a court-martial had several of the bravest of them disgraced or shot. But neither this nor a few inconsequent successes were sufficient to restore the prestige that Wallenstein had lost at Lutzen.

Nearly one hundred thousand corpses remained unburied on the field, and the plain all around was covered with wounded and dying.

It was not until the next day that the Swedes were able to find the body of their king; it was almost unrecognisable with blood and wounds, trampled by horses' hoofs, and naked. A huge stone was rolled by the soldiers as near as they could to the place where the royal corpse was found; it still rests where they left it, and is known as "The Stone of the Swede."

The Imperialists had stripped the body in their eagerness to preserve relics of the great Gustavus. Piccolomini sent his buff waistcoat to the emperor. His rings, spurs, and gold chain are still in possession of various families. A famous turquoise is supposed to have passed into the hands of a Roman Catholic bishop who desired a trophy of "Anti-Christ," as Gustavus was called by the Catholics.

The body was carried from the field in solemn state amid a procession of the whole army. It was taken to Weissenfels, and from thence to Sweden. There the whole nation mourned, knowing well that they should not have another monarch like Gustavus Adolphus.

Nothing has ever transpired to change the world's opinion of him as one of the world's greatest and best. Although the Thirty Years' War was not concluded for several years after his death, yet he was, nevertheless, the cause of its cessation. Through his agency alone the cause of the Protestant belief triumphed, and the effects of the great upheaval of the Reformation were not allowed to be obliterated in Germany.

Professor Smyth said of him: "It is fortunate when the high courage and activity of which the human character is capable are tempered with a sense of justice, wisdom, and benevolence; when he who leads thousands to the field has sensibility enough to feel the responsibility of his awful trust, and wisdom enough to take care that he directs against its proper objects alone the afflicting storm of human devastation. It is not always that the great and high endowments of courage and sagacity are so united with other high qualities as to present to the historian at once a Christian, a soldier, and a statesman. Yet such was Gustavus Adolphus, a hero deserving of the name, perfectly distinguishable from those who have assumed the honours that belong to it-the mere military executioners with whom every age has been infested."

Cust says: "Gustavus Adolphus is thought to have been the first sovereign who set the example of a standing army. The feudal association of barons with their retainers had given way in the previous century to a set of military adventurers, who made war a profession to gratify their license and their acquisitiveness, and who were commissioned by kings and leaders to collect together the assassins of Europe.

"These constituted at the very time of the Thirty Years' War the unprincipled and insatiate legions who harried Germany, who, without much discipline, were continually dissipated by the first disaster and collected together again, as it were from the four winds of heaven, to cover the face of the land again and again with terror, devastation, and confusion.

"Gustavus, who had witnessed this from afar, or experienced it in his Polish wars, had in him that spirit of organisation and order which signally distinguished him above every great leader who preceded him. He saw that a well-disciplined force of men to be commanded by a superior class of officers of high honour and intelligence, and who should constitute an armed body that might obtain the dignity of a profession of arms, would be more efficient and a cheaper defence of nations than the haphazard assembling of mere bloodhounds, and he first executed the project of having a force of eighty thousand men, part in activity and part in reserve, who should be constantly maintained well-armed, well-clothed, well-fed, and well-disciplined."

THE STORMING OF BADAJOZ

In studying the campaign in the Peninsula, one must remember first of all that the man who was made Earl of Wellington for the victory at Ciudad Rodrigo was not the great potentiality who, as the Duke of Wellington, influenced England after Waterloo. During the Peninsula campaign Wellington was afflicted at all times by a bitter and suspicious Parliament at home. They had no faith in him, and they strenuously objected to furnishing him with money and supplies. Wellington worked with his hands tied behind him against the eager and confident armies of France. We ourselves can read in our more frank annals how a disgruntled part of Congress was for ever wishing to turn Washington out of his position as head of the colonial forces.

Parliament doled supplies to Wellington with so niggardly a hand that again and again he was forced to stop operations for the want of provisions and arms. At one time he actually had been told to send home the transports in order to save the expense of keeping them at Lisbon. The warfare in Parliament was not deadly, but it was more acrimonious than the warfare in the Peninsula. Moreover, the assistance to his arms from Portugal was so wavering, uncertain, and dubious that he could place no faith in it. The French marshals, Soult and Marmont, had a force of nearly one hundred thousand men.

Wellington held Lisbon, but if he wished to move in Portugal there always frowned upon him the fortified city of Badajoz. But finally there came his chance to take it, if it could be taken in a rush, while Soult and Marmont were widely separated and Badajoz was left in a very confident isolation.

Badajoz lies in Spain, five miles from the Portuguese frontier. It was the key of a situation. Wellington's chance was to strike at Badajoz before the two French marshals could combine and crush him. His task was both in front of him and behind him. He lacked transport; he lacked food for the men; the soldiers were eating cassava root instead of bread; the bullocks were weak and emaciated. All this was the doings of the Parliament at home. But Wellington knew that the moment to strike had come, and he seems to have hesitated very little. Placing no faith in the tongues of the Portuguese, he made his plans with all possible secrecy. The guns for the siege were loaded on board the transports at Lisbon and consigned to a fictitious address. But in the river Sadao they were placed upon smaller vessels, and finally they were again landed and drawn by bullocks to Eloas, a post in the possession of the allies. Having stationed two-thirds of his force under General Graham and General Hill to prevent a most probable interference by Soult and Marmont, Wellington advanced, reaching Eloas on the 11th of March 1812. He had made the most incredible exertions. The stupidity of the Portuguese had vied with the stupidity of the government at home. Wellington had been carrying the preparation for the campaign upon his own shoulders. If he was to win Badajoz, he was to win it with no help save that from gallant and trustworthy subordinates. He was ill with it. Even his strangely steel-like nature had bent beneath the trouble of preparation amid such indifference. But on March 16 Beresford with three divisions crossed the Guadiana on pontoons and flying bridges, drove in the enemy's outposts, and invested Badajoz.

At the time of the investment the garrison was composed of five thousand French, Hessians, and Spaniards. Spain had always considered this city a most important barrier against any attack through Portugal. A Moorish castle stood three hundred feet above the level of the plain. Bastions and fortresses enwrapped the town. Even the Cathedral was bombproof. The Guadiana was crossed by a magnificent bridge, and on the farther shore the head of this bridge was strongly fortified.

Wellington's troops encamped to the east of the town. It was finally decided first to attack the bastion of Trinidad. The French commander had strengthened all his defences, and by damming a stream had seriously obstructed Wellington's operations. Parts of his force were confronted by an artificial lake two hundred yards in width.

The red coats of the English soldiers were now faded to the yellow brown of fox fur. All the military finery of the beginning of the century was tarnished and torn. But it was an exceedingly hard-bitten army, certain of its leaders, despising the enemy, full of ferocious desire for battle.

Perhaps the bastion of Trinidad was chosen because it was the nearest to the entrenchments of the allies. In those days the frontal attack was possible of success. On the night of the 17th of March the British broke ground within one hundred and sixty yards of Fort Picerina. The sound of the digging was muffled by the roar of a great equinoctial storm. The French were only made wise by the daylight, but in the meantime the allies had completed a trench six hundred yards long and three feet deep, and with a communication four thousand feet in length. The French announced their discovery by a rattle of musketry, but the allies kept on with their digging, while general officers wrapped in their long cloaks paced to and fro directing the work.

The situation did not please the French general at all. He knew that something must be done to counteract the activity of the besiegers. He was in command of a very spirited garrison. On the night of the 19th a sortie was made from the Talavera Gate by both cavalry and infantry. The infantry began to demolish the trench of the allies. The cavalry divided itself into two parts and went through a form of sham fight, which in the darkness was deceptive. When challenged by the pickets, they answered in Portuguese, and thus succeeded in galloping a long way behind the trenches, where they cut down a number of men before their identity was discovered and they were beaten back. General Phillipon, the French commander, had offered a reward for every captured entrenching tool. Thus the French infantry of the sortie devoted itself largely to making a collection of picks and spades. Men must have risked themselves with great audacity for this reward, since they left three hundred dead on the field, but succeeded in carrying off a great number of the entrenching tools.

Great rain-storms now began to complicate the work of the besiegers. The trenches became mere ditches half full of discoloured water. This condition was partly improved by throwing in bags of sand. On the French side a curious device had been employed as a means of communication between the gate of the Trinidad bastion and Fort San Roque. The French soldiers had begun to dig, but had grown tired, so they finished by hanging up a brown cloth. This to the besiegers' eyes was precisely like the fresh earth of a parallel, and behind it the French soldiers passed in safety.

Storm followed storm. The Guadiana, swollen past all tradition by these furious downpours, swept away the flying bridges, sinking twelve pontoons. For several days the army of the allies was entirely without food, but they stuck doggedly to their trenches, and when communication was at last restored it was never again broken. The weather cleared, and the army turned grimly with renewed resolution to the business of taking Badajoz. This was in the days of the forlorn hope. There was no question of anything but a desperate and deadly frontal attack. The command of the assault of Fort Picerina was given to General Kempt. He had five hundred men, including engineers, sappers, and miners, and fifty men who carried axes. At nine o'clock they marched. The night was very dark. The fort remained silent until the assailants were close. Then a great fire blazed out at them. For a time it was impossible for the men to make any progress. The palisades seemed insurmountable, and the determined soldiers of England were falling on all sides. In the meantime there suddenly sounded the loud, wild notes of the alarm-bells in the besieged city, and the guns of Badajoz awakened and gave back thunder for thunder to the batteries of the allies. The confusion was worse than in the mad nights on the heath in *King Lear,* but amid the thundering and the death, Kempt's fifty men with axes walked deliberately around Fort Picerina until they found the entrance gate. They beat it down and rushed in. The infantry with their bayonets followed closely. Lieutenant Nixon of the Fifty-second Foot (now the Second Battalion of the Oxfordshire Light Infantry) fell almost on the threshold, but his men ran on. The interior of the fort became the scene of a terrible hand-to-hand fight. All of the English did not come in through the gate. Some of Kempt's men now succeeded in establishing ladders against the rampart, and swarmed over to the help of their comrades. The struggle did not cease until more than half of the little garrison were killed.

Then the commandant, Gasper Thiery, surrendered a little remnant of eighty-six men. Others who had not been killed by the British had rushed out and been drowned in the waters of that inundation which had so troubled Wellington and so pleased the French general. Phillipon had estimated that the Picerina would endure for five days, but it had been taken in an hour, albeit one of the bloodiest hours in the annals of a modern army.

Wellington was greatly pleased. He was now able to advance his earthworks close to the eastern part of the town, while his batteries played continually on the front of Fort San Roque and the two northern bastions, Trinidad and Santa Maria.

But at the last of the month Wellington was confronted by his chief fear. News came to him that Marshal Soult was advancing rapidly from Cordova. It was now a simple question of pushing the siege with every ounce of energy contained in his army. Forty-eight guns were made to fire incessantly, and although the French reply was destructive, the English guns were gradually wearing away the three great defences. By the 2nd of April Trinidad was seriously damaged, and one flank of Santa Maria was so far gone that Phillipon set his men at work on an inner defence to cut the last-named bastion off from the city. On the night of the 2nd an attack was made on the dam of the inundation. Two British officers and some sappers succeeded in gagging and binding the sentinel guarding the dam, and having piled barrels of gunpowder against it, they lighted a slow-match and made off. But before the spark could reach the powder the French arrived under the shelter of the comic brown cloth communication. The explosion did not occur, and the inundation still remained to hinder Wellington's progress. On the 6th it was thought that three breaches were practicable for assault, and the resolute English general ordered the attack to be made at once. To Picton, destined to attach his name to the imperishable fame of Waterloo, was given an arduous task. He was to attack on the right and scale the walls of the castle of Badajoz, which were from eighteen to twenty-four feet high. On the left General Walker, marching to the south, was to make a false attack on Port Pardaleras, but a real one on San Vincente, a bastion on the extreme west of the town. In the centre the Fourth Division and Wellington's favourite Light Division were to march against the breaches. The Fourth was to move against Trinidad, and the Light Division against Santa Maria. The columns were divided into storming and firing parties. The former were to enter the ditch while the latter fired over them at the enemy. Just before the assault was to be sounded a French deserter brought the intelligence that there was but one communication from the castle to the town, and Wellington decided to send against it an entire division. Brigadier-General Power with his semi-useless Portuguese brigade was directed to attack the head of the bridge and the other works on the right of the Guadiana.

The army had now waited only for the night. When it had come, thick mists from the river increased the darkness. At 10 o'clock Major Wilson, of the Forty-eighth Foot (now the First Battalion of the Northamptonshire regiment), led a party against Fort San Roque so suddenly and so tempestuously that the work capitulated almost immediately. At the castle, General Picton's men had placed their ladders and swarmed up them in the face of showers of heavy stones, logs of wood, and crashing bullets, while at the same time they were under a heavy fire from the left flank. The foremost were bayoneted when they reached the top, and the besieged Frenchmen grasped the ladders and tumbled them over with their load of men. The air was full of wild screams as the English fell towards the stones below. Presently every ladder was thrown back, and for the moment the assailants had to run for shelter against a rain of flying missiles.

In this moment of uncertainty one man, Lieutenant Ridge, rushed out, rallying his company. Seizing one of the abandoned ladders, he planted it where the wall was lower. His ladder was followed by other ladders, and the troops scrambled with revived courage after this new and intrepid leader. The British gained a strong foothold on the ramparts of the castle, and every moment added to their strength as Picton's men came swarming. They drove the French through the castle and out of the gates. They met a heavy reinforcement of the French, but after a severe engagement they were finally and triumphantly in possession of the castle. Lieutenant Ridge had been killed.

But at about the same time the men of the Fourth Division and of the Light Division had played a great and tragic part in the storming of Badajoz. They moved against the great breach in stealthy silence. All was dark and quiet as they reached the glacis. They hurled bags full of hay in the ditch, placed their ladders, and the storming parties of the Light Division, five hundred men in all, hurried to this desperate attack.

But the French general had perfectly understood that the main attacks would be made at his three breaches, and he had made the great breach the most impregnable part of his line. The English troops, certain that they had surprised the enemy, were suddenly exposed by dozens of brilliant lights. Above them they could see the ramparts crowded with the French. These fire-balls made such a vivid picture that the besieged and besiegers could gaze upon one another's faces at distances which amounted to nothing. There was a moment of this brilliance, and then a terrific explosion shattered the air. Hundreds of shells and powder-barrels went off together, and the English already in the ditch were literally blown to pieces. Still their comrades crowded after them with no definite hesitation. The French commander had taken the precaution to fill part of the ditch with water from the inundation, and in it one hundred fusiliers, men of Albuera, were drowned.

The Fourth Division and the Light Division continued the attack upon the breach. Across the top of it was a row of sword-blades fitted into ponderous planks, and these planks, chained together, were let deep into the ground. In front of them the slope was covered with loose planks studded with sharp iron points. The English, stepping on them, rolled howling backward, and the French yelled and fired unceasingly.

It was too late for the English to become aware of the hopelessness of their undertaking. Column after column hurled themselves forward. Young Colonel Macleod, of the Forty-third Foot (now the First Battalion of the Oxfordshire Light Infantry), a mere delicate boy, gathered his men again and again and led them at the breach. A falling soldier behind him plunged a bayonet in his back, but still he kept on till he was shot dead within a yard of the line of sword-blades.

For two hours the besiegers were tirelessly striving to achieve the impossible, while the French taunted them from the ramparts.

"Why do you not come into Badajoz?"

Meanwhile, Captain Nicholas of the Engineers, with Lieutenant Shaw and about one hundred men of the Forty-third Foot, actually had passed through the breach of the Santa Maria bastion, but once inside they were met with such a fire that nearly every man dropped dead. Shaw returned almost alone.

Wellington, who had listened to these desperate assaults and watched them as well as he was able from a position on a small knoll, gave orders at midnight for the troops to retire and re-form. Two thousand men had been slain. Dead and mangled bodies were piled in heaps at the entrance to the great breach, and the stench of burning flesh and hair was said to be insupportable.

And still, in the meantime, General Walker's brigade had made a feint against Pardaleras and passed on to the bastion of San Vincente. Here for a time everything went wrong. The fire of the French was frightfully accurate and concentrated. General Walker himself simply dripped blood; he was a mass of wounds. His ladders were all found to be too short. The walls of the fortress were thirty feet in height. However, through some lack of staying power in the French, success at last crowned the attack. One man clambered somehow to the top of a wall and pulled up others, until about half of the Fourth Foot (now the King's Own Royal Lancaster Regiment) were fairly into the town. Walker's men took three bastions. General Picton, severely wounded, had not dared to risk losing the Castle, but now, hearing the tumult of Walker's success, he sent his men forth and thousands went swarming through the town. Phillipon saw that all was lost, and retreated with a few hundred men to San Christoval. He surrendered next morning to Lord Fitzroy Somerset.

The English now occupied the town. With their comrades lying stark, or perhaps in frightful torment, in the fields beyond the walls of Badajoz, these soldiers, who had so heroically won this immortal victory, became the most abandoned drunken wretches and maniacs. Crazed privates stood at the corners of streets and shot every one in sight. Everywhere were soldiers dressed in the garb of monks, of gentlemen at court, or mayhap wound about with gorgeous ribbons and laces. Jewels and plate, silks and satins, all suffered a wanton destruction. Napier writes of "shameless rapacity, brutal intemperance, savage lust, cruelty and murder, shrieks and piteous lamentations."

He further says that the horrible tumult was never quelled. It subsided through the weariness of the soldiers. One wishes to inquire why the man who was ultimately called the Iron Duke did not try to stop this shocking business. But one remembers that Wellington was a wise man, and he did not try to stop this shocking business because he knew that his soldiers vere out of control, and that if he tried he would fail.

THE BRIEF CAMPAIGN AGAINST NEW ORLEANS

(December 14, 1814 —January 8, 1815)

THE Mississippi, broad, rapid, and sinister, ceaselessly flogging its enwearied banks, was the last great legend of the dreaming times when the Old World's information of the arisen continents was roseate but inaccurate. England, at war with the United States, heard stories of golden sands, bejewelled temples, fabulous silks, the splendour of a majestic barbarian civilisation; and even if these tales were fantastic they stood well enough as symbols of the spinal importance of the grim Father of Waters.

The English put together a great expedition. It was the most formidable that ever had been directed against the Americans. It assembled in a Jamaican harbour and at Pensacola, then a Spanish port and technically neutral. The troops numbered about fourteen thousand men and included some of the best regiments in the British army, fresh from service in the Peninsula under Wellington. They were certainly not men who had formed a habit of being beaten. Included in the expedition was a full set of civilian officials for the government of New Orleans after its capture.

A hundred and ten miles from the mouth of the Mississippi, New Orleans lay trembling. She had no forts or entrenchments; she would be at the mercy of the powerful British force. The people believed that the city would be sacked and burned. They were not altogether a race full of vigour. The peril of the situation bewildered them; it did not stir them to action.

But the spirit of energy itself arrived in the person of Andrew Jackson. Since the Creek War, the nation had had much confidence in Jackson, and New Orleans welcomed him with a great sigh of relief.

The sallow, gnarled, crusty man came ill to his great work; he should have been in bed. But the amount of vim he worked into a rather flabby community in a short time looked like a miracle. The militia of Louisiana were called out; the free negroes were armed and drilled; convicts whose terms had nearly expired were enlisted; and down from Tennessee tramped the type of man that one always pictures as winning the battle-the long, lank woodsman, brown as leather, hard as nails, inseparable from his rifle, in his head the eye of a hawk.

The Lafitte brothers, famous pirates, whose stronghold was not a thousand miles from the city, threw in their lot with the Americans. The British bid for their services, but either the British committed the indiscretion of not bidding enough or the buccaneers were men of sentiment. At any rate they accepted the American pledge of immunity and came with their men to the American side, where they rendered great service. Afterwards the English, their offer of treasure repulsed, somewhat severely reproved us for allowing these men to serve in our ranks.

Martial law was proclaimed, and Jackson kept up an exciting quarrel with the city authorities at the same time that he was working his strange army night and day in the trenches. Captain John Coffee with two thousand men joined from Mobile.

The British warships first attempted to cross the sand-bars at the mouth of the river and ascend the stream, but the swift Mississippi came to meet them, and it was as if this monster, immeasurable in power, knew that he must defend himself. The well-handled warships could not dodge this simple strength; even the wind refused its help. The river won the first action.

But if the British could not ascend the stream, they could destroy the small American gunboats on the lakes below the city, and this they did on December 14 with a rather painful thoroughness. The British were then free to land their troops on the shores of these lakes and attempt to approach the city through miles of dismal and sweating swamps. The decisive word seems to have rested with Major-General Keane. Sir George Pakenham, the commander-in-chief, had not yet arrived. One of Wellington's proud veterans was not likely to endure any nonsensical delay over such a business as this campaign against a simple people who had not had the art of war hammered into their heads by a Napoleon. Moreover, the army was impatient. Some of the troops had been with Lord Ross in the taking of Washington, and they predicted something easier than that very easy campaign. Everybody was completely cock-sure.

On the afternoon of December 23, Major-General Gabrielle Villeré, one of the gaudy Creole soldiers, came to see Jackson at headquarters, and announced that about two thousand British had landed on the Villeré plantation, nine miles below the city. Jackson was still feeble, but this news warmed the old passion in him. He pounded the table with his fist. "By the Eternal!" he cried, "they shall not sleep on our soil!" All well-regulated authorities make Jackson use this phrase —"By the Eternal!" —and any reference to him hardly would be intelligible unless one quoted the familiar line. I suppose we should not haggle over the matter; historically one oath is as good as another.

Marching orders were issued to the troops, and the armed schooner *Carolina* was ordered to drop down the river and open fire upon the British at 7.50 in the evening. In the meantime, Jackson reviewed his troops as they took the road. He was not a good-natured man; indeed, he is one of the most irascible figures in history. But he knew how to speak straight as a stick to the common Each corps received some special word of advice and encouragement.

This review was quaint. Some of the Creole officers were very gorgeous, but perhaps they only served to emphasise the wildly unmilitary aspect of the procession generally. But the woodsmen were there with their rifles, and if the British had beaten Napoleon's marshals, the woodsmen had conquered the forests and the mountains, and they too did not understand that they could be whipped.

The first detachment of British troops had come by boat through Lake Borgne and then made a wretched march through the swamps. Both officers and men were in sorry plight. They had been exposed for days to the fury of tropical rains, and for nights to bitter frosts, without gaining even an opportunity to dry their clothes. But December 23 was a clear day lit by a mildly warm sun. Arriving at Villeré's plantation on the river bank, the troops built huge fires and then raided the country as far as they dared, gathering a great treasure of "fowls and hams and wine." The feast was merry. The veteran soldier of that day had a grand stomach, and he made a deep inroad into Louisiana's store of "fowls and hams and wine."

As they lay comfortably about their fires in the evening some sharp eye detected by the faint light of the moon a moving shadowy vessel on the river. She was approaching. An officer mounted the levee and hailed her. There was no answer. He hailed again. The silent vessel calmly furled her sails and swung her broadside parallel. Then a voice shouted, and a whistling shower of grape-shot tore the air. It was the little *Carolina*.

The British forces flattened themselves in the shelter of the levee and listened to the grape-shot go ploughing over their heads. But they had not been long in this awkward position when there was a yell and a blare of flame in the darkness. Some of Jackson's troops had come.

Then ensued a strange conflict. The moon, tender lady of the night, hid while around the dying fires two forces of infuriated men shot, stabbed, and cut. One remembers grimly Jackson's sentence —"They shall not sleep on our soil." No; they were kept awake this night at least.

There was no concerted action on either side. An officer gathered a handful of men and by his voice led them through the darkness at the enemy. If such valour and ferocity had been introduced into the insipid campaigns of the North, the introduction would have made overwhelming victory for one people or the other. Dawn displayed the terrors of the fighting in the night. In some cases an American and an English soldier lay dead, each with his bayonet sheathed in the other's body.

Bayonets were rare in the American ranks, but many men carried long hunting knives.

As a matter of fact, the two forces had been locked in a blind and desperate embrace. The British reported a loss of forty-six killed, one hundred and sixty-seven wounded, and sixty-four missing. In this engagement the Americans suffered more severely than in any other action of the short campaign.

On the morning of December 24, Sir George Pakenham arrived with a strong reinforcement of men and guns. Pakenham was a brother-in-law of Wellington. He had served in the Peninsula and was accounted a fine leader. The American schooners *Carolina* and *Louisiana* lay at anchor in the river firing continually upon the British camp. Pakenham caused a battery to be planted which quickly made short work of these vessels.

During the days following the two armies met in several encounters which were fiery but indecisive. One of these meetings is called the Battle of the Bales and Hogsheads.

Jackson employed cotton-bales in strengthening a position, and one night the British advanced and built a redoubt chiefly of hogsheads containing sugar and molasses. The cotton suffered considerably from the British artillery, often igniting and capable of being easily rolled out of place, but the sugar and molasses behaved very badly. The hogsheads were easily penetrated, and they soon began to distribute sugar and molasses over the luckless warriors in the redoubt, so that British soldiers died while mingling their blood with molasses, and with sugar sprinkling down upon their wounds.

Although neither side had gained a particular advantage, the British were obliged to retire. They had been the first disciplined troops to engage molasses, and they were glad to emerge from the redoubt, this bedraggled, sticky, and astonished body of men.

On the opposite bank of the river a battery to rake the British encampment had been placed by Commander Patterson. This battery caused Pakenham much annoyance, and he engaged it severely with his guns, but at the end of an hour he had to cease firing with a loss of seventy men and his emplacements almost in ruins. The damage to the American works was slight, but they had lost thirty-six in killed and disabled.

Both sides now came to a period of fateful thought. In the beginning the British had spoken of a feeble people who at first would offer a resistance of pretence, but soon subside before the victorious colours of the British regiments. Now they knew that they were face to face with determined and skilful fighters who would dauntlessly front any British regiment whose colours had ever hung in glory in a cathedral of old England. The Americans had thought to sweep the British into the Gulf of Mexico. But now they knew that although their foes floundered and blundered, —although they displayed that curious stern-lipped stupidity which is the puzzle of many nations, —they were still the veterans of the Peninsula, the stout, undismayed troops of Wellington.

Jackson moved his line fifty yards back from his cotton-bale position. Here he built a defensive work on the northern brink of an old saw-mill race known as the Rodriguez Canal. The line of defence was a mile in length. It began on the river bank and ended in a swamp where, during the battle, the Americans stood knee-deep in mud or on floating planks and logs moored to the trees. The main defences of the position were built of earth, logs, and fence-rails in some places twenty feet thick. It barred the way to New Orleans.

The Americans were prepared for the critical engagement some days before Pakenham had completed his arrangements. The Americans spent the interval in making grape-shot out of bar-lead, and in mending whatever points in their line needed care and work.

Pakenham's final plan was surprisingly simple, and perhaps it was surprisingly bad. He decided to send a heavy force across the river to attack Patterson's annoying battery simultaneously with the deliverance of the main attack against Jackson's position along the line of the Rodriguez Canal. Why Pakenham decided to make the two attacks simultaneously is not quite clear at this day. Patterson's force, divided by the brutally swift river from the main body of the Americans, might have been considered with much reason a detached body of troops, and Pakenham might have eaten them at his leisure while at the same time keeping up a great show in front of Jackson, so that the latter would consider that something serious was imminent at the main position.

However, Pakenham elected to make the two attacks at the same hour, and posterity does not perform a graceful office when it re-generals the battles of the past.

Boats were brought from the fleet, and with immense labour a canal was dug from Lake Borgne to the Mississippi. For use in fording the ditch in front of Jackson, the troops made fascines by binding together sheaves of sugar-cane, and for the breastwork on the far side of the ditch they made scaling ladders.

On January 7, 1815, Jackson stood on the top of the tallest building within his lines and watched the British at work. At the same time Pakenham was in the top of a pine-tree regarding the American trenches. For the moment, and indefinitely, it was a question of eyesight. Jackson studied much of the force that was to assail him; Pakenham studied the position which he had decided to attack. Pakenham's eyesight may not have been very good.

Colonel Thornton was in command of the troops which were to attack Patterson's battery across the river, and a rocket was to be sent up to tell him when to begin his part of the general onslaught.

Pakenham advanced serenely against the Rodriguez Canal, the breastwork, and the American troops. One wishes to use here a phrase inimical to military phraseology. One wishes to make a distinction between disinterested troops and troops who are interested. The Americans were interested troops. They faced the enemy at the main gate of the United States. Behind them crouched frightened thousands. In reality they were defending a continent.

As the British advanced to the attack they made a gallant martial picture. The motley army of American planters, woodsmen, free negroes, ex-convicts, and pirates watched them in silence. Here tossed the bonnets of a fierce battalion of Highlanders; here marched a bottle-green regiment, the officers wearing furred cloaks and crimson sashes; here was a steady line of blazing red coats. Everywhere rode the general officers in their cocked hats, their short red coats with golden epaulettes and embroideries, their skin-tight white breeches, their high black boots. The ranks were kept locked in the manner of that day. It was like a grand review.

But the grandeur was extremely brief. The force was well within range of the American guns when Pakenham made the terrible discovery that his orders had been neglected: there was neither fascine nor ladder on the field. In a storm of rage and grief the British general turned to the guilty officer and bade him take his men back and fetch them. When, however, the ladders and fascines had been brought into the field, a hot infantry engagement had already begun, and the bearers, becoming wildly rattled, scattered them on the ground.

It was now that Sir George Pakenham displayed that quality of his nation which in another place I have called stern-lipped stupidity. It was an absolute certainty that Jackson's position could not be carried without the help of fascines and ladders; it was doubtful if it could be carried in any case.

But Sir George Pakenham ordered a general charge. His troops responded desperately. They flung themselves forward in the face of a storm of bullets aimed usually with deadly precision. Back of their rampart, the Americans, at once furious and cool, shot with the quickness of aim and yet with the finished accuracy of life-long hunters. The British army was being mauled and mangled out of all resemblance to the force that had landed in December.

Sir George Pakenham, proud, heartbroken, frenzied man, rode full tilt at the head of rush after rush. And his men followed him to their death. On the right, a major and a lieutenant succeeded in crossing the ditch. The two officers mounted the breastwork, but the major fell immediately. The lieutenant imperiously demanded the swords of the American officers present. But they said, "Look behind you." He looked behind him and saw that the men whom he had supposed were at his back had all vanished as if the earth had yawned for them.

The lieutenant was taken prisoner and so he does not count, but the dead body of the major as it fell and rolled within the American breastwork established the high-water mark of the British advance upon New Orleans.

Sir George Pakenham seemed to be asking for death, and presently it came to him. His body was carried from the field. General Gibbs was mortally wounded. General Keane was seriously wounded. Left without leaders, the British troops began a retreat. This retreat was soon a mad runaway, but General Lambert with a strong reserve stepped between the beaten battalions and their foes. The battle had lasted twenty-five minutes.

Jackson's force, armed and unarmed, was four thousand two hundred and sixty-four. During the whole campaign he lost three hundred and thirty-three. In the final action he lost four killed, thirteen wounded. The British force in action was about eight thousand men. The British lost some nine hundred killed, fourteen hundred wounded, and five hundred prisoners.

Thornton finally succeeded in reaching and capturing the battery on the other side of the river, but he was too late. Some of the British war-ships finally succeeded in crossing the bars, but they were too late. General Lambert, now in command, decided to withdraw, and the expedition sailed away.

Peace had been signed at Ghent on December 24, 1814. The real battle of New Orleans was fought on January 8, 1815.

THE BATTLE OF SOLFERINO

"Italy," said Prince Metternich, "is merely a geographical expression."

The sneer was justified; the storied peninsula was cut up into little principalities for little princes of the houses of Hapsburg and Bourbon. The millions who spoke a common tongue and cherished common traditions of a glorious past were ruled as cynically as if they were so many cattle. The map of Italy for 1859 is a crazy-quilt of many patches. How has it come about, then, that the map of Italy for 1863 is of one uniform colour from the Alps to the "toe of the boot," including Sardinia and Sicily? We must except the Papal States, of course, still separate till 1870, and Venetia, Austrian till 1866, when the "Bride of the Sea" became finally one with the rest of Italy.

This was the last miracle that Europe had looked for. Unity in Italy! "Since the fall of the Roman Empire (if ever before it)," said an Englishman, "there has never been a time when Italy could be called a nation any more than a stack of timber can be called a ship." This was true even in the days of the mediaeval magnificence of the city-states, Venice, Genoa, Milan and Florence, Pisa and Rome. But in modern times Italy had become only a field for intriguing dynasties and the wars of jealous nations.

During the latter half of the eighteenth century Italy was strangely tranquil: Was she content at last with her slavery? Never that; the people had simply grown apathetic. Their spasmodic insurrections had always ended in a worse bondage than ever: their very religion was used to fasten their chains. Perhaps nothing could have served so well to wake them from this torpor of despair as the iron tread of the first Napoleon. The "Corsican tyrant" proved a beneficent counter-irritant —a wholesome, cleansing force throughout the land. It was good for Italy to be rid, if only for a little while, of Hapsburgs and Bourbons; to have the political divisions of the country reduced to three; to be amazed at the sight of justice administered fairly and taxation made equitable. But the most significant effect of the Napoleonic occupation was this, that the hearts of the Italians were stirred with a new consciousness: they had been shown the possibility of becoming a united race-of owning a nation which should not be a "mere geographical expression."

And although 1815 brought the bad days of the Restoration, and the stupid, corrupt, or cruel princes climbed back again on their little thrones, and the map was made into pretty much the same old crazy-quilt, still it was not the same old Italy: all the diplomats-at Vienna could not make things as they had been before. The new spirit of freedom came to life in the north, in the kingdom of Sardinia, that had made itself the most independent section of the country. In the beginning it was only Savoy, and the Dukes of Savoy, "owing," as the Prince de Ligne said, "to their geographical position, which did not permit them to behave like honest men," had swallowed, first, Piedmont; then, Sardinia; and then as many of the towns of Lombardy as they could. The restoration enriched the kingdom by the gift of Genoa, where, in 1806, Joseph Mazzini was born.

Mazzini, Garibaldi, Cavour-those names will be always thought of as one with the liberation of Italy.

Though frequently in open antagonism, yet the work of each of the three was necessary to the cause, and to each it was a holy cause, for which he was ready to make any sacrifice:

> "Italia! when thy name was but a name,
> When to desire thee was a vain desire,
> When to achieve thee was impossible,
> When to love thee was madness, when to live
> For thee was the extravagance of fools,
> When to die for thee was to fling away
> Life for a shadow-in those darkest days
> Were some who never swerved, who lived, and strove,
> And suffered for thee, and attained their end."

Of these devoted ones Mazzini was the prophet; his idealism undoubtedly made too great demands upon the human beings he worked for, but let us bear in mind that it needed a conception of absolute good to rouse the sluggish Italian mind from its materialism and Machiavellism. Mazzini wore black when a youth as "mourning for his country," and when his university course was at an end he took up the profession of political agitator and joined the Carbonari.

But the greatest service he ever did his cause was the organisation of a new society-on a much higher plane than the Carbonari and its like. The movement was called "Young Italy," famous for the spirit it raised from end to end of the peninsula. Among those attracted by Mazzini's exalted utterance was the young Garibaldi, who, taking part in Mazzini's rising of 1834, was condemned to death, and made his escape to South America. In constant service in the wars between the quarrelsome states he gained his masterly skill in guerilla warfare, which was afterwards to play so great a part in the liberation of his country. He did not return until it seemed as though the hour of Italy's deliverance was at hand, in 1848, which only proved to be the "quite undress rehearsal" for the great events of 1859.

Garibaldi has been called "not a soldier but a saint." Most great heroes, alas! have outlived their heroism, and their worshippers have outlived their worship; but Garibaldi has never been anything but the unselfish patriot who wanted everything for his country but nothing for himself. He has been described, on his return to Italy from South America, as "beautiful as a statue and riding like a centaur." "He was quite a show," said the sculptor Gibson, "every one stopping to look at him." "Probably," said another Englishman, "a human face so like a lion, and still retaining the humanity nearest the image of its Maker, was never seen."

The third of the immortal Italian trio, Count Camillo de Cavour, was, like Mazzini and Garibaldi, a subject of the Sardinian kingdom. There was no prouder aristocracy in Europe than that of Piedmont, but Camillo seems to have drawn his social theories from the all-pervading unrest that the great Revolution and Bonaparte had left in the air, rather than the assumed sources of heredity. In his tenth year he entered the military academy at Turin, and at the same time was appointed page to the Prince of Carignan, afterwards Charles Albert, father of Victor Emmanuel. This was esteemed a high honour, but it did not appeal to him in this light. When asked what was the costume of the pages, he replied, in a tone of disgust: "Parbleu! how would you have us dressed, except as lackeys, which we were? It made me blush with shame."

His attitude of contempt for the place occasioned a prompt dismissal. At the academy he was so successful with mathematics that he left it at sixteen, having become sub-lieutenant in the engineers, although twenty years was the earliest age for this grade. He then joined the garrison at Genoa, but the military career had no allurements for him. Taking kindly to liberal ideas, he expressed himself so freely that the authorities transferred him to the little fortress of Bard, till, in 1831, he resigned his commission.

Having by nature a "diabolical activity" that demanded the widest scope for itself, he now took charge of a family estate at Leri, and went in for scientific farming.

"At the first blush," he wrote, "agriculture has little attraction. The habitué of the salon feels a certain repugnance for works which begin by the analysis of dunghills and end in the middle of cattle-sheds. However, he will soon discover a growing interest, and that which most repelled him will not be long in having for him a charm which he never so much as expected."

Although he began by not knowing a turnip from a potato, his invincible energy soon made him a capital farmer; his experiments were so daring that "the simple neighbours who came trembling to ask his advice stood aghast; he, always smiling, gay, affable, having for each a clear, concise counsel, an encouragement enveloped in a pleasantry."

Besides agriculture, his interests extended to banks, railway companies, a manufactory for chemical fertilisers, steam mills for grinding corn, and a line of packets on the Lago Maggiore. During this time he visited England, and was to be seen night after night in the Strangers' Gallery of the House of Commons, making himself master of the methods of parliamentary tactics, that were to be of such value to Italy in later years.

In 1847 Cavour started the *Risorgimento,* a journal whose programme was simply this: "Independence of Italy, union between the princes and peoples, progress in the path of reform, and a league between the Italian states." As for Italian unity, "Let us," Cavour would say, "do one thing at a time; let us get rid of the Austrians, and then-we shall see." After returning from England in 1843. he wrote: "You may well talk to me of hell, for since I left you I live in a kind of intellectual hell, where intelligence and science are reputed infernal by him who has the goodness to govern us."

The king, Charles Albert, had called him the most dangerous man in the kingdom, and he certainly was the most dangerous to the old systems of religious and political bigotry; but his work was educational; gradually he was enlightening the minds of the masses, and preventing a possible reign of terror. In 1848 he wrote: "What is it which has always wrecked the finest and justest of revolutions? The mania for revolutionary means; the men who have attempted to emancipate themselves from ordinary laws. Revolutionary means, producing the directory, the consulate, and the empire; Napoleon, bending all to his caprice, imagining that one can with a like facility conquer at the Bridge of Lodi and wipe out a law of nature. Wait but a little longer, and you will see the last consequence of your revolutionary means-Louis Napoleon on the throne!"

Charles Albert, the king, who, as Prince Carignan, had been one of the Carbonari, and secretly hated Austria, has been accused of treachery and double dealing. (He explained that he was "always between the dagger of the Carbonari and the chocolate of the Jesuits.") But the time came when he nobly redeemed his past. In 1845 he assured d'Azeglio that when Sardinia was ready to free herself from Austria, his life, his sons' lives, his arms, his treasure, should all be freely spent in the Italian cause.

In February, 1848, he granted his people a constitution; a parliament was formed, Cavour becoming member for Turin.

In this month the Revolution broke out in Paris and penetrated to the heart of Vienna. Metternich was forced to fly his country; the Austrians left Milan; Venice threw off the yoke-all Italy revolted. The Pope, it is said, behaved badly, and left Rome free for Garibaldi to enter, with Mazzini enrolled as a volunteer.

Even the abominable Ferdinand of Sicily and the Grand Duke of Tuscany had been obliged to grant constitutions; all the northern states had hastened to unite themselves to Sardinia by universal plebiscite. At the very beginning Charles Albert fulfilled his pledge; he placed himself at the head of his army and defied Austria.

But it was too soon: Austria was too strong. On the 23rd of March, 1849, Charles Albert was crushingly defeated by Radetsky at Novara. There, when night fell, he called his generals to him, and in their presence abdicated in favour of his son, Victor Emmanuel, who knelt weeping before him. The pathos of despair was in his words: "Since I have not succeeded in finding death," he said, "I must accomplish one last sacrifice for my country."

He left the battle-field and his country without even visiting his home; six months later he was dead. "The magnanimous king," his people called him.

The young Victor Emmanuel began his reign in a kingly fashion; pointing his sword towards the Austrian camp, he exclaimed: "Per Dio! d'Italia sarà." It seemed at the time a mere empty boast-his little country was brought so close to the verge of ruin. The terms of peace imposed an Austrian occupation until the war indemnity of eighty million francs should be paid. Yet Cavour was heard to say that all their sacrifices were not too dear a price for the Italian tricolour in exchange for the flag of Savoy. It was not until July that Rome fell-Rome, where Garibaldi had established a republic and Mazzini was a Triumvir!

At the invitation of the Pope, Louis Napoleon, then president of the French republic, seeing the opportunity for conciliating the religious powers, poured his troops into Rome, and Garibaldi fled, with Anita at his side. The brave wife with her unborn child would not leave her hero, but death took her from him. In a peasant's hut, a few days later, she died, his arms around her. As for Mazzini, the fall of Rome nearly broke his heart. For days he wandered dazed about the Eternal City, miraculously escaping capture, till his friends got him away.

It was not until April of 1850 that Pius IX. dared to come back to Rome, where a body of French troops long remained, to show how really religious a nation was France. From his accession there had been a papal party in Italy, who, because of the good manners of the gentle ecclesiastic, had wrought themselves up to believe that Italy could be united under *him*. But as early as 1847 d'Azeglio wrote from Rome: "The magic of Pio Nono will not last; he is an angel, but he is surrounded by demons."

After the events of the 1848 rising, and his appeal (twenty-five pontiffs had made the same appeal before him!) to the foreigner against his own people, the dream of a patriotic pope melted into thin air.

And so Austria came back into Italy, and seemed again complete master there. It would be interesting to be able to analyse the sensibilities of these prince-puppets who were jerked back to their thrones by their master at Vienna. Plenty of Austrian troops came to take care of them. As for the bitter reprisals Italians had to bear, it is almost impossible to read of them. In certain provinces every one found with a weapon was put to death. A man found with a rusty nail was promptly shot. At Brescia a little hunchback was slowly burnt alive. Women, stripped half naked, were flogged in the market-place, with Austrian officers looking on. It was after his visit to Naples in the winter of 1850 that Gladstone wrote, "This is the negation of God erected into a system of government."

But Italy had now a new champion. When Victor Emmanuel signed his name to the first census in his reign, he jestingly gave his occupation as "Rè Galantuomo," and this name stuck to him for ever after. A brave monarch Victor Emmanuel proved, whose courage and honesty were tried in many fires.

When arranging negotiations with Radetsky after Novara, he was given to understand that the conditions of peace would be much more favourable if he would abandon the constitution granted by Charles Albert.

"Marshal," he said, "sooner than subscribe to such conditions, I would lose a hundred crowns. What my father has sworn I will maintain. If you wish a war to the death, be it so! My house knows the road of exile, but not of dishonour."

The Princes of Piedmont had been always renowned for physical courage and dominating minds. Effeminacy and mendacity are not their foibles. It is hinted by the Countess of Cesaresco, in her *Liberation of Italy,* that sainthood was esteemed the privilege strictly of the women of the family; but then sainthood is not absolutely necessary to a monarch. The Piedmont line had always understood the business of kings, —but none so thoroughly as Victor Emmanuel.

He was unpopular at first; the Mazzinists cried, "Better Italy enslaved than handed over to the son of the traitor, Carlo Alberto!" On the wall of his palace at Turin was written: "It is all up with us; we have a German king and queen" —alluding to the Austrian origin of his mother and of his young queen, Marie Adelaide.

These two-wife and mother-were ruled by clerics, and made his life melancholy when he began a course of ecclesiastical reform. One person in every two hundred and fourteen in Sardinia was an ecclesiastic, and the Church had control of all ecclesiastical jurisdiction and could shelter criminals, among other mediaeval privileges. To reform these abuses, the king, in 1849, approached the pope with deferential requests, but the pope absolutely refused to make any changes.

However, the work of reform was firmly pushed on, and a law was passed by which the priestly privileges were sensibly cut down, although the king's wife and mother wrung their hands, and the religious press shrieked denunciation. At this time Santa Rosa, the Minister of Commerce and Agriculture, died, and the Church refused him the last sacrament, though he was a blameless and devout member of the Roman Church. This hateful act of intolerance reacted on the clergy, as a matter of course, and gave an impetus to church reform.

When, in 1855, Victor Emmanuel was so unfortunate as to lose his wife, his mother, and his brother, within a month, and the nation as a whole mourned with him, his clerical friends embittered his affliction by insisting with venomous frankness that it was the judgment of Heaven that he had brought upon himself for his religious persecutions.

Strength was Victor Emmanuel's genius: he was not intellectual in any marked degree, but his ministers could work with him and rely upon him. A union between him and Cavour, the two great men of the kingdom, was inevitable. Up to this time Cavour had no general fame except as a journalist, but the king had the insight to recognise his extraordinary powers, and when Santa Rosa died (unshriven) Cavour in his place became Minister of Agriculture and Commerce. "Look out!" said the king to his prime minister, d'Azeglio, when this had come to pass, "Cavour will soon be taking all your portfolios. He will never rest till he is prime minister himself."

Under the régime of Cavour, railways and telegraph wires lined the kingdom in all directions; he took off foolish tariffs and concluded commercial treaties with England, France, Belgium, and other powers. "Milord Cavour" was a nickname showing the dislike aroused by his English predilections, but through him Piedmont repaired the damage of the war of 1848, and grew steadily in prosperity.

Cavour's brilliant intellectual powers seem to have been so limitless that it is rather a relief to think of him personally as only a dumpy little man with an over-big head. Although a born aristocrat, and living in the manner becoming one, he was capable of quite demonstrative behaviour. The occasion for this was a dinner given by d'Azeglio. Cavour, seated at table, joked the premier about his jealousy of Ratazzi; the premier replied angrily; whereupon the greatest of diplomats arose, seized his plate, lifting it as high as he could, and dashed it to the floor, where it broke into fragments. Then he rushed out of the house, crying:

"He is a beast! He is a beast!"

This quarrel, which sounds like an act from a nursery drama, led to a change in the cabinet, with Cavour left out. But a little later on d'Azeglio resigned, and Cavour was prime minister.

A marvellous stroke of statesmanship on behalf of his country was Cavour's intervention in the Crimean War in 1855, —three years after Louis Napoleon's *coup d'état*. It seemed an act of folly to send fifteen thousand troops from the little Italian state-which had no standing among European powers-to help England and France. The undertaking seemed to Sardinians an act of insanity; Cavour's colleagues were violently against him. But the king stood by him; so the troops were sent and the ministers resigned.

Never was an action more fully justified. At the close of the Crimean War Sardinia had two powerful allies-France and England; and for the first time she was admitted on terms of equality among the "Powers." A significant thing had been said, too, in 1855: "What can I do for Italy?" asked the Emperor Napoleon of Cavour. Cavour was not slow to tell him what could be done; he was convinced that he must look for aid to the vanity and ambition of Napoleon III.

No diplomatic pressure of his, however, availed. During the next two years the attitude of Austria became constantly more unendurable, but still Napoleon would make no move.

It proved to be the most unlikely of events that brought about a consummation of the wishes of Cavour.

On the evening of January 14, 1858, a carriage drove through the Paris streets on its way to the opera. With the appearance of its two occupants all the world is familiar; the wonderful Spanish eyes of the lady, the exquisite lines of her figure-who has not seen them pictured? The smallish man with her had been described by the Crown Prince of Prussia as having "strangely immobile features and almost extinguished eyes." His huge moustache had exaggeratedly long waxed ends, and his chin was covered with an "imperial."

The terrible crash of Orsini's bombs, thrown underneath their carriage, failed to carry out the conspirators' purpose. The emperor had a slight wound on the nose, and the empress felt a blow on the eye. That was all, except that her silks and laces were spattered with blood from the wounded outside the carriage. They continued their drive and saw the opera to its finish before they were told of the tragedy that had befallen. Eight people had been killed and one hundred and fifty-six wounded by the explosion.

The Empress Eugenie, it is said, showed the greatest composure over the event, but this was not true of her husband. Probably no man of modern times had had so many attempts made on his life as Louis Napoleon, and always, before, he made light of them; but this last one, resulting in such cruel slaughter, completely unnerved him. He now lived in a tremor, dreading the vengeance of still others of the revolutionary ex-friends of his youth; but he dared not relax the despotic grip with which he ruled his land. How could he placate them? He wore a cuirass under his coat; he had wires netted over the chimneys of the Tuileries, so that bombs should not burst on his hearth; a swarm of detectives were around him wherever he went, and always the question asked itself in his mind: What should he do to take off the curse of fear from his life?

Cavour, Victor Emmanuel, the whole of Italy, were filled with rage and disgust at the news of Orsini's attempt. Orsini-an Italian! That must be the end of all their hopes of help from France! But in the summer of 1848 Cavour was summoned to the emperor at Plombières, and during two days there the agreement was formulated by which France and Italy united against Austria. This was Louis Napoleon's solution of his problem-to help Italy at least sufficiently to annul the hate of every assassin on the peninsula. According to the Prince Regent of Prussia, he chose "la guerre" instead of "le poignard."

No written record was made of the bargain between Napoleon and Cavour; but we know that it gave Savoy and Nice to France, and made one innocent royal victim, the young Princess Clotilde, Victor Emmanuel's daughter, who was there betrothed by proxy to Prince Jerome Napoleon.

It was at Plombières that Napoleon with some naïveté said to Cavour: "Do you know, there are but three *men* in all Europe: one is myself, the second is you, and the third is one whose name I will not mention." Napoleon was not alone in his high estimate of Cavour. In Turin they said: "We have a ministry, a parliament, a constitution; all *that* spells Cavour."

At his reception on New Year's Day, 1859, Napoleon astounded every one by greeting the Austrian ambassador with these words: "I regret that our relations with your government are not so good as they have been hitherto." This ostentatious expression was equal to publication in a journal. Immediate war was looked for by every one. Piedmont, France, and Austria openly made bellicose preparations.

Although on the 18th of January, 1859, a formal treaty was made, by which France was bound to support Piedmont if attacked by Austria, Napoleon hesitated and tried to back out of his agreement. It will never be known by what tortuous system of diplomacy Cavour compelled Austria herself to declare war, but it was done, April 27.

Cavour's intrigues during these days were dazzlingly complicated; he had to deal on one hand with his imperial ally, and on the other with shady revolutionary elements-and to keep his right hand in ignorance of what his left hand did. He summoned Garibaldi to Turin; Garibaldi, in his loose red shirt and sombrero, with its plume, with his tumultuous hair and beard, struck dismay to the heart of the servant who opened the door. He refused to admit him, but finally agreed to consult his master. "Let him come in," said Cavour. "It is probably some poor devil who has a petition to make to me." This was the first meeting of the statesman and the warrior. When told of the French alliance, Garibaldi exclaimed: "Mind what you are about! Never forget that the aid of foreign armies must be, in some way or other, dearly paid for!" But his adherence was whole-heartedly given to Victor Emmanuel, and at the end of the short campaign Italy rang with his name.

For months past Austria had been pouring troops into Italy-there seemed no limit to them. Garibaldi, by the end of April, was in command of a band of Cacciatori delli Alpi, a small force, but made up of the iron men of North Italy, worthy of their leader.

On May 2 Victor Emmanuel took the command of his army; it comprised fifty-six thousand infantry in five divisions, one division of cavalry in sixteen squadrons, with twelve field-guns and two batteries of horse artillery. On May 12 the French emperor rode through the streets of Genoa amid loud acclamations; the city was hung with draperies and garlands in his honour. At Alessandria he rode under an arch on which was inscribed, "To the descendant of the Conqueror of Marengo!" In all he had one hundred and twenty-eight thousand men, including ten thousand cavalry.

It was a short campaign, but the weeks were thick with battles, and the battlefields with the slain.

The first engagement was at Genestrello, May 20. The Austrians, driven out, made a stand at Montebello, where, though twenty thousand strong, they were routed by six thousand Sardinians. The armies of the emperor and king forced the Austrians to cross the Po, and there retire behind the Sesia. On the 30th the allies crossed the Sesia and drove the foe from the fortified positions of Palestro, Venzaglio, and Casalino.

Next came Magenta—a splendid triumph for MacMahon; the Austrian loss was ten thousand men; that of the French between four thousand and five thousand. Meantime, Garibaldi had led his Cacciatori to the Lombard shores of Lake Maggiore, had beaten the Austrians at Varese, entered Como, routed the enemy again at San Fermo, and was now proceeding to Bergamo and Brescia with the purpose of cutting off the enemy's retreat through the Alps of the Trentino.

On the 8th of June Victor Emmanuel and Napoleon III. made their triumphal entry into Milan, from whence every Austrian had fled. Every one remembers how MacMahon, now Duke of Magenta, caught up to his saddle-bow a child who was in danger of being crushed by the crowd.

The emperor and the king soon moved on from Milan. By the 23rd their headquarters were fixed at Montechiaro, close to the site of the coming battle of Solferino.

On the day before the battle the lines of the allies lay near the Austrian lines, from the shore of the Lake of Garda at San Martino to Cavriana on the extreme right. On the evening of the 23rd there was issued a general order regulating the movements of the allied forces: Victor Emmanuel's army was sent to the extreme left, near Lake Garda; Baraguay d'Hilliers was given the centre in front of Solferino, which was the Austrian centre; to his right was MacMahon, next Marshal Niel, and then Canrobert at the extreme right, while the emperor's guards were ordered here and there in the changes of the battle.

The enemy, under Field-Marshal Stadion, held the entire line of battle strongly, with one hundred and forty thousand men.

Solferino has been the scene of many combats; it is a natural fighting-ground, and the Austrians had barricaded themselves at all the strong points of vantage.

At five in the morning of the 24th, Louis Napoleon sat in his shirt-sleeves, after his early coffee, smoking a cigar, when tidings came to him that the fighting had begun. In a few minutes he was driving at full speed to Castiglione, and on the way he said to an aide: "The fate of Italy is perhaps to be decided to-day." It was he indeed who decided it; whatever else is said of him, it was he who struck a great blow for Italy at Solferino.

It was the great day of Napoleon III.; he has never been considered a notable soldier, but throughout this day, in every command issued, he displayed consummate military ability.

The sun glared in the intense blue above with tropical heat, when, at Castiglione, Napoleon climbed the steeple of St. Peter's Church and beheld the expanse of Lake Garda, growing dim towards the Tyrolean Alps. There was the remnant of an ancient castle—a sturdy tower-guarding the village of Solferino, called the "Spy of Italy." Already a deadly fire from its loopholes poured on Baraguay d'Hilliers's men, who faced it bravely, but were falling in terrible numbers.

He could see the Austrian masses swarming along the heights uniting Cavriana with Solferino. The Piedmontese cannon booming from the left told that Victor Emmanuel was fighting hard, but his forces were hidden by hills. It was at once plain to him, from his church steeple, that the object of the Austrians was to divert the attack on Solferino-the key of their position-by outflanking the French right, filling up the gap between the Second and Fourth Corps, and thus cutting the emperor's army in two. Coming down from his height, Napoleon at once sent orders to the cavalry of the Imperial Guard to join MacMahon, to prevent his forces from being divided. Altogether the emperor's plan seems to have been clear and definite; his design was to carry Solferino at any cost, and then, by a flank movement, to beat the enemy out of his positions at Cavriana. Galloping to the top of Monte Fenil, the emperor beheld a thick phalanx of bayonets thrust its way suddenly through the trees of the valley; it was a huge body of Austrians sent to cut off the line of the French. There was not a minute to be lost; he sent orders to General Manêque, of the Guard, to advance at once against the Austrian columns. With magnificent rapidity the order was executed, and the Austrians —a great number-were beaten back far from the line of battle.

The Austrian batteries placed on the Mount of Cypresses and on the Cemetery Hill of Solferino were keeping up a deadly fire on the French.

Baraguay d'Hilliers brought Bazaine's brigade into action against the one, and the First Regiment of zouaves rushed up the other, only to be hurled back by the enemy as they reached the steep slope. A horrible confusion followed these two repulses, the zouaves and General Negrier's division being fatally mixed and fighting with each other like furies. But General Negrier kept his head and collected his troops, scattered all over the hillocks and valleys. Then, with the Sixty-first Regiment of the line and a battalion of the One Hundredth Regiment, he started resolutely to mount the Cemetery Hill. It was a deadly march; the enemy; holding the advantage, disputed every turn and twist of the ascent. Twice Negrier's troops rushed up along the ridge-like path, but the circular wall of the cemetery, bored with thousands of holes, through which rifles sent a scathing hail, was strong as a fortress to resist them. It was sheer murder to take his men up again; Negrier abandoned the attack.

The enemy's cannon-balls from the three defended heights fell thick and fast on Mount Fenil, where Napoleon and his aides breathlessly watched the progress of the drama.

Many of the Cent-Gardes who formed the imperial escort were shot down; the emperor was in the midst of death. The Austrians had been strongly reinforced, and held to the defence of Solferino more obstinately than ever.

But, notwithstanding this, the French were gaining ground; the left flank of the Austrians was at last broken by the artillery of the French reserve, and the whole army felt a thrill of encouragement.

A number of French battalions were now massing themselves about the spur of the Tower Hill of Solferino, but it was impossible to proceed to the attack while solid Austrian masses stood ready to pounce upon their flank.

A few fiery charges scattered the enemy in all directions, and a tempest of shouts rang out when Forey gave the order to storm the Tower Hill. The drum beat, the trumpets sounded. "Vive l'Empereur!" echoed from the encircling hills. "Quick" is too slow a word for French soldiers. The Imperial Guard, chasseurs, and battalions of the line rushed up with such fierce velocity that it was no time at all before the heights of Solferino were covered with Napoleon's men. Nothing could stand against such an electric shock-the Tower Hill was carried, and General Leboeuf turned the artillery on the defeated masses of Austrians choking up the road that led to Cavriana.

The convent and adjoining church, strongly barricaded, yielded after repeated attacks, and then Baraguay d'Hilliers and Negrier made a last attempt on the Cemetery Hill. The narrow path that led up to it was strewn with bloody corpses, but neither the dead resting in their graves nor these new dead could be held sacred. A strong artillery fire on the gate and walls stopped the rifles from firing through the holes, and in this pause Colonel Laffaile led the Seventy-eighth Regiment up. They burst in the gate of the cemetery, —there were not many there to kill! —they were soon on their way towards the village.

Their way lay through a checker-board of tiny farms and fields, separated by stone walls wreathed with ivy. Little chapels, dedicated to favourite saints, stood in every enclosure. Houses, walls, and chapels had all been turned into barricades by the Austrians. Douay's and Negrier's men had to fight their way to the village through a rain of bullets from unseen enemies. Now they took the narrow path winding up by the Tower Hill into the streets of the village; when nearly at the top the clanking of heavy artillery-wheels told them that the enemy were retreating and carrying off the very guns that had played such havoc on their ranks from the top of Tower Hill. It took but a short time to capture them, and then they were fairly in the village, chasing the last straggling Austrians through the streets.

Solferino was in the hands of the French; but the fate of the battle was not yet decided, for Cavriana was a strong position, and Stadion and his generals had made a careful study of its possibilities.

At two o'clock MacMahon's left wing was completely surrounded by the enemy, but moving forward on the right he boldly turned the Austrian front, and swept everything before him to the village of San Cassiano, adjoining Cavriana. The village was attacked on both sides and carried by Laure's Algerian sharpshooters; but the Austrians still held Monte Fontana, which unites San Cassiano to Cavriana, and repulsed Laure's men with deadly skill.

Reinforced, they made a splendid dash and took Monte Fontana, but the Prince of Hesse brought up reserves and won it back for the Austrians. Napoleon now ordered Mac Mahon to push forward his whole corps to support the attack, and as Manêque's brigade and Mellinet's grenadiers had succeeded in routing the enemy from Monte Sacro, they were ordered to advance on Cavriana.

Leboeuf placed the artillery of the Guard at the opening of the valley facing Cavriana, and Laure's Algerian sharpshooters after a prolonged hand-to-hand conflict with the Prince of Hesse's men carried Cavriana at four o'clock. Two hours later Napoleon was resting in the Casa Pastore, where the Austrian emperor had slept the night before. The sultry glare of the day had culminated in a wild, black storm; the wind was a hurricane, and it was under torrents of rain that the Austrians made their retreat, while the thunder drowned the noise of Marshal Niel's cannon driving them from every stand they made.

Such overwhelming numbers had been brought to bear on the French that day that their defeat would have been almost certain if it had not been for Napoleon's generalship and his modern rifled guns. These were new to the Austrians, who became panic-stricken at their effect.

The Piedmontese troops, under their "Rè Galantuomo," fought as nobly as their brilliant allies that day. The young Emperor Francis Joseph commanded in person at San Martino, but it was Benedek that Victor Emmanuel had to reckon with-the best general of all the Austrian staff. He beat him out of San Martino, and to the Italians the combat of June 24 is known as the Battle of San Martino to this day.

The scorching sun of next morning shone upon twenty-two thousand ghastly dead. It has been believed that the horrible sights and scents of this battlefield sickened the emperor and cut short the campaign; but who can tell? Was it perhaps Eugenie's influence-always used in favour of the pope? Or was it that he realised that the movement could now only end in the complete liberation of Italy —a consummation that he regarded with horror? All that is known is this: three days after the Austrians had been driven back to their own country, and while all Italy went mad with joy at the victory, while Mrs. Browning was writing her "Emperor Evermore" —a cruel satire on later events-it became known that Napoleon had sent a message to the Austrian kaiser asking him to suspend hostilities.

The two emperors met at Villafranca, a small place near Solferino. At the close of their interview Francis Joseph looked humiliated and sombre-Louis Napoleon was smilingly at ease. He, the parvenu, had made terms with a legitimate emperor, and was pleased with himself. He had arranged that Lombardy was to be united to Piedmont, while Venetia remained Austrian. When Victor Emmanuel was told of these terms he could only say coldly that he must ever remain grateful for what Napoleon *had* done, but he murmured "Poor Italy!"

And Cavour? Cavour was struck to the heart. Had he arranged such a finale as *this* with the upstart emperor-that he should leave the game when it suited his pleasure, and make terms with the Austrian emperor all by himself-insolently disregarding Victor Emmanuel? He wept with grief and anger. He left at once for the camp, and there he told the emperor his opinion of him in stinging words. He begged his king to repudiate the treaty and reject Lombardy, but Victor Emmanuel, although as bitterly disappointed as Cavour, felt that he must be prudent for his people's sake.

Angered at the' king's refusal, Cavour resigned his office and retired to his farms at Lèri, but after a few months he was back in his old place in the cabinet. All his hopes and ambitions came back-although physically the shock had broken him-and he laboured for Italy till his death in June of 1861. The whole Italian people, from king to peasant, knew that they had lost their best friend. But Cavour's life-work was nearly finished. Garibaldi had taken up the work of emancipation where Napoleon had abandoned it, and before he left him for ever, to Cavour was given the triumph of hearing his beloved master proclaimed King of Italy.

THE BATTLE OF BUNKER HILL

On the 12th of June, 1775, Captain Harris, afterwards Lord Harris, wrote home from the town of Boston, then occupied by British troops:

> "I wish the Americans may be brought to a sense of their duty. One good drubbing, which I long to give them, by way of retaliation, might have a good effect towards it. At present they are so elated by the petty advantage they gained the 19th of April, that they despise the powers of Britain. We shall soon take the field on the other side of the Neck."

This very fairly expressed the irritation in the British camp. The troops had been sent to Massachusetts to subdue it, but as yet nothing had been done in that direction.

The ignominious flight of the British regulars from Lexington and Concord was still unavenged. More than that, they had been kept close in Boston ever since by the provincial militia.

"What!" cried General Burgoyne when on his arrival in May he was told this news. "What! Ten thousand peasants keep five thousand King's troops shut up? Let *us* get in, and we'll soon find elbow-room!" "Elbow-room" was the army's name for Burgoyne after that.

A little later General Gage remarked to General Timothy Ruggles, "It is impossible for the rebels to withstand our arms a moment."

Ruggles replied: "Sir, you do not know with whom you have to contend. These are the very men who conquered Canada. I fought with them side by side. I know them well; they will fight bravely. My God, sir, your folly has ruined your cause!"

Besides Burgoyne, the *Cerberus* brought over Generals Clinton and Howe, and large reinforcements, so that the forces under General Gage, the commander-in-chief, were over ten thousand. By June 12 the army in Boston was actually unable to procure fresh provisions, and Gage proclaimed martial law, designating those who were in arms as rebels and traitors.

The *Essex Gazette* of June 8 says: "We have the pleasure to inform the public that the Grand American Army is nearly completed." This Grand American Army was spread around Boston, its headquarters at Cambridge, under command of General Artemas Ward, who had fought under Abercromby. The Grand American Army was an army of allies. Ward, its supposed chief, was authorised to command only the Massachusetts and New Hampshire forces, and when the Connecticut and Rhode Island men obeyed him it was purely through courtesy. Each colony supplied its own troops with provisions and ammunition; each had its own officers, appointed by the Committee of Safety.

To this committee, June 13, came the tidings that Gage proposed to occupy Bunker Hill, in Charlestown, on the 18th, and a council of war was held, which included the savagely bluff, warm-hearted patriot, General Israel Putnam, of the Connecticut troops; General Seth Pomeroy; Colonel William Prescott; the hardy, independent Stark; and Captain Gridley, the engineer-all of whom were veterans of the French and Indian war.

As a result of the meeting, a detachment of nine hundred men of the Massachusetts regiments, under Colonels Prescott, Frye, and Bridge, with two hundred men from Connecticut, and Captain Gridley's artillery company of forty-nine men and two field-pieces, were ordered to parade at six o'clock P.M., the 16th, on Cambridge Common. There they appeared with weapons, packs, blankets, and entrenching tools. President Langdon, of Harvard College, made an impressive prayer, and by nine o'clock they had marched, the entire force being under the command of Colonel Prescott.

A uniform of blue turned back with red was worn by some of the men, but for the most part they wore their "Sunday suits" of homespun. Their guns were of all sorts and sizes, and many carried old-fashioned powder-horns and pouches. Prescott walked at their head, with two sergeants carrying dark lanterns, until they reached the Neck.

The Neck was the strip of land leading to the peninsula opposite Boston, where lay the small town of Charlestown. The peninsula is only one mile in length, its greatest breadth but half a mile. The Charles River separates it from Boston on the south, and to the north and east is the Mystic River. Bunker Hill begins at the isthmus and rises gradually to a height of one hundred and ten feet, forming a smooth round hill.

At Cambridge Common, the night the troops started for Bunker Hill, Israel Putnam had made this eloquent address: "Men, there are enough of you on the Common this evening to fill hell so full of the redcoats to-morrow that the devils will break their shins over them."

At Bunker Hill the expedition halted, and a long discussion ensued between Prescott, Gridley, Major Brooks, and Putnam as to whether it would be better to follow Ward's orders literally and fortify Bunker Hill itself, or to go on to the lesser elevation south-east of it, which is now known as Breed's Hill, but had then no special name. They agreed upon Breed's Hill. They began to entrench at midnight. Prescott was consumed with anxiety lest his men should be attacked before some screen could be raised to shelter them. However enthusiastic they might be, he did not think it possible for his raw troops to meet to any advantage a disciplined soldiery in the open field.

So the pickaxe and the spade were busy throughout the night. It was silent work, for the foe was near. In Boston Harbour lay the *Lively,* the *Somerset,* the *Cerberus,* the *Glasgow,* the *Falcon,* and the *Symmetry,* besides the floating batteries. On the Boston shore the sentinels were pacing outside the British encampment. At intervals through the night Prescott and Brooks stole down to the shore of Charles River and listened till the call of "All's well!" rang over the water from the ships and told them that their scheme was still undiscovered.

At dawn the entrenchments were six feet high, and there was a great burst of fire at them from the *Lively,* which was joined in a few moments by the other men-of-war and the batteries on Copp's Hill, on the Boston shore.

The strange thunder of the cannonade brought forth every man, woman, and child in Boston. Out of their prim houses they rushed under trellises heavy with damask roses and honeysuckle, and soon every belfry and tower, house-top and hill-top, was crowded with them. There the most of them stayed till the thrilling play in which they had so vital an interest was enacted.

Meanwhile Prescott, to inspire his raw men with confidence, mounted the parapet of the redoubt they had raised, and deliberately sauntered around it, making jocular speeches, until the men cheered each cannon-ball as it came.

Gage, looking through his field-glasses from the other shore, marked the tall figure with the three-cornered hat and the banyan —a linen blouse-buckled about the waist, and asked of Councillor Willard, who stood near him —

"Who is the person who appears to command?"

"That is my brother-in-law, Colonel Prescott."

"Will he fight?"

"Yes, sir; he is an old soldier, and will fight as long as a drop of blood remains in his veins."

"The works must be carried," said Gage.

Gage was strongly advised by his generals to land a force at the Neck and attack the Americans in the rear. It was also suggested that they might be bombarded by the fleet from the Mystic and the Charles, and, indeed, might be starved out without any fighting at all. But none of this suited the warlike British temper; the whole army longed to fight-to chase the impudent enemy out of those entrenchments he had so insolently reared. The challenge was a bold one; it must be accepted. The British had the weight in all ways, but they also had the preposterous arrogance of the British army, which always deems itself invincible because it remembers its traditions, and traditions are dubious and improper weapons to fire at a foe.

At noon the watchers on the house-tops saw the lines of smart grenadiers and light infantry embark in barges under command of General Howe, who had with him Brigadier-General Pigot and some of the most distinguished officers in Boston. They landed at the south-western point of the peninsula.

When the intelligence that the British troops had landed reached Cambridge it caused great excitement. A letter of Captain Chester reads:

"Just after dinner on the 17th ult. I was walking out from my lodgings, quite calm and composed, and all at once the drums beat to arms, and bells rang, and a great noise in Cambridge. Captain Putnam came by on full gallop. 'What is the matter?' says I. 'Have you not heard?' 'No.' 'Why, the regulars are landing at Charlestown,' says he, 'and father says you must all meet and march immediately to Bunker Hill to oppose the enemy.' I waited not, but ran and got my arms and ammunition, and hastened to my company (who were in the church for barracks), and found them nearly ready to march. We soon marched, with our frocks and trousers on over our other clothes (for our company is in uniform wholly blue, turned up with red), for we were loath to expose ourselves by our dress; and down we marched."

After a reconnaissance, Howe sent back to Gage for reinforcements, and remained passive until they came.

Meanwhile, there were bitter murmurings among the troops on Breed's Hill. They had watched the brilliant pageant, —the crossing over of their adversaries, scarlet-clad, with glittering equipments, with formidable guns in their train, —and were conscious of being themselves exhausted from the night's labour and the hot morning sun. It was two o'clock, and they had had practically nothing to eat that day. Among themselves they accused their officers of treachery. It seemed incredible that after doing all the hard work they should be expected to do the fighting as well. Loud huzzas arose from their lips, however, —these cross and hungry Yankees, —when Doctor-or General-Joseph Warren appeared among them with Seth Pomeroy.

Few men had risen to a higher degree of universal love and confidence in the hearts of the Massachusetts people than Warren. He had been active in every patriotic movement. The councils through which the machinery of the Revolution was put in motion owed much to him. He was president of the Committee of Safety, and probably had been one of the Indians of the Boston Tea Party. But a few days before he had been appointed major-general. In recognition of this, Israel Putnam, who was keeping a squad of men working at entrenchments on Bunker Hill, had offered to take orders from him. But Warren refused, and asked where he might go to be of the greatest service. "Where will the onset be most furious?" he asked, and Putnam sent him to the redoubt. There Prescott also offered him the chief command, but Warren replied, "I came as a volunteer with my musket to serve under you, and shall be happy to learn from a soldier of your experience."

At three o'clock the redoubt was in good working order. About eight yards square, its strongest side, the front, faced the settled part of Charlestown and protected the south side of the hill. The east side commanded a field; the north side had an open passage-way; to the left extended a breastwork for about two hundred yards.

By three o'clock some reinforcements for General Howe had arrived, so that he now had over three thousand men. Just before action he addressed the officers around him as follows:

"Gentlemen, I am very happy in having the honour of commanding so fine a body of men. I do not in the least doubt that you will behave like Englishmen and as becomes good soldiers. If the enemy will not come out from their entrenchments, we must drive them out at all events; otherwise the town of Boston will be set on fire by them. I shall not desire one of you to go a step farther than where I go myself at your head. Remember, gentlemen, we have no recourse to any resources if we lose Boston but to go on board our ships, which will be very disagreeable to us all."

From the movements of the British, they seemed intending to turn the American left and surround the redoubt. To prevent this, Prescott sent down the artillery with two field-pieces — he had only four altogether-and the Connecticut troops under Captain Knowlton. Putnam met them as they neared the Mystic, shouting —

"Man the rail fence, for the enemy is flanking of us fast!"

This rail fence, half of which was stone, reached from the shore of the Mystic to within 200 yards of the breastworks. It was not high, but Putnam had said:

"If you can shield a Yankee's shins he's not afraid of anything. His head he does not think of."

Captain Knowlton, joined by Colonels Stark and Reid and their regiments, made another parallel fence a short distance in front of this, filling in the space between with new-mown hay from the fields.

A great cannonade was thundering from ships and batteries to cover Howe's advance. His troops, now increased to three thousand, came on in two divisions: the left wing, under Pigot, towards the breastwork and redoubt; the right, led by Howe, to storm the rail fence. The artillery moved heavily through the miry low ground, and the embarrassing discovery was made that there were only twelve-pound balls for six-pounders. H owe decided to load them with grape. The troops were hindered by a number of fences, as well as the thick, tall grass. Their knapsacks were extraordinarily heavy, and they felt the power of the scorching sun.

Inside the redoubt the Americans waited for them, Prescott assuring his men that the red-coats would never reach the redoubt if they obeyed him and reserved their fire until he gave the word. As the assaulting force drew temptingly near, the American officers only restrained their men from firing by mounting the parapet and kicking up their guns.

But at last the word was given-the stream of fire broke out all along the line. They were wonderful marksmen. The magnificent regulars were staggered, but they returned the fire. They could make no headway against the murderous volleys flashed in quick succession at them. The dead and wounded fell thickly. General Pigot ordered a retreat, while great shouts of triumph arose from the Americans.

At the rail fence Putnam gave his last directions when Howe was nearing him:

"Fire low: aim at the waistbands! Wait until you see the whites of their eyes! Aim at the handsome coats! Pick off the commanders!"

The men rested their guns on the rail fence to fire. The officers were used as targets-many of the handsome coats were laid low. So hot was the reception they met that in a few moments Howe's men were obliged to fall back. One of them said afterwards, "It was the strongest post that was ever occupied by any set of men."

There was wild exultation within the American lines, congratulation and praises, for just fifteen minutes; and then Pigot and Howe led the attack again. But the second repulse was so much fiercer than the first that the British broke ranks and ran down hill, some of them getting into the boats.

"The dead," said Stark, "lay in front of us as thick as sheep in a fold."

Meantime Charlestown had been set on fire by Howe's orders, and the spectacle was splendidly terrible to the watchers in Boston. The wooden buildings made a superb blaze, and through the smoke could be seen the British officers striking and pricking their men with their swords in the vain hope of rallying them, while cannon, musketry, crashes of falling houses, and the yells of the victors filled up the measure of excitement to the spectators.

Twice, now, the Americans had met the foe and proved that he was not invincible. The women in Boston thought the last defeat final-that their men-folk had gained the day. But Prescott knew better; he was sure that they would come again, and sure that he could not withstand a third attack.

If at this juncture strong reinforcements and supplies of ammunition had reached him, he might well have held his own. But such companies as had been sent on would come no farther than Bunker Hill, in spite of Israel Putnam's threats and entreaties. There they straggled about under hay-cocks and apple-trees, demoralised by the sights and sounds of battle, with no authorised leader who could force them to the front.

As for their commander-in-chief, Ward, he would not stir from his house all day, and kept the main body of his forces at Cambridge.

When General Clinton saw the rout of his countrymen from the Boston shore, he rowed over in great haste. With his assistance, and the fine discipline which prevailed, the troops were re-formed within half an hour. Clinton also proposed a new plan of assault. Accordingly, instead of diffusing their forces across the whole American front, the chief attack was directed on the redoubt. The artillery bombarded the breastwork, and only a small number moved against the rail fence.

"Fight! conquer or die!" was the watchword that passed from mouth to mouth as the tall, commanding figure of Howe led on the third assault. To his soldiers it was a desperate venture-they felt that they were going to certain death. But inside the redoubt few of the men had more than one round of ammunition left, though they shouted bravely:

"We are ready for the redcoats again!"

Again their first fire was furious and destructive, but although many of the enemy fell, the rest bounded forward without returning it. In a few minutes the columns of Pigot and Clinton had surrounded the redoubt on three sides. The defenders of the breastwork had been driven by the artillery fire into the redoubt, and balls came whistling through the open passage.

The first rank of redcoats who climbed the parapet was shot down. Major Pitcairn met his death at this time while cheering on his men. But the Americans had come to the end of their ammunition, and they had not fifty bayonets among them, though these were made to do good service as the enemy came swarming over the walls.

Pigot got up by the aid of a tree, and hundreds followed his lead. The Americans made stout resistance in the hand-to-hand struggle that followed, but there could be only one ending to it, and Prescott ordered a retreat. He was almost the last to leave, and only got away by skilfully parrying with his sword the bayonet thrusts of the foe. His banyan was pierced in many places, but he escaped unhurt.

The men at the rail fence kept firm until they saw the forces leaving the redoubt; they fell back then, but in good order.

A great volley was fired after the Americans. It was then that Warren fell, as he lingered in the rear—a loss that was passionately mourned throughout New England.

During their disordered flight over the little peninsula the Americans lost more men than at any other time of the day, though their list of killed and wounded only amounted to four hundred and forty-nine. The heavy loss of the enemy-ten hundred and fifty-four men-had the effect of checking the eagerness of their pursuit; the Americans passed the Neck without further molestation.

General Howe had maintained his reputation for solid courage, and his long white silk stockings were soaked in blood.

The speech of Count Vergennes, that "if it won two more such victories as Bunker Hill, there would be no more British Army in America," echoed the general sentiment in England and America as well as in France. So impressed were the British leaders with the indomitable resolution shown by the Provincials in fortifying and defending so desperate a position as Breed's Hill, that they made no attempt to follow up their victory. General Gage admitted that the people of New England were not the despicable rabble they had sometimes been represented.

Among the Grand Army itself many recriminations and courts-martial followed the contest. But Washington soon drilled it into order.

The most important thing to be remembered of Bunker Hill is its effect upon the colonies. The troubles with the mother country had been brewing a long time, but this was the first decisive struggle for supremacy. There was no doubt of the tough, soldierly qualities displayed by the Colonials; the thrill of pride that went through the country at the success of their arms welded together the scattered colonies and made a nation of them. The Revolution was an accomplished fact. "England," said Franklin, "has lost her colonies for ever."

Last Words

THE RELUCTANT VOYAGERS

CHAPTER I.

Two men sat by the sea waves.

"Well, I know I'm not handsome," said one gloomily. He was poking holes in the sand with a discontented cane.

The companion was watching the waves play. He seemed overcome with perspiring discomfort as a man who is resolved to set another man right.

Suddenly his mouth turned into a straight line. "To be sure you are not," he cried vehemently. "You look like thunder. I do not desire to be unpleasant, but I must assure you that your freckled skin continually reminds spectators of white wall paper with gilt roses on it. The top of your head looks like a little wooden plate. And your figure-heavens!"

For a time they were silent. They stared at the waves that purred near their feet like sleepy sea-kittens.

Finally the first man spoke.

"Well," said he, defiantly, "what of it?"

"What of it," exploded the other. "Why, it means that you'd look like blazes in a bathing-suit."

They were again silent. The freckled man seemed ashamed. His tall companion glowered at the scenery.

"I am decided," said the freckled man suddenly. He got boldly up from the sand and strode away. The tall man followed, walking sarcastically and glaring down at the round, resolute figure before him.

A bath-clerk was looking at the world with superior eyes through a hole in a board. To him the freckled man made application, waving his hands over his person in illustration of a snug fit. The bath-clerk thought profoundly. Eventually, he handed out a blue bundle with an air of having phenomenally solved the freckled man's dimensions.

The latter resumed his resolute stride.

"See here," said the tall man, following him, "I bet you've got a regular toga, you know. That fellow couldn't tell —"

"Yes, he could," interrupted the freckled man, "I saw correct mathematics in his eyes."

"Well, supposin' he has missed your size. Supposin' —"

"Tom," again interrupted the other, "produce your proud clothes and we'll go in."

The tall man swore bitterly. He went to one of a row of little wooden boxes and shut himself in it. His companion repaired to a similar box.

At first he felt like an opulent monk in a too-small cell, and he turned round two or three times to see if he could. He arrived finally into his bathing-dress. Immediately he dropped gasping upon a three-cornered bench. The suit fell in folds about his reclining form. There was silence, save for the caressing calls of the waves without.

Then he heard two shoes drop on the floor in one of the little coops. He began to clamour at the boards like a penitent at an unforgiving door.

"Tom," called he, "Tom —"

A voice of wrath, muffled by cloth, came through the walls. "You go t' blazes!"

The freckled man began to groan, taking the occupants of the entire row of coops into his confidence.

"Stop your noise," angrily cried the tall man from his hidden den. "You rented the bathing-suit, didn't you? Then —"

"It ain't a bathing-suit," shouted the freckled man at the boards. "It's an auditorium, a ball-room, or something. It ain't a bathing-suit."

The tall man came out of his box. His suit looked like blue skin. He walked with grandeur down the alley between the rows of coops. Stopping in front of his friend's door, he rapped on it with passionate knuckles.

"Come out of there, y' ol' fool," said he, in an enraged whisper. "It's only your accursed vanity. Wear it anyhow. What difference does it make? I never saw such a vain ol' idiot!"

As he was storming the door opened, and his friend confronted him. The tall man's legs gave way, and he fell against the opposite door.

The freckled man regarded him sternly.

"You're an ass," he said.

His back curved in scorn. He walked majestically down the alley. There was pride in the way his chubby feet patted the boards. The tall man followed, weakly, his eyes riveted upon the figure ahead.

As a disguise the freckled man had adopted the stomach of importance. He moved with an air of some sort of procession, across a board walk, down some steps, and out upon the sand.

There was a pug dog and three old women on a bench, a man and a maid with a book and a parasol, a seagull drifting high in the wind, and a distant, tremendous meeting of sea and sky. Down on the wet sand stood a girl being wooed by the breakers.

The freckled man moved with stately tread along the beach. The tall man, numb with amazement, came in the rear. They neared the girl.

Suddenly the tall man was seized with convulsions. He laughed, and the girl turned her head.

She perceived the freckled man in the bathing-suit. An expression of wonderment overspread her charming face. It changed in a moment to a pearly smile.

This smile seemed to smite the freckled man. He obviously tried to swell and fit his suit. Then he turned a shrivelling glance upon his companion, and fled up the beach. The tall man ran after him, pursuing with mocking cries that tingled his flesh like stings of insects. He seemed to be trying to lead the way out of the world. But at last he stopped and faced about.

"Tom Sharp," said he, between his clenched teeth, "you are an unutterable wretch! I could grind your bones under my heel."

The tall man was in a trance, with glazed eyes fixed on the bathing-dress. He seemed to be murmuring: "Oh, good Lord! Oh, good Lord! I never saw such a suit!"

The freckled man made the gesture of an assassin.

"Tom Sharp, you —"

The other was still murmuring: "Oh, good Lord! I never saw such a suit! I never —"

The freckled man ran down into the sea.

CHAPTER II.

The cool, swirling waters took his temper from him, and it became a thing that is lost in the ocean. The tall man floundered in, and the two forgot and rollicked in the waves.

The freckled man, in endeavouring to escape from mankind, had left all save a solitary fisherman under a large hat, and three boys in bathing-dress, laughing and splashing upon a raft made of old spars.

The two men swam softly over the ground swells.

The three boys dived from their raft, and turned their jolly faces shorewards. It twisted slowly around and around, and began to move seaward on some unknown voyage. The freckled man laid his face to the water and swam toward the raft with a practised stroke. The tall man followed, his bended arm appearing and disappearing with the precision of machinery.

The craft crept away, slowly and wearily, as if luring. The little wooden plate on the freckled man's head looked at the shore like a round, brown eye, but his gaze was fixed on the raft that slyly appeared to be waiting. The tall man used the little wooden plate as a beacon.

At length the freckled man reached the raft and climbed aboard. He lay down on his back and puffed. His bathing-dress spread about him like a dead balloon. The tall man came, snorted, shook his tangled locks and lay down by the side of his companion.

They were overcome with a delicious drowsiness. The planks of the raft seemed to fit their tired limbs. They gazed dreamily up into the vast sky of summer.

"This is great," said the tall man. His companion grunted blissfully.

Gentle hands from the sea rocked their craft and lulled them to peace. Lapping waves sang little rippling sea-songs about them. The two men issued contented groans.

"Tom," said the freckled man.

"What?" said the other.

"This is great."

They lay and thought.

A fish-hawk, soaring, suddenly turned and darted at the waves. The tall man indolently twisted his head and watched the bird plunge its claws into the water. It heavily arose with a silver gleaming fish.

"That bird has got his feet wet again. It's a shame," murmured the tall man sleepily. "He must suffer from an endless cold in the head. He should wear rubber boots. They'd look great, too. If I was him, I'd —Great Scott!"

He has partly arisen, and was looking at the shore.

He began to scream. "Ted! Ted! Ted! Look!"

"What's matter?" dreamily spoke the freckled man. "You remind me of when I put the bird-shot in your leg." He giggled softly.

The agitated tall man made a gesture of supreme eloquence. His companion up-reared and turned a startled gaze shoreward.

"Lord," he roared, as if stabbed.

The land was a long, brown streak with a rim of green, in which sparkled the tin roofs of huge hotels. The hands from the sea had pushed them away. The two men sprang erect, and did a little dance of perturbation.

"What shall we do? What shall we do?" moaned the freckled man, wriggling fantastically in his dead balloon.

The changing shore seemed to fascinate the tall man, and for a time he did not speak.

Suddenly he concluded his minuet of horror. He wheeled about and faced the freckled man. He elaborately folded his arms.

"So," he said, in slow, formidable tones. "So! This all comes from your accursed vanity, your bathing-suit, your idiocy; you have murdered your best friend."

He turned away. His companion reeled as if stricken by an unexpected arm.

He stretched out his hands. "Tom, Tom," wailed he, beseechingly, "don't be such a fool."

The broad back of his friend was occupied by a contemptuous sneer.

Three ships fell off the horizon. Landward, the hues were blending. The whistle of a loco-motive sounded from an infinite distance as if tooting in heaven.

"Tom! Tom! My dear boy," quavered the freckled man, "don't speak that way to me."

"Oh, no, of course not," said the other, still facing away and throwing the words over his shoulder. "You suppose I am going to accept all this calmly, don't you? Not make the slightest objection? Make no protest at all, hey?"

"Well, I—I—" began the freckled man.

The tall man's wrath suddenly exploded. "You've abducted me! That's the whole amount of it! You've abducted me!"

"I ain't," protested the freckled man. "You must think I'm a fool."

The tall man swore, and sitting down, dangled his legs angrily in the water. Natural law compelled his companion to occupy the other end of the raft.

Over the waters little shoals of fish spluttered, raising tiny tempests. Languid jelly-fish floated near, tremulously waving a thousand legs. A row of porpoises trundled along like a procession of cog-wheels. The sky became greyed save where over the land sunset colours were assembling.

The two voyagers, back to back and at either end of the raft, quarrelled at length.

"What did you want to follow me for?" demanded the freckled man in a voice of indignation.

"If your figure hadn't been so like a bottle, we wouldn't be here," replied the tall man.

CHAPTER III.

The fires in the west blazed away, and solemnity spread over the sea. Electric lights began to blink like eyes. Night menaced the voyagers with a dangerous darkness, and fear came to bind their souls together. They huddled fraternally in the middle of the raft.

"I feel like a molecule," said the freckled man in subdued tones.

"I'd give two dollars for a cigar," muttered the tall man.

A V-shaped flock of ducks flew towards Barnegat, between the voyagers and a remnant of yellow sky. Shadows and winds came from the vanished eastern horizon.

"I think I hear voices," said the freckled man.

"That Dollie Ramsdell was an awfully nice girl," said the tall man.

When the coldness of the sea night came to them, the freckled man found he could by a peculiar movement of his legs and arms encase himself in his bathing-dress. The tall man was compelled to whistle and shiver. As night settled finally over the sea, red and green lights began to dot the blackness. There were mysterious shadows between the waves.

"I see things comin'," murmured the freckled man.

"I wish I hadn't ordered that new dress-suit for the hop to-morrow night," said the tall man reflectively.

The sea became uneasy and heaved painfully, like a lost bosom, when little forgotten heart-bells try to chime with a pure sound. The voyagers cringed at magnified foam on distant wave crests. A moon came and looked at them.

"Somebody's here," whispered the freckled man.

"I wish I had an almanac," remarked the tall man, regarding the moon.

Presently they fell to staring at the red and green lights that twinkled about them.

"Providence will not leave us," asserted the freckled man.

"Oh, we'll be picked up shortly. I owe money," said the tall man.

He began to thrum on an imaginary banjo.

"I have heard," said he, suddenly, "that captains with healthy ships beneath their feet will never turn back after having once started on a voyage. In that case we will be rescued by some ship bound for the golden seas of the south. Then, you'll be up to some of your confounded devilment, and we'll get put off. They'll maroon us! That's what they'll do! They'll maroon us! On an island with palm trees and sun-kissed maidens and all that. Sun-kissed maidens, eh? Great! They'd —"

He suddenly ceased and turned to stone. At a distance a great, green eye was contemplating the sea wanderers.

They stood up and did another dance. As they watched the eye grew larger.

Directly the form of a phantom-like ship came into view. About the great, green eye there bobbed small yellow dots. The wanderers could hear a far-away creaking of unseen tackle and flapping of shadowy sails. There came the melody of the waters as the ship's prow thrusted its way.

The tall man delivered an oration.

"Ha!" he exclaimed, "here comes our rescuers. The brave fellows! How I long to take the manly captain by the hand! You will soon see a white boat with a star on its bow drop from the side of yon ship. Kind sailors in blue and white will help us into the boat and conduct our wasted frames to the quarter-deck, where the handsome, bearded captain, with gold bands all around, will welcome us. Then in the hard-oak cabin, while the wine gurgles and the Havana's glow, we'll tell our tale of peril and privation."

The ship came on like a black hurrying animal with froth-filled maw. The two wanderers stood up and clasped hands. Then they howled out a wild duet that rang over the wastes of sea.

The cries seemed to strike the ship.

Men with boots on yelled and ran about the deck. They picked up heavy articles and threw them down. They yelled more. After hideous creakings and flappings, the vessel stood still.

In the meantime the wanderers had been chanting their song for help. Out in the blackness they beckoned to the ship and coaxed.

A voice came to them.

"Hello," it said.

They puffed out their cheeks and began to shout. "Hello! Hello! Hello!"

"Wot do yeh want?" said the voice.

The two wanderers gazed at each other, and sat suddenly down on the raft. Some pall came sweeping over the sky and quenched their stars.

But almost the tall man got up and brawled miscellaneous information. He stamped his foot, and frowning into the night, swore threateningly.

The vessel seemed fearful of these moaning voices that called from a hidden cavern of the water. And now one voice was filled with a menace. A number of men with enormous limbs that threw vast shadows over the sea as the lanterns flickered, held a debate and made gestures.

Off in the darkness, the tall man began to clamour like a mob. The freckled man sat in astounded silence, with his legs weak.

After a time one of the men of enormous limbs seized a rope that was tugging at the stern and drew a small boat from the shadows. Three giants clambered in and rowed cautiously toward the raft. Silver water flashed in the gloom as the oars dipped.

About fifty feet from the raft the boat stopped. "Who er you?" asked a voice.

The tall man braced himself and explained. He drew vivid pictures, his twirling fingers illustrating like live brushes.

"Oh," said the three giants.

The voyagers deserted the raft. They looked back, feeling in their hearts a mite of tenderness for the wet planks. Later, they wriggled up the side of the vessel and climbed over the railing.

On deck they met a man.

He held a lantern to their faces. "Got any chewin' tewbacca?" he inquired.

"No," said the tall man, "we ain't."

The man had a bronze face and solitary whiskers. Peculiar lines about his mouth were shaped into an eternal smile of derision. His feet were bare, and clung handily to crevices.

Fearful trousers were supported by a piece of suspender that went up the wrong side of his chest and came down the right side of his back, dividing him into triangles.

"Ezekiel P. Sanford, capt'in, schooner 'Mary Jones,' of N'yack, N.Y., genelmen," he said.

"Ah!" said the tall man, "delighted, I'm sure."

There were a few moments of silence. The giants were hovering in the gloom and staring. Suddenly astonishment exploded the captain.

"Wot th' devil —" he shouted, "wot th' devil yeh got on?"

"Bathing-suits," said the tall man.

CHAPTER IV.

The schooner went on. The two voyagers sat down and watched. After a time they began to shiver. The soft blackness of the summer night passed away, and grey mists writhed over the sea. Soon lights of early dawn went changing across the sky, and the twin beacons on the highlands grew dim and sparkling faintly, as if a monster were dying. The dawn penetrated the marrow of the two men in bathing-dress.

The captain used to pause opposite them, hitch one hand in his suspender, and laugh.

"Well, I be dog-hanged," he frequently said.

The tall man grew furious. He snarled in a mad undertone to his companion. "This rescue ain't right. If I had known —"

He suddenly paused, transfixed by the captain's suspender. "It's goin' to break," cried he, in an ecstatic whisper. His eyes grew large with excitement as he watched the captain laugh. "It'll break in a minute, sure."

But the commander of the schooner recovered, and invited them to drink and eat. They followed him along the deck, and fell down a square black hole into the cabin.

It was a little den, with walls of a vanished whiteness. A lamp shed an orange light. In a sort of recess two little beds were hiding. A wooden table, immovable, as if the craft had been builded around it, sat in the middle of the floor. Overhead the square hole was studded with a dozen stars. A foot-worn ladder led to the heavens.

The captain produced ponderous crackers and some cold broiled ham. Then he vanished in the firmament like a fantastic comet.

The freckled man sat quite contentedly like a stout squaw in a blanket. The tall man walked about the cabin and sniffed. He was angered at the crudeness of the rescue, and his shrinking clothes made him feel too large. He contemplated his unhappy state.

Suddenly, he broke out. "I won't stand this, I tell you! Heavens and earth, look at the-say, what in the blazes did you want to get me in this thing for, anyhow? You're a fine old duffer, you are! Look at that ham!"

The freckled man grunted. He seemed somewhat blissful. He was seated upon a bench, comfortably enwrapped in his bathing-dress.

The tall man stormed about the cabin.

"This is an outrage! I'll see the captain! I'll tell him what I think of —"

He was interrupted by a pair of legs that appeared among the stars. The captain came down the ladder. He brought a coffee pot from the sky.

The tall man bristled forward. He was going to denounce everything.

The captain was intent upon the coffee pot, balancing it carefully, and leaving his unguided feet to find the steps of the ladder.

But the wrath of the tall man faded. He twirled his fingers in excitement, and renewed his ecstatic whisperings to the freckled man.

"It's going to break! Look, quick, look! It'll break in a minute!"

He was transfixed with interest, forgetting his wrongs in staring at the perilous passage.

But the captain arrived on the floor with triumphant suspenders.

"Well," said he, "after yeh have eat, maybe ye'd like t'sleep some! If so, yeh can sleep on them beds."

The tall man made no reply, save in a strained undertone. "It'll break in about a minute! Look, Ted, look quick!"

The freckled man glanced in a little bed on which were heaped boots and oilskins. He made a courteous gesture.

"My dear sir, we could not think of depriving you of your beds. No, indeed. Just a couple of blankets if you have them, and we'll sleep very comfortable on these benches."

The captain protested, politely twisting his back and bobbing his head. The suspenders tugged and creaked. The tall man partially suppressed a cry, and took a step forward.

The freckled man was sleepily insistent, and shortly the captain gave over his deprecatory contortions. He fetched a pink quilt with yellow dots on it to the freckled man, and a black one with red roses on it to the tall man.

Again he vanished in the firmament. The tall man gazed until the last remnant of trousers disappeared from the sky. Then he wrapped himself up in his quilt and lay down. The freckled man was puffing contentedly, swathed like an infant. The yellow polka-dots rose and fell on the vast pink of his chest.

The wanderers slept. In the quiet could be heard the groanings of timbers as the sea seemed to crunch them together. The lapping of water along the vessel's side sounded like gaspings. An hundred spirits of the wind had got their wings entangled in the rigging, and, in soft voices, were pleading to be loosened.

The freckled man was awakened by a foreign noise. He opened his eyes and saw his companion standing by his couch.

His comrade's face was wane with suffering. His eyes glowed in the darkness. He raised his arms, spreading them out like a clergyman at a grave. He groaned deep in his chest.

"Good Lord!" yelled the freckled man, starting up. "Tom, Tom, what's th' matter?"

The tall man spoke in a fearful voice. "To New York," he said, "to New York in our bathing-suits."

The freckled man sank back. The shadows of the cabin threw mysteries about the figure of the tall man, arrayed like some ancient and potent astrologer in the black quilt with the red roses on it.

CHAPTER V.

Directly the tall man went and lay down and began to groan.

The freckled man felt the miseries of the world upon him. He grew angry at the tall man awakening him. They quarrelled.

"Well," said the tall man, finally, "we're in a fix."

"I know that," said the other, sharply.

They regarded the ceiling in silence.

"What in the thunder are we going to do?" demanded the tall man, after a time. His companion was still silent. "Say," repeated he, angrily, "what in the thunder are we going to do?"

"I'm sure I don't know," said the freckled man in a dismal voice.

"Well, think of something," roared the other. "Think of something, you old fool. You don't want to make any more idiots of yourself, do you?"

"I ain't made an idiot of myself."

"Well, think. Know anybody in the city?"

"I know a fellow up in Harlem," said the freckled man.

"You know a fellow up in Harlem," howled the tall man. "Up in Harlem! How the dickens are we to-say, you're crazy!"

"We can take a cab," cried the other, waxing indignant.

The tall man grew suddenly calm. "Do you know any one else?" he asked, measuredly.

"I know another fellow somewhere on Park Place."

"Somewhere on Park Place," repeated the tall man in an unnatural manner. "Somewhere on Park Place." With an air of sublime resignation he turned his face to the wall.

The freckled man sat erect and frowned in the direction of his companion. "Well, now, I suppose you are going to sulk. You make me ill! It's the best we can do, ain't it? Hire a cab and go look that fellow up on Park-What's that? You can't afford it? What nonsense! You are getting-Oh! Well, maybe we can beg some clothes of the captain. Eh? Did I see 'im. Certainly, I saw 'im. Yes, it is improbable that a man who wears trousers like that can have clothes to lend. No, I won't wear oilskins and a sou'-wester. To Athens? Of course not! I don't know where it is. Do you? I thought not. With all your grumbling about other people, you never know anything important yourself. What? Broadway? I'll be hanged first. We can get off at Harlem, man alive. There are no cabs in Harlem. I don't think we can bribe a sailor to take us ashore and bring a cab to the dock, for the very simple reason that we have nothing to bribe him with. What? No, of course not. See here, Tom Sharp, don't you swear at me like that. I won't have it. What's that? I ain't, either. I ain't. What? I am not. It's no such thing. I ain't. I've got more than you have, anyway. Well, you ain't doing anything so very brilliant yourself-just lying there and cussin'." At length the tall man feigned to prodigiously snore. The freckled man thought with such vigour that he fell asleep.

After a time he dreamed that he was in a forest where bass drums grew on trees. There came a strong wind that banged the fruit about like empty pods. A frightful din was in his ears.

He awoke to find the captain of the schooner standing over him.

"We're at New York now," said the captain, raising his voice above the thumping and banging that was being done on deck, "an' I s'pose you fellers wanta go ashore." He chuckled in an exasperating manner. "Jes' sing out when yeh wanta go," he added, leering at the freckled man.

The tall man awoke, came over and grasped the captain by the throat.

"If you laugh again I'll kill you," he said.

The captain gurgled and waved his legs and arms.

"In the first place," the tall man continued, "you rescued us in a deucedly shabby manner. It makes me ill to think of it. I've a mind to mop you 'round just for that. In the second place, your vessel is bound for Athens, N.Y., and there's no sense in it. Now, will you or will you not turn this ship about and take us back where our clothes are, or to Philadelphia, where we belong?"

He furiously shook the captain. Then he eased his grip and awaited a reply.

"I can't," yelled the captain, "I can't. This vessel don't belong to me. I've got to —"

"Well, then," interrupted the tall man, "can you lend us some clothes?"

"Hain't got none," replied the captain, promptly. His face was red, and his eyes were glaring.

"Well, then," said the tall man, "can you lend us some money?"

"Hain't got none," replied the captain, promptly. Something overcame him and he laughed.

"Thunderation," roared the tall man. He seized the captain, who began to have wriggling contortions. The tall man kneaded him as if he were biscuits. "You infernal scoundrel," he bellowed, "this whole affair is some wretched plot, and you are in it. I am about to kill you."

The solitary whisker of the captain did acrobatic feats like a strange demon upon his chin. His eyes stood perilously from his head. The suspender wheezed and tugged like the tackle of a sail.

Suddenly the tall man released his hold. Great expectancy sat upon his features. "It's going to break," he cried, rubbing his hands.

But the captain howled and vanished in the sky.

The freckled man then came forward. He appeared filled with sarcasm.

"So!" said he. "So, you've settled the matter. The captain is the only man in the world who can help us, and I daresay he'll do anything he can now."

"That's all right," said the tall man. "If you don't like the way I run things you shouldn't have come on this trip at all."

They had another quarrel.

At the end of it they went on deck. The captain stood at the stern addressing the bow with opprobrious language. When he perceived the voyagers he began to fling his fists about in the air.

"I'm goin' to put yeh off," he yelled. The wanderers stared at each other.

"Hum," said the tall man.

The freckled man looked at his companion. "He's going to put us off, you see," he said, complacently.

The tall man began to walk about and move his shoulders. "I'd like to see you do it," he said, defiantly.

The captain tugged at a rope. A boat came at his bidding.

"I'd like to see you do it," the tall man repeated, continually. An imperturbable man in rubber boots climbed down in the boat and seized the oars. The captain motioned downward. His whisker had a triumphant appearance.

The two wanderers looked at the boat. "I guess we'll have to get in," murmured the freckled man.

The tall man was standing like a granite column. "I won't," said he. "I won't! I don't care what you do, but I won't!"

"Well, but —" expostulated the other. They held a furious debate.

In the meantime the captain was darting about making sinister gestures, but the back of the tall man held him at bay. The crew, much depleted by the departure of the imperturbable man into the boat, looked on from the bow.

"You're a fool," the freckled man concluded his argument.

"So?" inquired the tall man, highly exasperated.

"So? Well, if you think you're so bright, we'll go in the boat, and then you'll see."

He climbed down into the craft and seated himself in an ominous manner at the stern.

"You'll see," he said to his companion, as the latter floundered heavily down. "You'll see!"

The man in rubber boots calmly rowed the boat toward the shore. As they went, the captain leaned over the railing and laughed. The freckled man was seated very victoriously.

"Well, wasn't this the right thing after all?" he inquired in a pleasant voice. The tall man made no reply.

CHAPTER VI.

As they neared the dock something seemed suddenly to occur to the freckled man.

"Great heavens," he murmured. He stared at the approaching shore.

"My, what a plight, Tommy," he quavered.

"Do you think so?" spoke up the tall man, "Why, I really thought you liked it." He laughed in a hard voice. "Lord, what a figure you'll cut."

This laugh jarred the freckled man's soul. He became mad.

"Thunderation, turn the boat around," he roared. "Turn 'er round, quick. Man alive, we can't —turn 'er round, d'ye hear."

The tall man in the stern gazed at his companion with glowing eyes.

"Certainly not," he said. "We're going on. You insisted upon it." He began to prod his companion with words.

The freckled man stood up and waved his arms.

"Sit down," said the tall man. "You'll tip the boat over."

The other man began to shout.

"Sit down," said the tall man again.

Words bubbled from the freckled man's mouth. There was a little torrent of sentences that almost choked him. And he protested passionately with his hands.

But the boat went on to the shadow of the docks. The tall man was intent upon balancing it as it rocked dangerously during his comrade's oration.

"Sit down," he continually repeated.

"I won't," raged the freckled man. "I won't do anything." The boat wobbled with these words.

"Say," he continued, addressing the oarsman, "just turn this boat round, will you. Where in the thunder are you taking us to, anyhow?"

The oarsman looked at the sky and thought. Finally he spoke. "I'm doin' what the cap'n sed."

"Well, what in th' blazes do I care what the cap'n sed?" demanded the freckled man. He took a violent step. "You just turn this round or —"

The small craft reeled. Over one side water came flashing in. The freckled man cried out in fear, and gave a jump to the other side. The tall man roared orders, and the oarsman made efforts. The boat acted for a moment like an animal on a slackened wire. Then it upset.

"Sit down," said the tall man, in a final roar as he was plunged into the water. The oarsman dropped his oars to grapple with the gunwale. He went down saying unknown words. The freckled man's explanation or apology was strangled by the water.

Two or three tugs let off whistles of astonishment, and continued on their paths. A man dosing on a dock aroused and began to caper. The passengers of a ferry-boat all ran to the near railing.

A miraculous person in a small boat was bobbing on the waves near the piers. He sculled hastily toward the scene. It was a swirl of waters in the midst of which the dark bottom of the boat appeared, whale-like.

Two heads suddenly came up. "839," said the freckled man, chokingly. "That's it! 839!"

"What is?" said the tall man.

"That's the number of that feller on Park Place. I just remembered."

"You're the bloomingest —" the tall man said.

"It wasn't my fault," interrupted his companion. "If you hadn't —" He tried to gesticulate, but one hand held to the keel of the boat, and the other was supporting the form of the oarsman. The latter had fought a battle with his immense rubber boots and had been conquered.

The rescuer in the other small boat came fiercely. As his craft glided up, he reached out and grasped the tall man by the collar and dragged him into the boat, interrupting what was, under the circumstances, a very brilliant flow of rhetoric directed at the freckled man. The oarsman of the wrecked craft was taken tenderly over the gunwale and laid in the bottom of the boat. Puffing and blowing, the freckled man climbed in.

"You'll upset this one before we can get ashore," the other voyager remarked.

As they turned toward the land they saw that the nearest dock was lined with people. The freckled man gave a little moan.

But the staring eyes of the crowd were fixed on the limp form of the man in rubber boots. A hundred hands reached down to help lift the body up. On the dock some men grabbed it and began to beat it and roll it. A policeman tossed the spectators about. Each individual in the heaving crowd sought to fasten his eyes on the blue-tinted face of the man in the rubber boots. They surged to and fro, while the policeman beat them indiscriminately.

The wanderers came modestly up the dock and gazed shrinkingly at the throng. They stood for a moment, holding their breath to see the first finger of amazement levelled at them.

But the crowd bended and surged in absorbing anxiety to view the man in rubber boots, whose face fascinated them. The sea-wanderers were as though they were not there.

They stood without the jam and whispered hurriedly.

"839," said the freckled man.

"All right," said the tall man.

Under the pommeling hands the oarsman showed signs of life. The voyagers watched him make a protesting kick at the leg of the crowd, the while uttering angry groans.

"He's better," said the tall man, softly; "let's make off."

Together they stole noiselessly up the dock. Directly in front of it they found a row of six cabs.

The drivers on top were filled with a mighty curiosity. They had driven hurriedly from the adjacent ferry-house when they had seen the first running sign of an accident. They were straining on their toes and gazing at the tossing backs of the men in the crowd.

The wanderers made a little detour, and then went rapidly towards a cab. They stopped in front of it and looked up.

"Driver," called the tall man, softly.

The man was intent.

"Driver," breathed the freckled man. They stood for a moment and gazed imploringly.

The cabman suddenly moved his feet. "By Jimmy, I bet he's a gonner," he said, in an ecstacy, and he again relapsed into a statue.

The freckled man groaned and wrung his hands. The tall man climbed into the cab.

"Come in here," he said to his companion. The freckled man climbed in, and the tall man reached over and pulled the door shut. Then he put his head out the window.

"Driver," he roared, sternly, "839 Park Place-and quick."

The driver looked down and met the eye of the tall man. "Eh? —Oh —839? Park Place? Yessir." He reluctantly gave his horse a clump on the back. As the conveyance rattled off the wanderers huddled back among the dingy cushions and heaved great breaths of relief.

"Well, it's all over," said the freckled man, finally. "We're about out of it. And quicker than I expected. Much quicker. It looked to me sometimes that we were doomed. I am thankful to find it not so. I am rejoiced. And I hope and trust that you-well, I don't wish, to-perhaps it is not the proper time to-that is, I don't wish to intrude a moral at an inopportune moment, but, my dear, dear fellow, I think the time is ripe to point out to you that your obstinacy, your selfishness, your villainous temper, and your various other faults can make it just as unpleasant for your ownself, my dear boy, as they frequently do for other people. You can see what you brought us to, and I most sincerely hope, my dear, dear fellow, that I shall soon see those signs in you which shall lead me to believe that you have become a wiser man."

SPITZBERGEN TALES

THE KICKING TWELFTH

The Spitzbergen army was backed by tradition of centuries of victory. In its chronicles, occasional defeats were not printed in italics, but were likely to appear as glorious stands against overwhelming odds. A favourite way to dispose of them was frankly to attribute them to the blunders of the civilian heads of government. This was very good for the army, and probably no army had more self-confidence. When it was announced that an expeditionary force was to be sent to Rostina to chastise an impudent people, a hundred barrack squares filled with excited men, and a hundred sergeant-majors hurried silently through the groups, and succeeded in looking as if they were the repositories of the secrets of empire. Officers on leave sped joyfully back to their harness, and recruits were abused with unflagging devotion by every man, from colonels to privates of experience.

The Twelfth Regiment of the Line-the Kicking Twelfth-was consumed with a dread that it was not to be included in the expedition, and the regiment formed itself into an informal indignation meeting. Just as they had proved that a great outrage was about to be perpetrated, warning orders arrived to hold themselves in readiness for active service abroad-in Rostina. The barrack yard was in a flash transferred into a blue-and-buff pandemonium, and the official bugle itself hardly had power to quell the glad disturbance.

Thus it was that early in the spring the Kicking Twelfth-sixteen hundred men in service equipment-found itself crawling along a road in Rostina. They did not form part of the main force, but belonged to a column of four regiments of foot, two batteries of field guns, a battery of mountain howitzers, a regiment of horse, and a company of engineers. Nothing had happened. The long column had crawled without amusement of any kind through a broad green valley. Big white farm-houses dotted the slopes; but there was no sign of man or beast, and no smoke from the chimneys. The column was operating from its own base, and its general was expected to form a junction with the main body at a given point.

A squadron of the cavalry was fanned out ahead, scouting, and day by day the trudging infantry watched the blue uniforms of the horsemen as they came and went. Sometimes there would sound the faint thuds of a few shots, but the cavalry was unable to find anything to engage.

The Twelfth had no record of foreign service, and it could hardly be said that it had served as a unit in the great civil war, when His Majesty the King had whipped the Pretender. At that time the regiment had suffered from two opinions, so that it was impossible for either side to depend upon it. Many men had deserted to the standard of the Pretender, and a number of officers had drawn their swords for him. When the King, a thorough soldier, looked at the remnant, he saw that they lacked the spirit to be of great help to him in the tremendous battles which he was waging for his throne. And so this emaciated Twelfth was sent off to a corner of the kingdom to guard a dockyard, where some of the officers so plainly expressed their disapproval of this policy that the regiment received its steadfast name, the Kicking Twelfth.

At the time of which I am writing the Twelfth had a few veteran officers and well-bitten sergeants; but the body of the regiment was composed of men who had never heard a shot fired excepting on the rifle-range. But it was an experience for which they longed, and when the moment came for the corps' cry —"Kim up, the Kickers" —there was not likely to be a man who would not go tumbling after his leaders.

Young Timothy Lean was a second lieutenant in the first company of the third battalion, and just at this time he was pattering along at the flank of the men, keeping a fatherly lookout for boots that hurt and packs that sagged. He was extremely bored. The mere far-away sound of desultory shooting was not war as he had been led to believe it.

It did not appear that behind that freckled face and under that red hair there was a mind which dreamed of blood. He was not extremely anxious to kill somebody, but he was very fond of soldiering-it had been the career of his father and of his grandfather-and he understood that the profession of arms lost much of its point unless a man shot at people and had people shoot at him. Strolling in the sun through a practically deserted country might be a proper occupation for a divinity student on a vacation, but the soul of Timothy Lean was in revolt at it. Some times at night he would go morosely to the camp of the cavalry and hear the infant subalterns laughingly exaggerate the comedy side of the adventures which they had had out with small patrols far ahead. Lean would sit and listen in glum silence to these tales, and dislike the young officers-many of them old military school friends-for having had experience in modern warfare.

"Anyhow," he said savagely, "presently you'll be getting into a lot of trouble, and then the Foot will have to come along and pull you out. We always do. That's history."

"Oh, we can take care of ourselves," said the Cavalry, with good-natured understanding of his mood.

But the next day even Lean blessed the cavalry, for excited troopers came whirling back from the front, bending over their speeding horses, and shouting wildly and hoarsely for the infantry to clear the way. Men yelled at them from the roadside as courier followed courier, and from the distance ahead sounded in quick succession six booms from field guns. The information possessed by the couriers was no longer precious. Everybody knew what a battery meant when it spoke. The bugles cried out, and the long column jolted into a halt. Old Colonel Sponge went bouncing in his saddle back to see the general, and the regiment sat down in the grass by the roadside, and waited in silence. Presently the second squadron of the cavalry trotted off along the road in a cloud of dust, and in due time old Colonel Sponge came bouncing back, and palavered his three majors and his adjutant. Then there was more talk by the majors, and gradually through the correct channels spread information which in due time reached Timothy Lean.

The enemy, 5000 strong, occupied a pass at the head of the valley some four miles beyond. They had three batteries well posted. Their infantry was entrenched. The ground in their front was crossed and lined with many ditches and hedges; but the enemy's batteries were so posted that it was doubtful if a ditch would ever prove convenient as shelter for the Spitzbergen infantry.

There was a fair position for the Spitzbergen artillery 2300 yards from the enemy. The cavalry had succeeded in driving the enemy's skirmishers back upon the main body; but, of course, had only tried to worry them a little. The position was almost inaccessible on the enemy's right, owing to steep hills, which had been crowned by small parties of infantry. The enemy's left, although guarded by a much larger force, was approachable, and might be flanked. This was what the cavalry had to say, and it added briefly a report of two troopers killed and five wounded.

Whereupon Major-General Richie, commanding a force of 7500 men of His Majesty of Spitzbergen, set in motion, with a few simple words, the machinery which would launch his army at the enemy. The Twelfth understood the orders when they saw the smart young aide approaching old Colonel Sponge, and they rose as one man, apparently afraid that they would be late. There was a clank of accoutrements. Men shrugged their shoulders tighter against their packs, and thrusting their thumbs between their belts and their tunics, they wriggled into a closer fit with regard to the heavy ammunition equipment. It is curious to note that almost every man took off his cap, and looked contemplatively into it as if to read a maker's name. Then they replaced their caps with great care. There was little talking, and it was not observable that a single soldier handed a token or left a comrade with a message to be delivered in case he should be killed. They did not seem to think of being killed; they seemed absorbed in a desire to know what would happen, and how it would look when it was happening. Men glanced continually at their officers in a plain desire to be quick to understand the very first order that would be given; and officers looked gravely at their men, measuring them, feeling their temper, worrying about them.

A bugle called; there were sharp cries, and the Kicking Twelfth was off to battle.

The regiment had the right of line in the infantry brigade, and the men tramped noisily along the white road, every eye was strained ahead; but, after all, there was nothing to be seen but a dozen farms-in short, a country-side. It resembled the scenery in Spitzbergen; every man in the Kicking Twelfth had often confronted a dozen such farms with a composure which amounted to indifference. But still down the road came galloping troopers, who delivered information to Colonel Sponge and then galloped on. In time the Twelfth came to the top of a rise, and below them on the plain was the heavy black streak of a Spitzbergen squadron, and behind the squadron loomed the grey bare hill of the Rostina position.

There was a little of skirmish firing. The Twelfth reached a knoll, which the officers easily recognised as the place described by the cavalry as suitable for the Spitzbergen guns. The men swarmed up it in a peculiar formation. They resembled a crowd coming off a race track; but, nevertheless, there was no stray sheep. It was simply that the ground on which actual battles are fought is not like a chess board. And after them came swinging a six-gun battery, the guns wagging from side to side as the long line turned out of the road, and the drivers using their whips as the leading horses scrambled at the hill. The halted Twelfth lifted its voice and spoke amiably, but with point, to the battery.

"Go on, Guns! We'll take care of you. Don't be afraid. Give it to them!" The teams-lead, swing and wheel-struggled and slipped over the steep and uneven ground; and the gunners, as they clung to their springless positions, wore their usual and natural airs of unhappiness. They made no reply to the infantry. Once upon the top of the hill, however, these guns were unlimbered in a flash, and directly the infantry could hear the loud voice of an officer drawling out the time for fuses. A moment later the first 3·2 bellowed out, and there could be heard the swish and the snarl of a fleeting shell.

Colonel Sponge and a number of officers climbed to the battery's position; but the men of the regiment sat in the shelter of the hill, like so many blindfolded people, and wondered what they would have been able to see if they had been officers. Sometimes the shells of the enemy came sweeping over the top of the hill, and burst in great brown explosions in the fields to the rear. The men looked after them and laughed. To the rear could be seen also the mountain battery coming at a comic trot, with every man obviously in a deep rage with every mule. If a man can put in long service with a mule battery and come out of it with an amiable disposition, he should be presented with a medal weighing many ounces. After the mule battery came a long black winding thing, which was three regiments of Spitzbergen infantry; and at the backs of them and to the right was an inky square, which was the remaining Spitzbergen guns. General Richie and his staff clattered up the hill. The blindfolded Twelfth sat still. The inky square suddenly became a long racing line. The howitzers joined their little bark to the thunder of the guns on the hill, and the three regiments of infantry came on. The Twelfth sat still.

Of a sudden a bugle rang its warning, and the officers shouted. Some used the old cry, "Attention! Kim up, the Kickers!" —and the Twelfth knew that it had been told to go on. The majority of the men expected to see great things as soon as they rounded the shoulder of the hill; but there was nothing to be seen save a complicated plain and the grey knolls occupied by the enemy. Many company commanders in low voices worked at their men, and said things which do not appear in the written reports. They talked soothingly; they talked indignantly; and they talked always like fathers. And the men heard no sentences completely; they heard no specific direction, these wide-eyed men. They understood that there was being delivered some kind of exhortation to do as they had been taught, and they also understood that a superior intelligence was anxious over their behaviour and welfare.

There was a great deal of floundering through hedges, climbing of walls and jumping of ditches. Curiously original privates tried to find new and easier ways for themselves, instead of following the men in front of them. Officers had short fits of fury over these people. The more originality they possessed, the more likely they were to become separated from their companies. Colonel Sponge was making an exciting progress on a big charger. When the first song of the bullets came from above, the men wondered why he sat so high; the charger seemed as tall as the Eiffel Tower. But if he was high in the air, he had a fine view, and that supposedly is why people ascend the Eiffel Tower. Very often he had been a joke to them, but when they saw this fat, old gentleman so coolly treating the strange new missiles which hummed in the air, it struck them suddenly that they had wronged him seriously; and a man who could attain the command of a Spitzbergen regiment was entitled to general respect. And they gave him a sudden, quick affection-an affection that would make them follow him heartily, trustfully, grandly-this fat, old gentleman, seated on a too-big horse. In a flash his tousled grey head, his short, thick legs, even his paunch, had become specially and humorously endeared to them. And this is the way of soldiers.

But still the Twelfth had not yet come to the place where tumbling bodies begin their test of the very heart of a regiment. They backed through more hedges, jumped more ditches, slid over more walls. The Rostina artillery had seemed to be asleep; but suddenly the guns aroused like dogs from their kennels, and around the Twelfth there began a wild, swift screeching. There arose cries to hurry, to come on; and, as the rifle bullets began to plunge into them, the men saw the high, formidable hills of the enemy's right, and perfectly understood that they were doomed to storm them. The cheering thing was the sudden beginning of a tremendous uproar on the enemy's left.

Every man ran, hard, tense, breathless. When they reached the foot of the hills, they thought they had won the charge already, but they were electrified to see officers above them waving their swords and yelling with anger, surprise, and shame. With a long murmurous outcry the Twelfth began to climb the hill; and as they went and fell, they could hear frenzied shouts —"Kim up, the Kickers!" The pace was slow. It was like the rising of a tide; it was determined, almost relentless in its appearance, but it was slow. If a man fell there was a chance that he would land twenty yards below the point where he was hit. The Kickers crawled, their rifles in their left hands as they pulled and tugged themselves up with their right hands. Ever arose the shout, "Kim up, the Kickers!" Timothy Lean, his face flaming, his eyes wild, yelled it back as if he were delivering the gospel.

The Kickers came up. The enemy-they had been in small force, thinking the hills safe enough from attack-retreated quickly from this preposterous advance, and not a bayonet in the Twelfth saw blood; bayonets very seldom do.

The homing of this successful charge wore an unromantic aspect. About twenty windless men suddenly arrived, and threw themselves upon the crest of the hill, and breathed. And these twenty were joined by others, and still others, until almost 1100 men of the Twelfth lay upon the hilltop, while the regiment's track was marked by body after body, in groups and singly. The first officer-perchance the first man, one never can be certain-the first officer to gain the top of the hill was Timothy Lean, and such was the situation that he had the honour to receive his colonel with a bashful salute.

The regiment knew exactly what it had done; it did not have to wait to be told by the Spitzbergen newspapers. It had taken a formidable position with the loss of about five hundred men, and it knew it. It knew, too, that it was great glory for the Kicking Twelfth; and as the men lay rolling on their bellies, they expressed their joy in a wild cry —"Kim up, the Kickers!" For a moment there was nothing but joy, and then suddenly company commanders were besieged by men who wished to go down the path of the charge and look for their mates. The answers were without the quality of mercy; they were short, snapped, quick words, "No; you can't."

The attack on the enemy's left was sounding in great rolling crashes. The shells in their flight through the air made a noise as of red-hot iron plunged into water, and stray bullets nipped near the ears of the Kickers.

The Kickers looked and saw. The battle was below them. The enemy were indicated by a long, noisy line of gossamer smoke, although there could be seen a toy battery with tiny men employed at the guns. All over the field the shrapnel was bursting, making quick bulbs of white smoke. Far away, two regiments of Spitzbergen infantry were charging, and at the distance this charge looked like a casual stroll. It appeared that small black groups of men were walking meditatively toward the Rostina entrenchments.

There would have been orders given sooner to the Twelfth, but unfortunately Colonel Sponge arrived on top of the hill without a breath of wind in his body. He could not have given an order to save the regiment from being wiped off the earth. Finally he was able to gasp out something and point at the enemy. Timothy Lean ran along the line yelling to the men to sight at 800 yards; and like a slow and ponderous machine the regiment again went to work. The fire flanked a great part of the enemy's trenches.

It could be said that there were only two prominent points of view expressed by the men after their victorious arrival on the crest. One was defined in the exulting use of the corps' cry. The other was a grief-stricken murmur which is invariably heard after a fight —"My God, we're all cut to pieces!"

Colonel Sponge sat on the ground and impatiently waited for his wind to return. As soon as it did, he arose and cried out, "Form up, and we'll charge again! We will win this battle as soon as we can hit them!" The shouts of the officers sounded wild, like men yelling on ship-board in a gale. And the obedient Kickers arose for their task. It was running down hill this time. The mob of panting men poured over the stones.

But the enemy had not been blind to the great advantage gained by the Twelfth, and they now turned upon them a desperate fire of small arms. Men fell in every imaginable way, and their accoutrements rattled on the rocky ground. Some landed with a crash, floored by some tremendous blows; others dropped gently down like sacks of meal; with others, it would positively appear that some spirit had suddenly seized them by their ankles and jerked their legs from under them. Many officers were down, but Colonel Sponge, stuttering and blowing, was still upright. He was almost the last man in the charge, but not to his shame, rather to his stumpy legs. At one time it seemed that the assault would be lost. The effect of the fire was somewhat as if a terrible cyclone were blowing in the men's faces. They wavered, lowering their heads and shouldering weakly, as if it were impossible to make headway against the wind of battle. It was the moment of despair, the moment of the heroism which comes to the chosen of the war-god.

The colonel's cry broke and screeched absolute hatred; other officers simply howled; and the men, silent, debased, seemed to tighten their muscles for one last effort. Again they pushed against this mysterious power of the air, and once more the regiment was charging. Timothy Lean, agile and strong, was well in advance; and afterwards he reflected that the men who had been nearest to him were an old grizzled sergeant who would have gone to hell for the honour of the regiment, and a pie-faced lad who had been obliged to lie about his age in order to get into the army.

There was no shock of meeting. The Twelfth came down on a corner of the trenches, and as soon as the enemy had ascertained that the Twelfth was certain to arrive, they scuttled out, running close to the earth and spending no time in glances backward. In these days it is not discreet to wait for a charge to come home. You observe the charge, you attempt to stop it, and if you find that you can't, it is better to retire immediately to some other place. The Rostina soldiers were not heroes, perhaps, but they were men of sense. A maddened and badly-frightened mob of Kickers came tumbling into the trench, and shot at the backs of fleeing men. And at that very moment the action was won, and won by the Kickers. The enemy's flank was entirely crippled, and, knowing this, he did not await further and more disastrous information. The Twelfth looked at themselves and knew that they had a record. They sat down and grinned patronisingly as they saw the batteries galloping to advance position to shell the retreat, and they really laughed as the cavalry swept tumultuously forward.

The Twelfth had no more concern with the battle. They had won it, and the subsequent proceedings were only amusing.

There was a call from the flank, and the men wearily adjusted themselves as General Richie, stern and grim as a Roman, looked with his straight glance at a hammered and thin and dirty line of figures, which was His Majesty's Twelfth Regiment of the Line. When opposite old Colonel Sponge, a podgy figure standing at attention, the general's face set in still more grim and stern lines. He took off his helmet. "Kim up, the Kickers!" said he. He replaced his helmet and rode off. Down the cheeks of the little fat colonel rolled tears. He stood like a stone for a long moment, and wheeled in supreme wrath upon his surprised adjutant. "Delahaye, you d —d fool, don't stand there staring like a monkey! Go, tell young Lean I want to see him." The adjutant jumped as if he were on springs, and went after Lean. That young officer presented himself directly, his face covered with disgraceful smudges, and he had also torn his breeches. He had never seen the colonel in such a rage. "Lean, you young whelp! you-you're a good boy." And even as the general had turned away from the colonel, the colonel turned away from the lieutenant.

THE UPTURNED FACE.

"What will we do now?" said the adjutant, troubled and excited.

"Bury him," said Timothy Lean.

The two officers looked down close to their toes where lay the body of their comrade. The face was chalk-blue; gleaming eyes stared at the sky. Over the two upright figures was a windy sound of bullets, and on the top of the hill Lean's prostrate company of Spitzbergen infantry was firing measured volleys.

"Don't you think it would be better —" began the adjutant, "we might leave him until to-morrow."

"No," said Lean. "I can't hold that post an hour longer. I've got to fall back, and we've got to bury old Bill."

"Of course," said the adjutant, at once. "Your men got intrenching tools?"

Lean shouted back to his little line, and two men came slowly, one with a pick, one with a shovel. They started in the direction of the Rostina sharpshooters. Bullets cracked near their ears. "Dig here," said Lean gruffly. The men, thus caused to lower their glances to the turf, became hurried and frightened merely because they could not look to see whence the bullets came. The dull beat of the pick striking the earth sounded amid the swift snap of close bullets. Presently the other private began to shovel.

"I suppose," said the adjutant, slowly, "we'd better search his clothes for-things."

Lean nodded. Together in curious abstraction they looked at the body. Then Lean stirred his shoulders suddenly, arousing himself.

"Yes," he said, "we'd better see what he's got." He dropped to his knees, and his hands approached the body of the dead officer. But his hands wavered over the buttons of the tunic. The first button was brick-red with drying blood, and he did not seem to dare touch it.

"Go on," said the adjutant, hoarsely.

Lean stretched his wooden hand, and his fingers fumbled the blood-stained buttons. At last he rose with ghastly face. He had gathered a watch, a whistle, a pipe, a tobacco pouch, a handkerchief, a little case of cards and papers. He looked at the adjutant. There was a silence. The adjutant was feeling that he had been a coward to make Lean do all the grizzly business.

"Well," said Lean, "that's all, I think. You have his sword and revolver?"

"Yes," said the adjutant, his face working, and then he burst out in a sudden strange fury at the two privates. "Why don't you hurry up with that grave? What are you doing, anyhow? Hurry, do you hear? I never saw such stupid —"

Even as he cried out in his passion the two men were labouring for their lives. Ever overhead the bullets were spitting.

The grave was finished. It was not a masterpiece —a poor little shallow thing. Lean and the adjutant again looked at each other in a curious silent communication.

Suddenly the adjutant croaked out a weird laugh. It was a terrible laugh, which had its origin in that part of the mind which is first moved by the singing of the nerves. "Well," he said, humorously to Lean, "I suppose we had best tumble him in."

"Yes," said Lean. The two privates stood waiting, bent over their implements. "I suppose," said Lean, "it would be better if we laid him in ourselves."

"Yes," said the adjutant. Then apparently remembering that he had made Lean search the body, he stooped with great fortitude and took hold of the dead officer's clothing. Lean joined him. Both were particular that their fingers should not feel the corpse. They tugged away; the corpse lifted, heaved, toppled, flopped into the grave, and the two officers, straightening, looked again at each other-they were always looking at each other. They sighed with relief.

The adjutant said, "I suppose we should-we should say something. Do you know the service, Tim?"

"They don't read the service until the grave is filled in," said Lean, pressing his lips to an academic expression.

"Don't they?" said the adjutant, shocked that he had made the mistake.

"Oh, well," he cried, suddenly, "let us-let us say something-while he can hear us."

"All right," said Lean. "Do you know the service?"

"I can't remember a line of it," said the adjutant.

Lean was extremely dubious. "I can repeat two lines, but —"

"Well, do it," said the adjutant. "Go as far as you can. That's better than nothing. And the beasts have got our range exactly."

Lean looked at his two men. "Attention," he barked. The privates came to attention with a click, looking much aggrieved. The adjutant lowered his helmet to his knee. Lean, bareheaded, stood over the grave. The Rostina sharpshooters fired briskly.

"Oh Father, our friend has sunk in the deep waters of death, but his spirit has leaped toward Thee as the bubble arises from the lips of the drowning. Perceive, we beseech, Oh Father, the little flying bubble, and —"

Lean, although husky and ashamed, had suffered no hesitation up to this point, but he stopped with a hopeless feeling and looked at the corpse.

The adjutant moved uneasily. "And from Thy superb heights —" he began, and then he too came to an end.

"And from Thy superb heights," said Lean.

The adjutant suddenly remembered a phrase in the back part of the Spitzbergen burial service, and he exploited it with the triumphant manner of a man who has recalled everything, and can go on.

"Oh God, have mercy —"

"Oh God, have mercy —" said Lean.

"Mercy," repeated the adjutant, in quick failure.

"Mercy," said Lean. And then he was moved by some violence of feeling, for he turned suddenly upon his two men and tigerishly said, "Throw the dirt in."

The fire of the Rostina sharpshooters was accurate and continuous.

* * * * * * *

One of the aggrieved privates came forward with his shovel. He lifted his first shovel-load of earth, and for a moment of inexplicable hesitation it was held poised above this corpse, which from its chalk-blue face looked keenly out from the grave. Then the soldier emptied his shovel on-on the feet.

Timothy Lean felt as if tons had been swiftly lifted from off his forehead. He had felt that perhaps the private might empty the shovel on-on the face. It had been emptied on the feet. There was a great point gained there-ha, ha! —the first shovelful had been emptied on the feet. How satisfactory!

The adjutant began to babble. "Well, of course —a man we've messed with all these years-impossible-you can't, you know, leave your intimate friends rotting on the field. Go on, for God's sake, and shovel, you."

The man with the shovel suddenly ducked, grabbed his left arm with his right hand, and looked at his officer for orders. Lean picked the shovel from the ground. "Go to the rear," he said to the wounded man. He also addressed the other private. "You get under cover, too; I'll finish this business."

The wounded man scrambled hard still for the top of the ridge without devoting any glances to the direction from whence the bullets came, and the other man followed at an equal pace; but he was different, in that he looked back anxiously three times.

This is merely the way-often-of the hit and unhit.

Timothy Lean filled the shovel, hesitated, and then in a movement which was like a gesture of abhorrence he flung the dirt into the grave, and as it landed it made a sound-plop. Lean suddenly stopped and mopped his brow —a tired labourer.

"Perhaps we have been wrong," said the adjutant. His glance wavered stupidly. "It might have been better if we hadn't buried him just at this time. Of course, if we advance to-morrow the body would have been —"

"Damn you," said Lean, "shut your mouth." He was not the senior officer.

He again filled the shovel and flung the earth. Always the earth made that sound-plop. For a space Lean worked frantically, like a man digging himself out of danger.

Soon there was nothing to be seen but the chalk-blue face. Lean filled the shovel. "Good God," he cried to the adjutant. "Why didn't you turn him somehow when you put him in? This —" Then Lean began to stutter.

The adjutant understood. He was pale to the lips. "Go on, man," he cried, beseechingly, almost in a shout. Lean swung back the shovel. It went forward in a pendulum curve. When the earth landed it made a sound-plop.

THE SHRAPNEL OF THEIR FRIENDS.

From over the knolls came the tiny sound of a cavalry bugle singing out the recall, and later, detached parties of His Majesty's 2nd Hussars came trotting back to where the Spitzbergen infantry sat complacently on the captured Rostina position. The horsemen were well pleased, and they told how they had ridden thrice through the helterskelter of the fleeing enemy. They had ultimately been checked by the great truth, and when a good enemy runs away in daylight he sooner or later finds a place where he fetches up with a jolt, and turns face the pursuit-notably if it is a cavalry pursuit. The Hussars had discreetly withdrawn, displaying no foolish pride of corps at that time.

There was a general admission that the Kicking Twelfth had taken the chief honours of the day, but the artillery added that if the guns had not shelled so accurately the Twelfth's charge could not have been made so successfully, and the three other regiments of infantry, of course, did not conceal their feelings, that their attack on the enemy's left had withdrawn many rifles that would have been pelting at the Twelfth. The cavalry simply said that but for them the victory would not have been complete.

Corps' prides met each other face to face at every step, but the Kickers smiled easily and indulgently. A few recruits bragged, but they bragged because they were recruits. The older men did not wish it to appear that they were surprised and rejoicing at the performance of the regiment. If they were congratulated they simply smirked, suggesting that the ability of the Twelfth had been long known to them, and that the charge had been a little thing, you know, just turned off in the way of an afternoon's work.

Major-General Richie encamped his troops on the position which they had from the enemy. Old Colonel Sponge of the Twelfth redistributed his officers, and the losses had been so great that Timothy Lean got command of a company. It was not much of a company. Fifty-three smudged and sweating men faced their new commander. The company had gone into action with a strength of eighty-six. The heart of Timothy Lean beat high with pride. He intended to be some day a general, and if he ever became a general, that moment of promotion was not equal in joy to the moment when he looked at his new possession of fifty-three vagabonds. He scanned the faces, and recognised with satisfaction one old sergeant and two bright young corporals. "Now," said he to himself, "I have here a snug little body of men with which I can do something." In him burned the usual fierce fire to make them the best company in the regiment. He had adopted them; they were his men. "I will do what I can for you," he said. "Do you the same for me."

The Twelfth bivouacked on the ridge. Little fires were built, and there appeared among the men innumerable blackened tin cups, which were so treasured that a faint suspicion in connection with the loss of one could bring on the grimmest of fights. Meantime certain of the privates silently readjusted their kits as their names were called out by the sergeants. These were the men condemned to picket duty after a hard day of marching and fighting. The dusk came slowly, and the colour of the countless fires, spotting the ridge and the plain, grew in the falling darkness. Far-away pickets fired at something.

One by one the men's heads were lowered to the earth until the ridge was marked by two long shadowy rows of men. Here and there an officer sat musing in his dark cloak with a ray of a weakening fire gleaming on his sword-hilt. From the plain there came at times the sound of battery horses moving restlessly at their tethers, and one could imagine he heard the throaty, grumbling curse of the drivers. The moon died swiftly through flying light clouds. Far-away pickets fired at something.

In the morning the infantry and guns breakfasted to the music of a racket between the cavalry and the enemy, which was taking place some miles up the valley.

The ambitious Hussars had apparently stirred some kind of a hornet's nest, and they were having a good fight with no officious friends near enough to interfere. The remainder of the army looked toward the fight musingly over the tops of tin cups. In time the column crawled lazily forward to see.

The Twelfth, as it crawled, saw a regiment deploy to the right, and saw a battery dash to take position. The cavalry jingled back grinning with pride and expecting to be greatly admired. Presently the Twelfth was bidden to take seat by the roadside and await its turn. Instantly the wise men-and there were more than three-came out of the east and announced that they had divined the whole plan. The Kicking Twelfth was to be held in reserve until the critical moment of the fight, and then they were to be sent forward to win a victory. In corroboration, they pointed to the fact that the general in command was sticking close to them, in order, they said, to give the word quickly at the proper moment. And in truth, on a small hill to the right, Major-General Richie sat on his horse and used his glasses, while back of him his staff and the orderlies bestrode their champing, dancing mounts.

It is always good to look hard at a general, and the Kickers were transfixed with interest. The wise men again came out of the east and told what was inside the Richie head, but even the wise men wondered what was inside the Richie head.

Suddenly an exciting thing happened. To the left and ahead was a pounding Spitzbergen battery, and a toy suddenly appeared on the slope behind the guns. The toy was a man with a flag-the flag was white save for a square of red in the centre. And this toy began to wig-wag wag-wig, and it spoke to General Richie under the authority of the captain of the battery. It said: "The 88th are being driven on my centre and right."

Now, when the Kicking Twelfth had left Spitzbergen there was an average of six signalmen in each company. A proportion of these signallers had been destroyed in the first engagement, but enough remained so that the Kicking Twelfth read, as a unit, the news of the 88th. The word ran quickly. "The 88th are being driven on my centre and right."

Richie rode to where Colonel Sponge sat aloft on his big horse, and a moment later a cry ran along the column: "Kim up, the Kickers." A large number of the men were already in the road, hitching and twisting at their belts and packs. The Kickers moved forward.

They deployed and passed in a straggling line through the battery, and to the left and right of it. The gunners called out to them carefully, telling them not to be afraid.

The scene before them was startling. They were facing a country cut up by many steep-sided ravines, and over the resultant hills were retreating little squads of the 88th. The Twelfth laughed in its exultation. The men could now tell by the volume of fire that the 88th were retreating for reasons which were not sufficiently expressed in the noise of the Rostina shooting. Held together by the bugle, the Kickers swarmed up the first hill and laid on the crest. Parties of the 88th went through their lines, and the Twelfth told them coarsely its several opinions. The sights were clicked up to 600 yards, and, with a crashing volley, the regiment entered its second battle.

A thousand yards away on the right the cavalry and a regiment of infantry were creeping onward. Sponge decided not to be backward, and the bugle told the Twelfth to go ahead once more. The Twelfth charged, followed by a rabble of rallied men of the 88th, who were crying aloud that it had been all a mistake.

A charge in these days is not a running match. Those splendid pictures of levelled bayonets, dashing at headlong pace towards the closed ranks of the enemy are absurd as soon as they are mistaken for the actuality of the present. In these days charges are likely to cover at least the half of a mile, and to go at the pace exhibited in the pictures a man would be obliged to have a little steam engine inside of him.

The charge of the Kicking Twelfth somewhat resembled the advance of a great crowd of beaters who, for some reason, passionately desired to start the game. Men stumbled; men fell; men swore; there were cries: "This way!" "Come this way!" "Don't go that way!" "You can't get up that way!" Over the rocks the Twelfth scrambled, red in the face, sweating and angry. Soldiers fell because they were struck by bullets, and because they had not an ounce of strength left in them. Colonel Sponge, with a face like a red cushion, was being dragged windless up the steeps by devoted and athletic men. Three of the older captains lay afar back, and swearing with their eyes because their tongues were temporarily out of service.

And yet-and-yet, the speed of the charge was slow. From the position of the battery, it looked as if the Kickers were taking a walk over some extremely difficult country.

The regiment ascended a superior height, and found trenches and dead men. They took seat with the dead, satisfied with this company until they could get their wind. For thirty minutes purple-faced stragglers rejoined from the rear. Colonel Sponge looked behind him, and saw that Richie, with his staff, had approached by another route, and had evidently been near enough to see the full extent of the Kickers' exertions. Presently Richie began to pick a way for his horse towards the captured position. He disappeared in a gully between two hills.

Now it came to pass that a Spitzbergen battery on the far right took occasion to mistake the identity of the Kicking Twelfth, and the captain of these guns, not having anything to occupy him in front, directed his six 3·2's upon the ridge where the tired Kickers lay side by side with the Rostina dead. A shrapnel came swinging over the Kickers, seething and fuming. It burst directly over the trenches, and the shrapnel, of course, scattered forward, hurting nobody. But a man screamed out to his officer: "By God, sir, that is one of our own batteries!" The whole line quivered with fright. Five more shells streaked overhead, and one flung its hail into the middle of the 3rd battalion's line, and the Kicking Twelfth shuddered to the very centre of its heart, and arose, like one man, and fled.

Colonel Sponge, fighting, frothing at the month, dealing blows with his fist right and left, found himself confronting a fury on horseback. Richie was as pale as death, and his eyes sent out sparks. "What does this conduct mean?" he flashed out between his fastened teeth.

Sponge could only gurgle: "The battery-the battery-the battery!"

"The battery?" cried Richie, in a voice which sounded like pistol shots. "Are you afraid of the guns you almost took yesterday? Go back there, you white-livered cowards! You swine! You dogs! Curs! Curs! Curs! Go back there!"

Most of the men halted and crouched under the lashing tongue of their maddened general. But one man found desperate speech, and yelled: "General, it is our own battery that is firing on us!"

Many say that the General's face tightened until it looked like a mask. The Kicking Twelfth retired to a comfortable place, where they were only under the fire of the Rostina artillery. The men saw a staff officer riding over the obstructions in a manner calculated to break his neck directly.

The Kickers were aggrieved, but the heart of the colonel was cut in twain. He even babbled to his major, talking like a man who is about to die of simple rage. "Did you hear what he said to me? Did you hear what he called us? *Did you hear what he called us?*"

The majors searched their minds for words to heal a deep wound.

The Twelfth received orders to go into camp upon the hill where they had been insulted. Old Sponge looked as if he were about to knock the aide out of the saddle, but he saluted, and took the regiment back to the temporary companionship of the Rostina dead.

Major-General Richie never apologised to Colonel Sponge. When you are a commanding officer you do not adopt the custom of apologising for the wrong done to your subordinates. You ride away; and they understand, and are confident of the restitution to honour. Richie never opened his stern, young lips to Sponge in reference to the scene near the hill of the Rostina dead, but in time there was a general order No. 20, which spoke definitely of the gallantry of His Majesty's 12th regiment of the line and its colonel. In the end Sponge was given a high decoration, because he had been badly used by Richie on that day. Richie knew that it is hard for men to withstand the shrapnel of their friends.

A few days later the Kickers, marching in column on the road, came upon their friend the battery, halted in a field; and they addressed the battery, and the captain of the battery blanched to the tips of his ears. But the men of the battery told the Kickers to go to the devil-frankly, freely, placidly, told the Kickers to go to the devil.

And this story proves that it is sometimes better to be a private.

"AND IF HE WILLS, WE MUST DIE."

A sergeant, a corporal, and fourteen men of the Twelfth Regiment of the Line had been sent out to occupy a house on the main highway. They would be at least a half of a mile in advance of any other picket of their own people. Sergeant Morton was deeply angry at being sent on this duty. He said that he was over-worked. There were at least two sergeants, he claimed furiously, whose turn it should have been to go on this arduous mission. He was treated unfairly; he was abused by his superiors; why did any damned fool ever join the army? As for him he would get out of it as soon as possible; he was sick of it; the life of a dog. All this he said to the corporal, who listened attentively, giving grunts of respectful assent. On the way to this post two privates took occasion to drop to the rear and pilfer in the orchard of a deserted plantation. When the sergeant discovered this absence, he grew black with a rage which was an accumulation of all his irritations. "Run, you!" he howled. "Bring them here! I'll show them —" A private ran swiftly to the rear. The remainder of the squad began to shout nervously at the two delinquents, whose figures they could see in the deep shade of the orchard, hurriedly picking fruit from the ground and cramming it within their shirts, next to their skins. The beseeching cries of their comrades stirred the criminals more than did the barking of the sergeant. They ran to rejoin the squad, while holding their loaded bosoms and with their mouths open with aggrieved explanations.

Jones faced the sergeant with a horrible cancer marked in bumps on his left side. The disease of Patterson showed quite around the front of his waist in many protuberances. "A nice pair!" said the sergeant, with sudden frigidity. "You're the kind of soldiers a man wants to choose for a dangerous outpost duty, ain't you?"

The two privates stood at attention, still looking much aggrieved. "We only —" began Jones huskily.

"Oh, you 'only!' " cried the sergeant. "Yes, you 'only.' I know all about that. But if you think you are going to trifle with me —"

A moment later the squad moved on towards its station. Behind the sergeant's back Jones and Patterson were slyly passing apples and pears to their friends while the sergeant expounded eloquently to the corporal "You see what kind of men are in the army now. Why, when I joined the regiment it was a very different thing, I can tell you. Then a sergeant had some authority, and if a man disobeyed orders, he had a very small chance of escaping something extremely serious. But now! Good God! If I report these men, the captain will look over a lot of beastly orderly sheets and say —'Haw, eh, well, Sergeant Morton, these men seem to have very good records; very good records, indeed. I can't be too hard on them; no, not too hard.'" Continued the sergeant: "I tell you, Flagler, the army is no place for a decent man."

Flagler, the corporal, answered with a sincerity of appreciation which with him had become a science. "I think you are right, sergeant," he answered.

Behind them the privates mumbled discreetly. "Damn this sergeant of ours. He thinks we are made of wood. I don't see any reason for all this strictness when we are on active service. It isn't like being at home in barracks! There is no great harm in a couple of men dropping out to raid an orchard of the enemy when all the world knows that we haven't had a decent meal in twenty days."

The reddened face of Sergeant Morton suddenly showed to the rear. "A little more marching and less talking," he said.

When he came to the house he had been ordered to occupy the sergeant sniffed with disdain. "These people must have lived like cattle," he said angrily. To be sure, the place was not alluring. The ground floor had been used for the housing of cattle, and it was dark and terrible. A flight of steps led to the lofty first floor, which was denuded but respectable. The sergeant's visage lightened when he saw the strong walls of stone and cement. "Unless they turn guns on us, they will never get us out of here," he said cheerfully to the squad. The men, anxious to keep him in an amiable mood, all hurriedly grinned and seemed very appreciative and pleased. "I'll make this into a fortress," he announced. He sent Jones and Patterson, the two orchard thiefs, out on sentry-duty. He worked the others, then, until he could think of no more things to tell them to do. Afterwards he went forth, with a major-general's serious scowl, and examined the ground in front of his position. In returning he came upon a sentry, Jones, munching an apple. He sternly commanded him to throw it away.

The men spread their blankets on the floors of the bare rooms, and putting their packs under their heads and lighting their pipes, they lived in easy peace. Bees hummed in the garden, and a scent of flowers came through the open window. A great fan-shaped bit of sunshine smote the face of one man, and he indolently cursed as he moved his primitive bed to a shadier place.

Another private explained to a comrade: "This is all nonsense anyhow. No sense in occupying this post. They —"

"But, of course," said the corporal, "when she told me herself that she cared more for me than she did for him, I wasn't going to stand any of his talk —" The corporal's listener was so sleepy that he could only grunt his sympathy.

There was a sudden little spatter of shooting. A cry from Jones rang out. With no intermediate scrambling, the sergeant leaped straight to his feet. "Now," he cried, "let us see what you are made of! If," he added bitterly, "you are made of anything!"

A man yelled: "Good God, can't you see you're all tangled up in my cartridge belt?"

Another man yelled: "Keep off my legs! Can't you walk on the floor?"

To the windows there was a blind rush of slumberous men, who brushed hair from their eyes even as they made ready their rifles. Jones and Patterson came stumbling up the steps, crying dreadful information. Already the enemy's bullets were spitting and singing over the house.

The sergeant suddenly was stiff and cold with a sense of the importance of the thing. "Wait until you see one," he drawled loudly and calmly, "then shoot."

For some moments the enemy's bullets swung swifter than lightning over the house without anybody being able to discover a target. In this interval a man was shot in the throat. He gurgled, and then lay down on the floor. The blood slowly waved down the brown skin of his neck while he looked meekly at his comrades.

There was a howl. "There they are! There they come!" The rifles crackled. A light smoke drifted idly through the rooms. There was a strong odour as if from burnt paper and the powder of fire-crackers. The men were silent. Through the windows and about the house the bullets of an entirely invisible enemy moaned, hummed, spat, burst, and sang.

The men began to curse. "Why can't we see them?" they muttered through their teeth. The sergeant was still frigid. He answered soothingly as if he were directly reprehensible for this behaviour of the enemy. "Wait a moment. You will soon be able to see them. There! Give it to them." A little skirt of black figures had appeared in a field. It was really like shooting at an upright needle from the full length of a ball-room. But the men's spirits improved as soon as the enemy-this mysterious enemy-became a tangible thing, and far off. They had believed the foe to be shooting at them from the adjacent garden.

"Now," said the sergeant ambitiously, "we can beat them off easily if you men are good enough."

A man called out in a tone of quick, great interest. "See that fellow on horseback, Bill? Isn't he on horseback? I thought he was on horseback."

There was a fusilade against another side of the house. The sergeant dashed into the room which commanded that situation. He found a dead soldier on the floor. He rushed out howling: "When was Knowles killed? When was Knowles killed? Damn it, when was Knowles killed?" It was absolutely essential to find out the exact moment this man died. A blackened private turned upon his sergeant and demanded: "How in hell do I know?" Sergeant Morton had a sense of anger so brief that in the next second he cried: "Patterson!" He had even forgotten his vital interest in the time of Knowles' death.

"Yes?" said Patterson, his face set with some deep-rooted quality of determination. Still, he was a mere farm boy.

"Go in to Knowles' window and shoot at those people," said the sergeant hoarsely. Afterwards he coughed. Some of the fumes of the fight had made way to his lungs.

Patterson looked at the door into this other room. He looked at it as if he suspected it was to be his death-chamber. Then he entered and stood across the body of Knowles and fired vigorously into a group of plum trees.

"They can't take this house," declared the sergeant in a contemptuous and argumentative tone. He was apparently replying to somebody. The man who had been shot in the throat looked up at him. Eight men were firing from the windows. The sergeant detected in a corner three wounded men talking together feebly. "Don't you think there is anything to do?" he bawled. "Go and get Knowles' cartridges and give them to somebody who can use them! Take Simpson's too." The man who had been shot in the throat looked at him. Of the three wounded men who had been talking, one said: "My leg is all doubled up under me, sergeant." He spoke apologetically.

Meantime the sergeant was re-loading his rifle. His foot slipped in the blood of the man who had been shot in the throat, and the military boot made a greasy red streak on the floor.

"Why, we can hold this place," shouted the sergeant jubilantly. "Who says we can't?"

Corporal Flagler suddenly spun away from his window and fell in a heap.

"Sergeant," murmured a man as he dropped to a seat on the floor out of danger, "I can't stand this. I swear I can't. I think we should run away."

Morton, with the kindly eyes of a good shepherd, looked at the man. "You are afraid, Johnston, you are afraid," he said softly. The man struggled to his feet, cast upon the sergeant a gaze full of admiration, reproach, and despair, and returned to his post. A moment later he pitched forward, and thereafter his body hung out of the window, his arms straight and the fists clenched. Incidentally this corpse was pierced afterwards by chance three times by bullets of the enemy.

The sergeant laid his rifle against the stone-work of the window-frame and shot with care until his magazine was empty. Behind him a man, simply grazed on the elbow, was wildly sobbing like a girl. "Damn it, shut up," said Morton, without turning his head. Before him was a vista of a garden, fields, clumps of trees, woods, populated at the time with little fleeting figures.

He grew furious. "Why didn't he send me orders?" he cried aloud. The emphasis on the word "he" was impressive. A mile back on the road a galloper of the Hussars lay dead beside his dead horse.

The man who had been grazed on the elbow still set up his bleat. Morton's fury veered to this soldier. "Can't you shut up? Can't you shut up? Can't you shut up? Fight! That's the thing to do. Fight!"

A bullet struck Morton, and he fell upon the man who had been shot in the throat. There was a sickening moment. Then the sergeant rolled off to a position upon the blood floor. He turned himself with a last effort until he could look at the wounded who were able to look at him.

"Kim up, the Kickers," he said thickly. His arms weakened and he dropped on his face.

After an interval a young subaltern of the enemy's infantry, followed by his eager men, burst into this reeking interior. But just over the threshold he halted before the scene of blood and death. He turned with a shrug to his sergeant. "God, I should have estimated them at least one hundred strong."

WYOMING VALLEY TALES

I. —THE SURRENDER OF FORTY FORT.

Immediately after the battle of 3rd July, my mother said, "We had best take the children and go into the Fort."

But my father replied, "I will not go. I will not leave my property. All that I have in the world is here, and if the savages destroy it they may as well destroy me also."

My mother said no other word. Our household was ever given to stern silence, and such was my training that it did not occur to me to reflect that if my father cared for his property it was not my property, and I was entitled to care somewhat for my life.

Colonel Denison was true to the word which he had passed to me at the Fort before the battle. He sent a messenger to my father, and this messenger stood in the middle of our living-room and spake with a clear, indifferent voice. "Colonel Denison bids me come here and say that John Bennet is a wicked man, and the blood of his own children will be upon his head." As usual, my father said nothing. After the messenger had gone, he remained silent for hours in his chair by the fire, and this stillness was so impressive to his family that even my mother walked on tip-toe as she went about her work. After this long time my father said, "Mary!"

Mother halted and looked at him. Father spoke slowly, and as if every word was wrested from him with violent pangs. "Mary, you take the girls and go to the Fort. I and Solomon and Andrew will go over the mountain to Stroudsberg."

Immediately my mother called us all to set about packing such things as could be taken to the Fort. And by nightfall we had seen them within its pallisade, and my father, myself, and my little brother Andrew, who was only eleven years old, were off over the hills on a long march to the Delaware settlements. Father and I had our rifles, but we seldom dared to fire them, because of the roving bands of Indians. We lived as well as we could on blackberries and raspberries. For the most part, poor little Andrew rode first on the back of my father and then on my back. He was a good little man, and only cried when he would wake in the dead of night very cold and very hungry. Then my father would wrap him in an old grey coat that was so famous in the Wyoming country that there was not even an Indian who did not know of it. But this act he did without any direct display of tenderness, for the fear, I suppose, that he would weaken little Andrew's growing manhood. Now, in these days of safety, and even luxury, I often marvel at the iron spirit of the people of my young days. My father, without his coat and no doubt very cold, would then sometimes begin to pray to his God in the wilderness, but in low voice, because of the Indians. It was July, but even July nights are cold in the pine mountains, breathing a chill which goes straight to the bones.

But it is not my intention to give in this section the ordinary adventures of the masculine part of my family. As a matter of fact, my mother and the girls were undergoing in Forty Fort trials which made as nothing the happenings on our journey, which ended in safety.

My mother and her small flock were no sooner established in the crude quarters within the pallisade than negotiations were opened between Colonel Denison and Colonel Zebulon Butler on the American side, and "Indian Butler" on the British side, for the capitulation of the Fort with such arms and military stores as it contained, the lives of the settlers to be strictly preserved. But "Indian Butler" did not seem to feel free to promise safety for the lives of the Continental Butler and the pathetic little fragment of the regular troops. These men always fought so well against the Indians that whenever the Indians could get them at their mercy there was small chances of anything but a massacre. So every regular left before the surrender; and I fancy that Colonel Zebulon Butler considered himself a much-abused man, for if we had left ourselves entirely under his direction there is no doubt but what we could have saved the valley. He had taken us out on 3rd July because our militia officers had almost threatened him. In the end he had said, "Very well, I can go as far as any of you." I was always on Butler's side of the argument, but owing to the singular arrangement of circumstances, my opinion at the age of sixteen counted upon neither the one side nor the other.

The Fort was left in charge of Colonel Denison. He had stipulated before the surrender that no Indians should be allowed to enter the stockade and molest these poor families of women whose fathers and brothers were either dead or fled over the mountains, unless their physical debility had been such that they were able neither to get killed in the battle nor to take the long trail to the Delaware. Of course, this excepts those men who were with Washington.

For several days the Indians, obedient to the British officers, kept out of the Fort, but soon they began to enter in small bands and went sniffing and poking in every corner to find plunder. Our people had hidden everything as well as they were able, and for a period little was stolen. My mother told me that the first thing of importance to go was Colonel Denison's hunting shirt, made of "fine forty" linen. It had a double cape, and was fringed about the cape and about the wristbands. Colonel Denison at the time was in my mother's cabin. An Indian entered, and, rolling a thieving eye about the place, sighted first of all the remarkable shirt which Colonel Denison was wearing. He seized the shirt and began to tug, while the Colonel backed away, tugging and protesting at the same time. The women folk saw at once that the Colonel would be tomahawked if he did not give up his shirt, and they begged him to do it. He finally elected not to be tomahawked, and came out of his shirt. While my mother unbuttoned the wristbands, the Colonel cleverly dropped into the lap of a certain Polly Thornton a large packet of Continental bills, and his money was thus saved for the settlers.

Colonel Denison had several stormy interviews with "Indian Butler," and the British commander finally ended in frankly declaring that he could do nothing with the Indians at all. They were beyond control, and the defenceless people in the Fort would have to take the consequence. I do not mean that Colonel Denison was trying to recover his shirt; I mean that he was objecting to a situation which was now almost unendurable. I wish to record also that the Colonel lost a large beaver hat. In both cases he willed to be tomahawked and killed rather than suffer the indignity, but mother prevailed over him. I must confess to this discreet age that my mother engaged in fisticuffs with a squaw. This squaw came into the cabin, and, without preliminary discussion, attempted to drag from my mother the petticoat she was wearing. My mother forgot the fine advice she had given to Colonel Denison. She proceeded to beat the squaw out of the cabin, and although the squaw appealed to some warriors who were standing without the warriors only laughed, and my mother kept her petticoat.

The Indians took the feather beds of the people, and, ripping them open, flung the feathers broadcast. Then they stuffed these sacks full of plunder, and flung them across the backs of such of the settlers' horses as they had been able to find. In the old days my mother had had a side saddle, of which she was very proud when she rode to meeting on it. She had also a brilliant scarlet cloak, which every lady had in those days, and which I can remember as one of the admirations of my childhood. One day my mother had the satisfaction of seeing a squaw ride off from the Fort with this prize saddle reversed on a small nag, and with the proud squaw thus mounted wearing the scarlet cloak, also reversed. My sister Martha told me afterwards that they laughed, even in their misfortunes. A little later they had the satisfaction of seeing the smoke from our house and barn arising over the tops of the trees.

When the Indians first began their pillaging, an old Mr. Sutton, who occupied a cabin near my mother's cabin, anticipated them by donning all his best clothes. He had had a theory that the Americans would be free to retain the clothes that they wore. And his best happened to be a suit of Quaker grey, from beaver to boots, in which he had been married. Not long afterwards my mother and my sisters saw passing the door an Indian arrayed in Quaker grey, from beaver to boots. The only odd thing which impressed them was that the Indian had appended to the dress a long string of Yankee scalps. Sutton was a good Quaker, and if he had been wearing the suit there would have been no string of scalps.

They were, in fact, badgered, insulted, robbed by the Indians so openly that the British officers would not come into the Fort at all. They stayed in their camp, affecting to be ignorant of what was happening. It was about all they could do. The Indians had only one idea of war, and it was impossible to reason with them when they were flushed with victory and stolen rum.

The hand of fate fell heavily upon one rogue whose ambition it was to drink everything that the Fort contained. One day he inadvertently came upon a bottle of spirits of camphor, and in a few hours he was dead.

But it was known that General Washington contemplated sending a strong expedition into the valley, to clear it of the invaders and thrash them. Soon there were no enemies in the country save small roving parties of Indians, who prevented work in the fields and burned whatever cabins that earlier torches had missed.

The first large party to come into the valley was composed mainly of Captain Spaulding's company of regulars, and at its head rode Colonel Zebulon Butler. My father, myself, and little Andrew returned with this party to set to work immediately to build out of nothing a prosperity similar to that which had vanished in the smoke.

II.—"OL' BENNET" AND THE INDIANS.

My father was so well known of the Indians that, as I was saying, his old grey coat was a sign through the northern country. I know of no reason for this save that he was honest and obstreperously minded his own affairs, and could fling a tomahawk better than the best Indian. I will not declare upon how hard it is for a man to be honest and to mind his own affairs, but I fully know that it is hard to throw a tomahawk as my father threw it, straighter than a bullet from a duelling pistol. He had always dealt fairly with the Indians, and I cannot tell why they paled him so bitterly, unless it was that when an Indian went foolishly drunk my father would deplore it with his foot, if it so happened that the drunkenness was done in our cabin. It is true to say that when the war came, a singular large number of kicked Indians journeyed from the Canadas to re-visit with torch and knife the scenes of the kicking.

If people had thoroughly known my father he would have had no enemies. He was the best of men. He had a code of behaviour for himself, and for the whole world as well. If people wished his good opinion they only had to do exactly as he did, and to have his views. I remember that once my sister Martha made me a waistcoat of rabbits' skins, and generally it was considered a great ornament. But one day my father espied me in it, and commanded me to remove it for ever. Its appearance was indecent, he said, and such a garment tainted the soul of him who wore it. In the ensuing fortnight a poor pedlar arrived from the Delaware, who had suffered great misfortunes in the snows. My father fed him and warmed him, and when he gratefully departed, gave him the rabbits' skin waistcoat, and the poor man went off clothed indecently in a garment that would taint his soul. Afterwards, in a daring mood, I asked my father why he had so cursed this pedlar, and he recommended that I should study my Bible more closely, and there read that my own devious ways should be mended before I sought to judge the enlightened acts of my elders. He set me to ploughing the upper twelve acres, and I was hardly allowed to loose my grip of the plough handles until every furrow was drawn.

The Indians called my father "Ol' Bennet," and he was known broadcast as a man whose doom was sealed when the redskins caught him. As I have said, the feeling is inexplicable to me. But Indians who had been ill-used and maltreated by downright ruffians, against whom revenge could with a kind of propriety be directed-many of these Indians avowedly gave up a genuine wrong in order to direct a fuller attention to the getting of my father's scalp. This most unfair disposition of the Indians was a great, deep anxiety to all of us up to the time when General Sullivan and his avenging army marched through the valley and swept our tormentors afar.

And yet great calamities could happen in our valley even after the coming and passing of General Sullivan. We were partly mistaken in our gladness. The British force of Loyalists and Indians met Sullivan in one battle, and finding themselves over-matched and beaten, they scattered in all directions. The Loyalists, for the most part, went home, but the Indians cleverly broke up into small bands, and General Sullivan's army had no sooner marched beyond the Wyoming Valley than some of these small bands were back into the valley plundering outlying cabins and shooting people from the thickets and woods that bordered the fields.

General Sullivan had left a garrison at Wilkesbarre, and at this time we lived in its strong shadow. It was too formidable for the Indians to attack, and it could protect all who valued protection enough to remain under its wings, but it could do little against the flying small bands. My father chafed in the shelter of the garrison. His best lands lay beyond Forty Fort, and he wanted to be at his ploughing. He made several brief references to his ploughing that led us to believe that his ploughing was the fundamental principle of life. None of us saw any means of contending him. My sister Martha began to weep, but it no more mattered than if she had began to laugh. My mother said nothing. Aye, my wonderful mother said nothing. My father said he would go plough some of the land above Forty Fort. Immediately this was with us some sort of a law. It was like a rain, or a wind, or a drought.

He went, of course. My young brother Andrew went with him, and he took the new span of oxen and a horse. They began to plough a meadow which lay in a bend of the river above Forty

Fort. Andrew rode the horse hitched ahead of the oxen. At a certain thicket the horse shied so that little Andrew was almost thrown down. My father seemed to have begun a period of apprehension at this time, but it was of no service. Four Indians suddenly appeared out of the thicket. Swiftly, and in silence, they pounced with tomahawk, rifle, and knife upon my father and my brother, and in a moment they were captives of the redskins-that fate whose very phrasing was a thrill to the heart of every colonist. It spelled death, or that horrible simple absence, vacancy, mystery, which is harder than death.

As for us, he had told my mother that if he and Andrew were not returned at sundown she might construe a calamity. So at sundown we gave the news to the Fort, and directly we heard the alarm gun booming out across the dusk like a salute to the death of my father, a solemn, final declaration. At the sound of this gun my sisters all began newly to weep. It simply defined our misfortune. In the morning a party was sent out, which came upon the deserted plough, the oxen calmly munching, and the horse still excited and affrighted. The soldiers found the trail of four Indians. They followed the trail some distance over the mountains, but the redskins with their captives had a long start, and pursuit was but useless. The result of this expedition was that we knew at least that father and Andrew had not been massacred immediately. But in those days this was a most meagre consolation. It was better to wish them well dead.

My father and Andrew were hurried over the hills at a terrible pace by the four Indians. Andrew told me afterwards that he could think sometimes that he was dreaming of being carried off by goblins. The redskins said no word, and their mocassined feet made no sound. They were like evil spirits. But it was as he caught glimpses of father's pale face, every wrinkle in it deepened and hardened, that Andrew saw everything in its light. And Andrew was but thirteen years old. It is a tender age at which to be burned at the stake.

In time the party came upon two more Indians, who had as a prisoner a man named Lebbeus Hammond. He had left Wilkesbarre in search of a strayed horse. He was riding the animal back to the Fort when the Indians caught him. He and my father knew each other well, and their greeting was like them.

"What! Hammond! You here?"

"Yes, I'm here."

As the march was resumed, the principal Indian bestrode Hammond's horse, but the horse was very high-nerved and scared, and the bridle was only a temporary one made from hickory withes. There was no saddle. And so finally the principal Indian came off with a crash, alighting with exceeding severity upon his head. When he got upon his feet he was in such a rage that the three captives thought to see him dash his tomahawk into the skull of the trembling horse, and, indeed, his arm was raised for the blow, but suddenly he thought better of it. He had been touched by a real point of Indian inspiration. The party was passing a swamp at the time, so he mired the horse almost up to its eyes, and left it to the long death.

I had said that my father was well known of the Indians, and yet I have to announce that none of his six captors knew him. To them he was a complete stranger, for upon camping the first night they left my father unbound. If they had had any idea that he was "Ol' Bennet" they would never have left him unbound. He suggested to Hammond that they try to escape that night, but Hammond seemed not to care to try it yet.

In time they met a party of over forty Indians, commanded by a Loyalist. In that band there were many who knew my father. They cried out with rejoicing when they perceived him. "Ha!" they shouted, "Ol' Bennet!" They danced about him, making gestures expressive of the torture. Later in the day my father accidentally pulled a button from his coat, and an Indian took it from him.

My father asked to be allowed to have it again, for he was a very careful man, and in those days all good husbands were trained to bring home the loose buttons. The Indians laughed, and explained that a man who was to die at Wyallusing-one day's march-need not be particular about a button.

The three prisoners were now sent off in care of seven Indians, while the Loyalist took the remainder of his men down the valley to further harass the settlers. The seven Indians were now very careful of my father, allowing him scarce a wink. Their tomahawks came up at the slightest sign. At the camp that night they bade the prisoners lie down, and then placed poles across them. An Indian lay upon either end of these poles. My father managed, however, to let Hammond know that he was determined to make an attempt to escape. There was only one night between him and the stake, and he was resolved to make what use he could of it. Hammond seems to have been dubious from the start, but the men of that time were not daunted by broad risks. In his opinion the rising would be a failure, but this did not prevent him from agreeing to rise with his friend. My brother Andrew was not considered at all. No one asked him if he wanted to rise against the Indians. He was only a boy, and supposed to obey his elders. So, as none asked his views, he kept them to himself; but I wager you he listened, all ears, to the furtive consultations, consultations which were mere casual phrases at times, and at other times swift, brief sentences shot out in a whisper.

The band of seven Indians relaxed in vigilance as they approached their own country, and on the last night from Wyallusing the Indian part of the camp seemed much inclined to take deep slumber after the long and rapid journey. The prisoners were held to the ground by poles as on the previous night, and then the Indians pulled their blankets over their heads and passed into heavy sleep. One old warrior sat by the fire as guard, but he seems to have been a singularly inefficient man, for he was continuously drowsing, and if the captives could have got rid of the poles across their chests and legs they would have made their flight sooner.

The camp was on a mountain side amid a forest of lofty pines. The night was very cold, and the blasts of wind swept down upon the crackling, resinous fire. A few stars peeped through the feathery pine branches. Deep in some gulch could be heard the roar of a mountain stream. At one o'clock in the morning three of the Indians arose, and, releasing the prisoners, commanded them to mend the fire. The prisoners brought dead pine branches; the ancient warrior on watch sleepily picked away with his knife at the deer's head which he had roasted; the other Indians retired again to their blankets, perhaps each depending upon the other for the exercise of precautions. It was a tremendously slack business; the Indians were feeling security because they knew that the prisoners were too wise to try to run away.

The warrior on watch mumbled placidly to himself as he picked at the deer's head. Then he drowsed again, just the short nap of a man who had been up too long. My father stepped quickly to a spear, and backed away from the Indian; then he drove it straight through his chest. The Indian raised himself spasmodically, and then collapsed into that camp fire which the captives had made burn so brilliantly, and as he fell he screamed. Instantly his blanket, his hair, he himself began to burn, and over him was my father tugging frantically to get the spear out again.

My father did not recover the spear. It had so gone through the old warrior that it could not readily be withdrawn, and my father left it.

The scream of the watchman instantly aroused the other warriors, who, as they scrambled in their blankets, found over them a terrible white-lipped creature with an axe-an axe, the most appallingly brutal of weapons. Hammond buried his weapon in the head of the leader of the Indians even as the man gave out his first great cry. The second blow missed an agile warrior's head, but caught him in the nape of the neck, and he swung, to bury his face in the red-hot ashes at the edge of the fire.

Meanwhile my brother Andrew had been gallantly snapping empty guns. In fact he snapped three empty guns at the Indians, who were in the purest panic. He did not snap the fourth gun, but took it by the barrel, and, seeing a warrior rush past him, he cracked his skull with the clubbed weapon. He told me, however, that his snapping of the empty guns was very effective, because it made the Indians jump and dodge.

Well, this slaughter continued in the red glare of the fire on the lonely mountain side until two shrieking creatures ran off through the trees, but even then my father hurled a tomahawk with all his strength. It struck one of the fleeing Indians on the shoulder. His blanket dropped from him, and he ran on practically naked.

The three whites looked at each other, breathing deeply. Their work was plain to them in the five dead and dying Indians underfoot. They hastily gathered weapons and mocassins, and in six minutes from the time when my father had hurled the spear through the Indian sentinel they had started to make their way back to the settlements, leaving the camp fire to burn out its short career alone amid the dead.

III.—THE BATTLE OF FORTY FORT.

The Congress, sitting at Philadelphia, had voted our Wyoming country two companies of infantry for its protection against the Indians, with the single provision that we raise the men and arm them ourselves. This was not too brave a gift, but no one could blame the poor Congress, and indeed one could wonder that they found occasion to think of us at all, since at the time every gentleman of them had his coat-tails gathered high in his hands in readiness for flight to Baltimore. But our two companies of foot were no sooner drilled, equipped, and in readiness to defend the colony when they were ordered off down to the Jerseys to join General Washington. So it can be seen what service Congress did us in the way of protection. Thus the Wyoming Valley, sixty miles deep in the wilderness, held its log-houses full of little besides mothers, maids, and children. To the clamour against this situation the badgered Congress could only reply by the issue of another generous order, directing that one full company of foot be raised in the town of Westmoreland for the defence of said town, and that the said company find their own arms, ammunition, and blankets. Even people with our sense of humour could not laugh at this joke.

When the first two companies were forming, I had thought to join one, but my father forbade me, saying that I was too young, although I was full sixteen, tall, and very strong. So it turned out that I was not off fighting with Washington's army when Butler with his rangers and Indians raided Wyoming. Perhaps I was in the better place to do my duty, if I could.

When wandering Indians visited the settlements, their drunkenness and insolence were extreme, but the few white men remained calm, and often enough pretended oblivion to insults which, because of their wives and families, they dared not attempt to avenge. In my own family, my father's imperturbability was scarce superior to my mother's coolness, and such was our faith in them that we twelve children also seemed to be fearless. Neighbour after neighbour came to my father in despair of the defenceless condition of the valley, declaring that they were about to leave everything and flee over the mountains to Stroudsberg. My father always wished them God-speed and said no more. If they urged him to fly also, he usually walked away from them.

Finally there came a time when all the Indians vanished. We rather would have had them tipsy and impudent in the settlements; we knew what their disappearance portended. It was the serious sign. Too soon the news came that "Indian Butler" was on his way.

The valley was vastly excited. People with their smaller possessions flocked into the block-houses, and militia officers rode everywhere to rally every man. A small force of Continentals-regulars of the line-had joined our people, and the little army was now under the command of a Continental officer, Major Zebulon Butler.

I had thought that with all this hubbub of an impending life and death struggle in the valley that my father would allow the work of our farm to slacken. But in this I was notably mistaken. The milking and the feeding and the work in the fields went on as if there never had been an Indian south of the Canadas. My mother and my sisters continued to cook, to wash, to churn, to spin, to dye, to mend, to make soap, to make maple sugar. Just before the break of each day, my younger brother Andrew and myself tumbled out for some eighteen hours' work, and woe to us if we departed the length of a dog's tail from the laws which our father had laid down. It was a life with which I was familiar, but it did seem to me that with the Indians almost upon us he might have allowed me, at least, to go to the Fort and see our men drilling.

But one morning we aroused as usual at his call at the foot of the ladder, and, dressing more quickly than Andrew, I climbed down from the loft to find my father seated by a blazing fire reading by its light in his Bible.

"Son," said he.

"Yes, father?"

"Go and fight."

Without a word more I made hasty preparation. It was the first time in my life that I had a feeling that my father would change his mind. So strong was this fear that I did not even risk a good-bye to my mother and sisters. At the end of the clearing I looked back. The door of the house was open, and in the blazing light of the fire I saw my father seated as I had left him.

At Forty Fort I found between three and four hundred under arms, while the stockade itself was crowded with old men, and women and children. Many of my acquaintances welcomed me; indeed, I seemed to know everybody save a number of the Continental officers. Colonel Zebulon Butler was in chief command, while directly under him was Colonel Denison, a man of the valley, and much respected. Colonel Denison asked news of my father, whose temper he well knew. He said to me —"If God spares Nathan Denison I shall tell that obstinate old fool my true opinion of him. He will get himself and all his family butchered and scalped."

I joined Captain Bidlack's company for the reason that a number of my friends were in it. Every morning we were paraded and drilled in the open ground before the Fort, and I learned to present arms and to keep my heels together, although to this day I have never been able to see any point to these accomplishments, and there was very little of the presenting of arms or of the keeping together of heels in the battle which followed these drills. I may say truly that I would now be much more grateful to Captain Bidlack if he had taught us to run like a wild horse.

There was considerable friction between the officers of our militia and the Continental officers. I believe the Continental officers had stated themselves as being in favour of a cautious policy, whereas the men of the valley were almost unanimous in their desire to meet "Indian Butler" more than half way. They knew the country, they said, and they knew the Indians, and they deduced that the proper plan was to march forth and attack the British force near the head of the valley. Some of the more hot-headed ones rather openly taunted the Continentals, but these veterans of Washington's army remained silent and composed amid more or less wildness of talk. My own concealed opinions were that, although our people were brave and determined, they had much better allow the Continental officers to manage the valley's affairs.

At the end of June, we heard the news that Colonel John Butler, with some four hundred British and Colonial troops, which he called the Rangers, and with about five hundred Indians, had entered the valley at its head and taken Fort Wintermoot after an opposition of a perfunctory character. I could present arms very well, but I do not think that I could yet keep my heels together. But "Indian Butler" was marching upon us, and even Captain Bidlack refrained from being annoyed at my refractory heels.

The officers held councils of war, but in truth both fort and camp rang with a discussion in which everybody joined with great vigour and endurance. I may except the Continental officers, who told us what they thought we should do, and then, declaring that there was no more to be said, remained in a silence which I thought was rather grim. The result was that on the 3rd of July our force of about 300 men marched away, amid the roll of drums and the proud career of flags, to meet "Indian Butler" and his two kinds of savages. There yet remains with me a vivid recollection of a close row of faces above the stockade of Forty Fort which viewed our departure with that profound anxiety which only an imminent danger of murder and scalping can produce. I myself was never particularly afraid of the Indians, for to my mind the great and almost the only military virtue of the Indians was that they were silent men in the woods. If they were met squarely on terms approaching equality, they could always be whipped. But it was another matter to a fort filled with women and children and cripples, to whom the coming of the Indians spelled pillage, arson, and massacre. The British sent against us in those days some curious upholders of the honour of the King, and although Indian Butler, who usually led them, afterwards contended that everything was performed with decency and care for the rules, we always found that such of our dead whose bodies we recovered invariably lacked hair on the tops of their heads, and if worse wasn't done to them we wouldn't even use the word mutilate.

Colonel Zebulon Butler rode along the column when we halted once for water. I looked at him eagerly, hoping to read in his face some sign of his opinions. But on the soldierly mask I could read nothing, although I am certain now that he felt that the fools among us were going to get us well beaten. But there was no vacillation in the direction of our march. We went straight until we could hear through the woods the infrequent shots of our leading party at retreating Indian scouts.

Our Colonel Butler then sent forward four of his best officers, who reconnoitered the ground in the enemy's front like so many engineers marking the place for a bastion. Then each of the six companies were told their place in the line. We of Captain Bidlack's company were on the extreme right. Then we formed in line and marched into battle, with me burning with the high resolve to kill Indian Butler and bear his sword into Forty Fort, while at the same time I was much shaken that one of Indian Butler's Indians might interfere with the noble plan. We moved stealthily among the pine trees, and I could not forbear looking constantly to right and left to make certain that everybody was of the same mind about this advance. With our Captain Bidlack was Captain Durkee of the regulars. He was also a valley man, and it seemed that every time I looked behind me I met the calm eye of this officer, and I came to refrain from looking behind me.

Still, I was very anxious to shoot Indians, and if I had doubted my ability in this direction I would have done myself a great injustice, for I could drive a nail to the head with a rifle ball at respectable range. I contend that I was not at all afraid of the enemy, but I much feared that certain of my comrades would change their minds about the expediency of battle on the 3rd July, 1778.

But our company was as steady and straight as a fence. I do not know who first saw dodging figures in the shadows of the trees in our front. The first fire we received, however, was from our flank, where some hidden Indians were yelling and firing, firing and yelling. We did not mind the war-whoops. We had heard too many drunken Indians in the settlements before the war. They wounded the lieutenant of the company next to ours, and a moment later they killed Captain Durkee. But we were steadily advancing and firing regular volleys into the shifting frieze of figures before us. The Indians gave their cries as if the imps of Hades had given tongue to their emotions. They fell back before us so rapidly and so cleverly that one had to watch his chance as the Indians sped from tree to tree. I had a sudden burst of rapture that they were beaten, and this was accentuated when I stepped over the body of an Indian whose forehead had a hole in it as squarely in the middle as if the location had been previously surveyed. In short, we were doing extremely well.

Soon we began to see the slower figures of white men through the trees, and it is only honest to say that they were easier to shoot. I myself caught sight of a fine officer in a uniform that seemed of green and buff. His sword-belt was fastened by a great shining brass plate, and, no longer feeling the elegancies of marksmanship, I fired at the brass plate. Such was the conformation of the ground between us that he disappeared as if he had sunk in the sea. We, all of us, were loading behind the trees and then charging ahead with fullest confidence.

But suddenly from our own left came wild cries from our men, while at the same time the yells of Indians redoubled in that direction. Our rush checked itself instinctively. The cries rolled toward us. Once I heard a word that sounded like "Quarte." Then, to be truthful, our line wavered. I heard Captain Bidlack give an angry and despairing shout, and I think he was killed before he finished it.

In a word, our left wing had gone to pieces. It was in complete rout. I know not the truth of the matter; but it seems that Colonel Denison had given an order which was misinterpreted for the order to retreat. At any rate, there can be no doubt of how fast the left wing ran away.

We ran away too. The company on our immediate left was the company of regulars, and I remember some red-faced and powder-stained men bellowing at me contemptuously. That company stayed, and, for the most part, died. I don't know what they mustered when we left the Fort, but from the battle eleven worn and ragged men emerged. In my running was wisdom. The country was suddenly full of fleet Indians, upon us with the tomahawk. Behind me as I ran I could hear the screams of men cleaved to the earth. I think the first things that most of us discarded were our rifles. Afterward, upon serious reflection, I could not recall where I gave my rifle to the grass.

I ran for the river. I saw some of our own men running ahead of me and I envied them. My point of contact with the river was the top of a high bank. But I did not hesitate to leap for the water with all my ounces of muscle. I struck out strongly for the other shore. I expected to be shot in the water. Up stream, and down stream, I could hear the crack of rifles, but none of the enemy seemed to be paying direct heed to me. I swam so well that I was soon able to put my feet on the slippery round stones and wade. When I reached a certain sandy beach, I lay down and puffed and blew my exhaustion. I watched the scene on the river. Indians appeared in groups on the opposite bank, firing at various heads of my comrades, who, like me, had chosen the Susquehanna as their refuge. I saw more than one hand fling up and the head turn sideways and sink.

I set out for home. I set out for home in that perfect spirit of dependence which I had always felt toward my father and my mother. When I arrived I found nobody in the living room but my father seated in his great chair and reading his Bible, even as I had left him.

The whole shame of the business came upon me suddenly. "Father," I choked out, "we have been beaten."

"Aye," said he, "I expected it."

LONDON IMPRESSIONS.

CHAPTER I.

London at first consisted of a porter with the most charming manners in the world, and a cabman with a supreme intelligence, both observing my profound ignorance without contempt or humour of any kind observable in their manners. It was in a great resounding vault of a place where there were many people who had come home, and I was displeased because they knew the detail of the business, whereas I was confronting the inscrutable. This made them appear very stony-hearted to the sufferings of one of whose existence, to be sure, they were entirely unaware, and I remember taking great pleasure in disliking them heartily for it. I was in an agony of mind over my baggage, or my luggage, or my-perhaps it is well to shy around this terrible international question; but I remember that when I was a lad I was told that there was a whole nation that said luggage instead of baggage, and my boyish mind was filled at the time with incredulity and scorn. In the present case it was a thing that I understood to involve the most hideous confessions of imbecility on my part, because I had evidently to go out to some obscure point and espy it and claim it, and take trouble for it; and I would rather have had my pockets filled with bread and cheese, and had no baggage at all.

Mind you, this was not at all a homage that I was paying to London. I was paying homage to a new game. A man properly lazy does not like new experiences until they become old ones. Moreover, I have been taught that a man, any man, who has a thousand times more points of information on a certain thing than I have will bully me because of it, and pour his advantages upon my bowed head until I am drenched with his superiority. It was in my education to concede some licence of the kind in this case, but the holy father of a porter and the saintly cabman occupied the middle distance imperturbably, and did not come down from their hills to clout me with knowledge. From this fact I experienced a criminal elation. I lost view of the idea that if I had been brow-beaten by porters and cabmen from one end of the United States to the other end I should warmly like it, because in numbers they are superior to me, and collectively they can have a great deal of fun out of a matter that would merely afford me the glee of the latent butcher.

This London, composed of a porter and a cabman, stood to me subtly as a benefactor. I had scanned the drama, and found that I did not believe that the mood of the men emanated unduly from the feature that there was probably more shillings to the square inch of me than there were shillings to the square inch of them. Nor yet was it any manner of palpable warm-heartedness or other natural virtue. But it was a perfect artificial virtue; it was drill, plain, simple drill. And now was I glad of their drilling, and vividly approved of it, because I saw that it was good for me. Whether it was good or bad for the porter and the cabman I could not know; but that point, mark you, came within the pale, of my respectable rumination.

I am sure that it would have been more correct for me to have alighted upon St. Paul's and described no emotion until I was overcome by the Thames Embankment and the Houses of Parliament. But as a matter of fact I did not see them for some days, and at this time they did not concern me at all. I was born in London at a railroad station, and my new vision encompassed a porter and a cabman. They deeply absorbed me in new phenomena, and I did not then care to see the Thames Embankment nor the Houses of Parliament. I considered the porter and the cabman to be more important.

CHAPTER II.

The cab finally rolled out of the gas-lit vault into a vast expanse of gloom. This changed to the shadowy lines of a street that was like a passage in a monstrous cave. The lamps winking here and there resembled the little gleams at the caps of the miners. They were not very competent illuminations at best, merely being little pale flares of gas that at their most heroic periods could only display one fact concerning this tunnel-the fact of general direction. But at any rate I should have liked to have observed the dejection of a search-light if it had been called upon to attempt to bore through this atmosphere. In it each man sat in his own little cylinder of vision, so to speak. It was not so small as a sentry-box nor so large as a circus tent, but the walls were opaque, and what was passing beyond the dimensions of his cylinder no man knew.

It was evident that the paving was very greasy, but all the cabs that passed through my cylinder were going at a round trot, while the wheels, shod in rubber, whirred merely like bicycles. The hoofs of the animals themselves did not make that wild clatter which I knew so well. New York, in fact, roars always like ten thousand devils. We have ingenuous and simple ways of making a din in New York that cause the stranger to conclude that each citizen is obliged by statute to provide himself with a pair of cymbals and a drum. If anything by chance can be turned into a noise it is promptly turned. We are engaged in the development of a human creature with very large, sturdy, and doubly-fortified ears.

It was not too late at night, but this London moved with the decorum and caution of an undertaker. There was a silence, and yet there was no silence. There was a low drone, perhaps a humming contributed inevitably by closely-gathered thousands, and yet on second thoughts it was to me silence. I had perched my ears for the note of London, the sound made simply by the existence of five million people in one place. I had imagined something deep, vastly deep, a bass from a mythical organ, but found, as far as I was concerned, only a silence.

New York in numbers is a mighty city, and all day and all night it cries its loud, fierce, aspiring cry, a noise of men beating upon barrels, a noise of men beating upon tin, a terrific racket that assails the abject skies. No one of us seemed to question this row as a certain consequence of three or four million people living together and scuffling for coin, with more agility, perhaps, but otherwise in the usual way. However, after this easy silence of London, which in numbers is a mightier city, I began to feel that there was a seduction in this idea of necessity. Our noise in New York was not a consequence of our rapidity at all. It was a consequence of our bad pavements.

Any brigade of artillery in Europe that would love to assemble its batteries, and then go on a gallop over the land, thundering and thundering, would give up the idea of thunder at once if it could hear Tim Mulligan drive a beer waggon along one of the side streets of cobbled New York.

CHAPTER III.

Finally, a great thing came to pass. The cab horse, proceeding at a sharp trot, found himself suddenly at the top of an incline, where through the rain the pavement shone like an expanse of ice. It looked to me as if there was going to be a tumble. In an accident of such a kind a hansom becomes really a cannon in which a man finds that he has paid shillings for the privilege of serving as a projectile. I was making a rapid calculation of the arc that I would describe in my flight, when the horse met his crisis with a masterly device that I could not have imagined. He tranquilly braced his four feet like a bundle of stakes, and then, with a gentle gaiety of demeanour, he slid swiftly and gracefully to the bottom of the hill as if he had been a toboggan. When the incline ended he caught his gait again with great dexterity, and went pattering off through another tunnel.

I at once looked upon myself as being singularly blessed by this sight. This horse had evidently originated this system of skating as a diversion, or, more probably, as a precaution against the slippery pavement; and he was, of course, the inventor and sole proprietor-two terms that are not always in conjunction. It surely was not to be supposed that there could be two skaters like him in the world. He deserved to be known and publicly praised for this accomplishment. It was worthy of many records and exhibitions. But when the cab arrived at a place where some dipping streets met, and the flaming front of a music-hall temporarily widened my cylinder, behold there were many cabs, and as the moment of necessity came the horses were all skaters. They were gliding in all directions. It might have been a rink. A great omnibus was hailed by a hand under an umbrella on the side walk, and the dignified horses bidden to halt from their trot did not waste time in wild and unseemly spasms. They, too, braced their legs and slid gravely to the end of their momentum.

It was not the feat, but it was the word which had at this time the power to conjure memories of skating parties on moonlit lakes, with laughter ringing over the ice, and a great red bonfire on the shore among the hemlocks.

CHAPTER IV.

A terrible thing in nature is the fall of a horse in his harness. It is a tragedy. Despite their skill in skating there was that about the pavement on the rainy evening which filled me with expectations of horses going headlong. Finally it happened just in front. There was a shout and a tangle in the darkness, and presently a prostrate cab horse came within my cylinder. The accident having been a complete success and altogether concluded, a voice from the side walk said, "*Look* out, now! *Be* more careful, can't you?"

I remember a constituent of a Congressman at Washington who had tried in vain to bore this Congressman with a wild project of some kind. The Congressman eluded him with skill, and his rage and despair ultimately culminated in the supreme grievance that he could not even get near enough to the Congressman to tell him to go to Hades.

This cabman should have felt the same desire to strangle this man who spoke from the side walk. He was plainly impotent; he was deprived of the power of looking out. There was nothing now for which to look out. The man on the side walk had dragged a corpse from a pond and said to it, "*Be* more careful, can't you, or you'll drown?" My cabman pulled up and addressed a few words of reproach to the other. Three or four figures loomed into my cylinder, and as they appeared spoke to the author or the victim of the calamity in varied terms of displeasure. Each of these reproaches was couched in terms that defined the situation as impending. No blind man could have conceived that the precipitate phrase of the incident was absolutely closed. "*Look* out now, cawnt you?" And there was nothing in his mind which approached these sentiments near enough to tell them to go to Hades.

However, it needed only an ear to know presently that these expressions were formulæ. It was merely the obligatory dance which the Indians had to perform before they went to war. These men had come to help, but as a regular and traditional preliminary they had first to display to this cabman their idea of his ignominy.

The different thing in the affair was the silence of the victim. He retorted never a word. This, too, to me seemed to be an obedience to a recognised form. He was the visible criminal, if there was a criminal, and there was born of it a privilege for them.

They unfastened the proper straps and hauled back the cab. They fetched a mat from some obscure place of succour, and pushed it carefully under the prostrate thing. From this panting, quivering mass they suddenly and emphatically reconstructed a horse. As each man turned to go his way he delivered some superior caution to the cabman while the latter buckled his harness.

CHAPTER V.

There was to be noticed in this band of rescuers a young man in evening clothes and top-hat. Now, in America a young man in evening clothes and a top-hat may be a terrible object. He is not likely to do violence, but he is likely to do impassivity and indifference to the point where they become worse than violence. There are certain of the more idle phases of civilisation to which America has not yet awakened-and it is a matter of no moment if she remains unaware. This matter of hats is one of them. I recall a legend recited to me by an esteemed friend, ex-Sheriff of Tin Can, Nevada. Jim Cortright, one of the best gun-fighters in town, went on a journey to Chicago, and while there he procured a top-hat. He was quite sure how Tin Can would accept this innovation, but he relied on the celerity with which he could get a six-shooter in action. One Sunday Jim examined his guns with his usual care, placed the top-hat on the back of his head, and sauntered coolly out into the streets of Tin Can.

Now, while Jim was in Chicago some progressive citizen had decided that Tin Can needed a bowling alley. The carpenters went to work the next morning, and an order for the balls and pins was telegraphed to Denver. In three days the whole population was concentrated at the new alley betting their outfits and their lives.

It has since been accounted very unfortunate that Jim Cortright had not learned of bowling alleys at his mother's knee nor even later in the mines. This portion of his mind was singularly belated. He might have been an Apache for all he knew of bowling alleys.

In his careless stroll through the town, his hands not far from his belt and his eyes going sideways in order to see who would shoot first at the hat, he came upon this long, low shanty where Tin Can was betting itself hoarse over a game between a team from the ranks of Excelsior Hose Company No. 1 and a team composed from the *habitues* of the "Red Light" saloon.

Jim, in blank ignorance of bowling phenomena, wandered casually through a little door into what must always be termed the wrong end of a bowling alley. Of course, he saw that the supreme moment had come. They were not only shooting at the hat and at him, but the low-down cusses were using the most extraordinary and hellish ammunition. Still, perfectly undaunted, however, Jim retorted with his two Colts, and killed three of the best bowlers in Tin Can.

The ex-Sheriff vouched for this story. He himself had gone headlong through the door at the firing of the first shot with that simple courtesy which leads Western men to donate the fighters plenty of room. He said that afterwards the hat was the cause of a number of other fights, and that finally a delegation of prominent citizens were obliged to wait upon Cortright and ask him if he wouldn't take that thing away somewhere and bury it. Jim pointed out to them that it was his hat, and that he would regard it as a cowardly concession if he submitted to their dictation in the matter of his headgear. He added that he purposed to continue to wear his top-hat on every occasion when he happened to feel that the wearing of a top-hat was a joy and a solace to him.

The delegation sadly retired, and announced to the town that Jim Cortright had openly defied them, and had declared his purpose of forcing his top-hat on the pained attention of Tin Can whenever he chose. Jim Cortright's plug hat became a phrase with considerable meaning to it.

However, the whole affair ended in a great passionate outburst of popular revolution. Spike Foster was a friend of Cortright, and one day, when the latter was indisposed, Spike came to him and borrowed the hat. He had been drinking heavily at the "Red Light," and was in a supremely reckless mood. With the terrible gear hanging jauntily over his eye and his two guns drawn, he walked straight out into the middle of the square in front of the Palace Hotel, and drew the attention of all Tin Can by a blood-curdling imitation of the yowl of a mountain lion.

This was when the long-suffering populace arose as one man. The top-hat had been flaunted once too often. When Spike Foster's friends came to carry him away they found nearly a hundred and fifty men shooting busily at a mark-and the mark was the hat.

My informant told me that he believed he owed his popularity in Tin Can, and subsequently his election to the distinguished office of Sheriff, to the active and prominent part he had taken in the proceedings.

The enmity to the top-hat expressed by the convincing anecdote exists in the American West at present, I think, in the perfection of its strength; but disapproval is not now displayed by volleys from the citizens, save in the most aggravating cases. It is at present usually a matter of mere jibe and general contempt. The East, however, despite a great deal of kicking and gouging, is having the top-hat stuffed slowly and carefully down its throat, and there now exist many young men who consider that they could not successfully conduct their lives without this furniture.

To speak generally, I should say that the headgear then supplies them with a kind of ferocity of indifference. There is fire, sword, and pestilence in the way they heed only themselves. Philosophy should always know that indifference is a militant thing. It batters down the walls of cities, and murders the women and children amid flames and the purloining of altar vessels. When it goes away it leaves smoking ruins, where lie citizens bayoneted through the throat. It is not a children's pastime like mere highway robbery.

Consequently in America we may be much afraid of these young men. We dive down valleys so that we may not kow-tow. It is a fearsome thing.

Taught thus a deep fear of the top-hat in its effect upon youth, I was not prepared for the move of this particular young man when the cab-horse fell. In fact, I grovelled in my corner that I might not see the cruel stateliness of his passing. But in the meantime he had crossed the street, and contributed the strength of his back and some advice, as well as the formal address, to the cabman on the importance of looking out immediately.

I felt that I was making a notable collection. I had a new kind of porter, a cylinder of vision, horses that could skate, and now I added a young man in a top-hat who would tacitly admit that the beings around him were alive. He was not walking a churchyard filled with inferior headstones. He was walking the world, where there were people, many people.

But later I took him out of the collection. I thought he had rebelled against the manner of a class, but I soon discovered that the top-hat was not the property of a class. It was the property of rogues, clerks, theatrical agents, damned seducers, poor men, nobles, and others. In fact, it was the universal rigging. It was the only hat; all other forms might as well be named ham, or chops, or oysters. I retracted my admiration of the young man because he may have been merely a rogue.

CHAPTER VI.

There was a window whereat an enterprising man by dodging two placards and a calendar was entitled to view a young woman. She was dejectedly writing in a large book. She was ultimately induced to open the window a trifle. "What nyme, please?" she said wearily. I was surprised to hear this language from her. I had expected to be addressed on a submarine topic. I have seen shell fishes sadly writing in large books at the bottom of a gloomy aquarium who could not ask me what was my "nyme."

At the end of the hall there was a grim portal marked "Lift." I pressed an electric button and heard an answering tinkle in the heavens. There was an upholstered settle near at hand, and I discovered the reason. A deer-stalking peace drooped upon everything, and in it a man could invoke the passing of a lazy pageant of twenty years of his life.

The dignity of a coffin being lowered into a grave surrounded the ultimate appearance of the lift. The expert we in America call the elevator-boy stepped from the car, took three paces forward, faced to attention, and saluted. This elevator-boy could not have been less than sixty years of age; a great white beard streamed towards his belt. I saw that the lift had been longer on its voyage than I had suspected.

Later in our upward progress a natural event would have been an establishment of social relations. Two enemies imprisoned together during the still hours of a balloon journey would, I believe, suffer a mental amalgamation. The overhang of a common fate, a great principal fact, can make an equality and a truce between any pair. Yet, when I disembarked, a final survey of the grey beard made me recall that I had failed even to ask the boy whether he had not taken probably three trips on this lift.

My windows overlooked simply a great sea of night, in which were swimming little gas fishes.

CHAPTER VII.

I have of late been led to wistfully reflect that many of the illustrators are very clever. In an impatience, which was denoted by a certain economy of apparel, I went to a window to look upon day-lit London. There were the 'buses parading the streets with the miens of elephants. There were the police looking precisely as I had been informed by the prints. There were the sandwich-men. There was almost everything.

But the artists had not told me the sound of London. Now, in New York the artists are able to pourtray sound, because in New York a dray is not a dray at all; it is a great potent noise hauled by two or more horses. When a magazine containing an illustration of a New York street is sent to me, I always know it beforehand. I can hear it coming through the mails. As I have said previously, this which I must call sound of London was to me only a silence.

Later, in front of the hotel a cabman that I hailed said to me —"Are you gowing far, sir? I've got a byby here, and want to giv'er a bit of a blough." This impressed me as being probably a quotation from an early Egyptian poet, but I learned soon enough that the word "byby" was the name of some kind or condition of horse. The cabman's next remark was addressed to a boy who took a perilous dive between the byby's nose and a cab in front. "That's roight. Put your head in there and get it jammed —a whackin good place for it, I should think." Although the tone was low and circumspect, I have never heard a better off-handed declamation. Every word was cut clear of disreputable alliances with its neighbours. The whole thing was as clean as a row of pewter mugs. The influence of indignation upon the voice caused me to reflect that we might devise a mechanical means of inflaming some in that constellation of mummers which is the heritage of the Anglo-Saxon race.

Then I saw the drilling of vehicles by two policemen. There were four torrents converging at a point, and when four torrents converge at one point engineering experts buy tickets for another place.

But here, again, it was drill, plain, simple drill. I must not falter in saying that I think the management of the traffic-as the phrase goes-to be distinctly illuminating and wonderful. The police were not ruffled and exasperated. They were as peaceful as two cows in a pasture.

I remember once remarking that mankind, with all its boasted modern progress, had not yet been able to invent a turnstile that will commute in fractions. I have now learned that 756 rights-of-way cannot operate simultaneously at one point. Right-of-way, like fighting women, requires space. Even two rights-of-way can make a scene which is only suited to the tastes of an ancient public.

This truth was very evidently recognised. There was only one right-of-way at a time. The police did not look behind them to see if their orders were to be obeyed; they knew they were to be obeyed. These four torrents were drilling like four battalions. The two blue-cloth men manœuvred them in solemn, abiding peace, the silence of London.

I thought at first that it was the intellect of the individual, but I looked at one constable closely and his face was as afire with intelligence as a flannel pin-cushion. It was not the police, and it was not the crowd. It was the police and the crowd. Again, it was drill.

CHAPTER VIII.

I have never been in the habit of reading signs. I don't like to read signs. I have never met a man that liked to read signs. I once invented a creature who could play the piano with a hammer, and I mentioned him to a professor in Harvard University whose peculiarity was Sanscrit. He had the same interest in my invention that I have in a certain kind of mustard. And yet this mustard has become a part of me. Or, I have become a part of this mustard. Further, I know more of an ink, a brand of hams, a kind of cigarette, and a novelist than any man living. I went by train to see a friend in the country, and after passing through a patent mucilage, some more hams, a South African Investment Company, a Parisian millinery firm, and a comic journal, I alighted at a new and original kind of corset. On my return journey the road almost continuously ran through soap.

I have accumulated superior information concerning these things, because I am at their mercy. If I want to know where I am I must find the definitive sign. This accounts for my glib use of the word mucilage, as well as the titles of other staples.

I suppose even the Briton in mixing his life must sometimes consult the labels on 'buses and streets and stations, even as the chemist consults the labels on his bottles and boxes. A brave man would possibly affirm that this was suggested by the existence of the labels.

The reason that I did not learn more about hams and mucilage in New York seems to me to be partly due to the fact that the British advertiser is allowed to exercise an unbridled strategy in his attack with his new corset or whatever upon the defensive public. He knows that the vulnerable point is the informatory sign which the citizen must, of course, use for his guidance, and then, with horse, foot, guns, corsets, hams, mucilage, investment companies, and all, he hurls himself at the point.

Meanwhile I have discovered a way to make the Sanscrit scholar heed my creature who plays the piano with a hammer.

NEW YORK SKETCHES

STORIES TOLD BY AN ARTIST IN NEW YORK

A Tale about How "Great Grief" got His Holiday Dinner.

Wrinkles had been peering into the little dry-goods box that acted as a cupboard.

"There are only two eggs and a half of a loaf of bread left," he announced brutally.

"Heavens!" said Warwickson, from where he lay smoking on the bed. He spoke in his usual dismal voice. By it he had earned his popular name of Great Grief.

Wrinkles was a thrifty soul. A sight of an almost bare cupboard maddened him. Even when he was not hungry, the ghosts of his careful ancestors caused him to rebel against it. He sat down with a virtuous air. "Well, what are we going to do?" he demanded of the others. It is good to be the thrifty man in a crowd of unsuccessful artists, for then you can keep the others from starving peacefully. "What are we going to do?"

"Oh, shut up, Wrinkles," said Grief from the bed. "You make me think."

Little Pennoyer, with head bended afar down, had been busily scratching away at a pen and ink drawing. He looked up from his board to utter his plaintive optimism.

"The *Monthly Amazement* may pay me to-morrow. They ought to. I've waited over three months now. I'm going down there to-morrow, and perhaps I'll get it."

His friends listened to him tolerantly, but at last Wrinkles could not omit a scornful giggle. He was such an old man, almost twenty-eight, and he had seen so many little boys be brave. "Oh, no doubt, Penny, old man." Over on the bed Grief croaked deep down in his throat. Nothing was said for a long time thereafter.

The crash of the New York streets came faintly. Occasionally one could hear the tramp of feet in the intricate corridors of this begrimed building that squatted, slumbering and aged, between two exalted commercial structures that would have had to bend afar down to perceive it. The light snow beat pattering into the window corners, and made vague and grey the vista of chimneys and roofs. Often the wind scurried swiftly and raised a long cry.

Great Grief leaned upon his elbow. "See to the fire, will you, Wrinkles?"

Wrinkles pulled the coal-box out from under the bed and threw open the stove door preparatory to shovelling some fuel. A red glare plunged in the first faint shadow of dusk. Little Pennoyer threw down his pen and tossed his drawing over on the wonderful heap of stuff that hid the table. "It's too dark to work." He lit his pipe and walked about, stretching his shoulders like a man whose labour was valuable.

When dusk came it saddened these youths. The solemnity of darkness always caused them to ponder. "Light the gas, Wrinkles," said Grief.

The flood of orange light showed clearly the dull walls lined with scratches, the tousled bed in one corner, the mass of boxes and trunks in another, the little fierce stove, and the wonderful table. Moreover, there were some wine-coloured draperies flung in some places, and on a shelf, high up, there was a plaster cast dark with dust in the creases. A long stove-pipe wandered off in the wrong direction, and then twined impulsively toward a hole in the wall. There were some extensive cobwebs on the ceilings.

"Well, let's eat," said Grief.

Later, there came a sad knock at the door. Wrinkles, arranging a tin pail on the stove, little Pennoyer busy at slicing the bread, and Great Grief affixing the rubber tube to the gas stove, yelled: "Come in!"

The door opened and Corinson entered dejectedly. His overcoat was very new. Wrinkles flashed an envious glance at it, but almost immediately he cried: "Hello, Corrie, old boy!"

Corinson sat down and felt around among the pipes until he found a good one. Great Grief had fixed the coffee to boil on the gas stove, but he had to watch it closely, for the rubber tube was short, and a chair was balanced on a trunk, and then the gas stove was balanced on the chair. Coffee making was a feat.

"Well," said Grief, with his back turned, "how goes it, Corrie? How's Art, hey?" He fastened a terrible emphasis upon the word.

"Crayon portraits," said Corinson.

"What?" They turned towards him with one movement, as if from a lever connection. Little Pennoyer dropped his knife.

"Crayon portraits," repeated Corinson. He smoked away in profound cynicism. "Fifteen dollars a week or more this time of year, you know." He smiled at them like a man of courage.

Little Pennoyer picked up his knife again. "Well, I'll be blowed," said Wrinkles. Feeling it incumbent upon him to think, he dropped into a chair and began to play serenades on his guitar and watch to see when the water for the eggs would boil. It was a habitual pose.

Great Grief, however, seemed to observe something bitter in the affair. "When did you discover that you couldn't draw?" he said stiffly.

"I haven't discovered it yet," replied Corinson, with a serene air. "I merely discovered that I would rather eat."

"Oh!" said Grief.

"Hand me the eggs, Grief," said Wrinkles. "The water's boiling."

Little Pennoyer burst into the conversation. "We'd ask you to dinner, Corrie, but there's only three of us and there's two eggs. I dropped a piece of bread on the floor, too. I'd shy one."

"That's all right, Penny," said the other; "don't trouble yourself. You artists should never be hospitable. I'm going anyway. I've got to make a call. Well, good night, boys. I've got to make a call. Drop in and see me."

When the door closed upon him, Grief said: "The coffee's done; I hate that fellow. That overcoat cost thirty dollars, if it cost a red. His egotism is so tranquil. It isn't like yours, Wrinkles. He —"

The door opened again and Corinson thrust in his head. "Say, you fellows, you know it's Thanksgiving to-morrow?"

"Well, what of it?" demanded Grief.

Little Pennoyer said: "Yes, I know it is, Corrie, I thought of it this morning."

"Well, come out and have a table d'hote with me to-morrow night. I'll blow you off in good style."

While Wrinkles played an exuberant air on his guitar, little Pennoyer did part of a ballet. They cried ecstatically: "Will we? Well, I guess yes?"

When they were alone again, Grief said: "I'm not going, anyhow. I hate that fellow."

"Oh, fiddle," said Wrinkles. "You're an infernal crank. And besides, where's your dinner coming from to-morrow night if you don't go? Tell me that."

Little Pennoyer said: "Yes, that's so, Grief. Where's your dinner coming from if you don't go?"

Grief said: "Well, I hate him, anyhow."

* * * * * * *

As To Payment of the Rent.

Little Pennoyer's four dollars could not last for ever. When he received it he and Wrinkles and Great Grief went to a table d'hote. Afterwards little Pennoyer discovered that only two dollars and a half remained. A small magazine away down town had accepted one out of the six drawings that he had taken them, and later had given him four dollars for it. Penny was so disheartened when he saw that his money was not going to last for ever, that even with two dollars and a half in his pockets, he felt much worse than when he was penniless, for at that time he anticipated twenty-four. Wrinkles lectured upon "Finance."

Great Grief said nothing, for it was established that when he received six dollar cheques from comic weeklies he dreamed of renting studios at seventy-five dollars per month, and was likely to go out and buy five dollars' worth of second-hand curtains and plaster casts.

When he had money Penny always hated the cluttered den in the old building. He desired to go out and breathe boastfully like a man. But he obeyed Wrinkles, the elder and the wise, and if you had visited that room about ten o'clock of a morning or about seven of an evening you would have thought that rye bread, frankfurters, and potato salad from Second Avenue were the only foods in the world.

Purple Sanderson lived there too, but then he really ate. He had learned parts of the gasfitter's trade before he came to be such a great artist, and when his opinions disagreed with that of every art manager in New York, he went to see a plumber, a friend of his, for whose opinion he had a great respect. In consequence, he frequented a very great restaurant on Twenty-third Street, and sometimes on Saturday nights he openly scorned his companions.

Purple was a good fellow, Grief said, but one of his singularly bad traits was that he always remembered everything. One night, not long after little Pennoyer's great discovery, Purple came in, and as he was neatly hanging up his coat, said: "Well, the rent will be due in four days."

"Will it?" demanded Penny, astounded. Penny was always astounded when the rent came due. It seemed to him the most extraordinary occurrence.

"Certainly it will," said Purple, with the irritated air of a superior financial man.

"My soul!" said Wrinkles.

Great Grief lay on the bed smoking a pipe and waiting for fame. "Oh, go home, Purple. You resent something. It wasn't me, it was the calendar."

"Try and be serious a moment, Grief."

"You're a fool, Purple."

Penny spoke from where he was at work. "Well, if those *Amazement Magazine* people pay me when they said they would I'll have money then."

"So you will, dear," said Grief, satirically. "You'll have money to burn. Did the *Amazement* people ever pay you when they said they would? You're wonderfully important all of a sudden, it seems to me. You talk like an artist."

Wrinkles, too, smiled at little Pennoyer. "The *Established Magazine* people wanted Penny to hire models and make a try for them too. It will only cost him a big blue chip. By the time he has invested all the money he hasn't got and the rent is two weeks' overdue, he will be able to tell the landlord to wait seven months until the Monday morning after the publication. Go ahead, Penny."

It was the habit to make game of little Pennoyer. He was always having gorgeous opportunities, with no opportunity to take advantage of his opportunities.

Penny smiled at them, his tiny, tiny smile of courage.

"You're a confident little cuss," observed Grief, irrelevantly.

"Well, the world has no objection to your being confident also, Grief," said Purple.

"Hasn't it?" said Grief. "Well, I want to know."

Wrinkles could not be light-spirited long. He was obliged to despair when occasion offered. At last he sank down in a chair and seized his guitar.

"Well, what's to be done?" he said. He began to play mournfully.

"Throw Purple out," mumbled Grief from the bed.

"Are you fairly certain that you will have money then, Penny?" asked Purple.

Little Pennoyer looked apprehensive. "Well, I don't know," he said.

And then began that memorable discussion, great in four minds. The tobacco was of the "Long John" brand. It smelled like burning mummies.

A Dinner on Sunday Evening.

Once Purple Sanderson went to his home in St. Lawrence county to enjoy some country air, and, incidentally, to explain his life failure to his people. Previously, Great Grief had given him odds that he would return sooner than he had planned, and everybody said that Grief had a good bet. It is not a glorious pastime, this explaining of life failures.

Later, Great Grief and Wrinkles went to Haverstraw to visit Grief's cousin and sketch. Little Pennoyer was disheartened, for it is bad to be imprisoned in brick and dust and cobbles when your ear can hear in the distance the harmony of the summer sunlight upon leaf and blade of green. Besides, he did not hear Wrinkles and Grief discoursing and quarrelling in the den, and Purple coming in at six o'clock with contempt.

On Friday afternoon he discovered that he only had fifty cents to last until Saturday morning, when he was to get his cheque from the *Gamin*. He was an artful little man by this time, however, and it is as true as the sky that when he walked toward the *Gamin* office on Saturday he had twenty cents remaining.

The cashier nodded his regrets, "Very sorry, Mr. —er-Pennoyer, but our pay-day, you know, is on Monday. Come around any time after ten."

"Oh, it don't matter," said Penny. As he walked along on his return he reflected deeply how he could invest his twenty cents in food to last until Monday morning any time after ten. He bought two coffee cakes in a third avenue bakery. They were very beautiful. Each had a hole in the centre, and a handsome scallop all around the edges.

Penny took great care of those cakes. At odd times he would rise from his work and go to see that no escape had been made. On Sunday he got up at noon and compressed breakfast and noon into one meal. Afterwards he had almost three-quarters of a cake still left to him. He congratulated himself that with strategy he could make it endure until Monday morning any time after ten.

At three in the afternoon there came a faint-hearted knock. "Come in," said Penny. The door opened and old Tim Connegan, who was trying to be a model, looked in apprehensively. "I beg pardon, sir," he said at once.

"Come in, Tim, you old thief," said Penny. Tim entered slowly and bashfully. "Sit down," said Penny. Tim sat down and began to rub his knees, for rheumatism had a mighty hold upon him.

Penny lit his pipe and crossed his legs. "Well, how goes it?"

Tim moved his square jaw upward and flashed Penny a little glance.

"Bad?" said Penny.

The old man raised his hand impressively. "I've been to every studio in the hull city, and I never see such absences in my life. What with the seashore and the mountains, and this and that resort, I think all the models will be starved by fall. I found one man in up on Fifty-seventh Street. He ses to me: 'Come around Tuesday —I may want yez and I may not.' That was last week. You know, I live down on the Bowery, Mr. Pennoyer, and when I got up there on Tuesday, he ses: 'Confound you, are you here again?' ses he. I went and sat down in the park, for I was too tired for the walk back. And there you are, Mr. Pennoyer. What with trampin' around to look for men that are thousand miles away, I'm near dead."

"It's hard," said Penny.

"It is, sir. I hope they'll come back soon. The summer is the death of us all, sir; it is. Sure, I never know where my next meal is coming until I get it. That's true."

"Had anything to-day?"

"Yes, sir, a little."

"How much?"

"Well, sir, a lady gave me a cup of coffee this morning. It was good, too, I'm telling you."

Penny went to his cupboard. When he returned, he said: "Here's some cake."

Tim thrust forward his hands, palms erect. "Oh, now, Mr. Pennoyer, I couldn't. You —"

"Go ahead. What's the odds?"

"Oh, now."

"Go ahead, you old bat."

Penny smoked.

When Tim was going out, he turned to grow eloquent again. "Well, I can't tell you how much I'm obliged to you, Mr. Pennoyer. You —"

"Don't mention it, old man."

Penny smoked.

THE SILVER PAGEANT.

"It's rotten," said Grief.

"Oh, it's fair, old man. Still, I would not call it a great contribution to American art," said Wrinkles.

"You've got a good thing, Gaunt, if you go at it right," said little Pennoyer.

These were all volunteer orations. The boys had come in one by one and spoken their opinions. Gaunt listened to them no more than if they had been so many match-peddlers. He never heard anything close at hand, and he never saw anything excepting that which transpired across a mystic wide sea. The shadow of his thoughts was in his eyes, a little grey mist, and, when what you said to him had passed out of your mind, he asked: "Wha—a—at?" It was understood that Gaunt was very good to tolerate the presence of the universe, which was noisy and interested in itself. All the younger men, moved by an instinct of faith, declared that he would one day be a great artist if he would only move faster than a pyramid. In the meantime he did not hear their voices. Occasionally when he saw a man take vivid pleasure in life, he faintly evinced an admiration. It seemed to strike him as a feat. As for him, he was watching that silver pageant across a sea.

When he came from Paris to New York somebody told him that he must make his living. He went to see some book publishers, and talked to them in his manner-as if he had just been stunned. At last one of them gave him drawings to do, and it did not surprise him. It was merely as if rain had come down.

Great Grief went to see him in his studio, and returned to the den to say: "Gaunt is working in his sleep. Somebody ought to set fire to him."

It was then that the others went over and smoked, and gave their opinions of a drawing. Wrinkles said: "Are you really looking at it, Gaunt? I don't think you've seen it yet, Gaunt?"

"What?"

"Why don't you look at it?"

When Wrinkles departed, the model, who was resting at that time, followed him into the hall and waved his arms in rage. "That feller's crazy. Yeh ought t' see —" and he recited lists of all the wrongs that can come to models.

It was a superstitious little band over in the den. They talked often of Gaunt. "He's got pictures in his eyes," said Wrinkles. They had expected genius to blindly stumble at the perface and ceremonies of the world, and each new flounder by Gaunt made a stir in the den. It awed them, and they waited.

At last one morning Gaunt burst into the room. They were all as dead men.

"I'm going to paint a picture." The mist in his eyes was pierced by a Coverian gleam. His gestures were wild and extravagant. Grief stretched out smoking on the bed, Wrinkles and little Pennoyer working at their drawing-boards tilted against the table-were suddenly frozen. If bronze statues had come and danced heavily before them, they could not have been thrilled further.

Gaunt tried to tell them of something, but it became knotted in his throat, and then suddenly he dashed out again.

Later they went earnestly over to Gaunt's studio. Perhaps he would tell them of what he saw across the sea.

He lay dead upon the floor. There was a little grey mist before his eyes.

When they finally arrived home that night they took a long time to undress for bed, and then came the moment when they waited for some one to put out the gas. Grief said at last, with the air of a man whose brain is desperately driven: "I wonder —I —what do you suppose he was going to paint?"

Wrinkles reached and turned out the gas, and from the sudden profound darkness, he said: "There is a mistake. He couldn't have had pictures in his eyes."

A STREET SCENE IN NEW YORK.

The man and the boy conversed in Italian, mumbling the soft syllables and making little, quick egotistical gestures. Suddenly the man glared and wavered on his limbs for a moment as if some blinding light had flashed before his vision; then he swayed like a drunken man and fell. The boy grasped his arm convulsively, and made an attempt to support his companion so that the body slid to the side-walk with an easy motion like a corpse sinking into the sea. The boy screamed.

Instantly people from all directions turned their gaze upon that figure prone upon the side-walk. In a moment there was a dodging, peering, pushing crowd about the man. A volley of questions, replies, speculations flew to and fro among all the bobbing heads.

"What's th' matter? what's th' matter?"

"Oh, a jag, I guess!"

"Aw, he's got a fit!"

"What's th' matter? what's th' matter?"

Two streams of people coming from different directions met at this point to form a great crowd. Others came from across the street.

Down under their feet, almost lost under this mass of people, lay a man, hidden in the shadows caused by their forms, which, in fact, barely allowed a particle of light to pass between them. Those in the foremost rank bended down eagerly, anxious to see everything. Others behind them crowded savagely like starving men fighting for bread. Always, the question could be heard flying in the air. "What's th' matter." Some, near to the body, and perhaps feeling the danger of being forced over upon it, twisted their heads and protested violently to those unheeding ones who were scuffling in the rear: "Say, quit yer shovin', can't yeh? What do yeh want, anyhow? Quit!"

Somebody back in the throng suddenly said: "Say, young feller, cheese that pushin'! I ain't no peach!"

Another voice said: "Well, dat's all right —"

The boy who had been with the Italian was standing helplessly, a frightened look in his eyes, and holding the man's hand. Sometimes he looked about him dumbly, with indefinite hope, as if he expected sudden assistance to come from the clouds. The men about him frequently jostled him until he was obliged to put his hand upon the breast of the body to maintain his balance. Those nearest the man upon the sidewalk at first saw his body go through a singular contortion. It was as if an invisible hand had reached up from the earth and had seized him by the hair. He seemed dragged slowly, pitilessly backward, while his body stiffened convulsively, his hands clenched, and his arms swung rigidly upward. Through his pallid, half-closed lids one could see the steel-coloured, assassin-like gleam of his eye, that shone with a mystic light as a corpse might glare at those live ones who seemed about to trample it under foot. As for the men near, they hung back, appearing as if they expected it might spring erect and grab them. Their eyes, however, were held in a spell of fascination. They scarce seemed to breathe. They were contemplating a depth into which a human being had sunk, and the marvel of this mystery of life or death held them chained. Occasionally from the rear a man came thrusting his way impetuously, satisfied that there was a horror to be seen, and apparently insane to get a view of it. More self-contained men swore at these persons when they tread upon their toes.

The street cars jingled past this scene in endless parade. Occasionally, down where the elevated road crossed the street, one could hear sometimes a thunder, suddenly begun and suddenly ended. Over the heads of the crowd hung an immovable canvas sign: "Regular Dinner twenty cents."

The body on the pave seemed like a bit of debris sunk in this human ocean.

But after the first spasm of curiosity had passed away, there were those in the crowd who began to bethink themselves of some way to help. A voice called out: "Rub his wrists." The boy and a man on the other side of the body began to rub the wrists and slap the palms of the man. A tall German suddenly appeared, and resolutely began to push the crowd back. "Get back there-get back," he repeated continually while he pushed at them. He seemed to have authority; the crowd obeyed him. He and another man knelt down by the man in the darkness and loosened his shirt at the throat. Once they struck a match and held it close to the man's face. This livid visage suddenly appearing under their feet in the light of the match's yellow glare, made the crowd shudder. Half articulate exclamations could be heard. There were men who nearly created a riot in the madness of their desire to see the thing.

Meanwhile others had been questioning the boy. "What's his name? Where does he live?"

Then a policeman appeared. The first part of this little drama had gone on without his assistance, but now he came, striding swiftly, his helmet towering over the crowd and shading that impenetrable police face. He charged the crowd as if he were a squadron of Irish Lancers. The people fairly withered before this onslaught. Occasionally he shouted: "Come, make way there. Come, now!" He was evidently a man whose life was half-pestered out of him by people who were sufficiently unreasonable and stupid as to insist on walking in the streets. He felt the rage toward them that a placid cow feels toward the flies that hover in clouds and disturb its repose. When he arrived at the centre of the crowd he first said, threateningly: "What's th' matter here?" And then when he saw that human bit of wreckage at the bottom of the sea of men, he said to it: "Come, git up out that! Git out a here!"

Whereupon hands were raised in the crowd and a volley of decorated information was blazed at the officer.

"Ah, he's got a fit, can't yeh see?"

"He's got a fit!"

"What th'ell yeh doin'? Leave 'im be!"

The policeman menaced with a glance the crowd from whose safe precincts the defiant voices had emerged.

A doctor had come. He and the policeman bended down at the man's side. Occasionally the officer reared up to create room. The crowd fell away before his admonitions, his threats, his sarcastic questions, and before the sweep of those two huge buckskin gloves.

At last the peering ones saw the man on the side-walk begin to breathe heavily, strainedly, as if he had just come to the surface from some deep water. He uttered a low cry in his foreign way. It was like a baby's squeal or the side wail of a little storm-tossed kitten. As this cry went forth to all those eager ears the jostling, crowding recommenced again furiously, until the doctor was obliged to yell warningly a dozen times. The policeman had gone to send the ambulance call.

Then a man struck another match, and in its meagre light the doctor felt the skull of the prostrate man carefully to discover if any wound had been caused by his fall to the stone side-walk. The crowd pressed and crushed again. It was as if they fully expected to see blood by the light of the match, and the desire made them appear almost insane. The policeman returned and fought with them. The doctor looked up occasionally to scold and demand room.

At last, out of the faint haze of light far up the street, there came the sound of a gong beating rapidly. A monstrous truck loaded to the sky with barrels scurried to one side with marvellous agility. And then the black waggon, with its gleam of gold lettering and bright brass gong, clattered into view, the horse galloping. A young man, as imperturbable almost as if he were at a picnic, sat upon the rear seat. When they picked up the limp body, from which came little moans and howls, the crowd almost turned into a mob. When the ambulance started on its banging and clanging return, they stood and gazed until it was quite out of sight. Some resumed their way with an air of relief. Others still continued to stare after the vanished ambulance and its burden as if they had been cheated, as if the curtain had been rung down on a tragedy that was but half completed; and this impenetrable blanket intervening between a sufferer and their curiosity seemed to make them feel an injustice.

MINETTA LANE, NEW YORK.

Its Worst Days have Now Passed Away.
But its Inhabitants Still Include Many whose Deeds are Evil.

The Celebrated Resort of Mammy Ross.

Minetta Lane is a small and becobbled valley between hills and dingy brick. At night the street lamps, burning dimly, cause the shadows to be important, and in the gloom one sees groups of quietly conversant negroes, with occasionally the gleam of a passing growler. Everything is vaguely outlined and of uncertain identity, unless, indeed, it be the flashing buttons and shield of the policeman on his coast. The Sixth Avenue horse-cars jingle past one end of the lane, and a block eastward the little thoroughfare ends in the darkness of M'Dougall Street.

One wonders how such an insignificant alley could get such an assuredly large reputation, but, as a matter of fact, Minetta Lane and Minetta Street, which leads from it southward to Bleecker Street, were, until a few years ago, two of the most enthusiastically murderous thoroughfares in New York. Bleecker Street, M'Dougall Street, and nearly all the streets thereabouts were most unmistakably bad; the other streets went away and hid. To gain a reputation in Minetta Lane in those days a man was obliged to commit a number of furious crimes, and no celebrity was more important than the man who had a good honest killing to his credit. The inhabitants, for the most part, were negroes, and they represented the very worst element of their race. The razor habit clung to them with the tenacity of an epidemic, and every night the uneven cobbles felt blood. Minetta Lane was not a public thoroughfare at this period. It was a street set apart, a refuge for criminals. Thieves came here preferably with their gains, and almost any day peculiar sentences passed among the inhabitants. "Big Jim turned a thousand last night." "No-Toe's made another haul." And the worshipful citizens would make haste to be present at the consequent revel.

As has been said, Minetta Lane was then no thoroughfare. A peaceable citizen chose to make a circuit rather than venture through this place, that swarmed with the most dangerous people in the city. Indeed, the thieves of the district used to say: "Once get in the lane and you're all right." Even a policeman in chase of a criminal would probably shy away instead of pursuing him into the lane. The odds were too great against a lone officer.

Sailors, and any men who might appear to have money about them, were welcomed with all proper ceremony at the terrible dens of the lane. At departure they were fortunate if they still retained their teeth. It was the custom to leave very little else to them. There was every facility for the capture of coin, from trap-doors to plain ordinary knock-out drops.

And yet Minetta Lane is built on the grave of Minetta Brook, where, in olden times, lovers walked under the willows on the bank, and Minetta Lane, in later times, was the home of many of the best families of the town.

A negro named Bloodthirsty was perhaps the most luminous figure of Minetta Lane's aggregation of desperadoes. Bloodthirsty supposedly is alive now, but he has vanished from the lane. The police want him for murder. Bloodthirsty is a large negro, and very hideous. He has a rolling eye that shows white at the wrong time, and his neck, under the jaw, is dreadfully scarred and pitted.

Bloodthirsty was particularly eloquent when drunk, and in the wildness of a spree he would rave so graphically about gore that even the habitated wool of old timers would stand straight.

Bloodthirsty meant most of it, too. That is why his orations were impressive. His remarks were usually followed by the wide, lightning sweep of his razor. None cared to exchange epithets with Bloodthirsty. A man in a boiler iron suit would walk down to City Hall and look at the clock before he would ask the time of day from the single-minded and ingenuous Bloodthirsty.

After Bloodthirsty, in combative importance, came No-Toe Charley. Singularly enough, Charley was called No-Toe Charley because he did not have a toe on his feet. Charley was a small negro, and his manner of amusement befitting a smaller man. Charley was more wise, more sly, more round-about than the other man. The path of his crimes was like a corkscrew in architecture, and his method led him to make many tunnels. With all his cleverness, however, No-Toe was finally induced to pay a visit to the gentlemen in the grim, grey building up the river-Sing Sing.

Black-Cat was another famous bandit who made the land his home. Black-Cat is dead. Jube Tyler has been sent to prison, and after mentioning the recent disappearance of Old Man Spriggs it may be said that the lane is now destitute of the men who once crowned it with a glory of crime. It is hardly essential to mention Guinea Johnson.

Guinea is not a great figure. Guinea is just an ordinary little crook. Sometimes Guinea pays a visit to his friends, the other little crooks who make homes in the lane, but he himself does not live there, and with him out of it there is now no one whose industry's unlawfulness has yet earned him the dignity of a nickname. Indeed, it is difficult to find people now who remember the old gorgeous days, although it is but two years since the lane shone with sin like a new head-light. But after a search the reporter found three.

Mammy Ross is one of the last relics of the days of slaughter still living there. Her weird history also reaches back to the blossoming of the first members of the Whyo gang in the Old Sixth Ward, and her mind is stored with bloody memories. She at one time kept a sailors' boarding-house near the Tombs prison, and the accounts of all the festive crimes of that neighbourhood in ancient years roll easily from her tongue. They killed a sailor man every day, and pedestrians went about the streets wearing stoves for fear of the handy knives. At the present day the route to Mammy's home is up a flight of grimy stairs that are pasted on the outside of an old and tottering frame house. Then there is a hall blacker than a wolf's throat, and this hall leads to a little kitchen where Mammy usually sits groaning by the fire. She is, of course, very old, and she is also very fat. She seems always to be in great pain. She says she is suffering from "de very las' dregs of de yaller fever."

During the first part of a reporter's recent visit, old Mammy seemed most dolefully oppressed by her various diseases. Her great body shook and her teeth clicked spasmodically during her long and painful respirations. From time to time she reached her trembling hand and drew a shawl closer about her shoulders. She presented as true a picture of a person undergoing steady, unchangeable, chronic pain as a patent medicine firm could wish to discover for miraculous purposes. She breathed like a fish thrown out on the bank, and her old head continually quivered in the nervous tremors of the extremely aged and debilitated person. Meanwhile her daughter hung over the stove and placidly cooked sausages.

Appeals were made to the old woman's memory. Various personages who had been sublime figures of crime in the long-gone days were mentioned to her, and presently her eyes began to brighten. Her head no longer quivered. She seemed to lose for a period her sense of pain in the gentle excitement caused by the invocation of the spirits of her memory.

It appears that she had had a historic quarrel with Apple Mag. She first recited the prowess of Apple Mag; how this emphatic lady used to argue with paving stones, carving knives, and bricks. Then she told of the quarrel; what Mag said; what she said. It seems that they cited each other as spectacles of sin and corruption in more fully explanatory terms than are commonly known to be possible. But it was one of Mammy's most gorgeous recollections, and, as she told it, a smile widened over her face.

Finally she explained her celebrated retort to one of the most illustrious thugs that had blessed the city in bygone days. "Ah says to 'im, ah says: 'You-you'll die in yer boots like Gallopin' Thompson-dat's what you'll do. You des min' dat', honey. Ah got o'ny one chile, an' he ain't nuthin' but er cripple; but le'me tel' you, man, dat boy'll live t' pick de feathers f'm de goose dat'll eat de grass dat grows over your grave, man.' Dat's what I tol' 'm. But-law sake-how I know dat in less'n three day, dat man be lying in de gutter wif a knife stickin' out'n his back. Lawd, no, I sholy never s'pected noting like dat."

These reminiscences, at once maimed and reconstructed, have been treasured by old Mammy as carefully, as tenderly, as if they were the various little tokens of an early love. She applies the same black-handed sentiment to them, and, as she sits groaning by the fire, it is plainly to be seen that there is only one food for her ancient brain, and that is the recollection of the beautiful fights and murders of the past.

On the other side of the lane, but near Mammy's house, Pop Babcock keeps a restaurant. Pop says it is a restaurant, and so it must be one; but you could pass there ninety times each day and never know you were passing a restaurant. There is one obscure little window in the basement, and if you went close and peered in you might, after a time, be able to make out a small, dusty sign, lying amid jars on a dusty shelf. This sign reads: "Oysters in every style." If you are of a gambling turn of mind, you will probably stand out in the street and bet yourself black in the face that there isn't an oyster within a hundred yards. But Pop Babcock made that sign, and Pop Babcock could not tell an untruth. Pop is a model of all the virtues which an inventive fate has made for us. He says so.

As far as goes the management of Pop's restaurant, it differs from Sherry's. In the first place, the door is always kept locked. The wardmen of the Fifteenth precinct have a way of prowling through the restaurant almost every night, and Pop keeps the door locked in order to keep out the objectionable people that cause the wardmen's visits. He says so. The cooking stove is located in the main room of the restaurant, and it is placed in such a strategic manner that it occupies about all the space that is not already occupied by a table, a bench, and two chairs. The table will, on a pinch, furnish room for the plates of two people if they are willing to crowd. Pop says he is the best cook in the world.

When questioned concerning the present condition of the lane, Pop said: "Quiet! Quiet! Lo'd save us, maybe it ain't. Quiet! Quiet!" His emphasis was arranged crescendo, until the last word was really a vocal explosion. "Why, dish er' lane ain't nohow like what it uster be-no, indeed it ain't. No, sir. 'Deed it ain't. Why, I kin remember when dey was a-cuttin' an' a-slashin' long yere all night. 'Deed dey wos. My-my, dem times was different. Dat der Kent, he kep' de place at Green Gate cou't down yer ol' Mammy's —an' he was a hard baby —'deed he was-an' ol' Black-Cat an' ol' Bloodthirsty, dey was a-comin' round yere a-cuttin', an' a-slashin', an' a-cuttin', an' a-slashin'. Didn't dar' say boo to a goose in dose days, dat you didn't, less'n you lookin' fer a scrap. No, sir." Then he gave information concerning his own prowess at that time. Pop is about as tall as a picket of an undersized fence. "But dey didn't have nothin' ter say ter me. No, sir, 'deed dey didn't. I would lay down fer none of 'em. No, sir. Dey knew my gait, 'deed dey did. Man, man, many's de time I buck up agin 'em."

At this time Pop had three customers in his place, one asleep on the bench, one asleep on two chairs, and one asleep on the floor behind the stove.

But there is one who lends dignity of the real bevel-edged type to Minetta Lane, and that man is Hank Anderson. Hank, of course, does not live in the lane, but the shadows of his social perfections fall upon it as refreshingly as a morning dew.

Hank gave a dance twice in each week at a hall hard by in M'Dougall Street, and the dusky aristocracy of the neighbourhood know their guiding beacon. Moreover, Hank holds an annual ball in Forty-fourth Street. Also, he gives a picnic each year to the Montezuma Club, when he again appears as a guiding beacon. This picnic is usually held on a barge, and the excursion is a very joyous one. Some years ago it required the entire reserve squad of an up-town police precinct to properly control the enthusiasm of the gay picnickers, but that was an exceptional exuberance, and no measure of Hank's ability for management.

He is really a great manager. He was Boss Tweed's body-servant in the days when Tweed was a political prince, and any one who saw Bill Tweed through a spy-glass learned the science of leading, pulling, driving, and hauling men in a way to keep the men ignorant of it. Hank imbibed from this fount of knowledge, and he applied his information in Thompson Street. Thompson Street salaamed. Presently he bore a proud title: "The Mayor of Thompson Street."

Dignities from the principal political organisations of the city adorned his brow, and he speedily became illustrious.

Hank knew the lane well in its direful days. As for the inhabitants, he kept clear of them, and yet in touch with them, according to a method that he might have learned in the Sixth ward. The Sixth ward was a good place in which to learn that trick. Anderson can tell many strange tales and good of the lane, and he tells them in the graphic way of his class. "Why, they could steal your shirt without moving a wrinkle on it."

The killing of Joe Carey was the last murder that happened in the Minettas. Carey had what might be called a mixed-ale difference with a man named Kenny. They went out to the middle of Minetta Street to affably fight it out and determine the justice of the question.

In the scrimmage Kenny drew a knife, thrust quickly, and Carey fell. Kenny had not gone a hundred feet before he ran into the arms of a policeman.

There is probably no street in New York where the police keep closer watch than they do in Minetta Lane. There was a time when the inhabitants had a profound and reasonable contempt for the public guardians, but they have it no longer apparently. Any citizen can walk through there at any time in perfect safety, unless, perhaps, he should happen to get too frivolous. To be strictly accurate, the change began under the reign of police Captain Chapman. Under Captain Groo, a commander of the Fifteenth precinct, the lane donned a complete new garb. Its denizens brag now of its peace, precisely as they once bragged of its war. It is no more a bloody lane. The song of the razor is seldom heard. There are still toughs and semi-toughs galore in it, but they can't get a chance with the copper looking the other way. Groo got the poor lane by the throat. If a man should insist upon becoming a victim of the badger game, he could probably succeed, upon search in Minetta Lane, as indeed, he could on any of the great avenues, but then Minetta Lane is not supposed to be a pearly street of Paradise.

In the meantime the Italians have begun to dispute the possession of the lane with the negroes. Green Gate Court is filled with them now, and a row of houses near the M'Dougall Street corner is occupied entirely by Italian families. None of them seem to be over fond of the old Mulberry Bend fashion of life, and there are no cutting affrays among them worth mentioning. It is the original negro element that makes the trouble when there is trouble.

But they are happy in this condition are these people. The most extraordinary quality of the negro is his enormous capacity for happiness under most adverse circumstances. Minetta Lane is a place of poverty and sin, but these influences cannot destroy the broad smile of the negro —a vain and simple child, but happy. They all smile here, the most evil as well as the poorest. Knowing the negro, one always expects laughter from him, be he ever so poor, but it was a new experience to see a broad grin on the face of the devil. Even old Pop Babcock had a laugh as fine and mellow as would be the sound of falling glass, broken saints from high windows, in the silence of some great cathedral's hollow.

THE ROOF GARDENS AND GARDENERS OF NEW YORK.

A Phase of New York Life as Seen by a Close Observer.

When the hot weather comes the roof gardens burst into full bloom, and if an inhabitant of Chicago should take flight on his wings over this city, he would observe six or eight flashing spots in the darkness, spots as radiant as crowns. These are the roof gardens, and if a giant had flung a handful of monstrous golden coins upon the sombre-shadowed city he could not have benefited the metropolis more, although he would not have given the same opportunity to various commercial aspirants to charge a price and a half for everything. There are two classes of men-reporters and central office detectives-who do not mind these prices because they are very prodigal of their money.

Now is the time of the girl with the copper voice, the Irishman with circular whiskers, and the minstrel who had a reputation in 1833. To the street the noise of the band comes down on the wind in fitful gusts, and at the brilliantly illuminated rail there is suggestion of many straw hats.

One of the main features of the roof garden is the waiter, who stands directly in front of you whenever anything interesting transpires on the stage. This waiter is three hundred feet high and seventy-two feet wide. His finger can block your view of the golden-haired *soubrette*, and when he waves his arm the stage disappears as if by a miracle. What particularly fascinates you is his lack of self-appreciation. He doesn't know that his length over all is three hundred feet, and that his beam is seventy-two feet. He only knows that while the golden-haired *soubrette* is singing her first verse he is depositing beer on the table before some thirsty New Yorkers. He only knows that during the third verse the thirsty New Yorkers object to the roof-garden prices. He does not know that behind him are some fifty citizens who ordinarily would not give three whoops to see the golden-haired *soubrette*, but who, under these particular circumstances, are kept from swift assassination by sheer force of the human will. He gives an impressive exhibition of a man who is regardless of consequences, oblivious to everything save his task, which is to provide beer. Some day there may be a wholesale massacre of roof-garden waiters, but they will die with astonished faces and with questions on their lips. Skulls so steadfastly opaque defy axes, or any of the other methods which the populace occasionally use to cure colossal stupidity.

Between numbers on an ordinary roof-garden programme, the orchestra sometimes plays what the more enlightened and wary citizens of the town call a "beer overture." But, for reasons which no civil service commission could give, the waiter does not choose this time to serve the thirsty. No; he waits until the golden-haired *soubrette* appears, he waits until the haggard audience has goaded itself into some interest in the proceedings. Then he gets under way. Then he comes forth and blots out the stage. In case of war, all roof-garden waiters should be recruited in a special regiment and sent out in advance of everything. There is a peculiar quality of bullet-proofness about them which would turn a projectile pale.

If you have strategy enough in your soul you may gain furtive glimpses of the stage, despite the efforts of the waiters, and then, with something to engage the attention when the attention grows weary of the mystic wind, the flashing yellow lights, the music, and the undertone of the far street's roar, you should be happy.

Far up into the night there is a wildness, a temper to the air which suggests tossing tree boughs and the swift rustle of grass. The New Yorker, whose business will not allow him to go out to nature, perhaps, appreciates these little opportunities to go up to nature, although doubtless he thinks he goes to see the show.

One season two new roof gardens have opened. The one at the top of Grand Central Palace is large enough for a regimental drill room. The band is imprisoned still higher in a turreted affair, and a person who prefers gentle and unobtrusive amusement can gain deep pleasure and satisfaction from watching the leader of this band gesticulating upon the heavens. His figure is silhouetted beautifully against the sky, and every gesture in which he wrings noise from his band is interestingly accentuated.

The other new roof garden was Oscar Hammerstein's Olympia, which blazes on Broadway.

Oscar originally made a great reputation for getting out injunctions. All court judges in New York worked overtime when Oscar was in this business. He enjoined everybody in sight. He had a special machine made —"Drop a nickel in the judge and get an injunction." Then he sent a man to Washington for twenty-two thousand dollars' worth of nickels. In Harlem, where he then lived, it rained orders of the court every day at twelve o'clock. The street-cleaning commission was obliged to enlist a special force to deal with Oscar's injunctions. Citizens meeting on the street never said: "Good morning, how do you feel to-day?" They always said: "Good morning, have you been enjoined yet to-day?" When a man perhaps wished to enter a little game of draw, the universal form was changed when he sent a note to his wife: "Dear Louise, I have received an order of the court restraining me from coming home to dinner to-night. Yours, George."

But Oscar changed. He smashed his machine, girded himself, and resolved to provide the public with amusement. And now we see this great mind applying itself to a roof garden with the same unflagging industry and boundless energy which had previously expressed itself in injunctions. The Olympia, his new roof garden, is a feat. It has an exuberance which reminds one of the Union Depot train-shed of some western city. The steel arches of the roof make a wide and splendid sweep, and over in the corner there are real swans swimming in real water. The whole structure glares like a conflagration with the countless electric lights. Oscar has caused the execution of decorative paintings upon the walls. If he had caused the execution of the decorative painters he would have done better; but a man who has devoted the greater part of his life to the propagation of injunctions is not supposed to understand that wall decoration which appears to have been done with a nozzle is worse than none. But if carpers say that Oscar failed in his landscapes, none can say that he failed in his measurements of the popular mind. The people come in swarms to the Olympia. Two elevators are busy at conveying them to where the cool and steady night-wind insults the straw hat; and the scene here during the popular part of the evening is perhaps more gaudy and dazzling than any other in New York.

The bicycle has attained an economic position of vast importance. The roof garden ought to attain such a position, and it doubtless will soon-as we give it the opportunity it desires.

The Arab or the Moor probably invented the roof garden in some long-gone centuries, and they are at this day inveterate roof gardeners. The American, surprisingly belated-for him, has but recently seized upon the idea, and its development here has been only partial. The possibilities of the roof garden are still unknown.

Here is a vast city in which thousands of people in summer half stifle, cry out continually for air, fresher air. Just above their heads is what might be called a county of unoccupied land. It is not ridiculously small when compared with the area of New York county itself. But it is as lonely as a desert, this region of roofs. It is as untrodden as the corners of Arizona. Unless a man be a roof gardener, he knows practically nothing of this land.

Down in the slums necessity forces a solution of problems. It drives the people to the roofs. An evening upon a tenement roof with the great golden march of the stars across the sky, and Johnnie gone for a pail of beer, is not so bad if you have never seen the mountains nor heard, to your heart, the slow, sad song of the pines.

IN THE BROADWAY CARS.

Panorama of a Day from the Down-town Rush of the Morning to the Uninterrupted Whirr of the Cable at Night-The Man, and the Woman, and the Conductor.

The cable cars come down Broadway as the waters come down at Lodore. Years ago Father Knickerbocker had convulsions when it was proposed to lay impious rails on his sacred thoroughfare. At the present day the cars, by force of column and numbers, almost dominate the great street, and the eye of even an old New Yorker is held by these long yellow monsters which prowl intently up and down, up and down, in a mystic search.

In the grey of the morning they come out of the up-town, bearing janitors, porters, all that class which carries the keys to set alive the great down-town. Later, they shower clerks. Later still, they shower more clerks. And the thermometer which is attached to a conductor's temper is steadily rising, rising, and the blissful time arrives when everybody hangs to a strap and stands on his neighbour's toes. Ten o'clock comes, and the Broadway cars, as well as elevated cars, horse cars, and ferryboats innumerable, heave sighs of relief. They have filled lower New York with a vast army of men who will chase to and fro and amuse themselves until almost nightfall.

The cable car's pulse drops to normal. But the conductor's pulse begins now to beat in split seconds. He has come to the crisis in his day's agony. He is now to be overwhelmed with feminine shoppers. They all are going to give him two-dollar bills to change. They all are going to threaten to report him. He passes his hand across his brow and curses his beard from black to grey and from grey to black.

Men and women have different ways of hailing a car. A man-if he is not an old choleric gentleman, who owns not this road but some other road-throws up a timid finger, and appears to believe that the King of Abyssinia is careering past on his war-chariot, and only his opinion of other people's Americanism keeps him from deep salaams. The gripman usually jerks his thumb over his shoulder and indicates the next car, which is three miles away. Then the man catches the last platform, goes into the car, climbs upon some one's toes, opens his morning paper, and is happy.

When a woman hails a car there is no question of its being the King of Abyssinia's warchariot. She has bought the car for three dollars and ninety-eight cents. The conductor owes his position to her, and the gripman's mother does her laundry. No captain in the Royal Horse Artillery ever stops his battery from going through a stone house in a way to equal her manner of bringing that car back on its haunches. Then she walks leisurely forward, and after scanning the step to see if there is any mud upon it, and opening her pocket-book to make sure of a two-dollar bill, she says: "Do you give transfers down Twenty-eighth Street?"

Some time the conductor breaks the bell strap when he pulls it under these conditions. Then, as the car goes on, he goes and bullies some person who had nothing to do with the affair.

The car sweeps on its diagonal path through the Tenderloin with its hotels, its theatres, its flower shops, its 10,000,000 actors who played with Booth and Barret. It passes Madison Square and enters the gorge made by the towering walls of great shops. It sweeps around the double curve at Union Square and Fourteenth Street, and a life insurance agent falls in a fit as the car dashes over the crossing, narrowly missing three old ladies, two old gentlemen, a newly-married couple, a sandwich man, a newsboy, and a dog. At Grace Church the conductor has an altercation with a brave and reckless passenger who beards him in his own car, and at Canal Street he takes dire vengeance by tumbling a drunken man on to the pavement. Meanwhile, the gripman has become involved with countless truck drivers, and inch by inch, foot by foot, he fights his way to City Hall Park. On past the Post Office the car goes, with the gripman getting advice, admonition, personal comment, an invitation to fight from the drivers, until

Battery Park appears at the foot of the slope, and as the car goes sedately around the curve the burnished shield of the bay shines through the trees.

It is a great ride, full of exciting actions. Those inexperienced persons who have been merely chased by Indians know little of the dramatic quality which life may hold for them. These jungle of men and vehicles, these cañons of streets, these lofty mountains of iron and cut stone —a ride through them affords plenty of excitement. And no lone panther's howl is more serious in intention than the howl of the truck driver when the cable car bumps one of his rear wheels.

Owing to a strange humour of the gods that make our comfort, sailor hats with wide brims come into vogue whenever we are all engaged in hanging to cable-car straps. There is only one more serious combination known to science, but a trial of it is at this day impossible. If a troupe of Elizabethan courtiers in large ruffs should board a cable car, the complication would be a very awesome one, and the profanity would be in old English, but very inspiring. However, the combination of wide-brimmed hats and crowded cable cars is tremendous in its power to cause misery to the patient New York public.

Suppose you are in a cable car, clutching for life and family a creaking strap from overhead. At your shoulder is a little dude in a very wide-brimmed straw hat with a red band. If you were in your senses you would recognise this flaming band as an omen of blood. But you are not in your senses; you are in a Broadway cable car. You are not supposed to have any senses. From the forward end you hear the gripman uttering shrill whoops and running over citizens. Suddenly the car comes to a curve. Making a swift running start, it turns three hand-springs, throws a cart wheel for luck, bounds into the air, hurls six passengers over the nearest building, and comes down a-straddle of the track. That is the way in which we turn curves in New York.

Meanwhile, during the car's gamboling, the corrugated rim of the dude's hat has swept naturally across your neck, and has left nothing for your head to do but to quit your shoulders. As the car roars your head falls into the waiting arms of the proper authorities. The dude is dead; everything is dead. The interior of the car resembles the scene of the battle of Wounded Knee, but this gives you small satisfaction.

There was once a person possessing a fund of uncanny humour who greatly desired to import from past ages a corps of knights in full armour. He then purposed to pack the warriors into a cable car and send them around a curve. He thought that he could gain much pleasure by standing near and listening to the wild clash of steel upon steel-the tumult of mailed heads striking together, the bitter grind of armoured legs bending the wrong way. He thought that this would teach them that war is grim.

Towards evening, when the tides of travel set northward, it is curious to see how the gripman and conductor reverse their tempers. Their dispositions flop over like patent signals. During the down-trip they had in mind always the advantages of being at Battery Park. A perpetual picture of the blessings of Battery Park was before them, and every delay made them fume-made this picture all the more alluring. Now the delights of up-town appear to them. They have reversed the signs on the cars; they have reversed their aspirations. Battery Park has been gained and forgotten. There is a new goal. Here is a perpetual illustration which the philosophers of New York may use.

In the Tenderloin, the place of theatres, and of the restaurant where gayer New York does her dining, the cable cars in the evening carry a stratum of society which looks like a new one, but it is of the familiar strata in other clothes. It is just as good as a new stratum, however, for in evening dress the average man feels that he has gone up three pegs in the social scale, and there is considerable evening dress about a Broadway car in the evening. A car with its electric lamp resembles a brilliantly-lighted salon, and the atmosphere grows just a trifle strained. People sit more rigidly, and glance sidewise, perhaps, as if each was positive of possessing social value, but was doubtful of all others. The conductor says: "Ah, gwan. Git off th' earth." But this is to a man at Canal Street. That shows his versatility. He stands on the platform and beams in a modest and polite manner into the car. He notes a lifted finger and grabs swiftly for the bell strap. He reaches down to help a woman aboard. Perhaps his demeanour is a reflection of the manner of the people in the car. No one is in a mad New York hurry; no one is fretting and muttering; no one is perched upon his neighbour's toes. Moreover, the Tenderloin is a glory at night. Broadway of late years has fallen heir to countless signs illuminated with red, blue, green, and gold electric lamps, and the people certainly fly to these as the moths go to a candle. And perhaps the gods have allowed this opportunity to observe and study the best-dressed crowds in the world to operate upon the conductor until his mood is to treat us with care and mildness.

Late at night, after the diners and theatre-goers have been lost in Harlem, various inebriate persons may perchance emerge from the darker regions of Sixth Avenue and swing their arms solemnly at the gripman. If the Broadway cars run for the next 7000 years this will be the only time when one New Yorker will address another in public without an excuse sent direct from heaven. In these cars late at night it is not impossible that some fearless drunkard will attempt to inaugurate a general conversation. He is quite willing to devote his ability to the affair. He tells of the fun he thinks he has had; describes his feelings; recounts stories of his dim past. None reply, although all listen with every ear. The rake probably ends by borrowing a match, lighting a cigar, and entering into a wrangle with the conductor with an *abandon*, a ferocity, and a courage that do not come to us when we are sober.

In the meantime the figures on the street grow fewer and fewer. Strolling policemen test the locks of the great dark-fronted stores. Nighthawk cabs whirl by the cars on their mysterious errands. Finally the cars themselves depart in the way of the citizen, and for the few hours before dawn a new sound comes into the still thoroughfare-the cable whirring in its channel underground.

THE ASSASSIN IN MODERN BATTLES.

The Torpedo Boat Destroyers that "Perform in the Darkness. An Act which Is more Peculiarly Murderous than most Things in War."

In the past century the gallant aristocracy of London liked to travel down the south bank of the Thames to Greenwich Hospital, where venerable pensioners of the crown were ready to hire telescopes at a penny each, and with these telescopes the lords and ladies were able to view at a better advantage the dried and enchained corpses of pirates hanging from the gibbets on the Isle of Dogs. In those times the dismal marsh was inhabited solely by the clanking figures whose feet moved in the wind like rather poorly-constructed weather cocks.

But even the Isle of Dogs could not escape the appetite of an expanding London. Thousands of souls now live on it, and it has changed its character from that of a place of execution, with mist, wet with fever, coiling forever from the mire and wandering among the black gibbets, to that of an ordinary, squalid, nauseating slum of London, whose streets bear a faint resemblance to that part of Avenue A which lies directly above Sixtieth Street in New York.

Down near the water front one finds a long brick building, three-storeyed and signless, which shuts off all view of the river. The windows, as well as the bricks, are very dirty, and you see no sign of life, unless some smudged workman dodges in through a little door. The place might be a factory for the making of lamps or stair rods, or any ordinary commercial thing. As a matter of fact, the building fronts the shipyard of Yarrow, the builder of torpedo boats, the maker of knives for the nations, the man who provides everybody with a certain kind of efficient weapon. One then remembers that if Russia fights England, Yarrow meets Yarrow; if Germany fights France, Yarrow meets Yarrow; if Chili fights Argentina, Yarrow meets Yarrow.

Besides the above-mentioned countries Yarrow has built torpedo boats for Italy, Austria, Holland, Japan, China, Ecuador, Brazil, Costa Rica, and Spain. There is a keeper of a great shop in London who is known as the Universal Provider. If a general conflagration of war should break out in the world, Yarrow would be known as one of the Universal Warriors, for it would practically be a battle between Yarrow, Armstrong, Krupp, and a few other firms. This is what makes interesting the dinginess of the cantonment on the Isle of Dogs.

The great Yarrow forte is to build speedy steamers of a tonnage of not more than 240 tons. This practically includes only yachts, launches, tugs, torpedo boat destroyers, torpedo boats, and of late shallow-draught gunboats for service on the Nile, Congo, and Niger. Some of the gunboats that shelled the dervishes from the banks of the Nile below Khartoum were built by Yarrow. Yarrow is always in action somewhere. Even if the firm's boats do not appear in every coming sea combat, the ideas of the firm will, for many nations, notably France and Germany, have bought specimens of the best models of Yarrow construction in order to reduplicate and reduplicate them in their own yards.

When the great fever to possess torpedo boats came upon the Powers of Europe, England was at first left far in the rear. Either Germany or France to-day has in her fleet more torpedo boats than has England. The British tar is a hard man to oust out of a habit. He had a habit of thinking that his battleships and cruisers were the final thing in naval construction. He scoffed at the advent of the torpedo boat. He did not scoff intelligently but because, mainly, he hated to be forced to change his ways.

You will usually find an Englishman balking and kicking at innovation up to the last moment. It takes him some years to get an idea into his head, and when finally it is inserted, he not only respects it, he reveres it. The Londoners have a fire brigade which would interest the ghost of a Babylonian, as an example of how much the method of extinguishing fires could degenerate in two thousand years, and in 1897, when a terrible fire devastated a part of the city, some voices were raised challenging the efficiency of the fire brigade. But that part of the London County Council which corresponds to fire commissioners in United States laid their hands upon their hearts and solemnly assured the public that they had investigated the matter, and had found the London fire brigade to be as good as any in the world. There were some isolated cases of dissent, but the great English public as a whole placidly accepted these assurances concerning the activity of the honoured corps.

For a long time England blundered in the same way over the matter of torpedo boats. They were authoritatively informed that there was nothing in all the talk about torpedo boats. Then came a great popular uproar, in which people tumbled over each other to get to the doors of the Admiralty and howl about torpedo boats. It was an awakening as unreasonable as had been the previous indifference and contempt. Then England began to build. She has never overtaken France or Germany in the number of torpedo boats, but she now heads the world with her collection of that marvel of marine architecture-the torpedo boat destroyer. She has about sixty-five of these vessels now in commission, and has about as many more in course of building.

People ordinarily have a false idea of the appearance of a destroyer. The common type is longer than an ordinary gunboat —a long, low, graceful thing, flying through the water at fabulous speed, with a great curve of water some yards back of the bow, and smoke flying horizontally from the three or four stacks.

Bushing this way and that way, circling, dodging, turning, they are like demons.

The best kind of modern destroyer has a length of 220 feet, with a beam of 26½ feet. The horse-power is about 6500, driving the boat at a speed of thirty-one knots or more. The engines are triple-expansion, with water tube boilers. They carry from 70 to 100 tons of coal, and at a speed of eight or nine knots can keep the sea for a week; so they are independent of coaling in a voyage of between 1300 and 1500 miles. They carry a crew of three or four officers, and about forty men.

They are armed usually with one twelve-pounder gun, and from three to five six-pounder guns, besides their equipment of torpedoes. Their hulls and top hamper are painted olive, buff, or preferably slate, in order to make them hard to find with the eye at sea.

Their principal functions, theoretically, are to discover and kill the enemy's torpedo boats, guard and scout for the main squadron, and perform messenger service. However, they are also torpedo boats of a most formidable kind, and in action will be found carrying out the torpedo boat idea in an expanded form. Four destroyers of this type building at the Yarrow yards were for Japan (1898).

The modern European ideal of a torpedo boat is a craft 152 feet long, with a beam of 15¼ feet. When the boat is fully loaded a speed of 24 knots is derived from her 2000 horse-power engines. The destroyers are twin screw, whereas the torpedo boats are commonly propelled by a single screw. The speed of twenty knots is for a run of three hours. These boats are not designed to keep at sea for any great length of time, and cannot raid toward a distant coast without the constant attendance of a cruiser to keep them in coal and provisions. Primarily they are for defence. Even with destroyers, England, in lately reinforcing her foreign stations, has seen fit to send cruisers in order to provide help for them in stormy weather.

Some years ago it was thought the proper thing to equip torpedo craft with rudders, which would enable them to turn in their own length when running at full speed. Yarrow found this to result in too much broken steering gear, and the firm's boats now have smaller rudders, which enable them to turn in a larger circle.

At one time a torpedo boat steaming at her best gait always carried a great bone in her teeth. During manœuvres the watch on the deck of a battleship often discovered the approach of the little enemy by the great white wave which the boat rolled at her bows during her headlong rush. This was mainly because the old-fashioned boats carried two torpedo tubes set in the bows, and the bows were consequently bluff.

The modern boat carries the great part of her armament amidships and astern on swivels, and her bow is like a dagger. With no more bow-waves, and with these phantom colours of buff, olive, bottle-green, or slate, the principal foe to a safe attack at night is bad firing in the stoke-room, which might cause flames to leap out of the stacks.

A captain of an English battleship recently remarked: "See those five destroyers lying there? Well, if they should attack me I would sink four of them, but the fifth one would sink me."

This was repeated to Yarrow's manager, who said: "He wouldn't sink four of them if the attack were at night and the boats were shrewdly and courageously handled." Anyhow, the captain's remark goes to show the wholesome respect which the great battleship has for these little fliers.

The Yarrow people say there is no sense in a torpedo flotilla attack on anything save vessels. A modern fortification is never built near enough to the water for a torpedo explosion to injure it, and, although some old stone flush-with-the-water castle might be badly crumpled, it would harm nobody in particular, even if the assault were wholly successful.

Of course, if a torpedo boat could get a chance at piers and dock gates they would make a disturbance, but the chance is extremely remote if the defenders have ordinary vigilance and some rapid fire guns. In harbour defence the searchlight would naturally play a most important part, whereas at sea experts are beginning to doubt its use as an auxiliary to the rapid fire guns against torpedo boats. About half the time it does little more than betray the position of the ship. On the other hand, a port cannot conceal its position anyhow, and searchlights would be invaluable for sweeping the narrow channels.

There could be only one direction from which the assault could come, and all the odds would be in favour of the guns on shore. A torpedo boat commander knows this perfectly. What he wants is a ship off at sea with a nervous crew staring into the encircling darkness from any point in which the terror might be coming.

Hi, then, for a grand, bold, silent rush and the assassin-like stab.

In stormy weather life on board a torpedo boat is not amusing. They tumble about like bucking bronchos, especially if they are going at anything like speed. Everything is battened down as if it were soldered, and the watch below feel that they are living in a football, which is being kicked every way at once.

And finally, while Yarrow and other great builders can make torpedo craft which are wonders of speed and manœuvring power, they cannot make that high spirit of daring and hardihood which is essential to a success.

That must exist in the mind of some young lieutenant who, knowing well that if he is detected, a shot or so from a rapid fire gun will cripple him if it does not sink him absolutely, nevertheless goes creeping off to sea to find a huge antagonist and perform stealthily in the darkness an act which is more peculiarly murderous than most things in war.

If a torpedo boat is caught within range in daylight, the fighting is all over before it begins. Any common little gunboat can dispose of it in a moment if the gunnery is not too Chinese.

IRISH NOTES

I. —AN OLD MAN GOES WOOING.

The melancholy fisherman made his way through a street that was mainly as dark as a tunnel. Sometimes an open door threw a rectangle of light upon the pavement, and within the cottages were scenes of working women and men, who comfortably smoked and talked. From them came the sounds of laughter and the babble of children. Each time the old man passed through one of the radiant zones the light etched his face in profile with touches flaming and sombre until there was a resemblance to a stern and mournful Dante portrait.

Once a whistling lad came through the darkness. He peered intently for purposes of recognition. "Good avenin', Mickey," he cried cheerfully. The old man responded with a groan, which intimated that the lamentable reckless optimism of the youth had forced from him an expression of an emotion that he had been enduring in saintly patience and silence. He continued his pilgrimage toward the kitchen of the village inn.

The kitchen is a great and worthy place. The long range with its lurid heat continually emits the fragrance of broiling fish, roasting mutton, joints, and fowl. The high black ceiling is ornamented with hams and flitches of bacon. There is a long, dark bench against one wall, and it is fronted by a dark table, handy for glasses of stout. On an old mahogany dresser rows of plates face the distant range, and reflect the red shine of the peat. Smoke which has in it the odour of an American forest fire eddies through the air. The great stones of the floor are scarred by the black mud from the inn yard. And here the gossip of a country-side goes on amid the sizzle of broiling fish and the loud protesting splutter of joints taken from the oven.

When the old man reached the door of this paradise, he stopped for a moment with his finger on the latch. He sighed deeply; evidently he was undergoing some lachrymose reflection. For somewhere overhead in the inn he could hear the wild clamour of dining pig-buyers, men who were come for the pig fair to be held on the morrow. Evidently in the little parlour of the inn these men were dining amid an uproar of shouted jests and laughter. The revelry sounded like the fighting of two mobs amid a rain of missiles and crash of shop windows. The old man raised his hand as if, unseen there in the darkness, he was going to solemnly damn the dinner of the pig-buyers.

Within the kitchen Nora, tall, strong, intrepid, approached the fiery stove in the manner of a boxer. Her left arm was held high to guard her face, which was already crimson from the blaze. With a flourish of her apron she achieved a great brown humming joint from the oven, and, emerging a glowing and triumphant figure from the steam and smoke and rapid play of heat, she slid the pan upon the table, even as she saw the old man standing within the room and lugubriously cleaning the mud from his boots. "Tis you, Mickey?" she said.

He made no reply until he had found his way to the long bench. "It is," he said then. It was clear that in the girl's opinion he had gained some kind of strategic advantage. The sanctity of her kitchen was successfully violated, but the old man betrayed no elation. Lifting one knee and placing it over the other, he grunted in the blissful weariness of a venerable labourer returned to his own fireside. He coughed dismally. "Ah, 'tis no good a man gits from fishin' these days. I moind the toimes whin they would be hoppin' up clear o' the wather, there was that little room fur thim. I would be likin' a bottle o' stout."

"Niver fear you, Mickey," answered the girl. Swinging here and there in the glare of the fire, Nora, with her towering figure and bare brawny arms, was like a feminine blacksmith at a forge. The old man, pallid, emaciated, watched her from the shadows at the other side of the room. The lines from the sides of his nose to the corners of his mouth sank low to an expression of despair deeper than any moans. He should have been painted upon the door of a tomb with wringing willows arched above him and men in grey robes slowly booming the drums of death. Finally he spoke. "I would be likin' a bottle o' stout, Nora, me girrl," he said.

"Niver fear you, Mickey," again she replied with cheerful obstinacy. She was admiring her famous roast, which now sat in its platter on the rack over the range. There was a lull in her tumultuous duties. The old man coughed and moved his foot with a scraping sound on the stones. The noise of dining pig-buyers, now heard through doors and winding corridors of the inn, was a roll of far-away storm.

A woman in a dark dress entered the kitchen and keenly examined the roast and Nora's other feats. "Mickey here would be wantin' a bottle o' stout," said the girl to her mistress. The woman turned towards the spectral figure in the gloom, and regarded it quietly with a clear eye. "Have yez the money, Mickey?" repeated the woman of the house.

Profoundly embittered, he replied in short terms, "I have."

"There now," cried Nora, in astonishment and admiration. Poising a large iron spoon, she was motionless, staring with open mouth at the old man. He searched his pockets slowly during a complete silence in the kitchen. He brought forth two coppers and laid them sadly, reproachfully, and yet defiantly on the table.

"There now," cried Nora, stupefied.

They brought him a bottle of the black brew, and Nora poured it out for him with her own red hand, which looked to be as broad as his chest. A collar of brown foam curled at the top of the glass. With measured moments the old man filled a short pipe. There came a sudden howl from another part of the inn. One of the pig-buyers was at the head of the stairs bawling for the mistress. The two women hurriedly freighted themselves with the roast and the vegetables, and sprang with them to placate the pig-buyers. Alone, the old man studied the gleam of the fire on the floor. It faded and brightened in the way of lightning at the horizon's edge.

When Nora returned, the strapping grenadier of a girl was blushing and giggling. The pig-buyers had been humorous. "I moind the toime —" began the man sorrowfully. "I moind the toime whin yea was a wee bit of a girrl, Nora, an' wouldn't be havin' words wid min loike thim buyers."

"I moind the toime whin yea could attind to your own affairs, ye ould skileton," said the girl promptly. He made a gesture, which may have expressed his stirring grief at the levity of the new generation, and then lapsed into another stillness.

The girl, a giantess, carrying, lifting, pushing, an incarnation of dauntless labour, changing the look of the whole kitchen with a moment's manipulation of her great arms, did not heed the old man for a long time. When she finally glanced toward him, she saw that he was sunk forward with his grey face on his arms. A growl of heavy breathing ascended. He was asleep.

She marched to him and put both hands to his collar. Despite his feeble and dreamy protestations, she dragged him out from behind the table and across the floor. She opened the door and thrust him into the night.

II. —BALLYDEHOB.

The illimitable inventive incapacity of the excursion companies has made many circular paths throughout Ireland, and on these well-pounded roads the guardians of the touring public may be seen drilling the little travellers in squads. To rise in rebellion, to face the superior clerk in his bureau, to endure his smile of pity and derision, and finally to wring freedom from him, is as difficult in some parts of Ireland as it is in all parts of Switzerland. To see the tourists chained in gangs and taken to see the Lakes of Killarney is a sad spectacle, because these people believe that they are learning Ireland, even as men believe that they are studying America when they contemplate the Niagara Falls.

But afterwards, if one escapes, one can go forth, unguided, untaught and alone, and look at Ireland. The joys of the pig-market, the delirium of a little tap-room filled with brogue, the fierce excitement of viewing the Royal Irish Constabulary fishing for trout, the whole quaint and primitive machinery of the peasant life-its melancholy, its sunshine, its humour-all this is then the property of the man who breaks like a Texan steer out of the pens and corrals of the tourist agencies. For what syndicate of maiden ladies-it is these who masquerade as tourist agencies-what syndicate of maiden ladies knows of the existence, for instance, of Ballydehob?

One has a sense of disclosure at writing the name of Ballydehob. It was really a valuable secret. There is in Ballydehob not one thing that is commonly pointed out to the stranger as a thing worthy of a half-tone reproduction in a book. There is no cascade, no peak, no lake, no guide with a fund of useless information, no gamins practised in the seduction of tourists. It is not an exhibit, an entry for a prize, like a heap of melons or cow. It is simply an Irish village wherein live some three hundred Irish and four constables.

If one or two prayer-towers spindled above Ballydehob it would be a perfect Turkish village. The red tiles and red bricks of England do not appear at all. The houses are low, with soiled white walls. The doors open abruptly upon dark old rooms. Here and there in the street is some crude cobbling done with round stones taken from the bed of a brook. At times there is a great deal of mud. Chickens depredate warily about the doorsteps, and intent pigs emerge for plunder from the alleys. It is unavoidable to admit that many people would consider Ballydehob quite too grimy.

Nobody lives here that has money. The average English tradesman with his back-breaking respect for this class, his reflex contempt for that class, his reverence for the tin gods, could here be a commercial lord and bully the people in one or two ways, until they were thrown back upon the defence which is always near them, the ability to cut his skin into strips with a wit that would be a foreign tongue to him. For amid his wrongs and his rights and his failures-his colossal failures-the Irishman retains this delicate blade for his enemies, for his friends, for himself, the ancestral dagger of fast sharp speaking from fast sharp seeing-an inheritance which could move the world. And the Royal Irish Constabulary fished for trout in the adjacent streams.

Mrs. Kearney keeps the hotel. In Ireland male innkeepers die young. Apparently they succumb to conviviality when it is presented to them in the guise of a business duty. Naturally honest, temperate men, their consciences are lulled to false security by this idea of hard drinking being necessary to the successful keeping of a public-house. It is very terrible.

But they invariably leave behind them capable widows, women who do not recognise conviviality as a business obligation. And so all through Ireland one finds these brisk widows keeping hotels with a precision that is almost military.

In Kearney's there is always a wonderful collection of old women, bent figures shrouded in shawls who reach up scrawny fingers to take their little purchases from Mary Agnes, who presides sometimes at the bar, but more often at the shop that fronts it in the same room. In the gloom of a late afternoon these old women are as mystic as the swinging, chanting witches on a dark stage when the thunder-drum rolls and the lightning flashes by schedule. When a grey rain sweeps through the narrow street of Ballydehob, and makes heavy shadows in Kearney's tap-room, these old creatures, with their high mournful voices, and the mystery of their shawls, their moans and aged mutterings when they are obliged to take a step, raise the dead superstitions from the bottom of a man's mind.

"My boy," remarked my London friend cheerfully, "these might have furnished sons to be Aldermen or Congressmen in the great city of New York."

"Aldermen or Congressmen of the great city of New York always take care of their mothers," I answered meekly.

On a barrel, over in a corner, sat a yellow-bearded Irish farmer in tattered clothes who wished to exchange views on the Armenian massacres. He had much information and a number of theories in regard to them. He also advanced the opinion that the chief political aim of Russia at present is in the direction of China, and that it behoved other Powers to keep an eye on her. He thought the revolutionists in Cuba would never accept autonomy at the hands of Spain. His pipe glowed comfortably from his corner; waving the tuppenny glass of stout in the air, he discoursed on the business of the remote ends of the earth with the glibness of a fourth secretary of Legation. Here was a little farmer, digging betimes in a forlorn patch of wet ground, a man to whom a sudden two shillings would appear as a miracle, a ragged, unkempt peasant, whose mind roamed the world like the soul of a lost diplomat. This unschooled man believed that the earth was a sphere inhabited by men that are alike in the essentials, different in the manners, the little manners, which are accounted of such great importance by the emaciated. He was to a degree capable of knowing that he lived on a sphere and not on the apex of a triangle.

And yet, when the talk had turned another corner, he confidently assured the assembled company that a hair from a horse's tail when thrown in a brook would turn shortly to an eel.

III. —THE ROYAL IRISH CONSTABULARY.

The newspapers called it a Veritable Arsenal. There was a description of how the sergeant of Constabulary had bent an ear to receive whispered information of the concealed arms, and had then marched his men swiftly and by night to surround a certain house. The search elicited a double-barrelled breech-loading shot-gun, some empty shells, powder, shot, and a loading machine. The point of it was that some of the Irish papers called it a Veritable Arsenal, and appeared to congratulate the Government upon having strangled another unhappy rebellion in its nest. They floundered and misnamed and mis-reasoned, and made a spectacle of the great modern craft of journalism, until the affair of this poor poacher was too absurd to be pitiable, and Englishmen over their coffee next morning must have almost believed that the prompt action of the Constabulary had quelled a rising. Thus it is that the Irish fight the Irish.

One cannot look Ireland straight in the face without seeing a great many constables. The country is dotted with little garrisons. It must have been said a thousand times that there is an absolute military occupation. The fact is too plain.

The constable himself becomes a figure interesting in its isolation. He has in most cases a social position which is somewhat analogous to that of a Turk in Thessaly. But then, in the same way, the Turk has the Turkish army. He can have battalions as companions and make the acquaintance of brigades. The constable has the Constabulary, it is true; but to be cooped with three or four others in a small white-washed iron-bound house on some bleak country side is not an exact parallel to the Thessalian situation. It looks to be a life that is infinitely lonely, ascetic, and barren. Two keepers of a lighthouse at a bitter end of land in a remote sea will, if they are properly let alone, make a murder in time. Five constables imprisoned 'mid a folk that will not turn a face toward them, five constables planted in a populated silence, may develop an acute and vivid economy, dwell in scowling dislike. A religious asylum in a snow-buried mountain pass will breed conspiring monks. A separated people will beget an egotism that is almost titanic. A world floating distinctly in space will call itself the only world. The progression is perfect.

But the constables take the second degree. They are next to the lighthouse keepers. The national custom of meeting stranger and friend alike on the road with a cheery greeting like "God save you" is too kindly and human a habit not to be missed. But all through the South of Ireland one sees the peasant turn his eyes pretentiously to the side of the road at the passing of the constable. It seemed to be generally understood that to note the presence of a constable was to make a conventional error. None looked, nodded, or gave sign. There was a line drawn so sternly that it reared like a fence. Of course, any police force in any part of the world can gather at its heels a riff-raff of people, fawning always on a hand licensed to strike that would be larger than the army of the Potomac, but of these one ordinarily sees little. The mass of the Irish strictly obey the stern tenet. One hears often of the ostracism or other punishment that befell some girl who was caught flirting with a constable.

Naturally the constable retreats to his pride. He is commonly a soldierly-looking chap, straight, lean, long-strided, well set-up. His little saucer of a forage cap sits obediently on his ear, as it does for the British soldier. He swings a little cane. He takes his medicine with a calm and hard face, and evidently stares full into every eye. But it is singular to find in the situation of the Royal Irish Constabulary the quality of pathos.

It is not known if these places in the South of Ireland are called disturbed districts. Over them hangs the peace of Surrey, but the word disturbance has an elastic arrangement by which it can be made to cover anything. All of the villages visited garrisoned from four to ten men. They lived comfortably in their white houses, strolled in pairs over the country roads, picked blackberries, and fished for trout. If at some time there came a crisis, one man was more than enough to surround it. The remaining nine add dignity to the scene. The crisis chiefly consisted of occasional drunken men who were unable to understand the local geography on Saturday nights.

The note continually struck was that each group of constables lived on a little social island, and there was no boat to take them off. There has been no such marooning since the days of the pirates. The sequestration must be complete when a man with a dinky little cap on his ear is not allowed to talk to the girls.

But they fish for trout. Isaac Walton is the father of the Royal Irish Constabulary. They could be seen on any fine day whipping the streams from source to mouth. There was one venerable sergeant who made a rod less than a yard long. With a line of about the same length attached to this rod, he hunted the gorse-hung banks of the little streams in the hills. An eight-inch ribbon of water lined with masses of heather and gorse will be accounted contemptible by a fisherman with an ordinary rod. But it was the pleasure of the sergeant to lay on his stomach at the side of such a stream and carefully, inch by inch, scout his hook through the pools. He probably caught more trout than any three men in county Cork. He fished more than any twelve men in the county Cork. Some people had never seen him in any other posture but that of crowding forward on his stomach to peer into a pool. They did not believe the rumour that he sometimes stood or walked like a human.

IV.—A FISHING VILLAGE.

The brook curved down over the rocks, innocent and white, until it faced a little strand of smooth gravel and flat stones. It turned then to the left, and thereafter its guilty current was tinged with the pink of diluted blood. Boulders standing neck-deep in the water were rimmed with red; they wore bloody collars whose tops marked the supreme instant of some tragic movement of the stream. In the pale green shallows of the bay's edge, the outward flow from the criminal little brook was as eloquently marked as if a long crimson carpet had been laid upon the waters. The scene of the carnage was the strand of smooth gravel and flat stones, and the fruit of the carnage was cleaned mackerel.

Far to the south, where the slate of the sea and the grey of the sky wove together, could be seen Fastnet Rock, a mere button on the moving, shimmering cloth, while a liner, no larger than a needle, spun a thread of smoke aslant. The gulls swept screaming along the dull line of the other shore of roaring Water Bay, and near the mouth of the brook circled among the fishing boats that lay at anchor, their brown, leathery sails idle and straight. The wheeling, shrieking tumultuous birds stared with their hideous unblinking eyes at the Capers-men from Cape Clear- who prowled to and fro on the decks amid shouts and the creak of the tackle. Shoreward, a little shrivelled man, overcome by a profound melancholy, fished hopelessly from the end of the pier. Back of him, on a hillside, sat a white village, nestled among more trees than is common in this part of Southern Ireland.

A dinghy sculled by a youth in a blue jersey wobbled rapidly past the pier-head and stopped at the foot of the moss-green, dank, stone steps, where the waves were making slow but regular leaps to mount higher, and then falling back gurgling, choking, and waving the long, dark seaweeds. The melancholy fisherman walked over to the top of the steps. The young man was fastening the painter of his boat in an iron ring. In the dinghy were three round baskets heaped high with mackerel. They glittered like masses of new silver coin at times, and then other lights of faint carmine and peacock blue would chase across the sides of the fish in a radiance that was finer than silver.

The melancholy fisherman looked at this wealth. He shook his head mournfully. "Ah, now, Denny. This would not be a very good kill."

The young man snorted indignantly at his fellow-townsman. "This will be th' bist kill th' year, Mickey. Go along now."

The melancholy old man became immersed in deeper gloom. "Shure I have been in th' way of seein' miny a grand day whin th' fish was runnin' sthrong in these wathers, but there will be no more big kills here. No more. No more." At the last his voice was only a dismal croak.

"Come along outa that now, Mickey," cried the youth impatiently. "Come away wid you."

"All gone now. A-ll go-o-ne now!" The old man wagged his grey head, and, standing over the baskets of fishes, groaned as Mordecai groaned for his people.

"'Tis you would be cryin' out, Mickey, whativer," said the youth with scorn. He was giving his basket into the hands of five incompetent but jovial little boys to carry to a waiting donkey cart.

"An' why should I not?" said the old man sternly. "Me-in want—"

As the youth swung his boat swiftly out toward an anchored smack, he made answer in a softer tone. "Shure, if yez got for th' askin', 'tis you, Mickey, that would niver be in want." The melancholy old man returned to his line. And the only moral in this incident is that the young man is the type that America procures from Ireland, and the old man is one of the home types, bent, pallid, hungry, disheartened, with a vision that magnifies with a microscope glance any fly-wing of misfortune, and heroically and conscientiously invents disasters for the future. Usually the thing that remains to one of this type is a sympathy as quick and acute for others as is his pity for himself.

The donkey with his cart-load of gleaming fish, and escorted by the whooping and laughing boys, galloped along the quay and up a street of the village until he was turned off at the gravelly strand, at the point where the colour of the brook was changing. Here twenty people of both sexes and all ages were preparing the fish for market. The mackerel, beautiful as fire-etched salvers, first were passed to a long table, around which worked as many women as could have elbow room. Each one could clean a fish with two motions of the knife. Then the washers, men who stood over the troughs filled with running water from the brook, soused the fish until the outlet became a sinister element that in an instant changed the brook from a happy thing of gorse and heather of the hills to an evil stream, sullen and reddened. After being washed, the fish were carried to a group of girls with knives, who made the cuts that enabled each fish to flatten out in the manner known of the breakfast table. And after the girls came the men and boys, who rubbed each fish thoroughly with great handfuls of coarse salt, which was whiter than snow, and shone in the daylight from a multitude of gleaming points, diamond-like. Last came the packers, drilled in the art of getting neither too few nor too many mackerel into a barrel, sprinkling constantly prodigal layers of brilliant salt. There were many intermediate corps of boys and girls carrying fish from point to point, and sometimes building them in stacks convenient to the hands of the more important labourers.

A vast tree hung its branches over the place. The leaves made a shadow that was religious in its effect, as if the spot was a chapel consecrated to labour. There was a hush upon the devotees. The women at the large table worked intently, steadfastly, with bowed heads. Their old petticoats were tucked high, showing the coarse brogans which they wore-and the visible ankles were proportioned to the brogans as the diameter of a straw is to that of a half-crown. The national red under-petticoat was a fundamental part of the scene.

Just over the wall, in the sloping street, could be seen the bejerseyed Capers, brawny, and with shocks of yellow beard. They paced slowly to and fro amid the geese and children. They, too, spoke little, even to each other; they smoked short pipes in saturnine dignity and silence. It was the fish. They who go with nets upon the reeling sea grow still with the mystery and solemnity of the trade. It was Brittany; the first respectable catch of the year had changed this garrulous Irish hamlet into a hamlet of Brittany.

The Capers were waiting for high tide. It had seemed for a long time that, for the south of Ireland, the mackerel had fled in company with potato; but here, at any rate, was a temporary success, and the occasion was momentous. A strolling Caper took his pipe and pointed with the stem out upon the bay. There was little wind, but an ambitious skipper had raised his anchor, and the craft, her strained brown sails idly swinging, was drifting away on the first oily turn of the tide.

On the top of the pier the figure of the melancholy old man was portrayed upon the polished water. He was still dangling his line hopelessly. He gazed down into the misty water. Once he stirred and murmured: "Bad luck to thim." Otherwise he seemed to remain motionless for hours. One by one the fishing-boats floated away. The brook changed its colour, and in the dusk showed a tumble of pearly white among the rocks.

A cold night wind, sweeping transversely across the pier, awakened perhaps the rheumatism in the old man's bones. He arose and, mumbling and grumbling, began to wind his line. The waves were lashing the stones. He moved off towards the intense darkness of the village streets.

SULLIVAN COUNTY SKETCHES

FOUR MEN IN A CAVE.

Likewise Four Queens, and a Sullivan County Hermit.

The moon rested for a moment on the top of a tall pine on a hill.

The little man was standing in front of the campfire making orations to his companions.

"We can tell a great tale when we get back to the city if we investigate this thing," said he, in conclusion.

They were won.

The little man was determined to explore a cave, because its black mouth had gaped at him. The four men took lighted pine-knot and clambered over boulders down a hill. In a thicket on the mountainside lay a little tilted hole. At its side they halted.

"Well?" said the little man.

They fought for last place and the little man was overwhelmed. He tried to struggle from under by crying that if the fat, pudgy man came after, he would be corked. But he finally administered a cursing over his shoulder and crawled into the hole. His companions gingerly followed.

A passage, the floor of damp clay and pebbles, the walls slimy, green-mossed, and dripping, sloped downward. In the cave atmosphere the torches became studies in red blaze and black smoke.

"Ho!" cried the little man, stifled and bedraggled, "let's go back." His companions were not brave. They were last. The next one to the little man pushed him on, so the little man said sulphurous words and cautiously continued his crawl.

Things that hung seemed to be on the wet, uneven ceiling, ready to drop upon the men's bare necks. Under their hands the clammy floor seemed alive and writhing. When the little man endeavoured to stand erect the ceiling forced him down. Knobs and points came out and punched him. His clothes were wet and mud-covered, and his eyes, nearly blinded by smoke, tried to pierce the darkness always before his torch.

"Oh, I say, you fellows, let's go back," cried he. At that moment he caught the gleam of trembling light in the blurred shadows before him.

"Ho!" he said, "here's another way out."

The passage turned abruptly. The little man put one hand around the corner, but it touched nothing. He investigated and discovered that the little corridor took a sudden dip down a hill. At the bottom shone a yellow light.

The little man wriggled painfully about, and descended feet in advance. The others followed his plan. All picked their way with anxious care. The traitorous rocks rolled from beneath the little man's feet and roared thunderously below him. Lesser stone, loosened by the men above him, hit him on the back. He gained seemingly firm foothold, and, turning half-way about, swore redly at his companions for dolts and careless fools. The pudgy man sat, puffing and perspiring, high in the rear of the procession. The fumes and smoke from four pine-knots were in his blood. Cinders and sparks lay thick in his eyes and hair. The pause of the little man angered him.

"Go on, you fool," he shouted. "Poor, painted man, you are afraid."

"Ho!" said the little man. "Come down here and go on yourself, imbecile!"

The pudgy man vibrated with passion. He leaned downward. "Idiot —!"

He was interrupted by one of his feet which flew out and crashed into the man in front of and below. It is not well to quarrel upon a slippery incline, when the unknown is below. The fat man, having lost the support of one pillar-like foot, lurched forward. His body smote the next man, who hurtled into the next man. Then they all fell upon the cursing little man.

They slid in a body down over the slippery, slimy floor of the passage. The stone avenue must have wibble-wobbled with the rush of this ball of tangled men and strangled cries. The torches went out with the combined assault upon the little man. The adventurers whirled to the unknown in darkness. The little man felt that he was pitching to death, but even in his convulsions he bit and scratched at his companions, for he was satisfied that it was their fault. The swirling mass went some twenty feet, and lit upon a level, dry place in a strong, yellow light of candles. It dissolved and became eyes.

The four men lay in a heap upon the floor of a grey chamber. A small fire smouldered in the corner, the smoke disappearing in a crack. In another corner was a bed of faded hemlock boughs and two blankets. Cooking utensils and clothes lay about, with boxes and a barrel.

Of these things the four men took small cognisance. The pudgy man did not curse the little man, nor did the little swear, in the abstract. Eight widened eyes were fixed upon the centre of the room of rocks.

A great, grey stone, cut squarely, like an altar, sat in the middle of the floor. Over it burned three candles, in swaying tin cups hung from the ceiling. Before it, with what seemed to be a small volume clasped in his yellow fingers, stood a man. He was an infinitely sallow person in the brown-checked shirt of the ploughs and cows. The rest of his apparel was boots. A long grey beard dangled from his chin. He fixed glinting, fiery eyes upon the heap of men, and remained motionless. Fascinated, their tongues cleaving, their blood cold, they arose to their feet. The gleaming glance of the recluse swept slowly over the group until it found the face of the little man. There it stayed and burned.

The little man shrivelled and crumpled as the dried leaf under the glass.

Finally, the recluse slowly, deeply spoke. It was a true voice from a cave, cold, solemn, and damp.

"It's your ante," he said.

"What?" said the little man.

The hermit tilted his beard and laughed a laugh that was either the chatter of a banshee in a storm or the rattle of pebbles in a tin box. His visitors' flesh seemed ready to drop from their bones.

They huddled together and cast fearful eyes over their shoulders. They whispered.

"A vampire!" said one.

"A ghoul!" said another.

"A Druid before the sacrifice," murmured another.

"The shade of an Aztec witch doctor," said the little man.

As they looked, the inscrutable face underwent a change. It became a livid background for his eyes, which blazed at the little man like impassioned carbuncles. His voice arose to a howl of ferocity. "It's your ante!" With a panther-like motion he drew a long, thin knife and advanced, stooping. Two cadaverous hounds came from nowhere, and, scowling and growling, made desperate feints at the little man's legs. His quaking companions pushed him forward.

Tremblingly he put his hand to his pocket.

"How much?" he said, with a shivering look at the knife that glittered.

The carbuncles faded.

"Three dollars," said the hermit, in sepulchral tones which rang against the walls and among the passages, awakening long-dead spirits with voices. The shaking little man took a roll of bills from a pocket and placed "three ones" upon the altar-like stone. The recluse looked at the little volume with reverence in his eyes. It was a pack of playing cards.

Under the three swinging candles, upon the altar-like stone, the grey beard and the agonised little man played at poker. The three other men crouched in a corner, and stared with eyes that gleamed with terror. Before them sat the cadaverous hounds licking their red lips. The candles burned low, and began to flicker. The fire in the corner expired.

Finally, the game came to a point where the little man laid down his hand and quavered: "I can't call you this time, sir. I'm dead broke."

"What?" shrieked the recluse. "Not call me! Villain! Dastard! Cur! I have four queens, miscreant." His voice grew so mighty that it could not fit his throat. He choked, wrestling with his lungs for a moment. Then the power of his body was concentrated in a word: "Go!"

He pointed a quivering, yellow finger at a wide crack in the rock. The little man threw himself at it with a howl. His erstwhile frozen companions felt their blood throb again. With great bounds they plunged after the little man. A minute of scrambling, falling, and pushing brought them to open air. They climbed the distance to their camp in furious springs.

The sky in the east was a lurid yellow. In the west the footprints of departing night lay on the pine trees. In front of their replenished camp fire sat John Willerkins, the guide.

"Hello!" he shouted at their approach. "Be you fellers ready to go deer huntin'?"

Without replying, they stopped and debated among themselves in whispers.

Finally, the pudgy man came forward.

"John," he inquired, "do you know anything peculiar about this cave below here?"

"Yes," said Willerkins at once; "Tom Gardner."

"What?" said the pudgy man.

"Tom Gardner."

"How's that?"

"Well, you see," said Willerkins slowly, as he took dignified pulls at his pipe, "Tom Gardner was once a fambly man, who lived in these here parts on a nice leetle farm. He uster go away to the city orften, and one time he got a-gamblin' in one of them there dens. He wentter the dickens right quick then. At last he kum home one time and tol' his folks he had up and sold the farm and all he had in the worl'. His leetle wife she died then. Tom he went crazy, and soon after —"

The narrative was interrupted by the little man, who became possessed of devils.

"I wouldn't give a cuss if he had left me 'nough money to get home on the doggoned, grey-haired red pirate," he shrilled, in a seething sentence. The pudgy man gazed at the little man calmly and sneeringly.

"Oh, well," he said, "we can tell a great tale when we get back to the city after having investigated this thing."

"Go to the devil," replied the little man.

THE MESMERIC MOUNTAIN.

A Tale of Sullivan County.

On the brow of a pine-plumed hillock there sat a little man with his back against a tree. A venerable pipe hung from his mouth, and smoke-wreaths curled slowly skyward. He was muttering to himself with his eyes fixed on an irregular black opening in the green wall of forest at the foot of the hill. Two vague waggon ruts led into the shadows. The little man took his pipe in his hands and addressed the listening pines.

"I wonder what the devil it leads to," said he.

A grey, fat rabbit came lazily from a thicket and sat in the opening. Softly stroking his stomach with his paw, he looked at the little man in a thoughtful manner. The little man threw a stone, and the rabbit blinked and ran through an opening. Green, shadowy portals seemed to close behind him.

The little man started. "He's gone down that roadway," he said, with ecstatic mystery to the pines. He sat a long time and contemplated the door to the forest. Finally, he arose, and awakening his limbs, started away. But he stopped and looked back.

"I can't imagine what it leads to," muttered he. He trudged over the brown mats of pine needles, to where, in a fringe of laurel, a tent was pitched, and merry flames caroused about some logs. A pudgy man was fuming over a collection of tin dishes. He came forward and waved a plate furiously in the little man's face.

"I've washed the dishes for three days. What do you think I am —"

He ended a red oration with a roar: "Damned if I do it any more."

The little man gazed dim-eyed away. "I've been wonderin' what it leads to."

"What?"

"That road out yonder. I've been wonderin' what it leads to. Maybe, some discovery or something," said the little man.

The pudgy man laughed. "You're an idiot. It leads to ol' Jim Boyd's over on the Lumberland Pike."

"Ho!" said the little man, "I don't believe that."

The pudgy man swore. "Fool, what does it lead to, then?"

"I don't know just what, but I'm sure it leads to something great or something. It looks like it."

While the pudgy man was cursing, two more men came from obscurity with fish dangling from birch twigs. The pudgy man made an obviously herculean struggle and a meal was prepared. As he was drinking his cup of coffee, he suddenly spilled it and swore. The little man was wandering off.

"He's gone to look at that hole," cried the pudgy man.

The little man went to the edge of the pine-plumed hillock, and, sitting down, began to make smoke and regard the door to the forest. There was stillness for an hour. Compact clouds hung unstirred in the sky. The pines stood motionless, and pondering.

Suddenly the little man slapped his knee and bit his tongue. He stood up and determinedly filled his pipe, rolling his eye over the bowl to the doorway. Keeping his eyes fixed he slid dangerously to the foot of the hillock and walked down the waggon ruts. A moment later he passed from the noise of the sunshine to the gloom of the woods.

The green portals closed, shutting out live things. The little man trudged on alone.

Tall tangled grass grew in the roadway, and the trees bended obstructing branches. The little man followed on over pine-clothed ridges and down through water-soaked swales. His shoes were cut by rocks of the mountains, and he sank ankle-deep in mud and moss of swamps. A curve just ahead lured him miles.

Finally, as he wended the side of a ridge, the road disappeared from beneath his feet. He battled with hordes of ignorant bushes on his way to knolls and solitary trees which invited him. Once he came to a tall, bearded pine. He climbed it, and perceived in the distance a peak. He uttered an ejaculation and fell out.

He scrambled to his feet, and said: "That's Jones's Mountain, I guess. It's about six miles from our camp as the crow flies."

He changed his course away from the mountain, and attacked the bushes again. He climbed over great logs, golden-brown in decay, and was opposed by thickets of dark-green laurel. A brook slid through the ooze of a swamp; cedars and hemlocks hung their sprays to the edges of pools.

The little man began to stagger in his walk. After a time he stopped and mopped his brow.

"My legs are about to shrivel up and drop off," he said…. "Still if I keep on in this direction, I am safe to strike the Lumberland Pike before sundown."

He dived at a clump of tag-alders, and emerging, confronted Jones's Mountain.

The wanderer sat down in a clear place and fixed his eyes on the summit. His mouth opened widely, and his body swayed at times. The little man and the peak stared in silence.

A lazy lake lay asleep near the foot of the mountain. In its bed of water-grass some frogs leered at the sky and crooned. The sun sank in red silence, and the shadows of the pines grew formidable. The expectant hush of evening, as if some thing were going to sing a hymn, fell upon the peak and the little man.

A leaping pickerel off on the water created a silver circle that was lost in black shadows. The little man shook himself and started to his feet, crying: "For the love of Mike, there's eyes in this mountain! I feel 'em! Eyes!"

He fell on his face.

When he looked again, he immediately sprang erect and ran.

"It's comin'!"

The mountain was approaching.

The little man scurried, sobbing through the thick growth. He felt his brain turning to water. He vanquished brambles with mighty bounds.

But after a time he came again to the foot of the mountain.

"God!" he howled, "it's been follerin' me." He grovelled.

Casting his eyes upward made circles swirl in his blood.

"I'm shackled I guess," he moaned. As he felt the heel of the mountain about crush his head, he sprang again to his feet. He grasped a handful of small stones and hurled them.

"Damn you," he shrieked loudly. The pebbles rang against the face of the mountain.

The little man then made an attack. He climbed with hands and feet wildly. Brambles forced him back and stones slid from beneath his feet. The peak swayed and tottered, and was ever about to smite with a granite arm. The summit was a blaze of red wrath.

But the little man at last reached the top. Immediately he swaggered with valour to the edge of the cliff. His hands were scornfully in his pockets.

He gazed at the western horizon, edged sharply against a yellow sky. "Ho!" he said. "There's Boyd's house and the Lumberland Pike."

The mountain under his feet was motionless.

MISCELLANEOUS

THE SQUIRE'S MADNESS.

Linton was in his study remote from the interference of domestic sounds. He was writing verses. He was not a poet in the strict sense of the word, because he had eight hundred a year and a manor-house in Sussex. But he was devoted, at any rate, and no happiness was for him equal to the happiness of an imprisonment in this lonely study. His place had been a semi-fortified house in the good days when every gentleman was either abroad with a bared sword hunting his neighbours or behind oak-and-iron doors and three-feet walls while his neighbours hunted him. But in the life of Linton it may be said that the only part of the house which remained true to the idea of fortification was the study, which was free only to Linton's wife and certain terriers. The necessary appearance from time to time of a servant always grated upon Linton as much as if from time to time somebody had in the most well-bred way flung a brick through the little panes of his window.

This window looked forth upon a wide valley of hop-fields and sheep-pastures, dipping and rising this way and that way, but always a valley until it reached a high far away ridge upon which stood the upright figure of a windmill, usually making rapid gestures as if it were an excited sentry warning the old grey house of coming danger. A little to the right, on a knoll, red chimneys and parts of red-tiled roofs appeared among trees, and the venerable square tower of the village church rose above them.

For ten years Linton had left vacant Oldrestham Hall, and when at last it became known that he and his wife were to return from an incomprehensible wandering, the village, which for four centuries had turned a feudal eye toward the Hall, was wrung with a prospect of change, a proper change. The great family pew in Oldrestham church would be occupied each Sunday morning by a fat, happy-faced, utterly squire-looking man, who would be dutifully at his post when the parish was stirred by a subscription list. Then, for the first time in many years, the hunters would ride in the early morning merrily out through the park, and there would be also shooting parties, and in the summer groups of charming ladies would be seen walking the terrace, laughing on the lawns and in the rose gardens. The village expected to have the perfectly legal and fascinating privilege of discussing the performances of its own gentry.

The first intimation of calamity was in the news that Linton had rented all the shooting. This prepared the people for the blow, and it fell when they sighted the master of Oldrestham Hall. The older villagers remembered then that there had been nothing in the youthful Linton to promise a fat, happy-faced, dignified, hunting, shooting over-lord, but still they could not but resent the appearance of the new squire. There was no conceivable reason for his looking like a gaunt ascetic, who would surprise nobody if he borrowed a sixpence from the first yokel he met in the lanes.

Linton was in truth three inches more than six feet in height, but he had bowed himself to five feet eleven inches. His hair shocked out in front like hay, and under it were two spectacled eyes which never seemed to regard anything with particular attention. His face was pale and full of hollows, and the mouth apparently had no expression save a chronic pout of the under-lip. His hands were large and raw boned but uncannily white. His whole bent body was thin as that of a man from a long sick-bed, and all was finished by two feet which for size could not be matched in the county.

He was very awkward, but apparently it was not so much a physical characteristic as it was a mental inability to consider where he was going or what he was doing. For instance, when passing through a gate it was not uncommon for him to knock his side viciously against one of the posts. This was because he dreamed almost always, and if there had been forty gates in a row he would not then have noted them more than he did the one. As far as the villagers and farmers were concerned he never came out of this manner save in wide-apart cases, when he had forced upon him either some great exhibition of stupidity or some faint indication of double-dealing, and then this smouldering man flared out encrimsoning his immediate surrounding with a brief fire of ancestral anger. But the lapse back to indifference was more surprising. It was far quicker than the flare in the beginning. His feeling was suddenly ashes at the moment when one was certain it would lick the sky.

Some of the villagers asserted that he was mad. They argued it long in the manner of their kind, repeating, repeating, and repeating, and when an opinion confusingly rational appeared they merely shook their heads in pig-like obstinacy. Anyhow, it was historically clear that no such squire had before been in the line of Lintons of Oldrestham Hall, and the present incumbent was a shock.

The servants at the Hall-notably those who lived in the country-side —came in for a lot of questioning, and none were found too backward in explaining many things which they them-selves did not understand. The household was most irregular. They all confessed that it was really so uncustomary that they did not know but what they would have to give notice. The master was probably the most extraordinary man in the whole world. The butler said that Lin-ton would drink beer with his meals day in and day out like any carrier resting at a pot-house. It didn't matter even if the meal were dinner. Then suddenly he would change his tastes to the most valuable wines, and in ten days would make the wine-cellar look as if it had been wrecked at sea. What was to be done with a gentleman of that kind? The butler said for his part he wanted a master with habits, and he protested that Linton did not have a habit to his name, at least, none that could properly be called a habit.

Barring the cook, the entire establishment agreed categorically with the butler. The cook didn't agree because she was a very good cook indeed, which she thought entitled her to be extremely aloof from the other servants' hall opinions.

As for the squire's lady, they described her as being not much different from the master. At least she gave support to his most unusual manner of life, and evidently believed that whatever he chose to do was quite correct.

Linton had written —

> Black and bitter are her hating eyes,
> A cry the windy death-hall makes,
> O, love, deliver us.
> The flung cup rolls to her sandal's tip,
> His arm —"

Whereupon his thought fumed over the next two lines, coursing like greyhounds, after a fugitive vision of a writhening lover with the foam of poison on his lips dying at the feet of the woman. Linton arose, lit a cigarette, placed it on the window ledge, took another cigarette, looked blindly for the matches, thrust a spiral of paper into the flame of the log fire, lit the second cigarette, placed it toppling on a book and began a search among his pipes for one that would draw well. He gazed at his pictures, at the books on the shelves, out at the green spread of country-side, all without taking mental note. At the window ledge he came upon the first cigarette, and in a matter of fact way he returned it to his lips, having forgotten that he had forgotten it.

There was a sound of steps on the stone floor of the quaint little passage that led down to his study, and turning from the window he saw that his wife had entered the room and was looking at him strangely.

"Jack," she said in a low voice, "what is the matter?"

His eyes were burning out from under his shock of hair with a fierceness that belied his feeling of simple surprise. "Nothing is the matter," he answered. "Why do you ask?"

She seemed immensely concerned, but she was visibly endeavouring to hide her concern as well as to abate it.

"I —I thought you acted queerly."

He answered: "Why no. I'm not acting queerly. On the contrary," he added smiling, "I'm in one of my most rational moods."

Her look of alarm did not subside. She continued to regard him with the same stare. She was silent for a time and did not move. His own thoughts had quite returned to a contemplation of a poisoned lover, and he did not note the manner of his wife. Suddenly she came to him, and laying a hand on his arm said, "Jack, you are ill?"

"Why no, dear," he said with a first impatience, "I'm not ill at all. I never felt better in my life." And his mind beleaguered by this pointless talk strove to break through to its old contemplation of the poisoned lover. "Hear what I have written." Then he read —

"The garlands of her hair are snakes,
  Black and bitter are her hating eyes,
  A cry the windy death-hall makes,
  O, love, deliver us.
  The flung cup rolls to her sandal's tip,
  His arm —"

Linton said: "I can't seem to get the lines to describe the man who is dying of the poison on the floor before her. Really I'm having a time with it. What a bore. Sometimes I can write like mad and other times I don't seem to have an intelligent idea in my head."

He felt his wife's hand tighten on his arm and he looked into her face. It was so alight with horror that it brought him sharply out of his dreams. "Jack," she repeated tremulously, "you are ill."

He opened his eyes in wonder. "Ill! ill? No; not in the least!"

"Yes, you are ill. I can see it in your eyes. You-act so strangely."

"Act strangely? Why, my dear, what have I done? I feel quite well. Indeed, I was never more fit in my life."

As he spoke he threw himself into a large wing chair and looked up at his wife, who stood gazing at him from the other side of the black oak table upon which Linton wrote his verses.

"Jack, dear," she almost whispered, "I have noticed it for days," and she leaned across the table to look more intently into his face. "Yes, your eyes grow more fixed every day-you-you-your head, does it ache, dear?"

Linton arose from his chair and came around the big table toward his wife. As he approached her, an expression akin to terror crossed her face and she drew back as in fear, holding out both hands to ward him off.

He had been smiling in the manner of a man reassuring a frightened child, but at her shrinking from his outstretched hand he stopped in amazement. "Why, Grace, what is it? tell me."

She was glaring at him, her eyes wide with misery. Linton moved his left hand across his face, unconsciously trying to brush from it that which alarmed her.

"Oh, Jack, you must see some one; I am wretched about you. You are ill!"

"Why, my dear wife," he said, "I am quite, quite well; I am anxious to finish these verses but words won't come somehow, the man dying —"

"Yes, that is it, you cannot remember, you see that you cannot remember. You must see a doctor. We will go up to town at once," she answered quickly.

"'Tis true," he thought, "that my memory is not as good as it used to be. I cannot remember dates, and words won't fit in somehow. Perhaps I don't take enough exercise, dear; is that what worries you?" he asked.

"Yes, yes, dear, you do not go out enough," said his wife. "You cling to this room as the ivy clings to the walls-but we must go to London, you *must* see some one; promise me that you will go, that you will go immediately."

Again Linton saw his wife look at him as one looks at a creature of pity. The faint lines from her nose to the corners of her mouth deepened as if she were in physical pain; her eyes, open to their fullest extent, had in them the expression of a mother watching her dying babe. What was this strange wall that had suddenly raised itself between them? Was he ill? No; he never was in better health in his life. He found himself vainly searching for aches in his bones.

Again he brushed away this thing which seemed to be upon his face. There must be something on my face, he thought, else why does she look at me with such hopeless despair in her eyes; these kindly eyes that had hitherto been so responsive to each glance of his own. *Why* did she think that he was ill? She who knew well his every mood. *Was he mad?* Did this thing of the poisoned cup that rolled to her sandal's tip-and her eyes, her hating eyes, mean that his-no, it could not be. He fumbled among the papers on the table for a cigarette. He could not find one. He walked to the huge fireplace and peered near-sightedly at the ashes on the hearth.

"What, what do you want, Jack? Be careful! The fire!" cried his wife.

"Why, I want a cigarette," he said.

She started, as if he had spoken roughly to her. "I will get you some, wait, sit quietly, I will bring you some," she replied as she hastened through the small passage-way up the stone steps that led from his study.

Linton stood with his back still bent, in the posture of a man picking something from the ground. He did not turn from the fireplace until the echo of his wife's foot-fall on the stone floors had died away. Then he straightened himself and said, "Well, I'm damned!" And Linton was not a man who swore.

* * * * * * *

A month later the Squire and his wife were on their way to London to consult the great brain specialist, Doctor Redmond. Linton now believed that "something" was wrong with him. His wife's anxiety, which she could no longer conceal, forced him to this conclusion; "something" was wrong. Until these few last weeks Linton's wife had managed her household with the care and wisdom of a Chatelaine of mediæval times. Each day was planned for certain duties in house or village. She had theories as to the management and education of the village children, and this work occupied much of her time. She was the antithesis of her husband. He, a weaver of dream-stories, she of that type of woman who has ideas of the emancipation of women and who believe the problem could be solved by training the minds of the next generation of mothers. Linton was not interested in these questions, but he would smile indulgently at his wife as she talked of the equality of mind of the sexes and the public part in the world's history which would be played by the women of the future.

There was no talk of this kind now. The household management fell into the hands of servants. Night and day his wife watched Linton. He would awaken in the night to find her face close to his own, her eyes burning with feverish anxiety.

"What is it, Grace?" he would cry, "have I said anything? What is the reason you watch me in this fashion, dear?"

And she would sob, "Jack, you are ill, dear, you are ill; we must go to town, we must, indeed."

Then he would soothe her with fond words and promise that he would go to London.

This present journey was the outcome of those weeks of watching and fear in Linton's wife's mind.

* * * * * * *

Linton's wife was trembling violently as he helped her down from the cab in front of Doctor Redmond's door. They had made an appointment, so that they were sure of little delay before the portentous interview.

A small page in blue livery opened the door and ushered them into a waiting-room. Mrs. Linton dropped heavily into a chair, looking with a frightened air from side to side and biting her under lip nervously. She was moaning half under her breath, "Oh, Jack, you are ill, you are ill."

A short stout man with clean-shaven face and scanty black hair entered the room. His nose was huge and misshapen and his mouth was a straight firm line. Overhanging black brows tried in vain to shadow the piercing dark eyes, that darted questioning looks at every one, seeming to search for hidden thoughts as a flash-light from the conning tower of a ship searches for the enemy in time of war.

He advanced toward Mrs. Linton with outstretched hand. "Mrs. Linton?" he said. "Ah!"

She almost jumped from her chair as he came near her, crying, "Oh, doctor, my husband is ill, very ill, very ill!"

Again Doctor Redmond with his eyes fixed upon her face ejaculated, "Ah!" Turning to Linton he said, "Please wait here, Squire; I will first talk to your wife. Will you step into my study, madam?" he said to Mrs. Linton, bowing courteously.

Linton's wife ran into the room which the doctor pointed toward as his study.

Linton waited. He moved softly about the room looking at the photographs of Greek ruins which adorned the walls. He stopped finally before a large picture of the Gate of Hadrian. He travelled once more into his dream country. His fancy painted in the figures of men and women who had passed through that gate. He had forgotten his fear of the blotting out of his mind that could conjure these glowing colours. He had forgotten himself.

From this dream he was recalled to the present by a hand being placed gently upon his arm. He half turned and saw the doctor regarding him with sympathetic eyes.

"Come, my dear sir, come into my study," said the doctor. "I have asked your wife to await us here." Linton then turned fully toward the centre of the room and found that his wife was seated quietly by a table. Doctor Redmond bowed low to Mrs. Linton as he passed her, and Linton waved his hand, smiled, and said, "Only a moment, dear." She did not reply. The door closed behind them.

"Be seated, my dear sir," said the doctor, drawing forward a chair, "be seated. I want to say something to you, but you must drink this first." He handed Linton a small glass of brandy.

Linton sat down, took the glass mechanically, and gulped the brandy in one great swallow. The doctor stood by the mantel and said slowly, "I rejoice to say to you, sir, that I have never met a man more sound mentally than yourself" —

Linton half started from his chair.

"Stop!" said the doctor, "I have not yet finished-but it is my painful duty to tell you the truth-It is your WIFE WHO IS MAD! MAD AS A HATTER!"

A DESERTION.

The yellow gas-light that came with an effect of difficulty through the dust-stained windows on either side of the door, gave strange hues to the faces and forms of the three women who stood gabbling in the hall-way of the tenement. They made rapid gestures, and in the background their enormous shadows mingled in terrific conflict.

"Aye, she ain't so good as he thinks she is, I'll bet. He can watch over 'er an' take care of 'er all he pleases, but when she wants t' fool 'im, she'll fool 'im. An' how does he know she ain't foolin' 'im now?"

"Oh, he thinks he's keepin' 'er from goin' t' th' bad, he does. Oh, yes. He ses she's too purty t' let run round alone. Too purty! Huh! My Sadie —"

"Well, he keeps a clost watch on 'er, you bet. O'ny las' week, she met my boy Tim on th' stairs, an' Tim hadn't said two words to 'er b'fore th' ol' man begin to holler. 'Dorter, dorter, come here, come here!'"

At this moment a young girl entered from the street, and it was evident from the injured expression suddenly assumed by the three gossipers that she had been the object of their discussion. She passed them with a slight nod, and they swung about into a row to stare after her.

On her way up the long flights the girl unfastened her veil. One could then clearly see the beauty of her eyes, but there was in them a certain furtiveness that came near to marring the effects. It was a peculiar fixture of gaze, brought from the street, as of one who there saw a succession of passing dangers with menaces aligned at every corner.

On the top floor, she pushed open a door and then paused on the threshold, confronting an interior that appeared black and flat like a curtain. Perhaps some girlish idea of hobgoblins assailed her then, for she called in a little breathless voice, "Daddie!"

There was no reply. The fire in the cooking-stove in the room crackled at spasmodic intervals. One lid was misplaced, and the girl could now see that this fact created a little flushed crescent upon the ceiling. Also, a series of tiny windows in the stove caused patches of red upon the floor. Otherwise, the room was heavily draped with shadows.

The girl called again, "Daddie!"

Yet there was no reply.

"Oh, Daddie!"

Presently she laughed as one familiar with the humours of an old man. "Oh, I guess yer cussin' mad about yer supper, dad," she said, and she almost entered the room, but suddenly faltered, overcome by a feminine instinct to fly from this black interior, peopled with imagined dangers.

Again she called, "Daddie!" Her voice had an accent of appeal. It was as if she knew she was foolish but yet felt obliged to insist upon being reassured. "Oh, daddie!"

Of a sudden a cry of relief, a feminine announcement that the stars still hung, burst from her. For, according to some mystic process, the smouldering coals of the fire went aflame with sudden, fierce brilliance, splashing parts of the walls, the floor, the crude furniture, with a hue of blood-red. And in the light of this dramatic outburst of light, the girl saw her father seated at a table with his back turned toward her.

She entered the room, then, with an aggrieved air, her logic evidently concluding that somebody was to blame for her nervous fright. "Oh, yer on'y sulkin' 'bout yer supper. I thought mebbe ye'd gone somewheres."

Her father made no reply. She went over to a shelf in the corner, and, taking a little lamp, she lit it and put it where it would give her light as she took off her hat and jacket in front of the tiny mirror. Presently, she began to bustle among the cooking utensils that were crowded into the sink, and as she worked she rattled talk at her father, apparently disdaining his mood.

"I'd 'a come home earlier t'night, dad, o'ny that fly foreman, he kep' me in th' shop 'til half-past six. What a fool. He came t' me, yeh know, an' he ses, 'Nell, I wanta give yeh some brotherly advice.' Oh, I know him an' his brotherly advice. 'I wanta give yeh some brotherly advice. Yer too purty, Nell,' he ses, 't' be workin' in this shop an' paradin' through the streets alone, without somebody t' give yeh good brotherly advice, an' I wanta warn yeh, Nell. I'm a bad man, but I ain't as bad as some, an' I wanta warn yeh.' 'Oh, g'long 'bout yer business,' I ses. I know 'im. He's like all of 'em, o'ny he's a little slyer. I know 'im. 'You g'long 'bout yer business,' I ses. Well, he ses after a while that he guessed some evenin' he'd come up an' see me. 'Oh, yeh will,' I ses, 'yeh will? Well, you jest let my ol' man ketch yeh comin' foolin' 'round our place. Yeh'll wish yeh went t' some other girl t' give brotherly advice.' 'What th' 'ell do I care fer yer father?' he ses. 'What's he t' me?' 'If he throws yeh down stairs, yeh'll care for 'im,' I ses. 'Well,' he ses, 'I'll come when 'e ain't in, b' Gawd, I'll come when 'e ain't in.' 'Oh, he's allus in when it means takin' care 'a me,' I ses. 'Don't yeh fergit it either. When it comes t' takin' care 'a his dorter, he's right on deck every single possible time.'"

After a time, she turned and addressed cheery words to the old man. "Hurry up th' fire, daddie! We'll have supper pretty soon."

But still her father was silent, and his form in its sullen posture was motionless.

At this, the girl seemed to see the need of the inauguration of a feminine war against a man out of temper. She approached him breathing soft, coaxing syllables.

"Daddie! Oh, Daddie! O —o —oh, Daddie!"

It was apparent from a subtle quality of valour in her tones that this manner of onslaught upon his moods had usually been successful, but to-night it had no quick effect. The words, coming from her lips, were like the refrain of an old ballad, but the man remained stolid.

"Daddie! My Daddie! Oh, Daddie are yeh mad at me, really-truly mad at me!"

She touched him lightly upon the arm. Should he have turned then he would have seen the fresh, laughing face, with dew-sparkling eyes, close to his own.

"Oh, Daddie! My Daddie! Pretty Daddie!"

She stole her arm about his neck, and then slowly bended her face toward his. It was the action of a queen who knows that she reigns notwithstanding irritations, trials, tempests.

But suddenly, from this position, she leaped backward with the mad energy of a frightened colt. Her face was in this instant turned to a grey, featureless thing of horror. A yell, wild and hoarse as a brute-cry, burst from her. "Daddie!" She flung herself to a place near the door, where she remained, crouching, her eyes staring at the motionless figure, spattered by the quivering flashes from the fire. Her arms extended, and her frantic fingers at once besought and repelled. There was in them an expression of eagerness to caress and an expression of the most intense loathing. And the girl's hair that had been a splendour, was in these moments changed to a disordered mass that hung and swayed in witchlike fashion.

Again, a terrible cry burst from her. It was more than the shriek of agony-it was directed, personal, addressed to him in the chair, the first word of a tragic conversation with the dead.

It seemed that when she had put her arm about its neck, she had jostled the corpse in such a way, that now she and it were face to face. The attitude expressed an intention of arising from the table. The eyes, fixed upon hers, were filled with an unspeakable hatred.

* * * * * * *

The cries of the girl aroused thunders in the tenement. There was a loud slamming of doors, and presently there was a roar of feet upon the boards of the stairway. Voices rang out sharply.

"What is it?"

"What's th' matter?"

"He's killin' her!"

"Slug 'im with anythin' yeh kin lay hold of, Jack."

But over all this came the shrill shrewish tones of a woman. "Ah, th' damned ol' fool, he's drivin' 'er inteh th' street-that's what he's doin.' He's drivin' 'er inteh th' street."

HOW THE DONKEY LIFTED THE HILLS.

Many people suppose that the donkey is lazy. This is a great mistake. It is his pride.

Years ago, there was nobody quite so fine as the donkey. He was a great swell in those times. No one could express an opinion of anything without the donkey showing where he was in it. No one could mention the name of an important personage without the donkey declaring how well he knew him.

The donkey was, above all things, a proud and aristocratic beast.

One day a party of animals were discussing one thing and another, until finally the conversation drifted around to mythology.

"I have always admired that giant, Atlas," observed the ox in the course of the conversation. "It was amazing how he could carry things."

"Oh, yes, Atlas," said the donkey, "I knew him very well. I once met a man and we got talking of Atlas. I expressed my admiration for the giant and my desire to meet him some day, if possible. Whereupon the man said there was nothing quite so easy. He was sure that his dear friend, Atlas, would be happy to meet so charming a donkey. Was I at leisure next Monday? Well, then, could I dine with him upon that date? So, you see, it was all arranged. I found Atlas to be a very pleasant fellow."

"It has always been a wonder to me how he could have carried the earth on his back," said the horse.

"Oh, my dear sir, nothing is more simple," cried the donkey. "One has only to make up one's mind to it, and then-do it. That is all. I am quite sure that if I wished I could carry a range of mountains upon my back."

All the others said, "Oh, my!"

"Yes, I could," asserted the donkey, stoutly. "It is merely a question of making up one's mind. I will bet."

"I will wager also," said the horse. "I will wager my ears that you can't carry a range of mountains upon your back."

"Done," cried the donkey.

Forthwith the party of animals set out for the mountains. Suddenly, however, the donkey paused and said, "Oh, but look here. Who will place this range of mountains upon my back? Surely I can not be expected to do the loading also."

Here was a great question. The party consulted. At length the ox said, "We will have to ask some men to shovel the mountain upon the donkey's back."

Most of the others clapped their hoofs or their paws and cried, "Ah, that is the thing."

The horse, however, shook his head doubtfully. "I don't know about these men. They are very sly. They will introduce some deviltry into the affair."

"Why, how silly," said the donkey. "Apparently you do not understand men. They are the most gentle, guileless creatures."

"Well," retorted the horse, "I will doubtless be able to escape since I am not to be encumbered with any mountains. Proceed."

The donkey smiled in derision at these observations by the horse.

Presently they came upon some men who were labouring away like mad, digging ditches, felling trees, gathering fruits, carrying water, building huts.

"Look at these men, would you," said the horse. "Can you trust them after this exhibition of their depravity? See how each one selfishly —"

The donkey interrupted with a loud laugh.

"What nonsense!"

And then he cried out to the men, "Ho, my friends, will you please come and shovel a range of mountains upon my back?"

"What?"

"Will you please come and shovel a range of mountains upon my back?"

The men were silent for a time. Then they went apart and debated. They gesticulated a great deal.

Some apparently said one thing and some another. At last they paused and one of their number came forward.

"Why do you wish a range of mountains shovelled upon your back?"

"It is a wager," cried the donkey.

The men consulted again. And as the discussion became older, their heads went closer and closer together, until they merely whispered, and did not gesticulate at all. Ultimately they cried, "Yes, certainly we will shovel a range of mountains upon your back for you."

"Ah, thanks," said the donkey.

"Here is surely some deviltry," said the horse behind his hoof to the ox.

The entire party proceeded then to the mountains. The donkey drew a long breath and braced his legs.

"Are you ready?" asked the men.

"All ready," cried the donkey.

The men began to shovel.

The dirt and stones flew over the donkey's back in showers. It was not long before his legs were hidden. Presently only his neck and head remained in view. Then at last this wise donkey vanished. There had been made no great effect upon the range of mountains. They still towered toward the sky.

The watching crowd saw a heap of dirt and stones make a little movement and then was heard a muffled cry. "Enough! Enough! It was not two ranges of mountains! It is not fair! It is not fair!"

But the men only laughed as they shovelled on.

"Enough! Enough! Oh, woe is me-thirty snow-capped peaks upon my little back. Ah, these false, false men! Oh, virtuous, wise, and holy men, desist."

The men again laughed. They were as busy as fiends with their shovels.

"Ah, brutal, cowardly, accursed men; ah, good, gentle, and holy men, please remove some of those damnable peaks. I will adore your beautiful shovels forever. I will be slave to the beckoning of your little fingers. I will no longer be my own donkey —I will be your donkey."

The men burst into a triumphant shout and ceased shovelling.

"Swear it, mountain-carrier."

"I swear! I swear! I swear!"

The other animals scampered away then, for these men in their plots and plans were very terrible. "Poor old foolish fellow," cried the horse; "he may keep his ears. He will need them to hear and count the blows that are now to fall upon him."

The men unearthed the donkey. They beat him with their shovels. "Ho, come on, slave." Encrusted with earth, yellow-eyed from fright, the donkey limped toward his prison. His ears hung down like leaves of the plantain during the great rain.

So, now, when you see a donkey with a church, a palace, and three villages upon his back, and he goes with infinite slowness, moving but one leg at a time, do not think him lazy. It is his pride.

A MAN BY THE NAME OF MUD.

Deep in a leather chair, the Kid sat looking out at where the rain slanted before the dull brown houses and hammered swiftly upon an occasional lonely cab. The happy crackle from the great and glittering fireplace behind him had evidently no meaning of content for him. He appeared morose and unapproachable, and when a man appears morose and unapproachable it is a fine chance for his intimate friends. Three or four of them discovered his mood, and so hastened to be obnoxious.

"What's wrong, Kid? Lost your thirst?"

"He can never be happy again. He has lost his thirst."

"That's right, Kid. When you quarrel with a man who can whip you, resort to sarcastic reflection and distance."

They cackled away persistently, but the Kid was mute and continued to stare gloomily at the street.

Once a man who had been writing letters looked up and said, "I saw your friend at the Comique the other night." He waited a moment and then added, "In back."

The Kid wheeled about in his chair at this information, and all the others saw then that it was important. One man said with deep intelligence, "Ho, ho, a woman, hey? A woman's come between the two Kids. A woman. Great, eh?" The Kid launched a glare of scorn across the room, and then turned again to a contemplation of the rain. His friends continued to do all in their power to worry him, but they fell ultimately before his impregnable silence.

As it happened, he had not been brooding upon his friend's mysterious absence at all. He had been concerned with himself. Once in a while he seemed to perceive certain futilities and lapsed them immediately into a state of voiceless dejection. These moods were not frequent.

An unexplained thing in his mind, however, was greatly enlightened by the words of the gossip. He turned then from his harrowing scrutiny of the amount of pleasure he achieved from living, and settled into a comfortable reflection upon the state of his comrade, the other Kid.

Perhaps it could be indicated in this fashion: "Went to Comique, I suppose. Saw girl. Secondary part, probably. Thought her rather natural. Went to Comique again. Went again. One time happened to meet omnipotent and good-natured friend. Broached subject to him with great caution. Friend said —'Why, certainly, my boy, come round to-night, and I'll take you in back. Remember, it's against all rules, but I think that in your case, etc.' Kid went. Chorus girls winked same old wink. 'Here's another dude on the prowl.' Kid aware of this, swearing under his breath and looking very stiff. Meets girl. Knew beforehand that the footlights might have sold him, but finds her very charming. Does not say single thing to her which she naturally expected to hear. Makes no reference to her beauty nor her voice-if she has any. Perhaps takes it for granted that she knows. Girl don't exactly love this attitude, but then feels admiration, because after all she can't tell whether he thinks her nice or whether he don't. New scheme this. Worked by occasional guys in Rome and Egypt, but still, new scheme. Kid goes away. Girl thinks. Later, nails omnipotent and good-natured friend. 'Who was that you brought back?' 'Oh, him? Why, he —' Describes the Kid's wealth, feats, and virtues-virtues of disposition. Girl propounds clever question —'Why did he wish to meet me?' Omnipotent person says, 'Damned if I know.'"

Later, Kid asks girl to supper. Not wildly anxious, but very evident that he asks her because he likes her. Girl accepts; goes to supper. Kid very good comrade and kind. Girl begins to think that here at last is a man who understands her. Details ambitions-long, wonderful ambitions. Explains her points of superiority over the other girls of stage. Says their lives disgust her. She wants to work and study and make something of herself. Kid smokes vast number of cigarettes. Displays and feels deep sympathy. Recalls, but faintly, that he has heard it on previous occasions. They have an awfully good time. Part at last in front of apartment house. "Good-night, old chap." "Good-night." Squeeze hands hard. Kid has no information at all about kissing her good-night, but don't even try. Noble youth. Wise youth. Kid goes home and smokes. Feels strong desire to kill people who say intolerable things of the girl in rows. "Narrow, mean, stupid, ignorant, damnable people." Contemplates the broad, fine liberality of his experienced mind.

Kid and girl become very chumy. Kid like a brother. Listens to her troubles. Takes her out to supper regularly and regularly. Chorus girls now tacitly recognise him as the main guy. Sometimes, may be, girl's mother sick. Can't go to supper. Kid always very noble. Understands perfectly the probabilities of there being others. Lays for 'em, but makes no discoveries. Begins to wonder whether he is a winner or whether she is a girl of marvellous cleverness. Can't tell. Maintains himself with dignity, however. Only occasionally inveighs against the men who prey upon the girls of the stage. Still noble.

Time goes on. Kid grows less noble. Perhaps decides not to be noble at all, or as little as he can. Still inveighs against the men who prey upon the girls of the stage. Thinks the girl stunning. Wants to be dead sure there are no others. Once suspects it, and immediately makes the colossal mistake of his life. Takes the girl to task. Girl won't stand it for a minute. Harangues him. Kid surrenders and pleads with her-pleads with her. Kid's name is mud.

A POKER GAME.

Usually a poker game is a picture of peace. There is no drama so low-voiced and serene and monotonous. If an amateur loser does not softly curse, there is no orchestral support. Here is one of the most exciting and absorbing occupations known to intelligent American manhood; here a year's reflection is compressed into a moment of thought; here the nerves may stand on end and scream to themselves, but a tranquillity as from heaven is only interrupted by the click of chips. The higher the stakes the more quiet the scene; this is a law that applies everywhere save on the stage.

And yet sometimes in a poker game things happen. Everybody remembers the celebrated corner on bay rum that was triumphantly consummated by Robert F. Cinch, of Chicago, assisted by the United States Courts and whatever other federal power he needed. Robert F. Cinch enjoyed his victory four months. Then he died, and young Bobbie Cinch came to New York in order to more clearly demonstrate that there was a good deal of fun in twenty-two million dollars.

Old Henry Spuytendyvil owns all the real estate in New York save that previously appropriated by the hospitals and Central Park. He had been a friend of Bob's father. When Bob appeared in New York, Spuytendyvil entertained him correctly. It came to pass that they just naturally played poker.

One night they were having a small game in an up-town hotel. There were five of them, including two lawyers and a politician. The stakes depended on the ability of the individual fortune.

Bobbie Cinch had won rather heavily. He was as generous as sunshine, and when luck chases a generous man it chases him hard, even though he cannot bet with all the skill of his opponents.

Old Spuytendyvil had lost a considerable amount. One of the lawyers from time to time smiled quietly, because he knew Spuytendyvil well, and he knew that anything with the name of loss attached to it sliced the old man's heart into sections.

At midnight Archie Bracketts, the actor, came into the room. "How you holding 'em, Bob?" said he.

"Pretty well," said Bob.

"Having any luck, Mr. Spuytendyvil?"

"Blooming bad," grunted the old man.

Bracketts laughed and put his foot on the round of Spuytendyvil's chair. "There," said he, "I'll queer your luck for you." Spuytendyvil sat at the end of the table. "Bobbie," said the actor, presently, as young Cinch won another pot, "I guess I better knock your luck." So he took his foot from the old man's chair and placed it on Bob's chair. The lad grinned good-naturedly and said he didn't care.

Bracketts was in a position to scan both of the hands. It was Bob's ante, and old Spuytendyvil threw in a red chip. Everybody passed out up to Bobbie. He filled in the pot and drew a card.

Spuytendyvil drew a card. Bracketts, looking over his shoulder, saw him holding the ten, nine, eight, and seven of diamonds. Theatrically speaking, straight flushes are as frequent as berries on a juniper tree, but as a matter of truth the reason that straight flushes are so admired is because they are not as common as berries on a juniper tree. Bracketts stared; drew a cigar slowly from his pocket, and placing it between his teeth forgot its existence.

Bobbie was the only other stayer. Bracketts flashed an eye for the lad's hand and saw the nine, eight, six, and five of hearts. Now, there are but six hundred and forty-five emotions possible to the human mind, and Bracketts immediately had them all. Under the impression that he had finished his cigar, he took it from his mouth and tossed it toward the grate without turning his eyes to follow its flight.

There happened to be a complete silence around the green-clothed table. Spuytendyvil was studying his hand with a kind of contemptuous smile, but in his eyes there perhaps was to be seen a cold, stern light expressing something sinister and relentless.

Young Bob sat as he had sat. As the pause grew longer, he looked up once inquiringly at Spuytendyvil.

The old man reached for a white chip. "Well, mine are worth about that much," said he, tossing it into the pot. Thereupon he leaned back comfortably in his chair and renewed his stare at the five straight diamond. Young Bob extended his hand leisurely toward his stack. It occurred to Bracketts that he was smoking, but he found no cigar in his mouth.

The lad fingered his chips and looked pensively at his hand. The silence of those moments oppressed Bracketts like the smoke from a conflagration.

Bobbie Cinch continued for some moments to coolly observe his cards. At last he breathed a little sigh and said, "Well, Mr. Spuytendyvil, I can't play a sure thing against you." He threw in a white chip. "I'll just call you. I've got a straight flush." He faced down his cards.

Old Spuytendyvil's fear, horror, and rage could only be equalled in volume to a small explosion of gasolene. He dashed his cards upon the table. "There!" he shouted, glaring frightfully at Bobbie. "I've got a straight flush, too! And mine is Jack high!"

Bobbie was at first paralysed with amazement, but in a moment he recovered, and apparently observing something amusing in the situation he grinned.

Archie Bracketts, having burst his bond of silence, yelled for joy and relief. He smote Bobbie on the shoulder. "Bob, my boy," he cried exuberantly, "you're no gambler, but you're a mighty good fellow, and if you hadn't been you would be losing a good many dollars this minute."

Old Spuytendyvil glowered at Bracketts. "Stop making such an infernal din, will you, Archie," he said morosely. His throat seemed filled with pounded glass. "Pass the whisky."

THE SNAKE.

Where the path wended across the ridge, the bushes of huckle-berry and sweet fern swarmed at it in two curling waves until it was a mere winding line traced through a tangle. There was no interference by clouds, and as the rays of the sun fell full upon the ridge, they called into voice innumerable insects which chanted the heat of the summer day in steady, throbbing, unending chorus.

A man and a dog came from the laurel thickets of the valley where the white brook brawled with the rocks. They followed the deep line of the path across the ridge. The dog —a large lemon and white setter-walked, tranquilly meditative, at his master's heels.

Suddenly from some unknown and yet near place in advance there came a dry, shrill whistling rattle that smote motion instantly from the limbs of the man and the dog. Like the fingers of a sudden death, this sound seemed to touch the man at the nape of the neck, at the top of the spine, and change him, as swift as thought, to a statue of listening horror, surprise, rage. The dog, too-the same icy hand was laid upon him, and he stood crouched and quivering, his jaw dropping, the froth of terror upon his lips, the light of hatred in his eyes.

Slowly the man moved his hands toward the bushes, but his glance did not turn from the place made sinister by the warning rattle. His fingers, unguided, sought for a stick of weight and strength. Presently they closed about one that seemed adequate, and holding this weapon poised before him, the man moved slowly forward, glaring. The dog with his nervous nostrils fairly fluttering moved warily, one foot at a time, after his master.

But when the man came upon the snake, his body underwent a shock as if from a revelation, as if after all he had been ambushed. With a blanched face, he sprang forward, and his breath came in strained gasps, his chest heaving as if he were in the performance of an extraordinary muscular trial. His arm with the stick made a spasmodic, defensive gesture.

The snake had apparently been crossing the path in some mystic travel when to his sense there came the knowledge of the coming of his foes. The dull vibration perhaps informed him, and he flung his body to face the danger. He had no knowledge of paths; he had no wit to tell him to slink noiselessly into the bushes. He knew that his implacable enemies were approaching; no doubt they were seeking him, hunting him. And so he cried his cry, an incredibly swift jangle of tiny bells, as burdened with pathos as the hammering upon quaint cymbals by the Chinese at war-for, indeed, it was usually his death-music.

"Beware! Beware! Beware!"

The man and the snake confronted each other. In the man's eyes were hatred and fear. In the snake's eyes were hatred and fear. These enemies manœuvred, each preparing to kill. It was to be a battle without mercy. Neither knew of mercy for such a situation. In the man was all the wild strength of the terror of his ancestors, of his race, of his kind. A deadly repulsion had been handed from man to man through long dim centuries. This was another detail of a war that had begun evidently when first there were men and snakes. Individuals who do not participate in this strife incur the investigations of scientists. Once there was a man and a snake who were friends, and at the end, the man lay dead with the marks of the snake's caress just over his East Indian heart. In the formation of devices, hideous and horrible, Nature reached her supreme point in the making of the snake, so that priests who really paint hell well fill it with snakes instead of fire. These curving forms, these scintillant colourings create at once, upon sight, more relentless animosities than do shake barbaric tribes. To be born a snake is to be thrust into a place a-swarm with formidable foes. To gain an appreciation of it, view hell as pictured by priests who are really skilful.

As for this snake in the pathway, there was a double curve some inches back of its head, which, merely by the potency of its lines, made the man feel with tenfold eloquence the touch of the death-fingers at the nape of his neck. The reptile's head was waving slowly from side to side and its hot eyes flashed like little murder-lights. Always in the air was the dry, shrill whistling of the rattles.

"Beware! Beware! Beware!"

The man made a preliminary feint with his stick. Instantly the snake's heavy head and neck were bended back on the double curve and instantly the snake's body shot forward in a low, straight, hard spring. The man jumped with a convulsive chatter and swung his stick. The blind, sweeping blow fell upon the snake's head and hurled him so that steel-coloured plates were for a moment uppermost. But he rallied swiftly, agilely, and again the head and neck bended back to the double curve, and the steaming, wide-open mouth made its desperate effort to reach its enemy. This attack, it could be seen, was despairing, but it was nevertheless impetuous, gallant, ferocious, of the same quality as the charge of the lone chief when the walls of white faces close upon him in the mountains. The stick swung unerringly again, and the snake, mutilated, torn, whirled himself into the last coil.

And now the man went sheer raving mad from the emotions of his forefathers and from his own. He came to close quarters. He gripped the stick with his two hands and made it speed like a flail. The snake, tumbling in the anguish of final despair, fought, bit, flung itself upon this stick which was taking his life.

At the end, the man clutched his stick and stood watching in silence. The dog came slowly and with infinite caution stretched his nose forward, sniffing. The hair upon his neck and back moved and ruffled as if a sharp wind was blowing. The last muscular quivers of the snake were causing the rattles to still sound their treble cry, the shrill, ringing war chant and hymn of the grave of the thing that faces foes at once countless, implacable, and superior.

"Well, Rover," said the man, turning to the dog with a grin of victory, "we'll carry Mr. Snake home to show the girls."

His hands still trembled from the strain of the encounter, but he pried with his stick under the body of the snake and hoisted the limp thing upon it. He resumed his march along the path, and the dog walked, tranquilly meditative, at his master's heels.

A SELF-MADE MAN.

An Example of Success that Any One can Follow.

Tom had a hole in his shoe. It was very round and very uncomfortable, particularly when he went on wet pavements. Rainy days made him feel that he was walking on frozen dollars, although he had only to think for a moment to discover he was not.

He used up almost two packs of playing cards by means of putting four cards at a time inside his shoe as a sort of temporary sole, which usually lasted about half a day. Once he put in four aces for luck. He went down town that morning and got refused work. He thought it wasn't a very extraordinary performance for a young man of ability, and he was not sorry that night to find his packs were entirely out of aces.

One day Tom was strolling down Broadway. He was in pursuit of work, although his pace was slow. He had found that he must take the matter coolly. So he puffed tenderly at a cigarette and walked as if he owned stock. He imitated success so successfully, that if it wasn't for the constant reminder (king, queen, deuce, and tray) in his shoe, he would have gone into a store and bought something.

He had borrowed five cents that morning off his landlady, for his mouth craved tobacco. Although he owed her much for board, she had unlimited confidence in him, because his stock of self-assurance was very large indeed. And as it increased in a proper ratio with the amount of his bills, his relations with her seemed on a firm basis. So he strolled along and smoked with his confidence in fortune in nowise impaired by his financial condition.

Of a sudden he perceived on old man seated upon a railing and smoking a clay pipe.

He stopped to look, because he wasn't in a hurry, and because it was an unusual thing on Broadway to see old men seated upon railings and smoking clay pipes.

And to his surprise the old man regarded him very intently in return. He stared, with a wistful expression, into Tom's face, and he clasped his hands in trembling excitement.

Tom was filled with astonishment at the old man's strange demeanour. He stood puffing at his cigarette, and tried to understand matters. Failing, he threw his cigarette away, took a fresh one from his pocket, and approached the old man.

"Got a match?" he inquired, pleasantly.

The old man, much agitated, nearly fell from the railing as he leaned dangerously forward. "Sonny, can you read?" he demanded in a quavering voice.

"Certainly, I can," said Tom, encouragingly. He waived the affair of the match.

The old man fumbled in his pocket. "You look honest, sonny. I've been looking for an honest feller fur a'most a week. I've set on this railing fur six days," he cried, plaintively.

He drew forth a letter and handed it to Tom. "Read it fur me, sonny, read it," he said, coaxingly.

Tom took the letter and leaned back against the railings. As he opened it and prepared to read, the old man wriggled like a child at a forbidden feast.

Thundering trucks made frequent interruptions, and seven men in a hurry jogged Tom's elbow, but he succeeded in reading what follows: —

> Office of Ketchum R. Jones, Attorney-at-Law,
> Tin Can, Nevada, May 19, 18 —.
> > Rufus Wilkins, Esq.
> > Dear Sir, —I have as yet received no acknowledgment of the draft from the sale of the north section lots, which I forwarded to you on 25th June. I would request an immediate reply concerning it.
> > Since my last I have sold the three corner lots at five thousand each. The city grew so rapidly in that direction that they were surrounded by brick stores almost

before you would know it. I have also sold for four thousand dollars the ten acres of out-laying sage bush, which you once foolishly tried to give away. Mr. Simpson, of Boston, bought the tract. He is very shrewd, no doubt, but he hasn't been in the west long. Still, I think if he holds it for about a thousand years, he may come out all right.

I worked him with the projected-horse-car-line gag.

Inform me of the address of your New York attorneys, and I will send on the papers. Pray do not neglect to write me concerning the draft sent on 25th June.

In conclusion, I might say that if you have any eastern friends who are after good western investments inform them of the glorious future of Tin Can. We now have three railroads, a bank, an electric light plant, a projected horse-car line, and an art society. Also, a saw manufactory, a patent car-wheel mill, and a Methodist Church. Tin Can is marching forward to take her proud stand as the metropolis of the west. The rose-hued future holds no glories to which Tin Can does not —

Tom stopped abruptly. "I guess the important part of the letter came first," he said.

"Yes," cried the old man, "I've heard enough. It is just as I thought. George has robbed his dad."

The old man's frail body quivered with grief. Two tears trickled slowly down the furrows of his face.

"Come, come, now," said Tom, patting him tenderly on the back. "Brace up, old feller. What you want to do is to get a lawyer and go put the screws on George."

"Is it really?" asked the old man, eagerly.

"Certainly, it is," said Tom.

"All right," cried the old man, with enthusiasm. "Tell me where to get one." He slid down from the railing and prepared to start off.

Tom reflected. "Well," he said, finally, "I might do for one myself."

"What," shouted the old man in a voice of admiration, "are you a lawyer as well as a reader?"

"Well," said Tom again, "I might appear to advantage as one. All you need is a big front," he added, slowly. He was a profane young man.

The old man seized him by the arm. "Come on, then," he cried, "and we'll go put the screws on George."

Tom permitted himself to be dragged by the weak arms of his companion around a corner and along a side street. As they proceeded, he was internally bracing himself for a struggle, and putting large bales of self-assurance around where they would be likely to obstruct the advance of discovery and defeat.

By the time they reached a brown-stone house, hidden away in a street of shops and ware-houses, his mental balance was so admirable that he seemed to be in possession of enough information and brains to ruin half of the city, and he was no more concerned about the king, queen, deuce, and tray than if they had been discards that didn't fit his draw. He infused so much confidence and courage into his companion, that the old man went along the street, breathing war, like a decrepit hound on the scent of new blood.

He ambled up the steps of the brown-stone house as if he were charging earthworks. He unlocked the door and they passed along a dark hallway. In a rear room they found a man seated at table engaged with a very late breakfast. He had a diamond in his shirt front and a bit of egg on his cuff.

"George," said the old man in a fierce voice that came from his aged throat with a sound like the crackle of burning twigs, "here's my lawyer, Mr. er-ah-Smith, and we want to know what you did with the draft that was sent on 25th June."

The old man delivered the words as if each one was a musket shot. George's coffee spilled softly upon the tablecover, and his fingers worked convulsively upon a slice of bread. He turned a white, astonished face toward the old man and the intrepid Thomas.

The latter, straight and tall, with a highly legal air, stood at the old man's side. His glowing eyes were fixed upon the face of the man at the table. They seemed like two little detective cameras taking pictures of the other man's thoughts.

"Father, what d —do you mean," faltered George, totally unable to withstand the two cameras and the highly legal air.

"What do I mean?" said the old man with a feeble roar as from an ancient lion. "I mean that draft-that's what I mean. Give it up or we'll-we'll" —he paused to gain courage by a glance at the formidable figure at his side —"we'll put the screws on you."

"Well, I was —I was only borrowin' it for 'bout a month," said George.

"Ah," said Tom.

George started, glared at Tom, and then began to shiver like an animal with a broken back. There were a few moments of silence. The old man was fumbling about in his mind for more imprecations. George was wilting and turning limp before the glittering orbs of the valiant attorney. The latter, content with the exalted advantage he had gained by the use of the expression "Ah," spoke no more, but continued to stare.

"Well," said George, finally, in a weak voice, "I s'pose I can give you a cheque for it, 'though I was only borrowin' it for 'bout a month. I don't think you have treated me fairly, father, with your lawyers and your threats, and all that. But I'll give you the cheque."

The old man turned to his attorney. "Well?" he asked.

Tom looked at the son and held an impressive debate with himself. "I think we may accept the cheque," he said coldly after a time.

George arose and tottered across the room. He drew a cheque that made the attorney's heart come privately into his mouth. As he and his client passed triumphantly out, he turned a last highly legal glare upon George that reduced that individual to a mere paste.

On the side-walk the old man went into a spasm of delight and called his attorney all the admiring and endearing names there were to be had.

"Lord, how you settled him," he cried ecstatically.

They walked slowly back toward Broadway. "The scoundrel," murmured the old man. "I'll never see 'im again. I'll desert 'im. I'll find a nice quiet boarding-place and —"

"That's all right," said Tom. "I know one. I'll take you right up," which he did.

He came near being happy ever after. The old man lived at advanced rates in the front room at Tom's boarding-house. And the latter basked in the proprietress' smiles, which had a commercial value, and were a great improvement on many we see.

The old man, with his quantities of sage bush, thought Thomas owned all the virtues mentioned in high-class literature, and his opinion, too, was of commercial value. Also, he knew a man who knew another man who received an impetus which made him engage Thomas on terms that were highly satisfactory. Then it was that the latter learned he had not succeeded sooner because he did not know a man who knew another man.

So it came to pass that Tom grew to be Thomas G. Somebody. He achieved that position in life from which he could hold out for good wines when he went to poor restaurants. His name became entangled with the name of Wilkins in the ownership of vast and valuable tracts of sage bush in Tin Can, Nevada.

At the present day he is so great that he lunches frugally at high prices. His fame has spread through the land as a man who carved his way to fortune with no help but his undaunted pluck, his tireless energy, and his sterling integrity.

Newspapers apply to him now, and he writes long signed articles to struggling young men, in which he gives the best possible advice as to how to become wealthy. In these articles, he, in a burst of glorification, cites the king, queen, deuce, and tray, the four aces, and all that. He alludes tenderly to the nickel he borrowed and spent for cigarettes as the foundation of his fortune.

"To succeed in life," he writes, "the youth of America have only to see an old man seated upon a railing and smoking a clay pipe. Then go up and ask him for a match."

A TALE OF MERE CHANCE.

Being an Account of the Pursuit of the Tiles, the Statement of the Clock, and the Grip of a Coat of Orange Spots, together with some Criticism of a Detective said to be Carved from an Old Table-leg.

Yes, my friend, I killed the man, but I would not have been detected in it were it not for some very extraordinary circumstances. I had long considered this deed, but I am a delicate and sensitive person, you understand, and I hesitated over it as the diver hesitates on the brink of a dark and icy mountain pool. A thought of the shock of the contact holds one back.

As I was passing his house one morning, I said to myself, "Well, at any rate, if she loves him, it will not be for long." And after that decision I was not myself, but a sort of a machine.

I rang the bell and the servants admitted me to the drawing-room. I waited there while the old tall clock placidly ticked its speech of time. The rigid and austere chairs remained in possession of their singular imperturbability, although, of course, they were aware of my purpose, but the little white tiles of the floor whispered one to another and looked at me. Presently he entered the room, and I, drawing my revolver, shot him. He screamed-you know that scream-mostly amazement-and as he fell forward his blood was upon the little white tiles. They huddled and covered their eyes from this rain. It seemed to me that the old clock stopped ticking as a man may gasp in the middle of a sentence, and a chair threw itself in my way as I sprang toward the door.

A moment later, I was walking down the street, tranquil, you understand, and I said to myself, "It is done. Long years from this day I will say to her that it was I who killed him. After time has eaten the conscience of the thing, she will admire my courage."

I was elated that the affair had gone off so smoothly, and I felt like returning home and taking a long, full sleep, like a tired working man. When people passed me, I contemplated their stupidity with a sense of satisfaction.

But those accursed little white tiles.

I heard a shrill crying and chattering behind me, and, looking back, I saw them, blood-stained and impassioned, raising their little hands and screaming "Murder! It was he!" I have said that they had little hands. I am not sure of it, but they had some means of indicating me as unerringly as pointing fingers. As for their movement, they swept along as easily as dry, light leaves are carried by the wind. Always they were shrilly piping their song of my guilt.

My friend, may it never be your fortune to be pursued by a crowd of little blood-stained tiles. I used a thousand means to be free from the clash-clash of these tiny feet. I ran through the world at my best speed, but it was no better than that of an ox, while they, my pursuers, were always fresh, eager, relentless.

I am an ingenious person, and I used every trick that a desperate, fertile man can invent. Hundreds of times I had almost evaded them when some smouldering, neglected spark would blaze up and discover me.

I felt that the eye of conviction would have no terrors for me, but the eyes of suspicion which I saw in city after city, on road after road, drove me to the verge of going forward and saying, "Yes, I have murdered."

People would see the following, clamorous troops of blood-stained tiles, and give me piercing glances, so that these swords played continually at my heart. But we are a decorous race, thank God. It is very vulgar to apprehend murderers on the public streets. We have learned correct manners from the English. Besides, who can be sure of the meaning of clamouring tiles? It might be merely a trick in politics.

Detectives? What are detectives? Oh, yes, I have read of them and their deeds, when I come to think of it. The prehistoric races must have been remarkable. I have never been able to understand how the detective navigated in stone boats. Still, specimens of their pottery excavated in Taumalipas show a remarkable knowledge of mechanics. I remember the little hydraulic-what's that? Well, what you say may be true, my friend, but I think you dream.

The little stained tiles. My friend, I stopped in an inn at the ends of the earth, and in the morning they were there flying like little birds and pecking at my window.

I should have escaped. Heavens, I should have escaped. What was more simple? I murdered and then walked into the world, which is wide and intricate.

Do you know that my own clock assisted in the hunting of me? They asked what time I left my home that morning, and it replied at once, "Half-after eight." The watch of a man I had chanced to pass near the house of the crime told the people "Seven minutes after nine." And, of course, the tall, old clock in the drawing-room went about day after day repeating, "Eighteen minutes after nine."

Do you say that the man who caught me was very clever? My friend, I have lived long, and he was the most incredible blockhead of my experience. An enslaved, dust-eating Mexican vaquero wouldn't hitch his pony to such a man. Do you think he deserves credit for my capture? If he had been as pervading as the atmosphere, he would never have caught me. If he was a detective, as you say, I could carve a better one from an old table-leg. But the tiles. That is another matter. At night I think they flew in long high flock, like pigeons. In the day, little mad things, they murmured on my trail like frothy-mouthed weasels.

I see that you note these great, round, vividly orange spots on my coat. Of course, even if the detective were really carved from an old table-leg, he could hardly fail to apprehend a man thus badged. As sores come upon one in the plague so came these spots upon my coat. When I discovered them, I made effort to free myself of this coat. I tore, tugged, wrenched at it, but around my shoulders it was like a grip of a dead man's arms. Do you know that I have plunged into a thousand lakes? I have smeared this coat with a thousand paints. But day and night the spots burn like lights. I might walk from this jail to-day if I could rid myself of this coat, but it clings-clings-clings.

At any rate, the person you call a detective was not so clever to discover a man in a coat of spotted orange, followed by shrieking, blood-stained tiles. Yes, that noise from the corridor is most peculiar. But they are always there, muttering and watching, clashing and jostling. It sounds as if the dishes of Hades were being washed. Yet I have become used to it. Once, indeed, in the night, I cried out to them, "In God's name, go away, little blood-stained tiles." But they doggedly answered, "It is the law."

AT CLANCY'S WAKE.

Scene —*Room in the house of the lamented Clancy. The curtains are pulled down. A perfume of old roses and whisky hangs in the air. A weeping woman in black it seated at a table in the centre. A group of wide-eyed children are sobbing in a corner. Down the side of the room is a row of mourning friends of the family. Through an open door can be seen, half hidden in shadows, the silver and black of a coffin.*

Widow-Oh, wirra, wirra, wirra!

Children —B-b boo-hoo-hoo!

Friends (*conversing in low tones*) —Yis, Moike Clancy was a foine mahn, sure! None betther! No, I don't t'ink so. Did he? Sure, all th' elictions! He was th' bist in the warrud! He licked 'im widin an inch of his loife, aisy, an' th' other wan a big, shtrappin' buck of a mahn, an' him jes' free of th' pneumonia! Yis, he did! They carried th' warrud by six hunder! Yis, he was a foine mahn. None betther. Gawd sav' 'im!

(*Enter Mr. Slick, of the "Daily Blanket," shown in by a maid-servant, whose hair has become disarranged through much tear-shedding. He is attired in a suit of grey check, and wears a red rose in his buttonhole.*)

Mr. Slick-Good afternoon, Mrs. Clancy. This is a sad misfortune for you, isn't it?

Widow-Oh, indade, indade, young mahn, me poor heart is bruk.

Mr. Slick-Very sad, Mrs. Clancy. A great misfortune, I'm sure. Now, Mrs. Clancy, I've called to —

Widow-Little did I t'ink, young mahn, win they brought poor Moike in that it was th' lasht!

Mr. Slick (*with conviction*) —True! True! Very true, indeed. It was a great grief to you, Mrs. Clancy. I've called this morning, Mrs. Clancy, to see if I could get from you a short obituary notice for the *Blanket* if you could —

Widow-An' his hid was done up in a rag, an' he was cursin' frightful. A damned Oytalian lit fall th' hod as Moike was walkin' pasht as dacint as you plaze. Win they carried 'im in, him all bloody, an' ravin' tur'ble 'bout Oytalians, me heart was near bruk, but I niver tawt —I niver tawt —I —I niver —(*Breaks forth into a long, forlorn cry. The children join in, and the chorus echoes wailfully through the rooms.*)

Mr. Slick (*as the yell, in a measure, ceases*) —Yes, indeed, a sad, sad affair. A terrible misfortune. Now, Mrs. Clancy —

Widow (*turning suddenly*) —Mary Ann. Where's thot lazy divil of a Mary Ann? (*As the servant appears.*) Mary Ann, bring th' bottle! Give th' gintlemin a dhrink!...Here's to Hiven savin' yez, young mahn. (*Drinks.*)

Mr. Slick (*drinks*) —A noble whisky, Mrs. Clancy. Many thanks. Now, Mrs. Clancy —

Widow-Take anodder wan! Take anodder wan! (*Fills his glass.*)

Mr. Slick (*impatiently*) —Yes, certainly, Mrs. Clancy, certainly. (*He drinks.*) Now, could you tell me, Mrs. Clancy, where your late husband was —

Widow-Who-Moike? Oh, young mahn, yez can just say thot he was the foinest mahn livin' an' breathin', an' niver a wan in th' warrud was betther. Oh, but he had th' tindther heart for 'is fambly, he did. Don't I remember win he clipped little Patsey wid th' bottle, an' didn't he buy th' big rockin'-horse th' minit he got sober? Sure he did. Pass th' bottle, Mary Ann! (*Pours a beer-glass about half-full for her guest.*)

Mr. Slick (*taking a seat*) —True, Mr. Clancy was a fine man, Mrs. Clancy —a *very* fine man. Now, I —

Widow (*plaintively*) —An' don't yez loike th' rum? Dhrink th' rum, mahn! It was me own Moike's fav'rite bran'. Well I remember win he fotched it home, an' half th' demijohn gone a'ready, an' him a-cursin' up th' stairs as dhrunk as Gawd plazed. It was a —Dhrink th' rum, young mahn, dhrink th' rum! If he cud see yez now, Moike Clancy wud git up from 'is —

Mr. Slick (*desperately*) —Very well, very well, Mrs. Clancy. Here's your good health. Now, can you tell me, Mrs. Clancy, when was Mr. Clancy born?

Widow-Win was he borrun. Sure, divil a bit do I care win he was borrun. He was th' good mahn to me an' his childher; an' Gawd knows I don't care win he was borrun. Mary Ann, pass th' bottle! Wud yez kape th' gintlemin starvin' for a dhrink here in Moike Clancy's own house? Gawd save yez.

(*When the bottle appears she pours a huge quantity out for her guest.*)

Mr. Slick-Well, then, Mrs. Clancy, *where* was he born?

Widow (*staring*) —In Oirland, mahn, in Oirland! Where did yez t'ink? (*Then, in sudden, wheedling tones.*) An' ain't yez goin' to dhrink th' rum? Are yez goin' to shirk th' good whisky what was th' pride of Moike's life, an' him gettin' full on it an' breakin' th' furnitir t'ree nights a week hard-runnin'? Shame an yez, an' Gawd save yer soul. Dhrink it oop now, there's a dear, dhrink it oop now, an' say: "Moike Clancy, be all th' powers in th' shky, Hiven sind yez rist!"

Mr. Slick —(*to himself*) —Holy smoke! (*He drinks, then regards the glass for a long time.*) ... Well, now, Mrs. Clancy, give me your attention for a moment, please. When did —

Widow-An' oh, but he was a power in th' warrud! Divil a mahn cud vote right widout Moike Clancy at 'is elbow. An' in th' calkus, sure didn't Mulrooney git th' nominashun jes' by raison of Moike's atthackin' th' opposashun wid th' shtove-poker. Mulrooney got it as aisy as dhirt, wid Moike rowlin' under th' tayble wid th' other candeedate. He was a good sit'zen, was Moike-divil a wan betther.

Mr. Slick *spends some minutes in collecting his faculties.*

Mr. Slick (*after he decides that he has them collected*) —Yes, yes, Mrs. Clancy, your husband's h-highly successful pol-pol-political career was w-well known to the public; but what I want to know is-what I want to know —(*Pauses to consider.*)

Widow (*finally*) —Pass th' glasses, Mary Ann, yez lazy divil; give th' gintlemin a dhrink! Here (*tendering him a glass*), take anodder wan to Moike Clancy, an' Gawd save yez for yer koindness to a poor widee woman!

Mr. Slick (*after solemnly regarding the glass*) —Certainly, I —I'll take a drink. Certainly, M — Mish Clanshy. Yes, certainly, Mish Clanshy. Now, Mish Clanshy, w-w-wash was Mr. Clan-shy's n-name before he married you, Mish Clanshy?

Widow (*astonished*) —Why, divil a bit else but Clancy.

Mr. Slick (*after reflection*) —Well, but I mean —I mean, Mish Clanshy, I mean-what was date of birth? Did marry you 'fore then, or d-did marry you when 'e was born in N' York, Mish Clanshy?

Widow-Phwat th' divil —

Mr. Slick (*with dignity*) —Ansher my queshuns, pleash, Mish Clanshy. Did 'e bring chil'en withum f'm Irelan', or was you, after married in N' York, mother those chil'en 'e brought f'm Irelan'?

Widow-Be th' powers above, I —

Mr. Slick (*with gentle patience*) —I don't shink y' unnerstan' m' queshuns, Mish Clanshy. What I wanna fin' out is, what was 'e born in N' York for when he, before zat, came f'm Irelan'? Dash what puzzels me. I-I'm completely puzzled. An' alsho, I wanna fin' out —I wanna fin' out, if poshble-zat is, if it's poshble shing, I wanna fin' out —I wanna fin' out-if poshble —I wanna-shay, who the blazesh is dead here, anyhow?

AN EPISODE OF WAR.

The lieutenant's rubber blanket lay on the ground, and upon it he had poured the company's supply of coffee. Corporals and other representatives of the grimy and hot-throated men who lined the breastwork had come for each squad's portion.

The lieutenant was frowning and serious at this task of division. His lips pursed as he drew with his sword various crevices in the heap until brown squares of coffee, astoundingly equal in size, appeared on the blanket. He was on the verge of a great triumph in mathematics, and the corporals were thronging forward, each to reap a little square, when suddenly the lieutenant cried out and looked quickly at a man near him as if he suspected it was a case of personal assault. The others cried out also when they saw blood upon the lieutenant's sleeve.

He has winced like a man stung, swayed dangerously, and then straightened. The sound of his hoarse breathing was plainly audible. He looked sadly, mystically, over the breastwork at the green face of a wood, where now were many little puffs of white smoke. During this moment the men about him gazed statue-like and silent, astonished and awed by this catastrophe which happened when catastrophes were not expected-when they had leisure to observe it.

As the lieutenant stared at the wood, they too swung their heads, so that for another instant all hands, still silent, contemplated the distant forest as if their minds were fixed upon the mystery of a bullet's journey.

The officer had, of course, been compelled to take his sword into his left hand. He did not hold it by the hilt. He gripped it at the middle of the blade, awkwardly. Turning his eyes from the hostile wood, he looked at the sword as he held it there, and seemed puzzled as to what to do with it, where to put it. In short, this weapon had of a sudden become a strange thing to him. He looked at it in a kind of stupefaction, as if he had been endowed with a trident, a sceptre, or a spade.

Finally he tried to sheath it. To sheath a sword held by the left hand, at the middle of the blade, in a scabbard hung at the left hip, is a feat worthy of a sawdust ring. This wounded officer engaged in a desperate struggle with the sword and the wobbling scabbard, and during the time of it he breathed like a wrestler.

But at this instant the men, the spectators, awoke from their stone-like poses and crowded forward sympathetically. The orderly-sergeant took the sword and tenderly placed it in the scabbard. At the time, he leaned nervously backward, and did not allow even his finger to brush the body of the lieutenant. A wound gives strange dignity to him who bears it. Well men shy from this new and terrible majesty. It is as if the wounded man's hand is upon the curtain which hangs before the revelations of all existence-the meaning of ants, potentates, wars, cities, sunshine, snow, a feather dropped from a bird's wing; and the power of it sheds radiance upon a bloody form, and makes the other men understand sometimes that they are little. His comrades look at him with large eyes thoughtfully. Moreover, they fear vaguely that the weight of a finger upon him might send him headlong, precipitate the tragedy, hurl him at once into the dim, grey unknown. And so the orderly-sergeant, while sheathing the sword, leaned nervously backward.

There were others who proffered assistance. One timidly presented his shoulder and asked the lieutenant if he cared to lean upon it, but the latter waved him away mournfully. He wore the look of one who knows he is the victim of a terrible disease and understands his helplessness. He again stared over the breastwork at the forest, and then turning went slowly rearward. He held his right wrist tenderly in his left hand as if the wounded arm was made of very brittle glass.

And the men in silence stared at the wood, then at the departing lieutenant-then at the wood, then at the lieutenant.

As the wounded officer passed from the line of battle, he was enabled to see many things which as a participant in the fight were unknown to him. He saw a general on a black horse gazing over the lines of blue infantry at the green woods which veiled his problems. An aide galloped furiously, dragged his horse suddenly to a halt, saluted, and presented a paper. It was, for a wonder, precisely like an historical painting.

To the rear of the general and his staff a group, composed of a bugler, two or three orderlies, and the bearer of the corps standard, all upon maniacal horses, were working like slaves to hold their ground, preserve their respectful interval, while the shells boomed in the air about them, and caused their chargers to make furious quivering leaps.

A battery, a tumultuous and shining mass, was swirling toward the right. The wild thud of hoofs, the cries of the riders shouting blame and praise, menace and encouragement, and, last, the roar of the wheels, the slant of the glistening guns, brought the lieutenant to an intent pause. The battery swept in curves that stirred the heart; it made halts as dramatic as the crash of a wave on the rocks, and when it fled onward, this aggregation of wheels, levers, motors, had a beautiful unity, as if it were a missile. The sound of it was a war-chorus that reached into the depths of man's emotion.

The lieutenant, still holding his arm as if it were of glass, stood watching this battery until all detail of it was lost, save the figures of the riders, which rose and fell and waved lashes over the black mass.

Later, he turned his eyes toward the battle where the shooting sometimes crackled like bush-fires, sometimes sputtered with exasperating irregularity, and sometimes reverberated like the thunder. He saw the smoke rolling upward and saw crowds of men who ran and cheered, or stood and blazed away at the inscrutable distance.

He came upon some stragglers, and they told him how to find the field hospital. They described its exact location. In fact, these men, no longer having part in the battle, knew more of it than others. They told the performance of every corps, every division, the opinion of every general. The lieutenant, carrying his wounded arm rearward, looked upon them with wonder.

At the roadside a brigade was making coffee and buzzing with talk like a girls' boarding-school. Several officers came out to him and inquired concerning things of which he knew nothing. One, seeing his arm, began to scold. "Why, man, that's no way to do. You want to fix that thing." He appropriated the lieutenant and the lieutenant's wound. He cut the sleeve and laid bare the arm, every nerve of which softly fluttered under his touch. He bound his handkerchief over the wound, scolding away in the meantime. His tone allowed one to think that he was in the habit of being wounded every day. The lieutenant hung his head, feeling, in this presence, that he did not know how to be correctly wounded.

The low white tents of the hospital were grouped around an old school-house. There was here a singular commotion. In the foreground two ambulances interlocked wheels in the deep mud. The drivers were tossing the blame of it back and forth, gesticulating and berating, while from the ambulances, both crammed with wounded, there came an occasional groan. An interminable crowd of bandaged men were coming and going. Great numbers sat under the trees nursing heads or arms or legs. There was a dispute of some kind raging on the steps of the school-house. Sitting with his back against a tree a man with a face as grey as a new army blanket was serenely smoking a corn-cob pipe. The lieutenant wished to rush forward and inform him that he was dying.

A busy surgeon was passing near the lieutenant. "Good-morning," he said, with a friendly smile. Then he caught sight of the lieutenant's arm and his face at once changed. "Well, let's have a look at it." He seemed possessed suddenly of a great contempt for the lieutenant. This wound evidently placed the latter on a very low social plane. The doctor cried out impatiently, "What mutton-head had tied it up that way anyhow?" The lieutenant answered, "Oh, a man."

When the wound was disclosed the doctor fingered it disdainfully. "Humph," he said. "You come along with me and I'll 'tend to you." His voice contained the same scorn as if he were saying, "You will have to go to jail."

The lieutenant had been very meek, but now his face flushed, and he looked into the doctor's eyes. "I guess I won't have it amputated," he said.

"Nonsense, man! Nonsense! Nonsense!" cried the doctor. "Come along, now. I won't amputate it. Come along. Don't be a baby."

"Let go of me," said the lieutenant, holding back wrathfully, his glance fixed upon the door of the old school-house, as sinister to him as the portals of death.

And this is the story of how the lieutenant lost his arm. When he reached home, his sisters, his mother, his wife, sobbed for a long time at the sight of the flat sleeve. "Oh, well," he said, standing shamefaced amid these tears, "I don't suppose it matters so much as all that."

THE VOICE OF THE MOUNTAIN.

The old man Popocatepetl was seated on a high rock with his white mantle about his shoulders. He looked at the sky, he looked at the sea, he looked at the land-nowhere could he see any food. And he was very hungry, too.

Who can understand the agony of a creature whose stomach is as large as a thousand churches, when this same stomach is as empty as a broken water jar?

He looked longingly at some island in the sea. "Ah, those flat cakes! If I had them." He stared at storm-clouds in the sky. "Ah, what a drink is there." But the King of Everything, you know, had forbidden the old man Popocatepetl to move at all, because he feared that every footprint would make a great hole in the land. So the old fellow was obliged to sit still and wait for his food to come within reach. Any one who has tried this plan knows what intervals lie between meals.

Once his friend, the little eagle, flew near, and Popocatepetl called to him. "Ho, tiny bird, come and consider with me as to how I shall be fed."

The little eagle came and spread his legs apart and considered manfully, but he could do nothing with the situation. "You see," he said, "this is no ordinary hunger which one goat will suffice —"

Popocatepetl groaned an assent.

" —but it is an enormous affair," continued the little eagle, "which requires something like a dozen stars. I don't see what can be done unless we get that little creature of the earth-that little animal with two arms, two legs, one head, and a very brave air, to invent something. He is said to be very wise."

"Who claims it for him?" asked Popocatepetl.

"He claims it for himself," responded the eagle.

"Well, summon him. Let us see. He is doubtless a kind little animal, and when he sees my distress he will invent something."

"Good!" The eagle flew until he discovered one of these small creatures. "Oh, tiny animal, the great chief Popocatepetl summons you!"

"Does he, indeed!"

"Popocatepetl, the great chief," said the eagle again, thinking that the little animal had not heard rightly.

"Well, and why does he summon me?"

"Because he is in distress, and he needs your assistance."

The little animal reflected for a time, and then said, "I will go."

When Popocatepetl perceived the little animal and the eagle he stretched forth his great, solemn arms. "Oh, blessed little animal with two arms, two legs, a head, and a very brave air, help me in my agony. Behold I, Popocatepetl, who saw the King of Everything fashioning the stars, I, who knew the sun in his childhood, I, Popocatepetl, appeal to you, little animal. I am hungry."

After a while the little animal asked: "How much will you pay?"

"Pay?" said Popocatepetl.

"Pay?" said the eagle.

"Assuredly," quoth the little animal, "pay!"

"But," demanded Popocatepetl, "were you never hungry? I tell you I am hungry, and is your first word then 'pay'?"

The little animal turned coldly away. "Oh, Popocatepetl, how much wisdom has flown past you since you saw the King of Everything fashioning the stars and since you knew the sun in his childhood? I said pay, and, moreover, your distress measures my price. It is our law. Yet it is true that we did not see the King of Everything fashioning the stars. Nor did we know the sun in his childhood."

Then did Popocatepetl roar and shake in his rage. "Oh, louse-louse-louse! Let us bargain then! How much for your blood?" Over the little animal hung death.

But he instantly bowed himself and prayed: "Popocatepetl, the great, you who saw the King of Everything fashioning the stars, and who knew the sun in his childhood, forgive this poor little animal. Your sacred hunger shall be my care. I am your servant."

"It is well," said Popocatepetl at once, for his spirit was ever kindly. "And now, what will you do?"

The little animal put his hand upon his chin and reflected. "Well, it seems you are hungry, and the King of Everything has forbidden you to go for food in fear that your monstrous feet will riddle the earth with holes. What you need is a pair of wings."

"A pair of wings!" cried Popocatepetl delightedly.

"A pair of wings!" screamed the eagle in joy.

"How very simple, after all."

"And yet how wise!"

"But," said Popocatepetl, after the first outburst, "who can make me these wings?"

The little animal replied: "I and my kind are great, because at times we can make one mind control a hundred thousand bodies. This is the secret of our performance. It will be nothing for us to make wings for even you, great Popocatepetl. I and my kind will come" —continued the crafty, little animal —"we will come and dwell on this beautiful plain that stretches from the sea to the sea, and we will make wings for you."

Popocatepetl wished to embrace the little animal. "Oh, glorious! Oh, best of little brutes! Run! run! run! Summon your kind, dwell in the plain and make me wings. Ah, when once Popocatepetl can soar on his wings from star to star, then, indeed —"

* * * * * * *

Poor old stupid Popocatepetl! The little animal summoned his kind, they dwelt on the plains, they made this and they made that, but they made no wings for Popocatepetl.

And sometimes when the thunderous voice of the old peak rolls and rolls, if you know that tongue, you can hear him say: "Oh, traitor! Traitor! Traitor! Where are my wings? My wings, traitor! I am hungry! Where are my wings?"

But the little animal merely places his finger beside his nose and winks.

"Your wings, indeed, fool! Sit still and howl for them! Old idiot!"

WHY DID THE YOUNG CLERK SWEAR?
OR, THE UNSATISFACTORY FRENCH.

All was silent in the little gent's furnishing store. A lonely clerk with a blonde moustache and a red necktie raised a languid hand to his brow and brushed back a dangling lock. He yawned and gazed gloomily at the blurred panes of the windows.

Without, the wind and rain came swirling round the brick buildings and went sweeping over the streets. A horse-car rumbled stolidly by. In the mud on the pavements, a few pedestrians struggled with excited umbrellas.

"The deuce!" remarked the clerk. "I'd give ten dollars if somebody would come in and buy something, if 'twere only cotton socks."

He waited amid the shadows of the grey afternoon. No customers came. He heaved a long sigh and sat down on a high stool. From beneath a stack of unlaundried shirts he drew a French novel with a picture on the cover. He yawned again, glanced lazily toward the street, and settled himself as comfortable as the gods would let him upon the high stool.

He opened the book and began to read. Soon it could have been noticed that his blonde moustache took on a curl of enthusiasm, and the refractory locks on his brow showed symptoms of soft agitation.

"Silvere did not see the young girl for some days," read the clerk. "He was miserable. He seemed always to inhale that subtle perfume from her hair. At night he saw her eyes in the stars.

"His dreams were troubled. He watched the house. Heloise did not appear. One day he met Vibert. Vibert wore a black frock-coat. There were wine-stains on the right breast. His collar was soiled. He had not shaved.

"Silvere burst into tears. 'I love her! I love her! I shall die!' Vibert laughed scornfully. His necktie was second-hand. Idiotic, this boy in love. Fool! Simpleton! But at last he pitied him. She goes to the music-teacher's every morning. Silly Silvere embraced him.

"The next day Silvere waited at the street corner. A vendor was selling chestnuts. Two gamins were fighting in an alley. A woman was scrubbing some steps. This great Paris throbbed with life.

"Heloise came. She did not perceive Silvere. She passed with a happy smile on her face. She looked fresh, fair, innocent. Silvere felt himself swooning. 'Ah, my God!'

"She crossed the street. The young man received a shock that sent the warm blood to his brain. It had been raining. There was mud. With one slender hand Heloise lifted her skirts. Silvere leaning forward, saw her —"

A young man in a wet mackintosh came into the little gent's furnishing store.

"Ah, beg pardon," said he to the clerk, "but do you have an agency for a steam laundry here? I have been patronising a Chinaman down th' avenue for some time, but he-what? No? You have none here? Well, why don't you start one, anyhow? It'd be a good thing in this neighbourhood. I live just round the corner, and it'd be a great thing for me. I know lots of people who would-what? Oh, you don't? Oh!"

As the young man in the wet mackintosh retreated, the clerk with a blonde moustache made a hungry grab at the novel. He continued to read: "Handkerchief fall in a puddle. Silvere sprang forward. He picked up the handkerchief. Their eyes met. As he returned the handkerchief, their hands touched. The young girl smiled. Silvere was in ecstacies. 'Ah, my God!'

"A baker opposite was quarrelling over two sous with an old woman.

"A grey-haired veteran with a medal upon his breast and a butcher's boy were watching a dog-fight. The smell of dead animals came from adjacent slaughter-houses. The letters on the sign over the tinsmith's shop on the corner shone redly like great clots of blood. It was hell on roller skates."

Here the clerk skipped some seventeen chapters descriptive of a number of intricate money transactions, the moles on the neck of a Parisian dressmaker, the process of making brandy, the milk-leg of Silvere's aunt, life in the coal-pits, and scenes in the Chamber of Deputies. In these chapters the reputation of the architect of Charlemagne's palace was vindicated, and it was explained why Heloise's grandmother didn't keep her stockings pulled up.

Then he proceeded: "Heloise went to the country. The next day Silvere followed. They met in the fields. The young girl had donned the garb of the peasants. She blushed. She looked fresh, fair, innocent. Silvere felt faint with rapture. 'Ah, my God!'

"She had been running. Out of breath, she sank down in the hay. She held out her hand. 'I am so glad to see you.' Silvere was enchanted at this vision. He bended toward her. Suddenly he burst into tears. 'I love you! I love you! I love you!' he stammered.

"A row of red and white shirts hung on a line some distance away. The third shirt from the left had a button off the neck. A cat on the rear steps of a cottage near the shirt was drinking milk from a platter. The north-east portion of the platter had a crack in it.

"'Heloise!' Silvere was murmuring hoarsely. He leaned toward her until his warm breath moved the curls on her neck. 'Heloise!' murmured Jean."

"Young man," said an elderly gentleman with a dripping umbrella to the clerk with a blonde moustache, "have you any night-shirts open front and back? Eh? Night-shirts open front and back, I said. D'you hear, eh? *Night-shirts open front and back*. Well, then, why didn't you say so? It would pay you to be a trifle more polite, young man. When you get as old as I am, you will find out that it pays to-what? I didn't see you adding any column of figures. In that case I am sorry. You have no night-shirts open front and back, eh? Well, good-day."

As the elderly gentleman vanished, the clerk with a blonde moustache grasped the novel like some famished animal. He read on: "A peasant stood before the two children. He wrung his hands. 'Have you seen a stray cow?' 'No,' cried the children in the same breath. The peasant wept. He wrung his hands. It was a supreme moment.

"'She loves me!' cried Silvere to himself, as he changed his clothes for dinner.

"It was evening. The children sat by the fire-place. Heloise wore a gown of clinging white. She looked fresh, fair, innocent. Silvere was in raptures. 'Ah, my God!'

"Old Jean, the peasant, saw nothing. He was mending harness. The fire crackled in the fire-place. The children loved each other. Through the open door to the kitchen came the sound of old Marie shrilly cursing the geese who wished to enter. In front of the window two pigs were quarrelling over a vegetable. Cattle were lowing in a distant field. A hay-waggon creaked slowly past. Thirty-two chickens were asleep in the branches of a tree. This subtle atmosphere had a mighty effect upon Heloise. It was beating down her self-control. She felt herself going. She was choking.

"The young girl made an effort. She stood up. 'Good-night, I must go.' Silvere took her hand. 'Heloise,' he murmured. Outside the two pigs were fighting.

"A warm blush overspread the young girl's face. She turned wet eyes toward her lover. She looked fresh, fair, innocent. Silvere was maddened. 'Ah, my God!'

"Suddenly the young girl began to tremble. She tried vainly to withdraw her hand. But her knee —"

"I wish to get my husband some shirts," said a shopping-woman with six bundles. The clerk with a blonde moustache made a private gesture of despair, and rapidly spread a score of different-patterned shirts upon the counter. "He's very particular about his shirts," said the shopping-woman. "Oh, I don't think any of these will do. Don't you keep the Invincible brand? He only wears that kind. He says they fit him better. And he's very particular about his shirts. What? You don't keep them? No? Well, how much do you think they would come at?" "Haven't the slightest idea." "Well, I suppose I must go somewhere else, then. Um, good-day."

The clerk with the blonde moustache was about to make further private gestures of despair, when the shopping-woman with six bundles turned and went out. His fingers instantly closed nervously over the book. He drew it from its hiding-place, and opened it at the place where he had ceased. His hungry eyes seemed to eat the words upon the page. He continued: "—struck cruelly against a chair. It seemed to awaken her. She started. She burst from the young man's arms. Outside the two pigs were grunting amiably.

"Silvere took his candle. He went toward his room. He was in despair. 'Ah, my God!'

"He met the young girl on the stairs. He took her hand. Tears were raining down his face. 'Heloise!' he murmured.

"The young girl shivered. As Silvere put his arms about her, she faintly resisted. This embrace seemed to sap her life. She wished to die. Her thoughts flew back to the old well and the broken hayrakes at Plassans.

"The young girl looked fresh, fair, innocent 'Heloise!' murmured Silvere. The children exchanged a long, clinging kiss. It seemed to unite their souls.

"The young girl was swooning. Her head sank on the young man's shoulder. There was nothing in space except these warm kisses on her neck. Silvere enfolded her. 'Ah, my God!' "

"Say, young fellow," said a youth with a tilted cigar to the clerk with a blonde moustache, "where th'll is Billie Carcart's joint round here? Know?"

"Next corner," said the clerk fiercely.

"Oh, th'll," said the youth, "yehs needn't git gay. See! When a feller asts a civil question yehs needn't git gay. See! Th'll!"

The youth stood and looked aggressive for a moment. Then he went away.

The clerk seemed almost to leap upon the book. His feverish fingers twirled the pages. When he found his place he glued his eyes to it. He read:

"Then a great flash of lightning illumined the hall-way. It threw livid hues over a row of flowerpots in the window-seat. Thunder shook the house to its foundation. From the kitchen arose the voice of old Marie in prayer.

"Heloise screamed. She wrenched herself from the young man's arms. She sprang inside her room. She locked the door. She flung herself face downward on the bed. She burst into tears. She looked fresh, fair, innocent.

"The rain pattering upon the thatched roof sounded in the stillness like the footsteps of spirits. In the sky toward Paris there shone a crimson light.

"The chickens had all fallen from the tree. They stood, sadly, in a puddle. The two pigs were asleep under the porch.

"Upstairs, in the hall-way, Silvers was furious."

The clerk with a blonde moustache gave here a wild scream of disappointment. He madly hurled the novel with the picture on the cover from him. He stood up and said: "Damn!"

THE VICTORY OF THE MOON.

The Strong Man of the Hills lost his wife. Immediately he went abroad, calling aloud. The people all crouched afar in the dark of their huts, and cried to him when he was yet a long distance away: "No, no, great chief, we have not even seen the imprint of your wife's sandal in the sand. If we had seen it, you would have found us bowed down in worship before the marks of her ten glorious brown toes, for we are but poor devils of Indians, and the grandeur of the sun rays on her hair would have turned our eyes to dust."

"Her toes are not brown. They are pink," said the Strong Man from the Hills. "Therefore do I believe that you speak the truth when you say you have not seen her, good little men of the valley. In this matter of her great loveliness, however, you speak a little too strongly. As she is no longer among my possessions, I have no mind to hear her praised. Whereabouts is the best man of you?"

None of them had stomach for this honour at the time. They surmised that the Strong Man of the Hills had some plan for combat, and they knew that the best of them would have in this encounter only the strength of the meat in the grip of the fire. "Great King," they said, in one voice, "there is no best man here."

"How is this?" roared the Strong Man. "There must be one who excels. It is a law. Let him step forward then."

But they solemnly shook their heads. "There is no best man here."

The Strong Man turned upon them so furiously that many fell to the ground. "There must be one. Let him step forward." Shivering, they huddled together and tried, in their fear, to thrust each other toward the Strong Man.

At this time a young philosopher approached the throng slowly. The philosophers of that age were all young men in the full heat of life. The old greybeards were, for the most part, very stupid, and were so accounted.

"Strong Man from the Hills," said the young philosopher, "go to yonder brook and bathe. Then come and eat of this fruit. Then gaze for a time at the blue sky and the green earth. Afterward I have something to say to you."

"You are not so wise that I am obliged to bathe before listening to you?" demanded the Strong Man, insolently.

"No," said the young philosopher. All the people thought this reply very strange.

"Why, then, must I bathe and eat of fruit and gaze at the earth and the sky?"

"Because they are pleasant things to do."

"Have I, do you think, any thirst at this time for pleasant things?"

"Bathe, eat, gaze," said the young philosopher with a gesture.

The Strong Man did, indeed, whirl his bronzed and terrible limbs in the silver water. Then he lay in the shadow of a tree and ate the cool fruit and gazed at the sky and the earth. "This is a fine comfort," he said. After a time he suddenly struck his forehead with his finger. "By the way, did I tell you that my wife had fled from me?"

"I know it," said the young philosopher.

Later the Strong Man slept peacefully. The young philosopher smiled.

But in the night the little men of the valley came clamouring: "Oh, Strong Man of the Hills, the moon derides you!"

The philosopher went to them in the darkness. "Be still, little people. It is nothing. The derision of the moon is nothing."

But the little men of the valley would not cease their uproar. "Oh, Strong Man! Strong Man, awake! Awake! The moon derides you!"

Then the Strong Man aroused and shook his locks away from his eyes. "What is it, good little men of the valley?"

"Oh, Strong Man, the moon derides you! Oh, Strong Man!"

The Strong Man looked, and there, indeed, was the moon laughing down at him. He sprang to his feet and roared. "Ah, old, fat, lump of moon, you laugh! Have you seen my wife?"

The moon said no word, but merely smiled in a way that was like a flash of silver bars.

"Well, then, moon, take this home to her," thundered the Strong Man, and he hurled his spear.

The moon clapped both hands to its eye, and cried: "Oh! Oh!"

The little people of the valley cried: "Oh, this is terrible, Strong Man! He has smitten our sacred moon in the eye!"

The young philosopher cried nothing at all.

The Strong Man threw his coat of crimson feathers upon the ground. He took his knife and felt its edge. "Look you, philosopher," he said. "I have lost my wife, and the bath, the meal of fruit in the shade, the sight of sky and earth are still good to me, but when this false moon derides me, there must be a killing."

"I understand you," said the young philosopher.

The Strong Man ran off into the night. The little men of the valley clapped their hands in ecstacy and terror. "Ah! ah! what a battle will there be!"

The Strong Man went into his own hills and gathered there many great rocks and trunks of trees. It was strange to see him erect upon a peak of the mountains and hurling these things at the moon. He kept the air full of them.

"Fat moon, come closer," he shouted. "Come closer, and let it be my knife against your knife. Oh, to think that we are obliged to tolerate such an old, fat, stupid, lazy, good-for-nothing moon. You are ugly as death, while I —Oh, moon, you stole my beloved, and it was nothing, but when you stole my beloved and laughed at me, it became another matter. And yet you are so ugly, so fat, so stupid, so lazy, so good-for-nothing. Ah, I shall go mad! Come closer, moon, and let me examine your round, grey skull with this club."

And he always kept the air full of great missiles.

The moon merely laughed, and said: "Why should I come closer?"

Wildly did the Strong Man pile rock upon rock. He built him a tower that was the father of all towers. It made the mountains to appear to be babes. Upon the summit of it he swung his great club and flourished his knife.

The little men in the valley far below beheld a great storm, and at the end of it they said: "Look, the moon is dead." The cry went to and fro on the earth: "The moon is dead!"

The Strong Man went to the home of the moon. She, the sought one, lay upon a cloud, and her little foot dangled over the side of it. The Strong Man took this little foot in his two hands and kissed it. "Ah, beloved!" he moaned, "I would rather this little foot was upon my dead neck than that moon should ever have the privilege of seeing it."

She leaned over the edge of the cloud and gazed at him. "How dusty you are. Why do you puff so? Veritably, you are an ordinary person. Why did I ever find you interesting?"

The Strong Man flung his knife into the air and turned back toward the earth. "If the young philosopher had been at my elbow," he reflected, bitterly, "I would doubtless have gone at the matter in another way. What does my strength avail me in this contest?"

The battered moon, limping homeward, replied to the Strong Man from the Hills: "Aye, surely. My weakness is in this thing as strong as your strength. I am victor with ugliness, my age, my stoutness, my laziness, my good-for-nothingness. Woman is woman. Men are equal in everything save good fortune. I envy you not."

The End.

610

Other Short Stories:

The Black Dog

A Night of Spectral Terror

There was a ceaseless rumble in the air as the heavy raindrops battered upon the laurel thickets and the matted moss and haggard rocks beneath. Four water-soaked men made their difficult ways through the drenched forest. The little man stopped and shook an angry finger at where night was stealthily following them. "Cursed be fate and her children and her children's children! We are everlastingly lost!" he cried. The painting procession halted under some dripping drooping hemlocks and swore in wrathful astonishment.

"It will rain for forty days and forty nights, said the pudgy man, moaningly, "and I feel like a wet loaf of bread, now. We shall never find our way out of this wilderness until I am made into a porridge."

In desperation, they started again to drag their listless bodies through the watery bushes. After a time, the clouds withdrew from above them, and great winds came from concealment and went sweeping and swirling among the trees. Night also came very near and menaced the wanderers with darkness. The little man had determination in his legs. He scrambled among the thickets and made desperate attempts to find a path or road. As he climbed a hillock, he espied a small clearing upon which sat desolation and a venerable house, wept over by wind-waved pines.

"Ho," he cried, "here's a house."

His companions straggled painfully after him as he fought the thickets between him and the cabin. At their approach, the wind frenziedly opposed them and skirled madly in the trees. The little man boldly confronted the weird glances from the crannies of the cabin and rapped on the door. A score of timbers answered with groans, and, within, something fell to the floor with a clang.

"Ho," said the little man. He stepped back a few paces.

Somebody in a distant part started and walked across the floor toward the door with an ominous step. A slate-colored man appeared. He was dressed in a ragged shirt and trousers, the latter stuffed into his boots. Large tears were falling from his eyes.

"How-d'-do, my friend?" said the little man, affably.

"My ol' uncle, Jim Crocker, he's sick ter death," replied the slate-colored person. "Ho," said the little man. "Is that so?"

The latter' s clothing clung desperately to him and water sogged in his boots. He stood patiently on one foot for a time. "Can you put us up here until tomorrow?" he asked, finally. "Yes," said the slate-colored man.

The party passed into a little unwashed room, inhabited by a stove, a stairway, a few precarious chairs, and a misshapen table.

"I'll fry yer some po'k and make yer some coffee," said the slate-colored man to his guests.

"Go ahead, old boy," cried the little man cheerfully from where he sat on the table, smoking his pipe and dangling his legs.

"My ol' uncle, Jim Crocker, he's sick ter death," said the slate-colored man.

"Think he'll die?" asked the pudgy man, gently.

"No!"

"No?"

"He won't die! He's an ol' man, but he won't die, yit! The black dorg hain't been around yit!"

"The black dog?" said the little man, feebly. He struggled with himself for a moment. "What's the black dog?" he asked at last.

"He's a sperrit," said the slate-colored man in a voice of somber hue. "Oh, he is? Well?"

"He haunts these parts, he does, an' when people are goin' to die, he comes and sets and howls."

"Ho," said the little man. He looked out of the window and saw night making a million shadows.

The little man moved his legs nervously.

"I don't believe in these things," said he, addressing the slate-colored man, who was scuffling with a side of pork.

"Wot things?" came incoherently from the combatant.

"Oh, these —er — phantoms and ghosts and what not. All rot, I say."

"That's because you have merely a stomach and no soul," grunted the pudgy man.

"Ho, old pudgkins!" replied the little man. His back curved with passion. A tempest of wrath was in the pudgy man's eye. The final epithet used by the little man was a carefully-studied insult, always brought forth at a crisis. They quarreled.

"All right, pudgkins, bring on your phantom," cried the little man in conclusion.

His stout companion's wrath was too huge for words. The little man smiled triumphantly. He had staked his opponent's reputation.

The visitors sat silent. The slate-colored man moved about in a small personal atmosphere of gloom.

Suddenly, a strange cry came to their ears from somewhere. It was a low, trembling call which made the little man quake privately in his shoes. The slate-colored man bounded at the stairway and disappeared with a flash of legs through a hole in the ceiling. The party below heard two voices in conversation, one belonging to the slate-colored man, and the other in the quavering tones of age. Directly, the slate-colored man reappeared from above and said: "The ol' man is took bad for his supper."

He hurriedly prepared a mixture with hot water, salt, and beef. Beef-tea, it might be called. He disappeared again. Once more the party below heard, vaguely, talking over their heads. The voice of age arose to a shriek.

"Open the window, fool! Do you think I can live in the smell of your soup?"

Mutterings by the slate-colored man and the creaking of the window were heard.

The slate-colored man stumbled down the stairs, and said with intense gloom, "The black dorg'll be along soon."

The little man started, and the pudgy man sneered at him. They ate a supper and then sat waiting. The pudgy man listened so palpably that the little man wished to kill him. The wood-fire became excited and sputtered frantically. Without, a thousand spirits of the winds had become entangled in the pine branches and were lowly pleading to be loosened. The slate-colored man tiptoed across the room and lit a timid candle. The men sat waiting.

The phantom dog lay cuddled to a round bundle, asleep down the roadway against the wind-ward side of an old shanty. The specter's master had moved to Pike County. But the dog lingered as a friend might linger at the tomb of a friend. His fur was like a suit of old clothes. His jowls hung and flopped, exposing his teeth. Yellow famine was in his eyes. The wind-rocked shanty groaned and muttered, but the dog slept. Suddenly, however, he got up and shambled to the roadway. He cast a long glance from his hungry, despairing eyes in the direction of the venerable house. The breeze came full to his nostrils. He threw back his head and gave a long, low howl and started intently up the road. Maybe he smelled a dead man.

The group around the fire in the venerable house were listening and waiting. The atmosphere of the room was tense. The slate-colored man's face was twitching and his drabbed hands were gripped together. The little man was continually looking behind his chair. Upon the countenance of the pudgy man appeared conceit for an approaching triumph over the little man, mingled with apprehension for his own safety. Five pipes glowed as rivals of a timid candle. Profound silence drooped heavily over them. Finally the slate-colored man spoke.

"My ol' uncle, Jim Crocker, he's sick ter death."

The four men started and then shrank back in their chairs.

"Damn it!" replied the little man, vaguely.

Again there was a long silence. Suddenly it was broken by a wild cry from the room above. It was a shriek that struck upon them with appalling swiftness, like a flash of lightning. The walls whirled and the floor rumbled. It brought the men together with a rush. They huddled in a heap and stared at the white terror in each other's faces. The slate-colored man grasped the candle and flared it above his head. "The black dorg," he howled, and plunged at the stairway. The maddened four men followed frantically, for it is better to be in the presence of the awful than only within hearing.

Their ears still quivering with the shriek, they bounded through the hole in the ceiling and into the sick room.

With quilts drawn closely to his shrunken breast for a shield, his bony hand gripping the cover, an old man lay with glazing eyes fixed on the open window. His throat gurgled and a froth appeared at his mouth.

From the outer darkness came a strange, unnatural wail, burdened with weight of death and each note filled with foreboding. It was the song of the spectral dog.

"God!" screamed the little man. He ran to the open window. He could see nothing at first save the pine trees, engaged in a furious combat, tossing back and forth and struggling. The moon was peeping cautiously over the rims of some black clouds. But the chant of the phantom guided the little man's eyes, and he at length perceived its shadowy form on the ground under the window. He fell away gasping at the sight. The pudgy man crouched in a corner, chattering insanely. The slate-colored man, in his fear, crooked his legs and looked like a hideous Chinese idol. The man upon the bed was turned to stone, save the froth, which pulsated.

In the final struggle, terror will fight the inevitable. The little man roared maniacal curses and, rushing again to the window, began to throw various articles at the specter.

A mug, a plate, a knife, a fork, all crashed or clanged on the ground, but the song of the specter continued. The bowl of beef-tea followed. As it struck the ground the phantom ceased its cry.

The men in the chamber sank limply against the walls, with the unearthly wail still ringing in their ears and the fear unfaded from their eyes. They waited again.

The little man felt his nerves vibrate. Destruction was better than another wait. He grasped a candle and, going to the window, held it over his head and looked out.

"Ho!" he said.

His companions crawled to the window and peered out with him.

"He's eatin' the beef-tea," said the slate-colored man, faintly.

"The damn dog was hungry," said the pudgy man.

"There's your phantom," said the little man to the pudgy man.

On the bed, the old man lay dead. Without, the specter was wagging its tail.

A Tent in Agony

Four men once came to a wet place in the roadless forest to fish. They pitched their tent fair upon the brow of a pine-clothed ridge of riven rocks whence a bowlder could be made to crash through the brush and whirl past the trees to the lake below. On fragrant hemlock boughs they slept the sleep of unsuccessful fishermen, for upon the lake alternately the sun made them lazy and the rain made them wet. Finally they ate the last bit of bacon and smoked and burned the last fearful and wonderful hoecake.

Immediately a little man volunteered to stay and hold the camp while the remaining three should go the Sullivan county miles to a farm-house for supplies. They gazed at him dismally. "There's only one of you – the devil make a twin," they said in parting malediction, and disappeared down the hill in the known direction of a distant cabin. When it came night and the hemlocks began to sob they had not returned. The little man sat close to his companion, the campfire, and encouraged it with logs. He puffed fiercely at a heavy built brier, and regarded a thousand shadows which were about to assault him. Suddenly he heard the approach of the unknown, crackling the twigs and rustling the dead leaves. The little man arose slowly to his feet, his clothes refused to fit his back, his pipe dropped from his mouth, his knees smote each other. "Hah!" he bellowed hoarsely in menace. A growl replied and a bear paced into the light of the fire. The little man supported himself upon a sapling and regarded his visitor.

The bear was evidently a veteran and a fighter, for the black of his coat had become tawny with age. There was confidence in his gait and arrogance in his small, twinkling eye. He rolled back his lips and disclosed his white teeth. The fire magnified the red of his mouth. The little man had never before confronted the terrible and he could not wrest it from his breast. "Hah!" he roared. The bear interpreted this as the challenge of a gladiator. He approached warily. As he came near, the boots of fear were suddenly upon the little man's feet. He cried out and then darted around the campfire. "Ho!" said the bear to himself, "this thing won't fight – it runs. Well, suppose I catch it." So upon his features there fixed the animal look of going – somewhere. He started intensely around the campfire. The little man shrieked and ran furiously. Twice around they went.

The hand of heaven sometimes falls heavily upon the righteous. The bear gained.

In desperation the little man flew into the tent. The bear stopped and sniffed at the entrance. He scented the scent of many men. Finally he ventured in.

The little man crouched in a distant corner. The bear advanced, creeping, his blood burning, his hair erect, his jowls dripping. The little man yelled and rustled clumsily under the flap at the end of the tent. The bear snarled awfully and made a jump and a grab at his disappearing game. The little man, now without the tent, felt a tremendous paw grab his coat tails. He squirmed and wriggled out of his coat, like a schoolboy in the hands of an avenger. The bear howled triumphantly and jerked the coat into the tent and took two bites, a punch and a hug before he discovered his man was not in it. Then he grew not very angry, for a bear on a spree is not a black-haired pirate. He is merely a hoodlum. He lay down on his back, took the coat on his four paws and began to play uproariously with it. The most appalling, blood-curdling whoops and yells came to where the little man was crying in a treetop and froze his blood. He moaned a little speech meant for a prayer and clung convulsively to the bending branches. He gazed with tearful wistfulness at where his comrade, the campfire, was giving dying flickers and crackles. Finally, there was a roar from the tent which eclipsed all roars; a snarl which it seemed would shake the stolid silence of the mountain and cause it to shrug its granite shoulders. The little man quaked and shrivelled to a grip and a pair of eyes. In the glow of the embers he saw the white tent quiver and fall with a crash. The bear's merry play had disturbed the centre pole and brought a chaos of canvas about his head.

Now the little man became the witness of a mighty scene. The tent began to flounder. It took flopping strides in the direction of the lake. Marvellous sounds came from within – rips and tears, and great groans and pants. The little man went into giggling hysterics.

The entangled monster failed to extricate himself before he had frenziedly walloped the tent to the edge of the mountain. So it came to pass that three men, clambering up the hill with bundles and baskets, saw their tent approaching.

It seemed to them like a white-robed phantom pursued by hornets. Its moans riffled the hemlock twigs.

The three men dropped their bundles and scurried to one side, their eyes gleaming with fear. The canvas avalanche swept past them. They leaned, faint and dumb, against trees and listened, their blood stagnant. Below them it struck the base of a great pine tree, where it writhed and struggled. The three watched its convolutions a moment and then started terrifically for the top of the hill. As they disappeared, the bear cut loose with a mighty effort. He cast one dishevelled and agonized look at the white thing, and then started wildly for the inner recesses of the forest.

The three fear-stricken individuals ran to the rebuilt fire. The little man reposed by it calmly smoking. They sprang at him and overwhelmed him with interrogations. He contemplated darkness and took a long, pompous puff. "There's only one of me – and the devil made a twin," he said.

An Experiment in Luxury

The Experiences of a Youth Who Sought Out Croesus

IN THE GLITTER OF WEALTH

A Fuzzy Acrobatic Kitten Which Held Great Richness At Bay

LIFE OF THE WOMAN OF GOLD

Are there, After All, Burrs Under Each Fine Cloak and Benefits in All Beggars' Garb?

"If you accept this invitation you will have an opportunity to make another social study," said the old friend.

The youth laughed. "If they caught me making a study of them they'd attempt a murder. I would be pursued down Fifth avenue by the entire family."

"Well," persisted the old friend who could only see one thing at a time, "it would be very interesting. I have been told all my life that millionaires have no fun, and I know that the poor are always assured that the millionaire is a very unhappy person. They are informed that miseries swarm around all wealth, that all crowned heads are heavy with care, and--"

"But still--" began the youth.

"And, in the irritating, brutalizing, enslaving environment off their poverty, they are expected to solace themselves with these assurances," continued the old friend.

He extended his gloved palm and began to tap it impressively with a finger of his other hand. His legs were spread apart in a fashion peculiar to his oratory.

"I believe that is mostly false. It is true that wealth does not release man from many things from which he would gladly purchase release. Consequences cannot be bribed. I suppose that everyman believes steadfastly that he has a private tragedy which makes him yearn for other existences. But it is impossible for me to believe that these things equalize themselves; that there are burrs under all rich cloaks and benefits in all ragged jackets and the preaching of it seems wicked to me. There are those who have opportunities; there are those who are robbed of--"

"But look here," said the young man; "what has this got to do with my paying Jack a visit?"

"It has got a lot to do with it," said the old friend sharply. "As I said, there are those who have opportunities; there are those who are robbed--"

"Well, I won't have you say Jack ever robbed anybody of anything, because he's as honest a fellow as ever lived," interrupted the youth, with warmth. "I have known him for years, and he is a perfectly square fellow. He doesn't know about these infernal things. He isn't criminal because you say he is benefited by a condition which other men created."

"I didn't say he was," retorted the old friend. "Nobody is responsible for anything. I wish to Heaven somebody was, and these we could all jump on him. Look here, my boy, our modern civilization--"

"Oh, the deuce!" said the young man.

The old friend then stood vey erect and stern.

"I can see by your frequent interruptions that you have not yet achieved sufficient pain in life. I hope one day to see you materially changed. You are yet--"

"There he is now," said the youth, suddenly.

He indicated a young man who was passing. He went hurriedly toward him, pausing once to gesture adieu to his old friend.

The house was broad and brown and stolid like the face of a peasant. It has an inanity of expression, an absolute lack of artistic strength that was in itself powerful because it symbolized something. It stood, a homely pile of stone, rugged, grimly self reliant, asserting its quality as a fine thing when in reality the beholder usually wondered why so much money had been spent to obtain a complete negation. The from another point of view it was important and mighty because it stood as a fetich, formidable because of traditions of worship.

When the great door was opened the youth imagined that the footman who held a hand on the knob looked at him with a quick, strange, stare. There was nothing definite in it; it was all vague and elusive, but a suspicion was certainly denoted in some way. The youth felt he, one of the outer barbarians, had been detected to be a barbarian by the guardian of the portal, he of the refined nose, he of the exquisite sense, he who must be more atrociously aristocratic than any that he serves. And the youth, detesting himself for it, found that he would rejoice to take a frightful revenge upon this lackey who, with a glance of his eyes, had called him a name. He would have liked to have been for a time a dreadful social perfection whose hand, waved lazily, would cause hordes of the idolatrous imperfection to be smitten in the eyes. And in the tumult of his imagination he did not think it strange that he should plan in his vision to come around to this house and with the power of his new social majesty, reduce this footman to ashes.

He had entered with an easy feeling of independence, but after this incident the splendor of the interior filled him with awe. He was a wanderer in a fairy land, and who felt that his presence marred certain effects. He was an invader with a shamed face, a man who had come to steal certain colors, forms, impressions that were not his. He had a dim thought that some one might come tell him to begone.

His friend, unconscious of his swift drama of thought, was already upon the broad staircase. "Come on," he called.

When the youth's foot struck from a thick rug and changed upon the tiled floor he was almost frightened.

There was a cool abundance of gloom. High up stained glass caught the sunlight, and made it into marvelous hues that in places touched the dark walls. A broad bar of yellow gilded the leaved of lurking plants. A softened crimson glowed upon the head and shoulders of a bronze swordsman, who perpetually strained in a terrific lunge, his blade thrust at random into the shadow, piercing there an unknown something.

An immense fire place was at one end, and its furnishings gleamed until it resembled a curious door of a palace and on the threshold, where one would have to pass a fire burned redly. From some remote place came the sound of a bird twittering busily. And from behind heavy portieres came a subdued noise of three, twenty or a hundred women.

He could not relieve himself of this feeling of awe until he had reached his friend's room. There they lounged carelessly and smoked pipes. It was an amazingly comfortable room. It expressed to the visitor tat he could do supremely as he chose, for it said plainly that in it the owner did supremely as he chose. The youth wondered if there had not been some domestic skirmish to achieve so much beautiful disorder.

There were various articles left about defiantly, as if the owner openly flaunted the feminine ideas of precision. The disarray of a table that stood prominently defined the entire room. A set of foils, a set of boxing gloves, a lot of illustrated papers, an inkstand and a hat lay entangled upon it. Here was surely a young man, who, when his menacing mother, sisters or servants knocked, would open a slit in the door like a Chinaman in an opium joint, and tell them to leave him to his beloved devices. An yet, withal, the effect was good, because the disorder was not necessary, and because there are some things that when flung down, look to have been flung by an artist. A baby can create an effect with a guitar. It would require genius to deal with the piled up dishes in a Cherry street sink.

The youth's friend lay back upon the broad sat that followed the curve of the window and smoked in blissful laziness. Without one could see the windowless wall of a house overgrown with a green, luxuriant vine. There was a glimpse of a side street. Below were the stables. At intervals a little fox terrier ran into the court and barked tremendously.

The youth, also blissfully indolent, kept up his part of the conversation on the recent college days, but continually he was beset by a stream of sub-conscious reflection. He was beginning to see a vast wonder in it that they two lay sleepily chatting with no more apparent responsibility than rabbits, when certainly there were men, equally fine perhaps, who were blackened and mashed in the churning life of the lower places. And all this had merely happened; the great secret hand had guided them here and had guided others there. The eternal mystery of social condition exasperated him at this time. He wondered if incomprehensible justice were the sister of open wrong.

And, above all, why was he impressed, awed, overcome by a mass of materials, a collection of the trophies of wealth, when he knew that to him their dominant meaning was that they represented a lavish expenditure? For what reason did his nature so deeply respect all this? Perhaps his ancestors had been peasants bowing heads to the heel of appalling pomp of princes or rows of little men who stood to watch a king kill a lower with his cane. There was one side of him that said there were finer things in life, but the other side did homage.

Presently he began to feel that he was a better man than many-- entitled to a great pride. He stretched his legs like a man in a garden, and he thought he belonged to the garden. Hues and forms had smothered certain of his comprehensions. There had been times in his life when little voices called him to continually from the darkness; he heard them now as an idle, half-smothered babble on the horizon, he said, and, of course, there should be a babble of pain on it. Thus it was written; it was a law, he thought. And, anyways, perhaps it was not so bad as those who babbled tried to tell.

In this way and with this suddenness he arrived at stage. He was become a philosopher, a type of the wise man who can eat but three meals a day, conduct a large business and understand the purposes of infinite power. He felt valuable. He was sage and important.

There were influences, knowledges that made him aware that he was idle and foolish in his new state, but he inwardly reveled like a barbarian in his environment. It was delicious to feel so high and mighty, to feel that the unattainable could be purchased like a penny bun. For a time, at any rate, there was no impossible. He indulged in monarchical reflections.

As they were dressing for dinner his friend spoke to him in this wise: "Be sure not to get off anything that resembles an original thought before my mother. I want her to like you, and I know that when any one says a thing cleverly before her he ruins himself with her forever. Confine your talk to orthodox expressions. Be dreary and unspeakably commonplace in the true sense of the word. Be damnable."

"It will be easy for me to do as you say," remarked the youth.

"As far as the old man goes," continued the other, "he's a blooming good fellow. He may appear like sort of a crank if he happens to be in that mood, but he's all right when you come to know him. And besides he doesn't dare do that sort of thing with me, because I've got nerve enough to bully him. Oh, the old man is all right."

On their way down the youth lost the delightful mood that he had enjoyed in his friend's room. He dropped it like a hat on the stairs. The splendor of color and form swarmed upon him again. He bowed before thee strength of this interior; it said a word to him which he believed he should despise, but instead he crouched. In the distance shone his enemy, the footman.

"There will be no people here to-night, so you may see the usual evening row between my sister Mary and me, but don't be alarmed or uncomfortable, because it is quite an ordinary matter," said his friend, as they were about to enter a little drawing room that was well apart from the grander rooms.

The head of the family, the famous millionaire, sat on a low stool before the fire. He was deeply absorbed in the gambols of a kitten who was plainly trying to stand on her head that she might use all four paws in grappling with an evening paper with which her playmate was poking her ribs. The old man chuckled in complete glee. There was never such a case of abstraction, of want of care. The man of millions was in a far land where mechanics and bricklayers go, a mystic land of little, universal emotions, and he had been guided to it by the quaint gestures od a kitten's fury paws.

His wife, who stood near, was apparently not at all a dweller in though lands. She was existing very much in the present. Evidently she had been wishing to consult with her husband on some tremendous domestic question, and she was in a state of rampant irritation, because he refused to acknowledge at this moment that she or any such thing as a tremendous domestic question was in existence. At intervals she made savage attempts to gain his attention.

As the youth saw her she was in a pose of absolute despair. And her eyes expressed that she appreciated all the tragedy of it. Ah, they said, hers was a life of terrible burden, of appalling responsibility; her pathway was beset with unsolved problems, her horizon was lined with tangled difficulties, while her husband-- the man of millions-- continued to play with the kitten. He expression was an admission of heroism.

The youth saw that here at any rate was one denial of his oratorical old friend's statement. In the face of this woman there was no sign that life was sometimes a joy. It was impossible that there could be any pleasure in living or her. Her features were lined and creased with care and worriment as those of an apple woman. It was as if the passing of each social obligation, of each binding form of her life had left its footprints, scarring her face.

Somewhere in her expression there was terrible pride, that kind of pride which, mistaking the form for the real thing, worships itself because of its devotion to the form.

In the lines of the mouth and the set of the chin could be seen the might of a grim old fighter. They denoted all the power of machination of a genera, veteran of a hundred wondrously fierce effect, baleful, determined, without regard somehow to ruck of pain. Here was a savage, a barbarian, a spear woman of the Philistines, who ought battles to excel in what are thought to be the refined and worthy things in life; here was a type of Zulu chieftainess who scuffled and scrambled for place before the white altars of social excellence. And woe to the socially weaker who should try to barricade themselves against that dragon.

It was certain that she never rested in the shade of the trees. One could imagine the endless churning o that mind. And plans and other plans coming forth continuously, defeating a rival here, reducing a family there, bludgeoning a man here a maid there. Woe and wild eyes followed like obedient sheep upon her trail.

Too, the youth thought he could see that here was the true abode of conservatism-- in the mothers, in those whose ears displayed their diamonds instead of their diamonds displaying their ears, in the ancient and honorable controllers who sat in remote corners and pulled wires and respected themselves with a magnitude of respect and superstition. They were perhaps ignorant of that which they worshiped, and, not comprehending it at all, it naturally followed that the fervor of their devotion could set the sky ablaze.

As he watched. he saw that the mesmeric power of a kitten's waving paws was good. He rejoiced in the spectacle of the little fuzzy cat trying to stand on its head, and by this simple antic defeating some intention of a great domestic Napoleon..

The three girls of the family were having a musical altercation over by the window. The and later the youth thought them adorable. They were wonderful to him in their charming gowns. They had time and opportunity to create effects, to be beautiful. And it would have been a wonder to him if he had not found them charming, since making themselves so could but be their principle occupation.

Beauty requires certain justices, certain fair conditions. When in a field no man can say: "Here should spring up a flower; here one should not."

With incomprehensible machinery and system, nature sends them forth in places both strange and proper, so that, somehow, as we see them each one is a surprise to us. But at times, at places, one can say: "Here no flower can flourish."

The youth wondered then why he had sometimes surprised at seeing women fade, shrivel, their bosoms flatten, their shoulders crook forward, in the heavy swelter and wrench of their toil. It must be difficult, he thought, for a woman to remain serene and uncomplaining when she contemplated the wonder and the strangeness of it.

The lights shed marvelous hues of softened rose upon the table. In the encircling shadows the butler moved with a mournful, deeply solemn air. Upon the table there was a color of pleasure, of festivity, but this servant in the background went to and fro like a slow religious procession.

The youth felt considerable alarm when he found himself involved in conversation with his hostess. In the course of this talk he discovered the great truth that when one submits himself to a thoroughly conventional conversation he runs risks of being amazingly stupid. He was glad that no one cared to overhear it.

The millionaire, deprived of his kitten, sat back in his chair and laughed at the replies of his son to the attacks of one of the girls. In the rather good wit of his offspring he took an intense delight, but he laughed more particularly at the words of the son.

Indicated in this light chatter about the dinner table there was an existence that was not at all what the youth had been taught to see. Theologians had for a long time told the poor man that riches did not bring happiness, and they had solemnly repeated this phrase until it had come to mean that misery was commensurate with dollars, that each wealthy man was inwardly a miserably wretch. And when a wail of despair or rage had come from the night of the slums they had stuffed his epigram down the throat of he who cried out and told him that he was a lucky fellow. They did this because they feared.

The youth, studying this family group, could not see that they had great license to be pale and haggard. They were no doubt fairly good, being not strongly induced toward the bypaths. Various worlds turned open doors toward them. Wealth in a certain sense is liberty. If they were fairly virtuous he could not see why they should be so persistently pitied.

And no doubt they would dispense their dollars like little seeds upon the soil of the world if it were not for the fact that since the days of the ancient great political economist, the more exalted forms of virtue have grown to be utterly impracticable.

The Judgement of the Sage

A beggar crept wailing through the streets of a city. A certain man came to him there and gave him bread, saying: "I give you this loaf, because of God's word." Another came to the beggar and gave him bread, saying: "Take this loaf; I give it because you are hungry."

Now there was a continual rivalry among the citizens of this town as to who should appear to be the most pious man, and the event of the gifts to the beggar made discussion. People gathered in knots and argued furiously to no particular purpose. They appealed to the beggar, but he bowed humbly to the ground, as befitted one of his condition, and answered: "It is a singular circumstance that the loaves were of one size and of the same quality. How, then, can I decide which of these men gave bread more piously?"

The people heard of a philosopher who travelled through their country, and one said: "Behold, we who give not bread to beggars are not capable of judging those who have given bread to beggars. Let us, then, consult this wise man."

"But," said some, "mayhap this philosopher, according to your rule that one must have given bread before judging they who give bread, will not be capable."

"That is an indifferent matter to all truly great philosophers." So they made search for the wise man, and in time they came upon him, strolling along at his ease in the manner of philosophers.

"Oh, most illustrious sage," they cried.

"Yes," said the philosopher promptly.

"Oh, most illustrious sage, there are two men in our city, and one gave bread to a beggar, saying: 'Because of God's word.' And the other gave bread to the beggar, saying: 'Because you are hungry.' Now, which of these, oh, most illustrious sage, is the more pious man?"

"Eh?" said the philosopher.

"Which of these, oh, most illustrious sage, is the more pious man?"

"My friends," said the philosopher suavely addressing the concourse, "I see that you mistake me for an illustrious sage. I am not he whom you seek. However, I saw a man answering my description pass here some time ago. With speed you may overtake him. Adieu."

The Scotch Express

The entrance to Euston Station is of itself sufficiently imposing. It is a high portico of brown stone, old and grim, in form a casual imitation, no doubt, of the front of the temple of Nike Apteros, with a recollection of the Egyptians proclaimed at the flanks. The frieze, where of old would prance an exuberant processional of gods, is, in this case, bare of decoration, but upon the epistyle is written in simple, stern letters the word, "EUSTON." The legend reared high by the gloomy Pelagic columns stares down a wide avenue. In short, this entrance to a railway station does not in any resemble the entrance to a railway station. It is more the front of some venerable bank. But it has another dignity, which is not born of form. To a great degree, it is to the English and to those who are in England the gate to Scotland.

The little hansoms are continually speeding through the gate, dashing between the legs of the solemn temple; the four-wheelers, their tops crowded with luggage, roll in and out constantly, and the footways beat under the trampling of the people. Of course, there are the suburbs and a hundred towns along the line, and Liverpool, the beginning of an important sea path to America, and the great manufacturing cities of the North; but if one stands at this gate in August particularly, one must note the number of men with gun-cases, the number of women who surely have Tam-o'-Shanters and plaids concealed within their luggage, ready for the moors. There is, during the latter part of that month, a wholesale flight from London to Scotland which recalls the July throngs leaving New York for the shore or the mountains.

The hansoms, after passing through this impressive portal of the station, bowl smoothly across a courtyard which is in the center of the terminal hotel, an institution dear to most railways in Europe. The traveler lands amid a swarm of porters, and then proceeds cheerfully to take the customary trouble for his luggage. America provides a contrivance in a thousand situations where Europe provides a man or perhaps a number of men, and the work of our brass check is here done by porters, directed by the traveler himself. The men lack the memory of the check; the check never forgets its identity. Moreover, the European railways generously furnish the porters at the expense of the traveler. Nevertheless, if these men have not the invincible business precision of the check, and if they have to be tipped, it can be asserted for those who care that in Europe one-half of the populace waits on the other half most diligently and well.

Against the masonry of a platform, under the vaulted arch of the train-house, lay a long string of coaches. They were painted white on the bulging part, which led half-way down from the top, and the bodies were a deep bottle-green. There was a group of porters placing luggage in the van, and a great many others were busy with the affairs of passengers, tossing smaller bits of luggage into the racks over the seats, and bustling here and there on short quests. The guard of the train, a tall man who resembled one of the first Napoleon's veterans, was caring for the distribution of passengers into the various bins. They were all third and first-class.

The train was at this time engineless, but presently a railway "flier," painted a glowing vermilion, slid modestly down and took its place at the head. The guard walked along the platform, and decisively closed each door. He wore a dark blue uniform thoroughly decorated with silver braid in the guise of leaves. The way of him gave to this business the importance of a ceremony. Meanwhile the fireman had climbed down from the cab and raised his hand, ready to transfer a signal to the driver, who stood looking at his watch. In the interval there had something progressed in the large signal-box that stands guard at Euston. This high house contains many levers, standing in thick, shining ranks. It perfectly resembles an organ in some great church, if it were not that these rows of numbered and indexed handles typify something more acutely human than does a key-board. It requires four men to play this organ-like thing, and the strains never cease. Night and day, day and night, these four men are walking to and fro, from this lever to that lever, and under their hands the great machine raises its endless hymn of a world at work, the fall and rise of signals and the clicking swing of switches.

And so as the vermilion engine stood waiting and looking from the shadow of the curve-roofed station, a man in the signal-house had played the notes which informed the engine of its freedom. The driver saw the fall of those proper semaphores which gave him liberty to speak to his steel friend. A certain combination in the economy of the London and Northwestern Railway, a combination which had spread from the men who sweep out the carriages through innumerable minds to the general manager himself, had resulted in the law that the vermilion engine, with its long string of white and bottle-green coaches, was to start forthwith toward Scotland.

Presently the fireman, standing with his face toward the rear, let fall his hand. "All right," he said. The driver turned a wheel, and as the fireman slipped back, the train moved along the platform at the pace of a mouse. To those in the tranquil carriages this starting was probably as easy as the sliding of one's hand over a greased surface, but in the engine there was more to it. The monster roared suddenly and loudly, and sprang forward impetuously. A wrong-headed or maddened draft-horse will plunge in its collar sometimes when going up a hill. But this load of burdened carriages followed imperturbably at the gait of turtles. They were not to be stirred from their way of dignified exit by the impatient engine. The crowd of porters and transient people stood respectful. They looked with the indefinite wonder of the railway-station sight-seer upon the faces at the windows of the passing coaches. This train was off for Scotland. It had started from the home of one accent to the home of another accent. It was going from manner to manner, from habit to habit, and in the minds of these London spectators there surely floated dim images of the traditional kilts, the burring speech, the grouse, the canniness, the oat-meal, all the elements of a romantic Scotland.

The train swung impressively around the signal-house, and headed up a brick-walled cut. In starting this heavy string of coaches, the engine breathed explosively. It gasped, and heaved, and bellowed; once, for a moment, the wheels spun on the rails, and a convulsive tremor shook the great steel frame.

The train itself, however, moved through this deep cut in the body of London with coolness and precision, and the employees of the railway, knowing the train's mission, tacitly presented arms at its passing. To the travelers in the carriages, the suburbs of London must have been one long monotony of carefully made walls of stone or brick. But after the hill was climbed, the train fled through pictures of red habitations of men on a green earth.

But the noise in the cab did not greatly change its measure. Even though the speed was now high, the tremendous thumping to be heard in the cab was as alive with strained effort and as slow in beat as the breathing of a half-drowned man. At the side of the track, for instance, the sound doubtless would strike the ear in the familiar succession of incredibly rapid puffs; but in the cab itself, this land-racer breathes very like its friend, the marine engine. Everybody who has spent time on shipboard has forever in his head a reminiscence of the steady and methodical pounding of the engines, and perhaps it is curious that this relative, which can whirl over the land at such a pace, breathes in the leisurely tones that a man heeds when he lies awake at night in his berth.

There had been no fog in London, but here on the edge of the city a heavy wind was blowing, and the driver leaned aside and yelled that it was a very bad day for traveling on an engine. The engine-cabs of England, as of all Europe, are seldom made for the comfort of the men. One finds very often this apparent disregard for the man who does the work – this indifference to the man who occupies a position which for the exercise of temperance, of courage, of honesty, has no equal at the altitude of prime ministers. The American engineer is the gilded occupant of a salon in comparison with his brother in Europe. The man who was guiding this five-hundred-ton bolt, aimed by the officials of the railway at Scotland, could not have been as comfortable as a shrill gibbering boatman of the Orient. The narrow and bare bench at his side of the cab was not directly intended for his use, because it was so low that he would be prevented by it from looking out of the ship's port-hole which served him as a window. The fireman, on his side, had other difficulties. His legs would have had to straggle over some pipes at the only spot where there was a prospect, and the builders had also strategically placed a large steel bolt. Of course it is plain that the companies consistently believe that the men will do their work better if they are kept standing. The roof of the cab was not altogether a roof. It was merely a projection of two feet of metal from the bulkhead which formed the front of the cab. There were practically no sides to it, and the large cinders from the soft coal whirled around in sheets. From time to time the driver took a handkerchief from his pocket and wiped his blinking eyes.

London was now well to the rear. The vermilion engine had been for some time flying like the wind. This train averages, between London and Carlisle, forty-nine and nine-tenth miles an hour. It is a distance of 299 miles. There is one stop. It occurs at Crewe, and endures five minutes. In consequence, the block-signals flashed by seemingly at the end of the moment in which they were sighted.

There can be no question of the statement that the road-beds of English railways are at present immeasurably superior to the American road-beds. Of course there is a clear reason. It is known to every traveler that peoples of the Continent of Europe have no right at all to own railways. Those lines of travel are too childish and trivial for expression. A correct fate would deprive the Continent of its railways, and give them to somebody who knew about them. The continental idea of a railway is to surround a mass of machinery with forty rings of ultra-military law, and then they believe they have one complete. The Americans and the English are the railway peoples. That our road-beds are poorer than the English road-beds is because of the fact that we were suddenly obliged to build thousands upon thousands of miles of railway, and the English were obliged to slowly build tens upon tens of miles. A road-bed from New York to San Francisco, with stations, bridges, and crossings of the kind that the London and Northwestern owns from London to Glasgow, would cost a sum large enough to support the German army for a term of years. The whole way is constructed with the care that inspired the creators of some of our now obsolete forts along the Atlantic coast. An American engineer, with his knowledge of the difficulties he had to encounter – the wide rivers with variable banks, the mountain chains, perhaps the long spaces of absolute desert; in fact, all the perplexities of a vast and somewhat new country – would not dare spent a respectable portion of his allowance on seventy feet of granite wall over a gully, when he knew he could make an embankment with little cost by heaving up the dirt and stones from here and there. But the English road is all made in the pattern by which the Romans built their highways. After England is dead, savants will find narrow streaks of masonry leading from ruin to ruin. Of course this does not always seem convincingly admirable. It sometimes resembles energy poured into a rat-hole. There is a vale between expediency and the convenience of posterity, a mid-ground which enables men to surely benefit the hereafter people by valiantly advancing the present; and the point is that, if some laborers live in unhealthy tenements in Cornwall, one is likely to view with incomplete satisfaction the record of long and patient labor and thought displayed by an eight-foot drain for a non-existent, impossible rivulet in the North. This sentence does not sound strictly fair, but the meaning one wishes to convey is that, if an English company spies in its dream the ghost of an ancient valley that later becomes a hill, it would construct for it a magnificent steel trestle, and consider that a duty had been performed in proper accordance with the company's conscience. But after all is said of it, the accidents and the miles of railway operated in England is not in proportion to the accidents and the miles of railway operated in the United States. The reason can be divided into three parts – older conditions, superior caution, and road-bed. And of these, the greatest is older conditions.

In this flight toward Scotland one seldom encountered a grade crossing. In nine cases out of ten there was either a bridge or a tunnel. The platforms of even the remote country stations were all of ponderous masonry in contrast to our constructions of planking. There was always to be seen, as we thundered toward a station of this kind, a number of porters in uniform, who requested the retreat of any one who had not the wit to give us plenty of room. And then, as the shrill warning of the whistle pierced even the uproar that was about us, came the wild joy of the rush past a station. It was something in the nature of a triumphal procession conducted at thrilling speed. Perhaps there was a curve of infinite grace, a sudden hollow explosive effect made by the passing of a signal-box that was close to the track, and then the deadly lunge to shave the edge of a long platform. There were always a number of people standing afar, with their eyes riveted upon this projectile, and to be on the engine was to feel their interest and admiration in the terror and grandeur of this sweep. A boy allowed to ride with the driver of the band-wagon as a circus parade winds through one of our village streets could not exceed for egotism the temper of a new man in the cab of a train like this one. This valkyrie journey on the back of the vermilion engine, with the shouting of the wind, the deep, mighty panting of the steed, the gray blur at the track-side, the flowing quicksilver ribbon of the other rails, the sudden clash as a switch intersects, all the din and fury of this ride, was of a splendor that caused one to look abroad at the quiet, green landscape and believe that it was of a phlegm quite beyond patience. It should have been dark, rain-shot, and windy; thunder should have rolled across its sky.

It seemed, somehow, that if the driver should for a moment take his hands from his engine, it might swerve from the track as a horse from the road. Once, indeed, as he stood wiping his fingers on a bit of waste, there must have been something ludicrous in the way the solitary passenger regarded him. Without those finely firm hands on the bridle, the engine might rear and bolt for the pleasant farms lying in the sunshine at either side.

This driver was worth contemplation. He was simply a quiet, middle-aged man, bearded, and with the little wrinkles of habitual geniality and kindliness spreading from the eyes toward the temple, who stood at his post always gazing out, through his round window, while, from time to time, his hands went from here to there over his levers. He seldom changed either attitude or expression. There surely is no engine-driver who does not feel the beauty of the business, but the emotion lies deep, and mainly inarticulate, as it does in the mind of a man who has experienced a good and beautiful wife for many years. This driver's face displayed nothing but the cool sanity of a man whose thought was buried intelligently in his business. If there was any fierce drama in it, there was no sign upon him. He was so lost in dreams of speed and signals and steam, that one speculated if the wonder of his tempestuous charge and its career over England touched him, this impassive rider of a fiery thing.

It should be a well-known fact that, all over the world, the engine-driver is the finest type of man that is grown. He is the pick of the earth. He is altogether more worthy than the soldier, and better than the men who move on the sea in ships. He is not paid too much; nor do his glories weight his brow; but for outright performance, carried on constantly, coolly, and without elation, by a temperate, honest, clear minded man, he is the further point. And so the lone human at his station in a cab, guarding money, lives, and the honor of the road, is a beautiful sight. The whole thing is aesthetic. The fireman presents the same charm, but in a less degree, in that he is bound to appear as an apprentice to the finished manhood of the driver. In his eyes, turned always in question and confidence toward his superior, one finds this quality; but his aspirations are so direct that one sees the same type in evolution.

There may be a popular idea that the fireman's principal function is to hang his head out of the cab and sight interesting objects in the landscape. As a matter of fact, he is always at work. The dragon is insatiate. The fireman is continually swinging open the furnace-door, whereat a red shine flows out upon the floor of the cab, and shoveling in immense mouthfuls of coal to a fire that is almost diabolic in its madness. The feeding, feeding, feeding goes on until it appears as if it is the muscles of the fireman's arms that are speeding the long train. An engine running over sixty-five miles an hour, with 500 tons to drag, has an appetite in proportion to this task.

View of the clear-shining English scenery is often interrupted between London and Crewe by long and short tunnels. The first one was disconcerting. Suddenly one knew that the train was shooting toward a black mouth in the hills. It swiftly yawned wider, and then in a moment the engine dove into a place inhabited by every demon of wind and noise. The speed had not been checked, and the uproar was so great that in effect one was simply standing at the center of a vast, black-walled sphere. The tubular construction which one's reason proclaimed had no meaning at all. It was a black sphere, alive with shrieks. But then on the surface of it there was to be seen a little needle-point of light, and this widened to a detail of unreal landscape. It was the world; the train was going to escape from this cauldron, this abyss of howling darkness. If a man looks through the brilliant water of a tropical pool, he can sometimes see coloring the marvels at the bottom the blue that was on the sky and the green that was on the foliage of this detail. And the picture shimmered in the heat-rays of a new and remarkable sun. It was when the train bolted out into the open air that one knew that it was his own earth.

Once train met train in a tunnel. Upon the painting in the perfectly circular frame formed by the mouth there appeared a black square with sparks bursting from it. This square expanded until it hid everything, and a moment later came the crash of the passing. It was enough to make a man lose his sense of balance. It was a momentary inferno when the fireman opened the furnace-door and was bathed in blood-red light as he fed the fires.

The effect of a tunnel varied when there was a curve in it. One was merely whirling then heels over head, apparently, in the dark, echoing bowels of the earth. There was no needle-point of light to which one's eyes clung as to a star.

From London to Crewe, the stern arm of the semaphore never made the train pause even for an instant. There was always a clear track. It was great to see, far in the distance, a goods train whooping smokily for the north of England on one of the four tracks. The overtaking of such a train was a thing of magnificent nothing for the long-strided engine, and as the flying express passed its weaker brother, one heard one or two feeble and immature puffs from the other engine, saw the fireman wave his hand to his luckier fellow, saw a string of foolish, clanking flat-cars, their freights covered with tarpaulins, and then the train was lost to the rear.

The driver twisted his wheel and worked some levers, and the rhythmical chunking of the engine gradually ceased. Gliding at a speed that was still high, the train curved to the left, and swung down a sharp incline, to move with an imperial dignity through the railway yard at Rugby. There was a maze of switches, innumerable engines noisily pushing cars here and there, crowds of workmen who turned to look, a sinuous curve around the long train-shed, whose high wall resounded with the rumble of the passing express; and then, almost immediately, it seemed, came the open country again. Rugby had been a dream which one could properly doubt.

At last the relaxed engine, with the same majesty of ease, swung into the high-roofed station at Crewe, and stopped on a platform lined with porters and citizens. There was instant bustle, and in the interest of the moment no one seemed particularly to notice the tired vermilion engine being led away.

There is a five-minute stop at Crewe. A tandem of engines slid up, and buckled fast to the train for the journey to Carlisle.

In the meantime, all the regulation items of peace and comfort had happened on the train itself. The dining-car was in the center of the train. It was divided into two parts, the one being a dining-room for first-class passengers, and the other a dining-room for the third-class passengers. They were separated by the kitchens and the larder. The engine, with all its rioting and roaring, had dragged to Crewe a car in which numbers of passengers were lunching in a tranquillity that was almost domestic, on an average menu of a chop and potatoes, a salad, cheese, and a bottle of beer. Betimes they watched through the windows the great chimney-marked towns of northern England. They were waited upon by a young man of London, who was supported by a lad who resembled an American bell-boy. The rather elaborate menu and service of the Pullman dining-car is not known in England or on the Continent. Warmed roast beef is the exact symbol of a European dinner, when one is traveling on a railway.

This express is named, both by the public and the company, the "Corridor Train," because a coach with a corridor is an unusual thing in England, and so the title has a distinctive meaning. Of course, in America, where there is no car which has not what we call an aisle, it would define nothing. The corridors are all at one side of the car. Doors open from thence to little compartments made to seat four, or perhaps six, persons. The first-class carriages are very comfortable indeed, being heavily upholstered in dark, hard-wearing stuffs, with a bulging rest for the head. The third-class accommodations on this train are almost as comfortable as the first-class, and attract a kind of people that are not usually seen traveling third-class in Europe. Many people sacrifice their habit, in the matter of this train, to the fine conditions of the lower fare.

One of the feats of the train is an electric button in each compartment. Commonly an electric button is placed high on the side of the carriage as an alarm signal, and it is unlawful to push it unless one is in serious need of assistance from the guard. But these bells also rang in the dining-car, and were supposed to open negotiations for tea or whatever. A new function has been projected on an ancient custom. No genius has yet appeared to separate these two meanings. Each bell rings an alarm and a bid for tea or whatever. It is perfect in theory then that, if one rings for tea, the guard comes to interrupt the murder, and that if one is being murdered, the attendant appears with tea. At any rate, the guard was forever being called from his reports and his comfortable seat in the forward end of the luggage-van by thrilling alarms. He often prowled the length of the train with hardihood and determination, merely to meet a request for a sandwich.

The train entered Carlisle at the beginning of twilight. This is the border town, and an engine of the Caledonian Railway, manned by two men of broad speech, came to take the place of the tandem. The engine of these men of the North was much smaller than the others, but her cab was much larger, and would be a fair shelter on a stormy night. They had also built seats with hooks by which they hang them to the rail, and thus are still enabled to see through the round windows without dislocating their necks. All the human parts of the cab were covered with oilcloth. The wind that swirled from the dim twilight horizon made the warm glow from the furnace to be a grateful thing.

As the train shot out of Carlisle, a glance backward could learn of the faint yellow blocks of light from the carriages marked on the dimmed ground. The signals were now lamps, and shone palely against the sky. The express was entering night as if night were Scotland.

There was a long toil to the summit of the hills, and then began the booming ride down the slope. There were many curves. Sometimes could be seen two or three signal lights at one time, twisting off in some new direction. Minus the lights and some yards of glistening rails, Scotland was only a blend of black and weird shapes. Forests which one could hardly imagine as weltering in the dewy placidity of evening sank to the rear as if the gods had bade them. The dark loom of a house quickly dissolved before the eyes. A station with its lamps became a broad yellow band that, to a deficient sense, was only a few yards in length. Below, in a deep valley, a silver glare on the waters of a river made equal time with the train. Signals appeared, grew, and vanished. In the wind and the mystery of the night, it was like sailing in an enchanted gloom. The vague profiles of hills ran like snakes across the somber sky. A strange shape boldly and formidably confronted the train, and then melted to a long dash of track as clean as sword-blades.

The vicinity of Glasgow is unmistakable. The flames of pauseless industries are here and there marked on the distance. Vast factories stand close to the track, and reaching chimneys emit roseate flames. At last one may see upon a wall the strong reflection from furnaces, and against it the impish and inky figures of workingmen. A long, prison-like row of tenements, not at all resembling London, but in one way resembling New York, appeared to the left, and then sank out of sight like a phantom.

At last the driver stopped the brave effort of his engine. The 100 miles were come to the edge. The average speed of forty-nine and one-third miles each hour had been made, and it remained only to glide with the hauteur of a great express through the yard and into the station at Glasgow.

A wide and splendid collection of signal-lamps flowed toward the engine. With delicacy and care the train clanked over some switches, passed the signals, and then there shone a great blaze of arc-lamps, defining the wide sweep of the station roof. Smoothly, proudly, with all that vast dignity which had surrounded its exit from London, the express moved along its platform. It was the entrance into a gorgeous drawing-room of a man that was sure of everything.

The porters and the people crowded forward. In their minds there may have floated dim images of the traditional music-halls, the bobbies, the 'buses, the 'Arrys and 'Arriets, the swells of London.

Marines Signaling Under Fire at Guantanamo

THEY were four Guantanamo marines, officially known for the time as signalmen, and it was their duty to lie in the trenches of Camp McCalla, that faced the water, and, by day, signal the "Marblehead" with a flag and, by night, signal the "Marblehead" with lanterns. It was my good fortune – at that time I considered it my bad fortune, indeed – to be with them on two of the nights when a wild storm of fighting was pealing about the hill; and, of all the actions of the war, none were so hard on the nerves, none strained courage so near the panic point, as those swift nights in Camp McCalla. With a thousand rifles rattling; with the field-guns booming in your ears; with the diabolic Colt automatics clacking; with the roar of the "Marblehead" coming from the bay, and, last, with Mauser bullets sneering always in the air a few inches over one's head, and with this enduring from dusk to dawn, it is extremely doubtful if any one who was there will be able to forget it easily. The noise; the impenetrable darkness; the knowledge from the sound of the bullets that the enemy was on three sides of the camp; the infrequent bloody stumbling and death of some man with whom, perhaps, one had messed two hours previous; the weariness of the body, and the more terrible weariness of the mind, at the endlessness of the thing, made it wonderful that at least some of the men did not come out of it with their nerves hopelessly in shreds.

But, as this interesting ceremony proceeded in the darkness, it was necessary for the signal squad to coolly take and send messages. Captain McCalla always participated in the defense of the camp by raking the woods on two of its sides with the guns of the "Marblehead." More-over, he was the senior officer present, and he wanted to know what was happening. All night long the crews of the ships in the bay would stare sleeplessly into the blackness toward the roaring hill.

The signal squad had an old cracker-box placed on top of the trench. When not signaling, they hid the lanterns in this box; but as soon as an order to send a message was received, it became necessary for one of the men to stand up and expose the lights. And then – oh, my eye – how the guerrillas hidden in the gulf of night would turn loose at those yellow gleams!

Signaling in this way is done by letting one lantern remain stationary – on top of the cracker-box, in this case – and moving the other over it to the left and right and so on in the regular gestures of the wig-wagging code. It is a very simple system of night communication, but one can see that it presents rare possibilities when used in front of an enemy who, a few hundred yards away, is overjoyed at sighting so definite a mark.

How, in the name of wonders, those four men at Camp McCalla were not riddled from head to foot and sent home more as repositories of Spanish ammunition than as marines is beyond all comprehension. To make a confession – when one of these men stood up to wave his lantern, I, lying in the trench, invariably rolled a little to the right or left, in order that, when he was shot, he would not fall on me. But the squad came off scathless, despite the best efforts of the most formidable corps in the Spanish army – the Escuadra de Guantanamo. That it was the most formidable corps in the Spanish army of occupation has been told me by many Spanish officers and also by General Menocal and other insurgent officers. General Menocal was Garcia's chief-of-staff when the latter was operating busily in Santiago province. The regiment was composed solely of practicos, or guides, who knew every shrub and tree on the ground over which they moved.

Whenever the adjutant, Lieutenant Draper, came plunging along through the darkness with an order – such as: "Ask the 'Marblehead' to please shell the woods to the left" – my heart would come into my mouth, for I knew then that one of my pals was going to stand up behind the lanterns and have all Spain shoot at him.

The answer was always upon the instant: "Yes, sir." Then the bullets began to snap, snap, snap, at his head while all the woods began to crackle like burning straw. I could lie near and watch the face of the signalman, illumed as it was by the yellow shine of lantern light, and the absence of excitement, fright, or any emotion at all, on his countenance, was something to astonish all theories out of one's mind. The face was in every instance merely that of a man intent upon his business, the business of wig-wagging into the gulf of night where a light on the "Marblehead" was seen to move slowly.

These times on the hill resembled, in some days, those terrible scenes on the stage – scenes of intense gloom, blinding lightning, with a cloaked devil or assassin or other appropriate character muttering deeply amid the awful roll of the thunder-drums. It was theatric beyond words; one felt like a leaf in this booming chaos, this prolonged tragedy of the night. Amid it all one could see from time to time the yellow light on the face of a preoccupied signalman.

Possibly no man who was there ever before understood the true eloquence of the breaking of the day. We would lie staring into the east, fairly ravenous for the dawn. Utterly worn to rags, with our nerves standing on end like so many bristles, we lay and watched the east – the unspeakably obdurate and slow east. It was a wonder that the eyes of some of us did not turn to glass balls from the fixity of our gaze.

Then there would come into the sky a patch of faint blue light. It was like a piece of moon-shine. Some would say it was the beginning of daybreak; others would declare it was nothing of the kind. Men would get very disgusted with each other in these low-toned arguments held in the trenches. For my part, this development in the eastern sky destroyed many of my ideas and theories concerning the dawning of the day; but then I had never before had occasion to give it such solemn attention.

This patch widened and whitened in about the speed of a man's accomplishment if he should be in the way of painting Madison Square Garden with a camel's hair brush. The guerrillas always set out to whoop it up about this time, because they knew the occasion was approaching when it would be expedient for them to elope. I, at least, always grew furious with this wretched sunrise. I thought I could have walked around the world in the time required for the old thing to get up above the horizon.

One midnight, when an important message was to be sent to the "Marblehead," Colonel Huntington came himself to the signal place with Adjutant Draper and Captain McCauley, the quartermaster. When the man stood up to signal, the colonel stood beside him. At sight of the lights, the Spaniards performed as usual. They drove enough bullets into that immediate vicinity to kill all the marines in the corps.

Lieutenant Draper was agitated for his chief. "Colonel, won't you step down, sir?"

"Why, I guess not," said the gray old veteran in his slow, sad, always-gentle way. "I'm in no more danger than the man."

"But, sir – " began the adjutant.

"Oh, it's all right, Draper."

So the colonel and the private stood side to side and took the heavy fire without either moving a muscle.

Day was always obliged to come at last, punctuated by a final exchange of scattering shots. And the light shone on the marines, the dumb guns, the flag. Grimy yellow face looked into grimy yellow face, and grinned with weary satisfaction. Coffee!

Usually it was impossible for many of the men to sleep at once. It always took me, for instance, some hours to get my nerves combed down. But then it was great joy to lie in the trench with the four signalmen, and understand thoroughly that that night was fully over at last, and that, although the future might have in store other bad nights, that one could never escape from the prison-house which we call the past.

At the wild little fight at Cusco there were some splendid exhibitions of wig-wagging under fire. Action began when an advance detachment of marines under Lieutenant Lucas with the Cuban guides had reached the summit of a ridge overlooking a small valley where there was a house, a well, and a thicket of some kind of shrub with great broad, oily leaves. This thicket, which was perhaps an acre in extent, contained the guerrillas. The valley was open to the sea. The distance from the top of the ridge to the thicket was barely two hundred yards.

The "Dolphin" had sailed up the coast in line with the marine advance, ready with her guns to assist in any action. Captain Elliott, who commanded the two hundred marines in this fight, suddenly called out for a signalman. He wanted a man to tell the "Dolphin" to open fire on the house and the thicket. It was a blazing, bitter hot day on top of the ridge with its shriveled chaparral and its straight, tall cactus plants. The sky was bare and blue, and hurt like brass. In two minutes the prostrate marines were red and sweating like so many hull-buried stokers in the tropics.

Captain Elliott called out:

"Where's a signalman? Who's a signalman here?"

A red-headed "mick" – I think his name was Clancy – at any rate, it will do to call him Clancy – twisted his head from where he lay on his stomach pumping his Lee, and, saluting, said that he was a signalman.

There was no regulation flag with the expedition, so Clancy was obliged to tie his blue polka-dot neckerchief on the end of his rifle. It did not make a very good flag. At first Clancy moved a ways down the safe side of the ridge and wig-wagged there very busily. But what with the flag being so poor for the purpose, and the background of ridge being so dark, those on the "Dolphin" did not see it. So Clancy had to return to the top of the ridge and outline himself and his flag against the sky.

The usual thing happened. As soon as the Spaniards caught sight of this silhouette, they let go like mad at it. To make things more comfortable for Clancy, the situation demanded that he face the sea and turn his back to the Spanish bullets. This was a hard game, mark you – to stand with the small of your back to volley firing. Clancy thought so. Everybody thought so. We all cleared out of his neighborhood. If he wanted sole possession of any particular spot on that hill, he could have it for all we would interfere with him.

It cannot be denied that Clancy was in a hurry. I watched him. He was so occupied with the bullets that snarled close to his ears that he was obliged to repeat the letters of his message softly to himself. It seemed an intolerable time before the "Dolphin" answered the little signal. Meanwhile, we gazed at him, marveling every second that he had not yet pitched headlong. He swore at times.

Finally the "Dolphin" replied to his frantic gesticulation, and he delivered his message. As his part of the transaction was quite finished – whoop! – he dropped like a brick into the firing line and began to shoot; began to get "hunky" with all those people who had been plugging at him. The blue polka-dot neckerchief still fluttered from the barrel of his rifle. I am quite certain that he let it remain there until the end of the fight.

The shells of the "Dolphin" began to plow up the thicket, kicking the bushes, stones, and soil into the air as if somebody was blasting there.

Meanwhile, this force of two hundred marines and fifty Cubans and the force of – probably – six companies of Spanish guerrillas were making such an awful din that the distant Camp Mc-Calla was all alive with excitement. Colonel Huntington sent out strong parties to critical points on the road to facilitate, if necessary, a safe retreat, and also sent forty men under Lieutenant Magill to come up on the left flank of the two companies in action under Captain Elliott. Lieutenant Magill and his men had crowned a hill which covered entirely the flank of the fighting companies, but when the "Dolphin" opened fire, it happened that Magill was in the line of the shots. It became necessary to stop the "Dolphin" at once. Captain Elliott was not near Clancy at this time, and he called hurriedly for another signalman.

Sergeant Quick arose, and announced that he was a signalman. He produced from somewhere a blue polka-dot neckerchief as large as a quilt. He tied it on a long, crooked stick. Then he went to the top of the ridge, and turning his back to the Spanish fire, began to signal to the "Dolphin." Again we gave a man sole possession of a particular part of the ridge. We didn't want it. He could have it and welcome. If the young sergeant had had the smallpox, the cholera, and the yellow fever, we could not have slid out with more celerity.

As men have said often, it seemed as if there was in this war a God of Battles who held His mighty hand before the Americans. As I looked at Sergeant Quick wig-wagging there against the sky, I would not have given a tin tobacco-tag for his life. Escape for him seemed impossible. It seemed absurd to hope that he would not be hit; I only hoped that he would be hit just a little, little, in the arm, the shoulder, or the leg.

I watched his face, and it was as grave and serene as that of a man writing in his own library. He was the very embodiment of tranquillity in occupation. He stood there amid the animal-like babble of the Cubans, the crack of rifles, and the whistling snarl of the bullets, and wig-wagged whatever he had to wig-wag without heeding anything but his business. There was not a single trace of nervousness or haste.

To say the least, a fight at close range is absorbing as a spectacle. No man wants to take his eyes from it until that time comes when he makes up his mind to run away. To deliberately stand up and turn your back to a battle is in itself hard work. To deliberately stand up and turn your back to a battle and hear immediate evidences of the boundless enthusiasm with which a large company of the enemy shoot at you from an adjacent thicket is, to my mind at least, a very great feat. One need not dwell upon the detail of keeping the mind carefully upon a slow spelling of an important code message.

I saw Quick betray only one sign of emotion. As he swung his clumsy flag to and fro, an end of it once caught on a cactus pillar, and he looked sharply over his shoulder to see what had it. He gave the flag an impatient jerk. He looked annoyed.

Twelve O'Clock

I

"Where were you at twelve o'clock, noon, on the 9th of June, 1875?" – *Question on intelligent cross-examination.*

"EXCUSE *me*," said Ben Roddle with graphic gestures to a group of citizens in Nantucket's store. "Excuse *me*. When them fellers in leather pants an' six-shooters ride in, I go home an' set in th' cellar. That's what I do. When you see me pirooting through the streets at th' same time an' occasion as them punchers, you kin put me down fer bein' crazy. Excuse *me*."

"Why, Ben," drawled old Nantucket, "you ain't never really seen 'em turned loose. Why, I kin remember – in th' old days – when – "

"Oh, damn yer old days!" retorted Roddle. Fixing Nantucket with the eye of scorn and contempt, he said: "I suppose you'll be sayin' in a minute that in th' old days you used to kill Injuns, won't you?"

There was some laughter, and Roddle was left free to expand his ideas on the periodic visits of cowboys to the town. "Mason Rickets, he had ten big punkins a-sittin' in front of his store, an' them fellers from the Upside-down-F ranch shot 'em up – shot 'em all up – an' Rickets lyin' on his belly in th' store a-callin' fer 'em to quit it. An' what did they do! Why, they *laughed* at 'im! – just *laughed* at 'im! That don't do a town no good. Now, how would an eastern capiterlist" – (it was the town's humour to be always gassing of phantom investors who were likely to come any moment and pay a thousand prices for everything) – "how would an eastern capiterlist like that? Why, you couldn't see 'im fer th' dust on his trail. Then he'd tell all his friends that 'their town may be all right, but ther's too much loose-handed shootin' fer my money.' An' he'd be right, too. Them rich fellers, they don't make no bad breaks with their money. They watch it all th' time b'cause they know blame well there ain't hardly room fer their feet fer th' pikers an' tin-horns an' thimble-riggers what are layin' fer 'em. I tell you, one puncher racin' his cow-pony hell-bent-fer-election down Main Street an' yellin' an' shootin' an' nothin' at all done about it, would scare away a whole herd of capiterlists. An' it ain't right. It oughter be stopped."

A pessimistic voice asked: "How you goin' to stop it, Ben?"

"Organise," replied Roddle pompously. "Organise: that's the only way to make these fellers lay down. I – "

From the street sounded a quick scudding of pony hoofs, and a party of cowboys swept past the door. One man, however, was seen to draw rein and dismount. He came clanking into the store. "Mornin', gentlemen," he said, civilly.

"Mornin'," they answered in subdued voices.

He stepped to the counter and said, "Give me a paper of fine cut, please." The group of citizens contemplated him in silence. He certainly did not look threatening. He appeared to be a young man of twenty-five years, with a tan from wind and sun, with a remarkably clear eye from perhaps a period of enforced temperance, a quiet young man who wanted to buy some tobacco. A six-shooter swung low on his hip, but at the moment it looked more decorative than warlike; it seemed merely a part of his odd gala dress – his sombrero with its band of rattlesnake skin, his great flaming neckerchief, his belt of embroidered Mexican leather, his high-heeled boots, his huge spurs. And, above all, his hair had been watered and brushed until it lay as close to his head as the fur lays to a wet cat. Paying for his tobacco, he withdrew.

Ben Roddle resumed his harangue. "Well, there you are! Looks like a calm man now, but in less'n half an hour he'll be as drunk as three bucks an' a squaw, an' then . . . . excuse *me!*"

ON this day the men of two outfits had come into town, but Ben Roddle's ominous words were not justified at once. The punchers spent most of the morning in an attack on whiskey which was too earnest to be noisy.

At five minutes of eleven, a tall, lank, brick-coloured cowboy strode over to Placer's Hotel. Placer's Hotel was a notable place. It was the best hotel within two hundred miles. Its office was filled with arm-chairs and brown papier-maché receptacles. At one end of the room was a wooden counter painted a bright pink, and on this morning a man was behind the counter writing in a ledger. He was the proprietor of the hotel, but his customary humour was so sullen that all strangers immediately wondered why in life he had chosen to play the part of mine host. Near his left hand, double doors opened into the dining-room, which in warm weather was always kept darkened in order to discourage the flies, which was not compassed at all.

Placer, writing in his ledger, did not look up when the tall cowboy entered.

"Mornin', mister," said the latter. "I've come to see if you kin grub-stake th' hull crowd of us fer dinner t'day."

Placer did not then raise his eyes, but with a certain churlishness, as if it annoyed him that his hotel was patronised, he asked: "How many?"

"Oh, about thirty," replied the cowboy. "An' we want th' best dinner you kin raise an' scrape. Everything th' best. We don't care what it costs s'long as we git a good square meal. We'll pay a dollar a head: by God, we will! We won't kick on nothin' in th' bill if you do it up fine. If you ain't got it in th' house russle th' hull town fer it. That's our gait. So you just tear loose, an' we'll –"

At this moment the machinery of a cuckoo-clock on the wall began to whirr, little doors flew open and a wooden bird appeared and cried, "Cuckoo!" And this was repeated until eleven o'clock had been announced, while the cowboy, stupefied, glassy-eyed, stood with his red throat gulping. At the end he wheeled upon Placer and demanded: *"What in hell is that?"*

Placer revealed by his manner that he had been asked this question too many times. "It's a clock," he answered shortly.

"I know it's a clock," gasped the cowboy; "but what *kind* of a clock?"

"A cuckoo-clock. Can't you see?"

The cowboy, recovering his self-possession by a violent effort, suddenly went shouting into the street. "Boys! Say, boys! Come' 'ere a minute!"

His comrades, comfortably inhabiting a near-by saloon, heard his stentorian calls, but they merely said to one another: "What's th' matter with Jake? – he's off his nut again."

But Jake burst in upon them with violence. "Boys," he yelled, "come over to th' hotel! They got a clock with a bird inside it, an' when it's eleven o'clock or anything like that, th' bird comes out an' says, 'toot-toot, *toot*-toot!' that way, as many times as whatever time of day it is. It's immense! Come on over!"

The roars of laughter which greeted his proclamation were of two qualities; some men laughing because they knew all about cuckoo-clocks, and other men laughing because they had concluded that the eccentric Jake had been victimised by some wise child of civilisation.

Old Man Crumford, a venerable ruffian who probably had been born in a corral, was particularly offensive with his loud guffaws of contempt. "Bird a-comin' out of a clock an' a-tellin' ye th' time! Haw-haw-haw!" He swallowed his whiskey. "A bird! a-tellin' ye th' time! Haw-haw! Jake, you ben up agin some new drink. You ben drinkin' lonely an' got up agin some snake-medicine licker. A bird a-tellin' ye th' time! Haw-haw!"

The shrill voice of one of the younger cowboys piped from the background. "Brace up, Jake. Don't let 'em laugh at ye. Bring 'em that salt cod-fish of yourn what kin pick out th' ace."

"Oh, he's only kiddin' us. Don't pay no 'tention to 'im. He thinks he's smart."

A cowboy whose mother had a cuckoo-clock in her house in Philadelphia spoke with solemnity. "Jake's a liar. There's no such clock in the world. What? a bird inside a clock to tell the time? Change your drink, Jake."

Jake was furious, but his fury took a very icy form. He bent a withering glance upon the last speaker. "I don't mean a *live* bird," he said, with terrible dignity. "It's a wooden bird, an' – "

"A wooden bird!" shouted Old Man Crumford. "Wooden bird a-tellin' ye th' time! Haw-haw!"

But Jake still paid his frigid attention to the Philadelphian. "An' if yer sober enough to walk, it ain't such a blame long ways from here to th' hotel, an' I'll bet my pile agin yours if you only got two bits."

"I don't want your money, Jake," said the Philadelphian. "Somebody's been stringin' you – that's all. I wouldn't take your money." He cleverly appeared to pity the other's innocence.

"You couldn't git my money," cried Jake, in sudden hot anger. "You couldn't git it. Now – since yer so fresh – let's see how much you got." He clattered some large gold pieces noisily upon the bar.

The Philadelphian shrugged his shoulders and walked away. Jake was triumphant. "Any more bluffers 'round here?" he demanded. "Any more? Any more bluffers? Where's all these here hot sports? Let 'em step up. Here's my money – come an' git it."

But they had ended by being afraid. To some of them his tale was absurd, but still one must be circumspect when a man throws forty-five dollars in gold upon the bar and bids the world come and win it. The general feeling was expressed by Old Man Crumford, when with deference he asked: "Well, this here bird, Jake – what kinder lookin' bird is it?"

"It's a little brown thing," said Jake briefly. Apparently he almost disdained to answer.

"Well – how does it work?" asked the old man meekly.

"Why in blazes don't you go an' look at it?" yelled Jake. "Want me to paint it in iles fer you? Go an' look!"

III

PLACER was writing in his ledger. He heard a great trample of feet and clink of spurs on the porch, and there entered quietly the band of cowboys, some of them swaying a trifle, and these last being the most painfully decorous of all. Jake was in advance. He waved his hand toward the clock. "There she is," he said laconically. The cowboys drew up and stared. There was some giggling, but a serious voice said half-audibly, "I don't see no bird."

Jake politely addressed the landlord. "Mister, I've fetched these here friends of mine in here to see yer clock – "

Placer looked up suddenly. "Well, they can see it, can't they?" he asked in sarcasm. Jake, abashed, retreated to his fellows.

There was a period of silence. From time to time the men shifted their feet. Finally, Old Man Crumford leaned towards Jake, and in a penetrating whisper demanded, "Where's th' bird?" Some frolicsome spirits on the outskirts began to call "Bird! Bird!" as men at a political meeting call for a particular speaker.

Jake removed his big hat and nervously mopped his brow.

The young cowboy with the shrill voice again spoke from the skirts of the crowd. "Jake, is ther' sure-'nough a bird in that thing?"

"Yes. Didn't I tell you once?"

"Then," said the shrill-voiced man, in a tone of conviction, "it ain't a clock at all. It's a bird-cage."

"I tell you it's a clock," cried the maddened Jake, but his retort could hardly be heard above the howls of glee and derision which greeted the words of him of the shrill voice.

Old Man Crumford was again rampant. "Wooden bird a-tellin' ye th' time! Haw-haw!"

Amid the confusion Jake went again to Placer. He spoke almost in supplication. "Say, mister, what time does this here thing go off again?"

Placer lifted his head, looked at the clock, and said: "Noon."

There was a stir near the door, and Big Watson of the Square-X outfit, and at this time very drunk indeed, came shouldering his way through the crowd and cursing everybody. The men gave him much room, for he was notorious as a quarrelsome person when drunk. He paused in front of Jake, and spoke as through a wet blanket. "What's all this – monkeyin' about?"

Jake was already wild at being made a butt for everybody, and he did not give backward. "None a' your dam business, Watson."

"Huh?" growled Watson, with the surprise of a challenged bull.

"I said," repeated Jake distinctly, "it's none a' your dam business."

Watson whipped his revolver half out of its holster. "I'll make it m' business, then, you – "

But Jake had backed a step away, and was holding his left-hand palm outward toward Watson, while in his right he held his six-shooter, its muzzle pointing at the floor. He was shouting in a frenzy, – "No – don't you try it, Watson! Don't you dare try it, or, by Gawd, I'll kill you, sure – *sure!*"

He was aware of a torment of cries about him from fearful men; from men who protested, from men who cried out because they cried out. But he kept his eyes on Watson, and those two glared murder at each other, neither seeming to breathe, fixed like statues.

A loud new voice suddenly rang out: "Hol' on a minute!" All spectators who had not stampeded turned quickly, and saw Placer standing behind his bright pink counter, with an aimed revolver in each hand.

"Cheese it!" he said. "I won't have no fightin' here. If you want to fight, git out in the street."

Big Watson laughed, and, speeding up his six-shooter like a flash of blue light, he shot Placer through the throat – shot the man as he stood behind his absurd pink counter with his two aimed revolvers in his incompetent hands. With a yell of rage and despair, Jake smote Watson on the pate with his heavy weapon, and knocked him sprawling and bloody. Somewhere a woman shrieked like windy, midnight death. Placer fell behind the counter, and down upon him came his ledger and his inkstand, so that one could not have told blood from ink.

The cowboys did not seem to hear, see, or feel, until they saw numbers of citizens with Winchesters running wildly upon them. Old Man Crumford threw high a passionate hand. "Don't shoot! We'll not fight ye for 'im."

Nevertheless two or three shots rang, and a cowboy who had been about to gallop off suddenly slumped over on his pony's neck, where he held for a moment like an old sack, and then slid to the ground, while his pony, with flapping rein, fled to the prairie.

"In God's name, don't shoot!" trumpeted Old Man Crumford. "We'll not fight ye fer 'im!"

"It's murder," bawled Ben Roddle.

In the chaotic street it seemed for a moment as if everybody would kill everybody. "Where's the man what done it?" These hot cries seemed to declare a war which would result in an absolute annihilation of one side. But the cowboys were singing out against it. They would fight for nothing – yes – they often fought for nothing – but they would not fight for this dark something.

At last, when a flimsy truce had been made between the inflamed men, all parties went to the hotel. Placer, in some dying whim, had made his way out from behind the pink counter, and, leaving a horrible trail, had travelled to the centre of the room, where he had pitched headlong over the body of Big Watson.

The men lifted the corpse and laid it at the side.

"Who done it?" asked a white, stern man.

A cowboy pointed at Big Watson. "That's him," he said huskily.

There was a curious grim silence, and then suddenly, in the death-chamber, there sounded the loud whirring of the clock's works, little doors flew open, a tiny wooden bird appeared and cried "Cuckoo" – twelve times.

The Great Boer Trek

When, in 1806, Cape Colony finally passed into the hands of the British government, it might well have seemed possible for the white inhabitants to dwell harmoniously together. The Dutch burghers were in race much the same men who had peopled England and Scotland. There was none of that strong racial and religious antipathy which seems to make forever impossible any lasting understanding between Ireland and her dominating partner.

The Boers were more devoid of Celtic fervors and fluctuations of temperament than the English themselves; in religion Protestant, by nature hard-working, thrifty, independent, they would naturally, it seems, have called for the good will and respect of their conquerors. But the two peoples seemed to have been keenly aware of each other's failings from the first. To the Boers, the English seemed prejudiced and arrogant beyond mortal privilege; the English told countless tales of the Boers' trickery, their dullness, their boasting, their indolence, their bigotry. The burghers had transplanted the careful habits of their home in the Netherlands to a different climate and new conditions. In South Africa they were still industrious and thrifty, and their somewhat gloomy religion was more strongly rooted than ever. Although they lived nomadic lives on the frontier, yet they had made themselves substantial dwellings within the towns; the streets were blossoming bowers of trees and shrubs; their flocks and herds increased, their fields produced mightily. In the courts of law they had shown conspicuous ability whilst acting as heemraden; they had made good elders and deacons in their churches, and good commandants and field cornets in war – the ever-recurring conflicts with the Kaffirs.

Many observers have noted the strong similarity of thought and character between the Dutchmen and the Scotchmen. There is the same thrift which is often extreme parsimony, combined with great hospitality, the same dogged obstinacy, and the same delight in overreaching in all matters of business and bargain-driving. Moreover, their religious ideals bear the strongest resemblance one to the other. In his character as a colonist the Boer certainly showed magnificent qualities; he could work and endure and fight. But in spite of his dour sanctimoniousness, he was not a perfect person, any more than his brother Briton. The English missionaries objected to his treatment of the natives, but there was never any of the terrible cruelty practised that the Spaniards used toward the natives during their colonization of Mexico – nor that of various French, English and Portuguese adventurers in Africa during the seventeenth century. But the fact remains that the entire race of Hottentots has been modified through the Dutch occupation; it is said that no pure-blooded Hottentot remains. This amalgamation was treated by the Boers as a commonplace thing. That habit of theirs of producing scriptural authority for all their acts must have begun with their settlement in Cape Colony.

The "bastards," as they were openly called, were well treated, brought up as Christians and to lead a tolerably civilized life. The English missionaries were filled with disgust at this state of things, and the Boers were denounced from missionary platforms throughout England. Undoubtedly the missionaries were right, but the Boers, alas, are not the only white race who have taken this patriarchal attitude toward the natives of the country they were engaged in colonizing. The missionaries in their other charges were fanatical and ridiculous; they described the Boers as cruel barbarians, because they would not allow the vermin-haunted Hottentots to join them at family prayers in their "best rooms." The Colonial office acted on these representations, and refused to listen to any complaints of the Boers. As they numbered less than ten thousand, and English emigrants were constantly pouring into the colony, the Boers were considered of little importance to the government; it was not imagined that they could do anything effectual in the way of resistance. In short, they, who had been the ruling race in the colony for over a century, were now a subject race; they were hampered and restricted on every side.

The first grievance of the Boers was the attitude of the English missionaries. Some of these were men of really high religious ideals, but most of them were politicians. Mr. Vanderkemp and Mr. Read, missionaries of the London society, who had taken black wives, and announced themselves champions of the black race against the white, had sent to England reports of a number of murders and outrages said to have been committed upon Hottentots by the Dutch colonists. By order of the British government fifty-eight white men and women were put upon their trial for these crimes in 1812, and over a thousand witnesses, black and white, were called to give evidence. Several cases of assault were proved, and punished, but none of the serious charges was substantiated. In 1814 a farmer, Frederick Bezuidenhout, quarreled with his native servant, and refused to appear at a court of justice to answer the charge of ill treatment. A company of Hottentots was sent to arrest him; he fired on them and they shot him dead. A company of about fifty men joined an insurrection under the leadership of Bezuidenhout's brother Jan, but a strong force of Boers aided the government in putting down this rebellion; all surrendered but Jan, who was shot and killed.

Lord Charles Somerset, who drew a salary of ten thousand pounds a year, with four residences, was Governor at the time. He was arbitrary as a prince, and afterward suppressed a liberal newspaper and forbade public meetings. The prisoners taken were tried – they were thirty-nine in number – and six were sentenced to death, while the others all received some form of punishment. Somerset was entreated to annul the death sentence, but would do so only in one instance. The remaining five were executed in the presence of their friends, and the scaffold broke with their weight; they were all unconscious and were resuscitated. When they had been brought to consciousness their friends vehemently besought Somerset to reprieve them, but he was firm in his refusal and they were hanged again.

This event caused a lasting bitterness among the Boers; the place of execution is known as Slachter's Nek to this day. In 1823, the Dutch courts of justice were abolished with their landrosts and heemraden, and in the place of them English courts were established, with magistrates, civil commissioners and justices of the peace. The burgher senate was abolished, also, and notices were sent to the old colonists that all documents addressed to the government must be written in English. Soon after, a case was to be tried at the circuit court at Worcester, and one of the judges removed it to Cape Town because there was not a sufficient number of English-speaking men to form a jury, though the prisoner and the witnesses could speak Dutch only, and whatever they said had to be translated in court. The judges were divided in their opinion as to whether it were necessary for every juryman to speak English; in 1831 an ordinance was issued defining the qualifications of jurymen and a knowledge of English was not one of them. But in the mean time the Boers had been greatly embittered by their exclusion from the jury-box. They would not write memorials about it to the government, because they refused to write English.

During the years of English occupation the frontier aggressions of the Kaffirs were of frequent occurrence. The document called, "An Earnest Representation and Historical Reminder to H. M. Queen Victoria, in view of the Present Crisis, by P. J. Joubert," published a few months ago, contains this reference to the frontier wars: "Natives molested them [the Boers]; they were murdered, robbed of their cattle, their homes were laid waste. Unspeakable horrors were inflicted on their wives and daughters. The Boer was called out for commando service at his own expense, under command and control of the British, to fight the Kaffirs. While on commando, his cattle were stolen by Kaffirs. After, they were made to wait until troops re-took the cattle, which were afterward publicly sold as lost in the presence of their owners, the Boers being informed that they should receive compensation – not in money or goods, neither in rest nor peace, but instead, indignities and abuse were heaped on them. They were told that they should be satisfied at not being punished as the instigators of the disturbance."

As far back as 1809, Hottentots were prohibited from wandering about the country without passes, and from 1812, Hottentot children who had been maintained for eight years by the employers of their parents, were bound as apprenticed for ten years longer. The missionaries were dissatisfied with these restrictions; both of them were removed by an ordinance passed July, 1828, when vagrant Hottentots began to wander over the country at will. Farming became almost impossible; the farm-laborers became vagabonds and petty thefts took place constantly.

Early in 1834, Sir Benjamin D'Urban, called "the Good," was appointed Governor. A legislative council was then granted the colony, but its powers were not great.

The Boers had never been greatly in favor (many opposed it strongly) of slavery, but they had yielded to the general custom and over three million pounds was invested in slaves throughout the colony in 1834. Sir Benjamin D'Urban proclaimed the emancipation of the slaves, who had been set free throughout the British Empire, in August, 1833. This freeing was to take effect in Cape Colony on the 1st of December, 1834.

The news of the emancipation was felt to be a relief, but the terms on which it was conducted were productive of unending trouble. The slave-owners of Cape Colony were awarded less than a million and a quarter for their slaves – and the imperial government refused to send the money to South Africa; each claim was to be proved before commissioners in London, when the amount would be paid in stock. To make a journey of one hundred days to London was, of course, impossible to the farmers; they were at the mercy of agents who made their way down to the colony and purchased the claims, so that the colonist received sometimes a fifth, sometimes a sixth, or less, of the value of his slaves. The colonists had hoped that a vagrant act would have been passed by the Council when the slaves were freed, to keep them from being still further overrun by this large released black population, but this was not done.

In 1834, the first band of emigrants left the colony – forty-five men under a leader named Louis Triechard, from the division of Albany. He was a violent-tempered man, and so loudly opposed to the government that Col. Harry Smith offered a reward of five hundred cattle for his apprehension. He left then at once, being of the class of Boers on the frontier who lived in their wagons, as though they were ships at sea, and had no settled habitation. His party was joined, before it left the colonial border, by Johannes Rensburg. Together they had thirty wagons. They traveled northward. All but two of Rensburg's party were killed, and those of Triechard's party who escaped the savages reached Delagoa Bay in 1838, after terrible hardships, where they received great kindness from the Portuguese. But their sufferings had been so great that only twenty-six lived to be shipped to Natal. But before the emigration reached its height another Kaffir war came on. There was a tremendous invasion of savages, between twelve and twenty thousand warriors, who swept along the frontier, killing, plundering and burning. December, 1834, under Col. Harry Smith a large force was raised; they marched into Kaffirland, and defeated and dispersed the invaders, who were compelled to sue for peace. As a security for the future, Sir Benjamin D'Urban, who was also at the front, issued a proclamation, declaring British sovereignty to be extended over the territory of the defeated tribes as far as the Kei River. But while the people were still suffering from the effects of the invasion, an order came from Lord Glenelg – who became Secretary of State for the Colonies in April, 1835 – peremptorily ordering that the new territory must be immediately given up, on the ground that it had been unjustly acquired.

The Boers now felt that no security existed for life or property on the frontier; all the support of the British government was given – with a philanthropy stimulated by the missionaries – to the black races as against the Boer farmers. The feeling had now become general among them that they must escape British rule at any cost. They left their homes and cultivated fields and gardens – the homes of over a century's growth – and started into the wilds. Purchases of the vacated property were not frequent; a house sometimes was sold for an ox; many of them were simply left, with no sale having been made. All over the frontier districts the great wagons set out, loaded with household goods, provisions and ammunition, to seek new homes farther north. Each party had its commandant and was generally made up of families related to each other. When the pasturage was good, the caravans would sometimes rest for weeks together, while the cows and oxen, horses and sheep and goats, grazed. General Joubert declares that they were followed as far as the Orange River by British emissaries who wanted to be sure that they took no arms nor ammunition with them. However, he adds, the Boers were able to conceal their weapons – a fact that seems a very modern instance, indeed.

North of the Orange River the colonists regarded themselves as quite free, for Great Britain had declared officially that she would not enlarge her South African possessions.

The emigrants were ridiculed for leaving their homes for the wilderness – "for freedom and grass," and were called professional squatters. One English writer said: "The frontier Boer looks with pity on the busy hives of humanity in cities, or even in villages; and regarding with disdain the grand, but to him unintelligible, results of combined industry, the beauty and excellence of which he cannot know, because they are intellectually discerned, he tosses up his head like a wild horse, utters a neigh of exultation, and plunges into the wilderness."

The number of "trekkers" has been estimated at from five thousand to ten thousand. The tide of emigration (they went generally in small bands) flowed across the Orange River and then followed a course for some distance parallel with the Quathtamba Mountains. By this route the warlike Kaffirs were evaded, the only native tribes passed through being small disorganized bodies. Near the Vaal River, however, resided the powerful Matabele nation, under the famous Moselekatze, a warrior of Zulu birth, who had established himself there and brought into complete subjection all the neighboring tribes.

One band of emigrants under Commandant Hendrik Potgieter, a man of considerable ability, arrived at the banks of the Vet River, a tributary of the Vaal. Here he found a native chief who lived in constant dread of Moselekatze, who sold to Potgieter the land between the Vet and the Vaal Rivers, for a number of cattle, Potgieter guaranteeing him protection from Moselekatze. After a while, Commandant Potgieter, with a party, went to explore the country, and traveled north to the Zoutpansberg, where the fertility of the soil seemed encouraging. They also believed that communication with the outer world could be opened through Delagoa Bay, so that the country seemed to offer every advantage for settlement. In high spirits they came back to rejoin their families, but a hideous surprise awaited them; they found only mutilated corpses. Expecting an immediate return of the Matabele who had massacred his people, Potgieter made a strong laager on a hill, by lashing fifty wagons together in a circle, and filling all the open spaces, except a narrow entrance, with thorn-trees. Presently the Matabele returned, and with great shouts and yells stormed the camp, rushing up to the wagon-wheels and throwing assegais. But the Boers, with their powerful "roers," or elephant-guns, kept such a rapid and skilful fire, while the women kept the spare guns reloaded, that the Matabele were forced to retire, but they drove with them all the cattle of the party. They left one hundred and fifty-five dead, and one thousand one hundred of their spears were afterward picked up.

The emigrants in the laager were left without the means of transportation, and very little food, while they had lost forty-six of their people. But fortunately they were near the third band of emigrants under Commandant Gerrit Maritz, who encamped near the mission station at Thaba Ntshu, and now sent oxen to carry away Potgieter and the others. Also a native chief, Marroco, brought them milk and Kaffir corn, and pack-oxen to help them away. It was resolved to revenge the massacre, to follow up Moselekatze and punish him. One hundred and seven Boers mustered for this service, besides forty half-breeds, and a few blacks to take care of the horses. A deserter from the Matabele army acted as guide. The commando surprised Mosega, one of the principal military towns, and killed four hundred. Then setting fire to the kraal, they drove seven thousand head of cattle back to Thaba Ntshu. Potgieter's party then formed a camp on the Vet (they called it Winburg), which was joined by many families from the colony. Another band soon reached Thaba Ntshu, under Pieter Retief, a man of great intelligence. June 6th, 1837, a general assembly of Boers was held at Winburg, when a provisional constitution, consisting of nine articles, was adopted. The supreme legislative power was intrusted to a single elective chamber, termed the Volksraad, the fundamental law was declared to be the Dutch, a court of landrost and heemraden was created, and the chief executive authority was given to Retief, with the title of Commandant-General. One article provided that all who joined the community must have no connection with the London Missionary Society.

New bands of emigrants were constantly arriving, and some of them wished to go into Natal, although the condition of the camp at Winburg was very satisfactory. Pieter Uys, one of their leaders, had visited Natal before, and had been impressed with its beauty and fertility. Retief finally decided to go and see for himself if Dingaan, the Zulu chief, would dispose of some land below the mountain.

While he was gone, a second expedition against the Matabele set out, consisting of one hundred and thirty-five farmers, under Potgieter and Pieter Uys. They found Mosega with twelve thousand warriors, brave and finely trained, but at the end of nine days' warfare, Moselekatze fled to the north, after a loss of something like one thousand men. Commandant Potgieter now issued a proclamation declaring that the whole of the territory overrun by the Matabele, and now abandoned by them, was forfeited to the Boers. It included the greater part of the present South African Republic, fully half of the present Orange Free State, and the whole of Southern Bechuanaland to the Kalahari Desert, except that part occupied by the Batlapin. This immense tract of land was then almost uninhabited, and must have remained so if the Matabele had not been driven out.

Much has been written of the beauties of Natal, with its shores washed by the Indian Ocean, its rich soil, luxuriant vegetation and noble forests. When Pieter Retief first saw it from the Drakensberg Mountains, it was under the despotic rule of the Zulu chief Dingaan, who had succeeded Tshaka, the "Napoleon of Africa," the slayer of a million human beings. A few Englishmen, who were allowed to live at the port, gladly welcomed the emigrants, and took them to Dingaan's capital, called Umkungunhloon, acting as guides and interpreters. There was an English missionary clergyman living there, called Owen. Dingaan received them graciously and supplied them with chunks of beef from his own eating-mat, and huge calabashes of millet beer. But when Retief spoke about Natal, the despot set him a task, such as one reads of in folk-lore legends. Retief might have Natal for his countrymen to live in, if he would recover a herd of seven hundred cattle that had been recently stolen from him by Sikouyela, a Mantater chief. Retief accepted the condition, and actually made Sikouyela restore the cattle, which he drove back to Dingaan. The Boers at Winburg felt distrustful of Dingaan, and dreaded to have Pieter Retief trust himself again in the tyrant's hands. But in February, 1838, Retief started with seventy persons, armed and mounted, with thirty attendants. Again Dingaan received them hospitably, and empowered the missionary Owen to draw up a document granting to Retief the country between the Tugela and the Umzimvooboo. But just as the emigrants were ready to leave, they were invited into a cattle-kraal to see a war-dance, and requested to leave their arms outside the door. While sitting down they were overpowered and massacred, the horror-stricken Owen being a witness of the sight.

Immediately after the massacre, Dingaan sent out his forces against all the emigrants on the eastern side of the Drakensberg. Before daylight they attacked the encampments at Blaanwkrauz River and the Bush-man River – ten miles apart. It was a complete surprise and a terrible slaughter of the Boers, although a brave defense was made. The township which has since arisen near the scene of the conflict still bears the name of Weemen – the place of wailing.

As soon as the emigrants on the west of the Drakensberg heard of the disasters, they formed a band of about eight hundred men to punish Dingaan for his treachery. But they were led into ambush, and finally defeated by the Zulus, and forced to retreat after a tremendous loss of life. The condition of the emigrants was now one of terrible distress and privation. They had many widows and orphans to provide for. The Governor of Cape Colony sent word to them to return, and there were many who felt willing to go, but it was the women of the party who sternly refused to go back; they preferred liberty, although that liberty had cost them so dear. In November, 1838, Andries Pretorius arrived in Natal from Graaff Reinet and was at once elected Commandant-General. He organized a force of four hundred and sixty-four men and marched toward Umkungunhloon. He took with him a sufficient number of wagons to form a laager; wherever the camp was pitched it was surrounded by fifty-seven wagons; all the cattle were brought within the inclosure, the whole force joining in prayers and the singing of psalms. The army made a vow that if victorious they would build a church, and set apart a thanksgiving day each year to commemorate it. The church in Pietermaritzburg and the annual celebration of Dingaan's bear witness that they kept their pledge. They were not fighting for revenge. On three occasions the scouts brought in some captured Zulus, and Pretorius sent them back to Dingaan to say that if he would restore the land he had granted Retief he would enter into negotiations for peace.

Dingaan's reply came in the form of an army ten thousand or twelve thousand strong, which attacked the camp on December 16, 1838. For two hours the Zulus tried to force their way into the laager, while the Boer guns and the small artillery made dreadful havoc in their ranks. When at length they broke and fled, over three thousand Zulu corpses lay on the ground and a stream that flowed through the battle-field was crimson. It has been known ever since as the Blood River.

Pretorius marched on to Umkungunhloon as soon as possible, but Dingaan had set the place on fire and fled.

Dingaan, with the remainder of his forces, retired farther into Zululand. There, soon after, his brother, Pauda, revolted, and fled with a large following into Natal, where he sought the protection of the Boers. Another and final expedition was made against Dingaan in January, 1840, the farmers having Pauda with four thousand of his best warriors as an ally. By February 10th, Dingaan was a fugitive in the country of a hostile tribe, who soon killed him, and the emigrant farmers were the conquerors of Zululand. On that day Pauda was appointed and declared to be "King of the Zulus" in the name and behalf of the Volksraad at Pietermaritzburg, where the Boers established their seat of government as "The South African Society of Natal."

Four days afterward, a proclamation was issued at the same camp, signed by Pretorius and four commandants under him, declaring all the territory between the Black Imfolosi and the Umzimvooboo Rivers to belong to the emigrant farmers. "The national flag was hoisted," says a chronicler, "a salute of twenty-one guns fired, and a general hurrah given throughout the whole army, while all the men as with one voice called out: 'Thanks to the great God who by his grace has given us the victory!'"

Now that the "trekkers" had freed South Africa from the destructive Zulu power, and had driven the Matabele away, they wished to settle in Natal, and rest from the nomadic existence that had so long been theirs. But the British now came forward to hunt them on again. The Governor of Cape Colony, Sir George Napier, proclaimed that "the occupation of Natal by the emigrants was unwarrantable," and directed that "all arms and ammunition should be taken from them, and the port closed against trade."

What followed – the British bombardment of the port, the Dutch surrender, are well-known facts of history. May 12, 1848, Natal was proclaimed a British colony, and the emigrants again took to their wagons, crossing the Vaal.

A Dark-Brown Dog

A child was standing on a street-corner. He leaned with one shoulder against a high board-fence and swayed the other to and fro, the while kicking carelessly at the gravel.

Sunshine beat upon the cobbles, and a lazy summer wind raised yellow dust which trailed in clouds down the avenue. Clattering trucks moved with indistinctness through it. The child stood dreamily gazing.

After a time, a little dark-brown dog came trotting with an intent air down the sidewalk. A short rope was dragging from his neck. Occasionally he trod upon the end of it and stumbled.

He stopped opposite the child, and the two regarded each other. The dog hesitated for a moment, but presently he made some little advances with his tail. The child put out his hand and called him. In an apologetic manner the dog came close, and the two had an interchange of friendly pattings and waggles. The dog became more enthusiastic with each moment of the interview, until with his gleeful caperings he threatened to overturn the child. Whereupon the child lifted his hand and struck the dog a blow upon the head.

This thing seemed to overpower and astonish the little dark-brown dog, and wounded him to the heart. He sank down in despair at the child's feet. When the blow was repeated, together with an admonition in childish sentences, he turned over upon his back, and held his paws in a peculiar manner. At the same time with his ears and his eyes he offered a small prayer to the child.

He looked so comical on his back, and holding his paws peculiarly, that the child was greatly amused and gave him little taps repeatedly, to keep him so. But the little dark-brown dog took this chastisement in the most serious way, and no doubt considered that he had committed some grave crime, for he wriggled contritely and showed his repentance in every way that was in his power. He pleaded with the child and petitioned him, and offered more prayers.

At last the child grew weary of this amusement and turned toward home. The dog was praying at the time. He lay on his back and turned his eyes upon the retreating form.

Presently he struggled to his feet and started after the child. The latter wandered in a perfunctory way toward his home, stopping at times to investigate various matters. During one of these pauses he discovered the little dark-brown dog who was following him with the air of a footpad.

The child beat his pursuer with a small stick he had found. The dog lay down and prayed until the child had finished, and resumed his journey. Then he scrambled erect and took up the pursuit again.

On the way to his home the child turned many times and beat the dog, proclaiming with childish gestures that he held him in contempt as an unimportant dog, with no value save for a moment. For being this quality of animal the dog apologized and eloquently expressed regret, but he continued stealthily to follow the child. His manner grew so very guilty that he slunk like an assassin.

When the child reached his door-step, the dog was industriously ambling a few yards in the rear. He became so agitated with shame when he again confronted the child that he forgot the dragging rope. He tripped upon it and fell forward.

The child sat down on the step and the two had another interview. During it the dog greatly exerted himself to please the child. He performed a few gambols with such abandon that the child suddenly saw him to be a valuable thing. He made a swift, avaricious charge and seized the rope.

He dragged his captive into a hall and up many long stairways in a dark tenement. The dog made willing efforts, but he could not hobble very skilfully up the stairs because he was very small and soft, and at last the pace of the engrossed child grew so energetic that the dog became panic-stricken. In his mind he was being dragged toward a grim unknown. His eyes grew wild with the terror of it. He began to wiggle his head frantically and to brace his legs.

The child redoubled his exertions. They had a battle on the stairs. The child was victorious because he was completely absorbed in his purpose, and because the dog was very small. He dragged his acquirement to the door of his home, and finally with triumph across the threshold.

No one was in. The child sat down on the floor and made overtures to the dog. These the dog instantly accepted. He beamed with affection upon his new friend. In a short time they were firm and abiding comrades.

When the child's family appeared, they made a great row. The dog was examined and commented upon and called names. Scorn was leveled at him from all eyes, so that he became much embarrassed and drooped like a scorched plant. But the child went sturdily to the center of the floor, and, at the top of his voice, championed the dog. It happened that he was roaring protestations, with his arms clasped about the dog's neck, when the father of the family came in from work.

The parent demanded to know what the blazes they were making the kid howl for. It was explained in many words that the infernal kid wanted to introduce a disreputable dog into the family.

A family council was held. On this depended the dog's fate, but he in no way heeded, being busily engaged in chewing the end of the child's dress.

The affair was quickly ended. The father of the family, it appears, was in a particularly savage temper that evening, and when he perceived that it would amaze and anger everybody if such a dog were allowed to remain, he decided that it should be so. The child, crying softly, took his friend off to a retired part of the room to hobnob with him, while the father quelled a fierce rebellion of his wife. So it came to pass that the dog was a member of the household.

He and the child were associated together at all times save when the child slept. The child became a guardian and a friend. If the large folk kicked the dog and threw things at him, the child made loud and violent objections. Once when the child had run, protesting loudly, with tears raining down his face and his arms outstretched, to protect his friend, he had been struck in the head with a very large saucepan from the hand of his father, enraged at some seeming lack of courtesy in the dog. Ever after, the family were careful how they threw things at the dog. Moreover, the latter grew very skilful in avoiding missiles and feet. In a small room containing a stove, a table, a bureau and some chairs, he would display strategic ability of a high order, dodging, feinting and scuttling about among the furniture. He could force three or four people armed with brooms, sticks and handfuls of coal, to use all their ingenuity to get in a blow. And even when they did, it was seldom that they could do him a serious injury or leave any imprint.

But when the child was present, these scenes did not occur. It came to be recognized that if the dog was molested, the child would burst into sobs, and as the child, when started, was very riotous and practically unquenchable, the dog had therein a safeguard.

However, the child could not always be near. At night, when he was asleep, his dark-brown friend would raise from some black corner a wild, wailful cry, a song of infinite lowliness and despair, that would go shuddering and sobbing among the buildings of the block and cause people to swear. At these times the singer would often be chased all over the kitchen and hit with a great variety of articles.

Sometimes, too, the child himself used to beat the dog, although it is not known that he ever had what could be truly called a just cause. The dog always accepted these thrashings with an air of admitted guilt. He was too much of a dog to try to look to be a martyr or to plot revenge. He received the blows with deep humility, and furthermore he forgave his friend the moment the child had finished, and was ready to caress the child's hand with his little red tongue.

When misfortune came upon the child, and his troubles overwhelmed him, he would often crawl under the table and lay his small distressed head on the dog's back. The dog was ever sympathetic. It is not to be supposed that at such times he took occasion to refer to the unjust beatings his friend, when provoked, had administered to him.

He did not achieve any notable degree of intimacy with the other members of the family. He had no confidence in them, and the fear that he would express at their casual approach often exasperated them exceedingly. They used to gain a certain satisfaction in underfeeding him, but finally his friend the child grew to watch the matter with some care, and when he forgot it, the dog was often successful in secret for himself.

So the dog prospered. He developed a large bark, which came wondrously from such a small rug of a dog. He ceased to howl persistently at night. Sometimes, indeed, in his sleep, he would utter little yells, as from pain, but that occurred, no doubt, when in his dreams he encountered huge flaming dogs who threatened him direfully.

His devotion to the child grew until it was a sublime thing. He wagged at his approach; he sank down in despair at his departure. He could detect the sound of the child's step among all the noises of the neighborhood. It was like a calling voice to him.

The scene of their companionship was a kingdom governed by this terrible potentate, the child; but neither criticism nor rebellion ever lived for an instant in the heart of the one subject. Down in the mystic, hidden fields of his little dog-soul bloomed flowers of love and fidelity and perfect faith.

The child was in the habit of going on many expeditions to observe strange things in the vicinity. On these occasions his friend usually jogged aimfully along behind. Perhaps, though, he went ahead. This necessitated his turning around every quarter-minute to make sure the child was coming. He was filled with a large idea of the importance of these journeys. He would carry himself with such an air! He was proud to be the retainer of so great a monarch.

One day, however, the father of the family got quite exceptionally drunk. He came home and held carnival with the cooking utensils, the furniture and his wife. He was in the midst of this recreation when the child, followed by the dark-brown dog, entered the room. They were returning from their voyages.

The child's practised eye instantly noted his father's state. He dived under the table, where experience had taught him was a rather safe place. The dog, lacking skill in such matters, was, of course, unaware of the true condition of affairs. He looked with interested eyes at his friend's sudden dive. He interpreted it to mean: Joyous gambol. He started to patter across the floor to join him. He was the picture of a little dark-brown dog en route to a friend.

The head of the family saw him at this moment. He gave a huge howl of joy, and knocked the dog down with a heavy coffee-pot. The dog, yelling in supreme astonishment and fear, writhed to his feet and ran for cover. The man kicked out with a ponderous foot. It caused the dog to swerve as if caught in a tide. A second blow of the coffee-pot laid him upon the floor.

Here the child, uttering loud cries, came valiantly forth like a knight. The father of the family paid no attention to these calls of the child, but advanced with glee upon the dog. Upon being knocked down twice in swift succession, the latter apparently gave up all hope of escape. He rolled over on his back and held his paws in a peculiar manner. At the same time with his eyes and his ears he offered up a small prayer.

But the father was in a mood for having fun, and it occurred to him that it would be a fine thing to throw the dog out of the window. So he reached down and grabbing the animal by a leg, lifted him, squirming, up. He swung him two or three times hilariously about his head, and then flung him with great accuracy through the window.

The soaring dog created a surprise in the block. A woman watering plants in an opposite window gave an involuntary shout and dropped a flower-pot. A man in another window leaned perilously out to watch the flight of the dog. A woman, who had been hanging out clothes in a yard, began to caper wildly. Her mouth was filled with clothes-pins, but her arms gave vent to a sort of exclamation. In appearance she was like a gagged prisoner. Children ran whooping.

The dark-brown body crashed in a heap on the roof of a shed five stories below. From thence it rolled to the pavement of an alleyway.

The child in the room far above burst into a long, dirgelike cry, and toddled hastily out of the room. It took him a long time to reach the alley, because his size compelled him to go downstairs backward, one step at a time, and holding with both hands to the step above.

When they came for him later, they found him seated by the body of his dark-brown friend.

Manacled

IN the First Act there had been a farm scene, wherein real horses had drunk real water out of real buckets, afterward dragging a real waggon off stage, L. The audience was consumed with admiration of this play, and the great Theatre Nouveau rang to its roof with the crowd's plaudits.

The Second Act was now well advanced. The hero, cruelly victimised by his enemies, stood in prison garb, panting with rage, while two brutal warders fastened real handcuffs on his wrists and real anklets on his ankles. And the hovering villain sneered.

"'Tis well, Aubrey Pettingill," said the prisoner. "You have so far succeeded; but, mark you, there will come a time – "

The villain retorted with a cutting allusion to the young lady whom the hero loved.

"Curse you," cried the hero, and he made as if to spring upon this demon; but, as the pitying audience saw, he could only take steps four inches long.

Drowning the mocking laughter of the villain came cries from both the audience and the people back of the wings. "Fire! Fire! Fire!" Throughout the great house resounded the roaring crashes of a throng of human beings moving in terror, and even above this noise could be heard the screams of women more shrill than whistles. The building hummed and shook; it was like a glade which holds some bellowing cataract of the mountains. Most of the people who were killed on the stairs still clutched their play-bills in their hands as if they had resolved to save them at all costs.

The Theatre Nouveau fronted upon a street which was not of the first importance, especially at night, when it only aroused when the people came to the theatre and aroused again when they came out to go home. On the night of the fire, at the time of the scene between the enchained hero and his tormentor, the thoroughfare echoed with only the scraping shovels of some street-cleaners, who were loading carts with blackened snow and mud. The gleam of lights made the shadowed pavement deeply blue, save where lay some yellow plum-like reflection.

Suddenly a policeman came running frantically along the street. He charged upon the fire-box on a corner. Its red light touched with flame each of his brass buttons and the municipal shield. He pressed a lever. He had been standing in the entrance of the theatre chatting to the lonely man in the box-office. To send an alarm was a matter of seconds.

Out of the theatre poured the first hundreds of fortunate ones, and some were not altogether fortunate. Women, their bonnets flying, cried out tender names; men, white as death, scratched and bleeding, looked wildly from face to face. There were displays of horrible blind brutality by the strong. Weaker men clutched and clawed like cats. From the theatre itself came the howl of a gale.

The policeman's fingers had flashed into instant life and action the most perfect counter-attack to the fire. He listened for some seconds, and presently he heard the thunder of a charging engine. She swept around a corner, her three shining enthrilled horses leaping. Her consort, the hose-cart, roared behind her. There were the loud clicks of the steel-shod hoofs, hoarse shouts, men running, the flash of lights, while the crevice-like streets resounded with the charges of other engines.

At the first cry of fire, the two brutal warders had dropped the arms of the hero and run off the stage with the villain. The hero cried after them angrily. "Where you going? Here, Pete – Tom – you've left me chained up, damn you!"

The body of the theatre now resembled a mad surf amid rocks, but the hero did not look at it. He was filled with fury at the stupidity of the two brutal warders, in forgetting that they were leaving him manacled. Calling loudly, he hobbled off stage, L, taking steps four inches long.

Behind the scenes he heard the hum of flames. Smoke, filled with sparks sweeping on spiral courses, rolled thickly upon him. Suddenly his face turned chalk-colour beneath his skin of manly bronze for the stage. His voice shrieked. "Pete – Tom – damn you – come back – you've left me chained up."

He had played in this theatre for seven years, and he could find his way without light through the intricate passages which mazed out behind the stage. He knew that it was a long way to the street door.

The heat was intense. From time to time masses of flaming wood sung down from above him. He began to jump. Each jump advanced him about three feet, but the effort soon became heart-breaking. Once he fell, and it took time to get upon his feet again.

There were stairs to descend. From the top of this flight he tried to fall feet first. He precipitated himself in a way that would have broken his hip under common conditions. But every step seemed covered with glue, and on almost every one he stuck for a moment. He could not even succeed in falling down stairs. Ultimately he reached the bottom, windless from the struggle.

There were stairs to climb. At the foot of the flight he lay for an instant with his mouth close to the floor trying to breathe. Then he tried to scale this frightful precipice up the face of which many an actress had gone at a canter.

Each succeeding step arose eight inches from its fellow. The hero dropped to a seat on the third step, and pulled his feet to the second step. From this position he lifted himself to a seat on the fourth step. He had not gone far in this manner before his frenzy caused him to lose his balance, and he rolled to the foot of the flight. After all, he could fall downstairs.

He lay there whispering. "They all got out but I. All but I." Beautiful flames flashed above him, some were crimson, some were orange, and here and there were tongues of purple, blue, green.

A curiously calm thought came into his head. "What a fool I was not to foresee this! I shall have Rogers furnish manacles of papier-mâché to-morrow."

The thunder of the fire-lions made the theatre have a palsy.

Suddenly the hero beat his handcuffs against the wall, cursing them in a loud wail. Blood started from under his finger-nails. Soon he began to bite the hot steel, and blood fell from his blistered mouth. He raved like a wolf.

Peace came to him again. There were charming effects amid the flames. . . . He felt very cool, delightfully cool. . . . "They've left me chained up."

The Woof of Thin Red Threads

I

TWENTY-FIVE men were making a road out of a path up the hillside. The light batteries in the rear were impatient to advance, but first must be done all that digging and smoothing which gains no incrusted medals from war. The men worked like gardeners, and a road was growing from the old pack-animal trail. Trees arched from a field of guinea-grass, which resembled young wild corn. The day was still and dry. The men working were dressed in the consistent blue of United States regulars. They looked indifferent, almost stolid, despite the heat and the labor. There was little talking. From time to time, a government pack-train, led by a sleek-sided, tender bell-mare, came from one way or the other, and the men stood aside as the strong, hard, black-and-tan animals crowded eagerly after their curious little feminine leader.

A volunteer staff officer appeared, and, sitting on his horse in the middle of the work, asked the sergeant in command some questions which were apparently not relevant to any military business.

Men straggling along on various duties almost invariably spun some kind of a joke as they passed.

A corporal and four men were guarding boxes of spare ammunition at the top of the hill, and one of the number often went to the foot of the hill, swinging canteens.

The day wore down to the Cuban dusk in which the shadows are all grim and of ghastly shape. The men began to lift their eyes from the shovels and picks, and glance in the direction of their camp. The sun threw his last lance through the foliage. The steep mountain range on the right turned blue, and as without detail as a curtain. The tiny ruby of light ahead meant that the ammunition guard were cooking their supper. From somewhere in the world came a single rifle-shot. Figures appeared dim in the shadow of the trees. A murmur, a sigh of quiet relief, arose from the working party. Later, they swung up the hill in an unformed formation, being always like soldiers, and unable even to carry a spade save like United States regular soldiers. As they passed through some fields, the bland white light of the end of the day feebly touched each hard bronze profile.

"Wonder if we'll git anythin' to eat?" said Watkins, in a low voice.

"Should think so," said Nolan, in the same tone. They betrayed no impatience; they seemed to feel a kind of awe of the situation.

The sergeant turned. One could see the cool gray eye flashing under the brim of the campaign hat. "What in hell you fellers kickin' about?" he asked. They made no reply, understanding that they were being suppressed.

As they moved on, a murmur arose from the tall grass on each hand. It was the noise from the bivouac of ten thousand men, although one saw practically nothing from the low-cut roadway. The sergeant led his party up a wet clay bank and into a trampled field. Here were scattered tiny white shelter-tents, and in the darkness they were luminous like the rearing stones in a graveyard. A few fires burned blood-red, and the shadowy figures of men moved with no more expression of detail than there is in the swaying of the foliage on a windy night.

The working party felt their way to where their tents were pitched. A man suddenly cursed; he had mislaid something and he knew he was not going to find it that night. Watkins spoke again, with the monotony of a clock.

"Wonder if we'll git anythin' to eat."

Martin, with eyes turned pensively to the stars, began a treatise.

"Them Spaniards –"

"Oh, quit it!" cried Nolan. "What the piper do you know about th' Spaniards, you fat-headed Dutchman? Better think of your belly, you blunderin' swine, an' what you're goin' to put in it, grass or dirt."

A laugh, a sort of deep growl, arose from the prostrate men. In the mean time the sergeant had reappeared and was standing over them. "No rations tonight," he said, gruffly, and turning on his heel walked away.

This announcement was received in silence. But Watkins had flung himself face downward, and putting his lips close to a tuft of grass, he formulated oaths. Martin arose, and going to his shelter, crawled in sulkily. After a long interval Nolan said aloud, "Hell!" Grierson, enlisted for the war, raised a querulous voice. "Well, I wonder when we will git fed?"

From the ground about him came a low chuckle full of ironical comment upon Grierson's lack of certain qualities which the other men felt themselves to possess.

In the cold light of dawn, the men were on their knees, packing, strapping and buckling. The comic toy hamlet of shelter-tents had been wiped out as if by a cyclone. Through the trees could be seen the crimson of a light battery's blankets, and the wheels creaked like the sound of a musketry fight. Nolan, well gripped by his shelter-tent, his blanket and his cartridge belt, and bearing his rifle, advanced upon a small group of men who were hastily finishing a can of coffee.

"Say, give us a drink, will ye?" he asked wistfully. He was as sad-eyed as an orphan beggar.

Every man in the group turned to look him straight in the face. He had asked for the principal ruby out of each one's crown. There was grim silence. Then one said, "What fer?" Nolan cast his glance to the ground and went away abashed.

But he espied Watkins and Martin surrounding Grierson, who had gained three pieces of hard-tack by mere force of his audacious inexperience. Grierson was fending his comrades off tearfully. "Now don't be damn pigs," he cried; "hold on a minute." Here Nolan asserted a claim. Grierson groaned. Kneeling piously, he divided the hard-tack with minute care into four portions. The men, who had had their heads together, like players watching a wheel of fortune, arose suddenly, each chewing. Nolan interpolated a drink of water and sighed contentedly.

The whole forest seemed to be moving. From the field on the other side of the road a column of men in blue was slowly pouring; the battery had creaked on ahead; from the rear came a hum of advancing regiments. Then from a mile away rang the noise of a shot, then another shot; in a moment the rifles there were drumming, drumming, drumming. The artillery boomed out suddenly. A day of battle was begun.

The men made no exclamations. They rolled their eyes in the direction of the sound, and then swept with a calm glance the forests and the hills which surrounded them, implacably mysterious forests and hills which lent to every rifle-shot the ominous quality which belongs to secret assassination. The whole scene would have spoken to the private soldiers of ambushes, sudden flank attacks, terrible disasters if it were not for those cool gentlemen with shoulder-straps and swords, who, the private soldiers knew, were of another world and omnipotent for the business.

The battalion moved out into the mud and began a leisurely march in the damp shade of the trees. The advance of two batteries had churned the black soil into a formidable paste. The brown leggings of the men, stained with the mud of other days, took on a deeper color. Perspiration broke gently out on the reddish faces. With his heavy roll of blanket and the half of a shelter-tent crossing his right shoulder and under his left arm, each man presented the appearance of being clasped from behind, wrestler fashion, by a pair of thick white arms. There was something distinctive in the way they carried their rifles. There was the grace of an old hunter somewhere in it, the grace of a man whose rifle has become absolutely a part of himself. Furthermore, almost every blue shirt-sleeve was rolled to the elbow, disclosing forearms of almost incredible brawn. The rifles seemed light, almost fragile, in the hands that were at the end of these arms, never fat, but always with rolling muscles, and veins that seemed on the point of bursting. And another thing was the silence and the marvelous impassivity of the faces as the column made its slow way toward where the whole forest spluttered and fluttered with battle.

Opportunely, the battalion was halted astraddle of a stream, and before it again moved most of the men had filled their canteens. The firing increased. Ahead and to the left, a battery was booming at methodical intervals, while the infantry racket was that continual drumming which, after all, often sounds like rain on a roof. Directly ahead, one could hear the deep voices of field-pieces.

Some wounded Cubans were carried by in litters improvised from hammocks swung on poles. One had a ghastly cut in the throat, probably from a fragment of shell, and his head was turned as if Providence particularly wished to display this wide and lapping gash to the long column that was winding toward the front. And another Cuban, shot through the groin, kept up a continual wail as he swung from the tread of his bearers. "Ay – ee! Ay – ee! Madre mia! Madre mia!" He sang this bitter ballad into the ears of at least three thousand men as they slowly made way for his bearers on the narrow wood-path. These wounded insurgents were, then, to a large part of the advancing army, the visible messengers of blood-shed, death, and the men regarded them with thoughtful awe. This doleful sobbing cry, "Madre mia," was a tangible consequent misery of all that firing on in front, into which the men knew they were soon to be plunged. Some of them wished to inquire of the bearers the details of what had happened, but they could not speak Spanish, and so it was as if fate had intentionally sealed the lips of all in order that even meager information might not leak out concerning this mystery – battle. On the other hand, many unversed private soldiers looked upon the unfortunate as men who had seen thousands maimed and bleeding, and absolutely could not conjure up any further interest in such scenes.

A young staff officer passed on horseback. The vocal Cuban was always wailing, but the officer wheeled past the bearers without heeding anything. And yet he never before had seen such a sight. His case was different from that of the private soldiers. He heeded nothing because he was busy, immensely busy, and hurried with a multitude of reasons and desires for doing his duty perfectly. His whole life had been a mere period of preliminary reflection for this situation, and he had no clear idea of anything save his obligation as an officer. A man of this kind might be stupid; it is conceivable that in remote cases certain bumps on his head might be composed entirely of wood; but those traditions of fidelity and courage which have been handed to him from generation to generation, and which he has tenaciously preserved despite the persecution of legislators and the indifference of his country, make it incredible that in battle he should ever fail to give his best blood and his best thought for his general, for his men and for himself.

And so this young officer in the shapeless hat and the torn and dirty shirt failed to heed the wails of the wounded man, even as the pilgrim fails to heed the world as he raises his illumined face toward his purpose – rightly or wrongly his purpose – his sky of the ideal of duty; and the wonderful part of it is that he is guided by an ideal which he has himself created, and has alone protected from attack. The young man was merely an officer in the United States regular army.

The column swung across a shallow ford and took a road which passed the right flank of one of the American batteries.

On a hill it was booming and belching great clouds of white smoke. The infantry looked up with interest. Arrayed below the hill and behind the battery were the horses and limbers, the riders checking their pawing mounts, and behind each rider a red blanket flamed against the fervent green of the bushes. As the infantry moved along the road, some of the battery horses turned at the noise of the trampling feet and surveyed the men with eyes deep as wells, serene, mournful, generous eyes, lit heart-breakingly with something that was akin to a philosophy, a religion of self-sacrifice – oh, gallant, gallant horses!

"I know a feller in that battery," said Nolan musingly. "A driver."

"Damn sight rather be a gunner," said Martin.

"Why would ye?" said Nolan opposingly.

"Well, I'd take my chances as a gunner b'fore I'd sit 'way up in th' air on a raw-boned plug an' git shot at."

"Aw – " began Nolan.

"They've had some losses t'-day all right," interrupted Grierson.

"Horses?" asked Watkins.

"Horses, an' men too," said Grierson.

"How d'yeh know?"

"A feller told me there by the ford."

They kept only a part of their minds bearing on this discussion because they could already hear high in the air the wire-string note of the enemy's bullets.

The road taken by this battalion, as it followed other battalions, is something less than a mile long in its journey across a heavily wooded plain. It is greatly changed now; in fact, it was metamorphosed in two days; but at that time it was a mere track through dense shrubbery from which rose great, dignified arching trees. It was, in fact, a path through a jungle.

The battalion had no sooner left the battery in rear than bullets began to drive overhead. They made several different sounds, but as they were mainly high shots, it was usual for them to make the faint note of a vibrant string touched elusively, half dreamily.

The military balloon, a fat, wavering yellow thing, was leading the advance like some new conception of war-god. Its bloated mass shone above the trees, and served incidentally to indicate to the men at the rear that comrades were in advance. The track itself exhibited, for all its visible length, a closely knit procession of soldiers in blue, with breasts crossed by white shelter-tents. The first ominous order of battle came down the line. "Use the cut-off. Don't use the magazine until you're ordered."

Non-commissioned officers repeated the command gruffly. A sound of clicking locks rattled along the column. All men knew that the time had come.

The front had burst out with a roar like a brush fire. The balloon was dying, dying a gigantic and public death before the eyes of two armies. It quivered, sank, faded into the trees amid the flurry of a battle that was suddenly and tremendously like a storm.

The American battery thundered behind the men with a shock that seemed likely to tear the backs of their heads off. The Spanish shrapnel fled on a line to their left, swirling and swishing in supernatural velocity. The noise of the rifle bullets broke in their faces like the noise of so many lamp chimneys, or sped overhead in swift, cruel spitting. And at the front, the battle-sound, as if it were simply music, was beginning to swell and swell until the volleys rolled like a surf.

The officers shouted hoarsely.

"Come on, men! Hurry up, boys! Come on, now! Hurry up!" The soldiers, running heavily in their accouterments, dashed forward. A baggage guard was swiftly detailed; the men tore their rolls from their shoulders as if the things were afire. The battalion, stripped for action, again dashed forward.

"Come on, men! Come on!"

To them the battle was as yet merely a road through the woods crowded with troops who lowered their heads anxiously as the bullets fled high. But a moment later the column wheeled abruptly to the left and entered a field of tall green grass. The line scattered to a skirmish formation. In front was a series of knolls, treed sparsely like orchards, and although no enemy was visible, these knolls were all popping and spitting with rifle-fire. In some places there were to be seen long gray lines of dirt intrenchments. The American shells were kicking up reddish clouds of dust from the brow of one of the knolls where stood a pagoda-like house. It was not much like a battle with men; it was a battle with a bit of charming scenery, enigmatically potent for death.

Nolan knew that Martin had suddenly fallen. "What – " he began.

"They've hit me," said Martin.

"Hell!" said Nolan.

Martin lay on the ground, clutching his left fore-arm just below the elbow with all the strength of his right hand. His lips were pursed ruefully. He did not seem to know what to do. He continued to stare at his arm.

Then suddenly the bullets drove at them low and hard. The men flung themselves face down in the grass. Nolan lost all thought of his friend. Oddly enough, he felt somewhat like a man hiding under a bed, and he was just as sure that he could not raise his head high without being shot, as a man hiding under a bed is sure that he cannot raise his head without bumping it.

A lieutenant was seated in the grass just behind him. He was in the careless and yet rigid pose of a man balancing a loaded plate on his knee at a picnic. He was talking in soothing, paternal tones.

"Now don't get rattled. We're all right here. Just as safe as being in church. . . . They're all going high. Don't mind them. . . . Don't mind them. . . . They're all going high. We've got them rattled and they can't shoot straight. Don't mind them."

The sun burned down steadily from a pale sky upon the crackling woods and knolls and fields. From the roar of musketry, it might have been that the celestial heat was frying this part of the world.

Nolan snuggled close to the grass.

He watched a gray line of intrenchments, above which floated the veriest gossamer of smoke. A flag lolled on a staff behind it. The men in the trench volleyed whenever an American shell exploded near them. It was some kind of infantile defiance. Frequently a bullet came from the woods directly behind Nolan and his comrades. They thought at the time that these bullets were from the rifle of some incompetent soldier of their own side.

There was no cheering. The men would have looked about them wondering where the army was if it were not that the crash of the fighting for the distance of a mile denoted plainly enough where that army was.

Officially, the battalion had not yet fired a shot; there had been merely some irresponsible popping by men on the extreme left flank. But it was known that the Lieutenant-Colonel who had been in command was dead, shot through the heart, and that the Captains were thinned down to two. At the rear went on a long tragedy in which men, bent and hasty, hurried to shelter with other men, helpless, dazed and bloody. Nolan knew of it all from the hoarse and affrighted voices which he heard as he lay flattened in the grass. There came to him a sense of exultation. Here, then, was one of those dread and lurid situations which in a nation's history stand out in crimson letters, becoming tales of blood to stir generation after generation. And he was in it and unharmed. If he lived through the battle, he would be a hero of the desperate fight at – and here he wondered for a second what fate would be pleased to bestow as a name for this battle.

But it is quite sure that hardly another man in the battalion was engaged in any thoughts concerning the historic. On the contrary, they deemed it ill that they were being badly cut up on a most unimportant occasion. It would have benefited the conduct of whoever were weak if they had known that they were engaged in a battle that would be famous forever.

IV

Martin had picked himself up from where the bullet had knocked him, and addressed the Lieutenant. "I'm hit, sir," he said.

The Lieutenant was very busy. "All right, all right," he said, heeding the man just enough to learn where he was wounded. "Go over that way. You ought to see a dressing-station under those trees."

Martin found himself dizzy and sick. The sensation in his arm was distinctly galvanic. The feeling was so strange that he could wonder at times if a wound was really what ailed him. Once, in this dazed way, he examined his arm; he was the hole. Yes, he was shot; that was it. And more than in any other way it affected him with a profound sadness.

As directed by the Lieutenant, he went to the clump of trees, but he found no dressing-station there. He found only a dead soldier lying with his face buried in his arms, and with his shoulders humped high as if he was convulsively sobbing. Martin decided to make his way to the road, deeming that he thus would better his chances of getting to a surgeon. But he suddenly found his way blocked by a fence of barbed wire. Such was his mental condition that he brought up at a rigid halt before this fence and stared stupidly at it. It did not seem to him possible that this obstacle could be defeated by any means. The fence was there and it stopped his progress. He could not go in that direction.

But as he turned he espied that procession of wounded men, strange pilgrims, which had already worn a path in the tall grass. They were passing through a gap in the fence. Martin joined them. The bullets were flying over them in sheets, but many of them bore themselves as men who had now exacted from fate a singular immunity. Generally there were no out-cries, no kicking, no talk at all. They too, like Martin, seemed buried in a vague but profound melancholy.

But there was one who cried out loudly. A man shot in the head was being carried arduously by four comrades, and he continually yelled one word that was terrible in its primitive strength. "Bread! Bread! Bread!"

Following him and his bearers were a limping crowd of men, less cruelly wounded, who kept their eyes always fixed on him, as if they gained from his extreme agony some balm for their own sufferings.

"Bread! Give me bread!"

Martin plucked a man by the sleeve. The man had been shot in the foot and was making his way with the help of a curved, incompetent stick. It is an axiom of war that wounded men can never find straight sticks.

"What's the matter with that feller?" asked Martin.

"Nutty," said the man.

"Why is he?"

"Shot in th' head," answered the other impatiently.

The wail of the sufferer rose in the field, amid the swift rasp of bullets and the boom and shatter of shrapnel. "Bread! Bread! Oh, God, can't you give me bread? Bread!" The bearers of him were suffering exquisite agony, and often exchanged glances which exhibited their despair of ever getting free of this tragedy. It seemed endless.

"Bread! Bread! Bread!"

But despite the fact that there was always in the way of this crowd's wistful melancholy, one must know that there were plenty of men who laughed, laughed at their wounds, whimsically, quaintly, inventing odd humors concerning bicycles and cabs, extracting from this shedding of their blood a wonderful amount of material for cheerful badinage, and with their faces twisted from pain as they stepped, they often joked like music-hall stars. And perhaps this was the most tearful part of all.

They trudged along a road until they reached a ford. Here, under the eave of the bank, lay a dismal company. In the mud and the damp shade of some bushes were a half-hundred pale-faced men prostrate. Two or three surgeons were working there. Also there was a chaplain, grim-mouthed, resolute, his surtout discarded. Overhead always was that incessant, maddening wail of bullets.

Martin was standing gazing drowsily at the scene when a surgeon grabbed him. "Here! What's the matter with you?" Martin was daunted. He wondered what he had done that the surgeon should be so angry with him.

"In the arm," he muttered, half shame-facedly.

After the surgeon had hastily and irritably bandaged the injured member, he glared at Martin and said, "You can walk all right, can't you?"

"Yes, sir," said Martin.

"Well, now, you just make tracks down that road."

"Yes, sir." Martin went meekly off. The doctor had seemed exasperated almost to the point of madness.

The road was at this time swept with the fire of a body of Spanish sharpshooters who had come cunningly around the flanks of the American army, and were now hidden in the dense foliage that lined both sides of the road. They were shooting at everything. The road was as crowded as a street in a city, and at an absurdly short range they emptied at the passing people. They were aided always by the over-sweep from the regular Spanish line of battle.

Martin was sleepy from his wounds. He saw tragedy follow tragedy, but they created in him no feeling of horror.

A man, with a red cross on his arm was leaning against a great tree. Suddenly he tumbled to the ground and writhed for a moment in the way of a child oppressed with colic. A comrade immediately began to bustle importantly. "Here!" he called to Martin, "help me carry this man, will you?"

Martin looked at him with dull scorn. "I'll be damned if I do," he said. "Can't carry myself, let alone somebody else."

This answer, which rings now so inhuman, pitiless, did not affect the other man. "Well, all right," he said; "here comes some other fellers." The wounded man had now turned blue-gray; his eyes were closed; his body shook in a gentle, persistent chill.

Occasionally Martin came upon dead horses, their limbs sticking out and up like stakes. One beast, mortally shot, was besieged by three or four men who were trying to push it into the bushes where it could live its brief time of anguish without thrashing to death any of the wounded men in the gloomy procession.

The mule train, with extra ammunition, charged toward the front, still led by the tinkling bell-mare.

An ambulance was stuck momentarily in the mud, and above the crack of battle one could hear the familiar objurgations of the driver as he whirled his lash.

Two privates were having a hard time with a wounded captain whom they were supporting to the rear. He was half cursing, half wailing out the information that he not only would not go another step toward the rear, but was certainly going to return at once to the front. They begged, pleaded, at great length, as they continually headed him off. They were not unlike two nurses with an exceptionally bad and headstrong little duke.

The wounded soldiers paused to look impassively upon this struggle. They were always like men who could not be aroused by anything further.

The visible hospital was mainly straggling thickets intersected with narrow paths, the ground being covered with men. Martin saw a busy person with a book and a pencil, but he did not approach him to become officially a member of the hospital. All he desired was rest and immunity from nagging. He took seat painfully under a bush and leaned his back upon the trunk. There he remained thinking, his face wooden.

V

"My Gawd," said Nolan, squirming on his belly in the grass, "I can't stand this much longer."

Then suddenly every rifle in the firing line seemed to go off of its own accord. It was the result of an order, but few men had heard the order; in the main they had fired because they heard others fire, and their sense was so quick that the volley did not sound too ragged. These marksmen had been lying for nearly an hour in stony silence, their sights adjusted, their fingers fondling their rifles, their eyes staring at the intrenchments of the enemy. The battalion had suffered heavy losses, and these losses had been hard to bear, for a soldier always reasons that men lost during a period of inaction are men badly lost.

The line now sounded like a great machine set to running frantically in the open air, the bright sunshine of a green field. To the "prut" of the magazine rifles was added the under-chorus of the clicking mechanism, steady and swift as if the hand of one operator was controlling it all. It reminds one always of a loom, a great, grand steel loom, clinking, clanking, plunking, plinking, to weave a woof of thin red threads, the cloth of death. By the men's shoulders, under their eager hands, dropped continually the yellow empty shells, spinning into the crushed grass blades, to remain there and mark for the belated eye the line of a battalion's fight.

All impatience, all rebellious feeling, had passed out of the men as soon as they had been allowed to use their weapons against the enemy. They now were absorbed in this business of hitting something, and all the long training at the rifle ranges, all the pride of the marksman which had been so long alive in them, made them forget for the time everything but shooting. They were as deliberate and exact as so many watchmakers.

A new sense of safety was rightfully upon them. They knew that those mysterious men in the high far trenches in front were having the bullets sping in their faces with relentless and remarkable precision; they knew, in fact, that they were now doing the thing which they had been trained endlessly to do, and they knew they were doing it well. Nolan, for instance, was overjoyed. "Plug 'em!" he said. "Plug 'em!" He was aiming his rifle under the shadow of a certain portico of a fortified house; there he could faintly see a long black line which he knew to be a loophole cut for riflemen, and he knew that every shot of his was going there under the portico, mayhap through the loophole to the brain of another man like himself. He loaded the awkward magazine of his rifle again and again. He was so intent that he did not know of new orders until he saw the men about him scrambling to their feet and running forward, crouching low as they ran.

He heard a shout. "Come on, boys! We can't be last! We're going up! We're going up!" He sprang to his feet and, stooping, ran with the others. Something fine, soft, gentle, touched his heart as he ran. He had loved the regiment, the army, because the regiment, the army, was his life. He had no other outlook; and now these men, his comrades, were performing his dream-scenes for him. They were doing as he had ordained in his visions. It is curious that in this charge, he considered himself as rather unworthy. Although he himself was in the assault with the rest of them, it seemed to him that his comrades were dazzlingly courageous. His part, to his mind, was merely that of a man who was going along with the crowd.

He saw Grierson biting madly with his pincers at a barbed-wire fence. They were half-way up the beautiful sylvan slope; there was no enemy to be seen, and yet the landscape rained bullets. Somebody punched him violently in the stomach. He thought dully to lie down and rest, but instead he fell with a crash.

The sparse line of men in blue shirts and dirty slouch hats swept on up the hill. He decided to shut his eyes for a moment, because he felt very dreamy and peaceful. It seemed only a minute before he heard a voice say, "There he is." Grierson and Watkins had come to look for him. He searched their faces at once and keenly, for he had a thought that the line might be driven down the hill and leave him in Spanish hands. But he saw that everything was secure and he prepared no questions.

"Nolan," said Grierson clumsily, "do you know me?"

The man on the ground smiled softly. "Of course I know you, you chowder-faced monkey. Why wouldn't I know you?"

Watkins knelt beside him. "Where did they plug you, boy?"

Nolan was somewhat dubious.

"It ain't much, I don't think, but it's somewheres there." He laid a finger on the pit of his stomach. They lifted his shirt and then privately they exchanged a glance of horror.

"Does it hurt, Jimmie?" said Grierson, hoarsely.

"No," said Nolan, "it don't hurt any, but I feel sort of dead-to-the-world and numb all over. I don't think it's very bad."

"Oh, it's all right," said Watkins.

"What I need is a drink," said Nolan, grinning at them. "I'm chilly – lyin' on this damp ground."

"It ain't very damp, Jimmie," said Grierson.

"Well, it is damp," said Nolan, with sudden irritability. "I can feel it. I'm wet, I tell you – wet through – just from lyin' here."

They answered hastily. "Yes, that's so, Jimmie. It is damp. That's so."

"Just put your hand under my back and see how wet the ground is," he said.

"No," they answered. "That's all right, Jimmie. We know it's wet."

"Well, put your hand under and see," he cried, stubbornly.

"Oh, never mind, Jimmie."

"No," he said in a temper, "see for yourself."

Grierson seemed to be afraid of Nolan's agitation, and so he slipped a hand under the prostrate man, and presently withdrew it covered with blood. "Yes," he said, hiding his hand carefully from Nolan's eyes, "you were right, Jimmie."

"Of course I was," said Nolan, contentedly closing his eyes. "This hillside holds water like a swamp." After a moment he said: "Guess I ought to know. I'm flat here on it, and you fellers are standing up."

He did not know he was dying. He thought he was holding an argument on the condition of the turf.

"Cover his face," said Grierson in a low and husky voice, afterward.

"What'll I cover it with?" said Watkins.

They looked at themselves. They stood in their shirts, trousers, leggings, shoes; they had nothing.

"Oh," said Grierson, "here's his hat." He brought it and laid it on the face of the dead man. They stood for a time. It was apparent that they thought it essential and decent to say or do something. Finally Watkins said in a broken voice, "Aw, it's a damn shame."

They moved slowly off toward the firing line.

* * * * * *

In the blue gloom of evening, in one of the fever tents, the two rows of still figures became hideous, charnel. The languid movement of a hand was surrounded with spectral mystery, and the occasional painful twisting of a body under a blanket was terrifying, as if dead men were moving in their graves under the sod. A heavy odor of sickness and medicine hung in the air.

"What regiment are you in?" said a feeble voice.

"Twenty-ninth infantry," answered another voice.

"Twenty-ninth! Why, the man on the other side of me is in the Twenty-ninth."

"He is? . . . Hey there, partner, are you in the Twenty-ninth?"

A third voice merely answered wearily: "Martin, of C Company."

"What? Jack, is that you?"

"It's a part of me. . . . Who are you?"

"Grierson, you fat-head. I thought you were wounded."

There was the noise of a man gulping a great drink of water, and at its conclusion Martin said, "I am."

"Well, what you doin' in the fever place, then?"

Martin replied with drowsy impatience. "Got the fever, too."

"Gee!" said Grierson.

Thereafter there was silence in the fever tent save for the noise made by a man over in a corner, a kind of man always found in an American crowd, a heroic, implacable comedian and patriot, of a humor that has bitterness and ferocity and love in it, and he was wringing from the situation a grim meaning by singing the Star-Spangled Banner with all the ardor which could be procured from his fever-stricken body.

"Billie," called Martin, in a low voice, "where's Jimmie Nolan?"

"He's dead," said Grierson.

A tangle of raw gold light shone on a side of the tent. Somewhere in the valley an engine's bell was ringing, and it sounded of peace and home as if it hung on a cow's neck.

"An' where's Ike Watkins?"

"Well, he ain't dead, but he got shot through the lungs. They say he ain't got much show."

Through the clouded odors of sickness and medicine rang the dauntless voice of the man in the corner:

" . . . Long may it wave. . . ."

Made in United States
North Haven, CT
05 October 2024

58310195R00362